The Covenant

BEVERLY LEWIS

The Covenant

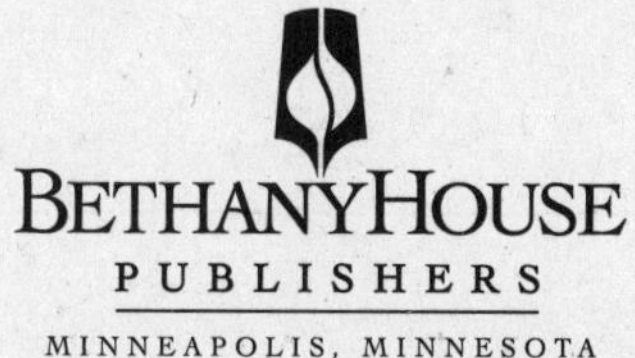

BETHANY HOUSE
PUBLISHERS
MINNEAPOLIS, MINNESOTA

The Covenant
Copyright © 2002
Beverly Lewis

Cover design by Dan Thornberg
Cover photo © Blair Seitz

Published by Bethany House Publishers
11400 Hampshire Avenue South
Bloomington, Minnesota 55438

Bethany House Publishers is a division of
Baker Publishing Group, Grand Rapids, Michigan.

Printed in the United States of America

ISBN 0-7642-2330-5 (Paperback)
ISBN 0-7642-2717-3 (Hardcover)
ISBN 0-7642-2718-1 (Large Print)
ISBN 0-7642-2719-X (Audio Book)

Library of Congress Cataloging-in-Publication Data

Lewis, Beverly
The covenant / by Beverly Lewis.
p. cm. (Abram's daughters ; 1)
ISBN 0-7642-2717-3 (hardback : alk. paper) — ISBN 0-7642-2330-5 (pbk.) — ISBN 0-7642-2718-1 (large print paperback)
1. Lancaster County (Pa.)—Fiction. 2. Sisters—Fiction. 3. Amish—Fiction. I. Title.
PS3562.E9383 C65 2002
813'.54—dc21 2002008665

Dedication

For

three devoted sisters:

Aleta Hirschberg, Iris Jones, and Judy Verhage.

My *aunties, ever dear.*

By Beverly Lewis

ABRAM'S DAUGHTERS

The Covenant

The Betrayal

The Sacrifice

The Prodigal

The Revelation

❖ ❖ ❖

THE HERITAGE OF LANCASTER COUNTY

The Shunning

The Confession

The Reckoning

❖ ❖ ❖

The Postcard

The Crossroad

❖ ❖ ❖

The Redemption of Sarah Cain

October Song

*Sanctuary**

The Sunroom

❖ ❖ ❖

The Beverly Lewis Amish Heritage Cookbook

www.beverlylewis.com

*with David Lewis

05B

BEVERLY LEWIS was born in the heart of Pennsylvania Dutch country. She fondly recalls her growing-up years, and due to a keen interest in her mother's Plain family heritage, many of Beverly's books are set in Lancaster County.

A former schoolteacher, Bev is a member of the National League of American Pen Women—the Pikes Peak branch—and the Society of Children's Book Writers and Illustrators. Her bestselling book *October Song* has received the Silver Award in the Benjamin Franklin Awards, and *The Postcard*, *Annika's Secret Wish*, and *Sanctuary* have received Silver Angel Awards. Bev and her husband have three grown children and one grandchild and make their home in Colorado.

Part One

◆ ◆ ◆ ◆

Therefore, on every morrow, are we wreathing
A flowery band to bind us to the earth.

—John Keats

Prologue

Leah

Growing up, I drank a bitter cup. I fought hard the notion that had I been the firstborn instead of my sister Sadie, my early years might've turned out far different. Fewer thorns over the pathway of years, perhaps. But then, who is ever given control over their destiny?

When I came along my parents already had their daughter—perty, blue-eyed, and fair Sadie. *Dat* needed someone to help him outdoors, so taking one look at me, he decided I was of sturdier stock than my soft and willowy sister. Hence I became my father's shadow early on, working alongside him in the fields, driving a team of mules by the time I was eight—plowing, planting, doing yard work and barn work, too, some of it as soon as I could walk and run. Mamma needed Sadie inside, doing "women's work," after all. And my, oh my, Sadie could clean and cook like a house a-fire. Nobody around these parts, or in all of Lancaster County for that matter, could redd up a place faster or make a tastier beef stew. But those were just two of Sadie's many talents.

Truth be known, my sister was at war with the world and its pleasures . . . and the Amish church. At eighteen, she was taking classes with Preacher Yoder, along with other young people preparing to follow the Lord in holy baptism, to make the lifetime vow to almighty God and the church. Yet all the while offering up her heart and soul on the altar of forbidden love.

Still, I kept Sadie's dreadful secret to myself. *Ach*, part of me longed to see her get caught and promptly rebuked. Sometimes I hated her for the unnecessary risks she seemed too willing to take, not just foolish but ever so dangerous. I was truly worried, too, especially since I was nigh unto courting age and eager to attend Sunday night singings myself when all this treachery began. What would the boys in our church district think of *me* if word got out about shameless Sadie?

"Promise me, Leah," she whispered at night when we dressed for bed. "You daresn't ever say a word 'bout Derry. Not to anyone."

Even though I wished Dat and Mamma *did* know of Sadie's worldly beau, I was sorely embarrassed to reveal such a revolting tale. I struggled to keep the peace between Sadie and myself, but against my better judgment. Soon, I found myself wondering just how long I could keep mum about my sister's sinful ways. Truth be told, I wished I knew nothing at all about the dark-haired English boy my sister loved beyond all reason.

In those early days I was forever worrying, so afraid I'd be stuck playing second fiddle to Sadie my whole life long. Living not only under the covering of my steadfast and God-fearing father, but daily abiding in the shadow of my errant elder sister. The cross I was born to bear.

Sometimes at dusk I would slip away to the upstairs bedroom I shared with Sadie. Alone in the dim light, I gazed into a small hand mirror, looking long and hard by lantern's light, yet not seeing the beauty others saw in me. Only the reflection of a wide-eyed tomboy stared back—a necessary substitute for a father's son, though I was a young woman, after all. And as innocent as moonlight.

Abram's Leah . . .

Clear up till my early twenties, I was identified by Dat's first name. To English outsiders, the two names together might've sounded right sweet, even endearing. But any church member around here knew the truth. *Jah*, the People were clearly aware that Leah Ebersol was dragging her feet about marrying the man her father had picked out for her. So because I was stubborn, I was in danger of becoming a *maidel*—in short, a maiden lady like Aunt Lizzie Brenneman, although she was anything but glum about her state in life. For most young women, not marrying meant denying one's emotions, but not Lizzie. She was as cheerful and alive as anyone I'd ever known.

As for Abram's Leah, well, I possessed determination. "Grit . . . with a lip," Dat often said of me. And I do remember that I had a good bit of courage, too. Never could just stand by tight-mouthed, overhearing the womenfolk speculate on "Abram's rough-'n'-tumble girl"—them looking clear down their noses at me just 'cause I wasn't indoors baking pies or doing needlework. Goodness, that's how Sadie spent *her* time . . . and Hannah and Mary Ruth, and of course, Mamma.

Puh! 'Twas Dat's fault I wasn't indoors making ready for supper and whatnot. I was too busy with farm chores—milking cows twice a day, raising chickens for both egg gathering and, later, dressing them to sell. Whitewashing fences, too. Oh, and sweeping that big old barn out in nothing flat every Saturday. I wasn't one to mince words back then. I was as hardworking as the next person. Just maybe more practical than most young women, I 'spect. Sometimes I even wore work trousers under my long dress so dust from the haymow or mosquitoes from the cornfield wouldn't wander up my legs of a summer. Come to think of it, my second cousin, Jonas Mast, was the boy responsible for sneaking the britches to me—promised to keep the deed to himself, too.

Ach, I was a lot of spunk in those days. A lot of talk, too. But now I try to mind my p's and q's, make apricot jam and pear butter for English customers, and get out and weed my patch of Zenith hybrid zinnias—purple, yellow, and green—in my backyard. More often than not, I find myself saying evening prayers without fail.

'Course now, nearly all that matters in life is the memories. Dear, dear Mamma and unyielding Dat. Kindhearted Aunt Lizzie. Happy-go-lucky Mary Ruth and her too-serious twin, Hannah—competitive yet connected all the same by invisible cords of the heart. And Sadie . . . well, perty is as perty does. The four of us, Plain sisters, attempting to live out our lives under the watchful eye of the Lord God heavenly Father and the church.

Ofttimes now before twilight falls, when the sun's last rays shift slowly down over the golden meadow, if I step outside on my little front porch and let my thoughts stray back, I can hear a thousand echoes from the years. Like a field sprinkled with lightning bugs, they come one by one. Bright as a springtime morning, radiant as a pure white lily. Others come tarnished, nearly swallowed up by blackness, flickering too hastily, overzealous little lights . . . then gone.

The night air seems to call to me. And though I am a sensible grown woman, I surrender to its urging. A vast landscape in my mind seems to reach on without end as I peer across the shadows into another world. Another universe, seems now. There I see a mirrored image that I treasure above all else—the reflection of a smiling, thoughtful young man, his adoring gaze capturing my heart on the day our eyes locked across a long dinner table, when all of us spent Second Christmas with Mamma's cousins over near Grasshopper Level. 'Twas a red-letter day, though Dat soon made me want to forget I had ever smiled back.

A lifetime ago, to be sure. These days, I simply breathe silent questions to the wind: *My beloved, what things do you recall? Will you ever know that I am and always will be your Leah? . . . daughter of Abram, sister of Sadie, child of God.*

Chapter One

SUMMER 1946

Gobbler's Knob had a way of shimmering in the dappled light of deep summer, along about mid-July when the noonday sun—standing at lofty attention in a bold and blue sky—pierced through the canopy of dense woods, momentarily flinging light onto the forest floor in great golden shafts of luster and dust, causing raccoons, moles, and an occasional woodchuck to pause and squint. The knoll, where wild turkeys roamed freely, was populated with a multitude of trees—maple, white oak, and locust. Thickets of raspberry bramble had sometimes trapped unsuspecting young fowl, stunned by the heat of day or the sting of a twelve-gauge shotgun during hunting season.

"*Steer clear of the woods*," the village children often whispered among themselves. They warned each other of tales they'd heard of folk getting lost, unable to find their way out. The rumors were repeated most often during the harvest, when nightfall seemed to sneak up and catch you unaware on the heels of a round white moon bigger than at any other season of year. About the time when all over Lancaster County, fathers came in search of plump Thanksgiving Day turkeys. But even before and after hunting season, children admonished their younger siblings. "*It's true*," they'd say, eyes wide, "*the forest can swallow you up alive*."

Certain mothers in the small community used the superstitious hearsay as leverage when entreating their youngsters home for supper during the delirious days of vacation from books and lessons.

One particular boy and his school chums paid no attention to the warnings. Off they'd go, scouring the forest regularly, day and night, in the eternal weeks of summer, playing cowboys and Indians near an old lean-to, where hunters found shelter from bone-chilling autumn rains and reloaded their guns and drank hot coffee . . . or something stronger. The lads promptly decided the spot where the run-down shelter stood was the deepest, darkest section of woodlands, where they whispered to one another that it was indeed true—sunlight never, ever reached through the mass of branches and leaves. There, among a maze of thorny vines and nearly impenetrable underbrush, everything was its own shadow with gray-blue fringes.

The area surrounding Gobbler's Knob, on all sides, was home to a good many folk, Plain and fancy alike. Soldiers, back from the war, were streaming home to Quarryville just seven miles southwest, to the town of Strasburg about five miles northwest, and to the village of Ninepoints a short carriage ride away.

Abram and Ida Ebersol's farmland was part and parcel of Strasburg Township, according to the map. Smack-dab in the heart of Pennsylvania Dutch country, the gray stone house had been built on seven acres bordering the forest more than eighty years before by Abram's father, the revered Bishop Ebersol, who now slumbered in his grave, awaiting the trumpet's call.

The "Ebersol Cottage," as Leah liked to call her father's limestone house, stood facing the east, "toward the rising of the sun," she would often say, causing Mamma to nod her head and smile. The house was surrounded by a rolling front lawn that became an expanse of velvety grass, where family and friends could sit and lunch on picnic blankets all summer long, the slightest breeze causing deep green ripples across the grass. Behind the two-story house, a modest white clapboard barn stabled two milk cows, two field mules, and two driving horses.

Inside, the front-room windows and those in the kitchen were tall and high with dark green shades pulled up at the sash. In fact, Leah had never remembered seeing the first-floor windows ever covered at all. Mamma was partial to natural light, preferred it to any other kind, said there was no need to block out the light created by the Lord God heavenly Father, whether it be a sunlit day or moon-filled night.

The second-story dormer windows were another matter altogether. Because the family's bedrooms were located on that particular floor, window shades were carefully drawn when the rooms were occupied, especially at dawn and dusk. Abram was adamant about his and Ida's privacy, as well as that of his growing daughters.

From their west-facing windows upstairs, Abram and Ida had a splendid view of the wide backyard, vegetable gardens, the barn and outhouse, the soaring windmill that pumped well water into the house, and beyond that the dazzling forest. What intrigued Ida more than the display of trees and brushwood were the songbirds that fluttered from tree to tree and trilled the sonnets of late spring and early summer, when open windows invited the outdoors in.

Meticulously kept and weekly cleaned, the farmhouse was in remarkable condition for its age. Abram and his family, as well as all who had come before, appreciated, even cherished, the warmth of its hearth and hallways, its congenial rooms. It was a house that when you were gone from it, you were eager to return. Leah often remarked upon arriving home from a visit to one relative or another that the front door and porch seemed to smile a welcome. This, in spite of the fact that she and the entire family always entered and exited the stately dwelling by way of the back door. Still, the pleasing exterior was like a shining beacon in a sea of corn and grazing land, forest and sky.

Whenever Abram's daughters happened to take the driving horse and family buggy over to Strasburg to purchase yard goods and whatnot, the sight of the four girls turned many a head. Thirteen-year-old Hannah and Mary Ruth were not quite as tall as Leah, sixteen in a few short weeks, but they were definitely experiencing a growth spurt here lately. Hannah's facial features—the pensive beauty of her brown eyes, thick lashes, and the delicate contour of her nose and chin—resembled blue-eyed Mary Ruth to some degree, but not enough for folk to automatically assume they were twins. Due to the vivid hue of their identical strawberry blond hair, Hannah and Mary Ruth did make a striking pair when tending the orange and yellow marigolds alongside the road together or looking after Mamma's vegetable-and-fruit stand.

But more times than not it was flaxen-haired Sadie—older than Leah by three unmistakable years—who caused young men to take special notice. Leah, the only brunette of the bunch, strove in her effort not to care that Sadie was often singled out. Still, she observed quietly how boys of courting age were drawn to her enticing older sister, especially now that it appeared Sadie was preparing to offer her lifetime covenant to God and the Amish church.

Seems the closer Sadie gets to her kneeling vow, the more foolish she becomes, thought Leah one hot and humid afternoon while helping Dat bring the mules in from the field. She wasn't one to wag her tongue about any of her sisters' personal concerns. Goodness knows, enough gossip went on in the community, mostly when womenfolk got together to quilt and gab at one farmhouse or another. Family stories—past and present—ideas, recipes, the weather, and ways of looking at things came flying out into the open then to be both heard and inspected. There were some *gut* forms of chatter, but most of it was a waste of time, she'd decided early on.

Leah herself had never been to a quilting frolic. Not once in her entire life. She'd heard plenty about it, more than she cared to, really, from Sadie and the twins. Such gatherings were fertile ground for tales, factual and otherwise, seemed to her. She preferred to engage in straightforward conversation, like the kind she occasionally got to enjoy with Dat out in the cornfield, plowing or cultivating the rich soil. Leah craved the succinct words of her father, his no-nonsense approach to life. After all, Sadie had Mamma's affection, and the twins garnered adequate consideration from both parents.

Here lately, Leah had had the nerve to think that she just might have an exceptionally level head on her mature shoulders and it was time she carved out a corner of credibility for herself. Especially with Dat, even though she and her father wholeheartedly disagreed on one thing, for sure and for certain. Her father had made up his mind years ago just whom Leah should one day marry, though if asked, he wouldn't have said it was by any means an *arrangement*—quite uncommon amongst the People.

The young man was Gideon Peachey, the only son of the blacksmith the next farm over. He was known as Smithy Gid, to tell him apart from other boys with the same name in the area. Gideon's father and Dat had long tended the land that bordered each other's property even before Leah was ever born. Truth was, when they were out working the field, Dat liked to say to Leah, pointing toward the smithy's fifteen acres to the east of them, "There now, take a wonderful-*gut* look at your future . . . right over there. Nobody owns a more beautiful piece of God's green earth than the smithy."

It was a knotty problem, to be sure, since Leah wanted to please her beloved Dat in the matter of marriage. And she was well aware of the benefits for the bridegroom, as well as for the lucky girl who would become Gideon's bride, since the smithy's son was to receive the deed to his father's sprawl of grazing land upon marriage. Of course, all this had, no doubt, played a part in the matchmaking, back when Leah and Gideon were youngsters. Not only that, but the smithy Peachey and Dat considered each other the best of friends, and Gideon was the son Dat wished he'd had.

Leah had no romantic feelings whatsoever for nineteen-year-old Gideon. Oh, he was nice looking enough with wavy brown hair that nearly matched her own and fair cheeks that blushed red when he smiled too broad. He was a good boy, right kind, hardworking, sincere and all. As a conscientious objector, he'd received an agricultural deferment, to the relief of his father and the entire community, just as had many other of their boys eighteen and older.

Leah and her sisters, and Gideon and his sisters, Adah and Dorcas, had grown up swinging on the long rope in the Peachey haymow together, and ice-skating, too, out on Blackbird Pond. She knew firsthand what a good-hearted boy Gideon was. And Adah . . . one of her own dearest friends.

Yet Leah's heart belonged to Jonas Mast and there was no getting around it. Of course, no one but Sadie knew, because things of the heart were carried out in secret, the way Leah's own parents had courted and their parents before them. Now Leah eagerly awaited the day she turned sixteen. At last she would ride home from Sunday night singing with Jonas in his open buggy, slip into the house so as not to awaken the family, hear the *clip-clopping* of the horse as he sped home in the wee hours, all the while dreaming the sweet dreams of romantic love. Jah, October 2 couldn't come anytime too soon.

The hilly treed area known as Gobbler's Knob had never frightened young Derek Schwartz, second son of the town doctor. He was well at home in the vast confines of the shadowy jungle, notwithstanding his own mother's warning. As a lad he had purposely sought out frozen puddles to break through with a single stomp of his boot. He insisted on defying most every periphery set for him growing up, and he proceeded to live as though he planned never, ever to die.

When Derek met up with Sadie Ebersol that mid-August night, he was instantly intrigued. It happened in the village of Strasburg, where two Plain girls, in the midst of their *rumschpringe*—the "running-around," no-rules teen years allowed by the People prior to their children's baptism into the church—were attempting to pull the wool over several English fellows' eyes. They'd abandoned their traditional garb and prayer caps and changed into cotton skirts and short-sleeved blouses for an evening out on the town. But Derek's friend Melvin Warner, sporting a pompadour parted on the side, said right away he knew the girls were Amish. "Just look at the length of their hair . . . all one length, mind you, not a hint of a wave or bangs like *our* girls."

Derek had taken note of the girls' thick, long hair, all right. He also noticed Sadie's roving blue eyes and the curve of her full lips when she smiled. "Doesn't matter to me if a girl's Plain or not," he told Melvin quickly. "I'm telling you, the blonde belongs to me." Almost before he'd finished his pronouncement, he rose from the table where he and his cronies—newly graduated from high school—sat drinking malted milk shakes, messing around, and waiting for some action. Standing tall, he strolled over to make small talk with the wide-eyed girls. Particularly Sadie.

Sadie never would've believed it if anyone had hinted at what might happen if she kept sneaking off to Strasburg come Friday nights. No, never. She had gone and done the selfsame thing several other times before this, discarding her long cape dress and black apron, even removing her devotional *Kapp*, unwinding her hair, parting it at the side instead of in the center, letting the weight of its length flow down over one shoulder. Ach, how many times in her most secret dreams had she wished . . . no, longed for a handsome young man such as this, and an *Englischer* at that? The tall boy headed her way, across the noisy café, had the finest dark hair she thought she'd ever seen. And, glory be, he seemed to be making a beeline right for her. Jah, as she waited, Sadie knew he was intent upon *her*! The look in his dark eyes was spellbinding and deep, and she could not stray from his gaze no matter how hard she might've tried. He seemed vaguely familiar, too. Had she known him during her years at the Georgetown School, when she and her sisters and their young cousins and Plain friends all attended the one-room public schoolhouse not far from their farm? Her mouth felt almost too dry, and pressing her lips together, she hoped he wouldn't notice how awful nervous she was being here in town, this far away from her familiar surroundings.

Quickly she glanced down at herself, still not accustomed to this fancy getup she wore, including what Englishers called bobby socks and saddle shoes. She wondered how she looked to such a young man, really. Did he suspect she was Plain beneath her makeup and whatnot? Would he even care if he knew the truth? By the sparkle in his eyes, she was perty sure her Anabaptist heritage didn't matter just now, not one iota.

Sadie felt her heart thumping hard beneath the sheer cotton blouse, the one she'd slipped on *under* her customary clothes so Mamma or Leah wouldn't suspect a thing if she ever happened to get caught leaving the house after she and her sister had headed on up to bed for the night. Excitement coursed through her veins. She lifted her head and tilted it just so, the way she'd practiced a dozen or more times, and smiled demurely her first hello to the well-to-do doctor's son, who, she would soon discover, much preferred the nickname his pals had given him—Derry—over Derek, the name his parents had chosen after his devout paternal grandfather, a minister of the Gospel.

For no particular reason, Leah awakened and saw that Sadie's side of the bed was empty. On a Friday night, yet. This was not a night for a scheduled Amish singing, she knew that for sure. *Sadie's flown to the world again*, she thought, wishing Mamma and Dat might've heard their wayward daughter leave the house after they'd all gone off to bed. *Why must she be so defiant, Lord?* Leah breathed her prayer into the darkness.

Slipping out of bed, she went and stood by one of the windows and pulled the shade away. She looked out at the glaring sky, almost white with the rising moon as its light lowered itself over the barnyard below. How had Sadie made her getaway *this* time? Sadie wasn't so handy outdoors, not at all—couldn't have just hitched up one of the driving horses to the family carriage without making a ruckus on such a silent, moonlit night. Ach, it wasn't possible for Sadie. *She must've gotten a ride with someone who owns a car.* Such harsh speculating made Leah feel nearly sick to her stomach. Surely Sadie wouldn't stoop so low as to do something like that. Why, such things would not only break their parents' hearts but bring awful shame and reproach to their family. Yet Leah feared that was just what her sister had gone and done. Ach, she shouldn't let herself worry so, not about the unknown. Not about things she had no control over.

Daylight would come all too early tomorrow, she knew.

Dat would appreciate her help with the five-o'clock milking. So she needed her rest. After all, *somebody* around here had to be responsible and get a good night of sleep on weekends.

Turning away from the window, Leah let the blind block out the moonlight and tiptoed back to bed. Refusing to dwell on a host of other shameful deeds her sister might be thinking of tonight, Leah sighed. She slipped back into bed and her head found the feather pillow. She longed for sleep. Truly she did.

The café radio blared the tune "Chiquita Banana," the calypso-beat jingle: *Pepsi-Cola hits the spot, twelve full ounces, that's a lot* . . . as Derek and his pal and the two Plain girls they had picked up headed for Melvin Warner's car. Soon they were speeding down Georgetown Road, laughing and joking, toward Gobbler's Knob. He had known almost immediately that Sadie Ebersol, his unexpected date for the evening, was not accustomed to modern ways. Not in any sense of the word. "Stop here," he told the driver of the car. "Sadie and I . . . we're getting out."

"You're *walking* her home, through the woods?" Melvin said from behind the wheel.

Sadie cast a wary look at him, the first time he had sensed any hint of alarm from her all evening. "Must we go thataway?" she asked.

"Trust me. I know the forest like the back of my hand." He opened the car door and helped her out.

"Aw, Sadie, are you sure?" the other Amish girl asked, sitting next to Melvin in the front seat, leaning toward them now, seemingly very concerned. "You know what they say . . . you might never find your way out again."

Derry nodded his assurance. "We'll be fine."

"Don't worry, Naomi." Sadie flung a small knapsack bundle through the open window and into her friend's lap. "Here, take care of this for me. I'll pick it up from you tomorrow."

Once the Jeep station wagon had rumbled down the road, Derry turned and offered Sadie a hand, helping her over the ditch that ran along the roadside, then through the underbrush that led to the knoll. "So you've never gone walking out here?" he asked, turning to look at her in the moonlight.

"Not on this side of the woods," she said. "I've visited . . . uh, the woman who lives in the log house at the far edge of the forest, though. I've gone there with my sisters, by way of the dirt road, over where the foxgloves grow."

He didn't know so well the flower-strewn side of the hillock. But on several occasions he had seen the woman Sadie mentioned, as well as the No Trespassing signs posted around the perimeter to alert hunters of her five-acre property. Smiling to himself, he thought, *Sadie must think I'm thick-headed. . . . That woman is Amish.* He remembered having seen her working in the flower gardens around the log cabin. "Is the woman a friend of yours?"

"Jah . . . er, yes." Sadie frowned for a moment, then turned to look at him, smiling. "Do *you* know Lizzie Brenneman?"

He shook his head. "I haven't met her formally, if that's what you mean."

"She likes living alone, always has. Loves that side of the woods . . . and the little critters that wander 'bout the forest."

"And she can't be too old," he said.

"Thirty-four, she is," replied Sadie, though it seemed she was holding back information, that maybe the woman was in all actuality a relative, maybe even Sadie's aunt. But he didn't press the issue. He had other more important things on his mind.

We'll be sure to avoid the area of the log cabin, he thought, glad Sadie had warned him, in so many words. He knew precisely where this late-night walk should take them. Nowhere near Aunt Lizzie, he'd see to that.

Sadie's inviting smile and the false air of innocence she seemed all too eager to exude spurred him on. "Ever kiss a boy on the first date?" he asked wryly.

Her warm and exuberant giggle was his delight. He knew he'd met his match. Hand in hand they ran deep into the seclusion of the dark timberland, where the light of the moon was thwarted, obscured by age-old trees, and the night was cloudless and still.

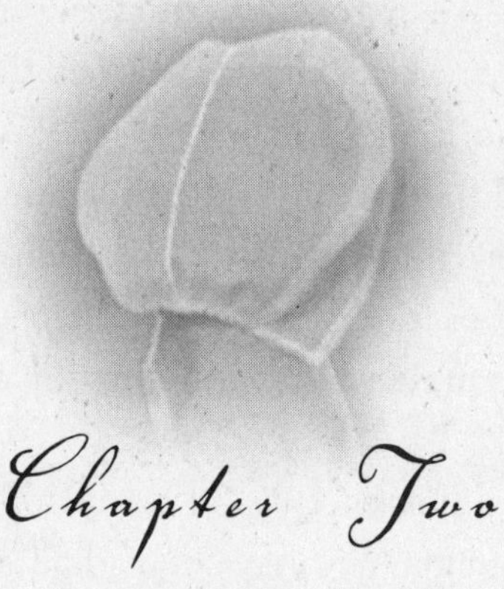

Chapter Two

Since she was a little girl, Hannah, the older of the Ebersol twins—by twenty-three minutes—sometimes contemplated death, wondering what it would be like to leave this world behind for the next. Such thoughts stuck in her head, especially when she was alone and tending the family's fruit-and-vegetable roadside stand. That is, if the minutes lagged between customers, and rearranging the table and checking on the money box were not enough to keep her mind truly occupied.

The plight of having only a handful of customers of a morning was not so common, really, once the decorative gourds and pumpkins and whatnot started gracing the long wooden stand in nice, even rows. Their bright harvest yellows and oranges caught the eye of a good many folks who would stop and purchase produce, enjoying the encounter with a young Plain girl. But this was August, and the baby carrots, spinach, and bush string beans were the big attraction, along with heads of lettuce and rhubarb.

Shy as a shadow, Hannah could hardly wait till the

Englischers made their selection of strawberries, radishes, or tomatoes and then skedaddled on back to their cars and were on their way. Jah, that's just how she felt, nearly too bashful to tend the roadside stand by herself. She figured, though, this was probably the reason she had been chosen to watch over the myriad of fruits and vegetables, because, as Mamma would say, "The more you do something, Hannah, the better you'll get at it."

Well, that might be true for some folk, Hannah often thought, but Mamma must have never had her knees go weak on her, her breath come in short little gasps at the thought of having to make small talk, in English of all things, with outsiders . . . strangers. She felt the same way about attending the one-room public school all these years, too. Thank goodness, Mary Ruth was her constant companion; otherwise, book learning away from home wouldn't have been pleasant at all.

But looking after the produce stand was even worse, really. The sight of a car coming down the road, slowing up a bit, non-Amish folk gawking and sometimes even pointing. Were they just curious about her long cape dress and black apron . . . her prayer cap, the way she parted her hair down the middle . . . was that why they chose to stop? And then the car pulling up smack-dab in front of the stand. Ach, it wasn't so bad if her twin hadn't any chores to tend to and came along with Hannah. Working the produce stand was easily tolerated at such times, if not enjoyed.

Tonight, though, she lay in bed next to Mary Ruth, aware of the even, deep breathing of her sister, thinking once again about heaven, since sleep seemed to escape her. She wondered what it was like when their grandmother on Dat's side—*Grossmammi* Ebersol—had breathed her last, six months ago now. Dat had not been present at his mamma's bedside the night of her passing, but several of the womenfolk had been, Mamma and three aunts, Dat's sisters. The comment had been made that Mammi's passing had been a peaceful one—whatever that meant. Hannah wished she knew. She couldn't quite understand how leaving your body behind and letting go of your spirit—that part of you that's supposed to live on and on through eternity—how that could be a pleasant experience. Not when just the opposite seemed to be true at the start of one's life, when you came hollering and fussing into the world. She'd witnessed enough home births to know *that* was true, for sure and for certain.

So she didn't know if saying someone's death had been a peaceful passing was quite the best way to describe such an event. Of course, now, she hadn't attended the death of anyone, not yet anyway. "You just haven't lived long enough, daughter," Mamma had said recently, when Hannah finally got up the nerve to say just how curious she was about the whole business of dying.

"*Himmel*—heavens, Hannah," Mary Ruth had reprimanded her over a bowl of snow peas, "don'tcha believe that the Lord God sends His angels to come and carry you over River Jordan . . . when the time comes? The Good Book says so."

Hannah had kept still from then on, not bringing up the subject again. Must be not everyone thought secretly about their own deaths the way she did. Maybe she was mistaken to just assume it all along.

Now, lying in the bed she shared with Mary Ruth, she couldn't help but wonder if her twin was just too cheerful for her own good. Jah, maybe that was the big difference between the two of them. Mary Ruth was unruffled, while Hannah looked at life through serious, worry-filled eyes. For as long as she could remember, that was how it was. Of course, they shared nearly everything, sometimes even finished each other's sentences—Dat got a laugh out of that if it happened at the dinner table. Same color hair, similar hankerings for food, and some of the same boys had caught both her and Mary Ruth's eye. Even though the two of them wouldn't be expected to start showing up at Sunday night singings for another three years—it wasn't proper for nice girls to do so before age sixteen—there were plenty of cute boys at Preaching service of a Sunday morning. Especially the Stoltzfus brothers—Ezra and Elias—close enough in age to almost pass for twins, though Ezra was the older by fourteen months. She had confessed in private to Mary Ruth that she wondered if some of those boys might not be thinking some of the same romantic thoughts about her and Mary Ruth. The laughter that had spilled out of Mary Ruth at the time was ever so warm, even comforting, when she admitted that she, too, had entertained notions about some of the same young men as Hannah. Mary Ruth answered, with a twinkle in her blue eyes, "We ain't too young to start filling up our hope chests, you know."

Hannah knew that, all right. She and Mary Ruth had spent many evening hours embroidering pillowcases and crocheting doilies. Hannah especially liked to embroider—with the lazy-daisy stitch—tiny colored flowers or a butterfly in the corners of simple square handkerchiefs Mamma bought over in Strasburg. Sometimes Hannah marked them "For Sale" out on the roadside stand, but mostly she enjoyed giving them away as gifts.

Mamma would often tuck one of Hannah's perty handkerchiefs up the sleeve of her dress. It came in handy for erasing a splotch of dirt from a young child's face—any number of nephews and nieces who came to visit—or just simply nose blowing for herself. One of the handkerchiefs Hannah had embroidered featured a row of six tiny people in the corner, one for each of her immediate family. That one happened to be both Leah's and Mamma's favorite, but Mamma usually won out having it in her pocket or wherever.

Much of what was already folded away in Hannah's pine hope chest could also be found in Mary Ruth's matching trunk. What one sister created, the other usually did, too.

Just now, turning in bed, Hannah stared into the serene face of her twin. Mary Ruth's eyelids were twitching rapidly. *What sort of dream is my sister having tonight?* she wondered.

She wished she might be so relaxed as to sleep through the sound of footsteps coming up the stairs. Was it Sadie coming home after midnight again? Hannah actually thought of slipping out of bed to catch her in the act of tiptoeing back to the bedroom. But, no, best not. Who knows what handsome and interesting Amish boy might catch *her* eye someday, if she ever broke out of her timid shell, that is. Who knows what risks she might take to spend time with a beau once she turned courting age.

Restless, with a hundred thoughts of her own future and that of her dear sisters, she rolled over and stared up wide-eyed at the dim ceiling, hearing Mary Ruth sigh tenderly in her sleep, utterly free from care.

Leah knew it was probably wrong to pretend to be asleep, when she was as wide awake as an owl and very much aware of Sadie's swift movements just now. Not to mention the loud getup her sister was wearing. Yet she trusted the dear Lord to forgive her for not sitting up right then and there, causing a scene in their quiet house.

Sadie had come silently into their room, moved quickly to the wooden chest at the base of the double bed, lifted the lid and secured it, then immediately removed her billowy, too-short skirt, then the sheer blouse and white ankle-length socks and saddle shoes.

Leah couldn't see now, and didn't try to, but she was fairly sure by the sound of it that Sadie was pushing the English clothes down into the depths of the trunk.

The rich, damp smell of the woods filled the room, that and a sprinkling of hyacinth, some cheap bottled cologne, maybe. Where on earth had Sadie found such clothes, not to mention the idea for the arrangement of her hair? It seemed that Sadie had become a frustrated artist and her golden locks, the canvas. Nearly every time she returned home late at night, her hairdo was different. Leah had no idea you could change your hair so many ways.

Saturdays were not so different from any other choring day amongst the People. Ida did notice, though, that Sadie seemed ever so sluggish this morning, lacking her usual vitality. Sadie's eyes were a watery gray. Gone the bright blue, and ach, such dark circles there were beneath her eyes. Was it possible her eldest had tossed and turned all night long? And if that was true, whatever could've plagued her dear girl's mind to torment her so? Was she ill?

"You seem all-in," she said as Sadie rolled out the pastry for pies. "Trouble sleeping maybe?"

Sadie was silent. Then she said something about maybe, jah, that could be, that she'd had herself a fitful sleep. "I'll hafta make up for it sooner or later, I 'spect."

"Anything I can do for you?" Ida replied quickly, thinking a nice warm herbal tea might help relax Sadie come bedtime tonight.

But Sadie seemed to bristle at the remark. "No need to worry, Mamma" came the unexpected retort.

"All right, then." Ida went about her kitchen work, sweeping and washing the floor. She began cooking the noon meal for Abram and the girls, knowing how awful hungry her husband, and Leah, too, would be when they came in from the barn around eleven-thirty or so, eager for a nice meal. Today it was meatball chowder, homemade bread and butter, cottage cheese salad, and chocolate revel bars, Abram's favorite dessert.

There was much work to be done in the house—plenty of weeding in the vegetable garden out back, too—more chores than Sadie seemed to have the energy for on this already muggy day. True, maybe her firstborn had merely suffered a poor night's sleep. But why on earth did she seem so nervous, almost jumpy? Didn't add up. Come to think of it, maybe Leah might know what was bothering Sadie, but Ida hadn't seen hide nor hair of the girl since Leah had gotten up with the chickens and gone out to milk cows with Abram before sunup. Besides, it was like pulling teeth to get Leah to share much of anything about Sadie or the twins. No, if Ida truly wanted to know why Sadie wore that everlasting half grin on her face, she'd have to wait till Sadie herself came confiding in her, which could be a mighty long time. Probably never.

Leah swept every inch of the barn that needed attention, whipping up a swirl of dust like never before. She couldn't help it, she simply felt like taking out her frustrations on the old broom and the barn floor. It was a good thing she'd hurried out here early this morning, so cross she was with Sadie.

An interesting discussion with Dat was about the only thing that might get her mind off her sister. She glanced over at him there in the milk house washing down the small room. He happened to catch her eye, and seeing her going about her chore with such vigor, he stopped what he was doing and hurried to her, digging deep into his trouser pockets for a clean blue kerchief. "Here, Leah, looks like you might be needin' this. It'll help keep your lungs free of grime, maybe," and he placed it over her nose and mouth, knotting it firmly behind her head.

"I'll surely scare the mules lookin' like this," she said, though awfully touched by her father's sympathetic gesture.

"Pay no mind to the animals. They've seen us both lookin' worse, ain't?"

"Guess you're right." Still, she felt awkward the way Dat's kerchief was tied around her head, pushing her devotional cap off center. So she quickened her pace, completing her job in the nick of time, just as Dat mentioned he was headed over to the welding shop. "Wouldja like to ride along? We'll be back before your mamma ever misses us," he said, already choosing his driving horse for the short trip.

"Jah, I'll go." She pulled off Dat's handkerchief. She'd much rather spend her morning with Dat than be anywhere near Sadie at the moment. No doubt in her mind! But she never let on to her father as they rode, the carriage swaying gently as the horse pulled them toward the welding shop.

"Preacher Yoder's thinking of hiring a driver to take him and his family out to Indiana for a short vacation, after the harvest is past."

"Why Indiana?"

"Well, it wouldn't surprise me if they're goin' to look for some grazing land while out there. Not for them to up and move, mind you, just to help one of his cousins who's thinking of getting married soon."

"To a girl in Indiana?"

Dat nodded. "Now don't that beat all?"

"Talk about long-distance courtship." She thought Dat might bring up Smithy Gid just then, try to blend the present topic with his ongoing anticipation of Gid marrying her; but he didn't. She was quite surprised that he refrained, especially when he easily could have slipped in a comment or two.

They rode along for a time enjoying the silence, aware of the hum of insects and chirp of birds. At last, Leah asked, "What do you think is the difference between being sorely tempted and yielding to it?"

"Well, all the difference in the world, far as the Scriptures say. We're admonished to watch and pray lest we fall into temptation."

"But how does a person avoid being tempted?"

" 'Tis by steering clear of those who may be tools of the enemy."

"You mean Englishers?"

The reins lay loosely in his lap, and he lifted his straw hat and scratched his head beneath. "Seems to me there's a time and a place to mingle with the outside world, but when it comes to making close friends or choosin' a mate, well, you know the best way is God's way."

She was trying not to think of Sadie now, afraid Dat might wisely see through her questions and suspect, maybe, why she was asking such things. They talked about the spirit being willing and the flesh awful weak at times. Dat brought up the pure conscience of the righteous and the battle that rages in every man . . . "every woman, too." He gave her a serious look. "But the most important thing 'bout temptation is knowing how to avoid it."

She fell silent then, soaking in all that Dat had said.

When Mamma wasn't looking, Sadie slipped into their large sunroom just off the kitchen, staring longingly out the windows, toward the barn and beyond to the dark woods. They'd made it through the dreadful maze—survived the denseness, the lurking shadows—just as Derry had said they would. He'd helped her find the way out, and she would tell Naomi so when she went to pick up her knapsack later on.

Why *had* she worried last night? With Derry by her side, she was safe in the forest. Safe anywhere at all, for sure and for certain.

Derry Schwartz. The most wonderful boy in the whole world. With a peculiar pang—part thrill, part anguish—she thought of his life and hers, how the two of them had seemed to collide unexpectedly, like an automobile appearing out of nowhere and hitting a horse and buggy—sort of like that. Of course, they had no business spending time together, none whatsoever. Yet they were drawn to each other, she for the sheer daring of a forbidden English boy who knew the outside world through and through and for the great love she truly believed he would soon have for her. And Derry . . . She didn't quite know yet. Maybe it was her wheat-colored hair and big blue eyes. Maybe he saw something in her other boys had missed. But find out, she must. She would fully discover what it was that the village doctor's son had appreciated in her, and in such a short time, yet . . . that he would ask to see her again, this very night! "Do you think you can meet me here in the woods? Would you be afraid?" he'd said after their joyful evening together. She'd said she didn't know—"It's ever so thick outside, confusing, too . . . with so much underbrush and all."

She had been careful not to admit to being fearful of the woods, just hoped he'd take the hint. And he had. He said he would be glad to meet her behind her father's barn at ten o'clock straight up.

"You could . . . wear your regular, uh, dress if you'd like," he'd added quickly, which took her off guard. "No need to pretend you're not Plain for my sake." So he'd known all along.

She could feel her cheeks growing warm. "You're sure?"

"Please don't risk getting caught in modern clothes that might, well, reveal that your boyfriend is modern."

Boyfriend . . . Her heart had leaped up at the thought. Derry must truly care for her already.

She decided right then that Derry was a very wise young man. For him to say outright that she didn't have to bother impressing him with fancy English clothing any longer. Jah, this was quite a burden lifted off her shoulders. She could be herself with him. Dress Plain, if he didn't mind. No more games to be played. Maybe she'd found the man of her dreams. Who knows, maybe he'd want to join church with her. Maybe he'd be asking more about life in the Plain community. Why else had he asked her to meet him for a second walk in the woods? Then again, maybe she would join *his* world and leave the Amish life behind.

She would know the answers soon enough. Now, if Mamma would just stop poking her head in the room, looking at her as if she was trying to figure out what in the world was twirling round in Sadie's head. No, she wouldn't go and spoil things by sharing her secret with either Mamma or Leah about the boy with dark wavy hair and shining brown eyes. Not just yet. Mamma would put her foot down hard about seeing a boy outside the church, heaven knows, especially when she was planning to be baptized here before too long. And Leah . . . well, she knew her sister would flat out tell her she was playing with fire. In the boundless forest, yet. Best keep all this to herself.

Mamma had often accused Mary Ruth, jokingly of course, that once she got started chattering she just didn't know when to quit. And she *had* been doing her share of talking this morning while helping Mamma cook breakfast.

I'll make a gut schoolteacher someday, she thought. *But Dat and Mamma would be alarmed if they knew.*

Her whole life, Mary Ruth had dreamed of becoming a teacher. But how could such a wonderful thing happen? Higher education—past the legal age of fifteen—was a no-no amongst the People, according to their bishop. Yet it was impossible to quiet her overwhelming desire to communicate learning skills to youngsters.

Mixing the pancake batter, she allowed her mind to wander. Tomorrow at Preaching service over at the Peachey place, there would be many little children in attendance. She hoped to spend time playing with some of them at the picnic following the church meeting. How many youngsters would the Good Lord give *her* and her future husband? And what sort of young man would share her love for books?

Eagerly, she looked forward to helping with the Lord's Day menu with Mamma and Sadie after breakfast. Unlike Sadie, she was only *slightly* interested in boys. As for Leah, well, that was the sister who captured her attention, especially when it came to Smithy Gid. He seemed to have his eye on their tomboy sister. Mary Ruth had suspected this for a year or so. Of course she hadn't, and wouldn't, utter a word to anyone. Leah was a very private sort of girl—practical, too—so there was no inkling of anything romantic in store, far as she knew.

Glancing over at Hannah setting the table, Mary Ruth could see that her twin was more curious about Sadie's glazed expression. It reminded Mary Ruth of the selfsame look in the eyes of worldly girls at the public one-room schoolhouse on Belmont Road, near Route 30, where she and Hannah attended. There, Amish, Mennonite, and English students recited their lessons together, and at recess some of the girls whispered about certain boys.

Mary Ruth didn't like the idea of comparing Sadie to worldly girls, though it was true that Sadie had attended the public high school over in the town of Paradise till she was seventeen. These days, Dat declared up and down it hadn't been such a gut idea for his eldest daughter to cultivate friendships with Englishers at school, an environment that promoted individuality so frowned on by the People. Had those years encouraged Sadie to have herself a wild rumschpringe?

It wasn't Mary Ruth's place to judge, really. She would bide her time, wait and see how the Lord God heavenly Father worked His will and way in each of her sisters' lives.

Pouring a cup of batter on the sizzling black skillet, she shook off the annoying blue feeling. She hummed a church song, doing what she could to lift everyone's spirits, as well as her own. It was high time to rejoice, for goodness' sake. The Lord's Day was ever so near.

Chapter Three

After the noon meal Leah helped Sadie wash and dry each one of the kerosene lamp chimneys in the house. The glass tubes had been rather cloudy last evening during Bible reading and evening prayers, and Leah and Mamma had both noticed the light was too soft and misty because of it. Dat hadn't complained at all, though he did have to adjust his reading glasses repeatedly, scooting close to the lamp in the kitchen, where they'd all gathered just before twilight, the back door flung wide, along with all the windows, coaxing the slightest breeze into the warm house.

"We really oughta clean these every day," Leah said, handing one to Sadie for drying. "No sense Dat struggling to see the Good Book, jah?"

Sadie nodded halfheartedly.

"Are you going out again tonight?" Leah whispered.

Sadie's eyes gave a sharp warning. "Ach, not now . . ."

Glancing over her shoulder, Leah saw that Mamma was dusting the furniture in the sunroom. "*Cleanliness is next to godliness*," Mamma liked to say constantly. Hannah and Mary

Ruth had run outside to hose off the back porch and sidewalk.

"You'll break Mamma's heart if you're sneaking out with English boys, ya know," she said softly.

"How do you know what I'm doin'?"

"I saw you come home last night—saw what you were wearing, too." But before she could ask where on earth Sadie had gotten such a getup, Mamma returned, and that brought a quick end to their conversation.

Leah washed the rest of the chimneys, turning her thoughts to the Preaching service tomorrow. *Will Gid single me out again before the common meal?* she wondered. He had been more than forthright with his intentions toward her before, though discreetly enough. Yet she knew he was counting the weeks till she was old enough to attend Sunday singings. And so was she, but for a far different reason. "I'll be first in line to ask you to ride home with me," he'd said to her out in the barnyard two Sundays ago, when it was her family's turn to have house church.

Speechless at the time, she wished the Lord might give her something both wise and kind to say. To put him off gently. But not one word had come to mind and she just stood there, fidgeting while the smithy's only son grinned down at her.

What she was really looking forward to was *next* Sunday—the off-Sunday between church meetings—when the People spent the day visiting relatives. Mamma was awful eager to go to Grasshopper Level and see the Mast cousins again. It had been several months.

Leah remembered precisely where she was standing in the barn when Dat had given her the news of the visit. Looking down, in the haymow, she'd stopped short, holding her pitchfork just so in front of her, half leaning on it while she willed her heart to slow its pace.

She smiled, fondly recalling the first time she'd ever talked with Jonas. The two of them had nearly missed out on supper, standing out in the milk house talking about birds, especially the colorful varieties that lived on Aunt Lizzie's side of the woods, near where the wild flowers grew. She had told him her favorite was the bluebird. Jonas had wholeheartedly agreed, his blue eyes searching hers. And for a moment, she nearly forgot he was three years older. He was Sadie's age. Yet, unlike any other boy, he seemed to know and understand her heart—who Leah truly was. Not a tomboy, but a real girl.

In all truth, she hadn't experienced such a thing with *anyone* ever in her life. Not with Sadie, for sure. And not so much with Mamma, though on rare occasions her mother had opened up a bit. Hannah and Mary Ruth had each other and were constantly whispering private conversations. Only with Aunt Lizzie and Adah Peachey, Gid's younger sister, could Leah share confidentially.

So she and Jonas had a special something between them, which was too bad. At least Mamma would think so if she knew, because young women weren't supposed to open up much to young men, unless, of course, they were being courted or were married.

Just now, Sadie glanced nervously toward the sunroom, where Mamma was still busy dusting. "Walk me to the outhouse," Sadie whispered to Leah.

"What for?"

"Never mind, just come." Sadie led the way, through the utility room and enclosed porch, then down the back steps, past the twins, who laughed as they worked.

Silently they walked, till Sadie said, turning quickly, "Listen, if ya must know, I think I'm falling in love."

"In love? Ach, Sadie, who with?"

"Shh! He lives down the road a ways. His name is Derry."

"So, I'm right then, a fancy boy." Leah wanted to turn around right now and head back to the house. She didn't want to hear another filthy word. "What's happened to you? English boys are big trouble. You oughta know from going to high school and all."

"You sound too much like Dat."

"Well, somebody's got to talk sense to you! Having a wild rumschpringe's one thing, Sadie, but whatever ya do, don't go outside the boundaries of the *Ordnung*."

Sadie's eyes were ablaze. "Say whatcha want, but zip your lip."

"Maybe I *should* tell."

Their eyes locked. Sadie leaned closer. "You have a secret, too, Leah."

"Are you threatening me?"

"Call it what you will, but if Mamma finds out about me, I'll know it came from you. And if you go and tell Mamma on me, I'll tell Dat on you. And if Dat finds out you hope to marry Jonas 'stead of Smithy Gid, he'll put a stop to it."

Leah's heart sank. Sadie had her, for sure.

Glaring at her, Sadie opened the door to the outhouse and hurried inside. The second Leah heard the door latch shut, she turned and fled for home.

Sadie emerged from the outhouse, and not seeing Leah anywhere, she headed toward the mule road. The dirt path led to the outer reaches of the northwest side of the woods, where Aunt Lizzie's perty little place stood. She felt the smooth dust against her bare feet, but her throat felt tight, almost sore. She regretted having told Leah anything at all about her English boyfriend. Might be nice to visit her aunt, get her mind off things.

When she neared the white front fence, Sadie spied Aunt Lizzie opening the screen door. Her aunt came running and waving a dishrag, her long purple dress and black apron flapping in the breeze. "Well, hullo there. If it ain't you, Sadie!" Lizzie wore the biggest grin on her suntanned face.

Sadie quickened her step. "Hullo, *Aendi*—Auntie."

"Come round the back and sit a spell," Lizzie said, leading her past the tall stone wall that rimmed the cabin—high enough to keep deer and other woodland critters out of her flowers—to the back porch, where three hickory rockers spilled out all in a row.

The little four-room bungalow was tucked into the edge of the woods, "half in and half out," Mamma liked to say. One could enjoy the benefit of both sun and sky, as well as towering shade trees flanking the back of the house. And there were ample sunny spots for Lizzie's beloved roses, lavender, lilies, clematis, and a variety of herbs. Her vegetable gardens, too.

Once they were seated on the back porch, Aunt Lizzie asked, "So . . . what brings you up here and all by yourself, yet?"

"Just out for a short walk."

" 'Tis a nice day for it."

"Jah, hope it'll be nice tomorrow, too." Sadie asked about Preaching service. "Are you comin' to Peacheys'?"

"Haven't missed a single meeting for ever so long. Don't plan to start now."

Sadie nodded, aware of Lizzie's curious gaze.

"I'm mighty blessed not to be prone to illness, seems."

"Must be all those herbs you grow in your garden. Mamma says they have healing qualities."

"The foxgloves, too." Lizzie pointed to an array of snowy white, crimson, and yellow snapdragons growing wild and a golden throng of buttercups vying for attention.

"Ach, how's that?"

"Them snapdragons open their little mouths and scare the sickness away." Lizzie burst into her jovial laughter.

"Oh, Auntie, they don't really, now, do they?"

Then Lizzie said unexpectedly, "You look a bit *bleech*—sallow. Not feelin' so well?"

Sadie was sure she didn't look any more washed-out than she usually did. After all, being a blonde, her skin was rather pale most of the time, except when she had a sunburn. "A little tired is all," she replied.

Lizzie scratched her dark head, her hazel-brown eyes serious now. "Looks to me like you skipped near a whole night of sleep."

"I was out a bit late," Sadie admitted.

"Then I 'spect you'll be heading for bed bright and early tonight?"

"Maybe so."

Lizzie stopped rocking and reached a hand toward her. "Best be awful careful who you spend your time with, Sadie dear," she cautioned.

The silence hung awkward and heavy in the hot air. This

was so peculiar, Aunt Lizzie poking her nose in where it didn't belong.

She was thinking what she ought to say, when who should show up just then but Hannah, carrying a loaf of bread. Her sister had appeared round the corner, grinning for all she was worth and coming up the porch steps.

"Mamma just baked some raisin-and-nut bread." Hannah planted a kiss on Lizzie's cheek.

Since there was only one rocker vacant, Hannah wandered over and sat next to Sadie, looking like a chipmunk chasing after an elusive acorn.

Not one to jump to conclusions, Sadie watched Hannah's rapt brown eyes. Just how long had her younger sister been standing round the corner of the cabin?

Hannah found it ever so hard to sit still and listen to Aunt Lizzie chatter about her plans to dig up yet another garden plot—this time for marigolds—when the talk had been far more interesting before. So what she suspected was true.

She wanted to say something about the fun they would all have tomorrow at the picnic on the grounds at the Peachey farm, but Aunt Lizzie kept prattling on about herbs and flowers. Sadie only stared; her eyes, pale and vague, were focused on the deepest part of the woods.

"Tell your mamma I'll lend her a hand with plantin' kale and broccoli on Monday," Aunt Lizzie said.

"We're always glad for extra help," Hannah replied.

"I'll be down right after breakfast."

"Oh, but Mamma will say to come have scrambled eggs and waffles with us, won't she, Sadie?" Hannah said, turning to her sister.

"Wha-at?" Sadie stumbled over herself.

Hannah rose, eager to get home. "We'll see you for breakfast on Monday, Aunt Lizzie." She leaned down and offered her best smile, hugging her aunt's neck.

Quickly Sadie stood and said her good-byes, too, and the two girls walked home, saying not a single word between them.

Chapter Four

"Out tempting the woods again." Henry Schwartz muttered his complaint to the wind. One by one, he proceeded to pick raspberry brambles out of his son's jeans cuffs, glad to help Lorraine, his wife, whenever he could. *Derek never could stay away from that forest*, he thought, wondering why his son had lied about going to Strasburg with friends when it was clearly evident where the boy had spent the bulk of his Friday evening.

Henry held high hopes for Derek, wishing he might grow out of his aimless fascination with so many young women. Couldn't he stay home once in a while like his older brother, an ex-GI back from the war? Except now that Robert was finally here safe and sound, he slept around the clock, and when he wasn't loafing in his bathrobe, he was staring at the new television set. He also seemed to have lost any incentive for job hunting, enjoying his membership in the "52–20 Club," his unemployment pay.

"Give him more time, dear. He'll get his bearings soon enough," Lorraine had said when he voiced his concern. "He survived D day, for pete's sake."

But Henry wasn't sure it was a wise thing to let a boy coast on his wartime merits. Discharged soldier or not. After all, young Derek had the next thing to a full-time job working for Peter Mast, an Amish farmer over on Grasshopper Level, and planned to join the military once he turned eighteen in December. Robert, at twenty, needed something to get him up and going in the morning. What would be so wrong with his elder son picking up the phone and asking Peter if he had need of another hired hand?

Gathering up the dirty jeans, Henry carried them into the house and down to the cellar, where he found Lorraine piling up damp clothes into the wide wicker basket at her feet. What a hardworking, devoted wife. He knew he was lucky to have married someone like her. She had helped him through most all the years of medical school, even stayed true to him during the year their marriage was sorely tested, looking after the needs of her trio of men. One of which Henry felt he must confront with last night's walk in the woods.

After lunch Mamma went off to her bedroom for a catnap, so Sadie decided now was as good a time as any to go to Naomi Kauffman's and pick up the knapsack she'd given her for safekeeping—and to cover her tracks a bit.

"Well, it's gut to see you made it out of the woods last night," Naomi said in the privacy of her bedroom. "I was so afraid you'd get swallowed up."

"I'm here, aren't I?"

"You were lucky this time. Just don't go back there again." Naomi leaned over and pulled Sadie's pack with its bunched-up clothing out from under the bed. "No one here suspects where we were last night, or what we were wearing. No one at all."

Be glad you don't have a sister named Leah, thought Sadie. "*Denki*—thank you."

"So . . . did you let him hold your hand the whole time?"

"For pity's sake, Naomi, he's a worldly boy."

"I'm not blind! I *saw* him reach for your hand when you got out of the car."

Sadie turned the tables. "Have I asked 'bout *your* English friend?"

Naomi squelched a smile. "Ach, and he was ever so good-lookin', too. Ain't so? We oughta sneak out again next Friday night. I hear there's a doin's over at Strasburg. Wanna go?"

"Might not be such a gut idea, for us . . . well, for *me*, at least, seein' as how I'm taking instructional classes for baptism, ya know."

"But I thought . . ."

"*Nee*—no, it's time I settled some things," Sadie insisted, hoping her friend wouldn't suspect.

"So, then, you're finished with running round? Ready to join church?"

That's not what she'd said exactly. Sure, she was taking baptismal classes and all, but she was just going through the motions so far. She hadn't decided whether or not she would follow through with the kneeling vow when the time came. Of course, she wouldn't be the first young person to change her mind this close to the sacred ordinance.

Sadie sighed. "How many times do you *really* think we

could go to Strasburg dressed up—painted up, too—like fancy girls and not get caught?"

"You never seemed worried before."

"I've been thinking. You'd best be goin' to Sunday night singings from now on. Let some nice Amish boy court you, settle down some, get married in a year or so."

Naomi was indignant. "Ach, you've changed your tune, Sadie Ebersol!"

"Well now, have I?" she said, turning toward the door. Naomi followed her into the hall and down the steps.

"You said before you wanted some excitement and fun—*adventure*—out in the modern world. Wanted to see firsthand what you'd been missin'."

Sure, she'd said that. Said it with a vengeance, nearly. But now? Now she had what she wanted—a boy named Derry—but she couldn't for all the world spill the beans to Naomi. No, such a thing would spread like a grass fire, and next thing she'd know, both Dat and Mamma would be talking straight to her, in front of Preacher Yoder, maybe. Or worse, the bishop.

"Things change." She was glad her friend stayed put at the end of the lane, Naomi's bare toes curled, digging hard into the dirt.

"Are *you* goin' to start attending singings again?" Naomi asked.

"We'll see." She turned to leave.

"Sadie . . . wait!" Naomi hollered, stumbling after Sadie as if her life depended on it somehow.

She kept walking. "Mamma's expectin' me home now," Sadie said without looking back. No, she'd keep on walking alone this time, her knapsack close to her heart. No sense in prolonging Naomi's disappointment. No sense lying outright, either.

During the hottest hour of the afternoon, while Sadie went out for a walk, Leah crept up to their bedroom, closed the door behind her, wishing for a lock for the first time ever. Like a curious kitten, she hurried to Sadie's hope chest and opened the lid. All day she'd thought of nothing more than wanting to have a closer look at the modern skirt and blouse Sadie had worn last night, and even the white-and-black two-toned shoes. She couldn't imagine wearing anything on her feet at all, not till the first hard freeze, for goodness' sake. Such things as shoes, of any kind, were much too confining.

Pushing down into the depths of the trunk, Leah felt for the shoes. She moved sheets and pillowcases, enough for three beds as was customary. There were towels and wash-cloths, too, along with tablecloths, hand-hooked rugs, and cushion tops. At last her hands bumped the shoes, and she pulled first one, then the next out, peering at each one, holding them gingerly by their white shoestrings the way Dat held dead mice he found in the barn by their tails. So peculiar looking they were. Ach, she felt almost sinful just touching them, studying the fancy shoes with disdain, knowing who had walked in them, and wondering all of a sudden who might've worn them even before Sadie. The cotton blouse still smelled of cologne and the forest. The skirt was a light russet color, cut with a flair at the hem. Not so worn that she might've suspected someone else of having owned the garment before Sadie. Not the blouse, either. So then, did this mean Sadie had actually gone into an English dress shop somewhere and purchased these clothes? And if not, how had the fancy outfit landed in her possession? Through one of Sadie's former high school chums, maybe?

She thought of Sadie's Plain girlfriends, those who were testing the waters, having their one and only chance to experience the outside world before deciding whether or not to become a full-fledged member of the Amish church. There were any number of girls who might influence Sadie in such a manner. Or, then again, maybe it was Sadie who was influencing them. Come to think of it, that was probably more likely . . . Sadie being the stubborn sort she was. Sometimes Leah felt sorry for her.

Leah recalled the time when Sadie had wanted to stay home and nurse a sick puppy back to health, missing Preaching service to do so. Mamma had said "*Nothing doin'*," but in the end, Sadie got her way. Leah, at the time, wasn't at all so sure her sister was actually going to sit at home and care for their new puppy dog. She had a feeling what Sadie really wanted was to hop in the pony cart and take herself out to the far meadow, spending time gathering wild daisies on the Lord's Day, yet. And Leah was perty sure that's just what Sadie had done, too, because she found a clump of limp buttercups in Sadie's top drawer later on. Besides all that, the sick puppy died that night. Hadn't been tended to at all.

Put out with herself, Leah honestly didn't know why she was thinking such things just now. She oughta be on her knees, praying for her willful sister, she knew, asking God to spare His judgment on dear Sadie.

Stuffing the defiled clothing and shoes back into Sadie's hope chest, she sighed, breathing a prayer, knowing it would take more than a few whispers sent heavenward to save her sister from sinful pleasures. Sadly, she hadn't the slightest idea how to rescue someone from the swift undercurrent of the world, especially when there was no sign of flailing arms or calling for help. Surely Sadie wouldn't just let herself go under without a struggle.

Leah shuddered to think that by keeping her sister's secret, she just might be helping Sadie drown. *Dear Lord, am I making a terrible mistake?*

Henry Schwartz had absolutely no success talking to his youngest son. First of all, Derek had made himself unavailable for the longest time, upstairs shaving. Then when Derek telephoned his friend Melvin Warner, he was interrupted several times by Mrs. Ferguson, who wanted to gab to her newly married daughter. But Derek put her off, tying up the party line they shared with twelve other families. Once his son did finish the phone call, Lorraine was signaling them to the dining room for breakfast.

Finally Derek had come dragging to the table, where Lorraine and Robert were engaged in a lengthy conversation, discussing such heartrending topics as "friendly fire," which had killed so many Allied soldiers, two hundred at sea alone. Robert had been only eighteen at the time of his enlistment, promptly being taken off to basic training in early 1944, just as the war was heating up, during the increasing attacks on Berlin.

Sitting quietly, watching his family down their breakfast, Henry wondered if it was such a good idea to confront Derek today regarding his most recent woodland excursion. His son was in a hurry, obvious by the way he wiped his mouth on his napkin and crumpled it onto the plate, then muttered "excuse me" and exited the room with little eye contact. His footsteps on the stairs were swift, as well, and Henry assumed he was rushing off to work at the Mast farm.

Recalling that his attempts to rein in *this* son had always failed in the past, he realized anew that Derek was a boy whom he had never been able to truly influence or oversee. Not at all like conscientious and honorable Robert, but to a certain extent similar to Henry himself, who had been rather reckless in his youth. No one, not even his father, the Reverend Schwartz, could manage him in those days.

Subsequently, like father like son. For Henry to acknowledge the fact was one thing; living with it on a daily basis was quite another. So he would wait for a more opportune time to sit down with Derek. If that moment presented itself at all.

It was the custom of the People to gather for Preaching at nine o'clock sharp on a Sunday morning. The day before, the menfolk removed the partitions that divided the front room from the big kitchen, creating an enormous space, enough for as many as one hundred fifty, give or take a few. Throw rugs were removed, decorative china washed and spotless. Furniture downstairs was rearranged and stoves polished and blackened. In the barn the manure had been cleared out and, in general, the stables cleaned up. Preaching service usually lasted three hours, ending in the common meal at noon and a time of visiting afterward. A day of great anticipation, to be sure.

Ida sat on the backless bench between Lizzie on her left

and Leah on her right. Sadie and the twins sat squarely in front of them, and Ida was taken yet again by the striking beauty of the girls' hair color, so similar to her own growing up. Hannah and Mary Ruth could scarcely be told apart when viewing them from this angle; the curve of their slender necks was nearly identical. Sadie, just a bit taller, was similar in build to her twin sisters, still mighty thin for being this close to the end of her teen years. Even so, Ida admired her girls lined up all in a row, when she should've been entering into an attitude of prayer in preparation for being a hearer of the Word.

She recalled that Leah had been much quieter than usual on the walk down their long lane and out to the road. As usual, Mary Ruth had been the one doing most of the talking, though Sadie had mentioned how awful perty the clouds were this morning. "All fluttery, they are," she'd said, which made Ida wonder what was *really* on her firstborn's mind, seeing as how she'd bumped into Sadie coming in the kitchen door at nearly one o'clock this morning. Ida had gone downstairs, suffering from an upset stomach. She didn't know why, really—hadn't eaten anything out of the ordinary. She was pouring herself some milk and nearly dropped the glass, startled to hear someone opening the back door at such an hour.

When she turned to see who it was, she gasped. "Sadie, ach, is that you?"

"Jah, Mamma. I'm home" was all Sadie said.

"Out all hours," Mamma said reprovingly.

Sadie was silent.

Now was as good a time as any to remind her daughter what the Scriptures taught. " 'What fellowship hath righteousness with unrighteousness? And what communion hath light with darkness?' "

"Still . . . it's my rumschpringe," Sadie muttered, then skittered past and hurried up the steps.

A faint timberland scent mingled with a fragrance Ida couldn't quite place as Sadie nearly fled from the kitchen. Ach, if only Abram had gotten their eldest a domestic permit, keeping Sadie home from the wiles of public high school after she finished eighth grade. Both Ida and Abram had erred and were paying for it dearly, exposing Sadie to higher education, her consorting with worldly teachers and students and all. After Sadie they'd gotten wise, requesting a permit for Leah to keep Abram's farmhand separated from the world once she turned fifteen.

Though, hard as it was not to rush after willful Sadie, Ida had just let things be. Her mother heart longed to interfere, if only for Sadie's well-being. Yet it wasn't the People's way. Better for her eldest to experience a bit of the world now, before her baptism, than to be curious about it afterward. So she didn't persist on the night before Preaching. No, the house was dark and still, and should remain so, even though she'd feared Sadie had been out wandering through the woods that late at night. And not alone, more than likely.

Then, of all things, Sadie had commented on the sky and the clouds as they'd strolled to church. Ida couldn't remember having heard her eldest talk thataway, as if she had suddenly come to appreciate the handiwork of Creator-God after all these years. No, it wasn't like her Sadie to pay the heavens any mind; she never had been as conscious of nature as either Leah or Lizzie.

Since the church meeting was just next door, so to speak, she and Lizzie, along with the girls, had all walked down the road together. Ida had taken her hamper of food over to the

Peacheys last evening in the carriage, so her hands were free. Early this morning, after milking and a hearty breakfast, Abram had gone to help the smithy with last-minute details.

Here they sat, the women and young children on the left side of the room, waiting to sing the first long hymn, while upstairs the ministers counseled amongst themselves, planning who would preach the *Anfang*—the introductory sermon, *Es schwere Deel*—the main sermon, and *Zeugniss*—the testimonies.

All the while Ida couldn't keep her eyes off the back of Sadie's dear head—the strings of her white prayer cap hanging loose over her graceful shoulders. Soon, jah, *very* soon Sadie would be making her covenant with God and the church. Ida caught herself sighing audibly. Sadie was so much like Lizzie had been during her youth, it seemed—though Ida hoped and prayed her eldest would tread lightly the path of rumschpringe, not follow its fickle corridors as far as Lizzie had. Ach, there was ever so much more than met the eye to the late teen years. For some it was the devil's playground—wild parties and whatnot. "A sin and a shame," Preacher Yoder often said in his Sunday sermons, admonishing the young people to "stay in Jesus." She must see to it that Sadie finished instructional classes for baptism and obeyed the Lord in that most sacred ordinance come September.

Lizzie gave Miriam Peachey and her daughter, Adah, a hand with preparations for the picnic on the grounds. She and several other women worked in Miriam's kitchen, arranging great platters of cold cuts, cheeses, and slices of homemade bread, all the while conscious of the growing number of young people milling about the barnyard; many were coming into the age of courting and their running-round years. She was a practical woman who had learned early on to curtail any lofty expectations for the youth of the church, not put hopes too high on certain ones in particular, knowing what she did. Keenly aware of human frailty, she'd stopped focusing too much on the future, rather concentrating on the present. The here and now. After all, what you did today, you had to live with tomorrow. Ach, she knew that truth all too well.

Silently she observed girls like Sadie and that buddy of hers, Naomi Kauffman. Lizzie could tell them a thing or two if they'd but listen. Yet they would pay her no mind. Not now. They were basking in the giddy blush of youth, along with many others, delighting in their youthful heyday. Oh, how she remembered having narrowly survived those years herself. And sadly, after those disturbing days, nothing had turned out the way she'd ever hoped. Goodness knows, she'd dreamed of marrying and having at least a handful of children by this time. Instead, the prospect of her own family was fading with every passing year.

Yet, in spite of it all, Lizzie was the last person to dwell on disappointments. She tried to live cheerfully, bringing as much joy into the lives of others as she possibly could. Take Ida's quartet of girls, for instance. Now, there was a right happy group of young women, especially round the dinner table when she was invited, which she was quite often. She wouldn't think of turning down a chance to spend time at her sister's place. Oh, how they laughed and told stories on each other, Ida in particular, recalling their girlhood days, growing up with a batch of siblings—one sister over in Hickory Hollow, who at the age of thirty-eight already had ten children and another on the way.

Sometimes Lizzie wished all her siblings had settled closer to Gobbler's Knob, where—from her midteen years on—she had such wonderful-gut recollections. Memories of dewy green Aprils and gingery Octobers, though such memories soon became entwined with painful ones, the way quilting threads of jade, sapphire, and cranberry interlock with strands of ebony and ash gray.

But on such a perty day as today, what with the sky the color of Dresden blue, Lizzie pasted a smile on her face, made her way outside, down the steps, and out to the long backyard, where picnic blankets were already being spread out in the shade of the linden tree, its thick heart-shaped leaves crackling in the heat of the day.

She refused to waste a speck more energy on feeling sorry for herself. Time to call the menfolk indoors to dish up, then the women and girls to follow soon after. She'd sit down on the large Ebersol blanket and eat lunch with Ida, Leah, and Hannah, too, while Mary Ruth ate and played with the little children, and Sadie and some of the older girls sat in a cloistered cluster a stone's throw away, clapping out their botching game. She would enjoy the fellowship, such a merry time, surrounded by so many folk who managed to be happy, come what may.

Chapter Five

The train that ran between Quarryville and Atglen could rarely be heard this far away from Route 372. Occasionally, though, in the dark morning hours, before the birds began their enthusiastic refrain at first light, its rumblings along the track traveled deep through the terrain, across the miles to Leah as she rose out of bed, stepping onto the wooden floorboards. She heard the faintest whistle, ever so distant and just now almost eerie, as the air was particularly still, with nary a breeze to speak of.

Preparing to slip into her brown choring dress and apron, Leah was still aware of the far-off train whistle. Dat would be surprised if she hurried out to the barn and got busy before he did on a Monday morning, but she felt strangely compelled to get an early start. She had an urgent, almost panicky feeling, wanting to get out of bed, remove herself as quickly as possible from Sadie, who slept peacefully now after yet another late night. How her sister managed to attend to daily chores with only a few hours' sleep, Leah didn't know.

Oh, how she missed the carefree days she and Sadie had

enjoyed as little girls. Such fond memories she had of playing hopscotch on a bright summer day, spending the night at Aunt Lizzie's, and playing hide-the-thimble on cold, rainy afternoons. They enjoyed pulling little wooden wagons round the barnyard with their faceless dollies wrapped in tiny handmade quilts no bigger than a linen napkin, extra-special things Mamma had sewn for each of them. And they'd promised one day, on a walk over to the Peachey farm, to be best friends for always; "*No matter what*," Leah had said. And Sadie had agreed, her deep dimples showing as she smiled, taking little Leah's hand.

Leah longed for the days when they shared everything, holding nothing back. But Sadie was sadly "betwixt and between."

On Monday mornings it was customary for Mamma and Sadie to get the first load of laundry washed and hung out on the line before they even started cooking breakfast. But from the barnyard Leah could hear Mamma calling for Sadie to get up. Then, a short time later, through open bedroom windows, similar pleas for Hannah and Mary Ruth to "rise and shine" came wafting down to Leah's ears.

Returning to the kitchen, she poured some freshly squeezed orange juice for herself. Then who should appear in the kitchen, ready to go down to the cellar to lend a hand, but her twin sisters.

"Sadie's under the weather," Mary Ruth volunteered as Leah gawked, surprised to see them doing their older sister's chores.

"Either that or just awful tired," Hannah said softly, her scrubbed face still bearing the marks of sleep.

Leah wasn't too surprised to hear it. She wondered when the time would come for Sadie to simply refuse to get up of a morning. And this the day Aunt Lizzie was coming to help Mamma with gardening.

Hurrying down the cellar steps, she announced that Aunt Lizzie would probably be here for breakfast perty soon. "Did you remember, Mamma?"

Looking a bit haggard herself, Mamma nodded. "Lizzie did say something at Preaching that she'd come over and help. She also said you girls had stopped by the other day. Wasn't that nice?"

"Jah, Sadie went," Leah said.

"And I took some raisin-nut loaf up there," Hannah said rather sheepishly.

"So *that's* where my sweet bread ended up," Mamma said, getting back to work sorting the clothes but without her usual chuckle.

"It's been too long since Aunt Lizzie came for breakfast," said Leah. "I wish she'd come more often."

"Well, now, your auntie practically lives here . . . most days," Mamma replied.

That was true. Still, Leah felt right settled round Lizzie. It was like the calm sweetness after a spring rain. Jah, Lizzie was more than just an auntie to her; she was a close friend, too.

Leah sat on the long wooden bench next to Aunt Lizzie at the eight-board table. Usually, their aunt, if present for a meal, would sit to Mamma's immediate left, with Dat at the head. Today Lizzie sat farther down the bench, between Leah and Mary Ruth. Sadie came dragging down the steps scarcely in time for Dat's silent blessing over the food and sat across the table, next to Hannah. Dat gave Sadie a stern sidewise glance before he bowed his head for prayer.

Such unspeakable tension in the kitchen now, and all since Sadie had come into the room. Dat and Mamma weren't totally ignorant of Sadie's behavior, Leah was fairly sure.

Not only was Leah uncomfortable, she was unfamiliar with this sort of strain, especially with someone seated at the table who wasn't part of their immediate family. Mamma's other siblings lived farther away, some over in Hickory Hollow and SummerHill, others in the Grasshopper Level area, but it was Lizzie they saw most often, since she lived just up the knoll, so near they could ring the dinner bell and she'd come running. Thankfully, Lizzie brought a joyous flavor to any gathering, and on this day Leah was more than grateful for her mother's youngest sister sharing their eggs, bacon, waffles, and conversation.

Over the years her aunt had taken time to introduce Leah, all the girls really, to God's creation, particularly the small animal kingdom. But it was Leah who had soaked up all the nature talk like a dry sponge. She recalled one summer afternoon long ago when Aunt Lizzie had shown her what squirrels could do with their tails. "Look, honey-girl," Lizzie had said when Leah was only three or four. "See how they fold them up over their little heads like an umbrella?" She was told that the umbrella-tail protected squirrels when the steady rains come, "which happens in the fall round here."

Lizzie continued as they sat in the shade of her treed

backyard. "Squirrels use their tails another way, Leah. They settle down onto their haunches and toss their tails over their backs like woolen scarves to keep them warm while they sit on the cold ground and eat."

Young Leah had found this ever so interesting, wanting her aunt to go on and on sharing such wonderful-gut secrets. So she pleaded for more while observing the many squirrels scampering here and there, up and down trees, over the stone wall.

"Well, now, have you ever felt lonely . . . in need of a hug?" Aunt Lizzie sometimes asked Leah peculiar questions, catching her off guard.

"I guess, jah, maybe I have," she'd replied, though it was hard to think of a time when she'd actually felt alone, what with three sisters in the house and more cousins than she could even begin to count.

"Squirrels get lonesome, too, don'tcha think?" And here Lizzie demonstrated with her own arms how squirrels used their tails to hug themselves, so to speak. "Ach, such a comfort it is to them."

At the time Leah wondered if her aunt was also a bit lonely. After all, she didn't have a husband to hug her, did she? She lived alone in the woods, well . . . not quite in the woods, but perty near. "You must like squirrels an awful lot, ain't so, Auntie?" Leah had said after thinking about the special things a squirrel's tail offered.

"Who *wouldn't* like such cute little animals? They look so contented with their bushy tails high over their heads or dragging behind them," Lizzie said quickly. "But the dearest thing is how their faces look like they're smilin'."

Leah had never thought of that. And every time she

spotted a squirrel from then on, she noticed not only what their tails were doing but also the humorous half smile on their furry little faces.

Just now, sitting next to Aunt Lizzie, Leah couldn't help but wonder if her aunt could use a nice hug, maybe. How long had it been since she'd spent time with her, just the two of them? Much too long it seemed. Goodness' sakes, Mamma was always one to hug her girls, and Dat and Mamma often embraced each other when Dat came in the house for supper. Surely Auntie needed hugs, too—maybe more so than all the rest of them put together. She didn't know why she would think such a thing just now, but she did. Which was why Leah decided then and there she'd take it upon herself to squeeze Aunt Lizzie's arm or hug her neck, for no particular reason today. Jah, she would.

Sadie felt her father's eyes on her throughout breakfast. And Mamma's, too. Had they heard her coming home late again last night? Did they suspect something?

Breathing in, she held the air a second or two, then exhaled, wondering if Leah had broken her word and talked to Mamma. Or maybe it was Dat who'd learned first from Leah the wicked secret they shared.

She was so tired she scarcely cared; in fact, she could hardly pick up her fork. So weak she was, nearly trembling as she sat at the table, the smell of the food turning her stomach. How many more hours before she could lie down and rest, take a quick nap? This afternoon, maybe, while Mamma, Hannah, and Mary Ruth headed down to the general store in Georgetown. Leah and Dat would be busy outside, so she'd have the house to herself, if Mamma didn't mind her staying home. She must have some time to herself here perty soon. A good solid hour or so of sleep would help a lot.

"Five more days before we visit Mamma's cousins," Mary Ruth was saying, all smiles. "Cousin Rebekah wrote me a letter, telling 'bout the Bridal Heart quilt she and the others are makin' for Anna. Seems it won't be long and there'll be a wedding on Mamma's side of the family."

The news didn't come as a surprise to anyone at the table, really. Both Sadie and Leah—probably Mamma, too—expected Mamma's cousin's oldest daughter and her beau, Nathaniel King, to be published soon in their own church district, come autumn. Of course, they'd all be invited to the November wedding.

Sadie squirmed with talk of Anna Mast and a possible wedding. According to age, she would be next in line for settling down, and rightly so. Sadie knew this, though she balked inwardly at the thought. Her attraction to Derry Schwartz was complicating things. What was she to do?

Inviting Aunt Lizzie for breakfast proved to be a mighty good idea. Leah felt nearly satisfied after Mamma's delicious eggs, scrambled up with diced cup cheese. After the bacon and toast, she had little room for waffles. She took one anyway, sipping black coffee to tone down the sweetness of the maple syrup. She observed Sadie, who wasn't herself at all, sitting nearly motionless across the table—not saying much—during the entire meal, her face pale, the color nearly gone from her eyes, too. Hannah was her usual quiet but smiling self, reddish blond hair gleaming on either side of the middle part, though she spoke occasionally, mainly to ask for second helpings of everything. Mary Ruth, bubbly and refreshed from a gut night's sleep, entered into the conversation with Mamma and Aunt Lizzie.

Dat said nary a word. Too hungry to speak, probably. As for Mamma, she looked happy to have her sister near, and she mentioned that maybe Lizzie would like to come along next Sunday "to visit Peter and Fannie and the children."

Lizzie seemed glad to be included in the outing to the Masts' orchard house and wore the delight on her bright face. "Jah, that'd be nice," she said.

"We'll be goin' to pick apples in a few weeks, soon as Fannie says they're ripe 'n' ready," Mamma said. "Why don'tcha come along then, too, Lizzie?"

"When we make applesauce—can Aunt Lizzie help us, Mamma?" asked Mary Ruth, leaning round their aunt to see Mamma's answer.

Leah hoped her aunt would agree to attend the work frolic. There was something awful nice about having Mamma's younger sister over. She was as cheerful and cordial as Sadie was sassy these days.

"The Masts grow the best McIntosh apples, jah?" Aunt Lizzie said between bites.

"Mm-m, such a gut apple for makin' applesauce," Mary Ruth spoke up.

"So's the Lodi . . . and Granny Smith apples, too," Hannah said, grinning at her twin.

Dat looked up at Sadie just then, as if all their talk had found its way to him, disrupting his thoughts. "Most folk have a preference for apples," he said. "Ain't so much the name as the quality and flavor."

Mamma continued where Dat left off. "Bruised apples, ones that fall from the trees, don't usually end up in applesauce, ya know. They're turned into cider."

Sadie frowned for a moment, her eyes blinking to beat the band. But she said nothing. It was Hannah who caught the subtle message, and when she did, her head was bobbing up and down, though she said not a word.

Aunt Lizzie must've sensed the tension and remarked that even apples used for cider could have a right sweet taste—if they were tended to carefully, spices added and whatnot. She seemed to direct her words to Sadie, because she was looking straight at her.

Leah understood what Lizzie was trying to say. In spite of falls from trees and bumps from the hard ground, your spirit—if it had been true and sweet to begin with—could be reclaimed in time and with the right kind of care.

Aunt Lizzie seemed to know what she was talking about, which was the thing most puzzling to Leah. Gathering up the dirty plates and utensils for Mamma, she thought sometime it would be nice to know something of Lizzie Brenneman's own rumschpringe, back when. Of course she wouldn't think of coming right out and asking; that wasn't something you did just out of the blue, not if you were as polite as Leah felt she was. Still, it would be nice to know.

It was midafternoon, and Sadie, stretched out on the bed, woke up from an hour-long nap. How nice to have this chance to relax before Mamma and the girls returned from the store. Leah, she knew, was out puttering in the barn or the potting shed—two of her favorite places to be, though Sadie never could understand Leah's unending attraction to the out-of-doors.

Sitting on the edge of the bed, she yawned drowsily. She

regretted having told Leah about Derry. She'd made a huge mistake in doing so and she knew it. She and Derry . . . well, their relationship was much too precious to be shared with a girl who had no idea what love was, probably, except for a smidgen of puppy love years ago. She recalled Leah's youthful account of an autumn walk with Cousin Fannie's oldest son. "Jonas says he wants to marry me someday," Leah had said with smiling eyes.

"Marry *you?*" Sadie had to snicker.

"I know, sounds silly. . . ."

"Sure does," and here she'd eyed Leah for a meddlesome moment. "You, at the ripe old age of ten, are secretly engaged to Jonas Mast?"

Leah had grinned at that, her face blushing shades of pink. "Jah, guess I am."

"You actually said you'd marry him?"

"I can't imagine loving any other boy this side of heaven," Leah had declared, her big hazel-gold eyes lighting up yet again at the mention of the Mast boy.

"Puh!" Sadie had exploded. But now she could certainly understand such romantic feeling. Back then she'd laughed out loud more than once at Leah's immaturity, so green her sister was! How could you possibly know who you wanted to spend the rest of your life with when you weren't even a woman yet? Such a big difference there was between herself and her spunky younger sister. There was not much, if anything, that could prompt Leah to ever think of straying from the fold.

Outside, she found Leah in the tidy little garden shed close to where the martin birdhouse stood ever so high, next to Mamma's bed of pink and purple petunias and blue bachelor's buttons. Near the tallest maple in the yard, where a white tree bench wrapped its white grape-and-vine motif round the base of the trunk. "Hullo," she called as she approached the entrance so as not to startle her sister. She couldn't risk getting off on the wrong foot for this conversation.

Leah turned only slightly, her fingers deep in potting soil. "Didja have a gut nap?"

Sadie nodded, bleary-eyed.

"What brings you out here?"

Sadie sensed a chuckle in Leah's voice. "Just thought we could chat, maybe. That's all," she replied.

Nodding almost knowingly, Leah smiled again. "Half expected you."

Leah's remark made it easy for Sadie to push ahead. "I hope you've kept things quiet, ya know, the way I asked you to."

"Haven't told a soul."

The pressure in her shoulders and neck began to ebb away, as if Leah's words had opened a tap in her, unlocking an inner serenity. "Not to *anyone*, then?"

"Not Aunt Lizzie; not Dat and Mamma neither."

Sadie was ever so glad. Knowing Leah as she did, she'd simply have to trust that the name Derry would forever be kept out of all family conversations from here on out. The Lord willing.

Chapter Six

Peter and Fannie Mast, walking arm in arm, strolled out to meet all of them as Leah, her mamma and aunt, and sisters stepped out of the carriage. "*Willkumm Familye!*" came the pleasant greeting. It was nearly one o'clock in the afternoon when they arrived; the blazing sun beat down, making all of them a bit droopy, though the Sunday ride had been only a half hour long.

Jonas and his seven brothers and sisters spilled out of the kitchen door into the backyard. Anna, Rebekah, Katie, and Martha Mast gathered round Sadie, Leah, and the twins, chattering in Pennsylvania Dutch, while Jonas, Eli, Isaac, and little Jeremiah Mast hung back a bit, arms conspicuously behind their backs, merely smiling.

Dat unhitched the tired horse and led him up to the barn to be watered, and Peter quickly turned and headed in that direction, too. Fannie invited everyone inside for spiced cold tea. "You children could take your glasses and sit in the shade under the willow," she said, grinning over her shoulder as they all followed her through the back door.

"Our mamma must want some quiet talk with your mamma and aunt," whispered Anna to Sadie. Leah had overheard and wondered what that was about.

"Might be cooler outside in the shade, anyways," Sadie replied. "Might catch an occasional breeze, ya know."

Leah didn't have to be coaxed. Far as she was concerned, it would be ever so nice to sit and chat with Cousin Fannie's children outdoors, though most of them were either in their teens or nearly twenty, so they were closer to being grown-ups than kids. Still, she hoped for an opportunity to speak with Jonas again after such a long time.

Before they left the kitchen for the backyard, Hannah passed round newly embroidered handkerchiefs to Cousin Fannie and each of her daughters. "Well, now, what a nice thing to do," said Fannie.

"*Denki*—thank you," Anna, Rebekah, Katie, and Martha said in unison.

Mamma's face was wrapped with a smile. "Hannah just loves to surprise folk with her handmade things."

" 'Tis better to give than to receive," Mary Ruth said, leaning her head on her twin's shoulder, and the twosome seemed to tilt toward each other like two birdlings in a nest.

Aunt Lizzie nodded in full agreement. Then, in spite of the white-hot air, they carried their iced-tea glasses outside, finding ample shelter beneath the towering tree in the far corner of the yard. Jonas and his younger brothers, including three-year-old Jeremiah, sat cross-legged in a jumble, off to themselves a bit but within earshot of the girls. Sadie and Anna sat together, leaving Leah, Hannah, Mary Ruth, and the four Mast girls to sit in a circle nearby.

"Won't be long and we'll all be goin' to Sunday singings,"

said Rebekah, eyes shining with expectation. "Now, ain't that something?"

Leah nodded. "How many are in your buddy group?" She asked the question of Rebekah, forgetting she was only fifteen.

"I'm not in any group just yet," Rebekah said, grinning. "Best be askin' Anna 'bout such things. Or Jonas, maybe. They go to singings all the time."

Hearing her name, Anna turned round, as did Sadie. "What didja say?" Anna asked, dark, loose strands of hair dangling below her prayer cap at her neck. She looked almost too young to be thinking of marriage this fall.

Rebekah wasn't shy and said quickly, "Leah just wanted to know how many youth go to the singings in our church district."

"More than I can count, it seems" came Anna's reply. "Just keeps growin' all the time."

Now Sadie was talking. "And you've got yourself a beau, jah?"

This brought a round of muffled laughter among the girls. Leah noticed the boys leaning back in the grass, chortling ever so hard. All except Jonas. He was staring right back at her, motioning his head just now, as if he was trying to get her attention . . . that he wanted her to go walking with him. Was that it? Or was he shooing a fly away from his sunburned face? She didn't think she ought to be looking back at him like this, no. But she couldn't help it, really. And, jah, he *was* motioning to her with his head. Of course, now, none of the others seemed to notice, so caught up in the mirth of the moment they were.

Mamma wouldn't approve, not one bit, of Leah going off

with Jonas by herself. It wasn't the time to be pairing off. Socializing was done at singings, where the church elders expected young folk to spend time talking, singing, and getting acquainted with each other—boys with girls—after sundown in one of the church member's barns. Not here, in broad daylight, with the family gathered round, and now Dat and Cousin Peter meandering back from the barn, talking slow in Amish, the way the menfolk often did, walking right past them, across the broad green lawn toward the big white farmhouse.

When Leah glanced over at Jonas again, he was busy with little Jeremiah; then he was talking to his brothers. She heard him say they should all play a game of volleyball . . . a *quiet* game, with no raising of voices, since it was the Lord's Day. The rest agreed, even though it was unbearably hot. Right there they divided up teams, under the dappled shade of the willow, and Leah wasn't surprised to be chosen on the side with Jonas, Eli, and their sister, eight-year-old Martha, along with Hannah and Mary Ruth.

"Six players on one side, five on the other. *Allrecht*—all right?" Jonas asked, and everyone nodded in agreement. "We'll play in the side yard." Smiling, he led his little brother up the back steps and into the house.

"Jeremiah must be tired," Anna remarked.

"Jah, it's time for his nap," Katie said.

Leah thought it was awful kind of Jonas, the oldest, to take time out for the youngest. *He'll make a wonderful-gut father someday*, she decided.

On the way round the house, past the well pump to the side yard, Leah hung back, walking alone. Because of that, she happened to overhear Rebekah ask Mary Ruth, "Would you and your sisters like to come over and help sew up the wedding quilt planned for Anna?"

"Sadie, Hannah, and I might," Mary Ruth replied. "But don't count on Leah comin'. She doesn't work on quilts, doesn't do much sewin' at all, really."

The look of surprise on Rebekah's face amused Leah. "Are ya sayin' Leah never quilts?"

Mary Ruth lowered her voice, but Leah considered her answer all the same. "Nee—no . . . Leah works outside with Dat."

"Doing *men's* work?"

"You didn't know?" Mary Ruth asked.

Rebekah shook her head.

"It's not like she gets callused hands—she doesn't. And Leah never lifts anything heavy. She's not built at all like a man, ya know. She just helps wherever she can, alongside Dat . . . keepin' him company. That's the way it's always been."

"Always?"

"Jah," said Mary Ruth.

Rebekah said no more, and Leah was truly glad. She felt awkward having listened in. She rather wished she'd walked on ahead, up with Anna, Sadie, and Hannah, and resisted the urge to eavesdrop. Truth be told, she felt pained—stung, really. Rebekah's startled reaction to her working with Dat made her feel less of a woman somehow. Caused her to think yet again that she was of less worth because she lent Dat a hand instead of helping Mamma with women's work. At least in Rebekah Mast's eyes, she was.

Why did she care what Rebekah, or anyone else, thought? It hadn't been her idea—not in the first place—to choose outdoor work over the chores Mamma and her sisters did. It wasn't that she couldn't cook or bake or clean house. She could easily do so, if need be. Yet, after all these years, she felt she didn't fit in at quilting frolics or canning bees. Sure, she enjoyed making apple butter or things like weeding the vegetable and flower gardens and helping Mamma with potted plants. There had been no question in her mind whether or not to consider changing ranks, so to speak. At least not till just now—this minute—listening to her sister and cousin discussing her place in life.

Still walking shoulder to shoulder with Mary Ruth, Rebekah spoke up suddenly. "I think Leah's right perty, don't you?"

Mary Ruth shrugged her shoulders. "Guess I never thought of her thataway."

"Well, she *is*," Rebekah insisted. "And I wouldn't be a bit surprised if more than one boy takes a likin' to her once she starts goin' to singings. You just wait 'n' see."

"Maybe so," Mary Ruth said softly.

Leah veered off to the right, making a beeline for the side yard, where the volleyball net was already set up and ready for play.

She preferred that neither Mary Ruth nor Rebekah know she had heard every word they'd said. What Jonas thought of her was all that really mattered. Did he find her attractive now, after all these years?

The volleyball game was not so much competitive as enjoyed for the fun of it. That, and for one another's company. Leah was especially pleased that Jonas kept setting up the ball for her to tap over the net. In fact, she found it curious just how many times that happened during the course of the afternoon. She had tried not to let Jonas distract her from playing well. For the sake of her teammates, she attempted to put aside the flutterings in her stomach, tried to ignore them so her feelings wouldn't show on her face, where just anybody might notice how much she cared for Jonas Mast.

Ida was ever so glad to have a peaceful yet short visit with Fannie, drinking ice-cold spiced tea with Lizzie, too, catching up on things here on Grasshopper Level. Abram and Peter had long since wandered into the front room, settling into a somewhat serene dialogue—voices subdued—man to man.

"Guess ya noticed all the celery we planted," Fannie said softly, leaning her chubby elbows on the trestle table.

"Can't say that I looked, really, but 'spose you're thinking of marryin' your daughter come November, jah?" She preferred not to be nosy over family matters, but Fannie had never been vague about things such as this.

"Jah, Anna's our bride-to-be, all right."

"Lizzie, the girls and I will be glad to help with whatever ya need for the wedding day," Ida offered. When her own daughters became marrying age, the favor would be returned.

"Won't be too much longer and we'll both be grandmothers, I 'spect." Fannie sighed as she fanned herself with the new handkerchief from Hannah.

"What a joyful day that'll be."

"How 'bout your Sadie . . . has she caught a young man's fancy yet?"

Ida flinched a little, though she hoped Fannie hadn't

noticed. She didn't know what to say to that, really. And Lizzie was keeping quiet—too quiet, maybe. Seemed it wasn't anybody's business that Sadie was spending far too much time outside the house come nightfall, two . . . sometimes three nights a week. She wasn't about to share that with Fannie, whose children hadn't given them a speck of trouble during their teen years. Not yet, anyways.

"Back when she turned sixteen, Sadie started goin' to singings, and she seemed to enjoy it for a time. Here lately she hasn't been going." Ida wished she might turn the topic of conversation to something else completely, talk of other relatives or recipes, anything at all.

"Well, why do you 'spose that is?" came Fannie's next question.

Lizzie rose and went to the back door, looking out.

Ida shook her head. "Can't always put much stock in some of the young people. You know how it is before they join church. They want to have their fun."

Some of the young people . . .

Why on earth had she clumped Sadie in with so many others thataway? Fannie would surely guess that something was amiss—after all, her cousin's wife wasn't so thickheaded. She was a bright woman, a few years younger than Ida, who'd seen her share of trouble amongst the young folk in the area during rumschpringe. Just probably hadn't bumped into any of her own daughters sneaking into the kitchen door in the middle of the night, carrying their fun much too far.

Ida glanced out the window, watching their youngsters playing a game of near-silent volleyball. Her gaze found Sadie—tall, slender, and beautiful. What a shame that such a girl wasn't nearly as perty on the inside. Sighing, she watched

Leah for a time. Quite the opposite was true of her tomboy girl. A lily white heart, for sure and for certain—as perty as can be, whose radiance shone through to her pleasing countenance. Ach, such an odd pair . . . complete opposites. Just the way she and Lizzie had been in their youth. Not so anymore. Life's hard knocks had a way of pushing you down on your knees. Both she and Lizzie had become prayerful women, almost like good Mennonites they were, talking silently to the Lord God heavenly Father about everybody and everything.

Fannie broke the silence. "Peter and I . . . we're gonna have us another baby next spring—end of March."

"Well, now, won't that be nice."

Lizzie turned, a grin on her face. "Ach, how nice!"

"Haven't told anyone just yet," Fannie said, eyes bright with the news. "Peter is ever so glad. And Jeremiah will have a playmate."

Ida was happy for Fannie. The new baby would be the very youngest of all her many first cousins' children. Jah, a wee one would bring joy to all, especially at their many family gatherings.

"Have you ever thought of having another baby, too—maybe a boy this time?" Fannie asked unexpectedly.

"Why, no, guess I haven't, really." She was a bit taken aback by Fannie's bluntness. "I'm movin' past childbearing years, I 'spect."

"After four girls, wouldn't it be awful nice for Abram to finally get his son?" came Fannie's too-quick reply. "To carry on the family name."

Ida thought it but didn't say that Leah had always been considered Abram's son. That was fairly common knowledge amongst the People. Of course, Leah was blossoming more and more as a young woman here lately. Chances were that someday Leah would get weary of the outdoor work and start wanting to prepare for marriage . . . learning to quilt and sew at long last.

She found it awkward that Fannie would talk so. The truth was, neither she nor Abram had ever worried their heads over the Ebersol name not being passed on. "We've always trusted the Lord for our children," she said. "If God wanted us to birth boys, well . . . I do believe we'd have some by now."

That silenced Fannie right quick, and Ida was more than relieved.

Sadie was startled when a car drove into the dirt lane, and she wouldn't have known who the driver was if she hadn't looked just then between plays. Her side of the volleyball net was rotating positions, getting ready for young Isaac to serve the ball, when a shiny gray car pulled up next to the house.

Once she realized who the driver was, she had to will herself to turn her attention back to the game. But she only half succeeded and watched Derry Schwartz get out of the car and hurry to the back door—as if he was family or something. His boldness further shocked her. Nobody but relatives and friends would knock at the back door of a Plain house. Anyone else used the front door. But Derry hadn't knocked on the door at all; he'd gone immediately inside, as though Peter or Fannie had been expecting him.

How odd, she thought. *Does Derry know Mamma's cousins?*

It wasn't but a few minutes and he came back out again, carrying a large basket.

That's when Jonas called to him from the server's position, "Hullo, Derek! Did you finally pick up the strawberry jam for your mamma?"

Derry paused before getting into the car. "I was out this way, so thought I'd drop by," he said, his hand on the door. "Need to make some brownie points at home."

Sadie had no inkling what Derry meant by that. And she was trying her best not to call attention to herself, when Jonas invited Derry to set the basket down and come meet some of his father's kin.

Derry still hadn't noticed her there; otherwise, she doubted he would have put the basket of preserves in the backseat of the car and come over to meet them at all. She was afraid she might breathe too quickly and pass out, so nervous she was.

When Jonas brought him over to her, Derry only smiled and said, "Nice to meet you, Sadie." Just as he had before when meeting Leah, Hannah, and Mary Ruth. He'd treated her the same, as if she wasn't his sweetheart-girl at all. Just a distant relative to Jonas Mast and his family, playing a game of volleyball on a hot Sunday afternoon.

She could hardly stand there and keep herself in the game, especially when Derry seemed to catch her eye for an instant as he turned the car round in the lane, slowing some as he waved out the window at all of them, heading for the road. Jonas had introduced her English beau to them as one of his father's hired help. So Derry was working for Mamma's cousin, Peter Mast. Doing what? And why hadn't he ever told her on their many woodland walks that he worked for an Amish farmer?

Her thoughts flew ahead to the next time she was to see Derry. Would he explain why he'd pretended not to know her today? Why he acted as if he was meeting her for the first time?

Leah collided midplay with Mary Ruth, both of them reaching high for the ball. Her sister wasn't hurt at all, but when Leah lost her balance and fell, she wrenched her ankle and lay there in the grass, unable to move her foot. Jonas rushed to her side first, asking whether or not she could walk. Then, while moaning and holding her foot—the pain was unbearable—she bravely tried to get up and see if she could take a step.

But before she could, Jonas reached down and scooped her up in his arms, carrying her across the yard toward the house. "I've got you, Leah," he said softly again and again. "You'll be all right."

She nestled her head against his blue shirt, embarrassed to have fallen, and feeling nearly as light as a pigeon feather the way Jonas was carrying her so confidently.

"I'm sorry . . ." she muttered.

"Ach, 'twas an accident, Leah."

The steady throbbing from her ankle may have clouded her ability to hear, but she almost thought Jonas had said "*my* Leah" as he strolled up the back steps with her and into the kitchen. So maybe he *hadn't* forgotten their childish secret engagement!

Ida, Fannie, and Lizzie all turned and looked at Jonas bringing Leah into the kitchen, carrying her, of all things, their conversation abruptly interrupted. Ida was rather relieved to have a diversion from the direction their talk was taking. But, goodness' sakes, she was sad to see Leah in so much pain. What on earth had she done to herself? And what was that odd look of triumph on Jonas's face?

"Leah's hurt her ankle," Jonas announced, still holding her.

Fannie fairly flew to Jonas, instructing him to put Leah there in the straight-backed chair near the wood stove. "Now . . . careful, that's right . . . don't jostle her too much."

Ida and Lizzie were close behind, kneeling quickly to tend to Leah's bruised ankle. "Best to get the pained foot iced," Ida said.

"And elevated above your heart, so the swelling can go down," Lizzie broke in.

"Jonas, go get some cold packs down cellar," said Fannie. Once he was out of earshot, she mumbled, "And make yourself useful, for pity's sake."

Ida frowned. Wasn't it clear that Jonas *had* done his part by bringing Leah inside? Holding Leah's swollen left foot in her right hand, she touched it lightly where black and blue streaks marked the painful area. Silently she prayed—for two things: that Leah's ankle was not broken, and that Jonas's intentions were simply helpful ones.

Yet, bristling at the memory, she recalled the snowy January day—nearly six years ago—when Abram and she had brought their young brood here to Peter and Fannie's for dinner to celebrate "Old Christmas," or Epiphany. Leah had been only ten at the time, and Jonas thirteen—a new teenager. She'd noticed them looking at each other across the table off and on during the meal, grinning to beat the band. But then later in the afternoon, she'd happened upon them outside in the milk house. Of course, they were only talking, but it was that rapt gaze in Jonas's azure eyes that worried her enough to mention something to Abram later after they returned home. Her husband, who had already decided that Leah should fall in love with the smithy's boy, was mighty quick to give the poor girl a tongue-lashing. Much later, in the privacy of their bedroom, Abram told Ida, "Nothin's getting in the way of Gideon Peachey becoming Leah's husband. Not even your cousin's eldest."

She shuddered, remembering the fury in Abram's voice and eyes. He had paced like a mad dog, back and forth across their upstairs room, stopping only to stare out the window for a moment, then turning, had paced some more, his hands pulling on his brown bushy beard, gray eyes flashing. "I'll be fleabit if Leah doesn't end up with Smithy Gid!" he'd said.

But, ach, this wasn't the time to dwell on such a day. Best to keep her attention on her dear girl's painful ankle, get Leah into the main-floor bedroom, have her recline so her wounded foot could be propped up higher than her heart, as Lizzie had said to.

Chapter Seven

After Bible reading and evening prayers that night, Leah hobbled up the stairs before anyone could offer to help her. She wanted to be alone—needed a reprieve from the events of the day. The one pleasant thing that still made her heart flutter was Jonas being concerned enough to carry her into the house thataway. She thought again of her face against his shirt, his strong arms holding her safe, his words of comfort and reassurance. Why hadn't he waited to see if she could walk after she'd stumbled to the ground? Thinking back on the accident, she felt she might've been able to limp to the house, given half a chance. But Jonas had been so impulsive, eager to help her himself.

In the stillness of the shared bedroom, she stood on one foot—her good one—and peered into the hand mirror, trying to find the beauty Rebekah had seen in her. But the reflection staring back just now wasn't near as perty as Sadie's or even Anna's face, not the way *she* thought of a girl being attractive. Maybe it was because her sisters had such light hair; could that be it? But no, she knew within her soul—made no difference that her hair was brown, she just didn't feel perty. Tomboys weren't supposed to be attractive. The truth came home to her yet again, pounding its way into her temples, causing pain in her head as well as her wounded ankle.

Mamma and Aunt Lizzie were mighty kind to her during the next few days, insisting she remain indoors, keep her left foot elevated either while in bed or on the downstairs couch. They brought her breakfast, dinner, and supper on a wooden tray, coaxing her to eat more than she needed, probably, but it was their way of demonstrating their love. Dat was short-handed outside, what with early potato digging and the second alfalfa cutting coming on real soon. But there wasn't anything she could do about it. Smithy Peachey and son Gid came over several times to help out during the week, but other than that, the work fell entirely on Dat's shoulders.

Aunt Lizzie said she was willing to walk to a nearby doctor, have him come take a look at Leah's ankle, tell whether or not it was broken. But Mamma didn't think it was, especially since Leah could move her foot—wiggle her toes, too—without causing her additional pain. So it was mutually decided that the ankle was just sprained. "Which," Lizzie reminded her, "can be as painful or worse than a break."

After the first few days Leah yearned for the outdoors, in spite of Hannah and Mary Ruth showing her how to embroider, Mamma giving her pointers on mending clothes by hand, and Sadie and Aunt Lizzie teaching her how to make the tiniest quilting stitches—things she might've never learned till now, since she was rather laid up. So, in some ways, her sprained ankle was turning out to be a blessing. Providential, she began to think, and she was more determined than ever to become a real woman. The kind of woman Jonas would be proud to have stand alongside him.

She enjoyed a good many unexpected visitors throughout that week. Two being Fannie and Rebekah Mast, which was awful nice of them to come all this way.

The next day Jonas Mast surprised her by dropping by with two blueberry pies and a burnt sugar cake for the family. While he was delivering the desserts from his mamma, Leah, who was reclining in the front room, happened to see him just where he stood in the kitchen. Of course, Mamma put her foot down about him going any farther than the doorway, only allowing him to call to her—"Hullo, Leah . . . hope your ankle's healing quickly"—before he was herded out the back way.

Adah Peachey stopped in one afternoon and stayed for two hours, reading the Bible and some of her own writings—she called them "personal essays on life and other things." Leah found her dear friend's sharing so interesting, even lovely, and told her so. "Mamma just won't let me do hardly anything till my ankle's better," she explained. "I'm ever so glad you came to visit."

They were upstairs in Leah's room, where Adah sat on the chair next to Leah, who was perched on top of the yellow-and-green quilted coverlet. "There's something else I'd like to read to you before I go," Adah said, her sea green eyes soft and glistening. She opened an envelope and removed the folded letter. "Well, on second thought, I 'spose you could read it for yourself."

Leah accepted the letter, and when she spied Gid's handwriting she knew Adah's brother, still sweet on her, had sent it.

"Go ahead, open it. My brother has a nice way with words," Adah encouraged her.

Honestly, she was tempted to push the letter back in the envelope.

"Aw, Leah, for goodness' sake, read the note."

Lest she hurt Adah's feelings, or worse—how would Gid feel if Adah recounted this moment to him later?—Leah opened the letter from the young man her father seemed to admire above all others. She began to read.

My dear friend Leah,

Greetings to you in the name of the Lord Jesus.

I happened to hear that you are under the weather, suffering an injured ankle. My sister Adah promised she'd deliver this letter to you in person, and I hope you will accept this heartfelt gesture as one of great concern and friendship. Please take care to stay off your bad foot and know that our family's prayers follow you daily.

Very soon, you will be up and around, going to the Sunday night singings—you, Adah, and I will be. Mend your foot quickly.

Da Herr sei mit du—May the Lord be with you.

Most sincerely,
Gideon Peachey

She was touched momentarily by the tender tone of the letter, but she knew she ought not to reveal this to Adah. No, she knew she must be very careful not to lead Adah to think her brother had a courting chance. "Denki," she said softly. "Tell Gid the letter was right thoughtful of him."

Adah's face shone with delight. "Jah, I'll be sure 'n' tell him."

Her heart sank just a bit seeing the look of near glee on Adah's face. So then, no matter what nice thing she might've said about Gid's note, his sister would have probably misunderstood, so hopeful Adah was. Ach, Leah felt she couldn't win for losing.

The afternoon could've easily been mistaken for early evening, so gray it was outside, with drenching rain coming down like Noah's flood. Not even the hearty fork-tailed martins who resided in the four-sided birdhouse next to the barn attempted to take flight this day. They preened their white torso feathers, waiting not so patiently for the sun to shine again.

Leah sat in the front room, her foot still propped up with cold packs, listening to the boisterous music of the rain on the roof. She didn't mind being alone, sitting there embroidering yellow and lavender pansies on a new pillowcase. Actually, she was beginning to enjoy the domestic "indoor" work of womenfolk and wondered what Dat might think if she joined ranks with Mamma, Sadie, and the twins. She knew she'd miss the infrequent yet meaningful chats with her father, would miss them terribly. Still, she couldn't help but feel she'd purposely been kept away from her mother and sisters all these years. Besides being the "sturdy girl" of the family, she didn't know, nor did she care to speculate, on the reasoning behind Dat's initial plan to keep her busy outdoors . . . except for the farm permit, so she wouldn't fall prey to higher education, as Sadie had.

Just as soon as her ankle was strong again, she'd be right back outside helping in the chicken house and elsewhere. Meanwhile, she found she rather liked the glide of the needle and thread weaving a path through the fabric. She hoped she might have more opportunities to sew and quilt, though not with a bum foot for company.

◆

Aunt Lizzie surprised her by coming for another visit the next day. Leah was pleased, hoping for some quiet time with her favorite aunt. With eight years between Lizzie and Mamma, Leah had often marveled that the two seemed closer than Mamma and her other siblings, though some were only a couple of years or so younger or older. Goodness, how the two of them loved to joke and laugh together while out gardening in either Mamma's or Lizzie's vegetable patches!

There had also been a few times when Leah, as a young girl, had happened upon them and they'd startled her a bit by ceasing their talk when they saw her—embarrassed her, really—acting as if they were still youngsters themselves . . . secretive little sisters playing house. Made her wonder, though she had no idea, really, just what they were whispering. Probably nothing at all about her. Yet such things had been going on for years, for as long as Leah could remember.

"Didja have a very long rumschpringe?" she asked when Lizzie and she were alone in the front room at last.

"Well, I wouldn't say *long* really." Her aunt offered her a plump strawberry from the bowl she held. "I can tell ya one thing . . . I'm not proud of those years. Not a bit."

"Oh? Didja tempt the devil?" The words flew out before she thought to stop them. "Like some young people do, I mean."

Aunt Lizzie sighed loudly and turned her face toward the window. The rain was still coming down hard, hammering against the roof. "I wish I could say I led a godly life during that time. Truth is, I went the way of the world for too long. I should've put my trust in the Lord instead of . . ." She stopped then, looking at Leah. "You're comin' into that time of your life, too, honey-girl."

Leah was surprised to hear her aunt use the nickname. How long had it been since Lizzie had called her that? She sighed. "Well, I don't want to make the mistakes many young folk do," she told her aunt.

"'Tis a gut thing to wholly follow the Lord no matter what age you are. My prayer for you is that one of our own boys will court you when it's God's will."

One of our own . . . The way Lizzie said it had Leah thinking, wondering if Lizzie knew something about Sadie. But no, how could she? As for the Lord God having anything to do with her courting days, well, she wondered if Aunt Lizzie had forgotten about Dat's plans—that Smithy Gid would be asking for Leah's hand in marriage sooner or later. How could the Lord God heavenly Father have any say in that?

She felt she had to ask, wanted to know more. "Did *you* fall in love with a Plain boy back then?"

A faraway look found its way into Lizzie's big eyes again. "Oh, there were plenty of church boys in my day, jah, there were. One was 'specially fond of me, but he ended up marryin' someone else when all was said and done. Can't blame him, really. *En schmaerder Buh!*—a smart fellow he was."

"To miss out on marryin' you, Aunt Lizzie? Why, how on earth could that be? I say he was *dumm*—stupid—if you ask me."

"No . . . no, I dawdled, sad to say. Fooled round too long. He had every right not to wait for me."

Leah wasn't so curious about the boy as she was annoyed that her aunt thought so little of herself. "I think you're ever so perty, Auntie," she said suddenly. "Honest, I do."

Eyes alight, Lizzie touched her hand. "Keep as sweet as you are now, Leah, will ya?"

She wanted to say right out that she'd never think of hurting Mamma and Dat—nor Aunt Lizzie either—the way Sadie was bound to if she kept on rubbing shoulders with the world. But she said none of what she was thinking, only reached over and covered Aunt Lizzie's hand with her own, nodding her head, holding back tears that threatened to choke her.

When the day was through, long after Aunt Lizzie had gone back up the hill to her own little house, Leah lay on her bed in the darkness. Positioning her still-painful ankle just so beneath the cotton sheet, she thought of her newfound joy—needlework and mending with her sisters and Mamma. Of course, she didn't dare tell Dat she thought she might prefer to work inside, where she rightfully belonged. No, she wouldn't just come right out and say something like that to him. She'd have to bide her time . . . wait for the right moment, then feel her way through, just the way she carefully gathered eggs of a morning, so the fragile shells wouldn't shatter in her gentle hands.

Leah sat out in the potting shed, glad the afternoon shower had held off till just a few minutes ago. After returning home from school, Hannah and Mary Ruth had helped her hobble out to help Mamma redd up the place a bit before it rained.

"This place has never been so filthy," Mamma said, using a dustpan and brush to clean off the counter that lined one complete wall. Several antique birdhouses sat there, waiting for spring. A collection of tools—hand rakes, gardener's trowels, hoes, and suchlike—and a bag of fertilizer were arranged neatly at the far end, along with the family croquet set and a box of quoits on the highest shelf. And the shared work apron, hanging on a hook.

"I'll wash the inside of the windows," she volunteered, happy to be of help. Today had been her first day outdoors in nearly two weeks. She'd gathered eggs in the chicken house and later scattered feed to a crowd of clucking hens and one rooster, who, come to think of it, had treated her like a stranger. She'd never considered her interaction with the chickens before and burst out laughing as she sat washing the dusty streaks off the shed window.

"Well, what's so funny?" Mamma asked.

Just now, looking at her mother, Leah noticed yet again that gleam of contentment. Mamma was always lovely to look at.

She began telling how the hens especially had behaved oddly, backing away from her as if they didn't know her.

"Hens are temperamental, that's all. Don't make anything of it, dear."

"It's funny, ain't so?"

Mamma seemed to agree, her blue eyes twinkling as she smiled. "They ate the feed, though, didn't they?"

That brought another round of laughter. "Jah, they did."

Still smiling, Leah was happy to share the amusement of the moment. Seemed to her that she and Mamma had made some special connection in the last couple of weeks. "Mamma, what would you think if I told Dat I want to sew and cook and clean, like you and Sadie do?" she asked.

An unexpected burst of sunlight streamed in through the newly washed window, merging with the dust Mamma was sweeping up. "Sounds like you've been thinking hard 'bout this."

"I have" was all she said, and she found herself nearly holding her breath, waiting to see what Mamma's answer might be.

"Jah, I think it's time you learned the womanly skills. It's all right with me."

She felt more than relieved with Mamma's response. After all, wouldn't be too many more years and she'd be married, keeping house for her husband, sewing clothes for her children. It was high time she caught up on her hope chest, which was fairly empty at the moment, except for the few quilts and linens Mamma, Aunt Lizzie, and several other relatives had given as gifts over the years.

"Wouldja like me to talk to your father?" asked Mamma.

Leah felt she wanted to do it herself. "Denki . . . but no.

Best for me to see how Dat takes to the notion. All right?"

Mamma shrugged her shoulders, going back to her sweeping. Leah felt some of the burden lift. Jah, in a few more days she'd get up the nerve to talk things over with Dat.

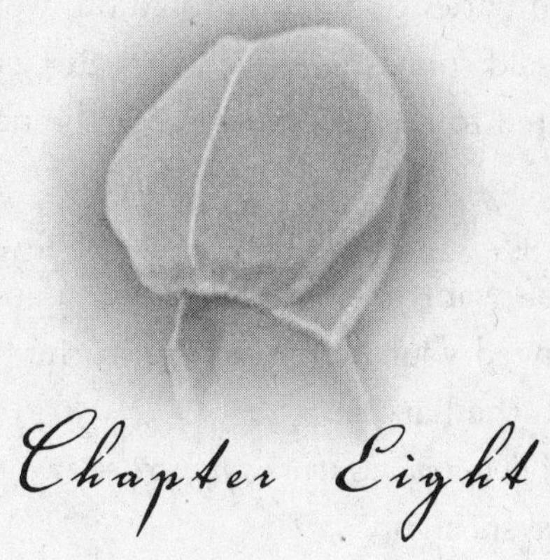

Chapter Eight

Leah's ankle had improved so much by now she was able to wash down the walls and floor of the milk house. She had to be mindful about where to place each step, hesitant to ask for help from the twins anymore, though her family was more than willing to rush to her beck and call. Stopping only to catch her breath, she gingerly climbed up the ladder to go sit high in the haymow. There she coaxed a golden kitten out of hiding and was stroking its soft fur, rubbing her hand gently down its back, when Dat opened the upstairs door and stood there with a serious look on his sweaty face. "Hullo, Leah," he said.

"Mind if we talk, Dat?"

He came and crouched in the hay, eyeing the kitten in her lap. Then slowly he removed his straw hat and wiped his forehead with the back of his arm. "Glad to have you back, Leah. Missed ya."

"Me too. I was just thinking . . ."

"I was hopin', now that your ankle's all healed up, that I could still count on you."

She waited patiently for him to go on, wondering now if Mamma had said something, even though Leah had made it clear she wanted to be the one to break the news to her dear father.

His eyes were flat, his ruddy face deadpan. "Truth is, Leah, as much as you want to help your mamma and sisters, that's how much I need your help out here in the barn . . . in the yard, and with the harvest."

Am I stuck doing men's work forever? she wondered, though she didn't dare speak up.

"If I thought you were going to marry in, say, a year or two, well then, I might think otherwise," Dat explained.

She was ever so glad he hadn't put Gid's name in the middle of things. "I don't even have my hope chest filled yet." The kitten's purr turned to a soft rumble in her lap. "What sort of wife would I be with no table linens or bed quilts? How could I keep a husband happy with no cookin' skills, not knowing how to make chowchow, put up green beans, or make grape jelly?"

"This you've been thinkin' through, jah?" A hint of a chuckle wrapped round Dat's words.

"Just since I hurt my ankle. Before then I was downright ignorant to what I was missing in the house." She filled her lungs for courage, smelling the sweet hay and the hot lather of the animals in the stalls below. "Now that I know how to stitch and mend, make Chilly Day stew, and bake date-and-nut bread—all the things Mamma enjoys—well, I'd like to have a chance to practice . . . be as skilled at keepin' house as every other girl in Gobbler's Knob."

Dat's jaw twitched a bit, but he looked straight at her, his honest eyes filled with understanding. "Are ya tellin' me that you're ready to be a daughter, too, 'stead of just a son?" A twinkle appeared in his eye.

"Aw, Dat . . . I—"

"What do ya say we make ourselves a deal?" He was more serious again.

She was all ears. After all these years, what would he tell her?

"What if you do the milkin' twice each day, gather the eggs, and if Dawdi Brenneman comes to live with us—and he needs help feeding and waterin' the barn animals—well, you could do that, too?"

Ach, she could think of a gut many things he'd failed to mention. Things like mowing and fertilizing the front, side, and back yards, shoveling manure out of the barn, washing the milking equipment, and much more. Did he mean to tell her that Dawdi might be up to doing all of that? Sure, what Dat had suggested was a place to start, so she spouted off what she thought he was getting to really. "Then, I 'spose the rest of the day I can work helpin' Mamma?"

Dat smiled weakly, nodding his head one slow time. He lifted his hat to his oily head and stood up, still looking her full in the face.

The kitten in her lap was not one bit interested in being moved or set free. Not when the sun's rays had found both Leah and the cat there in the haymow, where Dat had spoken some mighty important words, letting her know that *he* knew she was no longer a tomboy but a young woman. Truly, she was.

Goodness, she felt like jumping up and running round the barn. *Glory be!* she thought, grinning for all she was worth. Such gut news.

At sunset Gobbler's Knob was one of the pertiest places in all of Lancaster County, Sadie felt sure, with its view of the farmland below, dotting the landscape, shadowed in the gray-blue dusk.

She had become braver in her visits to the knoll, not waiting for Derry behind the barn any longer. She didn't feel the need to be led into the depths of the woods. After so many weeks, she knew the way to the hunters' shanty. Sometimes she arrived a half hour or so before Derry did, perched on the wooden ledge hewn into the wall. Or she might move to the windowsill, where she sat silently, peering out of the tiny square window, waiting for her beloved as darkness gathered over the forest. Often she remembered Derry's cautious yet compassionate remarks, told to her on one of the first nights they'd walked together amidst the brambles and undergrowth, all the things in the knoll that were dangerous, even deadly. Things like poison oak, wild orange mushrooms, a certain genus of herbs . . . and if you weren't careful, the way the darkness could creep up suddenly, almost out of nowhere, catch you unawares. "You can easily get turned around in here," he'd said, looking up at the dense trees, "or even lose your way completely." At the time she thought it was ever so kind of Derry to point out such things. She still did. It was as if he was looking after her, caring for her in a way that other boys wouldn't think to.

Oh, how she cherished everything he was to her, living for the hour when they—each of them—left their individual societies behind and sneaked away to the woods. To their secret place against an unforgiving world. They shared an unspoken pact now, a lovers' promise that she belonged to him and he to her. There was no one else for Sadie in all the world. And she was more certain than ever that Derry felt the same way.

Not even the coming rain, the wind high in the trees, disturbed her eagerness for the arrival of her beau tonight. When she and Derry Schwartz were together, she was able to forget who she was, really—to play a trick on herself and dismiss the truth that she was Abram and Ida Ebersol's firstborn, that sooner or later she would join church, marry within the confines of the Amish community, give birth to numerous children, carry on amidst countless work frolics with fifty or so other women, dress Plain forever, and live a life with strict rules and regulations set down by a bishop she scarcely knew.

Yet the reality of her future faded when she was with Derry. Then, and only then, was she free to be herself. Someone her own mamma would never even recognize, probably . . . a seething yet fragile spirit that knew no bounds. And when it came time for Derry and her to part, she attempted to grasp each precious moment, wishing she could lengthen the span of time, resenting the walk home alone, knowing she would gladly do anything he said, even run away with him, never looking back, she was convinced. She was frustrated at what she might have to face if Leah happened to be awake again when she tiptoed past their bed, slipped into her long white cotton nightgown, her beloved Derry long since having returned to his own separate world, his "I love you" still resounding deep within her heart.

You could lose your way. . . .

With trembling fingers, she traced the embroidered butterfly on the corner of her handkerchief, made by Hannah. She wished she might one day be like this butterfly and fly away, to just where, she didn't know. A place called freedom, maybe.

Counting the seconds now, she wondered how much longer before she'd see Derry running through the drenched woodlands, fast as can be, to her side. Would he ask her about her Plain life and heritage this time? Whisper of his anticipation for their future together? With all her heart, she truly hoped that maybe tonight he would.

The next day was a shining afternoon, and what a good opportunity to visit Leah's dear friend, once all the barn chores were finished. It felt wonderful-gut to have some mobility back, though her ankle was still tender certain ways she walked. Together she and Adah walked slowly through the moving meadow grass toward Blackbird Pond, out behind the Peachey barn and stables.

Leah shared her newfound joy of sewing and quilting, talking up a blue streak about all she'd learned in the last few weeks. Of course, she didn't share a thing of her hopes and dreams concerning Jonas, not with Adah thinking she might like to have her best friend for a sister-in-law and all.

"Wouldn't it be ever so much fun to live like real sisters?" Adah said. "Then I wouldn't feel so much like I'm the middle child, sandwiched in between Gid and Dorcas."

"I know how that feels," Leah replied, bypassing the real question. "Sometimes I think I'm nearly invisible in my own family."

"Ach, *you*, Leah?"

"Oh jah. I've always felt a bit lonely somehow. I don't rightly know how to explain it, really. Maybe it's . . . well, a little like the way Aunt Lizzie must surely feel."

"Seems to me middle children don't have any idea how important they are to their families," Adah said.

Leah bent down to pick a white snapdragon, growing wild in the expanse of grassland and flora, where meadow-foam grew to be five feet tall, striking the sky with pink cotton-candy-like blossoms in June. "Children comin' along behind the firstborn have their opinions, too, but seldom are heard . . . or understood," she said softly, unsure why she'd said such a thing.

" 'Tis awful sad to feel lost," Adah replied, reaching for Leah's hand. "You don't feel that way *now*, do ya?"

"Well, no . . . not when we're together." And this was ever so true. Leah and Adah were as close as any two sisters could hope to be. Sometimes she even wished Adah was a real sister to her. The *only* reason to even consider marrying Gideon, maybe.

Hand in hand, they came upon the glassy pond, where many a happy winter day had been spent skating and playing with the Peachey children. Even now, as teenagers, they would all be out sledding and skating here once winter's first hard December freeze came and stayed through February. Wouldn't be safe to skate on Blackbird Pond otherwise, since the water was mighty deep. Leah knew this was true, because Gid had held his breath for forty-five long seconds just so he could dive to the bottom and touch the muddy pond bed one summer when they all were little. "It's spring fed, for sure," he'd told them after a huge gasp of air, his face raspberry red from holding his breath longer than he ever had in his young life.

"We'll be together at our first singing soon," Adah spoke up.

"Jah, won't be long now."

Adah brightened. "We could ride to the local singing with Gid, in his open buggy."

"Best not."

"Well, now, what're you saying?" Adah demanded, letting go of Leah's hand.

"Just that I thought . . . well, that I'd like to go to a different one."

"Not *our* church district?"

"No, guess not."

"Well, we could still all ride together. Gid will take us wherever we want." Adah paused a moment. "Who you end up with after the singing . . . well, that's your business."

Still, Leah was worried Gid might think she would simply ride home with him, too. But that wasn't the way she'd planned things in her head. She must have a semblance of freedom, in case Jonas was in attendance, and she thought he would be, remembering how they'd talked together a week or so ago, when Dat and Mamma took all of them over to pick apples.

The morning spent in the orchard had started out ever so murky, she recalled, but by the time the Mast children and Cousin Fannie, along with Leah, her sisters, Mamma, and Aunt Lizzie had gone out to the apple trees with bushel baskets in hand, the fog had begun to lift slowly, allowing the sun to peek through. Leah had never had such a pleasant time picking apples, though they went to Grasshopper Level to do so every single year. She guessed her happiness had more to do with Jonas and his faithful observing of her all the while. Jah, that surely was the reason. Even now, as she remembered the day, her cheeks were warm with the memory.

Jonas had come right out and asked which of the October Sundays was she going to singing for her first time. And where? She had been at ease enough with him to tell him that the very first singing "after my birthday, I'll go. Prob'ly near Grasshopper Level." To this, Jonas had grinned, nodding his head, as if to say that was ever so fine with him. She'd taken his response as a not-so-subtle indication he'd be there himself, and if so, maybe he would ask her to ride home with him in *his* buggy. Well, if that happened, the way she thought it might, Smithy Gid would be out in the cold. Which, in her mind, was right where he'd been all along. Unknown to Dat, of course.

Sighing just now, she told Adah, "Denki for asking me, but I'll ride to singing with Sadie, prob'ly."

"So Sadie's goin' back to singings, then?" Adah seemed too eager to know.

Leah wasn't sure what was going to happen in the next weeks. Hoping against hope that Sadie might surprise everyone and follow through with joining church, Leah had thought of asking Sadie about Sunday singing here perty soon. Maybe she would tonight if Sadie stayed home for a change.

"I think you're gonna see a lot more of my big sister from now on." She said what she herself hoped might be true.

"Oh, at singings, you mean?"

"I have a feeling Sadie misses goin'. Honest, I do."

"Then, why'd she ever quit?"

Leah kept walking, didn't want to stop just because they'd come to the giant willow on the north side of the pond where she and Adah always liked to stand in its shade and skip pebbles, watching the ripples swell out across the blue-gray water. "Sadie's got her own opinions, same as we do" was all she said.

"I 'spect so," Adah answered. "It's all part of growing up, Mamma says."

"Ain't that the truth." With that, Leah tossed away the snapdragon she'd picked and sat down in the dirt beneath the willow tree.

"What're ya doin'?" Adah eyed her sitting there.

"Just come sit beside me . . . 'fore we grow up too quick."

Adah was nodding her head. "Jah, lest we forget who we are, who we *always* were."

Leah smiled, lifting her face to the sweet sunshine. Sitting here with Adah, she felt wonderful-gut all of a sudden, the cares of life falling off her back, tumbling into the plentiful grazing grass under the crooked willow and a wide blue sky.

At the corn-husking frolic that afternoon, Ida brushed off the remark made by Preacher Yoder's wife, Eunice, that Sadie had missed the next-to-last baptismal class. Seemed Ida's daughter's forgetfulness or downright apathy had caused more than one eyebrow to rise askance. Lest the gossip focus too much on her family, Ida quickly turned the women's attention to her most recent visit to Grasshopper Level. "Abram and I took all the girls—and Lizzie, too—over to pick apples at my cousins' orchard here lately. You should've seen us make quick work of 'em trees."

"What kind of apples?" asked one.

"McIntosh. Wonderful-gut for applesauce-makin', ya know." She went on, talking too much about the sweetness and texture of the apples found over at Peter Mast's orchard and felt downright peculiar going on so. Especially with all eyes on her, waiting . . . wanting a response to the preacher's wife's comment.

Their gaze was on her, boring ever so deep with unanswered questions. Why would a girl continue in her rumschpringe at the same time she was preparing for church baptism? Made no sense. Preacher Yoder—the bishop, too—would have every right to confront Sadie with simple laziness or even worse, indifference, if this wasn't nipped in the bud. The brethren might exclude her from baptism altogether. Ida knew that shoddy behavior and tendencies were to be reported, and goodness' sake, folk were already beginning to talk. She'd have to confide in Abram about this as soon as possible. Sadie's future in the community was in jeopardy.

Frightened, even distraught by her daughter's seeming lack of concern, Ida felt ever so lonely just now, yearning for Sadie to acknowledge her as a sounding board for whatever was ailing the girl spiritually. Not looking up at the women at all, she kept on husking ears of early sweet corn, hoping and praying there was some way to divert the conversation away from her *ferhoodled* and defiant daughter.

Chapter Nine

Leah couldn't help but recall the conversation she'd overheard between her cousin Rebekah Mast and her sister Mary Ruth that hot Sunday afternoon back toward the end of August. Seemed downright ironic that here she was driving horse and buggy over to help Anna Mast put together a wedding quilt on a Saturday, and both Mamma and Sadie sick in bed with stomach flu. It wasn't that she was filling in for either of them. She would've come along today, no matter. She was truly looking forward to her first quilting frolic.

A hint of fall was in the air. The horse snorted and *clip-clopped* along, and boastful blue jays shrieked at sunflowers growing near the road. Enjoying the short ride to Grasshopper Level, Leah was mindful of how this horse had been a balker back when Dat first bought him from Uncle Noah Brenneman. The steed had been doing fairly well the past year, especially when the reins were in Leah's able hands. Seemed he liked knowing Leah was in charge, which was a gut sign that her confident yet gentle ways with the animals hadn't been lost during the time she'd been laid up.

Leah was also very much aware of the quiet giggling of Hannah and Mary Ruth in the seat just behind her. "C'mon, now, isn't it 'bout time you two shared the joke with me?" Leah said, looking over her shoulder.

"Well . . . guess it ain't so funny, really," Mary Ruth spoke up.

"What's not?" Leah asked, thinking she knew now what had tickled the younger girls so.

"You sittin' up there in the driver's seat like Dat usually does," Hannah said at last.

Leah smiled. "So then, you're thinkin' you've got your very own driver?"

"Well, jah, could be." Mary Ruth leaped over the front seat and sat there next to Leah, still laughing. "There now, how's that?"

"What 'bout me?" Hannah leaned over Mary Ruth's shoulder playfully.

"There's room, if you want to squeeze in a bit," Leah replied.

"Jah, we'll make space for one more." And with that, Mary Ruth scooted over so close to Leah she could scarcely sit.

"Let's make ourselves right skinny," Leah said, holding the reins just so . . . holding her breath, too.

That brought another round of sniggers, and off they went—the three of them smushed together, but mighty happy about it—heading off to a daylong quilting bee.

"Too bad Mamma's under the weather," Hannah said as they made the turn off the main road. "Ain't like her to go back to bed after breakfast."

"Not Sadie, neither," Mary Ruth offered.

"Guess they must have the same bug. Or something they ate made 'em sick," Leah said, yet she wondered why the rest of the family were healthy as horses.

Going to the quilting bee turned out to be a wonderful-gut idea. Leah surprised herself, really, at how much she enjoyed sewing quilting stitches into Anna's Diamond-in-the-Square quilt. Come winter, the happy bride and groom would snuggle beneath its colorful woolen squares, cozy and warm. It made Leah wonder how much longer before Mamma might be saying they ought to start thinking about the number of quilts and coverlets Leah should have in her hope chest by year's end.

It was an exceptionally sunny day, which made for plenty of light shining in the front-room windows, the shades high at the sashes, as twelve women sat in short intervals round the large frame. Three of the quilters were Leah's first cousins from SummerHill—triplets, Nancy Mae, Sally Anne, and Linda Fay. Two of the older women, Priscilla and Ruth Mast, were also close cousins, by marriage, to Fannie Mast. Old acquaintances, longtime cousins, and friends all mixed together. Leah sat between her sisters, Hannah and Mary Ruth, near Cousin Fannie's three oldest girls, including Anna, who seemed to wear a constant smile these days, while eight-year-old Martha entertained little brother Jeremiah outdoors.

Still a bit unaccustomed to a sewing needle between her fingers, Leah was grateful to be here. Though nary a word was said about the fact that here she was on the brink of her sixteenth birthday, and yet this was her first-ever quilting frolic. She wondered if one of the older women might not mention something in passing as the hours ticked by. But the women were good-natured, seeing as how she was nearly a stranger to them—not by blood nor church ties, no. Only in respect to never having spent time at their frequent frolics and work bees.

Leah found herself settling into her usual comfortable silence, like the tiny green stitches she made that seemed to disappear into the jade background.

"Since America's war, ain't it harder to get nice material and dyestuff?" Fannie Mast said, across the frame from Leah. She asked this of Priscilla and Ruth.

"Jah, and the fabrics just don't hold up so well, neither," replied Priscilla.

Ruth nodded her head. "Colors just fade out in the wash."

"The sun fades 'em, too," Fannie added.

"I have seven quilts that are nearly wore out in just a few years," Priscilla agreed.

"Well, and such a shame, too, since some of my best stitchin's in them quilts of yours," Ruth said. This brought a peal of laughter all round.

When it was finished, Anna's new quilt would measure seventy-five by seventy-six inches. The border was nice and wide, and the corner blocks were big and bold. But what Leah liked best was the color contrast—green and scarlet against plum-purple. Such gay colors reminded her of a joyous celebration. Jah, that's what a wedding—a lifelong uniting of two cheerful souls—ought to be.

She was nudged out of her contemplation by Fannie's

cousin Ruth, who must've been talking about the fact that Ida was down sick with the selfsame illness as Sadie, "for goodness' sake." Then came the peculiar reference to Leah herself—"But we're awful glad to have Abram's Leah with us today."

All eyes met hers. *Abram's Leah* . . . Surely Ruth Mast hadn't meant that Leah was headed for a life of singleness, like Aunt Lizzie. She didn't see how they could be thinking such a thing today, now, would they? Not when she'd come to quilt with her sisters on her own accord and having such a wonderful-gut time of it, too. Till this moment.

The September day dawned breezy and a bit nippy, accompanied by a flat white sky. By midafternoon the heavens had turned indigo, a telltale sign that colder weather was on the way. Lizzie had gotten up at six o'clock, unable to stay in bed a second longer. An uneasy feeling had settled in round her, yet she couldn't put her finger on just why.

After a breakfast of fresh fruit, black coffee, and fried eggs, she set about cleaning her little house, going from the front-room parlor to the kitchen and back to her bedroom—redding up, dusting, sweeping, and changing the bedclothes on her big feather bed, bequeathed to her by her mamma. So grateful she was for the hand-me-down bed, glad for anything at all from her childhood home. Thinking on the goodness of the Lord, she returned to the kitchen and took a loaf of bread out of the oven, surprised at how quickly she was completing her chores this day.

"I'll have myself a nice long walk," she said, going to the pantry, which also doubled as a utility room. Finding her woolen shawl on the peg near the back door, she took it down and slipped it over her shoulders. Then she headed outdoors.

Large red-winged blackbirds fluttered from tree to tree, following her as she made her way toward the deepest part of the woods. Walking briskly now as she often did, Lizzie was conscious of scurrying animals, especially the graceful brown-red squirrels flitting up and down the trunks of flaming yellow oaks, playing hidey-seek with each other. In a couple of months, hunters would be up here combing through these woods, hoping for a nice plump turkey to take home for a Thanksgiving feast, and she'd have to find another spot to do her walking till all the shooting was done.

This time of year brought with it plenty of wistfulness, almost a feeling of homesickness. Her sisters, especially Ida, never seemed to pay much attention to the turning of the seasons the way Lizzie did. She actually looked forward to it, particularly the autumn when leaves danced and crackled, showing off their daring new colors. So she walked often through the woods—winter, spring, summer, and a scant few weeks in early fall, bundled up against the cold, somewhat sheltered by ancient trees that had become her constant companions.

She followed an unmarked path, one she sometimes took up to a little lean-to where turkey hunters rested and ate ham-and-cheese sandwiches sent along by their wives and sweethearts. A place where some of the men smoked cigars. She'd find the remnants discarded carelessly on the simple wood floor long after hunting season was over, having gone there to redd up the place a bit, even taking her own broom and dustpan sometimes. She liked things to be clean, even if the shanty was over a half mile from her own house.

Today she'd had no intention of sweeping out the old shelter, and she wouldn't have bothered to stop there at all if she hadn't heard what sounded like a raccoon or maybe a sick dog inside, whining to beat the band.

Pulling hard on the old door, she went in to see what all the racket was. And then she spied the most pitiful sight—a baby raccoon, tiny as can be, coming toward her as if it hadn't eaten for days, trapped in here away from its mamma. "Go on, s'okay, little one. Go home now." With that he scuttled past her, out the door, making a beeline for the woods. "Your family will be mighty glad to see you," she called after the downy, black-masked critter, wondering how on earth the poor thing had ended up inside instead of out in the forest where he belonged.

Standing in the doorway, she gazed after him till she could no longer see his bushy ringed tail. "Lord, please be ever mindful of your smallest creatures this day," she prayed softly.

Leaning against the door, she closed it behind her, knowing full well it would stick tight due to the current dampness, and soon she'd be prying it open with all her might when she was ready to leave. Still, she wanted to shut out the cold air and the sound of those raucous blackbirds high in the trees, no doubt waiting for her to walk home.

Suddenly overcome with fatigue, she went to sit on one of the wide wooden benches, noticing just how clean the place was since her last visit here. Noticing, too, how few human trappings littered the place. Usually she would find refuse in the corners—old newspapers, bottles of soda pop and beer, wadded-up paper bags and Baby Ruth candy bar wrappers, and the ever-present cigar stumps, smoked out. Looking round the small room, she had the feeling someone had taken extra care to redd up. It was uncommon for the place to be this free of rubbish. Someone *had* to have been here, taken their personal belongings, trash and all. Seemed ever so peculiar.

Not fully rested but ready to get home, knowing she had a long walk back to her cabin, she rose and straightened her shawl. As she did she noticed a white handkerchief lying on the floor beneath the bench, a delicate hemstitch round the edges. Leaning down, she picked it up, the cutwork embroidered butterfly catching her eye.

"Well, for goodness' sake," she whispered, recognizing Sadie's favorite hankie.

A metallic taste sprang into her mouth, the taste of fear. Slowly she brought the handkerchief to her heart, blinking back tears.

Lizzie took the short way home, through the thickest brambles; though, if she wasn't mistaken, there seemed to be a slight path cut through the wild brushwood, ever so subtle, as if a tall and willowy young woman had come this way on more than a handful of occasions. So then had her eyes *not* deceived her back several weeks ago? That half-moon night when she'd gotten up in the wee hours, too warm and restless to sleep. She'd thought she had seen someone running through the woods, past the foxgloves, past the high stone wall . . . a wispy likeness of a girl, lantern in hand. Though at the time Lizzie had wondered if she was just too sleepy eyed to put much faith in what she thought she saw.

Why must history repeat itself? she wondered, sorrowfully

making her way to the back porch of her house. *Why, oh why, dear Lord?*

The *caw-cawing* of the blackbirds was loud, if not merciless and grating. A swarm of them were so bold as to perch near her flower beds. But their heckling was not the answer she sought.

Sadie searched everywhere she could think of for her lost handkerchief. Unable to find it in any of her bureau drawers, she wondered if it might not be clinging to the inside sleeve of the dress she'd worn yesterday. But when she slipped her hand into the blue dress hanging on the wooden peg in her bedroom, she felt nothing. *Where'd I lose it* this *time?* she wondered, retracing her steps in her mind.

Then suddenly she knew. Sure as anything, she must've dropped it on the way up the knoll to the little hunters' shack, where she'd waited and waited for Derry last night. But he hadn't ever arrived, and she just assumed he had to work late for Peter Mast. Either that or something else important had come up. She didn't know for sure, though.

Now that she really thought on it, she was certain she'd taken the butterfly handkerchief along. And she worried that if she'd dropped it in the lean-to itself, someone might recognize her sister's stitching, so well known was Hannah's handiwork on tiny handkerchiefs amongst the People. If found, a body might put two and two together and know that one of the Ebersol girls had spent time there in the hunters' shack . . . and just why would that be? Especially since the drafty old place was supposed to be for grown men—Englishers—in need of a haven against the elements. A place to sit and drink a steaming hot cocoa or coffee. She'd noticed two abandoned thermoses on separate occasions recently.

To her the little shanty—*their* shanty—was a paradise of sorts. A home away from home; for when she was in Derry's arms, the world stopped spinning round, seemed to stand still just for them.

Now, in the dim light of the bedroom, she lay very still, awaiting Leah's steady, deep breathing that was sure to come. She stared across the room at the nearest window, where the tiniest crack of light from the moon had sifted beneath the shade like a silver splinter at the sill. She thought back to the night Leah had tearfully confided in her, telling of Dat's "arrangement" with Smithy Peachey. Gentle Leah was so close to her own rumschpringe. Just how would *she* handle her courting years? Would she submissively bend to Dat's wishes . . . be courted by the blacksmith's son—marry him and bear his children?

Sighing, Sadie wished she didn't have to change out of her nightclothes and scurry into the darkness. The evening breeze might chill her further. She'd felt so queasy and dizzy earlier. She stared at Leah next to her, almost asleep if not already. No need to have Leah wonder again where she was going at this late hour. No need to have more pointed questions asked of her. Not after the way Leah had lashed out earlier tonight.

Here, in the privacy of their shared room, her usually calm sister had gone much too far in her quest, asking . . . no, demanding that Sadie start going again to Sunday singings, spending more time with the church young people. "Why must you run off to the world for your fellowship?" Leah wanted to know, her eyes probing deep into Sadie's heart. Then her voice had softened suddenly, and she'd said,

"Won'tcha come along with me to my first singing, Sadie? *Sei so gut*—please?"

Sadie hadn't known what to say, so she'd said nothing. She was befuddled, torn between Leah's angry, accusing words, followed by the unexpected question, spoken with such tenderness. Oh, she wanted to be the kind of older sister Leah needed. She wished they might be as close as they had been in childhood. But now . . . *now* she was caught up in a world of her own making. She couldn't let go, even if she tried. She even struggled to breathe sometimes if she didn't see Derry every few days, wondering if this was how a girl felt when she'd met the boy of her life. A boy the Lord God surely intended to become her husband.

What seemed like an hour later, Sadie lifted herself silently out of bed, pulled on her choring dress and apron, and hurried outside, lantern in hand. Searching along the thin woodland path she'd carved out over the weeks, Sadie hunted for her hankie. *I must be more careful*, she told herself, mindful of a single oil lamp still burning in the back bedroom of Aunt Lizzie's cabin as she crept barefooted but a few yards away, through the soggy underbrush of Gobbler's Knob.

Out of breath, she finally arrived at the shanty, having not found the handkerchief along the way. She pushed hard on the door. Stuck! Turning, she set the lantern on the ground, then pressed her full weight on the door, leaning on it with all her might. When it gave way, she rushed inside, tripping over her long skirt. Brushing herself off, she went to retrieve the lantern and began to look for her handkerchief, hoping it might be somewhere near . . . where she might've accidentally dropped it.

She was beginning to think she'd made a wasted trip

when she spied something white over on the window ledge. The very spot where she'd sat and daydreamed, watching the rain drizzle down the windowpane, waiting for Derry. Hurrying to the wide sill, she found the butterfly hankie, folded ever so neatly, placed there for all to see . . . for *her* to see.

Someone else knows, she thought, her heart sinking. There was only one who would dare set out so far, past the clearing and into the depths of the knoll. Only one other person felt as comfortable in these dark woods as Derry Schwartz.

Part Two

◆ ◆ ◆ ◆

Their heart is divided; now shall they be found faulty. . . .
They have spoken words, swearing falsely in making a covenant:
thus judgment springeth up as hemlock in the furrows of the field.

—Hosea 10:2, 4

Chapter Ten

Sadie spent part of Saturday morning refilling the lamps and lanterns in the house with kerosene, in spite of her ongoing nausea. Mamma, who was still a bit pale, and Hannah and Mary Ruth were busy redding up the *Dawdi Haus*, the smaller addition connected to the main house, built on years ago when Dat's parents were still alive. But now Dawdi Brenneman was coming to live next door so Mamma could keep an eye on her widower father. It wasn't that Dawdi was being asked to leave his eldest son's place over in Hickory Hollow. The decision had come since Uncle Noah and Aunt Becky Brenneman were themselves getting up in years, and their youngest son and his wife were ready to take over the dairy farm.

So it was time for Dawdi John to come live in Gobbler's Knob. And all well and gut, for Sadie was fond of Mamma's father. At age seventy-seven, Dawdi wasn't the least bit ailing, and she felt sure he had many pleasant years ahead. Not even a trace of arthritis. Truth was, Dawdi seemed almost as spry as Dat on some days. Sadie hadn't thought of this before, but now she wondered if Leah had gone and pleaded with Dat to let her do less of the barn and field work and come inside to help Mamma. Jah, she thought that was probably true, though she didn't know just yet. Maybe that was even the reason why Mamma and Dat had eagerly agreed to have Dawdi come live here. Seeing as how he could help with the easy barn chores and whatnot in Leah's stead. Come to think of it, what better way for her sister to finally get her wish.

Sadie had to smile thinking of Leah's sudden interest in sewing and quilting, baking, cooking, canning, cleaning, all the many things the women were expected to do. Made her wonder if Leah might not be looking ahead to courting days and marriage here before too much longer. If so, she'd be attending baptism classes next year, from May to August, beginning after the spring communion, just as Sadie had.

As for the prospects of her own baptism, she'd suffered the embarrassing situation of having Dat quote to her Romans chapter twelve, verse two, all because Eunice Yoder had tattled that Sadie had missed meeting with the preacher for the next-to-last class.

A deep line of a frown marked Dat's suntanned face, and his gray eyes were as solemn as she'd ever seen them. " 'Be not conformed to this world: but be ye transformed by the renewing of your mind, that ye may prove what is that good, and acceptable, and perfect, will of God,' " he'd quoted. Out of the blue, he'd sat her down in the kitchen—with Mamma near—reminding her that the good and acceptable thing for her to do was to follow the Lord in holy baptism into the church, "as you planned to do." He went on to say that if she ever hoped for his and Mamma's blessing on her marriage, "whenever the time came," or on the *Haush-dier*—the house furnishings that fathers were expected to provide—then she'd best to *die Gemee nooch geh*—follow the church.

Humiliated and irked, she hardened her heart as Dat continued to lay down the law to her, and unbeknownst to her parents, she made a decision. Outwardly, she would meekly apologize to Preacher Yoder and attend the final Saturday session prior to baptism—where the articles were read to the members. The young candidates would then receive the consent and blessing of the membership into fellowship. The following day, Sunday—after the second sermon—Sadie would make her covenant to God, false as it was.

Wearing the weight of the world on her shoulders, she returned each of the oil lamps to their spots in the bedrooms, the front room, and kitchen. Back near the door in the utility room, she set down the big lantern on the floor for use if one of them made a quick trip to the outhouse after bedtime. Of course, Mamma preferred they used the chamber buckets; they were much handier than the outhouse when your eyes were groggy with sleep. And she would put lye soap shavings into each one, which kept the odor down but made for plenty of suds in the night.

Before heading over to the Dawdi Haus to see if her help was needed, Sadie sat down at the kitchen table and jotted a note to Derry. She didn't know when she'd be seeing him again, since he was working longer hours for Peter Mast, he'd said. Ach, how she hated the thought of missing him so. Why couldn't he simply meet her down at the end of their lane on the weekend, pick her up in his car, take her for a sandwich somewhere—spend just a little money on her? Or why wouldn't he think of taking her to the Strasburg café, where they'd first met? After all, it was coming up on one whole month since that wonderful-gut night of nights.

She wrote a quick note to send through the mail, hoping that just maybe he'd take the hint and return the favor. Oh, how she would treasure having a letter or card, something tangible from him. Something she could look at and be reminded of his love for her.

Dear Derry,

How are you? I'm doing fine here, helping round the house and looking after the roadside stand during the afternoons. I help Mamma get quilting squares ready for a quilting bee, coming up soon over at Grasshopper Level. That and fall housecleaning, which is always a busy time of washing down the walls, shining windows, and whatnot. My mother's father is coming to live on the other side of our house in two days—Monday afternoon. I'm looking forward to that.

Well, I must close now. But I miss you something awful. Thought I'd just say so and drop this in the mail to surprise you.

All my love,
Sadie

P.S. If you happen to have the time, would you like to drive over while I'm tending the produce stand next Wednesday? We could talk then while you pretend to be a customer. All right with you?

She didn't bother to read what she'd written. She was so eager to get the note folded and into the envelope, addressed and stamped. In the telephone book, she looked up Derry's home address, not knowing just where he lived. It was under the name Dr. Henry Schwartz that she located the correct mailing address, which was but half a mile away, up Georgetown Road to the northwest, then over on Belmont Road just a bit. Within walking distance, really.

Honestly, she felt she might do most anything to see

Derry again. Wanting to be alone with her beloved, she longed to be told yet again that she was the only girl for him, delight in his whispered adoration and his promise that "somehow, someday" they'd be together. Oh, she would willingly run the risk of losing her parents' blessing, even all that was rightfully hers, to spend time with the boy whose deep brown eyes held an irresistible sway over her, tugging at the core of her Anabaptist beliefs . . . at the underpinnings of her very soul.

Jah, she knew now what it was Derry had seen in her that first night. She wasn't just a perty face to him, no. They were cut from the same mold, sharing a common bond, in spite of their contrary cultures. In all truth, she was the murky, irreverent replica of him. He'd met his match, so to speak, and so had she.

Hurrying outside, she deposited the envelope in the mailbox at the far end of the lane. Come Monday, her beloved would hold her written words in his hands. What would he think of her invitation to drop by? Would he be pleased rather than put out with her being so *vorwitzich*—forward? Mamma would be ashamed of her if she knew. But Mamma *didn't* know, and if Leah even so much as hinted at taking back her word, well, Sadie would threaten her sister with spilling the beans to Dat—that Leah and Jonas Mast had made a silly childish pact between them. Jah, that would take care of that.

So Sadie had nothing to worry about, nothing at all, till Dat spied her and called to her, "Get your tail feathers over 'n' help your mamma and sisters!"

She didn't quite get why her father was so short with her just now, but she picked up her pace all the same and headed straightaway to the Dawdi Haus.

The chickens behaved much better this morning, the way they always had before Leah hurt her ankle. Jah, even the lone rooster was mighty pleased with her soft clucking as she stood there in the pen. Sometimes she actually liked to chatter to them, always quietly with a smile on her face. "Eat gut, now," she would coo at them. "Enjoy your dinner."

As soon as she finished her outdoor chores—less than half the farm duties she'd been used to—she planned to dash across the backyard to the Dawdi Haus and help Mamma and the twins, and Sadie, too, with the dusting and sweeping, washing down the walls and windows, getting the little house ready for Dawdi Brenneman. Ach, how Sadie's eyes had lit up at Dat's announcement yesterday that Dawdi was moving in. Far as Leah was concerned, it was a wonderful-gut thing he was coming to live so close. Because Sadie was in need of some wise counsel. Someone to take her under his sensible wing, since she didn't seem to heed Dat's admonition much anymore. Sadie did as she pleased these days. Take last night, when she must've thought Leah was deep in sleep, waiting ever so long to leave for the woods. Yet Leah had felt the bed heave, heard her sister shuffle across the room for her clothes, then head for the hallway and tiptoe all the way down the stairs. Listening for the creak of the back screen door, Leah must've fallen asleep before Sadie leaned low to pick up the lantern at the back door, stealing out of the house yet again. Headed to who knows where.

Mamma greeted Leah with a welcoming smile, though she looked rather tired and probably should've taken a nap instead of cleaning out the Dawdi Haus in a single day. "We can use your help, Leah. Why don'tcha go and strip the bed, then take all the rugs outside and beat them with a broom."

Hannah and Mary Ruth were cleaning the old wood stove in the center of the medium-sized kitchen, using plenty of elbow grease, though from where Leah stood, the stove didn't look dirty at all. The kitchen wasn't nearly as big as Mamma's. Still, it would serve Dawdi well if ever he wanted to take his meals separate from the family, though she'd be surprised if Mamma would hear of such a thing. There might well be times when Aunt Lizzie would come over and cook up a pot of oyster stew or Yankee bean soup. Jah, she was perty sure Lizzie would spell off Mamma a bit, take over some of the Dawdi Haus chores, probably. And here was yet another opportunity for Leah to practice her cooking and baking skills on someone who'd be happy, more than likely, to eat most anything she fixed. She had to smile, almost laughed out loud, and could hardly wait till Dawdi was just a hop, skip, and jump from their own back door.

Carrying the throw rugs down the steps, she saw Sadie coming up the sidewalk, looking for all the world as if she'd lost her only friend. "What'sa matter?" Leah asked, dropping the rugs in a heap on the grass.

"Nothin', really" came the hollow reply.

"Nothin', then?"

" 'S'what I said."

Leah bristled. "You sound miffed . . . are ya?"

Sadie shook her head. Leah picked up the first rug and went to hang it on the clothesline so she could beat it free of dust. "Sounds to me like you need a gut Sunday meeting."

"I'm gonna join church next Sunday," said Sadie.

"Didn't know you were thinkin' otherwise," Leah spouted, secretly thrilled.

"No . . . guess I wasn't."

"So, then, why're ya tellin' me this?"

Sadie shrugged. "Just thought I'd tell someone."

Someone . . . so is that what she'd become to Sadie? Just a someone, not the closest sister and best friend Sadie had ever had, before rumschpringe came along. "What's gotten into you anyhow?" she blurted without thinking. "What's *wrong* with you, Sadie?"

Sadie's eyes flashed anger. "I don't know what you're talking 'bout!"

"You most certainly do so!" Leah shouted back.

"Girls . . . girls, no need to raise your voices," Mamma rebuked them from the doorway.

Sadie turned and marched right past Leah, up the steps, and into the Dawdi Haus. Leah was left there, the mound of rugs at her feet.

"Didja think a yelling match was best, Leah dear?" Mamma said, walking toward her.

"Sorry, Mamma." She kept her eyes lowered, truly sad about what had just happened, though she didn't understand the extreme tension between herself and Sadie. Didn't like it one iota. Then, raising her head, she could see that Mamma didn't, either.

"Come along now . . . we'll have us a nice walk over to Blackbird Pond."

"But, Mamma . . ."

"I've waited long enough. It's time you told me what you know 'bout Sadie."

Leah's heart sank as sure as the clods of grass she, Adah, and Smithy Gid used to toss and let sink into Peacheys' pond. "Sadie's well into courtin' age, ain't so, Mamma?" She didn't have to remind her mother of the People's secretive courting tradition. What went on under the covering of night was always kept quiet till the last minute; then the second Sunday after fall communion in October, couples who planned to marry in November were "published" by the bishop. That's how it had always been in their Old Order circles, the way it had been nigh unto two hundred fifty years.

"Won'tcha consider confiding in me, Leah? I'm ever so worried."

"Well, I can tell you this . . . Sadie said she's joining church one week from tomorrow."

Such joyous news brought a flush of color to Mamma's cheeks, and she stopped walking and kissed Leah's face. "Denki for tellin' me. Oh, Leah!" With that, she promptly headed across the meadow.

Leah watched Mamma's skirt tail flapping in the breeze. *Sadie oughta be mighty glad I kept her secret all this time*, she thought.

Turning back toward the pond, she walked more slowly than before. She contemplated her mother's words to both her and Sadie a few years ago as they hung out the wash together. "*Remember, girls . . . purity at all costs*," Mamma had said. "*May be old-fashioned, but it's God's way . . . and the best way*." Mamma also said that a person with a pure heart could draw strength from prayer. The mention of God in such a personal way was odd, really, Leah had thought at the time.

Oh, she knew her mother prayed more than most womenfolk, probably. But talk of the Lord God heavenly Father wasn't something many of the People felt comfortable doing. Sacred things weren't discussed so much, except at church from the lips of Preacher Yoder and the deacon's Scripture readings.

Reaching the old willow tree, she sat down and watched dragonflies skim over the surface of the gray-blue pond, ever so glad she'd had something good to tell Mamma. What if Sadie and she hadn't exchanged heated words earlier? What if she hadn't known her sister was headed for the kneeling altar? But now Sadie would be making her covenant to the church, so surely Derry was out of the picture.

Thankful for that, Leah breathed a sigh of relief. Keeping Sadie's secret had tuckered her out but good, knowing that if something bad had happened to her sister, Leah herself would've borne the responsibility. Things were changing for the better, after all.

Chapter Eleven

Wednesday at the noon meal, Sadie volunteered to tend the vegetable stand by the road, "so Leah can help Mamma if need be," she'd said. Dat nodded his head, looking a mite bewildered at her eagerness. Mamma said that was all right with her, since Leah and the twins—once Hannah and Mary Ruth returned home from school—had other chores to see to later this afternoon. Mary Ruth had offered at breakfast to go out round four o'clock, "spell you off some," she'd said, but Sadie insisted she could easily look after things without any help. She didn't want sympathy just because she wasn't feeling so well these days.

So she was on her own, just the way she'd planned to be, having taken extra care to comb her hair back smoothly on the sides, tucking the loose strands tightly into the low bun at the nape of her neck. She'd worn Derry's favorite color, too. "The color of your eyes," he had said early on, after one of their first meetings. Now she sometimes wondered if he even noticed how closely the blue fabric matched her eyes on the sunniest days, as today definitely was. Temperatures had dropped slightly in the night, so she wore her clean white sweater over her cape dress, and though she'd come out to the roadside barefooted, she thought about returning to the house to pull on her high-top black shoes, first time the idea had crossed her mind since clear last spring. During the night there had been a trace of frost on the ground, maybe a bit soon for this early in September. Still, she remembered looking out the bedroom window this morning and seeing Dat's and Leah's footprints left behind on the thick green lawn. Now the sun stood high in the blue sky and there wasn't a breath of wind. The day had turned out much warmer than anyone might've expected. Who would've guessed the predawn hours had been so cold?

Farmers were in full swing, busy filling silos. Vegetable gardens were slowly emptying out and the corn was turning fast. "Buddies Day" came round perty often, when cookie-baking frolics and canning bees were plentiful, well attended by the younger women, especially. Sadie didn't mind so much making chowchow. Actually, she preferred cooking and canning bees over quilting, maybe because she sensed such scrutiny the past few times she'd been. She was glad Leah had gone in her stead recently to Anna Mast's quilting. Not that she was happy to be under the weather, no. Just hadn't felt like putting up with raised eyebrows and the unspoken questions that were surely being thought as she sat and stitched amidst a dozen or more women in fairly close proximity.

The last time she and Mamma had gone over to Hickory Hollow for an all-day frolic, *two* big quilts were in frames—the Sunshine-and-Shadow pattern for Mamma's friend Ella Mae Zook, the other the Log Cabin pattern for Ella Mae's twin sister, Essie King, both women distant cousins of Fannie

Mast. On another day the same group of women had gotten together at Ella Mae's to make a batch of fruit mush. Sadie's mouth watered at the memory just now, and she recalled that she and Mamma had returned home to find Leah turning the handle on the butter churn and feeling awful tired doing so . . . the closest thing to cooking she'd ever come.

Not so today. *This* morning, of all things, Leah had insisted on making breakfast for the family. *Erschtaunlich*—astonishing, really. Sadie had squelched a smirk, observing the look of delight on Mamma's face, the pleasant smiles from Hannah and Mary Ruth. But the fried eggs had turned out a lot harder than Mamma's usual "over easy," the way Dat liked his. As for the bacon, the long strips had gotten much too crisp, almost too hard to eat. Yet the family was as polite as could be and ate what was set before them, chewing longer and harder than they had in many a year.

Sadie was thankful for this time to be alone, out here near the road, wondering if Derry would come by or not . . . hoping he'd received her note. Going round to the front of the stand, she eyed the arrangement of long wooden shelves she and Leah had constructed late in the spring when early peas and head lettuce were first coming in. All told, there were three levels—bushel baskets of sweet potatoes and red beets on the first; bicolored pear-shaped gourds, as well as lime green, yellow, orange, and dark green gourds shaped like miniature bottles, eggs, and apples on the second shelf, along with acorn squash and butternut squash, late raspberries, strawberries, and blackberries. Turnips and tomatoes lined the third shelf. Occasionally, Hannah brought out a flat basket with embroidered handkerchiefs, offering them to the regular customers if they purchased more than a dollar's worth of produce. Of course, there were always the favorites—usually nearby neighbors—who insisted on purchasing the dainty hankies no matter how much produce they bought. Here lately, Mary Ruth had been baking a whole lot of pumpkin-nut loaf, which was selling out nearly as fast as she could bake it.

Just as her first customers for the afternoon drove up, Sadie moved back to the side of the produce stand. It was Mrs. Sauder and Mrs. Kraybill, two of their most frequent visitors, just down the road about a mile and a half to the southeast. Mrs. Sauder was always headed somewhere, like Strasburg, running errands with two preschool-age children in the backseat, "before my hubby gets home from work," she would say. Mrs. Kraybill was the Mennonite neighbor who drove Hannah and Mary Ruth to school three days a week. Dat, on the other two days, took the twins to school in his market wagon on his way up to Bird-in-Hand.

"What'll it be today?" Sadie asked, folding her hands and waiting while the women looked things over.

"Oh, I think I'll have several pints of strawberries and blackberries," said Mrs. Sauder.

"Makin' some pies, then?" asked Sadie.

"My husband loves his fruit pies. So do the children." Here, Mrs. Sauder motioned toward little Jimmy and Dottie, who were grinning up at Sadie from the car.

After Mrs. Kraybill chose her fresh vegetables for the week, a steady stream of folk began to stop by. It seemed to Sadie that the gourds and squash were in greatest demand, and by two o'clock, once she'd sold what was left of them, the berries and tomatoes were almost gone, too.

Standing there, reshuffling the remaining items, Sadie was

a bit surprised, yet very pleased, to look up and see Derry's gray automobile pulling onto the shoulder of the road. At once she noticed his plaid wool jacket and cuffed blue jeans as he strolled toward her. Usually when she saw him he was wearing a short-sleeved shirt and sometimes a nicer pair of trousers. But today he'd dressed as if he had made the trip just to see her instead of having come straight from work.

She looked at him and smiled, waiting for him to speak first.

"Hi, Sadie," he said.

"Hullo." Her eyes searched his.

"I almost didn't drop by today."

Was it the note she'd sent? Was he displeased?

"Well, I'm glad you did," she said. "Care for some sweet potatoes or turnips for your mother?"

Nodding his head, he dug his hand in his pocket, pulling out some change. "Here, take whatever you're asking for them."

"No . . . no, I didn't mean it thataway. I meant for you to take something home for supper, to your family, from me . . . to them."

He broke into a big smile then, warming her heart. "Thanks, but I can pay." He chose a turnip and a handful of yams.

"You'll enjoy a tasty meal tonight." She felt odd making small talk, aware of the awkward strain between them.

"I received your letter." His voice had turned suddenly flat. "My mother saw it first, in the mailbox."

"Oh . . . I'm sorry if—"

"From now on, it would be best if you didn't send anything through the mail. Wait until I contact *you*."

So she had been too bold. But with no telephone, no other way to keep in touch with him except the mail, how were they to communicate? Seemed to her the last couple of times they'd talked, it had been too easy to offend him, though she didn't know why . . . and it was much harder to make amends.

He turned to leave, heading back to his car, carrying turnips and sweet potatoes in the brown bag she'd given him. Should she say again that she was ever so sorry? Plead with him? Mamma would say no, plain and simple. It wasn't a gut thing to be *schandlos*—shameless—with a young man. Yet Sadie would like to hear him say good-bye to her at least. Anything at all. But something in her knew that if she dared to call out, she might not see him again. And she could never live with that. So she remained silent, the lump in her throat crowding out her very breath.

Please come back, she thought, fighting tears.

He started up the engine and drove slowly to the front of the stand, stopped, leaned his head down, and called to her through the open window on the passenger side, "Hop in, Sadie. Let's go for a spin."

A ride in his car? Ach, he still loved her!

She wanted to abandon her post and go with him, wherever he was headed. Yet what would her sisters think if she turned up missing? And worse, what would Mamma say if she left the remaining vegetables unattended? Then she knew what she could do. It was the clever thing Miriam and Adah Peachey did many a time when they were too busy with house or garden chores to just wait for customers. They made a sign, which was exactly what she did, too.

"I best be pricing the produce," she told him, overjoyed

that he wanted her with him. This day was turning out far better than she would've ever dreamed.

Reaching over, he opened the glove compartment of his car and took out a tablet of paper and a pen. "Here, price away."

She propped up one of the homemade signs against the turnips. It read, *Self-service today. Pay on the honor system.*

Suddenly she felt ever so merry. More than she had for quite some time. The afternoon would be wonderful-gut, she could just tell now by the glow in Derry's eyes. Jah, already the landscape looked brighter round them, as if someone had sprinkled golden sunbeams all over the cornstalks.

The school day was over promptly at three-thirty, and Hannah and her twin rode home with their Mennonite neighbors, whose children also attended the Georgetown School. As they made the turn off the road into their lane, Hannah noticed that the produce stand wasn't being looked after. *That's odd,* she thought.

The twins thanked Mrs. Kraybill for the ride, then headed into the house, kissed Mamma, and placed their school books on the kitchen table.

"How was your day at school?" Mamma asked in the midst of stirring up a chocolate dessert.

"Oh, we spent most of the day reviewing simple algebra," Mary Ruth said.

"Was it easy for *you*, Hannah?" asked Mamma.

"Not so much, no," Hannah answered. "Mary Ruth's much better at numbers, you know."

Mamma raised her eyebrows. "Algebra sounds like high school to me."

"It's required, is what the teacher says," Mary Ruth spoke up, and Hannah wished her sister would just leave it be. Mamma didn't need to know how awful exciting such hard problems were to Mary Ruth.

"Well, all I'll say is do your best . . . but don't be lookin' to go past the eighth grade. That's enough book learnin' for Plain girls." Mamma motioned to Hannah right then. "Run out and tell Sadie to come inside, will ya? I'm baking a triple batch of fudge meltaways, and I don't recall the creamy filling part."

"Does Sadie know?" Hannah asked.

Mary Ruth was nodding her head that jah, their big sister would definitely recall the ingredients for the filling.

"I'll see if I can fetch her, then," Hannah said, heading out the kitchen door.

So intent was she on finding Sadie, Hannah almost missed seeing the handwritten note propped against the turnips at the produce stand. "What's this?" she whispered, wondering where her sister might've gone, leaving a note for their frequent and loyal customers of all things. This wasn't satisfactory, not the way they were taught to do. Dat would be displeased, even though they knew of others who didn't bother to oversee a roadside stand for hours on end. But that just didn't seem considerate, somehow. Now what was she to tell Mamma, who'd sent her out here to trade off with Sadie?

Looking up and down the road, even going out on the hot pavement barefooted, she strained to see if her sister might've taken herself off for a short walk in either direction. But there were only acres and acres of corn, the golden brown tassels floating in the gentle breeze. And up the way, farmers threshing their golden wheat.

"Where could she have gone?" she said aloud. "Where?"

She shuddered to think that she'd have to tell Mamma about this. Turning, she ran back to the house to first tell Mary Ruth, who was raking the side yard, that Sadie had plumb disappeared. Then, realizing the seriousness of what this might mean, and having received an alarming reaction from her twin, the two of them rushed into the kitchen. There they found Mamma reciting the old recipe by heart, as if saying the ingredients out loud might help her remember every part.

"Mamma! Hannah says Sadie's gone—left the produce stand without tellin' a soul," Mary Ruth exclaimed.

Mamma's frown was hard against her forehead. "Hannah?" she said, looking right at her, all ears.

"Jah, Sadie left a sign for the customers." Hannah nodded her head. "I looked all round, but she's nowhere to be seen."

Mamma's shoulders slumped about two inches. "Well, she's gotta be *somewhere*, ain't so?"

But then and there, the plight of missing Sadie was dropped. Almost faster than Hannah could grasp, really. She was promptly sent back out to the road to remove the sign and stand there to greet folk and make change and whatnot. And Mary Ruth was the one chosen to help Mamma with the chocolaty coconut recipe. All the while Hannah kept thinking Leah didn't know about Sadie's being gone. Dat, neither. What would they think? Would they worry as Hannah was doing now? And as Mamma was, too, though trying to hide her concern. Surely Sadie hadn't been forced to leave against her will. Or had she?

Something truly peculiar had been happening the last full month; Hannah knew that for sure. Her big sister was off somewhere else, at least in her head she was, and most all the time. Maybe that was about to change, though, because from what Mamma had said recently, Sadie was headed for church membership in just four days. Jah, she'd be in the line for baptism come this Sunday, which made Hannah feel ever so much better now, thinking on it . . . even with Sadie gone from where she usually stood behind the hearty turnips and juicy red tomatoes.

Derry drove Sadie all the way out to Pinnacle Overlook, near Holtwood, where they stood high on a cliff and gazed out at the Susquehanna River, an expanse of greenish gray water beneath a robin-egg blue sky. He took her by surprise, whispering in her ear that he loved her and was sorry about what he'd said earlier . . . about his mother discovering the note in the mailbox and all. He seemed to want to make up for his hasty words and kissed her softly on the cheek when tears in her eyes threatened to spill down her face. He held her hand as they strolled along. All was forgiven again.

"Uncle Sam wants me after Christmas," he said when they were back in the car, speeding down the highway.

"Your uncle?"

He pursed his lips and motioned her over next to him. And she did. She slid across the front seat and sat right beside him, snuggling close when he put his arm round her shoulders. She listened carefully to his curious explanation that Uncle Sam actually stood for the United States—"Understand now, Sadie?" Ach, he could be so dear when he wanted to be.

But what he said next left her completely shaken. "You're gonna join up with the soldiers?" she said.

"That's right. I'm enlisting into the United States Army the minute I turn eighteen."

"But I thought—you and I . . ."

"Aw, Sadie, it won't be forever. You'll see."

"So, then, are you sayin' I'll know where you'll be?"

He turned toward her then, his breath sweet on her face. "Sure, I'll write to you twice a day."

His tender promise touched her deeply, so much so she nearly forgot his plans with the American uncle. She was more than willing to remove her prayer cap as they rode along, letting down her waist-length hair just for him. She took pleasure in the warm breeze coming in through the car windows, blowing her long locks back away from her face, breathing in the spicy scent of early autumn.

Derry was a fast driver but awful gut at it as he steered with one hand on the wheel, the other caressing her shoulder. If today he asked her to be his wife, she'd say she would marry him, let the chips fall where they may. Truth was, come Sunday she was joining church, so if she ran off and married him after that, she'd be shunned for sure. Even still, she had to go ahead with baptism for Dat's and Mamma's sake, if nothing else.

Such worry faded quickly with his kisses. She knew once again, in her heart of hearts, Derry was her one and only love, for always.

Chapter Twelve

The night of Leah's sixteenth birthday she dreamed of her hope chest, newly filled with birthday treasures, though still rather bare compared to Sadie's. In the dream, the daring sun peeked its golden head into each of the bedroom windows, shining forth a brilliant shaft at the foot of the double bed, where both girls' pine chests stood, side by side. Glancing at Sadie's, she found herself eager to look inside. She wanted to compare her gifts with the many items Sadie had made and received over the years. Leaning down, she opened the heavy wood lid, and there before her eyes were the beautiful contents of Sadie's years of hard work.

Still dreaming, Leah dug even deeper, suddenly startled to see all of her *own* perty birthday remembrances, each and every one . . . inside *Sadie's* hope chest. She lifted out the lovely hand-sewn pillow tops, crocheted doilies, and other linens she'd just received from Aunt Lizzie, Aunt Becky, and other aunts on both sides of the family, as well as from Fannie Mast and Miriam Peachey. She was especially delighted with Adah Peachey's embroidered floral pillowcases and the yellow quilted potholders and matching mitts from Mary Ruth and Sadie. Hannah had her own surprise for Leah. Seven perty handkerchiefs, one for every day of the week. Mamma, too, gave a useful gift—a complete set of sheets, with pillowcases to match, a woolen blanket, and a quilted coverlet. Here they were, all neatly folded inside her sister's chest.

"Ach, Sadie . . . what have you done?" She began to cry. Her sister had somehow taken away her few cherished gifts. The sky was a sudden gray, and she was terribly afraid.

Awakening, she sat straight up in bed, breathing ever so hard and looking round the dark room. It was nighttime, not noonday at all. And Sadie was next to her, sleeping quietly. Tempted to slip out of bed and investigate the two wooden chests, she was aware of the beating of her heart. But the longer she sat there, the more she realized the dream had only *seemed* real—the result of having a second helping of Mamma's dessert surprise. A wonderful-gut pineapple upside-down cake with fresh whipped cream. No need to think twice about such a dream. She turned on her side, facing away from Sadie, and hugged herself. *May my dreams be sweet now, Father God,* she breathed a prayer and closed her eyes, falling asleep once again.

◆

The morning of Sadie's baptism was as gloomy and rainy a Sunday as any she ever recalled. Seemed to her the heavens were already unleashing divine wrath upon her as she stood in the line, waiting with five other girls to take their places in the center section over near the minister's bench. Just now she felt an overwhelming need to *rutsche*—squirm—but her memory served her all too well. During many a Sunday Preaching service, when she was little and not able to sit as perfectly still as Mamma would expect her to, Sadie had received Mamma's firm pinch on her leg. She could almost feel the smarting pain even now, a bleak reminder of her indifference to those things her parents deemed sacred.

A holy hush came over the room. The applicants for baptism prepared to turn their backs on the world and all its pleasures, saying a resounding "Jah" to the Lord Jesus and the Ordnung—the unwritten rules for holy living.

Preacher Yoder had literally pounded away at the aspects of covenant making, as stated in the Old Testament, teaching them that a vow made had lifelong consequences if broken. "To disobey the church would mean death to the soul."

Obey or die. . . .

There had been exhortation from Dat, too, Sadie recalled. He'd sat her down just yesterday and read aloud from Genesis chapter fifteen, where Jehovah God made a covenant with Abram of old. The blood of a young heifer, goat, and ram, along with a dove and a pigeon, had been spilt. Then a blazing torch, representing the Holy One, had appeared and passed through the blood path, sealing the covenant. "Making a covenant with the Lord God heavenly Father is a very serious matter," Dat had said. Yet she had remained silent.

Kneeling before the bishop and his wife, Sadie battled in her spirit, caught betwixt right and wrong, good and evil. But she went ahead with her baptism, making good on her parents' hopes and wishes for her—paying merely lip service, so unable was she to deny her desperate love for Derry Schwartz.

A few weeks later Gideon Peachey and his father worked together, chopping and stacking wood, a backbreaking chore. Keeping his eye on the log, Gid swung the ax down hard in one mighty blow, splitting the log apart at the center, the way his pop had taught him to do.

Close to one o'clock Gid happened to look up and see Abram Ebersol coming across the pastureland, cutting through the side meadow and round the barnyard to where they worked, a long stone's throw from the barn. "Willkumm!" he and his father called at once.

Abram moseyed over and offered to lend a hand. Gid was glad for the extra help, since there was more wood to hew than he and Dat could possibly split in three hours' time, and the afternoon milking would be rolling round here before too long.

Nodding, Abram smiled stiffly. "Thought I could make myself useful."

Gid cheerfully gave Abram a spare ax, and the two of them worked on the pile of wood while Dat went to stacking. They kept at it for an hour and a half before Mam brought tall glasses of sweetened iced tea for each of them. Mopping his brow, Gid glanced at the man who might be his father-in-law someday. If Leah Ebersol would have him, that is. From the moment his father's and Abram's plan had been revealed to Gid, marrying Leah had appealed to him. He hadn't let on to either Dat or Abram that long before his school days he'd had his eye on the perty brunette girl who lived just across their grazing land. Of the four Ebersol sisters, Leah was the one who'd most caught his attention. Same thing once they started attending school together. Leah had been the kindest, most pleasant of all the girls in his class, which wasn't taking into account whatsoever that he thought she was downright beautiful—inside and out. Adah and Dorcas, his younger sisters, must've thought so, too, because the girls, especially Adah and Leah, had struck up an instant friendship back when they were just little.

Truth was, everyone who knew her spoke well of Abram's Leah. Gid could only hope he would be worthy of courting her. That she might allow him to accompany her home in his black open buggy come this Sunday night. Evidently Adah had already talked to Leah about driving to the singing together, the three of them. But Adah had said that Leah wanted to go a little farther away—over to the Grasshopper Level singing—which was right fine with him. It was the returning home part of the evening he cared most about.

According to Adah, she hadn't been able to pin Leah down about riding over with them. Seemed Leah preferred to go with Sadie. If so, would Leah meet up with Adah later? Did Leah mean to say she might give Gid a chance at being the young man to drive her home? The question had nagged him ever since Adah reported back about her quiet conversation with Leah out near the pond some days ago.

And what of the note he'd sent, delivered by Adah, where he offered his sympathy for Leah's hurting ankle? He would've gladly done more than simply pen a get-well message. If things weren't so downright awkward, what with both Dat and Abram plotting to set things up between himself and Leah, well, he might've gone over there to visit her awhile. Maybe even played a tune for her on his harmonica, having learned another new melody from Dawdi Mathias Byler. He and Dawdi Mathias liked to spend their evening hours practicing the mouth organ whenever they could. Dawdi would play his while Gid stumbled along, letting his ear tell him whether to slide up or down on the notes. Of course, the bishops wouldn't approve of their playing hoedown music at singings or whatnot, encouraging dancing and all. Still, it was all right for them to play in their homes, for their own enjoyment—"or our amazement," Dawdi Mathias would say with a chuckle and a twinkle in his eyes. Both Dawdi and Mammi Mattie Sue enjoyed having their grandchildren come for visits. "Come over whenever you like," Mammi always said, coaxing the three of them to spend the night on the Byler dairy farm, where they'd fall asleep to Dawdi's rhythmic serenade.

Thinking back to Leah, Gid was more than certain that Dawdi and Mammi would wholeheartedly approve of her, though he hadn't breathed a word of his affection to a soul, except to Adah, though ever so subtly, asking her to be a messenger girl just that once.

From now on, though, he planned to handle things on *his* terms. Very simply, he would have to draw Leah into conversation quickly at her first singing, be the only one to win her consent to see her home in his carriage. If not, he might lose his chance to court lovely Leah at all. With her winning smile and ways, she would be a magnet for any number of young men.

On the other hand, Sadie Ebersol—if she was to accompany Leah to the singing—was downright difficult to figure out. He honestly hoped Sadie might have other plans or be too busy at home to go along with Leah, which would give him a better prospect. Sadie just didn't seem to care much for him. Not romantically, of course, but just in general. She had looked down her nose at Gideon on several occasions lately, though he didn't know why. This struck him as odd, since both Hannah and Mary Ruth—and Abram and Ida, too—were as friendly and nice as Leah had always been. There was just something different about Sadie. Though she was ever so fair and had the most unusually blue eyes, well . . . he could almost surely put his finger on the root of the problem. Leah's older sister was plumb full of herself. She seemed to think rules were made to be broken, too. He'd heard tell from some of the youth; it was rumored that Sadie might be seeing someone outside the fold of the People. This was hard for him to accept, what with Sadie having bowed her knee before the bishop and the whole church membership after the Preaching service over at Moses Stolzfus's house several weeks ago. The sacred act firmly signaled the end of her rumschpringe. But none of this added up, not if Sadie was being untrue to her vows immediately after making them. But time would tell.

Secretly he had watched Leah while her sister was standing in line, ready to kneel and make her promises to God. Leah's perty face had twitched uncontrollably, as if she were fighting back tears. But why should she be sad at her sister's baptism? Were they tears of joy, maybe? He would never pry, wasn't his place, yet he did wonder sometimes what Sadie was thinking joining church when she seemed to lack the genuine goodness and spirit of honesty so evident in her sister Leah and others. Maybe someday dear Leah would share her feelings on all this. Then again, maybe not.

Sadie insisted to Leah that she was much too weary to attend singing on the following Sunday afternoon.

"Are ya sure?" Leah asked.

But Sadie only shook her head. No amount of pleading was going to change her mind. She said she planned to retire early this evening—a new twist for certain, Leah thought. And something Sadie ought to do more often, seeing as how she was awfully worn out. Yet she was staying home all the time, hadn't sneaked out of the house once lately. Leah was relieved and wondered if joining church *had* changed things for the better. Could it be?

Yet one thing still troubled Leah. She found it peculiar that she'd never heard an explanation for Sadie's disappearance that one afternoon, just days before her baptism. Where *had* her sister gone when she was supposed to be looking after the produce stand? No one—not even Dat and Mamma—seemed to know, or care. And if they did, they were keeping it hush-hush.

Well, all of that aside, the most important and blessed thing had happened at last. Sadie was an official member of the Old Order Amish church. Baptized and set apart.

Struggling not to be put out with Sadie for refusing to go to singing with her, Leah was determined to have some good fellowship, with or without her sister. Finished with both indoor and outdoor chores, she told Mamma where she was headed.

Then Leah hurried over to visit Adah round three o'clock, taking the shortcut through the meadow. She would have to find out from Adah if Gid really *would* drive them over to the Grasshopper Level singing.

But Adah seemed overjoyed at the idea that Leah should ride with them. "Such wonderful-gut news!" Adah said, beaming. "And don't worry about the little bit of distance. I'm sure Gid won't mind at all."

Giggling, they grabbed each other's hands and pranced round the bedroom Adah shared with Dorcas. And praise be, young Dorcas was nowhere in sight. Which was a very good thing, too. Leah surely didn't want to stir up any mistaken notions that she was soon to be courted by their only brother, who, just now, was out past the barnyard splitting logs with her own father and the smithy.

It turned out Leah and Adah rode in the second seat in the courting buggy, behind Gid, who wore a euphoric grin, reins in hand. She and Adah whispered to each other nearly all the way there. Gid was silent for the most part, joining in the conversation only occasionally to inquire of a particular male youth who might also have turned the appropriate age for the singings . . . but not a young *woman*, which Leah found interesting. It was as though Smithy Gid was bent on avoiding any talk of another girl having caught his fancy.

Of course, she kept her thoughts to herself about what Gid might be thinking. Wasn't her business to second-guess. He had every right to pursue any of the girls who might be in attendance tonight. She wouldn't stand in his way; that was certain.

Young people from several church districts were already gathering at the big barn when Leah and Adah stepped down from Smithy Gid's buggy. Almost immediately, Gideon unhitched the horse and led him up to the barn. Later, Adah told her, he would head off in the direction of a group of boys, playing the part of older brother not only for his sister Adah's benefit, but also for Leah's, since she had no brother to accompany her to the singing. There was the unspoken agreement that just because she had consented to ride with Gid and Adah didn't mean she was obligated to return home in the same buggy.

Leah's dearest hope was that Jonas Mast might show up tonight. She would be heartbroken if he didn't. Yet something within her assured her he *would* be here. And with a smile on his handsome face, just for her.

Ach, it was ever so nice to see so many young folk all in one place. And the boys, well, if they didn't look spiffy! It was as if they were attending preaching service, with hair clean and brushed, straw hats in hand, wearing long-sleeved white shirts, tan suspenders and black ties, and such fine black suits free of the slightest wrinkles or dust.

On the way up the lane, she'd taken special notice of the buggies lined up on the side yard, all shiny and neat. Some of the horses, she'd seen on the ride over, had too many reflectors on the bridles, just for show.

The girls were equally well-groomed for the occasion, many of them wearing their *for gut* blue or purple cape dresses, including a clean, long black apron. She had chosen her purple dress, just as Adah had.

"C'mon," Adah whispered to her, "let's gather round the table. It's time to begin, looks like."

Leah, feeling suddenly timid, followed her friend to a long table set up on the barn floor, swept clean for the evening.

The boys were expected to sit on one side and the girls on the other. So far, the girls were getting seated first. The boys were straggling over, three and four at a time, as if they might be sizing up the situation—seeing what new girls were here.

She felt prickly all of a sudden, a tingle of anticipation going up her spine. She still hadn't spotted Jonas, but Sadie, of all people, had cautioned her not to appear too eager for a particular boy. "If Jonas comes, you'll know he's lookin' to take *you* home and no other," Sadie explained. Leah assumed her sister was probably right.

The singing began almost before Leah realized what was happening. Several girls announced the first hymn, blew a pitch pipe, and got the melody going. They seemed to sing only the faster ones, and sometimes words were put to different songs than they sang at Preaching service. This was all new to Leah, but she caught on quickly and found herself joining in, singing heartily, just as Mamma always did in church, singing right in Leah's ear. Ever so joyful Mamma was at such times. Just as Leah was now, especially because Jonas Mast had just caught her eye, a long ways down the table.

Jonas is here! she thought, her heart gladdened. But she was careful not to look his way too often, lest both Adah, next to her, and Smithy Gid, directly across from her, might know there was really no chance she'd be riding home with the village blacksmith's son. None whatsoever. Yet she would be cautious not to hurt their feelings—his and her best friend's, both.

Between the selection of songs, there was enough time to talk to the boys across the table or, in Leah's case, to Adah and two other girls nearby. By the time ten o'clock rolled around, there were enormous bowls of popcorn brought in and soda pop and lemonade. Another whole hour would pass, with plenty of visiting and joking—and boys already doing their best to line up a girl to take home.

"If we instruct our children well, they won't forsake the truth." Mamma's words rang in Leah's ears as she sat there observing over a hundred young people, some moving away from the table, already pairing up.

Getting up, she looked around for Adah, who had disappeared. She was mindful of Gideon, but didn't want to be found standing alone, didn't want to be too available for Gid to approach her. Then she spied Adah way over on the other side of the barn, talking to a boy from their church district, of all things. So Adah had abandoned her for a boy on the first singing. But she didn't much care. Because, in the end, she was rather glad to be standing there alone, under the rafters where two cooing pigeons had perched high overhead.

Jonas sneaked up behind her and said in her ear, "Hullo, Leah."

She spun round and greeted him. "Nice to see you again," she said, grinning and wishing she might say more, but hoping they had the rest of the night to talk together.

"Saw you rode over with Adah Peachey and her brother," he said.

"Jah . . .'cause Sadie's not feelin' so well."

He showed some concern. "Is it the flu, then?"

"Must be. Both she and Mamma have it something awful."

Then he touched her elbow gently, guiding her to a more private spot under the haymow where they could talk without being overheard. "Leah, I was hoping . . ." His blue eyes were blinking fast. "What I mean is . . . would you like to . . . uh, will you allow me to see you home after a bit?"

Smiling, she gave her answer. "Jah, that'd be awful nice. Denki for asking."

His face lit up as if he wouldn't mind asking her the selfsame question for a good many singings to come. As if he was right now ready to leave and go driving with her. Of course, he shared with her what was expected. They would stand round and visit together, munch on popcorn and other snacks, watch some of the boys pull practical jokes on each other and other antics. Then, close to eleven o'clock, couples would pair off and head outside to the buggies for a nice, slow ride home under the stars.

Hearing from his lips how the evening was supposed to be, she could hardly wait for the rest of it. Yet it would be unthinkable to wish to rush the next full hour, knowing she had Jonas's full attention, and him right here by her side. Jah, her best dreams were coming true this very night.

Chapter Thirteen

In the morning Leah took charge of cooking breakfast, since both Mamma and Sadie were resting quietly, a rare thing for Mamma, at least. Sure was taking a long time for both of them to get back on their feet, Leah thought. But she was more than happy to help, to have another practice run at frying up the eggs and bacon, especially after the last time. Her family had been oh so polite, not saying a word about how awful bad the food tasted, sinking like a stone in the stomach. Come to think of it, maybe her sorry cooking had added to Mamma's and Sadie's digestive miseries. Could be. But today would be different. Maybe she would try her hand at poaching eggs for Sadie and Mamma instead of frying them. For Dawdi Brenneman, too. Might be more soothing. That and a bit of oatmeal.

She was setting the table, thinking back to last night's singing . . . and dear Jonas, when here came Aunt Lizzie, wanting to help. "Mamma's upstairs," she told her, "still not so gut."

"Ach, and Sadie?" asked Lizzie.

"Sadie, too. But this flu bug hasn't traveled through the house yet."

"Well, now, that's something to be thankful for, jah?" With that, her aunt headed up the steps, calling out softly, "Ida . . . are you presentable? It's your sister Lizzie."

Leah smiled, thinking how dear and close Mamma and Aunt Lizzie had always been. Sometimes Lizzie would show up clear out of the blue, without warning . . . no one telling her she was desperately needed or that something was up. No, she just seemed to know when to wander on down to them. And to tell the truth, Leah was awful glad to have Mamma's sister around this morning, because Leah was beginning to be stumped at what could be ailing her mother. As for Sadie, it was fairly obvious. She'd worn herself out running off to see her English boyfriend, Derry somebody. But, praise be, all that seemed to be a thing of the past. Now Sadie was merely catching up from all the nights she hadn't gotten a speck of sleep, probably.

When the poached eggs looked firm enough, she tested them with a fork. Sure enough, the yolk was only a little runny, the way Mamma liked hers. Leah found the wooden "sick" tray in the pantry and arranged it with a plate of eggs and buttered toast, a small bowl of warm oatmeal, and a cup of raspberry tea, awful gut for settling the stomach.

"Knock, knock," she called through the closed door at the top of the stairs, aware that Mamma and Aunt Lizzie were having themselves a quiet chat.

"C'mon in." Lizzie opened the door, her eyes wide when she spied the tray in Leah's hands. "Well, lookee here who's cooked up a right healthy-lookin' breakfast for you, Ida."

Ever so slowly, Mamma pushed herself up in bed at the

mention of food. Aunt Lizzie went over and helped prop her up with several more pillows. "How nice of you, Leah dear," her mother said.

"I trust this meal is tastier than the last one." She set the tray down on top of the covers over Mamma's lap once she was situated. "Is there anything else I can get you?"

"Well, why don'tcha look in on your sister Sadie, if you don't mind," Mamma said. Her face had a pasty look to it and her hair was still in a single long braid down her back.

"I'll check and see if she's feelin' hungry yet." But Leah wasn't really so keen on the idea of tending to her big sister. More and more, she felt it best they keep their distance. That way Sadie could work through whatever was bothering her here lately. Just maybe giving up her fancy man for the church was starting to sink in some. Jah, probably was, because Sadie wasn't nearly as cheerful as Leah had expected her to be after offering up her life and all her days to almighty God.

"Denki, Leah," said Mamma softly.

"Just tell Aunt Lizzie if there's anything else you need or want. Have her call it down to me, and I'll bring it on up for you." She felt almost like a short-order cook. A right nice feeling, really.

"Sure, I'll let Lizzie know," Mamma said, motioning to her sister to come sit on the bed. "You're awful gut to your old mamma, Leah."

Leah smiled. There was nothing old about her mother. Maybe she was just all tuckered out for some reason. Pulling the door nearly shut, she left it open a crack, then hurried down the hall to see about Sadie. She poked her head in the door. Her sister was stirring a bit but still in her nightclothes, stretched out in bed. "Will you be wanting anything to eat?" Leah asked softly.

Sadie, her hair in two thick, long braids, turned in bed and looked at Leah. "Maybe some tea, but that's all for now. Denki."

"You sure you wouldn't like some oatmeal? I made more than enough for Mamma."

"Later on, maybe." Sadie groaned a little, pulling the sheet up round her neck. "So Mamma's still under the weather, too?"

"Seems so."

"I wonder what *she's* got."

Leah shook her head. "Don't know."

"Well, whatever it is, I'm exhausted. Is Mamma, too?"

Leah recalled their mother's pale cheeks. They were usually a healthy, rosy hue. "Mam looks all washed out, same as you."

"Maybe after I eat a bite I'll feel better . . . like yesterday."

And the day before that, thought Leah.

She was on her way back down the hall when she heard what sounded like someone weeping softly. Stopping in her tracks, she heard Mamma talking, trying to tell Aunt Lizzie she thought she must surely be coming into the change of life.

"Well, if that's all 'tis, no need to fret so, Ida. If you ask me, I was wonderin' if you might not be in the family way."

Mamma laughed out loud. "Ach, don't be silly."

"Well, if you're right, then some raspberry tea oughta do the trick," said Lizzie.

Goodness' sakes, Leah had heard more than she cared to. Mamma going through the change at forty-two? She knew of other women getting teary eyed and sluggish come their mid-forties. It was just awful hard to think of her mother slowing down, when she'd always been one of the first to finish a chore at home or at a work frolic. Just couldn't be, could it?

Jonas Mast and his brothers, Eli and Isaac, found their father at the northernmost corner of the apple orchard just after breakfast. Mam had sent the three of them out with a thermos of hot coffee, "for later, if Dat gets chilled," and she shooed them out the back door. Jonas and thirteen-year-old Eli planned to help Dat gather up all the many apples that had fallen to the ground. Bruised apples made for gut cider, they knew. Isaac, who'd just turned eleven, said he'd stay for only a couple of hours, then he must return to his yard chores. That way, according to Mam, they could all sit down together for the noontime dinner.

Dat agreed. "You best work fast. No shirkin' today, son." To which Isaac nodded and set to work.

Picking up the fallen apples, Jonas's thoughts flew back to last night, where the sweetest girl of all had consented to ride home with him from singing. And what a buggy ride they'd had. Why, they had talked a blue streak, covering nearly every subject under the sun, too. The moon, really. Yet he had never tired of the lively conversation with his agreeable second cousin. On the contrary, she was one of the most interesting girls he thought he'd ever known, including his four sisters, and some of their first cousins, not to mention a whole bunch of girls in his church district—some had made it clear with either their enticing eyes or words that they wouldn't mind being courted by him.

The topic of their childhood promise had come up, but

neither of them was able to recall exactly what they'd said to each other years ago. Still, he knew he loved Leah *now* more than anyone else on God's green earth. And Lord willing, he would marry her one fine day.

Oh, what have I done? Sadie thought, pulling herself up to a sitting position in the bed. Tucking a pillow behind her, she let her tears fall freely. That thing she'd greatly feared had come upon her.

Thoughts of shunning filled her mind; ach, the sin and the shame of it all. Holding herself together, she was worried sick about Mamma's reaction once Sadie told her wicked secret. Dat might want to send her away, force her to give the baby up for adoption . . . she didn't know any of this for sure, but she fretted what would happen to her and the baby. As far as the church was concerned, she was an immoral young woman, an out-and-out lawbreaker. Unless she offered a kneeling repentance before the membership, she would be kicked out, forced to live separate from the community of believers.

Any joy she might've had, even for a moment—had she been a young bride instead of the way things were—faded quickly. Truly she was panic-stricken, unsure of just what she should do now. Or in due time. What would happen when her birth pangs began? Just who on earth would help deliver her baby? She couldn't think of contacting the Plain midwife; then for sure the word would get out.

Ach, a whole multitude of troubling questions clouded her mind.

Worst of all, she was alone, having to bear the blackness of sin's consequences. "Be sure your sin will find you out" was written in the Good Book, along with "The wages of sin is death."

And Dat wouldn't hesitate to remind her, no doubt. Soon as he knew.

By the noon meal Leah thought Mamma seemed to be feeling somewhat better. Aunt Lizzie had stayed through the morning to help redd up the house; then she'd peeled a pile of new potatoes for a big pan of scalloped potatoes. Hannah helped, too, since school was out for the English observance of Columbus Day. Mary Ruth was outside checking on the wash hanging on the line, seeing if some of the things might not be dry already. Soon she was bringing in an armload of clothes and had them all folded before Aunt Lizzie ever set the table.

Meanwhile, Leah's morning had been awful busy, too. She'd gathered the eggs from the chicken house, as well as emptied all the chamber buckets from each bedroom. Washing her hands now at the sink, she was glad *that* chore was completed. Of all her indoor responsibilities, it was the worst job of all. Mamma could never get Mary Ruth to help Leah with it, even if Leah pleaded and offered to do one of Mary Ruth's chores for her. Some things just had to be done . . . like it or not.

On her way out to call both Dat and Dawdi to dinner, she caught herself looking across the fields toward the smithy's farmhouse. Ach, she still felt a little sad inside—for Smithy Gid and what had happened last night. She hadn't known, really, how to tell him that she'd already been asked to ride home with Jonas when he came over to her, all red-faced and shy. Oh, she had tried to let him down ever so gently, even though she'd never promised or led him on in any way. Adah, thankfully, had been talking with a boy she liked; otherwise, it would've been even more awkward, Leah was sure. And poor Gid—she'd heard through the grapevine—had ended up driving his buggy home all alone. Hadn't bothered to ask another girl at all.

What could she do? Both boys were awful nice. And she could say, if asked, that she truly liked Gid. Such a friendly fella he was. Ever so loyal, it seemed. Which made her wonder just how faithful Jonas might've been if *he* hadn't asked her first. Would Jonas have ridden home alone, the way Smithy Gid had? She assumed so but didn't know. Not for sure.

Still, she felt blessed to have enjoyed the very best first singing a girl could ever hope to have. And she already had another date with Jonas to look forward to—in two weeks. The Saturday night before their off-Sunday, he wanted to take her riding again. This time their meeting was to be kept secret. So they were truly a courting couple. Glory be!

Chapter Fourteen

Hannah was anxious for a visit with Dawdi John, no school today and all. She knew he'd spent several hours working with Dat in the barn earlier, so he was sure to be tuckered out. An hour or so after the noon meal, she wandered over next door to find him waking from a nap.

Stretching a bit, he was sitting in his favorite wing-backed chair, all smiles. "Well, hullo, Hannah," he said, a light in his gray-blue eyes at the prospect of some company.

"Didn't mean to wake ya." She sat on the deacon's bench near the front-room window.

"Glad you come over."

Glancing out the window, she could see her father hurrying about the barnyard from where she sat. "Is Dat expecting you outside again?" she asked.

Dawdi laughed softly. "I 'spect your pop's had 'bout as much of me as he can stand in one day."

She didn't have the slightest notion what her grandfather meant by that. Sighing, she waited for him to say more. When he didn't, she asked if he wanted some hot coffee, because he was pulling his gray sweater closed just now, a bit chilly maybe.

"I'll have me some coffee, denki. Make it black."

"Jah, Dawdi, I remember," she called over her shoulder, heading out to his small kitchen. Next thing she knew, here he came, ambling out to sit at the little square table. Seemed he was as eager for a nice visit as she was.

One thing led to another—talk of the harvest, of upcoming doings over at Hickory Hollow, Dawdi reminiscing of days spent at Uncle Noah's place—and perty soon their chatter was focused on Gobbler's Knob. Hannah talked of growing up on this farm, having been the only place she'd ever known.

"Well, now, this here's the third house I've lived in," he said with a wry smile.

"That's right. First, 'twas your own farm . . . then Uncle Noah's, and now this Dawdi Haus."

He nodded. "Guess I'm tryin' to keep up with your aunt Lizzie."

"Oh, has she lived in several different places, too?"

"Three. Same as me."

Hannah clicked off in her head the places Aunt Lizzie had lived. "Hm-m, guess I only come up with two. Your house with Mammi when Lizzie and Mamma and their siblings were growin' up in Hickory Hollow, and later the log cabin. Was there another?" Far as she knew, Lizzie had gone directly from her parents' farmhouse to the log cabin, once she was considered a maidel.

Dawdi was nodding his head. "Didn'tcha know Lizzie lived right here in this little house?"

"Here, really?" Such peculiar news, though she didn't know what to make of it.

"Jah, for a time . . . shortly after her rumschpringe. Lizzie joined church here in Gobbler's Knob, coming to live near your mamma and pop."

"Aunt Lizzie and Mamma were always close, ain't so?" she said, knowing it was true.

Dawdi smiled at that. "Guess you could say Ida—your mamma—was Lizzie's second mother back then."

"That wonders me, what you said," Hannah spoke up. "Why should my aunt need a second mother if she was grown up enough to join church? And why didn't she ever marry, perty as she still is?"

Things got ever so quiet. In fact, Hannah thought she could hear the murmuring of a housefly's wings as it flew past her just now.

When Dawdi finally did speak, it was in a whisper. "Might not want to be askin' too many questions."

She was feeling more befuddled by the second. "But if Aunt Lizzie lived here once she was baptized, just when did she move to the cabin on the hill?"

"I 'spect once the place was built." Dawdi sighed, as if he was becoming restless. "Your pop and his brothers set to buildin' it for her."

"So she could live near Mamma?"

Dawdi rubbed his long gray beard. "Most maidels want a bit of independence, I 'spect. As I recall, Lizzie wanted that, jah. Yet here she could still be close enough for family activities and whatnot."

She thought on this. Aunt Lizzie *was* awful fond of them, which was mighty nice. And they loved her, too, same as all their aunts and uncles. "I'm glad Lizzie lives near us."

"Well, now, I am too," Dawdi declared.

His coffee needed warming up, so she got up from the table and poured some more for him without asking. "It's nice *you've* come to live here," she said.

"This way I can get to know my granddaughters better over in this part of the world."

She had to smile at that. Surely Dawdi must feel as if his children and grandchildren were scattered all round Lancaster County. And they were, come to think of it. Which was the reason Dat and Mamma hardly ever made the trip over to see Aunt Becky and Uncle Noah and all those cousins. Such a long way it was.

Suddenly she said, "You're the last of my *Grosseldere*—grandparents." Oh my! She hadn't meant to say it out in the open thataway. Still, she'd been thinking—pondering, really—the fact that both Dawdi and Mammi Ebersol had gone to heaven, and Mammi Brenneman, too. "So you're all I have left."

Dawdi smiled the kindest smile and reached out his hand to her. "Don't fret over such things or I'll hafta name you a worrywart. I've got lots of living to do yet, Lord willing."

Right away, she felt bad. "Mamma says I worry over things that will never come true."

Dawdi nodded. "Guess we all do, to some degree or 'nother."

"Still, we oughta enjoy every single day the Good Lord gives us, ain't so?" she replied.

Still holding her hand in his, Dawdi chuckled. "Don't be feeling sorry for me, Hannah. Living here is gonna be right fine. Already 'tis." There was a twinkle in his eyes. " 'Specially with so many interesting folk to talk to."

She felt better now. So Dawdi found her to be an interesting granddaughter. He didn't consider her to be a chatterbox, which he'd remarked in jest about Mary Ruth at the supper table last night. "We'll have us another chat here perty soon," she said, hearing Mamma calling to her from the other side of the house.

"Jah, I'd like that." He grinned up at her.

With that, she leaned down and kissed Dawdi's crinkly forehead.

Mary Ruth was glad for the near ceaseless flow of customers at the roadside stand all afternoon. She enjoyed selling a basketful of decorative gourds to Mrs. Ferguson, one of their many faithful customers. Then Mrs. Esbenshade arrived, almost before Mrs. Ferguson could get her spanking new green Nash sedan out of the way.

"I hear there's to be a wedding coming up soon in your family," Mrs. Esbenshade said.

The only family wedding she knew of was the Masts', and she mentioned Anna's name to the woman. "Do you know my second cousin, then?"

"Oh my, yes. I buy apples every year from Fannie and her girls." The woman's plump face brightened. "My neighbors' second son works for Peter Mast, doing odd jobs."

"We pick all our apples over there," Mary Ruth said, making small talk, what she loved doing best.

"When *is* Anna's wedding?"

"Third Tuesday in November. Anna and her beau were published in church right after the fall communion. That's our custom."

"So Amish weddings occur only in November and December?"

"Around Lancaster, jah . . . and once in a while late October or early January, if need be. There are only so many Tuesdays and Thursdays in a two-month period, ya know."

Mrs. Esbenshade smiled. "Well, I can't pretend to know much about your ways, Mary Ruth. I suppose I'll wait for a written invitation from Anna."

"A gut idea, I'd say." And with that, she tried to interest the English woman in some pumpkins, which were coming on real gut now.

"Oh, I'll come back tomorrow and pick out a nice big one for my nephew. He's seven this year and wants to carve a jack-o'-lantern all by himself."

"Tomorrow, then. Either Leah or Sadie will be here tending the stand, for sure." Mary Ruth knew nothing much about Halloween, only that it was a night English children went from door to door begging for candy. It wasn't a holiday the People had ever observed. The best thing about October was selling so many pumpkins, except the ones Mamma had already set aside to make pumpkin-nut cookies, pumpkin-spice cake, and pumpkin-chiffon pie, her specialty. So pumpkins were awful gut for business, and it seemed the more they planted each year, the more they sold.

A few minutes after Mrs. Esbenshade drove away, young Elias Stoltzfus rode up in his father's market wagon. He pulled off the road a bit and gave the horse a sugar cube before walking over to the produce stand. "Hullo there, Mary Ruth," he called to her, taking his straw hat off his head and completely ignoring the lineup of fruits and vegetables. Seemed he had a talk on, and that was right fine with her. "My pop says we might be goin' over to the Mast wedding next month. Now, what do you think of that?"

She liked the sound of it, sure did. And, so as not to be forward, she nodded her head slowly and smiled at the red-headed boy named for his father, a long-standing deacon in their church.

"What I'm getting to, Mary Ruth, is when it's time to sit down for the wedding feast, I hope you'll sit 'cross from me at the table."

"Jah, I'd like that, Elias." Her heart filled with joy at his invitation.

"I'll do all I can to make sure I'm lined up just right 'fore we sit down. Don'tcha worry none. We'll have us a wonderful-gut time."

Even though she was far from courting age—Elias surely knew that, and so was he—she liked the idea of being friendly anyways. Of course, she would be right sensible about boys, just as Leah had always been . . . and Mamma most surely had been back when. She wouldn't think of behaving the way Sadie had here the last year or so. Thank goodness her big sister had settled down and joined church. All for the better.

Elias didn't bother to purchase anything, just grinned, showing his teeth a little too much, and waved to her as he turned to go. "See ya tomorrow at school, jah?"

"Jah, at *recess*," she said, hoping he'd remember and come say hello to her maybe.

Running back to his horse and wagon, Elias got himself seated, then whistled loudly to alert the Belgian steed to pull out quickly. And he was on his way. Ach, and what a fast driver he was, Dat would surely say if he'd seen the way Elias handled the horse. But the Stoltzfus boy had always been like that, young and spirited, like his stallion. Yet there was something gentle and sweet about him, too, Mary Ruth knew. There was no getting round that.

She was mentally counting the years till her rumschpringe when another customer came calling. This time a fancy Englisher with the darkest hair and eyes she'd ever seen. A right handsome young man, really, as fancy boys go. His hair was groomed neatly and he wore pressed black trousers and a long-sleeved white shirt with a woolen red vest and black bow tie, as if he might be a Fuller Brush salesman. "How can I help you today?" she said, greeting him, thinking he'd surely have plenty of money to clean out the stand if he wanted to.

"I'm not interested in buying anything," he said bluntly. "I'm here to deliver a message to your sister. I assume you're related." He handed her an envelope.

"That depends on who you mean. I have three sisters, sir."

He smiled at her just then. "Please, you don't have to call me 'sir' . . . I'm not much older than you are."

She wasn't sure if he winked at her or not, but he was truly flirtatious. Glancing down at the letter in her hand, she saw it was addressed to Sadie Ebersol. "Jah, Sadie's my sister. I'll give it to her."

"I'd appreciate that." He nodded slightly, behaving again like a proper gentleman all of a sudden.

She slipped the letter into her pocket. "I'll see that Sadie gets it by suppertime, if that's all right with you."

"No hurry," he said. "So long." He turned and rushed back to his shiny gray car, then sped away like nobody's business.

She found it ever so curious that both boys had wanted to show off for her, one with a heavy hand on the reins, the other with a lead foot. Feeling for the letter in her dress pocket, she reminded herself to find Sadie as soon as she went inside, come suppertime.

It was well past dusk when they all sat down together for Bible reading and evening prayers in the kitchen. Sadie was glad to be keeping the glass chimneys on the oil lamps consistently clean; so much better it was for Dat when he read long passages from the Scriptures, which he did this night.

He read aloud in Pennsylvania Dutch from Luke chapter nine, beginning at verse twenty-three. " 'And he said to them all, If any man will come after me, let him deny himself, and take up his cross daily, and follow me. For whosoever will save his life shall lose it: but whosoever will lose his life for my sake, the same shall save it.' "

Dat continued to read, but Sadie's thoughts got stuck on the words "whosoever will save his life shall lose it." She wondered, was that what she'd done by making her kneeling vow before the bishop and the membership last month? Had she attempted to save her life . . . her very soul?

But what of the tiny life growing within her now? What was to become of Derry's baby once it was born into the Plain community? Would he love Sadie enough to marry her? She had no idea. She only knew that she was terrified and wished she might see Derry again very soon. She had to tell him that what she'd suspected for several weeks was absolutely true. And best she could calculate, by mid-June she'd be giving birth.

She could only imagine how hurt Dat and Mamma would be if they knew. Yet she couldn't bear to tell them today, not this week either. She didn't rightly know just when she could bring herself to reveal such a disgraceful thing as this. She recalled the church community's stand—and the consequences for the sinner—when a young girl had become pregnant back two years ago. Such a time that had been. And now here she was in the same jam! How? How could such a thing have happened to her?

Her thoughts continued to whirl as Dat's voice droned on. More and more she was thinking that if she weren't in danger of being shunned—would the bishop make an exception?—she could marry Derry and go fancy if he refused to join the community of the People. Save her family from *some* embarrassment, maybe. Though such ideas were truly hogwash, she knew. There was no getting round the *Ordnung*. It would be craziness to think otherwise. All she really knew, without a doubt, was that she had to share her startling news with her beloved. She could only guess what he would say or do. Surely he'd convinced her of his love—she could rely on that, couldn't she? He'd declared it outright so many times she dared not try and count. Truth was, her revelation might put them on dangerous ground. He could become angry at the least little thing.

She scarcely knew what to do first. Best keep this to herself for a while longer.

Mary Ruth rushed into the bedroom where Sadie and Leah were both in long cotton nightgowns, brushing their waist-length hair. "Ach, I forgot to tell you, Sadie," she exclaimed. "A young man—all dressed up—dropped by the roadside stand this afternoon. He asked me to give you this."

Sadie wondered what on earth Mary Ruth was talking about, and so excitedly at that. She saw her name printed on the envelope and her heart leaped up. Was this a letter from Derry? One of the very things she'd longed to see . . . to keep in her treasured things. Could it be?

Well, now that Mary Ruth had made her delivery, she wasn't leaving the room, wasn't leaving Sadie alone with this precious letter from her dearest one. "May I have some privacy?" she said at last.

Both Leah and Mary Ruth took the hint and left together, closing the door behind them. Moving to the small oil lamp atop the dresser, she stood there, fingers trembling, and opened the envelope.

Dear Sadie,

I hope you are well.

This may come as a surprise, but I hope you'll agree that the time has come for us to part. You are a baptized member of your church now, and I am preparing to enlist in the army, which will undoubtedly take me far away from Lancaster County. I realize we've discussed this already, that I promised to keep in constant touch with you during my military duty.

However, thinking about the potential problems of such a long-distance relationship, I have second thoughts about tying you down with no promise of marriage. I should not expect loyalty like that from you, and even if I did, it wouldn't be fair to either of us, would it?

I hope you have a happy life.

Sincerely,
Derek Schwartz

Sadie felt as though she'd been punched in the stomach. Was Derry saying good-bye to her for good? But how could that be? She couldn't begin to comprehend, after all they'd meant to each other. After *everything*. And now such a horrid letter when she needed him more than ever. Oh, she felt so ill . . . as if she might lose all her supper.

The time has come for us to part. . . .

Staggering to the bed, she clutched the letter, not caring to repress her sobs. Not realizing that now, as she buried her head in the pillow, Leah had slipped into the room, closed the door silently, and was leaning over her. "Aw, Sadie . . . my dear sister . . ." And then she felt Leah beside her, lying ever so near, wrapping her arms around her, holding her as if she were a little child. "There, there," Leah whispered. "Weep if you must."

"Ach, I loved him so," she cried. "I truly loved him. . . ."

Leah said no more, and somewhere between the blackness of night and the veil of bitter tears, Sadie slept.

Leah was torn between her sister's obvious grief and her own curiosity over the letter still clasped in sleeping Sadie's hand. So . . . Sadie *hadn't* ended her relationship with the English beau earlier, as Leah had hoped. No matter, it was over now. And though she felt terribly sorry for Sadie, she was mighty glad that Derry was gone once and for all. He'd broken things off in such a spineless manner! Well, the boy wasn't worthy of anyone's affections, let alone her sister's.

Leah purposely stayed awake, shifting her thoughts to Jonas. She had no reason to ever expect a coward's letter from *him*, now that she had proof of his keen interest in her, in his plan to court her. One year from now their wedding plans would be published in church, and by Thanksgiving Day they would be wed, probably. Jah, the year ahead would be the best one of her whole life . . . if Dat came to see the light, that is. Smithy Gid, too.

Sighing, she rose to pull up a lightweight quilt over her sister. Leah hoped and prayed that Sadie might enjoy the same depth of happiness she herself had found in dearest Jonas, only this time with a nice Plain boy.

But she worried, unable to sleep. Had Sadie's reputation been tarnished by the grapevine amongst the community of the People?

Chapter Fifteen

Derek Schwartz talked his brother into going out for a night on the town, to Harrisburg, thirty-eight miles away. Robert was a wet blanket when it came to having fun, particularly this Friday night, and Derek accused him in so many words as they drove to a downtown soda shop called The Niche.

After a near-silent supper they headed to the YMCA, where a bevy of girls were eager to dance to a live local band, and a Sinatra wannabe was crooning onstage and making time with the microphone. Derek was more than happy to oblige and danced with four different blondes before noticing Robert sitting over on the sidelines. This annoyed him, but he decided to keep his yap shut this time. Poor, miserable big brother, suffering the aftershock of war. Shouldn't he be content having survived Normandy's invasion with all his limbs and mental faculties? Some of the young guys his age had come back with a hook for a hand—or worse, in body bags. His father had told Derek in a whisper one night in the hallway connecting the small medical clinic to the house, "Your brother will need patience from all of us . . . time to adjust to civilian life again."

Even so, Derek could not muster up a trace of sympathy for Robert tonight. Why should he waste his dance-floor energy having to twist Robert's arm when the atmosphere was charged with pure exhilaration, perfumed and coiffed girls, and great music? Didn't the ex-GI know it was time to celebrate? He was alive, for pete's sake!

By the time they were back in the car and driving home, Derek was proud to have collected four phone numbers, all from blue-eyed blondes. One, a deep-dimpled girl, could have easily passed herself off as Helen O'Connell, sweet canary of Jimmy Dorsey's swing band. Yeah, the phone numbers were long-distance ones, but he didn't have to dial up all of them within the space of a week . . . or even a month. One thing was settled in his mind—he was ready for a new girl. Harrisburg, York, Reading, he didn't care. The fling with Sadie Ebersol had gone on way too long. He could kick himself for leading her on as he had, letting her believe he would keep in touch with her as an enlisted man. Or that he loved her at all. What got his goat was how innocent she had been . . . too trusting, too. He bristled now, recalling their furtive trysts in the woods. Memories of the past two months haunted him—the risks he'd taken—dragging off to work, too tired to pull his fair share.

Wisely, and in the nick of time, he had rid himself of Sadie with a tidy and to-the-point letter, which her cute—

and quite cheerful—younger sister had promised to deliver. By now, knowing Sadie as he did, she would have cried herself to sleep more than two nights in a row. Soon, though, she would be out flirting again, finding herself a good-looking but rowdy Plain boy, most likely, now that she was a bona fide member of that back-woodsy church. He made a mental note to be more discreet with his sugarcoated doublespeak in the future, having made empty promises repeatedly. His best move so far had been cutting things off before something happened to tie him down to her.

Robert broke the silence, intruding into Derek's reverie. "How can they do it?"

"Huh?"

"People act like things are fine. Don't those girls at the 'Y' know there's been a war? Our guys were blown to smithereens and they—you . . . *everyone*—acts like nothing happened."

Derek turned and looked at his brother. Robert was gripping the steering wheel with both hands, at ten o'clock and two, just as their father had taught them.

"How can things be the same here at home?"

In the four months since his brother's return, Derek had never heard him speak of his war experiences. He hadn't heard the edge of frustration, the intense anger in Robert's voice. "Maybe it's because some of us weren't there to see people get blown to kingdom come . . . that's how," Derek shot back, not sure why he felt so angry now himself.

Robert fell suddenly silent again, which made Derek uneasy. His brother's face was often as white as the sheets their father used to drape over a corpse from time to time. Robert proudly wore the mask of unwitting demise, which bothered Derek. It was as if this young war veteran had to experience death vicariously, here and now—after the fact—to somehow justify what his slaughtered best buddies had faced and lost. And now Robert was driving much too slowly on the highway as the turn-off for Strasburg came into view. What was really wrong? Derek wondered. Why was Robert driving like there was no need to get somewhere? Ever? Like he was in no hurry to arrive home, to crawl into bed and sleep in the safety of their father's home instead of a foxhole. Was he afraid he might endure the nightmarish dreams of the Normandy beaches all over again?

When the good doctor heard the knocking on the side door, he was slow to get up out of his comfortable chair to see who it was. The boys should be back soon, was his first thought. Maybe they'd forgotten the house key. But, no, when he opened the door he was met by the tear-streaked face of a young Amishwoman. "I'm ever so sorry to bother you," she said softly. "I was wonderin' . . . is Derry home?"

"Derek? You wish to see *my* son?"

"Jah, if that's all right."

He glanced around her, expecting to see a horse and buggy parked in the lane. "Did you come on foot?"

She nodded. " 'Tis important."

"Well, Derek isn't home," he said quickly, aware of her eyes in the porch light. Lovely, sad, faded blue eyes. "I wouldn't know when to expect him."

"I'd be willin' to wait."

Raking his hand through his hair, he wondered what he ought to say or do, wondering what was best for Derek. "Let me run you home. I can't say how late it might be before he—"

"Denki, but no. I must see Derry tonight."

She knows his nickname? What sort of relationship does this girl have with my boy? he worried.

Suddenly, he felt he must encourage her to visit tomorrow, or another day. But no amount of persuading could convince the girl that she should *not* sit outside on the porch step waiting, and she insisted on doing so. And now here was Lorraine, in her bathrobe, coming to see what all the commotion was, asking why Henry hadn't invited the poor dear inside.

"No . . . no, I can't do that," the girl said. "I wouldn't think of imposin' on you."

"But it's nothing," his wife insisted. "Please, do come in."

The girl, who gave her name simply as Sadie, was more stubborn than the two of them. She turned and planted herself on the second step of the side porch, determined to wait for Derek.

At last Henry closed the door on the girl, turning to Lorraine. "Why must you be so hospitable at this hour, when we don't even know the young woman?" he said, checking himself. It wouldn't do to protest . . . to make a mountain out of a simple molehill, most likely.

"She's surely a neighbor, Henry," his kind and compassionate wife said. "We have lots of Plain folk living up and down the road; you know that."

"But . . . an Amish girl asking for Derry?" He forced a chuckle. "How ordinary is that?"

The tension was ultimately diffused by their laughter, though he found himself checking out the window every fifteen minutes to see if the girl was still there, hoping for Derek's sake she might change her mind and walk back home. Where she belonged.

The highway was dark, the headlights the only source of light on the narrow road hemmed in by cornfields on all sides. Robert surprised Derry by breaking the silence. "Did Dad ever warn you about women?" Robert asked.

"Nope."

"Before I left for the war . . . at the train station, Dad said certain things."

Derek shook his head. "What're you getting at?"

" 'Stick to your own kind'—that's just what Dad said, slapping my back while the train chugged into view. And he seemed to feel strongly about it . . . even wrote letters warning me to keep my nose clean when it came to European girls. Dad said women were trouble."

"Not *all* women," Derry said. "Dad got lucky with Mom."

"Well, I didn't listen to him. I fell for a German girl named Verena." Robert stopped talking, having to cough several times.

"What happened?"

"She died in an explosion." His brother paused again. "Thank God she was asleep . . . it happened in the middle of the night . . . she never knew what hit her." Robert signaled and pulled over, then turned off the ignition and opened the window.

"Yeah? That's rough."

They sat there for the longest time, listening to the motor ticking.

Soon Derry was the one coughing. "Are we ever going home?"

Then Robert turned to face him, as if he were going to whine about the war some more. "This might sound weird to you, but I made a promise to God over there. When everyone around me was drowning or getting blown to bits . . . I prayed that if I got out of that hellish place alive, I'd give my life to Christ somehow. Do something big for Him."

"Like what?"

Breathing in audibly, Robert leaned his arm on the open window. "What would you think if I became a minister, like Grandpa Schwartz?"

Derry felt like laughing, but this wasn't the time or place. "Hey, it's your life. Mess it up if you want to."

"But . . . you didn't see how bloody—how unspeakably brutal the war was. Don't you understand I shouldn't be alive today? You should have a brother buried six feet under. . . ." Robert's voice trailed off to nothing.

"Well, don't let me be the one to tell you how stupid it could be to break a vow, or whatever, to God." Derry was sick and tired of all this talk from his big brother. All this religious talk . . .

It was time for Robert to quit spilling his guts and drive home. That's what. And when Derry said so, Robert stared back at him for a moment, then straightened and turned on the ignition, saying no more.

Sitting on the porch, having just met Derry's parents—Dr. Henry Schwartz and his friendly wife—Sadie waited for their son, thinking back to her childhood years here in Gobbler's Knob. For the longest time, she'd had a carefree, happy life . . . obeying the Ordnung and trying to do right. Dat and Mamma had brought her up in the ways of the Lord, no doubt of that. Yet here she was perched on the steps of strangers, really, their grandchild forming beneath her frightened heart.

Ach, she'd had to tell Leah *something*. After all, Leah had been by her side to comfort her after Derry's unexpected letter had clear knocked the wind out of her. She hadn't breathed a word about expecting a baby, though. Didn't want to share that news just yet, not with anyone. Only Derry should know. She had told Leah she wouldn't be seeing her English beau any longer but guarded the letter and didn't offer to share it.

Unable to slip away from the house, she'd waited all week to walk down the road a half mile or so because she didn't dare risk trying to hitch up the driving horse to the family buggy. Not at this hour. And now that she was here, Sadie felt even worse about the things Derry had written her. And awful sad it was, finding out he wasn't home tonight. She had hoped he might've stayed home, sorrowfully pondering the many days and weeks of their love. But now his being gone made her wonder if he had ever loved her at all, to be out having himself a nice time while she was still crying over him—over what might've been.

Or, now that she thought on it, what could *still* be. Did she dare tell him what was brewing in her mind . . . in her heart?

Henry wondered now if he might've been too hasty with the young barefooted woman. Why *hadn't* he invited her inside, welcoming her with the usual gracious bedside manner he was known for? Yet he was a man of his own opinions, and he pushed back alarm at the thought of a tear-streaked Amish girl on their doorstep.

He walked back to the front room, ears alert to what might unfold. The hour was late. Robert and Derek would surely be home any minute, and his second son was quite adept at handling things, whatever the girl's issue might be. This was not his concern, nor Lorraine's, yet he stood to peer out the window as Robert's car pulled into the lane.

Derek spotted Sadie instantly, hunched over on the porch step, as if she could fool him and not be noticed. Nevertheless, she was there, brazenly waiting for him. "What's *she* doing here?" he snapped.

"Who?" Robert asked.

"Never mind." He leaped out of the car, mad as a threatened dog, and walked partway up the walk toward her. "Come with me, Sadie," he barked, not waiting for her to get up and follow. Marching around the side of the house, toward the entrance to the medical clinic where his father treated patients, he waited for her to catch up, arms folded across his chest. "What were you thinking, coming here?" he demanded.

She inched her way closer to him, yet keeping her distance. It was then that he noticed she was barefooted beneath her long blue dress, as she always was, and in the dark coolness of the night, with only the porch lamp to cast a spell of light, he was taken once again with her beauty. "Derry, I'm sorry to bother you, but I must tell ya something," she said softly.

They stood like two statues engulfed in amber shadows.

"My letter," he muttered. "Is this about the letter?"

"Jah." Her voice quavered. "And . . . something else, too."

"Look, Sadie, I'm sorry about what happened between us. I wasn't thinking—"

"No," she interrupted, "but *I* have been." Then she said softly, almost in a whisper, "Derry, I'd thought you'd want to know . . . I'm in the family way."

Stunned, he took a step back as Sadie's words echoed in his brain. "Are you sure?"

"I wouldn't have told you if I wasn't."

An uncanny silence hung in the air, separating them like a damask curtain. His words were measured. "What're you going to do?"

"This isn't just *my* concern, Derry. This is your baby, too." Quickly she hung her head—not in shame, he was certain. After a time she slowly lifted her eyes to him. "If you loved me half as much as you said all those times before, you could save yourself from goin' off to serve Uncle Sam, ya know."

He did not immediately grasp her meaning. Then he did. She wanted him to marry her, give her baby a name and a home. Any girl would want that. She must think he was looking for an exemption from military duty, and Sadie wasn't simply hinting. He could see by her posture she was giving it to him straight. "What a wonderful-gut excuse to stay home, jah?"

"But I *want* to join the army."

She fell silent again.

He tried to avoid her eyes. Those beautiful eyes that had taunted him from the first night. "Let's talk about *you*." He didn't want to sound crass, but what choice did he have? "My father might know of someone in Philly who could take care of this problem—and soon. I'd drive you there myself."

"No," she said. "What's done is done." She stepped forward, coming face-to-face with him. "This wee one inside me, *our* baby together, was created out of love. 'Least, I thought so. You should be ashamed, Derry Schwartz, thinkin' that I'd do away with my own flesh and blood." She was crying. "I don't know you anymore. Maybe I never did." Turning, she ran across the lawn, heading for the road.

"Wait . . . Sadie!" he called after her. "Let me take you home."

She stopped abruptly, hands on her slender hips. "I'd rather walk ten miles in the blackest midnight than let you drive me anywhere. You're the cruelest human being the Lord God ever made!" With that pronouncement of his moral fiber, she sped off into the night.

Derek stood watching her at the edge of the lawn. "Dad was right. Women *are* trouble," he whispered, then spat on the ground.

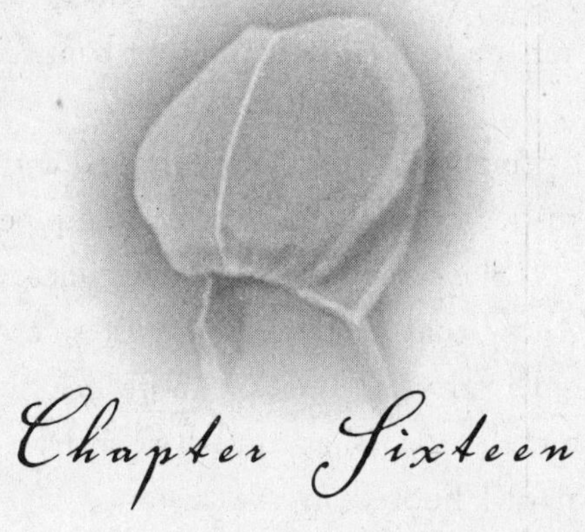

Chapter Sixteen

Leah remembered having placed a firm hand on Sadie's shoulder, hoping to talk sense to her, trying to stop her sister from going down the road to "talk to Derry, just this once."

"But . . . you've put the sins of the past behind, ain't so?" Leah had asked, aware of Sadie's glistening eyes. "Honestly, I don't mean to pry, but—"

"Then don't." Sadie had pushed away.

"Keep your vow to God" was all Leah could whisper before Sadie left their bedroom, rushing out into the night.

Now, alone in the room, Leah paced the floor, something she'd never done. Sadie was off somewhere talking to her former English beau . . . just why, she hadn't bothered to say. The letter that had brought such sad, sorrowful news days ago was buried deep in one of the dresser drawers—or Sadie's hope chest, maybe—Leah was awful sure, yet she wouldn't go searching for it. Would be wrong to read what Sadie had never offered to share.

But Leah wasn't about to take herself off to bed. Not till Sadie returned home, safe in their father's house again. She sat on the edge of the bed in her nightgown, praying silently and waiting for the tiptoed return of her baptized sister.

The biting smell of woodsmoke mingled with the autumn air as Sadie rushed home, indifferent to sharp pebbles tearing at her bare feet. She sometimes ran, sometimes walked on the two-lane highway that bordered the east side of the forest, where she and Derry had met on more occasions than she cared to count, the road that ran between Derry's home and her own. An owl hooted in the distance, the eerie sound coming from deep in the woods, though Sadie wasn't a bit scared to walk alone.

She thought of the toasty fire Aunt Lizzie surely had stoked all evening long, though at this hour the flames were no doubt reduced to smoldering embers, cooling now as she hurried toward home. Come to think of it, maybe Aunt Lizzie's place was the origin of the smoke that hung so heavily in the air, except that the little cabin was clear on the other side of the knoll. Just why was she thinking of her fun-loving maidel aunt on a night like this? Sadie knew how much Lizzie liked to walk in the woods. Sometimes even at night, especially when the moon was out. Aunt Lizzie said she could talk best to God at such times.

Sadie didn't know how she herself felt about the Lord God tonight. She'd built her whole future round Derry, only to have her hopes come crumbling down. She thought she might want to move to Hickory Hollow, live neighbors to some of her married cousins—Uncle Noah and Aunt Becky's grown children, maybe. Get away from not only the raised eyebrows that were sure to come, but the words of rebuke from Mamma, Dat, and eventually Preacher Yoder . . . all the way up to the bishop, if she didn't confess her terrible sin and come clean. Then, just as awful, she'd end up living alone, without the chance to marry. No Amish boy would want "secondhand goods." No more Sunday singings for her once she began to show, no more rides in an open buggy on a starry night, no more giggling at wedding feasts. Pairing up was a thing of the past. And tomboy Leah, of all things, would be the first of Abram's daughters to marry.

Sadie tied her prayer cap under her chin against the breeze, wondering what it would be like to live near her Hickory Hollow kinfolk. What had it been like for Lizzie, leaving all her friends and coming over here near Mamma? Especially when Lizzie had two sisters who were much closer in age than Mamma was, "and closer in spirit, too," Uncle Noah had said years back, one of the few times they'd visited Mamma's older brother and family. Of course, now it didn't seem to matter anymore. Lizzie was long settled in the Gobbler's Knob church community, a helper to Mamma, a caregiver for Dawdi Brenneman, and a woman of her own making. She'd never married, which often perplexed Sadie, and whenever the topic came up with either Leah or Mamma, one of them would say something like, "Some women seem content to live without a man." But Sadie didn't believe it, not for one minute. She'd noticed Aunt Lizzie at church picnics and whatnot, enjoying herself and everyone round her. Such a cheerful woman she was. Up until about five years or so ago, Sadie had wondered if Lizzie might not marry an older man—a widower, maybe—but no such opportunity had come along just yet.

Glancing over her shoulder at distant car lights coming fast, Sadie moved to the far left side of the road, near the grassy ditch where wild strawberry vines grew all summer long and lightning bugs could be seen flickering in June.

"I want to join the army. . . ."

Derry's words rang in her head. Thinking back to their dreadful conversation, she felt something snap way down inside her. No matter what Derry said or did from now on, she was going to cherish and care for their baby. The innocent child must be shielded from the murderous attitude of its own father.

Kicking at the road, she scraped her right foot but didn't care. *Der Derry Schwartz is en lidderlicher*—a despicable fellow—she thought. And the most frightening thing was she never would've guessed him to be anything but what she'd known of him these past months—kind and ever so loving . . . eager to see her as often as possible. What could've happened to change his mind about her? Had he found himself another girlfriend . . . in such a short time? Or was his decision to join up with the military the main reason? If that was true, why on earth would he refuse to write the letters he'd promised? Why?

A dozen questions or more gnawed at her peace. The car lights had caught up with her. She turned to see Derry waving his arm out the window. "Sadie! Stop right now and get in."

As soon as she knew who the driver was, she turned her head stiffly, still walking.

"Don't be stubborn," he was hollering at her. And now he'd stopped the car. She heard the door slam and his hard footsteps. Was he running after her to say he was ever so sorry, take her in his arms, tell her he didn't mean a word of what he'd said before? That they should be married right away, he'd changed his mind, decided not to go off with

Uncle Sam. He *loved* her, after all.

But no . . . his words rang out into the night. "Listen to me, Sadie!" She felt his hand on her shoulder now, turning her round to face him. "You can't go on like nothing's happened," he was saying. "You have to do something about the . . . baby."

"I'll do something. I'll be raising our child by myself," she answered, "and there ain't anything you can do 'bout it. Unless . . ." Looking past him, she saw his gray automobile sitting back there in the middle of the road, the door on the driver's side gaping wide just the way her life and her future felt to her—exposed for the world of the People to see and then condemn.

"Unless what?" He gripped her arms.

"Unless you change your mind."

"That's impossible," he said flatly. "Well, I guess there is adoption, but who's going to take a half-breed?"

She wondered if this might be the truest reason behind his rejection of their child. But she didn't think he'd be so uncouth as to put it into words. And such hurtful words they were. "Turn loose of me, Derry. I'm going home now."

He released her, though reluctantly, stepping back with defiance on his face. "Sadie Ebersol, I wish I'd never met you."

"Jah, well, I wish it more than you." She spun on her heels and began to run. She ran until her callused feet were numb to the sting of the hard pavement. She ran away from what might've been—all her wishes and dreams bound up in one horrible boy—and rushed toward her father's house, where she would do her best to hide her sin over the next months, sew her dresses and aprons ever wider, till she could no longer hide her secret. The People would then know the truth about her and her false covenant. They could either help her live as a maidel with a child, or they could reject her, cast her out—shun her. At this moment, she knew she was too stubborn to repent to a single soul.

Soon the rambling farmhouse came into view, and she quickened her pace, glad that Derry had chosen to turn round in the road and head back. She was sure she'd never see him again. She hoped so with all her might.

Leah heard Sadie coming up the stairs and stood in the doorway, waiting. "Gut, you're home at last," she whispered.

"I never want to see Derry again as long as I live."

Such a relief, thought Leah, but to Sadie she said, "I'm glad you're here, sister."

And then Sadie turned and looked at her, falling into her arms. Patting her sister ever so gently, Leah said no more, letting Sadie sob onto her shoulder, hoping her sister's cries were muffled enough to keep from waking Mamma.

Ida was put out with herself, having to get up several times in the night, rejecting the idea of the outhouse. She was thankful for the chamber bucket, especially here lately when her sleep was ever so deep. Like a rock, she felt, of a morning. Was this how her older sister-in-law, Becky Brenneman, felt come the change? She could talk right frankly with Becky face-to-face, she recalled. But it had been such a long time since Abram had agreed to drive all of them over there. "Too far to the Hollow," he'd said when she asked last week. "Not during harvest," he'd said just this evening. So she wouldn't be asking Abram again. Not till after the wedding season, but then it would be too cold, probably, too much snow on the road. Then his excuse would be the sleigh couldn't begin to hold all six of them. Seven, really, if Lizzie went, which she'd want to, Ida was awful sure.

Truth be known, Abram and Noah hadn't gotten along for the longest time. "We don't see eye to eye," Abram had often said. Which puzzled Ida when she thought of it, because there wasn't anyone else round the community who rubbed Abram the wrong way. He was a loyal and good friend to all the men in the church here. She sometimes wondered what peeved her husband about her elder brother. But, lying here in bed, she was grateful to have met and married such a man as Abram, who slept next to her breathing softly, not like many husbands, whose wives complained of their snoring. No, Abram's sleep was always placid. He could slumber through most anything, seemed to her. Even the mournful sounds coming from Sadie and Leah's bedroom just now.

What the world? she wondered. Sounded like Sadie crying, and when she leaned up to listen, jah, she was sure it was. Ach, she'd be ever so glad when all four girls were safely past their rumschpringe. To think that now Leah was coming into hers . . . and the twins not so far behind.

Dear Lord Jesus, help us through the comin' years. May we, each one, commit our ways to you, she began to pray.

When the sounds of sadness had ceased, she fell back into a stuporlike sleep where not a single dream invaded her serenity.

In the morning, before Abram rose to pull on his work clothes and go out to get started with milking, the wind swerved round to the northwest side of the house; and in those early-morning hours he lay next to dear Ida, who was sleeping soundly and, he noticed, snoring to beat the band.

Listening to the droning, whistling sound of a pending rainstorm, he thought of his father-in-law, John Brenneman, over in the Dawdi Haus. It hadn't struck him before, but here lately, John was beginning to remind him of Noah, his wife's outspoken oldest brother. Not always, just once in a while, the retired farmer would speak his mind to the point where Abram wished he'd keep his comments to himself.

Take yesterday, for instance, when the two of them were out working in the barn. John was pitching hay to the animals and Abram redding up the place a bit—something Leah had been doing till she decided she liked women's work better. Anyway, Abram had mentioned this fact about Leah.

Well, John spoke up, saying, " 'Tis time the girl made her own decisions, ain't?"

Abram didn't rightly know what to make of it, not really. Same thing had happened back some days ago, when he'd got to talking in confidence with John about Leah and Smithy Gid—that he thought the two of them would make a wonderful-gut match, and didn't John agree?

Well, about all John had to say was, "Let Leah be. If ya ask me, she oughta be allowed to fall in love as she pleases, same as you and Ida did."

Truth was, Abram regretted ever asking John's opinion. The man just seemed too eager to let his voice be heard about things that didn't concern him. Abram sure didn't want a steady diet of John's yap. He and Ida were doing the man a favor having him move to their neck of the woods . . . looking after him the way they were. And Lizzie was helping out, too. All the girls, really. Jah, everyone seemed to be fussing over the man.

Just now, thinking on all this, Abram wondered if it was such a good idea to take John with him today. That is, if the rain blew away and things dried out some. He and Smithy, along with several other men from the church, had hoped to go down the road a piece and help harvest their neighbor's corn crop. Wasn't such a smart thing to tax the older man, but then again, if John found out and wasn't included in the work frolic, well, Abram would catch it later.

So the more he thought on it, the more he was leaning toward asking John to go along. If his father-in-law tired out, he could always go inside with some of the womenfolk and have himself some hot coffee or a catnap, or both.

Gideon Peachey was glad for the blustery winds, which had already started blowing away the dark rain clouds. He had his harmonica tucked away in his pocket and was headed in his open buggy over to help Dawdi Mathias Byler put a new roof on his old shed out behind the house.

On his way he happened to glance over his right shoulder at Abram's big farmhouse and the expanse of land surrounding it. And, lo and behold, if he didn't see Leah come out on the front porch and shake out a long braided runner. He wanted to wave but realized she wasn't looking his way anyhow, so what was the use? And hadn't that been the story of his life with Leah, at least as long as he could remember? She was always looking off in a different direction completely.

He could kick himself for confiding in his father about Leah's refusal at the recent singing. He'd only wanted to share his disappointment with someone was all. Of course,

Dat's reaction wasn't so encouraging, really. "Best take yourself over to Ebersols' and do something to get Leah's attention," his father had said.

Do what sort of thing? he'd wondered, and why should he force the issue if Leah didn't feel the way he did about her?

So there she was beating rugs with a broom on a Saturday morning, and he'd missed the chance to wave her a greeting. But it wasn't his place to come between Leah and Jonas Mast. He'd seen the way they'd looked at each other over in the corner of the barn that night. Just wasn't the right thing to do, no matter what Dat said . . . Abram neither. It wasn't the way to win a girl's heart, Gideon didn't think, trying to vie for Leah's attention against her will. No, he'd let things play out between Leah and Jonas, let them decide if they were sweet on each other or not. So he'd wait his turn.

After about an hour or so, Abram knew he should've gone with his first hunch and left his father-in-law at home. Back where Ida and Lizzie could jump at his every beck and call. Wasn't so much that John needed attention this morning, he was just far too interested in Abram's conversation with Smithy, who said in passing that Gideon had been rebuffed by Leah.

"Well now, are you telling me Leah didn't ride home with Gideon?" asked Abram.

Smithy nodded his head hard. "That's what I'm a-sayin', all right."

John spoke up. "Did Gideon even ask her to?"

"Asked her right away," Smithy said. "But someone else got to her first."

"Did Leah ride home with *that* fella, then?" John asked.

"From what Gideon told me, jah, Leah did."

Abram didn't have to guess who that "someone else" was. The culprit was Jonas Mast. No doubt in his mind.

"The early bird gets the worm," announced John just then, having himself a good laugh.

Abram and Smithy didn't find it so amusing. And Abram tried to change the subject to the German shepherd pups Gideon was breeding for extra money, but John didn't show much interest.

"I'd say, if it was me, I'd set myself up with her long 'fore the next singing." John's eyes were beaming.

This irked Abram no end, but he held his tongue.

"Gid's not one to push himself off on folk, least of all girls," Smithy added. "There has to be a better way."

"Hoping the other fella sets his eye on 'nother girl, maybe?" John chuckled again.

"That other fella is none other than Peter Mast's son, Ida's cousin's eldest," Abram announced. There, he'd said it right out. See what they thought of *this* news.

"What're ya saying, Abram?" John's frown carved out deep lines on his already wrinkled brow. " 'S'nothing wrong with second cousins marryin'. Happens all the time."

Abram nodded. They all knew it wasn't something to bother disputing. However, here lately he'd heard of babies born with physical and mental problems, especially the offspring of married first and second Amish cousins. "Does raise the chances of deformity and other problems, though."

"Puh! That rarely happens round here," John retorted.

Abram shrugged. John could say what he wanted. What he really cared deeply about was Leah, Gideon, and their future offspring. He wanted only the best for his gentle yet hardworking girl, nothing less. And that sure wasn't Jonas Mast. Not in his book. Besides, Gid Peachey needed a strong, sturdy wife—like Leah—to help him raise beef stock on the grazing land he was to inherit someday.

Chapter Seventeen

Jonas Mast worked alongside Derek Schwartz boxing up potatoes, preparing them for market. Katie and Rebekah, his sisters, would sell many of them at the roadside stand out front, but the bulk of the potatoes was headed for Central Market at Penn Square, in downtown Lancaster. Anna, the oldest of his sisters, was making lists with Mamma, getting ready for her wedding in a month. Anna had been too busy to help with selling potatoes and apples this year. But she and Nathaniel King were planning on living just down the road from the Mast orchard, so Jonas knew he and Dat could count on Nathaniel for help with cultivating and whatnot next year . . . making up for their loss of Derek Schwartz.

"We'll miss you round here, come next summer and the harvest," Jonas told his English friend.

Derek nodded. "I'll be long gone by then."

"Pop wishes you didn't hafta sign up for the military." Jonas didn't need to remind Derek of the People's disapproval of violence and war. The doctor's son surely knew or had heard of the Anabaptist stand against aggression and revenge.

"I'm glad to be leaving here," Derek said unexpectedly, surprising Jonas as they worked.

"Why's that?"

Derek shrugged. "It's time for me to see the world. Get a new perspective. You know how it is, small-town boy meets big-time world."

Jonas didn't identify with Derek's twaddle, and, truth be told, he didn't care about either seeing or meeting the wide world. "You'll still be round here for Christmas, though, jah?"

"I leave sometime before the New Year."

"Where to?"

"Won't know until I receive my orders."

Receiving orders . . . leaving home . . .

All this made Jonas uneasy, really. He had no interest in giving up his present life or leaving the community of the People behind. The one and only thing that would make him even consider moving away from his father's house was marrying Leah Ebersol. And after several months of courting her—by year's end, maybe—he was fairly sure she'd be in agreement with him about their future together. Wouldn't do to rush things, though. He'd take his time winning her, but he had a feeling it wouldn't take much, seeing that bright smile on her perty face all the way home from singing. Jah, Leah was the girl for him, and he'd known it since he was thirteen and even before that.

"Say, Jonas," Derek said as they loaded the last crate of potatoes into the market wagon. "I was wondering . . . would you happen to know of an Amish family who might want to . . . well, adopt a baby?"

"A baby?" Jonas wiped his brow. He found this mighty curious, coming from Derek, who didn't impress him as having an ounce of paternal concern. "Wouldn't know offhand. Is this someone who's a patient of your father?"

Derek shook his head. "No . . . I just heard about a young girl who's in the family way."

"Well, then maybe you oughta ask your father, since he's in the business of family medicine and all. Maybe *he'd* know of a couple."

Jonas's response didn't seem to sit well with Derek. "Just forget it," Derek said quickly.

"Well, Mam's in the family way herself, so she'll have her hands full."

Derek shook his head. "I wasn't thinking of *your* mother."

"If it would help, I could ask her, though. She might know of a couple who could take in a baby . . . or folk who can't have any of their own."

"No . . . that's all right. Don't bother." And with that, Derek walked round the market wagon, said he needed a drink of water, and headed for the kitchen door.

Hannah had been dutifully following her twin around at school recess for quite a few days now, Mary Ruth having been convinced that Elias Stoltzfus wanted to visit with them. Of course, this was based on Elias's recent stop at their produce stand, Mary Ruth insisted. But they'd kept missing him, or he was involved in a baseball game or some activity with the other boys.

Watching for him today, Hannah spied him coming. He waved and ran over to say, "Hullo, Mary Ruth . . . and Hannah." He seemed happy to see both of them, yet Hannah felt like a third wheel and fell silent, which was how she preferred to be anyway round boys. She observed Mary Ruth's face brighten to a peach color and Elias, too, had a flushed face. Well, now, what was this? Were they embarrassed to talk together? Surely seemed so.

But, no, Elias was telling about his plans for fixing up an old pony cart his uncle was going to give him "here right quick," he said.

When the school bell rang and Elias dashed over to line up with the boys, Hannah whispered, "What was *that* all 'bout, Mary Ruth?"

"My guess is he's itchin' to have a way to get around. You know how Elias is when he drives his father's market wagon."

It was no secret that Elias Stoltzfus took a shining to anything that had some get up and go. His sisters all declared, up and down, if he was Mennonite he'd probably be out driving a fast car.

So the talk at afternoon recess—amongst the seventh-grade girls, anyways—was that Elias was going to have himself a pony cart.

"Maybe he'll hitch it up to his older brother Ezra," one of the girls said. That brought a big laugh.

Hannah could hardly wait to leave school and get home again. Who cared what Elias wanted with a secondhand pony cart? Truth be known, she was more interested in what *Ezra* had on his mind. Ach, but she was ever so shy. Too bashful to ever talk with a boy the way Mary Ruth could. All Hannah cared to do was busy herself with embroidery for the next few days. She wanted to give Anna Mast a special surprise. A blue cotton handkerchief with a white dove in the corner to carry in her pocket on the day she wed Nathaniel King.

Jah, Anna would be ever so pleased to receive such a gift, Hannah knew. She could hardly wait for that exciting day—

the Mast wedding. There she would see Ezra Stoltzfus yet again, if only secretly. Though, being fifteen and all, he surely had his eye on an older girl. More than likely, he did.

At half past nine Lizzie decided to walk down to Ida's for a bit. There she found both Leah and Ida in the kitchen, working shoulder to shoulder, companionably tending the wood stove. The cozy sight warmed her heart and she called out as she closed the back door behind her, "Yoo-hoo, anybody home?"

Leah and Ida looked up at the same time, smiles on their rosy faces. "Come in, come in, Lizzie," Ida said. "Nice to see ya, sister."

Lizzie felt special somehow, hearing Ida's usual warm greeting whenever she dropped by . . . as if Ida truly missed seeing her, even though it had been only a little over twelve hours since last evening's suppertime visit. Ida was a hospitable woman in every way, and Lizzie was mighty blessed to have such a dear big sister in her life. "Well, now, aren't the two of you lookin' chirpy," she said, making a beeline for the stove and sniffing at the kettles of homemade soup. "I take it you're feelin' better, Ida?"

"Oh my, ever so much better now." Ida's face lit up just then, and she turned back to the stove, where she busied herself with two big pots of soup, chattering instructions to Leah a mile a minute in Pennsylvania Dutch.

Lizzie looked round. "Where *is* everybody this morning?"

Leah spoke up. "The twins are at school, and Sadie rode along with Miriam Peachey over to Strasburg to purchase some yard goods."

"Jah, we need to get busy sewin' new dresses. The girls are

growin' like weeds, and it ain't even summer anymore." Ida laughed softly at her own remark.

Leah had a twinkle in her eye. "Mamma thinks we grow more when it's hot out."

"Ach, 'tis an old wives' tale," Lizzie said. She had a taste of the soup from the wooden ladle Ida held out for her, Ida's hand cupped beneath to catch any drips. "Mm-m . . . 's'gut. Real tasty, I must say." She stood there, hoping for more. "Do I have this recipe somewheres?"

"Oh, I'm sure ya do. It's just vegetable-oyster soup and salsify, with celery leaves for extra flavor." Ida dipped the spoon into the black kettle yet again. "Here, this is your last nibble till we eat."

"I'm invited to stay for dinner?" She was chuckling now.

Leah nodded her head, looking at her. "You're always invited, Aunt Lizzie. You oughta know that by now."

She knew, all right. And it was so comforting, too. Ida's family loved her—*liked* her—enough to include her in their day-to-day life. What had started out awkward and strained early on had turned out to be all right. And for everyone involved. Mostly because Ida and Abram had been so kind back then to invite her to come live here in Gobbler's Knob.

"Leah, can you tell me all the vegetable ingredients?" she asked, thinking it would reinforce what Ida was trying to teach Leah.

Eager to recite—at least it seemed so—Leah faced Lizzie. "There's diced potatoes, onions, shredded cabbage, ripe tomatoes, some carrots, one big stalk of celery, four ears of cut corn . . ." She stopped to think, whispering what she'd already said, touching her fingers lightly, counting as she went. "Mustn't forget the string beans, green and red peppers, lima beans, rice, and barley. Oh, and parsley leaves if you don't want to use celery leaves."

Lizzie clapped at such a wonderful-gut recitation and told Leah so. "You're catchin' on fast . . . isn't she, Ida?"

"Well, I should say." Ida went and sat down for a moment on the wooden bench beside the long table across the room. "She's come a long way in a short time. Even Abram says so."

Lizzie had to smile at that. Hardworking Abram, dear man. He was the reason she'd moved over from Hickory Hollow after her rumschpringe . . . built her a cabin to live in with his bare hands. Jah, such a gut man Ida had married. Lord willing, if she ever had the chance someday, wouldn't it be awful nice to meet a man just like that? Seemed single men were few and far between these days, what with her approaching forty here in a couple of years. Probably would never marry, though. Still, she wondered why the Lord God kept putting the longing for a husband in her heart. What was the purpose, really, if she was simply to hope and dream, living out her life under the covering of Abram and his family?

"When are the girls gonna be sewing, then?" she asked Ida.

"Tomorrow afternoon, prob'ly. Care to help?"

Leah went and sat next to Ida on the bench, still beaming, proud of herself, no doubt. "Jah, you should come, Aunt Lizzie. The house'll be a mess with all the material laid out and whatnot."

"I'd be happy to help," she said. "And just when are you planning to make something for Anna's wedding gift?"

Leah clapped her hand over her mouth. "That's right,

Mamma. We oughta be thinking about what we want to give as a family."

"Best find out from Fannie what the couple needs." Ida was fanning herself with the tail of her long black apron.

"I'd say they'll be needin' everything," Lizzie added. "Most young marrieds do."

Leah rose and headed for the back door. "Dat's gonna wonder why I haven't fed the chickens yet."

"Well, run along, then. Tell your father, if you see him, we'll be eating dinner round eleven o'clock."

"Jah, I will."

"Such a wonderful-gut girl," Lizzie said as she and Ida sat there watching Leah slip out the back door and head to the chicken house.

Ida touched her on the elbow. "I'm glad we're alone, Lizzie . . . I have something personal to share with you."

"Oh?"

Pausing a bit, Ida put her hand over her heart. "I'm going to have a baby."

Lizzie clasped her sister's free hand. "Ach, you are?"

"Jah," Ida replied, looking a bit sheepish. "Think of it, at my age, and just when I thought . . ."

Lizzie's heart leaped up. "Oh, Ida, this is such a surprise—what gut news, really 'tis." She couldn't help it; tears sprang to her eyes. "I'm awful happy for you. Does Abram know?"

"Not just yet. I'll tell him tonight, then the girls tomorrow . . . when they're all busy cuttin' out dress patterns and whatnot. Will you come over after the twins get home from school, then?"

She was ever so delighted. A new baby in the family! "I'll be sure'n come, Ida." She released her sister's hand. "You can count on me to help, just as I did when Hannah and Mary Ruth surprised all of us by bein' twins!"

"Well, I can only hope this one's a singleton." Ida fanned her face harder. "Don't know that I could handle more than one baby at this stage of life."

"Won't Abram be happy? And the girls, too?"

"I have a feeling it's another daughter," Ida said, "though how would I know?"

"Five girls would be just fine with me."

Ida went on to tell her what Cousin Fannie had said about them needing a son to carry on the family name. "Puh, I said we'd leave it up to whatever the Good Lord saw fit to give us."

Lizzie nodded, glad to have shared this private moment with Ida. "That's a right good answer, I daresay. When's the baby expected?"

"Best as I can tell, middle May."

"A springtime baby . . . *des gut*." Lizzie got up and went to the back door, looking out the window. She could see her father helping Abram lead the horses and mules out to pasture, and over there, across the barnyard, Leah was scattering feed to the chickens. *We'll have us another little one to love . . . and lead to you, Lord*, she prayed silently.

◆

Ida sat at the kitchen table after Lizzie left to go out for a short walk. Enjoying the rare solitude of the house, she decided to write a letter to Becky Brenneman, her sister-in-law, clear over in Hickory Hollow. Wouldn't Becky be shocked with Ida's news, just as Lizzie had been? Ida could see the look of amazement on her sister's face just now. For goodness' sake, who would've thought this could happen, the twins being thirteen, and all? Why, it would be almost like raising her grandchild, except this baby would be her *child*—her and Abram's—in their twilight years.

Pen in hand, she began to write.

My dear sister Becky,

It's been much too long since I've written. We've all been busy with vegetable gardens and canning and such . . . you too, probably. Dat is nicely settled in next door, and I do believe Abram enjoys having the extra set of hands to help out. (Leah's decided she wants to learn to cook, sew, and whatnot, which doesn't come as a surprise to me, really, since she's courting age now. I can hardly believe it . . . little Leah already sixteen.)

Well, now, how about you and Noah? How do you like living in the Dawdi Haus yourself? Won't be too much longer, I expect, and Abram and I'll be doing the same thing here—after Dat passes on to Glory.

She stopped writing just then, catching herself. There was no way in the world she and Abram would be moving over to their Dawdi Haus, even if her father should pass away within the next five to ten years. Not with a new baby coming on. What if she should give birth to a son? Being the baby of the family, and the only boy, *he* would end up farming this land, and a gut long time from now. Well, for pity's sake, this baby growing inside her just might upset the fruit basket, and wouldn't that be a perty sight? If the baby turned out to be yet another daughter, well, they'd still have to stay put and live on this side of the house, for the youngster's sake. There wasn't enough room in the Dawdi Haus for a growing family. A second family, at that!

She scratched out the last sentence of her letter, staring at the mess she'd made. *I'll start all over with a different letter to Becky*, she thought. Then, for no reason at all, tears sprang to her eyes, trickling down her face. She bowed her head and prayed for this precious new life within her—most truly unexpected.

Chapter Eighteen

The hours dragged on endlessly for Leah. Here it was only Thursday afternoon. She glanced at the farmland calendar hanging on the door that led to the cold cellar. *October twenty-first.* She had the rest of today and all day tomorrow to wait, then most of Saturday, before she'd see Jonas again. Nearly two and a half days!

She and her sisters set about laying out their homemade dress patterns and newly purchased yard goods across the long kitchen table. Leah thought of offering to do some of Mamma's chores later, as well as her own—get her mind off the upcoming secret meeting with Jonas this Saturday night. Mamma seemed to need more rest than ever before, and Leah sometimes wondered about what she'd overheard Aunt Lizzie say back that one time she'd listened into their conversation.

What had Mamma said? That she might be fast approaching the change of life? Well, Leah didn't know anything about that, really. Still, she could see the tired lines in her mother's face, the washed-out complexion. Wasn't like Mamma to look so wrung out.

"Hand me your scissors," Mary Ruth said to Hannah.

"What'sa matter with *yours?*" Hannah asked from across the table.

Mary Ruth looked down at the scissors in her hand. "Mine are awful dull."

"Well, take 'em out to the barn, to Dat," Leah suggested. "He'll sharpen 'em up for you."

Mamma came in the kitchen just then. "Girls . . . did I tell you, Aunt Lizzie's comin' over in a little bit to help us sew up your dresses?"

"Maybe Lizzie can take my place out at the produce stand later on, after Sadie's turn," Hannah said softly. "I'll do my *own* sewin'."

"But that's your job today, Hannah. Mustn't duck your duty." Mamma went to sit in the rocker.

Hannah wrinkled up her nose slightly, but said nothing more about her great reluctance to work at the roadside stand alone.

Mary Ruth piped up, eyes bright. "I wouldn't mind tending the stand till supper for Hannah. Really, I wouldn't, Mamma."

But their mother remained firm. "Ain't too many gourds or pumpkins left to sell, so I think Hannah can have her turn once more before the killing frost comes."

Aunt Lizzie came whistling up the back steps and into the house. "Good afternoon, everybody," she said. "What can I do to help?"

Mamma waved her hand, getting the girls' attention. "Before we do a speck of cuttin' and sewin', I have something to say. Somebody go out on the front porch and call Sadie in here real quick."

Mary Ruth scampered off to do Mamma's bidding.

Meanwhile, Leah turned and looked at her mamma. There was something different about the way she sat there, beaming now. What did she have to tell them on such a busy day?

Once Sadie was inside, Mamma said, "Girls, gather round."

They did so quickly. Sadie stood in the doorway, keeping an eye out for the road, no doubt. Leah and Hannah sat at Mamma's feet, and Mary Ruth leaned on Sadie's shoulder. "What is it, Mamma?" Mary Ruth asked.

Mamma rocked forward and back in the hickory rocker, then stopped. She folded her hands in her lap and looked up at them. "Ach, but I never thought I'd be saying such a thing. Not now . . ." She sighed audibly. "Well, girls, you're going to have yourselves a new little sister or brother."

At once Mary Ruth squealed, clapping her hand over her mouth. Sadie looked altogether startled, turning ashen. Hannah sat silently on the floor next to Leah, her face tilted in a question mark. But Leah felt great joy, a warmth filling her heart as she reached up for Mamma's hand and squeezed it. "Oh, Mamma, such wonderful news. What fun we'll have."

"How soon?" Sadie said rather glumly.

"Late spring . . . sometime in May, I think."

Hannah found her voice at last. "What's Dat have to say?"

Mamma nodded. "I told him last night, and he is . . . well, in shock I guess is the best way to put it."

"Surprised but happy?" Leah asked, glancing over at Aunt Lizzie, who looked as if the cat had gotten her tongue.

"It'll take some time getting used to," Mamma said, her eyes watering.

"Jah, seven more months," Mary Ruth said, trying her best to get Sadie to jig round the room with her, but Sadie wouldn't budge.

"We can take turns playing with our new sister," Hannah said.

"Who says it'll be a girl?" Leah spoke up. "Maybe Mamma and Dat will have a son."

"We'll see when the time comes," Mamma said wisely. "Now, don't we have some dresses to sew up today?"

Leah was truly glad for the news. Now she could think on something besides seeing Jonas again. Funny thing, though . . . Fannie Mast and Mamma both having babies. She wondered how long Mamma would be keeping her news quiet, just for the immediate family's ears. She didn't bother to ask. She was enjoying the prattle made by Mary Ruth and Aunt Lizzie. Hannah was her quiet self, but then so was Sadie. For some odd reason, her oldest sister was obviously silent. Could it be that all this fuss over a new baby coming bothered the firstborn of the family? But, no, Leah didn't think that could be. She'd never known Sadie to be the jealous sort. Maybe she was still wounded over whatever happened between her and that Derry fella. Jah, that was probably it.

Abram led the animals back from the pasture by himself. He'd spotted Lizzie up on the knoll, meandering down the mule road toward the barnyard. She was coming over to help with the girls' sewing bee, Ida had said last night after springing the news of a baby on him. And just before they retired for the night, yet. Did she think he'd be able to sleep after hearing such astonishing news? Well, he'd slept, all right, but only after mulling things over in his head for a gut hour or so.

With Smithy saying what he was about Leah turning down Gideon's offer at the last singing . . . well, Abram felt things were up in the air enough without the possibility of a son coming along way behind like this. A *real son*. Which was most likely what Ida would have, too. Wouldn't it be just like the Lord God heavenly Father to do such a thing, after all girls? Almost a practical joke, so to speak.

Removing his straw hat, he scratched his head. He wasn't sure he wanted to farm *that* much longer, not the way his arthritis had been acting up with every barometer change here lately. And his back ached some days like never before.

He turned and headed back to the barn, telling himself he ought not to worry so. What if the baby was another girl, after all? His main course of action, here and now, was to talk sense to Leah, get her to see that Smithy Gid was the best choice of a mate.

Still, he couldn't up and tell her not to see Jonas anymore, but he sure could try in a roundabout way. Jah, he sure could, and he would. First thing tomorrow, at the early-morning milking, when he and Leah could talk privately. Man to man, so to speak.

After the supper dishes were washed, dried, and put away, Ida sat down and wrote a short note to Fannie Mast, asking what Anna needed most in the way of handmade linens and such. Didn't take her long, though, and since she had plenty of space left on the lined writing tablet, she decided to share her news with Fannie, too.

> *P.S. I'd thought of telling you this the next time I visit there, but I don't know when that'll be, so I'm going to tell you now, and you can keep it under your hat for a while longer. Abram and I are expecting a baby come mid-to-late May. So your little one and ours will be ever so close in age. See what talking about babies in your kitchen did to me, Fannie? Ha, ha.*
>
> *Let me know as soon as you can about Anna's needs. I'll look forward to hearing from you soon.*
>
> *Lovingly, your cousin,*
> *Ida*

Rereading the letter, Ida knew she'd much rather be crocheting booties for her coming child than fussing over embroidering pillowcases and tablecloths or whatever it was that Fannie would say Anna needed. The reality of having a new baby was slowly sinking in . . . taking her over, really. Almost more than her joyful heart could hold. No more tears since yesterday. She wouldn't wish to turn back the clock, even if she could . . . no, she wouldn't think of going back to planning her and Abram's retirement years—the "slowing-down years," as Dat liked to say.

She hoped Abram might catch up with her delight here real quick, guessing it might take him longer than when she'd first told him about expecting their girls. He'd come round. Jah, in due time.

The next morning Leah sat sleepily on the milking stool, wiping down Bessie's underparts before she got started with hand milking. Dat had come over to her and said he'd help with Rosie. So Leah knew something was up. But she promised herself—if Dat's eagerness to chat was over her lack of interest in Smithy Gid—she wouldn't mention a word about her plans to meet Jonas Mast tomorrow after dusk at the end of the lane. She felt she must guard their secret courtship now more than ever.

About the time she began milking Bessie, Dat sat down on his own stool nearby. She heard the tinny *ping-ping* of Rosie's rich milk against the sides of the pail.

"I know I ain't 'sposed to ask . . . but you won't mind, will you?" Dat said.

She smiled. "Just what're you sayin', Dat?"

"Well, now . . . I was just wondering how you liked your first singing, is all."

She shrugged a little, cautious to keep things to herself. " 'Twas all right, really."

"Didja see anybody you knew . . . from our church district, I mean?"

Dat wasn't doing such a good job of fishing for information, but she played along. "Jah, I knew some boys there."

Two milk pails being filled was the only sound in the barn at that moment. So just why was Dat asking her such questions when he knew she was already into rumschpringe? Was it Smithy Gid he was so interested in?

She wanted to help Dat out a bit. "Gid was at the singing with his sister." Then she added quickly, "Adah and I sat together at the long table all during the songs."

"Oh, didja now?"

"She and I stuck right close to each other for a long time." She wouldn't go so far as to say that Gid's sister had ended up riding home with a boy other than her brother. That was all she best be saying. Who a girl paired up with was supposed to be kept quiet. Besides, Dat knew better than to ask.

"Didja happen to talk to Smithy Gid at the singing, then?"

Dat's question startled her. "Dat . . . I—"

"Oversteppin' my bounds, I 'spose. You know, Leah, I have such high hopes for you and the Peachey boy."

She thought on that. "You've been sayin' this for as long as I can remember. But . . . truth is, I like someone else. Always have."

Dat snorted a bit from the underside of his cow.

"Does it matter that I'm awful happy?" she asked. "Happy as you and Mamma?"

Silence.

"Dat?"

"Leah, I just don't know . . ."

"Are you put out with me, then?"

Dat stopped milking and leaned back on his stool, catching her eye behind the cow. "Just try to be choosin' wisely, won'tcha?"

"Which means I don't have a choice at all, jah?"

"You've got your mamma's tongue!"

"Sorry, Dat."

"Well, then?"

"Best not talk about this anymore," she said softly.

Dat's dear face disappeared behind ol' Rosie.

Ach, her father was sorely hurt. She wished she could see

his face again, see around the cow, see just how disappointed he must be.

Finally Dat spoke. "Still, as long as you ain't a married woman, I won't stop hopin'."

Sighing, Leah didn't know what to say. Looked as though there was no way to change Dat's mind. Not just yet. But someday she would. She and Jonas Mast would.

Truth be known, Sadie was pleased that Mamma was in the family way. The news had jolted her at first, but now that she'd had time to think, she realized it was wonderful-gut timing. This way all the fuss would be made over Mamma and her midlife baby, not Sadie's sad and sinful situation. She could hide behind Mamma's skirt tail, so to speak.

Meanwhile, she was beginning to feel a tender bond with the little one inside her, though no life flutters had occurred just yet. She wanted to shield her baby from the likes of Derry Schwartz. Such hateful remarks he'd made. How a young man could be so unlike his father—the village doctor, a man who helped folk get well—was beyond her. Sadie recalled the smiling, polite faces of Derry's parents. Such nice folk. Why, they'd even invited her inside, though they'd never laid eyes on her before. She could scarcely believe it still, when she thought back to that dreadful night.

Now her turn at the produce stand was over. Gladly she left things to Hannah, who never truly complained, just made it known by the way her nose twitched, eyes blinking, too, that she didn't so much care for being out here alone with English customers. "Remember what Mamma said," Sadie called over her shoulder. "If ya sell out everything, that'll be it till next spring."

"I heard what she said" came Hannah's gloomy reply.

"Well, I'm goin' for a walk . . . over to Blackbird Pond, if anyone wants to know." This she said because the last time she'd upped and disappeared, both Dat and Mamma had given her a scolding. None of her sisters had been privy to it. She'd endured the severe tongue-lashing, though at the time she wouldn't have traded those stolen hours with Derry for anything. Now . . . she would do most everything differently if she could, starting with sneaking off Friday nights with Naomi Kauffman. The two of them had spelled trouble all along, and there was no telling what would happen to Naomi if *she* didn't hurry up and join church.

"Best go in and help Mamma cook," Hannah called back to her.

But Sadie had no intention of heading straight indoors, where she was expected. Taking her time, she took the road down to the Peacheys' long dirt lane, then turned and headed toward their farmhouse, aware of the sun on her back. There was a coolness in the breeze, the first sigh of autumn. She breathed deeply, swinging her arms as she made her way past the smithy's house, through the barnyard, and out into the pastureland toward the pond.

She didn't expect to find anyone out there this afternoon. Both Adah and Dorcas were indoors cooking food ahead for Sunday, no doubt, same as Mary Ruth, Leah, and Mamma. Smithy Gid, more than likely, was helping his father in the blacksmith shop in the barn. She didn't care so much about farm work, or shodding horses, either. Maybe that was the reason she'd gone off to Strasburg, flirting with English boys come Friday nights. For as long as she could remember, she'd had no interest in marrying a farmer. Clear back to grade school days. Being Amish, though, what other choice did she have?

The area surrounding Blackbird Pond was deserted, and she was glad. She sat down in the shade of the twisted willow, the ground beneath her lumpy and cold. She remembered playing in this spot more times than she could count when she and Leah were little, watching Smithy Gid dive into the pond, catching tadpoles with his bare hands.

Just now, staring at the murky water, she wondered what it was—if anything—she could hope for. Besides being the best mamma a child could have, there wasn't much else to look forward to in her future. She had truly lost her way in the dark woods. All her own doing, too.

Leaning her head down on her knees, she gritted her teeth, knowing she ought to be sorry for all that had gone wrong in her life. But she was more angry than repentant. She wanted nothing to do with Derry, would never again darken the door of that wretched lean-to where they'd spent their late-night hours. She wished the turkey hunters, next month, would go and tear the place down, such an old shanty it was, really. Thinking back to the vast woods made her shudder. What had Derry warned her about the dangers lurking there? Yet he'd said she could trust him. Why *had* she been so gullible? So completely foolish?

She wished she could cry and release some of the tension inside. Might make more room for her baby to grow. Then she realized how awful silly that was. Getting better rest at night and eating her fruits and vegetables would assure her of a healthy son or daughter. Knowing so little about what she ought to do between now and when the baby was to be birthed, she'd hurried to the Strasburg library this past

Wednesday and checked out a book on such things while Miriam Peachey chose dress material. Then, so Miriam wouldn't know where she'd gone after making her own purchase of yard goods for her sisters' dresses, Sadie had hidden the book away under the backseat of the buggy. Suddenly it dawned on her. She could observe Mamma—eat what she ate, do what she did to have a healthy child. Come to think of it, her baby and Mamma's would grow up like siblings. Now, wasn't that peculiar?

She stood and walked the whole length of the side of the pond, seeing Gid's German shepherd, Fritzi, bounding toward her. "Here, girl," she called, happy for some company now. When the dog caught up with her, she knelt and rubbed its neck on both sides, where Gideon said she loved to be stroked. "Are you supposed to be out here, away from your new pups?" she whispered. "Whatcha doin' so far from the whelping box?"

Docile-eyed Fritzi looked up at her as if to say, *I needed to run free for a bit.*

"Jah, that's all right. Come along with me." So Sadie strolled clear round the opposite side of the pond, Fritzi at her side, a silent companion.

Looking up at the sky, she wondered how almighty God might choose to punish her for her transgressions. There were times when she remembered the Scripture Dat often read from the book of Romans—"And we know that all things work together for good to them that love God, to them who are the called according to his purpose."

She hadn't been devoted to God the way she should've, not in the least, otherwise she wouldn't be in this sad predicament. Having been called "according to his purpose," she'd willfully sinned . . . even after her baptism. Preacher Yoder, if he knew, would counsel her to make things right, and mighty soon. Well, repenting to the preacher and the deacons was one thing. Their going home and sharing the news of her immorality with their wives so they could spread the shameful word through the community at upcoming quilting bees . . . well, that was another thing altogether. Such potential gossip would not only hurt her chances of ever being courted again, but Leah's and the twins' reputations would be tainted, too. Yet once she became great with child, would it matter if she'd confessed to the brethren? The awful truth would be evident.

Oh, she hardly knew what to do these days. Didn't know what she believed in, either.

Chapter Nineteen

Jonas hurried the horse just a bit, eager to see Leah again. Her hazel eyes—the specks of gold in them—had brightened when he'd asked her, back on the night of their first singing, if he could come calling. "Jah, that'd be fine," she'd said, and he had walked back to the horse and open buggy with an extra spring in his heels.

Now, coming up over the hill, he spied Abram's flourishing acres of corn in the distance. Nearly half of it was harvested, he could see in the fading light. He might've offered to lend a hand if it wasn't that his own father needed him for the fall pruning of the apple orchard, some trees twenty feet high. The rigorous thinning process took hours of daily work, but it was best to press on and finish before the snow began to fly.

When he reached the spot where the long Ebersol lane met the road, he slowed the horse and pulled over onto the right shoulder. He glanced at the new dashboard, speedometer, and glove compartment he had installed just this week, hoping Leah would find his courting buggy to her liking and not too fancy. Truth be told, he took more than a little pleasure in knowing just how fast his horse pulled the open carriage. And the glove compartment, well, it was right nice for seeing Leah home from singings and whatnot, if she had any particular need of it.

Jumping down from his shiny black buggy, he stood near the horse, watching for Leah. Originally he had offered to come by much later in the evening—after Abram's house was dark—but she'd said she could easily meet him out here earlier, at the end of the lane. Being out late seemed to be of concern to her—just why, he hadn't the slightest notion. After all, tomorrow was the "off-Sunday," so courting couples could sleep in a bit. Had Abram spoken to her about not staying out too long? Jonas wanted to start things out on the right foot—wouldn't think of offending his dear girl's father, that is, if Leah had even revealed just who it was she planned to meet tonight. More than likely, she'd kept Jonas's name out of any conversation altogether.

He whispered to his horse, looking out over the golden serenity of the fall evening, his gaze wandering all the way round Abram's rolling front lawn, then over to the adjoining field. He'd heard the rumors about Abram's hopes of Leah and Smithy Gid uniting in marriage someday, though he dismissed them as mere tittle-tattle. Abram was a reasonable man. Surely he'd want Leah's say in the matter of a husband.

Tonight Jonas hoped to find out just how well he and Leah got along together. He had a nice surprise in store for her. They were going to drive over and visit his married cousin on his mother's side. Later on, Anna and her soon-to-be-husband were joining them there for pie and ice cream.

The gentle rustle of a breeze in the bushes made him

watch even more keenly for Leah, hoping she might appear at any minute. He started to walk down the lane to meet her halfway, and then there she was . . . he spied the white prayer cap atop her brown hair, and—if he wasn't mistaken—she wore a cheerful smile. "That you, Leah?" he called.

"Jah, 'tis. Hullo, Jonas."

He offered his hand as they walked across the road to the parked buggy. Giving her a slight boost, he waited till she was settled on the left side of the driver's seat, then, hurrying round to the other side, leaped into the carriage.

They rode down Georgetown Road a ways, talking all the while. He was struck yet again at how much he enjoyed the lively conversation. When there was a lull, he asked, "Does your dat know who you're out with tonight?"

"I didn't tell him."

He wanted to bring up the amount of time she expected them to be gone. "Didja want to return early, say before midnight?"

"Maybe closer to eleven," she replied. "Will that be all right with you?"

Jonas hated the thought of cutting their time short, because they wouldn't see each other again till next Sunday night at the singing, if Leah agreed to ride home with him again. "I'll have you back home early enough," he agreed.

When they got closer to his cousins' farm, he played a little game with Leah. "Can ya guess where we might be goin'?"

"To somebody's house?"

"Jah."

"Anyone I know?"

"You met 'em at the big family reunion several summers

back," he said, enjoying his clever pastime. " 'Twas when Mamma's distant cousins from Hickory Hollow came, too."

"Oh, now I remember. Let's see." She paused to think. "Is it a newly married couple?"

"Tied the knot just two years ago." He was sure she'd know from this additional tidbit.

"I think I know. Must be Bennie and Amanda Zook."

"That's right, and there's something else exciting." He lowered his voice, sounding even more mysterious. "Another couple is coming, too. Can you guess?"

"A courtin' couple or married?"

He was impressed with how sharp she was. "Courtin', that's all I best say."

She began naming off one young girl and boy after another. "Becky Lapp and John Esh? Mary Ann Glick and Jesse Stoltzfus?"

"Wouldja like another hint?" he asked at last.

"Just one clue, but a *little* one, jah?"

He leaned closer, a gut excuse to do so. "Their married name will rhyme with 'sing.' "

She thought for only a few seconds, then said, "Now I know. We're meeting your sister, Anna, and her beau, Nathaniel King!"

This was the moment he'd been waiting for. He slipped his arm around her and drew her near. "You're correct, my dear Leah." And with that, he kissed her cheek.

The harvest moon, yellow and full, rose slowly over the eastern horizon. Leah pointed and said the sight of it nearly took her breath away. Jonas was ever so glad, for he'd hoped she might think so . . . have some wonderful-gut memories of this, their first night as a courting couple, something special to tell their grandchildren in years to come.

The evening visit was filled with laughter, telling jokes and a few stories mixed in, but it was the chocolate-mocha pie and homemade vanilla ice cream that topped off the night. Both Leah and Anna decided it was the tastiest pie they'd ever had. Jonas was especially pleased to observe his sister and Leah getting along so agreeably.

At one point Nathaniel King whispered to him out of the girls' hearing that perhaps the two couples ought to have themselves a double wedding. Jonas was taken aback by the suggestion, though he assumed a casual attitude. "In less than three weeks? No, we've just started courtin'," he replied.

So the subject was dropped, since he was fairly sure the abrupt idea might scare off Leah. And if not her, then Abram, for sure and for certain. Jonas must prove himself over time, show himself to be deserving of Abram's daughter—his pick of the crop, far as Jonas could tell.

He took the long drive home, aware of the time, though it was only quarter of ten. Plenty of time for just the two of them. "Didja enjoy yourself?" he asked.

"Oh my, ever so much. Denki, Jonas."

"Anna and Nathaniel did, too, I think."

"Jah, they did. And I was glad to get better acquainted with your sister."

"Anna said to tell you it would be fun to do something else, the four of us . . . sometime."

"How does Nathaniel feel 'bout that?"

Jonas shook his head. "He's eager to have gut fellowship with us, too." Then he had the daring to ask her, right there and then, if she'd consent to riding home with him at the next singing.

"Why, sure, Jonas."

Right pleased with her response, he had to hold himself back a bit from moving too quickly, revealing the depths of his feelings for lovely Leah. After all, this was only their first time courting.

Enjoying the stillness, a trace of cinnamon in the fresh night air, he reached for Leah's hand and held it all the way home as they talked and laughed. Truly, they were so happy together!

Leah wished she'd never said a thing about Jonas having her home by eleven o'clock. Goodness' sakes, she was having the best time. And here they were, riding under a full moon, her hand in Jonas's, talking as comfortably as you please. She had built this night up in her mind, during the days between the last singing and now, yet how could she have known she'd feel almost sad to say good-bye?

Dat's cornfield was fast coming into view as the horse and buggy approached the Ebersol Cottage from the Peachey side. If only Dat could know how happy she was this night.

"I'll be countin' the days till I see ya again," said Jonas.

"A week and a day, jah?" She felt him squeeze her hand gently.

"My brothers and I will be workin' in the orchard 'tween now and then. Such a busy time it'll be."

"And I'll be helpin' Mamma finish up the canning and

doin' my outside chores for Dat, too." She didn't mention that her mother was in the family way, same as his mamma was. She just left that be. It was up to Mamma to share her news.

"We'll both be busy . . . so time'll fly, jah?" he said.

She nodded but didn't believe it for a second, knowing how the days had crawled along waiting for *this* night. And what if they both felt so strongly about missing each other? Just how many years would Jonas want to wait before they were married?

When it was time to say good-bye, he gave her a quick, awkward sort of hug. Oh, she wouldn't have minded letting him kiss her full on the lips, the way she felt just now . . . and the way he was looking at her, too. But she knew better. Mamma had taught her, "*Save your lip-kissin' for marriage*."

"God be with you, Leah." He held both her hands lightly now.

"And with you, Jonas." Though she said she could walk to the house on her own, he wouldn't hear of it.

Turning to tie up the horse, he then accompanied her down the lane that led to the barnyard. Yet another opportunity for Jonas to reach for her hand, and she had to smile, already having missed his tender touch.

Then, of all things, they got to talking again about how she had always worked outdoors with Dat, how that was just the way things had been. "I guess it happened 'cause Mamma and Dat were sorry they ever let Sadie go to high school, even though they could've gotten her a domestic permit when she turned fifteen." Leah had been hesitant to bring up her older sister tonight. She had no way of knowing just what rumors had been floating round . . . what Jonas might've heard of

Sadie's careless rumschpringe. "So when I finished eighth grade, Dat put his foot down . . . decided to keep me home, continue workin' outside with him."

Jonas stopped walking. "I'm so sorry, Leah. I wish you hadn't had to work that way . . . just to keep from goin' to school."

"I didn't mind, really. Dat and I get along just fine. And for the longest time, honestly, I didn't so much care for women's work . . . women's *talk*," she admitted.

"And now?" He was looking down at her, eyes searching hers in the moonlight.

"Oh, I don't know. I guess I never felt I fit in with the womenfolk. Wasn't like them, really." What she meant to say was that she didn't think she was as perty as the rest of them. But she dare not say such a thing. Jonas might think she was fishing for flattery.

"So you really *are* Abram's Leah?" whispered Jonas.

Her heart sank. "Where'd you ever hear that?"

"My sisters say it sometimes." He started walking again. "But I don't think it's right. To me, you're ever so perty. Maybe the pertiest girl I've ever known."

She wanted to say "no foolin'?" but she kept walking.

"Like a lovely bluebird, that's what you are," he said.

She could scarcely believe her ears. He had remembered her favorite bird from way back when! "I'd always thought of myself as a common brown wren."

"Well, if you're comparing yourself to Sadie, best not."

She swallowed hard, hoping he'd go no further.

"You've got it all over your older sister. You have such a gut heart."

"Well, that's awful nice of you, Jonas, but—"

"No, I *mean* it. You're *my* bluebird, Leah, and always will be."

His words startled her a bit. How could such a handsome boy be saying that *she* was perty? And besides, wasn't this too soon for him to offer such words of devotion?

But once Jonas was gone, and the clatter of carriage wheels on the road was but a memory, she was glad he'd spoken up like that. So they felt the same way about each other. After this many years, they still did.

At half past nine Sadie headed off to bed, not to sleep but to read her library book on pregnancy and childbirth. She had been careful to close the door securely, though there were no locks on any of the bedrooms—none in the house at all, not even the outside doors. So she sat in bed, the oil lamp propped up on a chair next to her, devouring every word, marveling at the information tucked away in one book. This, she thought, was a smart idea tonight, since Leah was gone with Jonas Mast—where she didn't know.

At ten-thirty she set the book aside, going to look out the window. No sign of Leah anywhere. At once she thought she might have to laugh, thinking that the tables were turned, her worrying over Leah this way.

Then, before creeping back to bed, she marked her place and hid the book deep in her hope chest, just as her secret was well hidden for now within her own body.

Yet she did not sleep, lying awake . . . waiting for the sound of footsteps on the stairs. And come along they would, fairly soon, she hoped. Leah had surely made it clear to Jonas that she wouldn't be staying out so late. Not on this, their first real courting night. Besides, Jonas would have a half-hour ride back once he brought Leah home. Because of the slightly longer distance between here and Grasshopper Level, Sadie wondered if Leah might not allow Smithy Gid to court her some, too, if for no other reason than for the sake of convenience. Most boys didn't care to drive too far to pick up a girl and take her home. She'd heard plenty of complaining about such things from some of her boy cousins, while waiting for the common meal after Preaching service. But no, Leah had her heart set on Jonas.

Sadie thought she just might go along with Leah to the next singing. Find out what was up. Wouldn't hurt none. Nobody at singing would have to know of her situation. Maybe, too, she'd find herself a nice boy. If she could get somebody to fall in love with her, then tell him her secret . . . well, if he consented to marry her even still, then her disgraceful state could come to an end. But who on earth would *that* boy be? Certainly not anyone she knew in their church district. No one she'd care to consider as a husband.

Putting out the lamp, she climbed out of bed and stood in the window looking down at the barnyard. So here *she* was, waiting for Leah to return, when she might've been out having some fun of her own on such a pleasant night. If only she hadn't been so foolish.

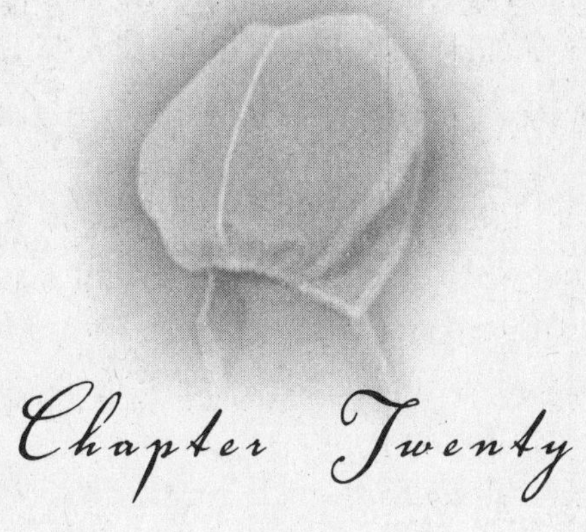

Chapter Twenty

The days passed quickly enough, just as Jonas said they would. Yet Leah often caught herself joyfully brooding over him, thinking ahead to the next wonderful-gut time, careful not to share too much with Sadie, who was ensnared in her own contemplation. The difference between them now was Sadie's tight-lipped response to most everything, while Leah could scarcely contain her happiness.

Mamma must've noticed, too, saying that Leah was nearly as *bapplich*—chatty—as Mary Ruth. This observation didn't seem to bother Mary Ruth at all, just made for livelier canning frolics in Mamma's big kitchen with Aunt Lizzie and Miriam and Adah Peachey.

Days grew shorter as the time neared for Anna Mast's wedding. One mid-November morning Leah awakened with the cold creeping in from outside, rousing her from deep slumber. Turning over, she saw that Sadie had pulled the heavy woolen quilts over to her side of the bed. Leah tugged at them, trying to get her fair share back, so she could at least sleep a bit longer before morning chores.

Here lately, though, Dat had said she didn't need to get up and come out in the cold for the first milking of the day. *Kind of him*, she thought, rolling over, her back against Sadie's.

Even after pulling her half of the quilts back over herself, Leah was still a bit shivery. But the weight of the heirloom quilts was always a comfort and a reminder of Mamma's love. Just as Jonas's wool throws kept her snug and warm in his open buggy each time they went riding.

At the last singing Sadie had surprised her by going along. They'd had such fun together, one of the first times recently—almost like their former days of childhood—though Sadie had latched on to her, hardly letting her talk with Jonas alone at all. And then, since Leah and Sadie had both ridden over with Smithy Gid and Adah, they had ended up riding back to Gobbler's Knob with Jonas, which was an interesting howdy-do.

Honestly, Leah had felt Sadie was spying on her and didn't appreciate it one bit. Jonas, on the other hand, took Sadie's presence in his stride, including her in their banter, paying nearly as much attention to Sadie as he had to *her*. Jah, Jonas had joked openly with Sadie, politely of course, who sat directly behind them in the second seat, clutching her own woolen lap robe. Such a peculiar thing, really—three in a courting buggy!

After that night, though, Sadie said she thought Leah ought to attend singings on her own. "Oh, why's that?" Leah had asked, sticking her neck out only for Sadie to wave her hand and say, "No reason. 'Tis just better for courtin' couples to be by themselves."

So now Sadie sat home nights while Leah entertained

Jonas in the kitchen, near the wood stove, after the family had gone upstairs to bed. And Leah was grateful that Jonas was not so much interested in the hops or hoedowns so frowned upon by the church yet attended by some of his "buddy groups." She felt he was ever mindful of the People's rules. The best beau, he was.

Two nights prior to Anna Mast's nuptials, Dr. Schwartz's wife reminded her family of the Amish wedding "this coming Tuesday."

Amidst obnoxious groans from Derek, Lorraine rose and went to the kitchen, returning with a tray of dessert and hot coffee. "It's a rare opportunity," she said, eyeing her husband for support. "One we will enjoy . . . *all* of us."

Henry spoke up quickly. "Derek, it is important that you honor your employer at his daughter's marriage ceremony."

The boy muttered something unintelligible and stabbed a fork into his baked berry pudding. About then Robert spoke up and asked Henry's permission to drive the family car to a church meeting in nearby Quarryville. "When will yours be in running order again?" Henry asked.

"The mechanic said tomorrow. So if you wouldn't mind, Dad . . ."

"Sure." Henry pulled the car keys out of his trouser pocket. "When shall your mother and I expect you home?"

"Nine-thirty, if not earlier," Robert replied, to which Derek snorted loudly.

Henry's eyes locked with Derek's. This unspoken

exchange was registered, and the belligerent son sat up straighter, his spine now flat against the dining room chair.

From the entryway, Robert called good-bye and waved to them and turned toward the coat closet. Henry was filled with paternal pride at the sight of Robert, tall and honorable. *Such dire things he's seen and survived*, he thought, disconcerted but not surprised by his son's sudden interest in the ministry.

Though not a religious man, Henry believed in a Creator-God, one who had the power to grant life and take it away. A God who dwelt in the heavens somewhere, afar off. Only once in Henry's life had he ever prayed, and that was out of desperation, nothing more—when Robert had sent word by letter of the bloodshed on the battlefields of Europe. Never had he done so since, not even to offer a heartfelt thanks for Robert's safe return.

Just this morning his son had enthusiastically mentioned that he hoped to attend a nearby Mennonite church meeting. Robert had even gone so far as to inquire of his mother about Grandpa Schwartz's ministry and life, to which Lorraine had responded by promptly leaving the room, only to return with a tattered scrapbook. She said it had been in the family for many years, though Robert avowed he had never laid eyes on it. He had looked at the pictures with great interest, making note of his grandfather carrying a Bible in one photo.

Presently, Henry watched Robert open then close the front door behind him. The war had certainly turned their young ex-soldier inside out. What would it take to get Derek on better footing in general? The upcoming stint in the army? Henry was banking on it.

Derek was undeniably closed to any discussion, and Henry

was breaking no new ground. "What's bothering you, son?" he asked, truly frustrated.

"I can't wait to get out of here" was the surly reply.

"You're looking ahead to the service, I assume?"

"Not just that . . . leaving Lancaster behind forever."

The remark cut deep. *Why should our boy feel this way?* Henry wondered.

Lorraine kept her distance, pinching off leaves from the many African violets in the far end of the parlor. Occasionally she glanced at him kindly. Henry and his dear wife had certainly had their times with Derek and might have had similar difficulties with Robert had he not come home from Europe a changed man.

Not a father to pry into the private facets of his sons' lives, Henry had concealed the fact that he'd silently witnessed the heated exchange between the Amish girl and Derek in the yard some weeks ago. Though he had heard nothing of what was said, he worried that something was amiss, even at stake, between the two of them. Then when Derek had bolted after the girl—who had taken off on foot—revving up his car like a maniac and racing down the road after her, Henry felt grave concern.

Now Derek's words agitated him further. "Besides, I want nothing to do with this stinking life—yours and Mom's!" His son leaped up from the table.

"Just a minute, young man. I've worked all these years to establish our good family name. I'll not have you speak—"

"Save it, Dad!" With that, Derek brushed past him.

Stunned at this outburst, Henry looked at Lorraine, who sadly shook her head. She came and placed her hands on his shoulders. "Incorrigible," he heard her say.

Then Henry stood up and reached for his wife, enfolding her in his arms. "I'm sorry you must suffer our son's antagonism, dear," he said. "It makes me realize what I must have put my own parents through."

"Derek will grow up soon enough, just as we all do." With that, Lorraine rose on tiptoe to kiss and hug him tenderly.

Leah and Jonas had been out riding about a half hour or so, meandering round the county roads, taking their time getting Leah home. The most picturesque farmhouses had a way of rolling down across the meadows and settling back a ways from the road. Jonas surprised her by asking what sort of house she'd want to live in when she was married, and, of course, she said a house something like Dat's . . . "a house that's been in the family for generations, you know."

"Something real old, then?"

"Oh, jah."

Turned out, Jonas agreed. So they were getting awful close to the topic that mattered most to Leah, and she was mighty sure to her beau, too—the subject of marriage, just when they might tie the knot, and all.

But as Jonas talked, she realized they weren't going to be discussing that subject just now, probably. At least not tonight. He was more interested in his sister's wedding in just two days. "Anna's awful ferhoodled," he said, laughing. "Both Mam and Pop just look at each other sometimes—I've seen 'em—like they can't believe how harebrained she is."

"What sort of young bride will she be, then?" Leah ventured, hoping she wasn't stepping on anyone's toes.

"Oh, Anna will be right fine, just as any newly married woman is . . . given time." And here he reached around her and drew her near. "Just the way *you'll* be someday."

" 'Cept for one thing," she spoke up quickly.

"What's that?"

"I know my way round a barnyard better than most brides!"

This brought the heartiest laughter she'd ever heard from Jonas. And he made no attempt to disagree with her.

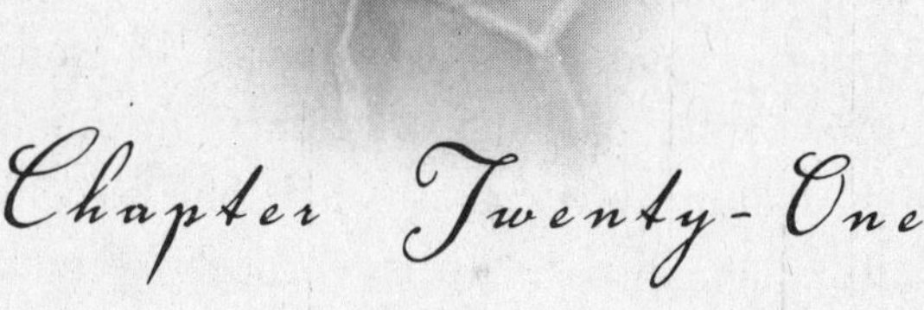

Chapter Twenty-One

The day of the Mast wedding dawned ever so bright. Sadie would have rather stayed home. But, of course, she didn't. The whole family—and Aunt Lizzie—piled into the family buggy and headed over to Grasshopper Level for the long day of festivities.

When they arrived at last, she and Leah walked up to a group of other girls their age waiting in the barnyard. They would remain there till they were given the signal to go inside for the service.

Naomi Kauffman and several other girls eyed her and smiled but stayed in their own little circle of fellowship. Sadie didn't let that bother her, though. What was troubling was seeing the Schwartz family drive up and get out of their car, the four of them walking up the lane toward the farmhouse.

For a fleeting moment, while glimpsing Derry, she wondered if her baby would resemble the Schwartz side more than the Ebersols. And how awful would that be!

She quickly dismissed the niggling thought. Yet seeing

Derry, even from afar, was sure to spoil her time at Anna's wedding. She scarcely could wait to get home again. Why had she come at all?

Quickly, before Anna's wedding service ever began, Hannah sneaked up to the bride's bedroom, knocked on the door, and handed the embroidered dove hankie to Anna herself. Hannah stared at the special handkerchief in Anna's hand. A dove stitched all in white against a pale blue background.

"Oh, Hannah, this is so perty!" the bride said. "I'll be needing the dove of peace on *this* day, what with all the doin's, ya know."

Hannah caught the meaning. Anna was obviously a bundle of nerves. "But you mustn't be anxious," she spoke up, surprising herself. "This is the day you and Nathaniel have been waiting for, to become husband and wife. Such a wonderful-gut day 'tis."

Then, quite pleased with herself, she kissed Anna's cheek, wished her "Happy day," and scurried down the back steps and through the summer kitchen. Outside, in the midst of the swell of wedding guests, she looked for Mary Ruth, swinging her arms just a bit. Not only had she given Anna Mast something to treasure for always, she'd offered a kind word to an anxious bride. Even though she'd had to exert herself a bit to do so.

After the main sermon, the bridal party—three young men and three young women—took their seats near the ministers' row in front. Then, toward the end of the three-hour meeting, in front of the bishop, Anna Mast agreed that she was indeed "ordained of God to be Nathaniel King's wedded wife." And Nathaniel was in agreement, too.

When they were pronounced husband and wife, plenty a tear was shed, especially after the words "till our dear God will again separate you from each other," pertaining to the duration of the couple's union under heaven. So solemn was this lifetime promise between two people.

Meanwhile, Sadie stuck close to Aunt Lizzie, steering clear of the likes of Derry Schwartz. Even so, the good doctor's gaze found her at one point, just as the fancy guests were preparing to leave before the wedding feast began. Sadie looked away quickly. Such embarrassment she felt, recalling how she'd made a fool of herself going over to the Schwartz home. Ach, she'd sat right down on their front porch steps, waiting to talk to their rat of a boy. She sometimes wondered what had gotten into her, going over there like that. But it had been the close of a final horrid chapter in her life. She hoped so, anyways, because she'd be paying dearly for her transgression once her secret was evident for all to see.

Now, though, she was being mighty careful to eat right—watching the sort of foods Mamma ate—and to get to bed at an early hour. Her body was in the beginning processes of making necessary changes, the baby growing ever so slowly at this point. All this was according to the helpful library book, which she had renewed one day here lately when she and Mamma drove to Strasburg for sewing notions and whatnot. She'd been allowed to keep the book for another three weeks and hoped by the time she had to relinquish it for good, such important things would be firmly fixed in her mind.

Gone were her actively sinful days, though she had never confessed her wickedness to a soul. Not even to Mamma. She'd pondered confiding in Leah, but what good would that do? Her sister couldn't redeem her. No one could. Unfortunately, her next younger sister was all caught up with Jonas, so dreamy eyed it was hard to get her attention during the day while she did her indoor chores. No, there was no need to spoil Leah's joy . . . not just now.

Mary Ruth was aware of Elias Stoltzfus's presence well before the wedding feast, especially when the young people were attempting to line up outside and some of the boys showed great timidity in pairing themselves up with a girl partner. Some were even grabbed and pulled to the door, where they had no choice but to stand beside a particular girl. Once they were in line, all struggling came to an end, and each youthful couple approached the wedding-supper table hand in hand, just as those in the bridal party did.

But Ezra Stoltzfus, who happened to be Hannah's partner, of all things, looked downright delighted to have managed to get in line, just so, to be precisely across from her twin. Mary Ruth couldn't help but think that somehow she and Hannah were *supposed* to be matched up with the Stoltzfus brothers for the wedding feast, recalling how spunky Elias had been about asking her if he could sit across the wedding table from her.

Thinking back on his unexpected visit at the produce stand, she felt her heart beat a little faster at what might become of their friendship. And at the years ahead, maybe. Then and there she decided to be the most cheerful wedding-feast partner to smiling Elias, who kept eyeing her in the lineup of girls, then quickly looking down his line of boys and bobbing his head, as if counting how many there were—and where he landed—making double sure he ended up being her partner.

Well, now, what a right fine day of days, thought Mary Ruth, overjoyed.

Abram felt he'd done a dance of sorts, trying his best to avoid Ida's brother, Noah Brenneman. Still, it seemed his brother-in-law was determined to confront him about the past. Yet another time.

The weathered farmer walked up to him after the feast. "You're avoiding me, Abram."

" 'Spect I am."

"Well, now that we've witnessed a blessed wedding and ate ourselves full, don'tcha think you could stand still for just a minute or two?"

"I'll see 'bout that." Abram wasn't surprised at the gray-bearded man's acute bluntness. Noah shot off his mouth this-away quite regularly; at least he had back years ago when the knotty problem between them had first reared its ugly head.

"Still holdin' a grudge, I see . . . after all these years," Noah said straight out.

"Jah, maybe so." Abram leaned on the well pump handle. "But you know the truth, same as me. What you had in mind for Lizzie . . .'twas awful wrong! That should be real plain to see now."

Noah stared him directly in the eye. "Maybe so, but I wanted to protect my family. I can't say the same for you, though. 'Tis a mighty big secret you're keeping, Abram. Mark my words. It'll blow up in your face one day."

"You leave that to Ida and me. That's our business."

"Don'tcha forget, Lizzie's *my* sister. What you and your family do affects all of us Brennemans." With that, Noah turned on his heel.

Abram shuddered. Noah's vicious remarks rang in his ears as Abram tuned out the frivolity, what with young people scampering round. He wished Noah would just keep to himself and his wife, Becky.

By gollies, he thought, *will we never see eye to eye?*

After supper that night the young people gathered in the Masts' big barn. There they had a singing of sorts, playing games till late.

Just before dusk, though, Leah and Adah Peachey left the games for a breather. They went for a quick walk by themselves, over in the high meadow behind the barn.

"I'm wore out," Adah said, reaching for Leah's hand as they made their way up the slope.

"A wedding day is always long. 'Tis understandable," Leah said.

"There's another reason I'm done in. My brother wants to know if you and Jonas are officially courtin'."

"And that's tiring you?" Leah said.

"Well, he keeps askin' . . . even though it's not his business to know."

"What do you say?"

"I tell him, 'open up your eyes . . . what do ya see happening at the local singings?' "

"Maybe he oughta go to a different singing," Leah suggested.

"I've told him that. Believe me." Adah sighed. "But it

does nothing. Gid's waitin' for you. He's stubborn thataway."

This puzzled her. "Why should Gid be marking time? He could be courtin' a girl of his own by now."

"Maybe so, but he cares for *you*, Leah."

The knowledge of this annoyed her. "Is this about something, well . . . that our fathers are wanting?" Leah had to know.

"Gid's future has been placed in his own hands now," Adah said, then became ever so quiet.

This was news to Leah. "Since when?"

"Just here lately."

"Are you sure?"

Adah nodded her head, letting go of Leah's hand to reach down and pick a dried-up wild flower. Gathering a bunch of them, Adah stood up and rubbed them together between her hands, letting the breeze scatter dead pieces into the air. "Pop told Gid the other day that love can be fickle. 'Tis best not to hang too high a hope on it," whispered Adah almost mysteriously. "My father told him to go ahead and court whoever he pleases."

Leah could hardly believe her ears.

Adah turned and gave her a strange little smile. "Why wouldn't you give my brother half a chance? I think you and Gid could've been a right gut pair is all I best say."

"I'm ever so sorry, Adah. Truly, I am." Leah wondered all the rest of the day if her father and the smithy had resigned themselves to her courtship with Jonas, which surely they knew from either Adah or Gid.

So most likely Dat knew about Jonas and had done absolutely nothing to stop them. Downright peculiar it was.

Chapter Twenty-Two

They attended one wedding after another all the rest of November and deep into the month of December. The ongoing weather could not have been more bitter—with snow-laden hills and dreary gray heavens, scattered with unsettled clouds. Wind and sleet visited them from the northeast, coming in with a vengeance from the Atlantic Ocean.

The forest behind the Ebersol Cottage seemed to grow darker with each passing day. Songbirds had long since flown south, and Ida especially missed hearing their cheerful warble as the babe within her grew. She looked ahead to spring with both a longing and a joy, and all who knew her said her face was simply "aglow" with radiance.

Though she was preoccupied with her coming child, she suspected something was terribly wrong with Sadie. But Ida would not allow her thoughts to stray down that path.

Leah was content to help her sisters and Mamma sew perty things for her own hope chest and others' and attend quilting bees and cookie frolics. Often she kept Aunt Lizzie company on the coldest afternoons, donning her snow boots and tromping up the hill to the cozy log cabin. Sometimes she would spend the night there by herself or with Sadie or Mary Ruth. Hannah never was one to care much for sleeping away from home, though. There at Aunt Lizzie's, they baked sweet breads and drank hot cocoa, or Lizzie's favorite hot drink, Postum. Leah enjoyed jotting down dozens of her aunt's recipes, asking for even more "for my own recipe files . . . come next autumn." That way Lizzie would know enough to quietly tell Mamma they'd need to sow a plentiful batch of celery next July for Leah's wedding feast in the fall. Lizzie's eyes lit up as the truth dawned on her, and she promised to keep Leah's plans quiet "till the time came."

Leah was ever so happy to entertain Jonas once each week all winter long, reading aloud to him from the book of Psalms and occasionally from *Martyrs' Mirror*—stories from seventeenth-century Christian martyrdom. Together they looked at colorful pictures in Jonas's book of birds, learning the voice and call of many different varieties.

One evening Jonas shared his keen interest in carpentry with Leah, telling her that some years ago he and his father had discussed the possibility of dividing up the Mast orchard and surrounding land if Jonas never had the opportunity to learn the trade of cabinetmaking. He and his bride could make their living growing apples and overseeing a truck farm, but Jonas wanted them to live close enough so Leah could be within walking distance to her sisters. Thus, living on Grasshopper Level wasn't an option, really.

They talked of joining Leah's church come next September, getting married early in November, settling down near the Ebersol Cottage, perhaps at first renting a little farm.

They discussed in whispered tones their future children and grandchildren, and at times played checkers into the wee hours.

Leah felt truly blessed to love and be loved in such a joyous way. She did sometimes worry, though, that she oughtn't to marry before Sadie, since that honor should go to the first daughter of their family. So she prayed that God would send along someone right quick for her older sister.

Sadie, who was becoming more self-conscious about her body as January came and went, promised herself she would somehow change her outlook on life. Without offering repentance—by sheer willpower—she made an effort to become a more obedient daughter and loving sister . . . especially to Leah, who had put up with far more than she herself might have tolerated from a sibling back last summer.

On the Saturday nights that Jonas Mast came calling, Sadie stole next door to visit Dawdi John, who enjoyed telling her—sometimes the twins, too—the familiar stories of his growing-up years. "The olden days," he'd say . . . how he learned to cut wood as a boy and catch fish with his own dawdi, and about the day he asked Mammi Brenneman to "get hitched" with him. If he happened to light up his old pipe and smoke by the fireside, the smell of sweet tobacco made Sadie feel a bit light-headed, took the edge off her deepest fears. At such times she came mighty close to letting her secret slip out, knowing full well she could trust Dawdi, but she never quite let herself go that far.

Sooner or later, though, she knew she'd be telling Leah. Time was passing and she had fallen in love with her baby, felt it was surely a boy, though she wouldn't have known how to explain such a thing. Yet she believed her precious unborn child would be the first male to grow up in this house in many years. Thankfully, she had never heard again from Derry and assumed he had gone to the army, nearly finished with his basic training by now.

Meanwhile, Mary Ruth poured herself into school studies, making the best grades she ever had through February. More and more she hungered for book learning, knowing full well how this might sit with Dat and Mamma when she finally had the nerve to tell them she wanted to attend high school. Then . . . college someday. Her twin was the only one who knew her true heart on this, and it pained her—the realization that one day their paths would surely have to part, knowing full well that Hannah intended to follow the Lord in holy baptism and join the Amish church.

Hannah had begun to write down her most personal thoughts in a journal every other day, starting back on New Year's Day. Some paragraphs—about certain boys—she could just imagine Mamma's eyebrows arching ever so high at what was being recorded. Her embroidered handkerchiefs had found a business outlet in a small gift shop in Strasburg. Hannah was saving her money toward helping Mary Ruth reach her secret goal of attending a teachers' college in the future. Yet the thought of living without her twin nearby was almost too painful to ponder.

Abram spent winter evenings reading the Bible in German and praying silent prayers with the family gathered near. Ida, who was putting on some extra pounds, sometimes complained that the wood stove put out too much heat for her liking. So they'd all get up and head to the front room, where the girls would shiver a little, all but Sadie, who seemed as comfortable in the cooler rooms as Ida.

If the topic of politics came up at all, which it sometimes did, he made a point of emphasizing to his family, especially his daughters, that he didn't have much use for America's new president. "Anyone who's bent on using such profanity, well . . . he ain't leadership material, not in my book."

But even more than Harry Truman's cussing, Abram was utterly annoyed by Jonas Mast's out-and-out determination to win Leah's hand. The smithy was none too keen on the idea, either, since Gideon hadn't shown the least interest in any other girl in the church yet. Leah was obviously Gid's one and only sweetheart girl, and he'd set his sights—and heart—on her, and nothing either Abram or the smithy thought about Jonas Mast made any difference. Far as Abram was concerned, his dear, dear girl was missing out on a gem of a boy while getting cozy with, even planning to wed, Ida's cousin's son. But if Leah loved him and he loved her, well . . . what was Abram to do? He couldn't demand his own way, could he? Why, no, he might push Leah away from his own heart, and then how could he live with himself?

Derek Schwartz never looked back once he'd packed his bags and headed for boot camp. His mother was teary eyed at the bus station, but his father appeared to be more serious than sad. Robert, not in attendance at Derek's farewell, had managed to beat his brother out of town, driving to Harrisonburg, Virginia, where he planned to find a part-time job and settle into an apartment, then begin second semester at Eastern Mennonite College. His father had been baffled at Robert's sudden interest in Anabaptist beliefs, in wanting to go into the ministry, too, but Mom had encouraged him to "follow your heart, Robert . . . wherever it may lead." It was typical of her, though he knew she hadn't taken too kindly to his brother's leaving home again.

Derek, on the other hand, figured it didn't matter as much what *he* did with his life. Mom would have turned irate—Dad, too—if either of them had known he was completely shirking his duty as a father-to-be, leaving naïve Sadie Ebersol to cope with raising their grandchild on her own. But no turning back now. Hadn't he offered to help her end the unwanted pregnancy? And she had refused in no uncertain terms. So there was nothing more for him to say or do. He had been smart, too, not falling for her ridiculous idea of marriage.

◆

It was on the day that Englishers celebrate love—Valentine's Day—that Sadie decided she could keep her secret no longer. She and Leah were putting on their flannel nightgowns, and Sadie was straining to see the side view of herself in the small mirror at the dresser. "Leah, do you think I'm gaining weight?" she asked.

"How could that be? You're as thin as a rail."

"But, no, seriously, look at me," she insisted, wondering if her sister would notice any difference in her shape. "Am I bigger . . . anywhere?"

Leah shook her head, laughing softly. "What're you getting at, sister? You look the same as always."

Sitting on the edge of the bed, Sadie breathed in deeply. Now was the time. She simply must tell Leah about the precious babe inside her. What should she say, and how to say it? After all, Leah hadn't had nearly five months to become accustomed to the idea of a baby as she herself had. So she must be more guarded, careful to express the regret, even grief, she'd felt at her first knowing, back in mid-October. But now . . . *now* she was ever so eager to hold her tiny baby in her arms, cradle him, rock him, whisper "I love you" in his little ears. Yet she wondered how Leah would take such news.

Well, she'd never know if she didn't get the nerve to speak up, and in the next minute or so. Leah was heading for the oil lamp now, ready to snuff it out. . . .

"Sister," she said softly. "There's something I want to tell you."

Leah turned, a frown on her face at first. Then when Sadie motioned for her to sit beside her, she came quickly, eyes animated. "What is it?"

"Just listen, Leah. . . ."

"Have you met a boy, someone who wants to court you?" asked Leah.

Sadie wasn't taken aback at that remark. After all, it was a natural thing for a younger sister to be thinking such things, really . . . for Leah to feel awkward at being nearly engaged and here Sadie was almost nineteen and without a beau, or even the promise of one.

Reaching for Leah's hand, she clasped it tightly. "What I'm goin' to say will be so awful hard for you to take at first. It was truly that for me." She paused, stroking Leah's innocent hand. "I have done wickedness, *sinned* in the eyes of the Lord and this family. Oh, Leah, my sweet sister, how do I tell you that I . . . am with child?"

The room was still, the light from a winter moon on the snowy landscape bright enough to show clearly Leah's stunned expression. "Ach, Sadie . . . what're you saying?"

"Do you remember that English boy I told you 'bout last fall? Well, we . . . he and I . . ." She could not make herself speak the words.

"Oh, this is too awful!" Leah blurted.

Sadie shushed her sister gently. "Best not alert the whole family to this just yet," she said, but she understood Leah's shock. She reached out and gathered Leah near. "I'm sorry you hafta know this . . . that you have such an immoral sister as I am," she whispered.

For the longest time Leah seemed unable to speak, struck dumb with anguish, weeping softly into the pillow. "How could you do such a thing, Sadie?" she said at last.

Then they curled up together in their childhood bed, beneath ancient quilts sewn by the honorable and just women on both the Ebersol and Brenneman sides. And Sadie, sapped of strength, said no more, realizing anew this evil thing she'd done to bring such shame on herself . . . and her dear family.

Abram was awake and had just come back from the outhouse, the light from the moon's reflection on the snow nearly blinding his tired eyes. Making his way up the stairs, he heard the sound of sniffling coming from the bedroom shared by Sadie and Leah.

Not pausing in the least, he headed straight to his and Ida's room, settling into bed next to his wife. He was awful sure it was Leah who was crying. Jah, it *was* Leah. But why?

He felt sudden wrenching guilt at what he'd gone and done just this afternoon, using a pay telephone in Strasburg to set a life-changing deed in motion. Of course, there was no way in the world Leah could know just yet, not *this* soon, that he'd placed a call to Fannie Mast's married cousin out in Ohio. Seemed easy enough when all was said and done. Jonas Mast would be getting a letter, being offered a job as a carpenter's apprentice in Holmes County.

If Leah ever found out what Abram had done, she'd be more than angry, beside herself with grief, which is how she sounded just now. But Fannie's cousin had vowed that no one would be told of his and Abram's quiet conversation this day.

So Abram let his thoughts drift toward sleep, knowing he'd stuck his neck out, more certain than ever of his choice of a mate for his most precious Leah.

It was pitch black in the haymow. Leah crept up the long ladder and hid herself away in the depths of the night while Sadie—expectant, *unmarried* mother—slept back in the house. As sisters, they had held each other till Leah slipped away, needing to be alone with her thoughts.

Fraught with worry, she sat there in the corner, where hay was stacked in even rectangular shapes, where only the sound of a mule's sighing broke the stillness. One of a half dozen barn cats found her and curled up in her lap.

It's all my fault—this horrid mess Sadie's in. I should've told on her while there was still time to save her purity. If only I'd known. . . .

Leah knew for sure . . . if she could simply turn back time, ach, she'd do it in a second—promptly run and tell Dat that her sister was in danger of hellfire.

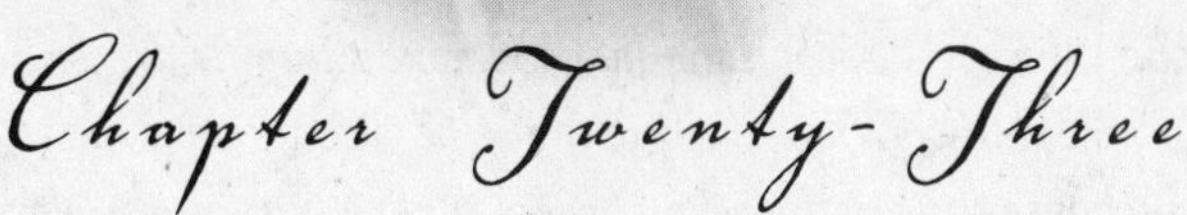

Chapter Twenty-Three

March 1, 1947

It's not so hard to believe that I've been writing in my new diary for two full months now. Mamma sometimes will glance into my bedroom through my open door, looking at me with a peculiar grin and see me writing away so fast in my little book. She mustn't worry that I'm practicing my hand at being a writer, trying to develop individuality, so opposed by the bishop. That's best done with my embroidery, if I must reach for creativity at all. Mamma doesn't have to worry over me, not like she'll have to with Mary Ruth after eighth grade, come next year.

Won't be much longer and we'll see if Mamma's baby is our sister or brother. I must admit, I won't begin to know what to do with a little brother. After four girls in the house . . . just how would that be?

Mamma's constantly happy these days. Dat's the one out of sorts more than ever before. And Leah is, too. Honestly, I don't know what's gotten into my older sisters. The eldest is so pleasant to me—and to Mary Ruth. Sadie has made a change in herself, I should say, now that she's through with rumschpringe. It's Leah who's so awful glum. Just how could they switch places like that?

But I'm thinking that Jonas will make Leah a right nice husband. He's over here visiting on Saturday nights, and I'm sure he's the boy bringing Leah home from the singings every other Sunday. He loves her a lot. I can see it in his eyes, before we get shooed out of the kitchen come nightfall. Mary Ruth and I hope Leah won't go getting married next autumn, like we suspect she might. Why? Well, it would be nice to have our happy little house snug with all four sisters staying put for a while yet. Of course, with a new little sibling coming along soon, things might just be a bit topsy-turvy anyways.

That's all for now.

Hannah Ebersol

Mary Ruth waited after school to chat with the teacher at the Georgetown School. "I'm wondering if I might get some extra assignments?" she asked. "I'm fascinated with mathematics."

"Well, let's see what I can do, Miss Ebersol." Flipping through her large math textbook, Miss Riehl found many pages of math problems. "Here . . . why don't you copy these down and work them at home?"

"Thank you ever so much!"

"I'll check your work when you're finished."

"I'll do them tonight," she promised.

"No need to hurry." The teacher sat down behind her desk.

"Oh, but there *is*." And Mary Ruth began to explain her goals for the future, pouring out her heart about her hope of becoming a schoolteacher someday. "But . . . please, will you keep this between us?"

Miss Riehl's face shone. She seemed to understand. "I'll help you all I can, Mary Ruth."

Saying thank-you yet again, Mary Ruth hurried to the door where Hannah was waiting. Together they walked to the small parking lot, watching for their ride.

"Well, didja do it?" Hannah asked, eyes smiling.

"You'll never believe how much extra work Miss Riehl gave me!"

"I'm so happy for you."

The girls exchanged tender glances. "I don't know how I'd manage sometimes if I didn't have you to share with," Mary Ruth told her twin.

Hannah nodded. "Will we always have each other?"

Mary Ruth heard her sister's sad desperation. The question came deep from Hannah's heart, from a girl who most likely would settle into the community of the People, never inquisitive about the outside world, while her twin sought to gain as much knowledge as her brain could hold.

The day the Ohio letter arrived in the Mast mailbox, Jonas was driving down their lane in the enclosed family buggy, running an errand over to Bart. He'd thought of simply bypassing the mail, letting one of his sisters come fetch it for Mamma . . . but stopping, he hurried to see just what might be in store for the family on this snowy end-of-March day.

Flipping through the mail, he noticed several from Willow Street and one from Ninepoints, notes from girl cousins and friends of Rebekah and Katie, probably, since his sisters enjoyed writing letters the most. Except for Mamma, who'd been writing a lot here lately, she'd told him, to Ida Ebersol—his future mother-in-law. Mamma had said just recently that the two families were getting much closer "just since the last get-together back in August." Well, he couldn't agree more, especially if Mamma and Dat had any idea just how many trips a month he made over to Gobbler's Knob to see his Leah.

The envelope that made him stand straighter, take notice, was one addressed to him, the postmark being from Millersburg, Ohio. "Who lives clear out there?" he muttered to himself, hurrying back to the carriage to get out of the cold.

Once inside, he closed the buggy door and scanned the contents, which revealed, to his great surprise, an invitation from his mother's cousin, David Mellinger, an expert carpenter. And . . . of all things, Jonas was being asked to consider coming there and working for David "till your pop's apples are ready for picking early next fall."

Six months away from home?

Instantly, his first thoughts were of Leah, how much he'd miss her for that long a time. What might his leaving do to their plans to take the required baptism instruction before the fall wedding season? He hated to think of telling Leah of this opportunity. Not that it wasn't one of the best kinds of offers a young man his age could receive from a seasoned carpenter and all. The very thing he'd always dreamed of doing!

But this letter coming now . . . well, it was just so untimely. Still, he couldn't dismiss Cousin David's invitation. He mulled over the ins and outs of such an adventure all the rest of the day.

Smithy Gid was well aware of the warm April morning "Sisters' Day" frolic happening at the house. Mam had invited all the Ebersol women, as well as their aunt Lizzie, over for a Saturday of making rag rugs. Adah and Dorcas had talked excitedly about the idea of doing such a thing for the past week, then last evening at the supper table had gently encouraged both him and Dat to "make yourselves scarce," the girls giggling too much at the remark for his liking.

But he'd followed their wishes, taking great pains not to go near the house after breakfast, tending to Fritzi and her second batch of pedigree pups, now three weeks old. He fed grain to the four Black Angus he and Dat were fattening for the butcher here in the next few weeks, then offered to help his father in the blacksmith shop. But Dat seemed preoccupied, saying he didn't need a hand. Not today, at least, which was downright peculiar, seeing as how Dat was *always* in need of something when it came to shoeing so many driving horses in the Plain community.

By Gid's calculations, his German shepherd pups were close to being weaned, in which case he could start contacting the folk who'd agreed to purchase at least five of the litter. The other two, well, he hadn't decided if he ought to advertise for them or not. He liked to amuse himself by thinking what Leah might do or say if he offered the gentlest one, with the pertiest markings, to her as a present, for no particular reason. He knew better than to step out of bounds with Leah Ebersol, but with word that Jonas Mast might possibly be heading out to Ohio for a time, working as a carpenter's apprentice . . . well, now, *this* news had surely come out of nowhere.

When he'd asked his father about it, the only thing said was "Don't know much of this, son. But . . . let's just see what comes of it." So it sounded like maybe Dat *did* know something, though Gid wasn't in the habit of questioning his father, even if only in his thoughts.

Leah felt ever so dismal. Her sister's words kept on ringing in her ears, even though now it had been nearly two months since Sadie's shocking revelation. She wished she'd never promised to keep quiet about Sadie and her English beau. Never!

Although Leah and Jonas shared most everything, Leah continued to keep her sister's secret from him. And from Dat and Mamma, too. Only once had she come close to sharing it with Aunt Lizzie, but she'd thought better of it, feeling it was Sadie's place to do so. Besides, there was nothing anyone could do.

Sadie would have to be the one to tell their parents, and perty soon, because she wouldn't be able to keep it from them forever. Leah had seen her sister's body slowly changing, especially in the soft glow of the oil lamp, when they dressed for bed at night.

Sighing, she laid down her scissors and left scraps of old fabric in a big basket on the floor. Excusing herself, she felt it was all right to go outside alone to the Peacheys' outhouse, though she might've asked Sadie or the twins to come along. It wasn't that she hoped to run into Gid on the way. She had no such thing in her mind, yet there he was over in the barn . . . stroking one of the new puppies in the whelping box. Quickly she turned her head and walked even more swiftly toward her destination.

Honestly, she felt almost sad for Gid these days—most all the time, really, clear back since her first singing that night in October. She wished he'd find himself a nice girl to court. After all, he was a right fine-looking fella himself, with a heart as pure as gold, Dat had always said. Far as she could tell, there had never been any reason to doubt it.

So when he called to her, after her return from the little house out near the barn, she turned and smiled, wondering what he had to say. "Leah, I've been thinking. . . ." Then he stopped and said no more, just held up a small dog with a reddish fawn coat with black overlay . . . sweet brown eyes and an almost curious smile. "Would you like to have him? He's yours for the taking."

"Oh, but I wouldn't think of—"

"No . . . no, I mean to say he's a gift. From one neighbor friend to another."

Gid's smile was so boyish just now. So eager to please her, he was. "I'm sure it's all right with your parents. Besides, I'm thinkin' you could use a gut watchdog over there."

With that, they both looked past the Peachey pastureland to the Ebersol Cottage, gazing on it from afar. Then Gid broke the silence. "If you're not so sure, why not ask your dat . . . see what *he* says?"

She couldn't argue with that. Then, reaching up, she touched the young pup in Gid's arms, and suddenly the dog began to lick her hand with his little pink tongue. "Oh, that tickles," she caught herself saying. "He's ever so cute."

"Well, now, I think he likes ya, Leah."

She had to laugh. "I think he does, too."

"I'd keep him for you. Then if or when you should decide to take him home, I'd be more 'n happy to bring him over."

"Aw, that's ever so nice of you. Denki." She hurried back to the house. A bright face like Gid's had cheered her up just a bit. She was sure his motives were honorable, though he would've had to be deaf not to have heard that Jonas was leaving for Ohio here right quick.

She'd been brave the night Jonas had shared this "rare opportunity" with her. Seeing his eyes light up at the makings of a dream come true, yet hearing the sadness in his voice, Leah knew she could not shed a tear in front of him. She had even wondered aloud if there was any way she might go along—maybe tend to an elderly relative or whatnot, so they could continue their courtship in person instead of by letter. Then, when the time came, they could return home and marry in the fall as planned.

She'd just have to trust the Good Lord—they both would—for the answers.

"I'll be back before the apple harvest next fall," he promised.

But when she'd shared this with Sadie, her sister said she ought not to count on such a pledge. "Best not to let him go at all," Sadie said. "If Jonas leaves, he might never return home. Remember Abe Yoder? He left poor Malinda for the lure of land in Ohio."

Sadie's words made Leah's heart ache. "I wouldn't think of speakin' up to Jonas like that. He has a right good head on his shoulders."

"Well, you might want to think twice 'bout keeping mum. At least tell him how much you'll miss him . . . let him know you'll pine for him."

Ach, she felt she knew her beloved, and if Jonas said he was going to come home before the harvest, then he would. For sure and for certain. And she'd told Sadie so. "You don't know my Jonas the way I do," she'd insisted.

By Leah's response and the heart-melting smile on her face, Smithy Gid was almost positive his gift offer—from his hand and heart to hers—had been an excellent idea, after all. So he wasn't one bit sorry about his impulsive deed, Jonas Mast aside. Leah was, after all, his longtime neighbor and childhood friend. If she chose to marry Jonas, well then, so be it.

Still, Gid had his hopes up that she might, at least, take the pick of Fritzi's litter and give the pup a home. Who knows, maybe a fond pet would be the start of something special between Leah and him. Then again, maybe not.

Chapter Twenty-Four

Abram was beside himself, downright befuddled. Jonas Mast had insisted on having a private meeting with him out in the barn after seeing Leah home rather early after the singing. The boy began by explaining some carefully thought out plans, it seemed . . . about his hopes to find a place for Leah to live and work near David Mellinger's home in Millersburg, Ohio. "I'm workin' on it and will have some answers in the next few days," Jonas said. "What would you think of that?"

Well, Abram wondered just what Jonas was afraid of—did Jonas honestly think Leah might start seeing someone else, maybe, if she stayed home on Gobbler's Knob? But no, when he quizzed the boy, Jonas said something about not wanting to go so long without seeing "my dear Leah."

"Well, then there's always letters, like anyone else in your situation," Abram advised. But deep down, he was shocked at Jonas's strong reluctance to leave Leah behind.

"I truly love her," Jonas confessed, eyes shining. "She's everything I live for. Leah's my dearest friend, too."

Nodding, Abram understood how a young man could be

smitten over Leah, sweet and gentle soul that she was. Still, he decided on the spot that his daughter was *not* going to Ohio. No matter what, she was staying put right here. Smithy Gid must have *his* chance to woo and possibly court Leah, too. Then, the way Abram saw things, his dear girl could make a choice between the two of them. And that was all he hoped to accomplish by Jonas's going away. Nothing more.

He tipped his straw hat as Jonas turned and left the barn, the boy full of hopes and dreams, obviously in love. It wasn't in Abram's thinking to wound him, no . . . not at all. But he knew in his heart of hearts he was altogether right about Smithy Gid and Leah. They must have their chance.

After the dishes were washed, dried, and put away that night, Sadie accompanied Dawdi John back to his side of the house, especially glad to go with him by herself. She hoped for yet another quiet evening with the wise older man.

Dawdi John was sure to give her a listening ear, and she was mighty glad to be here with him, away from the exciting talk next door, where Mamma, Leah, and the twins were still chattering about the Sisters' Day they'd enjoyed over at Miriam Peachey's. Leah was mostly interested in talking about a puppy dog Smithy Gid wanted to give her, "for the whole family, though," Leah was quick to say. "Go right on over there tomorrow and say you'll take the dog," Dat had said, wondering aloud why Leah had bothered to ask him, anyway.

So the whole family—the girls, especially—were beside themselves with glee, anticipating the arrival of Fritzi's perty little pup. Sadie could just hear it now—they'd be tossing round names for dogs for the next two hours or so till bedtime.

Once Dawdi was settled in his small front room, and Sadie had a nice fire blazing in the hearth, she asked him, "Dawdi, have you ever done something you were so ashamed of, you just couldn't bring yourself to confess to anyone?"

He regarded her curiously. "Well, now, I 'spect I have. We *all* have. There's nobody perfect, least that I know of."

She wasn't about to spill the beans on herself, lest Dat and Mamma would hear of her pregnancy secondhand. Of course, now, if she asked Dawdi to keep things in strictest confidence, he would. But wasn't that an awful burden to put on a man of his age, after all?

So she lost her courage and failed to share openly. He seemed to sense her need of comfort and amusement and recounted one story after another—mostly telling on himself as a youngster and into his teens.

Then his voice grew awful soft. "Listen here to me, Sadie. I want you to remember this saying as long as you live." He stopped talking to light his pipe, puffing on it just so to get the tobacco to ignite. When he was satisfied, pipe in hand, a thin puff of smoke spewed forth from his lips. "I care not to be judge of right and wrong in men," he said with a tender smile. "I've often lost the way myself and may get lost again."

Lost the way . . .

Well, she knew all about such things, dark and forbidden forest or no. Each time she had been with Derry Schwartz, she promised herself it would be the last, yet she longed to see him again and again. Such a feeble pact, one she hadn't been able to keep, loving him so.

But now part of her loathed him, and another part of her wondered how she could ever forget him, having conceived his baby. Could she ever truly release him from her heart?

"You know you're always welcome to talk to old Dawdi," her grandfather said, bringing her out of her musings.

"I'm awful glad of that," Sadie said, reaching for his wrinkled hand and holding it for a moment. But deep within, she knew this might be one of the last nights she'd have as an expectant mother. Very soon her baby would be nestled in her arms . . . and to think she'd kept it a secret so well from everyone, carefully sewing her dress seams thinner every time. Here lately, making her dress patterns a bit fuller through the waist was all she'd had to do.

Off and on all day she'd had the strongest cramping, almost made her want to bend over, the pain was so bad at times. The library book she'd nearly memorized hadn't mentioned a thing about the baby coming this way—not when she was only at the end of her seventh month of pregnancy, far as she could tell.

When the light bleeding started, getting heavier as the day wore on, she panicked and wondered what was happening to her. Was she going to lose her baby?

"Leah," she began long after supper, when they were preparing to dress for bed, "something's happening too soon, I fear. . . ."

"What do you mean?" Leah asked.

"I think the baby might be coming early."

"Well, then, I say it's time to tell Mamma!"

"No, no, not just yet," Sadie replied in lowered tones. "I need a doctor first."

Leah squinted at her, a fearful look on her face. "I can hitch up the horse right quick and take you to the midwife."

But that would be much too far away, and she didn't think she could bear all the jostling in the buggy. The nearest doctor was Derry's father, Sadie knew, but his clinic was the *last* place she wanted to be. "What about Aunt Lizzie? Maybe she can help," Sadie said. "You could tell Mamma we're going there to spend the night . . . for fun."

"That would be a lie," Leah said.

"It's the best way for now."

Leah winced but then agreed. "Jah, I 'spose, but what will you do when the baby *does* come? You won't be able to hide the truth then. You're not thinking clearly, Sadie."

Her sister was right about all that, but Sadie had no energy to argue. "I need help," she whispered, feeling ever so faint. "Just please get me to Lizzie's."

"Can you walk all the way up there, do you think?"

"If you're with me, jah, I believe I can."

"Then go slip on your woolen shawl. It's a bit nippy out," Leah said. "I'll poke my head in and tell Mamma we're headed to Aunt Lizzie's overnight. She won't mind one bit—may not even suspect a thing."

Sadie still had no idea what on earth would happen after she did give birth, if that's what was about to happen tonight. *If* the baby lived . . . goodness' sake, this was much too early!

And, ach . . . Aunt Lizzie would suddenly know everything. No getting around it now. Still, come to think of it, maybe this way was for the best. Lizzie could help break the startling news to both Dat and Mamma when the time came, when Sadie was ready to bring her baby home.

She leaned hard on Leah, making her way up the long hill

to Lizzie's log house—step by painful step—ever so glad her sister was near.

Lizzie bolted out of bed, hearing the pounding on the back door. She hurried to see who was coming to visit her after dark.

"For goodness' sake," she whispered, seeing Leah nearly holding Sadie up, both girls' faces wet with tears. "*Dummle*—hurry! Come in . . . come in."

She and Leah helped Sadie into the spare room. There they got Sadie settled, limp and pale as she was. Sizing up the situation, Lizzie could see that Sadie was definitely in the family way, just as she'd suspected for some weeks now. "How early is your baby, do you think?" she asked.

But Sadie wasn't responding except with occasional moans, so Leah did her best to fill in the details. My, oh my, Sadie needed help fast!

Lizzie hesitated to have anyone but an Amish midwife come to her house. Yet there was so little time, and the closest one lived three miles away.

Dear Lord, please help me know what to do, she prayed.

Sadie's face was turning a chalky gray, and she was all bunched up on the bed. Lizzie had no choice. An Englisher, Dr. Schwartz, would have to deliver this baby.

Turning to Leah, she said, "We can't do this alone." Lizzie gave directions to the medical clinic. "Run, fetch one of the horses—forget hitchin' up the buggy." Then guiding Leah into the doorway out of Sadie's hearing, she said, "You must ride the horse to the doctor's home . . . ride for your sister's and her baby's life!"

Frightened nearly to death, Leah ran all the way down the hill to the barn. She was glad that she, Smithy Gid, and Adah had once ridden bareback on their fathers' driving horses, years ago when they were but youngsters; otherwise, she wasn't so sure Aunt Lizzie's idea would've been such a wise thing. And, too, she knew it was not acceptable for horses to be used for such a purpose. But for an emergency—which by the look on Lizzie's face this surely was—she would obey her aunt and disregard the bishop's ruling about horseback riding. If her dear sister died tonight, Leah could never forgive herself if she chose to follow the letter of the law.

So she rode, clinging to the horse's neck and mane, her waist-length braids flying through the dreary night. Up Georgetown Road, past the woods on the knoll, to the home and clinic of the doctor Lizzie had suggested.

Henry's drowsiness fell away remarkably fast with the arrival of the stranger at his door. Without much ado, the Amish girl, calling herself Leah Ebersol, described a desperate situation—her teenage sister was in premature labor a half mile away.

With no time to waste, he grabbed his coat and hat and rushed outside. Meanwhile, the girl had tied up her horse in their backyard, promising rather apologetically to return for it later.

The drive took only a few minutes, and the young woman sat in the front seat and gripped the door handle. In spite of her great anxiety, Leah offered clear directions as to where to turn to get to the "mule road that leads to my aunt's cabin."

Getting out of the car, Henry hurried up the steps to a little log house, following Leah, whose gentle yet frightened eyes and faltering voice exposed her innocence to the whole ordeal of childbirth. He intended to do his best to save the lives of both her sister and the coming baby.

Quickly she led him to the room where her sister was writhing in pain. He set to work, evaluating the situation, noting the intense struggle on the part of the young mother, whose face was covered with beads of perspiration.

He spoke calmly to her, introducing himself. "I've come to deliver your baby, miss. If you do as I say, things will go more smoothly. Do you understand?"

She looked up at him and nodded weakly. At that moment he recognized her as the same young woman who had come looking for Derek one autumn night, the one who had then quarreled with his son and fled on foot. Whom he had seen at the Mast wedding, in fact. He saw the glint of recognition in her tearful eyes. She said her name was Sadie Ebersol, that she was unmarried, and that her parents did not yet know of her pregnancy.

Could this be Derek's child I've come to deliver? Henry wondered, the thought filling his soul with anguish.

No time to ponder the possibility. Instead, drawing on his medical expertise, he moved ahead with the task at hand. In the hallway, he heard the younger sister, Leah, call to someone in the kitchen, followed by the muffle of footsteps and a teapot whistling loudly. He checked his watch, timing the contractions, helping Sadie know how to breathe.

Seemingly terrified, Sadie fought the birth spasms every step of the way. Considering the circumstances, he was concerned that this delivery might be unlike any he had performed in recent years.

When the baby finally did come, Sadie lifted her damp

head off the pillow, and in an exhausted whisper asked, "Do I have a son?"

"Yes, a boy, but . . ." Henry could not get him to cry even after repeated smacks on the behind.

He paused, holding the infant in his arms, his mind racing. "I'm terribly sorry, Sadie, but . . . your baby is blue," he whispered. "No breath in him."

At this news, the young woman began to weep inconsolably. She called out to her sister, who came rushing into the bedroom. "He's dead, my dear baby's dead!" Sadie sobbed.

In the midst of the commotion, an older woman appeared in the doorway. Henry's gaze held hers for an instant. Her soft hazel-brown eyes seemed vaguely familiar, but he couldn't quite place her. Perhaps she had been one of his patients or someone he'd met along the road at a vegetable-and-fruit stand.

"You'll handle things for my niece, then?" The woman joined Leah at Sadie's bedside, where the two attempted to console the grief-stricken mother.

He looked down at the shriveled baby in his hands, a lump in his throat. "I'll take care of the remains . . . for you."

"Oh, thank you, Doctor," Sadie's sister spoke up.

Moving toward the bed, he offered, "I would be happy to look in on you tomorrow, Sadie. Make sure you're feeling better."

"That's kind of you," the girls' aunt replied, "but I'll see to her myself."

Then, from beneath the long sleeve of her nightgown, Sadie slowly drew out a tiny white handkerchief with an embroidered butterfly on the corner. Her fingers trembled as she opened it and gently laid it over the baby's face. "Fly away, my little one . . . rest in peace," she whispered.

Henry quietly extended his condolences again and headed for the door, the tiny, dead boy wrapped securely in the warmth of his coat, the bloody face covered with Sadie's handkerchief.

He placed the infant on the front seat of his car, keenly aware that he had most likely delivered his own stillborn grandson.

Mixed emotions swept over him, and he felt a sudden and inexplicable sense of loss. This was the little lad he would never have a chance to know, to play with, to watch grow into manhood. His own flesh and blood, though conceived in sin. His son's firstborn.

And yet . . . what would have happened if this boy *had* lived? Most assuredly Henry's reputation and that of his family would be tainted forever. If not destroyed.

He despised himself for his divided feelings and reached over and gently placed his hand on the dead babe's stomach. "Your mother's name is Sadie Ebersol," he said softly. The young Amishwoman's name would haunt him for years to come.

"And your father's name is . . ."

He thought of Derek. He and Lorraine had been excited by a recent letter, as they had not heard much since their boy's enlistment. Derek's note had been full of complaints about KP and acclimating to army life at Fort Benning, Georgia. He never inquired of either of them—of the home fires burning. And certainly not of the Amish girl he'd left behind. . . .

Lost in thought, Henry was aware of a faint whimper. Was it his imagination, or had the handkerchief over the infant's face fluttered slightly? And if so . . .

His hand still on the child's stomach, he felt the sudden rise and fall of the little chest. Then the infant's soft cry turned to a full-blown wail, as vigorous as any healthy newborn's.

What's this?

Evidently, he had accepted the child's death far too quickly. Medical journals documented rare cases such as this, infants who revived miraculously on their own.

Henry's pulse raced. Pushing the speed limit, he wasn't taking any chances. He must get Sadie's baby to the clinic—to an incubator. He tore into the driveway, then scooped up the infant, breathlessly carrying him inside.

Under the heat lamp, he washed its small face and body. Then he diapered him and wrapped the newborn preemie in a receiving blanket and settled him into an incubator. Even though the babe was breathing normally now, most likely he would be disabled either mentally or developmentally, having been deprived of oxygen at his birth—too tiny at the present to generate his own body heat. Later, he would even have to be taught to suckle for nourishment.

Henry hovered near, gazing into the now pink face of this child. Unmistakably evident—he recognized Derek's tuft of dark hair and the set of his eyes. This *was* his grandson!

Bewildered and torn, Henry took the soiled handkerchief—the one Sadie had placed over the infant's face—and rinsed it in cold water. Down the road, a grieving young mother wept in the night, totally unaware that her child was indeed alive.

He had the power to take her sorrow and replace it with joy, but in so doing he would bring shame to his own family's good name. Shame to her family's name, as well. What was he to do?

Back and forth he walked between the waiting room, his private office, and the infant nursery, muttering to himself, trying on every imaginable option. The right choice, of course, was to return the baby to its mother. Or he could simply arrange for an adoption, indeed saving Sadie's skin, who wanted to keep her Old Order Amish parents in the dark, for obvious reasons. Yet if he did so, he might never see his grandson again.

Long into the night Henry labored over a decision, rationalizing away all common sense.

◆

Leah felt weak with fatigue, drained of emotion. Still, she sat near Sadie in Aunt Lizzie's spare bed for several hours. She stroked Sadie's hair while she slept, exhausted from the pangs of childbirth, with nothing to show for her agonizing struggle.

Aunt Lizzie, asleep in the cane-backed chair nearby, had agreed that the girls should stay the night, as they often did. Leah was especially glad they'd cleared it with Mamma before ever leaving the house.

Meanwhile, Sadie rested fitfully, making sad, tearful sounds in her sleep. Leah didn't feel so well herself, though her wooziness came from spending half the night awake, either tending to Sadie after the doctor left or holding her and weeping along with her.

But then, once her sister fell into deeper slumber, Leah rose and walked back over to the clinic to leave the doctor's payment Lizzie had thrust in her hand. And she'd retrieved her horse at the same time, leading him back down the road to home long before dawn. Mindful of the bishop's decree, she'd hoped and prayed she might never have to break the church's rules for another emergency. Never again in her life.

Now, unable to rest or sit down, Leah walked the floor from one end of the cabin to the other, praying silently, asking God how this dreadful thing could have happened. But she felt she knew . . . would never tell her sister, though. The wretched sin of King David had been punished in a similar way. Why should Sadie's transgression be any different . . . or ignored by the Holy One? Surely, this was what the Lord God heavenly Father had allowed to befall her on this unbearable night. Divine chastisement.

Sadie had received just reward for disobedience. And Leah felt responsible for having kept quiet about her sister's sins.

Aunt Lizzie was more than a little reluctant about Sadie's plea not to tell Mamma. Truth was, Lizzie made an awful fuss, insisting that Mamma be told. Right then, Leah began siding with Sadie, begging Lizzie to leave things be. "What's done is done, and nothing good can ever come from Mamma and Dat knowing," she said.

At long last their aunt agreed never to utter a word of what had happened. Not unless Sadie spoke of it first.

So the three of them embraced the dark secret while a

heavy mist hung low to the ground outside, like a veil that would vanish at first light.

Soon as possible, Leah would have to tell Jonas that as much as she liked the idea of living in Ohio, being a mother's helper—while Jonas learned the carpentry trade in the Midwest—she simply couldn't see her way clear to leave Sadie. Not now. Sadly, she resigned herself to a courtship by mail. There was no other way.

Sisters came first, after all . . . even before a beau. Mamma had drilled this into all the girls, growing up. You stuck by family, no matter.

Chapter Twenty-five

Faithfully, Leah looked after Sadie in the days that followed, once Aunt Lizzie gave the go-ahead for Sadie to return home. Every so often Leah noticed Mamma eyeing Sadie curiously as they worked together in the kitchen, yet their mother did not question the sudden overnight stay. Nor the paleness of Sadie's face and her gaunt figure.

Soon Mamma's attention turned to her coming child, and Sadie began to regain strength, resuming all her daily chores.

Best of all, the girls had a cheerful time making a place for their new sibling in one corner of Dat and Mamma's big bedroom. What a flurry of sewing and whatnot went on. Sadie joined in, too, making a lightweight baby afghan for the spring and summer months, when the new babe would still be tiny and in need of an occasional wrap.

Leah winced, looking over at Sadie crocheting up a storm one afternoon, wondering how her sister was doing emotionally. Surely the loss of the baby and the heartache had taken its toll. But Sadie shared nothing at all, neither in the privacy of their room, nor when they happened to be alone downstairs, working together.

Sadie's ongoing silence worried Leah something awful. She felt strongly that if such a thing had happened to *her*, she would desperately need to confide in someone, share the wrenching sadness with a trusted sister or friend. But each time she made an attempt to open the door for such talk, Sadie abruptly changed the subject. It was ever so clear that her sister must be suffering terribly. But what to do? Leah wouldn't pry, for fear that might just push Sadie further away. Still, Leah couldn't imagine the loss Sadie must be feeling these days, especially now with all the talk of Mamma's baby coming soon.

A week later, nerves a-flutter, Leah hurried up the hill to visit with Aunt Lizzie, hoping to share some of the burden of concern. Lizzie met her at the door with a pained look in her perty eyes, though she did seem glad for the visit, serving up warm sugar cookies and cold milk. "Mm-m. You always have the best-tasting cookies," Leah said, settling down in the kitchen.

Lizzie's eyes brightened a bit. All of Leah's sisters made such remarks about their auntie's extraordinary baking talents. Mamma, too, would often say how nice and moist Lizzie's cookies were.

But soon Leah and Lizzie's talk turned to Sadie and how sick with worry both of them were. "My sister's too quiet all the time, scarcely ever speaks to any of us," Leah said, pouring out her heart. "I'm frightened, Aunt Lizzie. She's not herself, not one bit. And she takes off alone, walking out on the main road." Leah sighed. "What can we do to help her?"

Aunt Lizzie nodded, indicating that she, too, wished to

offer support somehow. "What's even more worrisome is your mamma's new baby comin' along in a few weeks now. How will *that* set with our Sadie?"

"Only the dear Lord knows. . . ." Leah felt there was little more to discuss. "But we can pray for God's help, ain't so, Auntie?"

"Jah, 'tis the very best we can do for now."

With that Leah felt a calm reassurance and thanked Lizzie for letting her bend an ear. "I best be getting home to help with supper." She kissed her aunt good-bye and hurried down the long hill toward the Ebersol Cottage.

One morning, after Dat gave his okay on the German shepherd pup, the girls were taking turns coming up with names. "Let's think of one that's not so common," Leah said. She knew by the markings that this was a special dog indeed. The way Smithy Gid handled the pet when he brought him over told her just how important this pup was.

The whole family was ever so glad to have a little watchdog in training nestled out in the barn in a box lined with sweet hay. And the girls each vied for the puppy's attention, taking turns feeding him milk from a bottle.

"I think he looks like a fuzzy peach," Mary Ruth spoke up. "Call him Peachy."

Hannah looked up, smiling, holding her sewing needle in midair. "You could name him Giddy Gid," to which they all broke out laughing. Even Mamma.

But none of the girls said why that was so funny. Still,

Leah caught it and hoped that by accepting Gideon's puppy dog she wasn't sending the wrong message. Surely not.

"You could name him *King*," said Mamma. "Since he's the only male round here besides Dat . . . so far."

"Jah, it's a wonderful-gut doggie name." So Leah took Mamma's suggestion, and King it was.

From time to time Sadie left the house and went walking down the narrow main road, beyond Dat's land and the adjoining acres belonging to Smithy Peachey. Sometimes ever farther . . . over toward the welding shop, a mile and a half from home, where she turned and headed past Naomi Kauffman's house. Of course, her friend Naomi was busy with her mamma and sisters, probably, so she wouldn't have seen Sadie wandering along, looking down in the mouth. Sadie didn't care how solemn she appeared these days. She was desperate for solitude, enduring her great loss in silence, for she dared not grieve openly. She made an effort to get outside every day or so, breathing in the fresh springtime air.

One afternoon she was out walking the same route, enjoying the fragrance of flowering trees and shrubs. The dogwoods were early this spring and so were the azaleas, the whole month of April having been much warmer than usual. She found it ever so amazing that this sliver of countryside was so pleasant, so out of the way, and yet speckled with interesting sights. And she'd never cared to notice before today that the road was winding in places, but best of all, it was free of summertime tourists who drove up and down Georgetown Road, hoping to catch a glimpse of a head covering or horse and buggy.

Oh, how she craved this time alone. Needed it desperately. Leah was getting on her nerves, asking questions and fishing to know how Sadie was coping—her arms empty and all. Of course, Leah was only trying to be kind, Sadie knew. Yet she resented her sister. Things had changed; tables were turned. She wished now for Leah's happy carefree life, since her own was in shambles. Too many church boys had heard—from Naomi, more than likely—that Sadie, too, had been awful wild during the years prior to church baptism. Such word, though whispered rumors, found its way to courting-age boys who might want to have a gut time for a while, but when it came to settling down and doing some serious courting, well, they much preferred someone innocent. Someone like Leah, who had *two* young men interested in her, of all things.

Sadie rejected Leah's repeated invitations to go to singings with her and Adah Peachey. If she went, she'd have to ride home with Jonas and Leah, which wasn't any fun for either of them, and certainly not for her. So Sadie had no one at all, not even her baby. God had taken away her precious infant son, allowing him to die before he could ever draw his first breath, before he could ever see the love in his young mamma's eyes. She wept bitter tears as she walked aimlessly along the road, feeling ever so light without her baby growing inside her, as if a wind might come up out of the north and simply blow her away.

Ach, how fair was it that Derry's life could just move forward, unfettered? Hers had come to a dead halt, beginning the night Derry suggested discarding their baby's life. She felt cut off from all that had previously meant anything to her, spending more time out on the road than round the house as the days grew longer, heading toward planting season. Soon they'd be knee-deep in vegetable gardens, including rows of celery to be served at Leah's wedding, and sowing early corn with Dat in the field. And soon a newborn baby would be living in the house, yearning for loving care, except Sadie wouldn't be its mamma.

The Lord God had dealt bitterly with her. Yet broken covenants required blood sacrifice. Dat's old German *Biewel* illustrated such truths, and Preacher Yoder was forever reminding them, especially the young people, what happened to people who broke their vows to God and the church.

Obey or die. . . .

She was reaping what she'd sown. Her world had completely collapsed. Losing her baby to death . . . it was the worst punishment any young woman could ever endure.

After lunch Hannah slipped off to her room and took out her writing notebook—her diary—while Mary Ruth sat at the kitchen table and wrote a letter back to her pen pal in Willow Street, and Mamma napped a bit.

April 23, 1947
Dear Diary,

I'm leery of putting my thoughts on paper today, lest they be read at some later time and be misunderstood. But I'd have to say (if asked) that Sadie is becoming ever so surly, distant to all of us. Even worse than a year ago. Mamma doesn't seem to know what to do about her, either. I can tell by the way our mother sighs and shrugs her shoulders. What with plowing and preparing the soil for planting, Dat isn't indoors all that much, except to eat, so he's not too aware of Sadie's behavior. If I didn't know better, I'd think she had been jilted by a beau, but just who that was or is none of us knows. And if Leah does, she ain't talking.

Putting down her pen, Hannah thought that even Leah's happiness seemed a bit tainted. But that was probably because Jonas Mast was leaving for Ohio very soon. Right perplexing it was, the similarity between Sadie and Leah these days.

And Hannah couldn't begin to understand what was causing such a feeling of calamity whenever Sadie walked into a room. She'd shared this with Mary Ruth privately, but her twin, not so sullen, had other things on her mind—excelling in mathematics, for one, saying that Miss Riehl was ever so proud of her accomplishments. Extra work completed and turned in for grading, too. Yet Mary Ruth seemed oblivious to the goings-on in the house. Ever typical, Hannah was the worried one, sensing the troubles of others.

Hannah was awful sure her twin was definitely on the path heading right out of Dat's house and away from the Amish community. If Mary Ruth kept up her thirst for learning, she most certainly would be. All the while, sisterly love prompted Hannah to sew more and more handkerchiefs, saving every nickel and dime toward making just such a dream come true for their someday schoolteacher.

While her girls assumed she was resting, Ida pulled a chair near the window, where the sun spilled in and the sky was dotted with high cloudiness. Sure enough, her little one began kicking and poking the moment Ida sat down. She smiled a bit, her gaze roaming over the barn roof, out past the windmill and toward the woods. It was then she noticed Sadie walking barefoot, up toward Lizzie's cabin. Ach, she'd been wondering a lot here lately, praying, too, for her eldest. Something just didn't sit right. Grouchy and aloof, Sadie had lost her smile; her confidence was all but gone. And, oddly enough, Lizzie seemed downright mum about it all.

And Ida had tried to talk with Sadie, too, on various occasions, but each time her daughter brushed her off, disinterested in any meaningful conversation, it seemed. No, everything was *hipperdiglipp*—slapdash—and almost hostile coming from Sadie these days.

Ida had voiced her concerns to Abram just last night. "What could be wrong with Sadie, do you think?" she had asked, fearing the worst.

"Now, what do you mean, dear?"

Well, if Abram hadn't noticed anything off-beam, then who was she to say anything and get him all stirred up? So she shrugged off the question and decided to look after her own needs for now. Though she wondered if Lizzie might know something and just wasn't saying. She'd seen Sadie out walking a lot this week, sometimes up the mule path between their barnyard and Lizzie's log cabin. Of course, she wouldn't press things with either Sadie or Lizzie. Time to think of the new little one, soon to be her babe-in-arms.

Aunt Lizzie's house was a one-level cabin that looked more like a perty cottage, one found in the pages of a magazine, at least inside it was. Set back amidst tall, budding trees and protected by flowering shrubs—lilac bushes and forsythia this time of year—the cozy place held a special, nearly sacred spot in Sadie's heart. Her darling baby had been born in Aunt Lizzie's spare room, yet the actual happenings that night were still so hazy in her mind.

"Come right in and make yourself to home," Lizzie said, meeting her at the back door.

"I shouldn't stay so long." But Sadie went in and sat down

right away, feeling awful weak suddenly.

"Well, why not catch your breath at least?" To this, Lizzie laughed softly. "You're here, Sadie. Might as well make it worthwhile. What can I get you to drink?"

"Oh, nothin' at all."

"Well, one look at you and I can see ya need something wet. What'll it be?"

Her aunt meant to coddle her, and she could certainly use some compassion today. Just as she'd needed Lizzie's listening ear the week after her baby son had been born, when she'd crept up here yearning to talk with someone. "All right then, I'll have what you like best . . . some Postum, maybe."

Aunt Lizzie must've seen right through her. "You never drink Postum, Sadie. How 'bout some nice cold lemonade instead?"

Too helpless to squabble, she nodded her head.

"I'll be right back. Now, don't go away, hear?" And with that Lizzie headed out to the kitchen.

Sadie shed her sweater and draped it over the back of the chair. From outside she heard the call of birds within the foxtail grass, way out past the stone wall surrounding the cabin. Getting up, she went to stand in the window, staring out at a mass of red-winged blackbirds, tussling for their territory. Who'd win? Would the strongest, biggest birds claim their spot?

She let her eyes go misty, daydreaming. And just who had won between Derry and herself? The boy going off to Uncle Sam had, no question. He'd gotten what he'd set out for, then up and left her. But now she was all the wiser for it.

Lizzie hadn't meant to startle her niece as she returned carrying a tray with two glasses of lemonade and a plate of oatmeal cookies. "Here we are. We'll have us a nice chat . . . a snack, too."

They sipped their drinks silently for a time, then ever so slowly Sadie opened up and asked the question that continually weighed on her heart. "Tell me again . . . didja see my baby after. . . ?" Unable to continue, she put her head down, fighting back tears.

"Aw, Sadie dear." Aunt Lizzie came and placed her hand on Sadie's back, saying her name over again.

"I just wish I knew what he looked like." She wept into her hands.

Lizzie tried to console her, saying, "It's all right to cry, truly it is."

And Sadie did cry. She sobbed till Lizzie thought the girl's heart might nearly dry up and break.

Then sitting back, Sadie began to talk in sputters. "Oh, I wish . . . I might've at least held him . . . just for a moment . . . before the doctor took him away."

"Jah. Still, some things are best as is."

"I shouldn't have let Dr. Schwartz leave so quick, prob'ly."

"What else could you do?" Aunt Lizzie sat down nearby. She was ever so uneasy about her niece, who needed such care at the present time, both physically and emotionally.

"All this just pains me something awful," Sadie said.

"Still, it's no surprise to see you distraught over such a loss."

Sadie nodded. "There are nights when I dream of nothing else but my baby, Auntie . . . that I still have him safe inside me. Then the nightmare starts all over again. . . ."

"Well, maybe a little time away might help get you back

on your feet again. A change of scenery can help a lot sometimes."

"But where could I go?" Sadie asked, sitting up a bit straighter.

"Most any place, really. Your mamma and I have cousins in Indiana and even up in New York State. Some kinfolk out in Ohio, too."

"How would I get there?"

"I have some money tucked away for emergencies. I could put you on a bus, maybe. How would that be?"

All this—every bit of it—seemed like music to Sadie's ears. And they spent the better part of an hour talking over the possibility of her living with a young family, cousins with a batch of children to look after, out in Millersburg, Ohio.

Lizzie made it clear that Sadie must go for only a short time, because to leave behind the church of her baptism for good would mean certain shunning. And so would being found out . . . about unrepentant sin. "What will your parents have to say about such a visit?" Lizzie asked. "Isn't it time you shared something—with your mamma at least?"

"No, I'd rather not just now. Maybe never . . ."

Oh, how Lizzie wished Sadie would openly share with her parents. Both Ida and Abram were right kind and caring folk, without a doubt. Was the dear girl afraid of being found out by the church elders? Well, if that were the case, Lizzie could attest to having seen the People rally round a wayward member. And once a wrongdoer repented, well, the arms of the community opened wide to welcome the church member right back into the fold.

Something was surely vexing Sadie. Perhaps it had to do with an unwillingness to repent. Truly, Lizzie wanted to ask why she didn't just offer her remorse privately to Preacher Yoder. But Lizzie kept her peace. Besides stubbornness, what on earth was holding the girl back? Was it the sin of pride, or was Sadie downright rebellious?

Then and there Sadie decided not to tell another soul about her plans to visit Ohio. She didn't know just how much longer she'd stay put here. Of course, with news that Jonas Mast was heading in the same direction, might be best to remain in Gobbler's Knob through the summer months till his return. That way, Leah wouldn't think she was running off after Jonas, for pity's sake. But if he *was* still in the area when she arrived, it sure would be nice to see at least one familiar face, though way off in Ohio.

So come next September, round the time Leah was to make her kneeling vow to God and the church, Sadie would simply slip off into the night . . . take herself away from Lancaster County for a while. And not a single Plain boy in Ohio would have any idea she'd disobeyed the Ordnung so totally. Nobody need know she'd allowed an English boy to court her, deceive her, and father her dead child. She'd be shunned, though, never truly welcomed back into her father's house if she stayed on. But what other choice was there?

Chapter Twenty-Six

The joyous birth of a daughter on May seventeenth had the Ebersol Cottage all abuzz with excitement. Aunt Lizzie rushed out of Mamma's bedroom to share the good news, letting the midwife have a chance to examine the pink, wailing newborn.

"It's a girl!" She passed the word to Hannah, who in turn, ran out to the garden rows, where Dat, Sadie, Leah, and Mary Ruth were planting pole snap beans, cucumbers, turnips, squash, and a variety of other vegetables.

"Well, looks like we're still just Abram's *daughters*," Hannah called, grinning at Dat and her sisters.

Dat stood up and wiped his forehead, eyes wide. "A girl, is it?"

"Jah, 'tis."

At that Leah and Mary Ruth came and hugged her, jumping up and down with glee. Sadie kept working, though, and Hannah didn't quite understand that. But then, maybe their big sister had been secretly hoping for a brother. Who knows?

The first few days, Ida chose Sadie the most to help her with Lydiann, especially during the morning and afternoon. She felt sure things might improve a bit for Sadie once she held her cuddly baby sister in her arms. Jah, there was something real comforting about holding a wee one. So the firstborn helped change and dress the baby of the family, walking the floor with her when she was a bit colicky of an afternoon.

After a full week of this, Sadie did seem to be settling down some. But not so much that she wanted to share with Ida. Not at all. *In due time, she will,* Ida decided.

Abram got a kick out of watching his new daughter make funny little face crinkles while she slept. He told Ida this was the pertiest baby he'd ever seen, which, if she remembered far enough back, he'd said the same of their other daughters when they were each brand-new.

Well, now they had five girls living under their roof, at least for now. Both Sadie and Leah would probably be wed here within the year, she guessed. Leah, for sure—to Jonas Mast. Lizzie had given her the word about the need for celery, thank goodness, so they'd best be planting some this summer, in mid-July.

Lo and behold, if Abram didn't have to worry over working the land after all, waiting so many years to hand over the farm to a son coming along behind. No, the Good Lord had taken care of that, seen fit to give them a daughter instead of a son. A right healthy girl at that.

So just whenever Dawdi John grew older and it was his time to go on home to heaven, she and Abram could simply move into the little Dawdi Haus with Lydiann—build on a bit, maybe—raise her over there, and let one of their sons-in-law tend to farming duties. Of course, by then both Hannah and Mary Ruth would be baptized church members and married, too, more than likely.

Thankfully, all things were working out wonderful-gut for those who love the Lord here on Gobbler's Knob. Seemed to be, anyways.

Ida put a kettle on to boil, hankering for a cup of raspberry tea with a spoonful of honey. Never mind the late hour. All day she had been so busy with her little one, she hadn't had a chance to sit down and read her cousin Fannie's long letter, which had come in the afternoon mail.

Wanting something in hand while she read, she waited for the water to boil, then let the tea leaves steep five minutes. Once she poured the simmering tea into her cup, she settled down in Abram's favorite hickory rocker. Glad for the stillness of the house, she knew all too well that Lydiann would be crying for nourishment here perty soon.

So with her ear attuned to the upstairs bedroom, where Abram slept soundly and their infant daughter was tucked into a handmade wooden cradle in the corner of the room, she began to read.

My dear cousin Ida,

Greetings from Grasshopper Level, where Peter and I are the happy parents of twins . . . a girl and a boy. No doubt you've heard through the grapevine of our double blessing. They arrived full-term, though the boy is somewhat smaller and not nearly as hearty as the girl. We named them Jacob and

Amanda—Jake and Mandie for short. And such a joyous sight the two of them are! Jake has Peter's dark hair and jawline, and Mandie has light brown hair and blue eyes like our Jonas and some of the girls.

We're ever so thankful to the Good Lord and continue to trust Him to see us through the first months of little or no sleep, as you must surely know by now yourself. I'm so happy to hear that you've had a healthy baby girl. Just whenever you have a free minute, I'd like to know how it is for you and Abram having a new baby after all this time.

Then one of these days, maybe come late summer, our families can visit again and enjoy seeing all three of our young ones lined up in a row. Such a perty sight that'll be.

Well, I hear little Mandie fussing for the next feeding. She cries and then both she and Jake get fed. Now, how about that?

Give my best to Abram and all the girls. (Lizzie, too.)

My love to you,
Cousin Fannie

Ida sighed, folding the letter. It was awful nice to sit and soak up the quiet, sipping tea late at night, almost old enough to be a *Grossmudder*, and here she was starting all over as a new mamma, yet. What was the Lord God thinking, anyways?

Of course, she knew she'd just be on her knees that much more, raising Lydiann clear at the tail end of the family, asking for divine wisdom and help along the way. God would continue to be their joy and their strength. Each and every day. Jah, she could count on that and never take such gifts for granted.

◆

Jonas had the use of one of his father's driving horses for the special occasion, this day Leah had dreaded to see arrive, yet she wouldn't have missed spending the afternoon hours with her beau. Not for the world. They'd taken to the road in Jonas's open buggy, diverting off from the main highway and heading toward White Oak Road, where the route curved round like a dusty ribbon under the hot sun.

One of the less-traveled paths, which they ended up following, shrank to a couple of furrows with a thin row of yellow dandelions running between, leading to a wide and open meadow. Thick green bushes, some thorny, others berry-laden, bedecked the roadside as they went. All the while Leah memorized the lush green acres and pungent farm smells around them, as well as the way the sunlight played on Jonas's light brown hair, listening intently as her dearest love shared his plans for their future.

"I'll return in late September or early October. For sure in time for apple picking." Jonas reached for her hand. "And I pray the time will pass quickly."

"Though I can't see how. . . ." Then she nodded, attempting to be brave. "But we'll both be ever so busy . . . so, jah, it oughta go fast."

"You should go ahead with your baptismal instruction, just as we'd planned. I'll do the same in Ohio."

"Ach, how will that all work out?" Leah had never heard of such a thing.

"I've already talked with my bishop. He's given me the okay, if I can find a conservative order in the Millersburg area."

Jonas slowed the horse as the buggy wheels *click-clacked* over a bridge made from old railroad ties, the creek rising and falling over giant stones beneath the old boards, some of them gaping too far apart for Leah's liking.

"I'll be countin' the days till I see you again," Jonas said, his voice husky now.

Oh no . . . don't say such things, she thought, having promised herself she wouldn't spoil the afternoon by shedding a tear. "We have all the rest of our lives, Lord willin', to enjoy our time together as husband and wife," she said.

He smiled at her then, his blue eyes alight with love. Leaning his head against hers briefly, he stopped the horse just as the road leveled out, past a slight incline. "Here's a good place to pick some wild flowers. Want to?"

Standing up quickly, she nodded. Jonas helped her out of the buggy to the grassy paddock, where flowing hills beckoned in every direction. "I'm planning a nice surprise for you," he said.

"Oh? What is it?"

"Well, now, it wouldn't be a surprise if I told you, would it?"

She was ever so inquisitive. "Just *when* will I know?"

He stood there, grinning at her to beat the band. "My dear girl, how will I get along without you by my side . . . even for such a few months?" Gently he pulled her near and brushed her cheek with a tender kiss. "You make it awful hard to keep a secret. Those big hazel eyes of yours."

She laughed softly as they strolled through the tall grass. "So . . . will you tell me, Jonas? Just what is it you have up your sleeve?"

"I'm going to try my hand at makin' you a big oak sideboard. What do you think of that?"

"Oh, such a wonderful-gut surprise! When will you have it finished, do you think?"

"When I return." He touched her face. "It'll be my wedding gift to you."

"I'll look forward to that day." She felt her throat close up and knew she couldn't have spoken more even if she'd wanted to.

"I love you, Leah." And with that, they spun round and round together. The whirling made her dizzy with delight, but she savored most the spot where she landed—in his strong arms. "Remember the day I hurt my ankle?" she said softly. "You picked me right up and carried me into your mamma's kitchen almost before I knew what you were doing!"

"Well, *someone* had to carry you, right?"

Aware of just how near she was to his heart, she laid her head against his white shirt and whispered back, "I love you, too, Jonas." And then she blushed. "Now, *I* have a secret. But I best not tell."

He reached over and cupped her face in his hands.

"Tell me or . . . well, I'll have to kiss you on the lips."

"If you do that, we'll spoil things."

Still, he held her face tenderly, moving closer. "What's your secret, Leah Ebersol?"

"Ach, must you be so impatient?"

"This minute . . . I must know, my dear one."

She breathed deeply, letting him cradle her in his arms once again. "I *always* loved you, Jonas. Even back when I was only ten. That's what."

He smiled down at her. "We both felt this way, didn't we? From the first time we met?"

"Jah—" she fought back tears—"and that we'd mean

much more to each other . . . go far beyond our childhood promises."

"And here we are, Leah."

"Did you ever think we'd be engaged, for sure and for certain?"

"I never doubted it," he said.

Then and there, she vowed their love must never become run-of-the-mill like other married couples. Theirs would be the strong and lasting kind, one that flourished well into old age, despite the strain of separation facing them now.

They walked hand in hand up to the crest of the hill, where they looked over grazing and cropland far below, watching butterflies drift up from the grasses. A single bluebird flew overhead, and Leah reached up happily.

"You're my bluebird . . . and always will be," her darling beau had said, back on their first night as a courting couple.

With Jonas by her side, she was right where she belonged—for always—certain no harm could befall two people so in love.

The Betrayal

BEVERLY LEWIS

The Betrayal

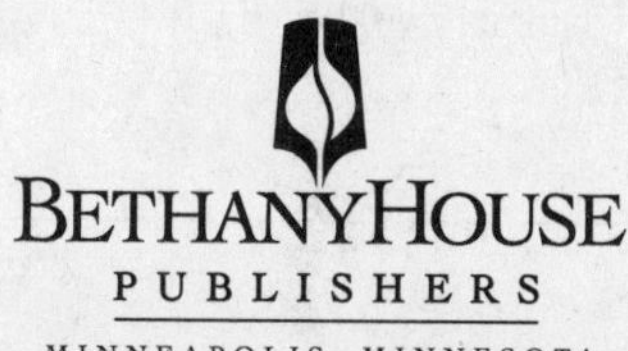
BETHANY HOUSE
PUBLISHERS
MINNEAPOLIS, MINNESOTA

The Betrayal

Cover design by Dan Thornberg

Note to Readers: Although *Martyrs Mirror* is an actual book, the account of Catharina Meylin is a creation of the author.

Published by Bethany House Publishers
11400 Hampshire Avenue South
Bloomington, Minnesota 55438

Bethany House Publishers is a division of
Baker Publishing Group, Grand Rapids, Michigan.

Printed in the United States of America

ISBN 0-7642-2331-3 (Paperback)
ISBN 0-7642-2807-2 (Hardcover)
ISBN 0-7642-2806-4 (Large Print)
ISBN 0-7642-2808-0 (Audio Book)

Library of Congress Cataloging-in-Publication Data

Lewis, Beverly
The betrayal / by Beverly Lewis.
p. cm. (Abram's daughters ; 2)
ISBN 0-7642-2331-3 (pbk.) — ISBN 0-7642-2807-2 (hardcover) — ISBN 0-7642-2806-4 (large print)
1. Lancaster County (Pa.)—Fiction. 2. Sisters—Fiction. 3. Amish—Fiction. I. Title. II. Series: Lewis, Beverly, 1949- , Abram's daughters ; 2.
PS3562.E9383B48 2003
813'.54—dc21 2002008665

Dedication

For

Pamela Ronn,

my "shadow twin"

and wonderful-good friend.

By Beverly Lewis

ABRAM'S DAUGHTERS

The Covenant
The Betrayal
The Sacrifice
The Prodigal
The Revelation

❖ ❖ ❖

THE HERITAGE OF LANCASTER COUNTY

The Shunning
The Confession
The Reckoning

❖ ❖ ❖

ANNIE'S PEOPLE

The Preacher's Daughter

❖ ❖ ❖

The Postcard · *The Crossroad*

❖ ❖ ❖

The Redemption of Sarah Cain
October Song · *Sanctuary**
The Sunroom

❖ ❖ ❖

The Beverly Lewis Amish Heritage Cookbook

www.BeverlyLewis.com

*with David Lewis

05C

BEVERLY LEWIS, born in the heart of Pennsylvania Dutch country, fondly recalls her growing-up years. A keen interest in her mother's Plain family heritage has led Beverly to set many of her popular stories in Lancaster County.

A former schoolteacher and accomplished pianist, Beverly is a member of the National League of American Pen Women (the Pikes Peak branch), and the Society of Children's Book Writers and Illustrators. She is the 2003 recipient of the Distinguished Alumnus Award at Evangel University, Springfield, Missouri, and her blockbuster novel, *The Shunning*, recently won the Gold Book Award. Her bestselling novel *October Song* won the Silver Seal in the Benjamin Franklin Awards, and *The Postcard* and *Sanctuary*, (a collaboration with her husband, David) received Silver Angel Awards, as did her delightful picture book for all ages, *Annika's Secret Wish*. Beverly and her husband have three grown children and one grandchild and make their home in the Colorado foothills.

August 9, 1947
Dear Jonas,

Honestly, you spoil me! I've saved up a whole handful of your letters, and only a few months have passed since you left for Ohio. It's all I can do to keep from running to the kitchen calendar yet again to count up the days till your visit for our baptism Sunday next month. How good of your bishop to permit you to join my church district. The Lord above is working all things out for us, ain't so?

Your latest letter arrived today in the mail, and I hurried out to the front porch and curled up in Mamma's wicker chair to read in private. I felt you were right there with me, Jonas. Just the two of us together again.

It's easy to see the many things you describe in Millersburg—the clapboard carpenter's shed where you're busy with the apprenticeship, the big brick house where you eat and sleep, even the bright faces of the little Mellinger children. How wonderful-good the Lord God has been to give you your heart's ambition, and I am truly happy for you . . . and for us.

Here in Gobbler's Knob (where you are sorely missed!), there isn't much news, except to say I know of four new babies in a short radius of miles. Even our English neighbors down the road have a new little one. Soon we're all going to Grasshopper Level to lay eyes on your twin baby sister and brother. I have to admit I don't know which I like better—feeding chickens and threshing grain, or bathing and playing with my sweet baby sister, almost three months old. Lydiann is so cuddly and cute, cooing and smiling at us. Dat laughs, saying I'm still his right-hand man. "Let Mamma and your sisters look after our wee one," he goes on. But surely he must know I won't be called Abram's Leah for too many more months now, though I haven't breathed a word. Still, I'm awful sure Mamma and Aunt Lizzie suspect we're a couple. Dat, too, if he'd but accept the truth of our love. Come autumn, the People will no longer think of me as my father's replacement for a son. For that I'm truly happy.

Oh, Jonas, are there other couples like us? In another village or town, hundreds of miles from here or just across the cornfield . . . are there two such close friends who also happen to be this much in love? Honestly, I can't imagine it.

I miss you, Jonas! You seem so far away. . . .

Leah held the letter in her hands, reading what she'd written thus far. Truly, she hesitated to share the one thing that hung most heavily in her mind. Yet Jonas wrote about everything under the sun in *his* letters, so why shouldn't she feel free to do the same? She didn't want to speak out of turn, though.

Should I tell Jonas about the unexpected visit yesterday from his father? she pondered.

Truth was, Peter Mast had come rumbling into the barnyard in his market wagon like a house on fire. In short order, he and *Dat* had gone off to the high meadow for over an hour. Sure did seem awful strange, but when she asked Mamma about it, she was told not to worry her "little head."

What on earth? she wondered. *What business does Cousin Peter have with Dat?*

Part One

◆ ◆ ◆ ◆

The daisy, by the shadow that it casts,
Protects the lingering dewdrop from the sun.

—William Wordsworth

◆ ◆ ◆ ◆

Never praise a sister to a sister,
in the hope of your compliments
reaching the proper ears.

—Rudyard Kipling

Chapter One

Dog days. The residents of Gobbler's Knob had been complaining all summer about the sweltering, brooding sun. Its intensity reduced clear and babbling brooks to a muddy trickle, turning broccoli patches into yellow flower gardens. Meadowlarks scowled at the parched earth void of worms, while variegated red-and-white petunias dropped their ruffled petticoats, waiting for a summertime shower.

Worse still, evening hours gave only temporary pause, as did the dead of night if a faint breeze found its way through open farmhouse windows, bringing momentary relief to restless sleepers. Afternoons were nearly unbearable and had been now for weeks, June twelfth having hit the record high at ninety-seven degrees.

Abram and Ida Ebersol's farmhouse stood at the edge of a great woods as a shelter against the withering heat. The grazing and farmland surrounding the house had a warm and genial scent, heightened by the high temperatures. Abram's seven acres and the neighboring farmland were an enticing sanctuary for a variety of God's smaller creatures—squirrels, birds, chipmunks, and field mice, the latter a good enough reason to tolerate a dozen barn cats.

Not far from the barnyard, hummocks of coarse, panicled grass bordered the mule road near the outhouse, and a well-worn path cut through a high green meadow leading to the log house of Ida's *maidel* sister, Lizzie Brenneman.

Ida, midlife mother to nearly three-month-old Lydiann, along with four teenage girls—Sadie, Leah, and twins Hannah and Mary Ruth—found a welcome reprieve this day in the dampness of the cold cellar beneath the large upstairs kitchen, where Sadie and Hannah were busy sweeping the cement floor, redding up in general. Abram had sent Leah indoors along about three-thirty for a break from the beastly heat. Ida was glad to have plenty of help wiping down the wooden shelves, making ready for a year's worth of canned goods—eight hundred quarts of fruits and vegetables—once the growing season was past. Working together, they lined up dozens of quarts of strawberry preserves and about the same of green beans and peas, seventeen quarts of peaches thus far, and thirty-six quarts of pickles, sweet and dill. Some of the recent canning had been done with Aunt Lizzie's help, as well as that of their close neighbors—the smithy's wife, Miriam Peachey, and daughters, Adah and Dorcas.

The Ebersol girls took their time organizing the jars, not at all eager to head upstairs before long and make supper in the sultry kitchen.

"I daresay this is the hottest summer we've had in years," Mamma remarked.

"And not only here," Leah added. "The heat hasn't let up in Ohio, neither."

Mary Ruth mopped her fair brow. "Your beau must be keepin' you well informed of the weather in Millersburg, *jah?*"

To this Hannah grinned. "We could set the clock by Jonas's letters. Ain't so, Leah?"

Leah, seventeen in two months, couldn't help but smile and much too broadly at that. Dear, dear Jonas. What a wonderful-good letter writer he was, sending word nearly three times a week or so. This had surprised her, really . . . but Mamma always said it was most important for the young man to do the wooing, either by letters or in person. So Jonas was well thought of in Mamma's eyes at least. Not so much Dat's. No, her father held fast to his enduring hope of Leah's marrying the blacksmith's twenty-year-old son, Gideon Peachey—nicknamed Smithy Gid—next farm over.

Sadie stepped back as if to survey her neat row of quart-sized tomato soup jars. "Writin' to Cousin Jonas about the weather can't be all *that* interesting, now, can it?" she said, eyeing Leah.

"We write 'bout lots of things. . . ." Leah tried to explain, sensing one of Sadie's moods.

"Why'd he have to go all the way out to Ohio for his apprenticeship, anyway?" Sadie asked.

Mamma looked up just then, her earnest blue eyes intent on her eldest. "Aw, Sadie, you know the reason," she said.

Sadie's apologetic smile looked forced, and she turned back to her work.

The subject of Jonas and his letters was dropped. Mamma's swift reprimand was followed by silence, and then Leah gave a long, audible sigh.

Yet Leah felt no animosity, what with Sadie seemingly

miserable all the time. Sadie was never-ending blue and seemed as shriveled in her soul as the ground was parched. If only the practice of *rumschpringe*—the carefree, sometimes wild years before baptism—had been abolished by Bishop Bontrager years ago. A group of angry parents had wished to force his hand to call an end to the foolishness, but to no avail. Unchecked, Sadie had allowed a fancy English boy to steal her virtue. *Poor, dear Sadie.* If she could, Leah would cradle her sister's splintered soul and hand it over to the Mender of broken hearts, the Lord Jesus.

She offered a silent prayer for her sister and continued to work side by side with Mamma. Soon she found herself daydreaming about her wedding, thinking ahead to which sisters she might ask to be in her bridal party and whom she and Mamma would ask to be their kitchen helpers. Selecting the hostlers—the young men who would oversee the parking of buggies and the care of the horses—was the groom's decision.

Jonas had written that he wanted to talk over plans for their wedding day when he returned for baptism; he also wanted to spend a good part of that weekend with her, and her alone. But on the following Monday he must return to Ohio to complete his carpentry apprenticeship, "just till apple-pickin' time." His father's orchard was too enormous not to have Jonas's help, come October. And then it wouldn't be long after the harvest and they'd be married. Leah knew their wedding would fall on either a Tuesday or Thursday in November or early December, the official wedding season in Lancaster County. She and Mamma would be deciding fairly soon on the actual date, though since Jonas didn't know precisely when he'd be returning home for good, she had to wait to discuss it with him. Secretly she hoped he would agree to choose an earlier rather than a later date.

As for missing Jonas, the past months had been nearly unbearable. She drank in his letters and answered them quickly, doing the proper thing and waiting till he wrote to her each time. It was painful for her, knowing she'd rejected his idea to spend the summer in close proximity to him out in Holmes County—a way to avoid the dreaded long-distance courtship. But for Sadie's sake, Leah had stayed put in Gobbler's Knob, wanting to offer consolation after the birth and death of her sister's premature baby. In all truth, she had believed Sadie needed her more than Jonas.

But Jonas had been disappointed, and she knew it by the unmistakable sadness in his usually shining eyes. She had told him her mother needed help with the new baby, the main excuse she'd given. Dismayed, he pressed her repeatedly to reconsider. The hardest part was not being able to share her real reason with him. Had Jonas known the truth, he would have been soundly stunned. At least he might have understood why she felt she ought to stay behind, which had nothing to do with being too shy to live and work in a strange town, as she assumed he might think. Most of all, she hoped he hadn't mistakenly believed her father had talked her out of going.

Today Leah was most eager to continue writing her letter the minute she completed chores, hoping to slip away again to her bedroom for a bit of privacy. When she considered how awful hot the upstairs had been these days, she thought she might take herself off to the coolness of the woods, stationery and pen in hand. If not today, then tomorrow for sure.

No one knew it, but here lately she'd been writing to Jonas in the forest. Before her beau had left town, she would never have thought of venturing into the deepest part, only going as far as Aunt Lizzie's house. But she liked being alone with the trees, her pen on the paper, the soft breezes whispering her name . . . and Jonas's.

Growing up, she'd heard the tales of folk becoming disoriented in the leafy maze of undergrowth and the dark burrow of trees. Still, she was determined to go, delighting in being surrounded by all of nature. There a place of solitude awaited her away from her sisters' prying eyes, as well as a place to dream of Jonas. She had sometimes wondered where Sadie and her worldly beau had run off to many times last year before Sadie sadly found herself with child. But when Leah searched the woods, she encountered only tangled brushwood and nearly impassable areas where black tree roots and thick shrubbery caused her bare feet to stumble.

Both she and Sadie had not forgotten what it felt like as little girls to scamper up to Aunt Lizzie's for a playful picnic in her secluded backyard. Thanks to her, they were shown dazzling violets amid sward and stone, demanding attention by the mere look on their floral faces . . . and were given a friendly peep into a robin's comfy nest—"but not *too* close," Aunt Lizzie would whisper. All this and more during such daytime adventures.

But never had Lizzie recommended the girls explore the expanse of woods on their own. In fact, she'd turned ashen on at least one occasion when seven-year-old Leah wondered aloud concerning the things so oft repeated. "*Ach,* you mustn't think of wandering in there alone," Lizzie had replied quickly. Sadie, at the innocent age of nine, had trembled a bit, Leah recalled, her older sister's blue eyes turning a peculiar grayish green. And later Leah had vowed to Sadie she was content never to find out "what awful frightening things are hiding in them there wicked woods!"

Now Leah sometimes wondered if maybe Sadie truly *had* believed the scary tales and taken them to heart, she might not have ended up the ruined young woman she was. At the tender age of nineteen.

At the evening meal Dat sat at the head of the long kitchen table, with doting Mamma to his left. Fourteen-year-old Hannah noticed his brown hair was beginning to gray, bangs cropped straight across his forehead and rounded in a bowl shape around the ears and neck. He wore black work pants, a short-sleeved green shirt, and black suspenders, though his summer straw hat likely hung on a wooden peg in the screened-in porch.

Before eating they all bowed heads simultaneously as the memorized prayer was silently given by each Ebersol family member, except baby Lydiann, who was nestled in Mamma's pleasingly ample arms.

O Lord God heavenly Father, bless us and these thy gifts, which we shall accept from thy tender goodness and grace. Give us food and drink also for our souls unto life eternal, and make us partakers of thy heavenly table through Jesus Christ, thy Son. Amen.

Following the supper blessing, they silently prayed the Lord's Prayer.

Meanwhile, Hannah tried to imagine how the arranged seating pattern might look once Leah was married. She worried her twin also might not remain under Dat's roof much longer, not if she stayed true to her hope of higher education. How Mary Ruth would pull off such a thing, Hannah didn't know, especially now with Elias Stoltzfus making eyes at her.

She gazed at her sisters just now, from youngest to eldest. The table *would* look mighty bare with only five of them present, counting Dat, Mamma and baby, Sadie, and herself. It wouldn't be long till Lydiann could sit in a high chair scooted up close. That would help round things out a bit . . . that and if Mamma were to have another baby or two. Anything was possible, she assumed, since Mamma was approaching forty-three. Not too terribly old for childbearing, because on the Brenneman side of the family, there were plenty of women in the family way clear into their late forties—some even into the early fifties. So who was to say just how many more Ebersol children the Lord God might see fit to send along? Honestly, she wouldn't mind if there were a few more little sisters or brothers, and Mary Ruth would be delighted, too; her twin was ever so fond of wee ones and all.

This made Hannah wonder how many children young and handsome Ezra Stoltzfus might want to have with his wife someday. She could only hope that, at nearly sixteen, he might find her as fetching as she thought *he* was. Here lately she was mighty sure he had taken more of a shine to her, which was right fine. Of course, now, he'd have to be the one to pursue her once she turned courting age. She wouldn't be flirting her way into a boy's heart like some girls. Besides, she wasn't interested in attracting a beau that way. She wanted a husband who appreciated her femininity, a man who would love her for herself, for *who* she was, not for attractiveness alone.

Hours after supper, alone in their bedroom, Leah offered to brush Sadie's waist-length hair. "I could make loose braids if you want," she said.

Sadie nodded halfheartedly, seemingly preoccupied. Leah tried not to stare as Sadie settled down on a chair near the mirrored dresser. Yet her sister looked strangely different. Sadie's flaxen locks tumbled down over her slender back and shoulders, and the glow from the single oil lamp atop the dresser cast an ivory hue on her normally pale cheeks, making them appear even more ashen. A shadow of herself.

Standing behind Sadie, she brushed out the tangles from the long workday, then finger combed through the silken hair, watching tenderly all the while in the mirror. Sadie's fragile throat and chin were silhouetted in the lamp's light, her downcast eyes giving her countenance an expression of pure grief.

Truly, Leah wanted to spend time with Sadie tonight, though it meant postponing the rest of her letter to Jonas. Tomorrow she would finish writing her long letter to him—head up to the woods to share her heart on paper.

She and Sadie had dressed for bed rather quickly,

accompanied by their usual comments, speaking in quiet tones of the ordinary events of the day, of having especially enjoyed Mamma's supper of barbecued chicken, scalloped potatoes with cheese sauce, fried cucumbers, lima beans, and lemon bars with homemade ice cream for dessert.

But now this look of open despair on Sadie's face caused Leah to say softly, "I think about him, too."

"Who?" Sadie whispered, turning to look up at her.

"Your baby . . . my own little nephew gone to heaven." Leah's throat tightened at the memory.

"You do, sister?"

"Oh, ever so much."

Neither of them spoke for a time, then Leah said, "What must it be like for you, Sadie? Ach, I can't imagine your grief."

Sadie was lost in her own world again. She moaned softly, leaning her head back for a moment. "I would've let him sleep right here, ya know, in a little cradle in this very room," she whispered. "I would have wanted to raise him like a little brother to all of us—you, Hannah, and Mary Ruth. Lydiann, too."

If Sadie's baby *had* lived, the disgrace on the Ebersol name would have been immense. But Sadie didn't need to be reminded of that at the moment.

Gently finishing up with her sister's hair, Leah began brushing her own, letting it hang long and loose, down past her waist. But quickly Sadie reached for the brush and said, "Here, it's *your* turn, Leah. Let me . . ."

Later, after Sadie had put out the lamp, they continued to talk softly in bed, though now about Mamma's plans to visit the Mast cousins soon. "I used to think it would be fun to have twins," Sadie said. "What about you?"

"If I could simply play with them all day, maybe so. But to cook and clean and garden, and everythin' else a mother must do, well . . . I just don't know how I'd manage."

"Oh, Leah, you're too practical, compared to me."

Leah had to smile at that. "I guess we *are* different thataway."

After a lull in their conversation, Sadie brought up the snide remark she'd made earlier in the day. "Honestly, I didn't mean to taunt you about writin' to Jonas," she said. "It was wrong of me."

" 'Tis not such a bad thing to write about the weather, jah?"

Sadie lay still next to her. "I'm thinking a girl oughta write whatever she pleases to a beau."

Whatever she pleases . . .

Inwardly Leah sighed. Wasn't that Sadie's biggest problem? Doing whatever she pleased had nearly destroyed her young life.

In the past Leah and Sadie had been like two pole beans on a vine, growing up under the same roof together.

What's happened to us? she wondered. Tender moments like tonight's were few and far between.

Sadie rested her head on the feather pillow just so, being careful not to muss her pretty braids. Tomorrow her hair bun would be a fairly wavy one, something Mamma wouldn't take too kindly to. Neither would Dat if he happened to notice. But Leah's fingers and the gentle brush on her hair had soothed her greatly. Sometimes it felt like old times, as if nothing had changed. A fond return to their friendlier days of sisterhood when they had shared every detail of each other's lives.

Her chin trembled and tears sprang to her eyes. Leah had always been a true and compassionate sister, but even more dear this summer. Forfeiting her own desire to spend time with Jonas, Leah had stayed home to comfort *her*.

Turning over, she fought hard to compose herself, lest she be heard sniffling again tonight. She did not pray her silent rote prayers. The desire to do so had long since left. She honestly believed the Lord God had seen fit to take away her tiny son instead of allowing her to love a baby conceived in sin, and the thought made her heart cold with aching.

Yet nearly every night—in a dream—she was with her own wee babe, who was ever so alive. And she and Derry were still desperately in love, sometimes even married, and always completely taken with their new little one, holding him . . . cooing baby talk at him.

Alas, upon waking each morning, Sadie was hit yet again with the ugly, hard truth. She had been punished for the sin of youthful lust. More than a hundred times she had recalled that hideous night, how Dr. Henry Schwartz had kindly said he would "take care" of the baby's remains. Now she regretted there was not even a small burial plot under the shade of ancient trees. Not a simple, respectable grave marker had been given her child, no grassy spot to visit in the People's cemetery, where she could grieve openly beneath a wide blue sky . . . where she could lie down under a tree and let her body rest hard against the earth. Her precious son had come into the world much too early, with "no breath in him," as the doctor had sadly pronounced.

Sometimes during the daylight hours it almost seemed as if the birth itself had never occurred, though she lived with a gnawing emptiness that threatened to choke her. Not having a place to mark the date and the event made the memory of that dark April night ofttimes shift in her mind, even distort itself. Sadie was back and forth about the whole thing—some days she treasured the memory of her first love; at other times she despised Derry for what he'd done to her.

Often she would stop what she was doing, painfully aware of a newborn's whimper. Was her imagination playing tricks? She would look around to see where her baby might be. Could Lydiann's frequent crying trigger this? She didn't know, yet the alarming sense that her baby still lived persisted no matter where she went these days—to Preaching service, to Adah and Dorcas Peachey's house, or to any number of Ebersol and Mast cousins' homes. The lingering feeling haunted her through every daylight hour, as acute as it was bewildering.

In spite of her depression, Sadie tried to look to the future, hoping someday she might have another baby to love, one whose father loved her enough to marry her in the first place. One with no connection to the Gobbler's Knob grapevine and who had no inkling of her wild days. Yet to meet a nice, eligible Amishman like that she would have to leave home, abandoning everything dear to her. It would mean enduring the shun.

The only other choice she had was a kneeling repentance

before the church brethren, but how could that ever solve her problems? It would never bring her baby back, nor Derry—neither one. Repenting could guarantee her only one thing: a lonely and miserable life.

Chapter Two

Leah hadn't realized before just how vulnerable she felt walking through the tunnel of trees that comprised much of the hillock. Even in the full sun of late morning, the light filtering through the webbing of leaves and branches seemed to die away the farther she headed into the woods.

Her best stationery folded neatly and pen in hand, she plodded onward, hoping to rediscover the same grassy spot where she'd spent a sun-dappled hour a few days ago. Beneath the feathery shade of a rare and beautiful thornless honey locust tree, she had written one of her love letters to Jonas. Never once did she think she'd have such difficulty finding the exact location a second time, so lovely it had been. Yet with hundreds of trees towering overhead, confusing her, how could she?

At the moment she thought the sun had set prematurely over distant green hills, she came upon a most interesting sight. She stopped in her tracks and wriggled her toes in the mossy path. "Well, what is this?" she whispered.

There, in a small clearing, a tiny shanty stood, though just barely. In all truth, it was leaning slightly to the left, and as she stepped back to take in the strange place, she could see it was quite old and in dire need of repair. Walking gingerly around its perimeter, she decided the wood shack was probably safe enough to enter. She did so and quickly, too, because the wind had suddenly come up, blowing hard from the north with an edge to it.

The sky *was* growing darker now, even as she pushed hard against the rickety door and hurried inside. Much to her surprise, she found a rather cozy, if untidy, room with exposed plank walls and overhead beams. Several wooden benches were scattered round, the only places to sit. A waist-high, makeshift counter stood in the back, along with a metal trash can. Still, nothing inside really hinted at what purpose the shack served.

Placing her writing paper down on one of the benches, she stood in the center of the little room and curiously looked around. It was in need of a good redding up, as Mamma would say. Both Mamma and Lizzie required cleanliness in all things, and had they come with her today, they would have immediately set to work picking up the paper debris and whatnot littering the floor. Never mind that the shack wasn't part of someone's house or barn; it needed some tending to. Even Mamma's potting shed was far neater.

Going to stand at the window, she leaned on the ledge and looked out at the wind beginning to whip through the shrubbery, bending the trees something fierce. She decided she might as well stay put for the time being, what with a storm rustling things up so. Not that she would complain about a blustery rain shower—not since the Good Lord had allowed this heat wave to encompass the region. Thirsty crops would drink up a downpour like this in short order.

She was ever so glad for even this unsteady shelter. The rain intensified, hammering wildly on the ramshackle roof. Settling down on a bench, Leah picked up where she'd left off with her letter to Jonas, putting her pen to the cream-colored paper.

There's one thing I should tell you in case you hear it through the grapevine. (I hope you won't feel bad about this.) Here lately I've had to help my father outdoors more than ever, since Dawdi John's hip gave out a few days ago. It's a pity seeing Mamma's father suffer. My sisters and I take our turns keeping him company, as does Aunt Lizzie. Sometimes to help Mamma, I take him over to the village doctor, Henry Schwartz, who's as kind as he can be.

As for working alongside Dat again, I've always known I was meant for the soil. Called to it, really. And once you and I are married, Dat will simply have to hire some extra help. Soon I'll be tending my own vegetable and flower gardens and cooking and keeping house for you while you build oak tables and chairs in your carpenter's shop nearby. We'll be happy as larks!

By the way, there's a small house with a For Rent sign in the front yard less than a mile from here—set back a ways from the road, even has an outbuilding on the property. Maybe Dat and I will go see about it if you agree we should.

I'll send this off right quick, then wait eagerly for your next letter.

All my love,
Your faithful Leah

She reread the letter, then folded the stationery. Leaning back, she stretched her arms and noticed a leak in the highest peak of the roof. Within seconds the droplets turned to a trickle; then a near-steady silver stream intruded upon her refuge against the cloudburst. Not a bucket was in sight, only the trash can overflowing with refuse. She searched for something else to catch the water but was startled to hear running footsteps outdoors and rushed to the window to look.

What's Aunt Lizzie doing out in this? she wondered.

The door to the shanty flew open, and there stood Mamma's younger sister soaked clean through to the skin. Lizzie's face turned instantly pale upon seeing Leah. "Well, I never—"

"Hurry and come in out of the squall, *Aendi*!"

The brunette woman leaned hard against the door, shoving out the wind and rain. "What on earth are *you* doin' here?"

"Oh, I'd hoped to find a comfortable spot under a tree somewhere . . . before the rain was makin' down so suddenly." She glanced over at her letter. "Caught me by surprise, really."

Lizzie nodded her head. "Seems the woods have a climate all their own, ain't so?"

Leah knew how much her aunt, even at thirty-five, enjoyed exploring the forest—truly, Lizzie's own backyard. Drawn to small woodland creatures, Lizzie often amused Leah and her sisters with animal-related stories. Leah sometimes wondered how it could be that Aunt Lizzie seemed so at home in the very woods she'd always warned against, knowing the name of each tall and dark tree at first glance. Lizzie's heart was as tender as the petal blossoms she cherished, and she doted on her nieces beyond all reason.

Outside, the rain was spilling fast over the eaves in elongated droplets, like the delicate, oval pearls Leah had seen on the bare neck of a worldly English woman in a Watt & Shand's department store newspaper ad. But inside, the stream from the unseen hole in the roof had taken up a rhythm all its own, predictable and annoying.

"Do you think you could help me find one particular tree if I described it? I mean, after the rain stops."

Aunt Lizzie smiled, pulling on the soaked-through purple sleeve that clung to her arm. Her long black apron and prayer cap were also sopping wet. "Which tree's that, honey-girl?"

"One where the grass is soft and thick and grows right up to the trunk. I must admit to thinkin' of the forest floor beneath it as my piece of earth." She went on to tell about the curious honey locust tree. "It has no thorns. And if ever I could find it once more, I believe I might somehow mark it so I could return there again and again."

"Oh . . .'twas a wonderful-*gut* place to daydream, jah?"

"Not dream so much as write a newsy letter," she confessed. "My sisters are awful nosy sometimes. They'd just love to know what I'm writin' to Jonas."

"Well . . . so *that's* what brought you here." Lizzie seemed somehow relieved as she spoke. She went and sat down on the closest bench, and Leah did the same.

"I never knew this place existed."

"Well, I daresay it's 'bout to come a-tumblin' down. Which, if you ask me, might be a gut thing."

"Oh, I don't know. Maybe with a little sweepin' and pickin' up it could be a right nice spot to—"

"No . . . no." Aunt Lizzie shook her head, turning to face the side window. "Best leave it for the turkey shooters, come Thanksgiving."

With Lizzie's quick remark, Leah felt she understood. So . . . the lean-to had been built long ago to provide shelter for small-game hunters. Nothing more.

"Since we're up here away from everyone," Leah said softly, "I can tell you I'm terribly worried 'bout Sadie."

Aunt Lizzie stared hard at the floor. "Jah, I fret over her, too."

"Must be somethin' we can do."

Aunt Lizzie nodded, removing her wet prayer bonnet. "I have to say I do miss her perty smile."

"And I think Mamma does, too."

"A cheerful countenance comes from the joy of the Lord God rising up from one's heart."

Leah wasn't surprised at this remark. Aunt Lizzie often spoke of the Holy One of Israel as if He were a close friend or relative. "What more can we do?" she asked.

"Nothin' short of haulin' Sadie off to the preacher or the deacon, I s'pose." Aunt Lizzie's face dropped with her own words. " 'Tis awful frustratin'."

"Honestly . . . I never would've promised to keep mum if I'd thought Sadie would remain stubborn for this long."

For a time Lizzie was silent. "Your sister would never trust you again. And she might not forgive me, neither."

"We can't just let Sadie lose her way. Can we, Aunt Lizzie?"

"Indeed. Seems to me somethin's got to break loose here 'fore long. Either that or she'll make a run for it."

Leah gasped. "Sadie would leave?"

"I'm afraid it was my idea. Last year I'd suggested a visit to Ohio might do her good, but I fear now she might never return."

Leah felt limp all over. She didn't know what to make of it. Sadie hadn't mentioned a word.

Aunt Lizzie continued. "I pleaded with her to stay put until at least your wedding. Perhaps by then she'll come to her senses. I pray so." She rose and went to the window. "I've talked to her till my breath is nearly all . . . to no avail. Still, I won't stop beseechin' the Lord God heavenly Father for her."

A stark silence followed, and Leah was mindful of the calm outside, as well. The summer shower had passed.

Chapter Three

The ground was soggy beneath their bare feet when Leah and Lizzie left the safety of the hunter's shack to hike down the hill toward home. Birds warbled a chorus of gladness, and the overcast sky steadily brightened as the sun finally succeeded in peeking out of the slow-moving gray clouds.

Lizzie put her nose up and sniffed. "Does the air smell sweet to you after a shower?"

Leah inhaled the clean, mintlike scent. "We could stand to have moisture like this every single day from now till Jonas and I . . ."

Lizzie offered a gentle smile. "Well, go on, Leah dear. I can keep quiet about your weddin' plans. You can trust me with the day Jonas will take you as his bride."

"Jah, I would, but . . . well," she sputtered a bit.

Lizzie must have sensed the awkwardness and attempted to smooth things over promptly. "What do you 'spect we'll do 'bout all that parched celery, honey-girl? You and your mamma will have a whole houseful of folk to feed at the weddin' feast, with no celery."

Mamma's celery stalks *had* been looking altogether pathetic, what with the intense heat and lack of precipitation, even with the additional hand watering they'd been doing lately.

Leah spoke up. "Maybe Fannie Mast's vegetable patch is farin' better than ours." She could only hope that was true, although with infant twins, Mamma's first-cousin Fannie would be hard-pressed to keep her one-acre garden going without help from daughters Rebekah, sixteen, and Katie, thirteen, and occasionally nine-year-old Martha.

Aunt Lizzie pushed ahead on the unmarked path, Leah following close behind, aware of the People's whispered tittle-tattle surrounding the wedding tradition of serving celery.

Taking a long breath, she held it a moment before letting the air out. "Mamma says it's, uh . . . necessary for the young couple to eat plenty of celery at their weddin' feast."

"For the sake of fruitfulness," Aunt Lizzie replied over her shoulder. "The Lord God put every plant—vegetable, fruit, and herb—on the earth for a purpose. Some have healin' properties, others aid in digestion and, well . . . getting young couples off to a right good start, ya know."

And that was the closet thing to a lesson on the birds and bees she knew she'd be getting from either Aunt Lizzie or Mamma. Of course, Sadie could easily fill her in to high heaven if she chose to, but Leah didn't care to ask. Not the way Sadie had gotten the cart long before the horse. Better to discover such things later, after Leah belonged to Jonas and he to her in the sight of the Lord God.

They had reached the place where something of a meandering dirt path appeared, descending into a grassy area with less underbrush to tangle one's bare feet. Lizzie's small house was in sight at last, up ahead on the left. This corner of God's green earth had a pungent fragrance, and its pleasantness made Leah suddenly think of Mamma—and an early-morning promise Leah had made. "Ach, I nearly forgot."

Lizzie turned quickly. "Forgot what?"

"Mamma's expectin' me home."

"Well, then, mustn't keep her waitin'. . . ."

Leah glanced at the sky. "We're going to bake up a batch of cherry pies . . . then after a bit Dat will be needin' me at milkin' time."

"You'll have to come visit me again soon."

Nodding, she said she would. "Or . . . better yet, why don't you come down tonight and have a piece of my pie? I'm determined for it to taste wonderful-gut."

"You'll do just fine. And when your dessert turns out to be ever so delicious, we'll compare notes, jah?"

"Mamma scarcely ever writes down recipes, you know. It's all up here." Leah tapped her head.

"Your mamma's one of the best cooks round here. She takes the cake, now, don't she?" Lizzie said, a hint of sadness in her eyes. Sadie's unwillingness to repent seemed to tinge nearly everything.

Leah hugged her, then broke free and headed on down the mule road toward home, turning briefly to wave to her dear aunt. But Lizzie was already gone.

Ida had been standing at the open window upstairs, having put the baby down for an early afternoon nap. Grateful for the coolness after the rain, she stepped back to allow a breeze into the bedroom. She could clearly see Leah up there in the woods, waving a fond good-bye to Lizzie. Then, here she came, bounding almost deerlike out of the trees as her long skirt swept the damp ground.

What's my sister filling Leah's head with today? she wondered, suspecting the pair had gone walking together, picking wild flowers, making a fuss over every little plant and animal. That was Lizzie's way—always had been. She was bent on soaking up every inch of the woodlands, introducing each of Ida's girls to the vast world of flora and fauna. Sadie had been spending all kinds of time up at Lizzie's during the past few months. Nearly all summer, really, until just the past week or so. More recently, Lizzie had singled Leah out.

She supposed Lizzie had every right to spend her spare time with whomever she pleased, but it irked her to no end. Truly, she wished Lizzie might keep her nose out of Abram's and her family's business. Lizzie and Peter Mast both. They'd all lived this long just fine. Some things were best left unsaid.

She exhaled sharply and headed downstairs, refusing to dwell on her fears for another minute. In the kitchen she laid out the flour, sugar, and all the necessary ingredients for the mouthwatering pies. As she did she thought ahead to the next Preaching service to be held here this weekend. Two hundred and more church members would come from a four-square-mile radius to gather where Abram's own father—the respected Bishop Ebersol—had raised this stone house as a shelter for his family and as a house of worship amongst the People. Hopefully, by then Lizzie's urgency could be put to rest. Ida made a mental note to talk with Abram about it once again.

Sadie, with a bucket of soapy water in hand, set about to wash down the bedroom walls, helping Mamma cleanse the house as was their custom, creating a holy place for the Sunday Preaching. "Might as well get a head start on some heavy cleanin'," she'd told Mamma at the noon meal.

" 'Tis a gut thing to make hay while the sun shines, too," Mamma had said in passing, somewhat inattentive.

Sadie was relieved to have the afternoon alone. Her twin sisters were downstairs dusting, sweeping, washing floors, and whatnot. These days it was best on her nerves to have absolute solitude, though that was next to impossible with seven people in the house. She had been suffering such a peculiar dull ache up and down her forearms, confiding it only to Aunt Lizzie earlier this summer.

What a surprise to discover Lizzie's remedy was to carry around a five-pound sack of potatoes, much the size of a wee babe. Lo and behold, when she did so, Sadie found it truly eased her pain. Accordingly, she clasped the potatoes quite often and ever so gently while spending time at Lizzie's away from Mamma's eyes.

Aside from frequent walks up to Lizzie's place, Sadie preferred to spend her "alone" hours cleaning for Mamma or hoeing and weeding the vegetable garden, along with visits next door to the *Dawdi Haus* to chat with Dawdi John.

Today she wholeheartedly threw herself into her work, stepping back now and again to see if she'd covered every square inch of the light gray walls. The bedroom windows were next on her list of things to do. She'd already decided to wash them single-handedly. No need asking for help from Hannah and Mary Ruth, not when they had plenty to keep them occupied downstairs. As for Leah, she'd hurried out the back door and headed up toward the mule road, as if going to visit Aunt Lizzie.

But Sadie was *schmaerder*. It didn't take much effort to figure out Leah these days. All of them assumed she was going off to the woods to write to her beau. Just so she kept her promise and didn't reveal Sadie's wild rumschpringe to Jonas Mast. Both Leah and Lizzie had vowed to keep quiet, but Sadie had heard recently that her former sidekick, Naomi Kauffman, was said to be weary of flirting with the world. She was even taking baptismal instruction right along with Leah, preparing to join church. Of all things!

Sadie didn't appreciate Naomi setting herself up as "holier than thou," which she certainly seemed to think she was here lately. And why? Just because she'd been far more careful than Sadie—or plain lucky—and hadn't gotten caught. Besides, Naomi's unexpected turn had more to do with Luke Bontrager, who was awful sweet on her, than most anything else. Of this Sadie was fairly sure.

If Naomi *was* to become the bride of the bishop's grandson, she had some fast confessing to do. Now, wasn't that a howdy-do? It was all fine and dandy for Naomi to make amends, turn her life around, and plan for a future as an upstanding young woman, so long as she kept Sadie out of it. Hopefully, Naomi didn't know the half about Sadie's fling, but what *did* she know? And if she started spilling the beans, what then? After all, Naomi had continued to see Derry's friend Melvin Warner after that first meeting at the Strasburg café. Derry had told Sadie this on several occasions, and she assumed it was true.

When Sadie was finished with the three upstairs bedrooms, she moved to the hallway and commenced to do the same—washing down walls, scrubbing mopboards, and mashing a few stray spiders as she went. Her thoughts flew to Aunt Lizzie as she worked. The past few weeks, Sadie had been discouraged. Not only had her aunt changed her mind and become adamant about her staying put, Lizzie was now saying she didn't think Sadie needed a change of scenery after all.

"Don't you see?" Lizzie had insisted. "Your father's covering and blessing are mighty important. If you would but confess to Preacher and the membership, you'd be pardoned by the People." Aunt Lizzie went on to quote her favorite Scripture. " 'Godly sorrow worketh repentance to salvation . . . but the sorrow of the world worketh death.' "

Obliged to listen, Sadie felt hot under the bonnet when Aunt Lizzie talked so pointedly.

Chapter Four

Too warm to stay indoors a second longer, Mary Ruth stepped outside for a breather on the back stoop. King, the German shepherd puppy, came scampering across the yard to greet Leah. Her skirt was mud spattered as she stooped to pet the dog, a curious yet kindly gift from Gid Peachey last spring. Observing this, Mary Ruth smiled as Leah hurried toward the house, the dog panting as he followed close on her heels.

"Hullo, Mary Ruth. I missed you!" Leah said.

Mary Ruth hoped Leah wouldn't go running off to help Dat. Not when she had a question to ask. "Didja get caught in the rain?"

Leah's face reddened. "No . . . I found shelter."

Sighing, Mary Ruth decided not to beat round the bush. "Does it bother you that Dat doesn't approve of you marryin' Jonas?"

Leah seemed a bit startled by the question, but she met Mary Ruth's gaze with a gentle smile. "Does it bother *you*?"

Pausing there, Mary Ruth was aware of Leah's sweetness

once again . . . her fine hazel eyes with tiny gold flecks, the dark curve of her long lashes, the way her expression seemed to radiate trustfulness, even goodness. Yet Leah was intent on ignoring Dat's wishes in order to become Jonas Mast's bride. None of it added up.

"Doesn't bother me in the least," she replied at last. "I'm just tryin' to understand."

Leah burst into a full smile. "That's what makes you so special. You have a gift of understanding, I daresay."

Mary Ruth couldn't help herself; she actually choked a little and tears welled up. "Much good that does me . . ."

Leah was staring now, wearing a concerned frown. "What is it, Mary Ruth? Why are you cryin'?"

"Just thinkin', I guess." She forged ahead and stuck her neck out. "I hope you'll follow your heart. Have the courage to marry the boy you love."

Leah's eyelids fluttered. "Didja think I might not?"

Turning quickly, Mary Ruth looked over her shoulder, toward the barn. "Dat, well . . . he's made it mighty clear here lately that it's Gideon Peachey who's the right beau for you. He's said as much to all of us."

"Dat has?"

"He said 'if only Leah knew Gid the way I know him.' Things like that. And he said he was weary of keepin' it to himself any longer—after these many years."

"Jah, I know *that* to be true, the years he's stewed about it."

She felt she ought to say one more thing. "Mamma's not so much in favor of Gid, though. Just so you know."

"You sure?"

"Mamma prefers Jonas, seems to me." Now she struggled to keep a straight face. "She thinks your children will be mighty handsome if you marry into the Mast family."

"And why's that?"

"Jonas has a right fine nose. Gut-lookin' all round, he is." Mary Ruth sighed. "I don't mean to say Smithy Gid *isn't* handsome. He's just more rugged lookin', I guess you could say. Whereas Jonas is—"

"Both handsome *and* strong—in body and mind? Is that what you mean?" Leah had her now, and her sister's eyes shone as if with glee. Sadie and Mamma sometimes grew weary of Mary Ruth's too-talkative nature, but Leah never seemed to mind.

Leah continued. "When it comes to certain things, no matter how defiant a choice might seem to others, if you know in your heart you were meant for somethin'—or someone—then, I believe, 'tis best to be true to that."

"You mean it?"

Leah nodded. "I've seen how you throw yourself into your schoolwork. You're a scholar, ain't? When the time comes, you'll have the courage to make the right decision. You'll simply have to put your hand to the plow and refuse to look back."

Mary Ruth's emotions threatened to overtake her again. "You're a true sister and friend, Leah," she managed through her tears.

"Always remember that." Leah smiled, reaching to hug her.

Sadie headed toward the kitchen for a glass of cold water, so awful hot it was upstairs. But before she stepped foot in there, she happened to overhear Leah talking to Mamma as they baked pies. Leah was saying she and Aunt Lizzie had taken shelter in a little hunter's shack on the hillock that morning. "The place was old and run-down like nothing you've ever seen," Leah said softly. "Right peculiar, I must say. Up there in the middle of nowhere, but it kept us safe and dry till the rain passed."

Sadie felt her throat constrict. Anguished memories rushed back and she was helpless to stop them. For all she cared, the shanty was good for one thing and only one: kindling.

Leah was frowning at Sadie now, catching her eye. "What? Did I say somethin' wrong?"

Himmel! she thought, not realizing how far she'd inched herself into the kitchen. There she was, standing in the doorway listening, evidently with a pained expression on her face. "Aw . . . no," she gasped. "I guess I'm surprised both you and Aunt Lizzie got caught in such a cloudburst, that's all. Usually, Lizzie can tell by smellin' the air if rain's a-comin'." She paused momentarily, then—"Looks to me like the bottom of your hem got awful grimy on your way back home."

Leah looked down at herself and seemed to agree she was in need of a good scrubbing. "But it won't do to wash up and change clothes now." She thanked Mamma for such helpful pointers with the pies, saying she hoped they tasted as good as they smelled, then scurried off toward the barn.

Sadie briefly followed after Leah. She stood in the open back door, staring out through the screen. She caught a glimpse of the bottom of her sister's bare feet as she ran to the barn. Milking the cows was something Sadie knew little about. Sure, she'd helped Dat here and there occasionally, but only in a pinch. Yet with Leah's wedding coming up soon, Sadie was worried sick she might have to take her tomboy sister's place outdoors with Dat. She was fond enough of her father, but there was no way she was willing to do the kind of dirty work Leah did—and cheerfully at that. Besides, *she* ought to have been marrying first.

Mamma broke the stillness. "Sadie, would you mind changin' Lydiann's diaper?"

She gasped inwardly. "Aw . . . must I, Mamma? I still have chores to finish. . . ." Her legs felt as rubbery as the inflatable tires on tractors, so forbidden by the bishop.

Mamma appeared to lapse into a gray mood, and her milky blue eyes seemed to look right through Sadie . . . to the dark of her heart. "Why is it you're not so lovin' toward your baby sister anymore?" Mamma's voice wavered. "When she was brand-new, you were ever so helpful then."

Back in May, when Lydiann was first born, Mamma had singled Sadie out as the elder sister most mindful of the new little one. At the time, she'd felt her mother truly suspected something was amiss and was hoping to force a confession. So Sadie had gone along with helping to care for Lydiann, hoping to hide the shocking truth.

Now, though, she went out of her way to avoid babies and the expectant mothers in the church community, especially during the common meals that followed Preaching service every other Sunday. At work frolics she sat on the opposite end of the quilting frame from the pregnant women. It just didn't seem fair other women were able to carry *their* babies to full-term. What was wrong with her?

Scarcely could she stand to be near Mamma anymore. She felt sure her mother was hovering and ready to report her to the ministers. If so, she would be required to offer repentance. *"Obey or be shunned"*—the People's endless refrain.

"A quick diaper change can't hurt none." Mamma's voice jolted her out of her musings.

"In a minute." She reached for a stack of plates to set the table.

When Mamma's back was turned, Sadie hurried outdoors, pretending to walk to the outhouse. She knew Dat and Leah were out milking and, more than likely, could observe her if they were but looking.

Once she reached the outhouse, she turned abruptly and ran to the meadow, dodging cow pies as she picked her way barefoot through the pastureland, muttering to herself all the while.

Kicking at a clump of wild grass, Sadie raised her head to the sky, studying the clouds and the way the sun shone too hard on the tin roof. Sniffling, she brushed away hot tears. *I'm the one black sheep of the family*, she thought.

The far-off clanging of the dinner bell gave her pause. She was sorely tempted to keep on walking, never to return. Simply walk away, just as she planned in due time.

Folding her arms tightly, she headed back toward the barnyard and the house, wondering which was worse—Mamma's disapproving mood . . . or her own restless heart?

Chapter Five

The liquid warble of several wrens out near the milk house awakened Leah. She hurried out of bed, whispering "time to wake up" to Sadie, who was still sleeping soundly. But Sadie only groaned and turned over, covering her head with the summer quilt.

Something was beginning to weigh on Leah's mind, and she wanted to talk with Sadie about it. It had to do with Naomi Kauffman and her outspoken new beau, Luke Bontrager, who had shown a different side than she'd expected. Especially here recently after the baptismal candidates had met with Preacher Yoder and Deacon Stoltzfus for the required instruction. Naomi had actually seen the error of her ways, making things right with the Lord God and Preacher Yoder—a mighty good thing. A girl just never knew when she might breathe her last lungful of air. Too many teenagers had lost their lives racing trains with horse and buggy or in farming accidents. Being Plain could be downright dangerous sometimes.

The deacon and the preacher had been admonishing them

mostly in High German that day, discussing at length the eighteen articles of faith from the Dordrecht Confession. Leah had a hard time understanding what was being taught, let alone how she should respond to the questions. She was brave enough to speak up—much to Luke's surprise—to ask if it would be all right for her parents to help her read the baptism chapter found in Matthew's gospel. Well, Luke had arched his eyebrows. "You ain't *studyin'* the Scriptures, now, are you?" he whispered her way.

"My father reads the German Bible to us in Amish each night, is all," she'd answered, not one bit ashamed. Besides, Dat's reading the Scripture aloud was far different than analyzing God's Word like some folk outside the community of the People were known to do. She might have added that Mamma often prayed without putting in many "thee's" and "thou's," like some Mennonites they knew who called upon the name of the Lord God. But by then she was cautious and didn't dare say that much. It wasn't anybody's concern how Dat and Mamma went about passing on the faith to their children, was it?

In the end Deacon Stoltzfus said he was in favor of Leah getting help from her parents, that it was all right for her to ponder these Scriptures—it wasn't as though they would be having an out-and-out Bible study like some church groups. "Your father can read you Matthew chapter twenty-eight, verse nineteen, as well as Mark chapter sixteen, verse sixteen . . . in English or Amish, either one. 'Tis long past time all you young folk understand fully the covenant making," said the deacon.

Preacher Yoder may have been less enthusiastic but gave

his blessing on Deacon's remarks. "Go ahead, Leah, speak with your father . . . if you have any questions about your kneeling vow a'tall."

Naomi had looked mighty eager to take Leah aside, which she did out in the barnyard after baptismal instruction. There Naomi had whispered to Leah that Luke had begun courting her, and to keep it quiet. " 'S'okay for you to tell Sadie I'm getting married, though," Naomi said unexpectedly. "She might be a bit surprised. . . ."

Which would have been the end of it if Adah Peachey hadn't come walking up to the two of them and said, "Hullo, Leah . . . Naomi."

For a while they stood there engaging in small talk. Then Naomi lowered her voice yet again, saying she'd like nothing better than if both Leah and Adah would consider being in her bridal party. Leah waited, expecting Naomi to correct herself on the spot and say she in fact meant *Sadie*—surely she would. But the uncomfortable silence was broken by Adah, who, all smiles, said she'd be right happy to be one of the bridesmaids.

"Well, Leah?" Naomi turned to her. "What about you?"

"I'm thinkin' maybe you'd want to be askin' Sadie, jah?"

"No, I asked *you*," Naomi replied, big eyes shining.

"Then, I'd like to talk it over with my sister, seein' as how you and she—well, you're close friends and all."

"Used to be."

The words had sounded so final, it pained Leah to remember them. "*Used to be*."

Now here she sat in the quietude of her bedroom, with Sadie beginning to stretch, there in the bed. Waiting for her sister to rise and shine, she felt quite uneasy. She let a few more minutes pass; then she spoke at last. "I want to ask you somethin', Sadie."

Suddenly she felt it might be a mistake to address the touchy issue. Yet it was better now than for Sadie to hear it elsewhere. "How would you feel if I stood up with Naomi on her weddin' day?" she blurted.

"That's up to you" came the quick and sleepy answer.

"You don't mind, then?"

"Not any more than I mind you goin' to her weddin' at all."

Leah sighed. "Well, aren't *you* goin'?"

"Not if I can help it." Sadie sat up in bed. "Friends and relatives are expected to attend the weddin'. I daresay I'm neither of those to Naomi."

Leah paused, then asked gently, "Can you say . . . uh, what happened between you and Naomi?"

"She has no business bein' baptized, is all." Sadie turned her head and was staring out the window.

"Then why do you s'pose Naomi's goin' ahead with it?"

"One reason, I 'spect."

"To marry Luke?"

Sadie clammed up, and Leah went to the wooden wall hooks next to the dresser and removed her brown choring dress from a hanger. Standing there, she felt awkward, as if she didn't truly belong in the shared room. " 'Tis a sorry situation, Naomi's . . . if what you say is true."

"Why must you be judgin' everyone?" Sadie snapped.

Leah was startled at her sister's biting words, but the conversation ended abruptly with Mamma's knock at the door.

"Time to begin the day, girls" came her soft call.

Hastily, they dressed in their choring dresses and brushed their hair into low buns at the nape of their necks. Then they put on their devotional caps and hurried downstairs to help—Sadie with kitchen duties and Leah with the first milking of the day.

That evening when Leah and Sadie were preparing to dress for bed, Sadie brought the matter up again. "You surely think the same of me as you do of Naomi," she said. "Ain't so, Leah?"

Leah wasn't prepared for this, even though Sadie's accusation—"*judgin' everyone*"—had echoed in her ears all day. "You know by now what I think," she said, getting up the nerve. "I think God will forgive anyone for sin. And so would Mamma. She's all for you, Sadie. She'd forgive you if you'd but ask."

"Mamma might, but not Dat."

"Ach, Sadie, how can you say that? If you went through the correct channels, bowed your knee in contrition before the People—"

"Might be best to save your breath, Leah."

Sadie's comment pained her. She feared her sister was farther from the Lord God and His church than ever before. And for this Leah felt truly sad.

Sadie continued to seethe with anger as she picked up the lantern at the back door and walked out into the night, past the well pump and through the barnyard. The moon wore a silver-white halo, the sky black as pitch. She might've used the chamber bucket under the bed, but she needed to breathe some fresh air. The night was exceedingly warm, despite the afternoon shower, maybe more so because of the humidity that hung like a shroud over the farm. Both she and Leah had thrown off the covers before ever settling into bed. Of course, it could be the harsh silence between them that was making Sadie feel warmer than usual. Even her fingertips were hot as she walked to the wooden outhouse.

Who did Leah think she was, ordering her elder sister around? All this fussing between them had left Sadie emotionally drained. To think her best friend, Naomi, had bypassed her and asked Leah to be a bridesmaid, of all things! Well, she hoped not to be anywhere near Gobbler's Knob by the time Naomi and Luke tied the knot.

On the return trip from the outhouse she made a stop in the kitchen to wash her hands and eat some graham crackers and drink a glass of milk. That done, she felt a little better and headed back upstairs only to discover that, lo and behold, Dat and Mamma were still awake and having a discussion in their room, behind closed doors. Sadie had never encountered this in all her born days because her parents were often the first ones to head for bed, especially with Lydiann waking up at three-thirty for her early-morning feeding.

Dat was doing the talking. "No . . . no, I tend to disagree."

"We ain't never goin' to see eye to eye—"

"Have you thought it over but good, Ida? *Have* you?" Dat

interrupted. "Do you realize what an upheaval this'll cause under our roof?"

"Indeed, I have. And I believe . . . if you don't mind me bein' so blunt, it's time we tell her."

Sadie froze in place. What on earth were her parents disputing? *Tell whom? Tell what?*

The conversation ceased altogether with Mamma's pointed remark, and Sadie assumed her parents had decided to retire for the night. As for herself, she was wide awake and crept back down the steps, hurried through the kitchen, then let herself out the back door without making a sound. Sitting on the back stoop, she stared up at a thousand stars.

"*Have you thought it over but good?*" Dat's words came back to haunt her. "*What an upheaval . . .*"

She slapped her hands over her ears, pressing tightly against her head . . . hoping to halt the memory of what she'd heard. Could it be they had been talking about her?

King came wandering over from the barn and sat on the concrete next to her, his long black nose pointed toward the moon. She reached down to rub his furry neck. "Something terrible's a-brewin'," she whispered, trembling now. "I feel it awful heavy in the air."

Chapter Six

Mary Ruth finished hoeing and weeding her patch of the family garden Thursday, along with the girls' separate charity garden. Standing up, she arched her back and attempted to relieve her aching muscles. Gazing at the sky, she noticed a bank of clouds drift across the blue at a mercilessly slow pace and felt a strange connection to them. Ever so restless, she despised the slow-poke pace of her days waiting for school bells to ring. In a little over a week!

With both her and Hannah off at school, Mamma would indeed suffer with less help around the house. Still, the law was the law, and Mary Ruth was happy to be required to attend through eighth grade. In one more year she'd be eligible for high school. The thought gave her chills of both delight and dread. She held no hope of Dat ever giving her the go-ahead; it would be next to impossible to obtain his blessing. He would simply quote the Good Book to her if she were brazen enough to share with him her deepest longing. "'For the wisdom of this world is foolishness with God'"—this said with Bible in hand. And that would be the end of their discussion, though sadly, it would never reach the phase of true discussion at all.

Even the term *high school* was not without reproach. It represented high-mindedness and pride, and she'd heard many times growing up that "*self-praise stinks*." Yet what was she to do about the inner craving? Was *she* the only one smitten with the problem amongst the People?

Hannah wandered over, hoe in hand. "What would ya think of goin' to Strasburg with me?"

"To stop by the little gift shop?"

"I have a batch more handkerchiefs to deliver."

"Okay, then we'll go right after lunch. And 'bout the time Mamma and Lydiann are up from a nap, we'll be back home."

Hannah nodded, all smiles. "Just the two of us?"

"Sounds gut to me." Mary Ruth hoped to squeeze in a visit to the public library while Hannah handled her consignment shop transactions. Getting a head start on her studies was heavy on her mind. If she had to, she could easily hide the newly checked-out books under the bed. Hannah could be persuaded not to tell.

It was clear Hannah was already counting the years till she made her covenant with the People and God. Unassuming and on the bashful side, especially around strangers, her sister would make a fine Amish wife and mother someday, which was just as appealing to Mary Ruth as the next girl—getting married and having children, that is. It was the unceasing hankering for books that got so dreadfully in the way. The thought of committing the sum total of her life to the People was troubling at best, and she was grateful to have a few more years till she had to decide one way or the other.

"You don't mind if I run across the street right quick . . . when we get to the gift shop?" Mary Ruth asked Hannah as they rode along in the enclosed carriage. She had chosen Dat's faster driving horse of the two, as well as the enclosed family buggy. With the gathering clouds and the increasing possibility of rain, it made good sense.

"Why not just say it outright?" Hannah said softly, almost sadly. "You're goin' to the library."

"Jah."

Hannah sat to her left, eyelids fluttering. "Truth be known, I prefer the summers. And you . . . well, you live for the school year."

"You know me awful gut." She paused, then added, "What do you think Mamma would do if she ever found my library books . . . hidden away?"

"Are you sayin' you honestly can't curb your appetite for readin'?"

"Books are like friends to me. Words come alive on the page."

Shrugging one shoulder slightly, Hannah said nothing.

"I s'pose I'm addicted, 'cause now I've started readin' other books, too," she ventured. "I don't mean *bad* books, don't misunderstand. But I must admit, I like readin' stories—things that are purely made up but that, well . . . *could* happen." She was somewhat hesitant for Hannah's reaction.

"Ach, I don't know what to think" was her twin's dismal reply. "I can accept you readin' geography books, imagining what it's like to travel round the continent and all, but made-up tales?"

Sighing, Mary Ruth wondered how to explain. "Here. This is what readin' stories is like to me. It's findin' a spring in the midst of a barren land. Just when I think I might up and die of thirst, I stumble onto this fresh, cold water, and I'm suddenly given new life 'cause I can—and do—drink to my heart's content."

Now Hannah was beside herself, seemed to Mary Ruth. She was staring down at the buggy floor, eyes blinking and glistening to beat the band.

"Aw, what's a-matter, Hannah?"

"I wish I could understand what you mean. That's all I best be sayin'."

The fact they didn't share a great love for reading was beside the point. Hannah was clearly pained by Mary Ruth's revelation that she was obsessed with books, especially fiction. *I wish I'd never said a word*, she thought.

She leaned over and tipped her head toward her twin's, their white prayer bonnets forming a double heart as the horse pulled them toward Strasburg.

While Mary Ruth hurried across the street to the library, Hannah made a beeline to the gift shop with her basketful of newly embroidered handkerchiefs in hand. Happily, she received her payment from the owner, Frances Brubaker, a short, petite woman in her thirties, Hannah guessed. Then she counted out forty more cotton hankies, a third of which showcased embroidered bumblebees this time. The rest were birds' nests with pale blue eggs nestled inside, and there were tiny baskets of fruit, too—all colors. She had decided it was time to stitch something different than the birds and multicolored butterflies of the last grouping.

While she was there, two English women came into the store, one more talkative than the other. Both were oohing and aahing over the various items, as if never having laid eyes on "handmade" things, which was the word they kept repeating, and this somewhat reverently. They spotted Hannah near the counter and took an immediate interest, peering over at her several times, unashamed at their curiosity. Each time, though, she had to look away, suffering the same uncontrollable feeling of shyness she had while tending to the roadside stand at home. Truth was, she felt self-conscious most of the time and wished Mary Ruth had stayed by her side, here at the store, instead of running off to her beloved books.

"An Amishwoman with several children in tow came into the shop the other day," Frances addressed her from behind the counter. "She was looking to buy a whole bunch of embroidered hankies. But she specifically requested *cutwork* embroidery, like the one she brought to show me."

Hannah was surprised at this. "What did it look like?"

"Well, it had a dainty emerald-and-gold butterfly sewn into the corner."

"And cutwork, you say?"

Frances nodded. "The customer was very interested in it, said nothing else would do. She said she wants to give a quantity of them away on her son's wedding day . . . that she'd stop by in a month or so. Could you duplicate a hankie like that to sell?"

"Maybe so if I could see it." Hannah found this more

curious than she cared to say. Truth was, she'd made only *one* such cutwork butterfly hankie in her life. *And awful pretty*, if she thought so herself. She'd given it, along with cross-stitched pillowcases, as a gift three years ago to Sadie on her sixteenth birthday. Sadie's reaction had been one of such joy Hannah decided it should remain extra special. Never again would she make the cutwork style on any of her other hankies, either for sale or for gifts, in honor of Sadie's turning courting age.

"I would make most anything else . . . just not a handkerchief like that." She wondered who the woman had been, asking about a handkerchief so surprisingly similar to Sadie's own. But she kept her peace and said no more.

Still, she couldn't stop thinking how peculiar this was and felt a bit crestfallen. *Had someone seen Sadie's special hankie and decided to copy it?* she wondered.

Back in the carriage on the ride home, Mary Ruth sat with her library books balanced on her lap as she attempted to hold the reins.

"How will you get all of them into the house?" Hannah asked, eyeing the books.

"Oh, I'll manage somehow, even if I have to sneak them in two at a time. Meanwhile, why don't you trade places with me?" She handed the reins over to Hannah, who promptly switched to the driver's seat.

They rode along for a time in complete silence. Mary

Ruth was glad to peek into the pages of the first book in her stack, *Uncle Tom's Cabin.* And by the time the horse turned off the narrow road at Rohrer's Mill, the water-powered grist mill, she'd already completed the first chapter. Her heart cried out with compassion for the slave girl Eliza and her handsome young son, Harry. With such strong emotions stirring, she wondered anew how she could ever give up this fascination with the printed page. Could she quickly devour oodles of books to satisfy her appetite, then join church, hoping that the wellspring of joy might linger on through the years, even though she'd never read again? She supposed it was one way to look at the problem, though she'd have to come clean to Preacher Yoder before ever taking her kneeling vow, especially with this new passion for fabricated stories.

She marked the page with her finger, then asked Hannah, "How old do you want to be when you get baptized?"

"Sixteen or so," Hannah said. "Seems to me we oughta join church together."

Just as she thought.

Hannah was quiet for a time, then she said, "If you end up goin' to high school—"

"Oh, I *will* go," Mary Ruth interrupted. "Somehow or other."

"Okay, then, what will you do 'bout Elias Stoltzfus?"

Mary Ruth paused. "I don't think that's somethin' to worry my head over, really, seein' as how neither of us is of courtin' age yet. Elias is just fourteen."

Hannah turned from her, looking away.

Mary Ruth leaned forward. "I'm sorry. Did I upset you?"

"It's nothin'," Hannah was too quick to admit. She sniffled

a bit, then straightened. "I just thought . . . well, that maybe Elias might change your thinkin', ya know. Maybe he'd make a difference in your future somehow."

Fact was, Elias *had* begun to upset the fruit basket. The more she ran into him at Preaching and whatnot, and the more she talked with him even briefly, the more she liked him. A lot . . . truth be told. It was like stepping barefoot on a nettle, seeing it tear away at the flesh of enthusiasm and desire. If she gave in to her attraction to him, and his to her, it wouldn't be but a few years and she'd be riding home from Sunday singings with him. He'd end up courting her . . . *and then what?* What if the same enormous hunger for books showed up in one or more of their children? Such a thing would bring heartache to both her and Elias's families.

No, she thought it best to nip her romantic interest in the bud, refuse his attention for the sake of her own ambition. She knew she was born to be a schoolteacher. In short, she could not deprive herself of the one true thing that mattered most to her on God's green earth.

When they arrived home, the sky had turned dark with threatening clouds. "It'll soon be makin' down," she said, working with Hannah to unhitch the horse from the buggy.

"A nice rain would help the crops," Hannah said, drawing in her breath loudly enough for Mary Ruth to hear. "Should I run inside and see where Mamma might be just now?"

Mary Ruth nodded, noting the look of dire concern on

Hannah's face. "Jah, go have a look-see. Meanwhile, I'll water and feed the horse."

Hannah strolled down to the house, calm as you please, but in a jiffy she returned with a big smile on her face. "Mamma's nursin' Lydiann upstairs," she whispered. "Best come now."

"Where's Dat, do you think?"

Hannah had a ready answer. "Both Dat and Leah are out back in the pasture, bringin' home the cows for milkin'."

"And Sadie?"

"Never mind her," Hannah replied, shaking her head. "She's nowhere round that I saw. Besides, she would hardly care, jah?"

So, confident as can be, Mary Ruth carried all seven books across the barnyard and into the house. Hannah led the way, glancing back at her every now and then as they hurried through the empty kitchen and up the long flight of stairs.

Once in their bedroom Mary Ruth separated the books and got down on her hands and knees, pushing a group of four, then three clear under the bed, far as she could reach.

"There," she said, rising up, "who's goin' to look *that* far under the bed?"

After supper Mary Ruth headed out toward the back porch. On the edge of dusk, the evening was still light enough for her to go walking. But on second thought she decided to go swing in the hayloft a bit. The long rope hung high on the rafters as a constant reminder of happy childhood days, and it was easy to ponder one's life out there amidst baled hay and weary animals moving slowly in the warm, dusty stable below. The mouse catchers were sure to keep her company, too.

On the way to the barn, she spotted Dat and Gideon talking in the cornfield. Dat placed his hand on Gid's shoulder for a time, thanking him, no doubt, for his afternoon help.

Dat's reeling in the smithy's son closer all the time, she thought. She was almost certain her father had a trick or two up his sleeve yet. But if that was true, he sure didn't have much time left to botch Leah's plans to marry Jonas Mast.

Besides that, if Dat did *not* succeed in getting Leah's eyes on Gid, something would have to give with farm chores when the time came for Leah and Jonas to set up housekeeping. Dat would definitely have to hire someone nearly full-time—more than likely Gid Peachy. But what a thorn in the side to poor Dat, who preferred to have Gid as his son-in-law, not as a hired hand. She could tell by the look on her father's ruddy face that he was much too partial to Smithy Gid, the way he spoke kindly of the brawny young man—used to be in Leah's hearing—which he didn't do so much anymore.

Still, she couldn't help feeling Dat just might keep Leah from marrying the boy she loved, one way or another. Mary Ruth clenched her jaw at the very notion, wishing she and her sisters weren't so hog-tied around here.

Chapter Seven

Friday dawned much cooler, and Abram, Ida, and the girls were grateful for the relief. While Mary Ruth took her turn tending the vegetable stand out front, Leah, Sadie, and Hannah weeded the enormous vegetable garden, spraying for insects so the family, not the bugs, could reap the benefit of their labors.

Leah worked tirelessly for hours, harvesting summer squash, carrots, peppers, and pounds of cucumbers. They'd already put up a bounty of pickles, both sweet and dill, and Mamma suggested they take even more cucumbers out to the roadside stand to sell. "Or give 'em away if you have to."

While doing her backbreaking gardening, Leah intentionally forced her thoughts away from Sadie to the inviting spot in the forest. The mental picture was even more delightful because Sadie and she were at odds—terribly so. And now that she'd stuck her foot in her mouth over Naomi's wedding request, well, Leah was at a loss to know what to say or do next.

All morning she suffered troublesome feelings toward her

elder sister. The silence between them became worse than annoying. Sadie harbored resentment toward her, that was clear. The slightest reference to Sadie's need for repentance had been met with disdain.

Once the gardening was done, Leah hurried up to Aunt Lizzie's, wanting to go in search of the honey locust tree. She hoped she could talk openly with Lizzie while tramping through the woods on their search. Surely Aunt Lizzie would not see this as an excuse to gossip—heaven forbid!—but rather take to prayer the things on Leah's heart. Such perplexing emotions made Leah wonder if her prayers might simply bounce off the bedroom ceiling instead of wending their way to the Throne of Grace.

With a hug, Aunt Lizzie met her at the back door wearing an old black cooking apron. Newly scrubbed, the small kitchen was awash in sunlight. The familiar, welcoming smell of freshly baked bread drew Leah to sit at the table and savor the aroma. "Smells wonderful-gut," she said.

"Thought I'd bake a dozen raisin cinnamon rolls and a loaf of oatmeal bread for the Nolt family, down yonder," Lizzie said, bringing a glass of iced tea over to Leah. "How would you like to ride along?"

Leah didn't have the heart to bring up the hoped-for excursion to the woods and discourage Lizzie from her kind and generous deed, especially seeing the bright look of happiness on her face. "Jah, I'll go," she was quick to say, still hoping to go to the woods with her aunt later.

It was during the buggy ride down Georgetown Road that Leah opened up and shared her heart. She told Aunt Lizzie of her recent conversation with Sadie, all the while Lizzie's gaze remained fixed on the road as she gripped the reins just so.

"Sadie's not interested in attending Naomi's wedding. Doesn't that seem odd to you?" asked Leah.

"Sounds to me like Naomi might not want her there."

Leah pressed further. "How can that be?"

Lizzie was slow to respond, taking a deep breath first. "Sometimes friends don't remain close for one reason or another. Honestly, I 'spect we should be awful glad Naomi and Sadie aren't so chummy anymore."

"Maybe so, but I have a strong feeling Naomi's turned away from the world completely. If it's not too blunt to say so, I believe she is more receptive to the church than ever."

Lizzie brightened at that. "I trust and pray what you say is true."

Then they chattered of this and that, especially of the flowers and vegetables growing in Lizzie's and Mamma's gardens. Soon, though, Leah asked, "I'm still thinking 'bout that uncommon honey locust tree. . . . Remember?"

"Well, honey-girl, I 'spect we might be able to walk right to it, once we get home again."

Leah was delighted. Leaning back a bit, she settled into the front seat of the buggy, gazing at the now colorless sky, ever so glad to have talked openly with dear Lizzie. Now, if the days would just pass more quickly till Jonas returned to her.

Hannah chased after two nasty flies in the front room. Mamma had ordered her to go inside from the garden to escape the midday heat because she looked "sallow and all done in." Well, here she was, though not sitting down in the kitchen with a tall glass of ice water or fanning herself, but downright eager to slap the annoying insects with the flyswatter. Truly, she had been suffering a headache off and on all week, not telling anyone but her twin. And what had Mary Ruth gone and done? She'd told Mamma, "Hannah needs some lookin' after."

Aside from the fact she was gripped with worry over school opening soon, there wasn't much ailing Hannah. *If only summer could last all year,* she thought. She and her sisters always busied themselves from late spring on with the necessary tasks of planting and harvesting, cooking and cleaning, and on and on it went. There was little else to occupy one's mind during this season, and that was just how Hannah liked it.

Suddenly feeling too tired to stand, she went to the kitchen and sat in the large hickory rocker near the windows. She had been happy to keep up her supply of consignment handiwork, especially her array of embroidered handkerchiefs and pillowcases, thankful for the extra money she was earning at both the Strasburg gift shop and the family's own roadside stand.

Hannah put the swatter down on the floor and leaned her head against the rocker. Just as she was becoming droopy eyed, here came Sadie indoors. "You look all in, Hannah," she said, going to the sink for some water.

"Oh, don't fret over me."

"Here," Sadie said, offering her the tall glass. "Mamma said you had a headache. Two glasses straight down will ease it a bit."

Hannah accepted the glass and began to sip, watching

Sadie return to the sink, now splashing water on her forehead and cheeks. Sadie patted her face dry with her apron, then reached for another glass. When she'd poured a drink for herself, she went to the table and sat down, her face as red as Hannah had ever seen it.

They were still for a time; then Hannah got up the nerve to say, "I was wondering . . . did you ever happen to show off that birthday hankie I made you, the green-and-gold butterfly one?"

Sadie seemed to stiffen at the question, frowned, and shook her head. "Why, no, I didn't."

Hannah, taken aback by her sister's sudden unease, forced a smile. "Just wondered if someone else in the area might've seen it besides our own family . . . and started making some like it to sell."

Sadie said nothing for the longest time. Then she whispered, "That hankie's gone forever, I'm afraid."

"Gone?" Hannah was startled. "But I made it special for you. How could you lose it?"

Sadie shook her head slowly. "I didn't say I did." Her voice was weak now, as if she'd just returned home from the funeral of a close relative, the emotion of the day sapping her strength.

"Then what—"

"Oh, Hannah, please don't ask me any more. I loved your handkerchief, but it's gone and I won't be getting it back."

Hurt over Sadie's seeming disregard for her gift, Hannah pondered her sister's strange reply. *Why would she do such a thing?*

She began to wonder if the woman who'd inquired of the

cutwork hankie might, in all truth, be the new owner of Sadie's birthday handkerchief. *Is that possible?* she thought sadly but said not another word to her sister.

Leah waited in the buggy, hand loosely touching the reins, while Aunt Lizzie hurried to the front door of the Nolts' red-brick house. Lavender statice and pale peach dahlias decorated the front yard of the fancy *Englischers'* house, neat as a pin and as tidy and well kept as the Amish neighbors' yards nearby.

Leah looked forward to this evening, when Dat planned to read to her from the family Bible, translating the verses highlighting baptism. Today at the noon meal Dat had suggested they do this "the sooner the better."

Gladdened, she felt secure in his fatherly love, in spite of his evident disappointment toward her approaching marriage. She was determined to make him proud, even though he was not so happy with her at present. The fact Dat was eager to open the Word of God and discuss the Scriptures meant he was rejoicing at least in her upcoming baptism—a requirement for marriage. In spite of himself, he was making it possible for her to marry Jonas.

She heard footsteps and turned to see Aunt Lizzie coming down the walkway, swinging her arms and smiling. Once settled into the driver's seat, Lizzie shared with her that the Nolts' baby was "as cute as a button."

Leah listened with interest. "I should've gone in with you."

"Another time, maybe." Lizzie clucked her tongue, and the horse pulled the buggy away from the curb. "The missus says she could use a bit of paid help round the house a few afternoons a week. Maybe Sadie—what do you think of that?"

"Just so you know," Leah said, "I think you should steer clear of askin' Sadie at all."

"Might do her some gut, don't you think?"

" 'Tween you and me, she's put off by our baby sister."

Lizzie nodded. "You think on it, honey-girl. Can you really expect she'd be any other way . . . considering everything?"

The notion was talked over till the horse made the turn off the road and pulled the carriage into Dat's long lane.

"So maybe Mary Ruth or Hannah, then?" Lizzie pulled back on the reins. "I'll clear it with your father first, though I doubt he'll be any too eager."

"Prob'ly he'll nix the whole idea . . . wouldn't surprise me."

Aunt Lizzie smiled, a twinkle in her eye. "You just leave that to me."

Leah was puzzled at Lizzie's confident response, but she said no more, hoping they'd take themselves off for a walk in the woods.

In the midafternoon light, they moved quickly up the hillock. Leah and Lizzie stopped for a moment to take in the sounds—every little crack and rustle they might expect to hear—garter snakes seizing centipedes, and other tiny creatures stirring beneath layers of brushwood and leaves teeming with life.

Standing there in the midst of the woods, Leah was struck with a startling thought, one she spoke right out. "What do you s'pose would've happened if Sadie had delivered her baby full-term . . . if her infant son had lived?" she asked. "How would Dat and Mamma have reacted—Sadie not havin' a husband an' all?"

Lizzie paused for a moment. "Well, now, that's not so hard to say."

Surprised, Leah studied Lizzie. "Would Dat and Mamma have taken it in their stride?"

"I didn't say that . . . just that I think in time they would've come to accept the baby—their flesh-and-blood grandson, after all."

"Something we'll never know for sure, prob'ly."

"But when all's said and done, the Lord knew best. He saw fit to call the precious little babe home to Glory."

"Just think how torn Sadie would've been her whole life long over the baby's father bein' fancy and all . . . not having him by her side."

"I doubt the lad much cared," Lizzie broke in, moving up the hill again.

Leah suddenly wondered who the father of Sadie's baby might've been. All she'd ever known was his first name—Derry. Even that made her squirm; it sounded to her like someone who might double-dare you to do something you'd later regret.

She matched her stride to Lizzie's, pleased to see the locust tree not four yards ahead. "You found it. How on earth?"

Lizzie hurried to pat the thick, grand trunk. Such an

immense and powerful tree. "Well, there aren't so many like this one, ain't so?"

"It's mighty special . . . even scarce, I'd say." She turned to look from whence they'd come. "How hard would it be to find my way home from here, do you think?"

"I'll mark the way back." Aunt Lizzie reached down for a medium-sized stone to mark the trees.

"Then, you won't fret over me coming here alone?"

Lizzie's smile faded. "Oh, I'll never say *that*."

The sun broke through the uppermost canopy, causing a thin stream of light to illuminate the grassy patch near their feet. "Lookee there!" Leah felt more confident than ever. "'Let there be light.'"

"Now, don't be thinkin' this is some heavenly sign or such nonsense."

At that Leah laughed along with Lizzie, yet she did wonder why the sunbeam had found them at that precise moment.

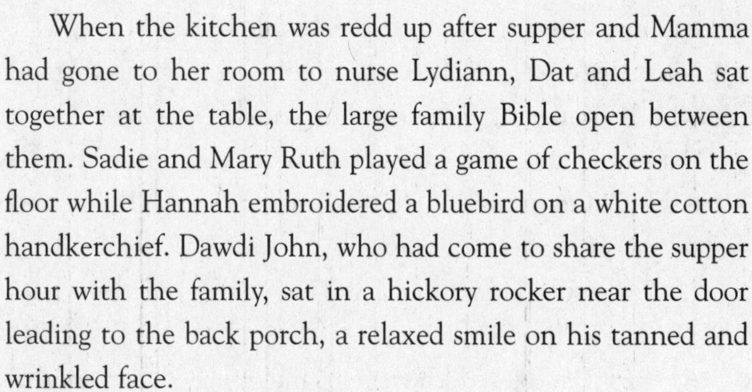

When the kitchen was redd up after supper and Mamma had gone to her room to nurse Lydiann, Dat and Leah sat together at the table, the large family Bible open between them. Sadie and Mary Ruth played a game of checkers on the floor while Hannah embroidered a bluebird on a white cotton handkerchief. Dawdi John, who had come to share the supper hour with the family, sat in a hickory rocker near the door leading to the back porch, a relaxed smile on his tanned and wrinkled face.

"We'll begin with the Lord Jesus being baptized by John," Dat said, his finger sliding down the page as he read. "'I indeed baptize you with water unto repentance. . . .'"

"Is that John the Baptist speaking?" Leah asked.

Dat nodded. "Our Lord set the example for us, even though He was the sinless Lamb of God."

Leah listened with rapt attention.

Dat continued. "Now, here's my favorite passage in this chapter. 'And Jesus, when he was baptized, went up straightway out of the water: and, lo, the heavens were opened unto him, and he saw the Spirit of God descending like a dove, and lighting upon him: And lo a voice from heaven, saying, This is my beloved Son, in whom I am well pleased.'"

Leah's ears perked up at the mention of a dove. Jehovah God had sent a gentle white bird, a symbol of peace, to rest on the Son of Man's head as a blessing.

"You must not take lightly this thing you're 'bout to do." Dat folded his callused hands on the Bible. "Membership in the church is a sign of repentance and complete commitment to the community of the People. It's also the doorway that leads to adulthood."

At this comment Leah noticed Sadie's head bob up as if she were listening, which was right fine. *'Specially now,* thought Leah, recalling their recent prickly exchange.

Dat began to quote Mark chapter sixteen, verse sixteen. "'He that believeth and is baptized shall be saved; but he that believeth not shall be damned.'"

"A divine pronouncement, and ever so frightening," Leah said, in awe of the Scripture.

At this Dat closed the Bible and reached for another

book, *Martyrs Mirror,* over eleven hundred pages in length. It was their recorded heritage of bloodshed and abuse—in all, seventeen hundred years of Christian martyrdom. "Obedience to God leads to a path of redemption, though it is exceedingly narrow . . . and few will ever find it," Dat said before beginning to read.

"We are a people set apart—we walk the narrow way, jah?"

Dat nodded reverently. " 'Tis our very life and breath."

"Without spot or blemish," Leah added, knowing the truth taught to her all the days of her life.

"Now I want to read to you about my mother's ancestor—a great-grandmother several times over." Dat turned the pages of *Martyrs Mirror* carefully, as if it were a holy book. He began to read the testimony of Catharina Meylin, who was fire branded on her fair cheek for her beliefs. " 'She held tenaciously to the doctrine of adult baptism,' " he read.

Leah struggled with tears for the courageous and devout mother of eleven children, wondering if she herself had that kind of commitment. *Am I willing to die for the Lord God?* At the very least she wanted to strive for strength of faith and character.

"Did she . . . live on?" Leah asked softly.

" 'Her feet were bound hard, and she was carried off to the convent prison, where she was given only bread and water for many weeks,' " Dat read in response.

He sighed loudly, glancing up. "She was allowed to write only one time—a testimonial letter to her grown children."

Leah listened intently. "Read the rest of the account, will ya?"

Her father nodded and followed the words with his finger. " 'Daily, Catharina was beaten, and when she would not deny her faith she was, in due time, delivered by the grace of God from her earthly bonds.' "

Starved and beaten to death? Leah wondered, though she felt too pained by what she had learned to ask. Truly, Dat's ancestor was a faithful servant of the Lord God.

Dat's voice wavered a bit. "She wrote this to her dear children: 'Henceforth there is laid up for me a crown of righteousness, which the Lord, the righteous judge, shall give me at that day: and not to me only, but unto all them also that love his appearing.' "

She gave up her life for what she believed. . . .

Leah felt ever so convicted. Was she worthy to present herself to the almighty One in baptism?

Dawdi John grunted out of the rocker, standing there all wobbly in the middle of the kitchen. Leah looked to Dat for a signal, and his brow crinkled slightly, letting her know the end of their study time had come.

"Come along, Leah," said Dawdi John at last, leaning hard on his cane.

She hurried to her grandfather's side, steadying him as they made their way to the front room and the connecting door to his little Dawdi Haus. Gladly she would ponder the Scriptures and Dat's great-grandmother's stalwart conviction, as well as the many important things Dat had said this night. For now she was thankful both Deacon Stoltzfus and Preacher Yoder had given consent for this discussion of the Scriptures. Something Sadie had never consulted Dat about, far as Leah knew.

Chapter Eight

The letters from Jonas continued to arrive in the Ebersol mailbox, and fast as she possibly could, Leah penned back a response. She still hadn't mentioned his father's visit to Dat. She tried not to ponder it too much, ignoring the gnawing nervousness that something might go awry.

Saturday, August 16
Dear Jonas,

Tomorrow we're having Preaching service here. Actually, Dat's thinking we ought to hold it in the barn, since it's a bit cooler out there. We've been having fairly regular afternoon showers now, which is nice for the ground but not so helpful for the workers—the third cutting of alfalfa is in full swing.

I've been spending several evenings a week with Dawdi John, who tells interesting stories of his youth. Might be nice for you to visit him when you return for baptism a month from now. We could go together, maybe.

I've agreed to be a bridesmaid in Naomi Kauffman's wedding, which is November 11. After observing her at baptismal instruction classes the past weeks, she seems to be ready to turn her full attention to serving the Lord God and the People. Maybe you and I will have some good fellowship with her and Luke once we're all settled in as young married couples.

Sometimes I worry about Sadie, with both Naomi and me being younger and soon to be married. It can't be easy for her.

I want to share something with you. Dat's allowing Mary Ruth to do some light housekeeping and cooking for our English neighbors, the Nolts—the new parents I wrote you about. It's puzzling to me because he was so steadfast about keeping us younger girls separate from the outside world after Sadie attended public high school. Do you think this is wise, letting one so young and innocent work for English folk?

As for me, I'm ready to follow the Lord in the ordinance of baptism and can hardly wait for that most holy of days when I will bow my knees before the bishop and the church membership.

Oh, Jonas, I can hardly wait to see you again! To think we'll be joining church together.

All my love,
Your faithful Leah

She folded the letter and slipped it into the envelope. In no hurry to leave the quiet woodland setting, she leaned her head against the locust tree and stared high into its leafy structure. Her life was about to change forever. No longer would she live under the protective covering of her father, though she would always love and respect him and Mamma both. Her place amongst the People would be that of Jonas's helpmeet and wife, and the mother of his children in due season.

Since Dat had read to her Catharina's final testimony of faith, Leah had been thinking constantly of the Anabaptist martyrs. She struggled with the thing that separated *her* from the dedicated church members right here in Gobbler's Knob—the terrible secret she kept locked away inside. She truly felt the Holy One of Israel was calling her to repent of the sisterly covenant made last year, though she dreaded what such a thing might do to her and Sadie's relationship.

In the end Dat would understand if she broke her vow to Sadie. With his concern about Sadie's rumschpringe, he would undoubtedly accept the dire revelation of his firstborn's misconduct as true, but would it cause him undue grief?

Mamma, though she would agree with Dat, would understand why Leah had made the covenant in the first place.

And what of Aunt Lizzie? Leah felt her cheeks burn, knowing Lizzie was unyielding when it came to the tie that binds. She'd made her promise to Sadie, as well.

The battle within Leah's heart between doing what she knew was the right thing and keeping her word to Sadie was causing her to lose her appetite. She found herself whispering rote but fervent prayers, not just at mealtime and bedtime, but all the day long.

Walking barefoot to the Nolts' house, Mary Ruth heard a pair of woodpeckers hidden in the trees that rimmed the road. Though she couldn't see them just now, she knew they were much larger than the bats Dat sometimes spotted in the barn rafters of a night. Their wedge-shaped tails steadied their black bodies as they flew from tree to tree, driving hard bills deep into tree bark in search of a succulent insect dinner.

She kept to the left side of the road, still baffled by her father's voluntarily allowing her to work for fancy folk. To be sure, Aunt Lizzie had played a part. Seemed most anything Lizzie wanted lately she got, especially if Dat had much to say about it.

Awful surprising, she thought as she headed off to her first day on the job with the nice Englishers and their infant son. When she'd gone to meet them with Aunt Lizzie yesterday after supper, she'd noticed right away the baby's dark hair, unlike his blond and blue-eyed parents, though neither of them seemed to pay any mind. Dottie Nolt had quietly shared with her that baby Carl was indeed adopted, not common knowledge. Now in their midthirties, the Nolts were pleased to have a little one to love as their own. Mary Ruth thought they must be churchgoers because Dottie had told her yesterday they were planning to have their baby dedicated to God in church soon. There was something awful special about knowing they wanted to raise their little one with the Lord God's blessings. It made her respect them, English or not, though she scarcely knew them.

"Hello again, Mary Ruth," Dottie greeted her at the front door.

"Hullo," she replied. Stepping into the thoroughly modern front room, Mary Ruth felt such gladness to be here again. She had an uncanny connection to the larger world here. It was just as some of her older girlfriends had described their first visit to downtown Lancaster—that unspeakable, somewhat delirious feeling of rumschpringe—being allowed to experience something other than the society of the People . . . truly the only thing she knew.

After she was offered a glass of lemonade, freshly squeezed just like Mamma's, Mary Ruth agreed to sweep and scrub both the entry hall and the kitchen floors. "I'll even get down on all fours like Mamma does at home," she told Dottie.

Her employer appeared somewhat surprised, eyebrows arching as she smiled. "I can see I'm going to become very spoiled with you around, Mary Ruth."

So she took extra care to reach far into all the corners and crevices, washing the floor by hand. When that chore was complete, she dusted the front room. Carefully removing knickknacks and magazines from the sofa tables, she hummed, enjoying herself far more than she'd ever dreamed possible—in a worldly home, of all things. Except she'd seen an open Bible in both the kitchen and now here, on what Dottie called the "coffee table." Interesting, to be sure.

Moving upstairs, she couldn't help but think of the extra money she was going to earn. What a good idea to put it away for future schooling needs. Dat would have a fit when he put two and two together and discovered what she was saving up for. Yet it wasn't as if she had sought out this work. The whole thing had fallen into her lap, thanks to Aunt Lizzie.

Hannah, on the other hand, had appeared startled about this opportunity. "How will ya keep up with your homework once school starts?" she had asked Mary Ruth in the privacy of their bedroom last night.

"Dottie Nolt wants me only two or three times a week. That's all."

"Twice oughta keep the house clean enough, seems to me," Hannah replied.

"Maybe so, but I want to please my first employer. I'll still have plenty of time to help Mamma at home."

So, after talking it over with Mamma, Mary Ruth agreed

that if the job interfered with schoolwork, she'd ask Sadie to fill in for a while. But she doubted that would work, what with Sadie seeming to recoil at the sight of her own baby sister. Mary Ruth truly wondered about that.

Just now, going into the darling nursery, she stopped to admire a framed wall painting above the dresser—a small boy with suntanned legs making chase after a lone orange-brown butterfly that appeared to be just out of reach. She'd seen bright-colored butterflies like that many times in the high meadow over near Blackbird Pond, out behind smithy Peachey's bank barn and blacksmith shop.

The painting made her smile, and she set to work dusting the dresser thoroughly before moving on to the oak rocker, cleaning the rungs beneath. A peek at the empty crib let her know baby Carl was either cradled in his new mother's arms or tucked away for a nap in the wicker bassinet near the kitchen. Such a wondrous thing, these folk opening their home and their joyful hearts to an orphaned baby.

Eager to complete her housekeeping chores in an acceptable manner, Mary Ruth attended to every detail. When the rocking chair was polished, she moved to the round lamp table nearby. To her surprise, there on the table lay yet another open Bible, same as the two downstairs. She saw that a verse from the Psalms was underlined in red—*As the hart panteth after the water brooks, so panteth my soul after thee, O God.*

Why so many copies of the Good Book in the house? she wondered. Was Dottie a follower of the Jehovah Lord? Were there Englishers who were also devout like the People? For sure and for certain, the idea of an open Bible in every room—and in a fancy home—was ever so curious.

Distracted and restless, Abram worked up a sweat redding up the barn for the Lord's Day gathering and the young people's singing that was to follow tomorrow evening. He'd made the decision to have the church benches set up on the threshing floor, where an occasional breeze might do some good keeping folk awake instead of the way it had been two weeks ago, when he and everyone else had been helpless to fight off the heat-induced stupor. And with Ida still tending closely to their infant daughter, the housework of removing all the rugs and rearranging the furniture would have fallen to the girls and Lizzie. Truly, it was better to have church in the barn, where he would plan the seating arrangement and direct the People to their seats.

He was mighty glad to have a strong helping hand this afternoon with the heavier duties. Far as he was concerned, Smithy Gid could easily become a necessary right arm to him, what with John suffering a hip ailment clear out of the blue.

Working with Gid, he shoveled manure out of the stable area. Then they raked and swept clean the widest area of the threshing floor, where the People would sit as hearers of the Word.

"'S'mighty gut of you to help," Abram said, pushing hard on the long-handled broom.

"Glad to do it."

"Ain't so certain how I'll manage here in a few weeks."

Gid nodded but kept working. "I wonder 'bout that, too,

Abram. But more and more Pop needs me to help him with some of the smithy work."

Abram knew that, all right. But there was no real need to address the event both men dreaded. The topic of Leah's impending marriage was something they avoided discussing altogether. Abram had witnessed firsthand Gid's feelings for Leah, saw the hopeless longing in the young man's eyes whenever she was anywhere near.

Abram's feeble attempt to get Jonas Mast out of town and off to Ohio had backfired. The time apart had served only to solidify their love, visible by the number of Ohio letters arriving each week. So Leah had fallen in love with the boy she believed was to be her life mate . . . although Abram would be surprised if she and Jonas ended up together.

He heard the sound of the horses and buggies now, the womenfolk arriving to help Ida make ready for the common meal tomorrow. Plenty of baking would take place in the Ebersol kitchen this day. *Will Leah and Lizzie be on hand to help Ida?* he wondered. The chummy twosome had gone to run an errand an hour or so ago.

Frankly, it was downright unnerving how Lizzie had inched her way deeper into their lives, all of them. First she'd gotten her grip on Sadie last year. Now Leah. Worst of all, Lizzie had pressed Abram to make a hasty decision over an English housekeeping job down the road a piece—giving him no breathing room. He had little choice but to do things Lizzie's way to keep her hushed up . . . for now. Alas, Lizzie Brenneman was railroading him down a path of her own choosing. Downright unbecoming of her.

Ida, on the other hand, wasn't much help, either. Seemed

his wife and her sister were out of check, and the bishop would tell him so if he sought out spiritual counsel. He was losing sway over his family in more ways than one, and growing weary before his time.

As for the upper hand, he also felt at a loss when it came to his father-in-law. It struck him as peculiar that John's bum hip, if real, had come on the heels of a fiery discussion concerning none other than Lizzie and her past blunders, though long ago confessed. Thus Ida's sister was causing strife at every hand. He'd have to put a stop to it before things spun completely out of control.

Turning his attention back to the barn cleanup, Abram knew he'd be tuckered out by this time tomorrow. No doubt he and Ida would rise early and dress for the Lord's Day right quick after Lydiann's early-morning feeding, around three-thirty. There was much to be organized before the membership began to arrive—two hundred thirty-eight strong, and many more wee ones on the way.

So he and the young man who he hoped might still become his son-in-law continued that most honorable and sacred task: making an acceptable place of worship in the sight of the Lord God and the People.

Chapter Nine

The morning mist took too long to burn off, revealing at last a cloudless, pure sky. By the time Dat and Leah had finished the milking, Sadie, Mamma, and the twins had cooked up a full breakfast of fried eggs and bacon, along with some fresh fruit, toast, jelly, and milk. "Best not dally," Mamma chided the girls, though they knew better than to linger on this Lord's Day. "There'll be folks arrivin' well before nine o'clock, to be sure."

Sadie didn't much care when the People came. They were all going to be sitting on the church benches in the smelly barn—the last place she'd like to be today. But go she must.

Her parents' closed-door conversation of four nights ago still rang in her ears. Pity's sake, she'd thought so long and hard about what she'd overheard she'd made herself sick. One thing was sure, she was convinced they knew *something* of her reckless year with Derry, that good-for-nothing boy who'd brought an everlasting stain on her life.

Thinking on all this, she decided then and there . . .

maybe she was just too ill to attend church today. She could take herself off to the high meadow and try to keep from being queasy. Dat might not believe her, but Mamma would—and so would Aunt Lizzie if it came to that.

Before the womenfolk were to file into the barn prior to Preaching, Leah was surprised to see Naomi come running over to join her and Adah Peachey, along with the twins and Mamma—babe in arms—and the Ebersol family cluster. The main thing on Leah's mind was Sadie, who wasn't where she was supposed to be just now. Boldly, her sister had gone up to the outhouse right quick before the service was close to beginning. *Never mind her,* thought Leah, dismissing her errant sister. *If she comes, she comes.*

Leah got herself into the line for church, behind the baptized single girls at the front. The earthy scent of cats and hay and cattle filled her nose. *Best smells on earth,* she thought, ever so glad to be alive as she shook hands with Preacher Yoder and the visiting minister from Ninepoints.

She noticed Ezra and Elias Stoltzfus turn their heads in unison when spotting Hannah and Mary Ruth, but the twins reverently walked toward the benches set up for the womenfolk and young children. Though Leah did not crack a smile, inwardly she was amused and gladly so. Someday her younger sisters might end up married to the deacon's boys. Who was to tell? But if so, her nieces and nephews, Hannah's and Mary Ruth's babies—the whole lot of them—now, wouldn't *they* resemble each other? Cousins, for sure, but even closer.

What a bright future they all had, including Sadie if she'd just get her tail feathers down here to settle in for the Preaching service. And not only did she need to hear the Word of the Lord . . . but Leah had just this minute decided Sadie might benefit from another straight talk. Life was too short to take risks with eternity, and her own conscience weighed ever so heavily.

The raucous come-hither trill of a group of blue jays cut the stillness at the end of the long, final prayer after the three-hour meeting. Once the People were seated again after kneeling, Deacon Stoltzfus rose and announced the location of the next Sunday Preaching, "in two weeks at smithy Peachey's place."

Then, when the meeting was opened up for any business to be conducted relating to church discipline, there was an issue involving "a reckless teenager," or so the member reported. That being the case, the closing hymn was sung and the youngsters began silently filing out of the barn, followed by the unbaptized, single young people. Another forty minutes or so of pointed discussion was to follow, including the humiliating possibility of the wayward youth having to confess before the People.

Leah shivered, wishing Sadie had been present at Preaching today. Aware of the secret members' meeting now going on, she felt sure it might have put the fear of God in her sister.

Mary Ruth hurried with Hannah to help Mamma, Leah, and Lizzie with a smorgasbord-style spread laid out on long tables in the sunny kitchen. Today being a perfect day for a picnic, the People would eat and fellowship on the grounds. Bread and homemade butter, sliced cheeses, dill and sweet pickles, strawberry jam, red beets, half-moon apple pies, and ice-cold lemonade—the standard light fare for a summer Sunday go-to-meeting. Not that a body could eat himself full on such a menu. It was merely intended to squelch growling stomachs till the People could ride horse and buggy back home.

"Has anybody seen Sadie?" Mary Ruth asked of Leah and Hannah.

"Sadie's sittin' up in the meadow, head between her knees like she's under the weather," Aunt Lizzie offered.

Mary Ruth joked, " 'Cept ain't it an awful *nice* day to—"

"Now, leave her be," Mamma spoke up.

At this Mary Ruth turned to Hannah and frowned.

"You heard Mamma," Hannah whispered.

Still, Mary Ruth wondered how Sadie could get by with skipping church, soaking up the sunshine instead. Unless she *was* ill. But if she was simply having a sulk, well, then it didn't make sense. Why would Sadie bring unnecessary shame to her parents on the day they hosted the church meeting?

After the noon meal, enjoyed on the rolling lawns, the young men gradually began to gather in the barnyard. There they congregated in one of two groups: the more pious teens—some baptized and some not—and the known rebels who typically ignored the rules of dress, conduct, and were all-round less serious minded.

Elias stood with the teens known for following the letter of the law, even though he was also *hipperdiglipp*—the type of fellow who rode his new pony cart to the limits of speed and daring.

On her way back from the outhouse, Mary Ruth stumbled upon Elias and had to swallow her nervousness. She'd never been this alone with him, except for that one time at the vegetable stand, nearly a year ago. Her resolve not to pay him any mind flew out the window. She was ever so eager to reply if he should happen to speak to her.

And speak he did, removing his straw hat. "Hullo, Mary Ruth. How *are* ya?"

Well, she might've thought the Lord God himself had descended and stood before her, she was that tongue-tied. "I . . . uh, hullo."

She wanted to say more, truly she did. Not lose her words in this hopeless stuttering, of all things. Should she try to talk again? She might not get a second chance today, and the next time to prove herself to be a bright and expressive young woman would be another two weeks away. *Be calm*, she told herself. *Breathe deep . . . stand tall.*

He scratched his tousled red hair and nodded. He was looking at her, sure as anything, and she tried ever so hard not to stare back. Yet his eyes drew her, pulled her like iron to a magnet. For what seemed like a full minute, he stood smiling down at her. "Awful nice seein' you again, Mary Ruth."

"*Denki*—thank you" was all she managed to say before he was on his way. Oh, she could just kick herself for being so jittery. Was this how it felt to be falling in love? She hoped not, because she absolutely must dismiss her feelings for Elias.

Her thoughts turned to the singing in the barn after nightfall. Of course she wasn't free to go. At just fourteen she longed to be older—an adult, to be sure. But she was too young for the true freedom she longed for and too old to be treated like a girl with hardly a care in the world. For truth, in spite of seeing Elias just now, she wasn't too sure she'd ever be happy living amongst the People forever, being treated the way the menfolk seemed to manage the womenfolk—under the thumb, so to speak.

Lately, though, she'd observed *one* woman whom she wouldn't mind imitating at all. Aunt Lizzie. Her aunt had a lip that wouldn't quit, and Mary Ruth knew it firsthand because she'd heard Lizzie talking mighty straight to Mamma just last night. "I'm telling you, time's running out for Abram," Lizzie said. "Put that in your work apron and mull it over, Ida. I'm fed up with him muzzling the ox." And with that Mary Ruth had darted back into the front room, hiding behind the doorjamb, changing her mind about heading straight for the kitchen. It wouldn't be wise to barge into such a squall.

For tonight she and Hannah would simply sit out on the back lawn, listening to the courting-age young people sing their "fast" songs, having themselves a good time.

Sadie wouldn't be going, either, not the way she'd kept herself away from the meeting today. No, Dat would see to it Sadie was nowhere near the barn singing. As for Leah, being engaged to Jonas would keep her away unless Adah Peachey or Naomi Kauffman talked her into going with them. Jah, tonight would be an interesting sight, with more than likely not a single one of Abram's daughters showing up at their own singing.

Dawdi John was a bit sluggish, but sharp as a nail. Tonight he wore his white "for good" shirt, tan suspenders, and black broadfall trousers, same as he'd worn all day. Because of the exceptionally warm evening, no coat was needed, and he'd left his black bowtie in his dresser drawer. His weak eyes, when he removed his glasses, were somewhat pained as he sat on a folding chair next to his granddaughters in the backyard.

"Nice to hear the young people lift their voices in song, ain't?" Leah was quick to say. Ever since she'd known of his hip problems, she'd gone out of her way to show extra kindness to Dawdi.

"They sing as heartily as the youth did back when I was a lad." He nodded, smiling.

Hannah and Mary Ruth were caught up in their own talk, sprawled out on a large green quilt, frayed round the edges. As for Sadie, she had been sent upstairs following the common meal to contemplate her irreverent behavior this morning. Dat had ordered her off to the hot and stuffy bedroom, called after her that she was "never, ever to feign sickness on the Lord's Day again!" and she was not allowed to leave the premises for a full week.

Leah couldn't blame Dat, really. Sadie had it coming, plain to see—although Mamma had actually winced when

Dat raised his voice. Even Hannah and Mary Ruth had put their heads down, squinting to beat the band. But Leah knew the punishment had come forth in such a fiery way due only to continual problems. Before supper tonight Sadie had refused to hold Lydiann, though their baby sister was as sweet as pudding. She wouldn't budge even when Mamma spoke directly to her. "Take your baby sister for me, please."

Sadie had actually backed away when Mamma held Lydiann out to her, shocking all of them. Mary Ruth came to Mamma's rescue, taking Lydiann in her own arms, and Sadie made a beeline to the back door, sobbing as she ran.

Leah, chagrined, had been sent out to fetch her sister, ordered to do so by Mamma, then Dat . . . then both her parents in chorus.

She hoped—and prayed often—that Sadie might snap out of her cantankerous mood. Unknowingly, Dat and Mamma were being pulled into the thick of it. *Won't Mamma, at least, put two and two together if Sadie keeps behaving in such a questionable manner?* she had wondered.

Just now she saw Adah Peachey running through the cornfield. Leah waved to her, noticing Gid was nowhere in sight.

"Won't ya come along with me?" Adah called to her.

"I'm keepin' Dawdi company," Leah replied.

"Aw, please come?"

Leah, wanting ever so much to accompany Adah, turned to ask Dawdi, "Will you be all right here for a bit?"

"Sure, go on, Leah. I'm just fine. Besides, Hannah and Mary Ruth will look after me, won'tcha, girls?"

The twins nodded, and Leah rose to meet Adah. Mary

Ruth hopped up from the quilt to claim Leah's vacant folding chair. "Have yourself a nice time," Mary Ruth said, plopping herself down.

Hurrying off with Adah, Leah realized suddenly that she hadn't bothered to dress for the singing, since she hadn't planned to attend. For sure and for certain, she would not impress any of the young men in attendance. No need to when she was engaged to marry Jonas in a few months. Adah, on the other hand, had combed her hair, taking care to wash her face, Leah noticed, because it was shiny from the scrubbing. "What're you thinking?" Leah asked as they stood in the gaping opening to the barn, peering in.

"Just that it's time you had yourself a bit of fun."

"Oh, I'm okay, really I am."

"You don't convince me." Adah smiled thoughtfully. "You look worried most of the time."

"I do?"

"Honestly, I've been wonderin' if you have second thoughts 'bout Jonas."

"What makes you think that?"

Adah fell silent suddenly as, one after another, the young folk made their way into the barn.

Leah waited for her friend to respond, but when she didn't, Leah added, "If I didn't know better, Adah, I'd think maybe it was *you* who's worried."

That got Adah talking again. "Whatever for?"

"I daresay you don't like the idea of us not bein' sisters-in-law, for one thing." As soon as Leah said it, she knew she'd been needlessly insensitive.

"Well, jah, 'tis ever so true. . . ."

Leah was deeply sorry. "What I meant to say was—"

"No . . . no, you should never have said such an unkind thing."

Beyond doubt she hated what had just happened; she'd had no intention of exchanging sarcastic words with her dearest friend. "I'm sorry, Adah, honest I am. I don't know what got into me."

"Well, I 'spect *I* do." Adah breathed in ever so deeply. "I think you're upset at Sadie. Naomi Kauffman told me the most revoltin' story the other day."

"You know I don't care to hear gossip," Leah replied.

"Ain't hearsay. Naomi says she knows what she's talkin' 'bout."

Leah panicked. Naomi probably *did* know something she oughtn't to be telling. Things concerning Sadie and their Friday-night adventures in the English world. "Is this so necessary to say?" she asked softly.

"Come with me." Adah led her away from the barn, up toward the mule road. "I'm not happy to be the one to tell you this, but . . ." She paused then, still walking hard. "I think you might already suspect as much. Could be the reason you're on edge."

"What's so important we have to walk clear away from the barn?"

"Your sister, that's what. Sadie took her baptism last year with an impure heart. If Bishop Bontrager knew of it, well, she'd be shunned for certain—at least the temporary *Bann*."

The words sprang to life in Leah, smarting her eyes. "Impure?"

"Sadie had herself an English boyfriend."

"I don't like what you're sayin'." She had to speak up. She couldn't just go along with Adah, yet she didn't want to let on she already knew.

"I'm only tellin' you in hopes you can talk sense to Sadie. Help her see the light before Naomi goes to Preacher with this."

Leah's heart sank. "What do you want me to do?"

"Talk openly, sister to sister. Let her know what Naomi's threatenin' to do."

Leah sighed loudly. "What if Sadie won't cooperate?"

"Just try, Leah. For the sake of your family . . . and to spare Sadie eternal punishment."

Leah looked now at Adah. She began to wonder if Adah wasn't actually relieved her precious brother was not romantically connected to the Ebersol family.

High above them, in trees silhouetted against a dark sky, whippoorwills called from unseen branches, and Leah felt sudden despair. The thing she had greatly feared had come to pass. Sadie had been found out. Just how much Naomi knew, she had no idea. But she intended to worm it out of her.

In a few minutes' time, she and Adah had walked all the way to the brink of the forest. Without speaking, they turned and stood there, looking down over the Ebersol Cottage, as Leah liked to call her father's house. In the near distance she spotted a single upstairs window aglow—Sadie's and her bedroom—where her bold and surly sister sat alone contemplating her Lord's Day misbehavior.

Meanwhile, their two-story bank barn was alive with light and music. Lightning bugs blinked yellow-white sparkles here and there over the field and beyond to the Peachey farm, making Leah think sadly of Smithy Gid. What a good thing he'd stayed at home and let his sister go it alone to singing this night. Indeed.

"Won'tcha come to the singing with me, *please?*" Adah asked.

"I'm not dressed for it," she said.

Adah looked her over, brushing Leah's apron off. "There, now."

Her dear friend's pleading eyes tugged at her heart. "S'pose I could go with you, but only for a little bit."

"Wonderful-gut!" Adah's face lit up and she reached for Leah's hand, and the two of them went running down the mule road toward the barn.

Gid caught himself breaking into a full grin, having just now spotted Leah Ebersol and his sister Adah come strolling into the barn, hand in hand. And just when he was starting to wish he'd stayed home to frisk with his new litter of German shepherd puppies. Soon he would be advertising again by word of mouth—the way he liked to, since it took nothing away from his growing savings account—letting folks know his full-bred pups were weaned and ready to purchase. His father had mentioned not two days before that he was well pleased with the amount of money Gid had saved over the past few years, thanks to the thriving side business. Gid would have liked to be looking to marry before too long, though the girl he really wanted to court was Abram's Leah, who was all caught up with a beau clear out in Ohio. Just what was Jonas Mast thinking, learning the carpentry trade? Gid wondered. But it wasn't his place to question. He knew there had been talk amongst the brethren—and this had come straight from his own pop—that Bishop Bontrager didn't take too kindly to young men who chose to make their way by doing something other than farming. Working the soil was the expected way in the eyes of the People. Anything else was "mighty English." Besides, there was ample farmland in Lancaster County.

Gid slowed his pace, hoping to appear relaxed as he approached Leah and Adah, who were talking off by themselves. Not wanting to barge in—he did and he didn't—he hoped to make Leah feel comfortable with his presence. Yet what was *she* doing here, where the singing activities were meant for coupling up? Surely Leah and Jonas Mast were secretly engaged by now. But that was anyone's guess . . . at least up until the second Sunday after fall communion, when the deacon named each couple in the district who planned to marry during the wedding season. After the publishing, Abram Ebersol would stand and invite everyone sixteen and older to the wedding, also announcing the day and month.

Gid had long thought he might have some reason for staying away from church that day. Wouldn't think of putting on like he was ill, though. Although, if he thought on it long enough, he *could* be. But he would try to put on a smile for the Ebersols, no matter what inner turmoil he would battle that day. Because wedding or not, Abram and his family were mighty special in his book.

"Hullo, Leah . . . and Adah." He stopped a few feet from them, forcing his gaze on his sister and away from Leah, who always seemed to draw his eyes to hers. How was it a girl could wear her sweet spirit on her face? It had always been that way with Leah.

"Oh, Gid, you're here!" Adah said, letting go of Leah's hand and gripping his arm.

He felt his face flush red. "I decided to come over at the last minute."

Adah turned to Leah. "Same as you did, Leah," his sister declared, eyes sparkling.

"Oh, Adah . . . for goodness' sake." Leah turned from Adah and looked at him, smiling pleasantly, not flirtatiously. "I came to keep your sister company, is all," she said.

" 'Twas my idea, for sure," Adah agreed.

"Well, I'm glad you're both here." Their talk quickly turned to King, Leah's dog, and it seemed she considered him a devoted pet.

"Dat likes having King round, too," Leah stated. "He's even said it might be nice to have one or two more dogs."

Adah brightened again. "Really?"

Leah was nodding. "Dat thinks havin' dogs on the property keeps outsiders honest."

"Not that he distrusts the English, I don't s'pose," Gid spoke up. He knew Abram well enough to know better.

Leah shrugged. "Dat sometimes worries over us girls . . . bein' there's only one man to do the protectin'." She must have suddenly caught herself, realizing what she'd said, because she looked quickly at Adah and turned too rosy in the cheeks.

Gid stepped closer and found himself forming a circle with the two of them. He thought he smelled a hint of homemade soap—probably Adah, who'd cleaned up right good for the evening. Still, there was a unique freshness about Leah, the way her eyes shone with joy, her surprising openness. She was as confident as any girl he knew; not shy at all, nor too frank like one of the girls here from the Grasshopper Level area. He hadn't seen her, but some of the fellows had said Jonas Mast's spunky sister Rebekah was in attendance, along with three other girls from that district. "Bold Becky" had shown up tonight to one of her first singings since she'd turned sixteen. He was careful not to concentrate too hard on Leah, dividing his attention between both her and Adah . . . though it was mighty difficult.

Chapter Ten

Monday morning after completing her milking duties, Leah hurried off on foot to pay a visit to Naomi Kauffman.

Arriving at Kauffmans' dairy farm, she hurried across the barnyard to the milk house. There she found Naomi looking mighty surprised to see her. "I hope you don't mind me comin' so early."

"Leah, what is it? Something happen over at your place?"

"Everything's just fine." She paused. "I have to talk to you." She went on to share in whispered tones what Adah had confided last night. "I'm worried sick 'bout Sadie—what might become of her if you . . . well, if you go to Preacher before she has a chance to repent on her own."

"She's had plenty of time, wouldn't you say? Nearly a year's passed since she started spendin' time with her worldly beau. And what's worse, she kept seein' him after she was baptized. I know she did 'cause Melvin Warner, Derry's English friend, told me so. 'Course, now, I was wild, too, 'cept not thinkin' on bein' baptized . . . not till recently." Naomi took a deep breath. "I just don't understand how Sadie could tempt the Lord God thataway. And she never made things right with the church brethren, neither." Naomi looked at her with stony eyes. "Has she confessed these things to you?"

Leah couldn't lie . . . not before God and her fellow baptismal candidate. "It's a touchy subject, the rumschpringe . . . so private it is, you know."

"Which is why Dat's been talkin' to Preacher Yoder and others about doin' away with it. Goodness' sake, I nearly got myself in a fix. Sadie and I . . . we went together clear up to Strasburg, seekin' out fancy fellas. We were *narrisch*—crazy. Truly we were."

"You don't have to come clean to me, Naomi. You've repented to God and Preacher, as we all must."

"Then, will you urge Sadie to do the same? Plead with her to go to the brethren."

"Why, so you won't have to?"

"Ach no, but ain't it true if a person knows of sin and doesn't encourage the sinner to own up . . . well then, they may be found to be just as guilty?"

Leah hated to think she, as well as Aunt Lizzie, was at fault right along with Sadie. Oh, they'd made futile attempts to get Sadie to express regret, pushing for her to at least tell Mamma what she'd done. Jointly and separately they'd done so, till they were blue in the face. But Leah couldn't reveal any of this to Naomi. It would never do to let *her* in on the fact that Leah had known all this for a long time.

"Jah, I'll do my best talkin' to my sister," Leah promised. "I'll tell her what you said. Or you could tell her yourself. Might be a gut thing for her to witness how you've turned your back on the world and all."

Naomi nodded. "Still, if she isn't willin' to ask for forgiveness, then I won't have any choice but to—"

"Talk to your beau's grandfather?"

Naomi blushed. "Has nothin' to do with Luke and me."

"Well, I surely hope not."

Squaring her shoulders, Naomi continued. "Listen, Leah, I'm bein' truthful with you. I couldn't live with my conscience if I didn't speak to *someone*. Don't you see? I want to present myself as a living sacrifice and follow the Lord Jesus in holy baptism with a pure heart."

Leah agreed. "Just as I do."

So it was settled. *Sadie's my sister, after all*, she thought.

Sadie would have one short month to offer atonement to her parents and, if she was willing, the church.

◆

At half past ten in the morning, the postman delivered the mail. Leah ran down the lane, eager to hear from Jonas. Just as she expected, there was a new letter from Millersburg.

Tearing the envelope open, she began to read.

My dearest Leah,

You are constantly in my thoughts and prayers! Just think, one month from now I'll hold you in my arms again. While I'm there for baptism, let's you and I talk over where we plan to live. We could have a look-see at the rental house you wrote about earlier.

Today as I worked in the carpentry shop, I had an interesting idea. I hope you might consider it. I realize there must have been an important reason for you to remain in Gobbler's Knob through the summer. But now, here we are in the middle of August, and I'd like for us to be in the same town together, at least for our final weeks as a betrothed couple. I want to court you in person, Leah. My heart longs for your smile, your sweet face . . . your dear, dear ways.

Let's think seriously about the possibility of you coming back to Ohio with me after we join church. My final weeks away from home will be much easier with you close by. If necessary, I will write to your father to get his blessing on the matter . . . or, better yet, I'll speak to him when I'm there.

By the way, David Mellinger's elderly mother, Edith, could benefit greatly from your help, if only for a short time. (They're inviting you through me.) You can stay in the Dawdi Haus with Edith. What do you think of this?

I'm also eager for you to meet the godly bishop here. The Scriptures have come alive for me—passages in the Bible I never knew existed. Here's one I must share with you today. Second Corinthians chapter three, verse eighteen: "But we all, with open face beholding as in a glass the glory of the Lord, are changed into the same image from glory to glory, even as by the Spirit of the Lord."

Leah, if you read this verse over again, the amazing truth will sink deep into your heart. To think our lives can be mirrors of God's goodness and grace, making it possible for others to see Christ Jesus reflected in us!

I should sign off and prepare for a long and busy day. I'm holding my breath to see you again!

All my love,
Jonas

She held the letter fondly, gladdened by his invitation. Jonas still wanted her to visit him in Ohio! She went to seek out Mamma with the news.

Mamma was far more understanding than Leah expected. "That's right nice of Jonas, but you'll have to see what Dat says, ya know," Mamma said, standing at the wood stove.

"Do you mean you could be in favor of it? If Dat is willin'?"

"Let's just see what he says"—Mamma's parting words on the matter.

She kissed her mother square on the cheek.

Obviously pleased, Mamma reminded her the "decision remains with Dat, ya must know."

"But still, I'm more hopeful 'cause of what you said."

This time it was Mamma who kissed *her*, high on the forehead, right where her middle part commenced.

Promptly Leah marched out to the barn, her heart in her throat, knowing full well what to predict from Dat. She found him caring for a nasty gash on the lower hindquarters of one of the mules. "Aw, the poor thing. You've got yourself some tendin' to do." She stood back a bit as Dat soothed the hurting animal.

"Jah, but never too busy for my girl. What's on your mind, Leah?"

That was just like Dat; he seemed to know her better than almost anyone. Now . . . how to say what was on her heart? Dare she risk Dat's temper after his recent flare-up with Sadie? "I guess I don't know where to start, really."

He looked up from his squatting position. "If this concerns

your aunt Lizzie, I'll be blunt with you—I have no time for it. That's all I best say."

"Aunt Lizzie? Why, no . . . it's about a letter from Jonas. Arrived just today." She pressed on, shaking inwardly as she told him what Jonas had in mind. "I really want to do this, Dat. I wouldn't risk annoying you if it didn't mean ever so much to me."

"You want to go an' visit Millersburg before you're married to Jonas?"

She explained she could stay with the master carpenter's mother to help with the widow's daily routine. "Jonas would reside where he is now, next door in the main farmhouse."

"A bit too familiar for my likin'."

"You know that would not be a concern." She was hoping to rule out all roadblocks. "This could be a special time for Jonas and me."

Abram turned away, lifting the mule's leg, manipulating it back and forth. "I don't see it that way," Dat said quickly.

She wanted to say, *I'm not like Sadie*, but bit her lip. Dat knew nothing of Sadie's past. And besides, it wasn't an issue of purity that seemed to irk him. He was just plain stubborn about preferring Gid Peachey.

"It's a closed subject," Dat added. "*Verschteh*—understand?"

She didn't dare argue with him. But she wanted to go to Ohio something awful. Breathing in hard, then exhaling, she turned and walked away, trying to keep still and not talk back. But she could hear Jonas's earnest plea in the words he'd written. Loving words—the compassion of her future husband. Jonas wanted to spend time with his bride-to-be. What was wrong with that? After all this time they'd been apart . . .

Suddenly she spun round and rushed back to the barn. "What if Jonas talks this over with you when he comes for baptism? Would that set better with you, Dat?" she entreated him, desperate for this one thing. "I scarcely ever ask for much, you know that. But this . . ."

Dat stood up just then and looked her full in the face. "My dear girl, how can you ever know what's in the deep of my heart? You are precious to me . . . since the first day I laid eyes on you. Tiny little thing, you were. A helpless infant, bawlin' your lungs out."

She was nearly embarrassed at his tender words. "Dat?"

"No, now listen to me, Leah. You're the light of my eyes, always have been."

For goodness' sake, Dat was being much too serious. She said, "I know you think of me more as a son than a—"

"No . . . no, you haven't any idea."

"Then, maybe . . . well, might you be willin' to change your mind? Could you reconsider . . . just this once?" All their years working the mules in the field, tending to a multitude of barn chores—always together—told her he might listen. After all, she *was* Abram's Leah, and she knew that, in his own stubborn way, he was attempting to save face. Known to be unyielding amongst the People, Dat wanted to give Leah what she most longed for. She was sure of it.

Sighing, Dat removed his straw hat and raked his thick fingers through his cropped hair. "For how long did you say?"

"A month or so is all."

"And you wouldn't ever think of marryin' anyone but this boy, your mamma's cousin's son?"

By now she couldn't begin to utter a response. How she loved the darling boy of her childhood! Dat knew this. *Why must he continually test me?* she wondered.

Dat gave her a long look before continuing. "If you love Jonas as much as you seem to, then can you find a way to get yourself out there? I won't be givin' you the money to ride a train or bus all the way to Ohio, just so you know."

Joyful tears sprang to her eyes. "Oh, I can't thank you enough!" Leah reached over and hugged his arm tightly. "I promise ya won't regret this."

Her father clasped her hand tight for a moment before they parted. Then, still grinning, Leah ran to tell Mamma the amazing news.

Chapter Eleven

At noon Mamma suggested the girls enjoy a long lunch break from their work. "We all need a bit of time off," she announced at the table.

Leah and the twins agreed, welcoming the idea with nods of the head. Sadie, however, went right back outside as if she hadn't heard.

Standing in the doorway, hand on the screen door, Leah watched Sadie work the soil. *She's punishing herself out in that sun. . . .*

Was now the time to approach Sadie? Such a ticklish position Naomi had put her in. Just how would Sadie react to Naomi's threat?

Sadie worked the hoe, all bent over, Leah noticed, making deep furrows in the vegetable rows to assist their hand-watering efforts. Some much-needed rain had come recently, but all through July and this far into August they'd supplemented by pumping well water up to the holding tank and using hoses in the garden. With constant care the girls had practically salvaged the entire celery crop. *A sign of gut things to come*, thought Leah.

Awful tired herself and wishing she could heed Mamma's suggestion to rest up, Leah opened the back door and stepped out. There was not a breath of wind to be felt, and the birds were silent. Uncanny, to be sure.

Taking a deep breath, she stepped past the narrow swath of red-and-white petunias lining the cement walkway on the right. Dat could be heard clear off in the cornfield, talking to either Gid or the smithy. The peculiar stillness gave Leah a sense of renewed courage, as if the earth were holding its breath along with her. *Best talk to Sadie right now*, she told herself, thinking again of Naomi's ominous warning.

Turning at the end of the whitewashed fence, she made her way to the family vegetable garden. Sadie was as pretty as ever, her golden hair shimmering in the sunlight through her white prayer bonnet. Leah was struck with the notion Sadie could pass for a heavenly messenger—an angel—so fragile and lovely she looked.

"Sister," she called softly, "why aren't you inside takin' a breather?"

"Don't need any time off" came the terse reply.

Leah didn't care to dispute that; no need starting another quarrel. "I saw you out here and thought maybe we could have us a quick chat."

"Seems you're the one who's most eager to talk."

Right away she felt put off by Sadie's remark, yet Leah rejected the urge to respond in kind. "I was hopin' we could discuss somethin' . . . without fussin' this time."

"All depends."

Leah reckoned if she brought up Naomi just now, Sadie might let out a holler. She wouldn't put it past Sadie, not the way her emotions had run unchecked lately. "Have you given any more thought to, well . . . what we talked 'bout before?"

"Don't mince words, Leah. Say what you mean."

"All right, then. Isn't it time . . . I mean, don't you feel you should unburden your heart to Mamma, at least?"

Sadie scowled.

Leah crouched down in the small irrigation ditch between the rows. "Honestly, Sadie, I'm scared someone else might know the truth—besides Aunt Lizzie and me—and report you to Preacher Yoder."

Sadie raised her voice, blue eyes glistening. "So . . . did you go an' tell?"

"Actually, Naomi told *me* a thing or two. She's decided to make a stand for virtue and hopes you'll repent. And mighty quick."

"Naomi has nothin' on me."

Leah whispered, "She didn't know you were in the family way?"

Sadie shook her head. "Only that I kept seein' Derry after my baptism, is all."

"Even so, I'm as worried for you as Naomi is. Unconfessed sin is treacherous." She remembered the Scripture Jonas had written in his last letter. *Beholding as in a glass the glory of the Lord . . .* If only she could share *that* just now, but her sister's heart was closed up; Leah knew by the hard look of frustration on Sadie's face.

Sadie rose and shoved the hoe deep into the ground. "I don't care anymore what happens to me."

"You're upset, that's all. You don't mean it."

"Oh, but I do."

"Sadie . . . sister, don't you want to obey the vows you made to the church . . . to God?"

"Don't fret over me. The covenant I made was false."

"I fear that's even worse."

"Let God be the judge of that."

Leah felt the breath go out of her. "I can't stand by and watch the brethren put the Bann on you. Oh, Sadie . . . I won't!"

"How are you goin' to stop them?"

"By pesterin' you till you agree to do what is right. Wouldn't you do the same if the tables were turned? Wouldn't you shake me but gut . . . help me see the error of my ways?"

"You're not me. Be ever so glad. . . ." She was quiet for a time, poking at the dirt with her toe. Then she said, "I'm countin' on you to keep your promise about my baby. Naomi thinks she has something to confess 'bout me, but it's you—and Aunt Lizzie—who know the worst of it."

Leah wished once more she'd never made her covenant with Sadie.

Again she opened her mouth and tried to explain her sense of urgency. "Naomi insists she wants to present herself to the Lord God without spot or blemish so she can partake in holy baptism."

"Am I s'posed to believe Naomi's motives are pure?" Sadie laughed bitterly. "You should've seen *her* with them English fellas."

"But Naomi's sins have been forgiven. She's put her wild days behind her."

" 'Tis hard to believe."

"She hopes the same for you, sister," Leah whispered. "I know this for truth."

"Naomi can't save me . . . neither can Preacher. No one can. Don't you see? It's too late for me. . . ." Sadie began to cry.

Glancing at the house, Leah hoped Mamma or the twins weren't witnessing this exchange. Tears sprang to her own eyes and she reached a desperate hand toward Sadie. Tall and stiff, Sadie remained aloof. "If I could take away your sadness and pain—all of it—even repent and bend my knee in your stead, I surely would," Leah said soft and slow.

"The People would set me up as an example. I'd rather be dead . . . like my baby boy." Sadie covered her face with her slender white hands, her shoulders rising and falling with the sobs.

Her heart breaking for her sister, Leah pressed on. "Won'tcha please talk to Dat and Mamma? They'll help you sort things out, help make things right with the church. Otherwise, Naomi will go an' talk to Preacher and his wife . . . in one month."

Sadie's hands flew up. "I won't . . . I *can't*, don't you see?"

"The People will not withhold forgiveness. So . . . why not confess?"

"Because I . . . I can't forgive myself, that's why" came the sorrowful reply. Sadie wrapped her arms round her own slender waist.

"Oh, Sadie . . ."

"One thing I would ask of Jehovah God if I could . . . and that would be to turn back time."

"Before your rumschpringe?" She hoped that's what Sadie meant.

"You're mistaken. I wouldn't trade those weeks and months, even though at times I loathe Derry for what happened." Sadie's tears spilled over her silky cheeks. "What I want more than anything is to hold my baby again . . . to bring my precious little one back from the dead. I have no right to seek God's forgiveness, don't you see?" Sadie turned abruptly and picked up the hoe, sniffling.

Astonished and pained by Sadie's words, Leah grasped a greater depth of her sister's agony. Sadie both despised and adored her former beau, and the departed baby was the only significant result of the forbidden union. No wonder Sadie was so terribly distressed.

"I'm thinkin' only of you, dear sister," Leah said softly.

"Haven't you done enough? You gave up your summer in Ohio for me."

"Isn't that what sisters do? Even if the People should shun you, which won't happen—will it?—you and I are sisters for always. Nothing can break that bond."

Sadie's expression softened. She leaned on the hoe, nodding. "But you mustn't try to carry the sorrow; it's mine alone."

"You know I'd do anything for you. Ev'ry night I pray for the balm of Gilead to soothe your poor, sad soul." Leah went to Sadie then, and Sadie received her as both girls fell into each other's arms.

"I'll think on what you said," Sadie said through her tears. "I'll think hard about confessin'. Honest, I will."

The flood tide was released. Leah wept in Sadie's arms for at least this glimmer of hope.

On the way out to the cornfield, carrying a tall Thermos of iced tea, Hannah heard Sadie and Leah talking in the vegetable garden. And of all things, it sounded like someone was weeping! *Well, what the world?* She turned to look over her shoulder and saw Leah standing near Sadie there between the rows, looking as if she, too, might be crying.

The sound of her sisters' sadness faded as Hannah distanced herself from the family garden and walked barefoot toward Dat in the field. The corn should have been knee-high by early in July. Sadly, much of it was only a little more than that tall now because of the long dry spell. Though, situated in a lower section of the field, a two-acre clump was thriving due to underground springs.

She turned to glance back at Sadie and Leah once more and decided not to vex herself about her sisters. She had enough to think on. For one, the secret stash of money she'd hidden away. She had no idea what would happen if Dat discovered she was planning to assist Mary Ruth in her quest for education, in spite of her own misgivings. With all the books piled up under their bed, she'd have to make sure no one but Mary Ruth helped move it away from the wall during early fall housecleaning!

Soon she was within earshot of Dat and the smithy Peachey. "Short of talking again to Gid, I have no idea where to go from here," the smithy was saying.

"I've done all I can and then some," Dat replied. "But let's not give up just yet."

Hannah called to her father. What an awkward situation. She hoped he might hear her and cease his discussion with the smithy.

Dat's expression changed when he saw Hannah and the Thermos. "Hullo!" he greeted her, shielding his eyes with one hand and waving big as you please with the other.

"Mamma sent some nice, cold tea—honey sweetened and sun brewed," she said, feeling the need to explain why she'd intruded on them.

"Denki, Hannah." He reached for the Thermos, exchanging glances with smithy Peachey, and right away he offered the cold drink to his neighbor and lifetime friend.

She turned to hurry back toward the house. The hillside was draped in purple clover, and in the sunlight the hue was at once as deep as it was radiant. She and Mary Ruth had often gone and rolled in the clover as little girls. Truth was, they still did sometimes at dusk when no one could see they were, indeed, still youngsters inside. But this day they wouldn't relax that way. She and Mary Ruth had an overabundance of chores to accomplish before supper, what with the garden bursting its vines with produce and the vegetable stand needing tending to. On top of that, Mamma had come to rely on both Hannah and Leah to spell her off with baby Lydiann. Mary Ruth wasn't much of a choice, though, since with someone *else's* house to look after, she wasn't around every day of the week. As for Sadie, she wasn't much of a sister *or* a nursemaid, neither one. Hannah had been writing down her thoughts about her surly sister on the lined pages of her diary, so perturbed she was at Sadie sometimes. And she wasn't the only one.

Just this morning when she was helping run the clothes through the wringer, Mamma had said she thought it might be wise for Sadie to go live with Aunt Lizzie for a spell, "till she gets herself straightened out some."

Hannah was stunned—such strong words falling from Mamma's lips. But when Mamma asked what she thought of that, the best Hannah could say was—"Ain't ever wanted any of my sisters livin' out from under Dat's roof. Not just yet."

"Well, I daresay none of them has ever had such a defiant streak." Mamma had frowned and shook her head. Clearly aggravated, she groaned a bit as she bent down to hoist the wicker hamper filled with damp clothing. She carried it out to the yard without even asking Hannah to lift a finger to help.

The two of them hung the clothes on the wash line, and all the while Hannah wished she might have had the wit to say something right quick—even important—like Mary Ruth would have for sure if *she'd* been there helping Mamma. Her twin was never shy about speaking her mind.

Sometimes Hannah was convinced Mary Ruth had gotten all the gumption. Come to think of it, maybe a problem ran in the family when it came to twins. After all, Cousin Fannie Mast had written Mamma recently saying one of *their* twins was behind the other in growth and development. But wasn't it a little silly to think just because you were a twin, one of you might have gotten greedy in the womb with the nourishment? Mary Ruth had never been a stingy sort of girl, in *or* out of their mother's belly. What's more, Mamma had always said they'd each weighed the same, and both had walked and talked on the exact same day.

Hannah decided that more than likely she was bashful by nature, not slow in her thinking, and her hesitancy wasn't the result of being a twin. And she felt she had at least one small gift from the Almighty. Though she would never think of boasting, she believed she had a right nice way of writing down words and phrases. Her diary was living proof.

Nearing the side yard, Hannah raised her head to look again toward the big garden, wondering if Sadie and Leah had talked out their problems. But her sisters were nowhere to be seen.

Chapter Twelve

Later that afternoon Leah hitched the slow horse to the family buggy, then returned to the house and helped Dawdi John limp across the walk. She still couldn't get over Dat having given her the go-ahead to spend a full month in Ohio, however reluctantly. Jonas would be mighty surprised and pleased, and this could go a long way toward bettering the relationship between her future husband and Dat. Now if she could just get together the money for her train ticket.

The sun hid behind a cloud as she and Dawdi rode toward the small medical clinic. Dawdi had complained all last week of his worsening hip, so Mamma had stopped in at Dr. Schwartz's last Friday on her way back from Strasburg and made an appointment.

More than happy to take her grandfather to see the doctor, Leah was equally glad for a bit of quietude—Dawdi being a peaceable man even when seriously ailing. Goodness knew, she needed a breather, and she felt herself relax some while she held the reins, letting the horse do the hard work. Such troubling things Sadie had blurted to her out in the garden.

Seemed, though, there might be a ray of hope for Sadie to confess. Truly, her sister's heart was broken and bleeding.

After their private talk Sadie had gone inside and created a fuss, all because Mamma had suggested Sadie take herself upstairs and lie down. "You look so hot in the face," Mamma had said sweetly, offering a concerned smile, no doubt noticing Sadie's swollen eyes.

"I'm all right, really," Sadie replied.

"Just thought a rest might do you good."

Then Sadie burst out crying. "I'll go out to the pasture if you say to—coax all the cows home for milkin'—do Leah's chores, but I *won't* be resting!"

Both Hannah and Mamma gasped, though Mamma the louder. "Such foolish words, Sadie dear. Time you behave like a baptized church member . . . and bite your tongue."

Sadie brushed her tears away, standing there silent now.

"You best go to your room," Mamma insisted. "'Tis not becomin' of you to disobey."

Suddenly Sadie brushed past Mamma and Leah, breaking into an all-out run. Out the back door and down the steps she went, toward the barnyard.

"Go now an' talk to Dat!" Mamma called after her, her face boiling red. She probably wanted to holler out in the worst way that Sadie best get inside this minute and do as she said.

But Sadie was already past the milk house and heading for the outhouse; Leah guessed she was flying off to Aunt Lizzie's—a good place for her, in Leah's opinion. Lizzie was the best one to calm down a distraught girl like Sadie, although Mamma might not think so.

For sure and for certain, just now Leah relished this peaceful time with Dawdi John. She looked over at him, hoping Dr. Schwartz could alleviate the severe pain, though at the moment Dawdi looked as relaxed as a sleeping baby, his head bobbing as the horse pulled them gentle and slow down the road.

"I hate Gobbler's Knob!" Sadie cried as she rushed into Aunt Lizzie's kitchen. "Mamma has it in for me. I know she does!"

Lizzie went to her. "Ach, your mamma loves you more than you know, Sadie dear." She led her to the front room and sat her down, loosening Sadie's prayer bonnet to stroke the top of her head. "You just listen here to your aunt Lizzie," she whispered low, beginning to hum a slow church song from the *Ausbund.*

Sadie felt an awful tightness in her neck and shoulders and thought she might burst apart, so distressed she was. Now that she was here, safe and secure in Aunt Lizzie's cozy house, she quite liked all this cooing and whatnot. Lizzie's soft arms and gentle touch made her feel as if, just maybe, the whole world wasn't going to fall apart.

After a time, when her sobbing slowed to a whimper, Sadie lay quietly with her head on Lizzie's lap, soaking up all the love, the soft humming, and an occasional "now there." At this moment she secretly wished Lizzie were her mother instead of merely her aunt. She could only wonder what life might be like living up here in the woods with Aunt Lizzie, not being the eldest sister to three, no, *four* girls, but rather a cousin-sister to Leah, the twins, and Lydiann. Goodness' sake, it was a trial putting up with Mamma's colicky baby crying all hours of the night. "Every time Lydiann wails, I feel like crying, too. 'Cept I do it inside."

"No wonder you weep," Aunt Lizzie said. "You have strong ties to the babe you carried close to your heart—right or wrong—and nothin' can take away the emptiness, now that he's not in your arms."

Sadie raised her head and looked into Lizzie's pretty hazel eyes. "So there's nothin' wrong with me?"

Lizzie smiled faintly. "No, my lamb. Don't be thinkin' thataway."

"Oh, Aunt Lizzie, what would I do without you to talk to?"

"Well, now . . . you'd prob'ly do like we all do, sooner or later, and be talkin' to the Good Lord about your trials."

"What's the point of prayin'?" Sadie asked. "I doubt the Lord would hear me, anyway."

"You may be thinkin' that, but believe me, there ain't a shred of truth to it."

She sat up, wiping away her tears. "Why's it seem so, then?"

"Your spirit's all closed up—like a rock-hard honeycomb. Back when you gave up your innocence, you hardened your heart to the gift of purity that's meant for your husband. You're altogether different now that you've been awakened to fleshly desires, the longings a wife has for her husband."

Sadie felt her pulse pounding in her stomach. She did yearn for Derry every day of her life. "You seem to know what I'm feelin', Auntie."

Lizzie turned to look out the window for a moment. Her

lip quivered slightly. "I'm guessin' it's about time I own up to you. You're plenty old enough now. . . ." She sighed. "Indeed, I do know what you're feelin'. Know it as sure as you sittin' here next to me."

"Whatever do you mean?"

Aunt Lizzie faltered, and if Sadie wasn't mistaken, there was a sad glint in her eyes. "As a young woman I committed a grievous sin against the Lord God, one of the reasons my father, Dawdi John, sent me here to Gobbler's Knob—to escape the shame that was sure to come in Hickory Hollow."

"Are you sayin' what I think?" Sadie asked, nervous to hear more.

"You must keep this between just us. Abram would not want me speakin' of this, not without his say-so."

"*Dat* wouldn't?" She was truly perplexed, yet the urgent look on Aunt Lizzie's face was nearly irresistible.

"He's an honorable man, Abram. Still, he is tight-lipped, and with all gut reason."

Sadie purposely turned to face Lizzie as they sat on the couch. She felt ever so drawn to her aunt now, desperately needing to concentrate on her gentle face, witness the haunting sadness and the truth-light in her eyes as Lizzie whispered tenderly, if hesitantly, of "the darlin' baby girl born to me when I was but a teen." Lizzie's eyes spilled over with tears, but she kept them fixed on Sadie.

"A *baby*?"

Lizzie nodded her head slowly.

"I never would've guessed. Not now, not ever," Sadie whispered, unable to speak in her normal tone, so stunned she was. Had Aunt Lizzie been required to live as a maidel for this reason?

"I've borne this secret these many years."

"Oh, Aunt Lizzie . . ."

"My dear girl, I've suffered the terrible consequence of my sin by not bein' able to raise my child as my own. But long ago I purposed in my heart to follow God in spite of what had happened to me."

"So . . . I'm not the only one to lose a child. . . ." She was aware of Aunt Lizzie's steady breathing. *No wonder I feel so close to you*, she thought, leaning her head against her aunt's shoulder.

Lizzie caressed Sadie's head, and for a moment they sat there, not speaking, scarcely moving.

After a time Sadie opened her eyes. Her heart was bursting with love and sympathy both, and she wondered just where Lizzie's daughter was now, all grown-up. Had one of Dat's or Mamma's many siblings stepped in to raise the little one? She didn't have the heart to ask just now, though she was dying to know.

Leah sat in the waiting room, hoping the doctor could help ease Dawdi's pain, his being the last patient of the day. Dat had said the strangest thing about the sudden onset of Dawdi's health problems the other day. He'd indicated Dawdi surely had something "all bottled up inside," and when she had asked just what that could be, Dat had brushed it off like it was nothing to worry over. Well, far as she was concerned, Dawdi wasn't putting on. She'd seen him shuffle along, nearly lame. She'd seen him wince as he stepped in and out of the buggy, too.

Reaching for a magazine on the lamp table, she opened to a full-page advertisement. A sense of guilt swept over her as she read the caption: *Which Twin Has the Toni?* She stared at the smiling faces of identical twin girls with matching home waves and bare necks. Englishers seemed bent on short hair, lots of curls, and too much skin, along with the many things their money could buy. She had come to this conclusion the few times she'd allowed herself a glance at the magazines displayed here in Dr. Schwartz's office. Convicted, she returned the magazine to the table.

Thinking now of Sadie, she hoped maybe her sister *had* run off to see Aunt Lizzie this afternoon after the spat with Mamma. Surely their aunt could help focus Sadie's mind on holy living—on obedience, too.

Getting up, Leah went to the window and stared out. The lone horse and buggy looked nearly out of place in the empty parking area, yet she was glad for Dr. Schwartz's willingness to see patients besides his English clients.

She pondered again the frightening night Sadie had given birth. She alone had been the reason the doctor had come to help Sadie, having ridden bareback on one of Dat's horses—a phantom ride through the midnight darkness, up the narrow road to the clinic. She recalled how reluctant she had been to travel back to the Ebersol Cottage and up the mule road with Dr. Schwartz in his fast automobile . . . yet she had. Gripping the door handle, she'd worried herself nearly sick at what might await them in Aunt Lizzie's log house.

Moving away from the window, she walked slowly about the room, noticing the many framed photographs on the light-colored walls. Pictures of people intrigued her, perhaps because she had been warned to avoid cameras, ever present in the summer when English tourists came calling. It was all right to display pastoral scenes on the walls, along with cross-stitched designs and floral or nature-related calendars. Bishop Bontrager permitted such things, but photographs of people were downright prohibited.

But here she was met by one smiling face after another, each framed in wood, all English folk. Nearly a whole wall of people dressed in fancy clothes, especially a woman with cropped and curled hair, seated on a white-wicker bench. Two young boys and a man encircled her, all smiling at someone's camera.

Looking closer, she recognized the man to be Dr. Henry Schwartz. *Is that his wife?* she wondered.

Several more photographs featured the foursome, no doubt posing at the photography studio she'd seen in downtown Lancaster, though of course she had never dared darken the door. The last in the lineup was a portrait of a boy with thick brown hair and exceptionally dark eyes, wearing what she guessed was a baseball team uniform, since there was a baseball bat in the youngster's hand.

She was drawn to the smiling face and saw the words: *Thanks, Dad . . . Love, Derry* in the bottom corner.

How peculiar to think someone would actually write on a photograph. But then she guessed that this, too, was another one of the strange customs of the English.

Derry . . .

Suddenly she began to shiver uncontrollably. Her scalp felt prickly as she stared at the boyish scrawl. She'd heard of only one such Englisher by that name in her life.

Her mind was spinning now. But no! This couldn't be Sadie's Derry, could it? *Did Sadie go and fall in love with one of Dr. Schwartz's sons?* she wondered.

Rejecting the notion, she went back and studied each of the framed pictures yet again, discovering one that was surely the same boy, only much older, possibly a graduating high-school senior. She moved back and forth between the two pictures, double-checking the young man's features against those of the child. She was desperate for something more to go on.

At last she spied gold lettering in the far corner and the name of the photo studio. *Gold Tone, 1946.*

Could this be the boy Sadie still wept for . . . the father of her dead baby? Going to sit on one of the several wooden chairs that lined the wall, she felt truly bewildered. If what she suspected was true, then Dr. Schwartz had delivered his own grandson last April.

Her heart was pounding. Her sister had been defiled by the good doctor's son!

She bit her lip, refusing the anger that threatened to overflow. She felt like running out the door and all the way home; she wanted to ease her exasperation but was ever so mindful of her surroundings. *I'll wait right here for Dawdi . . . I must hold my peace. . . .*

To stave off her fury, she turned and looked out the window yet again, across the yard to the road and the forested hillock beyond. She wanted to hurry home and ask Sadie if Derry Schwartz was, in fact, the father. On further reflection, she determined not to. She must not question her sister because it would be one more irritation between them. She was unwilling to further jeopardize their sisterhood.

When Dawdi emerged on the doctor's arm, still rubbing his thigh from the sting of a shot, she felt her head spin a bit. Carefully she rose and helped Dawdi John out the door and down to the horse and carriage. "Ach, I forgot to pay the doctor bill," Dawdi said once she had him settled.

"Not to worry, I'll return tomorrow," she replied, her thoughts in a flurry.

"Denki, Leah. You're such a gut girl."

Gut girl . . .

If only Sadie had been so. If only Sadie had refused the affections of an English boy.

Purposely Leah directed her attention to dear Dawdi, engaging him in slow conversation, attempting to soothe him, as well as to drive away the anger within herself.

Chapter Thirteen

After breakfast Mamma said she would be the one to go to Dr. Schwartz's clinic to pay Dawdi's bill from the day before. "I won't be but a minute," she announced before stepping out the back door.

Sadie was aware of Leah scurrying out to the chicken coop to feed the hens and the lone rooster while the twins kneaded two mounds of bread dough. It was Sadie's morning to tend the roadside stand, but instead of heading there she stood in the window and watched Mamma leave in the carriage. Aunt Lizzie's heartrending confession continued to fill her mind. To think both Lizzie and she had done the selfsame evil in the sight of God. During that troubling time, Mamma and Dat had taken Lizzie under their united wing, helping her through the pregnancy and delivery of a baby girl. But Lizzie had stopped short of telling the whole story, saying, when Sadie had asked at long last what happened to her baby, that the bishop decided the child should be given away. "To be adopted?" Sadie had said, horrified. Lizzie indicated it had been so with a solemn nod of her head. When Sadie pressed for more details, Lizzie assured her "'twas best for the baby, indeed."

Befuddled, Sadie hadn't even thought to ask how old Lizzie's daughter would be by now. She was astounded at the account Lizzie had given of her wild and youthful days. It wasn't any wonder why her wounded aunt was so understanding and kind toward her. Toward everyone whose life she touched, really.

Sadie went and asked Mary Ruth to cover for her out front at the roadside stand. "Just for a few minutes, would ya?" And Mary Ruth reluctantly agreed, washed the flour off her hands, and headed out the back door.

Sadie then crept up the stairs to the biggest bedroom, Dat and Mamma's room. There in the corner, snug in an oversized cherrywood cradle, Lydiann slept soundly. Last night had been a ruckus of sorts, a difficult one for the whole household. Lydiann's crying had kept Mamma and Dat from having much rest at all. Both Sadie and Leah had awakened to Dat's voice, then to his footsteps on the stairs as he headed outside for a spell, probably needing a bit of repose. Mamma had been the one to stay with Lydiann, humming and cajoling, finally getting her settled down again in the wee hours.

Standing over the pink-cheeked bundle, Sadie peered into the cradle. Lydiann's facial features, even her little head, were changing ever so quickly. Maybe all that crying and fussing made her grow faster. In no time at all she'd be sitting up, even crawling, talking . . . and before they knew it, she'd be off to singings, married, and a mamma herself; so the life cycle went. Goodness, Sadie had observed enough babies and toddlers growing up just that quickly in the church and at home, too, right under her nose.

She knelt beside the cradle, touching the side ever so lightly . . . rocking, rocking. She stroked the precious, dimpled hands, soft as cotton. "You're a perty baby girl," she whispered. "But you cry every night like your heart's a-breakin'. What an awful sad time it is round here. But you . . . just look at you. You're all right, Lydiann. You're alive . . . breathin' and growin'. . . ."

She leaned down and lifted the sweet-smelling bundle out of the cradle. Pacing the wide-plank floor in her bare feet, she gazed at the sleeping angel in her arms. *You . . . you're as sweet as a flower, but* my *baby's dead. You came to us just as I lost my own little one.*

She went and sat in the big rocker, across from the dresser, her arms warm with Lydiann's body so close to her. "A sorry excuse I am for a big sister," she whispered. "It's not that I don't love you, Lydiann . . . I do."

She began humming a mournful tune, something Gideon Peachey had played on his harmonica years ago. Back when they, all the girls and Dat and Mamma, had been invited by the smithy and his wife for a family picnic. And Gid, surrounded by his two younger sisters and the four Ebersol girls, had played the sad melody. Maybe he was outnumbered by girls and miserable, or he was secretly longing for a girlfriend, but Sadie had never forgotten the song. Nor the light in Gid's eyes for young Leah, who seemed oblivious to him, except that she nodded her head slowly to his melancholy music.

So Sadie hummed for Lydiann, thinking back over the years . . . all the happy days growing up here in Gobbler's

Knob, playing both in and near Blackbird Pond, swinging on the haymow rope, making grape jelly with Adah and Dorcas, watching Gid with his newest batch of German shepherd pups. . . .

Unexpectedly, the baby stirred, and lest the melody awaken her, Sadie stopped humming and began to rock more steadily. Then, once Lydiann had relaxed again and drifted back to sleep, Sadie talked to her, oh, so softly, scarcely able to stop. "I wish it weren't true, but you'll never, ever know your tiny nephew, my dead little baby. Not this side of the Jordan. You see, the Lord God took him away . . . before he ever had a chance to breathe or live or know how dearly loved he was."

She struggled, trying to hold back the tears lest they fall unchecked onto the tiny cotton nightgown. Besides, if she gave in to her urgent need to cry, she might not stop for a long time, like Lydiann did each and every night. But no, Sadie didn't want Mary Ruth and Hannah aware she was up here confessing her sins to a sleeping baby, of all things.

Confessing . . .

She sat there, rocking and sniffling. Leah's and Aunt Lizzie's constant urging echoed in her ears—and now Naomi threatening to tell if she didn't. . . .

She pondered what it might be like to tell the sorry truth of her sins to her parents and, eventually, to the church brethren . . . how she would kneel low on bended knee in front of the entire membership of the People. Such a hushed silence there would be in the house of worship, with the newly baptized young people staring at her, including the young men.

Awful difficult it was to imagine, yet she persisted. She would be required to speak up enough to be heard not only by the deacon and the preachers, but *all* the People must be able to hear what she and Derry had done in the private haven of the hunter's shack, in the name of love.

She felt the heat of her shame and reproach like the fires of hell licking at her feet. Sadie shuddered at the mental images—the sadness and shock on Mamma's face, the tense set of Dat's jaw, the accusing eyes of the People boring into her, the ministers asking repeated questions.

How could she go through it? How could she repent of loving her child? Repent of her anger toward God, who had *taken* her child, had killed him?

She looked down at Lydiann. The sweet peace of sleep on her wee face gave Sadie a sudden and terrible panic. She realized anew that repentance would mean the loss of everything she'd ever wanted. No boy in Gobbler's Knob would give her a second look, pretty as she knew she was. And worst of all . . . having a dear, precious baby of her own, one just like Lydiann, would be forever impossible.

Hannah felt uneasy standing there in the hallway. She had come upstairs to inform Sadie that Mary Ruth was getting more customers than she alone could handle at the vegetable stand. She preferred not to run out front herself but wanted Sadie to go instead, since it was Sadie's responsibility, anyway.

When she finally found her oldest sister, she almost called to her. But she was taken aback seeing Sadie sitting in Mamma's rocking chair, talking to Lydiann, who was sleeping right through it.

Listening, she overheard the most startling words. *Could it be? Ach no.* Sadie was surely making up a story—a sordid one at that—just talking slow and soft to soothe Lydiann. To be sure, their baby sister had been awful fussy since she came into the world. A person might whisper most anything to quiet down a tot like that. Still, Hannah had not heard Lydiann cry out or fuss at all this morning, not since Mamma left. *So what's Sadie doing up here?* she wondered.

Having listened in this long, she decided it wouldn't hurt to stand here a bit more. The English customers out front would just have to wait their turn with Mary Ruth. She locked her knees and leaned her ear, but what came next shocked Hannah no end. Sadie was cooing to Lydiann, her voice trembling as she spoke of another infant, though dead. "He was my own baby boy. The result of the worst sin I ever committed, yet I loved him so."

Hannah began to wonder just when on earth was it Sadie had been in the family way? If any of what she was babbling was even true.

But Hannah had heard enough. More than she cared to, really, yet she stood there nearly frozen in place, contemplating the meaning of Sadie's confession. Were Mamma and Aunt Lizzie privy to any of this? And what would Dat say or do if he knew? She could scarcely breathe at the thought.

Leah finished up with the chickens, gathering in the eggs before closing the door on their squawking. She hurried to the house as Mary Ruth came flying across the side yard. "It's Sadie's turn at the vegetable stand now," Mary Ruth said hastily. "I'm plumb wore out."

"Oh? What's Sadie doing?"

"I thought *you* knew where she was," Mary Ruth replied.

Leah had no desire to look for or exchange words with Sadie this morning. They'd said not a word to each other last evening as they undressed for bed. She must simply wait and pray Sadie would do the right thing.

She must not borrow trouble and worry over what might be. She turned her thoughts to Jonas. Time at last to write and tell him of her surprising chat with Dat, that her father's heart had softened. She would head up to the woods, to her favorite spot in the sun. No need telling anyone where she was going, not with the day so bright and blue and not a cloud in the sky.

Hurrying upstairs, she bumped into Hannah, who looked rather pale in the face. "Are you ill?" Leah asked.

Hannah shook her head no.

"Is Sadie around?"

Hannah pointed meekly toward Mamma's bedroom. "In there."

Leah turned to look just in time to see Sadie putting Lydiann down in the cradle. "What's she doin'?" she whispered.

"I wondered the same" came Hannah's reply.

Well, wasn't this an interesting turn of events? Sadie was tending to Lydiann without being asked. *What does it mean?* Leah wondered.

Leah turned to Hannah. "I'd like to talk with Sadie . . . alone."

Hannah nodded and headed down the steps.

Without delay, Leah went to Sadie, who was still staring

down at Lydiann. "Sister?" she said, standing near.

Sadie's cheeks were wet with tears.

"What's wrong?" Leah asked, touching her sister's elbow.

Sadie sighed, casting her sad gaze downward. Soon she looked up, her lower lip trembling uncontrollably. "I've been trying, Leah. Honestly, I've been thinking through my kneeling confession, and I can't do it."

For a moment Leah was at a loss for words. Sadie seemed unwavering in her decision. "Maybe later, then. Won't you give yourself a bit more time?"

"I'm simply markin' time now, waitin' with no purpose," Sadie replied. "Don't you see? There's no hope of a normal life for me here. Not anymore . . ."

"Oh, Sadie, that's not true. You're still grievin' for your baby. Things will certainly get better. Won't you reconsider?"

"Jah, things *will* be better, and soon, because I'm leavin' home."

Such unexpected words made Leah feel queasy. "Leavin'? But . . . I'm gettin' married soon. Won't you be here for that special day?"

"I'm awful sorry, Leah . . . truly I am." Sadie's eyes glistened with more tears.

"Where are you thinkin' of going?"

Sadie shrugged sadly. "Doesn't matter really. Anywhere. Maybe I'll set out on foot, then hitch a ride on the road."

Leah was horrified. "That's too dangerous."

"I just can't wait anymore." Sadie shook her head. "I thought I could stay put, but I can't. Once Naomi goes to the preacher 'bout me, the ministers will demand penitence . . .

and when I refuse, I'll be shunned. What's the point in stayin' any longer?"

Leah felt her throat close up. Yet she managed to ask, "Can't you talk to our parents, at least?"

"And tell them what? *Why* I'm leavin'? That I had a baby out of wedlock and I can't apologize to God?" Sadie looked over at Mamma's pretty blue go-to-meeting dress, hanging on the wooden peg. " 'Tis best I disappear."

Leah slipped her arm around her sister's waist. "Would you wait at least another day or so?"

Sadie looked pained. "Why? So you can tell everyone I'm goin'?"

Leah shook her head. "I promise not to, truthfully."

Sadie seemed to give it some thought. "All right." She sighed, her shoulders falling. "For you, I'll wait a bit. I can trust you, Leah. You and Aunt Lizzie."

"What about Dat and Mamma—you can trust them, too, ain't?"

"Maybe, 'cept they hold fast to the Old Ways. They'll never understand what's in my heart."

Leah breathed deeply, still vexed. "You won't just up and leave, then, not until we talk again?"

Sadie consented. "I'll say good-bye to you, jah. I promise."

Leah reached for her sister, who trembled in her arms. They clung to each other as Sadie quietly wept. *How much time do I have left with her?* she worried. *If Sadie leaves, the Bann will separate us . . . possibly forever.*

Sadie brushed away her tears and kissed Leah's face. Then she headed out to help mind the vegetable stand.

Watching Sadie go, Leah recalled her plans to write to

Jonas. Here, just a few moments before, she had been rejoicing with the good news she couldn't wait to share with him, that she would see him soon. And now? Everything had been colored by her dismal conversation with Sadie.

But wasn't her first responsibility to her beau? She had pledged her love and life to Jonas Mast. Sadie, on the other hand, was bent on making wrong choices, as seemed more evident with each day that passed.

Leah felt frustration toward her sister . . . yet at the same time, she felt ever so guilty for feeling so. Sadie had promised to stay for a few days longer, so perhaps Leah might have time to talk her out of running away. And if *she* couldn't reason with Sadie, maybe, just maybe, Aunt Lizzie could. Although the determined look in Sadie's eyes had frightened Leah no end.

Heaving a sigh, she headed down the hall to their bedroom, taking her best stationery pad and pen from her bureau drawer. Then she hurried back downstairs to the kitchen, where Hannah and Mary Ruth were busy scrubbing the floor on their hands and knees. "I'm goin' for a quick walk," Leah told them.

She dashed outside, looking toward the road as she went. She could now see that Sadie was busy with a customer. *'Tis gut,* she thought, glad everyone was accounted for, especially Sadie.

She spied Aunt Lizzie near the barn, hitching a horse to the carriage. "Are you headed somewhere?" she called to her.

"Over to Mattie Sue Byler's for a canning frolic," Lizzie said, smiling. "You?"

She remembered her promise to Sadie and decided not to

breathe a word. *How many more times must I make such promises to that sister?* Leah thought.

"My morning chores are done, so I'm off to write a letter," she said, hoping her voice didn't betray her stirred-up emotions.

Lizzie seemed to be in a hurry, but her eyes registered concern. "Watch closely for my tree markings, hear?"

"I know my way there and back."

"For certain?"

"No need to fret over me," she insisted. "I'll return well before the noon meal."

"All right, then." Lizzie waved and tore down the lane, the horse going too fast for Leah's liking.

Leah hiked up to the edge of the woods, eager to think about other things. This close to the end of August, she noticed the mornings felt cooler than even last week. Mary Ruth and Hannah would be starting school next Monday, the twenty-fifth. But today they would tidy up around the house, help weed the gardens, and maybe bake an apple dapple cake for supper. And they'd all be helping Mamma can plenty of pears and peaches this afternoon. Once she returned from writing her letter, she'd help Dat some, too, though it looked like Gid was already in the barn pitching hay to the mules.

Aunt Lizzie was right about these woods being daunting. The minute she stepped past the clearing and onto the densely treed hillock, she felt a foreboding, although it was probably just her distressed state of mind.

She looked for the first marked tree . . . there it was. The path led across furrows and hollows through the deepest brushwood. Then, when she reached a rather low summit, she caught glimpses of the horizon to the north, the blue of the sky like a wide ribbon woven through the trees.

She was alone. Not a single soul was within calling distance. Now she could sit beneath the honey locust tree and put aside her fear for Sadie. It was time to dwell on the fact Dat had said she could go to Ohio. Who would have thought it?

In this vast forest, she felt herself equal in smallness to the tiniest woodland creatures scurrying here and there as they sensed her presence. In the sight of the Lord God, was she like a little bird? A robin, a jay, a common wren? She understood from Dat's big Bible that the Lord was in all places at once—everywhere present—and all-knowing and wise, too. Could He see into her heart and know the things that concerned her? Did He see Sadie's sorrow, too?

She watched eagerly for the next tree marking, and the next, each put there so kindly by Aunt Lizzie. Walking quickly, she was eager to get to her spot, not taking time this day to pick up a pretty stone or a wild flower as she went.

At last she laid eyes on the enormous tree, a hint of yellow in the leaves welcoming her to the verdant place. Getting situated, she took a moment to orient herself, breathing in the rich, lovely scent of the forest. High in the canopy, squirrels leaped back and forth overhead and bees collected nectar.

She thought of Jonas's descriptions of Millersburg and longed to see it for herself. He had written of Killbuck Creek and its wide creek bed and clear waters, scurrying over rock and limb until it ran smack-dab through town. All the familiar trappings of the area came alive for her in his words, including the Swiss cheese factory near Berlin and the old Victorian house in Millersburg, considered a mansion in every way. An old general store was situated across from the majestic courthouse, Jonas had said, with its ornate stone exterior and unusual clock at the top of a tall turret. The historic building was surrounded on all sides by formal, well-manicured lawns, where courting couples liked to go and sit at dusk, ice-cream cones in hand. She assumed Jonas would take her there, too, when she went to visit him. Oh, if only the days till then would pass more quickly!

She began to write her letter, pouring out her heart to her darling, sharing all of her hope for the future—theirs together—putting it down on the page. She wrote how truly happy she would be to go to Ohio and meet David Mellinger, the man who had made Jonas's long-time dream come true, as well as the master carpenter's wife and family. She told Jonas she was beholden to them for the invitation to stay with their widowed mother, Edith, in the Dawdi Haus, and she kindly offered any help she might give to the ailing woman.

Such a pleasant time we'll have together, Jonas, in the days before our wedding. I'm also curious to learn more about the bishop there—the one you spoke so fondly of—and his teachings.

Referring to the Scripture Jonas had shared in his last letter, she couldn't help but think again of Sadie. Did her sister honestly think leaving Gobbler's Knob would make things better for her?

Suddenly a most unsettling notion came to her. Leah

sighed so loudly in response, she frightened a chipmunk nearby. Would sitting under the teaching of the Ohio bishop be of some benefit to distraught Sadie? According to Jonas, the man was well versed in New Testament Scripture, a rare thing amongst the Old Order.

Leah agonized, thinking of Sadie's delicate emotional state. She doubted her sister could survive on her own away from home. Even though Sadie might fancy herself a confident woman, Leah feared she might be harmed or taken advantage of—or worse yet, be pulled deeply into the English world, never, ever to return.

Placing her trembling hand on her heart, she breathed slowly. *Should I offer Sadie the chance to go to Ohio?*

Tears sprang to her eyes. This idea brewing in her heart—had it been put there by the Lord God? She wondered if she had any right to think like that. *What shall I do?*

She went back and forth in her mind, torn between what she desired for herself and Jonas, and what might possibly be best for Sadie. Yet another hurdle would be to convince her parents—for the sake of Sadie's right standing in the eyes of God and the church. Perhaps, too, Jonas could befriend Sadie without having to know the details of her sins, nor her persistent rebellion. He need only know she was desperate for a change of scenery, at least for a time. Then, when Jonas returned for the harvest, he could simply accompany Sadie back home. Surely by then she'd be ready to offer her repentance. The short time away would also spare Sadie from suffering even a temporary shunning, most likely.

The biggest obstacle was dear Mamma. She would grieve Sadie's leaving, no question. On the other hand, Dat would be relieved to have Leah's help for a while longer than he expected, but he'd certainly want to know why Sadie must go away. Therein was another knotty problem. But she knew enough to trust God, and the more she thought on it, the more she believed the idea *had* been planted in her heart by the almighty One. The crooked way would be made straight, and the rough places made plain.

Unwavering in her resolve, Leah began to tear her letter to Jonas in half, then in fourths, till she had a dozen or more pieces. They lay in the lush grass beside her, and she touched them gently as she wept. A second refusal from her to Jonas. *Will he have an understanding heart?* she wondered. Somehow . . . someway, she hoped he might.

A breeze came up and scattered the pieces out of reach before she could attempt to rescue them. She felt nearly helpless, watching them flutter through the trees as they came to light on moss and twig, like the haphazard markings of a lost soul.

Chapter Fourteen

Around eleven-thirty in the morning, Ida's dinner of veal loaf, baked macaroni and cheese, buttered lima beans, and fresh-tossed greens was ready to serve. She wanted Abram and the girls to come and sit down right away while the main course was still nice and hot. Since Sadie was tending the roadside stand and Ida hadn't seen Leah around all morning, she suggested Mary Ruth ring the dinner bell to alert the family.

The loud *dong-dong* brought Abram in promptly, and he headed for the sink.

"Is Leah on her way in?" asked Ida.

"You mean she's not in the house with you?" Abram glanced over his shoulder, rubbing soap over his big, callused hands.

"I thought she was outdoors. Have *you* seen her, Hannah?"

"She was standin' right here last I saw her," Hannah said, holding wide-eyed Lydiann, awake from a long morning nap.

"But that was hours ago. She said she was goin' for a walk somewhere."

Mary Ruth spoke up. "She and Aunt Lizzie were out talkin' together earlier."

"Before Lizzie left for Bylers'?"

"Jah, 'bout then." Mary Ruth placed hot pads on the green-checked oilcloth. "I daresay she might've hopped in the buggy with Aunt Lizzie, come to think of it."

Ida dismissed that comment; Lizzie had better sense than to allow that. Besides, Ida didn't think Leah would be interested in a canning frolic at Gideon Peachey's grandparents' place. For that reason alone, she was sure Leah had not gone with Lizzie.

She *had* noticed Leah picking at her food here lately and wondered if something was troubling her. *Is that why Leah isn't home for dinner?* she wondered.

"Ain't like her not to tell someone," Hannah said, handing Lydiann to Mamma.

Abram added, "Oh, she'll be along soon enough, I 'spect."

But by dinner's end, Leah still had not come. "Shouldn't one of the girls go lookin' for her?" Ida suggested, beginning to worry.

Abram pulled on his beard, squinting his eyes. "Maybe she got to talkin' to Adah over at the smithy's . . . and just stayed round there for lunch."

But Ida doubted that. Leah was being real careful not to run into Gideon Peachey too often these days. Abram's remark was downright silly, and he knew it.

They bowed their heads for the after-mealtime prayer, but Ida beseeched the Lord God heavenly Father for Leah's protection, especially if she'd taken herself off to the woods. Heaven knew, Leah ought not to be up there alone.

Completely off course, Leah pursued yet another direction. This time the way was even more densely overgrown with hedge and briar, leading to an outcrop of rocks and the sudden smell of animal carcass below. She shook her head, frustrated she'd gotten herself so disoriented after telling Aunt Lizzie she felt right confident. *What would Dat say if he knew?* But Dat hadn't any idea of her dilemma or that she'd even set off for the woods. None of the family did.

Why didn't I think to tell someone besides Aunt Lizzie? she thought.

The farther she went, the less visible the sun became, its light blocked by thick clusters of branches overhead, webbed and interlocked like an enormous barrier between heaven and earth.

By late afternoon Ida was beside herself with concern. Abram was out running errands, and she didn't dare try to set off looking for Leah on her own. She wouldn't consider sending her frail father to search, not with his bad hip, nor the twins. With Lizzie gone, the only other option was Sadie, but Ida didn't feel comfortable sending her eldest off to the dark woods. Until her rumschpringe Sadie had always been a home-body, and Ida hoped to nurture that in her again. Besides, it would never do if *two* of their girls got themselves lost up there.

Pacing back and forth between the barnyard and the kitchen door, she spied Gid strolling through the cornfield big as you please. "Say, Gideon!" she called to him, and the smithy's son came running. When she explained Leah had been gone since morning, "didn't even come home for the noon meal," Gid's face dropped and turned nearly ashen.

The young man sprang to life. "I'll take King along for some company," Gid said, calling to the German shepherd.

Ida was ever so glad; she felt she could rely on Gid to bring their girl home safe and sound. If anyone could, he could. She hoped and prayed it would be so.

The first signs of Leah were a few snippets of cream-colored stationery, torn to shreds. Gid picked up several, noticing the words *Dear Jonas* in Leah's own hand. Having attended school with her through eighth grade, he could have recognized her handwriting most anywhere. Truth be known, he was more than impressed with her neat writing, not to mention everything else about her, from as early as preschool days on. But lately he'd become more cautious, guarding his heart. He wouldn't allow himself to picture the day Abram's Leah tied the knot with someone other than himself because in his opinion she was the sweetest girl in the Gobbler's Knob church district. Sometimes he thought he might explore another district just once to see what other girls were available, but he hadn't been able to bring himself to do it, not yet. He couldn't imagine another as pretty and sweet as Leah, nor as kind.

Leah's dog sniffed the ground, as if trying to pick up her scent in the depth of the woods. The dog, though intelligent, had not been trained for tracking. Still, Gid was mighty glad for King's company today.

He glanced at the torn pieces of Leah's letter, feeling awkward with them in his hand. Had she changed her mind about something important, tearing up the letter this way? Gid pushed the idea aside. After all, Leah was a girl who knew what she wanted, always had. Just as he and Leah had been friendly since childhood, Leah and Jonas Mast had also been chummy, though even closer, evidently, or so the grapevine had it. Who was he to think otherwise?

Except now, with this torn letter . . .

Cupping his hands around his mouth, he began to call Leah's name loudly. He hoped she was safe, not hurt or frightened in any way. There were enough chilling tales associated with this forest; it wouldn't do for a young woman to come wandering up here alone, especially at night. And, best as he could estimate, dusk was less than three hours away.

He'd heard tell by his father—Abram's closest friend—that something terrible had happened to Lizzie Brenneman one night in the midst of her rumschpringe in these very woods. As a result, Lizzie had ended up with child, or so he thought the story went. Providentially, only a handful of folk had been aware of the circumstances at the time, and Bishop Bontrager had promptly ordered the whole thing hushed up.

But now, in the midst of his own "running-around years," Gid was surprised to discover more than a few young people held an alarmed apprehension of the enormous, dark Gobbler's Knob forest—especially the girls. It was as if Lizzie

Brenneman's secret had slowly trickled out over the years.

Leah, however, must not have heard the warnings, though he didn't see how, being Lizzie's niece and all. How was it possible for the Ebersol girls not to be privy to at least some of the dark rumors? For Lizzie's sake, he certainly hoped Abram's daughters *had* been protected from the truth. It wouldn't do to harp away on a close relative's painful past, even a shameful sin—though thoroughly repented of, to be sure.

When Gid finally found Leah, he had been tramping through the wilds for a good forty minutes or longer. There she was, perched forlornly on a fallen oak tree, a mystified frown on her pretty face. "Did you hear me callin' back to you?" she asked when she saw him. "I heard you a-hollerin' . . . heard King's barkin', too. Oh, I'm so glad you found me!"

He hurried to her side. "I heard you, all right. I'm glad you're safe."

"I'm just tuckered out, is all. I've been wanderin' round and round in these woods—for hours, seems to me."

"Do you know what time it is?" he asked, kneeling in the leaves.

"Past dinnertime, I'm sure."

Knowing Leah as he did, he was fairly certain she was being plucky for his sake. She must have been awful concerned . . . and hungry. Then he saw tears well up in her eyes. At once gone were his former intentions, his determined stand against getting too close. Where Abram's Leah was concerned, his heart was still tender, though he would have liked to think otherwise. "I could carry you home if . . . well, that is, if you're too wore out to walk."

"Oh, I think I'll manage." She looked at him and smiled, then glanced at her stationery pad in her lap.

"Your family is awful worried, Leah. We daresn't delay," he said, enjoying these stolen minutes more than he cared to admit.

"When I got lost this morning, I realized I'd mistakenly told only one person where I was goin' . . . Aunt Lizzie." She paused, looking at him with inquisitive eyes. "She must not be back from Grasshopper Level yet."

"Far as I know, she wasn't." He nuzzled King, too aware of the awkward silence between them. To break it, he said, "Your dog here is a mighty gut companion. And even though he ain't a trained hunter, he sure seemed to know where you were."

"He prob'ly followed the smell of the barn on me," she replied.

This brought a peal of laughter, and his heart was singing. Was there any chance for them? Any at all?

King went and licked Leah's face, and she put her head down and talked to him like he was one of the family. Then she looked up at Gid. "I'm so grateful to you," she said, still smiling. "And to your dog."

"He's *yours*, don't forget." He watched her face, the brightness in her eyes. *No*, he thought, groaning inwardly. *I must deny my affection for her. Soon she'll be married to another.*

For now it was enough to see Leah smiling, knowing she'd been found.

Sadie watched as Dat, Mamma, Dawdi John, and the twins all stood out in the backyard, eyes trained in anticipation on the woods beyond the barn. She had to wonder if such a fuss would be made over her once *she* turned up missing. The look of dire consternation in Dat's eyes just now was ever so telling.

"How long ago did you send Gid to search?" Dat asked Mamma, his right hand resting firmly on his lower back, as if in pain.

"More than an hour ago." Mamma shifted Lydiann in her arms.

"Why'd she have to go and get herself lost?" Sadie spoke up.

"Now, daughter . . ." Dat came walking toward her. He lowered his hat and his voice both at the same time. "You've done things twice as dumb as this," he said so only she could hear.

His remark took the breath clean from her.

She had nothing to say in response and wished she could run fast away. But she waited till they, one by one, headed inside for some cold drinks, Dat declaring up and down for her to holler right quick if she saw Leah or Gid, either one. She stared at the back door, her bare feet planted firmly in the grass as she peered past the screened-in porch and into Mamma's big kitchen beyond.

Once she was sure they were all preoccupied with ice-cold tea and whatnot, she stole away to the outhouse. Stopping to look back from that vantage point, she checked to see if they'd even noticed she was gone, then hurried on up the mule road, fast as she could go, to the woods herself.

Out of breath, she stopped for a moment near the old stone wall that surrounded Aunt Lizzie's vegetable and flower gardens. From far in the distance she heard the music of a harmonica and spirited laughter, and she caught a glimpse of Gid and Leah, the dog on their heels. Carefree-like, they made their way down the long rise together.

Sadie stared at the smithy's son and her own sister with unbelieving eyes. She never would've expected to see them like this. Not with Leah planning to marry Jonas here in a few months, if not weeks.

Yet there they were, Gid and Leah, holding hands and laughing and talking, looking like they felt awful cozy together.

She crouched behind the ivy-strewn barrier, making sure neither one could spot her.

Chapter Fifteen

The family gathered around Leah and Gid, making over Leah.

"The lost is found," Dat said, eyes shining. Mamma nodded, hovering near.

Hannah glanced around and noticed yet another sister missing. "Well, now, where's *Sadie*?" she asked Mary Ruth, who stood close by.

"I just saw her here. But maybe she's up there." Mary Ruth looked toward the outhouse.

Hannah didn't think so, but she kept silent. Instead, she continued to stew over Leah having disappeared for so long as all of them thanked Gid repeatedly for bringing her home safely.

Dat followed close beside Leah as they headed toward the house, his arm out slightly as if he might scoop her up and carry her inside. Once indoors, Mamma insisted on sitting Leah down in Dat's hickory rocker in the kitchen and giving her some fresh-squeezed lemonade. Then she poured some for everyone.

All the while, Gid's face kept changing colors from pink to red and back again, and Hannah wondered what *that* meant. She kept her eyes wide open, noting how he spoke ever so kindly, if not tenderly, to Leah. And she knew, right then and there, why Dat had set his sights on Gid Peachey for Leah. Such a thoughtful young man he was. *What's kept Leah from losing her heart to Gid?* she pondered. *Did Jonas simply catch her attention first?*

Just then Gid began to recount how he'd found Leah in the woods. "King, here, sniffed his way to her, just like a trackin' dog."

"But we know he ain't that!" Dat said, having himself a hearty laugh, surely aware even the dog was fond of Leah, just as they all were.

Especially Gid, Hannah noticed again.

Except for Sadie now being the absent one, it looked as if things might return to normal this evening. She hoped so because she didn't ever want to endure another day like this. She wanted her family, each one, to remain sheltered and altogether free from care. It wasn't good for a body to get as worked up as they all had been.

A few hours after Leah's return, Aunt Lizzie and Sadie came wandering into the kitchen together. Smithy Gid had been gone for quite some time, and the rhythm and routine of the family was as expected, even though supper was to be served much later than usual.

Leah was relieved to be home. Gladly, she helped Mamma and the twins with the cooking and took turns keeping Lydiann occupied and happy.

Due to her own difficult decision made while in the woods, Leah felt her joy had evaporated—her month-long visit to Ohio was not to be. Yet she believed her idea was Sadie's best and only hope.

The minute she and Sadie were alone in their room, she revealed Jonas's written invitation and their father's unexpected decision. "Dat gave me his blessin'," she said, then paused. "But now . . . I'm startin' to think it might be best if I don't go at all. Why don't you go instead?"

Sadie, suddenly wide-eyed, stared at her. "You want *me* to?"

"Jah, and stay with the Mellingers' elderly mother—you'd have a right nice visit."

"You're giving up your time with Jonas?"

Slowly at first, Leah opened her heart to her sister, sharing what she felt was of the greatest importance. "The bishop there might help you, Sadie."

"You really think this is a gut idea?" Sadie rose and walked the length of the room and then turned to face her sister. "Do you honestly think Dat might agree to this—me tradin' places with you?"

Leah's heart sank. "It would keep me on here longer—helpin' him outdoors and all."

"I wasn't goin' to tell you this, but I had once thought of headin' to Ohio." Sadie paused a moment before continuing. "Aunt Lizzie got me thinkin' that way last spring, said she'd give me money for a bus ticket. . . ." Her voice trailed off.

Leah remembered her conversation with Lizzie in the hunter's shack. "But this is better; it's the perfect situation," she said. "And you'll be back before too long."

Leah spoke up again quickly, sharing what Jonas had said of his bishop being so knowledgeable about the Scriptures. "Now, what do you think of that?"

To this Sadie nodded. "I wouldn't mind attendin' the Mellingers' church."

Leah was startled, really, at how easy it had been for the light to dawn in Sadie's heart. But wouldn't Dat and Mamma nix the idea? Unless they didn't have a chance to. . . .

Why not help Sadie leave secretly . . . not tell a soul? she thought. But how could that happen, and with what money?

"How soon can you be ready to leave?" she asked Sadie.

"By tomorrow if need be." Sadie's reply was not only swift but certain.

"That quick?" Leah asked, quite startled. Seemed her sister would be gone before Leah even got accustomed to the idea.

◆

After milking the next morning, Leah returned to the house from having used the telephone at Dr. Schwartz's clinic to call Jonas. Right quick she sought out Mary Ruth, knocking on the twins' bedroom door.

"Hannah, is it you?" asked Mary Ruth.

When Leah opened the door, she found Mary Ruth dressed, all but her long apron. Her face registered surprise.

"Oh, it's you, Leah. I thought maybe Hannah forgot somethin'," she said.

Leah got to the point. "I need to borrow some money. I could pay you back in a few months. Is that agreeable?"

Promptly Mary Ruth went to the bureau, opened the second drawer, and pulled out her pay for the past several days. "Here, take what you need."

Leah was both stunned and grateful that the way for Sadie's leaving seemed to be ever so smooth. Thus far.

If Sadie *had* to go, at least she'd be safe with the Mellingers. And perhaps she'd have a change of heart while there in Millersburg. Leah could only pray so, because nothing changed the fact that if Sadie didn't return, the People here would shun her—for sure and for certain. Leah hung on to the hope that a short time away from Gobbler's Knob, with Jonas and his minister, was the best thing for her troubled sister. After all, she believed the whole idea had been given her by the Lord God.

Chapter Sixteen

At this time of year—less than a week before the school year resumed—everyone was so keen on cooler weather they wanted to taste it in the form of Strasburg Bakery's famous and exceptionally delicious sweet rolls. "Sticky buns," as they were commonly referred to, were always added to the specials board every year just before September, and at a discount. Any number of Sadie's relatives and neighbors might have easily made up a batch of them, but there was something special about going to the cheerful shop to eat them.

But this Thursday was not a typical day for either Sadie or Leah. Long before Dat or Mamma had awakened, Sadie had taken her suitcase out to the buggy, and shortly afterward, she and Leah had slipped away to the quaint village of Strasburg, which was a good, long ride in the dark.

By the time they arrived, the sun had begun to peek over the eastern hills. The window shades on the bakery shop had been raised, inviting early risers inside to enjoy the freshly brewed coffee and a variety of pastries.

Entering the bakery, Sadie noticed the place was already

buzzing with folk. Word of mouth was always the best advertisement for both English bakeries and Amish roadside stands. She and Leah stood in the line and waited their turn, knowing full well they had plenty of time before the Strasburg trolley left for Lancaster.

She eyed a large wall poster. *Annie Get Your Gun, an Irving Berlin musical* were the words most prominent. "Annie," who must be Ethel Merman, the woman named on the poster, was all decked out in glittering western attire, staring back at her from the wall as the line to the counter inched ahead.

Once their purchase was made, they found a vacant table, talking softly all the while in their common language, Pennsylvania Dutch, to guarantee the privacy of their conversation—precisely how Sadie preferred it this day. While she and Leah wondered aloud about Mamma's and Dat's ultimate reaction to her unexpected leaving, not to mention Leah's assistance, other customers around them had their own concerns.

At a nearby table there was hushed, somber talk of war casualties, even this long after America's boys had returned to the homeland. The enormous loss of life continued to be on the minds of those whose families had been ravaged by war's calamity, though the community of the People in Gobbler's Knob had scarcely been touched by the horror. At another table, plans for building a new shed were being discussed, and at yet another, women spoke of sewing new Girl Scout uniforms.

Sadie briefly considered asking Leah about Gid Peachey and seeing them in the forest the day before, but she quickly dismissed the idea. This wasn't the time or the place to ask

Leah such a question. Surely she and Gid were simply friends, as Leah had always declared.

After sipping coffee and relishing their sweet rolls, the sisters sat without speaking for a moment. Then Leah licked her fingers before reaching into her pocket to hand a wad of bills to Sadie. "You'll need part of this for your trolley fare and again in Lancaster when you purchase your ticket at the train depot. Be sure to save the rest for your return trip in October."

I won't be comin' back, Sadie thought, a lump in her throat. She mustn't let on, though. She must keep her chin from quivering when they said good-bye.

Sadie felt thankful for her younger sister's unmistakable gentleness, noticing for the first time the beauty that radiated from her smile and the way she sat tall and slender in the chair. Her hazel eyes shone with tenderness. Strong both in body and spirit, Leah was the kind of young woman a person could entrust her life to. Sadie felt she was doing just that by allowing herself to be secretly whisked off to Ohio.

Sadie and Leah sat together in the family buggy on Main Street, waiting for the trolley. "I guess this is *Hatyee*—so long—for a little while," Leah said, smiling sadly. "'Tis hard to believe you're goin'."

Sadie thought of the many miles that would eventually separate them. "My head's still spinnin', so quick you were to arrange things. I don't know how I'll ever thank you."

"Jonas was a big help with the plannin' . . . though he

knows nothin' at all about what you did during rumschpringe." Leah looked downright glum. "He'll be the one to meet you in Millersburg. Stay alert when you change trains in Pittsburgh, jah? Don't be shy about askin' for directions. It'll be wonderful-gut for you to get away."

They embraced ever so tightly. Sadie hung on to her sister longer than she might have under different circumstances. It was next to impossible to think of saying good-bye forever. "Oh, Leah, thank you for keepin' my awful secret—you and Aunt Lizzie both. You're a dear sister."

Leah's face turned ashen just then. She seemed at a loss for words.

"You'll tell Mamma and Aunt Lizzie I love 'em, won't you? After they realize I'm gone and all. Same for Hannah and Mary Ruth . . . and Dat, too."

"I'll be sure and tell everyone."

Sadie reached for her suitcase. "Don't worry 'bout me, hear?"

Leah nodded. "I've been wantin' to ask you somethin', Sadie. Will you still consider bein' one of my bridesmaids, come November?"

"Well, I—" She fought hard the tears. Truth was, long before then Naomi would have gone to the brethren with her revelation of Sadie's sins. And if so, Sadie could be in Leah's wedding only if she was willing to confess, and they both knew it. Still, she couldn't blame Leah for asking. "It'll be a wonderful-gut day for you and Jonas."

"I really want you to stand up with me," Leah persisted. "Will you think on it?"

"I'll send you a letter in due time." They hugged again.

"I'll be missin' your baptism, too," Sadie said, torn with emotion.

" 'Tis all right."

This was torture, now that she was this far into her flight away from home. To think she might never lay eyes on Leah—on any of her family—ever again.

Sadie did not delay. Climbing down from the carriage, she waved one last time, tears threatening to spill down her cheeks.

"Safe trip!" she heard Leah call.

Turning to look once more, she saw her sister stand, waving to her from the buggy. The horse started a bit, and Leah sat down quickly, still holding the reins tightly in her hands.

The image of Leah, looking so forlorn, even anxious, remained with Sadie during the trolley ride past the Strasburg Mennonite Church and cemetery and down Route 222 to Lancaster.

Once she was settled on the train, she kept to herself, not once speaking to the passenger next to her. She warded off the ever-present stares of the English while covertly looking around herself. Two women with bobbed hair wore interesting dark suits with collared jackets that hugged the bodice, then flared slightly below the waistline. One woman powdered her nose and applied bright red lipstick before opening her book, *The Egg and I* by Betty MacDonald. Sadie wondered how the author had come up with such a peculiar title.

The passenger across the aisle and up one seat was reading a page from *The New York Times*. A half-page advertisement for something called *A Streetcar Named Desire* caught Sadie's attention, but she had no idea what such a thing as Broadway was.

Turning toward the window where she sat, she realized just how excited she was to be on a train for the first time—going *anywhere,* really—as the rhythmic sway of the passenger car lulled her into thinking she was indeed doing the right thing. To think it was Leah, of all people, who had made it possible for her to take the train, which ran from Pittsburgh west to Orrville, Ohio, before heading south to Millersburg.

Already, Sadie was missing home. Dear Mamma and Dat, her sisters, and Aunt Lizzie, along with the deceased baby she'd birthed—missing *him* every day she lived. She must dry her endless tears and attempt to make a new life for herself, leaving the old behind, including her constant thoughts of the love she'd shared with Derek Schwartz. Hard as it was to forsake the only folk she'd ever known, she must set her mind on meeting a good Amish boy and becoming his wife someday. Nothing else would do.

The more Mary Ruth read from the book *Uncle Tom's Cabin,* the more outraged she became. She thought constantly about the enslavement of helpless black folk—during her chores, on the way to house church, and while she prayed silent prayers at night. *What a torturous life poor Tom led in the south!* she thought sadly.

Sometimes her imagination ran unchecked, and she wondered if somewhere in the world there were other men as cruel as plantation owner Simon Legree. *Never in Pennsylvania Amish country*, she assumed. Her world was far different; she was safe here.

She would not think of breathing a word of this book, or any like it, to her family. Not even to Hannah, though she had heard last year from several students at the Georgetown School that the book was required study in high school. That being the case, she'd done herself a favor by devouring it ahead of time.

When she scurried downstairs to help Mamma with breakfast, she was startled to find Sadie nowhere around. To top it off, Dat was just now coming in from the barn, asking, "Ida, have ya seen Leah?"

Mamma's red and swollen eyes told a sad story.

◆

Abram locked his legs deliberately where he stood, there in the lower portion of the barn where he milked, fed, and watered his cows daily. He listened with ears to hear, but he did not comprehend—not immediately—the things Leah was telling his weeping Ida and him. "What do you mean, you helped Sadie leave home?" Bewildered, he took off his hat. "Why would you do such an impulsive thing, daughter?"

Leah hung her head.

"Ain't like you, Leah," Ida spoke up.

At last Leah raised her head. "Sadie was . . . well, afraid you wouldn't give her your blessin' to go away."

Ida was rocking back and forth as she sat on a milk stool.

"Your sister's wants and wishes haven't influenced you before. How could you act on your own judgment, without your father's say-so?"

"Truth be told, Sadie was plannin' to sneak away on her own."

"And you felt you ought to help her?" Abram felt the ire rising in him and struggled to keep his temper in check. Then, before Leah could respond, he added, "I thought it was you who was lookin' to go out to Millersburg."

"I was, but I honestly thought it wiser for Sadie to be the one. There she'll be welcomed by shirttail cousins—looked after, too. I guess you could say she and I traded spots."

"Just a short trade, I hope," Ida said, her jaw set as she leaned against a bale of hay. Her blue eyes looked faded, as if her tears had washed away some of the color.

"Jah, 'tis what both Sadie and I thought she needed—a new outlook on life for a little while," Leah replied, looking as sheepish as Abram had ever seen her.

"And was this turn of events disappointin' to Jonas? Sadie goin', 'stead of you?" he couldn't help asking.

"Jonas seemed to understand when I called from Dr. Schwartz's office."

"You used Dr. Schwartz's telephone?" Ida was obviously disappointed.

"I left money beside the phone," Leah said. "I know it sounds awful forward, Mamma, but there was no other way to make plans quickly. And since Jonas took the train out there, I knew he could give me advice for Sadie's trip."

"Why on earth was it necessary to do all this so quick-like?" Ida folded her arms over her ample bosom.

Looking up at him, Leah captured Abram's heart anew. "I wonder, Dat . . . and Mamma, did you ever happen to hear Sadie weepin' in the night?"

Ida's sad eyes gleamed and she nodded her head.

Abram didn't own up to having heard any such goings-on. He was more interested in knowing the real reason for Sadie's wanting to up and leave . . . and where on earth she'd gotten the money.

"I believe gettin' away for a bit will help my sister." Leah turned her head and stared at the hayloft.

Scant as it was, that was all the explanation she appeared willing to give for now. Yet he was almost sure Leah knew more than she was letting on. "You must go to Preacher Yoder with whatever you're not tellin' us," he said. "Tell *him* why Sadie's in Ohio."

"But . . . Dat, I love my sister" came the soft protest.

Abram felt he might burst, so frustrated was he. " 'Tis best you confide in Preacher if you care 'bout her at all."

"Sisters may come before a beau," Ida added, "but not before the Lord God or the church." She was growing tearful again. "Oh, what'll we do round here without Sadie?" she whimpered.

He felt right sad for his wife, surely he did. He understood how she felt because he felt the selfsame way toward Leah. Going over, he placed a gentle hand on Ida's shoulder. "Might be this is gut timin', seein' how rebellious Sadie's been lately." It was mighty hard to erase from his mind Sadie's repeatedly unruly ways.

"Maybe she'll appreciate home more once she returns," Leah offered.

Ida wiped her eyes. "Meanwhile, what'll we tell the twins?"

"Best let me think on this and discuss it tonight at supper," Abram spoke up.

Ida nodded in agreement. So it was settled. Hannah and Mary Ruth would be told something—just what, he didn't know yet. He was thankful to have Leah still here living under his roof, that much was certain. Could it mean her affection for Jonas was beginning to fade? He would continue to hold out hope to that end.

"Sadie's visiting some of Fannie Mast's cousins in Ohio for a few weeks," Abram said when they'd all gathered at the table. The twins had begun eating Ida's Swiss steak and rich gravy, but when realization set in, their fair faces drooped identically, as if they'd each lost their best friend.

"This surely is awful sudden, ain't so?" Mary Ruth spoke up. "But Sadie did seem dreadful sad, I daresay. Maybe she'll be happier there."

"Will Sadie be looked after . . . out there, so far away?" Hannah asked shyly.

Abram was glad to reassure his gentle Hannah. So much like Leah, this twin was. Mary Ruth, on the other hand, reminded him of Sadie—a troubling thought, to be sure. "Sadie will be just fine, and you'll hear of Millersburg in her letters."

Leah was nodding at that. "Sadie said she'd write. I 'spect

we'll be hearin' something in a few days."

Mary Ruth looked up from her plate and gazed at Leah just then. Abram noticed the knowing glance exchanged between the two. *Just as I guessed,* he thought. *Mary Ruth provided the money for the train ticket.*

Later, during Bible reading, he read from the Ninety-first Psalm to comfort his family. " 'He that dwelleth in the secret place of the most High shall abide under the shadow of the Almighty. I will say of the Lord, He is my refuge and my fortress: my God; in him will I trust.' "

Besides him, Mary Ruth was the only one not sniffling as he finished up the chapter.

Lizzie paced back and forth in her kitchen, wishing she'd had a chance to stop Leah from doing what she'd gone and done. She was downright annoyed to hear the news from Abram of Sadie's leaving, much preferring Leah or Sadie to have told of their plans.

Sighing, she was awful sure they'd never see hide nor hair of their pretty Sadie again. *Ach, the pain of it all,* she thought. She stepped out onto her back porch and went to lean on the banister, taking comfort in her colorful garden flowers, nearly too many to count. It was as she leaned hard against the railing that she was struck anew how this whole terrible idea of Sadie's—to forever keep such a secret—was so wrong. She, of all people, knew what it was like to have a secret burning a hole in your heart. And with the knowing came the heartbreak . . . and the praying.

Chapter Seventeen

The day after Sadie's departure, Ida carried sleeping Lydiann to the wooden crib, recently passed down from her sister-in-law Nancy Ebersol, Abram's younger brother's wife. "Sleep tight, little one." She kissed the sweet face, then gently lowered the tiny girl onto the small mattress.

With Lydiann snug for her first long nap of the day, Ida had the idea to get a head start on some fall cleaning. She had to do something with herself to get her mind off her eldest slipping away without thinking enough of them to say something ahead of time. Ever so sneaky, it was. And Abram's Leah . . . goodness' sake, what was *she* thinking by helping Sadie do such a thing?

It wasn't enough for Leah to tell her side of the story hours after Sadie had already left Lancaster by train; Sadie should have spoken for herself. Leah revealed she had gone so far as to contact Jonas Mast to make plans by ringing the telephone David Mellinger kept out in the woodworking shop—ever so surprising *that* was. So . . . the Mellingers were much less conservative folk, it seemed, if they were allowed a telephone on the property. She did know of a family who had urgent need of a phone for emergencies—a child allergic to beestings, she recalled. So maybe David had gotten permission from his bishop for some such reason. A rare thing, indeed. Whatever the circumstances were, the ministers *here* felt strongly that telephones were not to be had by "a holy generation." Let the Mennonites have their telephones, electricity, and automobiles.

Ida much preferred the strict teachings of *their* church district, where the People were encouraged to carry the truth within them, hour by hour, and simply write letters or go visiting whenever they could. After all, they were working toward the highest goal: to get to heaven some sweet day.

Most disturbing was that both Sadie and Leah had taken matters into their own hands. Such behavior was typical of the teen years, though Sadie had already joined church and wasn't considered to be running around any longer. Ida would be ever so glad once all her girls had joined church, safely within the Fold . . . and settled down as young wives. So surprising it was that her pretty eldest daughter hadn't yet chosen a life mate. If only Sadie could be married first, before her younger sister.

She sighed and got to thinking about making ready for heavy-duty housecleaning. *With Hannah and Mary Ruth going off to school next Monday, why not have all the girls pitch in and help?* she thought. Standing at the top of the stairs, she called down to the twins. "Hannah . . . Mary Ruth . . . can you hear me?"

When she received no answer, she assumed they were outdoors, so she headed downstairs herself, to the utility room where she kept her many mops. Back upstairs, she hurried to the twins' bedroom, eager to eliminate any and all cobwebs that might be hiding from view. Though she could not move the heavy double bed herself, she got down on the floor and lifted up the quilt, peering beneath. Pushing the dry mop as far back against the wall as she could, she felt satisfied. Then she rose and went to do the same on Mary Ruth's side of the bed.

This time the dry mop bumped into something, and she raised the quilt even farther. Getting down to look, she was surprised to see books—a good many of them. "Well, what's this?" she whispered, stretching to reach them.

Mary Ruth knew right away she was in hot water when Mamma singled her out upstairs following the noon meal. "I need to ask you something," her mother said.

Gesturing for her to go into the big bedroom, Mamma went and pulled out the bottom drawer of her wide dresser and brought out Mary Ruth's library books. "I dust mopped your room," she said, waving *Uncle Tom's Cabin* at her, "and I found these under your side of the bed. I s'pose they belong to you?"

By the way Mamma's brow knit into a frustrated frown, Mary Ruth knew she was in big trouble. Probably more so, now that Sadie was gone from home and Mamma missed her so. "They belong to the public library," Mary Ruth answered.

"Why is it you have to go behind my back—mine and Dat's?"

"I *like* books, Mamma. I enjoy stories that take me to places I can only hope to see . . . and the story people, ever so different than me." *And some not so different, too,* she thought, thinking of poor Eliza, the slave girl who had very few choices in life, except to mind her mistress. She couldn't go on to say that looking forward to reading a book was one of the best things about getting up in the morning. Could she?

"You ain't so much studyin' with this sort of book but readin' lies, Mary Ruth, don't you see?" Mamma meant, of course, the novels, the made-up stories Hannah had spoken out against, too.

"Books like that have plenty of truth in them. Sometimes it's what the characters learn from goin' through a trial; other times it's—"

"My dear girl," Mamma interrupted, "you best be holdin' your tongue."

"Aw, but, Mamma, you could see for yourself." She hurried to her mother's side and removed Harriet Beecher Stowe's book from the pile. "Just look." She opened the pages to the beginning, hoping against hope Mamma might give her an opportunity to explain.

Her mother gave her a stern look. "You must return the books before they start you thinkin' like the English."

"All the books, Mamma?"

"If they ain't for studyin', then I'm 'fraid so."

That was the last word on the subject. Mary Ruth knew better than to continue to argue. She collected the four novels from Mamma's hands. Suddenly she thought of a place she might store them till it was time to return them to the library. Would Dottie Nolt mind if she kept some books at her house? Since she was headed to the Nolts' after the noon meal tomorrow, the timing was altogether perfect.

"Will you be tellin' Dat?" Mary Ruth hoped to be spared his wrath.

Mamma's eyes softened. "Your father has enough on his mind now, what with Sadie off in Ohio. As long as there are no more books like that kind in this house, he won't know this time."

Sighing, Mary Ruth thought yet again of Dottie, who was as understanding a woman as any she'd known—even if Dottie was an Englisher.

Leah took Dawdi John to another appointment with Dr. Schwartz late in the afternoon. If she got the chance today, she would thank the doctor yet again for allowing her to use his office telephone before clinic hours to make her long-distance call to Jonas. He had even been kind enough to step out of the small room, giving her a bit of privacy. Carefully following Sadie's instructions to tell the phone operator David Mellinger's name and home address, Leah had thought placing the call had been nearly as easy as preparing a picnic. She had been rather astonished at how much Sadie knew about the English world, though in this case, her sister's understanding of the telephone had turned out to be downright helpful.

Until Dawdi would return to the waiting room, Leah

wandered over to the bulletin board near the receptionist's alcove. There she scanned the many personal ads—baby-sitting needed, lost dog, and suchlike.

It was the typewritten notice regarding fall cleaning, a request for window washing, that caught her eye. When she looked closer, she saw the person posting it was none other than Dr. Schwartz. Then and there, she decided if he was willing to hire her to wash the clinic windows, she could earn back the money she'd borrowed from Mary Ruth. In short order, maybe. Truth be told, she was also downright curious about the doctor, who seemed altogether kind and gentle—a far cry from his son, if it was his Derry who had fathered Sadie's baby.

When Dawdi John came out of the examining room leaning on the doctor's arm, she quickly went over and asked what she must do to apply for the job. She turned and pointed to the bulletin board.

Dr. Schwartz lowered his glasses and smiled, narrowing his gaze to focus on her alone. "I'd like to think I'm a man who knows an honest face when I see one." He turned to Dawdi. "Can you vouch for your granddaughter?"

Dawdi John beamed from ear to ear. "Leah's one responsible young woman."

"Then, I say she has the job."

"When would you want me?" she asked, feeling good about this already.

"This Saturday, first thing."

She said she must first help her father with the morning milking but that she could arrive shortly thereafter. "Is that agreeable to you?"

He seemed pleased. "I'll look forward to having clean windows."

"Awful nice of you to lend me your telephone before," she remembered to say as she helped Dawdi to the door.

"Anytime," the doctor replied.

On the ride home, Dawdi asked, "Do you think your father will approve of you working for Dr. Schwartz? He's English, after all."

"Well, why not?" she replied quickly. "Mary Ruth is lots younger, and Dat lets *her* work for Englishers. Besides, it's just a one-time job, not every week like Mary Ruth's work at the Nolts'."

That evening when Leah approached her father about the job at the clinic, Dat said he didn't mind if she wanted to earn a bit of pocket change. She was both glad and relieved, for she desired to continue her peaceable working relationship with Dat. But, more and more, she felt it wrong to hold out on both him and Mamma regarding Sadie's plight.

Her baptism day was soon upon her—hers and Jonas's—and it was time to be honest with herself about just what sort of girl she truly was, deep down. Far as she was concerned, she'd had no right to speak out pointedly to Sadie about repenting, not with her own heart so tainted.

She swept out the barn, then went out to the pasture, fixing to bring home the cows for milking. All the while she battled within herself, feeling more wicked with each passing hour. Here she was learning from the ministers all the Scriptures pertaining to baptism, even memorizing the articles of faith, and what was she doing but concealing a secret sin. Not her own, true, but in a way it might as well have been. The secret pact she'd made with her sister had come between herself and the Lord God. This she knew, sure as the harvest.

Almost immediately on this first full day in Millersburg, Sadie made the surprising discovery that the area postman delivered the mail at four o'clock of an afternoon—the Mellinger spread being the last house on his route. The Widow Mellinger had written out a list of chores for Sadie to do, "once you're settled in a bit." One of the things expected of her was to bring in from the mailbox the widow's many letters coming from Sugarcreek and Walnut Creek, Ohio, and even some from Shipshewana, Indiana. Edith loved hearing from her Friendship Circle, all of them Plain, including several Old Order River Brethren women. Sadie didn't blame Edith—after all, the woman could scarcely move about the Dawdi Haus, what with her asthma acting up. Still, Edith Mellinger went at her correspondence as if her very existence were in jeopardy if she would but dally only a few hours before responding to her beloved pen pals.

David and Vera Mellinger's farmhouse was laid out much like the Ebersol house, with several exceptions, one being a connecting doorway between the large kitchen in the main house and the small kitchen in the Dawdi Haus, where

David's mother, Edith, resided. Back home, the connecting doorways were between the two front rooms, making it a longer trek for Dawdi John to get from his rocking chair to Mamma's table.

Sadie's bedroom was situated on the second floor of Edith's Dawdi Haus—a secluded sanctuary, to be sure, since Edith could barely negotiate the main-level rooms, let alone the stairs. Once Sadie ascended the wood staircase in the evening, she felt as if she were heading off to a vacation of sorts, and glad of it.

Graciously, Vera had urged her to come over "next door" any time at all and help herself to whatever she could find in the icebox. Sadie had felt altogether comfortable around both David and Vera from the start. The three Mellinger children were as delightful and well behaved as any youngsters she'd known. Jonas, too, seemed to be going out of his way to be kind, beginning with his warm smile when he greeted her at the pint-sized train depot.

Today she had just opened the icebox to get some ice cubes for the sun tea Vera had set out on the back porch when here came Jonas into the kitchen. "Would you care for some tea?" she asked.

He nodded. "How'd you know that's what I wanted?"

"By the thirsty look on your face." She felt a little silly saying so.

He chuckled at that. "David sent me in for a Thermos full."

"I'll be glad to fill it for you anytime," she offered.

He stood there, still smiling. "First time away from home?" he asked.

The peace of Millersburg had caught her off guard, and so had Jonas Mast. "Well, jah, I s'pose it is."

"Anytime you're homesick and want to take a walk, just let me know. After all, we're soon to be brother and sister, ain't?"

She was a bit startled by his disarming smile and cordial ways. "Denki," she managed to say. "I'll let you know."

◆

Weary from a long and busy day cleaning the clinic windows, Leah headed upstairs after evening prayers and was quite surprised to discover a small notebook lying open on her bed.

"What's this?" she whispered, picking it up and realizing it was the makeshift diary Hannah wrote in most every day. The note, attached with a paper clip, caught her eye.

Dear Leah,

I feel anxious and peculiar asking you to read one of my recent diary entries, but when you do, I hope you'll understand. I've wanted to share this with you for a few days now, but I've been back and forth with the notion . . . ever so confused, really.

Maybe we should talk privately after you read this.

With love,
Your sister Hannah

Well, she'd never encountered this before. What could be so important her shyest of sisters should invite a peek at her secret musings?

Dear Diary,

This is a sad day for our family. How awful strange not to know what to think or do first. So I'm writing what I know, or believe to know, in this notebook.

To begin with, I innocently overheard my eldest sister say some frightening things to baby Lydiann this morning while Mamma was gone from the house. Sadie was holding Lydiann in her arms, talking ever so softly about another baby. A baby boy Sadie had supposedly birthed—but he had died for some reason, she said. I'm guessing I must've heard wrong. Surely none of this is true. Is my Sadie suffering in the head? I'm ever so worried for her!

Now I fear I must tell Mamma . . . or Leah, maybe. Otherwise, I cannot live with this knowledge. Please, dear Lord God heavenly Father, may Sadie understand that by my recording these words here, I am doing what I believe to be right for her sake. Not for any other reason would I reveal any of this.

Respectfully,
Hannah Ebersol

Leah looked around the room she'd shared with Sadie her whole life. The place seemed too empty just now. *What am I to do?* she wondered.

But she knew she must nip in the bud those things Hannah had overheard. She took the diary notebook with her and headed down the hall to Hannah and Mary Ruth's bedroom.

Leah knocked and poked her head in after one of them said, "Come in." Turned out both twins were dressed for bed, and Mary Ruth had begun brushing her strawberry blond locks.

Hannah was sitting on the cane chair near the dresser,

removing her white head covering. "What is it?" she asked, glancing nervously at Mary Ruth.

Leah motioned with her finger, trying not to call too much attention to herself, carefully keeping Hannah's diary behind her back. "Can you come to my room for a minute?" She hoped Mary Ruth wouldn't trail along as she often did. Where one twin went, the other seemed content to follow.

Once Leah had quietly closed her door, she opened Hannah's notebook to the revealing page. "I just read this. You did the right thing, sharin' with me this way."

Hannah was silent, brown eyes blinking.

"Best keep mum about this for now." She paused. "No need worryin' Mamma and Dat."

Hannah nodded, seemingly willing to keep both her diary closed and her lips locked tight.

Such a sorry situation this was. Not only did Naomi Kauffman and Adah Peachey know something of Sadie's sin, but now Hannah knew—and knew the worst part of it. *Goodness' sake*, Leah thought, *it won't be long before everyone knows!*

Chapter Eighteen

Ida sat next to Abram in the front seat of the open spring wagon, brooding over Sadie, now absent more than a week. The sun was exceptionally warm for the second to the last day of August, and there was precious little breeze as they rode to Grasshopper Level for a Saturday afternoon visit with Peter and Fannie Mast. Ida was awful glad to have received word from Millersburg, though not directly from Sadie. Vera Mellinger, David's wife, had taken time to pen a quick note, saying, *All is well here with your eldest. We'll take care to see she attends church with us, as well as Bible study on Wednesday nights.*

Neither Ida nor Abram had figured Jonas was involved in such a forward-looking church. The Amish here shied away from organized study of the Bible. So now Sadie, too, would be attending a more open-minded community. Still, Leah had said Jonas spoke favorably of the bishop there, so Ida tried to set aside her concerns and simply look forward to Sadie's return in time for the Mast-Ebersol wedding. She would pray all was well with her dearest girl.

In the second seat of the wagon, Leah and Aunt Lizzie sat together, with Hannah and Mary Ruth on the bench behind them. The wide cart was still full despite having a bit more breathing room, given Sadie was absent and Dawdi John had decided to stay home and rest. In no time Lydiann fell asleep in Mamma's arms, lulled by the swaying and the peaceful *clip-clopping* of the horse's hooves.

Leah watched the landscape drift slowly by—plentiful trees, songbirds, grassy fields, and acres of cornstalks standing sentry. She wished she might relive the day she'd gotten herself so mixed-up in the forest—embarrassingly lost. Thinking back on it, she felt downright peculiar about Gid making over her like he had. She hoped to goodness he hadn't gotten the wrong notion from her. Still, it was awful kind of him to find her and help her home, weary as she'd been.

Sighing, her thoughts flew to Sadie, as they often did now, and her sister's final words to her at the Strasburg trolley. *I'll be missing your baptism. . . .* Sadie had said it so convincingly, as if it truly mattered she wouldn't be a witness to Leah's life covenant.

She wondered how long before a letter from her sister might arrive. After all, Sadie had offered to write, and Leah was glad about that. She felt she might burst into tears, the whole of it was such a troubling thing, even now.

Aunt Lizzie touched her arm, patting it gently. "Best not fret, Leah," she whispered.

Leah knew she must trust in the Lord God heavenly Father on behalf of Sadie. She would try harder to pray more often for her sister. That and encourage Jonas—in her very next letter—to look after Sadie, though there was little time before he'd be home for his baptism. She could hardly wait! Having Jonas back even for a weekend would lift their spirits—all of them—for he would surely tell how Sadie was getting along at the Mellingers'.

As the minutes wore on she watched the clouds glide across the sky. How eager she was to see and hold Cousin Fannie's twin babies. She and Mary Ruth would be the ones most captivated by the twins' sweet babyhood, she was sure. Hannah, on the other hand, was somewhat unsure of herself around young ones, infants especially.

Mamma must have been thinking along the same lines, for she said, "Girls, be extra careful if you hold either of Fannie's babies. 'Specially Jake. He's not nearly as robust and healthy as his sister Mandie. Nor Lydiann, neither one."

"We promise to be gentle, Mamma," Mary Ruth quickly replied from the back of the spring wagon.

Once they arrived Dat let them off within a few yards of the back door, then drove up to the barn. Peter Mast was waiting there to help unhitch and water the horse. "Hullo, Abram. I see you've got one less mouth to feed," Peter was heard to say.

Leah paid little mind to his comment and walked across the yard and up the back steps, along with Mamma, Aunt Lizzie, and the twins. Cousin Fannie, all rosy cheeked, greeted them splendidly as always. Leah had to grin, wondering why they didn't visit here more often, so pleasant it was. Fannie, her mother-in-law-to-be, was smiling at each of them, offering some ice-cold peppermint water for "whoever's thirsty." Imagining the wedding-day feast they'd be putting on before long, Leah clasped Fannie's outstretched hands.

"Just look at you," Fannie said, eyes aglow. "How's our next young bride?"

Leah felt her cheeks turn instantly warm, and Mamma spoke up right softly. "Best not be sayin' such things just yet."

Fannie gave a nod of the head. Leah, ever so glad none of the Mast boys were within hearing distance, went and sat at the table with her cousins Rebekah and Katie. Young Martha came over quickly and perched herself on the edge of the long bench, eyes alight with curiosity. Surely Jonas's family had some idea of their plans to marry, though it wasn't their custom for couples to speak openly of their engagement this many weeks before the wedding season.

"Didja pick your bridesmaids?" Rebekah piped up, surprising them all.

Thankfully Mamma intervened yet again. "Now, Becky . . ." Her eyes turned solemn and her voice a bit prickly.

Aunt Lizzie added more tenderly, "Let's just wait on that," with a peculiar, even restrained, smile.

Jonas and the upcoming wedding aside, the high point of the visit was all of them tiptoeing upstairs to have a look-see at Jacob and Amanda. "Ach, they're but wee ones," Aunt Lizzie was first to say, reaching with outstretched arms for fair-haired Mandie. She received her from Fannie and set to cooing like a contented mamma chick. Mamma's arms were full up with Lydiann, who looked nearly twice as big as Fannie's twins, though she was younger.

Leah was hesitant to step up when Fannie held up the next bundle, one a mite smaller—tiny Jake. "Do you mind if I hold him first?" she asked Hannah and Mary Ruth.

Fannie clucked warmly at this, and Mary Ruth frowned, as if impatient for her turn.

Jake's awful cute, Leah quickly decided, cradling him and looking down at his miniature button nose, closed eyes, and wee, oval-shaped mouth. His fingers were the smallest she'd ever seen, his nails nearly the size of raindrops.

"He's small but mighty," Fannie spoke up, coming over to touch his wrinkled brow with her pointer finger. "His squeal can rouse me out of the deepest slumber—right up out of bed and onto my feet! Peter thinks he'll catch up with his twin sister in no time." She paused for a moment, then—"We were a bit worried at the outset, truth be told."

"Oh, why's that?" Mamma was next to Aunt Lizzie, with Lydiann blinking her bright little eyes at her youngest girl cousin.

"He had quite a lot of trouble . . . couldn't suckle so well—just awful tiny—didn't seem ready to face the world. Yet the twins weren't said to be premature."

Leah noticed Hannah's eyes grow wider with Cousin Fannie's every remark. "Do you think . . . um, Mandie took away some of the nourishment from Jake . . . that is, before they were born?"

Since Hannah scarcely ever spoke up, all of them turned their heads toward her at once. "Well, now, I gather that's altogether possible," Fannie replied. "I never thought of it thataway."

Mamma nodded in agreement. "Jah, there are times when one twin snatches the food away from the other during the developing. But such was not the case with you and Mary Ruth."

Leah couldn't help but smile. Mamma's eyes sparkled with love just now.

Quietly Leah slipped out of the room and into the hallway, still holding Jake, who was beginning to stir. Aunt Becky Brenneman in Hickory Hollow had once said—and quite adamantly—that talking about an infant in front of him or her "makes for a self-conscious and shy child," and she felt she ought to spare baby Jake.

"Just look at you," she whispered, smiling down at him, his eyes blinking up at her. "I think you're right handsome myself . . . ev'ry bit as healthy as any baby round here. So what if you're small. Babies are s'posed to be, ain't so?"

He gurgled at her, wiggling, too. She wandered down the hallway, cooing all the while, thinking it providential Sadie was in Ohio instead of here with Fannie's babies.

"My turn." Mary Ruth tapped her on the shoulder.

"Aw, I just got him," Leah protested but reluctantly handed over the sweet bundle. "Careful, now."

Mary Ruth nodded. "Didja forget already that I help with Lydiann . . . and Carl Nolt?"

"I know," she replied, still eyeing the full head of brown hair framing Jake's miniature face. Her heart was ever so drawn to the delicate boy, and she wished she could help protect him somehow, though it wasn't her place. Still, if she and Jonas lived at all closer, she had the feeling she would be over here quite often.

"In all gut time I 'spect you'll have your own little ones to love, jah?"

Leah truly hoped so. Many a bride gave birth nine months after the wedding day. But whenever the Good Lord saw fit to bless her future union was right fine. Truth was, she wouldn't mind having a son first, someone to carry on the respected Mast name and help with Jonas's carpentry work or yard work. But then again, she refused to do as Dat had done, wishing too hard for a boy and getting another girl—like when she came along after Sadie. No, she would be grateful for any son *or* daughter the Sovereign Lord chose to give her once she and Jonas were wed.

They had all gone walking, the five of them—Leah, the twins, and Rebekah and Katie Mast. They talked and strolled barefoot across a low ridge near the barn, past the windmill, and up to the high meadow, leaving the farmhouse far behind.

Right off they talked about piling into the pony cart for a laughing good time. But both Katie and Rebekah suggested they best not be too rowdy, what with the Lord's Day just around the bend. Leah could hardly disagree, and they heeded the call of prudence and headed toward the apple orchard for a lighthearted romp through the trees.

Rebekah was grinning as she asked, "When do you's start goin' barefoot over in Gobbler's Knob—in the spring, I mean?"

"Whenever it's warm enough." Mary Ruth was first to answer.

"My feet are so callused it scarcely matters," Katie spoke up.

"Well, let me tell you when Mamma says *we* can run

barefoot," Rebekah said, walking just ahead of Leah and Hannah, with Katie and Mary Ruth on either side of her. "We wait till the bumblebees fly," Rebekah announced as if it were some important revelation. "You know, the big, fat ones?"

"*Our* mamma says the same," Mary Ruth added.

Leah agreed. "Jah, 'cause too soon in the season, and your toes might get frostbit."

To this, the girls let out a peal of unrestrained laughter. They felt a convincing sense of freedom out here, far from the ears and eyes of their elders.

"Looks like we'll be seein' each other several times this year . . . with Jonas and Leah's weddin' coming up," said Rebekah, glancing at Leah.

" 'Course, us girls—and Dat and Mamma, too—are s'posed to be in the dark about it," said Mary Ruth, grinning now. "But as fast as Jonas's letters keep comin', well, we'd all have to be blind not to see the handwritin' on the wall."

"Just think," Katie spoke up, "once they marry, our parents will be in-laws together 'stead of just cousins. But what will that make us girls?"

Mary Ruth clapped her hands. "Second cousins and then some, I'm thinkin'. Glory be!"

Leah smiled with delight. The Mast girls were evidently eager to be as closely connected as they could be. After all, Cousin Peter and Fannie Mast, along with their ten children, were soon to become her second family. Five more sisters. And four *brothers*—a first!

When they'd quieted down a bit, Rebekah asked, "What's Sadie doin' out in Ohio?"

Leah's heart jolted. She bit her lip and remained silent.

She would wait for either Hannah or Mary Ruth to say what Dat had shared with all of them. She guessed Mary Ruth would be the one to answer.

And Mary Ruth it was. "Most everyone, at one time or 'nother, needs some thinkin' time. Sadie will be home soon, you'll see."

Leah was relieved. Seemed Mary Ruth most certainly had accepted their father's explanation—hook, line, and sinker.

"But ain't it strange she should be livin' so near to *your* beau, Leah?" Rebekah said, turning around and looking right at her.

"How do you know this?" Leah asked, standing still with the others.

Rebekah seemed eager to volunteer the information. "Vera Mellinger, Mamma's cousin's wife, wrote and said how worried she was over Sadie."

"Jah, Sadie cries most ev'ry night, Vera writes," Katie added, joining arms with older sister Rebekah. "Just why would that be?"

"Could be she's missin' home, but if so, why'd she go all the way out there in the first place?" Rebekah asked, eyes wide.

Leah shook her head and was starting to speak when Mary Ruth said, "There's nothin' wrong with Sadie that a little rest won't help. And that's all there is to it."

"The same kind of rest your aunt Lizzie Brenneman needed back when *she* was a teenager?" said Rebekah.

Perplexed and uneasy, Leah said, "Seems to me we're talkin' foolishness now. What can you possibly mean?"

"Well, if you don't know, I best not be the one to say."

With that Rebekah spun around and headed on her way.

"Come back!" Mary Ruth called to her, exchanging bewildered glances with Hannah and Leah.

"There's only one reason your parents would send a courting-age daughter away!" Rebekah hollered back. "Think on *that*."

Heartsick anew, Leah suggested she and the twins return to the house. "Let Rebekah say what she will," she said softly. "Come, let's go."

Mary Ruth and Hannah followed, but Katie Mast turned and bounded after Rebekah, deep into the orchard, the opposite direction from the house. "What do you s'pose she meant to imply about Aunt Lizzie?" Mary Ruth asked.

"I wonder . . ." said Hannah.

Leah felt she ought to put a halt to this. "Sadie needs our understandin', not hearsay."

For a short while they trailed the creek as it fell over rock and twig, looping past small oak trees and patches of moss.

Then, when the house and barn were again in sight, Hannah stopped walking. "Last year Dawdi John told me the strangest thing," she said. "Did either of you know Aunt Lizzie lived in our Dawdi Haus at the tail end of her rumschpringe?"

Mary Ruth looked startled. "You sure?"

"Since Dawdi has a clear mind and wouldn't think of lyin', I tend to believe him," Hannah replied. "He said Lizzie joined church in Gobbler's Knob 'stead of the Hickory Hollow district."

"News to me," Leah said. "Did Dawdi say why that was?"

"I guess 'cause for a time, Lizzie needed Mamma's love to

get her through some rough days. Just what . . . I don't know." All at once Hannah turned pale.

"What is it?" asked Leah, her own mouth suddenly dry.

"You don't s'pose . . . the reason Aunt Lizzie never married was—"

"Uh, don't let's be speculatin'!" Mary Ruth interrupted, her face crimson red.

"I should say." Leah deliberately took the lead and began walking faster than they had before, hoping her sisters might follow her back to the house—and quickly at that.

Chapter Nineteen

Sunday, following Preaching service, Sadie climbed into the Mellinger family two-horse carriage. She sat in the second seat with Edith Mellinger. Edith's grown son, David, his wife, Vera, and their young family—Joseph, Mary Mae, and Andy—sat up front, the two smaller children perched on their parents' laps.

The ride back to the Mellingers' farmhouse dragged on and on. She had already sat through the main sermon, which was miles long, much like the Preaching service back home. Yet today she'd felt the hot pangs of conviction from the first hymn and *Zeugniss*—testimonies—till the benediction. The passages of Scripture read were some not so emphasized by either Bishop Bontrager or Preacher Yoder. Today's main sermon had been about Galatians, chapter six, verse eight—*For he that soweth to his flesh shall of the flesh reap corruption*—which put the fear of the Lord God in her. Did this mean "sowing wild oats," like she had done during rumschpringe and beyond? The part about the flesh reaping corruption had her stumped, really. Did it mean she could be punished further for her immorality, even more than she had been already, losing her baby and all? Ofttimes she worried God might not allow her to have more children if she was ever to marry. Oh, she trembled at the thought!

The minister had also preached on the latter half of the verse: *but he that soweth to the Spirit shall of the Spirit reap life everlasting*. That part had caught her attention but good, and she pondered it still.

She didn't know what it was about the church out here. Honestly, she wished she might put her finger on it, might know exactly why she'd felt so disgraceful sitting there with the other women—even corrupted, just as the Scripture stated. Was this what both Leah and Aunt Lizzie had been talking about for so many months?

Thinking back to Leah's repeated pleas for her repentance, and today's meeting, Sadie fought hard a feeling of utter sadness. But out here in the fresh air and sunshine, her guilt was beginning to lessen again. She had thoroughly enjoyed the common meal and some good fellowship with the young people. Just today she'd met two handsome young men, Ben Eicher from Walnut Creek and John Graber from Grabill in Allen County, Indiana, both here for oat harvesting and shocking. Recalling their spontaneous smiles, she felt she just might manage through yet another Lord's Day this far from home.

Does Mamma miss me? Does Leah? She thought of picking up a pen and finally writing letters to them. *Tonight I will*, she decided.

"How long are you gonna visit?" David's youngest son brought her out of her musing. The little boy, a miniature of his father complete with a wide-brimmed black felt hat, turned round in the front seat and was smiling at her with inquisitive blue eyes.

"Now, Andy, that's not polite to ask." His mother helped turn the towheaded youngster back around in his seat, saying, "Our boy's awful sorry, Sadie."

"No, I *ain't* sorry, Mamma," said Andy outright. "I like Sadie, and I hope she stays put here for a good long time."

So do I, she thought, smiling in spite of herself. She was not eager in the least to return to Lancaster County with Jonas in October. How could she go back only to witness her younger sister's wedding service before her own? Of course, Sadie knew that if she'd chosen to, she could have been courted by a respectable boy from Gobbler's Knob. It was her own fault that when Jonas had first started courting Leah, Sadie herself was secretly seeing an English beau.

'Tis past history, she thought. Now there was only one thing to cling to: her recurring dream of being happily married and coddling her baby boy. Before coming here she had been hopeful the sound of a crying infant might cease once she got settled into her new surroundings, but it had continued, haunting her wherever she went—if not stronger than before. However, she was fully convinced now that what she'd been "hearing" was no more than her imagination.

Sitting next to her, Edith made a slight moan. Sadie turned to look at the snoring woman, her long chin nearly bumping the cape of her dress as she slept.

In order to stay on here, I'll have to live with poor, ailing Edith, she thought. Not much of a life, really, till Sadie got married. If she ever did.

Once she was alone in her room, Sadie began to write her promised letters, beginning with Mamma's.

Sunday evening, August 31
Dearest Mamma,

Greetings to you and Dat from Ohio. I should've written sooner, but the Widow Mellinger needs near constant looking after. Honestly, I don't know how much time Leah would've had to spend with Jonas if she was doing what I do here. Except courting couples always tend to make time for each other, no matter.

How is everyone? Are the twins enjoying school? I hope all of my kitchen duties haven't fallen on your shoulders, Mamma.

I'm guessing Lydiann is rolling over already, ain't so?

With the mention of her baby sister, she felt overcome with sadness. She was beginning to miss little Lydiann, missed working alongside Mamma, too. And Leah? A close and caring sister could never be replaced, that was sure. The evening hours had always been best, when they talked most personally in their bedroom.

She continued her letter.

The Preaching service here is a lot like at home, but the Scriptures are new to me. The ministers here say teaching from the whole Bible is necessary for us to reside quietly in Christ, so I guess it's time I learned more about the sayings of God's Son. Bishop Bontrager might take issue with this, espe-

cially since he preaches the same favorite Scriptures sermon after sermon.

She felt she best not go on too much about that. If Mamma shared the letter with Dat, which she more than likely would, such news might stir up even more concern about her being gone from home.

No doubt you were upset when I disappeared with Leah's help . . . and I ought to be saying how sorry I am if this caused you stress, Mamma. I'm thinking long about many things here while I keep busy with Edith, as well as having fun with the Mellinger children.

Tell Leah I'm still considering hard her request I be one of her bridesmaids. Next letter I'll say for sure, one way or the other.

I'll write again soon. Tell Dat I love him, too!

With loving affection,
Your daughter Sadie

Finished, she folded the letter and left it on the little writing desk near the window. Then, too tired to think of writing yet another letter, she undressed quickly for bed.

I'll write my sister soon enough, she decided, feeling certain Mamma would share this letter around with the family.

On Monday evening Leah accompanied Dawdi John next door after supper. Unable to dismiss Hannah's haunting words about Aunt Lizzie, she wanted to ask a tactful question or two of Dawdi.

For a time they sat quietly in his front room. She lingered there awkwardly till he spoke at last, worrying aloud over the prospect of colder weather setting in "here 'fore too much longer." Nodding, she listened with the hope of putting him in a favorable mood.

After a solid half hour of weather talk, she rose and went to his alcove of a kitchen just a few steps away and poured a glass of water for herself. "Would you like somethin' to wet your whistle?" she asked.

"I'm fine, Leah. Come sit with me." His voice seemed suddenly strained.

She brought with her the glass of cold well water and hurried back to sit across from him on a cane chair. "What is it, Dawdi?"

He leaned his head back as if glancing at a particular spot on the ceiling. For the longest time he sat that way, his untrimmed gray beard cascading down to his chest. Then, ever so slowly, he lowered his somber eyes to meet hers. "I mayn't be the smartest soul on earth, but I know when my granddaughter's fit to be tied." He paused, still holding her gaze, then continued. "Truth is, you've been wantin' to talk with ol' Dawdi for some time now. Ain't?"

She wondered how he knew. "Guess I have."

"Your perty face gives you away. Them hazel-gold eyes of yours, well . . ." He smiled then, a slow, soft smile that made his gray eyes shine.

She decided to forge ahead. "I *have* been thinking an awful lot about Aunt Lizzie. For the longest time, I've wondered why she never married. She's fun lovin' and kind—would make a right gut wife and mother."

"Well, why not ask her all this?" Dawdi said.

"In so many words, I s'pose I have."

" 'Tis safe to say not every maidel ends up married. Sometimes just ain't enough husbands to go round."

She decided to press the issue further. "But there were plenty of young men durin' Aunt Lizzie's courtin' years. She told me so." Truth was, lots of church boys had been interested in Lizzie. In fact, there was one special boy who had declared his love for her, but he didn't wait for Lizzie to settle down from rumschpringe.

"I'll admit, there were several interested fellas," said Dawdi. "In Hickory Hollow, 'specially. I wished to goodness she'd paid more attention to some of them. . . ."

Leah waited, hoping Dawdi might say more, but his voice faded away. They sat there together in awkward silence a few minutes.

Finally Leah felt she must speak up once more before returning to the main part of the house. She had to stick her neck out just a bit farther, since she didn't know when she'd ever have another opportunity. Not with both Hannah and Mary Ruth vying for Dawdi's attention after the evening meal, too. Come dessert time, the twins always seemed to get to their grandfather before Leah could here lately. She didn't know what it was, but Hannah, especially, and now Mary Ruth was awful eager to spend time with Dawdi.

She breathed deeply, then asked, "Is it true . . . well, that Aunt Lizzie came to live here in this addition when she was a youth?"

Dawdi nodded his head without catching her eye. "Jah, 'tis."

"And was there . . ." She faltered, then managed to continue. "Um . . . was there somethin' wrong that . . . required Mamma's attention?"

Dawdi reached for his old German *Biewel* on the table nearby and opened to a marked page without speaking. She was aware of the whistling sound in his nose as he breathed in and out. And she had a peculiar feeling Dawdi was, right now, preparing to give her a message from the Lord God. If that wasn't true, then why were his eyes so intent on hers as he held the Good Book in his gnarled hands?

He opened his mouth and began to read. " 'When my father and my mother forsake me, then the Lord will take me up. Teach me thy way, O Lord, and lead me in a plain path, because of mine enemies.' " Dawdi sighed, and if Leah wasn't mistaken, there was a tear in his eye. "Your aunt Lizzie was taken in by Abram and Ida 'cause she had need to be."

Leah didn't quite understand what Dawdi meant to say. Why didn't he speak his mind clearly? "I'm ever so puzzled," she admitted. "Did you and Mammi Brenneman . . . well, did you send Lizzie away from Hickory Hollow?"

He closed the Bible as slowly as he'd opened its fragile pages. "I don't s'pose I can explain this to you without stirrin' up even more questions." He paused, his wrinkled hands folded atop the Good Book. "Lizzie and her older brother, your uncle Noah, simply did not see eye to eye back then."

She was staring at him now, grasping for some meaning. Why had he read such a startling psalm to her?

For truth, she couldn't begin to imagine why Aunt Lizzie

would have come from her home in Hickory Hollow all the way to Gobbler's Knob to live absent from her immediate family. Unless . . . could it possibly be what Cousin Rebekah Mast had hinted at in the apple orchard? Could it be Lizzie *was* with child back then?

Nee. She rejected the notion. Not good-hearted and decent Aunt Lizzie.

Feeling terribly uneasy, she said at last, "Is it possible Aunt Lizzie thought of Uncle Noah as her enemy, like in the psalm you just read?"

"Best to simply say the plain path of the Lord God led Lizzie here to Gobbler's Knob . . . and to her sister's arms."

She watched as Dawdi's lips moved, the whites of his eyes glistening. Somewhere between what Dawdi was trying to tell her and what she'd observed all her life in Aunt Lizzie, a line of unspoken truth had been drawn. Surprisingly, what was and what seemed to be appeared even more mystifying than before.

Abram spent the evening with his nose in the Good Book. He refused to go sour faced on Ida, who sat darning an old sock while Lydiann slept in the crook of her arm. He might have allowed his emotions to run unchecked, getting the best of him, because Leah was next door with Dawdi this very moment. From what he remembered saying to his father-in-law just this afternoon, well, there was no way anything good could come of such a visit. Not the way John had laid into him earlier, threatening to "blow the top off this whole family hush-hush!" not so many hours before.

He'd done his best—what he could, at least—urging John to "hold his tongue" till he and Ida could discuss things further. But then, somehow or other, Leah had wormed her way over to Dawdi immediately following Ida's dessert. She'd gotten to him first, offering her arm to steady his gait long before either of the twins had, which was downright disheartening, since he'd taken both Hannah and Mary Ruth aside not so many weeks back and told them to look after their Dawdi right close after supper—"'tis mighty important," he'd said. Mary Ruth had frowned, no doubt questioning his urgency—she had that way about her—but Hannah, thankfully, had succumbed to his request, ready obedience alight in her soft brown eyes.

All in all, the twins had been doing a right fine job of scurrying over to John the second he wiped his mouth on his handkerchief after eating the last morsel of Ida's apple crumb cake or whatnot.

Till tonight. And now Abram was ever so anxious over what things were being said from the lips of an impatient grandfather to his naïve and softhearted granddaughter.

Hannah hurried upstairs to the bedroom she shared with Mary Ruth. There she began to pour out her anxieties onto the pages of her diary notebook.

Monday, September 1
Dear Diary,

I shouldn't be writing this, probably, but Dat's fretful about something. He wore the concern on his dear face tonight after Leah helped Dawdi John next door after supper. Still can't quite understand Dat telling Mary Ruth and me to "hurry over to help Dawdi, following the dessert." And he insists we do this every night till he says otherwise. So strange it is!

I miss Sadie something awful, and Mary Ruth's much too busy with the Nolt family and her schoolwork these days for my liking.

Leah spends more time indoors with Mamma now, so there's scarcely any chance for my sister and me to talk privately. I have a hunch Leah had something to do with Sadie going to Ohio. Maybe it's the sad look in Leah's eyes every now and then, especially since there've been no letters from Sadie. I thought by now she would've sent Mamma one, at least.

What an emptiness is in me when we sit down for a meal anymore. Sadie is off in another state, mourning the loss of her baby—or at least imagining she had one. Oh, it wonders me if she's in her right mind or not.

Honestly, I can't say which way I would feel most sorry for Sadie, really. If she's not right in the head . . . that's terrible. But if she was immoral and birthed a dead baby, then that's heartrending. Nothing less.

Respectfully,
Hannah Ebersol

More than two weeks after she'd sent her letter to Mamma, Sadie was returning to the Mellingers' large farm, having taken one of the buggies to the general store to purchase some items for Edith. Looking up, she noticed the sky was a resplendent blue, nearly the color of a spanking new piece of blue cotton fabric, the shade of Leah's soon-to-be wedding dress.

Pausing at the back stoop, she again stared up at the heavens, wondering if the same hue might also be evident in the sky in Gobbler's Knob, where Jonas was headed come this time tomorrow. She felt her heart beating its muffled, secret throbs, wishing she could be a fly on the wall, privy to the things Jonas might soon be saying to Leah. But would Leah let on she'd spent time in the woods with Gid Peachey after getting lost for hours on end? Sadie couldn't imagine *that* being discussed. Still, she'd seen Leah and Gid with her own eyes, coming down out of the deep of the forest together.

Since arriving here, and on the long train ride, she'd thought several times of what she'd seen that day—so confusing it had been. Hadn't Gid taken a shine to Leah all these years? They *had* been holding hands the day she'd spied them, laughing and having themselves a mighty nice time together. What could it mean?

She'd thought of asking Leah about it later that night, and then again as they said their good-byes at the trolley, but she hadn't. Now she wished she had.

Pity's sake, Leah had nearly pushed her out the door to Millersburg. Why? Was it for the reason she said . . . or to stay home for Gid?

Impossible, Sadie thought. *Not the Leah I know.*

She was altogether nervous. The kernel of doubt remained. If true—if Leah *was* two-timing her beau—well, then Jonas deserved better. Much better.

Yet another thought crossed Sadie's mind. Could it be that even at this late date, Leah was having second thoughts about Jonas? Was she leaning toward doing Dat's bidding, after all?

She could only guess at Leah's true motive for sending her here, but she did wonder a little if something wasn't fishy.

As for Jonas, he had been right kind since her arrival here. An outgoing sort of fellow, he occasionally gave Sadie a welcoming smile across the kitchen table when the family gathered there, especially if the subject of his return to Pennsylvania for baptism rose out of a mix of conversation that included the weather, the next canning frolic, and which of the farm families in their area was growing oodles of celery these days. This during the Mellinger family's eventide hours when David read aloud from the Good Book while katydids chirped in the fields. If she interpreted Jonas's thoughtfulness correctly, she wondered if he felt sorry for her being there, so far removed from her family. Did he assume she was homesick? Maybe that was the reason for his wide-eyed gaze on her from time to time, since he had no knowledge of her past sins. Surely not. And she'd just as soon keep it that way.

Part Two

◆ ◆ ◆ ◆

They that sow in tears shall reap in joy.

—**Psalm 126:5**

Chapter Twenty

On Friday, September 19, Leah stood waiting out at the end of the long lane at dusk. She watched with devoted eyes for Jonas to come riding down the road in his open buggy, his dashing steed brushed spanking clean for the occasion.

Her heart thumped fast and hard, and she felt she might not be able to stand there much longer, so jittery she was. In his last letter from Ohio, he had written he could arrive in Gobbler's Knob at twilight on this night. *Will you be waiting for me, dear Leah . . . near the road?*

Over the shadowy hills a splinter of a moon crept up; its cambered rim cast an ancient white light over the fertile valley below. She gazed at the hollow band of road, feeling all trace of time was lost. Gone—the ache of days, the summer of loneliness, endless weeks of missing her beloved's smile, the touch of his hand on hers, his strong but tender embrace.

And then she spied him, his horse and carriage two shadowy silhouettes moving in the distance, heading in her direction. She felt her heart might burst with growing joy.

"Oh, Jonas," she whispered to the honeysuckle-scented air even before he jumped down from the courting carriage and ran across the road to her. They fell into each other's arms.

"Dear Leah . . . Leah, it's you at last!" He held her so close she felt his breath on her neck. "I missed you so," he said, not letting her go.

Her tears fell onto his shirt as she clung to him. "Jonas . . ."

"I was crazy, out-of-mind missing you." Gently he released her, but only for a moment, his eyes searching hers. "My darling girl . . . perty as a bride on her weddin' day."

The horse let out an impatient neigh, tossing his mane back in the fading light. "Whoa, steady there," Jonas called softly over his shoulder.

Leah found it both comical and comforting—Jonas's unruffled tone attempted to soothe the horse as if he were talking to a human. She fell in love with her beau all over again, appreciating his tender heart toward even an animal.

"Wouldja like to go for some ice cream?" he asked.

"Where you are, that's where I want to be," she replied. And before she could protest, he reached down and lifted her up into his shining carriage.

She couldn't stop smiling as he set her down on the front seat, then fairly flew round the buggy and leaped up into the driver's seat to her right. "Ice cream it is!" He paused, smiling at her. "Guess I oughta pay attention to the road," he said at last, turning slowly to pick up the reins. "We have all night, ain't so?"

"Just so I'm home in time for a few winks before milkin'," she reminded him, though she wished she didn't have to say a word about what tomorrow's duties required of her, including the final meeting with Preacher Yoder prior to baptism. With her whole heart, she would much rather ride off with Jonas, never to come down to earth again, so to speak.

She thought of her husband-to-be's name in front of her own—Jonas's Leah—and it brought such gladness. She whispered it right then and there.

"Didja just say what I think?" he asked, reaching for her hand.

She nodded, unable to repeat it.

"Remember, that's who you'll be for always . . . *my* Leah."

They rode slowly all the way to Strasburg, where he bought ice-cream cones for them. They sat high in the carriage, enjoying the treat in an out-of-the-way spot in the parking lot, away from cars.

When her ice cream was half eaten, Leah brought up the subject of her sister. "How's Sadie doin' in Ohio, would you say?"

"I guess she's all right. She does seem awful dreary, though. Must be she's pining for your family."

His comment startled her. "Jah, that could be. . . ."

"Then, she's not there for her health?"

She felt the awkward hesitancy of his words. Surely he didn't suspect Sadie might be in the family way? Yet there was that unspoken concern in his eyes. She mustn't let on that her sister had indeed experienced such dreadful heartache already, in both her soul and her body. She refused to expand on the scant information.

"Sadie needs a little time away, is all." She considered

what she might say further. Then she knew. "My sister needs a friend, I daresay."

"I've had only a little contact with her, which is the way I prefer it, Sadie bein' single and all."

She felt he was being overly serious. "Aw, Jonas, you're not timid around my sister, are you?"

His face broke into a warm smile. "You mustn't worry on my account. I'm going to marry *you*."

His words hung in the air, a promise for a lifetime. She could rest in such a pledge, and this made her think about the vow they would be taking on Sunday. "It's awful nice of you to be baptized with me."

"We'll mark the day," he said, blue eyes shining.

"Jah, for sure and for certain."

He nodded, holding his now dripping ice-cream cone in his right hand. "Just as we'll commemorate our weddin' day for always."

Silently she finished her own melting ice cream, her heart racing as fast as when she'd first spied him tonight, coming up the road in his handsome courting buggy.

"What wouldja think, Leah, for us to marry on the last Tuesday in November, the twenty-fifth? Would that suit you and your family?"

The combination of ice cream and the lump of happiness in her throat kept her from answering promptly. At last she managed to speak. "Jah, that will be a wonderful-gut day of days. With all of my heart, I'm lookin' forward to bein' your wife."

He must have sensed the anxiety of a young bride-to-be.

"Are you also a little bit nervous?" he asked softly, drawing her near.

"More relieved than anythin', really." And she confided in him how eager she was to discuss the date with Mamma.

They talked of this and that, Jonas sharing something of his work with David Mellinger. "I'm tryin' to complete a year's worth of apprenticeship in six months or thereabouts so I can return to help my father in the orchard at harvest time. That bein' the case, Cousin David expects me to be in the wood shop as early as if I were milkin' cows of a morning, workin' alongside him. David's mighty helpful, but let me tell you, he makes me earn my keep."

She felt it was all right to bring up something else, the way they were sharing so openly and all. "How is it you ended up learnin' the carpentry trade clear out in Ohio?"

"Nothing less than providence is how I look at it," Jonas said. "The Lord God heavenly Father works all things together for our gut. Believe me, it was downright perfect timing."

"Has your mother's cousin always known of your keen interest in carpentry? Is that why he contacted you in the first place?"

Jonas shook his head. "I can't say it was, really. I scarcely knew of David and Vera Mellinger."

Then, how was it Jonas had been invited to do an apprenticeship with a distant relative? Unless, could it be David had heard of Jonas's lifelong dream to be a carpenter through the Amish grapevine? If so, how had it gotten all the way to Ohio, and right around the precise moment the two of them were betrothed last spring? She had always wondered about that, though she'd never told a soul.

"What is it, love?" he asked.

"Oh, I'm all right." She put a smile on her face. But the hard facts were that Jonas was to be the only young man round these parts who chose to earn his living doing something other than farm related. Practically unheard of for the firstborn son of a farmer not to follow in his father's own footsteps. Having hinted at her curiosity in a letter, she was eager to ask all this of Jonas, but she held her peace. For now, she would cherish their time together, wanting nothing to spoil this night.

Chapter Twenty-One

One more day till baptism, Leah thought as she awakened early Saturday morning. Her time with Jonas the evening before lingered fresh and sweet in her mind, yet she worried her beau must surely suspect something was amiss with Sadie.

With Naomi counting the hours until she talked to Preacher Yoder today, and with Gid's sister Adah wondering what in the world Sadie was doing so far away, Leah dreaded Jonas might get wind of something. After all, unsuspecting Hannah had learned the *full* truth from Sadie's own lips. Wasn't it just a matter of time before Sadie's secret leaked out?

For sure and for certain, the things Naomi would tell Preacher at the final instructional class paled compared to what Leah knew of Sadie's wild side. *Naomi doesn't know the half of it,* she thought, embarrassed anew. Her heart beat heavily in her chest.

She felt the Lord God's urging ever so strong and could no longer resist on the side of honoring her sister's wishes. She must cast aside her promise, difficult as that would be, to answer a holy call.

Making her way to the barn in the predawn hour, she found Dat busy watering the driving horses and the field mules. "'Mornin', Leah," her father said, glancing over his shoulder at her.

"'Mornin', Dat." She forced her bare feet to move quickly, lest she lose heart and falter. "I need to talk with you," she blurted.

He looked at her with solemn eyes. "What's on your mind?"

When she didn't answer immediately, Dat rubbed his beard. "Your mamma and I feel you may have done the right thing by Sadie, after all . . . if that's weighin' on your mind."

"Then, you aren't so upset?" she asked.

"'Tis not easy, all this happenin' so suddenly. Heaven knows . . ." He paused for a moment, looking back at the house. "And your mamma's goin' to need some extra attention from you—all of us, really."

"I 'spect so. . . ." How easy it would be to simply go and wash down the cows' udders and dismiss what she'd set out to do. "I . . . uh . . . must speak with you about something else," she said, stepping forward. "It's about my baptism . . . makin' ready for it in my heart."

Dat removed his black wide-brimmed hat, holding it in both hands. "'Tis all right, Leah. If something's causin' a stir in ya, 'tis best to air it."

She nodded, aware of a lump in her throat.

"Are you prepared to follow the Lord in holy baptism?" he came right out and asked. "Or is there some resistance on your part . . . about the ordinance?"

"I simply want to ask your forgiveness, Dat."

"Well, now, whatever for?"

She paused, the tug-of-war awful strong, then plunged forward. "I need to tell you I've known of somethin' . . . of a terrible sin Sadie committed and had me promise not to tell."

Dat stood mighty still just then. "How terrible do you mean?"

She glimpsed the pain that registered in her beloved father's eyes and had to look away. "Sadie had a baby," she whispered, reliving the frightening truth of it. "I was there the night she birthed a baby boy. And if Aunt Lizzie hadn't helped, well, I hate to think what might've happened. Sadie was in such an awful bad way."

Dat's face grew ever more solemn. "Lizzie was on hand, you say?"

"She had a part in savin' Sadie's life." She went on to describe how she'd ridden bareback on one of the horses "to fetch Dr. Schwartz, though I knew ridin' thataway was a sin of my own makin'—and I'm right sorry 'bout it. There was just no other choice to make . . . unless 'twas to let my sister die."

Dat stared down at his hat, moving it slowly around in his hands. "Do you mean to say Lizzie knew Sadie was in the family way?"

Leah was afraid of this. Dat seemed miffed, even angry. "Sadie didn't tell Aunt Lizzie till the night the baby came. Ach, don't be upset at Lizzie, Dat. She did only what she had to."

"And what of the baby? What became of *him*?" Dat's

words hung in the air for a moment before she could answer.

"The poor little thing gave up the ghost . . . and died." Fighting back tears, she pressed on. "Oh, Dat, with all of my heart, I had to tell you these things. I've waited much too long, I fear."

His eyes, wide and moist, were fixed on her. But he said no more.

"When I make my confession of faith and join church, I want to present myself a clean and willin' vessel. . . ."

He surprised her by reaching for her right hand and holding it in both of his.

"May I have your mercy for keepin' this dreadful secret?" she asked.

A single, slow nod came from him, and she knew he was offering his understanding, even forgiveness, at her burning request.

Hours later Leah met with both Preacher Yoder and Deacon Stoltzfus, along with Jonas and the other baptismal candidates. Upon first entering the Yoders' farmhouse, she caught a glimpse of Naomi talking quietly with Preacher in the front room. As expected, Sadie's former best friend had followed through with her warning. More than likely, Naomi was reporting Sadie's misconduct and deceit this minute.

Naomi turned to look at her, and the blood instantly drained from her face. Sadie's former best friend had come clean, all right.

Leah waited her turn to speak with Preacher Yoder, not willing to call attention to herself. It was true, there had been plenty of time for Sadie to repent on her own. But today, before Leah filed into the Preaching service with the other candidates and offered her life as a "living sacrifice" to the Lord God heavenly Father, she, too, must open her mouth and confess. She and Sadie—Aunt Lizzie, too—had made a hasty, even unwise covenant last year; it was past time to set things right between herself and God. Because if the day ever came that Sadie bowed her knee at last, she would realize what Leah was about to do was right and good in the sight of the Lord. When all was said and done, this act of obedience on Leah's part might just turn things around more quickly for Sadie.

When it was her turn to speak to Preacher Yoder, he offered her a handshake that could make a man out of a boy, she decided, careful not to wince. She began to acknowledge her sins of omission. "It is my understanding certain transgressions have been committed by my baptized sister. . . . Sadie Ebersol. For some time now, I've known of them," she began. "Yet I have failed to bring them to light. . . ." She went on to tell all she knew of Sadie's sinning, grievous as it was.

Here the minister glanced at the deacon and nodded his head slowly. "I commend you, Leah," he said. "May you find your forgiveness in Jesus Christ, our Lord and Savior."

Now, upon Sadie's return from Ohio, there would be a serious confrontation with the brethren. She would be given a chance to confess or be shunned. Sadie would no longer have the consolation of simply biding her time. Her sin had found her out.

When the final instructional meeting got under way, the ministers discussed with great sobriety the difficulty of "walking the straight and narrow way." Leah soaked up every word, steadfast in her decision. She and the other applicants were given ample opportunity to turn back from the baptismal covenant, but she sat tall in her chair and said jah with confidence when asked.

Jonas answered with a similar assent. When the young men were asked if they would pledge to accept the duties of a minister if the lot should ever fall to them, Leah noticed he was emphatic in his affirmative response.

The heaviness she'd carried for nigh unto a year was lifted, and she felt as light as a driving horse without its harness. Only one nagging worry remained: How would her confession affect Sadie?

Ida felt so awkward, there in the cramped phone booth. The fact that Abram was squeezed in with her made it even more confining. Abram was still smarting over the truth of Sadie's iniquity, having shared with Ida Leah's confession in the barn this morning. Both were suffering, truth be known.

Now here they were in the one-horse town of Georgetown. They felt it of great necessity to speak to Sadie without delay, and to use an English telephone, of all things. Ida found it altogether curious Abram already had David's woodworking shop number in his possession. Leaning around her, he wasted no time in dialing.

When David answered, Abram told who he was and that he wanted to speak to Sadie "right away, if at all possible." Ida thought he might've at least chatted some about the weather, not been so quick to get off the phone with the man who was making it possible for their Sadie to have a roof over her head.

"Hullo, daughter? Jah . . .'tis your mamma and me callin'," Abram said.

There was a short pause; then Abram asked, "How're you getting along there?"

Abram waited for Sadie's answer.

"We're fine, just fine," he said back to her.

Then Ida heard him get right to the point. "It's sadly come to our attention that you were guilty of improper courtship practices. Is this true, Sadie?"

Ida held her breath for the longest time. She simply couldn't bear to listen to only one side of the conversation. And about the time she felt she could no longer contain her frustration, Abram turned and held out the phone to her. "Sadie's cryin' . . . wants to talk to you."

She put the black receiver to her ear. "My dear girl . . ." So eager she was to hear her daughter's voice again. *Please come home to us*, she thought.

"Oh, Mamma . . ." was all she heard from Sadie, then a bit of sniffling.

"We best talk over some things. Can you speak freely?"

More sniffles. Then, "Jah, I can."

"It's come to light since you've been gone that you were . . . well, that you birthed a child," she managed to say.

"Did . . . Leah tell you . . . this?" Sadie sputtered.

"I best not say just yet."

"Well, I won't go before the ministers. I hope you didn't call to ask me to—did you, Mamma?"

"It's the only way, the only thing to do." She inhaled, looking to Abram for moral support. "You wear a stiff upper lip, Sadie, but I've heard you weepin' in the late-night hours. Dat and I . . . we both hope you'll return home and make things right."

"I don't see how . . . not now."

Ida ignored the comment. "This pain you carry . . . let it lead you to repentance, Sadie."

"I'm a lot like Aunt Lizzie, ain't so, Mamma?"

It was Ida's turn to sputter. "What—whatever do you mean?"

"Lizzie sinned in the selfsame way." Sadie was silent for a moment, then—"It's ever so foolish for me to repent."

" 'Tis foolish *not* to. If you refuse, then I'm sorry to say, but Dat and I—oh, it'll be ever so difficult—we'll have no choice but to go along with *die Meindung*—the shunning—if it should come to that."

The shun . . . Ida went cold at the thought. Surely such harsh discipline could be prevented.

"I don't care." Sadie's words echoed in her ear. "Let the People do as they must."

Ida began to weep and Abram comforted her as best he could, the two of them nearly nose to nose in the cramped space.

"This is all my sister's doin'," Sadie said. "I'll never speak to her again!"

"Oh, Sadie . . . no." The dreadful words tore at Ida's heart, and she could talk no longer.

Abram kindly took the telephone and spoke slowly into the receiver. "We best be sayin' *Da Herr sei mit du*—the Lord be with you, Sadie. Good-bye."

Then he hung up.

Sadie was distraught as she returned the phone to its cradle. It was a good thing David Mellinger had made himself scarce while she spoke on the phone. Hearing Dat's voice on the telephone line seemed mighty peculiar. But nothing could compare to the realization Leah had betrayed her!

Mamma, no doubt, would hope to shield Hannah and Mary Ruth from the pitiless reality. This, when Sadie thought of it, gave her the slightest bit of comfort, except she wondered how long the twins could be kept in the dark.

Such a blight she was on her family name, in more ways than one. Even so, her father had offered a blessing before he'd said good-bye. This, along with Mamma's pressing remarks—from a compassionate and concerned heart—helped to quell Sadie's anger.

But it was the knowledge Leah had broken her promise that was most troubling. Resentment lingered long after supper, deep into the night.

Chapter Twenty-Two

At first rosy dawn, Leah was awakened by robins tweeting out a "Lord's Day . . . Lord's Day" pronouncement. Dozing off and on, she dreamed that upon arrival at Preaching, she discovered Jonas gone. Cousin Peter Mast was there, telling the ministers his son had changed his mind and returned to Ohio. Brokenhearted even amidst her grogginess, Leah lay in bed, tears trickling over the bridge of her nose as she struggled to escape this partial wakefulness. She felt herself brush away the tears, fully awake now. Such peculiar and troubling imaginings on this most reverent day!

Truly, she could not conceive of Jonas leaving Gobbler's Knob without following the Lord in joining church. What the sacred ordinance meant to her, it also meant to him. Baptism was the essential next step in being allowed to marry with the blessing of the People. This was nothing more than a fuzzy-headed predawn stupor.

She sat upright in the bed, shaking her head and pushing sleepiness and the alarming dream aside. Reaching over, she placed her hand on her wayward sister's pillow. *Will you understand what I had to do?* she wondered, missing Sadie.

Leah chased away her troublesome thoughts and embraced this most blessed day.

Almost immediately upon dressing for church, after milking and breakfast were finished, Leah heard a knock at her door. Quickly she went to see who was there.

"Do ya have a minute for your ol' auntie?" Lizzie said, standing there smiling wistfully.

What with this being an extra-special Sunday, Leah wasn't too surprised to see her. "Come in, come in. And since when are you old?" She reached for Lizzie's hands and pulled her gently into the bedroom.

Strangely enough, Lizzie closed the door firmly behind her. Then she turned back to face Leah. "I'm old, jah . . . when my nieces have grown up enough to join church and give themselves to the Lord God. Ain't so?"

"No . . . no, no. You're as young as you've always looked to me."

Apparently there was more on Lizzie's mind than talk of growing older. "I'm here to offer a heartfelt blessin' to you, Leah."

She sighed. "If only Sadie were here to witness the day."

Aunt Lizzie nodded. "I daresay we should never have promised to keep that wretched secret of hers."

"What's done is done," Leah said. "Now we must forgive

ourselves, just as the Lord God has forgiven us through Jesus Christ."

"Abram told me you confessed quietly of Sadie's baby boy," Lizzie said.

Leah had wondered when Dat might reveal this to Aunt Lizzie. He surely had not wasted any time.

Sighing deeply, Leah continued. "I must tell you I feel ever so light now—a burden's lifted from me, truly. Yet in the selfsame way, I bear such heaviness in my heart for Sadie."

"Surely our Sadie knows how dearly loved she is," Aunt Lizzie said, embracing her.

"And I pray my confession will bring her heart home to the People, once and for all," Leah replied.

Suddenly tears welled up in Lizzie's eyes. "Let me look at *you.*" She paused, reaching for Leah's hands. "Oh, my dear girl, I've waited so long for this day of days, when you would choose to follow in obedience the path of righteousness. The way of the People. May the almighty One bless you abundantly."

Leah was greatly touched by her aunt's thoughtfulness and, most of all, by her unexpected blessing—something a father ordinarily bestowed upon his son or daughter.

"Oh, Aunt Lizzie, it's good of you to come up here just now." She was at a loss for more words.

" 'Tis a day to 'come out from among them, and be ye separate,' " Lizzie quoted the well-known Scripture. She continued. " 'Be a light to the world,' honey-girl. Without spot or wrinkle."

"With the help of the Lord above, I will," Leah replied.

Then, as quickly as she'd come, Aunt Lizzie turned, opened the door, and hurried down the hall to the stairs.

Downright edgy, Mamma brushed Dat's black felt hat as Leah and the twins gathered in the kitchen. Mary Ruth insisted on making a fuss over Leah's freshly ironed white organdy *Halsduch*—a triangular piece of cloth, also called a cape—and the long white apron over her long black dress. Mamma kept looking at Leah, an odd glint in her eyes. And all the more when Lizzie went and stood right next to Leah.

It wasn't long, though, and they heard Dat calling to them to "come now, and let's be goin' to the house of worship."

They heeded the call and hurried out the back door.

Leah stooped to pet her dog quickly, wondering how awkward things might be for Smithy Gid *this* day. Undoubtedly, he'd be watching—and praying, too—when Leah filed into the service with the other girls who were to be baptized.

She spied Dat standing near the horse, talking low and soft to the animal, the way he often did, while the family stepped into the spring wagon for the short ride.

"*Be a light to the world. . . .*" Aunt Lizzie had said upstairs.

"Mustn't keep the ministers waitin'," Dat was heard to say as Leah climbed into the backseat with Aunt Lizzie.

She prayed silently as they rode along a bit faster than was a typical Sunday go-to-meeting pace. Dat must be eager to get her into the Fold, she thought, lest something should surface to keep that from happening. No doubt he was terribly upset over Sadie's wrongdoings—probably hoping Leah would remain pure before the Lord God.

Looking out at the pre-autumn landscape—tobacco fields reduced to green stubble and cornstalks rising to new heights—she thought of the personal matters she and Jonas had discussed well into the night on Friday. For one, he was planning to approach her father—this very afternoon—about the possibility of purchasing a corner of his land to build a house, possibly in the spring of next year. As newlyweds they wouldn't need a place to call their own just yet. Jonas wanted to follow the Old Way of doing things. They would simply visit amongst their many relatives, staying with different ones for the first six months after marriage. During this time they would be given free lodging, as well as an assortment of wedding gifts at each house, as was the People's custom. Just yesterday Mamma had hinted she hoped they might spend their wedding night in the spare bedroom downstairs.

Naturally the biggest hurdle of all would be whether or not Jonas and Dat saw eye to eye on the matter of land. The more she thought on it, the more she felt embarrassed Dat had not initiated such a plan, offering to *give* his son-in-law and daughter a bit of land as a dowry . . . a blessing on their marriage. But she had an irksome hunch Dat was still holding out for something to go wrong between Jonas and herself . . . even at this late date.

Sometime this afternoon they would know one way or the other what Dat's reaction to Jonas's request might be. She hoped her years of working closely alongside Dat might somehow make a difference.

In contrast to last year's baptism Sunday, which was overcast and gray—when Sadie had been one of six girls baptized—*this* Lord's Day the sky was a spotless blue with no indication of a single cloud. A good sign.

And now here were this year's applicants, eight girls and six boys—Jonas being the only one who had not grown up in the Gobbler's Knob church district. Leah was grateful to Bishop Bontrager for making it possible for Jonas to be baptized along with her. She hoped to have the opportunity to tell the bishop so at some point, when the time was right and with Dat by her side.

The massive barn doors gaped wide, propped open for the Preaching service to allow for additional ventilation. The People poured into the meeting place, some with additional family members and friends from other church districts for the special ordinance. Latecomers were assigned to sit on the back benches, near stacked bales of hay, which often poked the spine—a sure incentive not to be tardy.

With head bowed, Leah sat on the middle bench with the other girls, up front near the ministers. Across from them on a wooden, backless bench, the boys sat, their spines straight as ladders, while the next hymn was sung in unison by the People.

Seven ministers entered the area set up amidst the long granary and alfalfa bales, including Bishop Bontrager, Preacher Yoder, Preacher Lapp, Deacon Stoltzfus, and three other visiting ministers and deacons. They removed their large black hats and shook hands with different folk nearby, on their way to the ministers' bench.

After two sermons were given, each an hour long, Bishop

Bontrager stood and offered personal remarks directed to the candidates. This was Deacon Stoltzfus's cue to leave the meeting and bring back a pail of water, along with a tin cup.

The bishop continued. "You are to be reminded that your lifelong vow is being made to the Most High God . . . not only to the ministers here and this church membership."

Fully aware of the meaning of the covenant—what it required of her all the days of her life—Leah was eager to go to her knees when the bishop said, "If it is still your intention to be baptized and become a member of the body of Christ, then kneel before Almighty God and His church to obtain your salvation."

As she knelt, Leah prayed silently for the strength to take this holy step.

The bishop asked the first question. "With the help and grace of our Lord God heavenly Father, are you each willing to renounce the world, your own flesh, and the devil and to be obedient only to God and His church?"

The repeated jah was heard as each of them answered.

"Now, can you promise to walk with Christ and His church and remain faithful through life and until your death?"

Again the answer came in a stream of jahs.

"Do you confess that Jesus Christ is the Son of God?"

When it came Leah's turn, she said, "I confess that Jesus Christ is the Son of God."

The membership and children in the congregation stood for prayer after the last vow was audibly sealed. Leah and the others had been instructed to remain in a kneeling position, in an attitude of humility. The deacon's wife untied the ribbons of Leah's prayer cap; then the bishop laid hands on her bare head as Deacon Stoltzfus poured water into Bishop Bontrager's cupped hands. She felt the water dripping onto her hair and running down her face and neck, and at that moment she wept.

"May the Lord God in heaven complete the good work He has begun in each of you and strengthen and comfort you to a blessed end," prayed the bishop. He reached out a hand to Leah. "In the name of the Lord God and the church, we extend to you the hand of fellowship. Rise up, Leah Ebersol."

She rose, struck by the solemn responsibility she now had to the People under God Almighty. The deacon's wife greeted her, then offered the Holy Kiss. Leah and the other newly baptized church members took their seats, and each girl retied her prayer veiling once again.

Leah sat motionless, mindful of the lifetime commitment she had just made. Understood within the vow was the promise she would help to uphold the *Ordnung*—rules and order—and forsake not the exceptionally strict church of her baptism.

Chapter Twenty-Three

Mary Ruth felt more at ease today than she had the last time she'd stumbled upon Elias Stoltzfus after Preaching. Today the People had gathered at Uncle Jesse Ebersol's farmhouse. Though older than her father, Uncle Jesse was on hand after the meeting to pump well water to quench the thirst of a good many folk while a half-dozen women headed for the house to help with the common meal. Mary Ruth and Hannah helped Leah and some of their girl cousins set out the food—bread and butter, two kinds of jam, sweet and dill pickles, red beets, fruit pies, and black coffee. She knew they'd be setting and resetting the table three or four times, and the youngest children would eat last.

Still, encountering Elias had occurred quite unexpectedly—out in the barnyard, once again on her way to the outhouse. Not so embarrassed this time, she had been the first to say, "Hullo!" And he had returned the smile and greeting in kind.

She was more than pleased when he said he'd seen her walking on the Georgetown Road several different times in the past weeks. "Wouldja ever let me take you to where you're goin'?" he asked.

She was markedly aware of other people milling about the backyard. "I . . . well, do you think that's a wise thing?"

"Why, I'm thinkin' it's a mighty gut idea. It'll save your feet, for one thing."

She had to cover her mouth quickly to halt the laughter that managed to break loose anyway. They stood there, both of them laughing.

"I s'pose I can take your smile as a jah?" he asked, still grinning, his black hat off and resting flat in his hands.

Goodness' sake, this is abrupt, she thought. What would Dat say if he knew she was agreeing to let Elias take her to the Nolts' house in a pony cart?

"When will ya be out and 'bout again?" he asked, not one bit shy.

"In a couple-a days."

He returned his hat to his head and gave it a pat. "Well, then, I'll just plan to be happenin' by of an afternoon."

She felt her face grow warm. "I'd say if you were to be around the stretch of road 'tween my house and 'bout a mile west of there—round four o'clock or so—you might see me walkin'."

He nodded. "Done!" he said and was on his way.

"What have I gone and agreed to?" she whispered to herself.

"Hullo, Dawdi!" Leah called to her grandfather where he sat rocking on the small, square porch at home.

Dawdi John's eyes lit up as Leah and Jonas walked toward him across the backyard an hour or so after the common meal at Uncle Jesse's place.

"Well, now, who's that you got with ya?" he said, grinning.

"Jonas Mast . . . my beau. And one of the few young relatives you've yet to meet."

Jonas leaned down and extended his hand to Dawdi. "I'm mighty pleased," he said.

"John Brenneman's my name. I hail from Hickory Hollow, the reason I've never laid eyes on you, I daresay." Dawdi slowed down his rocking. "Welcome to the family."

"This is Mamma's father," Leah told Jonas. "Soon to be your grandfather-in-law."

Slipping his arm around her, Jonas stood tall, eyes beaming, as the three of them exchanged comments about the weather and, soon after that, the baptism. " 'Twas a right nice group of young folk this year," said Dawdi. "I daresay all of 'em will be hitched up by December."

Leah smiled at his bluntness. "Now, that's not the *only* reason to join church, is it?" Even though it might appear Amish young folk had marriage on their collective mind when thinking through their lifelong covenant, they best be heeding the promises made for more than just the purpose of marriage. She felt ever so sure about that.

"Well, it won't be long and the two of you will be man and wife, jah?"

Jonas smiled down on her. "Not long at all."

"Where do you young ones plan on livin', come next spring?" asked Dawdi.

Leah expected her grandfather to ask this. "Jonas and Dat plan to talk through that in just a bit."

"Well, I have a notion Abram won't make it any too easy for you, Jonas . . . just a warnin' from your ol' Dawdi-to-be." With that he winked at them both. "Used to be a Lancaster County bride could expect her father to offer expensive gifts, but anymore—"

"Dawdi! Remember, Dat's got to be prudent in the matter," Leah interrupted but quickly covered her mouth, realizing what she'd done.

"Go on, speak your mind, honey-girl." Dawdi lifted his black hat and scratched his head underneath. "What were you sayin'?"

"Sadie should be the recipient of such a gift, really—bein' the eldest daughter. And the twins are comin' along close behind . . . and someday, Lydiann. If Dat gave each of us girls a parcel of land, wouldn't be long and there'd be none left for him to farm."

Dawdi was nodding his head, pulling on his gray beard. "You've got a point there, but I doubt Abram will use that as his excuse today." Here he looked up with wise and gentle eyes. "Best steel your heart, young man. Don't expect anything from Abram Ebersol, and you won't be disappointed."

Leah's hopes fell a bit. Truly, she didn't want her Jonas feeling the same way. After their visit with Dawdi, Leah walked with Jonas out to the bank barn. They headed all the way around the back, where the second-level door opened up to the haymow. They stood outside, some distance from the gaping entrance, lest Dat overhear them.

"Dawdi John makes Dat sound like a hardhearted man. Dat can be difficult, to be sure, but he's also compassionate," she said.

Jonas nodded, reaching for her hand. "It's not necessary for me to ask anything of Abram. I'm a frugal sort; we can manage fine without land."

She felt ever so glum. "Maybe it's best to wait an' see if Dat offers on his own." That was unlikely. Dat would want to hold on to as much land as he possibly could for all the reasons she'd given earlier. Maybe it *was* wise for Jonas to forget about talking to Dat—at least this afternoon.

"We can always rent the house you wrote about," Jonas suggested. "Save up our money and buy land later to build on."

"Jah," she said, still wanting her father to treat her as special as she'd always felt she was to him.

Looking up, she noticed Aunt Lizzie running down the mule road, waving and calling to them. "Oh, look who's comin'," she told Jonas. "You remember my aunt Lizzie, don't you? Come, let's chat with Mamma's sister."

Before Lizzie, Jonas, and Leah could greet one another there in the barnyard, here came Dat hurrying out of the stable toward them, and Mamma running out the back door, skirt on the wing.

Leah found it both humorous and odd as they stood in a small but not so cozy circle in the barnyard. High in the sky behind the barn, the windmill creaked and whispered as Leah reintroduced Jonas to her aunt. "You remember Jonas from our visits to Grasshopper Level, jah?"

Aunt Lizzie grinned. "Why, certainly I do."

Mamma nodded, forcing a smile. Dat looked green around the gills, and Leah wondered what on earth that was all about. She felt the mood was severely strained, with most of the tension coming from Dat, though Aunt Lizzie's face looked awful pink, too.

After a while Dat suggested he and Jonas "walk out to the field for a spell," and with that, Mamma, Leah, and Lizzie strolled toward the house, the three of them linking arms.

"I have a feelin' Abram might talk to Jonas concernin' a dowry," Mamma whispered as they went.

"Can you be sure?" Lizzie asked.

"Well, I s'pose not, but I wouldn't be surprised."

"I'd say 'tis past time for Abram to show some charity," Lizzie piped up.

Leah glanced at her aunt and gave her a frown.

"Honestly, I'm wonderin' . . . what's Abram been waitin' for? After all, Jonas is the man of Leah's hopes and dreams," Aunt Lizzie continued, talking now more to Mamma than Leah.

Mamma pursed her lips like she wasn't sure what to say, and Leah was ever so glad her mother was quiet. If Mamma got started, no telling where any of this might lead.

Glancing over her shoulder, she saw Dat and Jonas heading for the tallest stalks of corn, Dat moving slowly as he went, and Jonas swinging his arms carefree-like. They walked together a ways; then—much too abruptly—they stopped and faced each other, silhouetted like two tall blackbirds against rows and rows of corn.

It might not have been the best timing for this man-to-man talk with Jonas. For some months, Abram had been calculating the risks, wondering just when he ought to take the lad aside. Should he speak straight from the hip this far removed from the wedding season, as Peter Mast had demanded back in August? Or wait till closer to November, maybe? What was best?

The risks were ever so many. His relationship with Leah was on the line, not to mention his and Ida's. And what a lip his wife could have at times, though he knew she had every right to be outspoken about *this* matter.

All that aside, he wanted to know what Jonas Mast was made of—if the boy had a speck of grit in him. He wanted to observe this blue-eyed boy Leah had fallen for when she was but a girl, witness for himself the kind of reaction the startling truth, so long held, might trigger in Jonas. And if Leah's beau hightailed it for the hills, all the better.

"No doubt the two of you have picked your weddin' date," he began as they walked.

Jonas nodded. "Leah and I discussed it Friday night."

"I 'spect Leah will be talkin' to her mamma 'bout all of that."

"Seems so."

They meandered to the edge of the cornfield and turned and stood there, still wearing black hats and Sunday-go-to-meeting black trousers and frock coats, the long sleeves of their white shirts rolled up.

A waft of wind came up, and cornstalks hissed as the two slipped through the golden fringe. They followed a narrow path single file through a maze of straight rows.

When they were completely cloaked by tall shoots of near-ripened corn, Abram stopped walking. Jonas, barely a yard away, looked almost too young to be taking Leah as his bride. "The time has come to speak bluntly," Abram began.

Another current of air rustled the stalks so strongly they thrashed against the wide hat brims the men wore. Quickly Abram secured his with one hand while Jonas tilted his head against the gust, his hands still deep in his trouser pockets.

"The dear girl you have chosen to be your bride is not who you may think," he continued.

Jonas fixed a silent gaze on him.

Where had the wonderful-good years flown? It was mind-boggling that he should be standing here, on the verge of revealing this momentous news to Leah's young beau.

He straightened a bit and pressed on. "When Lizzie Brenneman was in her rumschpringe, she was found to be with child." With his next breath, he laid out the truth. "For nearly seventeen years now, my wife and I have raised Leah as our own."

Eyes blinking steadily, Jonas scarcely moved. "Why do you tell me this?"

" 'Tis only fair that you know. And . . . if this truth in any way discourages you from marryin' the girl who believes herself to be Ida's and my daughter . . . well, then, I give you this chance, here and now, to reconsider."

"I love Leah" came Jonas's emphatic words. "This information doesn't alter how I feel."

Abram expected as much.

Just then thousands of blowing cornstalks threatened to flatten him. He leaned his head back and looked up at the sky, blue as the ocean, with flimsy white cotton for clouds. *Oh, Father in heaven, help this your defenseless servant. . . .*

Attempting to compose himself, he looked directly at Jonas. "Ida and I will talk with Leah tonight concerning this."

"Do you mean to say my Leah is unaware of her own mother?"

My Leah . . .

Put off by Jonas's quick tongue, Abram said, "She looks to Ida as her mamma . . . so I ask you not to speak of this to her." He paused, reflecting on the precarious circumstance. "Do you plan to spend more time with Leah today?"

"Maybe so . . . to say my good-byes."

"It was Lizzie's hope Leah be spared this knowledge till she reached the age of accountability. Which has now come, her bein' a baptized member of the church." He didn't go so far as to reveal the recent stress between himself and Lizzie and, more recently, Ida regarding the how and when of telling Leah. That was of no concern to Jonas.

Removing his hat, Jonas ran his long fingers through his light brown shock of hair. "Are Leah's sisters also in the dark 'bout this?"

"In due time they will know." He paused, then—"I repeat myself: If this causes you grave concern—Leah's life havin' issued forth from a corrupt union—speak now or forever hold your peace."

Jonas inhaled and appeared to grow an inch or more taller. "I won't be speakin' my mind on this issue just now. There'll be plenty of time for Leah to share with me her feelin's. . . ."

Abram was perplexed. "By letter, do ya mean to say?" Such a weighty matter for written correspondence.

Jonas nodded. "Until that time comes, I'll be makin' this a matter for prayer." He returned his hat to his head and said, "Is there more to discuss?"

"You have not asked for my blessing on the marriage."

"I have my Father's blessing," Jonas said. "And if Leah is strong enough to follow through with our wedding, I will ask for your blessing, as well." With that he turned and headed straight out of the cornfield, toward the house.

Abram suffered a sudden and fleeting light-headedness. He had lost this round with Peter Mast's son, that was clear. Wishing for a piece of straw to put in his mouth, he yanked on a cornstalk instead, bending it and pulling off a handful of tassel. Staring down at it, he frowned and changed his mind. He tossed it onto the ground, then stamped his hard shoe on it, muttering as he did.

Jonas had felt downright sure of himself while being sheltered by lofty cornstalks. But now, as he walked over the grazing land toward the house to Leah, he was somewhat befuddled. He could see her where she was sitting on the front porch, beside the woman whom she'd known all her life as her aunt Lizzie but who, in all truth, was her biological mother. And also next to her was Ida Ebersol, who had taken Leah in as her very own baby daughter but who was, in brief, her aunt.

How *would* Leah take such shocking news? He hoped his sweetheart would not be distressed—and to think he would not be anywhere near when Abram broke the news. He would be too far away to offer any reassurance, too far to hold her when she cried for all the years her family had deceived her.

Certainly, he did not know all the particulars or just why it was Abram and Ida had abided by Lizzie's wishes and withheld the truth from Leah. It might not be such a good idea for him to second-guess the wisdom of it.

Leah spied him from her cozy spot on the porch and stood to wave. My *dear girl*, he thought, waving back. Oh, the urge to run to her was nearly uncontrollable, yet he kept his pace, lest Ida and Lizzie notice how compelling his attraction was to Leah. Yet, here she came running across the rolling green turf to him, her bare feet flashing white beneath her long skirt.

Darling Leah . . .

"Did Dat offer us a bit of land?" were the first words out of her mouth.

He had completely forgotten she expected her father to have discussed the dowry. This the supposed reason for their walk in the first place.

Before he could admit no such topic had been brought up, she was nestled in his arms. He embraced her gladly, noting Ida and Lizzie must have slipped inside, for they were now nowhere to be seen.

"What did Dat say?"

He hadn't actually promised not to tell Leah the truth of her parentage, yet he would honor the elder man's request. "Let's go for a ride," he said, taking her hand.

"Where to?"

"Somewhere quiet—away from here—where we can walk and talk awhile." He wanted to hold her close and never let her go, to shield her from the coming revelation.

"I'll go an' get my shawl." She pulled away from him and scurried to the house.

While hitching up the horse, he struggled with the reality of Abram's words. Leah was the outcome of Lizzie Brenneman's youthful lust. What would his family think? Would Dat advise him against marrying his second cousin . . . if *he* knew? And Mamma, would she weep with the news? Or did she have the slightest inkling? After all, Mamma and Ida Ebersol had been fairly close through the years, sending letters back and forth occasionally, and Abram and Peter were known to put their heads together at farm auctions and the like.

A stern yet somewhat compassionate man, Abram had given his life for a secret, possibly turning a dreadful situation into a seemingly happy one for all concerned. Till now.

What *would* become of Leah once she was told? He'd have to await her letter—surely by this coming Wednesday he would have some indication. Such a dear she was about writing and sharing her thoughts with him. Soon enough Jonas could expect to know her heart on this.

Chapter Twenty-four

Leah and Jonas spent what was left of Sunday afternoon sitting side by side in a grassy, unfenced area not far from the perimeter of smithy Peachey's farm. Long and unpaved, the one-lane road had led them to a vast meadow with a small pond in the north corner of the property. Seemingly, this area was not used for grazing land, though Leah wondered why.

"Who owns this acreage?" asked Jonas.

"I don't know, really. For as long as I remember, no cows or horses have ever been on it." Her mind wasn't fully on Jonas's question just now. She was thinking about him leaving tomorrow . . . and what, if anything, Dat had said to Jonas earlier. But she'd decided while running to the house to get her shawl that she would be patient and not press for answers. Knowing Dat, it was possible he'd had other things on his mind than the dowry.

"Most any piece of property can be had for a price." Jonas leaned forward, resting his arms on his knees.

So . . . Dat must not have offered Jonas land as a wedding gift, she thought sadly. Just looking at Jonas, she knew. The brightness was gone from his eyes. Something was troubling him, all right.

"Do you think the smithy might know who owns the land we're sittin' on?" he asked.

"Maybe. You could ask, if you want."

He turned to her and smiled hesitantly. "Well, no, that could be awkward, ain't?"

She knew what he was getting at, of course. Gid's father, if he owned this land—well, then, they were trespassing—and Jonas was thinking it would be right tricky to approach the blacksmith, given the circumstances. "Did you want me to find out?" she asked.

He picked a blade of grass and held it between his fingers, staring hard at it. "I'll think on it."

Not only troubled, Jonas seemed a bit aloof, too . . . and this just since his talk with Dat. She'd watched for him to come back from the rows of corn with Dat, wondering why they'd had to go in so deep she couldn't see them at all. To talk man to man? But she stuck to the promise she'd made herself—she wouldn't put her nose where it didn't belong.

Jonas let the long piece of grass fall from his hand and looked at her. "Will you write to me . . . like before?" he asked suddenly.

"Jah, and will you, too?"

He nodded and was quiet for the longest time. Turning back to gaze toward the southern horizon line, he sat there amidst the grassland and a thousand insects, some of which kept crawling up her legs. She remembered the time when Jonas, but a boy, had slipped her a pair of his work trousers, bringing them out in a makeshift backpack to his father's milk house. She had asked if he had a pair he'd outgrown, some she could borrow for the summer because she hated being bit by mosquitoes and other insects, working out in the fields with Dat. Besides, back then, she'd felt more like a boy than the girl she was. Nobody, not even Sadie, ever knew of the trousers. One of the silliest things she'd ever done. But even then she'd recognized the irresistible bond between herself and her second cousin.

After a time Jonas turned to look at her again, searching for her hand. Finding it, he smiled with both his mouth and his eyes. She felt the sweet warmth of his hand; then he lifted it to his lips and kissed the back of her wrist, oh, so gently. She had to smile; he was ever so dear and certainly not distant now. Not in any way. "I truly wish you were comin' back to Ohio with me." He pressed her hand against his face.

"Mamma couldn't begin to manage with both Sadie and me gone. It's best for Sadie. . . ." She paused, biting her lip. "I'm sorry, Jonas, honest I am. I wish things had worked out differently."

"You never said why it was more important for Sadie to go than you." His eyes were trusting, yet questioning.

"Someday . . . things will become more clear" was all she dared say.

That seemed to satisfy him, and he sat there enfolding her hand in both of his. "I'll count the hours till I see you again." He turned and gathered her into his arms. "Oh, Leah . . ."

Leaning her head on his shoulder, she felt both happy and sad. "November twenty-fifth will be our day for always," she whispered.

Then, she didn't know quite how it happened, but his head was close to hers, ever so near. "My precious girl," he whispered. "Dearest Leah." He nuzzled her nose slowly, yet playfully with his own, and before she could resist, his tender lips found hers. She was startled at first but did not pull away. The kiss was sweeter than she'd ever imagined, and, oh, she longed for more. No wonder Mamma had said to save lip-kissing for after the wedding!

When briefly they pulled away from each other, the longing in his eyes could not be denied. Truly, he adored her.

His arms encircled her yet again, and she was enraptured by his affection, even fervency, as she snuggled near. His second kiss led to yet another, till she felt breathlessly woozy.

"Oh, Jonas . . ."

"Are you all right?" He touched her cheek.

"Maybe not."

They smiled then, faces aglow. She laughed a little shyly and leaned away from her darling beau. "I love my husband-to-be," she told him.

His eyes were intent on her, and he shook his head slowly. "I am the happiest man on earth." He caught her hand in his and looked down at their entwined fingers.

She thought she might cry. "Nothin' dreadful will come of this, I hope."

"Ach, Leah . . . never. No . . . no. How can it be? We've sealed our engagement with three kisses, our mutual promise to wed." He was frowning now, his eyes searching hers. "Don't you agree?"

"So . . .'tis not a bad omen, then?"

He shrugged his shoulders. "I honor and respect you, dear.

You're the light of my eyes. I can't say I believe in omens, really."

"Well, gut," she said, and because she was convinced what he said was true, she leaned over and kissed *him* square on the lips.

"Let's walk," he said, standing now. He lent a hand and pulled her up, and they went strolling happily together, talking over the ins and outs of their wedding day soon to come. A warm breeze caressed their faces, and Jonas leaned down and picked a wild yellow daisy. "What a happy day it will be," he said, giving the flower to her.

"Jah, ever so happy." She lifted the delicate petals to her cheek.

They walked a bit farther, and Jonas pointed out a curious, rectangular-shaped mound. "What is that, not three yards away? Do you see it?"

She squinted, looking hard in the direction of his hand, quickening her pace to match his.

"How peculiar." He stooped to examine what looked to her to be a small grave. "Someone must've buried either a little child or a pet dog here," Jonas said.

She saw where the ridge of grass had been cut away, and the slight rise. "But who would bury someone here and not in a cemetery? 'Tis awful strange."

Jonas agreed. "And seems to me, a private burial place would require at least a simple marker."

"You'd think so, jah."

"But why a grave dug here in the middle of a deserted pasture?" he mused aloud.

"This is wasted grazing land," she spoke up. "I can't

imagine it should become a cemetery, can you?"

Jonas shook his head. "Hardly. But fancy folk do the strangest things sometimes, ain't so?"

She wondered why Jonas now assumed the owner was English. Right surprising it was, really.

Jonas drove Leah home and walked with her to the back door. They said their good-byes rather swiftly—no lingering, so the family had no opportunity to observe, the way of the Old Order. Serious courting was done in secret, under the covering of night.

Not wanting to shed a tear in front of him, she waved and hurried inside, bypassing any conversation with Mamma and the twins, who were rushing to get supper on the table. She headed straight to her bedroom and lay down, thinking back on her afternoon with Jonas and their kisses, hoping the Lord God would not punish them for disobeying Mamma's strict wishes.

Recalling the warmth of Jonas's embrace—his face ever so near—a small part of her began to understand how it was Sadie had succumbed to forbidden hours with the Schwartz boy, one thing leading to another till she'd found herself in an awful bad way.

Leah was most thankful Jonas was an upstanding young man and that they were now baptized church members. They had made their promises to God and *her* church this very day. Realizing the reality anew, she felt even worse for having lip-kissed on the day of holy baptism.

She went to the window and looked out toward the woody hillock, wishing she might visit with Aunt Lizzie. But in a few minutes Mamma would be calling for supper. For now she must put on a smile or else her family might wonder what she'd been up to. Kissing Jonas, beau or no, would not be fitting supper talk. Besides, Leah wanted to be a shining example to Hannah and Mary Ruth, who would experience similar feelings in the not-so-distant future.

'Tis a gut thing Jonas and I will be married soon, she thought, blushing as she hurried down to the kitchen. *I must tell Mamma the date we've chosen for the wedding.*

Jonas hurried his steed toward Grasshopper Level. He hadn't spent much time at all with his family this visit, though his twin baby brother and sister held great fascination for him. His married sister, Anna, and her husband, Nathaniel King, had been vying for his attention, as well as Mamma. Next month when he returned, he hoped to make up for lost time. Along with Dat, his brother-in-law, Nathaniel, and younger brothers Eli and Isaac, they would all help bring in the apple harvest, as planned. There would be plentiful time for some good fellowship then. He hoped he might be able to complete the apprenticeship he and David had agreed upon—a few weeks shy of seven months. Though he was working diligently to make that happen, if he could not, he would simply extend his stay in Ohio and trust his father could make do without him during harvest. If so, his final return home would fall very close to his wedding day.

Tonight, however, he looked forward to an enjoyable time

around the long kitchen table. Mamma, more than likely, would put on a big spread for him, another sure reward for riding all that way on the train and back. At supper he must let Dat know there was a slim chance he might not make it back home by apple-picking time.

The horse whinnied and he settled back in the carriage. He thought of Leah's vague comment about Sadie, made without so much as a blink of an eye: *Someday . . . things will become more clear. . . .*

He was somewhat apprehensive, having heard a few rumors over the years about Lizzie Brenneman—all confirmed this day. Could it be Sadie suffered a related problem? Certain sins ran in families, his father often said.

It wasn't fair to point fingers, if only in his mind, not the way his own passions had flared this afternoon. He should have stopped with a single kiss, yet Leah's eager response had taken him by surprise. She loved him greatly, that much was clear.

So his sister's unexpected letter a month back, warning him of Leah's interest in Gideon Peachey, had to be false. Still, he planned to speak to Rebekah tonight, hear her out about whatever she thought she'd witnessed at the August singing in Abram Ebersol's barn. Not that he had ever given her foolish letter a second thought, anyway.

He let the reins rest loosely across his knees. Recalling the afternoon's pleasures, the time he'd spent with his darling girl, he determined it *was* best, even wise, that Leah remain here in Gobbler's Knob for the next four weeks or so. A separation of hundreds of miles was a good idea for now. He could not imagine anything more embarrassing than having to answer no to the deacon's appointed question, "Have you remained pure?" prior to the wedding service. At all costs, he must protect and keep as sacred his love for Leah.

Abram sat at the head of the table and bowed his head. He took his time saying the Lord's Prayer in his mind, following the silent blessing for the meal Ida had cooked for them. He knew full well his time had run out. Lizzie had been demanding the truth be revealed ever since Leah turned courting age. And because Jonas Mast was now aware of it, Abram could no longer put off what he had to do. Tonight the story of Lizzie's sorry rumschpringe was to unfold.

Sometime after supper he and Ida would arrange to speak privately to the girl they considered to be their second child. To Abram, she was all a daughter should be—everything he and Ida could hope for and more. And considering the shameful path their firstborn, Sadie, had chosen, having to talk to Leah weighed even more heavily on him.

Short of asking her to go with them to the barn or for a walk over to Blackbird Pond, behind the smithy's barn . . . well, he didn't know how things would play out. Still, he could wait no longer; otherwise, Lizzie might take matters into her own hands, jump ahead, and talk to Leah about the circumstances of her birth.

His father-in-law would be of no help with any of this, Abram knew. It had been John's desire ever since he'd come to live in the Dawdi Haus last spring for Abram to "face up to the hard facts, and the sooner the better." John's attitude hadn't set well with Abram, and as a result they'd exchanged some heated words, the last of which seemed to cause a flare-up in John's bad hip. No longer could he lift a hand to harvest or to fill silo. With Leah soon to be hitched, Abram hadn't the slightest idea how he was going to keep the farm running at all, let alone soundly.

Mary Ruth broke the silence. "Please pass the mashed potatoes, Mamma."

Ida did so quickly, then handed the large platter of baked pork chops to Abram. "Your favorite," she said with a quick smile.

Abram looked to see where Ida had put Lydiann, who usually spent the supper hour in Ida's arms. "Is the baby upstairs sleepin'?"

"Jah, she has a low-grade fever. . . ."

"End of summer flu?" Mary Ruth asked.

"Oh, I hope not," Hannah spoke up.

"No, no, no." Ida was adamant. "Lydiann's just trying to cut her first tooth."

Leah had slumped down in her seat, awfully quiet—more so than usual. Abram observed her discreetly between bites of meat. *Did Jonas defy me today and speak to Leah about Lizzie?*

He shuddered at the thought.

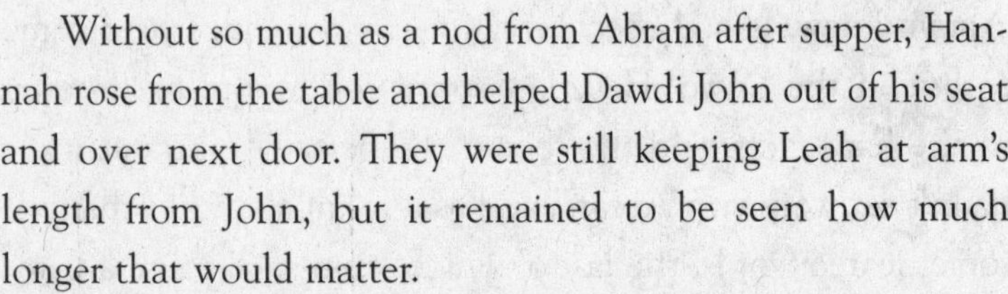

Without so much as a nod from Abram after supper, Hannah rose from the table and helped Dawdi John out of his seat and over next door. They were still keeping Leah at arm's length from John, but it remained to be seen how much longer that would matter.

Abram breathed deeply. John's relationship with his granddaughter Leah would not change one iota once she was told of her true beginnings. As for himself, Abram's parental status would be reduced to merely *Onkel*. With that woeful thought, he curled his toes inside his shoes.

He got up from the table and found *The Budget*, a newspaper published in Sugar Creek, Ohio, and distributed by mail to the Old Order communities. Meanwhile, Leah and Mary Ruth cleared the table and cleaned up the dishes.

After a bit Leah said she was feeling "awful tired tonight" and turned to leave the kitchen.

"I hope you're not cutting teeth like the baby," Mary Ruth teased.

This brought a peal of laughter from Mamma, as well as Hannah, who'd just now returned from the Dawdi Haus.

"Ach, Mary Ruth, best leave your sister be," Abram spoke up in Leah's defense.

Leah smiled weakly, even gratefully, and headed upstairs.

Hearing from Leah's lips that she was under the weather gave Abram pause. Tonight just might not be the best time to reveal such life-altering information, after all.

He drew a sigh and settled back in his hickory rocker. *One more day won't hurt none*, he decided.

But what if Leah had already been told by Jonas? The thought continued to nag him through the evening and later as he lay down on his bed and had to contend with Ida's steady snoring. His back pained him enough to make him restless. He stared out the window at the moonlit sky, afraid that once Leah was told of her roots, he and Ida would never regain what they'd lost.

Sadie helped Edith off to bed early, as was the older woman's custom. "Lanterns out" usually came by eight o'clock of an evening, which gave Sadie plenty of time to read or think. But this night she planned to write a letter.

Sunday, September 21
Dear Mamma,

Hello from Millersburg.

I suppose Leah and Jonas are glad to have joined church today. You and Dat must surely be grateful. Was there a big crowd?

She wondered when or if she might hear that a letter from Preacher Yoder had been sent to the Millersburg preacher. Or worse, from Bishop Bontrager to the Ohio bishop. Church discipline, after all, followed closely on the heels of the unrepentant soul. Naomi Kauffman, if she'd kept her word, had already set things in motion for Sadie to be disciplined, at least in the Gobbler's Knob church. With Leah having spilled the beans to Dat and Mamma, as surely she had, no doubt Preacher Yoder had gotten an earful from her, too.

You might think me uncaring, Mamma, if I say Leah shouldn't count on me to be a bridesmaid. You can tell her for me. There's so much going through my mind now. Better to ask Hannah and Mary Ruth. Or . . . Adah Peachey, since she and Leah have been bosom friends. Yet I daresn't be so bold as to suggest whom Leah ought to pick, for goodness' sake. Still, I'm awful angry at her these days.

Mamma, I know it was ever so awkward for you and Dat to use the telephone yesterday. I know, too, that your words—both of yours—were meant to encourage me to confess. Truly, they have gone round and round in my head. And, if I'm to be honest, in my heart.

I best be signing off for now. Write when you're able. I hope Jonas Mast might tell me of his and Leah's baptism.

With love,
Your daughter Sadie

Chapter Twenty-five

Abram rose and dressed in his work clothes before the rooster's first crow. He rolled up his sleeves and headed promptly to the barn, where he wiped down the bloated udders of his two milk cows before sliding the wooden stool up to Rosie.

Leah was late in getting out to help, which was unusual for her on a Monday morning—if she was coming at all, considering her departing words in the kitchen last evening. Ida would surely alert him if Leah was, in fact, ill.

The last time one of his daughters had been said to be "under the weather," no one guessed she was expecting a child. Sadie had been both immoral and successful at concealing it for a time. Even now, thinking about Sadie's deception made him want to go out and find the *Lump* who'd done her wrong. He hadn't asked who had been the father of the baby. Best not to know.

The unexpected clatter of a carriage coming up the long lane caused him to crane his neck to look; Abram was flabbergasted to see Preacher Yoder in the faint morning light.

"*Wie geht's*," the brawny man called to him from the side yard.

"Hullo! I'm in the barn milkin'."

"I know where you are, Abram" came the reply, reminiscent of the Lord God calling Samuel of old.

He looked up and saw Preacher walking at a brisk pace, following the outline of the barnyard where the gravel met the back lawn. "Looks to be another mild day on the way," Abram said, keeping on with his hand-milking chore beneath Rosie.

"Better weather I haven't seen for September twenty-second."

"We mark this day?" he asked, puzzled. "What's on your mind, Preacher?"

Not only stocky, but taller than most Plain men in the area, Preacher had a fearsome way of filling up the space he occupied. Young folk, mainly those in danger of church discipline, often whispered that the strength of Jehovah God was sketched on Preacher's countenance. He had been only thirty-two years old when the lot of ordination fell on him; it was soon after that he became the divinely appointed shepherd for the Gobbler's Knob flock. Now he was fifty-five and as forthright as ever. "Leah spoke with me on Saturday mornin', just so you know, Abram. Are you privy to what she had to say?"

He nodded. "That I am."

"Then you know your eldest—soon as she returns home—will have to face Deacon Stoltzfus, Bishop Bontrager, and myself." Preacher stepped back as if eager to exit. "When do you expect the girl back?"

The girl . . . not "your daughter." Preacher Yoder was making a severe point, and Abram should have expected as much. Preacher, along with Bishop Bontrager, was known to dig in his heels. Little or no mercy was the rule, and baptized church members were fully aware of the consequences of missing the mark.

"Sadie is visiting in Ohio. As far as I know, she'll return in a few weeks. When she does I'll instruct her to follow the Ordnung in submission to the church."

"That is your word on this, Abram?"

"Jah, 'tis."

Standing at the upstairs window, Leah had seen Preacher Yoder's buggy through the lane and into the barnyard. She decided it best not to head out to the barn, what with somber talk of Sadie going on. Must be the reason why Preacher had come here so early of a morning. She'd half expected him to come calling yesterday afternoon, even while Dat and Jonas had gone to talk privately in the cornfield. But Preacher Yoder had his own way of doing things, and no one ever questioned the time of day he chose to drop in.

She carried around in her at least a speck of hope. After all, Sadie hadn't yet turned down her request to be a bridesmaid in the wedding, an honor Sadie knew was wholly tied to a confession. Now, with the church brethren involved, it might be that the way was paved for her sister's redemption.

After Preacher Yoder left the barn to return to his carriage and hurry out to the road, Abram finished the milking and stumbled across the barnyard, heading for the house. The tantalizing aroma of bacon sizzling and Ida's scrambled eggs with cheese welcomed him, discouraged as he was.

"Abram?" His rosy wife met him at the back door.

Before she could say more, he was nodding his head. He sensed her concern. "Jah, Sadie best be gettin' herself home. And mighty soon."

"Then, she's in danger of the shun?"

"If she doesn't hurry and confess, she is."

"Ach, what'll we do?" asked Ida, hovering near as he hung his hat on the wooden peg in the utility room.

"When it comes to our daughters, we never give up on 'em."

Ida gave him an encouraging smile, then leaned on the crook of his elbow as they headed for the kitchen. "I'll keep this in my prayers."

He wanted to ask about Leah in the worst way but held his peace. The fact she wasn't anywhere around led him to think she might be upstairs tending to Lydiann.

About the time he might have asked, here came Leah carrying his wee daughter. "Let me have that baby of mine," he said, sitting down at the table.

Leah, smiling now, gently offered Lydiann to him. "She's dry and ever so happy."

"Then her tummy's full, too?" He glanced over at Ida, who was scooping up the eggs and dishing them onto an oval platter.

"Oh my, did she ever eat." Ida came over, carrying the platter. She set it down and gave him a peck on the forehead, then smooched Lydiann's tiny cheek, making over their little one. "Can you believe how fast she's growin'?"

Abram touched Lydiann's soft face with his thumb. "Who's she take after, do you think?"

"Hard to say, just yet," Ida replied. "But I daresay Lydiann's most like our Leah."

Our Leah . . . How much longer will she be considered ours alone? he wondered. Everything within him resisted telling Leah now. If ever.

Leah's eyes shone with delight at Ida's comment. She hurried to set the table, catching his eye. "Sorry I didn't get out to help you this mornin', Dat. What with Hannah and Mary Ruth dressin' round for school and all, Mamma needed my help with the baby."

Just then the twins rushed to take their places at the table. "Aw, lookee there," Mary Ruth said, grinning at Lydiann in Abram's arms. "She's her father's baby girl, ain't so?"

This brought plenty of smiles, and Abram figured he knew why. Truth was, he'd spent hardly any time at all with Lydiann. Not because he didn't want to. He was just far busier than he'd hoped to be at this phase of his life. Looking to slow down some, he'd been hoping for the longest time Smithy Gid might take over the heavy farming duties once married to Leah. But Jonas Mast had seen to it those plans had gone awry.

"No . . . no, I say Lydiann's *Mamma's* girl," said Ida, cooing now and taking the baby from Abram. "I daresay she'll be mighty content to sit on my lap while you feed your face, dear."

Quickly Leah and Ida took their seats. When Abram

bowed his head for the blessing over the meal, he added an additional prayer. *O Lord God, may your watch care rest on our Sadie. . . .*

He breathed in audibly, signaling the end of the prayer.

Leah reached for the platter of eggs near her and noticed Mary Ruth helping herself to three long strips of bacon across the table. "Won'tcha save some for the rest of us?" she joked.

Mary Ruth gave her an apologetic look. "Sorry. Guess I thought I needed plenty of energy today."

Hannah nodded her head.

"And why's that?" Dat asked.

"We're havin' the first test in mathematics," Mary Ruth explained, all smiles. "I s'pose to see what each pupil recalls from last year."

"In arithmetic, you say?" Dat said.

"It's hard work," Hannah said softly. "Takes a lot out of certain pupils." She smiled at Mary Ruth and they tittered.

"If a *certain* daughter of mine didn't fret so over grades, I doubt she'd need any extra bacon a'tall." Dat chuckled a bit. "Ain't so, Mary Ruth?"

Mamma looked up just then, jostling Lydiann, who was reaching for the nearby breakfast plate. "Better learn all you can this year, girls. Next year I'll be puttin' you both to work here at home."

Mary Ruth's smile faded instantly. Leah suspected it was an indication of how her sister's heart had just sank, to be sure.

Feeling like it might be a wise thing to change the subject, Leah stuck her neck out and asked, "Dat, would smithy

Peachey happen to know who owns the grassland northeast of his property line?"

"*I* know who does," Dat replied. "That land belongs to the good doctor."

"Dr. Schwartz?"

"Henry Schwartz has done nothin' with it all these years. Why do you ask?"

Leah was caught like a driving horse in the path of a reckless automobile. "Jonas and I were there yesterday afternoon, is all."

"So then you know it's perfect grazing land and a cryin' shame not to put animals on it." Dat shoveled another spoonful of eggs into his mouth. While chewing, he managed to say, "You were trespassin' if you's were over there."

She recalled Jonas had suspected as much. How peculiar that an English doctor, of all people, wanted to let that land just sit there with no intended purpose.

Then it struck her hard as a bushel of potatoes falling on her head. Dr. Schwartz owned the land where someone had dug a tiny grave. Awful strange!

She reached for her glass and drank down half of the creamy milk, straight from Rosie to Mamma's table. Could it be? But no, surely not. Had *Derry's* father buried Sadie's blue baby in his own field?

"What is it, Leah?" Mamma was asking, staring at her.

"I guess I'm not feelin' so gut right now." She slid off the bench and rushed out of the kitchen.

She heard Dat say as she headed upstairs, "Goodness' sake, Leah was sick last night, too."

Well, she couldn't help how she was feeling. She had to

take herself off to her room for a while. She needed to breathe slowly . . . think this over carefully. Besides, what *could* she say was wrong with her later, when she went out to hose down the milk house, feed the chickens, gather the eggs, and mow and fertilize the yards? How could she begin to say that Dr. Henry Schwartz must have buried his own grandson—and Dat's, too—on that fertile plot of land? How could she confess that Sadie had conceived the dead baby with the doctor's wicked son?

Nearly worse than all of that, Dr. Schwartz hadn't had the decency to tell Sadie about the burial. He could have done so in confidence, one way or another. Mercy knows, this might have helped ease Sadie's desperation and suffering, even given her a place to privately kneel and ponder her great loss.

Henry Schwartz was a licensed physician and a trusted family friend. She'd seen the framed certificates on the wall at his medical clinic, felt the steadfastness in his handshake. So why should such a smart doctor give a stillborn, premature baby a burial? If he indeed had done so. Made hardly any sense.

She felt helpless and sad at once. Helpless to know what to think . . . and awful sad for Sadie, who knew nothing of this, and just as well.

Chapter Twenty-Six

Lizzie was helping Ida put up the late cabbage the Tuesday after Leah's baptism, making sauerkraut in her sister's kitchen. "'Twas my understanding you and Abram were plannin' to speak openly to Leah two days ago." With both Hannah and Mary Ruth away at school and Leah safely outside with Abram, she felt at ease bringing this up.

"We changed our minds, is all," Ida explained. "Leah wasn't feeling so well."

"Oh? Leah's ill?"

Ida nodded, absentmindedly it seemed. "Abram decided we should wait a bit."

Wait longer?

Lizzie didn't like the sound of this. Both Ida and Abram had used the selfsame remark as an excuse too many times over the past months. Honest to goodness, she didn't think it fair to wait one more day. After all, Leah was old enough to be courted and marry, so why not acknowledge her maturity in *this* important matter?

"I say it's past time" was what she felt like saying, and did so flat out.

"Well, now, Lizzie, is it your decision to make, do you think?" Ida's blue eyes could grow dark with displeasure on occasion, and this was clearly one of those times.

"If you're draggin' your feet—scared of what Leah's response might be—well, I'm willin' to tell her myself."

"I'm sure you are." Ida straightened and then continued to stir the wilting cabbage in the kettle of boiling water. "But I think you best be waitin'."

"Waitin's all I've been doing Leah's whole life long." Lizzie wished to push back the years. Back to when her daughter was but a toddler—so cute Leah was—and Lizzie wished she might whisper it was *she* who was Mamma. But with the help of Bishop Bontrager, the three of them had made an agreement to last until Leah reached courting age. Lizzie had stuck by her word, keeping the hardest promise of her life.

"Just when do *you* think Leah should know 'bout me?" Lizzie asked hesitantly.

"Soon as Abram says" came the expected answer.

Wanting to say more, she bit her tongue. She was distressed these days, even worried, knowing the wedding season was just round the bend—desperate, really, to share her maternal affection with Leah. Not that she hadn't always demonstrated her love to her birth daughter—to all of Abram's daughters, really.

Abram's daughters . . .

Oh, there she'd gone and forgotten the truth yet again. One of the Ebersol girls was really *her* daughter. Would heart and head never agree?

Honestly Sadie had been glad to see Jonas Mast return to Millersburg. She didn't let on to anyone, and certainly not to Edith, who nearly every day now was telling about one "nice Amish boy" or another, several of whom had come in from surrounding counties for the potato and corn harvests. "All kinds of young fellas are here. My goodness, Sadie Ebersol, you picked a right gut time to visit!" The frail woman had a clacking tongue, except when she was deep in slumber for the night or napping during the day, which was much of the time, depending on what was happening in the house.

"What sort of lookin' boys are they—the ones from surrounding counties?" Sadie found herself asking.

"Oh, blond or dark haired, it don't matter none. All of 'em be mighty attractive, same as you," the widow said. "You'll see for yourself if you go to one of the singings. That's where the lookin' gets the strongest, ya know." Edith sighed, her slight chest heaving. "I daresay the most wonderful-gut thing on God's green earth is a match well made."

"I s'pose so" was all Sadie said in response.

A rumble was heard next door in the main house, and Sadie went to see if one of the children had fallen. But Vera signaled all was well—"just a bit of confusion 'tween Joseph and Mary Mae" was the excuse. Which meant there must have been a scuffle, a battle of wills common to any household with children.

Vera Mellinger had her hands full with three lively youngsters and another on the way. Young Andy suffered with severe asthma, the reason a telephone was permitted in the woodworking shop. As if she weren't busy enough, Vera often hosted Bible studies for the church women, too. Sadie had repeatedly been invited to attend but felt she should look after Edith next door, a right good excuse for not sitting a full hour while reading Romans or Corinthians, epistles written by the apostle Paul the People here liked to study.

So many things were different here in Millersburg. She was still becoming accustomed to the pitch-black color of the buggies, instead of the gray color of Lancaster County, not to mention the curious shape of the carriages. Men's hat brims were only three inches wide, and the single, baptized young men grew beards right away, instead of waiting till they were married, like in Gobbler's Knob. Here, too, the men's hair was medium-length and notched—squared off at the ear—compared to the bowl-cropped, shorter style back home.

The local women wore their bodice capes more frequently, and their prayer caps had numerous ironed pleats in the back. She was the only girl with a pleasant-looking, even pretty, heart-shaped head covering, she realized. This fact alone attracted plenty of attention from young men—also, that she was visiting the Mellingers, a well-respected family.

The flourishing countryside reminded her of home, for sure and for certain, except there were more rolling hills. Once chores were done, Sadie often walked the back dirt roads, dodging the deep grooves made by the metal wagon wheels and looking out over the miles and miles of ripening corn.

She felt like a foreigner with a name like Ebersol. More common were the surnames Schlabach, Hershberger, and

Stutzman, and she sometimes wondered why Mamma had never mentioned David Mellinger's family was connected to Fannie Mast's side or that their ancestors had put down early roots here.

If asked, Sadie might have said she liked being round a whole houseful of shirttail cousins who doted on her at times, embarrassingly so. It was as if they felt somewhat sorry for her but at the same time liked her for who she was. Still, if they'd had any idea what she'd done and refused to repent of, they might have packed her up and sent her home promptly. She was awful sure of that, seeing as how they were forever discussing Scripture—sometimes even in heated debates, which she found to be curious.

One such conversation had taken place last night, when Jonas returned from Pennsylvania. He and Cousin David were having themselves a fine time disputing the cut of a man's hair. "The rounded style looks mighty fancy to me," David had said, staring at Jonas's bowl-shaped cut.

"Not to me, nor to the brethren back home."

"But there's a problem with it, I'd have to say," said David, looking serious. "For one thing, if you were ever stuck out in the middle of nowhere and had no way to shape the curved ends, you'd be in a pickle, jah?"

Jonas's eyes had brightened. "I guess I can see your point, but I'd have to say the notched style would be that much harder to keep up . . . if you were away from civilization, so to speak."

This had brought rousing laughter. Even Vera and droopy-eyed Edith were smiling.

"What about the length?" Jonas asked. "Ain't it a solid issue in the Bible?"

David got up and went to get the Good Book. Then, sitting back down at the table, he began to read. " 'If a man have long hair, it is a shame unto him.' "

"I agree, 'tis a sin and a shame," Jonas said, a twinkle in his eye. "The longer the hair is, the more shame, I'd say."

David had agreed with a smile, his own hair at least two inches longer all around than Jonas's cropped style.

Sadie wondered if the Lord God paid any attention to a Plain man's hair. Wasn't it a person's heart that made the difference? That's what Dat and Mamma had always said. Maybe four inches or more too long was an issue if a man wanted to follow hard after the Word of God. But two inches?

She tried to imagine Dat sitting here talking over such things, but she knew her father had no use for nitpicking Scripture.

Jonas, though, had seemed to enjoy the debate. *Such fun I'd have with him as my brother-in-law,* she thought, knowing she'd never have the chance to enjoy the relationship because the Bann and eventual shunning would put a wedge between her and Jonas, as well as her entire family.

The afternoon found Sadie on her way downtown to the old general store, where Vera and other Amishwomen sold their handmade wares. This day there was a whole batch of potholders, aprons, sunbonnets, and embroidered dish towels to deliver.

The air had the slightest chill to it, and she was glad she'd worn Vera's navy blue sweater, though she missed her shawl from home. Being it was now toward the end of September, she should have planned for the change in weather. But she'd packed quickly to come here, so fast she hardly had much of anything to choose from. Soon, though, she would be sewing more dresses, and she'd have to figure out a way to bring in some spending money for fabric and sewing notions. She couldn't expect Vera and David to pay her way in life, though she was providing a live-in care service for their mother.

Rain was forecast, so she hurried the horse just a bit, eager to get where she was going.

It was on her way back to the Mellingers' that an almost eerie wobble made the buggy shake and groan . . . then *bang*! Somehow the hitch either broke or came loose, and she sat helplessly while the horse, complete with its harness dragging, kept on going, trotting away in spite of her calling, "Come back! Ach, you mustn't leave me here like this."

Still, the mare hightailed it down the road, paying her no mind. So there she was, cockeyed in the wagon, fortunately on a dusty side road where scarcely any automobiles dared to venture.

At first she considered getting out of the now slanted buggy, its front pitched forward so that it was impossible to sit in the seat. She thought of getting out to walk the long way back. Too far. Still, she couldn't just sit there and wait for night to fall.

Gazing out at the fields of corn on all sides so similar to

those back home, Leah came to mind. What nerve, her younger sister sending her off on a train to the Midwest, then telling Dat and Mamma on her once she was gone! How could Leah up and betray her like that?

Irritated to no end, Sadie managed to climb down out of the horseless carriage. She went and balanced herself on the split-rail fence by the side of the road. She knew it wouldn't be right to abandon David's family carriage—wasn't the kind of thing a visiting relative, though awful distant, would do. Sooner or later she hoped someone would miss her and begin to wonder where she was, especially come suppertime, which, best as she could guess, was in another two hours or so.

Sadie might have sat and fumed for the rest of the day about her situation if Jonas Mast hadn't happened along in David's market wagon an hour later.

"Well, now, where's your horse, Sadie?" He jumped down and hurried over to her.

She told him what had happened, and he was surprisingly calm. "Wasn't your fault," he said. "I'll get you back to the Mellingers', then go lookin' for the horse. David can help fix the hitch."

Glad for his kindness, she got settled into the wagon. She was ever so relieved and anxious to talk to him, but she wanted to be careful about appearing too forward. "Your baptism—and Leah's—was the weather nice for it?"

" 'Twas a sunny day . . . and the best day of my life, so far," he said, holding the reins. "Aside from weddin' Leah, I can't think of anythin' I'd rather do than kneel before the bishop and promise my life to the Lord God and the church."

His answer got her goat; she wasn't prepared for this. Yet she should expect him to say such things, shouldn't she? After all, he was just as devout as Leah seemed to be. Maybe more so.

"How was Leah? Did she shed a tear?"

He clucked his tongue, urging the horse to hasten along. "Leah was ever so happy. Too bad you weren't there for the ordinance yourself."

"Jah." Suddenly she was at a loss for words. The People would have expected her to be present at her sister's baptism, no question. But soon enough they'd all know why she'd left—and why she was never going back.

They rode along in silence, except for the chirping of the birds, too loud for her liking. She longed for the quietude of Edith's back porch, where no one could bother her and the barn cats could roam up and purr their soft contentment while she held them in her lap.

It was then that Jonas spoke again. "Next week I plan to drive Sarah Hershberger, next farm over, to the Sunday singing. A girl with not a single brother to drop her off. I'm doing it only as a favor for her father, a carpenter friend of David's. She's about your age, I'd guess. How would you like to ride along?"

She had to laugh a little. Jonas was as kind as he was well-mannered, acting as a big brother to David's close friend . . . and to her, as well. She liked the idea of going somewhere in the coming week, so she said, "Jah, I'll go," and left it at that.

On Wednesday Jonas received Leah's first letter since their baptism. He wasted no time in beginning to read it, hoping she might indeed share her thoughts on what she'd learned Sunday night from Abram and Ida. But surprisingly, there was no mention of anything out of the ordinary. Had Abram decided against telling her? For what reason would he not?

One thing was quite interesting: Leah had written that the local doctor was the owner of the property where they'd spent the sunniest part of Sunday afternoon.

> *Dat says Dr. Henry Schwartz, down Georgetown Road a mile or so, owns the land. We best not go back because it's trespassing, just as you said.*
>
> *Lydiann is babbling a lot now, and today I almost thought she said, "Mamma." Sadie won't know her when she returns home next month.*
>
> *I asked Mamma if she thought November twenty-fifth was all right for our wedding, and she agrees it will be just fine.*
>
> *I'm missing you already, Jonas. Something awful, truly!*

Reading this, he almost wished he'd stayed on in Lancaster County. How could he have left his sweetheart-girl to deal with the harsh reality of her birth without his loving support? She might think him coldhearted, though by his kisses she knew better.

Without a doubt, he felt all but guilty for knowing what Leah did not. His bride-to-be was Lizzie Brenneman's own daughter! Once Abram and Ida revealed the truth to her, she would be sorting through a gamut of feelings. Alone.

Mary Ruth had been anxious for the chance to see Elias again. Scarcely had she stepped out the front door of the Nolts' house when here he came in his pony cart. Nearly flying down the road, his black felt hat was high in the air as he waved and beamed a smile at her. *He likes me*, she thought, her heart racing as she walked barefoot along the road.

"Hullo, there, Mary Ruth!"

"How are you, Elias?" she said, feeling oh, so comfortable with him.

He leaped down and went around to help her into the small cart, which wasn't at all necessary, since it was considerably lower to the ground than a buggy.

"Didja think I'd remember?" he asked cheerfully.

She wanted to say, "I knew you would," but instead replied, "I'm glad you did."

The russet pony pulled them much faster than she thought possible. Too fast, maybe, but it wasn't her place to say so. She must learn not to talk so much, to let others speak their minds, especially a young man as interesting as this jovial boy next to her.

"When will you turn sixteen?" he asked, as if he didn't know.

She smiled, keeping the laughter inside for now. Once she got home, she'd tell Hannah all this, and they'd giggle together. "Well, not till February tenth, year after next."

He wasn't a bit shy about his answer. "I'll be waitin' for that, Mary Ruth."

"Hannah will be sixteen the same day," she offered, wondering if he might think to include his older brother, Ezra, in his plans—whatever they might be—so far ahead in time.

"I hope you like ice cream." He made a high-pitched sound that his pony recognized as a signal to speed up even more.

"Jah, I do. Mamma makes it homemade. Do you?"

"Sometimes, if we have blueberry pie to go along with it."

She didn't know why that sounded funny to her. "A little pie with your ice cream, then?"

"That's right, Mary Ruth." His pony was working up a lather, and she felt a bit uneasy, the two of them speeding along in the cart. Yet she kept her peace, not wanting to spoil the delight of this special afternoon.

Chapter Twenty-Seven

After leading the animals out to pasture, Leah helped Dat shovel manure, then mowed the front, side, and back lawns—fertilizing them for the final time this year.

That done, she followed Aunt Lizzie's markings, heading for the honey locust tree, a letter from Jonas in hand.

Friday morning, October 3
Dearest Leah,

I am always glad to receive your letters, and I cherish each one. Often I read them over again before drifting off to sleep after a long day of work; that way I can be sure you will show up in my dreams.

Even so, there are times when I wish I received only one letter each week from you. Why, you may ask? In all truth, it is difficult for me to bear your sweet letters because they fill me with longing for you, dear Leah. Especially now, when the memory of our kisses still lingers. . . .

My heart beats only for you. There is no other way to put it.

Now, I hesitate to tell you this, but I've just been offered the prospect of establishing a partnership with David Mellinger here in Millersburg. This may be God's providence at work, and I wanted you to hear this good news directly from me.

I don't mean to alarm you, but what would you think of us living in Ohio after we're married? We would have to get Bishop Bontrager's permission and blessing on such a thing, but we'll cross that bridge later.

I look forward to your next letter!

All my love,
Jonas

Leah's hand shook as she finished reading. Jonas was surely excited, and his words—*this good news*—clearly indicated her beau was more than willing to pull up stakes and leave Pennsylvania permanently.

Yet how could *she* leave her family behind? Jonas knew firsthand how close she was to her sisters . . . and to dear Dat and Mamma. Aunt Lizzie, too. And how empty would her life be without her lifelong best friend, Adah Peachey? Besides, at the time of baptism, she'd made her promise to both her father and the bishop that she would never permanently leave the Gobbler's Knob church district—as had Jonas.

A graceful lark swooped down from high overhead before it soared up again, disappearing from view over the treetops and toward the densest area of the forest. She pondered what to write to him, how to share her heart yet not hold back on her happiness for him—for this remarkable chance to own a carpentry business. Most any girl would be thrilled at such a prospect, were it not for leaving everything she knew and loved behind. Except for Jonas, of course.

Ach, what can I say to you, my beloved? A woman's obedience to her husband came first after her submission to almighty God and the church. This had been ingrained in Leah since childhood, having been taught by Mamma's example and in nearly every sermon.

It was kind of Jonas to ask her in such a manner as to make her feel she had a choice. But truly, Leah knew she had none at all. Only one way could she possibly reply; this she knew instinctively. She must write back quickly and say she was ever so glad for him, that if he was able to obtain the bishop's go-ahead and blessing, and he believed the Lord God was leading them to live and raise their future children in Ohio, then so be it.

Jonas had begun to think perhaps Abram was counting on a measure of moral support—waiting till Jonas made Leah his wife—before revealing Lizzie to be Leah's mother. It seemed strange to him that Leah had not written a word about it. Her silence on the matter was unlike her. Undoubtedly, Abram would have informed Leah that he'd also told Jonas the facts regarding Lizzie—on their baptism Sunday, no less. And Leah would just assume he was waiting for some word from her, wouldn't she? Unless there was some other reason she seemed so evasive.

He'd thought of writing Abram to inquire, but that might put his future father-in-law on the spot. No need to open the door to a clash. There was enough potential for that, with

Smithy Gid still lurking in the wings and Abram Ebersol all for it.

Was it possible Abram had confided in Jonas hoping the news of Leah's parentage might cause him to abandon his wedding plans, leaving Leah in the dust? Was it for the purpose of running him off? If so, this would definitely make room for Smithy Gid. But Jonas rejected the notion as absurd.

Based on the things his sister Rebekah had told him the last evening he was home, he might have had reason to think hard and long about getting right back to Lancaster County to spend his final weeks as a single man closer to Leah. But the memory of his darling girl's fervent kisses persuaded him otherwise.

Still, he put enough stock in Rebekah's observations to be somewhat concerned. He did hope to question Sadie soon, when he helped her with some chores tomorrow evening. They would go downtown together in the market wagon to make a delivery of quilted goods for Vera. This time he hoped the wagon might stay hitched to the horse. It wouldn't do for him to get stuck somewhere at dusk with Leah's beautiful blond sister. People talked. Everyone here rumored he was betrothed to marry a girl from back home . . . and that the girl was not Sadie, but her younger sister.

◆

Leah gathered eggs and fed the chickens the next day before helping Mamma with the washing that hadn't been completed on Monday washday. Yesterday the skies had darkened, making down rain, and she'd rushed to take in the near-dry clothing. Because of the change in weather, Mamma had decided to break with the schedule and wash the rest of the clothing today.

"Cousin Fannie wrote me a nice letter," Mamma said as they worked together at the hand-wringer. "She wants to invite you and me to a quiltin' bee in your honor."

"Really?"

"I guess this is Rebekah's idea—hers and Katie's."

Leah couldn't help but recall the last time she'd spent time with Fannie's daughters. Downright uncomfortable, it had been . . . such pointed questions about Sadie and all. She'd had a difficult time dismissing the cutting remarks, especially from Rebekah.

"Why do you think they want us to quilt with them?" she asked.

"They're welcomin' you into the family as a sister." Mamma gave her a smile. "We'll make whatever quilt pattern you like."

So Rebekah and Katie wanted to make amends—was that it? How awkward, otherwise, to marry their brother with such unsettled feelings. "I'll go, sure. Sounds to me like fun."

"The first week in November it is," said Mamma, holding on tight to a pair of Dat's work pants as the wringer did its work.

"Won't be long after the quiltin' frolic and Jonas and I will be wed." She remembered, too, that Naomi's wedding service was coming up soon. Naomi had said no more about it, but Leah had heard from Mamma that Luke was putting pressure on Naomi to see a doctor. Leah didn't quite understand what Mamma had meant by that. But when she asked, Mamma indicated in hushed tones the bishop himself had taken steps to determine just how pure the young woman who was to become his grandson's bride really was. Evidently, he had taken to heart Naomi's rumschpringe with Sadie.

Leah blushed to think the bishop had that much say. Dat had often indicated by dropping hints along the way that this "minister with full power" ruled somewhat mercilessly amongst the People. But this? She didn't care to dwell on it. She assumed it remained to be seen whether or not Naomi Kauffman would end up becoming Naomi Bontrager.

"When do you think our bishop will contact the Ohio ministers?" she asked softly, thinking now of Sadie.

Mamma could not respond. She simply shook her head, eyes filling with tears.

By this reaction from dear Mamma, Leah understood the letter of warning had most likely already been written and sent. The wheels of excommunication and shunning had been set in motion. The People did not slap the Bann on a church member easily or swiftly unless the nature of the offense allowed for no other alternative. In Sadie's case, once she returned home, the six weeks probationary shunning would go into effect so she could have a taste of it and want to repent of her sins. Whether Sadie returned home or remained in Ohio, if she did not repent, she would end up shunned. Just as Leah and Jonas would be if they left Gobbler's Knob and Bishop Bontrager did not rule on the side of leniency.

Leah's greatest dread was that Sadie might simply decide never to come home.

Promptly at four o'clock the mail arrived, and Sadie hurried out to bring in the bundle of letters. She made her stop on David and Vera's side of the big brick house, depositing a third of the mail in the designated spot on the corner of the kitchen counter. She noticed yet another letter from Leah to Jonas and shoved it down toward the bottom of the pile. Then she hurried to the Dawdi Haus to bring great joy to Edith with five letters bearing the widow's name. Edith had begun to share many of her pen-pal letters with Sadie. One of the women she wrote to had a grandson, a courting-age boy Edith wondered if Sadie might like to get to know. Even though courting amongst the People was kept secret, it seemed to Sadie that Edith was bound and determined to play matchmaker.

Sadie also held a letter from Leah to her, along with one from Mamma. She was fairly sure Mamma's letter would carry the same urgent message she'd stated by telephone. Precisely, Mamma was making a determined, obvious plea for Sadie to *come home immediately and repent. Spare yourself the shame of the ministers there having to contact you. Oh, Sadie, my dear girl, you must do this! Dat has also requested this of you.*

She cast aside Mamma's letter in favor of the one from Leah. The first letter her sister had bothered to write to her . . . another sure sign Leah had helped to get her out here, only to betray her once she was gone. What both Mamma and Leah didn't know was that there were plenty of interested fellows here, something she could never now hope for in

Gobbler's Knob. Both Ben Eicher and John Graber had scrapped amongst themselves to get Sadie's attention at the last singing. She'd ended up riding home with Ben, having secretly promised John her presence at the following singing. Either of them would do just fine for her to marry. She didn't mind that Ben lived over in Walnut Creek or that John made his home much farther away in Allen County. Indiana, Ohio—wherever she ended up meant she didn't have to be a *Pennsylvania* maidel. It would be all right with her not to be within earshot of either Leah or Mamma—especially Leah, though Sadie did miss Aunt Lizzie terribly. One of these days she must write Lizzie a long letter.

Seeing the smile on Edith's face, Sadie helped open each of the pen-pal letters for the old woman, then excused herself to the light and airy bedroom that was for now her home away from home.

The second-floor bedroom was smaller than the one she'd shared with Leah back home. Still, it was all her own, with a double bed to stretch out in and a wide oak dresser with plenty of space for her few clothes. She had already started sewing some new dresses and aprons for the coming autumn using the dress patterns from the Millersburg church district, with Vera's input on style and cut. Easily, she had stitched up the long seams of two blue dresses in short order. Since Vera was soon to give birth, Sadie felt she ought to do this sewing herself, as well as some for Edith.

Now she pulled the only chair in the room over next to the tall window and tore open the letter from her sister.

Dearest Sadie,

How are you? All of us here are all right, except we miss you something awful. I've waited to hear from you, but when you didn't write, I worried you were miffed. And rightly so.

I did not tell Mamma about your baby on a whim. Honestly, it was the hardest thing I've ever done, breaking my promise to you. You must believe me. In one way I despised it, but in doing so I felt the burden of guilt lift from me. Our sisterly covenant was ever so wrong. I see it clearly now. Oh, Sadie, I can hardly ask your forgiveness.

For all the time I did keep mum, I thought hard about those things you shared with me, especially that day in the garden. I weep sad tears, knowing how you struggle to forgive yourself, dear sister. And I pray you will let God, our loving Father, restore you to the church. He alone can grant grace and mercy.

I know (and you do, too) that soon you will be called upon to make things right with the brethren here, and I'm worried this will cause a terrible rift between us. Surely you must live in fear of the shun; I myself tremble to think of it. It seems all of Preacher Yoder's sermons nowadays call us to live as a holy generation. How could I possibly do so while carrying a heavy weight of deceitfulness?

One thing I hope to accomplish in this letter is to let you know, once again, that I love you and will never stop. What I did I would expect you to do if ever I strayed from the narrow way. Oh, please come home and make amends, dearest Sadie.

Will you write soon?

With much love,
Your sister Leah

Sadie slumped back in her chair, sighing. Obviously her sister had taken great care to write such a heartfelt letter. Torn between fond memories of their early days together and blaming Leah for spilling the beans on her, Sadie let the letter slip from her fingers and drift to the floor.

Chapter Twenty-Eight

The stately trees lining the road had already begun to turn to golden, red, and orange hues. Because of this and the fact he felt rather glum, Jonas did not rush the mare to his final destination. As a boy he had often gone out this time of year, past his father's orchard to where giant maples and oaks dropped their leaves in such abundance he liked to gather up a select few, choosing the most colorful to press between the pages of the largest book in the house, *Martyrs Mirror*.

His mother had once discovered a red sugar maple leaf marking the page where the account of "four lambs of Christ"—a brother and three sisters—had been sentenced to death as heretics, though they were indeed followers of Christ. He was stunned when he read the middle sister came to her death singing, then prayed aloud, "Lord, look upon us, who suffer for thy word. Our trust is in thee alone." All four commended their spirits into the hands of the Lord God, offering up their blood sacrifice, their very lives, for their unfaltering faith.

From that day forth, he had often wondered if he, too,

might be given the heralded "martyr's grace" if ever he were to come to such a fate. For that reason, he had purposed to give his life fully to spreading the goodness of the Lord above, wherever his feet may trod.

This evening, though, there was no need for that kind of grace. But empathy, perhaps. Sitting next to him was a young woman who seemed as sad as she was lonely. The sooner he got her back home the better.

Sadie said not a word as they rode along, evidently waiting for him to do the talking. He held the reins too high, tense as can be. "What do you know of Smithy Gid?" he blurted out his question.

She replied softly. "He's the only son of my father's closest friend, the blacksmith. Our neighbor, as you know."

Jonas contemplated how to phrase his next question. Or should he?

They rode along, too quiet for several minutes. At last he brought up the August Sunday singing held in Abram's barn. "Did you happen to see Leah and Gid together there?"

"I didn't go to the singin' that night." He noticed out of the corner of his eye that she turned to look at him. "I did see Leah and Gid walking through the cornfield over to his house after attendin' the singing."

He could only guess why Leah had even gone to the singing, let alone left with Gid. Nevertheless, this information wasn't earthshaking enough that he should be concerned. Although it did seem odd for a betrothed young woman to spend time with a single man.

"Do you have any reason to believe Leah might be interested in Gid?" Everything within him rebelled against asking such a thing—Rebekah's report made not one lick of sense. He knew Leah was as devoted to him as he was to her. And yet the tone of her last letter made him wonder if something wasn't amiss.

"I saw them . . . one other time, too," Sadie added somewhat hesitantly.

"When was this?"

"Not too many days before I left for here."

Tension spread down from his jaw to his neck and now his shoulders. "Are you sure you saw *Leah* with Gid?"

She sighed, fidgeting now. "It happened the day Leah got herself lost in the woods. When she didn't come home for the noon meal, Mamma sent Gid out lookin' for her, with the German shepherd—a gift to Leah from Gid last spring."

He tried to recall if Leah had ever mentioned the dog. Inhaling, he held his breath before continuing. "Does your father hold out hope for the two of them gettin' together?"

"Oh my . . . ever so much."

That fact still did not establish a reason to suspect Leah of being unfaithful. "Can you be more specific about what you saw the day Leah got lost?" he asked.

"Well, they were walkin' out of the deepest part of the woods. Gid was playin' his harmonica for Leah, and they were laughin' together. And . . . I'm not sure I ought to say much more."

"Go on, please. . . ." he said, her hesitancy causing his heart to pound. "What is it?"

"I . . . I saw them holdin' hands." She paused. "I had an awful hard time believin' it then, but it was so."

He clenched his jaw. No! This *had* to be purely innocent

on Leah's part. Then he remembered how Leah had refused his two invitations to come here . . . to be near him this summer. Why had Leah sent her sister instead?

He had never thought to address the question, not in connection to Leah wanting to stay home for Smithy Gid. She'd indicated her mother needed help with the new little one, though at the time, he *had* wondered why Sadie or the twins couldn't have pitched in, freeing Leah up to make the visit.

Keeping his gaze on the road, he never once looked at Sadie to his left. Could she be trusted? He wasn't certain. Why *was* she here and not Leah?

I'll write to Leah immediately about this, he thought. *I must know her side of things*.

Observing the road ahead as far as he could see, he followed the line of every ridge and valley, each soaring tree, till his eyes found the sky. He was struck by the coming nightfall—something of a lemon color—not the predictable rosy hue of setting sun.

'Tis the end of summer, he thought, hoping it was not also signaling the end of Leah's affection for him. Yet with each dying moment, summer ebbed toward autumn . . . and there was nothing he could do to slow its progress.

When Leah received Jonas's letter, she didn't have time to read it in sweet solitude. Dat expected her to help with as many of his barn chores as possible, more than usual this week since smithy Peachey and several other farmers nearby needed his help digging potatoes. Due to severe back pain, he'd finally given in and paid a visit to Dr. Schwartz "to get me some pain pills." Being able to offer his help with the harvest had always been of utmost importance to her father. He enjoyed the make-work-fun mentality of the People, wanting to be counted on by the neighboring farmers.

She hurried upstairs to her room right after dinner, knowing she must not dawdle. There she read the letter from Jonas.

Right away she determined something was wrong: Jonas wanted to know if she'd "spent time with Gid Peachey at a singing in August" . . . and could she explain his gift of a German shepherd?

I hope to hear from you as soon as possible, Leah. Since we are betrothed and plan to marry in a few short weeks, I trust you will clear this up for me.

Surely it is nothing more than a misunderstanding. I pray so!

I'll watch eagerly for your letter.

With love,
Jonas

Oh, her heart ached for him. None of this had any bearing whatsoever on their love. She must answer him immediately, even take time tonight to write before going to bed. For dear Jonas's sake, she would write long into the wee hours if necessary.

To think that someone—who?—wanted to cause a falling-out between them this close to their wedding day! She could not imagine how such a thing had come about.

She slipped the letter into the top dresser drawer and

hurried downstairs to help with kitchen cleanup so Mamma could nurse Lydiann.

All of a sudden, a distressing thought occurred to her. Was it possible Sadie had something to do with this?

Getting Edith settled this night was a chore and then some. Edith wanted to sit by lantern's light in the front room and read one pen-pal letter after another aloud—this humorous happening and that event—till Sadie was plain tuckered out. On top of that, she was having trouble giving the woman her full attention, recalling how miserable Jonas looked since their trip to town. He was nearly silent at mealtime, not engaging so much with either David or Vera in the good-natured sort of conversation they'd obviously enjoyed all summer long. Even Mary Mae and Andy, the two younger Mellinger children, weren't successful in getting him to play evening games, she noticed.

Daylight hours were growing shorter, and the family—Edith and Sadie included—spent more and more time together following supper. Edith wasn't in a hurry to be helped back to the Dawdi Haus; she liked to sit in one of the old rockers in Vera's kitchen and listen to the after-meal talk or ask David to read yet another chapter from the Good Book.

Sometimes Sadie slipped into her daydream world, thinking about Ben Eicher or John Graber while helping Vera with dishes, looking forward to the next singing. Neither boy could hold a candle to fair-faced and handsome Jonas Mast, who she was beginning to think was the most desirable young man anywhere. Still, as much as she admired Jonas, she couldn't just out and out steal him away from Leah, could she? The rational side of her pondered this continually, but the compelling desire to lash out and have her revenge made Jonas most enticing. Ever more so as each day passed.

Two days later Sadie found herself sitting on the front porch, waiting to bring in the mail.

She walked down the sloping lawn to the mailbox and thanked the postman for the delivery, then thumbed through the pile of letters on her way up to the house. Right away she noticed an envelope addressed to Jonas from Leah. Seeing her sister's handwriting and name in the upper left-hand corner made her heart pound hot and hard.

Leah broke her vow. She promised to keep my secret forever! she thought. *She doesn't deserve to be happy. . . .*

Quickly, without thinking ahead to what sadness this might cause Jonas, she slipped the letter into her dress pocket. Then, hurrying into the house, she headed to Vera's kitchen and deposited the stack of letters on the counter as usual.

Glad no one was anywhere around, she pulled Leah's letter out of her pocket. Holding it in both hands, she stared at it, aware of the heat in her face, the rage in her heart.

Leah belongs with Smithy Gid, she told herself. *Dat knows it, so maybe 'tis best. . . .*

Vera's trash receptacle was kept under the sink, and Sadie

reached down to open the cabinet door. Jittery with a guilty conscience, yet flush with anger, she held Leah's letter over the waste can, took a deep breath, and let it drop into the rubbish.

Chapter Twenty-Nine

The day came and went with no mail back from Leah, although Jonas was glad for a letter from his mother. She had written of being extra busy with Jake and Mandie. *They bring us great joy, times two*. There was also a cheerful letter from his brother-in-law, Nathaniel, and one from his next-youngest brother, Eli, with talk of the apple harvest.

Jonas was aware, on some level, of the singular squeak of a car's brake as the postman stopped in front of the house each day. Ankle-deep in sawdust out back in the carpentry shop with David, he imitated the master carpenter's every movement, taking great care to craft each desk or chair into a shining example of excellence. All the while he was mindful of the hammering of his own heart.

What's keeping Leah? he wondered.

Thinking back to her response to his earlier letter raising the subject of them living here after the wedding, he wished now he hadn't put the question to her in writing. He should have waited to talk with her in person about the prospect once he returned home. Her return letter, he recalled, had been one of loving words, even of encouragement. She wanted him to be happy in his life's work, as long as Bishop Bontrager would sanction such a thing. She wanted what *he* wanted, *with the blessing of our sovereign Lord and the church.*

Despite her seemingly positive approach to moving, he had sensed an underlying hesitancy, even disappointment. He decided to reread that particular letter tonight. First, though, he must take good care in making the dovetail joints on the dresser drawers for one of David's regular clients. After that he planned to sweep out the workshop and redd up before going to the house for supper.

With no word back from Jonas, Leah began to think something must be wrong. Surely he had understood the things she'd written to him, that she and Gid were merely friends, neighborly and all, as one would expect when families in close proximity work together. *Nothing more,* she had written, still shocked Jonas had been led to believe otherwise. She'd explained why she had been present at the singing, how she'd gone with Adah at her request. Also, she'd told Jonas in no uncertain terms that King belonged to the *whole* family, not just to her . . . and she'd even asked Dat's approval, wondering how prudent it was to accept such a gift.

Even so, in spite of all she'd written him, she felt something was terribly amiss. A single day turned into an agonizing two . . . then three. Jonas was clearly ignoring her letter. But why? Had he read between the lines of her earlier letter? Had he sensed her reluctance to live in Ohio? Surely he did not question the bishop's stern stance on keeping to home or that they had both promised to live amongst the People of Gobbler's Knob, vowing so at baptism.

Worse, had Jonas chosen to believe the near accusations about Smithy Gid and herself?

Truth be known, she had begun to wonder if their premature affection—kissing as they had—might have been a bad omen, indeed, just as she had brought up to Jonas that very day. Yet he'd brushed it off.

She went about her work in a fog. Never having been one to question herself, she began to question everything. She recalled the tiniest details of her life with Jonas, the joyful snatches that had begun with their earliest days and family visits to Grasshopper Level: picnics on the lawn, romps in the meadow, daisy picking, volleyball games—all of it—including their most recent Sunday afternoon together, soaking up sunbeams in Dr. Schwartz's empty meadow.

She decided to send yet another letter to her beloved, to make one more attempt to convince him she was, and had always been, trustworthy—his faithful Leah. She would not cover the old ground previously written—that Smithy Gid had merely found her in the forest and walked her home, that both she *and* Adah had gone with Gid over to the Peacheys' house after the singing that night.

The letter she intended to write this time was meant to state once more how she felt in the deep of her heart, recalling their youthful promises—made so long ago, it seemed—as well as the loving words exchanged during courtship's dearest days.

Do you remember helping me catch that hop toad the

Sunday we were out by the creek all alone? My mamma raised her eyebrows when we returned, awful muddy from having such fun together. I guess she thought at my tender age of eleven I had no business falling in love with you. But Mamma didn't know what we knew, did she? We truly cared for each other, even then. And still we do . . . I do. How can I not write you again to tell you these things within my heart?

Yet you remain ever so silent. Are you displeased, Jonas? Have I offended you? I would return the dog in a short minute if you say the word.

My love always, for you alone.
Your faithful Leah

Desperate to resolve whatever had caused this breach, she scanned her letter before sealing it shut, hoping . . . *praying* Jonas might read her words . . . and see through to the love in her heart.

It was well before sunrise when Jonas set out running. Frustrated to no end, he sprinted for a full mile without stopping on a level dirt road near Killbuck Creek. A pain in his side caused him to slow up, so he resorted to walking.

Not a speck of traffic was here so early in the morning. He was glad for the peace before he and David were to head out for Berlin to eat breakfast at Boyd and Worthman's Restaurant and General Store.

With still no word from Leah, he wondered if their plans for marriage were on shaky ground. Was it possible she did care for Gid Peachey and had never had the courage to tell him? But if so, what about their afternoon together, kissing and sharing their hearts so openly in the flower-strewn pasture . . . and their talk of the wedding?

He walked more briskly, getting his wind back. The thought crossed his mind Leah might possibly have some of the same inclinations Lizzie Brenneman had as a fickle and lustful youth. Was it possible—could it be—Leah was in any way similar to her birth mother? There had never been any indication of that. Leah had convinced him of her love, that she was true blue.

He picked up his pace and began to run again, soon turning to head back to the Mellingers' place just as dawn broke over distant hills. Desperately he tried to outrun the exasperating thoughts, such wretched ones they were.

Leah awakened feeling all wrung out, so scarcely had she slept. She had argued with herself all night, going back and forth about whether or not to send the last letter she'd written to Jonas, dear to her as it was.

She got up and dressed, brushed her hair, and pinned it back in a tight bun, finally setting her prayer cap on her head. Forcing herself down the stairs and out to the barn, she decided to wait till after breakfast to think more about the letter. Dat had always said never to make an important decision on an empty stomach. Mundane as it was, she felt she needed sustenance—some of Mamma's scrambled and cheesy eggs, maybe—to hold her together. With still not a single letter arriving from Jonas, she felt short of breath, concerned she might not be able to perform her many outdoor chores this day.

Plain and fancy men alike were feeding their faces at the well-known Berlin restaurant. Some sat at the long counter, others settled in toward the back, sitting around tables. The atmosphere was charged with farm talk and the coming cold snap, a change of pace to be sure. But David seemed to have more than home cooking on his mind. "Something's bothering you, Jonas," he said.

"Is it that obvious?"

David smiled quickly. " 'Tis all over your face."

Jonas couldn't say what was on his mind, couldn't reveal the torture he'd lived with each day the mail came and went with no word of explanation from Leah. "I'm thinkin' I might need to cut short my apprenticeship, if that's agreeable to you."

David nodded. "Well, now, you've come a mighty long way in nearly six months, to be sure. We'll miss you round here, but jah, that's all right in my book."

Jonas paused, staring down at his plate. "I need to get home right quick." He wasn't so keen on saying what was on his mind just now. He could think only about seeing Leah again, talking with her face-to-face . . . hearing the truth directly.

"We've had gut fellowship since you've come here," David said, his eyes registering sympathy. He poured two heaping teaspoons of sugar in his black coffee, stirred it, and slurped the hot drink. "I hope things are all right 'tween you and your sweetheart back home," he said.

Jonas drew a deep breath. "Jah, I hope so, too." He stopped for a moment, then continued. "And while we're speaking bluntly, I've been wonderin'—do you have any idea how my apprenticeship came about? Any inkling at all?"

David nodded. "I shouldn't say . . . prob'ly. But between you, me, and the fence post, 'twas your father-in-law-to-be who set it up with me."

"*Abram* did?" Jonas was taken aback.

David had another drink of his coffee. "He called on the telephone to tell of your keen interest in carpentry and wondered if I might not take you on—help you get your feet wet."

His head was spinning. "When was this?"

"Round the end of March."

Just as I began to seriously court Leah, he thought. *So Abram wanted me gone all along.*

Leah happened to meet up with Gid, of all people, as she was closing the door on the chicken coop, having just gathered the eggs.

He removed his black hat as he came near, offering a boyish grin. "Bein' more careful in the woods these days, Leah?" He slowed a bit and glanced toward the forest.

She had to smile. "Jah, I am that," and she thanked him again for rescuing her that awful day.

"Well, I best be gettin' back to work," he said, heading off in the direction of the mule road.

She stood there, basket of eggs in hand, observing his long stride. He reached up and put his hat back on his head, going up toward Aunt Lizzie's. Probably to clean out her chimney flue before the cold days set in, Leah assumed. Lizzie had been saying as much, though Leah hadn't expected her to ask Gid to do it. Lizzie would insist on offering him something for his work, of course. More than likely, it would be a nice, plump fruit pie or suchlike, instead of money.

Carrying the eggs carefully to the house, she wished Jonas could have seen her just now with Gid, seen there was nothing except pure friendship between them. She placed the basket on the kitchen counter and hurried upstairs to her bedroom. From her dresser drawer, she pulled out her latest letter to Jonas. Still unsure of what to do, she read it again.

Finished, she refolded the letter. She knew she must not further plead with him to believe what he surely already knew in his heart. If he didn't trust her by now, when would he ever?

She pushed the letter back into the drawer. Hurt and discouraged, she headed downstairs.

Will we ever be truly happy again? she wondered. *Will I?*

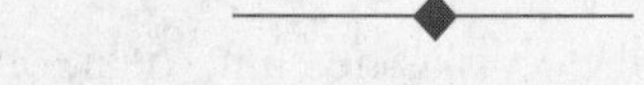

David was already in the workshop hand sanding a table leg when Jonas arrived promptly at six-thirty the morning after their talk in Berlin. The day felt slightly cooler than yesterday's dawning hour, and he smelled woodsmoke lingering in the air, a sure sign of autumn.

Jonas greeted the master carpenter and set to work, using a doweling jig on the eight-inch oak boards, soon to be a trestle-table top. He was anxious to throw himself into the work to drown, if possible, the disappointment that cut away at him. He must help David catch up on a half dozen or so projects for eager customers, enduring the wait till his father got word back to him with some dependable answers regarding Leah.

Feelings of near despair had begun to set in during the past week. The letter he had written to his darling girl had offered him no solution, having been met only with maddening silence. Though he could hardly hold back his urgency, he knew it was not prudent to assume the worst or to be impulsive and rush home unannounced. Instead, he'd written a letter to his father asking him to pave the way for the unplanned visit with Leah. He'd spelled out his dire concerns, pleading with Dat to get a feel for the situation with Abram Ebersol—*because I can't go on this way, not knowing for sure about my Leah.*

He had sent the letter off in yesterday's mail. *Dat won't ignore my request,* he thought. *He'll go right away to Gobbler's Knob. I know he will.*

Now he must attempt to be patient till he received word back regarding Leah and his impending trip. The hours stretched long before him.

Chapter Thirty

It was chilly in the barn, even with the wide doors all closed up this morning. After a short time Abram went back into the house for his work coat while Leah milked Rosie.

Returning to the barn, he heard a horse and carriage rattle into the lane. Walking over to the side yard, he was surprised to see Peter Mast waving a greeting to him. "Hullo, Abram!"

"*Willkumm!*" he called back.

Peter got out and tied the horse to the post. They exchanged a few words about the change in weather, then they walked toward the barnyard, where Peter asked if they could speak privately.

"Oh?"

" 'Tis concerning your daughter and my son." Peter sounded downright serious all of a sudden. "Ain't the first time we've been mighty plainspoken, as you recall."

"Leah's within earshot," Abram replied, jigging his head in her direction. "Why don't we mosey up to the pasture?"

Instead of taking things slow, they walked at a hurried

pace, Abram noticed, all the way out past the barn to where the windmill stood guard over his prized property. He looked toward the woods and thought he saw Lizzie out sweeping her front porch, a thin line of smoke curling up from the log house chimney.

Peter seemed overly eager to get to the point. "It's come to my attention, namely from Jonas, that Leah and the smithy's son may be carryin' on romantically."

Abram bristled and Peter stopped talking, glancing at the ground, as if to let the information settle in. *How could Jonas suspect such a thing?* Abram wondered. *Why is Peter here on the boy's behalf?*

This made no sense, but he waited for Peter to continue, hard as it was not to spew forth the questions rapidly gathering in his mind.

"Now, Abram, I know you and I know Ida, but I can't vouch for Leah . . . and I think you can guess what I'm gettin' at here."

Can't vouch for Leah . . .

Abram suppressed the fire in his bones. What kind of nerve! Peter and Fannie Mast had known from the beginning of Lizzie's unwed pregnancy, even though the bishop had put the shush on things early on for little Leah's sake. Still, it wasn't Peter's place to throw around insults like this.

"You best be speakin' straight with me, Peter," he urged.

"All right, then—is Smithy Gid warmin' up to Leah?"

Abram set his chin. He was tempted to give Peter what for, and then it came to him . . . the *real* reason Peter was here. Well, now, wasn't this curious? Jonas must be having second thoughts about marrying Lizzie's illegitimate daughter after all. Most likely, Peter was here to help Jonas wiggle out of his betrothal, using as an excuse what Abram had shared with Jonas man to man. If that was the case, then he *had* found out what Peter's son was made of, and none too soon. "Who's askin' this—you or Jonas?" Abram said.

"I'm here at my son's request. But I have a stake in this, too."

Abram straightened, recalling the day Gid had gone in search of Leah in the woods, bringing her home wearing an unmistakable grin. "Seems to me Gid would be a right fine man for my Leah," he replied. "Ain't no secret how I feel 'bout that. If he wants to spend time with Leah, I have no problem with it."

"So . . . it's true, then?"

"Gid's awful fond of her. As for courtin', well, 'tis hard to be exact about what goes on under the coverin' of night."

"Gideon Peachey has your blessin', is that what you're sayin'?" Peter's face had turned as red as a ripened beet.

"He's had the go-ahead since he turned sixteen." There, he'd said it all, though clouded over with a shade of gray.

"Then, I guess that's that." Peter turned tail and headed back through the paddock without so much as a good-bye grunt or a tip of his black hat.

Heading toward the barn, Abram felt torn. He was fully persuaded Gid was Leah's best chance for happiness. Even so, he could not bear to see her heart broken. He was caught between his dear girl's hopes and wishes and what a father knew best. Downright angry he was at Jonas Mast for instigating a breakup. No doubt in his mind—Peter's boy had made a deliberate turn away from Leah, starting that day in the cornfield.

The telephone in the woodshop was jangling as Jonas hurried to answer it. David was nowhere around, so he picked up the phone. "Mellingers' Carpentry."

"Jonas? Is that you?"

He perked up his ears. "Dat?"

"Jah, thought I'd make a quick call to you, son."

"Gut to hear back from you." He wondered if his father had some important news. Why else would he resort to using a telephone?

"I don't want you to waste any more time troublin' yourself over the likes of Leah Ebersol."

The words slapped him in the face. "You spoke to Abram?"

"This morning . . . and, believe me, you're better off this way than findin' out your girl was disloyal after you married her."

Jonas was aware of the pounding of his heart. His precious Leah untrue? His throat went dry. How could this possibly be?

He recalled again Leah's decision not to spend the summer here with him. How frustrating it was not having solid answers for why she had refused. Yet he'd trusted her, respecting her right to remain in Gobbler's Knob as she wished. Then, when he'd invited her a second time, what had she done but call him on the telephone, of all things, to ask if he could make arrangements for Sadie to come in her stead! Just why *had* Leah sent Sadie to him? He could only imagine.

Feelings of total frustration flooded him, and he knew not what to say or think. Knowing Leah through all the years of their friendship, he would never have thought she might purposely set out to betray him. Such a thing was unthinkable, truly.

"Son, are you there?"

He drew in a breath and expelled it suddenly. "I can't begin to understand this, Dat."

"'Tis essential for you to come home. You made a covenant with the Gobbler's Knob church. . . ."

I can't think of living anywhere near Leah if I can't be with her myself, he thought. But to his father he said, "David's offered me a partnership and perhaps I oughta be thinking on that."

"Jonas . . . son, you'll be shunned if you don't return."

Bishop Bontrager was one of the most austere ministers in all of Lancaster County, the spiritual head of the Gobbler's Knob and Georgetown church districts. Responsible for recommending excommunication and shunning, the man of God had the power to seal Jonas's fate.

"I'll write to him and plead my case if I have to," he said. "But if he refuses, I'll make a life here for myself without Abram's Leah. . . . Somehow, I will. With God's help."

His father continued to argue for Jonas to return home, saying he couldn't think of going on without him.

When the time came to say good-bye, Jonas offered, "God be with you, Dat. Tell Mamma I love her . . . and my brothers and sisters, too."

"Son, please think hard about this. You mustn't throw

away your life. . . ." There was great heaviness in Dat's voice. Then he said, "I'm through with the Ebersols, kin or not, for what they've done to us!"

Jonas stared at the telephone after hanging up. It seemed unbelievable. Leah must have given in to Abram's wishes . . . and now preferred Gid.

It was going to be a warm afternoon, much nicer than the morning had started out to be; this was clear to Sadie by well past the noon meal. She helped not only Edith with some light cleaning but also Vera, offering to dust the front room and bake a pie for supper while Vera read to Mary Mae and Andy before putting them down for a nap.

With the cherry pie nestled safely in the oven, she hurried back to the Dawdi Haus through the connecting door. She saw Edith dozing in her rocking chair, white-gray head tilted back, mouth gaping open. Tiptoeing past her, Sadie headed for the stairs.

In her room, she sat near the window, looking out. She felt at once guilty and even sad for having thrown away Leah's letter to Jonas. But the very next morning, after a sleepless night, she had gone to look through the kitchen trash, only to discover someone had gathered up the refuse in the house and taken it out to the large trash bin. When she inquired of Vera about the trash pickup, she was told the county collectors had already come and hauled it away.

For more than a week, she struggled immensely. She'd had

no business taking Jonas's letter, nor should she have thrown it in the trash. Angry or not, though, she could reason Leah had it coming—her telling on Sadie and all. She honestly felt she could overlook, even forgive Naomi Kauffman for going to Preacher Yoder to rid herself of sin prior to baptism. Naomi's knowledge of Sadie's rumschpringe was scant in detail compared to what Leah was privy to. Besides, sisters were supposed to keep vows of the heart. And Leah had not.

What misery I've caused Jonas, she thought, having daily witnessed his despair firsthand. And the act of tampering with mail was a crime, she knew. The all-seeing eyes of the Lord God heavenly Father roamed to and fro over the earth. Her list of sins was ever lengthening.

She had wrongly interfered in the fate of two people's lives, delving into the most personal regions of the heart. Yet she felt helpless to confess her wrongdoing to Jonas, though she knew she must. She was worried sick what he would think of her.

By being in the kitchen when Jonas came in for a refill on his Thermos of iced tea, she might force herself to come clean. She was prepared to confess the whole thing, and she'd calculated the timing of their encounter, hoping he was punctual with his afternoon break. Since Vera had gone upstairs with the children, this was Sadie's best opportunity.

Now here he came, hurrying across the lawn and up the steps into the house. "Hullo," he said flatly, the smile gone from his face.

His greeting distressed her; she was at fault. Even so, no matter how solemn he looked, she must follow through. "I, uh, wonder if I might talk to you right quick." She leaned hard against the kitchen sink.

"In fact, I'm awful glad I bumped into you," he said, taking her off guard. His eyes were red-rimmed yet unwavering, and he glanced about, as if checking to see if they were alone. "You were right, Sadie. It's true what you told me . . .'bout Leah and Gid. They *are* a couple."

She didn't know what to think and felt her face go flush. "Are you sayin' you heard from someone back home?"

Jonas nodded and told of his father's telephone call. Then he startled her by saying, "I owe you much gratitude."

She could hardly believe what she was hearing. So she *had* been right about what she'd seen in the woods that day? She could see by the stricken look in his eyes that here was a young man in need of comfort.

"I'm ever so sorry, Jonas," she said in a tender voice.

He smiled then, a shattered kind of smile that did nothing to disguise his hurt. "No, no. This is not for you to worry over."

She glanced at the oven. "I baked a cherry pie hopin' to cheer you up at supper."

He attempted to force another smile, she could see. "I'll look forward to your pie," he said. Then he returned to his work.

She watched him hurry toward the back door. *I spared Jonas by discarding Leah's distressing letter,* she thought in amazement. *And surely it was that, because there are no more coming.*

Hours later Sadie was outside sweeping the little box of a back porch to the Dawdi Haus when she saw the ministers walking toward her across the yard.

They've wasted no time, she thought, noting the stern look in both the preacher's and the deacon's eyes. Suddenly she felt as if she were headed to the gallows.

Chapter Thirty-One

Leah came in the kitchen door and saw Mamma sitting at the table, her face stained with tears. "Ach, what is it?" She rushed to her mother's side.

"I worried something like this might happen." Mamma looked down at the letter in her lap. "It's the worst news ever."

"What is?"

Mamma shook her head. "Sadie's not comin' home. Already she's had a visit from the brethren there. But everythin' hinges on her willingness to repent."

"S*till* she refuses?"

"Awful sad, 'tis." Mamma pulled out one of Hannah's embroidered hankies hidden beneath her sleeve and wiped her eyes. Her voice faltered. "If the Bann is put on her—even a short-term shunning—Bishop Bontrager might put a stop to her letters."

"Then we'll lose touch with her. . . ." Leah felt strangled. She laid her head on her mother's soft, round shoulder, keenly aware of her own grief but even more so of Mamma's trembling.

When Dat came indoors for a drink of water and spotted them there, his mouth dropped open. "What's wrong, Ida . . . somebody up and die?"

Mamma said nothing, holding up the letter for him to see.

Removing his hat slowly, Dat planted himself in the middle of the kitchen, his eyes moving back and forth across the page. His lips formed every silent word.

When he finished reading, he frowned. "If Sadie's diggin' her heels in about comin' home, then I 'spect there might be a reason for it." His words sounded convincing, but his voice was right wobbly.

Leah held her breath and Mamma said, "Just what could that be, Abram?"

He folded the letter, staring down at it. "Who's to say, really. But I'm a-thinkin' . . . could be Sadie has herself a new beau."

"Who'd have her if she's to be shunned?" asked Mamma.

Dat fell silent for a time. When he looked up, his eyes were awful watery. Leah felt her skin go prickly. "Maybe Jonas, for one," he said.

"Ach, Abram!" Mamma clasped a hand to her heart.

Leah was devastated at Dat's remark, though the idea *had* crossed her mind. Could it be Sadie was the reason for Jonas's ongoing silence, the reason why his letters had ceased? *Surely not*, she hoped, her mouth going dry.

"What'll become of our Sadie?" Mamma asked, sniffling.

Dat glanced at Leah somewhat ruefully. Unexpectedly, he went and sat next to Mamma at the table. Slipping his arm around her, he stared at the checked oilcloth. "We do as the Lord God calls us—to live as a holy example. . . . Sadie knows the way, Ida."

Leah felt as distressed as Dat and Mamma looked. She leaned hard against the table, wishing the stillness might be broken—if not for happy talk, at least for her burning question.

Finally she asked, "What'll happen if Preacher Yoder has already written and told the preachers there . . .'bout Sadie's iniquity?"

Dat raised his head and looked at her. "Seems to me, they'll want to keep all that tomfoolery under their ministerial hats," he said. "In fact, I 'spect they'd prefer to keep it hush-hush, them eager to bring new blood to the community and all."

"What about the Proving?" asked Mamma. "Won't Sadie be watched closely for a time?"

Dat nodded his head. "If she passes scrutiny for six months, she'll be welcomed into the Ohio fellowship, as long as they hold to believers' baptism, separation from the evil world, and reject going to war. Far as I understand, anyway."

Leah had heard tell of the Proving. She'd also heard of certain church districts where the People intermarried so frequently the children born to such unions suffered physical problems—sometimes mental.

So, in the process of time, if she repented there, Sadie would be allowed to join the Millersburg church district. But she'd be shunned in Gobbler's Knob.

Mamma spoke up. "Ach, the worst is our girl will be cut

off from us—unless she has a change of heart and comes home."

"Not likely now, I'm afraid," Dat said, getting up.

"What'll happen to Jonas?" asked Leah quietly.

Pulling at his beard, Dat eyed Mamma. "I daresay he must've gotten special permission from the Grasshopper Level bishop to take his apprenticeship out of state."

"Jah, he did," Leah said. "Jonas told me so last spring before he left." She sighed, wondering if she ought to say more. Then she could hold the words back no longer. "Will he be shunned, too, if he doesn't return?"

"That'll be for his bishop to work out with both Bishop Bontrager and the Ohio brethren." His eyes showed deep concern toward her.

A groan escaped Leah's lips.

Dat went on. "Unless Jonas gets himself home by the end of next month, he'll be subject to the vote of the People. But . . . I'd say there's still hope he'll be spared the shun."

Not if Sadie's caught his eye, she thought, cringing inwardly. *I was naïve, sending my beautiful sister to Millersburg in my stead!*

Leah could no longer deny her sorrow. How on earth could she sit here while Dat speculated, when her future with the only boy she'd ever loved was at stake? She wondered if she should now make some attempt to contact Jonas besides her letter. Should she hurry to a telephone and call him?

No, that was much too bold on her part. She wouldn't put Jonas on the spot. Indeed, he must have a reason for not writing, though she couldn't imagine what. Patience . . . and a meek and gentle spirit were of the utmost importance. No respectable Amishwoman would behave otherwise. Hard as it would be, she must allow him to get in touch with her on his own terms.

Without saying more to either Dat or Mamma, she hastened out the back door, hurrying down the lane to the road. She ran so hard she lost track of where she was going, and by the time she slowed to catch her breath, she'd come upon the boundary line where Peacheys' land and Dr. Schwartz's empty field met up—where she and Jonas had exchanged their first kisses not so long ago. What could have gone wrong in such a short time?

Weary now, she sat on a nearby rock, indifferent to trespassing. Moments crept by and it felt that the world—*her* world—had come to a halt. She looked out over the fertile grassland to the approximate area of the small grave, though she could not see it from here. The lonely place, without even a marker, lay in the tall grass, representing the death of everything she had come to hold dear.

There lies my future without Jonas, she thought, realizing just how terribly depressed she felt.

Then, quite unexpectedly, another sad thought crossed her mind. For all she knew, Sadie's little baby lay lifeless and cold in that grave. Such a devastating turn of events this all was, beginning with the sins of Sadie's rumschpringe. Everything—*everything*—had spun out of control, shattering their lives, from Sadie's first curious look at a worldly English boy.

Heavyhearted, she rose and labored back up the long road toward the Ebersol Cottage, as she'd always called her father's abode. The limestone house with its grand front door and wide porch seemed to smile a welcome to friend or foe alike. If the things Dat said were true—and no doubt they were—

the family home would remain a place of refuge for her well into a bleak and lonely future. Not the house of her wedding service, nor her wedding night. Not the happy dwelling place where she and Jonas came for visits with their new babies. . . .

She would remain Abram's Leah for a long time to come. Maybe forever.

After outside chores were done, Leah kept busy sewing a blue bridesmaid's dress for Naomi's upcoming wedding—when she wasn't helping Mamma. In spite of her busyness, she could not get her mind off Jonas as each day passed and no more letters arrived.

She and Adah spent their leisure time sewing together. But, though Leah tried to conceal her sadness, she couldn't fool her best friend.

"Oh, Leah, as much as I would like to have you as my sister-in-law, I can see clearly how much you love Jonas."

They had been working side by side at Adah's mother's trestle table, stitching by hand the side seams. With no one in the kitchen except the two of them, it was a rare and quiet moment, indeed.

Leah looked into Adah's pretty green eyes and sweet face. "You'll always be like a sister to me, no matter. . . ."

Adah stuck her needle into the pincushion and stopped her sewing. "If you ask me, I'd say you should go find a pay telephone and call your Jonas."

Leah gasped. "Ain't proper."

"But you can't live without knowin' for sure, can you? I'd be glad to go with you. Honestly, you *must* call him!"

She stared at her friend. "Surely you don't mean it."

"You said you two could talk 'bout anything, jah?"

For sure and for certain, that was true. At least that *had* been the case before his letters stopped.

"So, will you call him?"

Leah sighed. Adah was right: She had to know something one way or the other.

Leah didn't feel the need to take Adah up on her offer to go to the pay telephone booth with her. Not wanting to let either Dat or Mamma know what she was up to, she agreed to borrow some loose change from Adah to place the call, awkward as it was. She had used up all her window-washing pay from Dr. Schwartz to reimburse Mary Ruth. And rightly so.

Having already gone through the process of getting David Mellinger's woodworking shop number before, she felt much more self-confident making a long-distance call this time.

When a grown man's voice came on the line, she realized it was the master carpenter himself. "Uh, jah, I wonder if I might be speakin' to . . . Jonas Mast?" she sputtered.

"Well, I'm sorry to say he's not here just now."

"Oh, I don't mean to bother you," she said.

"No trouble a'tall."

"When would you be expectin' him?"

"Well, can't say that for sure. No tellin' when they'll be back from the singing."

They?

"Do you mean to say. . . ?" She stopped, scarcely able to finish. "Are you speakin' of Sadie Ebersol, maybe?"

"Why, that's right. Sadie and Jonas left here not five minutes ago."

She leaned back against the glass of the phone booth, feeling faint. *So it is true! Just as Dat supposed. Jonas is now seeing Sadie!*

"Is there a message I might give Jonas?" The question jolted her, and she was so hurt and befuddled she found herself shaking her head instead of giving a verbal response.

"Hullo? Are you there?"

"Uh . . . there's no message. I'm sorry." She felt stiff, scarcely able to place the receiver back in its cradle.

I'm sorry. . . .

Why had she said that? Sorry was for a faithless boy like Jonas Mast to be saying to her, for goodness' sake! But sadly, she might never hear those words uttered from her former beau's lips.

Oh, she rued the day she'd ever let him kiss her, especially the fervent way he had. *They* had.

She slapped the reins a bit too hard once she climbed back into the buggy, sending the mare swiftly forward. Only one person she cared to see just now, what with this dreadful pain churning inside. Only one, because Aunt Lizzie must have felt the selfsame stabbing pain when the boy she'd loved had walked out on her, too.

She must get to Lizzie right away. She must sit across from

Lizzie at her little kitchen table and sip some warm, honey-sweetened tea, letting the tears roll down, stopping only to ask what a girl could do when her heart hurt this awful bad.

"Lizzie's over in Strasburg buyin' fabric for your weddin' quilt," Mamma told Leah when she asked.

"When will she be back?" she asked, feeling worse than glum.

"In time for supper," Mamma said, handing Lydiann off to her. "Could you entertain your baby sister a bit?"

Poor, dear Mamma. She'd been wrung out lately, largely due to Sadie. But what would Mamma think if she knew Sadie had beguiled yet another young man? This time Leah's own beau.

Jonas was all mine for ever so long, Leah thought tearfully, holding Lydiann close.

She kissed her baby sister's head, got two spoons for Lydiann to play with, and put her down on the floor. Then, lifting her long skirt to the side, she got down and sat next to the active baby.

Watching Mamma stir a great pot of beef stew, she breathed in the aroma of onions and celery cooking. The smell reminded her of one of the few times they'd ever invited the Mast family over for a Saturday supper. Jonas had sat directly across from her, as he often did—no, come to think of it, as he *always* did. Right from the start, she'd been naïve enough to believe he was as smitten with her as she was him!

Would every smell from now on point her to memories of Jonas? Would it always be so?

"I hope Lizzie can use the fabric for somethin' besides my weddin' quilt," she heard herself saying. In that moment she felt as if she were buried in a straw stack, trying to find an air hole, yet suffocating all the while.

"Aw, Leah, you mustn't . . ." Mamma turned to look at her.

Slowly, Mamma's expression withered as she stood there, potholder in one hand, wooden spoon in the other. "Oh, honey-girl." She set them both down quickly and hurried to kneel on the floor. It was the first time Leah had ever heard Aunt Lizzie's special nickname for her come pouring out of her mother's mouth.

"Oh, Mamma," she cried. "There's not goin' to be a weddin' after all." She told what she'd done at the pay telephone booth and, worse, what David Mellinger had said. "Sadie's gone and taken Jonas from me."

Mamma leaned over and wrapped her comforting arms around her, saying over and over, "My dear, dear girl . . ."

When at last Mamma released her, Leah felt as limp as a dry tobacco leaf. Without saying a word, she picked up Lydiann and carried her upstairs to Mamma's bedroom and closed the door. She lay down with her on their parents' bed while Mamma finished cooking downstairs. Placing her hand gently on her sister's tiny chest, she searched to feel the soft yet steady beat of the baby's heart.

"You must never suffer so," she whispered.

Chapter Thirty-Two

It had come to Ida's attention, by way of Miriam Peachey, that the gossip vine was spreading itself along, heralding the news that Jonas Mast and their own Sadie were a rather odd partnership. And it had all happened so suddenly. Naturally, none of the talk had started with either herself or Leah, but *someone* had gotten the grapevine swinging with the news.

The saddest thing was not only were Sadie and Jonas both in danger of long-term estrangement from the local church community, but they'd never again enjoy the warmth of their families, unless individually they could get Bishop Bontrager to lift the Bann in due time. So both young people were in the same boat, though Sadie's shunning was imminent, Ida knew, and would more than likely be enforced only in Pennsylvania. Jonas, on the other hand, still had time on his side.

Even so, Peter and Fannie Mast, though kin, were clearly not on speaking terms with either Abram or Ida. Fannie no longer answered Ida's letters, and Abram didn't seem to mind one iota. It was as if the two families had shunned each other, and Ida despised it something awful.

Sadie was nearly finished setting the table when Vera let out a sharp cry. "Go and call David," Vera said, pointing toward the back door with one hand and holding her stomach with the other. "Tell my husband to ride quick an' get the midwife!"

Doing as she was told, Sadie scurried out the door and down to the woodworking shop to inform David his fourth child was on the way.

While David took the carriage and hurried down the road, Vera was upstairs preparing to give birth. The task of feeding supper to Joseph, Mary Mae, and Andy now fell to Sadie. And, she just realized, Jonas would also be present at the table.

Somewhat nervous at the prospect of carrying on a conversation with the young man her sister had jilted, she set about dishing up the food, calling for the children to wash their hands and "come to the table."

Fortunately a good portion of the meal was already on the stove or in the oven. She smiled, glad she could truly take credit for the homemade noodles and gravy, and dried-corn casserole . . . if Jonas happened to ask.

Joseph and Mary Mae came quickly. Mary Mae held up her chubby hands for Sadie's inspection before she took her place at the table. "Did I wash 'em clean enough?" she asked, blue eyes shining.

Sadie assured Mary Mae she had done an excellent job of it. Then she said quickly that their mamma would soon introduce them, each one, to a new baby brother or sister. "Won't be long now."

"Best be a boy," Joseph said suddenly. He wore a slight frown, as though worried about the sounds coming from upstairs.

"Your mamma will be just fine," she said in his ear, guiding him around the table to his place.

It was little Andy who dawdled at the sink, sliding the round stool over and stepping up to wash his hands. Jonas glanced at Sadie, then at the food, steaming hot on the table. His eyes seemed to say, *You're handling things very well.*

She caught the message and rose to help the four-year-old dry his hands and get seated. "Now I believe we're ready for the table blessing," she said, looking to Jonas to bow his head and take David's place in all of this.

While her head was bowed, she thought how strange, yet awful nice, this unexpected situation was—she and Jonas the only grown-ups at the table, surrounded by three young ones. She felt she was being given a glimpse of what life might be like as a young wife and mother. Married to Jonas Mast, maybe? Well, that would please her, for sure and for certain . . . if the handsome boy across the table could get her sister out of his head long enough to notice *her*.

Jonas made the quick sound in his throat, just as both Dat and David Mellinger always did, to signal the end of the silent prayer. They all sat up straight, and Sadie passed the food to Jonas first; then she began to serve the children.

While they ate, she waited for Jonas to bring up an interesting topic for conversation, but she wasn't so ready for his remark when he finally did. In fact, she had to stop to think of what to say, she was that cautious.

He spoke to her while the children occupied themselves with feeding their faces. "I saw you had unexpected visitors recently." His voice was rather quiet, softer than usual.

She did not wish to call more attention to herself over this. Thankfully, Edith had snoozed all through the ministers' conversation that day. Still, Sadie was sure both Vera and David had been alerted to the men arriving in the preacher's buggy. It was hard not to stand up and take notice of the sober-looking men wearing their black trousers and frock coats with straight collars. "Evidently, word's gotten out that I intend to stay on here," she said.

Joseph let out a belch and Andy tried to mimic him.

Sadie continued, saying she'd discussed her idea with Edith and the widow was absolutely delighted with the prospect of an ongoing companionship.

"What about your family . . . and your home church?" Jonas held his glass of water, not drinking. "How do the Gobbler's Knob brethren look on it?"

"Bishop Bontrager has issued a warning, is all." She shared with him what she had been told, that, eventually, she could join the church here, "though more progressive than at home." She didn't tell him that Bishop Bontrager had mercifully spared her by not revealing to the Ohio ministers the details of her past transgressions.

"I'd hate to see you shunned for simply stayin' put here."

She said no more, hoping his curiosity had been satisfied. Truth be told, she wanted to keep Jonas's attention on *her*, not on problems relating to church rules and regulations. "I'll be all right," she replied. "You'll see."

Leah spent her after-supper hours alone in her bedroom following silent evening prayers and Bible reading. Night after night, her room seemed to grow ever larger, what with Sadie gone. When she finally did allow herself to lie down and sleep some, she often awoke with tears in her eyes, trying to comprehend how it was Jonas no longer was coming home. How could it be possible her beau was now courting her sister?

Sitting by her bedroom window late into the night, having long since snuffed out the oil lantern, she stared up at the dark sky. She didn't care that some folk were saying things like "Abram's Leah is pining away, a bride-to-be without a beau" or "just look at Abram's Leah—ach, she grows old before our eyes."

She glanced briefly in the hand mirror on the dresser and observed how awful gray her face was. Gone the rosy cheeks, the bright eyes. She was only seventeen and appeared to be dying. Then and there, her thoughts strayed to Catharina, the martyred Ebersol great-grandmother who had lost everything to follow the Lord God.

Leah couldn't go so far as to think that she, too, had given up all to do God's bidding. But she *had* followed her heart at the prompting of the Holy One, breaking her pledge to Sadie . . . to give her life to the Amish church.

On the day of Naomi Kauffman's wedding, Leah felt as if

she were floating through all the necessary motions, saying all the expected things. She assumed Naomi's doctor must have given the bride a clean bill of health, so to speak, which no doubt pleased Luke Bontrager. Not to mention the bishop. Leah despised the tittle-tattle that went around amongst the womenfolk. For the sake of Naomi's future as a God-fearing wife and mother, she was glad Sadie's former friend hadn't fallen near as far as some young people did during rumschpringe.

Upstairs, arranged on Naomi's bed, many wedding gifts were on display. Mostly kitchenware for Naomi and farm tools for Luke. Careful to show interest in the bride's gifts, Leah went upstairs to look with Naomi before the wedding service began. "What a joyous day," she said.

Naomi smiled, eyes brimming with happy tears. "All's well, now."

Leah was much relieved Naomi did not once mention Sadie's name.

Later, during the preaching, Leah sat next to Naomi, along with Adah—the three young women all in a row, wearing their new blue dresses and white aprons—while Bishop Bontrager gave the main sermon. He focused on the Old Testament marriages, beginning with the story of Adam and Eve, up through Isaac and Rebekah, and concluding with a story from the Apocrypha about Tobias heeding his father's counsel and choosing a bride from his own tribe.

Leah sat still as could be, trying not to dwell on the fact that two short weeks from now, she and Jonas had planned to be standing before the bishop, making their lifelong vows to each other. Her eyes dimmed at the thought. Hard as it was, she was following through with her promise to Naomi, being a dutiful wedding attendant. She hoped no one suspected her pain, though she assumed all of them had heard by now, one way or another.

She took in several breaths and attempted to paste on a permanent smile as Naomi and Luke agreed they were "ordained of God for each other" and would remain so till such time as death should separate them.

Leah and Adah had decided beforehand they would not stay for the barn games, geared toward the single youth and courting couples. Adah had suggested they return home together with Leah's family so she could spend the rest of the afternoon and evening with Leah, helping her through "such a hard day."

Gid sat with the menfolk, unable to keep his eyes off Leah. He wished he might do something to ease her sorrow, which was plainly evident. Leah was a plucky one, but knowing her as he did, he felt sure she was suppressing her grief. At least for the moment . . . for Naomi's happiness.

What a girl! To think she'd lost her beau to her own fickle sister. The thought stirred him up, even though it meant the girl he'd always admired and cared for would not be marrying this month after all. Leah would still live neighbors to him under the covering of Abram's roof. Yet he felt sick to his stomach, enduring some of the pain that such a dear girl must be experiencing this moment as she stood tall and pretty next to the bride and groom.

Dat agreed there was plenty of room for Adah to ride home with them, and Leah was ever so glad. They didn't say much as they rode together in the back of the spring wagon, with Lizzie and the twins in the next seat up, and Mamma, Lydiann, and Dat up front.

Once home Adah followed her upstairs so Leah could change into an everyday dress and apron. " 'Twas nice to see Naomi lookin' so happy, jah?" Adah said.

Leah had to agree. "To think what might've turned out to be." She didn't much care to discuss the aftermath of a reckless rumschpringe.

She hung up her new dress and apron, and the girls hurried downstairs and out the back door, both draped in their warm shawls. They headed through the rows and rows of brown stumps that had once been a cornfield, to Adah's house. There, Adah slipped out of her nice, new dress and hung it up for the next Preaching service. "I'm sorry you had to suffer through today, Leah," Adah said.

"I'm glad you were right beside me," Leah replied quickly. "Such a comfort it was. You just don't know."

Adah suggested they not attend many of the weddings this year. "I can think of plenty of things to do besides goin' from one weddin' to another all November long."

Leah appreciated her friend's thoughtfulness. "Mamma said she heard there were some spillin' over into December."

"No one should expect you to go to all of them . . . or any, for that matter." Adah reached for her hand.

"Still, I'd hate to see *you* miss out, Adah. There'll be plenty of nice boys there, eager to play the barn games and whatnot. You really should go with your sister . . . and Gid."

Adah, it was plain to see, was reluctant to say she would or wouldn't go. Leah knew that if Adah waited too long, she might miss out on having herself a beau. It wouldn't be fair for Adah Peachey to be Gid's age and still single, waiting for the "right one" to come along.

Jonas worked extra hard in the wood shop, recalling Leah was to be a bridesmaid in Naomi Kauffman's wedding this day. He set to sawing with such fervor that David looked up and gave notice, raising an eyebrow, before he returned to staining a table.

Stopping to wipe his face on his sleeve, he shuddered to think Abram had succeeded in getting his first choice in a beau for Leah. So Gid had stolen his bride. Still baffled as to why he hadn't known, or at least surmised as much, he found himself shaking his head in utter dismay. Leah had chosen to let him down by simply not responding to his important letter—by not coming right out and saying that, jah, she wanted to obey her father's wishes.

There was only one thing to do now: try his best to forget her, that and the pain she'd caused him . . . and his family. Best leave the past right where it belonged—behind. Yet that was anything but easy with Leah's beautiful and wide-eyed sister practically living under the same roof. She was a constant reminder of what he'd lost.

Leah and Adah had been walking out near Blackbird Pond and beyond for over an hour. Even though Adah insisted they rest near the willow tree, Leah refused to stop. She had such pent-up energy, yet was nearing collapse at the same time. She wanted to calm down but wouldn't let herself. "How will I ever forget Jonas?" The question poured out of her like vinegar mixed with honey.

She welcomed Adah's gentle touch on her shoulder, and they fell back into their silent, somber walk. The two friends had shared both sadness and joy through their years together, but today Leah's despondency was far more intense than any time she could remember.

"Love must be disappointing at times," Adah said. "I 'spect you'll never forget him."

They walked in silence till Adah spoke up again. "Mamma sometimes says, 'Love is faith with its work clothes on.'"

Leah had heard that said, too. "It's all I can do to rise in the morning, missin' him . . . missin' the life we'd planned. I have no hope in me, Adah." She wouldn't go so far as to reveal that as children she and Jonas had made a love covenant of sorts. It was pointless to talk about, let alone consider now . . . especially with Gid's sister.

"I s'pose after some time passes, you'll delve deep into your heart and find forgiveness there for what Jonas and Sadie have done to you."

"Forgiveness warms the heart and soothes the sting," Leah said softly. "Aunt Lizzie has said that my whole life, growin' up. Easier said than done."

"The Good Lord will help you, Leah. I'll do my part, as well."

Giving Adah a quick smile, she slipped her arm around her best friend, and they walked one more time around the large pond.

◆

Tuckered out, Leah said good-bye to Adah at last and headed across the field to the barn. She went around the back way, toward the earthen barn bridge leading to the second level. The haymow beckoned her.

She stepped inside, taking in the familiar and sweet scent. Looking around, she made herself a spot to nestle in and sank down into the warm hay. Fatigued as she was, she called to mind her conversation with David Mellinger yet again.

Jonas and Sadie . . .

Together.

Jonas's name connected to her sister's. Why? How? *Oh, Lord God heavenly Father, please help this weary soul of mine!* she prayed.

She drifted off to tearful sleep and dreamed she was pitching hay, the raked pile seemingly never ending as she gripped the pitchfork. Her arm muscles and clenched fist throbbed with the intensity of the chore, and she roused herself slightly, only to relax once again and return to sleep.

In search of a shovel, Smithy Gid climbed the ladder to the hayloft and was thunderstruck to see Leah there, fast asleep. Several gray mouse catchers had positioned themselves around her like miniature guards, but by the look of their relaxed and furry bodies, getting forty winks was uppermost in their feline minds.

Lest he disturb Leah's peaceful slumber, he decided against tramping through the hay just now and would have immediately descended the ladder if he hadn't noticed Leah's tear-streaked face. Unable to move away, he stared unashamedly at the curve of her eyelashes, the blush of peach on her cheeks, the relaxed expression on her lips.

Most precious she is. . . .

His heart wrenched and his breath caught in his throat. He would move heaven and earth if he could to let her know, in the appropriate time, that he was eager to offer his hand of friendship. If it should take years, he would wait. For goodness' sake, Leah must not live life as a passed-over maidel due to the outright heartlessness of Jonas Mast.

Two cats awakened and blinked their green eyes at him, staring him down. Pressing his finger to his lips, he hoped to ward off any piercing meows; then he realized how futile the gesture was. Cats cried, even screeched, as they desired. A body could simply look at a barn cat and a ruckus could follow if the cat's mood was just right.

He stood motionless, hoping the cats in question might run off or return to their dozing. *Just keep still*, he thought.

Again shifting his gaze to Leah, he found himself wanting to lean forward, stretch just enough to touch her face . . . even gently press the loose strand of her brown hair between his fingers. But he held fast to the ladder.

Gid struggled, knowing he had always been a distant second in Leah's mind. *Can I persuade her otherwise?* He recalled the coolness of her hand in his that day in the woods. Several times during their difficult trek down the entangled hillock, he had reached for her innocently—steadying her, keeping her from stumbling or worse.

But now it appeared she *had* fallen, having succumbed to the cruelly twisted jumble of her life. And though he was willing, he had been unable to keep her from doing so.

Chapter Thirty-Three

A solid half hour came and went as Leah napped quietly. She stirred in and out of a dream, aware of voices below her.

"No . . . no, Leah can't handle this now. I've just lost one daughter; I won't lose another!"

It was Dat's voice . . . in her dream? But no, she was right here in the hay.

Lost in a sleepy stupor, she tuned her ears to whatever she thought she'd heard.

"Time's run out, Abram. There are people who know the truth. . . ."

Aunt Lizzie? Was she nearby, too? She wondered what on earth Dat and Aunt Lizzie were doing in the barn together.

"There's no need to be rushin' ahead with this, 'specially with the wedding called off," Mamma said. "And 'tis a difficult time for the family just now, what with Sadie soon to be shunned."

"I agree," Aunt Lizzie said. "But wouldn't *you* rather tell her than have her find out through the grapevine?"

Leah rose and shook the hay off her dress and apron, the cats scattering as she did so. Bewildered, she walked to the edge of the loft and peered down. "Dat? Mamma?" she called softly, surprised to see all of them in a huddle by the feed trough.

Dat turned and spotted her, his face paling instantly.

Their eyes held. An awkward silence fell between them, and Leah saw that both Mamma and Lizzie were befuddled, too. Lizzie's hand flew to her mouth; Mamma's eyes glistened, her face quivering.

At last Dat broke the stillness. "Leah, how long have you been up there?"

"I don't know . . . must've fallen asleep." She moved toward the ladder and made her way down.

"Come here to me, child." Mamma opened her arms to embrace her.

She felt the breathless heaving of her mother's bosom and wondered why her heart beat so fast.

Dat turned to Aunt Lizzie, his mouth open as if he wanted to speak, but the words wouldn't come.

Mamma held fast to Leah. "I think 'tis best for Abram and me to be alone with Leah for now, Lizzie. You understand, ain't?"

Eyes downcast, Aunt Lizzie sighed audibly, and Leah observed the intense struggle between what Dat and Mamma were wanting—whatever it was—and what Lizzie must have been hoping for. Lizzie seemed to shrink in size just then. For an agonizing moment her aunt stood next to Mamma, saying not a word, looking forlorn and alone.

When Aunt Lizzie raised her head, she fixed her sad eyes on Leah.

"Sister?" pleaded Mamma softly.

Slowly turning away, Aunt Lizzie wandered slump shouldered over to the wide barn door, leaning hard against it as it inched open.

Leah felt the rush of cool air as her dear auntie headed outside.

Once they were alone, Dat sat down on a square bundle of alfalfa. He looked at her, beard twitching to beat the band. "It's time you heard the truth, Leah." He placed his big hand on the spot beside him. "Come, sit beside ol' Dat."

Just the way he patted the baled forage made Leah tremble.

Lizzie was beside herself. Why had they sent her out of the barn? In all truth, she had every right to be present when her honey-girl heard the story for the first time.

She stumbled up the mule road toward home, continuing to worry. Had they made a mistake deciding to tell Leah? Poor thing, she'd been through so much lately. Lizzie had seen how washed out and frail Leah looked as a bridesmaid in Naomi's wedding this morning. A wonder she'd managed to get through the wedding service at all!

Heartsick as she was, Leah didn't need to learn that Lizzie, not Ida, was her real mamma . . . not this day. *How awful selfish of me*, Lizzie thought.

Hurrying to the back door of her house, she pushed it open and went straight to the wood stove to begin boiling water. Some strong mint tea would help calm her, if that was possible. She scarcely knew peace at all anymore.

Standing over the pot of hot water, she forced her thoughts away from Leah to Abram's flesh-and-blood daughter. How relieved she was; Sadie's secret was out in the open at last. In spite of the shun the dear girl might be able to get herself some much-needed spiritual help in Millersburg . . . especially if there *was* a godly bishop, as Leah had indicated from Jonas's previous letters. *If only Sadie had never left home,* she thought. If only she'd been repentant *here*, none of this dreadful thing between Sadie and Jonas would have happened.

What gall of Sadie! She poured the water into her prettiest cup and walked to the front room window. Sipping her tea, she looked out toward the depths of the forest, where Sadie had, no doubt, conceived *her* love child.

Lizzie was overcome with despair yet again, recalling the night of her own rumschpringe madness. Things had gotten clean out of hand, beginning with her decision to seek out some New Year's Eve excitement. She had gone to a beauty parlor to have her waist-long hair cut to chin length and parted on the side, with finger waves like the young woman in a Coca-Cola ad she'd seen. Brazen and fun loving, she was ready for anything.

All her life, she had been warned to stay close to home—to avoid fancy Englishers' automobiles—yet defiantly she had tucked a pack of Chesterfields in her pocketbook and walked up to Route 340, thumbing a ride. The handsome young man who picked her up had no idea she was Amish, let alone underage. Grinning a warm greeting, he drove her around Lancaster County, eventually heading to Gobbler's Knob, where he parked his Niagara Blue Roadster near the ditch along the road and shared some moonshine. They laughed and talked and drank too much, then hiked into the cold woods. There, in a hunters' shack hidden deep in the trees, she willingly gave up her viture.

Leah's life began in the shanty that winter night—the worst possible thing that could have happened to young Lizzie, discovering she was with child. Both her mother and father, as well as her older brother, Noah, brought the fact up to her continually, till she thought she might lose her wits. Noah even threatened to haul her away to a big city and force her to abort her baby. "Such a disgrace you are to this family!" he'd said time and again, the color in his face rising to a bright purple.

In desperation, she had written a letter to her big sister, Ida, pleading for help. The next day Abram and Ida came with toddler in arms—fair-haired Sadie—to Hickory Hollow, having ridden all the way from Gobbler's Knob.

A serious scuffle took place in the barn, she learned later. Abram stood up to Noah—even held up his fists—and said under no circumstances was Noah to compound Lizzie's sin with *two* wrongs.

In short order a pact was made involving Abram, Ida, and herself. That very night, Lizzie rode to her new home in Gobbler's Knob.

Lizzie held no grudge toward the handsome stranger. Conceiving his child had been just as much her fault as his. Yet October 2, 1930, the date of Leah's birth, had burned its way into her memory for always.

Abram took her and Ida to talk privately with Bishop

Bontrager, who welcomed Lizzie into the church after she freely repented. She was baptized a year later, along with a number of unsuspecting youths.

So the secret was set, and Leah was raised as Abram's and Ida's own. Altogether plump, Ida didn't have to make much excuse for this new baby showing up three years after Sadie. Only a handful of folk knew much of anything at all, though rumors flew like lightning bugs when Lizzie moved into the Ebersols' Dawdi Haus till her little log house could be built up behind the bank barn.

Lizzie turned away from the window and went to sit for a spell. She was ever so tired all of a sudden. Her head spun with the memory of years.

Setting the teacup down on the floral saucer, she sighed and leaned back a bit, wishing she'd never, ever breathed a word to Abram today, nor this week for that matter. What had she been thinking? Poor Leah needed a respite from sadness and pain. Not a revelation that could cause her further grief.

Closing her eyes, she breathed a prayer for what must surely be happening in Abram's barn this very moment—her dear Leah was being presented with such untimely news.

Tears sprang to her eyes. *What'll happen when Leah hears the truth? Will she distrust me? What of Abram and Ida? Will our girl view us as betrayers, all these years?*

Just how long she had been resting there, she didn't know. Maybe only a few minutes when she heard someone calling in the distance.

"Aunt Lizzie!"

Getting up out of her chair, she flew to the southeast-facing window in the spare bedroom and looked out. There, running up the mule road, was Leah, skirts flying like a kite in a windstorm.

"Aunt Lizzie!" her daughter called.

Oh, Lizzie thought she must be seeing things. Her heart leaped into her throat. How would Leah react to such jolting news?

Lizzie ran to get her shawl and hurried out the back door, down the narrow porch, and past the flower beds, finished for the season. Over the grassy yard she went, past the stone wall and down the hill to the edge of the woods, where the light broke free, clear as glass.

She kept going, fast as she could, though young Leah's pace was far quicker. "Are you all right?" Lizzie called to her, nearly out of breath.

Leah's feet pounded hard against the dirt path, and if Lizzie wasn't mistaken, her face was marked with tears.

And then they were in each other's arms, Leah sobbing and whimpering. "Oh, Aunt Lizzie, it was you all along . . . all these years, 'twas *you*."

Stunned at what she was hearing, she kissed Leah's soft, wet cheek. "The Lord God be praised," she said, breathing much easier now. To think how Leah *might have* responded to the news. Well, she dared not dwell on that. Not now. She wanted to soak up all the love, capture the brightness in Leah's eyes, the pure delight she saw in them, reflected in her own. Truly, she was more than relieved; she was brimming with utter gladness.

Leah stepped back and fixed her eyes on Lizzie. "Ach, I can scarcely believe it . . . you gave me life, Aunt Lizzie. How on earth could it be that I never guessed such a wonderful-gut thing!" Then she threw her arms around Lizzie again.

Why, oh why, did I ever worry? Lizzie thought, truly grateful. "How I love you, Leah." This she whispered, clinging to her daughter for dearest life.

Then, arm in arm, they strolled toward the log house, all the while Lizzie feeling her heart might burst apart. "I could only pray you might feel this way," she managed to say. "Honestly, I have to say I worried you might—"

"But how else *could* I feel? Goodness, I've loved you all along—nearly like a daughter loves her mamma, ya must surely know," declared Leah. "Of course I told Mamma and Dat, 'I am and always will be your girl, too.' " Leah was wearing the first true smile Lizzie had seen on her pretty face in weeks.

"Well, of course, you're theirs for always." She was unable to keep from looking . . . no, staring at Leah's lovely face.

"And I'm *your* honey-girl, Aunt Lizzie. To think I've had two mammas all along. Guess I'm double-blessed, ain't?"

Lizzie agreed wholeheartedly. *O Lord God, thank you for making it so.*

On November 25, the Tuesday she and Jonas had planned to wed, Leah skirted a sharp, rock-strewn bank scattered here and there with moss, picking her way through the woods. She rather liked the feeling of being overwhelmed by age-old trees and their intertwined branches above, along with the leafy labyrinth below.

Once again, she found herself pondering Catharina Meylin, slain at the hands of God's cruel enemies. Dat's ancestor had given up her life freely for her devout faith. Leah wondered, *Did I lose Jonas in exchange for my obedience to the Lord God?*

For sure and for certain, she hadn't lost her physical life . . . but she felt as if she'd lost her heart. Daring to do what was right and good in the sight of the Almighty, she'd made her lifelong covenant with the church, regardless of the harsh consequences.

Locating the honey locust tree, she stood tall and determined beneath its cold and leafless branches, leaning back to peer up through the web of bough and stem to the blue sky. Somehow, her future would be bright with or without Jonas. If they must be apart—no matter what lay before her—she was determined to trust in God.

Aunt Lizzie had often talked of "praying from one's heart." But not until this moment had Leah ever attempted to do so. She bowed her head, faltering at first, and began to address her heavenly Father. "O Lord, I stand here . . . heartbroken before you. Hear my prayer, dear God."

She poured out her sorrow, even her bitterness, in the timbered stillness. She went so far as to speak aloud Sadie's name . . . and the betrayal, placing it all before the Throne of Grace. "I must find the strength to forgive both my sister—"and here she stopped, struggling with tears—"and . . . Jonas. O Lord and heavenly Father, help me to do this difficult thing."

Drawing in a deep breath, she began to feel an undeniable peace. She wept with strange relief, confident that the God of Moses, who had parted the roaring waves of the Red Sea, could make a path where there had been none before. This same Jehovah God would make plain and straight the path of her own life, wherever it might lead.

Walking toward home, she looked ahead to the wood's edge, where beams of sunlight flooded the opening that led to Dat's pastureland . . . and the mule road. Then and there she knew she was no longer Abram's Leah, although the People would continue to reckon it so. Neither was she Jonas's Leah. In this clear moment of understanding, she knew she was wholly the Lord's. From tip to toe.

"I belong to you, Lord God," she whispered, quickening her pace. "Forever and always, I am your faithful Leah."

Acknowledgments

The procedure for the baptismal service described in this book was adapted from the Amish ministers' manual, *Handbuch*. I am especially thankful for Plain church members in both Lancaster, Pennsylvania, and Holmes County, Ohio, who were willing and gracious, indeed, to verify essential information regarding baptismal instruction and the baptism service itself.

I offer my truest gratitude to Carol Johnson, my editor and dear friend, along with Rochelle Glöege, Barbara Lilland, and David Horton, all vital members of Bethany's expert editorial team.

My deep appreciation also goes to my husband, David Lewis, who encourages me daily with his prayers, love, and keen interest in my many writing "journeys."

My brother-in-law, Dale Birch, was a wealth of information regarding the work of a master carpenter. And an unexpected blessing came from Larry Quiring, retired U.S. postal worker, who eagerly answered my questions regarding mail delivery in 1947.

To my partners in prayer, a heartfelt thank you! I value your ongoing spiritual encouragement. May the Lord bless you abundantly for your faithfulness.

For readers who wish to probe deeper into the Plain culture, I recommend the following books:

Amish Society, by John A. Hostetler

The Riddle of the Amish, by Donald B. Kraybill

Strangers at Home, Amish and Mennonite Women in History, edited by Kimberly D. Schmidt, Diane Zimmerman Umble, and Steven D. Reschly

Plain and Amish, An Alternative to Modern Pessimism, by Bernd G. Langin

Martyrs Mirror of the Defenseless Christians, or The Bloody Theatre, compiled by Thieleman J. van Braght

---

Watch for ABRAM'S DAUGHTERS Book Three, *The Sacrifice*, at your local bookstore!

The Sacrifice

Beverly Lewis

The Sacrifice

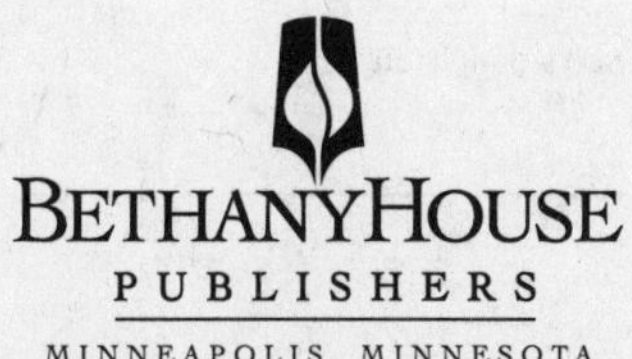

BethanyHouse Publishers
Minneapolis, Minnesota

The Sacrifice

Cover design by Dan Thornberg

The portion of a poem cited in chapter thirty-four is as quoted in *A Joyous Heart* by Corrie Bender, published by Herald Press of Scottdale, Pennsylvania, in 1994. The author of the poem is unknown.

Published by Bethany House Publishers
11400 Hampshire Avenue South
Bloomington, Minnesota 55438

Bethany House Publishers is a division of
Baker Publishing Group, Grand Rapids, Michigan.

Printed in the United States of America

ISBN 0-7642-2872-2 (Paperback)
ISBN 0-7642-2875-7 (Hardcover)
ISBN 0-7642-2876-5 (Large Print)
ISBN 0-7642-2877-3 (Audio Book)

Library of Congress Cataloging-in-Publication Data

Lewis, Beverly, date-
The sacrifice / by Beverly Lewis.
p. cm. — (Abram's daughters ; 3)
ISBN 0-7642-2875-7 (hardcover : alk. paper) —ISBN 0-7642-2872-2 (pbk.) —ISBN 0-7642-2876-5 (large-print pbk.)
1. Lancaster County (Pa.)—Fiction. 2. Amish women—Fiction. 3. Young women—Fiction. 4. Sisters—Fiction. 5. Amish—Fiction. I. Title II. Series: Lewis, Beverly, date. Abram's daughters ; 3.
PS3562.E9383S23 2004
813'.54—dc22 2003028149

Dedication

For

Jeannette Green,

wonderful friend and "sister."

Beautiful in every way.

By Beverly Lewis

ABRAM'S DAUGHTERS

The Covenant
The Betrayal
The Sacrifice
The Prodigal
The Revelation

THE HERITAGE OF LANCASTER COUNTY

The Shunning
The Confession
The Reckoning

ANNIE'S PEOPLE

The Preacher's Daughter

The Postcard · *The Crossroad*

The Redemption of Sarah Cain
October Song · *Sanctuary**
The Sunroom

The Beverly Lewis Amish Heritage Cookbook

www.beverlylewis.com

*with David Lewis

05C

BEVERLY LEWIS, born in the heart of Pennsylvania Dutch country, fondly recalls her growing-up years. A keen interest in her mother's Plain family heritage has led Beverly to set many of her popular stories in Lancaster County.

A former schoolteacher and accomplished pianist, Beverly is a member of the National League of American Pen Women (the Pikes Peak branch) and the Society of Children's Book Writers and Illustrators. She is the 2003 recipient of the Distinguished Alumnus Award at Evangel University, Springfield, Missouri, and her blockbuster novel, *The Shunning*, recently won the Gold Book Award. Her bestselling novel *October Song* won the Silver Seal in the Benjamin Franklin Awards, and *The Postcard* and *Sanctuary* (a collaboration with her husband, David) received Silver Angel Awards, as did her delightful picture book for all ages, *Annika's Secret Wish*. Beverly and her husband have three grown children and one grandchild and make their home in the Colorado foothills.

Prologue

Summer 1949

Come June, the first song of the whippoorwill reminds me of berry picking . . . and bygone days. Although it has been over two years since Jonas Mast left for Ohio, I still wonder about him, along with my older sister, Sadie, and am able to pray for their happiness more readily than at first.

Especially now, at summer's onset, when strawberries are ripe and ready for pies and preserves, I think of Jonas. He loved strawberry-rhubarb pie like nobody's business, and both his mamma and mine made it for him with sugar *and* raw honey, so it was nothing short of wonderful-good. "Desserts are s'posed to be plenty sweet," Mamma has said for as long as I can remember. This, with her irresistible wide-eyed smile. These days Sadie is the one baking such delicious fruit pies for Jonas.

Now and again I feel almost numb for the way things turned out between Jonas, Sadie, and me. Close as I was to each of them, it seems they should have cared enough to send some word early on—prior to Bishop Bontrager's strict decree—offering an explanation. Anything would've been better than this dreadful silence. It's the not knowing how things got so *verkehrt*—topsy-turvy—that causes the most frustration in me. The lack of word from Ohio confirms my worst fears. I expect even now Sadie probably wonders if I have any idea she is married to Jonas, or that I feel strongly she stole him away from me. How on earth does she live with herself?

I'm slowly accepting the split between my beau and me, since it would be wrong to pine for a man who belongs to another. Most folk just assume I've passed the worst of it and am moving on with life. They will never know truly, because I tend to go about things rather cheerfully . . . and, too, so much time has passed since that devastating autumn. It does still puzzle me, if I think on it, how one minute we were so happily planning our wedding, and then, clear out of the blue, a most peculiar letter arrived saying Jonas suspected Gideon Peachey of carrying a torch for me. Even though I promptly wrote to reassure him of my devotion and love, I never again heard from him. Downright baffling it is.

Of course, if Jonas were privy to my *present* friendship with Smithy Gid, he might have a little something to go on. But, back then, nothing was further from the truth. Fact was, my heart belonged wholly to Jonas, and nothing and no one could make me think otherwise. Not Smithy Gid, nor his sister Adah, my closest friend. Not even dear *Dat* and Mamma, though my father has long hoped Gid might one day win my affections.

With the revelation of Aunt Lizzie's secret to me—to Mary Ruth and Hannah, too—my father's and grandfather's health seems much improved and both Mamma and Aunt

Lizzie have a new spring in their step, in spite of the vacant spot at the supper table. Sadie's absence is a constant source of worry, especially since she's been shunned from the Gobbler's Knob church. And Dat was right; the bishop—after a reasonable time—insisted Sadie's letters be returned unopened. It's no wonder she stopped writing along about Christmastime after leaving for Ohio. I wish to heavens I might've been allowed to read those things she wrote to us.

Some days it seems as if my sister has been away for years on end. But if that were true, I'd be thought of as a *maidel* by now, which I'm surely not. I am still only nineteen—a few years under the limit of the expected marrying age—though if Smithy Gid had his way, he and I would be hitched up already.

The berry patch calls to me even now as I help Dat with morning milking. Seems there's something nearly sacred about creeping along the mounded rows, the blissful buzz of nature in my ears, long runners tripping at my bare feet as the blistering sun stands high and haughty in the sky and the tin bucket steadily fills with plump red fruit. Being out there alone with the birds and the strawberry plants, beneath the wide and blue heavenly canopy, soothes my soul and sets my world aright. At least for a time . . .

Part One

◆ ◆ ◆ ◆

What doth the Lord require of thee,
but to do justly, and to love mercy,
and to walk humbly with thy God?

—Micah 6:8

Chapter One

The morning Mamma quietly announced her baby news, Leah hung back a bit, standing near the kitchen door, while her twin sisters, especially Mary Ruth, were overjoyed at Mamma's being in the family way again. Many of the Old Order viewed it as shameful to share such things with unmarried children, but both Mamma and Dat felt otherwise and didn't hesitate to include their four eldest daughters, though discreetly.

"Since Lydiann's a toddler and not so little anymore, it'll be fun to have a baby around again," declared Mary Ruth.

"And wonderful-*gut* for Lydiann to have a close-in-age brother or sister." Hannah's smile stretched from ear to ear as she seemingly took the news in her stride, much as Dat must surely have, too, when Mamma told him in private earlier.

Leah had suspected nothing of this from Dat, although he'd had plenty of opportunity to say something during early-morning chores. Her father had never been one to speak of personal things; she knew this firsthand, because, for some time now, she had been asking for information relating to her own birth, to no avail. "For goodness' sake, Leah," he would say each time she brought it up, "be grateful the Good Lord made you healthy and strong, that you were born headfirst. What else wouldja care to know?"

But there were certain things she *did* ponder, such as who her first father might be. Lizzie, however, seemed unable to discuss the subject. *Is it too hard to dredge up the past?* Leah wondered. Or was Lizzie simply unwilling to bring it up for fear of implicating a member of the Hickory Hollow Amish church, miles away? There were also nagging questions concerning the day Leah was born in the Ebersol Cottage, but she couldn't bear to ask them of Lizzie.

Mary Ruth broke the stillness, glancing furtively at Leah as she said, "Maybe Dat will finally get a *real* son."

"Aw, pity's sake," Mamma said, shaking her head at Mary Ruth. She went to sit on the wooden bench next to the kitchen table, fanning herself with the hem of her long black apron. Her round face was flushed from the heat of the wood stove, where she had two strawberry pies baking.

"But . . . if the baby is a girl," Hannah spoke up, "there'll be less sewing to do."

Leah spoke at last. "Only if we get busy and make plenty of little afghans 'tween now and December. Lydiann was a spring baby, don't forget."

At this Leah caught Mamma's sweet and gentle smile. "That's my Leah, always leaning toward the practical."

Mary Ruth continued to chatter, asking where Lydiann would sleep once the wee one came.

Quickly Hannah suggested, "Why, she can sleep with us. Ain't so, Mary Ruth?"

Mamma laughed at that. "I daresay there wouldn't be much sleeping goin' on. Not as wiggly as that one is!"

Leah turned and slipped outdoors, going to the hen house, where she scattered feed to the chickens. Inside, she leaned against the rickety wall, watching them peck the ground near her bare feet. "Honestly," she said right out, "I don't know whether to be happy or sad about a new baby."

The hens paid her no mind, but the lone rooster cocked his head and eyed her curiously. In all truth, she had forced a smile about Mamma expecting a little one come next Christmas. Here, with only the chickens for company, she recalled the months before two-year-old Lydiann came into the world. Mamma had been ever so tired . . . nauseated, too. At close to forty-five, she was not nearly as energetic and strong as in years past, but there *were* a good many women that age or older in the family who had no trouble birthing babies. Leah was glad her mother came from a long line of such women. Indeed, she was happy at the prospect of Dat's having his first son should the baby turn out to be a boy.

Heading out of the hen house toward the barnyard, Leah was suddenly aware of Smithy Gid calling to her from the brink of the cornfield. "*Wie geht's*, Leah. Do ya have a minute?"

Out of habit, she glanced toward the back door, curious if Mamma or one of the twins was observing her with Gid, who was not only breathless from running, but his eyes were strangely aglow. "What is it?" she asked.

He grinned down at her. "I've got a whole new litter of German shepherd pups, and I think there's another dog Abram—your pop—might just take a shinin' to."

It was common knowledge Dat wanted a third dog, after having purchased from Gid his second German shepherd, Blackie, well over a year ago. "With a houseful of women folk, another male dog might be worth thinkin' about. 'Least I won't be so outnumbered anymore," he'd said that very morning, chuckling heartily.

She walked alongside Gid to the barn, listening as he described the various puppies' coloring.

"Does Dat know about the recent pups?" she asked.

"He oughta, 'cause I ain't been talkin' to myself all these weeks." They both laughed at that; then Gid added, "I believe Abram's just waitin' for the gut word."

She felt her cheeks warm. "Then you best be tellin' *him.*"

His eyes lit up. "Well, now, I wanted to tell you, Leah."

She held her breath, scared he might take this opportunity to say more, them alone this way.

And he did, too . . . at least started to. "I've been wantin' to ask ya something."

She took a small step back. In fact, she had been inching away from him, romantically at least, her whole life long, and for all good reason. She had always loved her second cousin Jonas, though she had made a conscious effort to bury her bitter sadness, hiding it from her family and especially from Smithy Gid, who remained a right good friend as he'd always been—even more so lately. Yet Leah shuddered at the thought of Gid showing kindness to her out of mere pity. Surely their friendship was more special than that. But she had no intention of leading him on just because he was clearly fond of her.

Ach, she groaned inwardly, wishing someone—*anyone*—

might come flying into the barn. But no one did, and not even the barn doves, high in the rafters, made a sound as the smithy's son reached for her hand. "Uh, Gid . . ." What she really wanted to tell him was *please don't say another word,* but the words got trapped in her throat. She knew all too well the ache of rejection, and the way his eyes were intent on hers just now, it would be downright unkind to hurt him.

He was still holding her hand as the slow creaking of the windmill behind the barn broke the stillness. "Adah and her beau are going for supper in Strasburg next Saturday night. I thought it might be fun if you and I rode along."

No two ways about it, *riding along* simply meant double courting and Gid knew it. Sighing, she gently pulled her hand away, staring down at her toes. *What should I say?*

"If you want to talk it over with Adah, I don't mind." His words were like thin reeds in a swamp compared to his usual self-assured manner. Inside, Smithy Gid was most likely standing on tiptoes. Furthermore, she suspected he had been ever so eager to spend an evening with her for quite some time, hoping to double up with her first cousin Sam Ebersol, Uncle Jesse's youngest son, along with Gid's sister Adah. But Leah also knew Gid wouldn't be asking her twice. If she didn't give her answer now, she'd have to seek him out in the next day or so. Because at twenty-two—three years her elder—Smithy Gid was to be treated with the respect he deserved.

"I'll think on it." She trembled, afraid he might take her reply as a *maybe.*

Truth be told, she figured he was working his way to ask her to go "for steady," and right soon. To be true to herself, she knew she ought to refuse. Yet looking on the bright side, allowing Gid to court her would convince the People, especially Mamma and Aunt Lizzie, that she'd regained her balance, so to speak, that her shattered heart was on the mend. Wasn't it about time for that, anyway? Jonas was happy with someone else; why shouldn't *she* marry, as well? And, too, it had been ingrained in her all her days that to follow the Lord God's will for her life, she must marry and bear many children, as many as the Good Lord saw fit to give her and her future husband.

One thing was sure, Leah enjoyed her barn chats with Gid while pitching hay to the field mules or redding up the haymow for summertime Preaching services. It was downright pleasant to have a young man of Gid's reputation thinking of her as a good friend. Other times, she almost wished he might fix his gaze on a girl whose heart was truly available, like, for instance, any number of her cousins—dozens of Ebersols to choose from in Gobbler's Knob alone.

Naturally Gid wanted to marry well before his sister Adah. Even his youngest sister, Dorcas, was seeing someone seriously, or so Adah had confided in Leah recently. A knotty problem for Gid, being the eldest of the family and the only son and still unmarried, though it was clear thus far he'd set his cap for no one other than Leah.

Daily this weighed heavily on her mind, especially because Smithy Gid was such a fine young man. Why should she forfeit having a family of her own just because things between her and Jonas had fizzled? She could simply marry the farm boy who'd waited for her all these years, couldn't she?

She watched Smithy Gid walk back through the cornfield, holding her breath and not knowing for sure the right answer to his invitation. *I'll ask Mamma what to do*, she thought and headed out the barn door.

Leah found Mamma in the potting shed, fanning herself. "Another hot day, ain't?"

To this her mother nodded, and Leah began to share her uncertainty. "Smithy Gid invited me to go ridin' with him, Mamma. What do you think 'bout that—if you were me, I mean?"

Mamma moved the potting soil around in the earthen jar before speaking. She stopped her work and looked at Leah with a fond expression. "Seems to me if you care the least at all for him, why not see where it leads? He's a right nice young man."

" 'Tis easy to see Dat thinks so," Leah offered. She wouldn't ask for a comparison between Gid and Jonas; Mamma had made it known years ago how fond she was of Jonas.

"Far as I can tell, Gid's been sweet on you for a long time."

She thought on that. "Honestly there are times I think it *would* be fun to go somewhere with Gid, at least with another couple along."

Mamma's blue eyes grew more serious, and she set about cleaning the potting soil off the wooden work counter with a hand brush and dustpan. "Sometimes I wonder if you care for Gid simply because his sister is your dearest friend. Have you ever considered that?"

"Adah has little to do with Gid's and my friendship," Leah said quickly. The smithy's son had happily befriended her during her darkest days. They had even gone walking at dusk several times, but mostly their conversations took place in the cow pasture. She worried if allowing herself to warm to his winning smile might in some way betray the depth of love she'd had for Jonas.

"Just so Gid understands where your heart is," Mamma said.

Light streamed in through the windows, casting sunny beams onto the linoleum floor.

Where your heart is . . .

Leah sighed. "Whatever do you mean?"

Mamma sat tall and still, her gaze intent on Leah. "I think you know, dear. Deep within you, a voice is whispering what you should or should not do."

"I can't come right out and tell Smithy Gid that I don't love him as a beau, can I? How cruel that would be."

"You might say instead you think of him as a close brother."

Knowing Gid as she did, if she revealed this truth, he might take it as a challenge to try harder still to win her. "Oh, Mamma, I don't know what to say, honest I don't."

"Then say nothing . . . until you're sure. The Lord will give you the right words when the time comes. God holds the future in His hands . . . always remember this."

Mamma was as wise as any woman she knew—Mamma and Aunt Lizzie both. She thanked the Lord above for allowing her to grow up close to such women, though if she'd had her druthers, she would have preferred to know early on that

Lizzie Brenneman was the woman who'd birthed her. But to dwell on this was futile.

Mamma's words nudged her back to the present. "Why not ask Adah how *she* thinks her brother might react."

"I've thought of that, but I can't bring myself to open my mouth and say what I oughta."

Mamma frowned momentarily. "That's not the Leah *I* know."

Leah forced a smile. Maybe what Mamma was trying to say was *Don't settle for a Gideon Peachey if your heart longs for a Jonas Mast.*

Still, she refused to let Mamma or anyone see the depth of bewilderment that plagued her. It was as if her feet had sprouted long tendrils, like the runners that sometimes tripped her in the berry patch, making it impossible to move forward, tangling her way, keeping her from progressing on the path of her life.

"Are you afraid I'll never marry . . . if I pass up Gid's affection?" she asked suddenly.

"Not afraid, really," Mamma replied. "Just awful sorry if you're not happy in your choice of a husband. 'Tis better to be a contented maidel—like your aunt Lizzie—than a miserable wife, ya know."

Leah had heard similar remarks at the quilting frolics she and her twin sisters attended with Mamma; seemed there was an overabundance of spontaneous advice from the women folk nowadays. But the overall bent of Amish life, at least for a woman, was to marry and have a large family. Anything less was a departure from what the People expected.

All of a sudden she felt overcome with fatigue. The

potting shed had trapped the hot air, and she longed for the cool mossy green of the shaded front yard.

Politely she offered to help Mamma with the rest of her planting, but her mother shook her head.

"Go and have yourself some time alone," she said. "Goodness knows, you must need a rest."

Leah kissed Mamma's cheek and walked around the southeast side of the house, admiring the clear pink hydrangea bushes flourishing there. She sat on the ground and rested in the shadow of an ancient maple, daydreaming that Jonas had never, ever left Gobbler's Knob for his carpentry apprenticeship in Ohio.

Everything would be so different now. . . .

Yet she refused to give in to her emotions. Something as innocent as a daydream was wrong, she knew. Jonas belonged to Sadie now, and she to him.

"God holds the future in His hands." Mamma's confident words echoed in her mind.

Mosquitoes began to bite her ankles, and the sound of the noontime dinner bell prompted her to rouse herself and paste on yet another pleasant face. Leah rose and trudged toward the house.

Chapter Two

Sunday evening the air was so fresh and sweet it was hard for Mary Ruth to imagine a better place to be on such a fine night. She rode next to Hannah down Georgetown Road in the family buggy, chattering on the way to the singing. Once again, Aunt Lizzie had offered to drive, drop them off, and return home with the carriage, since there were no brothers to do the favor. Ever since February, when they turned sixteen and became eligible to attend Sunday singings, Lizzie had been kind—even eager—to drive them.

It had crossed Mary Ruth's mind to ask Leah to take them to the singing, but with Leah past her *rumschpringe* and a baptized church member, she was no longer expected to go to the barn singings, though she was welcome if she desired to, since she *was* still single. Mary Ruth couldn't help but wonder if Leah might have an awful slim chance of marrying now, unless, of course, she succumbed to Smithy Gid.

Mary Ruth felt sure Leah was still in mourning for Jonas, despite that everlasting smile of hers; her sister's cheerful mood didn't fool Mary Ruth one bit.

All in all, Aunt Lizzie was a much better choice for taking them to singings. One thing annoyed Mary Ruth, though—their aunt seemed a little too interested in who rode home with whom. Especially here lately, since the Stoltzfus boys had been bringing the twins home long past midnight every other Saturday. The grown-ups in the house were supposed to play dumb; the age-old custom of turning a deaf ear and a blind eye.

"Do you think Ezra and Elias will bring only one courting buggy to singin' again?" Mary Ruth whispered to her twin, eyes wide with anticipation. "It's such fun double courting, ain't so?"

To this Hannah smiled, shrugging her shoulder and looking nervously at Aunt Lizzie.

Hundreds of lightning bugs blinked over the cornfield like stars fallen glittery white from the heavens as the carriage headed downhill toward Grasshopper Level. A lone doe crept out at dusk and stood on the edge of the woods and watched them pass, as though hesitant to cross a road just claimed by a spirited steed.

"Elias has eyes only for you," Hannah whispered back. "If ya didn't know already."

Mary Ruth reached for her sister's hand and squeezed it. "I should say the same for you 'bout Ezra."

Aunt Lizzie turned her head just then and smiled. "What're you two twittering about?"

"*Ach*, best not to say, *Aendi*," Mary Ruth said quickly.

"Well, s'posin' I try 'n' guess," Aunt Lizzie taunted jovially, wispy strands of her dark hair loose at the brow.

Mary Ruth frowned. "Let's talk 'bout something else."

Their aunt caught on and clammed up, and that was that. Truth was, neither Mary Ruth nor Hannah felt comfortable telling Lizzie that the Stoltzfus boys were ever so fond of them. Since Ezra and Elias were less than a year and a half apart, it was fascinating they should be double-courting. "It's almost like we're going 'for steady' with twin boys, they're so close in age," Mary Ruth had declared to Hannah in the privacy of their bedroom last week.

"Not only that, but if we end up married . . . our children will be double cousins." Shy Hannah's pretty brown eyes had danced at that.

Yesterday afternoon, while stemming strawberries and, later, picking peas, Mamma had hinted she'd heard only a single buggy bringing her dear girls home here lately. Which, of course, could mean just one thing: the boys were either the best of friends and using the same open buggy . . . or they were brothers.

Naturally, with the secrecy surrounding the courting years, their mother knew better than to mention much else. Yet she'd said it with a most mischievous smile and out of earshot of Dat. At the time Mary Ruth had noticed how pretty Mamma looked, her face beaming with joy. Was it because she was with child once again? The women folk often whispered at canning bees and such that a woman in the family way had "a certain glow."

Or . . . maybe it had more to do with Mary Ruth showing an interest in a nice Amish boy; maybe that's what made Mamma smile these days. If so, then surely their mother wasn't nearly as worried as she had been at the end of the twins' eighth grade, a full year ago. The evening of graduation from the Georgetown School, Mary Ruth had out-and-out declared, "I want to attend high school next year!"

However, the very next day Dat had surprised her by taking her aside and talking mighty straight. "Hold your horses now, Mary Ruth." He'd asked her to wait until her rumschpringe to decide such a thing, so this past year she had continued to work three days a week for their Mennonite neighbor, Dottie Nolt, doing light housekeeping and occasional baby-sitting for the Nolts' adopted son, Carl. Along with that, she helped Mamma, as did Hannah and Leah, tending to the family and charity gardens, cleaning house, keeping track of busy Lydiann, and attending quilting frolics. Now that she was courting age, she was also going to Sunday singings with Hannah, who was taking baptismal instruction without her—a terrible sore spot between them.

Since she was "running around" now, Mary Ruth was able to openly read for pleasure, as well as study books at home, but the novelty of getting together with other Plain young people, especially fine-looking boys, had tempered her intense craving for escape into the world of English characters and settings. If she wanted to experience the modern world, she didn't have to rely on fiction any longer. Besides, it was great fun spending time with Elias Stoltzfus, who was as much a free spirit as she, within the confines of the Plain community, of course. She loved riding in his open courting buggy through Strasburg and the outskirts of Lancaster, soaring fast as they could through the dark night—though always in the company of Hannah and Ezra.

"How's Dottie Nolt these days . . . and her little one?" Aunt Lizzie asked unexpectedly.

"Carl moves right quick round the house. Dottie has to watch him awful close," Mary Ruth readily replied.

"I 'spect so. He's what—two now?"

She nodded. "A delightful child, but he's definitely on the go."

The horse turned off the road and headed down a long dirt lane, coming up on the old clapboard farmhouse. Aunt Lizzie pulled on the reins, and the carriage came to a stop. "Well, it certainly looks like a nice gathering of young folks."

Mary Ruth was happy to see the big turnout. What a wonderful-good night for a barn singing, not to mention the ride afterward under the stars with Elias. "Come along, Hannah." She hopped down out of the carriage. "*Denki*, Aunt Lizzie!" she called over her shoulder.

"Don't worry a smidgen 'bout us," Hannah said more softly to Lizzie.

Mary Ruth waited for Hannah to catch up, and then they walked together toward the two-story bank barn in their for-good blue dresses and long black aprons. "Why'd you say that?" asked Mary Ruth. "Do you really think Lizzie worries?"

"Well, I 'spect Mamma does, so I wouldn't be surprised if Aunt Lizzie does, too."

"They ought to know how nice the Stoltzfus family is," Mary Ruth spoke up in defense of Ezra and Elias. "Everybody does."

"*Jah* . . . but our eldest sister's wild rumschpringe days must surely haunt Mamma."

"Our sister was ever so foolish," Mary Ruth said, being careful not to mention Sadie's name outright. They had been forbidden to do so by Dat and the bishop following the *Bann*.

"Foolish, jah. And downright dreadful . . . stealing Leah's beau."

Mary Ruth didn't want to worry herself over things that couldn't be changed. She was caught up in the excitement of the moment and tried hard not to gawk at the many courting buggies lined up in the side yard. *Which one belongs to Elias?* she wondered, a thrill of delight rushing up her spine.

Abram sat next to Ida on the front porch swing, watching the stars come out. He also noticed the lightning bugs were more plentiful than in recent summers, maybe due to frequent afternoon showers. " 'Twas right kind of Leah to settle Lydiann in for the night," he said.

Ida nodded, sighing audibly. "Jah . . . even though she's as tuckered out as I am, prob'ly. She's such a dear . . . our Leah."

"That, she is."

Ida leaned her head gently on his shoulder. At last she said, "We did the right thing treatin' her as our very own all these years."

Hearing his wife speak of their great fondness for Leah made him realize anew that his own affection for Lizzie's birth daughter was as strong as if Ida had given birth to her. For a moment he was overcome with a rare sadness and remained silent.

Their flesh-and-blood Sadie was a different story altogether. Her defiance in not returning home after all this time had stirred up more alarm in him than he cared to voice to beloved Ida.

"The Good Lord's hand rests tenderly on us all," Ida said softly, as if somehow tuned in to his thoughts. "I daresay we'd be in an awful pickle otherwise."

He had to smile at that and reached over to cup her face in his callused hand. Sweet Ida . . . always thinking of the Lord God heavenly Father as if He were her own very close friend.

"Where do you think our twins are tonight?" He stared at the seemingly endless cornfield to the east of the house, over toward smithy Peachey's place.

"Don'tcha mean *whom* the girls are with?"

He let out a kindly grunt; Ida could read him like a book. She continued. "Deacon's wife told me in so many words that two of her sons are spending quite a lot of time with Hannah and Mary Ruth."

"Which boys . . . surely not the older ones?"

"I'm thinkin' it must be Ezra and Elias." Ida snuggled closer.

"A right fine match, if I say so myself. I best be givin' my approval to Deacon here 'fore long."

He heard the small laugh escape Ida's lips. "Best not get in the way, Abram. Let nature take its course."

"I s'pose you're thinkin' I shouldn't have interfered with Jonas and Leah back when."

Ida sat up quickly and looked at him, her plump hands knit into a clasp in her wide lap. "Leah would be happily married by now if you hadn't held out for Smithy Gid."

"Are ya blamin' *me* for what went wrong?" he said.

Ida pushed her feet hard against the porch floor, making the swing move too fast for his liking. When she spoke at last, her voice trembled. "None of us truly knows what caused their breakup."

He inhaled and held his breath. Ida didn't know what had caused the rift between Jonas and Leah, but *he* knew and all too well. Abram himself had gotten things stirred up but good by raising the troublesome issue of Leah's parentage with Jonas. He had never told her that, at Peter Mast's urging, he'd put Jonas to a fiery test of truth, revealing Lizzie's carefully guarded secret. When all was said and done, Jonas had failed it miserably. "Best leave well enough alone. Jonas is married to our eldest now."

"Jah, and worse things have happened," Ida whispered, tears in her eyes. "But I miss her something awful."

Abram didn't own up to the same. "What's done is done," he said. "Thing is we've got us a son-in-law we may never lay eyes on again. Could be a grandchild by now, too."

"All because our daughter was bent on her own way. . . ."

He leaned back in the swing and said no more. At times an uncanny feeling gnawed at him, made him wonder if Ida—who seemed to know more about Sadie than he did—might've disregarded the bishop and read a few of their eldest's early letters, after the law was laid down about returning them unopened.

But no, now was not the appropriate time to speculate on that. Clearly Ida needed his wholehearted companionship and understanding this night.

Chapter Three

Hannah was surprised how warm the night was, with little or no breeze. Her eyes kept straying toward the moon, and she was grateful for the hush of the evening hour, especially after having sung so robustly. Now she sat eating ice cream in the front seat of the open carriage with Ezra Stoltzfus, who wore a constant if not contagious smile.

She hoped Elias was not able to wrestle the reins away from Ezra tonight. It seemed both boys liked to trade off sitting in the driver's seat of the shiny new carriage. In fact, she was fairly sure they were actually sharing ownership of the courting buggy, though she'd never heard of this done in other families with many sons. As keenly interested as the deacon's boys had been in Mary Ruth and herself for the past several years, it was no wonder Ezra and Elias might share a single buggy now that the foursome were courting age.

Hannah's heart leaped with excitement. She was truly fond of auburn-haired Ezra, but more than that, she was most happy to see Mary Ruth putting aside her dream of becoming a schoolteacher. At least it appeared to be so in the presence of her dashing young beau. If Elias was the reason for Mary Ruth to set aside her perilous goal, then all was well and good and Hannah could simply use the money she'd saved from selling handiwork for something else altogether. If Mary Ruth didn't end up needing the money for future college expenses, maybe several pretty wedding quilts would do.

Thinking about this, Hannah felt she could accept Ezra's affections if for this one reason alone—to keep the double courting going full speed ahead, for the sake of a peaceful household and for Mary Ruth's future as a baptized church member. The latter she knew their parents wished for above all else.

"Let's find another courtin' couple to race," Elias said nearly the minute they were finished eating ice cream.

"Not tonight," Ezra replied firmly.

Hannah bit her tongue. She hoped her beau got his way, being older and all.

"Aw, lookee there. It's Sam Ebersol and Adah Peachey." Elias pointed to an open buggy some distance behind them, then waved his arms, trying to get the couple's attention.

"*I'm* driving," Ezra said at once.

But Elias persisted. "C'mon, it'll be fun. What do you say, Mary Ruth?"

"Sure, why not?" her twin was quick to say.

Hannah grew tense. The last time Elias persuaded his brother to let him race, they'd nearly locked wheels with another courting carriage on the way to a railroad crossing down on Route 372. In the end, Hannah had let out a squeal . . . and Elias had stopped. He'd apologized promptly, saying he hadn't meant any harm by it. He had also said,

"There's plenty other things to do to have fun after singing."

Plenty other things is right, thought Hannah. She figured at the rate he was going, Elias wouldn't be ready to settle down and farm, probably, or marry, for another couple of years. But she'd seen the love-light in her twin's eyes for the redheaded and handsome young man, and in his for pretty Mary Ruth. Sooner or later, the both of them would start thinking about joining church.

Just then Sam and Adah pulled up beside them. "What's goin' on?" asked Sam.

"Thought you might wanna race," Elias called to them from the backseat.

Sam looked at Adah, then answered, "Oh, that's all right. We've got some talking to do, Adah and I."

"Okay, then," Elias said, sitting down.

Hannah was relieved and felt herself relax against the seat. Sam hurried his horse, passing them, and she was glad to see Ezra let Sam gain on him. Ezra, after all, was most steady and dependable. At nearly eighteen, he was taking baptismal instruction classes and might be looking to settle down and marry within a year or so. Hannah wondered if she was truly mature enough, though, to accept if he should ask her to be his wife. Was *she* ready for the duties of home and motherhood? Mamma's sisters had married young. All except Aunt Lizzie, of course. And Mamma, who, though she'd been but seventeen when first she'd met Dat, had waited until her early twenties to tie the knot.

Behind her, she heard Elias whispering to Mary Ruth, probably with his arm draped around her shoulder; they'd done their share of snuggling, for sure.

As for herself, the rest of the night would be most pleasant—watching for shooting stars with Ezra, playing Twenty Questions, and letting him reach for her hand as they slowly made their way back home before dawn.

Once Leah had safely nestled Lydiann into her crib for the night, she crept toward the stairs. Having just kissed the little girl's tiny face, she realized sadly that Sadie might never know about Mamma's coming baby—their new sibling-to-be.

Downstairs, she spotted the tops of her parents' heads through the front room window. She wouldn't think of disturbing them. Much of their energy, too, went into thinking of Sadie; Leah was sure it had been so since her sister's shunning.

Turning from the room, she decided it was best to leave Dat and Mamma be. They deserved some quiet time together.

She went to the kitchen and poured a glass of water, thinking now of Smithy Gid. More than likely, he could be found in his father's big barn playing with the new brood of pups. "Tonight's the night," she said to herself, "ready or not."

Slipping out the back door, she headed past the barnyard and through the cornfield. She'd kept Gid waiting long enough—too long, really, as he'd made his thoughtful invitation to her two days ago. She mustn't be rude and keep him guessing by the hour. She'd had several opportunities to speak privately with him yesterday, but she had still been uncertain, though she knew Gid was as stalwart in his soul as he was in his frame. He wasn't just "as good as gold," as Dat liked to say; Gid was superior to Dat's proverbial gold, and the girl who consented to be his wife would be truly blessed.

Is it to be me? she wondered. *Can I trust the Lord God to guide my faltering steps?*

In vain, she tried to imagine being held in his strong arms. Would she be gladdened by his tender affection . . . ready for their courting days to begin? All these things and more Leah contemplated as her bare feet padded the ground on her way to find the blacksmith's son before Dat and Mamma wondered where on earth she'd taken herself off to on a night set apart for singings.

She found Smithy Gid in the haymow, amusing himself with a new pup. "Hullo," Leah called up to him.

Quickly he rose and made his way down the long ladder to her, carrying the tiny dog. "I wasn't expecting to see you tonight, Leah." He looked at her with gentle eyes. "But it's awful nice," he added with a warm smile.

They stood there looking at each other by lantern light, Leah feeling ever so awkward. She glanced down for a moment, breathed a sigh, and then lifted her face to his. "I'm ready to give you my answer," she said softly.

"Jah?"

"I'll go along to Strasburg with you . . . with Adah and Sam, come Saturday night."

Gid's face lit up like a forbidden electric light bulb. "Wonderful-gut! Denki for comin' here to say so."

She realized at that moment the power her decision had over him. If she'd said otherwise, she could just imagine the look of disappointment that would have transformed his ruddy face. "I best be headin' home," she said.

"Aw, must ya?" His eyes implored her to stay.

"Dat and Mamma don't know I'm gone. I wouldn't want them to fret." She didn't go on to say they were worried enough over Sadie. No doubt he was aware of that; it was to be expected with Gid's mother and Mamma close neighbors and bosom friends. Miriam Peachey had surely heard tell of Mamma's sleepless nights.

"Well, then, I 'spect it's best you return *schnell*—quickly."

At that she moved toward the barn door. "*Gut Nacht*," she said as Gid strolled alongside her.

"Good night, Leah."

She nodded self-consciously and turned to go, walking briskly toward her father's cornfield. Hundreds of stars beckoned her, and she found herself wondering if anyone had ever tried to count them, at least those twinkling over the Ebersol Cottage.

Staring up at the sky, she pondered her decision to go with Gid this one time . . . and his near-gleeful response. *Did I do the right thing?*

The last place Gid wanted to be, now that Leah had told him her good news, was back up in the lonely haymow. He returned the puppy in hand to the whelping box and hurried out behind the barn, toward Blackbird Pond. He had to keep looking at the ground, now murky in the early evening hour, to see if his feet were really touching the grassy path that led through the pastureland and beyond to the lake.

With great joy, he began to count the hours till he would see Leah again, not in Abram's barn or out in the field . . . no, what he most anticipated was their first *real* date. The long ride to Strasburg was nothing to sneeze at as far as time on the road; he must make sure he took along a light lap robe, in case the evening had a chill to it. They would enjoy a fine meal in town with Adah and Sam, then leisurely return to Gobbler's Knob, a round trip of nearly ten miles. All in all, the night would not be so young when he returned Leah to the covering of her father's house.

Gid's heart sang as he picked up his pace and began to run around the wide lake. *Will Leah accept my love at last?*

Chapter Four

Dr. Schwartz plodded upstairs to the second-floor bedroom, where, in the corner of the large room, he found his wife reclining on the leather chaise, sipping a cup of chamomile tea. *Lorraine's nerves must be ragged again tonight*, he thought. He'd learned not to address her when she was in such a state. In the past, when he had attempted to engage her in conversation, she withdrew further still.

As for Henry, he was much more practiced at concealing his misery; he prided himself in his ability to do so. Even Lorraine had no knowledge of his ongoing despair, he was quite certain. On the exterior, his life was as fulfilled now as he had ever hoped it to be—faithful wife, grown sons, and a flourishing medical clinic. With their boys gone from home, he and Lorraine had sufficient time to do as they pleased, which most evenings meant sitting in easy chairs and reading silently, enjoying baroque music, or discussing eldest son Robert's zealous letters and spiritual ambition. Lorraine was increasingly anxious, though, and he had begun to recognize the fact around the time the boys spread their proverbial wings. Continually she invited him to attend church with her and their neighbors, Dottie and Dan Nolt and their toddler-age son. Without exception, he refused, adding to his wife's dejection. Having attended church only sporadically during their adult years, he was by no means interested in jumping on Lorraine's recent religious bandwagon. To her credit, his wife was a woman who knew how to blend persuasion with loving consideration. This fact, over the years, had helped keep their marriage intact.

His misery had not so much to do with Robert's search for God, nor Derek's enlistment in the army and detachment from the family, as his bleak memory of a dark April night when his own frail grandson had experienced both life and death in the space of a few hours. That fateful night had altered Henry's very existence.

Accordingly, each Sunday before Lorraine awakened and the sun rose, he crept downstairs and got into the car, driving down Georgetown Road, past the Ebersol and Peachey farms, turning onto a dirt lane east of the smithy's spread of land. That narrow byway led to the ten acres he'd inherited from his father, Reverend Schwartz. Having decided against ever building a house there, Henry had held on to the grazing land, letting it appreciate in value over the years. More recently, he had thought of offering to sell it to the local blacksmith, if the Amishman was so inclined. Lorraine, however, had suggested the parcel of land remain in the family, perhaps to be given at the appropriate time to Robert as a wedding gift.

Getting out of the car, Henry would go and tend to a small grave unmarked by a headstone, trimming the tall grass away with hand clippers. When finished, he stood in deep contemplation, the little mound of earth his altar and the clipped grass his pew, surrounded by a choir of insects and birds.

Just this morning he had visited the site and stared down at the memorial of his own making, recalling the momentous night he had hauled to the spot a shovel in the trunk of his car. Having paced the ground, he had made a frantic determination for the location of a proper burial. The hollowness in his soul had been undeniable as he pushed hard and deep into the ground—the ball of his foot on the shovel, his arms lifting out the soil one heaping pile at a time. Grave digging was harder work than he had anticipated, both physically and otherwise, but the burial itself had been excruciating. And when the task was complete, the lifeless body of an infant boy lay in the broken earth.

There it was that Henry presented himself to the Creator-God on Sunday mornings, each and every one since that very first, refusing Lorraine's invitation to a church with walls of stone and mortar. Nowhere else drew him like the open-air cathedral where he was the one and only parishioner, the lone visitor to a child's tiny grave.

Startled out of his musing by Lorraine's gentle voice, Henry jerked his head, a piece of mail slipping out of his hands and onto the floor.

"Dear," she said, "be sure to read Robert's letter."

Lorraine had left a pile of their personal mail from Saturday afternoon lying on the dresser for him. He had been much too busy at the clinic to bother thumbing through the bills and such. He stooped now to reach for his eldest's latest letter. "How are things going for him?" he inquired for Lorraine's sake. Hard as it was for him to admit, son Robert was looking for absolute truth—strangely finding it in a group of Bible-believing Mennonites.

"He's planning to come home for Thanksgiving," Lorraine offered, still seated with cup poised in midair.

"Oh?" He nodded absentmindedly. Late November was the perfect time for a visit with his strapping son. Perhaps Robert would consider arriving a few days early so that they might join the enthusiastic turkey shooters over on the wooded hillock across the road. *We'll surprise Lorraine with a plump turkey for our Thanksgiving feast*, he thought, wishing that Derek, too, might be inclined to desire connection with family. Regrettably there had been no word from Derek in the past year, a fact that continued to grieve them. *Yes*, thought Henry. *Our younger son is long gone in more ways than one.*

He settled down with Robert's letter, adjusting his eyeglasses and leaning his head close to the linen stationery in order to follow every line and curve of his firstborn's penmanship.

Thursday, June 16

Dear Mom and Dad,

Thanks for writing, Dad. I received your last letter in the Wednesday mail. And thanks, Mom, for the care packages. Several of my campus friends have gratefully helped me devour your chocolate-chip cookies and banana-nut breads. Because of your delectable gifts, I'm one of the best-fed—and most popular—fellows I know!

I hope to make a trip home for Thanksgiving weekend. Any chance Derry might show up? He continues to snub my letters, but I'd like to see him again . . . it's been too long.

Well, I must head to class. I'll look forward to hearing from you soon.

With love to you both,
Robert

Sighing, Henry blurted out, "What do you make of that, Lorraine?"

"Sounds to me Derry has no intention of keeping in touch with *any* of us." Her voice wavered.

Henry felt sure he knew why; no doubt Derek was suffering a severe bout of old-fashioned guilt, and no wonder. He'd gotten an Amish girl pregnant, only to promptly leave Gobbler's Knob for the army. His son's misbehavior and indifference were an embarrassment. How could Derek ruin the girl's life and simply abandon her?

Henry folded the letter, returning it to the envelope. When it came to guilt, he could relate to having made a few serious mistakes in life—some more earthshaking than others.

"We must celebrate the prospect of seeing Robert again," he said suddenly as he prepared to retire for the night. "We can't go on mourning Derek's appalling attitude."

"Sometimes that's far easier said than done," Lorraine replied, dabbing at her eyes.

He acknowledged the grim fact with a nod of his head. *What else is there to do?*

Soon after Leah started working part-time at the village clinic, she began to recognize her interest in children, especially the youngest ones with obvious injuries. She loved to console or distract them in the waiting room by using the sock puppets Hannah had knitted. She often did the same at home while caring for Lydiann, who, at times, seemed rather accident prone—scraped knees, brush-burned elbows, and all.

Leah had surprised herself with her immediate like for the doctor and his wife; she felt sure she'd met good solid folk, although worlds apart from her in culture and upbringing. There was not one iota of plainness about Henry and Lorraine, but that didn't stop Leah from enjoying their company. The doctor's infectious laughter, though seemingly forced at times, and Lorraine's delicious specialty cakes and breads she set out for the clinic staff during short breaks in the flow of patient traffic made Leah feel most welcome.

This Monday morning she hurried into the clinic and made coffee for the receptionist, as well as the coming patients. That done, she did a bit of dusting, which, before today, had not been one of the things expected of her. Till now she had swept and washed the floors and windows, making doubly sure the examination rooms and miniscule restroom were sanitary, along with sweeping the steps and sidewalk. In many ways she was considered the clinic's sole housekeeper.

Lorraine had recently hinted *she* might need a bit of help, especially with the large kitchen floor and the many knickknacks that accumulated dust in both the living and sitting rooms of the Schwartz residence. So far Leah hadn't jumped at the opportunity to assist Lorraine with additional tasks, mainly because Mamma's strawberries were coming on awful fast now and there would be plenty to sell at the Ebersols' roadside stand. In fact, at this moment, Mamma and Miriam Peachey were out in the hot sun picking berries while Hannah and Mary Ruth completed the washing. And Lydiann, more than likely, was babbling to Dawdi John next door in the Dawdi Haus. Only occasionally did Mamma ask her father to watch her youngest, but since Leah was expected home in time for the noon meal, Lydiann would be in Dawdi's charge only a short time. After that Leah herself would help tend to her baby sister, along with her afternoon chores outside. By taking Lydiann along with her to the barn and whatnot, she hoped to develop a strong love of the land and the farm animals in the wee toddler. And, too, it wouldn't be long and Lydiann would be someone to talk to while working outdoors—someone besides Gid, that was, and Sam Ebersol's older brother, twenty-year-old Thomas, recently hired by Dat to help with fieldwork part-time.

During a lull between patient appointments, Leah got up the nerve to mention the doctor's grazing land, "not so far from the Peacheys' place," interested to see what Dr. Schwartz might say about it.

When there was little or no direct response to her comment, she forged ahead. "Have you ever thought of putting cattle out there? Such nice grazing it would be."

The good doctor scratched his head and looked nearly disoriented for a few seconds. Then he said, "I've thought of different things over the years. Everything from building a house and barn on it . . . to putting up a stable for horseback riding. In the end, I always come back to its being too great an effort to bother with putting cattle or anything else on it, though."

She paused to study him. Tall and lean, he was a man with plenty of options flitting in his head. But he fell silent, and in a short time another patient came up the walk and in the door.

Leah was surprised to see her mother's cousin Fannie Mast, with young Jake and Mandie in tow. She at first felt sheepish standing there, then pained, remembering Fannie was to have been her mother-in-law. Without meaning to, she found herself gawking at the twins; she hadn't seen them in two years and they'd grown so much.

This woman, equally as plump as Mamma now, if not more so, had always been a bubbly hostess when the Ebersols visited the Mast orchard house on Grasshopper Level, not but a thirty-minute buggy's ride from Gobbler's Knob. Today, though, when Fannie caught Leah's eye, her mouth drooped and she turned away, taking the twins' hands and guiding them to the far corner of the waiting room.

Undaunted, Leah slipped into the short hall, hoping to watch her little cousins toddle with their mamma to one of the examination rooms. She stood behind the doorjamb and peered out as the threesome made their way.

Jake was tall and skinny, much like his big brother Jonas, though his hair was a deep brown and he limped slightly as he tottered along. Leah couldn't tell if he'd hurt himself or if he was still discovering his own stride as a two-year-old. She recalled the first time she'd held him, how she had sensed his helplessness as an infant—a frail one at that.

But it appeared his mother's nurturing touch had made all the difference, just as it had for the sickly lambs and struggling houseplants Fannie was known to nurse back to health.

Dr. Schwartz appeared in the hallway and called Jake's name, then scooped him up in his arms. He touched the top of Mandie's head, speaking quietly to Fannie.

Observing Mandie now, Leah was taken with her dainty features, though altogether different from Jake's—her blue eyes and blond hair showing hints of highlights the color of honey, much lighter than Jonas's.

Attempting to redirect her thoughts from her former beau, she wondered how Fannie must feel seeing her here after all this time, knowing—surely she did—how devoted her firstborn son had been to Leah from his earliest teen years. Until he'd turned his attention to Sadie, of course. Did Fannie have any knowledge of Jonas and Sadie, perhaps where they were living in Ohio? Would she even care to say if Leah got up the nerve to ask?

Having been in attendance at the required membership meeting where Bishop Bontrager called for a vote for or against shunning Jonas—most excruciating for her—she understood fully that he had been cut off from his family as entirely as the rest of the People. Unless he returned and repented for breaking the strict covenant, Jonas would be estranged from both the communities of Gobbler's Knob and Grasshopper Level all the days of his life. Leah felt strongly that the bishop had found fault with him because of his keen interest in carpentry. For Jonas to abandon the idea of farming was near heresy!

Sighing now, she was tormented with the image of the smiling Mast children, as well as the solemn face of Fannie, Mamma's once bright and happy relative. *Why is she sour toward me?* she wondered. *Does she blame me for the shun on her son?*

It was Lizzie, not Ida, who spent a good part of the morning picking strawberries with Miriam Peachey when she came to lend a hand. Ida remained indoors, trying to keep herself cool, and all for the best since she had complained of nausea today. Lizzie was more than a little concerned about her sister.

She was glad for the white-pleated candlesnuffer-style sunbonnet Hannah had presented to her just this morning after the twins had hung out the clothes to dry.

"It'll keep the sun off your face," Hannah had said sweetly, entering the kitchen wearing a green choring dress.

"So your nose won't peel something awful . . . like last summer's sunburn," Mary Ruth had added, glancing approvingly at her twin.

Since Ida had already taken herself upstairs, Lizzie felt she ought to see who was doing what chores, both indoors and out. Mary Ruth spoke up, declaring she would be the one to look after Lydiann while the clothes dried, and then she'd single-handedly fold everything neatly after the noon meal, once Lydiann was down for a nap. Hannah, on the other hand, volunteered to hoe the large family vegetable garden after the dishes were washed and dried.

With Leah gone for the morning at the clinic, it seemed they might've been a bit shorthanded with Ida resting, but thanks to Miriam, the morning duties would be accomplished in a timely manner.

"Awful kind of you to come over," Lizzie said as she and Miriam moved through the strawberry patch. "Did you suspect Ida might be suffering another bout of mornin' sickness?"

Miriam nodded. "Jah, and she has no business bein' out here in the hot sun."

"Aside from that, I'd have to say she's feeling perty well. She's a strong one, Ida."

They worked together without saying much more for a time. Then Miriam asked softly, looking over her shoulder, "Ida bears most of her pain in silence . . . what with her eldest gone, ain't so?"

"Oh my, ever so much. The girl's shunning has taken its toll. None of us understands why she refused to repent here in Gobbler's Knob. The silence and separation is almost a punishment for all of *us*, too."

Miriam stretched a moment, then resumed picking. "On top of that, Ida tells me she gets ever so blue not hearin' a speck from Fannie." She shook her head sadly. "Why she keeps on writing letters, I just can't figure. If it were me, I'd plain quit."

Lizzie knew well why her sister continued to send letters over to Grasshopper Level. "Bless her heart, she hopes Fannie might write back with some word of our wayward girl . . . though the Masts must be in the dark as much as we are."

"How awful sad for Abram and Ida, having no contact with either their eldest or their only son-in-law," Miriam replied. "And the Masts have kept mighty tight-lipped. Surely something will give sooner or later."

"I can only imagine what it might take to get the two families talking again." Lizzie's pail was nearly full now, and a glance at Miriam's let her know now was as good a time as any for them to hurry inside and cool off a bit with a nice tall glass of iced tea.

Chapter Five

Hannah stole away to the bedroom during the hottest hour of the day and took from the bureau drawer her makeshift writing journal, a simple notebook with yellow lined paper. She wanted to catch up on her diary before it was time to dress around for a double date with Ezra, and Mary Ruth and Elias.

Saturday afternoon, June 25
Dear Diary,

I haven't put my thoughts down on paper every other day like I'd set out to. Now, more than ever, I ought to be recording the events as they happen to my dear twin and me. If Ezra Stoltzfus and his younger brother Elias are to become my and Mary Ruth's husbands someday, it would be an awful shame not to have faithfully written about our double courtship. Goodness knows, my children and grandchildren might one day wish I had.

So . . . I am making an attempt to be more thorough, beginning with what happened today. Mary Ruth confided she has been seriously considering extending her rumschpringe for several more years. This is such a disappointment; I'd hoped she would join church with me. We've done everything else together. Why not this?

Life is ever so unpredictable—makes me wonder if Elias, too, is thinking along the same lines. Obviously he isn't headed toward making his kneeling vow before the membership this fall, since he's not taking baptism classes with Ezra.

Naturally I pleaded with Mary Ruth not to tell another soul, "not till you think gut and hard." Such news would hurt Mamma and Dat even worse than they already are. And Leah . . . oh my, I hate to think what it would do to her if Mary Ruth stalled too long and ended up going her own way. Leah has had more than her share of heartache.

Come tonight, I'm hoping Elias and Mary Ruth sit in the front seat of the courting buggy. They might not be so inclined to smooch that way . . . though it's more awkward for Ezra and me, sitting behind them and having to see what's going on.

When all's said and done, liking a boy so much that you turn your back on the Lord God and the People isn't worth a hill of beans all summer. Knowing Mary Ruth, I expect she'll come round sooner or later.

Respectfully,
Hannah

She closed the notebook and placed it back in the drawer, concealing it with several woolen scarves. Then she went to fill the washbasin with water to freshen up for supper and her evening with Ezra, who had suggested going to Strasburg for some store-bought ice cream. The thought of seeing him again made her feel light inside, and a peace settled over her.

Leah was content with the quietude of the house. Lydiann was napping while Mamma read the Good Book in the big bedroom. Aunt Lizzie worked downstairs in the kitchen, cooking as silently as she could, and Mary Ruth and Hannah were down the hall in their room, most likely preparing to go riding in someone's courting buggy.

Standing at the window, Leah looked down, appreciating the bright green of the enormous trees and the meadow. Dashes of color from the wild flowers scattered here and there caught her eye, and she wondered, *What's Gid thinking? Is he counting the minutes till we sit side by side in his open buggy?*

Slowly she turned from her window, wandered to the corner of the room, and sat in the single cane chair, leaning her elbows hard on her legs, palms cupping her chin. With a great sigh, she began to remove her head covering and the pins in her bun. She shook out her hair, untangling it with her fingers and going over and over the length.

As she began to brush her hair vigorously, she recalled the many times she had brushed or combed Sadie's beautiful blond locks. Often the two of them had taken turns doing so at day's end.

When she was satisfied all the snarls were out, she rose and walked to the bed—the one she and Sadie had shared from the time they were but tiny girls, once Leah was able to sleep in a bed and not roll out.

Do you miss me, sister, as sorrowfully as I miss you?

She felt the strength drain from her legs, and she was compelled to lie down. A short rest might rejuvenate her for the long night ahead. Almost immediately her muscles relaxed as she stretched out on the bed. Sadie's plump pillow was a constant reminder of their many late-night talks, sharing dreams of the future as schoolgirls and on into the early teen years . . . and finally rumschpringe. They had always talked of living neighbors to each other as married women. "Our babies will grow up together just like brothers and sisters," Sadie had promised in the fading light.

Leah couldn't bear to think of the children Sadie would give birth to. Such things were too painful still. Reaching over, she slid her hand beneath her sister's pillow, aware of its utter coolness to the touch. *Will I ever see you again?* she wondered. The thought left her torn, and tears came all too fast . . . missing Sadie yet not wanting to truly know about her life as Jonas's wife. *No, 'tis best you stay wherever you are. . . .*

When it came time to go out and hitch his horse to the courting buggy, Gid simply told his mother he had "some business in town." It was a common phrase used among the young men in the community on a Saturday night before the no-church Sunday. This, to explain the reason for having cleaned up, put unruly hair to order with a comb, and dressed around in clean black trousers and colorful shirts, though Plain parents all over Lancaster County were mindful it was courting night.

"Oh?" his mamma said, her face shining her delight. "Well, have yourself a good time, hear?"

Pop nodded slowly, smiling faintly before recovering his solemn look. Gid was downright certain his father had at least an inkling Leah would also be going along "to tend to business."

"We won't be waitin' up for you, son," Mamma said, a twinkle in her eyes.

Pop agreed they'd be "goin' to bed with the chickens," so Gid felt assured of their trust, just as all young Amishmen did on such a night. Though he knew they would not interfere with his choice of a girlfriend, he would attempt to guard his relationship with Leah, whatever it was to be, from the eyes and ears of the People as a whole for as long as possible. In fact, he must remind Adah once again to keep quiet about Leah going along with them tonight, just as he wouldn't think of breathing a word that Leah's cousin Sam was seriously courting Adah and, more than likely, soon to marry her. The age-old custom of secrecy was so ingrained into the ritual of courtship, Gid felt sure no one would guess whom he was engaged to when the time finally did come. No, he must woo and win Leah's heart and require his sister to vow absolute secrecy.

Nothing must go wrong, he thought. *I must do things the respectable and right way. Beginning tonight.*

Locusts sang a percussive song as Smithy Gid's best horse pulled the open buggy west from Gobbler's Knob, past the dense woods on the north, heading toward the town of Strasburg. Gid's sister pointed out how pretty the sky was, and Sam Ebersol said he wouldn't be surprised if there was a downright beautiful sunset tonight.

To Gid's left, Leah sat straight and stiff in the seat, as if she wasn't wholly committed to being there. Or, more than likely, she was uneasy with double courting, what with Adah and Sam nearly engaged already. How awkward for her—for them, really. *Yet I'm determined for her to have a right nice time,* thought Gid, holding the reins. *Leah must feel comfortable not only with me, but with my sister and her beau.*

Surely the sweet fragrance of honeysuckle, the shimmer of the first evening star shortly after sunset, and the fact Leah's best girlfriend was along for the ride would enhance her first outing in his black courting buggy. Gid dared not to go so far as to think his mere presence might make the evening altogether pleasant for her.

Behind them in the second seat, Sam began to tell a joke to Adah. Both Adah and Sam laughed out loud when the tall story was over. Gid felt like letting loose with hearty laughter himself, but Leah was only smiling, not laughing at all, so he remained silent. He was, in general, much too self-conscious. He wanted to be himself, to relax and enjoy the ride, the night air so warm and agreeable for such a trip. Frankly he felt nearly helpless to wind down, and it was obvious Leah felt the same.

He was indeed thankful for Sam's wholehearted chortle, which continued for several more jokes, at least until well past Rohrer Mill Road. Soon the horse turned north at Paradise Lane, taking them closer to the Strasburg Pike and then west, past the railroad depot and into the town of Strasburg.

"Did ya hear of the boy who attended his first singing, hooked up with a wild bunch, drank himself full of moonshine, and passed out on the front seat of his own carriage?" Sam asked.

"Ach, what happened?" Adah asked innocently.

"From what I heard—and this is true—his horse simply trotted on home, the drunk youth sleepin' all the while in the buggy."

Gid had heard such stories, too, and he said so but added quickly that there were "some fatal accidents happening under those kinds of circumstances, too." He didn't especially want to be a wet blanket, but, truth was, several young men had been killed that way when their horses galloped right through a red light at a dangerous intersection, the carriage hit broadside by an unsuspecting automobile.

His comment stirred up some talk from Leah, and a few minutes later Sam jumped in with more jokes. With an inward sigh, Gid realized the evening was going to turn out just fine. He felt the tension drain from his jaw, and when he could do so discreetly, he saw that Leah, too, seemed much more tranquil now, her hands not so tightly clasped in her lap.

It was on the ride home from Strasburg, as they made the bend onto Georgetown Road, that Gid spotted two open buggies riding side by side at a fast pace. "Look at that!" he said.

Both Leah and Adah gasped.

"Pity's sake, what're they doin'?" Adah hollered.

Leah held on to the seat with both hands. "Somebody's a *Dummkopp!*"

"Worse than a blockhead," Gid added.

"I should say!" Adah said.

"Let's not get too close, in case. . . ." Leah's voice trailed off.

"Don'tcha worry none," Gid reassured her, wanting to touch her hand but refusing to take advantage of the harrowing situation. Instead, he steered the horse onto the right shoulder and slowed down, allowing some distance between his buggy and the two speeding carriages ahead.

Suddenly he heard a girl's voice from one of the buggies. "Elias, stop!"

"Ach no," Leah whispered.

"What?" Gid leaned near. "Do you recognize someone?"

"My sister . . . Hannah." She turned in her seat now that they had rolled to a halt. "She may be dating one of the deacon's sons."

"Then he oughta know better!" Adah was standing up behind them now for a better look.

The deafening sound of a car horn pierced the stillness. Quick as a wink, one of the buggies fell behind the other, and Gid breathed a sigh of relief. "Too close for comfort."

"You can say that again." Leah put her hands on her throat.

Gid waited a few more minutes, then clicked his cheek and his horse pulled forward. "We could follow the buggy your sister's in," he suggested.

"Gut idea," Adah said.

"Jah, let's follow 'em!" Sam said.

Leah said no more, and Gid wondered if she was worried the Stoltzfus boy might feel threatened somehow, that trailing them might cause a rift between herself and her younger sisters. He certainly understood if she was thinking that way. Leah might've told him, if the two of them had gone riding alone, that Abram's other daughters—she and Sadie, at least—had surely endured enough strain between them to last a lifetime.

Chapter Six

Hannah said not a word to Mary Ruth as they slipped into the house through the kitchen door. She was so upset with Elias—and Mary Ruth for egging him on—all she wanted to do was hurry and undress for bed. *At least in my dreams I won't be ridin' with the likes of Elias Stoltzfus!* she thought, heading for the stairs.

Once the two of them were situated in bed, scarcely needing even a sheet, with the room so stuffy and warm, she was careful to sigh ever so lightly, hoping Mary Ruth wouldn't mention anything. She felt done in from having clung to her seat for dear life, and literally, too! Goodness, she was fairly sure the driver of the car coming straight at them tonight scarcely had enough time to sound the horn, let alone pray that the wild buggy driver could get out of his way.

"I know what you're thinkin'," Mary Ruth whispered on the pillow next to her.

Hannah inhaled and held her breath for a moment, then let it out gradually. "Honestly, I felt I saw my whole life flash in front of my eyes tonight."

"I don't think we were ever in any real danger, Hannah. For pity's sake!"

"Oh, but we *were!* Didn't you see how close that car came to hitting us?"

Mary Ruth was quiet, stirring only enough to turn her back to Hannah.

"Weren't you frightened, Mary Ruth?"

"I *did* feel the hairs on my neck stand straight up, but that was only from excitement, nothin' more. Frankly it was lots of fun." Mary Ruth pulled on the sheet, leaving little for her twin. "Besides, Elias is a right gut driver, really he is."

Hannah thought her sister was sadly mistaken. "Well, if that's what you call fun, then maybe we'd best not go double courting anymore."

"If that's what you want" came the empty reply.

She has no sense of good judgment, Hannah thought. Maybe Mary Ruth preferred to court alone, after all. If so, Hannah didn't quite know how she felt about that, though it *would* give her and Ezra more time to get to know each other. That might be a good thing; however, she wasn't so sure it would be wise to encourage Mary Ruth and Elias to court alone. She hated to think of her twin ending up the way Sadie had . . . and like Aunt Lizzie evidently, too, according to Mamma's account of things most private.

Leah was becoming more and more eager to get home, back to the comfort of her soft bed. The carriage seat felt awful hard now, and Gid seemed too eager to keep driving around in circles. Adah and Sam were silent in the second seat behind them, and she wondered if Adah had dozed off on Sam's shoulder. Surely they weren't smooching, knowing Adah.

Looking to her left, away from Gid, Leah recalled her first-ever kiss. Jonas had shown no hesitancy whatsoever, and as much as she had delighted in the feel of his lips on hers that afternoon in the meadow, she'd also heard clearly Mamma's admonition: *Save lip-kissin' for your husband. . . .*

Well, obviously she and Jonas had been only betrothed, not married, so according to Mamma, she had no business yielding to his embrace. And every day that passed, she pushed away the warm thoughts of her former beau, wishing to high heavens she'd waited to let her husband be the first to kiss her, whoever that was to be.

She had been meaning to ask Aunt Lizzie about all this, or Mamma. If they knew, would they say her disobedience had caused her to lose Jonas in the end? Might Mamma admit such a thing? Was the lip-kissing rule passed down from all the People's mothers to their daughters as keenly important as that? She knew of a good many young married couples that never kissed till their wedding day; some stricter groups even forbid holding hands before marriage.

Wishing the road was better lit than by an occasional yard light whenever they passed the English farmhouses, Leah wondered what time it was and how much longer she'd have to wait to return home.

Out of the blue, Smithy Gid got a talk on, and as tired as she was, she thought it best to lend her ear . . . show respect. "What would you think of going to Strasburg again sometime?" he said.

She wasn't sure if he meant to ask if she enjoyed the visit

to the neighboring village or if he was asking her for another date. So, not to confuse him, she mentioned the nice supper they'd had, how awful kind it was of him to include her.

"Didja like the food?" he asked.

"Right tasty, it was. Denki."

" 'Twas my first time eating there. Sam has been tellin' me off and on for several weeks that we oughta go."

"So Sam knew of it, then?"

He nodded cheerfully. "That's how I heard of the place."

She was feeling sorry for Gid, truly; he was trying to draw her out of her shell, wanting to make good conversation. "I liked it just fine," she said, putting on a smile. "As gut as home cooking, really."

She saw him glance down to see where her hands were just then, and she was glad she'd folded them on her lap. No sense making things more complicated than they already were, him wanting more than mere friendship and her content with things as they were. For now.

"How would you feel 'bout going to the next singing?" he asked.

"I haven't been for the longest time. Might seem peculiar."

"Maybe you and Adah could ride together, and then . . . I'd be happy to bring you home."

She didn't know what made her say it, but without thinking twice, she simply said, "Sure, Gid. That'd be fine." She hoped they might not end up with Adah and Sam again, though. It was awful complicated riding around the countryside with them when all they talked about was renting or building a house, what they needed in the way of furnishings, and whatnot—typical talk for a serious couple. Surely Gid must either know or strongly suspect this about his sister and Sam.

She looked off toward the horizon line to the west, her thoughts straying hard to Ohio . . . wondering if Sadie and Jonas were still living there. Were they happy as larks? Was it even possible for Sadie to find joy with Leah's first and only love? Quickly she felt ashamed, because it was wrong to begrudge her sister and Jonas anything.

"Sometimes you seem almost lost without your older sister," Gid said unexpectedly.

"Is it that noticeable?"

They rode along in silence for a ways. He surprised her when he slipped his arm around her shoulder, barely touching her as he did. "It pains me so . . . you must know this, Leah."

Then and there, she felt the oddest twinge. She turned and looked at him—really looked. Such compassion in his face, his eyes much too serious now. Usually he was easy to talk to, but this minute she felt awkward, unable to speak. She wanted to please him, to let him know how grateful she was for his caring about her, yet what should she say? What *could* she say?

Slowly he drew her near, letting go the reins and reaching for her ever so gently. "Oh, Leah. I'm awful sorry for what you've been through. . . ."

She couldn't help herself as she began to cry, at once glad Adah and Sam were asleep sitting up in each other's arms. "You're so nice to me, Gid. You've always been so."

He held her fast, and she was surprised at how good it felt to rest in the strength of his arms. Like he was truly a dear and trusted friend, not an anxious young man wanting to get on with courting, hoping she might fall in love with him so he could marry before his younger sisters. No, there was a genuine consideration in his warm embrace, and she laid her head against his burly shoulder.

Two long, sad years had come and gone, and she'd behaved nearly like a widow, never attending singings or corn huskings where young men and women paired up, so distraught she was. She had made up her mind all she wanted was the love of the Lord God and whatever He had in store for her life. She'd even turned her back on the idea of marrying, thinking that if Aunt Lizzie could be happy as a maidel, then why couldn't she?

But now, with these familiar feelings stirring within, what was she to do? Yet, when all was said and done, Leah *was* free to love again. *If I choose to,* she thought, surprising herself.

Sitting this close to Gid, she felt genuinely cared for, looked after . . . even cherished. She was wary of the feeling—she'd missed it so desperately after she and Jonas split up. Now she was afraid it might overcome her, because as they rode along, she suddenly knew she wanted more, wanted to drown her resentment toward Sadie in Gid's loving arms.

When they neared the turnoff to the Peachey farm, he asked, "Do you mind if I walk you home? We could cut through the field, if that's all right with you."

She said she didn't mind, and right then she realized how glad she was. This happy night had completely changed her outlook. Gone was her impatience to get home. Something tender that had died in her was beginning to revive, and at this moment, she felt she might at last be able to cast aside the stranglehold of sadness and animosity hindering her path. *Just look at the smithy and Miriam Peachey . . . how happy they are*, she told herself. If Gid's father was as loving to his mother as Leah had always observed him to be, then Gid would also be a compassionate husband, wouldn't he? How foolish of her to pass up the chance to be loved so dearly, to be so completely adored.

She found herself thinking ahead to what it might be like to accept Gid's hand, to live with him and cherish him, to care for their little ones . . . to be his devoted helpmeet. As thoughtful and kind as he was, how hard would it be to follow her heart—if truly her heart *was* coming round, as it seemed to be?

Lest Leah was getting ahead of herself, she chased such thoughts away, but she was altogether pleased she and Gid had yet another few minutes to spend together this night.

They were enveloped in the green scent of jagged grass and the dank smell of cow pies as they strolled through the wide field between the Ebersol and Peachey farms.

The roof of her father's barn caught Leah's eye, the brilliant reflection of the moon dousing the silvery tin with its whiteness. She heard what she thought was one of their mules braying. Mules weren't nearly as stubborn as some folks seemed to think. They could be coaxed, not easily, but persuaded nevertheless to work the narrowest sections of the field. And mules required less feed and had greater fortitude than horses.

Gid glanced over at the barn. "What's the racket over there?"

"Must be a bat tormenting the livestock." She looked up at Gid. "Ever see one lunge at a mule?"

To this they both laughed, and she welcomed his hand finding hers. His companionably firm clasp made her own hand seem small and almost fragile, and once again she was startled at the long-dormant stirring within. She moved along at his side, keeping pace with his stride.

"Speaking of mules," Gid said halfway across the field, "didja ever hear of certain long-ago ministers sayin' it was offensive to mix God's creatures because our heavenly Father didn't create such an animal in the first place? Like breeding a horse and a donkey to produce a mule."

"Jah, Dat's said as much . . . but we all have mules these days, ain't? So what do you make of that?"

"Sure beats trying to get the field horses to go into steep places or some of the more narrow spots in the field," Gid replied.

They talked slowly as they walked, both seemingly hesitant to call it a night now that they were getting on so well. Now that they were alone with only the moon, the stars, and the blackness of the sky.

Leah's impression of the last full hour with Gid had grown as a little garden in her heart. Never in the most secret landscape of her soul could she have foreseen the joy she felt as she walked with Gid Peachey, picking her way through the thick grazing land, her hand snugly in his.

"What would you say if I told you this is the happiest night of my life?" he came right out and said.

A lump crept into her throat, and she was afraid she might cry again. She dared not try to answer.

He must have understood and squeezed her hand, turning to face her. His wavy light brown hair seemed almost colorless in the glow of the moon. "I hope it's not too forward of me. . . ."

She wondered what he might say and, composing herself, she asked, "What is it, Gid?"

He paused but for a moment. "I'd like to court you, if you . . . well, if you might agree."

She didn't once glance sheepishly at the Ebersol Cottage as she often did when talking with Gid here lately. No, she kept her gaze on him, studying the rugged lines of his face, the unabashed attraction he displayed for her as he leaned slightly forward.

She knew she'd traversed the gamut of feelings, from reluctance at the outset of the evening to this strange yet wonderful sincerity, the way she felt at this moment—surely it wasn't the moonlight and gentle sweet breeze of the wee hours, was it?

Smithy Gid's invitation was hard to resist. "Jah, I'll go for steady with you," she replied.

Then and there, he picked her up and swung her around and around. Her joy knew no bounds, because she had been so sure—in that most secret room of her heart—she would never, ever feel this way again. Yet here she was . . . and she did.

Chapter Seven

June's fair weather swept into the soaring temperatures of midsummer, and Mamma's lilies flourished, amassed in a solid bed of eye-catching pink.

On her way to the outhouse, Mary Ruth happened to brush past them, deep in thought, not paying any mind that her for-good purple dress had gotten some of the golden red pollen smeared on it. When she did notice it, she tried to brush it off with her hand, setting the stain but good. Realizing what she'd done, she hurried back to the house and told Mamma.

"Ach, you must always use adhesive tape to get lily pollen off," Mamma said.

"That or wipe it off with an old rag . . . anything but your hands," Aunt Lizzie said, explaining the natural oils from the skin set the stain.

Mamma continued. "If the stain stays put after using the rag, let the sun bleach it out."

Mary Ruth sighed and looked down at the smudged mess. "Well, now I have nothing to wear to the singing. My other good dress is too snug through the middle."

Aunt Lizzie shook her head. "Then you may just have to stay home and sew a new one tomorrow."

"What?" Mary Ruth didn't catch on to Aunt Lizzie's kidding at first.

Lizzie's face broke into a smile. "Come, let me see what I can do."

Mamma left the kitchen to tend to Lydiann, who was wailing upstairs, and while Aunt Lizzie scrubbed with an old rag, Mary Ruth bemoaned the fact that Hannah was refusing to double court with her. "My twin's not herself," she confided.

Lizzie seemed to perk up her ears. "Why would that be?"

Mary Ruth wouldn't go so far as to say more than "Hannah's persnickety these days . . . been so all summer, really."

"Well, in some cases, that's not such a bad thing," Lizzie said, still scrubbing. "All depends on what a person's bein' particular about, ain't so?"

Good point, thought Mary Ruth. "Still . . . ever since Hannah started taking baptismal classes, she seems aloof."

"For gut reason, I 'spect." Aunt Lizzie stepped back to look over the pollen stain and Mary Ruth herself.

"Why do you think that?"

"I daresay if you consider it carefully, you prob'ly already know."

She knew, all right. She just hated to admit it to anyone, especially Aunt Lizzie. For the longest time it seemed Hannah had been too quiet, almost downhearted. Was it the absence of Sadie . . . the unending silence from Ohio? Or was Hannah peeved at her for not following the Lord in holy baptism as

Hannah herself hoped to do come fall? No one but her twin knew that Mary Ruth had refused, of course. It wasn't something you went around telling, not amongst the People. The women folk would frown and carry on something awful if they knew the Ebersol twins—close in looks and upbringing—might be heading in different directions, one certainly not in the Old Ways of their forefathers.

Aunt Lizzie was still scrubbing the spot awful hard, and Mary Ruth wondered if she might be attending the singing with a hole in her best dress—or, just as bad, a smeared stain.

"Have you asked Hannah to loan you one of *her* dresses?" Aunt Lizzie's question cut through the stillness.

She hadn't thought of that. "I best not be askin' her for anything."

Lizzie's hands rested hard on her slender hips. "Pity's sake, the two of you have shared nearly everything since you were both just little ones." She frowned and cocked her head, looking awful curious.

"If you promise not to tell, I'll say why," she whispered back.

But Aunt Lizzie surprised her—startled her, really—by backing away and waving her hands in front of her. "No . . . I'm not interested in hearin' or keepin' any more secrets. I've learned a mighty hard lesson."

Aunt Lizzie's response made Mary Ruth feel even more alone and made her want to tell her aunt all the more. But it was no use to plead. Truth was, contrary to what Hannah might say or think, Mary Ruth hadn't fully decided whether or not to join the Amish church. What was the rush, anyway? Hannah could make her covenant this September if she chose, without Mary Ruth tagging along just because they were twins and all. Then, when Mary Ruth was good and ready, she'd decide, and not one moment before. Meanwhile, she wanted to take her time with rumschpringe, just as Dat had said to do back last year. Joining church, after all, was for a lifetime, so it could wait . . . for now. She had too much fun ahead of her to get bogged down with required membership meetings where the People sat and voted on weighty issues like shunning wayward and sinful folk. No, she didn't think she was ready for that kind of responsibility. And, if the full truth were known, she sometimes resented the People for ousting Sadie the way they had when all the girl had gone and done was fall in love with the wrong boy. Sure, Sadie had known better, but putting her under the Bann for life was so awful harsh, wasn't it? Unforgiving too. Mary Ruth wasn't certain she could set herself up as a holy example amongst the People . . . not the powerful way she longed for Elias's hugs and kisses, though Mamma would have a fit if she knew. With Hannah and Ezra courting on their own, the temptation would be stronger for her when with Elias, especially when the moon was as bright and beautiful as it would be tonight.

"If you won't ask Hannah for a clean dress, what 'bout Leah?" Aunt Lizzie suggested.

"Gut idea . . . just might solve the predicament," Mary Ruth said and reached for her aunt, gave her a grateful hug, and hurried out the back door in search of Leah.

Lizzie could see Ida needed to give extra attention to Lydiann, who was awful fussy following supper, so Lizzie stayed to clean up the dishes, then dropped off Hannah, Mary Ruth, and Leah at the barn singing over at Abram's brother Jesse Ebersol's place. It was right nice to see Leah participating in the activities with the young folk again; Lizzie's heart was truly glad.

When she returned from the trip, she took her time unhitching the horse and carriage, in no hurry to head toward the house. The evening was pleasant, and what with having taken the girls to the singing, she was feeling a slight bit sorry for herself. Not like her, really. She knew she ought not to allow her thoughts to stray back to her own courting years, but Abram had told her rather falteringly on several occasions that Leah had been asking questions of him, wanting to know about her father—namely who he was. If Lizzie had her druthers, she'd just as soon never say.

Straightening now, she looked toward the woods and her log house, put there by Abram and his brothers back when she was in such a bad way, expecting Leah and scarcely but a girl herself . . . not knowing anything about her baby's father. At least, not back then. And now didn't it beat all for Leah to be so interested in knowing?

Just what *was* she to tell Leah? She certainly couldn't bring herself to make known the whole story—how she'd run around something terrible as a teenager, thumbing a car ride with a complete stranger, an *Englischer* at that. Oh, the idea of revealing such a thing to precious Leah made her feel queasy with embarrassment. She almost wished to roll back the calendar, thinking it might've been better to leave things as they had been, with Leah thinking Ida was her one and only mamma.

If I could relive the worst of my youth, what would I do differently? she wondered, shuddering at the sudden thought. If she had not had her hair cut or her face made up on New Year's Eve back when—and drunk far too much moonshine—dear sweet Leah would never have been conceived. Truly, the Lord God had wrought a miracle of life and joy out of her great sin.

Feeling glum, she found herself heading toward the Ebersol Cottage, hoping she might offer to help Ida with something, anything at all, as an excuse to stay. At the moment she could not face her own empty house.

She discovered Ida giving Lydiann a bath in the middle of the kitchen in the big galvanized tub. "Here, let me do that for you." She knelt down to splash her little niece while Ida rose and went to sit across the room in Abram's hickory rocker.

"I'm all in," Ida admitted, fanning her face with her apron.

"You just rest there, sister." And to Lydiann, she said, "Now, ain't that right? We'll let your mamma be for a bit while you get all soaped up and clean." She couldn't help it; the baby talk came flying fast out of her mouth as she enjoyed bathing the adorable toddler.

Soon Abram clumped indoors to wash his hands. He made over Lydiann, still sitting in four inches or so of water that had been warmed by the kettle on the wood stove. Lydiann tapped a wooden spoon on the water's surface, making more and more bubbles.

"Well, now, Ida, looks like we've got ourselves a tidy

youngster," said Abram, standing near the tub and watching.

"Soon it'll be Ida's turn in the bath, jah?" Lizzie said, glancing at Ida, who was grinning at her wee daughter, lathered up from head to toe.

"I should say so," Ida replied. "Goodness knows, I must smell like a pig, what with the awful heat this week."

Lizzie offered to tuck Lydiann in for the night, but the girl cried up a storm when she went to pick her up. "Aw, you wanna play longer?" She set her back down.

Abram chuckled. "You're spoiling the child; that's plain to see."

"She's only two once, ain't?" Ida said, beaming with love from the rocking chair.

Going to sit on the bench, Abram leaned back against the table, his elbows spread behind him. "You's oughta guess who I ran into this morning," he said.

"Who?" Lizzie said.

"Peter Mast." On any given day, Abram would have avoided all discussion about the Masts, quickly looking at the floor if they were mentioned in conversation, as if merely hearing the name caused him distress.

"Did he speak to ya?" Ida asked, leaning forward.

"Not a word." Abram shook his head. "'Tis the oddest thing, really."

"Jah" was all Ida said.

Lizzie had an idea—maybe not such a bright one, but she shared it anyway. "Has anyone thought of taking some fruit pies over to Fannie Mast?"

Ida clasped her hands and brought them up as if praying.

"I've considered doing so any number of times as a goodwill gesture."

"A peace offering?" Abram frowned, clearly not sure if this was something to ponder, let alone pursue.

"What if you sent the twins over to deliver the pies?" Lizzie suggested.

"Certainly not Leah," Ida said.

Nodding in agreement over that, Abram rose and wandered into the dark front room, and Lizzie heard him sink down into a chair.

"Well, what do ya say?" she asked Ida, who came and threw a towel over her shoulder and lifted out Lydiann. The toddler's soft bottom looked as shriveled as a prune.

"It would be nice to get things smoothed over with the Masts, but I'm sure Abram will want to think on it some more," Ida said as she wrapped Lydiann, bawling and squirming, in the towel before marching out of the room and upstairs.

A couple of tasty pies just might begin to repair the breach, Lizzie thought, removing her wet black apron and going to hang it up in the utility room. If so, how foolish of them to have waited all this time.

Chapter Eight

The next day was a no-church Sunday, a day set aside not for Preaching service but for rest, reading the Good Book, and visiting relatives and friends.

Mary Ruth held the reins while Hannah sat to her left, silent as a rock. "Dat and Mamma must've thought this over for a gut long time, us goin' to Grasshopper Level with pies for the Masts," Mary Ruth muttered.

"Two long years Mamma's been thinking of what to do, I 'spect," Hannah said softly.

"Aunt Lizzie baked till late last night is what I was told. Must've been a hurry-up job."

"While we were at singing, maybe," Hannah replied.

Mary Ruth scratched her head. "By the way, did you happen to see who Leah rode home with last night?"

"I thought 'twas Gid, though I can't be certain."

"Won't Dat be happy if it was?"

Hannah made a little sound, then spoke. "Mamma prob'ly will be, too, seein' Leah's been hurt so awful bad . . . the way Jonas did her wrong."

"Wasn't all Jonas's fault, don't forget. Takes two, ya know." Mary Ruth felt she had to remind Hannah.

"Wouldn't *any* parent be pleased to have Smithy Gid as a son-in-law?"

"Can you see Gid and Leah as husband and wife? Honestly, can you?" asked Mary Ruth.

Hannah sighed. "Maybe so," she said in almost a whisper. Then abruptly she changed the subject. "Mamma's nothin' short of wonderful-gut. She never once thinks of Leah as her niece, now, does she?"

Mary Ruth found this turn of topic rather interesting. They had spoken behind closed doors of Lizzie's being Leah's birth mother after Mamma had shared with them, almost two years ago, the story of their aunt's wild days. Occasionally the twins would rehash their feelings, so great had been their surprise. "Seems to me, Leah is just as much Mamma's as you and I are." Mary Ruth meant this with all of her heart. "I wouldn't want things to change with Leah just because we know the truth 'bout Aunt Lizzie."

"Me neither." Hannah smoothed out her long green dress.

"Anyway, I could never think of Leah as merely our first cousin, even though she is that. The heart ties that unite are so strong, ain't so?" She surprised herself saying as much. "We'll always be sisters."

The tie that binds . . .

Now was as good a time as any for Hannah to bring up the knotty fact they were no longer double courting with the Stoltzfus boys . . . that there was a sort of estrangement between the two of them.

But Hannah said nothing, and they rode on in silence for the last mile.

As the twins pulled in the lane at the Masts' farmhouse, Mary Ruth noticed several of the younger Mast children scampering about. But when the youngsters spotted who was driving up in the carriage, they quickly disappeared into the house.

"Just as I expected," Mary Ruth said. "Now what?"

"We could end up sittin' here till the cows come home if we don't get out and make our delivery," Hannah replied.

"I wish Aunt Lizzie had come 'stead of us." Mary Ruth felt not only embarrassed but put out at having to come here when the Masts had chosen of their own accord to shun them.

Hannah was the one to stand up first, taking hold of the pies neatly placed in Mamma's wicker food hamper. "I'm not afraid of Cousin Fannie. I never did her wrong." With that she climbed down out of the buggy.

Taken aback by her sister's uncharacteristic boldness, Mary Ruth breathed in deeply and stepped out, too. "Which of us is goin' to knock on the back door?"

"Why, both of us. That's who" came Hannah's quick answer.

Mary Ruth wasn't so sure any of this was such a good idea, yet she was shocked at the way Hannah's feet pounded against the ground. Sure was a first, far as she could remember—

Hannah spouting off without uttering a word, using only her feet to do the talking!

Not to be outdone, Mary Ruth knocked on the kitchen screen door, wishing the whole ordeal were over. She could see past the screened-in porch and into the long kitchen, part of the bench next to the table showing. But there was no one in sight, which was downright peculiar on a "visiting" Sunday.

"Your turn to knock," she told Hannah, who promptly did so.

They waited, but the house remained apparently uninhabited. The call of birds seemed louder than before.

"How much longer should we wait?" Hannah asked.

Mary Ruth glanced over her shoulder, looking for any sign of life, but there were no sounds coming from the barn nor, naturally, from the fields, it being the Lord's Day and all. "I say we leave," she said at last.

"But . . . what 'bout the pies?" It was Hannah who was wide-eyed now.

"We'll have 'em for supper ourselves."

"What'll Mamma say?"

Then, just as Hannah was speaking, here came Cousin Fannie shuffling along toward the door like she really didn't want to at all. She poked her head out.

Before Fannie could speak, Mary Ruth said quickly, "We brought you something from Mamma and Aunt Lizzie."

A frown flickered across Fannie's face as she eyed the pies. "I'm sorry, but we can't accept them." She started to close the screen door.

"Oh, but Aunt Lizzie wants you to have them. She made them special for you and Cousin Peter," Mary Ruth explained, feeling awkward having to beg someone to accept such delicious gifts.

But Fannie soundly latched the screen door, then backed away, shaking her head before turning and walking to the kitchen.

"Well, I declare!" said Mary Ruth, tugging on Hannah's sleeve. "Come along, sister. They don't deserve Aunt Lizzie's pies!" With that they hurried to the buggy and got in. The horse pulled them slowly up to the widest section of the barnyard, then circled around to come back down the lane.

Mary Ruth spotted two small heads peering out the back door. "Look," she whispered. "Isn't that Mandie and Jake?"

"Sure looks like them to me," Hannah agreed.

"So . . . we've been out-and-out refused. Well, isn't this a fine howdy-do!"

"Something to talk about at supper tonight," Hannah said.

"Won't Mamma be irked?"

Hannah nodded. "Irked and offended both."

"It's really too bad our families can't make amends." Mary Ruth was certain both Mamma and Dat would have a reaction to this. Aunt Lizzie, too.

"What if we give them one more chance—try 'n' break the ice, so to speak," Hannah suggested.

"And do what?"

"We could both write to Rebekah and Katie one last time . . . see what comes of it. See if they'll reply."

"What a waste of time and stationery. But go ahead, if you want."

"I say, best ask Mamma what *she* thinks." Hannah seemed

to make a to-do of crossing her arms and sighing.

"Well, now, why are you upset at me, Hannah? I'm not the one ignorin' your letters." Mary Ruth paused. "Whoever said twins had to be baptized into the church the same year, anyway?" There—she'd said exactly what was on her mind.

Hannah began to sniffle, which turned into a full-blown sob in a hurry. Mary Ruth had no desire to offer one bit of comfort. If Hannah wanted to cry her eyes out right here on the road, in plain sight . . . well, let her.

Half a mile later, she spotted Luke and Naomi Bontrager riding in their enclosed carriage. "You best dry your eyes," she cautioned. "Here comes the bishop's grandson. Word might get back that you looked mighty sour today."

Hannah turned to face her, quick as a wink. "What do I care? Truth is, the bishop himself already knows what you're up to!"

"What do you mean?" Mary Ruth didn't want to believe her ears.

"Bishop Bontrager has been askin' why you aren't joinin' church with me."

"And what're you sayin' to that?"

"Seems to me that's your problem."

Mary Ruth bit her lip. Luke and Naomi were smiling and waving now as they approached on the opposite side of the road. "Wave back," she whispered to Hannah.

Meekly Hannah did so, and Mary Ruth called to them, "Hullo, Luke and Naomi!"—waving and grinning for all she was worth. *Can't make things any worse . . . might actually help some*, she reasoned.

"Couldn't you offer a smile with your wave?" she asked Hannah.

"Didn't feel like it," Hannah said when the other buggy had passed by.

Mary Ruth knew she could easily say the wrong thing if she opened her mouth just now, so she pressed her lips shut.

Hannah, however, couldn't seem to drop the argument of Mary Ruth joining church. "'To him that knoweth to do good, and doeth it not, to him it is sin.'" Hannah stated the pointed verse oft quoted amongst the People.

Without a shadow of doubt, Mary Ruth knew Hannah was altogether peeved at her about rejecting baptism this year. It was beginning to cloud nearly everything, even something as innocent as a ride in the family carriage. *I won't cut short my rumschpringe!* she thought. *I'll join church when I feel like it.*

On Sunday, July 17, Leah met up with Naomi Kauffman Bontrager in Deacon Stoltzfus's barnyard. She, along with Mamma, Aunt Lizzie, and the twins, had been milling about with the other women folk, waiting for the ministers to arrive before Preaching service.

"Hullo, Leah, nice to see ya," Naomi greeted Leah warmly, taking both her hands and squeezing them gently. "I've been wishin' we could talk."

They strolled away from the large group of women and young children. "Everything all right, Naomi?"

There was a distinct dampness to the day, which put a bit

of a wave in Naomi's hair—the wispy strands at the nape of her neck, at least.

"Oh, jah, things are fine." Naomi's eyes lit up. "I've been meaning to tell ya my news. I'm in the family way. Come this December, Luke and I will have us our first wee babe. Close to Christmas . . . when your mamma's baby is due."

"This is gut news and I'm ever so happy for you." She kissed Naomi's cheek. "Luke must be awful excited, too."

"He's holdin' his breath for a son, naturally."

"Maybe you'll get *two* boys," Leah replied, recalling that twins seemed plentiful on Naomi's mother's side. In fact, there was a set of triplet boys.

"I s'pose I wouldn't mind several babies at once. Whatever the Good Lord gives us will be all right."

"I'm glad I heard directly from you," Leah said as they walked back toward the women. She was truly happy for Sadie's former girlfriend, and hearing the news from Naomi got her thinking of her own future and the possibility of many children. After all, Mamma was expecting this baby in her midforties. Leah counted the years, thinking ahead. *If I were to marry Gid by next year, I'd have plenty of childbearing years ahead of me. . . .*

But she knew it was better not to think in terms of what might be . . . or worse, *what might have been* where Jonas was concerned. No, she would trust the Lord God, just as she had promised to do at her baptism. She would honor the Almighty One all the days of her life, and He alone would lead her. If God willed that she should marry and have children, then so be it. If not, she would try to be as cheerful and content with her lot as Aunt Lizzie.

Thinking of her aunt, she spied Lizzie chattering with the deacon's wife and had to smile. *Aunt Lizzie's a sly one, she is . . . talking to Ezra and Elias's mother, of all things!*

It was fairly common knowledge among Dat, Mamma, and Aunt Lizzie that two of the Stoltzfus boys were awful sweet on Hannah and Mary Ruth. Mamma had confided this to Leah, who, in turn, had mentioned something to Dat in the barn last week. Dat, bless his heart, had tried to act like he didn't know too much about it, but Leah could see the helpless smile of delight on her father's face. Since they all knew who was who and what was what, it was best they keep quiet now and allow the courting process to take over. Could be, as soon as a year from this fall, Hannah might be wed.

As for Mary Ruth, she'd most likely missed out on also marrying then. Much better to take her time and be sure than to rush into something and be sorry later, thought Leah. She guessed she ought to think likewise about her courtship with Smithy Gid, because he was visibly smitten . . . and, truth be known, she was falling for him, too.

Could it be Hannah and I will marry during the same wedding season? she wondered, spotting Gid's shock of light brown hair above the throng of men preparing to go inside the barn for the Sunday meeting. Her heart skipped a little as he caught her eye and then turned discreetly, pretending not to have seen her. The People's way . . .

Mamma might faint if she knew how fond Gid is of me . . . how often he says he loves me. I have yet to tell him, though. I must be ever so sure.

Chapter Nine

Lorraine Schwartz had been so deeply moved by the previous Sunday's sermon that she readily agreed to go with the Nolts to the midweek service. She had not a hunch how Henry would take this, but she was altogether eager to attend the Mennonite house of worship again, and she told him about it just as he was sitting down for supper on Wednesday night. "I hope you won't mind if I go out this evening for a few hours." She went on to say what she was planning.

He was slow to speak, evidently tired. "Are you trying to keep up with your son?"

She hadn't thought of it in that light, but now that Henry had mentioned it, she assumed Robert's quest for the spiritual might have influenced her, as well. "Why don't you come along?" she suddenly suggested. "You might be surprised and enjoy yourself."

"My desk is piled high with paper work." The tone of his voice caught her off guard; he was insulted.

"Are you all right with this, Henry?"

He looked across the table, his brow creased. "Go, if you must."

Fortunately their suppertime talk took a turn when Henry admitted he was toying with the idea of expanding the clinic, perhaps offering an internship to a medical student and building on to make room for more patients.

This was news to her, but she liked the idea. Henry, though he was close to his forty-fifth birthday, had aged considerably in the past year—virtually before her eyes. She speculated it was due to keeping himself busy with an overabundance of patients, more than enough for one country doctor, and she sometimes worried about his frequent lethargy. Even so, he had much to teach anyone interested in medicine.

Henry's need to extend himself to new blood coming up in the ranks surely had something to do with his sons' lack of interest in the medical profession—Derek having chosen a soldier's life and Robert, more recently, the Lord's work. She was almost certain Robert's abrupt fork in the road had affected Henry more than he realized.

"Any hope of Derek getting leave time for Christmas?" she asked, changing the subject.

"He'll have off two weeks, I would presume."

"Have you written him lately?"

"I did a week ago," said Henry.

Good, she thought. Her husband was keeping in touch with their younger son in spite of Derek's stubborn silence.

Henry shook his head and reached for his coffee. "Deep down, our boy *does* have a beating heart."

She was glad to hear this from Henry's lips and watched as he drank his coffee. Slowly she finished off her carrot cake and ice cream. If only Henry might consent to go with her to church, even a single time, she believed the pockets of stress under his eyes might soften and the spring in his step might return.

Hannah could scarcely wait to show Mary Ruth the letter from Grasshopper Level. They were already in their cotton nightgowns, each having brushed the other's hair, when Hannah asked her twin to "guess who'd written."

Mary Ruth shrugged. "I'm too tired to care, really." She slipped under the sheet and snuggled into bed.

"Well, listen to this," Hannah said. "It's a letter from our cousin Rebekah Mast!"

"What?"

"I saved it till just now."

Hopping out of bed, Mary Ruth hurried to peer over Hannah's shoulder. "Quick, read it to me."

Dear Cousin Hannah,

This is the last letter I'm planning to send to you! I haven't even told Mamma I'm writing, but you need to know she's awful peeved you and Mary Ruth would come here. We don't need no pies and no letters, neither, from you Ebersols.

If I sound upset, I am. After all, your sister Leah got our brother Jonas shunned by talking him into joining church over there in your neck of the woods. I won't say everything that's on my mind, but we wish to goodness he'd never laid eyes on her!

Please don't bother to answer this letter. We have nothing to say to each other. Only one good thing came out of this awful mess—Sadie and Jonas have found some true happiness out west. That's all I best be saying.

So long,
Rebekah Mast

"Well, I declare!" Mary Ruth said a bit too loudly.

"Shh! You'll wake up the whole house." Hannah shoved the letter into the envelope and stuffed it in her drawer. "What a horrible cousin."

"You can say that again." Looking mighty gloomy now, Mary Ruth headed back to her side of the bed.

"I didn't think Rebekah had it in her to be so rude."

Mary Ruth pulled up the sheet and muttered, "No doubt Becky's echoing what Cousins Fannie and Peter are sayin' and thinking 'bout us."

Hannah put out the oil lamp on the dresser and crawled into bed. "I knew she was bossy and liked to talk a big talk, but this . . ." She almost wished she'd never bothered to open the envelope, especially not at night. Now the cutting words would encircle her thoughts, and she needed her sleep. Tomorrow she planned to help Leah mow all the yards—front, back, and side—then burn the week's trash. That alone would take nearly the whole morning.

"Don't worry yourself over Becky Mast," said Mary Ruth, reaching over and stroking her hand. "Just consider the source."

"Jah, I s'pose."

They lay quietly for a time; then Mary Ruth spoke again. "Aunt Lizzie and I will be canning quarts and quarts of pickles tomorrow. Who's gonna look after Lydiann?"

Hannah shared with her what she planned to do, laughing a little. "Maybe Dawdi John will come over and look after our baby sister."

"That's not such a gut idea, do you think? Not as quick on her feet as Lydiann is gettin' to be." Mary Ruth had a point there.

"Jah, he may be hard-pressed to keep up with our baby sister; it's a good thing Dawdi John's hip has improved with Dr. Schwartz's help."

Hannah was anxious for sleep to come.

Mary Ruth yawned and turned to face her. "Do you ever wonder who it was Lizzie must've loved enough to give up her innocence before marryin'?"

"I hate to admit it, but I've thought about the same thing. . . ." She didn't want to speculate, but she guessed Leah's birth father must surely be the son of one of the Hickory Hollow ministers. And, if so, well . . . wouldn't it be interesting to know just who? "Best be sayin' good night now," she said, hoping to turn off the chatter.

Ida found herself standing in the hallway where she had stood that first morning twenty years ago now—here, at the top of the stairs, where the window looked out to the southeast, to the Peacheys' fine-looking spread of land. Tonight, though, she did not care to admire the smithy's acres and acres of corn and grazing land. No, she was looking up, high overhead. The stars captured her attention this night.

Bless the Lord, o my soul: and all that is within me, bless his holy name. She paused to rest her hands on her middle. O

Father God, place your hand of blessing on this babe of mine, growing so restlessly within, she prayed silently.

Here she stood, suffering twinges in her stomach on the very spot where so long ago she had accidentally overheard Abram telling young Lizzie what she must do about *her* baby. Lizzie had begun to soften from the near-rebellious state she was in when she and Abram brought her home to live with them. Ida recalled, too, that Abram had repeatedly questioned Lizzie to no avail that same day. "Your baby's father . . . who is he?" Her sister could only weep, not once mentioning the young man's name.

Surely she'll want to share the truth with Leah someday, Ida thought, still staring at the sky strewn with stars. But deep inside, in that near-sacred place where a woman frets silently over her dear ones, Ida was fearful. Nervous for Lizzie and Leah both, for what such a revelation might do to the good solid relationship they enjoyed. But, most of all, she worried for Abram. If Leah were ever to know her blood father, would Abram lose his rightful, even special place in Leah's eyes? She could only imagine what hurt this could cause him and the girls. All of them, really.

She moved away from the window, wincing as she caressed her stomach . . . her unborn child, wondering if Leah's natural father even knew he had a daughter. She ambled down the hall, stopping at the first bedroom to look in on Leah, sound asleep, then on to Hannah and Mary Ruth's room, where they, too, slept peacefully, like two small kittens nearly nose to nose.

Checking, observing, loving . . . her beloved family of girls, minus one. Would the hands of time turn things around for Sadie? Would the grace and goodness of God—the blessed Holy Spirit—woo her to Him faster than the People's shun? She prayed it would be so.

How she loved her girls, all of them equally, and she prayed as she walked the hallway, speaking to the Lord silently, imploring Him for each one's future. Ida longed for them to walk uprightly, to know the Holy One of Israel not only as their heavenly Father, but to embrace the atonement of His Son, the Lord Jesus.

Bring peace to this house . . . to my heart, she prayed without speaking. At last she headed back to the bedroom where Lydiann slept in a wooden crib in the corner and Abram lay sound asleep, not knowing she had been walking softly and praying earnestly. Not knowing that all too often, of late, the wee hours were filled with sharp pain, and sleep was far from her.

Chapter Ten

July stepped gingerly into August, and soon after September came in on wild turkeys' feet, surprising the local folk with much cooler temperatures and buckets of rain. The unsuspecting gobblers wandered brazenly out of the woods, becoming unwelcome visitors to the cornfield, as if daring someone to shoot them before small-game hunting season.

Mamma observed her forty-fifth birthday on the second day of September without much ado other than a card shower from the women folk. Leah said the hydrangea bushes near the house had seen fit to mix their brilliant hues with some deep bronze on cue for Mamma's special day, the first hint of long and lazy autumn days leading the way for the harvest and silo filling.

October's gleaming red and yellow apples rapidly turned to applesauce, cider, and strudel, and the musty scent of wet leaves led smack-dab into November's wedding season and the glory of deepest autumn.

It was the Sunday evening before Thanksgiving Day when Leah consented to ride along with Smithy Gid to visit his ailing uncle Ike. She was glad for the heavy woolen lap robe protecting them, since the open carriage provided no shelter from twilight's falling temperatures.

Gid held the reins with one hand and steadied his harmonica in the other, playing one tune after another as they rode along. In between songs, he whistled, as cheerful as she'd ever known him to be.

We're practically betrothed, she thought but instead quickly brought up the subject of his uncle. "Has a doctor seen him for his pneumonia yet?"

"Aunt Martha wants to call in the hex doctor, but Uncle Ike won't hear of it. Seems they're at a standstill, but I'm sure my uncle will have his say-so."

Leah thought on this. "What do *you* think of powwowing, Gid?"

"I don't rightly know. Pop says there ain't nothin' wrong with having the hex doctor have a look-see when somebody's sick, but *Mamm,* now, there's a whole 'nother story."

"She goes to the medical doctor, then?"

"I believe Mamm would rather die than have white witchcraft goin's-on in our house. And that's just how she says it, too."

White witchcraft? Leah pondered that. Seemed her own mamma lined up with Miriam Peachey on this matter. Dat, now, he didn't seem to care one way or the other—neither did Dawdi John. Aunt Lizzie, though, liked to have had a fit when Leah mentioned it some time back in regard to the day she was born. "Was there an Amish midwife or hex doctor on hand?" she'd asked, to which Lizzie had replied, "No midwife . . . not the powwow doctor, neither one," turning an indignant shade of peach when Leah mentioned the latter.

"What do the ministers say 'bout powwowing?" she asked.

Gid shook his head. "They'd prob'ly say they have more important things to think about."

Seemed to her the brethren ought to have an opinion one way or the other. Still, such a topic would never be preached on in any Sunday sermon.

Recalling that Jonas used to write her about certain Scriptures not being used in sermons here in Gobbler's Knob, she thought of asking Gid what he thought of *that*. But she kept her peace, not wanting to touch on the past—good or bad.

The road from Quarryville was particularly deserted this evening. Most folk were indoors keeping warm on such a brisk night, Robert Schwartz assumed. He wanted to surprise his parents by arriving early for Thanksgiving but had been just as eager to attend the Oak Shade Mennonite Church before heading northeast to Gobbler's Knob.

The minister had begun by speaking slowly to the congregation in an almost conversational tone. As time passed, though, his discourse had become swift and strong in its delivery, and Robert had been enthralled by the message, "Finding God's Plan for Your Life."

"As sons and daughters of Christ Jesus, we have an obligation to seek out His will and live it," the preacher had instructed. "We must delve into the Word of God for answers. What would God have *you* do with your remaining days on earth? Will He send you forth into the field, for it is white unto harvest?"

White unto harvest. The words had seeped into Robert's

heart, taking hold. To think what he might have accomplished for God in the weeks and months leading up to the invasion at Utah Beach in Normandy. The Allied air forces had dropped all those bombs . . . twenty thousand tons on France alone. Too many of his buddies had died on those bombing missions. And he'd lost his sweetheart, a true flower of a girl, though an unbeliever. *If only I'd known the Lord then*, he thought sadly as he remembered Verena.

Tonight he had gladly received the preacher's fervent words. They, along with many months of Bible study at the Mennonite college, had converged in an overwhelming epiphany, clinching his decision to become a country preacher. Truly, he wished he might have known God on some significant level during the war. What comfort and support he might have offered to his comrades and others had he been a believer then. Certainly the chaplains weren't the only ones imparting spiritual consolation during those horrendous days and nights. He recalled there had been a few Christian boys who had shared the Good News among the young, yet hardened soldiers. He would have joined ranks with them had he known then what he knew now. To think he might have saved a life or two, or more . . . for God. Instead, he had aided in the death of many enemies of the Allied forces—a martial victory, true, but a defeat for eternity, nevertheless.

Now, on the drive home, the words of the seasoned minister continued to resound in his thinking. He felt nearly euphoric as he drove the forsaken back road. Something was compelling him to follow through, to get his license to preach despite his father's disapproval, which was ongoing and would surely be voiced during the coming holiday. Still, his spirit had been touched in a way unlike any he had ever felt in the village church where his parents had infrequently attended through the years. There parishioners dutifully congregated Sunday mornings to hear a social gospel that trumpeted Jesus' humanitarian accomplishments, with few references to the true and living Word of God. If Robert was not mistaken, the small edifice with its numerous stained-glass windows was coming up here fairly soon on the left side of the road.

I'm here to answer your call, O Lord, he prayed, gripping the steering wheel as the road narrowed and the dense woods closed in on either side.

◆

They had been talking about the fact that neither of them was well versed in the Holy Scripture when Leah first heard a siren in the distance. The wail came closer as Gid's horse pulled the courting buggy back from Uncle Ike's farmhouse toward Gobbler's Knob.

"Ach, Gid," Leah said, clutching her throat. "Someone nearby must be hurt."

The ambulance was approaching fast behind them, and Gid skillfully reined the horse onto the dirt shoulder and stopped while the shrill siren pierced their eardrums.

"Wanna follow and see if we can be of some help?" Gid asked after the ambulance had sped by.

"Sure, if we can catch up."

The accident, as it turned out, was less than a mile away, but by the time they arrived, the ambulance had already arrived and left. Two patrol cars blocked the road in both directions, so Gid parked the buggy a distance away, leaving Leah holding the reins. "I'll be back right quick." He jumped out of the buggy. "Will you be all right here alone?"

She said she would, but up ahead the sight of a car crisscross in the road, its headlights shining across the mowed cornfield, frightened her no end. A lame horse, which looked to be awful young—more like a pony, really—was being led limping off the road by one of the policemen.

Then she noticed a young Englisher sitting in the backseat of one of the police cars. Could it be he was the driver of the car? Had he caused the accident, maybe startling the young horse?

Heart pounding, she stood up for a better look and saw the splintered remains of what looked to be a pony cart. On the east side of the road, a farmhouse stood way back snuggled against tall trees. She wasn't so sure in the dark, but she thought this might be the homestead of Deacon Stoltzfus and his large family.

She did think it peculiar that, by now, none of the family had come running down the lane to offer assistance. Then it dawned on her that maybe—hopefully not—one of their children had been riding in the crumpled pony cart, in which case the deacon and probably his wife and some of the youngest children would have gone along in the ambulance, leaving the oldest girls to look after the rest. The older boys, Leroy, Gideon, Ezra, and Elias, most likely were out riding around with their girlfriends, unaware of the dreadful accident.

A lump caught in her throat. *Dear God, please help whoever was hurt here tonight*, she prayed.

The distinctive ripeness of late autumn closed in around

her, and when a sudden wind came up, Leah felt its eerie chill and drew her shawl near. Oh, she wished Gid would hurry back and tell her what on earth had happened.

"The pony and cart shot out from the lane onto the road, you say?" the police officer quizzed Robert.

Pointing to the concealed treed lane, Robert explained, "Over there, leading down from the farmhouse. The cart appeared out of nowhere, right in front of me . . . before I could ever stop." He felt sick with the memory of the youth lying unconscious in the road, broken and bleeding. "My car hit it broadside."

The policeman filled out an accident report, scrutinizing Robert's driver's license, then inquired about his father. "Is Doc Schwartz your old man?"

"That's right."

The policeman looked him over. "Say . . . aren't you the son who fought in the war?"

He felt his shoulders tense. "I . . . well, sir, God must have been watching out for me overseas." That's all he could say about the past when the present—and possibly the future—was staring him hard in the face.

Returning his attention to the accident report, the officer added, "The lad's Old Order Amish, so I doubt there will be charges filed against you, although it's clear you weren't in the wrong. If this goes the way most accidents do involving them, you'll never hear boo from anybody. The Amish practice non-resistance."

Nonresistance . . .

Robert swallowed hard, hoping the boy would survive the

accident for both the boy's sake and his family's. He had certainly put into practice every first-aid technique he'd ever learned from his father in tending to him—his body crushed and bleeding—trying his best to save the kid's life.

"You were driving the speed limit or less?" he was asked.

"Yes, sir." He waited as the policeman finished filling out the accident report, feeling a desperate coldness steal over him. Robert shuddered in the darkness as the reality of what had happened here sunk in. "Can someone please phone me later? I'd like to know the boy's name and where I might visit him," he said.

A visit to the hospital was the least he could do; he wished he could do more. No doubt there would already be Amish friends and relatives gathering at the hospital, as was their custom. They would not want the boy and his family to suffer through the dark night alone.

"Someone from the station will be in touch with you, Mr. Schwartz." The policeman's voice startled him. "Take care, son."

"Why . . . thank you," he heard himself say. Robert's words, though sincere, sounded hollow and distant even to his own ears.

Due to the lateness of the hour and the heavy cloud cover, the road leading home was even darker now as Robert headed down the final stretch. His memory haunted him as he replayed the accident scene again and again. The shattered pony cart, the moaning boy lying in the road, the mournful neigh of the wounded horse . . .

"O Lord in heaven . . . please let the boy survive. Please, let him live," Robert implored. He slowed the car to a near crawl as he rounded the bend and saw the yard light on at his parents' house. *How can I begin to tell my family what has happened this night . . . what I have done?*

"It was a terrible mess up there," Gid told Leah when he returned at last, somewhat out of breath. "If somebody didn't die in that wreck, I'd be mighty surprised."

"Anyone we know?" She was unnerved.

Gid seemed dazed as he took the reins from her, sitting there for the longest time without speaking. And then finally he did. "*Himmel,* this slaughter on the roads—cars and carriages—just keeps . . . happening." His voice faltered.

Leah was shaking. What if one of her own kin was in such an accident? The People reckoned tragedies as being God's sovereign will, yet she shuddered to think of losing a sister to death.

"The pony cart belonged to young Elias Stoltzfus," Gid said at last. "He was severely injured tonight . . . if not mortally."

Leah gasped. *Not Mary Ruth's beau!* Suddenly she was panic-stricken at the thought of her own sister. *Was she riding along with Elias tonight?* she wondered. *Was she?*

"Was there anyone else in the cart?" Leah managed to ask.

"I don't know."

"Are you certain it was Elias who was hit?"

Gid nodded slowly, his expression sad.

If the boy did not survive, many of the People would

gather as a compassionate community for the wake at the Stoltzfus house, offering to help in any way possible. Leah determined that if the worst were to be, she would volunteer to help with the milking and whatnot. Anything to assist and by so doing lessen the immediate pain of loss.

Leah arrived home, where she was relieved to learn Mary Ruth was safe. Hours later she witnessed firsthand how much Mary Ruth cared for Elias—the whole family did. When they saw the tall figure of Leroy, the oldest Stoltzfus boy, on the back step, face drawn, eyes red . . . coming to deliver the death message, Mary Ruth burst out sobbing and fled from the kitchen.

Her heartrending cries were heard all through the house, and the pitiful sound struck Leah at the core of her very heart, for she knew too well something of the sting of Mary Ruth's loss.

Leah, Hannah, and Mamma offered their sympathy as best they could, but Mary Ruth would not be comforted. Her weeping continued as Leah sat on the side of the twins' bed, stroking Mary Ruth's hair while Hannah lay next to her twin, her slender arm wrapped around her. Mamma, after a time, kissed each of them good night, then slipped off to her own room, sniffling every bit as much as Leah recalled her doing the weeks following Sadie's shunning.

Miserable and helpless to know what to say or do, Leah decided now was a good time to pray—not the familiar rote prayers of their childhood, but one that came directly from her heart. The kind she knew Mamma and Aunt Lizzie often prayed, and the kind of earnest prayer she herself had offered in the woods, following her heartbreak over Jonas.

Sitting in the darkness, she silently pleaded for divine comfort for her grief-stricken younger sister, as well as the brokenhearted Stoltzfus family.

Chapter Eleven

Restless and unable to sleep, Mary Ruth tiptoed down the stairs after midnight, leaving the warmth of her bed to hurry outdoors. The night was as still as the animals resting in the stable area of the barn. Deftly she reached for the sides of the old wooden ladder and climbed to the hayloft without making a sound, wanting to sit alone in the midst of the baled hay.

She anguished at the memory of her last conversation with Elias in the barnyard following Preaching service yesterday. He had asked her to go "on a lark, for some fun before going to the singing." Ezra, it seemed, had gotten first dibs on the courting buggy and was planning to spend time with Hannah again, just the two of them. So Elias had wanted to use his pony cart.

If Ezra had included Elias and me, she thought, *my dear beau might still be alive!*

Now in spite of Elias's fondness for her and hers for him, he was gone forever, soon to be buried in the People's cemetery not so far away. Her own beloved.

Too exhausted to ponder further what might've happened

if things had been much different this night, she pulled the long black shawl about her and wrapped her arms around her knees. Sassy, the new pup—short for Sassafras—soon found her. The droopy-eyed pet comforted Mary Ruth by licking her salty cheeks, remaining by her side as she wept till close to dawn.

Hannah stared at the new handkerchief she had quickly made for Elias's grieving mother. Somehow, she hoped to find a way to slip it to the poor woman, though seeing the crowd of mourners gathered at the Stoltzfus house, she didn't know how or when that might be possible.

Just now, though, standing in the backyard with the other women of her family, waiting to enter the farmhouse, Hannah couldn't shake the fear of death knocking on her own door, coming too soon, before she was ready for it. She'd long struggled this way. Like Elias had been, she felt she was much too young to die, though if such a thing should happen, even prematurely, the People believed it was the divine order of things. Hannah had been taught this from her childhood, and being a baptized church member now, having made her kneeling vow back in September with Ezra, she felt she, too, must embrace the Lord God's supreme plan for each of His children. Yet she still battled the horror of death—when it was to come and how it might happen . . . and, most of all, how difficult it might be to get to the other side. She felt her neck grow exceedingly warm with the worry.

Just what *did* the Lord God heavenly Father want with

young Elias up in heaven when there was so much left for him to do down here? She guessed there must be some mighty important work waiting for him in Glory Land—maybe something that required lots of time. *Jah, maybe* that's *why he was taken so early*.

Robert was reduced to sitting in the backseat, a passenger in his father's car as he and his parents traveled down the road to the Amish funeral on Tuesday morning. Not able to sleep or eat since the accident, he had thought of staying home and would have preferred to, but his mother had slipped into his room after breakfast and attempted to console him, reminding him the mishap was simply not his fault. "Any driver might have hit the boy. It was impossible for you to see him," she'd insisted. Then she had encouraged Robert to "come along with us, in spite of the accident. Share your sadness with the Amish community. The entire Stoltzfus family will be there, I am sure."

And they were, all thirteen of them—eleven remaining sad-faced children, some teenagers, and their somber parents. Robert had gone immediately with his father to the hospital, following the accident, but he had not had the chance to see Elias. Sadly the young man had been pronounced dead on arrival, and Robert could merely offer his condolences to the solemn parents. How very taxing that had been. He instantly deemed himself a murderer, however unintentional the act. Most difficult for Robert was knowing full well that if he had never gone to the Quarryville church meeting and had driven straight home from college in Harrisonburg, Virginia, he might have been home this morning reading or watching television, and young Elias would have been alive.

How does this nightmarish thing fit into God's plan? he agonized. What exactly would the dynamic Mennonite preacher have to say about the circumstances Robert so unpredictably found himself in? The policeman at the collision scene had been correct in his assessment; no charges had been discussed with Robert nor filed. He had been driving well under the speed limit, so there was no question of a reckless driving charge. He felt he should be somewhat relieved, but he was nothing of the kind. A sense of despondency encompassed him, and he was miserable with the knowledge that, however blameless, he was responsible for snuffing out a young life.

Staring out the car window, he was aware of the blur that became one Amish farmhouse, then pastureland, cornfields, and another farmhouse, and so on, one after another. He had survived the horrors of war on foreign soil only to come home and accidentally kill an innocent civilian.

Stunned with grief and struggling to sit through the long funeral in the house of worship—*house of sorrow,* Mary Ruth thought—she attempted to keep her hands folded, yet every so often she noticed she had been unconsciously wringing her handkerchief. At one point Hannah leaned close to her and whispered, "I believe that's the driver of the automobile."

She sighed ever so deeply, her breath coming in ragged gasps as she fought tears and looked over at the man Hannah assumed to be Robert Schwartz. The mere thought of a car plowing into Elias's vulnerable pony cart made her wince; it was next to impossible for a person to survive such an impact. She battled the urge to despise the Englisher. *Who does he think he is, coming to the funeral?*

Somehow, as the service progressed, she was able to deny her tears, having spent all day yesterday and Sunday night, too, wearing herself out in distress over her beau. Through sheer will, she had managed to go with Leah and Aunt Lizzie to the Stoltzfus farm early yesterday morning to help with some of the cooking, cleaning, and tending to the small children, just as other church members had.

Presently she was in desperate straits, trying hard to listen to the first sermon, thirty minutes long and given in Pennsylvania Dutch, followed by Scriptures read in High German, which she did not understand. Who of the People did? Most of the old-timers perhaps, but none of the youth.

She was suddenly stirred, then and there, wishing she might comprehend the words Preacher Yoder read from the Old German *Biewel*—wanting to know what was being said at her beau's funeral, for pity's sake!

During the second sermon, she noticed Robert Schwartz sitting tall and stately, yet weeping silent tears that coursed down his solemn face. Strangely, he made no attempt to brush them away. Mary Ruth found this curious, never having seen a grown man shed tears in public, let alone at a large gathering. She felt compelled to glance his way every so often but only with her eyes, never moving her head.

Goodness knows what he must be feeling, she thought, but her heart was bound up with fond memories of dear Elias, as well as her own great sadness. How could she ever forget how he'd made it a point to put off joining church to run around a bit longer? What did this mean for his everlasting soul?

The People were admonished to live righteous lives, as

one never knew when his or her "day of reckoning" might come. The second minister spoke on this subject for nearly an hour, urging young people to think carefully about joining church. "Do not put off the Holy Ordinance. It has the power to seal your eternal fate."

Mary Ruth felt a quiver run up her spine as the minister continued preaching. She wondered, just then, if what had befallen Elias was connected in any way to his decision to postpone church membership "till another year," as he'd said. But no, she couldn't allow herself to be that superstitious.

She *did* wonder if Elias had died in his sins. Since he was not baptized at the time of the accident, were the ministers right? Was her beloved standing *outside* the gates of Glory?

During the brief obituary reading in German by Preacher Yoder, Mary Ruth considered the idea of wearing her black mourning garment for a full year, as if she were Elias's widow-bride. She knew Mamma would not approve, but at this moment of determined loyalty to her beau, she didn't rightly care what anyone thought.

While the coffin was being moved outside so the People could view the body, Leah noticed Dr. Schwartz and his wife, Lorraine, walking toward their car. It seemed they were scarcely able to put one foot in front of the other, so downtrodden they and their son Robert looked. She had recognized him from seeing his pictures several places in the Schwartz house, as well as on the wall of the clinic waiting room.

Watching them cross the yard together, arm in arm, she

felt a deep measure of sympathy and wondered if Dr. Schwartz would say something to her about this awful sad day come Friday, when she was scheduled to do some cleaning at the clinic. She wouldn't be so rude as to bring up the topic of Elias's death herself. Still, she wondered how the Schwartz family would manage to cope.

When she turned back toward the house, she noticed Mary Ruth hovering near the coffin, now situated on the front porch for the final viewing before burial. She wondered if her sister was out of her mind with grief, as sometimes happened to couples if one or the other was taken early. Then she knew for sure Mary Ruth was suffering unspeakably, for her sister leaned down and touched Elias's face—her last chance to see him ever so close. But when she bent lower and kissed him, Leah cried. *She's saying farewell,* she thought, wishing she, too, might have had that opportunity, though keenly aware how tragically different a situation *this* was.

Later, in the *Graabhof*, her father stood next to Smithy Peachey, black felt hat in his rough hands, as they glanced now and then at the coffin-shaped hole in the earth. Small grave markers were scattered here and there in unpredictable rows within a makeshift fence. For a moment the wire barrier made her feel captive to the People, and she thought of Sadie and her endless shunning.

Leah's gaze drifted to the brethren—the ministers and grown men, farmers all—who set forth the unwritten guidelines for living. *The* Ordnung *rules our very lives*, she thought, missing her elder sister anew. The faces of the men looked pale in spite of their ruddy, sunburned complexions, she noticed, and women and girls dabbed handkerchiefs at their eyes, trying not to call attention to themselves. Yet how could they stop their tears when the deacon's red-haired young son—once spirited and smiling—lay lifeless in a simple walnut box?

Four pallbearers used shovels to fill the grave once the coffin had been lowered into the previously dug tomb by the use of long straps. Deacon Stoltzfus stood near his remaining sons, their jaws clenched, lower lips quivering uncontrollably; Ezra, especially, looked ashen faced. Elias's mother, grandmothers, aunts, and many sisters clustered together, some of them holding hands and crying, but none of them wept aloud. It was not the People's way to wail and mourn conspicuously, and Leah was glad for that. The sadness she felt for these dear ones spilled over into her own spirit, and she hung her head as if in prayer.

Once the grave was nearly filled, the pallbearers ceased their shoveling and Preacher Yoder stood tall and read a hymn from the *Ausbund*. The People did not sing on this most sobering occasion, and every man and boy in attendance removed his black hat.

Leah could scarcely wait for the sunset, hours from now, that would bring an end to this heart-wrenching day. The prevailing gloom triggered the familiar helpless feeling she had often wrestled with in the black of night as she lay quiet as death itself, wishing for sleep to come and rescue her from her memories of Jonas. Of course, there was far less of that these days than before she and Smithy Gid had begun spending time together. If things went as she assumed they might, she and the smithy's son would be husband and wife come next year; she felt sure Gid was looking toward that end. As for herself, she understood fully why her father had been adamant about Gid being a "wonderful-gut young man," not to mention his first choice as a husband for her. What was to fear?

Hannah put her hand over her heart, taking short little breaths as the soil was mounded. The burial complete, she felt like she might break into a sob, and just then Mamma reached over and found her hand, holding it for the longest time. Listening intently, perhaps too much so, she was scarcely able to draw a breath as Preacher Yoder admonished the People, "Be ready when your time comes."

She could only hope that she would be . . . if or when her number should be called. *How can I or anyone be ready for that day?* she pondered, not knowing in the slightest.

She felt she should talk to Mamma about her worries. After all, she'd heard her mother praying beside her bed several times—typically in the late-night hours, when Mamma surely must have assumed her girls were fast asleep. Honestly it seemed maybe both Mamma and Aunt Lizzie knew more about the Good Lord than they were ever allowed to let on, and it was time for her to ask a few important questions. With Elias's funeral taking up much of this day, she hoped to find some time soon to talk quietly with Mamma before Thanksgiving. They wouldn't be observing the day as an all-out holiday the way the English did, nor with prayer and fasting as Plain folk in Ohio did. They were taught to be grateful for every day as it came, though they did gather as families around a bountiful feast table, especially because it was their season of weddings. Attending this funeral of her sister's beloved at such a normally joyous time was the most difficult thing Hannah had ever done.

The afternoon crept along ever so slowly for Mary Ruth, particularly during the shared meal. About three hundred mourners had returned to Deacon Stoltzfus's home, passing by the location of the actual calamity there on the road at the end of the long dirt lane. Mary Ruth had refused to look; she'd kept her head tilted back, eyes on the stark tree branches lining the way.

She observed Ezra sitting at the table with his younger brothers. His face was swollen, and the stern set of his jaw betrayed something of his pain, making her flinch. Their custom of eating a meal with the family of the deceased created a strong sense of comfort and belonging for all of them, to be sure, yet she was painfully aware of the hole in the very middle of her heart. Elias had brought energy and excitement into her life. His keen attention had given her even more reason to spring out of bed each morning and, if she were truthful with herself, was equal to her pleasure in book learning.

But now . . . what was she to do? She'd completely missed joining church with Hannah this year, deciding to put it off because she and Elias wanted to enjoy rumschpringe longer. Much longer, truth be known. Now it surely seemed as if Hannah and Ezra were the wiser.

Mary Ruth felt herself sinking into a gray despair such as she had never known.

Chapter Twelve

Dejected and in urgent need of prayer, Robert left his father's house and drove to Quarryville for Wednesday prayer meeting the night following Elias's funeral. At the church, he prayed silently before the service began, pouring out his great woe to God. When he raised his head, anticipating the beginning of the meeting, he was aware of a number of Amish youth gathered there—serious, distraught young people more than likely searching for consolation on the heels of the startling death of Elias. Yet their attendance was highly unusual, to be sure.

Following the singing of hymns, the pastor invited those with a testimony of grace to stand and "give a witness." One church member after another praised the Lord publicly, expressing the ways they believed God was at work in their hearts.

When a short lull ensued, Robert felt compelled to stand. Turning to face the people, he directed his solemn remarks primarily to the Amish youth. He began by sharing his anguish and then faltered. "I humbly beg . . . your forgiveness . . . for having been the driver of the car last Sunday night. I pray you might find it in your hearts—all of you here—to forgive me for accidentally killing your own Elias Stoltzfus." Shuddering as he spoke, he was aware of sniffling and then a single sob. Unable to go on, he sat down, fighting back tears. His feelings of guilt over not having been charged with involuntary manslaughter or even a lesser charge continued to preoccupy his thoughts, although Reverend Longenecker had kindly pointed out when he had met with him privately before the service that Robert's guilt was unfounded. Nevertheless, the minister's words had not lessened the fact Robert sincerely wished the Stoltzfus family had not let him off scot-free.

When the minister stood behind the pulpit and began to pray, not a sound was heard except his earnest voice. "Our Father in heaven, we come this night, carrying our burdens to you, O Lord. . . ."

Mary Ruth volunteered quickly when Mamma asked for someone to take one of two batches of graham-cracker pudding over to the Peacheys' the Thursday following Elias's funeral. Glad for an excuse to clear her head in the chilly air, she headed across the cornfield to the neighbors', low in spirit and dressed in the black garb of a mourner. Spying Adah's younger sister driving into the lane, she hurried to deliver the pudding to Miriam, then returned to help Dorcas unhitch the horse from the carriage.

"Are ya doin' all right, Mary Ruth?" asked Dorcas, who

reached for and squeezed her hand.

"No . . . not so gut. Not at all, to be honest."

"I'm ever so sorry for ya, truly I am." Dorcas let go of her hand and looked around like she wanted to say something private. "Have ya heard tell of the meeting last night in Quarryville?" she asked.

Mary Ruth had not.

Dorcas leaned closer and whispered now. "You could go 'n' see for yourself."

"How's that?"

" 'Cause there's another gathering tonight. I wish I could go again, but maybe *you* could. Might help ya some."

She urged Dorcas to tell her more and was surprised to hear the Englisher who'd hit and killed Elias had stood up in the meeting and made a sober apology. "Ever so odd it was, yet awful sad, too. I mean, we Amish just wouldn't think of holdin' a grudge against someone, yet there he was, talkin' like that. I tell ya it made us all cry. Every one of us."

Mary Ruth didn't bother to ask who all from Gobbler's Knob had gone, but she assumed from what Dorcas was saying that a sorrowing bunch of the youth had made the trip, seeking for something more than the Amish church could offer.

By Thanksgiving night, the very evening following Robert's apology, the Mennonite meetinghouse had filled to capacity simply by word of mouth—the local Amish grapevine was evidently lightning quick. Robert was surprised to see an even larger group of Old Order youth there to mourn their friend Elias and hear of God's goodness and grace—some for the first time, he was certain.

When Reverend Longenecker asked Robert to stand and give his testimony, he did so with confidence. Later, when the minister gave the altar call, ten more Amish young people came forward to open their hearts to the Lord Jesus.

◆

The first Saturday after Elias's death, Leah happened to overhear Mary Ruth squabbling with Dat out in the barn. "I need to take the family buggy tonight," she was insisting.

"Where to?" Dat asked.

"Quarryville."

"What's down there?"

"A gathering of young folk, is all."

"Amish youth?"

"No."

Dat drew in an audible breath. "I forbid you to go, then."

She wondered if he, too, might've heard all the talk—the reports of a throng of Amish young folk finding God at the Mennonite church. "Well, I'm goin', anyway. One way or the other, I am!"

"Just 'cause you're in the midst of rumschpringe . . . doesn't mean you should be back-talkin' your father!" Dat shot back and rather loudly at that.

"Well, if I'm old enough to run around with boys, shouldn't I be allowed to speak my mind 'bout *some* things?"

Leah felt terrible about standing there behind the wall of the milk house, just off the main part of the barn. Yet she hardly knew how to make her presence known. And, truth be told, she wasn't sure she wanted to.

Mary Ruth didn't wait for Dat to give his answer; she simply ran out of the barn, crying as she went.

Leah scarcely knew what to do or say, though she hurt something fierce for both Dat and Mary Ruth. She also felt awkward to know how to get herself out of the milk house without Dat spotting her and wanting to know what the world she was doing sneaking around like that, listening in on a private conversation.

So she set about cleaning out the place once again, sweeping, then rinsing down the floor, stopping only when she happened to realize Dat had come in and was standing there staring at her, for who knows how long, waiting.

"Your sister's bent on havin' her own way, as you already know. Might be best, next time—should there be a next time—to cough or sneeze or something, Leah. Eavesdropping is out-and-out deceitful. Best be more respectful from this time forth."

Before she could speak, he turned and left, his work boots making powerful clumps against the ground. She was glad he'd left, in a way, because she would not have been able to defend herself, nor did she want to. Truth was, she felt nearly as innocent as the dogs—King, Blackie, and Sassy—who'd also been privy to Dat's wrath and Mary Ruth's foolhardy determination.

Put out with herself and, if she dared admit it, with Dat, too, Leah hurried to the house, her father nowhere in sight. She could hear Lydiann wailing her lungs out. "There, there," she said, running upstairs to rescue the napped-out tot. "Did you get left up here all by your lonesome? Did Mamma forget 'bout ya?"

Such a thing was no way near the truth. Mamma had probably gone to the outhouse. Hannah, meanwhile, was redding up her and Mary Ruth's bedroom, and Mary Ruth was right now running pell-mell down the lane, heading toward the road. Just where she thought she was going was anybody's guess. Leah *was* concerned about her grieving sister and wished she might help in some way, do something to ease not only the tension between Dat and Mary Ruth, but lessen the ache in Mary Ruth's heart.

"Let's go downstairs and see what Dawdi John's doin'," she whispered to Lydiann. The tiny girl's eyes were wide and bright from awakening, though tears still glistened from her attention-getting cries. "Your grandfather hasn't seen you yet today, so it's time we go over and visit, ain't so?" She continued to coo as she carried her sister down the stairs, through the front room, and over to the small attached home built onto the main house. The Dawdi Haus was a refuge for elderly or single relatives. For Leah, it was a comfort to be able to go and sit with Mamma's father in his cozy front room, situated close enough to the cook stove in the tiny kitchen to keep it warm on even winter days.

"There, now." She set Lydiann down near Dawdi.

"Did you come to see your ol' Papa?" He reached for her and Lydiann held up her chubby arms.

"That-a girl," he said, putting her on his knee and bouncing her gently. "Here's a horsey, a-trottin' and a-goin' to market . . . to market."

Her sister giggled, and Leah sat down across from them,

watching with pleasure the joy Lydiann brought to Dawdi—to all of them, for that matter. Soon, within another full month, there would be a baby sister or brother for them to hold and love . . . for Lydiann to grow up with, too.

How nice for all of us, 'specially Dawdi, she pondered, knowing he was slowing down more all the time, even though his health had greatly improved and his good days seemed to be very good.

She pondered whether to ask the question she was almost too curious about—and how to ask it without causing a stir.

"Dawdi," she began, "I sometimes wonder . . . I mean, what do you know 'bout my father?"

A serious look on his face, her grandfather replied, "Well, now, I've been workin' with your father all morning, Leah."

"Ach, you know what I mean, don'tcha?" she said.

He grew more somber. "I know you've had yourself some difficult times, getting adjusted to who the mother was that birthed you. Guess you feel like you have two mammas, ain't?"

"Sometimes, jah, I s'pose I do, though I can't say I think on that so much."

He tilted his head, gazing lovingly at Lydiann. As he did, Leah noticed his beard was thinner than she'd remembered and whiter, too. "I wish it could stop right there. Wish you could be content with simply knowing 'bout your first mamma, Lizzie, and the woman who raised ya as her very own. Seems to me the rest of it, well, ain't all that important."

"Is there more to Lizzie's secret than she's willin' to share? I don't know . . . she seems almost closed up about it."

Dawdi said softly, "Or is it something else altogether?"

Her heart quickened and she sat there in the tiny room, not taking her eyes off Dawdi, hoping this might be the moment of revelation. "Do *you* know who my blood father is?"

He began to shake his head back and forth, slowly at first, and then faster. Then he stopped abruptly and looked straight into her face . . . into her heart, too, it seemed. "I just never thought you'd care a speck 'bout Lizzie's wildest days. 'Tis long forgotten . . . why dig up the shameful past?" He sighed loudly. "And 'tis hurtful, I must say, dear girl."

"For Lizzie, too?"

"Above all."

She considered this moment here with Dawdi and the soft babble of Lydiann as the moment when she felt she understood something of her grandfather's love for herself and for Lizzie. No matter which woman she claimed as her mother, Dawdi John Brenneman was her devoted grandfather, and nothing she could do or not do, know or not know, would change that. Dawdi John was her flesh-and-blood grandfather for always, and what he might know about her paternal origins no longer concerned her. She had asked and not received the information she desired.

She must simply wait for it to unfold before her, as surely it would in time.

All day Mary Ruth waited for the tension to diminish between herself and Dat. At the noon meal she found the strain even harder to bear, as her father refused to ask her to pass the potatoes and gravy, even though they were clearly in front of her. Instead, he asked Hannah or Leah, making it seem as if she wasn't even present at the table.

Is this what it's like to be under the Bann? she thought.

She could not get used to the fact her own father did not come close to understanding her. Not only did he not understand or attempt to, she felt he was too harsh in his stance.

When dusk fell and she was still wishing to attend the nighttime church meeting, she asked Dat once again if she might borrow the family buggy. This, after supper dishes were cleared off the table, washed, and put away. She attempted to soften her voice and her approach, though she felt as if she might boil over with eagerness. "I'll take gut care, Dat, honest I will. If you'll just think 'bout letting me go . . ."

"You should not be goin' alone after dark," Dat said.

"I could take Hannah, if you'll let her come along." She wondered momentarily how that would set, since Hannah was already a baptized church member.

"What's the urgency to go all that way?" he asked.

She refused to confess the rumors that Plain teenagers were getting religion. "I'll know better once I get there," she said best as she could muster. "Ach, just say I can go."

"Why not stay home, help your mamma bathe Lydiann and whatnot?" He wasn't budging.

"Please, Dat, won'tcha let me take the buggy and Hannah, too? We won't be gone long."

He turned beet red and pulled hard on his beard, making his lower lip protrude. "I'm not in favor of it; no way, no how." He stared at her, a frown crossing his brow. "But . . . I s'pose 'tis better to have ya goin' in my family carriage than out runnin' round with empty-headed boys all hours."

He was referring to Elias's reckless buggy driving, no doubt, before it got him killed. But she kept her mouth closed. Stunned that she was actually allowed to go, however reluctantly Dat had granted permission, she did not voice her gratitude. She took off running to the barn to get the horse and carriage hitched before he could change his mind.

Mary Ruth had unconsciously retained the image of tall young Robert Schwartz from Elias's funeral, and when she saw him sitting on the men's side of the meetinghouse, her anger was rekindled. Yet she was strangely conscious of his demeanor, his compelling and kind, yet sad eyes. The minister introduced the young man as having a zealous testimony of God's forgiveness and grace before asking him to rise and stand behind the pulpit. Already this was not at all like an Amish preaching service.

Beside her, Hannah fidgeted, glancing at Mary Ruth, probably wishing she hadn't come along now that they were settled into the seventh row on the left side with the other women. Surprisingly there were numerous youth present, a good many of them from their own church district.

When Robert read his sermon text in English, she wondered how this could possibly be. She had never known a gathering where the Scripture was read, and so freely, not from the High German but in a language understandable to all present. And to think that *this* young man was the preacher tonight!

" 'Wherefore lay apart all filthiness and superfluity of naughtiness, and receive with meekness the engrafted word, which is able to save your souls. But be ye doers of the word, and not hearers only, deceiving your own selves.' " He read the text from the epistle of James, chapter one. The doctor's son went on to say it was "high time for men and women to stand up and be counted for the Lord. We are called to do His work. But in order to make our bodies a living sacrifice to this high calling—to be used of Him in the harvest fields of souls—we must first present ourselves to the Most High God. Do not wait until it is too late to 'Give of your best to the Master. Give of the strength of your youth.' "

Mary Ruth intently listened to words and phrases from sections of the Bible she was completely unfamiliar with, and she hungered for more.

The engrafted word, which is able to save your souls . . .

The young preacher continued. "We—all of us—are lost, and we're inclined toward sin and the self ruin that follows. From our birth onward, we yearn to be set free. We long for someone to take away our burden of sin and sadness. Our sin-sick souls crave to be reborn, renewed."

She felt a strange tugging in her heart, something ever so new. She had been taught there was no assurance of salvation in this life. A person had to die first and then only on the Judgment Day could the words—"Well done, thou good and faithful servant," or "Depart from me, ye workers of iniquity"—ever be spoken.

But evidently the Bible stated your soul could be saved here and now, while you were still alive and breathing; the verses just read confirmed this clearly.

She had thought of asking someone about the Scriptures that had been read in High German at Elias's funeral. Now that she was here, inside a church *building*, of all things—her first time ever—she wished there was someone to help her understand.

"O Lord," the young speaker began to pray, "look into our shattered hearts this night. Heal our brokenness and soothe our sorrow. Let us understand fully the price you paid for our salvation, for each of us assembled here. You have redeemed us for yourself with your precious blood spilled on Calvary's tree, and we are forever grateful. In Jesus' blessed name. Amen."

Those gathered in this most reverent place began to sing softly a hymn Mary Ruth had never heard before, yet the words tugged at her heart. "Fightings and fears within, without . . . O Lamb of God, I come, I come." The heartfelt song so perfectly described this night and clinched her longing for the Lord Jesus.

◆

All the way home, Mary Ruth chattered to Hannah, who wasn't at all interested in discussing "forbidden Scriptures," as her twin put it. "But didn't the preacher's words stir up something in you, sister . . . didn't they?"

"The young man speaking tonight killed Ezra's brother" was Hannah's harsh response. "That's all I could think of, though it's not my place to judge. I'm surprised it's me thinkin' this and not you!"

Mary Ruth was suddenly outraged, though she'd felt the

selfsame way as Hannah at Elias's funeral just days before. "I happen to believe Elias died as a result of an accident, pure and simple. An *accident*. Why do you question the sovereignty of God?"

Hannah shook her head, glaring at her. "The young preacher-man *slaughtered* your beau with his automobile, that's what. Such modern things are of the world and are therefore a sin. That's how I see it. So should you."

Mary Ruth felt as if she might burst out crying again, reliving the shocking news of that horrid night, but she wouldn't give in to the grief she had endured. Besides, Hannah had redirected her thoughts with her comments. Truly, Elias's death was a woeful thing and the reason she would wear her long black cape dress and apron for as long as they felt right to her. Yet tonight she had stumbled onto something amazing: the renewal of life and the spirit. Hers. This renewal was something altogether foreign to her, yet she yearned for it like someone dying of thirst yearns for water.

"You saw him, Hannah. . . . Did Robert Schwartz look like a man who would intentionally run his automobile into a pony cart? Did he sound like it as he read the Word of God?"

"Ach, you talk nonsense," Hannah said. "What's got into you?"

She ignored her sister's barbed remark. "Best keep your thoughts to yourself, 'cause I have no intention of staying home tomorrow night. If the meetings continue on, I'm gonna be there."

"Best count *me* out. I made my vow to God and the Amish church. Ain't no room for Mennonite gatherings in my future."

"I'll go with or without you, then," Mary Ruth said, surprised at Hannah's outburst; wasn't like her twin to give voice to such frustration and so strongly, too. She, on the other hand, had been venting her thoughts far too often. "If I have to get the Nolts to drive me in their car, I'm goin' back. I'm empty in my soul, Hannah, ya hear? The Amish church can't even tell me Elias is in heaven. I want to know God the way the doctor's son described Him. I may not always have known it, but I've been lookin' for this my whole life."

That hushed Hannah up quicklike, for which Mary Ruth was ever so glad; she'd had about all she could take. The hour was awful late, and she felt nearly too limp to attend to the reins. Yet such a hankering she had to know and hear more of God's Word.

I will return tomorrow night, she promised herself. *No matter.*

Chapter Thirteen

Mary Ruth stood in the shadow of the springhouse, waiting for Dat to head to the barn. She knew he was indoors talking up a storm to Mamma, probably saying how the twins had come dragging in mighty late last night. Maybe, too, he was letting off steam about the many Gobbler's Knob young folk "out lookin' for the Lord God in all the wrong places."

She wouldn't put it past her father to say something like that. Then Mamma might speak up and say how she felt, or simply nod her head and remain quiet this time.

It certainly didn't matter to Mary Ruth whether or not Mamma voiced her opinion. Truth was, she felt strongly enough about what she'd heard at the church in Quarryville to convince her entirely. Scarcely could she wait to speak to Dat, who was just now hurrying out the back door and making a beeline for the barn.

She waited a bit, then took out after him, willing her feet to walk not run. *Slow down, Mary Ruth . . . take your time.*

Once inside the barn, she sought out her father, noting his disheveled appearance—hair mussed and oily from a week of hard work. He pushed his tattered black work hat onto his head, securing it with dirty and callused hands.

She called to him and, getting his attention, hurried in his direction. "I best be talkin' with you, Dat." Quickly she began to share those things she'd heard from the Mennonite pulpit and had been pondering overnight.

As soon as her comments focused on the assurance of salvation, a change came over her father's countenance—a hardening in his eyes, a frown on his face.

"I have no time for such talk!" he replied.

She fought hard the urge to holler out her aggravation in the stillness of the barn. "Don't you see, there are Scriptures to help us get to heaven? We can *know* we're goin' there! We've been kept in the dark all these years."

Dat was just as adamant. "It smacks of pride for a person to say they've received salvation. You know the story of creation by heart, Mary Ruth. The all-powerful, all-knowing God fashioned all things, both on the earth and in the heavens. Then the evil one, Satan, was cast out of heaven for the ultimate sin of pride, and tempted Eve into thinking she could be 'better than God,' which is exactly what you're sayin' when you claim salvation."

Here Dat paused a moment, then went on. "Must I take you to the bishop himself to discuss these things you know already?"

She decided then and there, Bishop Bontrager ought to be told the truth of the Holy Scriptures. After all, he was the chief authority and responsible under God for the Gobbler's Knob church district. "That's a wonderful-gut idea," she shot back. "We could open the Bible to the selfsame verses preached on last night."

Dat's eyebrows came together in a dark ripple. "Then you knew all along where you were headed—to the Mennonites." He shook his head in disgust. "You cause strife in our midst, daughter."

She felt the hot stain of embarrassment on her cheeks, yet she would not submit; she had absolutely nothing to lose. She must fight for what she believed the Lord God had allowed her to hear and witness in a strange church, because in the span of a single night, her world had been altered more than she could say.

As much as she respected her Amish upbringing, and as much as she missed her dear Elias, Mary Ruth now realized she must follow her heart to higher education, that one thing the Lord had implanted deep within her.

"Dat, I don't mean to cause trouble. I've waited a full year—and more. Why should I wait any longer to go to high school? I'm old enough to do as I please; anybody knows that."

"We had this all worked out, Mary Ruth. You agreed to stay home with your mamma and help . . . till you married, whenever that time came." Dat's voice sounded nearly breathless.

"But all that's changed . . . don't you see? Everything's different now."

"Just 'cause Elias died?"

"Since my beau was . . . *taken* from me." Mary Ruth was angry and sorrowful all mixed up together. "Nobody knows this, but Elias and I were goin' to be wed . . . one day."

"I'm awful sorry 'bout his death, daughter. Truly, I am."

"Oh, Dat!" she sobbed. "If you mean it, then won'tcha give me your blessing to get my education? This is the only thing I really want now in life."

A long silence ensued. Sadly she knew pursuing the dream would eventually lead her away from her parents' church. Unknowingly she had been searching for something deeper her whole life . . . for true wisdom. Losing Elias had uncovered the emptiness in her spirit, and the obvious lack on the part of Bishop Bontrager and the brethren to fill it.

When Dat did not respond to her fervent plea, she spoke again. This time with an even more fiery edge to her words. "Blessing or not, I'm goin' to get my high school diploma . . . as soon as I can get myself enrolled. Even if I have to do it by correspondence or whatnot, I must follow God's bidding."

"How on earth can ya know such a thing?" Dat asked.

"Can't explain it, really. All I know is the Almighty put it there . . . my desire to teach young children." She paused, contemplating what she must say next. "And I want to read and study the Bible."

"Study, ya say?"

"Jah, and no wonder the Quarryville church has room only to stand at the back. The place is packed, and you and Mamma . . . you should go and see for yourself. *Hear* the words of the Lord God preached in such a way as you've never known."

She knew her father faithfully read Scripture, but he did not pause and ponder any of it or ask questions of anyone about what he read. Usually he did so silently in High German, seven chapters at a time, and, when asked, he would read in Pennsylvania Dutch to the family. But at no time would he have admitted to formally studying the verses. That was thought to be haughty and high-minded . . . and far from the ways of the People.

No wonder Mamma had been opposed to the library books once hidden beneath Mary Ruth's bed. Was she worried Dat might discover Mary Ruth also desired to study the Holy Bible, perhaps in English? Begin poring over it the way she did every other book?

"Mamma reads the Bible for herself, even says some of the verses over and over again. I know she does." Mary Ruth said it too quickly, and she worried she may have mistakenly pulled her mother into the center of the storm.

"Ain't your concern a'tall." Dat turned away, removing his black hat and raising it ever so high off his head, as if preparing to shoo a fly, but there was no fly in sight. Downright mad he was, and she knew it.

Then, nearly as swiftly as he'd lost his temper, he somehow managed to regain it and pushed the hat back square on his mashed-down hair. He turned to face her. "I'm tellin' you this here minute, if you are so *schtarrkeppich* as to insist on your way—to ignore my rightful authority as your father—I'll have no choice but to go to the brethren about this matter."

"What can *they* do?" she retorted. "I'm not baptized."

"No . . . but Hannah is, and the two of you are bound by unbroken cords of blood and spirit." He was surely grasping at straws.

She felt put upon, as if she'd done something terribly wrong against her twin. *Bound by unbroken cords . . . well, for pity's sake*. Baptism was up to the individual, not a mandate of the People.

Dat shrugged, then walked away.

She could see it was no use trying to continue the heated debate; Dat's mind was made up. Now she would have to follow his wishes or suffer the consequences—rumschpringe or not.

Still, she could not squelch the hankering to know more. She despised the feeling of having been kept from things that truly mattered—essential truths found in the Holy Bible. After all, there must be some important reason why folk called it the *Good* Book. Mary Ruth didn't rightly know how she would get to Quarryville again, but one way or another she was going tonight. If she had to run down the road to the Nolts' place, she would.

Leah was out searching and calling for a wayward cow, up in the high meadow and clear back toward the woods on the north side. She couldn't help but think as she wandered the field that the cow was truly the smart one. The day was awful pretty, what with the skies as blue as one of her for-good dresses, and not a single cloud. Such late autumn days wouldn't stay nice like this much longer. It was highly unusual for the twenty-seventh of November to be this mild.

We're having us a fine Indian summer, she thought, tramping through the tall grass, wearing shoes for the first time that autumn on feet swollen from months of going barefoot.

At long last Leah located Rosie under a stand of trees, the

boughs void of leaves now but still sturdy enough to provide a bit of shade. Munching away and minding her own business, the cow appeared to be content this far from the bank barn. "I'd say you went explorin' today, didn'tcha?" Leah slapped Rosie's hindquarters playfully. "Let's go on home now."

On the walk back, Leah spoke coaxingly to King and Blackie, who ran together more often now that the pup, Sassy, had come to live with them. *Three's an odd partnership*, Mamma liked to say. Leah was seeing it firsthand, for the younger pup preferred to stay close to home, begging for handouts at the back door. It was easy to see Mamma was spoiling that one.

"When will the first snow fly?" She reached down, petting King and Blackie both as they went. Then she had to direct the cow away from the temptation of going belly deep in a clear creek nearby. "Can you sniff the air and forecast a change in weather like Aunt Lizzie does?"

She had to smile. Her blood mother, bless her heart, was the sweetest, dearest Aendi she had, and there were plenty on both sides of the family. Leah was looking forward to seeing more of Mamma and Lizzie's sisters again over in Hickory Hollow come next Saturday. It had been a good long time since Dat had actually consented to take the family to the old Brenneman homestead, where Dawdi John and Mammi—gone to heaven—had lived and raised their brood of children. This visit they planned to see Aunt Becky and Uncle Noah Brenneman, the man Dat had often tried to avoid at all costs, before the truth of Lizzie's past had finally come to Leah's ears.

"Nearly time for milkin'," Leah said, nearing the corral and following Rosie into the barn. She was eager for winter weather, because once the windmill started clanging its tinny song and strong gusts of cold air swept up from the distant hills, piling snow up high against the north side of the barn, Dat wouldn't need her so much outdoors. No, Dat was awful kind that way, and he was beginning to be even more considerate these days, now that he suspected Leah was seriously seeing Gid.

Funny how that is, she thought, preparing the cows for milking. *When Dat's happy, everybody else is bound to be, too.*

She wondered how things would go when the smithy's son asked Dat for her hand. That day couldn't be too far off, and she felt almost breathless with excitement. She looked forward to long winter days of quilting, when she would once again be included in the community of women folk, something she enjoyed more than ever.

Is it because I am soon to become a wife? She didn't quite know why her attitude toward work frolics was changing. Scarcely could she wait to see what pattern and colors would be used in sewing the next quilt. This one, she knew, was meant to be given to Deacon Stoltzfus's wife for her birthday, come Christmas. Everyone knew the reason behind the gesture was to bring a bit of cheer to the grieving woman. She had looked awful peaked last Sunday at Preaching service, Leah recalled, her heart going out not only to Elias's mother but to the whole family.

When Dat came shuffling into the barn, she greeted him. "Just in time for milkin'," she said. But he surprised her by heading right back outside without saying a word.

Something's awful wrong, she thought, hoping it wasn't more bickering with Mary Ruth. Still, she couldn't help wondering, because just before she'd gone looking for missing Rosie, Hannah had dashed through the barnyard, running hard down the lane after Mary Ruth, hollering, "Come back, sister. Won'tcha please come back?"

She pressed the cow's teat, milking by hand as she always did, and was nearly startled at the strength of the first spritz of creamy milk. "Good girl, Rosie," she said softly. "Glad *someone's* content round here."

◆

Robert Schwartz held the obituary in his hands—a paper memorial. He had cut out the small square of newsprint last Wednesday, tucking it in his personal possessions to take back to college. Something tangible to forever remind him . . .

He sat in the dark, in the formal front room, where he could contemplate the events of the last week without interruption. Life-altering days when opinions and perceptions had radically changed. How could one twenty-four-hour period be so drastically different from the next?

He replayed the entire week from Sunday to Sunday in his head. Visions of Elias's body sprawled pitifully out on the road . . . recollections too painful to ponder. Elias's mother at the funeral, how she looked as if her knees might give out, leaving her too weak to stand. The Deacon Stoltzfus, as he had been reintroduced to Robert prior to the service, had worn a solemn face, sitting erect with his sons, the weight of the world on his back. Robert had recognized the invisible burden, because he, too, carried one linked to all the misery of the day.

He had heard the sniffling of one young woman in particular. She was surely not more than a teenager, likely Elias's own age, perhaps younger. A girl with a look-alike sister, possibly a twin—both with strawberry blond hair—had struggled through the endless funeral service, even leaning, at one point, on the shoulder of the other girl. *Elias's sweetheart*, he had surmised at the time, for no other woman, apart from the mother, had appeared to be as distraught.

Robert had noticed the same girl and her sister at the Quarryville church. On the final night of meetings, just last evening, he had spoken with her briefly as she made her way out the door with Dan and Dottie Nolt and their son. Dan had introduced her to him as "Elias's former bride-to-be, who came along with us tonight." He wanted to say how very sorry he was, say the accident was the worst thing that had ever happened to him, but any words of sympathy he might have offered remained locked behind his lips. He could not recall the few words he'd said in response to Dan's brief introduction, but he remembered offering his hand and shaking hers quite gently, lest it break, requesting forgiveness with his eyes.

Thinking back, he suddenly realized there would have been no spontaneous meetings at all—no rejoicing of the heavenly hosts when dozens of grieving, repentant Amish young people came to the Lord Jesus—had he driven home last Sunday night without incident. "*Things happen for a reason*," one of his professors often stated with conviction. "*Therefore the sovereignty of God can be wholly trusted. You can throw your life on His mercy. . . .*"

Contemplating these things in the quietude, he was startled when his father wandered into the darkened room and sat on the leather chair, put his feet up with a sigh, and merely sat silently for more than a full minute. Robert felt obliged to be the first to speak, and he began by simply saying he wondered if the whole village of Gobbler's Knob hadn't turned out for the funeral of Elias Stoltzfus . . . as well as the revival meetings that followed.

His father frowned disapprovingly, changing the subject to the weather. Not to be daunted, Robert rose and offered to pour some freshly brewed coffee. To this his father agreed. Robert hurried from the parlor, toward the kitchen, glad for some common ground, inconsequential as it was.

Chapter Fourteen

Ida, now at the end of her eighth month of pregnancy, had not slept soundly for three nights straight. She shared this in passing with Leah, who had come in from the barn. "Catch your breath a bit, dear," she said. "And I will, too."

Leah settled down nearest the window with a cup of tea. "Soon we'll be using the one-horse sleigh to get to and from Preaching and market and all."

Ida sighed, glad for this rare quiet moment. "And we'll soon have us another sweet babe to hold and warm us in the midst of our winter. I'm ever so eager. Can't help but thinkin' this one might be Abram's first son."

"Oh, Mamma, really?"

She didn't want to make too much of it, Leah having been Dat's longtime sidekick for these many years. But if she were forthright, she'd have to admit this baby was mighty different from his sisters. He kicked harder and poked deep into her ribs at times. He jumped and leaped and ran in place all night long, chasing sleep away. "What shall we name him if he's to be a boy?"

"Well, the name Abram *does* come to mind." Leah smiled broadly.

Ida had thought of that, too. "Well, now, 'tween you and me, I think there's room for only one Abram under this roof." She paused momentarily before continuing. "What would ya think if we named the baby Abe?"

"It sounds similar to Abram, for sure. Like a wee chip off the old block." Leah glanced up at the ceiling like she was thinking it through. When her gaze drifted back down, she offered another smile. "I think Abe's a right fine name. So why not see what Dat says to it?"

"Jah, Abram might enjoy namin' his boy." She went and poured herself some hot tea, stirring two teaspoons of honey into the steaming brew. Ida knew Leah was right. It was fitting to include Abram in all the excitement of a new little one. He'd gotten somewhat lost in the shuffle with the previous births, except for the day Leah came into the world.

She sipped her tea and recalled the autumn day, suddenly feeling compelled to tell Lizzie's first and only child the events surrounding the day of her birth. Rather impulsively, she began. "I understand from Abram you're quite curious 'bout your birthday—your very first one, that is."

Leah's hazel-gold eyes brightened instantly. "Jah, Mamma, what can you tell me?"

"Only as much as I know," she said. "That October day was a busy one, what with potato diggin' in full swing. As I recall, the sun was warm and the skies were clear, although we'd had the very first frost of the season—quite heavy, in fact. That morning I thought of all the weeds blackened by the killing frost, not one bit sad 'bout that. But . . . the flowers, well, I was awful sorry to see their perty heads all wilted overnight.

"Lizzie and I had awakened quite early. She'd come down from her log house to eat breakfast with us here, and after a bit we decided to make some apple dumplings, then redd up the kitchen.

"Several hours after I'd gone to help Cousin Fannie with her fall housecleaning, Lizzie's labor began. There was no way for Abram to get word to Grasshopper Level 'bout Lizzie without leaving her alone, and she was fairly terrified, puttin' it mildly. He hollered for the smithy and Miriam, but the Peacheys were out diggin' potatoes clear on the other side of their barn. So poor Abram, if he wasn't beside himself, wonderin' what the world to do.

"Then things began to happen awful fast, and there was no time to call for the Amish midwife, not the doctor, neither one. By the time I arrived home, late in the afternoon, you had already made your entrance into the world."

Stopping to catch her breath, Ida felt again some of the surprise and excitement of that day. She drank a little more of her tea. "Abram was the one who came to our Lizzie's rescue, bless his heart, and helped with your birth. He delivered his little niece—you—and we raised you as our own second daughter. And, 'course, you know all the rest." She felt she might cry now as she remembered Abram's account of the special day.

"Dat, you see, was the first to hold you and speak softly to you—'welcome home,' he said—and kiss your little head, covered with the softest brown peach fuzz. Oh, how Abram loved you, Leah. Right from the start he did. Honestly, I believe he fixed his gaze on you like no other man might have, maybe 'cause your own birth father was nowhere to be found . . . or, far as we knew, even known." She reached over and covered Leah's hand with her own.

Leah was still now, eyes wide. "Oh, Mamma, no wonder Dat took me under his fatherly wing. No wonder . . ."

"Jah, 'tis for certain. And not only that, but Dat had it in his head that he'd spared your life back when, after Lizzie first knew she was carrying you, which was prob'ly true, too. It was during that time your outspoken uncle Noah was bent on sending Lizzie away to end her pregnancy."

Leah clasped Ida's hand. "Mamma, why is it Dat has never wanted to talk 'bout my birth to me?"

She'd wondered if Leah might press further. "I daresay he may be embarrassed, really, recounting all the day entailed, ya know. . . ."

"I just thought there was more to it, that's all."

She shook her head. "You now know all I know, Leah. If it's your first father you're thinkin' of, well, I don't know a stitch more than I've already said."

Leah glanced out the window and Ida slipped her hand away. "You mustn't ever think you weren't longed for or dearly wanted by Lizzie . . . and Dat and me. Just 'cause, well, you know—"

"Because Lizzie didn't have a husband? Is that what you mean?"

Neither of them spoke for a time. The warmth from the wood stove encircled them like a sheer prayer veiling as both women brought their teacups to their lips.

Ida set her cup down and leaned on the table, studying

Leah. "I'd like you to know something," she said at last. "You comin' into the world, the moment you did . . . well, it turned my wayward sister round right quick . . . away from the lure of worldly things. She had a change of heart even while she was expecting you. You gave her purpose to live a holy and upright life. She nursed and tended to you—with plenty of help from me—and began to seek after the Lord God and His ways." Here she couldn't help but sigh, remembering. "Lizzie became nearly childlike in her faith. Truly, the grace of God was upon her. She wanted to learn how to pray . . . and I taught her, just as Abram's mother had taught me long ago."

"So Lizzie wasn't content with the memorized prayers of the People?"

"She had a yearning to share from her heart is the best way I can explain it. She wanted to learn to listen more to the Lord, as well."

Leah's eyes widened at that. "Ach, Mamma, whatever do you mean?"

She wondered how to describe the deep longing in both her heart and Lizzie's. "I s'pose at one time or 'nother, most all of us yearn after the Lord Jesus in a way that may be difficult to understand." She hoped her comments might whet Leah's appetite to walk with the Lord God heavenly Father in a similar manner.

"I promised, at the time of my baptism, to uphold the Ordnung." Leah fiddled with the oilcloth on the table before going on. "You're not sayin' you go beyond what the brethren teach at Preaching service in the prayers you speak of . . . are ya?"

"To honor the unwritten code of behavior amongst the

People is all well and good, but it's equally important to obey God's Word, the Holy Bible."

Leah looked up just then, catching Ida's eye. "Aunt Lizzie taught me to talk to God from my heart, as she likes to say. After Jonas and I . . . after we didn't end up getting married, when I was ever so brokenhearted, Lizzie helped pick up the pieces of my life by showing me the way to open up my spirit to the Holy One."

"I pleaded with her to do so," Ida admitted. "I felt this was something you and she could share—mother and daughter, ya know."

Leah got up abruptly and came around the table. She sat next to her and leaned her head on Ida's shoulder. "Oh, Mamma, I don't know what I ever did to deserve two such loving women in my life. You and Lizzie . . ." She brushed away her tears. "I'm mighty grateful . . . and I hope ya know."

Drawn anew to Leah, she patted her girl's face. "The way I look at it, God must've loved Lizzie and me a lot to give you to *both* of us. Such a dear one you are."

At this Leah straightened and reached around her and gave a gentle squeeze. "I'm all the better for it, Mamma."

"All three of us are," Ida declared, getting up to warm her tea.

"In case you're wonderin', it makes no difference when it is that I find out who was my first father. I've decided to be patient in this and simply wait till Lizzie's ready to share with me . . . and not before."

You may have to wait forever on that, Ida thought but did not voice it.

Leah hurried to the cellar to help Mamma run the clothes through the wringer between Monday morning milking and breakfast. Hannah and Mary Ruth were already working in the kitchen, and Leah was glad for that. She could stay put near Mamma, aware of an extra-special closeness on this dawning of a new day, wanting to continue the conversation from last night.

"Why don't the ministers teach us to pray the way you and Aunt Lizzie do?" Leah asked when it appeared they might be alone for a while longer.

Mamma glanced toward the stairs. " 'Tis best you keep such things to yourself."

"Why's that?" She felt strangely intrigued, as if sharing something forbidden.

"The brethren need not know of this." Mamma looked a bit worried now. "There are different ways of lookin' at things, far as I'm concerned. If a body wants to speak directly from the heart to the Almighty—not use the rote prayers—then who's to stop him or her?" She nodded her head. "This happens to be one of those big issues that, sad to say, is downright niggling. Divisive, even, amongst the People."

"Hinnerlich?"

"Oh my, ever so troublesome, jah."

She wondered what other things Mamma might be referring to; the not knowing caused even more of an urge to question. Still, she was obedient and held her peace, trusting God to bring things to light in His own timing and way.

◆

When lunch had been cleared away, Mamma sent Leah over to Miriam Peachey's with a large casserole of Washday Dinner, consisting of a hearty layer of onions, an ample coating of sliced new potatoes, tomato juice, and sausages.

"Mamma heard you were under the weather," Leah said, handing the meal to the smithy's wife, her someday mother-in-law, Lord willing.

Miriam's face warmed with the gesture as she accepted the tasty offering with a smile and a joyful "Denki!" then asked, "Tell me, how's your mamma now?"

"Oh, she has her energy back and is doin' all her regular work—and keepin' up with Lydiann, too," Leah assured her.

Miriam nodded her head and thanked Leah once more. "I'll return the favor next week."

"No need to, really. Mamma's feelin' wonderful-gut. Has some trouble sleepin' at night but that's all." Leah turned to go, noticing Gid in his father's blacksmith shop, running the blower, stirring up the coals to make the forge hotter. She wouldn't bother him by going over to say a quick hello when it was obvious how occupied he was just now.

Returning home, she found herself imagining how busy Smithy Gid would be as her husband, managing his blacksmithing obligation to his father, as well as his work with Dat, which would take Gid back and forth between the Peachey and Ebersol farms. Not to mention his own work hauling and splitting wood for the cook stove and mowing and keeping things tidy outdoors, wherever he and she might end up living. She wondered if Aunt Lizzie might possibly move down to the Dawdi Haus to care for Dawdi John at some point, making it possible for Leah and Gid to live as newlyweds in the little log house half in and half out of the woods. No one had ever suggested such a thing, but she smiled at the idea, thinking how much fun it would be to get her pretty things out from her hope chest, making a home at last for herself and Gid . . . and, eventually, their children.

She wondered if Lizzie had ever stopped to think about her own future, back when she was Leah's age. *Was she at all like me when she was young? Did she think some of the same thoughts as I do now?* She tried to imagine Lizzie Brenneman wandering outside as a young girl, talking quietlike to a favorite dog—like Leah often did to companionable King—or looking up at the black night sky, speckled with bright stars, and wishing she could count them, so many there were.

Just who will I be? Leah wondered. *In the future, will I be satisfied with the choices I make now? Who will I become in the eyes of the Lord, and will He be pleased with me?*

Nobody knew it, but the night Leroy Stoltzfus had come into the kitchen to tell the news of Elias's accident, Mary Ruth had felt her heart turn nearly hard as a stone. She could scarcely hear what Leroy was saying—only the words *Elias died tonight* had broken through.

It was as if she had willingly stopped up her own ears somehow. She didn't know for sure if the tuckered-out feeling she had just now was a delayed reaction to the funeral, this being the eighth day since the shocking news had come. She felt heavy inside as she headed upstairs and sat on her side of the bed, on top of the colorful handmade quilt made by Mamma and Mammi Ebersol years before.

She ought not to have been surprised when, nearly thirty minutes later, Leah tiptoed near, settled on the floor near the bed, and leaned her head against the mattress, her hand resting on Mary Ruth's. "You can cry for Elias all ya want, but I won't have you up here cryin' alone."

Tears continued to seep out of the corners of her eyes, spilling down the bridge of her nose. "Oh, I miss him so . . . I just can't say how awful much."

"Mary Ruth, honey . . . I believe I understand," Leah replied.

She knows 'cause she lost Jonas . . . just not to death, thought Mary Ruth, at least glad of the latter for poor Leah. "But I can't begin to know how *you* must've felt, Leah . . . you-know-who doin' what she did."

They fell quiet, the two of them there together, both acquainted with similar sorrow.

When Mary Ruth got the strength to speak again, it was a whisper. "Would you help me talk to Dat 'bout getting my education? He's ever so fired up these days."

A flicker of a frown creased Leah's brow. "Well, I don't know."

"Please, sister? See if you can gain some ground for me."

Leah sighed. "All right, I'll do whatever I can."

"You'll go and speak to him, then?" She wanted to get up, she felt that much encouraged, but she sat there without moving, still exhausted.

"I'll do what I'm able." This was Leah's promise to her.

"That's ever so gut and I'm grateful." She gripped Leah's hand. "I don't like shouting matches," she declared. "Not one little bit."

"Then why do it?" came the quick reply. "Dat wants only what's best for you."

"I s'pose I'm too quick to say what I'm thinkin' is all. You know me—everyone knows how much I like to talk. Gets me in hot water more than I can say; more than I *should* say. And sometimes the talkin' gets mixed up with the thinkin', and that's when I have the most trouble."

Leah smiled sweetly. "Seems to me you could do more thinkin' and less, well . . . *you* know."

"I'll keep that in mind."

To this they both smiled. Mary Ruth felt more hopeful and cared for when Leah was near and she told her so. What she did not say was that she had run off to Dottie Nolt, mad as all get out, and discovered another sympathetic ear down the road. No, it was best Dat or anyone else not know she was talking to the "enemy," so to speak, though the Nolts were the nicest, kindest Englishers she'd ever known, and she sincerely liked them. Still, if Dat knew they'd invited Mary Ruth to come live with them, well, he'd raise the barn roof—for sure and for certain.

Chapter Fifteen

Leah was out helping Dat split wood the morning after her heart-to-heart with Mary Ruth when she got up the nerve to say something about her grieving sister's zeal for education. "I know you've already talked this out with Mary Ruth some time back, but she's more determined than ever to attend high school."

Dat avoided her gaze, raising his ax clear behind his head and back, then bringing it forward to meet the log. "She oughta know better than to put you up to this," he grumbled when he'd sliced through the piece of wood with a single blow.

"I just thought—"

"How can you, Leah?" he interjected. "Why must ya think your sister will benefit in any way from stubbornly lusting after the world?"

"She'll probably do it, anyway. Why not give her the go-ahead just as you allowed both of us girls to work outside the home?" she replied softly.

He leaned hard on the ax, the blade next to the soil. "If I

let her attend public high school, she might end up like . . ." He stopped short of uttering Sadie's name.

Leah had scarcely felt like speaking up in defense of something she herself did not believe in, yet she'd dared to, knowing of Mary Ruth's torment over wanting something she could not have. Leah was stuck, it seemed, loving Mary Ruth and wanting to honor Dat and do the right thing.

He looked at her, eyes blazing. "I say if you're to be Mary Ruth's mouthpiece, then tell her this for *me*. Tell her she is no longer welcome in this house if she chooses to disobey her father!"

Oh no, Dat . . . no. This was the worst thing for Mary Ruth, because surely now she *would* leave; she was just that stubborn. Without Elias alive to keep her linked to the People and her Amish roots, she would most certainly fly away to the world.

Leah tried to get Mamma to sit down and rest in her big bedroom. She had asked Hannah to play with Lydiann for a while, hoping to coax Mamma off her feet and into bed. Terribly distressed at the news of Mary Ruth packing her clothes, Mamma began to weep.

"Maybe she won't like high school," Leah suggested, doubting it herself.

"No . . . no . . . no," sobbed Mamma. " 'Tis wrong, ever so wrong, to push her out of the nest too soon like this."

Feeling awkward about hearing Mamma voice her disapproval of Dat's decision, Leah hovered near. Mamma was standing in defiance, looking out the bedroom window. "Best talk to Dat 'bout all this," whispered Leah.

"I'll talk all right!" Mamma turned and suddenly fell into Leah's arms. "Oh, what's to become of us? First my eldest daughter, now Mary Ruth."

"Preacher Yoder says all is not lost till it's truly too late. 'As long as there's breath there is hope,' he says, ya know."

"Life and hope, jah. I just don't want to see Mary Ruth sent away like this. We all love her so!" She began to cry again. "What'll dear Hannah do, bless her heart? They're close twins, for goodness' sake."

Leah felt like sobbing, too, but she needed to be stronger than poor Mamma. Wordlessly she helped her mother over to the bed to stretch out a bit, then closed the door and tiptoed down the stairs to the kitchen, where she would start supper soon. First, though, Leah must tend to sad Hannah, check on Lydiann . . . and pray fervently for God's grace and mercy to fill this too-empty house.

Leah, Lydiann, and Aunt Lizzie piled into the second seat of the buggy the Saturday of the planned visit to Hickory Hollow. Mamma and Dat sat up front. Hannah, having volunteered her companionship, stayed home with Dawdi John, who was suffering a head cold and a sore throat. Leah was fairly sure the real reason Hannah had stayed behind was to steal away to the Nolts' for a good long visit with Mary Ruth; that way Dat wouldn't have to know about it and neither would Mamma, who was beginning to worry Leah and Lizzie both.

Lizzie had made a fuss about Mamma making the long trip today, but her pleas had fallen on deaf ears. "I don't need pamperin'," Mamma said in response to Lizzie's entreaty.

Besides that, Dat didn't look too kindly on Lizzie interfering with the set plans for this brisk, yet sunny afternoon. "I'll see to Ida. You see to yourself," he snapped, startling Leah.

All during the ride to Hickory Hollow, Dat sat stiff and aloof, holding the reins. Leah felt awful sorry for Mamma and wished she could be sitting next to her, patting her hand if need be. Dear, dear Mamma . . . two of her girls were gone from the house . . . and the Fold.

Of course, none of them knew for sure if Sadie had ever gained acceptance into an Ohio church community, so Leah guessed she ought not to jump to conclusions. Still, they all assumed Bishop Bontrager would have heard something if Sadie *was* a repentant member of a "high" church, one with a more relaxed discipline—in short, just plain more worldly.

Leah pondered this while taking in the sky and trees, now bare of leaf and stark as could be against the wispy clouds and fiercely blue sky, hinting of gloomy gray days, blowing snow, and icy winds. Soon heavy snows would put everything into slow motion once again.

She shivered suddenly, eager for Mamma's newborn babe, knowing full well the great joy an infant could offer a wounded soul. In the eyes of her heart, though, she could not imagine ever holding her own baby, hard as she tried. "Oh, that'll come, surely it will, once you and Smithy Gid are husband and wife," Aunt Lizzie had assured her the other day when she'd confided this.

Once I am a wife . . .

The words still seemed somewhat foreign to her, yet she knew her heart was ready to both give and receive love again. *"Once you're married, you'll forget you ever loved Jonas,"* one quilter had cheekily whispered in her ear during a break for coffee and sticky buns.

Leah didn't see how she'd ever quite forget the relationship she'd had with Jonas, maybe because he had been her girlhood love. But, in due time, Mamma had recently insisted, Leah's injury of the heart would mend "a hundred percent."

When they neared Cattail Road, tired from traveling, Dat announced they were coming up on Hickory Hollow.

Leah liked the sound of the small place and wondered how it got its name. She knew what a hollow was—a holler the People called it—but just why was the nearly invisible dot on the map named Hickory? Was it because of the many hardwood trees growing nearby, most originating from the walnut family? She'd heard her father speak of a farmer there who made hickory rockers as a hobby. Dat had purchased several rocking chairs some years back from the older gentleman. Whatever the source of the name, Leah was eager to lay eyes on the well-forested landscape once again.

Once they arrived, Dat jumped out and hurried around the carriage to help Mamma down, seemingly more compassionate toward her than at the outset of the trip.

Now for some good fellowship, Leah thought, breathing a relieved sigh at having safely reached their destination, as well as at Dat's improved mood. They all could use a carefree afternoon, what with Mary Ruth gone to live with Englishers.

During the ride up, Aunt Lizzie had talked softly to Leah, who was glad to cradle sleeping Lydiann in her arms. "Noah and Becky will be mighty glad to see us," Lizzie had said. " 'Specially Lydiann, I would think."

"Much too long since we've visited, ain't?"

Lizzie had nodded. "We ought not to be so distanced from relatives."

Immediately Cousins Peter and Fannie Mast came to mind. Leah shook herself, not so much physically as mentally. She dared not allow herself to think about the Mast family.

Now she leaned down and kissed the tip of Lydiann's tiny nose. Her little sister's eyes blinked open. "Lookee where we are now. You slept nearly all the way, dear one."

She continued to hold Lydiann close for a moment, till the wee girl awakened. Then she rose and got down out of the buggy herself, still carrying her sister.

"What a nice December day!" Lizzie commented as they followed Becky and Noah into their Dawdi Haus, filling up nearly all the places for sitting in the small front room.

Aunt Becky served hot spiced cider to each of them, except for Lydiann, who seemed glad to sit off away from the others at the small kitchen table, drinking a cup of chocolate milk. Leah pulled out a chair to be near Lydiann, noticing Lizzie and Mamma's sister-in-law, Becky, was moving slower, even limping on occasion. Uncle Noah, with his long graying beard, was, too.

Goodness, they look older than I thought they might. She wondered how long it would be before Dat and Mamma began to show their age and slow down. Uncle Noah was lots older than Lizzie, for sure, and a number of years ahead of Mamma, too. She observed Aunt Becky, who had seemed to be trying very hard not to stare at Mamma's swollen stomach.

She probably thinks Mamma shouldn't be out in public, thought Leah. After all, there were probably only three weeks left before they'd know if Abram's daughters would be welcoming a brother at long last. *At least two of us will be on hand to help Mamma with the new one.* Leah was thinking of Aunt Lizzie and herself; naturally Hannah and Lydiann would be nowhere near the birthing room. Just then she wondered if Dat would ban Mary Ruth from the house even on the joyous day of Mamma's delivery.

Mamma's voice drew Leah back to the moment. "A new baby will help keep my *Mann* and me young longer," she said right out. "Ain't so, Abram?"

Dat appeared sheepish now and said nothing.

Leah found his lack of response intriguing. "Well, now, that's the truth," she whispered playfully to Lydiann, reaching over to tickle her head as the toddler reached up and grabbed Leah's fingers with an unexpectedly strong grip.

"*Schweschder* . . . Lee—ah," Lydiann surprised her by saying.

"Jah, that's right. I *am* your sister." She laughed softly. Wouldn't Mamma enjoy hearing about Lydiann's sweet words? She would be sure to tell her on the ride home to Gobbler's Knob.

After sitting and talking about the weather and whatnot, as well as asking about both Hannah and Mary Ruth, Aunt Becky brought out a small tray of crackers and several kinds of cheeses, along with sliced apples. "Help yourself," she said, tottering about the room while balancing the tray in one hand. Her wooden cane had made its appearance, but no one said a word about it.

Uncle Noah and Aunt Becky talked of their own friends and relatives, including one Ella Mae Zook. "The dear woman's known for her mint tea and mighty lovin' heart," Aunt Becky said. "She's even got herself a nickname."

"Oh? What's that?" asked Mamma.

"Some folk nowadays are callin' her the Wise Woman."

Uncle Noah grimaced and made a peculiar sound in the back of his throat. "What women don't go 'n' think up. . . ." Leah thought she heard him mutter.

But the real news from Hickory Hollow that day was about Sadie. "I hear Sadie's in the family way," Aunt Becky said, grunting as she sat down.

Mamma's face at once brightened and then instantly sagged. Dat right away turned and stared hard at the window. Leah didn't know if he was struggling with the mention of his firstborn's name or just what.

She kept waiting for someone, anyone at all, to make a reminder that there was to be no mention of Sadie's name in the midst of the Gobbler's Knob folk by Bishop Bontrager's decree—and Dat's own wishes. Of course, the Bann did not include Hickory Hollow.

"When did ya hear?" Mamma managed to say.

"Just yesterday," Aunt Becky replied.

Right then it seemed Mamma and Becky Brenneman were the only two in the room and communing on some cherished level.

"Who told ya?" Mamma asked, eyes wide.

"A cousin of a friend of Ella Mae's."

"Anything I can read for myself?" Mamma said, shocking Leah and evidently Aunt Lizzie, too, as Lizzie's hands flew to her throat.

Aunt Becky shook her head. "No. Sorry, Ida."

"Simple hearsay, then?"

"Either she's expecting a baby or she ain't," Aunt Becky replied, accompanied by a severe stare from Uncle Noah.

"No more!" Abram's head was bowed low, as if in prayer. Raising his face to them, he spoke again. "Best leave things be."

Glancing around the room at Dat and Mamma . . . and Aunt Lizzie, too, Leah saw pain mirrored on their faces. She felt the urge to speak up like Mary Ruth had been doing lately. Trembling, she had to will herself to remain silent and simply let the news of Sadie's first baby as a married woman sink into the hollows of her mind. Seeping slowly, surely into her splintered heart.

Chapter Sixteen

Ida went about her washday routine the Monday after the Hickory Hollow visit, washing and hanging out clothes with help from Leah and Hannah, who took turns tending to Lydiann throughout the morning hours. Ida refused to give in to the jagged pain that wracked her middle. Surely this was nothing more than the result of too much brooding over Mary Ruth moving out so awful sudden . . . and the disquieting news of Sadie being with child—and lo, at the selfsame time as Ida again. *Same as when I was carrying Lydiann.* What was it about her firstborn and herself? Was it the tie that binds, as Lizzie so often referred to regarding mothers and daughters?

It wasn't wise to waste time wondering or worrying when she had plenty to accomplish, just as she did every day but Sunday. Her "vacation" was nigh upon her, and that would be all well and good once her baby arrived. She knew instinctively this was to be her last child, just as Lizzie seemed to always know when the weather was changing and rain or snow was headed their way. For her own sake, she must not dwell on either Sadie or Mary Ruth any longer, though it was mighty hard not to, especially when Mary Ruth showed up later that afternoon, long after the noon meal.

"I need to speak with you, Mamma," she said, her pretty face close to the screen door.

Ida hurried to the back door. *What'll Abram say if he catches her sneaking round here?* She didn't care so much to be finding out.

" 'S'okay if I come in?" Mary Ruth was *rutsching* around, squirming to beat the band.

"Well, jah, all right," Ida said, not going all the way to the door, but motioning quickly to her.

They scampered like frightened cats upstairs to what was now Hannah's bedroom. "I *had* to see you," Mary Ruth said. "Even if it means I get a tongue-lashin' from Dat." Then she began to cry. "I want, more than anything, to share what's happened to me. I just never thought . . ."

"Now, now, dear girl," Ida said, cradling her. "I know your heart's taken over, that's all. We all struggle so at one time or 'nother."

"Then you *do* understand, Mamma? You don't hate me for what I must do?"

She shook her head. "Believe me, there is not a speck of anything but love in me for you and your sisters. Never doubt that, Mary Ruth."

"I hope Dat will allow me to visit sometimes, see the new baby, too. I'm not under the Bann, for pity's sake." Mary Ruth was sitting on the side of the bed where, till now, she'd always slept.

"That, you're not." Ida felt all in now, wondering whether or not to say what she wanted to. And then she did, surprising herself. "This should never have happened—you bein' sent away. Your father is of the old school, so to speak. And, well, s'posin' I am, too, 'cause I'm married to him. He's mighty determined not to let his opinions slip to the side—not 'bout higher education nor spending time with Mennonites, neither one."

They looked at each other, basking in the love only a mother and daughter can know. "So then, I'm bein' shunned by Dat alone?"

"Sad to say, but seems so. No reason for it, really . . . you aren't baptized yet."

Mary Ruth hung her head. "I can't put aside my hopes and dreams—and my newfound joy in the Lord Jesus." She began to share the arrangement she had with Dan and Dottie Nolt. "They want to help me with my studies; then next semester—beginning in January—I'll start school at Paradise High School."

"These plans of yours, they've been simmerin' inside ya for ever so long." Ida knew this was true. Oh, the light of adventure filled every part of her talkative girl.

"I'm ever so happy in one way . . . and awful sad in another."

"Jah, I 'spect so, but there's nothin' to be done 'bout it, now, is there?" she said, feeling the tightness in her stomach again.

" 'Tis awful nice that I live within walkin' distance of you and Dat." Mary Ruth's pretty blue eyes glistened and filled with tears once more. "I can only hope and pray Dat will see the light of God's Word, that he'll understand I must follow the Lord's call. Honestly, Mamma, I've found such *life* at my new church. And, oh, the preaching! I hesitate to say the things I feel . . . that I know without a scrap of doubt. I wish you could know this same peace and joy—this overflowing love for everyone round me."

A tight throat kept her from acknowledging that she, too, fully understood and had long embraced this sacred hope—had opened her heart wide to it long ago, though out of necessity keeping it secret.

At last she found her voice. "I have prayed this might come to you, dear one. For all my children, really. And now I see that it has. Oh, Mary Ruth!"

Mary Ruth's eyes, bright with tears, lit up again. "Then, are you sayin' you walk and talk with the Lord just as I do?"

Ida was eager to say she, too, was a believer and in every sense of the word saved—set free from her sins. Openly she told Mary Ruth these things, sharing her belief that people can "stand up and be counted for the Lord" no matter where they find themselves. "Yet just 'cause I've opened my heart to God's truth and attempt to live it out day by day, I don't feel I must leave the community of the People behind. I want to be a shining light right here in Gobbler's Knob."

"Oh, Mamma, you're a beacon! You surely are." Mary Ruth gripped her hand and rose when Ida did.

"'Tis best to pray and not boast of this salvation, just as I do not. The Lord sees your yielded heart and mine. That's what matters most."

Mary Ruth nodded. "Does Dat know of this?"

"Your father is content with the Old Ways." That's all Ida had best be saying. She would not share everything she and Abram had discussed through the years; some of it would no doubt be as troubling to Mary Ruth as it was to her. It was pointless to reveal too much, lest she discourage her daughter's boundless joy, profoundly registered on her lovely face.

Hannah didn't like the thought of winter setting in here before too long; the cold and bleak season had always reminded her of her own mortality. She found herself wondering what it had felt like for Elias to die so suddenly out on the road. Had he endured excruciating pain? Was that the thing that killed a person . . . took a soul from this world to the next?

As for winter, the season was good only for missing the smell of air-dried clothes on the wash line, the sun beating down on her back as she tended the roadside stand, the sound of birds—the same songbirds Mamma loved. But the worst of it was Mary Ruth leaving home in the month of Christmas, of all sad things. And just as Mamma was close to her delivery date, leaving only Hannah and Leah to help with Lydiann and soon another baby sister or brother. Not much for tending to children, Hannah supposed she best get used to holding babies, what with Ezra Stoltzfus having dropped some strong hints about getting married sometime next year. Here lately, though, she didn't know for sure where he stood on the matter . . . or where *she* did. He hadn't gone to the singing last night, hadn't let her know he wouldn't be there, either, and he hadn't contacted her to go riding with him next Saturday after dark. Most likely he was still taken up with mourning the loss of his brother. Understandably so.

Still, something in the back of her mind wondered her about Ezra. He might need a lot more time to get back on his feet. She would wait till he felt more sociable again. But that wasn't her biggest worry.

She was far more concerned over her twin's peculiar comments about their visit to the meetinghouse last week. Seemed mighty odd to hear Mary Ruth go on so about the Scripture readings. In the deep of Hannah's heart, she feared she and her sister might lose the closeness they'd always had growing up. Mary Ruth's passionate interest in "salvation through grace," as she put it, was the worst of it.

Curling her toes, she flinched at the thought. She ought not to have gone, for had she refused, Mary Ruth might never have gone herself. But she had succumbed to her twin's persuasion—Mary Ruth ever so good at pleading, making things seem urgent and all. Hannah wished she'd stood her ground and stayed home. Of course, riding along to Quarryville meant she was on hand to assist Mary Ruth in case there was trouble with the carriage or the horse. Other than that, she had not enjoyed her experience at the strange gathering and had even felt guilty for being there. Her first, and hopefully last, breach of the Ordnung. Yet according to Mary Ruth, Dat had not put his foot down about their going. He'd even given a halfhearted blessing, though not knowing precisely where they were headed.

Quickly she set the table while a kettle of oyster stew simmered on the cook stove. She couldn't help but wonder how much longer Mamma would insist on leaving an empty spot where Sadie had always sat at the table, as if for someone deceased. Mary Ruth's place was empty, too, and not to be filled by another family member. The family had shrunk down to near nothing—the pain of it especially evident in Mamma's eyes at mealtime. Wouldn't be long and Leah's place would also be vacant, once she married Smithy Gid, which she surely would do. Made no sense to be a maidel if a nice boy like Gideon Peachey was asking.

When Mary Ruth returned to her new home away from home, she felt nearly wrung out with the effort she'd put forth to steal in and out of the Ebersol Cottage. She could imagine the fury in Dat if ever she was caught visiting Mamma or her sisters—Aunt Lizzie, too.

For now she could put that worry behind her. She found Dottie in the kitchen peeling yellow delicious apples for drying. Not eager to expend additional energy telling of her visit with Mamma, she asked if Carl was awake from his nap.

"If he isn't, he oughta be," Dottie said, her hair tied back in a ponytail that made her look younger than her years. "Why don't you go and wake him, if you'd like."

Mary Ruth agreed. "I'll check and see if he's stirring. If he's awake, I'll keep him company for a bit."

Dottie nodded her consent. "He'll be glad to see you. I think he's becoming very attached."

He'll mistakenly think I'm his big sister before too long, she thought, wondering if that was such a good thing, being that she didn't know how long she would be living here.

In Carl's nursery, she tiptoed to the pint-sized bed and was delighted to see the beautiful boy lying very still but smiling up at her with shining eyes. "Well, hullo, sweetie," she said, standing over him. "Do you want to play with Aunt Mary

Ruth?" She smiled at the name she'd just assigned to herself.

"Ma-ry," he said, sitting up.

"That's right." She helped him escape from under the tucked-in sheet and blanket.

Together, they found the box of blocks and began to pile them up in a tower, only for Carl to take absolute glee in knocking them down with a swift sweep of his small hand.

Later she took him downstairs to Dottie, and while Carl sat in his high chair and fed himself pieces of orange and banana, Dottie began to tell of the "miracle that occurred when Dr. Henry Schwartz called with news of a baby boy."

Mary Ruth listened with eagerness, thankful for the obvious hand of the sovereign Lord on the Nolts' home, especially because they had longed for a child for a good long time before Dr. Schwartz's phone call had come. "God knows our hearts' cry—our deepest desires" was all Mary Ruth was able to express for the lump in her throat.

Intuitively Gid recognized there was something downright gritty about early December that made him contemplate the future and prospects for having a family of his own. Fields had already turned brown and the mouth-watering apples had been picked—a few rotten ones languished on the ground, and red fox, scavengers at twilight, came searching them out, devouring them in quick *chomps*. Farmers were twiddling their thumbs following the corn harvest, looking ahead to the first farm sale of the season and finding excuses to gather in the barnyard, smoking pipe tobacco and chewing the fat, watching teenage boys play cornerball while waiting to bid on a piece of farm equipment. Such happenings turned Gid's thoughts to hearth and home, helped along by the scent of cinnamon pervading the kitchen as spicy pumpkin pies appeared supper after supper on the family table.

Perhaps it was the nearness of Christmas that got him thinking, as well. Complete with the annual program at the one-room school, as well as the feast day, the Lord's birthday was the most celebrated of all the holidays among the People, no doubt because it centered around kith and kin. Second Christmas, observed January 6—known as Epiphany by some—was also a time for families to gather and eat and play games indoors and out. Seemed to him every young man *his* age had already married and was expecting a baby come next summer. Even Adah had settled down and married Leah's cousin Sam in the past few weeks. Dorcas, his younger sister, would follow in Adah's footsteps in another year or so, most likely.

As it was, Gid would have to go through another long and cold winter without a mate to warm him, since the wedding season was all but past. If Leah would have him, they would wait till next autumn to marry.

These were a few of the reasons he felt urged to ask Leah to be his wife while they rode together in his open carriage on a courting Saturday night. A wistful winter night of nights, chilly enough for a woolen lap robe and his protective arm around his dear girl.

What with all Smithy Gid's talk of plans to help his uncle butcher hogs next week, Leah hardly felt much in a romantic mood, yet she listened intently as he talked of sharpening knives and scouring the enormous iron kettle.

"There'll be plenty of youngsters there," he told her, "takin' turns working the sausage grinder, ya know."

She knew all right from her own childhood days. Several times Dat had allowed both her and Sadie to miss school for a butchering day, saying the event was "mighty educational," so she'd had ample experience in just what butchering a hog entailed. Everything from heating the water to scalding in the black kettle situated in the washhouse, to hanging the carcasses up and, later on, squaring the middlings and trimming the hams and shoulders. Sadie had always said the stench was awful, and she didn't see why she had to watch when she much preferred to stay home with Mamma and cook or clean or sew.

For Leah, the whole process was intriguing; she especially liked watching the men hoist up the large hams and shoulders, hanging them from the smokehouse crossbeams till they were completely cured and flavorful. Sometimes she'd chase after the younger girls, who collected the silken pigs' ears, and she giggled as the little boys took the tails for souvenirs of the day, pretending to fasten them to one Dawdi or another. Naturally for the women there was the fun of visiting and planning the next work frolic, while men talked of divvying up the meat, daydreaming, no doubt, about the tender sausages, tasty fried bacon, and home-cured baked-ham dinners their wives were sure to prepare.

Sadie said the best part was knowing the rendered lard

would make for yummy doughnuts. Thinking of that, just now, helped put Leah in a sweeter mood as Gid slowed the horse's gait.

"I've been thinkin' an awful lot." His tone was gentle as could be. "What would ya say 'bout becomin' my wife . . . come next year?"

She'd honestly wondered if Gid might ask her tonight, but she hadn't expected the important question to come on the heels of the hog-butchering talk. "We *have* been seein' a lot of each other lately," she said.

He paused before continuing. "If you agree, we could marry in late October next year. Be one of the first couples to marry during the wedding season."

She was glad to be snug and warm under the lap robe, her hands hidden from Gid's touch. That way his words and his eyes did the talking, and his fingers couldn't cloud her thinking, putting pressure on her to say jah.

"Would it be all right if we pray privately 'bout this? Ask almighty God to bless our union?"

He nodded, seemingly taken back a bit by the unexpected reply. "No need to hurry up with your answer," he was kind enough to say—kind as he always had been for as long as she'd known him.

It wasn't that she thought she needed time to consider Gid as her husband-to-be, her betrothed. She honestly couldn't stop thinking about recent talks with Mamma, who seemed to want to speak to the Lord about most everything. *So why not pray about her response to a possible mate?*

She assumed it best if she not say what was going through her mind. Clearly Gid was eager to move on now, discuss something else. She hoped he wasn't miffed. It was just that most couples who'd spent time courting this long would probably go walking in the woods somewhere, hand in hand, watch the moon from a high vantage point, then talk of their wedding day. She had no idea what she and Gid would talk about for the rest of the evening, now that she hadn't answered with a quick reply to his heartfelt question.

Settling back, she breathed in the fresh and crisp night air, glad Gid had simply begun to play his harmonica, sweet and low, surprising her with his unruffled repose. One tune after another, he played, seeming to her as a kind of loving serenade to a nervous sweetheart.

As he played, she thought back to all the years of his unwarranted faithfulness to her, years of uncertainty. Yet he'd responded with sheer loyalty, patiently waiting for her, and now he was asking her to be his wife, the mother of his children, making it possible for her to do that thing she was called to be and do. What Amish girl would refuse such a true and sincere gesture? Gid loved her immeasurably; she knew that beyond doubt.

A stir of affection for him welled up in her. When he stopped playing his cheerful tune, he clicked his cheek to send a signal to the horse to speed to a trot, and she brought her hand out into the cold air and touched his arm. "Gid, I don't need more time to think on your question."

He waited without speaking, eyes fixed on her.

"I would be ever so glad to be your wife." At that very moment she truly cherished her own words.

Chapter Seventeen

If any former blemishes had been evident on the rolling front yard and surrounding landscape of her father's house prior to the thick blanket of snow, the present winter scene was so breathtakingly perfect that Leah found herself staring at the Ebersol Cottage as she made the turn into the lane leading to the barnyard and back door.

She had stolen away in the predawn hour of Christmas Eve day to Grasshopper Level, choosing the faster of Dat's two driving horses. At the Masts' orchard house, she dropped off a basket of goodies and fruit for little Jeremiah and the twins. Once there she got out of the carriage and made her way through the ice and snow to the back stoop, depositing the bright basket with its red ribbon on the top step.

Only Aunt Lizzie was aware of her "splendid idea," as she'd put it, to spread cheer to relatives who'd shunned them for much too long. Not even Mamma knew of the furtive trip, and Leah hoped to keep it that way. Together, she and Lizzie had made a big batch of peanut-butter balls dipped in melted chocolate, several dozen sand tarts, candied dates, and crystal stick candy at Lizzie's house yesterday. They'd had a laughing good time doing so. The best part of all was there were still plenty of sweets to go around, even having shared a considerable portion with Cousin Peter and Fannie's family.

Dat would more than likely devour a half dozen or more himself before the weekend was over. Unhitching the horse and buggy in the barnyard, she was glad to bring such happiness to his heart with the surprise. This, along with the fact she'd purposely let slip her intention to marry his choice of a mate, come next year.

Their neighbors down the road, including the Schwartzes and Nolts, had already taken axes to the dense woods and found attractive trees to chop down and set in a prominent place in their houses. Tonight, following Christmas Eve supper, most English families would carefully decorate fir or spruce with strung popcorn, colorful glass balls, bubbling lights, and tinsel strands.

The Ordnung did not allow for a tree to become an idol in the way of the Englishers. Instead, the People would happily celebrate the birthday of the Son of God tomorrow by attending Preaching service and sharing a common meal. Since Christmas fell on Sunday this year, much visiting would go on throughout the week. Folk would look into the faces of dear family members and friends, enjoying their precious nearness while sharing feasts at noon on Christmas Eve Saturday and sitting around the wood stove afterward to tell stories and recite poetry, giving and partaking of homemade candy, cookies, and other sweets. Dat would also read aloud certain passages from the Good Book to all who gathered there. Others would wait till Monday to celebrate, being Sunday was church.

Leah *had* seen the Nolts' tree twinkling from their front windows in the two-story clapboard house where Mary Ruth now lived and worked. They must have been eager to put it up and decorate before Christmas Eve this year, maybe because Mary Ruth was living there, and, too, because young Carl would enjoy all the merriment.

As for the Schwartz family, Leah had observed the enormous tree the doctor and his two sons dragged from the forest across the street just yesterday, when she dusted the furniture and washed the floors for Lorraine. She was certainly glad not to have been formally introduced to the younger Schwartz boy, Derry, whom Sadie had said such horrid things about—though Leah might have *had* to meet him if she'd stayed much longer at the Schwartz abode. Fact was, Leah had purposely finished up her duties in a jiffy, having clearly recognized Derry as she watched the threesome tugging on the nine-foot tree from the dining-room window, hoping against hope to avoid either shaking his hand or looking him in the eye.

Miraculously she had. She'd called rather softly, "Happy Christmas," over her shoulder to Lorraine, not wanting to draw a smidgen of attention to herself, then hurried out the door. Too nervous to look back, she found herself rushing down Georgetown Road, heart in her throat. She was most afraid she might not be able to temper what things came flying out of her mouth if she encountered Sadie's former beau.

Thank goodness she's nowhere near Gobbler's Knob, Leah thought, awful anxious for Dat's farmhouse to come into view.

But now, as she slipped into Mamma's toasty-warm

kitchen, she spotted the pretty presents wrapped and waiting on the sideboard for the family to gather on the day after Christmas, when they planned to celebrate with the Peacheys. After the Monday meal, following Aunt Lizzie's desserts of nut loaf, apple pie, and hot-water sponge cake, they would exchange simple gifts, fewer than any other year before. Mary Ruth's absence would add to the pain of Sadie being gone yet another blessed Christmas. But Mamma, great with child, was the next best blessing of all. Leah could scarcely wait to hold the newborn babe, coming so close to the Lord's own birthday.

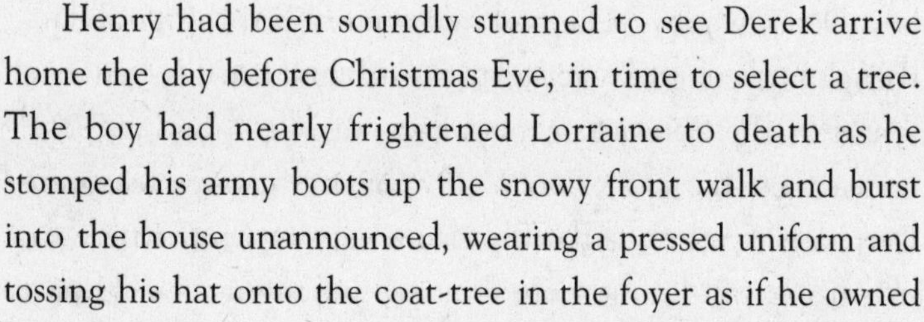

Henry had been soundly stunned to see Derek arrive home the day before Christmas Eve, in time to select a tree. The boy had nearly frightened Lorraine to death as he stomped his army boots up the snowy front walk and burst into the house unannounced, wearing a pressed uniform and tossing his hat onto the coat-tree in the foyer as if he owned the place.

For months, Henry had written letters requesting, nearly pleading, for Derek to return home for the holidays. *Your presence would cheer your mother greatly*, he had penned in his most recent note. It appeared his persuasive efforts had paid off famously; their wayward son was seated at his mother's Christmas table of lace and fine china as Henry said a traditional grace, offering thanks for the bounty with which they had been blessed this year.

When Henry raised his head, he noticed Derek had neither closed his eyes nor bowed his head, and his hand held the fork, poised to dig in.

Has he learned nothing from his time in the military? Henry wondered. For a moment he wished he might have saved his time, ink, and stationery. But as the day wore on, things seemed to lighten up and Henry had a change of heart *and* mind, especially as he observed Lorraine smiling and even laughing from time to time, less in her hostess mode than usual and more relaxed overall. In fact, Henry observed, the day almost seemed as pleasant as many Christmases before it—this as they sat together exchanging gifts in the shadow of the fine Christmas tree ablaze with lights. From the radio, Bing Crosby crooned "Here Comes Santa Claus," backed up by the Andrews Sisters.

After gifts were opened and bows and wrapping paper lay scattered on the floor, Lorraine spoke softly, saying she wished to share a short reading. "From the New Testament . . . Luke's account of the birth of my Lord and Savior."

Henry happened to catch Derek's dismayed look. The boy stood abruptly and, without excusing himself, left the room. Heavy footsteps were heard echoing from the hall, and when the back door slammed, Lorraine jumped.

Robert pulled out a pocket Testament from his sports coat. "Here, Mother," he said. "Don't worry over Derek . . . I have an idea the Lord is at work where his heart's concerned."

More ill at ease than he had been in some years, Henry braced himself for the Scripture verses Lorraine appeared determined to share.

Until this moment, Mary Ruth wouldn't have admitted to missing her parents and sisters dreadfully during the past weeks, but she felt an overwhelming sadness as she helped redd up the kitchen for Dottie. She felt sluggish this Christmas Day, slow to gather up scraps of wrapping paper and odds and ends of boxes from the front room. "I'd be happy to take the trash out," she called to Dottie, who was putting Carl down for his afternoon nap.

Meanwhile, Dan was out back gathering up dry cut wood from the timber box to add to the embers in the front room fireplace as Mary Ruth headed for the front door. Scarcely had she tossed the rubbish and closed the top on the trash receptacle than she heard a pounding of feet on the road. Looking up, she noticed a dark-headed young man running in a military uniform of some sort, though she couldn't be sure, as she'd never before seen a soldier.

She wouldn't have stood there watching, but the young man's angry movements caught her attention—the fierce way he swung his arms as he ran, as if ready for a fighting match.

Mary Ruth felt so curious beholding this peculiar sight, she didn't catch the sneeze that crept up on her, calling attention to *her,* and for that she was perturbed.

Immediately the stranger halted in his tracks, his dark, dark eyes inching together as he frowned hard. When he spoke, she instinctively stepped back. "Hey . . . I know you, don't I?" The frown faded and a smile took its place. "Aren't you Sadie's little sister?"

At once she was no longer startled, because she recognized him as the boy who'd stopped by the vegetable and fruit stand years back; this same fancy fellow with the handsome features had handed her a letter for Sadie on that day. Just why was he carrying on like a madman out there on the road, and on Christmas Day yet?

"Jah, I'm Mary Ruth." She took a step forward to show her confidence. "And who are you?"

He blinked his eyes, holding her gaze. "An old friend of Sadie's."

She shook her head. "If you say your name, I might just recognize it."

"Name's not important. Truth is, I'm home for the holidays—a wounded soldier." Here he leaned down and began to roll up his left pant leg. "Let me show you—"

"No, no, I believe you." She noticed his short hair cut on the side above his ears, beneath his uniform-style hat, so what he'd said was probably true. "Sorry you got yourself hurt."

"Maybe you could help me . . . so I won't have to go all the way down the road to visit Sadie, after all." He pushed his trouser leg back down where it belonged and leaned hard on the other good leg, his right hand on his hip now.

"Just what did you have in mind?" She stood her ground, no longer frightened by him, though she still wondered what business he had with Sadie.

"I've been thinking . . . wondering how she's doing. That's all. Is she well?"

His question sounded strange. *How would I know?* "My sister's not ill, far as I know." The words popped right off her tongue. Besides, if Sadie were still living here in Gobbler's Knob, what would she want with a fancy Englisher . . . and on Christmas?

"Well, I haven't seen her in a while. Thought I might

catch her outdoors milking cows, maybe . . . present myself to her as a sort of surprise."

She sighed. "Oh, well, if it's my sister you're after, you best be savin' your steps, 'cause she's married out in Ohio."

He ran his hand straight down the middle of his hat, smiling at her in a way that suddenly made her feel uncomfortable. "Isn't that a pity. She was the prettiest Amish girl I ever laid eyes on." Then, stepping back, he added, "But now that I'm here talking to you, I think you've got my Sadie beat all to pieces."

My Sadie . . .

Something sprang up in her that instant, and she felt she best return to the house. "I oughta be goin' now." She turned to leave.

But he followed on her heels. "Wait! No need to be afraid. Don't you know who I am, Mary Ruth?"

She stopped walking and turned around and looked him over. Now that she was beginning to put two and two together, this was probably the boy who'd put her big sister in the family way—the young father of Sadie's dead baby.

He limped toward her a bit. "You mean to say she never told you about me?"

Her mind leaped to a final conclusion. "So . . . you must be. . . ?"

"That's right. I'm the old man, and I mean to lay eyes on my son or daughter." He breathed in and rubbed his knuckles against his chest, displaying a sickening conceit. "Boy or girl, which is it?"

Silently she prayed; she felt she needed God's help lest this man standing before her begin to thrash his arms yet again, directing his anger toward her. And, come to think of it, his limping was downright deceitful, because she had seen him *running* to beat the band before she'd ever let out her sneeze. "I take it . . . you must not know what happened. Oh, it's awful sad, really."

"Well . . . *what?*"

Filling her lungs with air, she told him. "Sadie's baby died 'fore it ever had a chance to live."

"Stillborn, you say?" To this he appeared rather stunned, but gradually his surprise turned to obvious relief. Without so much as a good-bye, he walked away, leaving Mary Ruth standing there.

Ach, what a wretched soul! How on earth did Sadie ever fall in love with such a boy? she wondered. She could not comprehend in the slightest. Encountering him as she had, she hoped and prayed the Lord had heard her sister's cries of repentance. Surely by now dear Sadie had called out to God for help and forgiveness. *Dear Lord Jesus, please be near and dear to my Ohio sister this day*, Mary Ruth prayed.

Chapter Eighteen

The day following Christmas, Leah insisted on Mamma resting after the big noon meal. Even though their close neighbors, the Peacheys, along with Adah and husband Sam, had come to share the feast, Mamma excused herself at Leah's urging and went to lie down.

Leah followed her to the upstairs bedroom, watching as she sat on the bed. "Here, let me help you," Leah said, getting a blanket out of the chest at the foot of the bed. "Are ya in need of more warmth?"

"No, no . . . I'm just fine now, denki." Mamma leaned back and sighed, closing her eyes. "Will ya see to our guests while I nap?"

Leah nodded. "Of course. You have nothin' to worry 'bout." She leaned down and kissed Mamma's cheek, then quietly slipped out the door.

Downstairs, she found Miriam and Aunt Lizzie playing a game of checkers while Dat, Smithy, and Sam sat around the wood stove, rocking slowly and talking low. Adah was playing peekaboo with Lydiann, and Hannah and Dorcas were visiting quietly in the corner of the kitchen.

Meanwhile, Gid sat on the floor near the wood stove, reading *The Budget*, pausing to chuckle every so often at one humorous story or another. "Listen to this." He held up the paper, and Dat and Gid's father both leaned in to hear better. "Some folk over in New Holland had a letter the other day sayin' they were gonna be getting a buggy full of company for supper, but it says right here they don't have any idea who it'll be." Gid looked up, a grin on his face. "So they're lookin' forward to seein' just who's coming . . . and wonderin' if their guess is correct."

"That *is* funny," Dat agreed.

Smithy Peachey nodded, rocking harder now. "Seems to me whoever wrote oughta have had the courtesy to say who they was!"

"You'd think so, ain't?" Dat glanced at Leah, a quick frown on his brow. He motioned for her to come over, and Leah was glad to tell him Mamma was resting.

"She's all right now. Don't worry."

She went and sat on the floor on a round braided rug next to Gid as he read silently from the Sugarcreek, Ohio, newspaper. After a time he whispered, "Here, Leah, read this." He pointed to a report from Lititz.

I went downtown and got myself a nice haircut last Tuesday, the Amish scribe had written. *That afternoon Barbara Zimmerman and myself answered jah to several questions asked us by our old bishop. Then, quick as a wink, he changed Barbara's name from Zimmerman to Wert. I'm awful glad she said yes, and she's ever so glad I got me a haircut!*

Leah couldn't help but think next year around this time

her name would be Leah Peachey. When she glanced at Gid, he smiled and winked at her. Leah's cheeks flushed and her heart did a little flip-flop, and she wondered if he might give her his Christmas gift outside. Gid was pretty good at thinking of reasons to take her outdoors today. Still, Dat was the only one who knew anything of their engagement, except maybe the smithy and Adah. Neither Mamma nor Hannah suspected anything, she didn't think, though she could be wrong.

Aunt Lizzie looked her way and Leah ducked her head, hiding behind *The Budget*, hoping Lizzie wouldn't see what was probably written all over her face. Truth was, Leah was awfully fond of Gid and was enjoying herself this sweet Christmastide.

"Best be headin' out for milkin'," Gid said just loud enough for the two fathers' benefit.

That was Leah's cue to get up and go along with him. After all, there was no need for Dat to leave his best friend and nephew, nor the warmth of Mamma's kitchen, anytime soon. This, then, was her gift to her father . . . so Gid could present *his* to her.

After Mamma's long nap and once Leah and Gid had finished the milking, they all sat down again for a light supper of leftovers. Mamma kept her hand on the meat platter, ready to dish up well before anyone might request seconds. That was Mamma, Leah thought, always eager to serve her family and others.

The meal over, Aunt Lizzie, Hannah, and Dorcas cleared off the table while Mamma and Miriam settled into chairs near the wood stove and Sam and Adah bundled up and went out for a walk, like newlyweds so often do.

Dat and Smithy headed outside to get the toboggans out of the barn and ready for some snow fun. Gid and his sister Dorcas and Leah and Hannah carried the sleds back behind the barn, to the banked bridge connecting the lower level to the upper. Gid and Dorcas were the first to go flying down the slope amidst squeals of delight from the girls.

With Leah at the helm, Leah and Hannah piled on the second toboggan, and they had themselves a turn. In nothing flat, Gid got the idea to race the sleds down the hill. They did that three times, with Gid and his sister winning each run.

"Ach, it ain't fair. You've got more weight with Gid on." Leah pointed out the reason.

"Jah, that's why," Dorcas said, smiling at Leah.

"Try it with Gid alone," Hannah suggested, "and the three of us girls."

"If all of us can even fit on one," Leah said, laughing.

In the end, the girls beat Gid soundly. And when a stiff wind blew up out of the north, Dorcas and Hannah said they were cold and headed for the house, leaving Gid and Leah alone once again.

"I wanted to tell you, Leah . . . you've made this the best Christmas for me." He leaned down and kissed her cheek.

She reached up and hugged his neck, but he didn't let her go quickly; he held her close, his rough cheek against her cold face. "Next year we'll be husband and wife," he said. "Lord willin'."

"A blessed Christmas to you, Gid," she replied, happy to be nestled in his strong arms, grateful for his present—a pretty wall hanging of a special calendar that could be used over and over, the days marked in with a calligraphy pen. She could hardly wait to start filling it in.

"Once we're published at the Preaching service next year, I'll show you the pine chest I plan to make for you—an engagement gift soon to come."

She was overjoyed. What a happy day of days!

◆

Gentle snowflakes fell as Leah took Hannah along to deliver the birthday quilt to Elias's mother after supper. She had been hoping for this chance to take the one-horse sleigh down the snow-packed road, to get all bundled up again in earmuffs and mittens, hot bricks at her feet.

Hannah was more talkative tonight than usual, perhaps because she missed Mary Ruth something fierce.

They stopped in at the Stoltzfus family's, staying longer than planned because the deacon's wife wanted to warm them up with hot chocolate topped with whipped cream, also offering a plateful of oatmeal-raisin cookies for them to nibble during the ride home. "Share the rest with your whole family," she insisted.

There are fewer of us Ebersols all the time, Leah thought while standing with her back to the wood stove, sipping cocoa. She glanced at Hannah, noting her sister seemed rather aloof, her face too pale. Soon enough Leah understood as she spotted Ezra . . . his back to them at the kitchen table.

He never even turned round when we came in, she thought, suspecting something was terribly wrong between him and Hannah. But she said nothing, waiting for Hannah to mention his peculiar behavior later on the ride home—if at all.

"I have an idea," Leah said now, hurrying the horse just a bit. "Let's stop by and wish Mary Ruth a happy Christmas. What would ya say to that?"

"Oh, sister, could we?" Hannah's eyes glistened in the moonlight.

"We can . . . and we will!"

She wanted Hannah to end the day happily, and seeing Mary Ruth was sure to put a smile on her face. Besides, Leah was lonesome for Mary Ruth . . . as was Mamma—possibly the reason their mother had looked so gray around the eyes and all washed out earlier. If only Dat had been more patient, even merciful toward Mary Ruth, Christmas could have been far less somber this year. Mamma would've had her spirits up, for sure and for certain.

With this in mind, Leah strained to see the bend in the road and the corner lot where the Nolts lived . . . where Mary Ruth now resided, a boarder to Englishers, of all things.

Hannah choked back sad tears, downright grateful to be with Leah tonight, though the evening was freezing to the bones. She'd actually thought she might become ill back there in Ezra's mamma's kitchen.

Ezra. What on earth had made him change so? His brother's death—could it be? Was he so angry at God he was taking his rage out on her?

She had no idea what to think. Ezra was downright

standoffish and hadn't been showing his face at recent singings. Was he staying away to avoid seeing her? She hoped not. For her, it was hardly worth going to the barn singings anymore—a waste of time to ask Lizzie to take her and drop her off. There was only one reason to go at all: in hopes of being asked to ride home with Ezra in his courting buggy.

Deliberately Hannah turned her attention to seeing Mary Ruth again, though she also felt a bit distanced herself when it came to her twin. It wondered her, as she and Leah rode in the sleigh, what Leah might make—if she knew—of the things spoken about at the Quarryville church that had added fuel to the fire for Mary Ruth. Her recent switch to the Mennonites, along with her renewed determination to get an English education, had set things off the beam between Dat and her twin.

Sighing, Hannah felt her breath literally freeze in midair. To think their father would send Mary Ruth away because of her stubbornness—and during rumschpringe, no less, when Amish parents typically let their youth run free, if not wild. It made not a bit of sense. *Has to be more than that,* thought Hannah. *Dat's ire is up about Mary Ruth going to high school!*

She settled against the buggy seat, reflecting on this day—the love and the laughter of the earlier time with family and the Peacheys—wishing she had brought along the embroidered pillowcases she'd sewn for Mary Ruth. She felt strangely empty, like a tall glass half full.

The lights from a Christmas tree brightened the window at the Nolts' house as the horse pulled the sleigh into their driveway. "Ach, is it such a gut idea to stop so late like this?" she asked Leah.

"Mary Ruth's bound to be homesick tonight," Leah answered. "C'mon, a visit will do us all good." She paused. "But we best not tell 'bout the fun we had tobogganing with Peacheys, jah?"

Hannah nodded. She struggled with guilt at having spoken out so boldly to Mary Ruth after going with her to Quarryville that single night. "I wouldn't think of adding more sadness to her," she mumbled as they picked their way over the snow and ice to the back door. *Not one little bit.*

Hannah embraced Mary Ruth in the entryway of the Nolts' fine house. "Oh, how I miss you, sister!" she whispered.

"I miss *you*," Mary Ruth said, clinging to her.

Leah wrapped her arms around both twins, and the three of them stood hugging and weeping.

After a time Mary Ruth showed them into the front room, where the tree stood alight with shimmering tinsel strands and tall bubbling lights. They spoke softly to each other, Mary Ruth doing most of the talking, as usual. "How's Mamma feeling?" she asked.

"She had to rest awhile following the noon meal," Leah offered, "but she was back up again before supper and had herself a right nice time." Then Leah began to share the news of Naomi and Luke Bontrager's baby boy, born six days ago.

Mary Ruth asked, "I wonder who could get word about Naomi's first baby to our sister?" Leah knew she meant Sadie but had politely refrained from mentioning the forbidden name. After some discussion, none of them felt the urgency to force the issue.

There was an awkward pause, and then Hannah spoke up, "The smithy's whole family came to our house today." She seemed eager to change the subject. "Adah and Sam sure are an awful cute couple."

Leah nodded, eyes fixed on the sparkling tree while Mary Ruth sat with her hands folded against the black of her mourning dress and apron.

Hannah recalled Adah and Sam's wedding, where Leah and Dorcas had stood up as bridesmaids, along with Adah's same-age cousin, Rachel Peachey. What a joyful day it had been. Leah herself had been absolutely radiant—almost like a bride.

Suddenly Hannah felt sorry all over again for Mary Ruth, having lost her beau to death. *I shouldn't have mentioned Adah and Sam*, she thought, chagrined.

Quickly Hannah said, "If I'd known we were goin' to stop by here, I would've brought the present I made for you. Aw, that's too bad."

Leah shook her head, her hazel eyes shimmering with tears. "The idea to surprise you popped in my head on our way back from taking the birthday quilt to Deacon Stoltzfus's wife."

"Oh jah . . . and how nice of you," Mary Ruth said, filling in as both Hannah and Leah brushed tears away. "S'pose Mrs. Stoltzfus was awful glad to have it."

"She was," Leah spoke up. "I hope it brought some cheer to the house, 'cause it was awful hard seeing them . . . all of them lookin' so forlorn."

"How did Ezra seem to you?" asked Mary Ruth.

The reference to his name sliced through Hannah's heart. "He ain't himself a'tall," she managed to say.

"Well, and no wonder," Mary Ruth said softly. "I ran into his older brother Leroy the other day at Central Market in downtown Lancaster. He told me how worried he was . . . that Ezra's not so sure anymore 'bout staying Amish. Feels the Lord God took away his best brother."

They were silent for a time and then Leah said softly, "We'll pray Ezra changes his mind and doesn't get himself shunned."

Hannah stiffened at her sister's words but said nothing.

"He'll need time to grieve, of course." Mary Ruth reached for Hannah's hand. "I say you're right, Leah. We'll pray."

Standing up, Hannah went to the Christmas tree and stood before it, hoping not to hear further talk of her beau. Her eyes were dazzled by the brightness and vivid colors. "How can ya think of stayin' on here, sister?" she asked finally. "Livin' with Englishers 'n' all? Can't ya make things right with Dat and come on home?" Tonight would be the perfect timing for such a thing, she thought. "It's so near to Christmas, after all."

She was surprised to find Mary Ruth at her side just that quick. "Jah, but it's not in my heart to leave behind my new-found faith. It's the Lord's birthday we celebrate."

"You don't need to tell *us*." Leah joined them beside the tree.

"No, I 's'pose not. It's just that . . . I've opened my heart to the Lord Jesus and His ways. I feel brand-new inside, truly I do."

Leah was nodding her head, as if to say she agreed.

Somewhat startled, Hannah stared at the tree. "Seems to me you've embraced the beliefs of Englishers. You're goin' backward 'stead of forward in the faith of our Anabaptist forefathers."

"You're upset because I found mercy and grace at a Mennonite church, ain't so?" Mary Ruth asked. "And 'cause I'm living here with fancy folk, too. Isn't that your biggest worry, really?"

Hannah tried her best to share the things that troubled her deeply—possibly living forever apart from Mary Ruth—but her twin was closed up to the Old Ways, it surely seemed. Mary Ruth insisted she'd found a "precious *new* thing," and nothing Hannah could say made a bit of difference.

She and Leah trudged through the snow to the sleigh and horse. Hannah felt awful glum as they rode into the crisp and icy night, back to the Ebersol Cottage. Truth be told, she almost wished they'd gone straight home after the Stoltzfus visit.

Chapter Nineteen

Leah, come inside quick!" Aunt Lizzie called to her from the doorway.

Leah and Hannah hurried into the kitchen. "What is it?" Leah asked, fear gripping her. She and Hannah followed Lizzie upstairs.

"Is Mamma all right?" Hannah asked softly.

Leah tiptoed into her parents' bedroom, shocked to see Mamma thrashing about, crying out with her wrenching pains.

"This is like nothing she's ever experienced before," Lizzie told them in hushed tones, eyes wide with concern. "She's never uttered a single cry in childbirth . . . never!"

Dat sat off to the side of the room as was customary, though Leah noticed the agitation written on his face as he kept the newspaper raised high to shield his view.

Lizzie asked Hannah, who was still standing in the hall, to wait downstairs. "And, Leah, won't you go 'n' boil some water?"

"Jah," said Leah, her heart in her throat.

"Please close the door behind you," Lizzie said over her shoulder.

Mamma's in trouble! Leah rushed downstairs to put a kettle of water on the wood stove. Swiftly she headed back upstairs to stand at Mamma's bedside. Her heart broke as she watched Mamma struggle so. She wanted to do something to help—take Mamma's pulse, perhaps, while Dat counted the seconds steadily. *Jah, this one thing I can do!*

Tenderly she held her mother's weak arm, feeling the pulse . . . much too slow. Mamma's heartbeat was fading in strength even as Leah pressed her fingers against the white wrist.

"Hannah must ride immediately to get the midwife," Leah said, reliving the night Sadie had travailed with the birth of her dead son.

"No . . . no, it should be the *Hexedokder*," said Dat, still hiding behind his paper. "We daresn't take any chances."

Mamma tried to lift her head. "No, Abram, not . . ." Her voice trailed off.

"Ida does *not* want the powwow doctor settin' foot in this house," Lizzie insisted, clearly speaking on behalf of Mamma. "Better to call for Anna Mae Yoder, the midwife. She'll know what to do."

"Well, whoever Hannah gets, tell her to make it snappy!" demanded Dat, lowering his newspaper momentarily.

Reluctant to leave Mamma's side, Leah turned and fled the room yet again.

"What's happened . . . to my prayer . . . veiling?" Ida

asked, reaching her right hand up and finding her head bare as she lay in her bed. She felt utterly dismayed at this discovery, her long hair having come loose from its bun. Such prolonged labor . . . never ending it seemed. She tried hard to form the words, make them sound sensible, understandable, yet her lips would not cooperate. Ever so frustrating when she wanted to communicate this needful thing.

"My dear, your head covering's unnecessary just now," Abram said, his face close to hers. She smelled pipe tobacco on his breath, sweet and soothing, and she longed for him to hold her in his arms.

"I'm sinking, Abram. Oh, Lizzie . . . help me. I fear I'm a-fallin'."

"You're right here, dearest sister." It was Lizzie's voice, soft and gentle. "The midwife will be on her way soon. Press on, Ida. Don't give up."

"Find my . . . prayer veiling," she said again, yearning for it. She made an excruciating effort to open her eyes. "Please do this thing . . . I ask."

She was aware of Abram's hand on hers, the gentle dabbing of a damp towel at her forehead. "Ida . . . dear one," he said.

She fell into what seemed to be a deep sleep, suddenly free of stabbing pain. In her stupor, she felt the loving hands of either Lizzie or Leah placing her head covering atop her head, and then tying it tenderly beneath her chin.

"*Da Herr sei mit du* . . . the Lord be with you," said Lizzie and kissed her forehead.

A blissful warm nothingness overtook her, and she was helpless to resist.

Hannah felt she was nearly flying in the family sleigh, hurrying the mare as best she could. After dropping the midwife off at home, she turned right around and rode up the road to the Nolts' place. There she timidly knocked on the door, only to stand on the porch, waiting. In her dire need for a quick response, she remembered it was growing quite late and looked to see if the Christmas tree was still blazing merrily in the front window. She stepped to the side of the door and saw the front room was dark; not a light was on anywhere on the main level of the house that she could tell. Thinking she best hurry, she pressed the doorbell and stepped back, hearing the *ding-dong-ding* of the chime, feeling terribly intrusive and wishing there was a way to alert Mary Ruth without waking up the entire family.

As it turned out, Dan Nolt came to the door in his long bathrobe and slippers. She told him why she'd come at such an hour, apologizing. "Shall I call for Dr. Schwartz?" the man asked with concern in his eyes.

"The Amish midwife is with Mamma now" was all she said.

"Very well," he said. "But if you have any qualms at all . . . the doctor is just around the corner. It would be no trouble at all to summon him."

Hannah wasn't sure what to do; with both Aunt Lizzie and the midwife tending to Mamma, surely all would be well. "Denki, but no," she said shyly. It was terribly unnerving to be speaking about Mamma's care with the head of this English household, of all things!

Soon she found herself upstairs in the grand house, waiting for Mary Ruth in her fine-looking bedroom. Her twin quickly dressed around, anxiety in her eyes. And together the two of them hurried home.

"My friend and sister in the Lord."

Rousing herself, Ida recognized the dim voice as Annie Mae Yoder's. The midwife and her black bag were present at last—Annie Mae would help spare her life and her baby's, too.

Annie Mae examined her and immediately said she would attempt to reposition the baby. "It's breech," she said, placing gentle hands on Ida's abdomen, attempting to begin the forward roll, moving the baby up and out of the pelvic bones. She did this several times, but there was no change in the baby's position, she said.

"The child lies directly across the uterus," Annie told them.

"Horizontal?" Lizzie asked. "'Tis dangerous, ain't so?"

"Jah," said Annie Mae softly, "the shoulders will lead the way into the birth canal . . . if I can't reposition the baby."

"Well, keep tryin'," Abram insisted.

Annie said meekly, "I fear Ida bleeds too much for that."

Ida, in her haze, took Annie's words to mean real trouble. She'd heard of rare breech positions. But this. *Oh, my dear babe's life is in jeopardy. Father in heaven, help Annie Mae know what to do!*

The intense contractions began again. She held on to the twisted sheet, desperately wanting to control her cries but to no avail.

"My dear Ida, the baby and you . . . both are in an awful bad way," the older woman said when the birth pangs abated momentarily.

"Help my wife live," Abram said. "This I beg of you."

No . . . no, Abram . . . the baby's life is most important. Life for this our son.

But try as she might, she could not verbally express her urgent wish. She squeezed Abram's hand—the simple yet difficult squeeze of her fingers on his callused flesh.

"She understands you. Now, get on with it!" said her husband.

Ach, Abram, be ever so kind, she thought.

"Work with me, Ida. Help me deliver this child."

"Why not try turning the baby once more?" Lizzie was saying, ever near.

"Ida's hemorrhaging strongly" came the solemn answer. "I scarcely feel her pulse."

In a haze of confusion, Ida did her best to follow Annie's instructions, attempting to be stoic, as she'd always been in the past. In the far recesses of her mind, she strangely recalled that never before had she needed a speck of coaxing or help. Not even with the delivery of twins.

Such a dreadful pain exploded through her, wounding her, lingering longer than before. Deadly. It continued, shuddering its fury within her till she felt she might break asunder. O *Lord Jesus, I call upon your name.*

"Do something!" Abram commanded. "Spare my wife!"

Annie Mae made the offer of ether. "Just a sedative whiff."

"Denki . . . but no. I must hear . . . my baby's cries," Ida managed to say.

"Please let Annie help you, Mamma," Leah urged.

Ida could feel Annie Mae's breath on her cheek now, replacing Abram's. She was aware of the midwife's grip on her weak hand. She felt at once like a small girl again . . . she saw the four-sided Martin birdhouse in Hickory Hollow, where she'd grown up in her parents' big farmhouse . . . the white birdhouse shooting up tall from a yellow daisy-strewn meadow. Martins flew together in family units, going to warmer climes come autumn. Staying together . . .

She felt torn between this world and the next, weary of this pilgrim way, drawn—no, pulled ever so gently, even lovingly—and, oh, she longed to allow herself to simply let go. To fly away to Glory Land, that home of her Lord and Savior where her heart, her spirit, her very being craved to be.

But something held her fast. Her dear baby was on his way. His little body was hankering for life, for air to breathe. This wee boy would grow up without his mamma; she knew this in her bones. He was going to grow under the influence of Abram, to learn to plow and cultivate the soil. *The good earth . . . Oh, this son I am giving life to.*

An image of a pond glistened as a breeze made the sun's kisses sparkle on the surface. Then, away in the distance, a youthful figure came walking toward her.

Oh, Mamma . . . I see you. You're coming for me!

"My darling mother," Leah was saying.

But Ida was confused by her daughter's words, mixed up with her own mother's image near the radiant pond.

"Hang on, Ida," Abram said from the corner of the room.

A surge of energy she had not known in hours filled her completely. She raised her head, leaning on her elbows, and opened her eyes to see Leah and Lizzie on her right and Annie Mae on her left. Dear, dear gray-headed Annie. How many babies had she safely seen into this world?

"Lie back, sweet Ida. Rest now," Annie whispered.

Abram's newspaper closed quickly and she heard him rise from his chair. Once again he came to sit on the bed. His kisses were on her face, her lips, mingled with salty tears. "You stubborn woman," he said. "*Ich lieb dich* . . . still, I love ya so."

The midwife spoke again, encouraging her to birth the babe before giving in to the sinking end. "I'll help ya through this hard valley."

"Oh, Mamma . . . no!" Leah sobbed and the bed trembled.

Leah's tearstained face became less and less visible, but Ida continued to hear the dear girl's voice. Lizzie's, too, now and then. Somewhere along the way, she knew Abram must have slipped out into the hallway. Faintly she heard his voice along with Mary Ruth's and Hannah's, as the sounds drifted in and out of her consciousness.

I bless your name, Lord Jesus. . . .

The bewildering falling sensation came, plunging her down again. Yet she knew she must cling to the thread of life, not let it slip from her grasp until she heard the first birth cries.

My life is in your hands, Lord.

Soon they came. Loud and pitiless, her newborn baby heralded his arrival with a strong set of lungs.

"It's a boy, Ida! Praise be, as healthy as they come," announced Annie Mae.

Thank you, dear Lord. She longed to see her baby, to lay eyes on this miracle of life. Her and Abram's love . . . in the form of a tiny man-child. She looked but saw only blackness.

Then, suddenly, he lay in her arms, nestling against her, moving, searching . . .

"Mamma, can you hear me?" Leah pleaded. Precious girl . . . ever so concerned. Should she be on hand, attending the death of her mother?

Ida nodded, though weakening as the seconds sped by.

Oh, my motherless son . . .

"Don't struggle so, Ida," said Lizzie. "Rest now. Rest . . ."

Ida began to shake her head, back and forth slowly. *No . . . no!* The battle cry continued in her brain. *Someone must care for this baby and his sister Lydiann,* she longed to say but could not.

Hard as she might, she fought to live now, changing her mind. She must survive to care for her only son. She must live for him to suckle, bond, be nourished . . . and he did so as she lay there. Clawing at the walls of life—her happy sweet life—she gasped for her final breaths, her very lifeblood seeping away.

"I love you, Mamma," Leah said, lying down on the bed.

She felt the warmth of Leah's slender body and her loving arms slipping beneath her, cradling both her and the baby.

"I'm here . . . right here with you," Leah said quietly.

Ida could scarcely whisper, "Raise him as your own, Leah. Lydiann, too."

"Oh, Mamma . . . you needn't worry over that just now.

Beseech the Lord God to let you live instead."

Ida felt she might be left hanging in the balance between earth and heaven if she did not know what was to become of her little ones. "Promise me this thing?"

Leah paused; she was silent for too long. Then slowly she said, "I promise, jah . . . to look after Abe, and I'll care for Lydiann till she's grown, Mamma." Leah whispered the words, kissing her face repeatedly. "But only if need be."

Little Abe . . . Lydiann. You'll be greatly loved with Leah. Oh, be safe . . .

The power in the dying was too strong to oppose, yet she labored against it—an unmistakable desire kept her alive and living—till that "acceptable time."

Her baby nursed, making the familiar sucking sounds she cherished. *Stay alive*, she told herself. *Let little Abe have this important start.*

Annie Mae touched her wrist, checking her pulse again. She heard muffled words . . . fading fast away. "I'm so sorry, my sister and friend. May the Lord be with you."

Yet again Ida was keenly aware of her mother's voice . . . closer, it seemed, than before. She felt the cool touch of her mamma's gentle hand, guiding her along. She felt more than she could see, vividly aware of the cross, Jesus' sacrifice made on Calvary's hill for her sins, for all humanity . . . for the People lost in a web of rules and tradition. For her family, for young Lydiann, and now her only son . . . Abe.

Tears slipped down her cheeks, yet she was too weak to brush them away. Leah was seeing to that, darling girl. Lizzie's first and only child, here, caring for *her* in these fragile moments . . . connected to Ida as closely in death as Sadie had been in life. Leah, filling her elder sister's shoes. Beautiful Leah, inside and out.

Sadie . . . share your burdens with the Lord Jesus. She breathed the prayer.

The babe in her arms went limp, resting . . . full of life-giving sustenance . . . for now. He would sleep soundly, she knew.

Bless this child, Lord. Make him a blessing all of his days. . . .

"I'll help you go to Jesus, Mamma," Leah said, wet face against her own.

"Tell Mary Ruth I love her . . . that I wish . . ."

"Jah, Mamma, I will. And I'll tell Hannah, too."

"But M*ary* . . . ach—"

"Mary Ruth knows, Mamma. She's known all along."

Abram whispered trembling words in her ear. "Ida . . . dear wife of mine."

"Oh, Abram . . . be there. When the Lord . . . calls you, be ready." She felt his strong arms beneath her, intertwined with Leah's. "I'll be . . . waitin' . . ."

Breathing her last, she relinquished her grasp on the mortal and utterly gave in to overwhelming love, the purest discerning of it. The Lord Jesus was present, standing next to her own mamma, His nail-pierced hands extended to her. "Welcome home, child," she heard ever so clearly.

And all was well.

Chapter Twenty

More crucial than Leah sitting through the solemn two-day wake with Miriam Peachey and dozens of Ebersol and Brenneman relatives was planning how to care for and feed newborn Abe, keeping her promise to Mamma hour by hour.

She followed Aunt Lizzie's suggestion and gave the baby a small bottle of sugar water the first full day. On the second day she fed him goat's milk diluted with sterile well water, purchased from a meticulous family who shaved their goats for exceptional cleanliness and flavor. Tiny Abe took to it with much eagerness, as if to say, I'm mighty hungry for *life!*

Leah felt honored to look after Abe and Lydiann, tending to them as she might have her own wee ones. She suppressed sorrowful tears during the daylight hours, only succumbing to deepest grief in the privacy of her room after nightfall.

The raw memory of her helplessness and the utter desperation of Mamma's final moments distracted Leah in all her domestic and, now, motherly duties. She would never forget the earnest plea in her mother's sunken eyes, as if calling out to be surrounded by their love.

Ever so near. As close as Leah had ever dared to be, paying no mind to the midwife or Dat when she followed her heart and slipped into the deathbed alongside Mamma. She had felt irresistibly pulled to do so, wanting to help her beloved mother die peacefully.

On the day of the funeral Leah sat with Aunt Lizzie and the other women folk and raised her voice in song as best she could, singing the old familiar Ausbund hymns with over two hundred souls gathered in their home. She pondered the strength it would take to carry out her new role. *I must be strong today*, she thought, refusing to cry as she held Lydiann on her lap while Abe slept soundly upstairs in his cradle.

The ache in her throat threatened to choke her midway through the second long sermon. She'd spotted the back of Smithy Gid's head just now, and the unexpected mission of raising Mamma's babies weighed heavily on her mind, accompanied by her great sorrow at their loss. The future, indeed, seemed to stretch beyond her reach.

My help cometh from the Lord, she reminded herself. *Please let it be so, O God.*

As the service drew to a close and the People began making their traditional line to await the viewing, she was keenly aware of her own weakened spirit. It was painfully obvious to her that Peter and Fannie Mast and their family had not cared enough to attend Mamma's funeral service. The news would have easily traveled to their ears over in Grasshopper Level, she knew; nonetheless, far as Leah could tell, Mamma's cousins were nowhere to be seen today. She did not crane her neck in hopes of finding them.

With steadfast heart, she squared her shoulders in reliance upon God, clinging to the hope that one day, Lord willing, the two families might somehow be reunited.

In the week that followed Mamma's death, Leah knelt at her bedside at dawn and dusk, calling on the Lord God heavenly Father for help and strength. But when Hannah came privately to confide her most secret concern, Leah felt nearly powerless to know what to say.

"I hesitate to speak my heart on this," Hannah began, her face ashen as she stood against the bedroom door. "Yet I must say it, or I fear I'll burst apart."

Leah reached for her sister's cold hands. "Don't mince words . . . please, what is it?"

"Don't know how to put this, really."

"Start with a deep breath. It'll come out better that way."

Hannah began again, faltering a bit. "Could it be . . . do ya think Mary Ruth's leavin' home was partly the cause of Mamma dyin'?" she asked. "Did Dat's wrath cause mortal trauma in our mother?"

Honestly Leah didn't think so—at least she didn't *want* to think such a thing. Poor sorrowful Dat needed their kindness, not their finger-pointing. Besides, Mamma had struggled all during this pregnancy, Leah reminded Hannah. "She truly did."

When Leah hinted of Hannah's worries to Lizzie, her aunt

was adamant in her response. "Seems to me Abram has a mighty gut chance to redeem himself by askin' Mary Ruth back home. That's what *I* think."

Leah was surprised. "Do you mean to say you think Dat would actually do that?"

Lizzie stood at the cook stove, wearing her long black apron over a purple cape dress. "Well, why not? 'Tis a mighty big man who looks back on a bad decision and has a hankerin' to make things right."

Aunt Lizzie had hit the nail smack-dab on the head. But just *who* among them was going to bring this up to Dat? Leah shivered a little, contemplating the conflict that was sure to arise.

Holding Abe, who was tightly swaddled in a soft blanket, she went to sit at the table next to Lydiann. She watched as her little sister made broad red crayon strokes on the paper.

"Where's my mamma?" Lydiann looked up at her with big blue eyes.

Right then she thought of Sadie's poor baby, gone to heaven. All those months of her sister's deep grief, her loss . . . never having held her son close as Mamma had so tenderly before her death.

"Our mamma's in heaven." Leah forced a smile.

"I want her *here*," Lydiann said, making a round circle with her crayon.

Leah sighed. This was ever so difficult, yet she must be strong for her youngest sister. "I know, dear one. I miss Mamma, too."

Lydiann put down her crayon and leaned against Leah.

Leah signaled for Aunt Lizzie to take tiny Abe, then lifted

Lydiann up onto her lap. She rocked her gently and whispered, "I'll be your second mamma for as long as you need me."

This brought a little smile to Lydiann's face, though Leah didn't know how much Lydiann comprehended.

Turning, Lydiann clung to her, and Leah rose with the toddler still wrapped in her arms and carried her into the front room. From the window, she drank in the white splendor of snow and ice . . . the stark blackness of tall trees against a merciless gray sky.

The Lord is thy keeper; the Lord is thy shade upon thy right hand. She thought of one of Mamma's favorite psalms.

Then she whispered a promise, "We'll have us a happy life, dear one."

"Happy . . . with Mamma Leah." Lydiann snuggled hard against her.

She hummed a hymn and pondered the future. Just how would the Lord aid her efforts? She knew not the answer. She had only to listen to God's voice one day at a time. *I must not fear the morrow. . . .*

With a kiss on the head, she put Lydiann down, and the two of them wandered back to the kitchen. Abe slept in his cradle not far from the cook stove, where Aunt Lizzie was frying up some chicken.

"There's something I've been thinking 'bout." Lizzie's voice startled her.

"What's that?" Leah turned slightly, watching Mamma's sister at the stove.

"You oughta get out some this week. Goodness' sake, for a girl who nearly grew up outdoors—"

"It's all right, really 'tis. Dat's got himself two hired hands, so I'm not much needed outside anymore. Besides, Hannah's right happy to help Dat some these days, seems to me." She stared down at Abe's smooth forehead, his light tuft of hair. *Liewi Boppli* . . . "As for me, I like bein' with these beloved babies."

"Smithy Gid won't be able to help Abram near as much once the two of you get hitched, ain't so?" Aunt Lizzie was looking down at the frying pan—and rightly so. "Don't ya go sayin' you ain't marryin' him . . . I see how the two of you look at each other."

Leah said nothing. Let Aunt Lizzie say what she wanted. Truth was, she needed to talk to her beau here before too long—needed to share with him the important promise she'd made to Mamma. Pledges, nay, even covenants made to a dying parent could not be taken lightly. She would keep her word and raise Lydiann and Abe as her own. But the more she thought on it, the more the problem increased in her heart and mind. She did not want to hurt Gid, nor herself by parting ways with the man who planned to marry her. Yet she had no idea how to make Mamma's wishes come to pass in light of that.

To soothe herself, she reached down into the cradle and picked up Abe, enjoying his sweetness tucked so close to heart. *What am I to do?*

Following the suppertime meal, Dat took Leah aside before evening prayers. "I know you have your hands busy with the little ones, but when you have a breather tomorrow, could you begin sorting through your mother's things?" he asked, puffy eyes betraying his mournful spirit.

She suspected Dat privately grieved out in the barn, when he was alone with the animals and his somber thoughts, remembering all the years spent as his wife's confidant and lover.

"Jah, I'll see to it, Dat, first thing tomorrow." She touched his arm gently. "You must know . . . I miss Mamma, too. Something awful."

He nodded quickly, then straightened and went to the corner cupboard, where he picked up the big German Bible. His voice sounded dreadful this night, a husky monotone. She knew his heart was not in the reading of God's Word.

First, last, and foremost, Leah thought of herself as a compliant sort; except for the years given to her dream of marrying Jonas Mast, she had generally obeyed her father's bidding. But she felt rather bold when Dat asked her not only to go through Mamma's personal effects but to "discard everything but her old Bible . . . and her clothing, which can be given away to friends and older relatives." She spoke up, telling Dat there might be certain other things she or the twins might wish to save, perhaps as keepsakes. But observing the unyielding look in Dat's swollen eyes, she held her peace and said no more.

The night of Mamma's passing, she and Hannah had moved both Lydiann's little bed and Abe's cradle into Hannah's and Leah's respective bedrooms. At night Leah was comforted by the soft sounds of Abe's breathing as she tucked him in, and his gurgling as she fed him every three hours or so around the clock. This arrangement also made it possible for Dat to have himself a good night's sleep—if he was able. Thankfully Abe wasn't nearly as fussy as Lydiann had been during her infancy. For this Leah was glad, not so much for herself as for poor Dat, who was obviously aging with each passing day. Without Mamma to seemingly soften his harsher side, Leah worried he might swiftly grow into a cranky old man.

After Dat rose early the next morning, Leah got up and checked on Abe, who slept soundly, then hurried to do the difficult work of sorting through her mother's clothing. She pulled out one drawer after another, folding Mamma's things and making small piles on the bed. Opening the bottom drawer, she discovered a woolen gray scarf and matching knitted mittens, something she hadn't seen Mamma wear in the longest time. *She must've made these long ago, when Dat was courting her.*

Lovingly, Leah slipped her own hands into the scratchy mittens and wrapped the long scarf about her neck, tears clouding her vision. Would Dat rethink his desire to dispose of these precious things? But no. Best to simply give the scarf and mittens to Miriam Peachey or another of Mamma's friends, what with Dat behaving somewhat crossly these days. Better yet, she could slip them to Aunt Lizzie for safekeeping;

that way they could ultimately remain in the family.

She didn't know if she ought to be thinking that way, yet she questioned Dat's demand to discard all that had belonged to their darling mother. She felt even more strongly when her hands discovered a grouping of many letters from Cousin Fannie written to Mamma over the years. And another letter hidden away, farther back in the drawer—this one with Sadie's handwriting clearly on the envelope.

"What's this?" she said aloud.

Did Mamma go against the bishop and keep one of Sadie's early letters?

She could not stop looking at the postmark. She *had* to know.

Going to the dresser, she held the letter under the gas lamp and saw it had been sent in late December of 1947, not so long after Bishop Bontrager decreed Sadie's letters be returned unopened. Dat had laid down the law, as well, saying it was imperative to follow the "man of God on the matter of the shun."

Why would Mamma disregard both the bishop's and Dat's final word on this?

Leah battled right and wrong, holding the envelope, turning it over and noticing it was open already. *Oh,* she groaned inwardly. *I have to know what Sadie was writing to Mamma.*

Hastily she stopped herself and pushed it back, closing the drawer soundly. The notion that Mamma might have been also writing to Sadie crossed her mind. If so, did that mean Mamma's soul was hanging in eternal balance? Had her spirit gone to the Lord God in heaven or not? She shuddered to think Mamma would willingly disobey the Ordnung and risk her everlasting reward. Could it have been a misunderstanding that allowed this letter to find its way into Mamma's drawer?

She felt she knew her mother through and through—Mamma would have confessed such a thing before passing from death unto life. Surely if Mamma viewed keeping and reading Sadie's letter as a sin, she would never have disobeyed. *Niemols!*

Coming to this conclusion, Leah decided if Mamma could read the letter and hide it away—and die peacefully—then why couldn't *she* read it, too? Taking a deep breath, she reopened the drawer and reached for the letter, hurrying out of Dat's bedroom to her own. There she put it away in her bureau, where it would remain till she could take her time to read it—to savor and pore over every word and phrase, hoping for some clue as to what on earth had happened between Jonas and herself.

Chapter Twenty-One

"You oughta reconsider this, Abram." Lizzie was glad to have cornered him in the milk house. "Mary Ruth is your daughter!"

"You have no right to order me around!"

She inhaled and held her breath in, then let the words come gushing out. "Ain't it awful clear you were wrong 'bout Mary Ruth?"

His face reddened. "Don't go sayin' I'm responsible for Ida's death 'cause of Mary Ruth's leaving home. Don'tcha dare."

Sighing, she said more softly now, "Seems I don't *have* to, now, do I?"

He slumped and went to the window, looking out through the streaked old glass. "I don't know how a thing like this—Mary Ruth's stubbornness and goin' to live with Englishers—can happen to God-fearin' folk like us."

She was more careful in choosing her words this time. "We let the bishop think for all of us, that's how. The preachers and Bishop Bontrager tell you how to feel 'bout your own dear ones . . . your own Mary Ruth."

Abram muttered something about ministers being chosen—ordained by God. But when he began to cough, he couldn't seem to quit, and she worried he might vomit, so distraught he was.

"I'll leave you be," she said. "I didn't mean to upset you so."

"You best be goin' indoors. Check on that son of mine," Abram said it low but decisively.

He needed some time alone, probably, out here where he sometimes wept so loudly she wondered if he might be making himself ill. But then she, too, was acquainted with such dreadful sadness. Anyone who had lived as long as either she or Abram knew full well the pain of disappointment. She wished she might say he was merely passing through this life, that this old earth was not his eternal home and the treasures of truth were laid up in Glory for him—for all of them. *We've got our eyes fixed on what's all around us*, she thought. *Mistakenly so.*

"Jah, I'll look in on Abe, but Leah's doing a right gut job of taking care of him and Lydiann." She turned to leave, glad to have sobbed away her initial grief, having cried herself to sleep plenty of nights following her sister's funeral. To suffer was a part of living; how well she knew it. Best to simply move on, make the best of life, and trust the Lord, as she had learned to do. And love what family they had left.

Hannah sat in her bedroom with her diary in her lap while Lydiann napped on the side of the bed where Mary Ruth had always slept.

With pen in hand, she began to write, reliving the night of Mamma's death.

Tuesday, January 3, 1950
Dear Diary,

One week and one day have passed since Mamma breathed her last. For me it is the worst pain I've known. I wish I'd agreed to Dan Nolt's suggestion—calling in Dr. Schwartz might have spared Mamma's life. I feel fairly responsible, but I have shared this with no one. If only I had given a simple nod of my head that night at the Nolts' front door! Oh, what a difference a single choice might have made.

Leah says Mamma's passing was serene, that she did not seem to fight the final throes of death but embraced it, once she knew Abe was healthy and had cuddled him near. It breaks my heart that my baby brother will never know our mother.

The night Mamma died, I rode to get Mary Ruth to bring her home with me, thinking it necessary. Dat must not have thought so, for he met us in the hallway just outside their bedroom door. When he greeted me but did not speak to Mary Ruth—not at first—it pained me nearly as much as to think of Mamma struggling terribly in childbirth. Mary Ruth spoke up, though, inquiring of Mamma's condition . . . and the unborn babe's. And she offered a heartfelt apology for having spoken disrespectfully to Dat prior to his sending her away.

Obviously bewildered, Dat said nothing about my fetching Mary Ruth to the house. Honestly I'd hoped he might've opened his arms to her and welcomed her back. But such was not the case, and we stood quietly, tears glistening, as Mamma's cries became fainter.

If Dat doesn't feel he caused Mamma great distress in the last days of her carrying wee Abe, I don't understand. Truly, the upset between him and Mary Ruth must have played some part. If my twin still lived here, she would surely have her say; then again, maybe not. Things are awful tense when it comes to Mary Ruth claiming salvation "full and free" while living under a worldly roof . . . not to mention her membership at an English church.

All that aside, I'm beginning to wonder if Ezra will ever attend another singing. He doesn't come to Preaching anymore, either. What's to become of him? I've told no one this, but I saw him on Main Street in Strasburg recently when I went to deliver more embroidered hankies to Frances Brubaker at her consignment shop. Ezra was dressed in blue jeans and had his hair cut like an Englisher—and was smoking a cigarette!

I worry for his dear mother. What she must be going through, losing two sons: Elias to death and Ezra to the world—the flesh and the devil. If Ezra doesn't soon get back on the right path, he'll be in danger of the shun, just as Sadie was.

Along with the guilt I bear for Mamma's death, I also wish to goodness I'd stuck my neck out and talked to her about how to be ready to meet one's Maker. I could kick myself, because I missed my chance forever. Who can I ever share my heart with now?

Oh, I fear I might worry myself sick, and I might, too, if Dat didn't need me helping with the milking and other outdoor chores. Such work helps me a lot, and I do enjoy working alongside Smithy Gid. He has a right gentle way, and it'll be ever so nice when he marries into our family, probably next year, I'd guess. Leah deserves some happiness, and, at long last, I'll have me a big brother. I ought to be counting my blessings more, but it's hard these days. What an awful way to welcome a new year with Mamma gone from us.

Each day I observe Leah going about her responsibilities—

rising before dawn to cook breakfast and on her feet all day long, up several times in the night with Abe. A shining example, for certain. Never does she complain, and I know she must be tuckered out each and every night as we head upstairs to bed. When I can, I help her with Lydiann, but Leah's fulfilling a labor of love. Not only is she a wonderful-good big sister to Abe and Lydiann, she is becoming a tender and loving mamma to them, too. The light in her hazel eyes when she tends to Abe, especially, gives me hope during these dark sad days.

Sorrowfully,
Hannah

Hours before supper Leah hurried out to the barn and found Dat sweeping, looking somewhat dazed. Her heart went out to him, and she wondered if she ought to wait to speak with him later, giving him more time to grieve before she unburdened her soul.

She started to turn to leave when Dat stopped his sweeping. "Somethin' on your mind, daughter?"

She contemplated simply leaving him be but found herself nodding. "Jah," she said slowly. "I was thinkin' I best be talkin' to Gid 'bout my promise to Mamma. But I wanted to speak to you first."

"Well, what's to say?"

Leah went on to tell him she assumed Smithy Gid would urge they now marry quickly, merely going before Preacher Yoder to make their lifelong promises to God and each other. "I'm fairly sure he'll offer to help me raise Lydiann and

Abe . . . the two of us, as a family." She couldn't help but wonder how Dat would feel, this coming from her.

"Gid's a right fine man," Dat began, "but I'll be raisin' my children myself, and no two ways 'bout it."

She wasn't surprised. Dat was fiercely possessive when it came to his family.

"I say you should go ahead with plans to marry Gid when the time comes and let Lizzie or Hannah look after Abe and Lydiann here."

"But Mamma asked *me* to raise them."

Dat sighed loudly. "Your mamma was awful befuddled with the pain of childbirth. I daresay she'd never expect ya to keep such a promise. Besides, you made your betrothal vow to Gid before the one to Mamma, ain't so?" At that he set about pushing hard his wide broom again, making a rhythmic swooshing sound.

Mamma knew my heart, thought Leah. *She trusted me to do the right thing for Abe and Lydiann . . . befuddled or not.*

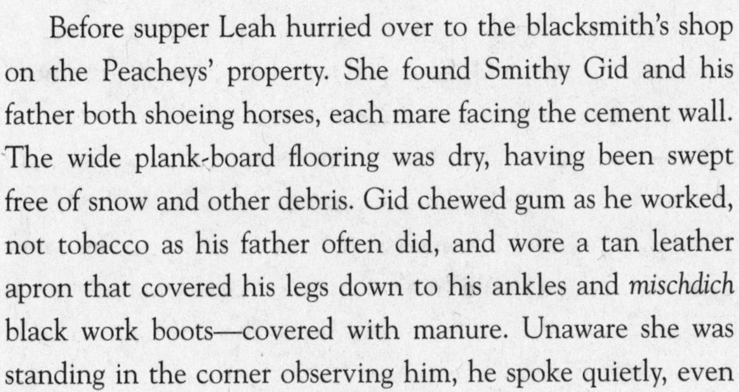

Before supper Leah hurried over to the blacksmith's shop on the Peacheys' property. She found Smithy Gid and his father both shoeing horses, each mare facing the cement wall. The wide plank-board flooring was dry, having been swept free of snow and other debris. Gid chewed gum as he worked, not tobacco as his father often did, and wore a tan leather apron that covered his legs down to his ankles and *mischdich* black work boots—covered with manure. Unaware she was standing in the corner observing him, he spoke quietly, even gently, to the mare, bringing the animal's leg up between his own, clamping his thighs against it as he positioned the new shoe, hot from the forge, with the end of a rasp. Gid's hair was disheveled as he leaned over, his toes pointing in slightly to better keep his balance.

Glancing at the square-shaped brick forge, she saw the opening, where the blower kept the cinders hot. Smithy Peachey was almost too busy juggling his many Amish clients—and occasionally an Old Order Mennonite customer, too—most of them on an eight-week schedule. Because of this, his father sought out Gid's help several days a week, and Leah was fairly certain he was hoping to pass on his livelihood to his only son.

She waited to let him know she was present till Gid was finished with all four hooves and had accepted the exact amount of money from the farmer. Gid waved a cheerful farewell as Old Jonathan Lapp led the animal away, an obvious shine on the new horseshoes. The older man hitched his mare to a long sleigh and was gone.

While Gid organized the long tongs, hoof nippers, rasp, and other smithing tools, she moved out of the shadows and, coughing a little so as not to startle him, said, "Hullo, Smithy Gid."

"There ya are, girl. How're you today?" His grin was as infectious as ever, and she hoped for a lull between customers.

"Do ya have time to talk?" she asked.

"Why, sure. Always have plenty-a time for my girl." He removed his heavy leather blacksmithing apron and brushed his hands off on his trousers; then he went to get his work coat, which hung on a hook near the wide door, and slipped it on. "Let's walk a bit." Smiling, he reached for her hand and rubbed it between his own.

"I need to tell you something, Gid," she began. "Mamma asked me to raise her babies . . . as she lay dyin', and I said I would."

Smithy Gid nodded his head as if he'd suspected as much.

"I can't go back on my word," she said. "I wouldn't even if I could."

"No . . . no, you oughtn't be thinkin' thataway." He continued. "We could go to the preacher and have us a short wedding as soon as this weekend, if you'd want to. You and I could live in my folks' empty Dawdi Haus, bring up the little ones there as our own."

She figured he'd suggest that. "Just today I talked to Dat 'bout this, and he wants to do *his* part raising Lydiann and Abe."

He turned and gazed at her. "Surely ya know I would do whatever it took to make ya my bride." There was a strange hesitancy in his voice. "But, Leah, I want to have my own family with you . . . make a home separate from our parents. Don't you?"

" 'Course I do, but things have changed now since Mamma died." Breathing deeply, she stared ahead at Blackbird Pond, where they'd played as youngsters. "I just . . ." She felt she couldn't go on.

"What is it, dear?"

She felt his arms around her unexpectedly. "Living apart from Abe and Lydiann just doesn't fit with my promise to Mamma."

"But we're meant for each other," he broke in, fervor in his words. "I love ya so."

She tried not to cry. "Honestly I don't know what to do,"

she said softly. She didn't tell him she'd moved Abe's cradle into her own bedroom, that she knew clearly her infant brother had bonded with her . . . that she couldn't imagine passing the responsibility nor the maternal love off to either Aunt Lizzie or Hannah, as Dat had suggested.

"I've waited this long for ya, Leah. Surely I can get Abram to see the light—to let us raise his little ones in our own house."

"My father won't change his mind on this," she replied sadly. "I know that for sure."

They clung fast to each other, there beneath the lone willow tree, where the recent snow weighed down each slender branch and the pond was frozen over rock hard. Where they, their sisters, and parents had ice skated, built bonfires on the shore, and played hockey on sunny winter days.

"How can I let you go?" Gid caressed her face. "I'd be crazy to."

"Oh, Gid," her voice trembled.

"There must be some other way."

"Surely there is," she whispered. "Surely."

Sitting at the supper table, Gid stared hopelessly at the meat loaf, marbled mashed potatoes, and scalloped asparagus. He could hardly bring himself to pick up the serving dishes when they were passed.

"Something botherin' you, son?" Mamma eyed him curiously.

He would have to make himself eat. There was no sharing

his and Leah's problem tonight. Romantic difficulties were never spoken of to parents, though at times, he felt such a tradition was to an extent ridiculous, especially when his older and wiser father might have some powerful-good advice to offer.

Somehow or other, something *had* to give. If it meant talking privately with Abram, he would. He couldn't simply let his engagement to Leah come to an end. Nothing must be permitted to put a wedge between them . . . not even a dying mother's plea!

Robert Schwartz paced the college corridor, eager for posted results of a pre-Christmas theology exam. He recoiled at the memory of both Thanksgiving and Christmas: Elias Stoltzfus's death . . . and Derek's surprise visit. Still, the Plain young man's passing had caused a tremendous religious stir among Elias's own people. God had reached down in goodness and grace, turning the tragedy into a spiritual victory.

Robert wished he could say the same of his brother's brief return home. Christmas Day had been a far cry from his boyhood memories of baked-ham dinners and laughter as the family gathered to decorate the tree on Christmas Eves. Derek had been not only irritable but dreadfully sullen after coming home from a "long walk," as he'd put it, and no amount of persuading on either Dad's or Mother's part could bring him around. He'd wanted "something strong to drink" when he stormed back into the house. After not having seen him for much of the afternoon, their parents spent a miserable evening waiting for the prodigal to return, which did not happen until long past midnight.

Robert had been reluctant to leave Dad and Mother alone, but he wanted to get away and pray for a time. Following supper, he drove to Quarryville and found solace in the stillness of the vacant church, pleading for God's help on behalf of his lost brother . . . and the grieving Amish family who had suffered the greatest loss of all.

Leah could think of nothing else but her talks with both Dat and Gid as she dressed Abe in his tiny pajamas, kissing each little hand as she guided it through the sleeve opening. She was truly glad for Hannah's offer to help with combing Lydiann's hair and getting her ready for bed, though she knew dear Hannah had her share of things to do in the kitchen and elsewhere. *She has a knack for sensing my mood*, Leah thought, grateful for Hannah and missing her other sisters terribly.

The house feels too empty, she pondered, carrying Abe downstairs to warm his milk bottle. *Having Smithy Gid live here surely would fill up the place . . . and Dat wouldn't be so outnumbered.*

Yet she'd seen the look of disappointment in Gid's eyes, and she knew she couldn't take away his rightful place as head of his household. Besides, their own babies would most likely come along soon enough, and how complicated would it be for Gid to assume the fatherly role for his flesh-and-blood children but not for Lydiann and Abe? The problem nagged at her till she was altogether weary of it.

As soon as Abe was nestled in his cradle and asleep, Leah closed the bedroom door and went to the bureau. Taking out Sadie's letter to Mamma, she curled up on the bed and hugged her sister's former pillow as she read.

December 15, 1947
Dearest Mamma,

I hope at least one of the letters I've written ends up being read by you eventually. Christmas is coming soon and the Mellinger children are ever so happy. David and Vera's new baby is already a month old and as sweet as can be.

Jonas loves playing with the little ones, maybe more so than some young men I know. He's been so kind to me, Mamma—you just don't know. I think it's because he wants things to turn out well for me. I suppose I should tell you that I broke down one night and cried out my woes to him—about having a baby out of wedlock with an Englisher and all. He'd offered to go walking with me after supper, and I just couldn't keep the truth inside any longer. You probably wonder how I could tell him such a thing, especially when I wanted to keep it a secret from everyone else back home.

When all was said and done, I did the right thing by sharing with Jonas that I was "damaged goods." He said he wanted to help me, felt sorry for me . . . wanted to make sure I was cared for. That I should be looked after by a kind and good husband. I thought he meant himself . . . and he did. He said he would marry me then and there.

Of course, I argued it might be too soon, what with his having been in love with Leah and engaged and all, but he insisted we get married following my six-week Proving time. We talked a lot about that, too, and how the brethren here seemed to understand my plight, not sharing my sinful past with the People. Honestly I felt the Lord God must be looking out for my sin-weary soul. So in my next letter to you, I'll be writing to say I am a happily married woman. Jonas's Sadie, I'll be. I know you don't approve, Mamma, but I had to share these things with you.

I trust you, Dat, and Aunt Lizzie are all right. Don't cry for me, Mamma. God has a way of leading wayward souls to Him. Write to me again, please? I miss you so . . . and my sisters, too.

I know you can't tell Dat or anyone else in the family how much I love them—if you read this letter, that is—but I surely do. I hope there might come a day when we will see each other again face-to-face.

All my love,
Your firstborn, Sadie

Holding the letter, Leah stared at it, unseeing. The welcoming curve of the familiar handwriting blurred all too quickly. Sadie had shared her sinful ways with Jonas, as well as the news of her stillborn baby, after having resisted doing so to the brethren here, when and where it was most necessary. How was it so easy for her to do that in Ohio? Had she fallen for Jonas's dear smile, his gentle eyes?

Not wanting to dwell on this, she let her angry tears flow freely, pushing the pillow aside. Had Sadie somehow used her wicked past to purposely play on Jonas's sympathy, kind and compassionate man that he was? *My sister dared to combine her sin with yet another—stealing my beloved beau! How could she?*

Reaching over, she pulled Sadie's pillow toward her and rose, carrying it with her. She thought of pushing it under the bed where cobwebs and clumps of dust formed faster than she could keep up, especially now that she was busy caring for a newborn, as well as a two-and-a-half-year-old. Beneath the bed was a good idea, because she would not have to look at the pillow hidden there, recalling the nights she and Sadie had shared their fondest hopes and dreams, lying side by side, their heads resting happily on their pillows.

But no, she'd had enough of those memories. Breathing hard, Leah carried the pillow all the way downstairs to the cold cellar, where she stuffed it deep into the heart of Sadie's old hope chest, giving it a good solid pounding before closing the lid. *I never want to see this again!*

With that she felt she was also willing to live out her whole life long without ever seeing Sadie again.

Back upstairs, she took the letter and began to rip it into as many as pieces as her anger would allow. *I do this for poor Mamma*, she thought, giving in to a rising resentment she'd thought she had long put to rest. *And this is for Dat and Aunt Lizzie . . . for Hannah and Mary Ruth . . . Lydiann and Abe.*

Stopping, Leah realized she was shaking uncontrollably. *I must surely despise Sadie*, she thought, realizing it was true. She continued on, tearing the small pieces into even tinier ones. *This is for Abram's Leah . . . who surely I will be forevermore.*

Chapter Twenty-Two

Before her baby brother awakened for the morning, Leah hurried to pen a note to Vera Mellinger in Millersburg, Ohio, hoping to get word of Mamma's passing to her older sister. Halfway through the letter, after sharing the joyous news of tiny Abe's birth and his good health in spite of the trauma, she noticed her jaw was clenched.

Leaning back against the headboard of her bed, she deliberately tried to relax. *Calm yourself,* she thought, but doing so was a whole different matter. The horrid way she felt about Sadie after reading her letter yesterday, well, she'd just as soon let her older sister continue on in her ignorance, not knowing one speck about Mamma. But such an attitude was cruel, even spiteful, and she knew better than to harbor bitterness. So Leah made herself continue writing, ending with a plea for Vera to write back as soon as she could. *Please tell me how to get word to my sister Sadie.*

She signed off the way Mamma had taught her and quickly wrote her full name. Sealing the envelope, she placed the stamp in the proper place and hurried downstairs to don her woolen cape and snow boots. At the mailbox in front of the house, she pushed the letter inside and looked about her, momentarily glad for the predawn darkness.

The serenity soothed Leah, and she breathed in the icy air, relieved to have accomplished washing and drying the family's laundry two days ago, on Monday's washday. With Hannah and Lizzie's help, she'd hung out the many baby items on the line, though it had been quite tedious in the wrenching cold. Miriam Peachey had come over, bringing a large pot of corn chowder, which everyone enjoyed at noon, especially Dat and Dawdi John. And she'd asked Aunt Lizzie to keep Mamma's old knit scarf and mittens at her house—conceal them, really. Surely Dat would overlook Leah's momentary boldness when he came around—years down the road—and realized how important it had been to hang on to at least one item of Mamma's.

I will lift up mine eyes unto the hills, from whence cometh my help, she thought silently while trudging back to the house.

She knew she must go talk with Dr. Schwartz sometime soon—possibly with Lorraine, too. They must be told that although she wished to keep her part-time job, she was needed nearly twenty-four hours a day here at home. The idea that maybe Mary Ruth might come and take care of Abe and Lydiann for several hours of a Saturday dropped into her mind. But then again, there was the problem of Dat's determined stance—Mary Ruth was not at all welcome in the house. *Nix that idea.* She might ask Aunt Lizzie, though . . . see what ideas *she* might have.

On the way around the back to the kitchen door, she happened to hear her aunt's boots clumping down the snow-covered mule road. "Hullo, Leah!" Lizzie called.

"'Mornin', Aendi!" Leah called back, standing near the back stoop, waiting and shivering, too. *What would we do without sweet Lizzie? Life would be ever so empty without Mamma's sister near.*

Once she and Lizzie were back indoors, she opened the grate on the wood stove and they warmed their hands and feet together. Lizzie asked, "Are ya feelin' all right, honey-girl?"

Leah nodded. "I feel numb when I think of Mamma. But when I'm holding Abe and Lydiann, things tend to change in me . . . some."

"'The Lord giveth and the Lord taketh away.'" Lizzie put her arm around Leah.

Ain't that the truth. She thought again of Sadie's revealing letter to Mamma.

She sighed and went to the window near the long table. "I found something in Mamma's drawer," she began, "when I cleared out her personal things for Dat."

Lizzie came and sat at the head of the table, where Dat always sat at mealtime.

"Seems to me Mamma may have hidden one of Sadie's letters away on purpose." She turned and looked at Lizzie. "What do ya make of that?"

"I shouldn't be surprised, I guess."

She felt the tightness in her chest, wondering if she ought to say what she'd read. Would that be as sinful as Mamma's own disobedience? She didn't know. "So then you must think Mamma disregarded the bishop . . . and Dat, too," Leah said nearly in a whisper.

"Honestly she didn't much care for the do's and don'ts of the Old Ways. She honored the Ordnung as best she could . . . walked a line, s'pose you could say. She read the Good Book from cover to cover nearly every year. She told me she'd shared some of these things with Sadie, Hannah, and Mary Ruth . . . and with *you*, most recently."

Leah clearly remembered the conversation. "But what 'bout *Gelassenheit*—submission to God and to the People? What was Mamma's view on that?"

Lizzie nodded her head. "Sadly that was the biggest issue—the push and pull of it all. Abram wanted to live by the letter of the law, following the bishop's and the preachers' every whim. This annoyed my sister no end. 'Tween you and me, I think when the end came, she was eager to go home to Glory."

"Not 'cause of Dat, I hope."

Lizzie paused a moment, then went on. "She simply yearned to see the Lord Jesus."

"'Best to be in heaven's lap than caught in the world's grasp,'" Leah whispered.

Lizzie patted the bench. "Come and sit. You have a big day ahead."

She smiled. "Every day's thataway."

"You're doin' a wonderful-gut thing, Leah. Never forget," Lizzie said.

Abe's cries were heard just then, so Leah quickly excused herself and ran upstairs to comfort her mamma's precious boy.

The first day of the new school semester, Mary Ruth followed a group of fancy students into Paradise High School. She was happy to ride the school bus with other Mennonite youth, glad she wasn't the only conservative girl on board. Naturally she wasn't nearly as Plain now as she had been, what with her floral-print dress, though long to her ankles.

Thankfully Dottie Nolt had driven her to the school a week earlier, when she had enrolled for the remainder of the year and taken her placement tests. To her delight, she discovered she was ready for *second*-semester tenth grade, even though she'd completed only eight years at the Georgetown School—staying home with Mamma for two years after that. All told, she was well on course to graduate by the time she was nineteen—a full year older than most high school graduates, but that didn't bother her in the least. The main thing was to prepare herself for teacher's college. And, here lately, she believed God was calling her to attend a Christian college someday. She was on her way!

Busy hallways were disconcerting at first, and changing classrooms and having different teachers for each subject was also confusing. After a few days, though, she felt she would become accustomed to the schedule. Still, the sight of girls wearing knee-length wool skirts with bare legs clear down to the tops of their white ankle socks made Mary Ruth feel as if she were in a foreign land.

Getting her locker open was another discouraging situation, but, in the end, the problem had its reward. An attractive boy with brown hair and green eyes noticed her plight and came over to help. "I'm Jimmy Kaiser," he smiled. "You're new, aren't you?"

She nodded, afraid she'd say jah and scare him off, which she certainly didn't want to do, not with those big bright eyes looking right at her.

"If you ever run into a snag with your combination lock, look me up," Jimmy said, pointing toward his own locker. "I'm only five lockers down from yours on the other side of the hallway. Don't be bashful, all right?"

"Nice to meet you, Jimmy."

"Welcome to Paradise . . . *High School*, that is!" Grinning, he turned and hurried away.

Well. She was entirely pleased with the first student she'd met. *Pleased as punch*, she thought. *Does this mean I'm beginning to forget Elias?* She wondered that plenty.

Surely it was a good sign, her experiencing a slight flutter when a good-looking boy like Jimmy made the effort to cross the hall and make her feel welcome.

Another surprise was the first reading assignment given in American literature class: her beloved *Uncle Tom's Cabin*. She knew the book inside and out, perhaps better than the other students in the class because she identified in part with Eliza, the black slave girl, though Mary Ruth had never been abused physically. All the same, the book reopened certain sore spots for her, and she longed to see oppressed people released from spiritual bondage.

That afternoon following school Mary Ruth slipped away to her lovely bedroom at the Nolts' to do her homework, writing carefully the assigned essays and working the geometry problems. When she was finished, she knelt to pray, asking the Lord to help her forgive the brethren, especially Bishop Bontrager, who ruled with an iron hand, much the way Simon

Legree did in Harriet Beecher Stowe's classic novel. The man's shunning of Sadie had altered her family members' lives for the worst, she was sure. She also asked the Lord to forgive her for smooching so awful much with Elias, not having saved lip-kissing for her husband . . . and to guide her life as a Christian young woman.

Following Elias's death, she had initially decided to wear a black dress for a good long time, but recently she'd changed her mind and put aside her mourning clothes. Her newfound joy in the Lord Jesus had turned every part of her life around, including the slightest details. No longer did she part her hair down the middle; she simply brushed it straight back and gathered it into a higher bun, and, like Dottie, she wore the many-pleated formal head covering unique to Mennonite women, with the strings hanging loose and untied. Not quite as Plain, true, but nevertheless not worldly, either.

Getting used to electricity and automobiles had been the easiest adjustment of all, though she knew she would gladly ride in Dat's family carriage if invited.

Perhaps Elias's death had been God's way of giving her a heavenly sign she was never intended to join the Amish church. Truth was, she enjoyed having modern conveniences at her fingertips, and what she was experiencing under Dan and Dottie's roof—and in attending church with them—was pure freedom. For the first time in her life, she could breathe easily, free from bondage, ever ready to honor the Lord in everything she put her hand to do, all the days of her life.

In due time, Leah received word back from Vera Mellinger that Sadie and Jonas no longer lived in Millersburg. Vera wrote that she hadn't heard from them in "quite some time" and said she was "ever so sorry" to hear of Mamma's passing.

Passing. Why was it folk avoided the word *death*? Was it easier to think of a person going from one place to the next, moving forward as their soul surely did at the point of death, instead of lying still in a coffin? The Scriptures taught the passing of the soul from this life into eternity, from "death unto life."

She felt both sorry and thankful having read Vera's letter, and she took it out to the barn, where Hannah and Dat were cleaning out the lower stable area. She regretted Sadie having no way of knowing their mother was dead, yet she was secretly relieved her sister wouldn't be rushing home over the sad news—though Leah did wonder how such news would have affected Jonas if *he* had known of it. But no, she couldn't let herself wonder about that. Too much time had flown to the wind.

Outdoors, she found Hannah wearing old work boots, Leah's own. When Dat was free enough, she handed Vera's letter to him. He stood with his legs braced apart and read it quickly. "Well, if that ain't a fine howdy-do," he said, waving the note once he finished. "She runs off so we can never find her . . . even if it's her own mamma who's died."

Hannah blinked her eyes fast and Leah wondered if she was trying not to cry. But Hannah surprised her by saying, "You did the right thing, Leah, but maybe our shunned sister doesn't wanna be found."

Dat nodded in agreement. "Long gone . . . she is."

"Should I write to Cousin Fannie next? See if *she* has any knowledge of our sister's whereabouts?" She held her breath, unsure what Dat might say to do.

Dat hung his head. "Where the Masts are concerned, we're as gut as dead."

She took that as a no and accepted the letter back from Dat. Heading toward the house, she was eager to check on Lydiann, who was napping, and Abe, who was lying on a quilt spread out on the kitchen floor, the warmest room in the house. She almost wished Dat hadn't sided with Hannah just now, saying Sadie was "long gone." Had he given up on her ever repenting here in Gobbler's Knob?

Mamma's prayers while she lived surely still follow my sister now, she thought.

Abram had seen to it that his work boots were cleaned of caked-on mud and mule droppings before hitching up the horse to the sleigh. It might've been that he'd have made less a spectacle of himself had he simply gone walking to Daniel Nolt's place, but now as Abram reined in his horse in the driveway of the fine house, he sat there, not sure what to do next.

Just why he'd come, he wasn't altogether certain. He knew it had to do with the short letter from Ohio that Leah'd had him read. Something mighty sorrowful about it, he'd decided, and it had prompted him out of his lethargy. Not that he had been digging in his heels about visiting Mary Ruth; no, he just felt it might be the right time to make an attempt to see how his daughter was doing these days.

He got down from the sleigh and let the reins lie loose on the seat; the well-mannered horse would be fine here for a few minutes. Next thing he knew he was standing on the front porch of a stranger's house.

When Mary Ruth came to the door with a bright-eyed youngster in her arms, he was taken aback and found himself sputtering a greeting. She was mighty kind and invited him inside—even brought him some hot black coffee on a fancy tray. They sat and talked in the front room, pretty Mary Ruth and himself, no doubt as foolish sounding as he felt.

"I came to say I was wrong . . . and so were you, daughter," he started the conversation. "But now . . . well, I want you to consider coming home. Wouldja think on that for ol' Dat?"

She was quiet, not responding right off the way she normally did, which surprised him. Instead, she stroked the boy's dark hair, whispering something—he didn't know what—in his tiny ear.

"Your sisters—Leah and Hannah—would be downright happy. And . . . sorry to say, but you haven't properly met your new baby brother, Abe."

"Named after *you*, Dat." Her eyes seemed to light up at the mention of the baby.

"Jah, Leah and . . ." He had to pause. The mere thought of Ida still choked his words.

"Mamma and Leah's choice for a name, then?" She was helping him along. Mary Ruth, ever dear; the daughter who had never lacked for a comment.

He nodded, still composing himself.

"I wished I might've comforted you, Dat, at Mamma's

funeral. . . . Still hurts to think on it." She was silent for a moment; then she continued. "I just felt so far removed from my family. I wish things were better between us."

The punishment *had* been severe; he knew that. "I'd do plenty-a things different . . . now."

"I s'pose all of us would." But in the end, she refused his invitation to move back home. "I'd be a terrible thorn in your flesh, Dat," she admitted. "You see, I started high school—just yesterday, truth be told."

He hung his head. Things were spinning away from him. Nearly every day more things floated out of his reach. First Mary Ruth's odd declaration of salvation, then Ida's passing. He'd even received a fierce tongue-lashing from his father-in-law, of all things. Just yesterday John had given him what for about running Mary Ruth off. To top it all off, John had outright declared he wanted to go back to Hickory Hollow to live with one of his "sensible" grown grandchildren, where he didn't have to look at "the likes of you, Abram Ebersol, day in, day out."

Holding fast to the Old Ways was costing him dearly, but he felt toothless to change. With Ida dead and gone, it remained to be seen just how entrenched he would become over time, unwilling to stand up to Preacher Yoder or the bishop, neither one. Ida had found her strength in the Lord, she'd always said. As for himself, he couldn't see getting down on his knees and speaking words to the Almighty into the air. Lizzie, on the other hand, wasn't afraid to say she set ample time aside each day to do so. "You oughta try it once," she'd told him the day after Ida's funeral, when she'd found him coughing and weeping beside the feed trough as if his life was over. She'd been awful bold and said right out, "Prayer will help ya, Abram. I know this to be true."

Stubborn as he was, he had not followed her suggestion and had no intention of talking to Creator-God that way. Honest to Pete, what was this old world coming to when a man was nagged on mercilessly by his deceased wife's sister?

"I love you, Dat." Mary Ruth interrupted his musings. "I'll come visit, all right?"

"Jah, come see us. Hold your baby brother some, too."

When she reached for him, he didn't hug her back, only grunted. Surely she'd understand it wasn't in him today to be embracing her or anyone else. His heart felt more cold and deserted as each minute ticked by without his Ida.

Be there, his darling had said on her deathbed. *When the Lord calls you, be ready*. Saint that she was . . . Ida had put up with him all these years.

He said his good-byes to Mary Ruth and pressed his black hat down hard on his head. Leaning into the frosty evening, he made haste to return to Leah, Hannah, and his little ones.

On the way, he recalled Ida's funeral and burial service. So many people had come to bid a fond farewell. Even Dr. and Mrs. Schwartz and their elder son, Robert, had come to pay respect. They, along with other Englishers, including Henry and Lorraine's neighbor, Mrs. Ferguson; Mrs. Kraybill, who'd taken Hannah and Mary Ruth to the Georgetown School in her car all those years; and Mrs. Esbenshade, a frequent customer of their roadside stand.

Such a time to bury someone . . . in the cold and miserable ground, he thought, lamenting that his wife had to pass away so near Christmas. *Too near . . .*

For all his remaining days on the earth, Abram would regret not having insisted on calling for the Hexedokder. Any hex doctor would have known what to do to turn the baby within Ida; the awful bleeding could have been stopped, no matter how far his wife had slipped away. But Ida had made her most holy choice, her final stand—she who had rejected the powwow practices all their married life. Even unto death, he'd wrongly let her have her say.

Chapter Twenty-Three

Piercing cold temperatures lingered through January. Roads became miserably icy and snow-packed as one blizzard followed another, with grooves from horse-drawn sleighs and the occasional buggy becoming deeper and harder to avoid as the days wore on. Power lines up and down White Oak Road were weighed down by thick ice, causing power outages for Englishers in a radius of several miles. But the lack of electricity did not affect Leah and her family, nor their surrounding Amish neighbors.

Leah was thankful for Dat's unexpected willingness to allow Mary Ruth a weekly visit on Saturday mornings, since it gave her opportunity to continue working at Dr. Schwartz's clinic once a week. The doctor reacted kindly when Leah shared her predicament, wholeheartedly approving the hours best suited for her. "We don't want to lose you," he told her, to which Lorraine agreed emphatically.

"If you're ever in a jam, you can always bring the little ones here," she'd said. "I'll gladly entertain them."

Harder than juggling her life with its added responsibilities was the gnawing within—the intense knowing that it was imperative for her to find some sensible resolution to the problem of her promise to Mamma . . . and her betrothal to Gid. She had been somewhat relieved that he had seemed to understand how important her vow to Mamma was—how critical it would be day to day and year by year.

With that in mind, she agreed to talk privately with him when Gid knocked on the kitchen door one afternoon. Cordially they talked things out every which way in the stillness of the barn, only for Gid to conclude they must go their separate ways, releasing her from her betrothal promise.

Such a hopeless situation. *Gid's right about this*, Leah thought, dread filling her soul. Yet she knew for sure her husband would have felt terribly trapped, surrounded by an extended family he had no say about and having to kowtow to Dat on a daily basis.

In the very place where they had spent so many hours working together, tending to the farm animals' needs, Gid removed his black hat and reached for her hand. Struggling to speak, he said softly, "'Tis such a hard thing . . . I'm ever so sorry. Truly, I am." His eyes were intent on hers. "One thing's sure." His voice grew stronger. "You have my truest friendship, Leah—for as long as ya live."

"And you have mine, too. For always." She choked back tears. "We'll . . . see each . . . other, jah?" she sputtered, realizing how awkward it would be to occasionally bump into him.

"As good friends . . . you can count on that."

She felt ever so blue as they parted, and then again a few hours later, when the finality of his decision and their good-byes struck her anew as she stood at the window and saw him crossing the barnyard, heading for home. He caught her eye and waved to her, but she couldn't mistake the look of despair on his face.

Then and there, she believed the best thing to ward off further misery for them both was not to interact at all, though it wouldn't be easy, since Gid was still working part-time for Dat. The winter season while the ground was resting would be the simplest time to maintain a distance. The spring and summer plowing and planting, along with the fall harvest, would be much more awkward, since Gid would be quite visible on the property.

So the dismal expression on Gid's usually cheerful face made Leah want to turn away. Yet it wasn't anyone's fault what had become of them, really. After all, she couldn't help that she had been the one Mamma asked to raise her babies; it was for Leah to accept her lot with a smile. Truly, she couldn't imagine otherwise . . . for the sake of the children.

◆

Gid kept his hands busy every day except the Lord's Day so his loss of Leah wouldn't overtake him. He spent each waking minute shoeing horses or clearing out the fencerow of small trees. Diligently tending to another new litter of German shepherd pups also took plenty of time, as did pruning his father's grapevines, keeping up with chores for Abram, and doing whatever Dawdi Mathias needed done over at his place.

He could not be angry with Abram for wanting to raise

his own children. It just wasn't in him. Leah was doing the right thing by her little sister and brother . . . the right thing by Ida, too. Under God, Gid couldn't fault her or Abram, neither one, although he suspected Abram no longer felt an urgency for Leah to marry, not with a healthy baby boy growing up under the Ebersol roof. Once Abe reached the age of five, he would be out helping his father. Wouldn't be but a few short years and Abram's little boy would find the fieldwork he was meant for.

Still, Leah was the kind of girl Gid had always wanted to marry—someone who loved the soil and didn't mind getting her fingernails dirty, who even helped with plowing and planting some if need be. If he hadn't had his heart so set on her since youth, this setback wouldn't be as devastating. He suspected Leah had never quite committed herself to him—not as she had to Jonas so long ago.

He was in love with a girl he could never have. Quite stuck, he had marked time for much too long and was now nearing the limit on age for attending Sunday night singings—too late to ever hope to find a Leah replacement, if that were even possible.

So Gid toiled long and hard, hoping to lose himself in his labor, burying his lifelong wish to take Leah as his beloved wife.

Now and again Abram insisted on helping with some of the baby-related chores, things he knew Leah was altogether surprised about, such as holding out the towel and drying off his baby son after a warm bath. Once Abe was dressed for the night in his miniature white nightclothes, Abram put his face down right close and talked to him. He told his infant boy all about his deceased mamma as the sleepy bundle lay quietly in his arms, whispering, too, what Abe's new mamma had given up to care for him and Lydiann. He figured since Ida was gone, the least he could do was spend plenty of after-supper time with Lydiann and Abe, which was a most pleasant task. Fact was, he wished now he'd done the same with his older daughters when they were small.

One such evening following a meal of pork chops and savory rice, he took Abe from Leah while she and Hannah did the dishes. Dawdi John and Lizzie were with him around the wood stove while he balanced both youngsters on his lap.

Lydiann giggled when he tickled her nose with the length of his soft beard.

"Do it to Abe," Lydiann said playfully.

When he did, his beard made Abe, who was lying in the length of his lap, sneeze.

"Do it again!" Lydiann said, her eyes bright, even mischievous. For a fleeting moment he seemed to be looking into Sadie's little-girl eyes. "Dat . . . will ya?"

Sighing, he was more careful to be gentle this time and held the back of his infant son's hand up to his own face. Then, moving his head slightly, he tickled Abe, much to Lydiann's delight—and to his own.

It was as Abram chuckled and played with his wee ones that he caught Leah's eye across the kitchen. For the first time in many weeks, his heart was full, gladdened beyond words.

As the winter days wore on, Leah and Hannah took turns caring for the babies, trading off working outside with Dat to grease and mend the harnesses. Smithy Gid and Thomas Ebersol were out slaughtering meat animals at both the Peachey and Jesse Ebersol farms, which meant Leah felt more at ease to go about her chores. Knowing she wouldn't run into Gid made her feel at once relieved and as blue as could be.

The occasional sound of red-winged blackbirds reminded her of previous rambles to visit her "piece of earth" and the rare thornless honey locust tree growing deep in the forest behind Aunt Lizzie's log house. But she dared not return there lest she be reminded of her first love and the many letters written to him.

The excitement of upcoming March farm sales brought plenty of chatter from Dat and Dawdi John, especially at mealtime. Even Hannah seemed happy about going along this year, one of the first times Leah remembered her younger sister being interested in such community events. Leah would miss seeing what machinery, cattle, household items, and odds and ends were up for sale, as well as the occasional entire farm on the auction block. Men, women, and children attended, and sometimes the schools closed for the day. It was a wonderful-good time to see dozens of cousins and lifelong friends and anticipate the coming spring, but this year Leah knew her place was snug at home with Lydiann and Abe. Truth be known, she much preferred to be with them than spending all day at a farm sale, anyway.

How things had changed. She contemplated the fact

while peeling potatoes on a Wednesday afternoon at the end of February, recalling the many years she'd rushed out to milk the cows each day at four o'clock, before suppertime. Today she glanced at the day clock, thinking ahead to Dat bringing the cows home. What a cozy, even warm spot the barn was with the animals all inside, waiting for their supper of silage and grain. Even on a bitter cold day like today, Leah missed tending to the animals, their breath warming the air. The Lord God had certainly handpicked a pleasant place for His Son to be born.

On a Saturday in mid-March Leah went on foot to the clinic, having arranged for Mary Ruth to spend a full day baby-sitting Abe and Lydiann. Walking up the sidewalk to the front entrance, she noticed a small white handkerchief. When she stooped to pick it up, she was surprised to see Sadie's butterfly handkerchief, the one with the embroidered cutwork. "What on earth?" she muttered, carrying it inside.

Dr. Schwartz was shuffling through paper work when she arrived at eight-thirty that morning, so she set to work sweeping and washing the floors, dusting, and then shaking out all the rugs, deciding not to bother him just yet. But around nine-fifteen, before the few Saturday patients were scheduled to arrive, she knocked on his open office door.

He looked up, smiled, and waved her inside. "Pull up a chair, Leah."

She removed the handkerchief from her pocket. "I found this lying on the walk. It belonged to my older sister."

His smile faded quickly, and he was silent for a long awkward moment. When he spoke, his voice sounded low and somewhat strained. "Are you sure of this?"

"Completely," she replied. "This is the hankie my sister placed over her dead baby's face the night you delivered him." She paused a moment to breathe. Then she added, "I'm sure you remember, Dr. Schwartz, because, if you don't mind my sayin' so, it was *your* grandson born—and died—that April night, ain't?" She found his expression odd—so peculiar, in fact, that she felt queasy. "It's the *only* handkerchief Hannah ever made like this. A special one indeed."

"Well, if it's Sadie's, as you say, I wonder how it found its way to the ground," he said rather defensively.

"I thought you might've tucked it in with the dead . . . baby—whatever it is a doctor does with a blue baby born too early." Right then, in a rush of memory, Sadie's heartbreaking labor and delivery came to her and caught her off guard. Leah couldn't go on—not this close to Mamma's death. Her heart felt suddenly cold, her nerves shot. She didn't know how she would manage the cleaning tasks ahead of her. "I'm sorry," she said at last. "That awful night still pains me so."

Dr. Schwartz reached out his hand, as though attempting to comfort her from where he sat. "Leah, you are correct about your sister's baby being mine and Lorraine's grandson, though my wife knows nothing of it."

She stared at him in disbelief. "You . . . never told her?"

He shook his head, hands now firmly clasped on the desk. "The news would have caused her tremendous sadness . . . even embarrassment. I saw no need for that."

The thought came to her. *He trusts me not to tell.* "You

must have kept my sister's special handkerchief, then . . . somewhere safe, in case she returned from Ohio?"

"No doubt, I *should* have given it back," he confessed, sighing loudly. "Now you have it in your possession. I suppose it's too late to send it off to Sadie."

"We have no way of contacting her." Then she found herself opening up, sharing her deep sense of loss over both Sadie's severe shunning and Mamma's death.

The doctor listened, removing his glasses and seeming to pay exceptionally close attention. When she was nearly spent, he admitted to her, "I did not keep the handkerchief in a safe place, as you suppose. I guess that's of little consolation to you, and I'm sorry."

Leah's mind was in a whirl. How *could* a warm and caring doctor overlook such a sensitive thing?

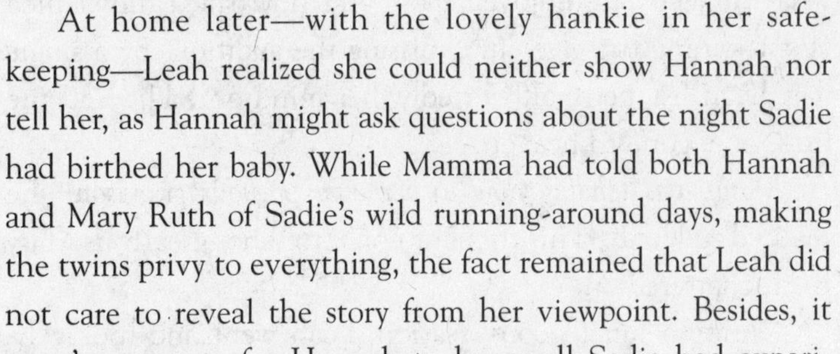

At home later—with the lovely hankie in her safekeeping—Leah realized she could neither show Hannah nor tell her, as Hannah might ask questions about the night Sadie had birthed her baby. While Mamma had told both Hannah and Mary Ruth of Sadie's wild running-around days, making the twins privy to everything, the fact remained that Leah did not care to reveal the story from her viewpoint. Besides, it wasn't necessary for Hannah to know all Sadie had experienced that night.

In the privacy of her room, she caressed the emerald-and-gold butterfly hankie and noticed not a single bloodstain. Dr. Schwartz must have washed it thoroughly in cold water following the birth. Folding it carefully, she placed the delicate item deep in her hope chest, deciding that was the best place for it.

Moved to tears, she knelt beside the bed and asked the Lord to calm her nerves, then offered thanksgiving for the discovery of the handkerchief—the one truly important item of Sadie's she had in her care. She also prayed for God's protection and grace on her wayward sister, "Wherever she might be."

That done, she headed downstairs and turned her attention to Lydiann and Abe, who were in the kitchen being supervised by Mary Ruth. *I must put on a cheerful face*, she thought. *Please, Lord, help me.*

"Did it go well at the clinic?" asked Mary Ruth, warming a bottle for Abe while Lydiann sat at the table trying to string up a dozen or more empty spools.

"Jah, just fine."

Mary Ruth seemed anxious to talk about her schooling—what subjects she enjoyed most and how she'd dillydallied about joining the glee club, missing the auditions by a single day. Leah listened halfheartedly, her mind on Sadie and the little one, gone to heaven.

Mamma is tending now to her own precious grandson! she realized suddenly. This thought comforted her greatly as Mary Ruth chattered on.

During a lull in conversation, Leah went and took Abe from Mary Ruth and held him close. She looked into the tiny face of Mamma's handsome little boy—hair the color of sheaves of grain and those shining blue eyes—and battled both her own quivering lip and the tears that threatened to spill.

Chapter Twenty-Four

Almost before Leah could comprehend it, a full year had passed, taking flight on wings of love. Her hands found plenty to do, and she did it with all her might—kneading and baking daily loaves of bread, scrubbing floors, washing diapers, and helping with the canning. When the after-supper hours rolled around, she often spent time playing with Mamma's babies.

Gradually her keen affection for Smithy Gid began to fade as she became more and more caught up in the routine of caring for a now four-year-old and an eighteen-month-old. Busier days she had never known.

Aunt Lizzie helped some, regularly looking in on Dawdi John due to his age. Dawdi was slowing down quite a lot and hadn't shown any interest in getting out in the fields for plowing or planting this year. Still more telling, he no longer cared for sitting outdoors once the warm days crept up. Truth was, he had become almost as much a homebody as Leah, and she enjoyed his company, taking the little ones next door quite often.

Dawdi had quit his fussing about wanting to return to

Hickory Hollow to live there, what with Mary Ruth's frequent visits. Since Aunt Lizzie continued to dote on him like he was a child, Dawdi John had himself a right nice setup. There were even times when Gid and the smithy came over to chew the fat with him, especially now that warmer weather was upon them. All around, the Ebersol Cottage had somehow managed to get back on an even keel without Mamma's pleasant disposition and her wonderful-good pies, though Leah was mighty glad to have caught up on nearly all of both Mamma's and Aunt Lizzie's recipe files. Gid and his family often benefited from this, as well, since Hannah liked to take an extra pie or two over to the Peachey farm from time to time; a blessing from Leah's hand to her former beau and his kin is the way she thought of it—the least she could do to bring a smile to Smithy Gid's kind face.

Abram asked Leah if she thought Lydiann was old enough to go with him to market and was right surprised to be given the go-ahead. All the way to Strasburg, Lydiann chattered beside him, sitting with her little hands folded in her lap. "I wanna be a gut cook like Mamma Leah," she said, eyes alight as she shared a list of recipes she wanted to learn.

He had to chuckle, but not so loudly she might mistakenly think he was making fun. "You follow your big sister round, and not only will ya be a fine cook but also a careful gardener, plower, sower, and harvester."

"Mamma can do *all* them things?"

He nodded. "All that and more."

Lydiann ducked her chin a bit, like she was taking it all in and rather amazed at the talents of her mother figure.

"Someday I'm sure Leah will teach you how to milk a cow," he volunteered.

Lydiann looked up at him, eyes blinking. "She already did. Just the other morning she sat me down on a stool, smack-dab under Ol' Rosie."

"Did she, now?"

"Jah, and it was the funniest thing." Lydiann sighed, unfolding her hands and adjusting her small bonnet. "Mamma Leah says I'll be out milking every mornin' once I turn six."

"Is that so?" He smiled more to himself than to his young daughter. Seemed Leah was bound and determined to create another outdoor girl, which was right fine with him. The world could definitely benefit from more than one Leah Ebersol, he decided then and there. Reaching around Lydiann, he pulled her into a bear hug to a stream of giggles.

Gid was more than willing to help move Ivan and Mary Etta Troyer and their brood of ten children—newly transplanted from Sugarcreek, Ohio—into the farmhouse down the road from the Kauffmans' spread. Glad for a mild and sunny day, he carried heavy boxes into the large farmhouse, as well as the trestle table and kitchen benches. All the while he thought of Leah, wondering how to approach her with his news. After all, they had enjoyed a long-standing friendship nearly their whole lives, one that had even weathered the sad yet necessary end of their engagement. While he and three other young men from the church district got the new family settled, he considered stopping by the Ebersol home to visit with Leah after a bit. *Out of courtesy to such a dear friend.*

When he was free to leave, he headed up Georgetown Road in his open buggy, turning a sharp right into Abram's long drive. He noticed young Abe toddling about in the side yard, doing his best to chase after a red squirrel. The boy pointed a curious finger at the tree branch where the small creature had decided to perch. Abram came around the corner and scooped his son up into his arms, standing there with Abe still pointing and jabbering.

"Hullo!" Abram called to him.

Getting out of the carriage, Gid waved and hurried across the yard. "Catch any squirrels yet, Abe?" He tousled the towheaded youngster's thick hair.

"He's most interested in things that move," Abram explained. "Leah has her hands full watching *this* young'un."

"I see that."

"Well, let's go, Abe," Abram said as he carried him out toward the barn. Abram turned to look over his shoulder. "You here to see—?"

"Leah," Gid said quickly, making his way to the back door.

"Don't bother to knock," Abram called back to him. "Just give a holler. She's inside makin' supper."

He crept in the door furtively, quite aware of his own breathing. He called out her name. "Leah . . . it's Gid."

Turning, she looked at him from where she stood at the counter. She offered that warm and lovely smile of hers, and he wondered if it might disappear once she heard his confession. "Got a minute?" he asked.

She nodded. "What's on your mind?"

He knew full well that Hannah and Lydiann were out on the mule road together, for he'd seen them rolling a big ball on the ground, back and forth, as he'd come up the lane. He must not waste any time before sharing his heart. "I've been meaning to talk with ya."

She wore a slight look of worry on her face.

"I think it best you hear directly from me. Not through the grapevine . . ." He was conscious of the heat of his long-sleeved shirt for the first time today, and he tugged on the cuff absentmindedly. "You see, I've become quite fond of your sister Hannah," he started again. "I plan to speak to Abram 'bout the possibility of courting her. If, well . . . if it seems all right with you."

Her eyes were suddenly brighter than before. "All right? Oh, Gid, of course, it is. Really 'tis!" Then she surprised him by reaching for his hand. "This is wonderful-gut news, truly."

For a moment he thought he might hug her. But he refrained from doing so, squeezing only her hand. "Denki, Leah. This means a lot to me."

Pulling back, he stood there, gazing at her, his former love. His first and only sweetheart . . . till now. What an unexpected surprise that his heart should be reawakened with love for another when he hadn't thought such a thing possible. He was glad to have taken time to talk with Leah, just as Abram had encouraged him to do. Thoughtful as always, Leah had given him a most precious gift—reassurance that all was well.

Lizzie's nose was but a few inches from the damp earth. She'd gone tramping through the woods, needing a chance to clear her head, what with being cooped up too much these days in the Dawdi Haus with her ailing father. Bent nearly double, she laughed at herself, glad she was still as spry as ever. She pulled herself up from the barely visible trail and brushed off her long dress and apron. *Goodness me*, she thought, cracking a twig underfoot as she rose to stand. How she'd ever gotten her foot tangled in the underbrush, she didn't know. After all, she knew these vast woods like the back of her hand and wasn't any too shy about saying so.

They were, after all, her woods—hers and God's. Smiling, she turned and headed back east toward Abram's house. Springtime humidity hung in the air, making the moss grow faster on tree trunks around her. Creepers adorned the spruce and maples, leaving a welcome impression in her mind. Breathing deeply, she found herself thinking of her brother-in-law. He *had* begun to soften toward Mary Ruth, and this made Lizzie sit up and take notice. Ida's widower was also noticeably less gruff in general. Lizzie didn't know what to make of it, but she knew she liked working alongside him in the barn and elsewhere a whole lot more than ever before. Deciding right then she would not let up on her talk of the Lord, nearly daily now it seemed, she pushed on and made her way toward the clearing.

There she spotted Smithy Gid in the distance, climbing into his open buggy. *Same courting buggy he's had all these years, poor fella.* Seeing his carriage parked in Abram's lane set her mind to racing. While she had long suspected Gid of being sweet on Hannah, she wondered why he was showing up here in broad daylight.

Making her way down the mule road, she happened to see

Leah waving through the kitchen window at him. *A dearer boy there never was*, she thought, happy for Hannah but a little sad for Leah, who would never fully know Gid's love. Or any man's, for that matter.

Dear Lord, bless Leah today, she prayed. *Bless our faithful girl with your tender grace.*

◆

With another summer came opportunities for getting Lydiann and Abe outdoors, and Leah was glad of it. She liked to spread an old blanket out on the back lawn and sit and play with the children, sometimes feeding them small pieces of apple and orange. King, Blackie, and Sassy wandered over to investigate the fruity treats amid squeals of delight from the children, especially from Lydiann, who was nearly as fond of the dogs as she was her baby brother. Now and then Dat would stop what he was doing and make over the tots, paying closest attention to Abe.

It was late morning and Abe was fussy, ready for a nap. Hannah had just returned from the barn and came running over and plopped down on the blanket. "'Tis a right nice day, ain't?"

"One of the best times of year," Leah replied. "Wild roses are awful perty, farmers are makin' hay, and honeysuckle never smelt sweeter."

"And . . . young scholars can say, 'no more papers, no more books . . . no more teacher's tetchy looks,'" Hannah chanted the familiar verse. "Sure am glad *I'm* not in school anymore."

"Your thoughts must be with Mary Ruth today," said Leah.

"S'pose they are." She skimmed the palm of her hand across the blades of grass, and Sassy came and playfully nipped at Hannah's fingers. "The house seems so quiet sometimes, is all."

"How can that be, with the children growin' up under our noses?"

Hannah sighed. "You know what I mean."

Leah nodded; she knew, all right.

They sat there enjoying the warm weather and a hint of a breeze every so often, the scents of summer all around. The big leaves of the linden tree quaked gently outside the window.

"What's *really* on your mind, sister?" Leah said at last.

Hannah twitched her nose, looking at Lydiann. "How long before our little sister understands certain things?"

"Whatever do you mean?"

She leaned over and whispered in Leah's ear. "I need to talk to you . . . in private sometime."

"Well, why not say what's on your mind in English 'stead of Dutch? That'll keep Lydiann in the dark, if that's what you want." Leah rose and carried Abe to the back door while Hannah took Lydiann's hand and led her inside.

"I'll put Abe down for his nap," said Hannah while Leah sent Lydiann upstairs to find her dolly and a cradle.

When Hannah returned, her face was flushed. "Ach, but this might seem strange to you"—here she guided Leah through the kitchen to the screened-in back porch. "I don't know how you'll feel 'bout this. . . ."

"What is it, Hannah?" She studied her sister's eyes. Big

and brown, they were, and dancing like she'd never seen them.

"What I'm tryin' to say is, what would ya think if I told ya I like Smithy Gid? Not as just a friend, I mean."

Leah couldn't help herself. So . . . Gid had already talked to Hannah about the possibility of going for steady. She smiled and clapped her hands. "Well, it's clearly all over your face. I couldn't be happier for you—both of you."

"You mean it?"

"I can't think of a better match for Gid than my own precious sister."

Hannah kissed her good-bye. "I best not be gone too long, or Dat will wonder what's become of me." She turned and hurried away.

"Jah, go on now. But be back for dinner at straight-up noon," Leah called after her. She headed to the kitchen. Hannah deserved to have an attentive beau like Smithy Gid, dear soul that she was. No need to think twice on it. And she was the perfect choice for Gid, as well. To think Dat just might get his son-in-law of choice, after all!

As for Hannah, she'd been through a wringer of sorts, what with Ezra Stoltzfus's leaving the Amish church behind, getting himself shunned so soon after baptism. The grapevine had it that he'd upped and gone *ferhoodled* or worse after the death of Elias, as wild as if he'd never knelt his knee in baptism. So Hannah was better off, his dropping her like a hot potato and all, making it possible for Gid to have his chance.

Leah found Lydiann talking Dutch to her little faceless doll. She was saying it might not be so long and they'd all be going fishing with Dat and "Smitty Gid" over at Blackbird Pond . . . and wouldn't that be such fun?

Lydiann would enjoy the benefits of growing up with a brother; something Leah had always felt she'd missed. *She* had been the boy of the family, so to speak, but those days were gone for good. She was truly the woman of the house, not only Mamma to Lydiann and Abe, but the matriarch in charge of seeing that the household ran smoothly, including the Dawdi Haus. She no longer felt she'd missed out on certain joy by not marrying, as her friend Adah and most every other girl her age in the church community had. Goodness, Naomi Bontrager was already expecting her second baby.

In all of this, Leah did not feel she was fooling herself; after all, being a maidel was evidently her lot in life, and her role in helping raise Abe and Lydiann was a good one. She had dealt with her resentment toward Sadie and moved forward with life, ever so glad to be a mother to her youngest siblings. Truly it was God who had seen fit to bless her with these two adorable children.

After the noon meal, Abram was right pleased to see Leah outdoors with Abe and Lydiann in tow. He stopped to pump some well water, quenching his thirst while he fanned himself with his beat-up straw hat. He sure could use a new one. His father-in-law hadn't minced words about it, complaining to high heavens about how "awful ratty that old hat looks." John seemed to pick at near everything Abram did or didn't do these days. He'd become a rather cantankerous sort, living alone without his wife of many decades and losing his daughter Ida, all in the space of a few years. Still, Abram could relate all too keenly to John's hopelessness. In other ways, though, John had mellowed some recently, especially when it came time for Mary Ruth's visits.

With that in mind, he thought he ought to pay John a visit himself before too long.

Chatter from Abe brought his attention back to the present. "Thirsty?" he asked Leah.

Lydiann spoke up before Leah could, asking for a nice cold drink herself. Leah looked right pleased, watching Lydiann hold the dipper and sipper, the excess water dripping down her plump cheeks. Of course, now Abe was grousing for equal treatment.

Once the little ones were satisfied, they wandered about the lawn barefooted and laughing, soaking up the afternoon sunshine. His heart swelled with pride, glad for this moment to pause and reflect on the good thing his Leah had done . . . was *doing*. "Denki, Leah . . . for bein' such a gut mamma to the children." He wished he'd said this a long time ago.

"Dat . . . that's all right." Leah gave him a warm smile. "I love seein' them grow up like this."

"You've given up everything for my little ones." They both knew he was talking about Smithy Gid in particular.

"I'm happy with my life. Honestly." She paused, turning to check where Abe and Lydiann had disappeared to. Then she continued, "I prob'ly shouldn't say this, but you surely know Gid's sweet on Hannah." She said it nearly in a whisper.

"Oh, jah." He was careful not to react too cheerfully, wanting to be sensitive to any open wounds remaining from Leah and Gid's breakup. He looked her over but good. "Well, now . . . how do *you* feel 'bout it?"

She smiled again. "It's 'bout time you got the son-in-law you've been waitin' for!"

He studied her mighty hard at this instant, wondering . . . hoping . . . then, beyond all doubt, he knew she was quite sincere. Eagerly so, it seemed by the look of delight on her pretty face.

He called to Abe, who came running and jumped high into his arms. "Come along," he said, offering a hand to help up Leah. "Let's ride over to Georgetown and have us all some ice cream."

This brought an even bigger smile to Leah's face. To the words *ice cream*, Lydiann and Abe clapped with delight, which made Abram feel right pleased with himself. The Good Lord was surely shining down His blessings. *In spite of myself*, thought Abram.

Chapter Twenty-five

Leah was anxious to attend the July Sisters Day at Adah's house, two miles away. Thanks to Aunt Lizzie volunteering to baby-sit Lydiann and Abe, Leah was freed up to go with Hannah. Lizzie had been insisting all week long that it was high time for Leah to be around other adults. "You're in the house too much," she kept saying.

Leah had laughed, recognizing what her aunt said was true and looking forward to the outing. The women folk did share a gift of close friendship, even though she'd never much cared for their work frolics growing up.

"Friendships are the core of our lives, ain't so?" she said, enjoying the carriage ride.

Hannah nodded. "And sisters are always the best of friends."

"I should say." Leah wondered if Hannah was maudlin about her twin again, although Mary Ruth had been coming to see them three or four times a week lately. Aunt Lizzie, Dawdi John, and even Dat enjoyed seeing her, as well, and yearned for the delicious dishes Mary Ruth sometimes brought to share with the family, though she was reluctant to stay and eat, out of respect for Dat.

"We're mirrors to the past, in a way," Hannah said softly. "We look into each other's faces and remember what we know. . . ."

"Well, now, you're sounding like a dreamer today."

Hannah laughed. "Guess maybe Mary Ruth's rubbin' off on me some."

"But what you say is true. There *is* such deep understanding between sisters."

Hannah nodded and fell silent. Leah was thankful for this time alone, just the two of them. Scarcely did they ever have the opportunity to go out riding or to a work frolic like this. The sky seemed a prettier blue today and little robin red breast sang stronger because Hannah was here to share the day.

Once they arrived at Adah's house, Leah was happy to see Adah's younger sister, Dorcas, as well as Adah's five sisters-in-law, Ebersol cousins all. The kitchen was full up with sisters of every shape and size, peeling tomatoes at the sink, boiling water in large pots, preparing to stew the red fruit, as well as make soup and spaghetti sauce—an all-day affair. Several were expecting babies, including Adah herself. Leah found this sight, here in Adah's cozy kitchen, not only joyful on behalf of her dear friend, but she was excited for Adah to join yet again the maternal realm. "We're sharing the joys of motherhood after all, you and I," she whispered to her.

Adah flashed a quick sad look, but Leah squeezed her hand to reassure her all was well. Truly, it was.

Hannah helped mash a mountain of cooked tomatoes. After a time the mushy red color and strong odor made her feel queasy, and she wondered how she'd ever manage attending such canning frolics as Smithy Gid's wife someday. His mother's side of the family was tomato crazy, putting up anything and everything with the fruit in it. Far as she could tell, though, that was the one and only drawback to her marrying into the Peachey family one fine day.

She tried holding her breath as she crushed the nasty red fruits, but that didn't work, either, because when it came time for her to breathe again, she had to fill her lungs even more deeply with the fragrant aroma.

"Is Leah doin' okay, really?" Adah asked her, unaware Hannah was the one struggling at the moment, though not emotionally.

"She seems fine to me," she replied, glad to raise her head and her nose out of the immediate vicinity of the tomatoes. "Leah's the sweetest mother to Lydiann and Abe," she offered. "You should see her with them."

"I've seen her all right; I just can never tell for sure if Leah's all right *inside*," Adah persisted.

"Jah, I believe she is." Hannah wanted to put Adah's fears to rest. After all, she and Adah were soon to be sisters by marriage. She'd told no one just yet, but, short time that it had been since he'd declared his feelings for her, darling Gid had not only begun to court her but had already proposed marriage. He wasn't wasting any time, which was right fine with her, being she'd known him her entire life and Dat, Dawdi John, and Aunt Lizzie were all for it. "Long as it won't hurt Leah further," Lizzie had been quick to say.

"If there's ever any doubt, Hannah, you'll let me know 'bout Leah, jah?" asked Adah, clearly still devoted after all these years.

Adah, precious friend to Leah—always thinking of others, just as Leah was known to. *And that nearly to a fault*, Hannah thought. *Sometimes my sister is better to others than to herself.*

While Gid waited to shoe his next horse, he set about redding up. Suddenly thirsty, he finished sweeping the floor and ran to the house for some cold lemonade. Oddly enough, the kitchen, fragrant with the scent of freshly baked muffins, was empty. He walked to the window and stood watching for his customer, glad for the solitude. Gulping down a tall glass, he returned to the icebox and poured another. He then went and perched himself on the long bench next to the table, sitting there with his glass in hand.

All the while he daydreamed of pretty Hannah. There was something about the way she looked at him that made him think she was not just pretty but truly lovely. *She's very young*, he thought, realizing anew how peculiar it had seemed—but only at first—to meet up with fair Hannah Ebersol at a Sunday singing, though he'd seen and talked to her plenty of times out in Abram's barn. More than hesitant that particular night, he soon found his voice and discovered her to be nearly as easy to talk to as Leah, if not more so. Attentive and sweet, Hannah had won his heart in a matter of a few buggy rides home.

Right this minute he wondered if the Lord God might've had all this planned from the foundations of the earth, giving back the years he'd lost while waiting for Leah. Was it heresy to think about the heavenly Father that way? Gid had no intention of deliberating the notion, but it was true that Hannah, at only eighteen, had a good many childbearing years ahead of her as his loving wife. They would have themselves a wonderful-good time raising their brood, and if their babies looked anything like Hannah, he would be a very blessed and happy man.

He removed his straw hat and scratched his head. The Almighty certainly worked in extraordinary ways, seemed to him. Downright mystifying it was.

The clatter of carriage wheels brought him to his feet, and he left his glass half full on the table as he hurried outside to greet both horse and client.

It was on the ride home from Adah's that Leah and Hannah got to talking heart to heart. Weary from being on her feet for much of the day, Leah was content to sit back and relax, let Hannah rein down the horse to a slow walk, and, of all things, do much of the talking. She was getting to be nearly as chatty as Mary Ruth. *Nice to see her coming out of her shell little by little*, Leah thought, listening to her prattle about this and that.

They were coming up on the corner where a left-hand turnoff would lead to Naomi's parents' farmhouse when Hannah stopped talking and began humming a hymn from the Ausbund.

Smithy Gid came to mind and Leah said, "I think you and Gid are a right nice match."

"Oh?"

"Both of you enjoy music so."

"Jah, he plays his harmonica all the time." She paused, blushing a little.

"Not *all* the time, I hope."

"Oh, Leah . . . you know what I mean." At this they began to giggle.

Just then two old codgers rode toward them, their white beards as long as any Leah had ever seen. They were leaning back against the seat, downright relaxed, just taking their sweet time. "Like there's no tomorrow," she whispered to Hannah.

The presence of another carriage made them quickly gather their wits and stop the tittering, since the men were within earshot. Once they'd passed, Hannah resumed their conversation. "If you feel comfortable 'bout it, I'd like you to be one of my bridesmaids, Leah."

"That's awful nice of you," Leah replied, meaning it.

"So you'll stand up with me?"

"'Course I will."

"'Tis awful sad Mary Ruth has no chance of being my bridesmaid."

Leah felt sorry, too. "Jah, but I wouldn't think of askin' Dat's permission on that. I can imagine what he'd say."

"Ain't that the truth."

"Be glad Mary Ruth will at least be in attendance," Leah reminded Hannah.

"Jah, that I am."

Leah, eager to cheer her sister, continued on a positive note. "Just think how happy Mamma would be over your upcoming marriage," she said. "She always liked Gid, ya know."

Hannah sighed. "We'll all miss her at the wedding, ain't so?"

Leah agreed and closed her eyes, thinking of dear Mamma.

Hannah stirred her back to the present. "I wish with all of my heart one certain sister could be on hand to witness my marriage, too."

Drowsily Leah reached over and patted Hannah's hand. "I know, dear sister. I know."

They rode quietly now, surrounded by the twitter of birds and the scent of new-mown hay and early harvest apples ripening in orchards. Leah found herself wondering how many more times she might be asked to be a bridesmaid. Naturally, as time went on, she would be passed over; no bride in her right mind would invite an old maidel to stand up with her. Maybe this *would* be the last time, which was quite all right. What with both Sadie and Mary Ruth having flown the nest, she could be Hannah's supportive and gentle right hand. Knowing her, dear Hannah would need a close sister-friend on her wedding day.

Evident in Hannah's eyes was her deep fondness for Smithy Gid. Leah was fully aware how much in love her sister and Gid were. *The love they share is the kind Jonas and I had together,* she thought. *The kind both Gid and Hannah deserve.*

While she had cared a great deal for Gid, lately she had come to the realization her love for him had not been the same as her love for Jonas. She had made this conscious discovery simply by watching Hannah's face when she spoke of

Gid, and, on one occasion, by observing them from afar as they held hands and walked together, Hannah leaning her head against Gid's strong arm. The adoring way they seemed to bend toward each other, even as they walked and talked, brought back a rush of memories. *So like the way Jonas and I always did. . . .*

Upon their return home, Leah let Hannah unhitch the horse and lead him to water in the barn, as she had so kindly offered to do. Leah tried to swallow the lump in her throat but did not succeed. Hastily she headed to the house, more eager than ever to hold Lydiann and Abe—*her* little ones—close to her heart.

Part Two

◆ ◆ ◆ ◆

There is no greatness where there is

no simplicity, goodness and truth.

—Leo Tolstoy

◆ ◆ ◆ ◆

Truth, crushed to earth, shall rise again.

—William Cullen Bryant

Chapter Twenty-Six

Spring 1956

The month of May arrived in misty splendor. Yellow daffodils, along with purple and red tulips, raised their radiant heads to the sky. Creeks were swollen and burbling, and it seemed to Leah every song sparrow, robin, and meadowlark must be joining in the springtime chorus.

She stood out near the hen house, watching Lydiann scatter feed, talking soft and low to the chickens and the solitary rooster. *The way I always did,* she thought, smiling. Leah was glad school doors were closed for summer vacation, the last day having been Friday, the eighteenth, one day following Lydiann's ninth birthday.

Tall for her age, Lydiann reminded Leah of Sadie as a child. Though rather lanky like Leah, the energetic youngster had outgrown her topsy-turvy tendency to fall over not only herself but also occasional buckets of fresh milk, half-gallon pails of shelled peas, and whatnot. Both Dat and Leah were thankful for Lydiann's zeal for assisting with outdoor chores, what with Hannah busy mothering two small girls—Ida Mae, named for Mamma, and baby Katie Ann. Smithy Gid and

Hannah lived snug and contented in Aunt Lizzie's former log house, while Lizzie had moved down to the Dawdi Haus to care for Dawdi John after Gid and Hannah had tied the knot at a late autumn wedding four and a half years ago.

Cheerful and hardworking, Abe was almost six and a half and his father's shadow. Leah felt truly blessed to witness the close father-son relationship unfolding daily.

"That rooster's poutin', ain't so, Mamma Leah?" Lydiann said, frowning.

"I daresay you could be right 'bout that."

"He's mighty pushy, too . . . whatever's botherin' him?"

She went to stand near Lydiann. "Seems to me he wants some attention."

"From one of the hens . . . or from me?" Lydiann's sweet voice still retained its childlike appeal.

Leah smiled. "*All* the hens, prob'ly."

Laughing, Lydiann grinned at her. "Ach, Mamma, you're pullin' my leg. He don't want *all* them hens a-lookin' at him preenin', does he?"

"Well, maybe not." She put her hand on Lydiann's slender shoulder. They stood rooted to the spot, watching the chickens peck and scrap over their dinner, amused at their antics.

Abe came hollering out of the barn, running toward them. "Mamma! Lydiann! You's must come have a look-see!"

"What on earth?" Leah hurried to follow him back to the barn, with Lydiann close behind.

Abe made haste, climbing as fast as his short legs would take him, up the ladder to the hayloft. Getting to the top, he set about catching one of many cats. When he'd done so, he held it up by the nape of its neck and pointed to its hind end. "See, she's missin' her tail!"

Leah didn't know whether to laugh or cry at such a sorry sight.

Lydiann spoke up first. "She got it cut off during the harvest last year's my guess."

"Either that or the fellas got her on a lark—durin' a pest hunt," volunteered Abe.

Leah flinched. Abe was much too young to be aware of such things; he was just out of first grade, for goodness' sake! Truth was, some of the young men in the community were a bit too rowdy for her liking. They chose up sides nearly every night during harvest, giving themselves points for snuffing out the life of farm pests, a practice that kept teenage boys in the midst of rumschpringe busy in Gobbler's Knob instead of out smoking or chasing after worldly girls in Lancaster. Each side collected heads and tails for points, everything from rats and sparrows, to hawks and starlings. The group with the most points was rewarded with a baked-ham dinner.

"Does it hurt anything for a cat not to have a tail?" asked Lydiann.

"Makes it hard to keep the flies off her, I'd think," Abe spoke up, his dark blue eyes twinkling, framed by long thick lashes.

"Why did a cat get picked as a pest, I wonder?" Lydiann peered closely at the spot where the tail had been severed.

"Too many kitties can be looked on as a problem by some folk," Leah answered, wishing to switch to another subject. She'd known of farmers who drowned or shot their excess feline population, but if she had her way, there'd be a house cat or two living *inside* the Ebersol Cottage. Mamma never cared much for indoor pets, though, and neither did most of the women folk in the community, for that matter. These days, Dat had better things to do than argue for or against having a favorite cat, and Leah had decided not to pursue the matter.

"This one must've wandered over to the Peachey farm last fall, ain't?" Abe said, eyes still wide.

"Sad to say." Leah turned to head toward the ladder, hoping the children would follow and leave the subject of the poor cat be.

"I heard from brother Gid that Smitty asked for a pest hunt." Abe put the cat down and shuffled across the haymow. "Too many sparrows were diggin' holes in the straw stacks and roostin' in there. Them boys sewed some big ol' blankets together and trapped the birds inside the stacks. Once they got too hot or stopped breathing, the fellas just went in and cut off their heads."

Lydiann shrieked. "Mamma, make him stop talkin' 'bout that!"

Leah waited for Abe to bound down from the ladder, then placed a firm but gentle hand on his head. She stroked his blond hair, the color of the straw stacks he'd just described. "Best not be wishin' your youth away, young man," she said. "There's plenty of time for goin' on a lark with the boys."

"I s'pose" was all he said, and they headed back outside.

Lydiann tugged on her brother's black suspenders. "Lookee up there," she said, pointing at the sky. "Now *that's* a sight worth talking 'bout."

And it surely was. Leah noticed sunbeams threading a

pathway through a wispy patch of clouds, thankful for Lydiann's keen interest in the more pleasant side of nature. Abe, of course, was all boy with an ongoing appetite for food and otherwise and far louder than any of Abram's daughters had ever been, full of pep and broad grins. He was always mighty eager to find the first bumblebees come spring, which meant it was finally time to shed shoes and run barefoot. He also loved to take his fishing pole to the nearby creek or Blackbird Pond, sometimes joined by both Gid and Dat, but mostly—Leah knew this all too well—taking off to his favorite fishing hole without ever telling a soul where he was headed.

Just now he looked downright ornery with his front tooth missing—a true disheveled schoolboy with cropped hair. Scarcely, though, did Abe ever wear the straw hat expected to be worn by all men and boys starting at age two. *Hat or not, he's ever so dear,* she thought, wishing Mamma might have lived to see this day. These precious beautiful children were having the best time of their young lives, soaking up summertime.

God doeth all things well. . . .

She and Lydiann headed into the house. Without being told, Lydiann scrubbed her hands, and then set the table while Leah took the roasted chicken, stuffed with bread dressing, out of the oven.

Thinking again of Mamma, she asked Lydiann if she'd like to take a long walk after dinner. Bobbing her blond head, Lydiann said she would. Abe would be going over to Smithy Gid's grandfather's place with Dat this afternoon because Mathias Byler, Miriam Peachey's father, needed a hand with transplanting young tobacco plants into the field. Abe especially liked to go to "Dawdi Byler's," as Gid encouraged him to address the older gentleman, since young Abe got a kick out of hearing both Gid and Gid's grandfather play their harmonicas together.

After dishes were washed and dried, she and Lydiann made their way down the long lane toward the road, heading past the Peachey farm, clear out to the turnoff to the Kauffmans'.

Down the road a ways, they turned and climbed over a vine-filled ditch and then up a slight embankment, heading to the Amish cemetery protected by giant shade trees.

"Dat's parents are buried here somewhere," Leah said softly.

"They passed on before I was born, ain't?"

She nodded, looking down at Lydiann. "You would've loved Dawdi and Mammi Ebersol . . . a lot."

"What were they like?"

"Dawdi was kind and fun loving, yet he had his own ideas, I guess you could say."

"Bullheaded, ya mean?" Lydiann surprised her by saying.

"Ach, that doesn't become you, child."

"*Es dutt mir leed.*" Lydiann hung her head.

"You best be sorry," Leah was quick to say, reminding herself of Mamma, who had never approved of her daughters speaking out of turn, calling folk names.

"Mammi Ebersol was sweet as cherry pie . . . never said an unkind word 'bout anyone. Not her whole life."

"I could be that sweet—even as honey," Lydiann said, looking up at her with innocent, yet spirited eyes.

"Jah, that you can certainly be." *When you want to,* she thought.

With that Lydiann reached for her hand, and they walked for a while amidst the headstones and trees. Leah was aware, once again, of the birds' exhilarating song. "Did you ever hear this verse from the Good Book? 'The flowers appear on the earth; the time of the singing of birds is come . . .'?"

"Can't say I have. Where'd *you* hear it?"

"Mamma told it to me once. She loved to listen to the birds, 'specially early in the morning."

Lydiann's eyes suddenly looked bluer. "What else did Mamma love?"

"That's easy." She turned and knelt down in the soft woodland grass. "She loved *you.* I wish you could remember her carryin' you here and there, talkin' to you in Dutch and English both, hopin' you'd grow up to respect the land and listen for the song of nature all round you."

"Aunt Lizzie does that, too, ain't so?"

"Maybe more than all of us."

"Even more than Mamma did?"

She hugged Lydiann close. "Each sister had certain things she enjoyed about God's green earth. For Mamma it was the birds and the way the sky could paint itself all kinds of colors. She saw the Lord God clearly in all of His creation, just as Aunt Lizzie does. Lizzie especially likes trampin' through the hillock up behind the house where Hannah and Gid live now."

"That's awful gut of Aunt Lizzie, givin' up her house and moving in with Dawdi."

"I should say, but it's the way of the People, ya know." She rose and looked around, wishing she could walk straight to Mamma's grave, without getting lost as she had the previous time. It had been months since her last visit, as she had rejected the inclination to visit the graveyard during the frost and cold of winter—such a severe time to think of dearest Mamma lying cold in the ground. She was ever so glad that six feet under wasn't the end of things. According to Aunt Lizzie, Mamma's spirit was with the Lord Jesus. Her body was simply the unique shell of her, housing her spirit.

Leah located the small white marker with the few words etched in its stone:

Ida Brenneman Ebersol
B. September 2, 1904
D. December 27, 1949

"Will we ever see Mamma again?" Lydiann asked.

Leah was a bit taken aback by Lydiann's question. Truly, she did not wish to step on Dat's toes, because Lydiann was *his* daughter. "Jah, I happen to believe we will someday," she said hesitantly, longing to share the eternal truth as she understood it.

"But Dat says it's up to the Lord God on Judgment Day whether we go to heaven or to the *bad* place," Lydiann spoke up. "He says we can't know if we're saved just yet."

For sure, just as all the brethren were, Dat was adamant about that Day of Days being the first and only time a person would know where he or she was to spend eternity. Still, she knew there were some who believed differently amongst the People, as she did. Silent believers, Aunt Lizzie liked to call them.

"Always remember this, Lydiann—the Lord Jesus came as a baby to give us life. And not only while we're alive here on earth. In heaven, too."

"For certain, Mamma?" Lydiann asked, eyes wide with the hearing.

"Sure as God's love . . . that's the honest truth."

Lydiann seemed satisfied and turned to scamper around the cemetery, peering down at the small markers, reading the names and dates aloud in Pennsylvania Dutch.

Meanwhile, Leah sat beside her mother's grave. *We all miss you, Mamma,* she thought. *Except for Dat, I daresay I miss you most of all.*

The wild ferns growing close to the road were nearly ankle-deep as Leah and Lydiann walked leisurely home from the cemetery. Leah pointed out one bird after another and yellow buttercups growing in clusters with no rhyme or reason.

"Why do ya think the Lord God made such perty colors every place?" asked Lydiann.

"Well, just think of all the different colors of people there are—red and yellow, black and white . . . we're all precious in His sight."

"That's the song Mary Ruth sings to me, ain't so?"

Leah nodded. She'd heard Mamma singing "Jesus Loves the Little Children," too, but Lydiann couldn't have remembered since she was only two when Mamma died. Mary Ruth, on the other hand, had sung it all the time to Lydiann and

Carl Nolt when he was little. Here lately Mary Ruth had been saying she thought it was a shame young Carl and Lydiann hadn't gotten acquainted as playmates, since they were neighbors and all, but truth was, Dat had no interest in either Lydiann or Abe rubbing shoulders much with Englishers. When all was said and done, Mennonites surely were Englishers, at least in Dat's book. Preacher Yoder's, too.

Thinking about the highly revered minister, she recalled he hadn't been able to attend Preaching service several times in a row. Word had it he was suffering from a bad heart—that, and some serious problems with asthma, which she guessed only worsened his heart ailment.

She and Lydiann had been walking for a while, working up a sweat, when Lydiann began to count the tiny white moths that fluttered here and there. Enjoying the sun and warm breeze, Leah happened to look off to the north and, lo and behold, if she didn't spy Dr. Schwartz's automobile parked in the field just down from Peacheys' property.

Curious, she strained to see, but what she saw startled her so much she stopped in her tracks. *Why's he kneeling in the grass . . . near that little mound of dirt?* she wondered, recalling the day she and Jonas had stumbled upon the peculiar plot.

"What're we stoppin' for?" asked Lydiann.

Promptly Leah started walking again, lest her young charge continue to ask questions or, worse, realize who was over there tending a grave with hand clippers and ask to go and talk to her *Dokder*.

"Come along, now." She picked up the pace. "You and I best be getting home for milkin'." She pointed out the Kauffmans' farm on the left side of the road, hoping to distract

Lydiann from *whatever* was going on over on the right. She succeeded, or thought she had, saying they ought to go visit Naomi and Luke here before too long, down near Ninepoints, where the couple had built themselves a nice new house with plenty of room for their growing family of young sons.

Thankfully they were nearing home when Lydiann piped up. "That was our doctor in the field, jah?"

Leah didn't say it was or wasn't; she simply hurried up the lane leading to the barnyard.

When they approached the house, Lydiann asked again.

"Dr. Schwartz owns that field" was all Leah cared to say.

Chapter Twenty-Seven

Hannah must've wanted to talk to Leah in the worst way, because she followed her up to the outhouse. "I know something 'bout Mary Ruth, but you can't tell a soul," she said, hurrying to keep step.

Leah had made several promises in her life that had cost her dearly, so she was rather hesitant for Hannah to say more. "Happy news, I hope?"

Hannah's face shone with the secret. "You'll be so surprised, I'm thinkin' . . . and jah, it's right happy. Wanna guess?"

"I'm afraid I'm too tired for that."

"Ach, don't go spoilin' my fun." Hannah looked hurt.

Leah couldn't have that. "I *do* want to hear what's on your mind. It's just, well . . . I'm not so interested in hearsay, ya know."

With a most sincere smile on her face, Hannah said, "This came straight from the horse's mouth, so ya don't have to worry none." She stopped to bend down and pull a weed out from between her toes. "Mary Ruth must've forgiven the English driver."

"Who?"

"You know . . . the young man who hit and killed Elias Stoltzfus."

Robert Schwartz? Leah suddenly felt tense.

"She's seein' the doctor's son, that young minister she and I heard preach in Quarryville years back, remember?"

"Are you certain of this?" She knew she must sound like a mother hen talking so straight, but, if true, this *was* interesting news!

"Mary Ruth told me . . . and agreed only you could know, too. Ya know, if Robert Schwartz should end up marryin' our sister, well, she could be a schoolteacher *and* a preacher's wife someday. Now, don't that beat all?"

Actually, Leah was somewhat startled at Hannah's apparent enthusiasm. "I didn't think you cared two cents 'bout Mennonite beliefs. So . . . why are *you* happy?"

"After Elias died so young and all, I'm awful glad Mary Ruth's not grieving anymore," Hannah said. "She's lookin' ahead to her future."

"The doctor and his wife are fine folk," Leah said. "I would hope their older son is just as nice, 'specially if he's a preacher. But can you imagine him falling for an Amish girl?"

"Well, she ain't so Amish anymore."

"Jah, 'tis true." Leah couldn't help but think how odd it was that another one of the doctor's sons had fallen for a Plain girl.

"Mary Ruth says Robert's completed his Bible studies in Virginia and has been offered a part-time job at the Quarryville church. I guess he'll fill in for the head pastor at times and teach Sunday school some, too. Mary Ruth will see him plenty . . . gut enough reason to attend services." To this Hannah laughed softly.

"I wonder if she realizes what might be required of her if they were to, well . . . marry," Leah said.

"I s'pose that remains to be seen. But for now she's all smiles. For sure and for certain."

Leah pondered the news. If Mary Ruth continued to see Robert, more than likely she'd never return to join the Amish church. Dat would be awful disappointed over that. Mamma, on the other hand, wouldn't care one bit up in heaven. But then again, a crush wasn't much to worry about, was it?

Robert sat behind the wheel, waiting for the gas station attendant to wash and dry the car's front and rear windows. He made some quick notes for his upcoming sermon, and when the time came to pay the bill for the gasoline, he dug into his pants pocket for the required cash while the tall attendant stood patiently.

On the ride home, his thoughts turned to Mary Ruth Ebersol, the young lady he was presently dating. It was she who had once loved and lost Elias Stoltzfus, the boy he had accidentally struck and killed nearly seven years ago. Though trusting the Lord for victory over his intense struggle, in all truth, recurring nightmares of the accident continued to haunt him. To think he had fallen hard for young Elias's intended, a homegrown Old Order Amish girl who'd converted to the Mennonite church of her own volition. Yet his association with her, pleasant and even exciting as it was, caused him to have to face the catastrophe yet again.

Redirecting his thoughts to his sermon outline, Robert pondered the Lord's own Sermon on the Mount, taking comfort in its promises. *Blessed are the meek: for they shall inherit the earth.*

Leah's bare feet took her across the cornfield to the Peacheys' house. Dat, Lydiann, and Abe had all gone fishing, and with some unexpected hours to herself, she had a hankering to see Miriam today. She felt nearly carefree enough to skip across the way.

When Miriam saw her from the porch swing, she called out, "Hullo, Leah!"

"Wie geht's?" she asked, happy to see Miriam looking so well.

"Oh, I'm fair to middlin'. Come sit with me here on the swing." Miriam slid over to make room. "It's awful pleasant today, but this weather won't last. The heat of June is just round the bend. We'll be tryin' to escape the sun in a few weeks."

"And the mosquitoes will be out in full force."

"How are your little ones, Leah?"

She smiled. "They're sweet as strawberry jam." Seemed everyone considered Lydiann and Abe *hers* now. Too soon, though, they'd be itching to try out their wings and fly, to create their own families; it was the way God set things in motion for humankind. Leah wasn't sure where she'd live or what she'd do once that time came, though it could be she'd end up living in the Dawdi Haus with Aunt Lizzie once Dawdi John passed on. But since no one but the Lord God knew the end from the beginning, there was no need to worry over the future.

She remembered, quite unexpectedly, Mamma saying the same thing to Hannah, especially when the twins were younger. Even Aunt Lizzie liked to point out that "Worryin' 'stead of trustin' just ain't the way of God's children." Leah sometimes wished she could be consistently cheerful, more like happy-go-lucky Lizzie. *Someday I will be . . . if I live long enough.*

"What can I do for ya?" Miriam asked.

"I'm curious 'bout one of Mamma's old recipes. It's not written down anywhere, since Mamma knew it by heart, but she's not here and . . ."

Miriam glanced at her and gripped her hand. "Aw, honey. You miss her, of course ya do. We *all* miss Ida so."

She hadn't come here just to ask about a recipe, nor to get sympathy—neither one. Truth was, she enjoyed talking to Miriam, and though she saw her several times a week from afar and at church twice a month, there were certain times when Leah felt she simply needed to look into Miriam's eyes and see and know the understanding Mamma had always found there.

"Which recipe are ya thinkin' of?" asked Miriam.

"Mamma's pineapple upside-down cake. I can't seem to remember how much of the shortening, baking powder, or vanilla. All the pinches of this and that tend to get stuck in my head."

"Seems to me that happens to all of us at one time or 'nother. Come inside. I'll try 'n' write it down so you'll have it."

"Denki." She followed her into the big spotless kitchen. Waiting for her to get a pad of paper and pen, Leah felt suddenly warm inside, most pleasantly so. Having this special recipe in her possession would be yet another connection to Mamma.

At precisely that moment she realized why Mamma might've risked disobeying, keeping back the forbidden letter from Sadie. *It's about losing and trying desperately to hold on*, she thought.

Even all these years later, she felt almost too glad to have destroyed the evidence, lest Dat, the preachers, or the bishop had gotten wind of it and thought less of Mamma than she deserved. Truly, coming to visit Miriam this day was one of the best things Leah could've done for both herself and her memory of Mamma.

Even the meadowlarks sang more sweetly as she accepted the cake recipe from Miriam and hugged her good-bye, heading back across the cornfield toward home.

Chapter Twenty-Eight

Mary Ruth insisted on helping Robert's mother set the table for the evening meal. "You mustn't treat me like a guest," she told Lorraine as they moved about the table, placing linen napkins and silverware in their proper places.

"Since you're Robert's steady girlfriend, you're nearly family," Lorraine replied, smiling across the table.

Robert strolled into the dining room. "What's this whispering I hear?" Mary Ruth caught his flirtatious wink.

Dr. Schwartz came in and stood behind his chair at the head of the table. "Are we ready for supper, dear?"

Lorraine's rosy cheeks seemed brighter than usual. "Please, be seated . . . and you, too, Mary Ruth. I can manage just fine."

Mary Ruth sat on one side of the table with Robert directly across from her. Having enjoyed one other fine spread at this grand old house, Mary Ruth knew what to expect. The lovely lace tablecloth reminded her once again that she had turned fancy rather quickly following Elias's death—so long ago now it seemed. Never had she questioned her chosen teaching profession, even though she knew it aggrieved her father no end; that, and the fact she'd abandoned the People. Surprisingly the tension had lessened somewhat over the years, and for this she was grateful. She could come and go as she pleased at the Ebersol Cottage, thanks in part to Leah and Aunt Lizzie. Maybe seeing Lydiann and Abe grow up, having little ones around again, had prompted Dat to be more flexible. Maybe, too, God was at work in his heart. This, she prayed for daily.

"Here we are," Lorraine said, carrying a tray of roasted chicken surrounded by an array of cooked vegetables—onions, cauliflower, broccoli, and new potatoes. She disappeared again and returned with a Waldorf salad and homemade applesauce sprinkled generously with cinnamon.

Once his wife was seated, Henry looked to Robert for the blessing. "Son?"

Robert bowed his head, as did the others. "Thank you, Lord, for these bountiful blessings laid out here before us. Bless the hands that prepared the food, and make us ever mindful of your love and grace, and your suffering and death on the cross for our sins. In Jesus' precious name. Amen."

"Thank you, Robert," Lorraine said, looking at her son with obvious affection. Then she directed Henry to pass the large platter to Mary Ruth.

The matching silver candlesticks with twinkling white tapers graced the meal, as well as the evening, and by the time the dessert was served, Mary Ruth felt almost too full, but grateful for this time spent with Robert's parents.

Sadly Henry and Lorraine had slim hope of having good fellowship with their younger son. Robert had shared that they scarcely ever heard from Derek. Mary Ruth found this to be distressing, especially because it was clear how fond Robert was of his parents. Just then she wondered if the opportunity would ever present itself for her to tell Robert what she knew of Derek—his illicit relationship with Sadie. *Too soon yet*, she decided.

When it came time to say their good-byes, Robert offered to walk with her over to the Nolts' house. On the way, he asked, "What do you plan to do with yourself all summer?"

"Oh, I have a few ideas." She told him how she had been lending a hand in Leah's vegetable garden. "And on washday, I help her heat up the water and whatnot. Of course, I *do* enjoy my little sister and brother, as well, so spending time with them means Leah can rest once in a while."

"I like the sound of this," he said, reaching for her hand. "Have yourself a good time with Leah . . . dear sister of yours."

"Do you pity her, Robert?"

"I didn't say that."

"I just thought . . . well, maybe I heard it in your voice."

He paused. "Your sister's an example for us all. A measure of a person's character is what's done in run-of-the-mill daily life, when no one is watching."

"Sounds like you could write that into one of your sermons."

"I just might."

She was aware of the sound of their shoes on the road but said no more.

At last Robert spoke again. "In your opinion, how did it happen that Jonas Mast left Leah behind, jewel that she is?"

"He was a fool, that's how." The words flew from her lips.

"I mean . . ." She caught herself. *I mustn't say such things. It's not becoming of me*, she thought. "I guess when it comes to my sisters and Abe, I have to say I have a tendency to be outspoken. I'm very sorry."

It wasn't until later, after she'd said good night and was nestled into bed, that it dawned on her how she must have come across to Robert. Still, she felt he must surely know her well enough to understand she wasn't as docile as some young women, though she *was* trying to mellow . . . on a day-by-day basis, with the Lord's help.

Her biggest struggle was thinking ahead to how things might work out if Robert kept looking at her the way he did . . . if he happened to ask her to marry him someday. Just how would such a thing affect her relationship with her family? Would they turn their backs on her, the way they had Sadie? She knew they would never shun her, but she was almost sure the wedge between her and Dat would grow.

On top of that, sometimes she had second thoughts about Robert because of his younger brother, Derek, and what she knew of *his* loose morals. What kind of boy would do such a thing to an innocent girl—that is, if Sadie had been innocent. Only the Lord knew such things. Even so, the more time she spent with Robert and the Schwartz family, the more Mary Ruth found herself pondering these things.

◆

The day after her evening with the Schwartzes, Mary Ruth was delighted to see Hannah standing at the front door of the Nolts' house. Before her sister could knock, Mary Ruth scurried to the screen door and opened it wide. "Aw, where are the little ones?" she asked, faintly disappointed Hannah hadn't brought her children.

Hannah smiled a bit wearily and stepped inside. "I took Aunt Lizzie up on her offer to stay with the girls awhile."

"Some grown-up talk should help some." Mary Ruth understood the amount of energy it took keeping up with youngsters. "It's draining being round children all day, although I must say I enjoy being a teacher as much as I thought I would."

Hannah smiled as they sat at Dottie's kitchen table. "You look awful gut, sister. I didn't want to come over too soon, not with school just out 'n' all. Thought you might need a week or so to catch your breath, prob'ly."

"That's considerate of you, but I'm always glad to see you."

Mary Ruth poured lemonade for them both and settled into their contented chitchat. "How's Lizzie's cottage in the woods working out for the four of you?" she asked.

"Just fine for now, but"—and here Hannah paused—"there's gonna be *five* of us in a little while."

"Another baby to love! How wonderful."

Hannah's face clouded over. "Come December," she said. "My next baby's due at Christmas, same as young Abe's birthday."

Mary Ruth reached over and squeezed her hand. "Now, you mustn't worry. You're *many* years younger than Mamma was with Abe, and the circumstances of his birth were highly unusual."

"Poor Mamma," Hannah whispered, sniffling. "She loved Abe ever so much."

"She loved us all." Mary Ruth observed Hannah, wondering if this was the right time to say more. They fell silent for a moment, and then she said, "And . . . Mamma loved the Lord Jesus, too. She opened her heart wide to His love and forgiveness."

Waiting to continue, she hoped Hannah might not turn away. Thankfully this time she did not get up and leave the table as she often did when Mary Ruth spoke either of Mamma's or her own spiritual perspective. "The decision to walk with Jesus is not so much a mental one as it is a yielding of the heart . . . to God's plan for our lives." She thought she might break down with emotion, so strongly she felt about this.

Hannah bobbed her head and fought her own tears. "I wish to goodness I'd asked Mamma certain things before she died," she admitted. "I waited much too long."

Mary Ruth's heart was tender toward her. "I had a private talk with Mamma not too long before she died . . . after Dat kicked me out of the house. She said she, too, was a believer, though a silent one, following Jesus and living out her days as best she could, considering the Ordnung . . . and Dat."

"Mamma?"

"Jah, and it's easy to see, too, isn't it? She had such a long-suffering, joyful way 'bout her, ya know. Mamma could forgive at the drop of a hat; a sure sign of her deep faith, I'd have to say."

"I miss her terribly." Hannah looked across the table and out the window beyond. For the longest time she sat there still as could be; then she whispered, "I've always been frightened of death. . . . Always."

"Oh, sister. Truly, there's no need to be." She rose and hurried to Hannah's side. Stroking her back, she said, "When she was nearing the end, Mamma wasn't afraid to pass over Jordan's banks to Glory. Leah said as much."

"Jah, I remember hearing that." Hannah sighed. "But when Mammi Ebersol died and we were just thirteen, honestly that was 'bout all I could think of—day in, day out. Such a worrywart I was then."

"And not *now?*"

Hannah smiled through tears, hugging her hard. "Sure, I worry too much. Gid, bless his heart; he's tryin' to help me with that."

"Smithy Gid's a fine man. I see it clearly in his eyes when he looks at you and your girls."

Hannah nodded in agreement. "You just don't know how wonderful-gut he is to me. Being his wife, I've experienced a lightness, an odd sort of peace."

"Then we're both happy, seems to me."

"Very happy," Hannah echoed.

"Who would have guessed I'd end up being courted by a Mennonite preacher—a doctor's son, at that."

"Your eyes sparkle with this path you've chosen, Mary Ruth. Truly, I'd always hoped you'd come back and be Amish with me, but it seems you've found something more befittin' you."

She smiled, thinking how dear it was of Hannah to say such a thing; despite their very different lives, her twin's heart was still warm toward her. "It's a good thing I *didn't* join church with you and then left, or we wouldn't be enjoying such close fellowship today." She got up and poured more lemonade for them.

"Do you ever think of our big sister?" Hannah asked.

"Oh, every day."

"Honestly, I worry 'bout Leah, having lost her close-in-age sister for life."

Mary Ruth sipped her lemonade. "I can't imagine us growing old and not knowing something about her. It's painful to consider."

"I wonder if she has more than the one child we'd heard she was expecting . . . back years ago."

Mary Ruth often wondered the same. "Let's hope she has a houseful by now. For our sister's sake—Jonas's too—being cut off from family as they are."

"Speakin' of wee ones, I best be thinkin' of returning home here perty soon. Lizzie's got her hands full."

"So does Leah," Mary Ruth said. "I'm going to help her as much as I can this summer. Such a cute little sister and brother we have. God was so good to Dat, don't you agree?"

Hannah wore a brighter smile now. "Such joy they bring to our wounded sister, too."

"The children do seem to comfort her. Leah's been known to keep things bottled up inside her, ya know."

She followed Hannah through the back door and outside, at once missing her horse-and-buggy days as Hannah got herself situated into Gid's fine gray family carriage. "The Lord be with you," she called.

"And with you!" came the familiar reply.

Mary Ruth was grateful for her sister's unexpected receptiveness to her words today. She would continue sowing seeds of the gospel into Hannah's precious heart. "Fertile soil," as Robert liked to say.

Robert. He had secretly admired her long before they'd ever actually gone on a real date. Then he had patiently waited to court her while she finished up her teaching certificate. Because he had been so patient, she had been able to focus on her studies, made possible, in the long run, by Hannah, who'd helped her out of a financial bind, surprising her with a secret hankie savings fund—a humbling gift, to say the least. Because of this gesture of kindness, Mary Ruth had been able to complete her college education with nary a debt, boarding with the Nolts and working for them several evenings a week, as well as waiting on tables at a Strasburg restaurant on the weekend. Hannah, in the end, had refused any talk of repayment.

The Lord had worked all things together for good, giving Mary Ruth the desire of her heart, teaching young children—the *passion* of her heart, really. She hoped to continue at the rural elementary school for English children. Her first calling, for now.

She stood in the yard, giving Hannah one long wave as the horse pulled the buggy out of their lane and onto the narrow road.

Hannah's fingertips felt numb from picking, shelling, and canning peas the day following her visit to Mary Ruth. She, Leah, and Lydiann would be doing the same again tomorrow while Aunt Lizzie again kept a watchful eye on Hannah's daughters. Peas took time and tallied up ever so slowly, but the work, though tedious, meant time spent with her sisters.

Now that evening had come, she and Gid stood alone on the back porch, looking up at the stars. "'Tis the best time of the day . . . right now," he whispered in her ear.

"Jah, just the two of us. The way it all started out, ain't?"

With the girls sound asleep, she was eager for his warm embrace and fervent kisses. But he seemed to want to talk, and she was willing to listen. "Just so ya know, our horse has the strangles, and we'll have to borrow one of Abram's for a while."

She breathed in the smell of the night as she leaned against the porch rail, Gid's arm around her waist. "Hope you and Dat can cure it soon enough."

"The disease is right contagious, so we'll have to isolate this one horse, for sure. 'Tis best to let the infection run its course, though."

"Isn't there something you can do?" she asked.

"Penicillin shots will only lengthen the disease, but Abram's goin' to give his drivin' horses shots to prevent it." Gid continued, talking of making hay all day and how he, Dat, and Sam Ebersol would be working together tomorrow. "Pop is best stayin' with shodding horses, I'm a-thinkin'. It gets harder and harder for him to make hay or fill silo every year that goes by. I'm just glad to be able to help him. Sam is, too."

"I'm afraid the same goes for Dat."

Gid nodded. "'Cept the difference 'tween my father and yours is Abram's battlin' hard growing old . . . wants to stay as young as he can for Lydiann and Abe's sake, prob'ly."

"I see the fight in him, too."

"On the other hand, my pop's back keeps goin' out on him. Don't know how much longer he'll be able to do his blacksmithing duties, really."

"What'll happen then?" She'd worried some about this off and on the past year.

"Right now, Sam is gut 'bout helping, so let's not cross that bridge 'fore we have to, dear."

Her concerns had run away with her yet again. No need to get Gid thinking too hard on that—the People took care of their own. Mamma would have said that when the time came, the Lord God heavenly Father would give them the strength and the grace they needed—just as it had been for Aunt Lizzie tending to Dawdi John and Leah caring so lovingly for Lydiann and Abe. She hoped it was true.

"You all right, Hannah?"

"Just thinkin', is all." She leaned against Gid's sturdy arm.

"Counting your blessings, jah?"

She nodded, not wanting her husband to wonder if her fears were taking her over once again. "Ever so many blessings," she managed to say.

Chapter Twenty-Nine

Sure is wet for July," Dawdi John said at midday. Leah, along with Lydiann and Abe, sat taking a quick breather in Dawdi's front room.

"It's July the *twelfth*," insisted Abe.

"What's the date matter?" Lydiann piped up.

"Matters to *me*," said Abe.

"Goodness," said Leah. "Aren't you lippy today."

Her boy nodded. "I'm getting myself ready for school here 'fore too long, fixin' to surprise my teacher."

"How's that?" Dawdi asked.

" 'Cause I can make heads 'n' tails of the calendar," Abe replied.

Leah ruffled his hair, taken once again by Abe's clever remarks. "That's not all she'll be pleased 'bout, I daresay. You've been workin' your arithmetic this summer . . . with some help from Lydiann and Dat."

Dawdi nodded his head, twitching his nose. "Right smart ya both are. Take after your mamma."

Abe's eyes lit up. "Mamma *Leah?*"

Dawdi leaned back with laughter. "Well, now, she's a bright one, too."

Lydiann was too quiet, Leah happened to notice. "Everything all right, Lyddie?"

She shook her head, her eyes filling with tears.

"Well, now, honey, what's wrong?" Dawdi asked.

"I . . . can't remember what my first mamma looked like no more."

Abe was quick to speak. "Me neither, Lyddie. But that don't mean I have to go 'n' cry 'bout it."

"Aw, now, Abe . . . don't act so," Dawdi John said. "Come here and sit on my knee." He put down his cane and Abe hopped up on his lap. "Let me tell you 'bout your mother who birthed ya."

"Your daughter, ain't?" Abe said.

Dawdi nodded. "She had the pertiest blue eyes I ever did see. Just look at your sister over there; she has your mother's eyes."

"What did *I* get of Mamma's?"

Somewhat comically, Dawdi scrutinized Abe. "Let me see . . ." He pulled on his long beard, frowning; then a smile spread across his wrinkled face. "I know. You have her spunk. I see it in your eyes—awful mischievous they are. And—"

"It's in his voice, too." Lydiann smiled at her brother.

"And what else?" Abe asked.

Leah felt compelled to speak up. "If ya ask me, you both have Mamma's pretty hair. Light as the color of wheat . . . even blonder than your aunt—" She almost said "Sadie" but stopped herself.

"What were you gonna say?" asked Abe.

Dawdi must have surmised her thoughts and intervened. "There are plenty-a light-headed relatives in the family, young man."

"So Abe's got Mamma's hair and eyes and her spunk," Lydiann said, looking right at her brother. "That oughta keep ya quiet for now."

Leah had to smile. *Ach, how they love to bicker*. Just as she and Sadie had as girls; same as Hannah and Mary Ruth, too. *They'll grow out of it one day*, she thought.

Dawdi began to tell a humorous story from his boyhood, quickly getting the children's attention by describing how rainy and muddy it had been one long-ago summer. "My boot got stuck on the mule road over in Hickory Hollow, where I lived in an old farmhouse with my parents, your young mamma, Aunt Lizzie, and a whole bunch of your great-aunts and great-uncles. Well, I pulled and pulled and could not get my boot out."

Lydiann grinned from ear to ear. "What'd ya do, Dawdi?"

"I decided I'd best just pull my foot out and leave my boot stuck there."

"You did, really?" Abe said.

"Jah, and I walked all the way down the road in the mud to the well, pumped out some water, and rinsed off my sock and foot. And that was that."

"What happened to your boot?" asked Lydiann.

"It stayed right there overnight till we got more rain, which turned the mud into stew . . . and I lugged the boot out."

This brought a round of giggles, egging Dawdi on but good.

Leah's mind wandered while the storytelling continued, back to early days when she, Sadie, Hannah, and Mary Ruth would sit at their father's knee, listening to him read *The Budget*. Aunt Lizzie and Mamma, ever near, would sit inches away doing their knitting or crocheting. Now and then, Mamma would make a little sound, and Dat would look her way, smile, and return to reading. It was as if they were connected by a fine and loving thread that wove the family together, night after night, day after day.

How she missed those times! Still, she wouldn't think of going back, even if she could—not with the children needing her so. Yet if she had to live her youthful days over again, she might choose to return to autumn hayrides and the snipe hunts she and Jonas, along with all their siblings, enjoyed so much. Back then she had been the age Lydiann was now; such an innocent, happy time.

The best part of those autumns had been the bright blue weather, warm and wistful during the days with a nip to the night air. Once she'd sat all alone out behind the barn in the high meadow just staring at the night sky, gazing at the big harvest moon, counting the stars, and wondering about her future—whom she might marry when she grew up . . . and how many little ones she and her husband would have one day.

The children's laughter, mingled with Dawdi John's, brought her back to the business at hand. "Best finish cookin' supper," she said, getting up.

Lydiann and Abe followed, giving Dawdi a hug before

they left. "We'll see ya at the table soon," Lydiann said with a mischievous smile. "Mamma and I are makin' a surprise for everyone."

Leah lifted her finger to her lips. "Now, Lydiann, don't spoil things by sayin' too much."

"Ach, girls can't keep no secrets," Abe spouted off.

Dawdi chuckled and Leah shooed the children toward the connecting door, back to the main house.

Leah glanced out the window, making note of the fine summer day as she and the family, except for Aunt Lizzie and Dawdi John, all sat down to breakfast.

Immediately following the silent prayer, Abe announced too loudly, "Today's Friday the thirteenth!"

Dat quickly linked the date to superstition. "So 'tis best to be extra alert and careful, 'least till sundown."

Mamma would not have approved of Dat saying such a thing, yet he joked about it anyway, though he surely knew better. Good thing Aunt Lizzie hadn't joined them for eggs and pancakes. She would've spoken up but quick, putting an end to the nonsense talk. Lizzie had been cut from the same mold as Mamma, and for this Leah was glad.

Once Dat was finished eating, he left the table for the barn. It was then Leah told Lydiann and Abe both there was nothing to worry about. "Don't worry yourself about the date. We're not so superstitious, really—never have been."

Abe looked puzzled, glancing over his shoulder toward the back door. "But Dat said—"

"I know what your father said." She was struggling, not sure how to preserve respect for Dat while teaching the children what she knew to be true—what she knew her mamma and Aunt Lizzie would have said. She didn't want to out-and-out discredit her father, but she felt troubled deep in her soul each time Dat talked about such dark things.

Just last week he had suggested the hex doctor come take a look at Lydiann when she'd gotten bit up by mosquitoes and welts had come out all over her legs. Had it not been for Aunt Lizzie prevailing, Leah would have been at a loss to handle things. Dat, after all, was Lydiann's father. She, on the other hand, was merely a substitute mother with little say—at least it seemed so at times like this.

"Do you remember where we're goin' today?" she asked Lydiann and Abe, changing the subject as gracefully as possible.

"To see the doctor!" Lydiann said merrily. She liked having her "ticker checked," as Dr. Schwartz called it when he listened to the children's hearts with his stethoscope.

"In one hour we must leave," she told them, pointing for Lydiann to clear the dirty dishes from the table, and then directing Abe toward the back door to go and offer Dat some help in the barn.

"Dawdi John was mighty happy with our supper surprise last night," Lydiann said, getting up from the table.

Abe smacked his lips. "So was I. Dawdi and Dat both liked your pineapple upside-down cake, Mamma."

"There's some left for dinner today," Lydiann told him. "Now, how 'bout that?"

To this Abe went running outside, hollering the happy

news to Dat. Leah stood at the back door and watched him go, glad all the talk of Friday the thirteenth was past for now.

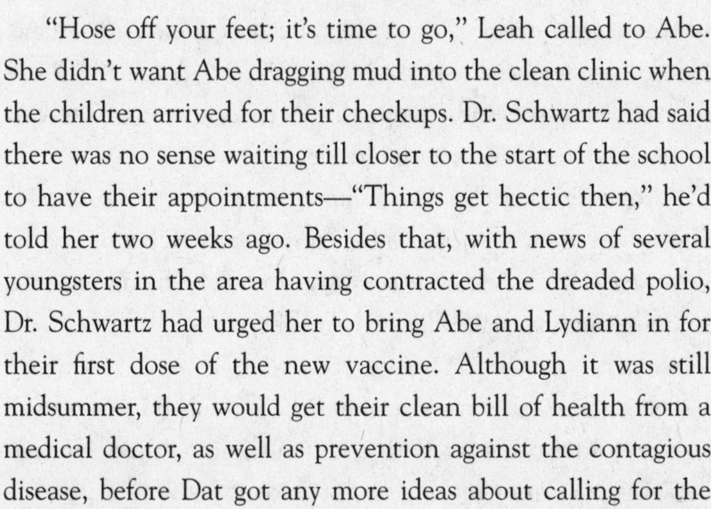

"Hose off your feet; it's time to go," Leah called to Abe. She didn't want Abe dragging mud into the clean clinic when the children arrived for their checkups. Dr. Schwartz had said there was no sense waiting till closer to the start of the school to have their appointments—"Things get hectic then," he'd told her two weeks ago. Besides that, with news of several youngsters in the area having contracted the dreaded polio, Dr. Schwartz had urged her to bring Abe and Lydiann in for their first dose of the new vaccine. Although it was still midsummer, they would get their clean bill of health from a medical doctor, as well as prevention against the contagious disease, before Dat got any more ideas about calling for the powwow doctor.

The horse hitched up to the carriage easily, and in no time at all they were headed down the one-mile stretch to the clinic. "I wonder how much I weigh *this* year," Abe said, sitting to the left of Leah in the front seat.

Leah waited for Lydiann to say something either funny or snooty, but she was silent in the second seat. Glad for the peace, Leah focused on the steady rhythm of the *clip-clopping* of the horse.

Soon Lydiann began to hum rather forcefully "Jesus Loves Me," the song Mary Ruth had often sung to the children.

"For the Bible tells me so . . ." Abe joined in, his voice cracking.

When they came to the part, "Little ones to Him belong . . . they are weak . . ." Leah winced, recalling how tiny Sadie's baby had been at his birth. She hummed along with the children, hoping to dispel her momentary gloom.

Arriving well before the appointment, Leah noticed another horse and buggy waiting ahead of them in the lane. Not knowing who was parked there, she decided, since it was so pretty out, she and the children would just sit in the carriage till closer to time to go inside.

Promptly, though, Abe jumped down from the carriage and moseyed over to the other gray buggy. Relaxing in the front seat, she decided not to hinder him from being sociable, since it came so naturally to him. She closed her eyes for a moment.

Next thing she knew, Lydiann had climbed out and run over to join Abe. With both children standing there chattering away, she reluctantly got out and tied the horse to the post, then walked slowly to the other buggy.

"Mamma, this here's Mandie and Jake Mast," Lydiann said quickly when she saw her coming.

"Well, hullo . . . children." She was flabbergasted to see Fannie's twins sitting there by themselves.

Mandie explained. "Our mamma's inside . . . has a nasty flu."

"Jah, she's been terrible sick." Jake nodded his head as he spoke.

Mandie's blond hair was pure contrast to Jake's dark head and eyes. "We're goin' straight home once Mamma gets herself some medicine," she said.

"She needs to feel better and right quick," Jake added.

They don't know of their parents' stand against us Ebersols, thought Leah, finding it rather curious to be here talking so freely with Jonas's baby sister and brother. She savored the special moment; these twins would have been her brother- and sister-in-law had she and Jonas married.

"What's *your* name?" Mandie asked her, blue eyes twinkling.

"I'm Cousin Leah," she said, not revealing her last name. "And this is Lydiann and Abe."

"Abe already told us his name." Jake smiled broadly, showing his white teeth. A wider grin she'd never seen.

"Leah's a right perty name," Mandie said. "And . . . you're our cousin?"

She straightened, repeating that she was indeed. *They've never heard tell of their eldest brother's first love.*

Suddenly Jake jumped down out of the carriage. "Let's see how tall I am next to you, Lydiann."

"Jake, what on earth are ya doin'?" Mandie scowled from the carriage. "She's a girl, for pity's sake."

"She's our *cousin*, for pity's sake!" Jake hollered over his shoulder.

"No need to yell, children," Leah found herself chiding them, watching in disbelief as Jake and Lydiann simultaneously turned themselves around and stood back to back, head to head.

"I'm taller, ain't so, Mamma?" asked Lydiann, staring straight ahead, holding still as could be.

Observing the childish scene play out before her eyes, she was intent on the irony of the unexpected meeting—Cousin Fannie inside paying a visit to the doctor for a summer flu;

the twins out here. "Well, it's hard to say, really . . . but jah, I s'pose you are. But only by a hair."

To this Lydiann giggled. Jake, on the other hand, looked terribly concerned, if not upset.

"See, Jake? I *am* taller than you!" Lydiann said a bit too gleefully.

"That can't be," Jake insisted, his hands on his slender hips.

"Come along, now," Leah said, turning to go while Abe and Lydiann said good-bye to their newfound cousins.

"Won'tcha come to Grasshopper Level 'n' visit us?" Jake asked.

"That'd be fun," Lydiann said, waving.

"See ya later!" called Mandie.

Obviously Abe and Lydiann were quite taken with the cute twins. When at last they joined Leah, they hurried up the long walk toward the clinic.

Glancing over her shoulder at Cousin Fannie's youngsters, Leah had mixed feelings about the encounter. For as obstinate as the Masts were toward the Ebersols, there was little or no hope they would ever see hide nor hair of Jake and Mandie again.

Chapter Thirty

Leah quickened her pace to keep up with Lydiann and Abe, delighting in their chatter as the three of them walked down the road to the schoolhouse this second week of school. Abe was in second grade this year, looking splendid in his lavender shirt, black broadfall trousers, and suspenders. Today, for a nice change, he wore his straw hat firmly on his head. Lydiann was pretty as a picture in her green dress and crisp black apron, her small hair bun hidden beneath her white prayer veiling.

Leah had been mighty busy sewing several new sets of clothes for each child during the final weeks of August, and she had volunteered to help clean up the schoolhouse with other parents in preparation for the start of school, as well.

"Won'tcha come back for our school picnic today?" Lydiann asked her.

"*Please*, Mamma," Abe begged, hopping up and down.

"Do ya really want me to?" she said, knowing full well the answer.

"'Course we do!" Abe shouted.

"The pupils from the school over on Esbenshade Road are joinin' us today, too," Lydiann said.

"A *wunderbaar Picknick!*" said Abe.

In her busyness, she'd completely forgotten the combined school event. Mandie and Jake Mast attended the other school that served the conservative Mennonite and Amish children in the Grasshopper Level area. What fun it would be for Lydiann and Abe to see their Mast cousins again. "Sure, I'll return at eleven-thirty with the horse and buggy," she said.

"Will ya stay for story time after lunch recess?" Abe asked, swinging his lunch pail.

"We'll see." She wanted them to enjoy their classmates, feel at liberty to make friends, not be too dependent on her.

"Aw, won'tcha, Mamma?" she whined.

"None of the other mothers stay, do they?"

Abe shook his head. "But you ain't like them," he said. "You're younger than most."

"Pertier too." Lydiann reached for her hand and held it tight.

Quickly Leah directed their attention to the various trees, different kinds of birds, and other familiar landmarks along the road. It was a good long walk, but it was a fine way to extend her day with them. They never seemed to tire of her presence, as if they required her more than some children needed their mammas.

Back home again, Leah canned seven quarts of peaches, then made up a large batch of catsup, with help from Lizzie.

While making a sandwich to take back with her to the children's school, a decisive knock came at the back door. The smithy had "sorrowful news to bear" of Preacher Yoder's passing. "Happened just hours ago." Their longtime minister had died of a heart attack.

"We're in need of a new preacher," Aunt Lizzie said as the two women watched smithy Peachey scurry out to the barn to tell the news to Abram and Gid.

"I 'spect we'll be having an ordination service 'fore too long," Leah said.

"We best start prayin' for God's will in the selection of a new minister," Aunt Lizzie said reverently.

"Does Dat ever pray thataway?" asked Leah.

"What do ya mean?"

"Does Dat beseech the Lord God heavenly Father for divine will in all things the way you do?" *The way Mamma always did*, she thought.

Aunt Lizzie's face brightened at Leah's question. "I believe the Lord is definitely at work in Abram's heart," she replied softly, yet confidently. "You wait 'n' see. He'll come round to the saving grace."

Lizzie's remarks wondered Leah. "I hope you're right 'bout that," she found herself saying. "Maybe then there won't be so much talk of hex doctors anymore."

"Oh jah . . . all that white witchcraft talk will fly out the window. You'll see."

Lizzie's words went round and round in Leah's head. Even as she hitched up the horse and headed back to the little one-room school for lunch, the words "you'll see" continued to echo in her brain.

Actually, she was glad for a reason to be gone over the noon hour, what with plans for the minister's wake no doubt taking shape. *Lizzie's far better at such things*, she thought as she rode down Georgetown Road.

When she arrived, the school yard was bustling with children, girls eating their sack lunches on the grass, boys eating theirs on the merry-go-round.

Lydiann looked awful sad when Leah found her. "Our Mast cousins didn't come," she said. "All the other pupils did . . .'cept not them."

They must've told their mamma about meeting Lydiann and Abe, Leah decided. *Cousin Fannie's shunning the youngest Ebersols through her twins!*

Leah had to offer some sort of explanation to distract poor Lydiann, though in all truth, a mere girl didn't need to know such spiteful things. "Maybe Jake and Mandie are under the weather," she offered as a possible excuse.

"That can't be it," Lydiann piped up. "The teacher said their mamma kept them home today."

On purpose . . . in case they might have themselves another good time with Abe and Lydiann, thought Leah. *Will this never end?* She was tempted to ride over to the Masts' orchard house and storm up to the back door to give Cousin Fannie a good tongue-lashing. It was one thing to punish the Ebersol grown-ups, but this!

Following the news of Preacher Yoder's death, Lizzie promptly hurried across the field to visit Miriam Peachey. They spent a few minutes at the kitchen table making a list of food items necessary for supplying the grieving family; then she and Miriam said good-bye and Lizzie ambled back to the house to prepare roast-beef sandwiches for her father and Abram.

At the noon meal she was mindful to stay out of their table conversation as the two men discussed the Yoder family wake and the subsequent funeral and burial services.

When they were finished eating, Abram bowed his head for the silent prayer; then she cleared the table and washed and dried the dishes. That done, she swept the kitchen floor, and then the back porch and sidewalk. All the while, she contemplated her earlier exchange with Leah. Was it possible Abram would indeed embrace the Lord as Savior? Lizzie *had* seen strong indications he was softening, little cracks of light slowly penetrating his gritty soul.

Privately she continued to share with him what she'd learned over the years through time spent on her knees in prayer and by reading Scripture. *Faith cometh by hearing, and hearing by the word of God.* Tenaciously she clung to this passage in Romans whenever Abram became resistant. Yet she felt sure the frequency and the fervency of her witness was getting through to him, touching the deep of his heart.

"Mamma? Are you upset?" Abe asked hours after the picnic, sitting next to Leah in the front seat of the carriage as she drove them home.

Leah hadn't realized it, but here she was groaning, disturbing the children.

She gathered her wits. "I'm all right."

Lydiann began to rehash the day. "S'posin' *I* should be upset, too, since our own cousins didn't come to the picnic."

Abe shook his little head. "When will we see them again, Mamma?"

Before Leah could answer, Lydiann suggested they invite Jake and Mandie to Abe's birthday, "come December."

Abe's eyes shone. "Jah, and maybe Christmas dinner, too!"

Late that night, Leah was too fidgety to sleep. So . . . the Mast twins *had* told their mother of meeting Cousin Leah. Oh, to have been a fly on the backseat of the buggy!

She struggled to put into practice what the Scriptures taught about forgiveness, for the Masts surely needed to be forgiven, didn't they?

Sitting up in bed, she stared into the darkness of her room. She wished she could be at peace with all men—*and* women—including kinfolk like Peter and Fannie and their children.

Dear Lord, drive my anger far from me, she prayed.

Chapter Thirty-One

The letter from Sadie to the bishop was a single page long, and Abram's first reaction was to walk away and ignore it.

Bishop Bontrager, large man that he was, stood near the hay baler in Abram's own barn, blocking the setting sun's horizontal rays from coming through the door. "Go ahead, Abram, have a look-see." The bishop pushed the letter into his hands, apparently eager to hear what Abram made of it.

Fairly torn, Abram felt pressured to read his long-lost daughter's letter. At the same time he was curious to know why she'd written in the first place. Walking toward the doorway, he held the page up to the last vestiges of daylight.

Friday, September 14, 1956
Dear Bishop Bontrager,

Greetings from Nappanee, Indiana, where I have been living for eight years.

I am writing to ask your kind permission to return to my family. This would be ever so helpful to me, even necessary at this distressing time. You see, I am a widow as of two weeks ago, due to a silo-building accident in Goshen.

Since I am under the Bann in my home church, I thought it best to contact you directly. I hope you might pave the way for this request. It has been a long time since my baptism and my leaving, and since then I have been a God-fearing woman and made my peace with the Lord God and with a church here in Nappanee, as well as the Millersburg, Ohio, district, where first I confessed my sins privately to the ministers.

Will you allow me to make things right with this letter? I want to return home to look into the faces of my dear father, mother, and sisters with the shunning lifted from me.

Respectfully,
Sadie (Ebersol)

Abram scarcely knew what to say. Sadie wanted to come home, wanted to repent. "So much she doesn't know 'bout us," he said. "She has no knowledge of Ida's passing . . . is unaware of her little brother."

My firstborn . . . a young widow, he thought, pained.

Before Abram was fully ready to relinquish the letter, the bishop reached for it and quickly stuffed it back into the envelope. "I have half a mind to say she ought not return. Simply puttin' words on a page is not enough for me to give a shunned woman the go-ahead to come home."

Abram's heart sank. "Then, ya must not believe she's sincere?"

"Sincerely *wrong*, she is. Your eldest ain't above the Ordnung, though she might think so. If she wants to live with you and Leah and the rest of the family, she'll have to offer a kneeling repentance before the entire membership. Nothin' less." The bishop tapped the envelope on the palm of his callused hand. "If she should be stupid enough to make an attempt at returning without takin' the proper steps, you and Leah will be shunned, too."

Caught coming and going, Abram thought, realizing he was contemplating the same things Ida used to say—and Lizzie would now. It made little sense to slap the Bann on a family just because they had a shunned relative, and one obviously in need. But he kept his opinion to himself, not wanting to jeopardize an opportunity to see his daughter and possibly young grandchildren. What an awful long time had passed since Sadie had left home, and now she was living in Indiana. Evidently Jonas couldn't make it as a carpenter in Ohio. Abram wasn't too surprised at that; not with the bishops out there and here frowning hard on young men who thumbed their noses at farming. *Seems mighty English to do otherwise*, he thought.

But now Jonas had been killed building a silo. Such risky, even dangerous work—anybody knew that. *Especially for a scrawny carpenter!*

Poor Sadie lived with the same familiar pain of loss as he did. The realization swept over him, and he felt sorry for his ambivalent feelings toward his own flesh and blood . . . even after all these years of her absence and her defiant refusal to make recompense here at home, where it most mattered.

"Will ya write and remind her of what she must do?" he asked the bishop.

The burly man leaned on the baler and looked him straight in the face. "I'm sure you miss her and I can't blame ya for it. I'll write her what's expected. If she's yielded and agreeable, I'll let you know."

Stunned at the change in the bishop's attitude, Abram nodded. "I'll wait to hear from you. Denki!"

The older man headed out toward the sinking sun. Then, almost as if he'd forgotten to say what was still on his mind, he turned and asked, "How will this affect Leah, do ya think? And your young children, too?"

Abram inhaled sharply. "Once you hear back from my eldest, I'll speak with Leah, break it to her . . . somehow. Then she and I will decide what to tell Lydiann and Abe."

"I'll drop by again. I 'spect it'll be soon."

Sadie needs us now, he thought. *Surely she'll abide by the Ordnung this time.*

He watched as the bishop made his way toward his buggy, wondering how to go about telling Leah, when it was time. *I have some fences to mend*, he thought ruefully.

Leah sat down in the kitchen with Dat, who had come in from the barn midafternoon, removed his straw hat, and placed it slowly on the table. "I have some news for ya, Leah." Breathing deeply, he sat next to her on the wooden bench. "Your sister's comin' home with the bishop's blessing. She says she wants to repent."

"My sister?" Her heart leaped up. *Sadie's returning to us!*

Dat continued, explaining the letter and visit of a week ago, the bishop's follow-up—all of it. Leah hung on every word, yet wondered why her father's somber face did not match his joyful words. "What's wrong, Dat? Why are ya sad?"

He faltered just then, staring long at the floor. When he

looked up, the color had drained from his face. "Truth is, she's comin' back a widow."

The thorny words narrowly stuck in her mind. *My sister, a widow?*

She studied Dat, struggling with the meaning of this. *So Jonas must be dead.*

Dat was talking again, but she scarcely heard a word. Something that had been buried so long ago broke free within her. Years of innocent pretense, of hoping and striving . . . wanting to forgive Sadie and praying it was so. All of it simmered to the surface in that moment, and no longer could she hold back the tide. She put her head down and sobbed on her arm.

Dat reached out to comfort her. "There, there, my lamb," he said, the way Mamma always had. "This, too, shall pass."

Powerless to think of anything but her own loss of Jonas, she raised her head, eyes clouded with tears. "*Nee*—no!" she sobbed. "My sister took my beau . . . *my* beloved. Don't you see? She stole the years that were meant for me—for Jonas and me! Now he's dead, gone forever!"

Dat's face fell, plainly dumbfounded at her outburst. "Leah. . . ?" His eyes were intent on her, a concerned frown on his face.

Beneath his gaze, she felt as foolish as a young child. Yet she was crushed to near despair.

Abram, taken aback by Leah's outburst, had never seen her so distraught, neither so outspoken. Promptly he stopped trying to calm her, feeling inadequate to do so. *I should've asked Lizzie to be on hand,* he thought.

Never had he felt comfortable when it came to a weeping woman. Here Leah was, unable to dry her tears, beside herself with fresh grief over Sadie's betrayal. Just when he had been so sure she was long past her anger and sadness.

He wondered how to make things better, how to place the ultimate blame where it belonged. He contemplated telling her of his conversation with Jonas, the two of them hidden away in the cornfield the day of Leah's and Jonas's baptisms. Such a confession might redirect Leah's resentment—and rightly so.

He rose to stretch his legs and move about the kitchen, to give himself a chance to think how he ought to reveal his deception, beginning with his furtive phone call to David Mellinger clear back when Jonas first began courting Leah, when she was merely sixteen. And . . . ending with Peter Mast's visit over a year later, when Abram had spoken half-truths, not putting to rest the rumor that there was something more than innocent friendship between Gid and Leah. All of his subtle scheming to keep Jonas away—far removed from Leah. For what purpose? So Smithy Gid could have his chance, nothing more. Clearly from Leah's apparent anguish, he had been decidedly wrong on all counts.

Inhaling slowly, he felt he must open up to her, to confess at least in part. "There's something you oughta know. I should've told ya, oh, so long ago."

She looked at him, visibly puzzled, eyes red.

"I'm mighty sorry," he began again. "From the deep of my heart, I am."

She remained silent.

"Jonas marrying your sister was partly my fault," he said.

"Your fault? How can that be?"

He was pacing now. *I regret the day I ever meddled with her future*, he thought. *Leah's a maidel now because of me.*

"Dat? What is it?" Leah asked, her pretty brow lined with deep concern.

"*Narr,*" he began. "I was a fool. . . ."

A bewildered look crossed her face, yet it was evident she wanted to understand, to hear him out. "Whatever do ya mean, Dat?"

He stood near the wood stove, feeling mighty chilled; he didn't dare consider sitting at the table any longer, so far from the slow fire in the belly of the stove. No, he needed the warmth. As it was, he could barely relax the muscles in his jaw enough to speak, to make his mouth form the words that must finally be said.

Chapter Thirty-Two

Not only was Leah perplexed at the idea of Sadie's returning home, she was dismayed to think Dat had created feelings of doubt in Jonas regarding her faithfulness to him, shedding more than a little suspicion on Leah's companionable association with Gid!

She recalled the alarming letter Jonas had sent so long ago, asking her pointed questions about Smithy Gid. Poor Jonas had gotten his doubts about her from Dat, of all people. Still, what part had Sadie played in this? Leah had not fully understood the ins and outs of Peter Mast's visit here that autumn day as described by Dat, and she wondered if her father was holding back other things he'd rather not say; she could only imagine what they might be.

Nevertheless, Sadie was soon to be traveling home, and Leah needed to make some necessary sleeping arrangements. She asked Dat if he'd mind moving downstairs to the spare bedroom off the front room, and he agreed immediately, giving up the largest of the bedrooms to Leah and Lydiann, who didn't mind sharing the room over the kitchen, the warmest in the house. Even if Sadie had more than one or two children to bed down, in no way did Leah feel comfortable handing over Dat and Mamma's bedroom to their disobedient daughter and her offspring. *Jonas and Sadie's little ones . . .*

Hannah and Mary Ruth's former bedroom would become Sadie and her children's, since it was the farthest removed from Leah's new bedroom—*a good idea,* she thought. Abe, bless his heart, would have Leah's old room, with its lovely view of the barnyard and the woods.

So it was decided, and she was glad Dat never questioned her one iota. Each of them would have a place to call his or her own, and Leah would still be near enough to Lydiann and Abe, to look after them a bit.

Lizzie helped her wash down the walls and redd up the spare room for Dat, and he promptly moved his clothing and personal items the next day. When all the changes had been made and the rooms were ready on Saturday, Leah put a pot of chicken corn soup on the stove for supper, then asked Lydiann to watch and stir it every so often.

She noticed a whole flock of wild turkeys—two dozen or more—strutting around the barnyard and even more of them in the cornfield, finding leftovers from the harvest, as she headed up to the woods to visit Hannah. Once there, she was happy to see petite and sweet Ida Mae who, at almost three, was as chatty and fair as Mary Ruth had always been. "She even looks like your twin when she was tiny!" Leah said, to which Hannah agreed.

Katie Ann, the other wee dishwasher in the making, was said to be napping. "She does so twice a day now, which is right nice," Hannah said, pushing back a loose strand of strawberry blond hair.

Leah got down on the floor and played with Ida Mae, who was talking to the knitted-sock hand puppet Hannah had made. It was one Leah had used through the years to soothe hurt or ailing children at Dr. Schwartz's medical clinic.

"Should we plan something special for our lost sister when she returns?" Hannah asked.

She would not share with Hannah how despairing she felt about Sadie. "Maybe so" was all she said.

"Wouldn't it be fun? A right nice welcome home."

Leah rose and headed for the door, struggling with the lump in her throat.

"You just got here," Hannah called to her. "What's your hurry?"

"I thought of walking in the woods, that's all." She didn't say she needed some time alone, that she felt all this pressure in her chest might cause her to suffocate.

"Aw, Leah, come back. Are ya sad over Preacher Yoder's passing?"

"I . . . I'll see ya later." Right then she felt sorry about being short with Hannah, but she couldn't stay a minute longer, not if she didn't want to be seen weeping.

Hurrying out the back door, she rushed past the stone wall and gardens, noticing that the recent killing frost had put an end to Hannah's late-summer flowers. But Leah didn't dare stop to sit there and try to calm herself. She hastened on, trying in vain to locate her cherished honey locust tree, but too many years had come and gone since the bliss-filled hours spent beneath its trunk.

She pressed on, looking anxiously for her favorite tree, aware of geese overhead, honking their way south for the winter. Eventually unable to find her way to her former piece of earth, she headed up a ways to the crest of the hillock, to the old hunter's shanty, surprised it was still standing—though barely that.

Deciding against going inside, she wandered around and looked for a place to sit where she could be alone with the towering trees and the dense foliage, soaking up the peace here. She found a cluster of boulders, recalling this to be the spot where Smithy Gid had found her the day she'd wandered here and gotten herself lost. Not worried that such a thing would occur again, she sat herself down. *So Hannah wants to have a party, but Sadie deserves no such thing.*

A scampering squirrel stopped to look at her, his tiny head slightly cocked as if to say, *Hullo, lonely Leah. What're you doing here in my woods?*

She realized she still had an imagination, probably thanks to the strong influence of the children—her children. How she loved them! Cheerful yet outspoken Lydiann . . . and Abe, who was always caring, eager, and confident. Both seemed mighty glad to have her as a mamma and often said so.

But she best not think on such prideful things; she didn't need the children's reassurance. She just needed to simmer down like the kettle full of soup at home.

I've lost Jonas twice. She let the harsh truth seep into her bones. *Once to Sadie and now to death, both in the space of nine years.*

She felt she'd aged in just a few days of grieving Jonas's

death. Holding her slender hands out before her, she peered at small veins protruding through pale skin. *It's a good thing Smithy Gid woke up and married Hannah,* she thought, feeling at once sorry for herself, yet knowing what a happy couple Gid and Hannah were.

Looking up, she tried to see the sky, but only the tiniest dots of light shone through the canopy. She was taken anew by the quietude and suddenly missed her youth, gone with the years.

When she heard whistling, she turned to see where the sound hailed from, and there was Aunt Lizzie tramping toward her. "Hullo, honey-girl!"

"Out for an afternoon walk?" she asked, glad to see her.

"Been trampin' through these woods for a gut many years now; don't 'spect I'll quit anytime soon." Lizzie came and sat next to her on the boulder. "I daresay *you* aren't walkin' so much as thinkin'."

She knows me through and through.

"Your sister's comin' home and you're beside yourself, ain't?"

"That'd be one way of puttin' it."

"Well, best get it out of your system before she arrives." Lizzie mopped her brow with the palm of her hand.

"How would ya say I oughta go 'bout that?"

Lizzie straightened a bit, pushing her work shoes down deep into the leaves and vines. "Lean hard on the Lord, honey-girl."

Wondering, she voiced the question aloud. "Does God truly know how I'm feelin' just now?"

Lizzie started a little and looked Leah full in the face. "He knows this time of suffering you're goin' through . . . that it's awful hard. But this must be His plan for you, as difficult as that is to understand. Life ain't a bed of roses; it's downright painful at times. But I 'spect if ya get your eyes off yourself and look at your sister, you'll see she's in need of our love now more than ever. A widow and not even thirty yet, for pity's sake."

"I *do* love her," Leah said softly. "I've prayed for her all these years. But now I just don't know how I can . . ." She stopped because she simply couldn't go on.

"Sooner or later, you'll have to forgive her, Leah. The path of unforgiveness is a thorny one." Aunt Lizzie had known all along what it was eating away at her.

"I wish I didn't have to go to the membership meeting, witness my sister kneelin' before the Lord God and the brethren, confessing aloud her past sins." All this time she'd yearned for this very thing for Sadie's sake; yet here it was nearly the eve of such a meeting, and all she wanted to do was run far from it. She didn't care to hear the words of repentance that would ultimately lift the Bann from Sadie. The shunned one would be welcomed back, profoundly so, into the warmth of Dat's home, *her* refuge.

"I see now I can't begin to think of voting to accept her back into the fellowship. I just can't, Lizzie." She wept sad tears in her birth mother's arms.

"There, there, you go 'n' cry it out. Then, when you're through, we'll head on home for supper. We'll see this through together, you 'n' me."

Leah wept good and long. When she'd had her cry, she wiped her face dry with the edge of Lizzie's apron, startlingly aware of the bitterness within—sorrowful remnants of the past.

Somewhere along the way, they had silently agreed not to talk while milking cows, which was exactly how it was Monday morning. Leah felt she had little to say to Dat.

They finished the milking, and while her father carried away the cans of fresh milk to the milk house, Leah headed back to her indoor chores. From now on, she decided, Abe, or Sadie—once she arrived—could help with the milking. She, on the other hand, was in charge of the house and by no means ready to give up her place of responsibility and authority, under God and Dat, to her elder sister. Sadie did not deserve that place of honor. She'd abandoned this family to have her own will and way with her life. And now, if she was to come home, Leah felt strongly about making sure Sadie knew where things stood—certainly no longer could she hold the honored place of Abram's eldest daughter. No, Sadie had forfeited that standing, no two ways about it.

Late in the afternoon Adah surprised Leah by stopping by, once all her wash had been dried and folded. She came alone, all smiles, with a "wonderful-gut idea. Let's have a card shower for your sister." Her eyes were bright with the suggestion. "If ya want, I could help out with some cold cuts and whatnot, turn it into a coming-home party and invite as many of the women folk who'd wanna come." She offered, as well, to spread the news.

"Well, since we don't know exactly *when* she's comin', why not wait to see if she actually does."

Adah frowned quickly. "Do ya mean to say she might change her mind?"

Leah shrugged her shoulders. "How should I know? It's been a long time. . . ."

Nodding, Adah patted her arm. "We'll bide our time, if that's what you want to do."

Leah didn't have the heart to say much more, and she couldn't help but wonder how Mamma would expect her to treat Sadie after all this time. Sooner or later, like Aunt Lizzie had said, Leah knew she would have to unearth the merciless and bitter root deep within and look at it for what it was. *Whatever pain may come of this, for Mamma's sake, I must choose to be kind.*

Chapter Thirty-Three

Leah spied her first—Sadie plodding up the long lane, carrying only a tan suitcase. She looked smaller somehow, weighed down by the cares of life and her bulky luggage. Her dress hung too loosely, as if she'd lost weight suddenly, and her hair was blonder than Leah remembered, the gleam of it peeking out from beneath her prayer veiling. But then again, maybe it was simply the light cast by the sun at high noon.

Leah paused where she was, standing nearly like a statue, bewildered to witness this moment alone. *Where's Dat?* she wondered, thinking she ought to call for him and Dawdi John or Aunt Lizzie—all of them, really.

But she felt the sound of her own voice would have heightened the peculiarity of the moment, making her feel weak, even powerless. She battled against her own reluctance but could not call out even a welcome to her sister; instead, she managed to raise a hand in a feeble wave. Here was the sister she had thought she'd forgiven. Good thing Sadie hadn't looked up right then, noticed her standing there in her old brown choring dress and apron, wearing a pair of

Mamma's worn-out shoes. Good thing, because she'd probably be wondering why Leah wasn't tearing down the path, throwing her arms around her, saying over and again, "Oh, I missed ya ever so much, I did. Wonderful-gut to have you home. . . ."

She swallowed the lump in her throat and wondered where Sadie's children were, or at least the one. Had she left them behind in Indiana with close church friends or Jonas's family, maybe? If so, did this mean she was merely coming for a visit, nothing more? Surprised at the sense of calm that came over her at the latter thought, Leah inhaled deeply and willed herself to move forward.

One step at a time, she made her way down the lane, her legs as stiff as solid planks.

Sadie, seeing her now for the first time, hesitated, then dropped her suitcase and hurried forward. Her arms were outstretched like those of a doll, and her eyes glistened as her embrace found Leah. The bittersweet moment nearly overtook her, so fervently did Sadie enfold her.

"I missed ya so, Leah . . . oh, you just don't know."

"It's been . . . a long . . . time" was the best Leah could muster. To mimic the tender words that came from Sadie's lips would have been false and ever so wrong.

Sadie stepped back and, drying her tears, asked, "Where's Smithy Gid?"

A bit surprised, Leah said, "Oh, he's fillin' silo with Sam Ebersol—you remember our uncle Jesse's youngest boy? Sam and Adah Peachey are married now."

Sadie nodded, seemingly a bit dazed.

"Didja have to travel long?" asked Leah, bending to pick up the suitcase.

"First by bus, then by train; then from Lancaster I rode the trolley back to Strasburg." She stopped and caught her breath. "After that, I hired a taxi driver to bring me on home."

Leah said nothing as Sadie took in the house, the grounds, the barn, and milk house. "So you and Gid, are ya livin' in the main house now? Are Dat and Mamma snug in the Dawdi Haus?"

She felt the air go out of her. "What do ya mean Gid and me?"

"You and your *husband*, Smithy Gid."

"Why, no. He's married to Hannah."

"Hannah?" A quick frown crossed Sadie's brow and she stumbled.

"Watch your step," Leah offered, reaching out a hand.

Sadie grasped it and they walked hand in hand.

"Where are your children?" Leah asked. "We heard you were expecting a baby back some time ago."

Sadie was quiet as they made their way toward the house. "Stillborn babies were all I ever birthed, Leah . . . same as my first wee son, so long ago."

As sorrowful as Sadie appeared just now, Leah thought she best be thinking how she should tell her sister of Mamma's passing. Sadie must hear the heartrending news before ever encountering either Dat or Aunt Lizzie. It was the compassionate thing to do.

When they approached the back door, Leah knew she must speak up. She paused on the sidewalk and turned to look at Sadie. "There's something you oughta know . . . in case you didn't hear. Believe me, I tried to get word to you."

Sadie's countenance turned nearly gray.

As upset as Leah was, her heart went out to her sister. "I'm awful sorry to be the one to tell ya, but someone ever so dear passed away a while back. Someone we all loved very much."

Sadie's eyes welled up with tears, and she shook her head. "Not Mamma. Please, say it's not my mamma."

Leah breathed in some air for courage. "Jah, Mamma's gone to Jesus."

Sadie collapsed on the back stoop, her hands over her eyes, head down, sobbing, knees up close to her face. She began to rock back and forth. "Dear, dear Mamma."

Leah felt compelled to explain further, wanting to comfort her sister in this moment; yet she stood without moving, arms held stiffly behind her back. "Mamma's been gone for many years now. She passed away giving birth to Abe."

Looking up, Sadie blinked her eyes, tears staining her face. "Ya mean to say, Mamma had another child after Lydiann?" Sadie frowned with wonder. "I have a baby brother?"

Leah honestly wished there was a better way to catch her up on things than standing here on the back stoop. "Well . . . Abe's not such a baby anymore. He's nearly seven—will be, come Christmas." She wished to say more, wanted to set the record straight. Abe wasn't just Sadie's baby brother. In all truth, he was Leah's son, only not by birth, just as she had been Mamma's daughter in every way that truly mattered.

But hadn't Sadie, travel weary, taken in enough information in the past few minutes? Maybe too much for having just arrived home. That the gaunt young woman before her had suffered more than her share of pain was clearly etched on her face, beautiful as it still was.

"Come in and rest. I'll make you some sweet tea." Leah opened the door and held it, then led the way into the kitchen.

"That'll hit the spot. Goodness knows, I need something to pick me up." Sadie dried her tears and, sighing loudly, sat down on the bench beside the table.

"Once you've had a sip or two, you'll want to go next door and say hello to Dawdi John and Aunt Lizzie. Dawdi's up in years and doesn't go out much, but he still tells us some mighty interesting stories. He and Lizzie both are excited to see you, of course. Dat, too, but he must be over at the smithy's, or he would've shown his face by now."

"That's all right. I'll take my tea quietly." Sadie accepted the warm cup and held it between her hands, staring at Leah. "Didja . . . well, I mean, should I ask . . . if you ever married?"

Please don't ask this, she thought, unsure how to share any more of the essential things. Leaning her head back, she began. "Long after we heard you were married, nearly two years later, Smithy Gid did court me, but only for a time. When Mamma was dying, she asked me to raise Lydiann and Abe. Honestly, maybe you'd rather not—"

"No, no . . . I want to know about you, sister. It's been the hardest thing, me bein' separated from my own family for all these years."

Leah continued on, telling how she had made the promise to care for Mamma's little ones and how that promise had sealed her future as a maidel due to Dat's eagerness to raise his own son and daughter, instead of allowing Gid and Leah to do so. But she didn't care to say much more. It was enough . . . almost, to have Sadie sitting here in the kitchen, sipping brewed tea with her, like old times. Enough to have those sad blue eyes staring and searching hungrily, as if looking for meaning in Leah's gaze, longing to know what she had missed here in her own family's home.

Leah didn't have the heart to go on, though she wished she might tell Sadie how sorry she was Jonas had died so terribly young, leaving her a widow. *Awful sorry . . .*

Leah felt nearly too ill to attend the required membership meeting the Sunday following Sadie's arrival, but she went anyway, sitting clear in the back, thus allowing herself no *visual* memory of repentant Sadie kneeling before the People. But her ears surely witnessed Sadie's embarrassing, even frank words of confession—the repeated meetings in the hunter's shack in the woods, the loss of her illegitimate son. . . . She cringed, wishing to stop up her ears, as well, but surely . . . *surely*, Sadie's heart was pure before God and the People. Surely Sadie hadn't come home to repent just because she was a widow and all alone in the world.

Leah, nevertheless, had become quite ill with an early autumn flu. The stress of having to vote to receive her shunned sister back into the fold had made her absolutely green round the gills, but she did her duty as a church member in good standing. *Good thing the ministers can't see into my heart*, she thought, despising her own reluctance to forgive and forget.

After the common meal at Uncle Jesse Ebersol's place, where house church had been held, several couples and their families followed Dat's carriage back home for a visit. Naomi and Luke Bontrager came with their little boys, as well as Hannah and Gid and their girls.

Mary Ruth joined all of them after church, as well, just as she'd quickly come to visit on the first evening of Sadie's arrival.

Leah felt some better later in the afternoon and joined the cheerful group, though she kept to herself, not stepping into her usual role as hostess. No doubt sensing her difficulty, dear Lizzie filled her shoes instead, and Leah pulled up a chair, relieved to simply sit and not lift a finger.

Abe hovered near, evidently not interested in playing with his cousins. Leah was glad for his company and that he stood protectively beside her chair for the longest time. Lydiann, however, was her outgoing self, readily engaging the laughter and attention of the big sister she'd never known. Because of the severity of the shunning, neither Lydiann nor Abe could remember hearing Sadie's name uttered in their lifetime. So there was much catching up to be done, and everyone, especially Sadie, seemed to enjoy the spontaneous get-together. They all stayed and talked till milking time, and then disbanded outdoors with Naomi and Sadie weeping in each other's arms, best friends reuniting under the canopy of heaven.

Dear Lord, please give me the grace I need, Leah pleaded. But the tearful scene was too much for her, and she slipped back into the house to soothe herself yet again.

Chapter Thirty-four

Soon the daily routine—Monday washday, Tuesday ironing and cleaning—took precedence as the newness of Sadie's return began to wear off, at least for Leah. Lydiann, on the other hand, was rather taken with Sadie and followed her around the house incessantly, Leah noticed.

Early Wednesday morning, while Leah was still making the bed in her room, a firm knock came at the door. "Who's there?" she called, reckoning who it might be.

"It's Sadie."

Stopping what she was doing, Leah moved toward the door and opened it slowly.

Before her stood her sister, the blue gone from her eyes, washed away by tears. "May I come in?" she asked.

"If it's important enough for you to be cryin', then I 'spect we ought to go outside," she surprised herself by saying. Honestly, she didn't much care to hear Sadie tell of her widowed sorrow, not in the privacy of Leah's bedroom. Not this near-sacred place where Mamma had given up her life for Abe . . . and where Leah had made her important promise.

"I'm not meanin' to box your ears," Sadie said suddenly. "But the way ya talk, you'd think we were gonna have it out between us."

Leah hadn't meant to be reckless with her words. "I'll meet you out front, where we can speak plainly without bein' overheard."

Sadie frowned, seemingly surprised. "All right, then."

Leah closed her door. She took her time finishing up the bed making, even set the green shades straight, eyeing them carefully so they each matched in length across the three windows on the side facing the woods. All this before ever leaving the house to meet Sadie.

"Truth be told, you act like you wish I'd stayed away forever," Sadie said when they were alone amidst the trees on the rolling front lawn. "And don't be sayin' otherwise."

There was nothing to add, really. Leah felt if she couldn't say anything nice, she ought not to say anything at all.

"What's wrong, Leah? Why do you seem to detest me?"

She filled her lungs with air. "Best not talk 'bout it, I'm thinkin'."

"Why? Does it annoy you that I assumed you were married to Smithy Gid? If so, I was only saying what Jonas told me years back."

"He told you *that?*" She was as bewildered now as she had been the day his strange letter arrived, followed by total silence once she promptly responded, writing him the truth.

"Several times, jah."

"But there was nothing tender between Gid and me, 'least not while I was engaged to Jonas." She paused. "Are you rememberin' things correctly—did Jonas really say that?"

"Why, sure he did. Even his father confirmed to Jonas that Gid was sweet on you, that Dat had given his blessing for him to court you. All this while you were betrothed to Jonas—just as he was completing his carpentry apprenticeship and preparing to travel home for your wedding."

So this was what Peter Mast and Dat had secretly discussed—the two of them had destroyed her future with Jonas!

"Frankly," Sadie went on, "at the time, I found it downright surprisin', but I assumed you'd decided to follow Dat's wishes in the end and marry Gid instead."

"That's ridiculous. You of all people knew how much I loved Jonas!"

"Jah, I thought I knew that, but I was altogether befuddled when I saw you and Gid holdin' hands in the woods that day you got yourself lost up there. Remember?"

"You saw *what?*" She couldn't believe her ears. Sadie was off in the head!

Her sister went on, describing the day Gid had gone in search of Leah, at Mamma's urging. Sadie told how she herself had gone into the forest, up to the low stone wall rimming Aunt Lizzie's log house. "Smithy Gid and you were holding hands and laughin' together. I saw it with my own eyes, so you can't deny it."

"You must've told this to Jonas," Leah said, not recalling the hand-holding incident whatsoever. "You made me look unfaithful . . . was that what you did?"

Sadie shook her head, blinking back tears. "I simply told

him once he asked what I knew 'bout Gid, and only after that. You must believe me, Leah. He'd heard, but not from me, that you'd gone to a summertime singing in our barn where you'd linked up with Gid, then walked home with him through the cornfield."

Again, she was wholly baffled. "I believe I recall that evening, but Adah and I went *together* to the singing. She and I, along with Gid—the three of us—walked over to the Peacheys' afterward . . . innocent as the day is long."

Sadie touched her elbow. "Ach, Leah, I don't care to bring up the past. That's not why I say these things. I only wondered why you hadn't married Smithy Gid after Jonas and I had believed it so strongly."

They were still for a moment as the sun rose higher through the trees from its dawning place. "I s'pose there's nothin' to be gained by rehashing all this," Leah said, grappling with her own words. "We oughta be thinking of *you* now, sister. Your needs . . . your great loss." She looked at her brokenhearted sister, sharing the intense sorrow. "How sad to have lost Jonas that way—in the silo accident. I feel right sorry for you . . . him so young and all."

A shadow swept over Sadie's face. "Didja say . . . Jonas?"

Leah nodded, unable to go on, wishing not to visualize the fatal fall from such a height.

Sadie shook her head slowly. "Oh, Leah . . . no wonder. You're sadly mistaken. I haven't seen Jonas in years."

Leah's breath bounded out of her lungs. *What on earth . . . how can this be?* "You mean you didn't . . . you never married Jonas at all?" She held herself around the middle, thinking she might be sick then and there.

Shaking her head, Sadie appeared as flabbergasted as Leah felt. "Why, no. I married Harvey Hochstetler . . . from Indiana." Sadie began to explain how Jonas had taken care to befriend her after she'd shared with him the tale of her wild rumschpringe. He had gone so far as to begin to date her, "solely out of a sense of duty, not love. He and I went our separate ways the following spring, after I met a boy named John Graber, who introduced me to Harvey."

"And what of Jonas? Where is he?"

Sadie shook her head sadly. "I don't know."

"When was the last you heard of him? Where was he then?" She felt nearly panic-stricken, suddenly aware of the horrid string of deceit coupled with misunderstandings. Unspeakable, for sure and for certain.

"I last saw Jonas in Millersburg. He was preparing to move, though he never said just where. I assumed he was hoping to set up his own carpentry shop somewhere in Ohio, but I can't be sure." Sadie went on. "Bein' shunned ruined his life, he said. It changed everything . . . made it impossible for him to continue his ties with his family and friends. Jonas once told me he felt like a man without a country. I surely understood that."

"So he just disappeared . . . is that what you're sayin'?" Leah sat right down in the grass, her legs incapable of supporting her. She held her hands over her heart, no longer able to deny her tears. "Oh, Sadie, I can't bear to hear any more," she cried. "Please stop. I . . . loved him so."

Sadie knelt next to her, wrapping her arms around her. "I'm sorry for comin' between you and Jonas," she whispered, leaning her head against Leah's. "I should've known you and

Smithy Gid were merely good friends. I should've known. . . ."

Like a breeze blowing the memory of that day gently back, the treacherous hike out of the deepest part of the woods became clear in Leah's mind. She recalled well-meaning Gid reaching for her hand several times, steadying her when she felt nearly too weak to walk, having strayed through the immense tangle of the woods, wandering for hours. He had merely protected her as a big brother. Nothing more.

But there were no words now to speak the truth of it to Sadie. Instead, she wept in her big sister's arms—for the lost years, for her resentment toward Sadie, who had been caught in a maze of misconceptions. Her heart ached, as well, for the long-ago sweetheart she would never see again. Dear Jonas . . . gone forever. Leah felt as if her very life was being driven from her.

Whispering now, Sadie said, "Do you remember what Mamma used to tell us? 'God knows the end from the beginning.' "

How on earth could the Lord God know such a thing, as Mamma had ofttimes said, and yet allow what had happened to take place? The end from the beginning. Leah had missed being Jonas's loving wife by a series of errors. Nothing more.

After a time, when the sadness and disbelief had spilled forth in a great veil of tears—Sadie comforting her through it all—Leah dried her eyes and kissed her sister. "The grapevine had it all wrong 'bout you and Jonas," Leah said softly, still puzzled by the absolute certainty of the news they'd received over the years.

Sadie spoke up, attesting to the fickleness of gossip. "No

wonder you've despised tittle-tattle your whole life," she remarked, to which Leah could only nod her throbbing head.

Together, the two of them rose slowly and walked hand in hand toward the house. *Sadie's return is both an end and a beginning for us all,* Leah thought, hoping it would be so when all was said and done. She was mindful to breathe deeply, willing her headache away. The children would be hungry for breakfast soon, and she must wear a smile for them.

But it was Sadie who was smiling broadly now. "What do ya say if I help Dat and Lydiann with the milkin' from here on out?"

"Well, now, are ya sure, sister?"

"That's one chore you should never have to do again. After all these years."

Leah was surprised but pleased. "Sounds quite all right to me. I'll be glad to cook breakfast and pack the children's lunch pails." With Sadie's offer to do the milking chores, Leah realized they'd reversed roles from childhood. Not only that, but she and Sadie were both single women, without husbands or hope of any. *Together under the same roof,* she thought, finding the notion almost humorous in a strange sort of way, recalling the saying, "Too many cooks spoil the broth."

With that she carried stacked firewood for the cook stove into the kitchen, where she was met by the sound of Lydiann's expressive voice. Sitting at the table, Lydiann carefully practiced the poem she was expected to recite at school today.

"'My Father, what am I that all Thy mercies sweet, like sunlight fall so constant o'er my way? That thy great love should shelter me, and guide my steps so tenderly through every changing day?' "

Leah could not simply stand there and overhear the truth of the rhymed verse, spoken so clearly by her young charge. Honestly, she couldn't help herself; she smiled. Quickly pushing the wood into the belly of the stove, she hurried to Lydiann's side. "God's mercies *are* new every morning, ain't so?" she found herself saying as she slipped her arm around her.

Looking up at her with shining eyes, Lydiann said, "You must've heard me sayin' my poem, Mamma."

"Indeed I did, and I hope you never forget those perty words, 'cause they're ever so true." Leah's heart was filled anew with love for her dear ones. She kissed her girl's forehead and rose to make pancakes, eager for this shining new day.

Epilogue

It's nearly Christmastide again, and Hannah continues to worry about her new little one coming so close to Abe's seventh birthday—Mamma's going-to-Glory date. I wish she would trust the Good Lord more. Fortunately Sadie's homecoming *has* seemed to help Hannah some. Actually, all of us are better in spirit since Sadie's return to Gobbler's Knob.

Dat and I had a much-needed talk following her return. Both hurt and befuddled, I expressed my disappointment over the role he had played in Jonas's and my breakup. His keen desire for Smithy Gid "to have his chance" was the culprit . . . the one and only motivation for my father's deception. Ever so adamant about my choice of a mate, he sadly shared with me that he had lost his head to dogged aspiration, and one wrong turn had simply led to another. In the end, Dat pleaded my pardon, and I surrendered to his open arms, with a clearer picture of the past. Some might say I have every right to carry a grudge, but an unforgiving spirit eventually destroys the soul, and I have better things to do.

This week Dat and Smithy Peachey are out chopping

wood with a group of other men, filling up the woodsheds round Gobbler's Knob while the women folk have been swapping dozens of cookies and recipes, everything from snowballs and coconut cookies to snickerdoodles and whoopie pies.

I try never to think of Jonas any longer. Knowing him, he's happily married and busy with his carpentry work, with plenty of little mouths to feed. I have to admit I'm glad he didn't end up with Sadie, because then, who knows, he might've been helping to build that silo, same as Harvey Hochstetler was the day he died. Who's to know really, except the Lord. *He* knows the end from the beginning and sees Jonas Mast and his dear ones wherever they are. 'Tis not for me to ponder.

The gray pallor of grief has flown away; I know this to be true. There was a spring in my step early this morning as I donned my boots and trudged through the snow to scatter feed for the small birds that stay with us during winter. While out in the crisp air, I noticed the hydrangea bushes bare against the side of the house. How Mamma loved their colorful summertime clusters! Yet each autumn they shed their pretty pink blossoms, and next year's buds lie dormant on the bough, waiting to burst forth and bloom again.

As for Aunt Lizzie's remark to me in the woods, I'm making a conscious effort to keep my eyes off myself and what I had viewed as a rather bleak future as a maidel, once Lydiann and Abe are grown, that is. I'm looking more compassionately on Sadie—helping her walk through yet another Proving because of our severe bishop. He's setting her up as an example for other young people, just as she always worried he would.

Preacher Yoder's death left a mighty big hole in our midst. We had ordination for the new minister back in October, a week following Sadie's kneeling confession. The divine selection—the lot—fell on Smithy Gid, so he's become Preacher Peachey now, which gets Lydiann's tongue tied up at times. I told her to simply call him Brother Gid, and she does.

Dat's standing up more and more to the bishop and beginning to talk to the Lord on his own, is what Aunt Lizzie tells me. She and Dat still go round and round sometimes, fussing over the least things. I guess she feels she must keep Mamma's beliefs alive with her own voice.

Yesterday Abe came bouncing home from school with a Scripture verse on his lips. " 'Be not conformed to this world,' " he said, eyes big as buttons. To which Sadie nodded her head, genuinely in agreement. *Her* motto these days, and she tells it to the children every other minute seems to me, is " 'For the wages of sin is death; but the gift of God is eternal life.' "

Come spring and the first song of the robin, I will go in search of the honey locust tree. I'll take Lydiann and Abe along and introduce them to the beauty and the tranquility of the deep forest—make some new memories. And when berry-picking time creeps up on us again, we'll go and pick a pail of juicy ripe strawberries and bake some strawberry-rhubarb pies for no other reason than that they taste so wonderful-gut. After all, desserts are supposed to be plenty sweet.

Lately I find myself staring far less at the night sky, contemplating the number of stars, than I do counting the smiles on Lydiann's and Abe's faces, the dear ones Mamma gave to me. Providence, some might say. I call it love, plain and simple.

Acknowledgments

I offer heartfelt thanks to each research assistant and prayer partner, for each helpful encounter, and for each wonderful person who gave expert advice in the thrilling journey-mission of writing this book.

Fondly I think of Eli and Vesta Hochstetler of Berlin, Ohio, who opened their hearts and delightful bookstore to me last fall, and who drove me to visit a working blacksmith shop deep in Amish country. Thank you! Great appreciation also goes to the young Amish smithy who gave a crash course in the art of shoeing horses.

Hank and Ruth Hershberger were a tremendous help, inviting me to their lovely Sugar Creek home and answering numerous questions, including Amish ins and outs of "going on a lark" and "pest hunts." I am truly grateful!

Monk and Marijane Troyer discovered information regarding the horse disease the "strangles," as well as other vital information. Thanks for inviting me to a joyful evening of food and fellowship with your newlywed son and daughter-in-law. I enjoyed every minute of Monk's storytelling, as well.

My thanks to Sandi Heisler, who graciously offered medical information regarding home births and midwives.

A big thank-you to Aleta Hirschberg and Iris Jones, my Kansas aunties, who shared their memories of Saturday-night baths in a large galvanized tub. And to Priscilla Stoltzfus, who helped with many Amish-related questions.

As always, to my devoted friends in Lancaster County Amish country who help with research but who wish to remain anonymous . . . I am forever indebted. May the Lord bless each of you abundantly!

I am so appreciative of my publisher, Gary Johnson, whose wit and wisdom brighten our days, and whose ongoing vision and prayers make books like this one possible.

Many thanks to my superb editors. To Carol Johnson, who knows my readers as well as anyone and who is a treasured friend indeed. To Rochelle Gloege, a remarkable editor who makes my writing sing. And to David Horton, whose astute perspective and attention to the nitty-gritty details are so vital.

To Steve Oates, Bethany's VP of Marketing, and his amazing team, an enormous thank you for the earnest prayers, the behind-the-scenes work that gets my books into the hands of readers, and for Steve's perpetual humor, a welcome relief from the stress of writing deadlines!

To my faithful (and affectionate) readers, who offer a wealth of encouragement. Every letter and email message is read with keen interest and appreciation.

My dear family is my underpinning of support. Much love and gratitude to my husband, Dave, for his tender encouragement and practical help. To Julie, Janie, Jonathan, and Ariel for their infectious smiles, energizing food, and solid editorial input. And I'm ever grateful to my wonderful parents, Herb and Jane Jones, whose life and ministry of faith are the heritage that has brought me this far. Thanks for your persistent prayers, Dad and Mother, so critical to my writing journey.

Finally I offer up my heart anew to my dear Lord Jesus, who has called me to walk with Him all the days of my life.

BEVERLY LEWIS

The Prodigal

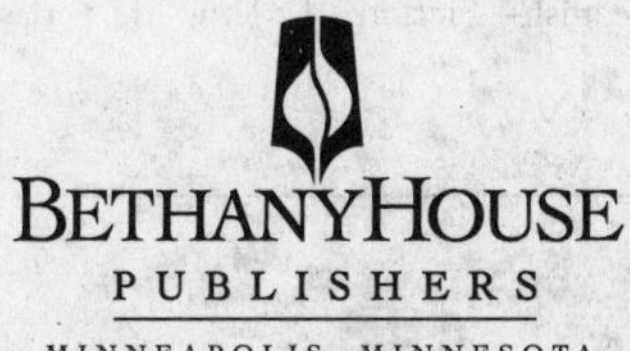

BETHANY HOUSE PUBLISHERS
MINNEAPOLIS, MINNESOTA

The Prodigal

Cover design by Dan Thornberg

Published by Bethany House Publishers
11400 Hampshire Avenue South
Bloomington, Minnesota 55438

Bethany House Publishers is a division of
Baker Publishing Group, Grand Rapids, Michigan.

Printed in the United States of America

ISBN 0-7642-2873-0 (Paperback)
ISBN 0-7642-2878-1 (Hardcover)
ISBN 0-7642-2879-X (Large Print)
ISBN 0-7642-2880-3 (Audio Book)

Library of Congress Cataloging-in-Publication Data

Lewis, Beverly, date–
The prodigal / by Beverly Lewis.
p. cm. — (Abram's daughters ; 4)
ISBN 0-7642-2878-1 (hardcover : alk. paper) — ISBN 0-7642-2873-0 (pbk.) — ISBN 0-7642-2879-X (large-print pbk.)
1. Lancaster County (Pa.)—Fiction. 2. Amish women—Fiction. 3. Sisters—Fiction. 4. Amish—Fiction. I. Title II. Series: Lewis, Beverly, date . Abram's daughters ; 4.
PS3562.E9383P76 2004
813'.54—dc22 2004012014

Dedication

For

Carolene Robinson,

with happy memories

of our "baby days" . . .

and laugh-out-loud Mark Twain nights.

By Beverly Lewis

www.beverlylewis.com

ABRAM'S DAUGHTERS

The Covenant
The Betrayal
The Sacrifice
The Prodigal

❖ ❖ ❖

THE HERITAGE OF LANCASTER COUNTY

The Shunning
The Confession
The Reckoning

❖ ❖ ❖

The Postcard
The Crossroad

❖ ❖ ❖

The Redemption of Sarah Cain
October Song
*Sanctuary**
The Sunroom

❖ ❖ ❖

The Beverly Lewis Amish Heritage Cookbook

*with David Lewis

Beverly Lewis writes for younger readers, too! See back of book for details.

04C

BEVERLY LEWIS, born in the heart of Pennsylvania Dutch country, fondly recalls her growing-up years. A keen interest in her mother's Plain family heritage has led Beverly to set many of her popular stories in Lancaster County.

A former schoolteacher and accomplished pianist, Beverly is a member of the National League of American Pen Women (the Pikes Peak branch) and the Society of Children's Book Writers and Illustrators. She is the 2003 recipient of the Distinguished Alumnus Award at Evangel University, Springfield, Missouri, and her blockbuster novel, *The Shunning*, recently won the Gold Book Award. Her bestselling novel *October Song* won the Silver Seal in the Benjamin Franklin Awards, and *The Postcard* and *Sanctuary* (a collaboration with her husband, David) received Silver Angel Awards, as did her delightful picture book for all ages, *Annika's Secret Wish*. Beverly and her husband have three grown children and one grandchild and make their home in the Colorado foothills.

Prologue

Winter 1956

Sometimes in the midst of gray fog and drizzle, especially at this time of year, it's difficult to tell where the day ends and the night begins. Alas, mud clings to nearly everything—buggy wheels, horses' hooves, and work boots. But in a few short days, when the predicted cold snap arrives in Gobbler's Knob, all this sludge will freeze hard, and hopefully everyone's footing will be safer once again.

Yet even now the long night of separation is past. My repentant sister, Sadie, has returned to the open arms of the People, and my heart is tender with love for her. Nine-year-old Lydiann privately asks me why Sadie ever left us to live in the Midwest. 'Tis a prickly subject with little hope of being understood by a girl so young and one who scarcely knows Sadie. I can only pray that dear Lydiann will set aside her curiosity and enjoy her eldest sister for who she is now . . . for who she is becoming.

Little by little, Sadie and I have completed the task of sewing her new dresses and aprons—all black for the one-year mourning period—since the few she brought home in her suitcase definitely reflected the style and pattern she wore while living in Nappanee, Indiana. Even the head coverings are quite different out west compared to here in Lancaster County—lots more pleats to iron than we have in our prayer veilings. We boxed up all of Sadie's former clothing and sent it back to Nappanee, hoping some of her deceased husband's family might be able to put it to good use. For sure and for certain, she intends never to need it again.

Along with tending to my youngest sister and only brother, I have been going to plenty of quilting frolics, where joyous fellowship fills the day now that I've learned to tune out the tittle-tattle and simply concentrate on making tiny quilting stitches. With Adah Peachey Ebersol, my best friend and cousin by marriage and, at times, Aunt Lizzie by my side, I am ever so content. Aunt Lizzie has an amazing ability to swiftly sew many little stitches, and straight ones at that. Sometimes she and I make a game of seeing who can sew the smallest ones, and she always wins with seven or eight per needle. Naturally she would; she's been quilting for many years longer than I. Yet it seems to me finishing well in this life is not so much about who is the best or greatest at something, but rather who embraces lowliness of heart. Laying down one's rights—meekness—is a blessed virtue, one that must surely come straight from the Throne of Grace.

In the nearly seven years since Mamma's death, Aunt Lizzie has become a mother to me, though I have yet to refer to her as Mamma. Still, in my heart she is now just that, and I know she senses the affectionate tie that binds the two of us.

On quilting days, Aunt Lizzie and Sadie take turns staying home to cook and clean and look in on *Dawdi* John, our elderly maternal grandfather, who still lives in the cozy Dawdi *Haus* adjoining our farmhouse. But neither Sadie nor Aunt Lizzie will ever consider letting *me* stay behind, and they're rather outspoken that I should be the one getting out of the house, even though winter is surely creeping up on us. I don't have to remind them that I do have ample opportunity to leave the Ebersol Cottage and have a change of scenery, since I work for the English doctor, Henry Schwartz, and his wife, Lorraine. Truth be told, sometimes I think Lizzie is concerned that too much of my free time is spent with fancy folk, though she brings this up only rarely. Probably in the back of her mind—and *Dat*'s, too—is Mary Ruth's leaving the community of the People behind for the Mennonite church, though I believe Dat has begun to temper his displeasure with Mary Ruth, speaking out less strongly here lately. Dawdi John, too, says he's seen "a whole other side" to Dat in recent days.

Secretly I've been reading Mamma's old Bible and searching out the underlined passages, coming to understand why dear Mamma was so patient and kind—walking the way of true humility. Such qualities seemed to come second nature to her, as she had a servant's heart, just as I desire to have before the Lord. If I continue to follow diligently the path God has set before me, though sometimes as prickly as nettles when I find myself alone, I believe I will be most joyful.

Patience is yet another virtue, one that grows stronger through the practice of waiting, and I've done much of that in recent years, come to think of it. I often linger near the school yard for Lydiann and Abe, whom I happily view as my own little ones. Young Abe, surrounded as he is by a houseful of women folk, is dearly treasured by each of us. He brings such delight to our lives that it's truly painful to contemplate how terribly close we came to losing him along with Mamma on the day of his birth.

I must also admit to waiting, with some measure of hope, for a letter from Grasshopper Level, praying that one day Mamma's cousins Peter and Fannie Mast might wake up and realize they have a whole family of folk who love them here. And it would be wonderful-good, if the Lord wills, to get word from someone—anyone at all—telling of Jonas Mast and his faraway life and family.

Most of all, I longingly wait for Sadie's six-month Proving to come to an agreeable end. Bishop Bontrager's choice of an older woman to oversee her during this time is Mamma's dearest friend, Miriam Peachey. The Proving means my sister can't be alone with a man for the time being, except male relatives. Of course this means she's not allowed to be courted until next April. Still, though she's but twenty-eight, I can't imagine her even being interested in another man—or at least not for a good long time.

So there is nothing to do but go along with the minister's stern decree and look ahead to a happier season—next springtime—when Sadie will be reinstated as a member in good standing, if she keeps her nose clean. We can only hope and pray she will; otherwise, she will no longer be welcome in Dat's house or the community of the People. As harsh as her shunning was, what with no letters allowed all those years she was gone, I sincerely hope the severity of this second Proving has not caused further distress in my widowed sister.

Before long the shortest day will darken the hours at both ends of the clock, the celebration of the Lord's birthday will come and go . . . and soon after, our little Abe will observe his seventh birthday. Then, too, my sister Hannah will bear her third wee babe. All of this in the space of a few short days, Lord willing.

For now I'm content to push split logs into Mamma's old wood stove and help Sadie and Aunt Lizzie cook and bake the family recipes, though in doing so, I am ever mindful of the constant ache in me, living life without dear Mamma. Keeping busy is one way of getting by, I daresay. Although Sadie now shares our parents' former room with me, it is in the night hours, when the rest of the family is snug in their own beds, that I am most threatened by profound loneliness as a *maidel*. Nonetheless, I remember always to count my blessings, moment by moment . . . day by day.

Part One

◆ ◆ ◆ ◆

The entrance of thy words giveth light . . .

—Psalm 119:130

Chapter One

Early morning winds pressed a row of saplings nearly flat to the ground, and the stark contrast between a dreary sky and the eerie whiteness of a snow-sleek earth created a peculiar balance of light.

Leah pulled her woolen shawl tightly against her as she made her way back to the house from the barn, where she'd gone to take a tall Thermos of hot coffee to her father and brother-in-law, Gid.

" 'Tis terrible cold out," she told Sadie, making a beeline into the kitchen, eager to warm her chapped hands over the wood stove.

Sadie looked up from Dat's favorite rocking chair, her needlework in her lap. " 'S'pose the men were glad for the coffee, *jah*?"

Leah nodded. "I like seein' the smiles on their red faces. Besides, it's the least I can do for Dat and our new preacher, ya know." She smiled. Truth was, Dat needed a bit of fussing over, still floundering at times without Mamma. So did Gid, what with Hannah so great with child she could scarcely shuffle to the kitchen to cook a meal for their growing family. Both Lizzie and Sadie had been taking turns carrying hot dishes up to the log house on the edge of the woods, helping out some. "What do ya think Hannah will have this time—girl or boy?" asked Leah.

"I'm sure Gid's hopin' for a son, just as Dat did all those years back. But it wouldn't surprise me if Hannah has another daughter. Girls seem to run in the Ebersol family," Sadie said.

"Jah, prob'ly so." Leah didn't care one way or the other. So far, young Abe was the only male offspring, and a right fine boy he was.

Hours later, when the time came to call the family together for dinner, Leah headed to the front room, where Lydiann was dusting the corner cupboard. Stopping to watch, Leah was struck by how sweet the girl's face was. Nearly heart shaped, truly, and pretty blue eyes much like Sadie's. She sighed, thinking what a handful Lydiann could be, yet at the same time, she brought a wealth of affection to the whole family. Lydiann was especially attentive to young Abe, her only close-in-age sibling.

"Sadie says the stew's ready," Leah said softly, so as not to startle her.

Turning, Lydiann smiled. She laid the dust rag on the floor and fell in step with Leah, slipping her arm around her waist. "Our big sister has that certain touch, ain't so?" Lydiann sniffed the air comically. "I daresay her cookin' oughta bring her another fine husband someday."

"Now, Lyddie," Leah chided her.

"Well, Mamma," whispered Lydiann, "you know what I mean."

"S'posin' I do, and Sadie does have that special something every cook yearns for." Leah went to the back door and rang the dinner bell while Lydiann washed her hands at the kitchen sink. Quickly Leah pulled the door shut, keenly aware of the bone-chilling cold, the bitter kind that crept up through long skirts and long johns both.

The present cold snap was expected to linger for a while, according to the weather forecast, which wasn't always so reliable. Dat, however, took both the weatherman and *The Farmer's Almanac* quite seriously most days, especially here lately. Leah wondered if her father simply needed something to hang his hat on, but the weather was the last thing a body could count on, as unpredictable as winter was long.

She went to help Sadie carry the food to the table. Along with stew, there were cornmeal muffins, a Waldorf salad, and a tray of carrot sticks, pickles, and olives, with plenty of hot coffee for the adults and fresh cow's milk for Lydiann and Abe. The children much preferred the taste of the milk when the cows were barn fed instead of pasture fed, so she knew they'd be draining their glasses tonight.

By the time Dat and young Abe dashed indoors, got themselves washed up, and sat down at the table, Dawdi John and Aunt Lizzie had come over from the Dawdi Haus, commenting on the delicious aroma of Sadie's stew. Lydiann was swinging her legs beneath the long table, clearly restless as Leah slipped in next to her on the wooden bench.

"What's takin' everyone so long?" Lydiann whispered to her.

"You must be awful hungry," Leah replied. "But how 'bout

let's be willin' to wait, jah?" She bowed her head as Dat motioned for the traditional silent prayer.

After the table blessing, Leah noticed Dat's gaze lingering a bit longer than usual on Aunt Lizzie, who was smiling right back at him. *Well, now, what on earth . . . Is it possible?* For a moment she contemplated the idea Dat might be taking a shine to Mamma's younger sister. She couldn't help wondering how peculiar she'd feel if Dat were actually sweet on her own birth mother.

And what might precious Mamma think?

Sadie dished up generous portions of the stew as each person in turn held a bowl to be filled. Abe's eyes were bright, apparently pleased at the prospect of his favorite—"plenty of meat and potatoes." He smacked his lips and dug a spoon deep into his bowl.

"I'll be takin' Abe with me to the farm sale come Thursday," Dat said, glancing at Leah. "Just so ya know."

"Yippee, no school for *me*!" Abe exclaimed, his mouth a bit too full.

"Aw, Mamma . . ." Lydiann complained, looking at Leah with the most pitiful eyes. "Can't I—"

"No need askin'." Lovingly, she leaned against Lydiann.

"But *you* always went with Dat to farm auctions growin' up, Mamma," Abe said, surprising her. "Ain't so, Dat? You told me as much."

Their father had to struggle to keep a grin in check, his whiskers wriggling slightly on both sides of his mouth. Truth was, Abe was quite right, and Leah was somewhat taken aback that Dat had told about those days when she had been her father's substitute son.

"Jah, Leah was quite a tomboy for a *gut* many years." Here

Dat turned and, for a moment, looked fondly at her. Feeling the warmth in her cheeks, she lowered her head. It had been the longest time since Dat had said such a thing in private, let alone in front of everyone.

"I daresay our Leah has herself a higher callin' now," Aunt Lizzie spoke up.

"She's our sister *and* our mamma," Abe said, grinning from ear to ear.

Lydiann muttered something, though just what, Leah cared not to guess. Best not to make an issue of it. No, let Lydiann simmer over having to attend school on the day of the farm sale. She needed not to miss any more school, having recently suffered a long bout with the flu. Even if Lydiann hadn't missed at all this year, there was no reason for her to go traipsing off to the all-day farm sale with Dat, Abe, and Gid when her place was at school or home.

Mamma must've thought that of me, too . . . all those years ago.

"You go 'n' have yourself a fine day of book learnin' on Thursday, Lydiann," Dat said just then. "And no lip 'bout it, ya hear?"

Dat must have sensed the rising will in his youngest daughter. He was becoming more in tune with his family's needs as each year passed, in spite of the grief he carried over him like a shroud.

Lydiann buttered her cornmeal muffin and then asked meekly for some apricot jam. Sadie hopped right up from the table to get it, and Dawdi John smiled broadly at the preserves coming and asked for a second helping of both stew and muffins. "Won't be a crumb of leftovers." He patted his slight belly.

This got Abe laughing and leaning forward to look down the table at their grandfather. "Maybe Dawdi oughta be goin' with us to the sale," Abe said. "What do ya think of that, Dawdi John?"

Dat murmured his concern. It was anybody's guess whether or not Dawdi, at his feeble age, could keep up with the menfolk, since a full year had passed since Dawdi had made any attempt at going. In fact, Leah recalled clearly the last time Lizzie's elderly father had decided to push himself too hard and go down to Ninepoints, where an Amish farmer was selling everything from hayforks to harnesses to the farmhouse itself. Dat had soundly reprimanded Aunt Lizzie for suggesting that her frail father go. Leah knew this because she'd unintentionally overheard them talking in the barn that day. Turned out poor Dawdi had gotten right dizzy at the sale, sick to his stomach, and later that night, he'd suffered with a high fever and the shakes. The illness had put an awful fear in not only Dat, but all of them.

Thankfully Dawdi was now saying no to young Abe's request, his white beard brushing against the blue of his shirt as he shook his head. "*Ach*, you and Abram go for the day. Leave me here at home with the women folk."

Once again Leah felt a warm and welcome relief, and she realized anew how deep in her heart she carried each one of her family members.

◆

Sadie and Dat hitched up the open sleigh to the horse the next morning, which took far less time than the usual half hour or so when the job was to be accomplished by only one person. With weather this nippy, Sadie couldn't see letting Leah start out with frozen fingers and toes from having to hitch up and then drive Lydiann and Abe to school, stopping for all the neighborhood children who attended—Amish and English alike. It had been her idea to surprise Leah, getting Dat from the barn so the two of them could prepare the sleigh.

Since returning home in October, she hadn't found the courage to open her mouth and tell the whole truth to her sister, but she *was* awful sorry about the part she'd played in keeping Jonas from marrying Leah. The letter from Leah to her beloved, the one Sadie had deliberately and angrily discarded so long ago, continued to haunt her. But she worried that it might cause another rift between herself and her dear sister if she were to confess the wicked deed. Meanwhile, she simply tried to find ways to help lift the domestic burden for Leah—anything to lessen her sense of guilt.

Leah's face shone with delight when she came out of the house, her pleasure evident at not having to face the chore single-handedly. She rushed to Sadie and hugged her but good while Dat grinned and waved and headed back to the barn. "Ach, Sadie . . . and Dat, you didn't have to do this."

Sadie rubbed her hands together. "We wanted to."

Just then Lydiann and Abe came flying out the back door, lunch buckets in hand. "One more day of school till the farm sale," Abe hollered over his shoulder, beating Lydiann to the sleigh.

Sadie saw Lydiann pull a face. Then both children laughed and hopped up into the sleigh. Turning to face her, they waved as Leah twitched the reins, pulling out and heading down the long lane to the road.

Sadie, aware of the bitter cold, stood there longer than need be, watching the horse's head rise and fall as the sleigh, soon to be filled with schoolchildren, slipped away from view.

I might've had a sleigh full of my own little ones.

Slowly she made her way toward the house, up the sidewalk shoveled clean of new snow. *'Tis nearly Christmas and I ought to be happy.*

"Oughta be a lot of things," she muttered as she reached for the back door and hurried inside. She didn't move quickly to the wood stove to warm her ice-cold hands and feet. She went and stood at the window, looking out over the side pasture, her gaze drifting all the way to the edge of the woods. Deep in that forest, there were deer hunters probably right now resting and warming themselves in an old, run-down shanty. She wished to goodness the place had fallen down in disrepair, wished Aunt Lizzie might have discovered the flattened shelter on one of her many treks through the woods, its walls of decaying wood lying flat on the snow-glazed ground, just asking to be hauled away.

Sadie recognized anew the one reason she'd ever hesitated to write to Bishop Bontrager telling of her widowhood and of her desire to return home to her father's house: the sordid memories here of the sin she had allowed herself to get caught up in as a teenager, the wickedness she'd shared with the village doctor's younger son. Although she had safely passed the Ohio church Proving and eventually married an upstanding young man, Harvey Hochstetler, there were times when thoughts of Derek Schwartz still haunted her. Did he even know she'd given birth to a stillborn son?

Derry . . . the boy who'd stolen her virtue. No, that was not true and she knew it. She had willingly given up her innocence to a virtual stranger, a heathen, as Dat often said of Englishers. She had known firsthand that Derry was just that, but he had not been a thief those nights in the hunters' shack.

Now, though, having heard that Mary Ruth was seeing Derry's older brother, Robert, Sadie couldn't help but feel squeamish at the wretched possibility of having to meet him one day. This made her tremble, and she hoped such a meeting might be months, even years away. She just felt so helpless at times, missing Harvey something awful, even more so now that she was safely home again, snug in Dat's big farmhouse. Yet the knowledge of that horrid shanty, the place where she had conceived her first child, illegitimate at that, caused her to draw her black shawl around her chin as she looked out toward the dark woods.

If the bishop knew my thoughts, he'd surely be displeased. She knew she ought not to dwell on the past. She ought to think on the good years she'd spent with Harvey, the kind and loving husband the Lord God heavenly Father had granted her . . . for a time. Still, coming home had stirred everything up again. Sometimes she wondered if the almighty One had withheld His favor even though she had turned from her rebellious ways, with the help of the Ohio ministers to begin with . . . and thoughtful Jonas. She had completed her Proving time in Millersburg well before ever meeting Harvey and moving to Nappanee.

All the babies I carried, she thought. *All of them lost to me . . . to Harvey, too. All the blue-faced wee ones I birthed . . .*

Silently she questioned if the reckless willfulness of her early sin had made divine judgment most severe. Here she was, all this time after, stuck in a mire of doubt and hopelessness, a woman longing for her dead children and husband. The awareness that Bishop Bontrager had set her up as an example to the young people did not make things any easier.

She had long wished for Dat to have known Harvey, for her sisters to have enjoyed her husband's hearty laugh and interesting stories told around the hearth. And yet in spite of the congenial and closely knit family she had shared with Harvey, she had often felt she was marking time clear out there in Indiana, far away from home. There had always been a feeling of waiting to undo what had been already done. She had sometimes cried herself to sleep, longing for Mamma's loving arms and nighttime talks with Leah. All of this unbeknownst to her husband.

I'm home now. Regardless of her initial reservations, she was glad to be living in a big family once again, with Dat and Leah, Aunt Lizzie and Dawdi John, and the eager-faced Lydiann and Abe—finally getting to know her youngest siblings. Most of all, it was fun watching her young sister and brother growing up underfoot, seeing their wide-eyed devotion to Leah. She wouldn't let herself envy Leah for having what she did not—a close bond with children, the memory of having held Lydiann and Abe ever so near as infants, rocking them to sleep in their tiny cotton gowns, rejoicing over their first toddler steps. Constantly, though, Sadie noticed every young one who was the age her children would have been had they lived . . . especially her dead son.

Still, it did seem a bit unfair that Leah was a mother without having given birth, while Sadie had given birth but was not a mother. Yet she wouldn't allow herself to contemplate that too much, not wishing to usurp Leah's position in Lydiann's and Abe's eyes.

Moving away from the window, she trudged to the utility room just off the kitchen. There, she removed her shawl and hung it on the third wooden peg. The first peg belonged to Dat, of course, and she had noticed right away upon her return home last fall that Leah's shawl now hung where Mamma's always had. So, even though there was still a vacant place at the table for Mamma, Leah must have felt no need to leave the wooden peg empty.

Chapter Two

When the nine o'clock auctioneer's chant began, Abram was ready. He and Abe had taken plenty of time to scrutinize all the farm equipment, as well as the field mules up for sale. Abe followed him around, never leaving his side, and Abram was downright pleased.

Dozens of men milled about in the snow and mud, most of them wearing black felt hats, the telltale sign of an Amishman. They stood around chewing the fat and telling jokes, some of them spitting tobacco. Each potential customer eyed the enormous array of farm tools, woodworking implements, livestock, milking equipment, and odds and ends of things—old green medicine bottles, two martin birdhouses, woolen mufflers, work boots and gloves, and a pile of garden rakes—all the men hoping for a bargain price. Their sons and grandsons were off playing cornerball or sitting over on the split-rail fence like black-capped chickadees perched on a wire.

When the time came, Abram raised his head slowly, signaling his first bid on a good-sized box of saws, drills, and sandpaper. The auctioneer scanned the crowd shrewdly, obviously spying another interested farmer. Up another dollar. Abram flickered his eyebrow at the local auctioneer, older than some but known for keeping the crowd loose.

"Who's biddin' against us, Dat?" whispered Abe, jumping up and down, trying to see over the crowd.

Abram put a hand on the lad's shoulder, not wanting to miss his chance at the saws and drills. A few more blinks of the eye and the bidding was done. The other fellow hadn't wanted them as much as Abram had. "Come on, now," he said to Abe. "We got ourselves some right nice handsaws."

He guided his boy through the crowd to claim the goods, saying it was Old Jonathan Lapp who'd dropped out of the bidding when he saw how quickly Abram kept coming back with a higher bid.

"When can I start makin' such bids?" Abe asked as they carried the box of saws and things to the carriage.

"When you're earnin' money." Abram had to smile at Abe's innocent sincerity.

"Just when will *that* be?"

"In due time" was all he said. There was plenty of food to go around, but when it came to cash there was less to speak of these days, what with Sadie living at home now. Leah, on the other hand, put every dime she made from her work at the Schwartz clinic into the family pot. Even so, Abram couldn't afford to pay his young son for his field and barn work before and after school and on weekends. He wouldn't think of doing so until Abe was closer to courting age, a good decade away.

He and his boy spent several more hours at the farm sale following Abram's only purchase. They stood in the barnyard talking with the men, but when Abe's nose and ears began to look mighty red, almost purple, he knew he best be taking this one home to warm up.

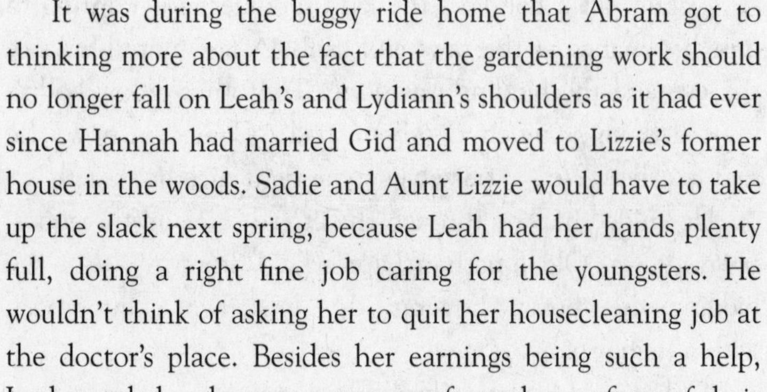

It was during the buggy ride home that Abram got to thinking more about the fact that the gardening work should no longer fall on Leah's and Lydiann's shoulders as it had ever since Hannah had married Gid and moved to Lizzie's former house in the woods. Sadie and Aunt Lizzie would have to take up the slack next spring, because Leah had her hands plenty full, doing a right fine job caring for the youngsters. He wouldn't think of asking her to quit her housecleaning job at the doctor's place. Besides her earnings being such a help, Leah needed a chance to get away from the confines of their four walls. He'd heard from the doctor that his missus felt she couldn't manage without Leah, so not only had she impressed them with her hard work, Leah had endeared herself to them, as well.

Thoughts of the Schwartzes led his mind to Mary Ruth, who was rather taken with their firstborn, presently studying to be a preacher. Having not met "honorable" Robert as of yet, he had only Mary Ruth's word to go on. Someday, if they continued to spend time together, he'd have to do the mannerly thing and meet his daughter's Mennonite boyfriend.

Lest his thoughts run away with him, he asked Abe, sitting to his left, what he thought of exchanging names in the family this Christmas. He didn't go so far as to say this approach would save some of the family's money, though.

"I'd like to draw Mamma Leah's name, if we put the names in a hat." Abe's blue eyes shone as he turned to look at Abram. "Either Mamma's or Lydiann's."

"Not Gid's, then?" He was taken aback by the serious tone of Abe's remark.

Abe shook his head. "Gid oughta be gotten by Hannah or one of their girls. Ain't so?"

Clicking his tongue, Abram urged the horse onward toward home. Ida's boy was as discerning and devoted as he was youthful. Abram reached down and patted Abe on the knee and nodded, mighty glad to have such fine company this brisk winter day.

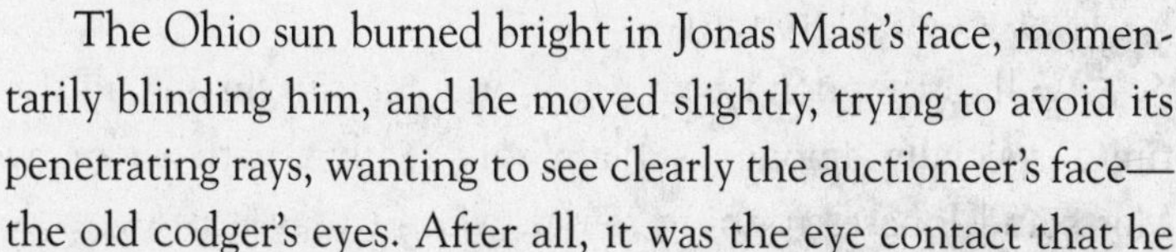

The Ohio sun burned bright in Jonas Mast's face, momentarily blinding him, and he moved slightly, trying to avoid its penetrating rays, wanting to see clearly the auctioneer's face—the old codger's eyes. After all, it was the eye contact that he wanted, having upped his bid this high already.

Dark blue and fluted, the carnival glass vase was the object of his steady bidding, and he would not let up, for he knew he had stumbled upon the best choice of a present for dear Emma. He could just imagine the look of sheer joy on her face when he gave it to her on Christmas Day.

He'd come to the distant farm sale interested in purchasing additional woodworking tools, having heard tell of the auction through the Amish grapevine. But while wandering about, he'd discovered antique dishes, quilts, and other old household items laid out in the front room of the house, set just up from the barn on a slope.

If I can just get the final bid, he thought, raising his eyebrows again to signal the auctioneer he had not lost interest.

The pretty vase was being held high in the air just now, and his pulse sped up when he heard the word "Sold!"

But the auctioneer shielded his eyes from the sun and, with a mystified look, peered into the crowd. "I daresay you ain't from round here."

"Name's Jonas Mast," he replied quickly, slightly embarrassed, with the crowd having turned to stare his way. "From up north a ways."

"Well, fine and dandy. Sold to our gut neighbor Jonas."

He had claimed his prize and turned to head back toward his horse and carriage when an old Mennonite farmer came up to him, leaning on his wooden cane. "Couldn't help overhearin', but you're Jonas Mast, ya say?"

Jonas offered a tentative nod.

"Well, if that don't beat all. World's gettin' smaller all the time, 'specially among us Plain folk . . . but with so many Masts and Jonases running round, who's to say if it *was* you, really."

"I'm sorry . . . have we met somewhere?"

"Doubt it," the older man replied, squinting his bleary eyes. "But then again, who knows? Ever live in Millersburg?"

Jonas felt surprise. "Why do ya ask?"

Such a long time ago . . .

With renewed excitement, the old farmer continued. "My cousin and I were reddin' out an old shed yesterday and happened to stumble onto a tattered old letter—unopened, as I recall—with a faded name written prettily on it."

Jonas was downright curious, though unsure if the white-haired man even knew what he was talking about. "Whom was the letter addressed to?"

"*Ach*, to *you*, of course."

"Hmm . . . you don't say." He was altogether befuddled. "Was there a return address?"

The old fellow removed his hat and scratched his head. "Honestly, paid no mind to that."

Jonas found all the talk of a letter puzzling—certainly the man's guess that he had once lived in Millersburg was right, but the rest of the story was downright odd. He stepped closer to the elderly man, noticing a hint of moonshine on his breath. "S'pose I best be headin' on home now," said Jonas, clinging to the antique vase. "Have a gut day!"

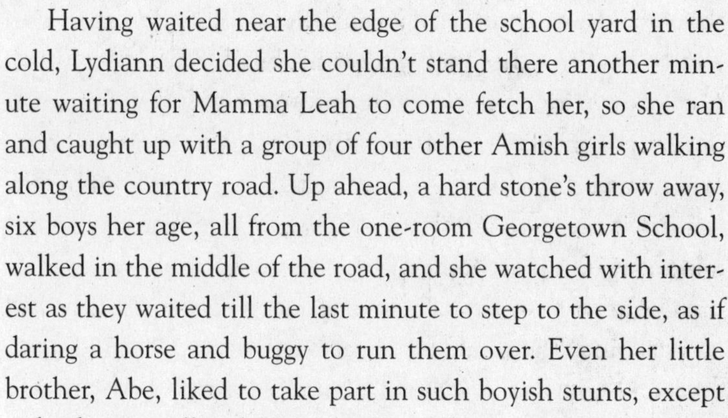

Having waited near the edge of the school yard in the cold, Lydiann decided she couldn't stand there another minute waiting for Mamma Leah to come fetch her, so she ran and caught up with a group of four other Amish girls walking along the country road. Up ahead, a hard stone's throw away, six boys her age, all from the one-room Georgetown School, walked in the middle of the road, and she watched with interest as they waited till the last minute to step to the side, as if daring a horse and buggy to run them over. Even her little brother, Abe, liked to take part in such boyish stunts, except today he was off with Dat at a farm sale.

She listened as the girls jabbered in Pennsylvania Dutch, not joining in their conversation about the Christmas play, where she was to be Mary, the mother of baby Jesus, come this Monday, Christmas Eve afternoon.

The boys shifted to the right side of the road as a car came toward them, and she noticed the dark-haired Mennonite boy, Carl Nolt, scramble to safety more quickly than either of the three Amish and two English boys. The only child of Dan and Dottie Nolt whistled as he scurried along. The Nolts owned the house where Lydiann's older sister Mary Ruth, a schoolteacher at an all-English school, lived and worked part-time.

"Carl's gonna make *en feiner* Joseph, ain't?" one of the girls said, all smiles.

This brought a round of snickers and "shhs!" but Lydiann pretended not to hear just what a fine Joseph he would be. *Carl has the brownest eyes I've ever seen,* she thought, wondering right then which of his natural parents had passed down the dark eyes to him and why on earth they hadn't kept him.

It was Mary Ruth, who was more like a big sister to Carl than she'd ever been to Lydiann, who'd confided that Carl had been adopted promptly after his birth. Since Mary Ruth was known for sometimes saying too much, Lydiann had never spoken of the matter with Carl. Still, she was pretty sure he had a good heart—at least she thought so from having rehearsed the nativity play during lunchtime recess yesterday and today. But pretending to be Mary to a Joseph who was no more Amish than the man in the moon sent a strange chill up her spine. She would never let on as much, though, for the sake of Mary Ruth, who had been bringing Carl with her when she came to the Ebersol Cottage to visit each week. It seemed Mary Ruth was a little too eager to include Carl in the games played near the wood stove with both Lydiann and Abe. Right peculiar it was, especially since Dat had made it clear he did not approve of Mary Ruth living with folk who had "electric." Such a blight it was, losing one of their own to Mennonites.

Lydiann suspected kindhearted Aunt Lizzie of having

something to do with Dat welcoming Mary Ruth, as well as Carl. Aunt Lizzie had a way of poking her nose in and having her say, and Dat didn't seem to mind this much at all. Ever so amazing, really.

Up ahead, riding in a one-horse sleigh, came Mamma Leah. Lydiann quickened her pace, glad to see her. "Come! Have yourself a ride home!" she called to the other children.

The girls responded by hurrying to catch up with her, passing the boys, who lagged behind—all but Carl. "Mind if I come along?" he asked no one in particular.

"Hop on," Mamma said, her cheeks bright pink.

Carl hesitated, looking back toward the boys.

"It's all right," Lydiann said, hoping he might sit right beside her, though she suspected he would keep his distance.

Carl smiled and climbed aboard, sitting closer to Mamma Leah than to any of the girls.

"When are you comin' with Mary Ruth for a visit again, Carl?" Mamma asked, and Lydiann paid attention to what he might say.

He shrugged his shoulders and said nothing for a moment. Then, when he finally found his voice, he said, "Mary Ruth says we might have all of you over for New Year's Eve . . . if it's agreeable with your father."

"How kind of you, Carl," Mamma replied before Lydiann could speak up.

Carl looked more comfortable now, and Lydiann wondered if he had been bashful before getting on the sleigh because of the boys. Maybe he worried what they might think of him riding with a group of girls.

"Where's Abe today?" he asked. Lydiann nearly missed the question, so caught up she was in her thoughts.

Once again Mamma Leah beat her to a reply. "Oh, he's off to a farm sale with his father."

"Lookin' to buy anything particular?" asked Carl.

Prob'ly some milkin' equipment and whatnot, thought Lydiann. But she didn't say what she was thinking and instead nodded her head and watched the relaxed way Carl sat cross-legged on the hay, wrapped in one of the woolen blankets Mamma Leah had brought along.

"Oh, I 'spect they might just find something worthwhile," Mamma said, looking back over her shoulder. "They usually do."

"I think my uncle went to that sale, too," Carl said. "He used to be Amish, so he likes to go where the Old Order farmers gather."

Lydiann found this interesting. So . . . somewhere in Carl's adopted family there had been at least one Amishman. *Did he leave the church before baptism, or was he shunned like Sadie?* Since Carl said no more, she wasn't about to follow up on the subject. Shunning was much too close to home, what with Sadie going through her Proving time now. Shunnings divided families, turning sisters and brothers into strangers . . . even if the shunned one repented and returned home.

Poor Sadie, pretty as the day was long. What on earth had she done to be treated so?

The smell of pecan pies baking drifted in from the doorway between the front room and the Dawdi Haus, and the familiar aroma reminded Sadie of Mamma, who had loved the Christmas season more than any other. Drawn by the delicious scent, Sadie headed next door to find Dawdi John napping in his rocking chair—head back, mouth open, and sawing logs rather loudly.

Where's Aunt Lizzie?

Tiptoeing through the small front room to investigate the smaller square of a kitchen, she quickly realized Aunt Lizzie was nowhere to be seen. She glanced at Dawdi, who remained oblivious to her presence, and opened the door leading to the stairs. Instead of calling up to her and risking awakening Dawdi, Sadie stepped lightly, heading upstairs.

She found her aunt sitting in the window of the first bedroom, Lizzie's own, reading the Bible. "Oh, hullo there, Sadie."

"Mind if I sit with you?"

Lizzie nodded. "Make yourself comfortable."

"Couldn't help but smell the pies."

Lizzie smiled. "Thought I'd surprise everyone and serve 'em for supper."

"Abe and Lydiann will like that, for sure and for certain." Sadie grew quiet.

Aunt Lizzie put her finger in the Bible, closing it, and tilted her head just so, looking hard at her now. "Something's on your mind, child. I can nearly hear it from here."

She thought how much better it might be if she didn't give in to the urge to open herself up and instead simply sat there, basking in the love her aunt so effortlessly offered. But Lizzie was altogether correct that there was much on her mind. "I miss talkin' to ya, *Aendi.* And I want to speak about my husband, Harvey, with somebody . . . with you, maybe, if you'd like to hear."

"Well, sure I would," Lizzie insisted.

Sadie related that she wished her family might have had the opportunity to know her husband. "Harvey kept folk in stitches, tellin' one story after 'nother whenever we invited relatives or friends over for meals or whatnot. Among other things, I sorely miss his laughter."

Aunt Lizzie leaned back, relaxing in her chair. "I daresay there is much to miss. I wish to goodness I might've known your Harvey."

Sadie felt suddenly eager to share something of her married years with Lizzie, having kept fairly mum since her return home, her loss having been too recent. She talked of their Christmases together, happily surrounded by Harvey's extended family, as well as the church folk. "Ach, we had the kindest bishop. I often wished he might've met Bishop Bontrager somehow, ya know." She was ever so careful not to step too hard on their bishop's toes here, but there *had* been many times when she felt sorry for Dat and Mamma and other members of the Gobbler's Knob church district, as well as herself. But, lest she show disrespect now for the Lord's anointed, she kept her peace. Aunt Lizzie need not know her private opinion of Bishop Bontrager. Besides, Lizzie had never admitted to having a problem with him.

"I'm glad you had such a fine husband and church in Indiana," Aunt Lizzie said after a while, giving Sadie's knee a pat. "We best be checking on the pies."

Sadie followed her downstairs and helped her set the pies out to cool. They then looked in on Dawdi John, who was still sleeping, before Lizzie motioned Sadie back upstairs. "There's something I've been thinkin' on," her aunt said in hushed tones. "And it's best ya hear it from me."

Sadie wondered if this heart-to-heart talk might involve Leah and her maidel status, or some such sad thing. *Can it be she senses I've kept mum about some of my own meddling in that?*

But Lizzie readily made it clear she had other things on

her mind. "When I was but a teenager, I got myself in some terrible trouble, as you already know." She stopped, as if to catch her breath. "I never told you all there was to the story . . . and now I feel you oughta know the daughter I gave birth to is your sister Leah—in all truth, your first cousin." Aunt Lizzie's face was slightly flushed. "Leah has known this since her baptism, and before the Lord took your mamma, she shared this with Mary Ruth and Hannah. I thought it was high time you knew, too."

Aunt Lizzie is Leah's mother? Sadie felt the air go clean out of her. "Leah's your . . . your own daughter?"

Lizzie nodded her head, a tear glistening in her eye.

Struggling to take in this bewildering revelation, Sadie whispered at last, "How does Leah feel 'bout this?"

"Oh, we never speak of it anymore, just as the People do not speak of the shun once a person repents," said Lizzie.

Sadie found this news not only curious but altogether unnerving. Lizzie had given Leah to Mamma and Dat to raise, yet her child had grown up at arm's length, where Lizzie could observe and love her.

A shiver of sadness flew up her back, and Sadie, for a fleeting moment, recalled with dread the days and nights she had frequently heard the cries of a phantom baby, a constant reminder of her first wee one.

"I don't know what to say, really," she confessed, choking down the lump in her throat at the thought of Leah's unexpected bond with the aunt Sadie so admired. "To think you and Leah . . . well, I guess I might've wondered all those years why Leah was the only dark-haired one in the family. But I never would've guessed this."

Aunt Lizzie went on to say that, at the time of Leah's

conception, she had been so caught up in her youthful rebellion she hadn't cared what anybody thought. "I just did as I pleased."

Same as I did, Sadie thought ruefully.

"Thankfully, your parents took me in as their own for a time, even as they did Leah when she was born."

"So the young man, Leah's father, never wanted to marry you or care for you?" The question slipped out effortlessly, though as soon as Sadie had voiced it, she felt suddenly sorry. "Uh, that's not at all for me to ask."

"No . . . no, it's to be expected, really 'tis."

But when Lizzie did not offer to say more about Leah's blood father, Sadie knew better than to press the question now burning in her mind.

Just who is Leah's real father?

Chapter Three

Gid says might just be a gut idea if the hex doctor's on hand for this baby," Hannah told Aunt Lizzie in the privacy of her cozy kitchen on Christmas Eve day. "He thinks we should've had him here for the first two, just to be safe."

She had been pouring tea for herself when who but Lizzie had come knocking at the back door. Having felt awful sluggish all day, Hannah was glad for a chance to sit down and share a nice cup of tea with Lizzie. They'd gotten on to the topic of Hannah's choice of an Amish midwife when Hannah felt she ought to speak up about her fears.

"Dat still feels strongly that Mamma would be alive today if he'd had his way about callin' in the powwow doctor." She watched Aunt Lizzie closely, hoping for some further explanation as to why Lizzie, like Mamma, was so opposed to the sympathy healers.

Lizzie's hazel-brown eyes appeared more earnest now; it was surprising to see her usually cheery aunt turn suddenly solemn. She poured a rounded teaspoon of sugar into her teacup and stirred slowly before looking up at last. "I hesitate to talk much about so-and-so's stubborn stand on this subject, but if I do . . . well, please don't say anything."

"You have my word, Aendi."

Lizzie took several sips of hot tea. Then, setting the pretty floral cup down lightly on its matching saucer, she continued. "This has been a sore point with your father and me for much too long, I must admit. Here lately, though, I think he may be coming round 'bout the things your mamma believed in. I pray so."

Hannah found this admission hard to understand. What was Lizzie saying? That she and Dat had started to see eye to eye on the Amish doctors? If so, what would it mean for her and Gid . . . and the baby soon to be born? Would Dat interfere, try to convince Gid otherwise?

She shuddered to think of risking her baby's life as Mamma had done, only to lose her own. It was a miracle young Abe was as sturdy and smart as he was. Any of the women folk, if they were privy to all that Leah said poor Mamma had gone through to birth Abe, might still be bracing themselves, waiting for something wrong to show up either mentally or physically in her little brother. For Dat's sake and Abe's, too, Hannah sincerely hoped Abe would be healthy his whole life long.

"Are ya sayin' Dat would be opposed to having a hex doctor assist the midwife?"

Aunt Lizzie raised her eyebrows. "Why in heaven's name would you want to do such a thing, Hannah? Your mamma never did. She wanted nothing to do with the powwow doctors."

Sometimes Hannah just wished to goodness she could simply share her opinion without Aunt Lizzie raising a stink, especially when Ida Mae and Katie Ann were napping not so far from the kitchen. Knowing Lizzie as she did, Hannah wouldn't put it past her aunt to speak her mind and then some. Truth was, this minute she didn't feel strong enough to argue her side of things and regretted bringing up the subject. Sure, Lizzie had her view, but so did Hannah. And now that she was Gid's wife, shouldn't she take into account *his* feelings? After all, the growing babe within her belonged to her and Gid, not to Lizzie.

"I'd rather be safe than sorry, is all," she whispered, tears springing to her eyes.

Aunt Lizzie placed a soft hand on hers. "Well, now, Hannah, what's to worry? You had no trouble birthing Ida and Katie."

Hannah nodded. " 'Tis quite true."

"Why do ya feel the need to invite a spirit of evil into this house?"

Hannah gasped. *What's Lizzie saying? Does she actually believe the Amish doctor is of the devil?*

She'd heard such whispered things from one of Mamma's Mast cousins—either Rebekah or Katie—years ago when Dat and Mamma were still on friendly terms with Cousins Peter and Fannie, but never before from Aunt Lizzie.

"I don't think you understand," Hannah began quietly at first, but she felt the ire rise in her as she went on. "I want to have a safe delivery . . . and I want to live to see this new one grow up—same as Ida and Katie. Why should you want to stand in my way?"

"And why would ya put your trust in someone other than the Lord God? Powwowing is nothing short of white witchcraft. Your mamma said the same." Aunt Lizzie pursed her lips, then stared down at the cup of tea before her, fiddling with the handle.

Hannah shook her head in disagreement but said no more. Something within her wanted to say, *We'll decide for ourselves*. But there was another urging deep inside her, prompting her to think long and hard about this, even suggest that Gid discuss it with Dat himself.

"Death haunts me, Aunt Lizzie," she surprised herself in saying.

Lizzie reached over to pat her hand again. " 'Cause of your mamma?"

"Maybe so . . . and Mary Ruth's first beau, Elias. One just never knows. . . ."

Lizzie fell silent as she stroked Hannah's hand.

Hannah felt the need to fill the stillness, though. "Seems nobody knows for sure and for certain what's waitin' for us on the other side."

Lizzie frowned. "Over Jordan?"

Hannah nodded. "I wish this wasn't so troubling." She continued on, sharing that she'd struggled privately since childhood with the issue of death. "Some days I wish we could simply live forever, the way Adam and Eve were created to."

"Without aging?" Here Aunt Lizzie broke into a winning smile. "Just think, Dawdi John's beard might be dragging on the ground if that's the way the dear Lord intended things to be for us now . . . since Adam fell from grace."

"Guess it was fallin' from grace that turned ev'rything topsy-turvy, ain't? If only Adam and Eve had obeyed God in the first place, things sure would be lots easier."

"Obedience, jah." Aunt Lizzie leaned forward. "Let me tell ya what I think."

For the next half hour or so, Hannah listened as her aunt shared things she'd never heard from an Amishwoman before, except for the one time she'd accidentally stumbled onto Mamma saying late-night prayers. Now she was fairly sure that what Lizzie believed about the Lord Jesus coming to earth to die to offer eternal life was precisely what Mamma had also believed. Hearing Aunt Lizzie say that we *can* be saved and know it without falling into the sin of pride, that the "Good Book teaches this," Hannah wondered what Gid might think if he knew. And she worried if Gid and the brethren got wind of Lizzie's beliefs, that her newly ordained husband would feel obligated to speak about them to Bishop Bontrager.

Could dear Aunt Lizzie be in danger of the shun? A cold shiver flew up Hannah's back.

Nearly as excited as the children had been at breakfast, Leah rode along in Dat's sleigh to Georgetown School after lunch. Sadie, too, had been invited to attend the Christmas play, but she'd awakened with sniffles and decided to stay home. Aunt Lizzie and Dawdi John had also been given homemade invitations, but the children didn't expect Dawdi to make the effort to venture out on such a blustery day—none of the family did. And Aunt Lizzie had felt she ought to stay put in case Hannah went into early labor, as she had with the first two little ones. Fortunately, she was only a holler away in the little log house.

"Lydiann said she was awful nervous 'bout the play when I took her and Abe to school this morning," Leah said as they rode along.

Dat made his familiar grunt, which meant he'd heard but was somewhat preoccupied.

"There'll be lots of parents on hand, I'm sure." She made yet another attempt to have conversation with her father, since they scarcely ever found themselves alone anymore.

"I hope we won't be expected to sing the *weltlich* carols," Dat said, glancing at her.

"Well, why not the more lighthearted ones?" She found this interesting.

He kept his face forward just now, and Leah thought she saw the corners of his mouth twitch.

"Dat? Did I speak out of turn?"

His chest rose at the question. "No . . . no, that's fine."

She wished he'd talk about whatever was bothering him. Was he missing Mamma still, just as *she* was? Leah wouldn't be so bold as to bring up such a thing. All the same she wondered, though Mamma's home-going seemed a distant memory to her.

"I'm sure Lydiann and Abe are havin' trouble keeping their minds on their schoolwork right now," she said.

"They're prob'ly getting the schoolhouse ready, I'd guess."

"Jah, puttin' up string across the room to hang up letters spelling out 'Merry Christmas to Everyone!'" she said, glad Dat was talking freely.

He sighed. "Abe said he was mighty happy with the name he drew for Christmas."

"I hope he didn't tell ya who." She had to smile at this. "Abe's quite the little man . . . as thoughtful as any child I've known."

"But he speaks his mind when he wants to."

She knew this was so.

Dat kept the horse going at a steady pace—just right for a quiet talk on a snowy afternoon.

"Sadie seems to be settling in here again, ain't so?" she asked, sticking her neck out a bit.

"I daresay she's missin' her husband something awful." Dat paused, bent his head low, and then continued. "She and I have something in common for the first time."

Leah hadn't thought of it quite like that. But Dat was right. Both he and Sadie shared a great sense of sorrow.

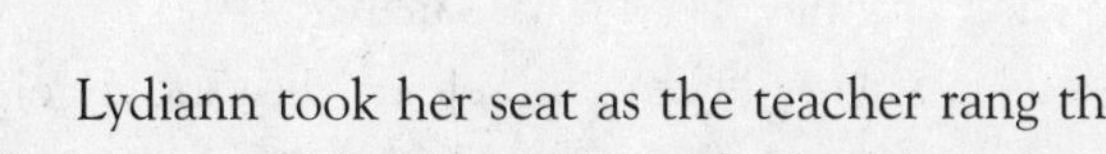

Lydiann took her seat as the teacher rang the bell on her desk. She couldn't keep a straight face, because Dat and Leah were right here in this very room, sitting in the back with lots of other folk—parents, grandparents, aunts, uncles, cousins, and babies. It looked to her as if nearly all of Gobbler's Knob had turned out for the school play.

Her first-grade cousin, Essie Ebersol, stood at the front of the room and began to recite a poem. "'Baby Jesus, meek and mild . . .'"

When Essie returned to her seat, Lydiann knew it was time for a group of older boys to perform their skit. Following that, the boys sang "The First Noel" quite nicely, she thought. *For boys with squeaky voices*.

Soon the teacher started another carol, "Hark! The Herald Angels Sing," and everyone joined in heartily. Lydiann turned quickly and spied Mamma Leah with Dat, both of them singing and smiling.

What a wonderful-gut time of year, she thought. Looking over a few rows, she noticed Abe twiddling his fingers but singing, nonetheless. She couldn't remember ever hearing her little brother's voice in song—at Preaching service, Abe always sat on the side with the menfolk, next to Dat.

She squirmed in her seat a bit, thinking ahead to what was to come. Would Carl remember his lines? *Will I?*

When the final note was sung, the teacher nodded to her and Carl, and to all the angels, shepherds, and wise men. Quickly the angelic host lined up behind Joseph and Mary, and the teacher brought out a wooden manger containing a small sack of potatoes wrapped in a blanket.

"Christ is born!" announced one of the shepherds.

"He is the King of kings," said a wise man.

Carl took a deep breath. "Let us all rejoice with the angels this day."

"Come see the place where the Christ child lay," added Lydiann, feeling a flutter of excitement as she reached down and lifted the holy bundle into her arms. She was thankful their teacher had wrapped the potatoes very tightly. This way, she could hold the "baby" on her lap.

They went on to recite their rhymed verses, and Lydiann was pleased because she—and Carl—remembered every single word.

When the play was over, each student gave a gift of fruit or a candy cane to every other student, and to the teacher. But getting a big hug from Dat and a kiss on the cheek from Mamma Leah was the best gift of all. Both Lydiann and Abe climbed happily into the second seat of Dat's sleigh and called to their friends, "Merry Christmas!"

"Same to you!" their friends called back.

When they returned home, it was time for Lydiann to assist Mamma in cooking supper. Sadie was all wrapped up in a blanket, sitting on the rocking chair near the wood stove, so she wasn't feeling well enough to help. If Lydiann wasn't mistaken, it looked to her like her eldest sister had been crying.

She went and offered Sadie a big round orange. "*En hallicher Grischtdaag!*—a merry Christmas to you."

Sadie looked up and smiled, accepting the gift. "*Denki*," she said softly.

And with that, Lydiann knew for sure and for certain Sadie wasn't only suffering from the sniffles.

Chapter Four

A midnight gale had come up and temperatures plummeted. Upon awakening to the dawn of Christmas, Leah was surprised at the thick layer of frost on the window as she lifted the green shade. Unable to peer out, she stared at the pretty pattern Jack Frost had painted. Once the sun rose over the eastern hills and its rays reached the house, the crust of ice would melt quickly. Then she would be able to see from this upstairs lookout what snowy new shapes the overnight drifting had created in the barnyard and beyond.

For now, though, she was eager to dress and hurry downstairs to make a special breakfast, one that would include baked oatmeal and raisins, baked eggs, and chocolate waffles with a homemade syrup of brown sugar and melted butter.

She lightly touched Sadie's sleeping form. "Merry Christmas to you, sister," she said softly, waiting for Sadie to rouse a bit. When she did, Leah asked if she felt well enough to help with milking, offering to take her place if she was still under the weather. But Sadie shooed her out of the room, saying she was just fine. Leah was surprised that Sadie was so adamant and determined to go out in the cold, especially when she'd felt too ill to attend the school play yesterday.

Making her way down the long stairs, she recalled Dat's remark about Abe and the drawing of names for today's gift exchange. She couldn't help but notice how gleeful her boy had been the past few days, but then he was downright happy most of the time. And, too, she was quite aware that both Lydiann and Abe had been slipping over to the Dawdi Haus a lot recently, and Aunt Lizzie and Dawdi John had been secretive about whatever the children were doing.

Going to the back door, she discovered the same hard coating of frost on the windowpane and knew there was no way to know what she might discover outside unless she yielded to curiosity and opened the door. When she did so, she was amazed at the sweeping, arclike hollows beneath the base of each tree and the odd-shaped swells of white along the lane that led around to the bridge of the bank barn, where Dat and Gid had evenly placed large stones to rim the way. "Ach, somebody needs to shovel a path to the barn," she said to herself, surprised Dat wasn't up yet.

I'll make some coffee right quick, she decided, closing the door to get a fire going in the wood stove. Reaching for the bundle of wood Dat had conveniently stacked in the utility room, probably before heading off to bed, she realized suddenly just how cold it was in the house. Why she hadn't noticed before, she didn't know.

Lydiann will be shivering . . . and won't be shy about saying so, she thought, wondering if Aunt Lizzie was up already next door, stoking the fire so Dawdi John would awaken to warmth.

Making haste to get the fire going in the wood stove now,

she smiled at whose name *she* had drawn. What delightful surprises this day held for all. She did wonder, though, how Hannah, Gid, and the girls would make it down the long, snow-drifted hill to join them for the noon feast. More than likely, Dat would have to take the horse and sleigh up there to fetch them. She just hoped Hannah's baby wouldn't decide to come early, what with the main roads nearly impassable. *But no, I daresn't worry. Besides, Hannah's baby isn't due quite yet.*

When Dat still hadn't wandered into the kitchen fifteen minutes later, Leah decided to check on him to see if he had overslept. Making her way through the front room, she noticed his bedroom door was closed.

She hesitated to bother her father, but thinking he might be ill, she put her hand to the door and tapped gently. "Dat?" she called softly.

A slight shuffling sound followed, and then she heard his voice. "That you, Leah?"

"Jah."

"I'll be right out," he said, and she scurried back to the kitchen.

When the oatmeal had been poured into a greased pan and slid into the oven, Dat entered, looking somewhat disheveled. She offered him a cup of hot coffee, and he took it, blowing on it as he stood near the sink.

Abe joined them in the kitchen. "Looks like I'm not the only late riser," Dat said with a quick smile. "Merry Christmas to ya both."

"And to you, too, Dat," she said, returning his enthusiasm.

Abe's eyes twinkled and he hurried to get his coat.

Sadie came downstairs at that moment, wearing a green choring dress and black apron with a rather bedraggled-looking navy blue sweater. "It'll be right nippy in the barn," she said, glancing down at the buttoned-up sweater, as if to explain the old wrap.

"Want some coffee?" Leah asked. "Or I can make hot cocoa, if you'd rather."

Sadie shook her head. "Coffee's fine."

"Did ya hear the wind howlin' last night?" Leah said as she poured a second cup of coffee, aware of Abe still tinkering around in the utility room.

Sadie nodded, glancing away, but not before Leah noticed a glistening in her sister's eyes. She suddenly felt sad and wondered if this first Christmas as a widow would be as hard on Sadie as Dat's first without Mamma had been.

She set about making hot cocoa for Abe and called to him when the hot drink was ready. He came immediately, face shining. "It's a right special day," he said with mischievous eyes. He reached for the cup. "Denki, Mamma."

Mamma . . . The name never ceased to warm her heart.

When they'd drained their cups, Sadie and Dat bundled up and headed outdoors with Abe. Dat shoveled a path as Sadie and Abe came behind with their brooms. Leah watched momentarily from the utility room, having closed the interior door to the kitchen so as not to allow heat to escape. *Please, Lord God, be ever near to my sorrowing sister this day.*

While the oatmeal baked, she hurried to Dat's room to redd up and make his bed. But before she did, she went to the narrow bookshelf and reached for Mamma's Bible, not the big German family Bible stored in the corner cupboard in the kitchen, but the one Mamma had read repeatedly through the years. Leah noticed the leather wasn't as cold as she might have expected it to be on such a chilly day and wondered if Dat might have been holding this Bible in his strong hands . . . for quite some time, too, maybe.

Heartened at the thought, she moved to the window and read the underlined final verse in chapter fifty-four of the book of the prophet Isaiah: *No weapon that is formed against thee shall prosper; and every tongue that shall rise against thee in judgment thou shalt condemn. This is the heritage of the servants of the Lord, and their righteousness is of me, saith the Lord.*

The verse puzzled her no end, though she had read it repeatedly since first discovering Mamma's pen had marked it. What had this particular underlined passage meant to her mother? Leah was anxious to know.

Closing the Bible, she returned it to its place on the shelf. Then she smoothed out Dat's bedcovers, top quilt and all, and left to return to the kitchen. There she prepared the baked eggs, using Mamma's old muffin tins, placing the round pieces of toast, moistened with milk, inside and then breaking the eggs over the tops.

All the while she pondered the meaning of the verse, finding it peculiar Mamma would have contemplated it in such a way as to take pen to the Holy Bible. Was it possible Mamma had come under some verbal attack, possibly by the church brethren? If so, wouldn't Aunt Lizzie know?

Every tongue that shall rise against thee . . . Those words especially disturbed her. She knew she best cast aside her musings. *'Tis Christmas Day, for pity's sake.*

Sighing, she went to the foot of the stairs to check on Lydiann, only to see her standing at the top, fully dressed, hair combed and pulled back in a bun. "Happy Christmas, dear girl," Leah greeted her.

Lydiann smiled broadly. "Merry Christmas to you, Mamma." Then she added, "'Twas awful cold when my feet touched the floor."

Leah nodded and had to smile. "Well, speakin' of cold, it might not be a bad idea for you to run out and take Sadie's place after a bit to let her come in and warm up. I'd hate for her to catch an even worse cold."

Lydiann headed down the steps toward her, eyes concerned. "Is Sadie gonna cry again today, do ya think?"

"Well, I hope not. We must be especially considerate toward her on our Lord's birthday," Leah replied, walking with Lydiann to the kitchen. She hurried to prepare the waffle batter, setting the big black waffle iron on the cookstove.

Leah felt at such a loss to explain Sadie's absence for all those years; the People simply did not speak of a shunning after the fact. She hoped Lydiann's curiosity over Sadie might soon subside. *Not just for my sake, but for all of us.*

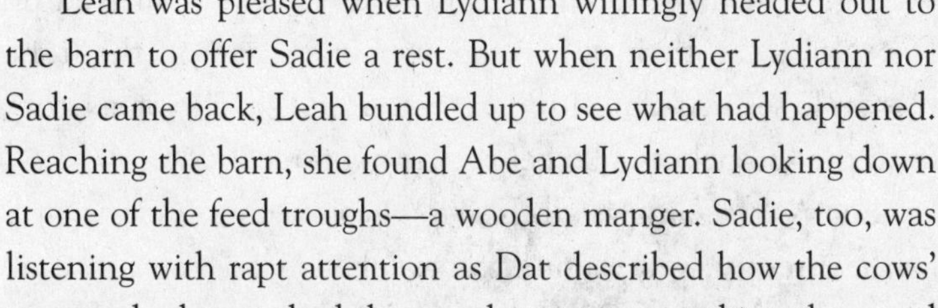

Leah was pleased when Lydiann willingly headed out to the barn to offer Sadie a rest. But when neither Lydiann nor Sadie came back, Leah bundled up to see what had happened. Reaching the barn, she found Abe and Lydiann looking down at one of the feed troughs—a wooden manger. Sadie, too, was listening with rapt attention as Dat described how the cows' tongues had smoothed the wood over time, making the wood of the manger "nice and smooth . . . fit for baby Jesus."

Surprised at her father's words, Leah stood quietly as she

observed the little gathering, which included their three German-shepherd dogs—King, Blackie, and Sassafras—in the nearly balmy atmosphere of the barn's stable area.

"God put the notion in the animals' heads?" Abe asked, touching the glistening wood with the full palm of his hand, clearly intrigued.

"Jah, I believe so." Dat stooped down, tugging on his long beard.

Lydiann looked up at Sadie just then, and Sadie put her arm around her young sister, who said, "The Lord God must've planned way ahead of time for Jesus to be born in a barn, ain't so?"

Dat nodded, even chuckled. "The Lord doeth all things well, and I daresay this is one of them."

Leah continued to watch silently as Dat spoke openly with the children. *A long time comin'*, she thought, ever so glad.

Hours later, after Dat had gone to fetch Gid, Hannah, and their girls in his sleigh, and after Mary Ruth had arrived by Dan Nolt's car, their father had everyone gather in the front room. He seemed almost too eager to read the Christmas story from the Gospel of Luke before the noon meal.

But as intriguing as all this was, Leah was most captivated by the attentive way Aunt Lizzie watched Dat during his reading of the old Bible. *Can it be she has feelings for Dat, too?*

After the noontime feast, and once all the dishes and utensils were washed, dried, and put away, the family was ready for the gift exchange Lydiann and Abe had been awaiting so patiently.

They assembled in the front room once again, and Abe promptly marched to Dat's side and presented his gift of a handwritten, homemade book. Dat smiled when he turned to the first page and saw the printed names and birth dates of each family member, along with several Scripture verses, all in Abe's own hand. "I learnt them from Aunt Lizzie," the boy explained, looking over at Lizzie and grinning.

Next Lydiann approached Leah. "I drew *your* name, Mamma," she said, holding out her gift.

"Oh, Lyddie, how perty!" Leah accepted the embroidered handkerchief.

"I made it myself," whispered Lydiann, "but with Aendi's help."

Leah hugged her girl close. "Denki, dear one . . . I'll treasure it for always."

"Look at the butterfly," Lydiann said, pointing to a fanciful green butterfly suspended over a yellow rosebud.

"I see . . . and it's very nicely done." For a moment Leah likened it to the butterfly handkerchief hidden deep in her hope chest, although this one featured a simple embroidery stitch, not the elaborate cutwork style that Hannah had long-ago made for Sadie.

Glancing now at her elder sister, who was seated next to Hannah with eighteen-month-old Katie Ann on her lap, Leah wondered when or if she might return the beautiful hankie to Sadie. But no, the connection to Sadie's stillborn son might easily mar the holy day, and that would be heartless. She dismissed the idea quickly, at least for the time being.

When Aunt Lizzie was not so occupied with Dawdi John,

Leah slipped to her side and gave Lizzie the gift she'd purchased. "I had your name," she whispered, handing her a small case filled to the brim with many colored spools of thread and sewing notions.

Lizzie was pleased. "Oh, just what I needed!" she said, giving Leah a kiss on the cheek. "Thank you ever so much."

Hannah and Gid's oldest daughter, three-year-old Ida Mae, giggled as she licked a candy cane. Squirming out of Sadie's lap, Katie Ann toddled to big sister, Ida, for repeated tastes. "That's awful nice of you to share your treat," Hannah said, touching Ida's chubby cheek.

Gid sat with his arm protectively draped behind his wife's chair, looking mighty pleased about the box of saws and other items given him by his father-in-law. Leah suspected Abe wanted to tell—in the worst way—how Dat had "kept at it" to win them at the auction.

"Now, don't be tellin' stories out of school," Dat was heard to say to his exuberant son.

Abe frowned comically and went to sit beside Leah. "My mouth's gonna get me in trouble yet," he told her softly.

She patted his arm. "You're just fine."

The merriment continued on through a good half of the afternoon, till time for milking rolled around again. Gid rose with Abram at four o'clock and told both Sadie and Abe to "stay put."

Not putting up a fuss, Sadie smiled her thanks, and the two men left the house for the barn.

"I wonder if the manger is even smoother now," Abe whispered to Leah. "For baby Jesus' birthday, ya know."

Leah was touched by her boy's remark, and she pulled him into her arms. "Come here—and don't be sayin' you're too old for a big hug," she said, her heart truly gladdened by the day.

Chapter Five

On the walk to the barn, Abram was suddenly aware of the heavy moisture content of the recent snow. Every tree branch, every shrub, and even the roof of the old corncrib sagged with the weight. Several large limbs had snapped under the burden, and he made a mental note to turn them into firewood tomorrow.

Meanwhile, he and Gid had the afternoon milking to tend to, and feeling the cold creep through his work jacket and trousers, Abram quickened his pace toward the barn, as did his son-in-law.

Inside, they washed down the cows' udders, pushed tin buckets beneath, and perched themselves on low wooden stools, talking in quiet tones as they milked by hand. The dogs, all three of them, rested in the hay nearby—Blackie eyed them fondly and wagged his long tail—while Abram listened without commenting as Gid mentioned their desire to have a hex doctor at the birthing of their third child. "Not in place of a midwife, mind you . . . just in case something goes wrong. What do ya think of that?"

"Why ya askin' me?"

"Well, 'cause Hannah said she and Aunt Lizzie had been talkin' it over."

Abram was fairly sure if Lizzie and Hannah had hashed it out, as Gid said, that Lizzie would've had her say and then some. Still, he didn't want to butt in since Gid was Hannah's husband and the man of his house. Abram saw no point, really, in speaking his mind, because far as he knew, Gid had heard through Lizzie what his stand on powwowing was.

"You don't need my two cents' worth."

"No . . . no, Hannah and I want your opinion."

He toyed with saying straight out they ought to have as much help with Hannah's delivery as possible, especially if she was feeling nervous for any reason. If that meant having the powwow doctor, then all well and good. He certainly didn't want to be held responsible for their making a bad decision, still too mindful of all that had gone wrong when Ida birthed Abe.

He went ahead and told Gid how he'd kicked himself for not having the Amish doctor on hand for Ida that terrible night. "I'd do things completely different now if I could." *Anything to have saved Ida's life. . . .*

Yet his wife's feelings had mattered, too. Ida's opinion had always mattered to him, thus the reason he'd let her have her say now and again, although he had managed to rule his roost, keeping the upper hand for the most part. Sadly that sort of approach had caused great strife and despair for his family, as he had seen all too clearly for some time now. Looking back, he realized how rigid he'd been about Leah's choice of a mate, and he kicked himself every time he thought of her being a maidel. He had been equally harsh with Mary Ruth, insisting on his own way when it appeared Hannah's twin was as content as can be—teaching English schoolchildren, boarding with the Nolts, and attending the Mennonite church. The truth pained him, making it difficult for him to stand by and watch the circumstances unfold. On the other hand, he believed in the deep of his heart that his daughter had somehow found her intended way, although the path she trod no longer embraced the teachings of the Amish church. It wasn't that she didn't look Plain any longer; she did. But the manner Mary Ruth talked about the Lord God heavenly Father was somewhat foreign to his way of seeing things, though not to his Ida's . . . nor to Lizzie's. More and more, he was making the discovery that Ida's Lord was the same as Mary Ruth and Lizzie's, having spent many early morning hours reading and rereading his wife's well-loved Bible, particularly the passages she'd taken time to underline. Truth be known, he was learning far more than he'd ever expected from such an undertaking.

"Should I take this question up with the bishop?" Gid's voice broke the stillness.

Abram knew better than to encourage Gid to speak with Bishop Bontrager on the matter. Why, the whole thing could blow up in Gid's face . . . in all of their faces, really. The issue of sympathy healers was troublesome amongst the Amish—had the power to divide the church district right down the middle.

"Make up your own mind and stick with it. Do what you think is best for *your* family."

Gid went on to say that his mother was downright opposed and didn't think "white witchcraft" had any business being invited into the sacred places of their home. "*Mamm* has spoken out quite adamantly 'bout keepin' the hex doctors far from our door."

Abram nodded, considerate of Gid's position—stuck between the opinion of his wife and his mother. Not a good place to be for a young man of Gid's character and calling. Abram suggested Gid and Hannah talk further on it.

"Then you must not view powwowing as of the devil, like my mother does."

Gid had him there, and there was no telling how far this conversation might drift from its origins. "What's the Good Book say on it?" Abram surprised himself by asking but felt sure Gid knew him well enough not to hold such a question against him.

"I don't know. Haven't stumbled onto anything just yet."

Abram grunted, wishing he had something pertinent to add, but he didn't.

In the end, Gid would have to decide for his family. Even so, Abram wondered what difference it made if the blue cohosh herb was used to induce labor when needed, nor did it bother him if a bit of necessary chanting went on. No bother at all. On the other hand, he couldn't get Ida's view on the matter out of his mind.

Mary Ruth sat with Hannah in the front room, near Lydiann and Abe, who were playing with their games at Leah's feet while snacking on the popcorn balls and hard candies they'd received as presents from their neighbors, the Peacheys. Mary Ruth was delighted to hold sweet little Katie Ann on her lap, especially because the toddler's usually bright eyes were looking mighty droopy just now, and Mary Ruth hoped the dear girl might give in to sleep right there in her arms. Oh, how she enjoyed Hannah's little ones, and the joy of being around them stirred up such eagerness as she looked ahead to the day when she might marry and become a mother herself. She wouldn't dare to think too far into the future, though, because she strongly believed the Lord had called her to teach. She was living the life she'd long wished for, sharing her book knowledge with youngsters who had thirsty minds, ever glad to be able to share the love of the Lord Jesus with her students through word and deed.

Holding Katie Ann and listening to Ida Mae's childish chatter helped fill the hours, as did spending the day with her sisters. She was rather relieved to see how well Sadie was doing now that she had been home these two months, and Leah, too, was smiling more genuinely than she had been at past Christmases, at least that Mary Ruth could recall.

" 'Tis awful nice of Gid to help Dat with milkin'," Leah told Sadie.

Sadie nodded, glancing at Abe. "Looks like more than one of us got to stay in where it's warm, ain't?"

To this, Abe looked up from his checkers and grinned. "I wouldn't have minded goin' out in the cold," he said. "I'm a strong one, I am."

This brought a round of "ohs," and Abe put his head down, visibly embarrassed.

"Won't be long and you'll be takin' Sadie's place all the time at milkin'," Lydiann spoke up, pausing in her play with her two faceless dolls.

"Now, Lyddie, that ain't for you to say," Sadie pointed out.

Mary Ruth found the exchange between Abe and Sadie to be amusing and, looking down, discovered Katie Ann had fallen limp in her arms. "Look who's tuckered out." She nudged Hannah.

Hannah smiled. "You've got a tender touch."

Mary Ruth scooted back in her chair, being careful not to relax too much lest the crook of her arm not support her precious niece.

Some time later Lydiann's remark about Carl Nolt made Mary Ruth pay closer attention yet again to the conversation. Lyddie was mentioning Carl's New Year's Eve invitation— "He said his parents want all us Ebersols to have supper with them. Carl told me himself yesterday after the school play," Lydiann happily announced. "I know he meant it, because he's the sort of boy who doesn't fib. You can just tell."

"You're absolutely right about that," Mary Ruth spoke up, certain Dottie must've shared this with Carl.

"Could ya ask about this, Mary Ruth?" Lydiann pleaded.

Leah stirred, appearing somewhat uncomfortable. "Well, dear one, I think we best wait to see if an invitation comes directly from Carl's parents."

"Jah, I think that's wise," Mary Ruth said, backing Leah up. "Wouldn't be right to just assume it."

"But you don't understand," Lydiann broke in. "Carl was sure . . . I *know* he was!"

Leah reached down and put a hand on Lydiann's shoulder, patting her. "Best not fret. There'll be plenty to do here at home this week while school's out."

"Plenty gut things to eat, too!" Abe piped up a bit too loudly.

Mary Ruth couldn't help but smile. Leah surely had her hands full with these two—that was easy to see—yet her sister seemed as content as ever she'd known her to be. For this, Mary Ruth was most grateful.

Sadie wandered out to the kitchen while the happy gathering continued in the front room. She poured fresh cow's milk into a saucepan and set it on the fire, stirring the milk slowly lest it scald. She would surprise her sisters and the children with hot chocolate.

From where she stood at the wood stove, she could see past the utility room, through the back door window, and out to the white expanse of snow in the barnyard. *When will I see Miriam Peachey again?* Miriam had been so compassionate to her through the scrutiny thus far. Though Sadie was expected to spend time with the older women in the church district whenever she left the house, it was primarily Miriam who had been appointed to oversee her comings and goings. This meant she couldn't go much of anywhere alone, except to visit Hannah and the children, or across the pasture and field to the Peacheys'. She terribly missed her long jaunts on foot, feeling like a caged bird at times.

Presently she stared at the snow weighing down the treetops. The bitter cold would surely visit them again tonight, and she thought of bringing in some wood to stack. Maybe she would tiptoe downstairs in the night to add some logs to the wood stove, like Dat used to before he moved to the downstairs bedroom at the quiet far end of the house. Now he no longer awakened at midnight or after, which meant the upstairs grew cold by morning, and Lydiann's sharp yelps could be plainly heard when she first stepped out of bed. Abe, on the other hand, was all boy—*strong*, as he had declared to all of them this afternoon, and afraid of nothing, least of all ice-cold plank flooring. He climbed jagged tree trunks and rough stone walls, even crawling halfway up the silo one day last October, to Leah's dismay and Dat's forced laughter, though Dat's face had turned ever so pasty. *Some boys are just born tougher than others*, Dat had said with a healthy dose of pride, but Sadie decided, then and there, that Dat viewed Abe's daring from the standpoint of previously having raised only girls.

All that aside, both Lydiann and Abe were the happiest of children, and their cheerful faces reminded her of earlier days growing up in this old farmhouse, when she and Mamma had been ever so close, spending all day together cooking and baking, cleaning and talking . . . as fond of each other as Lydiann and Abe were of Leah now.

"Anybody for hot chocolate?" She sang the question as she carried the tray into the front room.

"Ach, we'll come to you," Leah said, meeting her halfway. "No need to risk spills with youngsters."

That was Leah, always thinking on the practical side. No wonder Mamma had chosen her to raise Abe and Lydiann. No wonder Aunt Lizzie looked ever so kindly on Leah; each time Sadie happened to glance at her aunt, she was aware of that deep admiration.

Tuesday, December 25, 1956
Dear Diary,

I feel sure it won't be long now and our new baby will make his or her entrance into this world. Goodness, it would be awful nice if we'd have a boy to help Gid and Dat and young Abe with the outdoor work. Leah encourages Lydiann to be out in the barn and whatnot more than I see necessary. But, more and more, Leah and Dat are having equal say in the raising of Lydiann and Abe, seems to me. I suppose that is both good and bad, although I'd have to agree with Gid that Leah dotes on Abe rather too much. She's awful protective of him, even saying he isn't old enough to go ice fishing with Dat, Gid, and Smitty come this Saturday, but Abe begged and pleaded and got Dat to intervene but quick. So they're all planning to go over to Blackbird Pond early that morning, more than likely as soon as milking's through. I hope I have this baby before then. Most uncomfortable I'm becoming!

Gid and I have together decided there's nothing whatsoever wrong with having the Hexedokder *wait in the front room when I go into labor with this one. Just knowing that, I'm already feeling much better . . . whether or not my mother-in-law's in favor of this. She's beginning to irk me some, what with all the say-so she's been given—by the bishop, no less—in overseeing Sadie's Proving. Give some folk a bit of authority and they crave even more. I hope Sadie behaves herself, truly I do, but it's hard to know what's going on in her head, let alone her heart. She seems more brooding than I remember her to be . . . and no wonder, given what she's gone through.*

Last night I had a troubling dream, one I don't know what to make of. All of us were gathered, sniffling, in a small, dark room, surrounded by unrecognizable sounds. Dat's face was drained of color, and he was struck dumb, unable to speak. Leah, though I recognized only her form, stood tall, like a beacon of light in the dimness. Since I don't normally have such dreams, I wonder if this was a result of all the sweets I've been nibbling on this week. Then again, I hope it's not a bad omen. For sure and for certain, we've had our share of heartache round here.

Respectfully,
Hannah

Chapter Six

Midmorning Thursday Abram and Gid cut down the dead branches left dangling by the heavy snows, spending a good part of the sunny but cold morning dragging chopped limbs into the woodshed to dry. Abram enjoyed working with his son-in-law and he told him so. "You just don't know how lonely an old man I'd be without ya workin' by my side."

Gid looked at him cockeyed, as if to indicate he wasn't used to hearing such soft words from a man. "You ain't old, Abram."

"Oh, but I feel my age ev'ry morning when I rise. Besides that, my baby boy is seven today."

Gid went about stacking the branches, remaining silent, as if waiting for him to continue.

"Next farm auction, you and I oughta go together. Abe will prob'ly jump at the chance to miss a day of school, too, 'cept Leah will frown on that." He rambled on, saying how well both Abe and Lydiann were doing in their studies. "I can only hope they don't get the notion to seek after higher education like Mary Ruth did."

Abram wouldn't admit to worrying like an old hen some days about losing more of his family to the fancy English world. No way, nohow, did it look like Mary Ruth would ever give up her new life, with its electricity, fast cars, and Bible studies. Fact was, she was getting herself in deeper all the time, what with spending nearly all her free time with the doctor's elder son, Robert. Well, he had no intention of letting his mind wander in that direction, so he straightened himself and asked Gid what he thought about asking Gid's brother-in-law Sam Ebersol to join them for ice fishing on Saturday.

Gid nodded his assent.

"I'll ride over there and talk to Sam this afternoon, then," Abram said. "We'll have us some tasty fish to fry up for supper this weekend." The thought of the catch and the time of fellowship sent his spirits soaring.

Following the noon meal, Sadie dried and put away the dishes and utensils, then headed to the front room, where she sat to finish stitching a floral design on a set of pillowcases that had arrived a month ago in the trunk containing her wedding gifts and small household linens from Indiana. When the sudden sound of knocking came at the front door, she was surprised to see the mailman standing on the porch.

"Good afternoon," the man wearing the familiar postal hat said. "Sorry to bother you on this cold day, but I thought it best to be extra careful with *this* letter delivery." He held out to her a stained envelope with the words *Return to sender* stamped across the front. "Looks like this here got lost somehow or other," he said, pointing out the October 1947 postmark, "nine years ago now."

Sadie nodded her astonished thanks and stood at the door holding the letter marred and frayed by the years. Upon careful examination of its terribly faded writing, she was stunned to realize it was an unopened letter from Leah to Jonas Mast. Somehow it had found its way to the Ebersol Cottage.

Could this be the letter I threw away?

Turning it over, she saw the envelope was soiled, as if it had, indeed, been in a pile of rubbish at one time. Yet how on earth had it resurfaced after nearly a decade?

Impossible, she thought, noticing the letter was still sealed shut.

Having attempted to bury the shameful deed deep within her forgetfulness, she felt convicted as she stared at the envelope, evidence of her wrongdoing.

What should I do now?

She and Leah had forged a new relationship these months since Sadie's return, and she was far too hesitant to open up an old and hurtful wound. Besides, there'd been many letters flying back and forth between Leah and Jonas when this letter was written.

She'd thrown it away once in the heat of anger; why not discard it again? Better yet . . . burn it. Coming clean about this dreadful thing would serve no purpose now. Best to leave things be, let the truth remain concealed and her sin covered up once and for all.

Or, better still, she could simply slip the letter into the mailbox for Leah to discover on her own. No confession required. Even though Leah might wonder why Jonas had never opened the letter, or why it was being returned all these years later, Sadie's part in its disappearance would remain undiscovered. Besides, wasn't she already paying for past sins? The imposed Proving was proof, and she could never ever go back and right all the wrongs.

Nagging thoughts tormented her as she paced the floor. After all, this letter was by no means her property. Leah deserved to have it returned to her with a full apology.

What will good-hearted Leah think of me? Will she despise me? She cringed at the prospect of the confession Leah surely deserved.

Yet the fact Leah seemed so jovial, what with today being Abe's birthday and all, made Sadie feel her sister might take the news of the long-lost letter awful hard.

Not today, she thought. Nothing good would come of the truth this day. Heart pounding, she slipped the letter into her dress pocket and hurried upstairs, where she deposited it between several layers of clothing in her own drawer in the tall bureau.

Feeling justified in her choice to ignore this for the time being, with Leah's best interest at heart, Sadie hurried back downstairs and picked up her sewing with trembling hands.

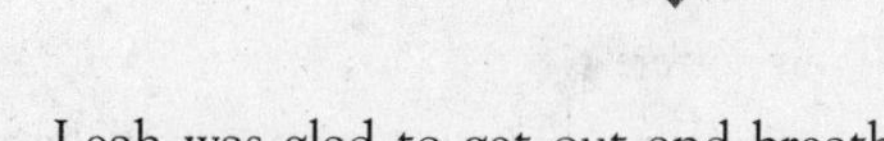

Leah was glad to get out and breathe some fresh air that afternoon. Abe and Lydiann were filled with chatter during the buggy ride to visit Uncle Jesse Ebersol and his family, and Leah was hoping her dearest friend, Adah, might be on hand, as well. Sadie had also agreed to come along, though not as eagerly as Leah would have thought, seeing as they'd all been rather cooped up in the house. For her part, Aunt Lizzie had looked a bit droopy in the face when Leah announced they were heading over to Jesse's for an afternoon visit. Lizzie felt she ought to stay home with Dawdi John—something it seemed to Leah was becoming her lot in life. Leah felt a twinge of sadness at the thought of Aunt Lizzie once again missing out on an opportunity to do the kind of visiting she so thoroughly enjoyed, and Leah promptly decided she would offer to stay behind next outing.

"Too bad Lizzie couldn't join us," Dat said when they were about halfway there.

"She's such a kindhearted soul, never complains 'bout tending to Dawdi's needs," Leah agreed.

Dat turned and smiled at her full in the face. "Sounds like someone else I know." He clicked his tongue and the horse sped up some.

"Oh, for goodness' sake," Leah said, catching on.

Sadie, sitting to Leah's left, patted her sister's shoulder. "Jah, 'tis for goodness' sake!"

Dat said no more, and Leah was suddenly conscious of Lydiann's voice in the seat behind her. "You daresn't tell nobody," Lydiann was saying, soft and low, to her brother.

"I won't promise not to tell," Abe said. "That's girl talk."

"No . . . no, now you listen to me," Lydiann's voice grew louder for a moment, then softer.

From that, Leah assumed Lydiann was cupping her hand around Abe's ear. Evidently she was not to be privy to the rest of this furtive conversation, and she wasn't so sure she cared to be, especially when the name of Carl Nolt was mentioned several times in the space of the next few seconds.

Leah remembered what she had been thinking and doing as a girl Lydiann's age. Nearly all her waking hours had been spent working around the animals—feeding and watering them, cleaning the stalls, working with Dat in the fields, too. Thankfully Mamma had birthed Abe, which meant Lydiann could learn to cook and sew at a young age, unlike Leah, who had never attended a quilting frolic till she was nearly sixteen. She smiled, recalling that first quilting, how she'd pulled up a chair to the enormous frame where the colorful Diamond-in-the-Square pattern was to be stitched. So much water had passed under the bridge since that September day. Truly now she was her own person, with the Lord God's help, and mighty glad of it, too. Gone were the days of longing for what she didn't have, and she was as content as when she had been growing up under Dat's and Mamma's watchful eyes on their peaceful farm.

Sadie startled her out of her reverie. "Oh, lookee there, Leah. Adah's come."

Sure enough, dear Adah was getting down out of the family carriage, her two young sons already scurrying about as she turned to wave.

She looks so happy, thought Leah. Adah's husband, Sam, Leah's first cousin, was a hardworking and kind man, and as Sam and Adah picked their way through the snow toward the big clapboard farmhouse, Leah recognized again how nice it was that Adah was now her cousin, as well as her closest friend.

"If Adah and Sam are here, don't ya think Smitty and Miriam might just show up, too?" Leah asked, hoping so for Sadie's sake, since heavy snow had kept any of them from tromping through the drifts to visit the Peachey farm the past few days. Smitty had driven over in his sleigh to deliver pretty bags of hard candy and nuts for Lydiann and Abe on

Christmas Eve, but none of them had ventured out on foot to take baked goods to Miriam Peachey, who, she'd heard, was looking ahead to vacating the main farmhouse and moving into the Dawdi Haus come spring. Dorcas, their youngest, and her husband, Sam Ebersol's best friend, Joseph Zook, and little ones planned to take over the Peachey farm. From what Dat had told Leah, Smitty wasn't quite ready to throw in the towel and fully retire; he would keep a hand in shoeing horses, gradually turning over more of his customers to Gid as time went by.

As Dat brought the horse to a stop, Lydiann broke the stillness, telling Abe what Carl had recently told her at school. "A two-year-old Amish neighbor boy named Johnnie Weaver drank some kerosene and had to be rushed to the emergency room last week," she said.

"No foolin'?" Abe replied.

"I guess he was okay once he got some oxygen."

"Why'd he want to drink something so awful?" asked Abe.

To this Leah said nothing, enjoying the innocent exchange as she hopped down from the buggy and fell in step with Sadie.

"It's beyond me why," said Lydiann. "But you can ask Carl 'bout it when we see him on New Year's Eve."

Lydiann may be sadly disappointed, thought Leah, fairly sure that even if they were invited to the Nolts' place for a meal, Dat would decline.

Sadie noticed Uncle Jesse's face light up when he came to the back door and saw who was there. Her uncle grabbed Dat and slapped him on the back, mighty glad indeed to see his younger brother. And right away she spotted Miriam Peachey over at the table, whispering to Aunt Mary Ebersol, pointing their way. *Perhaps they've come to celebrate Abe's birthday, too,* thought Sadie.

Sadie's guess turned out to be true when Aunt Mary brought out a bowl of butterscotch pudding, as well as a rich chocolate pie, hermits, and pecan drops. Sadie helped Aunt Mary and Miriam set out a stack of plates and the necessary utensils, but when it came time to serve the desserts, only Lydiann, Abe, and Adah's boys, along with the women folk, sat down to eat. The men—Uncle Jesse, Dat, Smitty, and Sam—all stood around the wood stove talking Dutch. Sadie didn't wish to eavesdrop, but she couldn't help but hear Dat inviting Uncle Jesse and Cousin Sam to join in Saturday's ice-fishing outing.

Sadie couldn't see what was so appealing about that. *What's the point of sitting outside and freezing yourself for a couple of fish?*

Miriam slid in next to her on the wooden bench, reaching for the butterscotch pudding. "Your mamma loved her puddings," Miriam said, glancing at Sadie but then looking over at Lydiann and Abe, across the table.

"Did she have a favorite?" asked Abe.

Miriam paused and frowned a moment. "Well, now, I'll bet your big sister Sadie might know that."

Sadie smiled, recalling many happy hours making a variety of custards and puddings in Mamma's big kitchen. "She loved the smell of chocolate pudding, that's for sure. But a favorite? I guess I'd have to say either graham-cracker or date pudding."

"Oh jah," added Miriam. "Your mamma loved her date pudding, she did."

Lydiann had both her elbows on the table now as she

stared across at Miriam. "Our first mamma was your best friend, ain't so?" she said.

Miriam blushed all shades of red. "Well, I'd have to say I thought of her as my closest friend, jah."

"And I'd have to say my best friend's a boy," Lydiann piped up in response. "A Mennonite boy!"

Abe clapped his hand over his mouth, looking at Lydiann, who must have realized how she'd sounded. "Best be eatin' more and talkin' less," he said, repeating one of Dawdi's sayings as he poked her in the ribs.

Adah's little boys were busy with their bowls of pudding and too small to have caught the embarrassing banter between Abe and Lydiann. But Miriam hadn't missed it, not one iota; Sadie knew this because she'd heard a gasp escape Miriam's lips.

"Are ya havin' a happy birthday, Abe?" Miriam asked, her voice pitched higher than usual.

Sadie felt as though she might lose her composure and start laughing, although she was ever so sure such an outburst might not be the wisest thing for a widow in mourning. Besides that, Miriam was sitting only a few inches away from her. What would she say if she also knew of Sadie's reluctance to return Leah's letter and make a heartfelt apology?

Thoughts of the rigid period, penance for her sins, calmed her quickly, and she sat back and became an observer, immersing herself in the cheerful chatter, especially between the birthday boy and his next-oldest sister. Sadie's gaze drifted to Leah. To think she had, all those long, sad years, assumed Sadie had been married to Jonas, yet she showed Sadie not a hint of past bitterness now. Today especially, Sadie found herself wishing for a tongue-lashing from her sister, if not worse.

Truly, Leah exemplified a forgiving spirit, just as Mamma had all her days, but surely there were limits even for someone like Leah.

There, in the midst of the laughter and the celebrating, Sadie felt as sad as could be, missing both her husband and mother. She'd thought she would have a lifetime with Harvey, and here she was a widow. Had she taken their wedded happiness for granted? She felt torn between longing for Harvey and believing she'd squandered Mamma's final years, yet had she stayed put in Gobbler's Knob with Mamma, she never would have met and fallen in love with her Harvey. Oh, sometimes there was just no sorting through emotions so raw and unnerving.

When the dishes were cleared away, washed, and dried, Sadie sat in the front room with Miriam, glad to be alone with Mamma's bosom friend. "How are ya feelin' this week, it bein' Christmas and all?" asked Miriam, touching the back of Sadie's hand.

"Well, it's not the happiest Christmas I've ever had," she admitted. "But it's *wunderbaar*-gut being back home in Gobbler's Knob. I've been enjoying the fun with Lydiann and Abe."

Miriam nodded, her eyes intent on Sadie. "But ya must be thinking 'bout your loss, too."

Sadie looked down at her black apron, so much a part of her daily attire. It was cut from the same bolt of fabric as her mourning dress, making it difficult to tell where one began and the other ended. "Some days I think I might wear black the rest of my life." *For all the deaths . . .* She didn't say what she was really thinking, because she'd confided only in Leah regarding the many stillbirths.

" 'Course you'd be thinkin' thataway," Miriam said, sighing. "Harvey's passing is still fresh in your mind."

"He was a good man," Sadie said. "He never lost his temper that I know of, not once. He spoke kindly of everyone, and he got along famously with all his siblings."

Miriam listened, her gaze not straying from Sadie's. "How many brothers and sisters?"

"Five brothers and three sisters." Lest Miriam wonder why Harvey's siblings hadn't invited her to live with one of them, Sadie explained that, after his death, she had felt the Lord God was calling her home to Lancaster County.

"Oh, such a blessed thing to hear, Sadie! Does our bishop know of this?"

"No . . . I said not a word." She wouldn't reveal she cared not one whit for Bishop Bontrager, not as far as she was into the Proving now. If he knew the full truth about her, would he consider even this punishment too slight? Surely he would, but Sadie couldn't bear much more, most days wishing she could simply blend into the mopboards.

"I'm thinkin' he oughta know," Miriam was saying. " 'Tis high time."

"Please, no. . . . Let's just keep that between us . . . and my family. No need to tell the bishop." She felt so strongly about this, tears sprang up.

"Ach, Sadie, I'm ever so sorry I said a word." Miriam leaned forward. "I'm just awful glad you're back with us, and I'm sure your father feels the same."

All Sadie could do was nod, her heart heavy under a weight of her own making.

Chapter Seven

There was a special quietude at the midafternoon hour Lorraine Schwartz had always taken pleasure in, especially in summertime when the heat of the day required a catnap or, at least, a rest from the fierce sun. This Friday, though, was not to be compared in the slightest with the dog days of late July or August. The old year was dying fast, and she had drawn the curtains and curled up by the roaring fire Henry had kindly built for her in the handsome tiled fireplace not too many feet from her easy chair. With a cup of chamomile tea in hand, she had been reading the Scriptures until the telephone's ringing prompted her to rise and pick up the black receiver.

"Schwartz residence. Lorraine speaking."

"Hello, Lorraine. It's Dottie Nolt."

"Oh, how are you today?"

"We're just fine, thanks. How was your Christmas?"

"Quiet . . . but very nice. You?"

Dottie shared how she and Dan had enjoyed watching Carl unwrap his presents and that their son had been especially pleased at receiving a new sled. "But the reason I'm calling is to invite you and Henry for supper on New Year's Eve."

"Well, how thoughtful of you." Lorraine knew they had no plans whatsoever. "I'll check with my husband, but I think it's safe to say we'll accept. Thank you, Dottie. What can I bring?"

"Just yourselves. This is Dan's and my treat. We're inviting several neighbors, and Mary Ruth will be here, as well, so please extend the invitation to your son Robert."

"I will indeed."

"We also plan to invite Mary Ruth's family."

"That'll be nice to get better acquainted," said Lorraine.

Minutes later, when Henry came in from the clinic, she shared with him Dottie's kind invitation.

He stiffened visibly. "You didn't accept, did you?"

"Well, yes, I did." She was puzzled by his response.

Henry shook his head. "Call back and decline . . . say we have other plans."

"But we don't, dear. We would simply be alone on New Year's Eve, unless, of course, Robert should decide to stay home and not spend the evening with Mary Ruth. But I hardly think he'll want to do that."

Again Henry shook his head, frowning deeply. "Please call Dottie back, Lorraine."

His words reached her ears, but it was her memory that served her best. Henry was resistant, most likely, because the Nolts were mainly responsible for her renewed interest in church.

It was Robert's arrival at the front door that brought the conversation to a quick end, for which Lorraine was grateful. And when the first thing out of his mouth was "Dottie Nolt's having a New Year's Eve dinner party, and we're all invited," she was secretly relieved.

That said, Henry dropped his opposition.

Good, she thought, *no need for me to embarrass myself with a return phone call to Dottie*. Robert obviously had more influence over Henry than she ever would.

Gid paced the floor in the front room of the log house, stopping now and then to keep Ida Mae and Katie Ann occupied with their toys. He was nearly tempted to stand with his ear to the door of the birthing room, where he felt sure Hannah was in the final throes of labor. Against his mother's wishes, he had summoned one of the men hex doctors, who sat not but a few yards from him on a rocking chair, watching the girls play. Hannah had been disappointed to discover that Old Lady Henner, the most powerful Amish doctor in the area, no longer made house visits, so they'd had to settle for this solemn-looking man.

At least he's someone to talk to, he thought, carrying *The Budget* over and offering a section of the newspaper to the older man. "Got any relatives out in Ohio?" he asked, hoping to make small talk.

"Two cousins."

"Ever go 'n' visit?"

"Nope."

Not so keen on conversing with a brick wall, Gid wandered to the kitchen, poured himself a tall glass of water, and stood at the back door, staring out at the open woods, deprived now of leaves. The sky had opened up some, and he was grateful for the light, conscious as he was at this moment of the seasonal rhythms of his own life.

This waiting was difficult, a good test of his patience, and he contemplated the Old Ways: the father-to-be hiding behind a newspaper, uninvolved, or pacing the floor somewhere in the house. Hannah had once told him there were some women who simply slipped behind a bush of a summer and had their wee babes unattended. He flinched at the thought of darling Hannah having to birth *her* babies that way. Not as long as he could ride for a midwife—and, in this case, the hex doctor, too—would his wife give birth alone. Leah had planned on being on hand, as well, but hearing of Hannah's insistence on having the hex doctor come, Leah had hastily changed her mind, to Hannah's disappointment.

When the cries of a newborn pierced the air, he felt strangely relieved that the midwife had managed to deliver his son or daughter without the help of the man in the sitting room.

Hurrying to the bedroom door, Gid waited for word to come from the midwife. When it did, he was told he and Hannah had a third daughter. "She's a rosy one," the midwife said, motioning for him to enter the room.

He made a beeline for his wife, leaning down to kiss Hannah's brow, then cupping her chin in his hand. "*Ich lieb dich*, Hannah." He pushed back a wispy strand of her strawberry-blond hair.

"Oh, Gid, I love *you*." She held up his new daughter, now wrapped in a thin blanket. "Awful perty, she is."

"Have ya thought of a name?"

Hannah smiled up at him sweetly from the bed. "I think it's your turn."

He had been pondering this and asked what Hannah thought of Miriam, after his mother. "We could call her Mimi for short."

Nodding, Hannah said it was a wonderful-good name. "I like it."

So it was settled, and although he'd hoped for a son this time around—with the name Mathias all picked out to honor Dawdi Byler—Gid was most grateful Hannah and the baby were all right. Truth be told, he was altogether ready to thank the hex doctor for his time and send him on his way.

Leah was overjoyed at the news, heralded by Gid himself, of the birth of little Mimi Peachey, and by Saturday morning Leah had held Hannah's darling baby several times already. Now she sat in the kitchen near the wood stove with Aunt Lizzie while Dat, Abe, and a group of men headed over to Blackbird Pond for a morning of ice fishing. She had cautioned Dat, privately, to keep his eye on adventuresome Abe, this being the boy's first such wintertime experience.

"Oh, he'll be just fine," Aunt Lizzie had said when Leah told her of her concern.

"I s'pose I worry too much."

"Jah, but then all mothers do," Lizzie replied with a knowing smile.

She had noticed for some time now that Aunt Lizzie no longer called her "honey-girl," as she had all her growing-up years and beyond. Did she think Leah too old for the nickname? She didn't know and dismissed the thought as they settled into their study of Scripture, reading aloud the entire fifty-fourth chapter of the book of Isaiah. When Leah came to the final verse, the one she'd found underlined in Mamma's old Bible, she asked Aunt Lizzie about it. "Do you have any idea why Mamma would have marked this one?"

Lizzie looked down for a time, then, raising her face, she said slowly, "My sister Ida—your dear mamma—was rebuked harshly by Preacher Yoder, a good many years back." She paused and sighed, her hand at her throat, and then continued. "Your mamma went to speak with Deacon Stoltzfus one day, unbeknownst to any of us—"

"Not even Dat?"

"Abram would've put a quick stop to it had he known."

"Why'd Mamma go to speak to the brethren?"

Lizzie put her finger in the Bible to mark the page. "Well, she had oodles of questions . . . passages in the Good Book puzzled her no end."

"Did she share this with you?"

Lizzie nodded. "Oh, we had our talks, just the two of us."

Leah held back a bit, not wanting to push too much. "I hope Mamma got her answers."

Lizzie straightened in her chair and slowly opened the Bible yet again. "That she did . . . and then some."

Leah inhaled deeply and reread the underlined passage. *No weapon that is formed against thee shall prosper; and every tongue that shall rise against thee in judgment thou shalt condemn.*

According to Aunt Lizzie, Mamma had gone over Dat's head, taking her issues to the preacher, of all things, who apparently admonished her to remain silent. Mamma had been judged for her curiosity . . . no, for her intense hunger for the Lord Jesus, a hunger Leah now shared for "the living Bread" as she read through Mamma's cherished Bible.

"The worst of it," Lizzie added, "was that Ida lost her peace."

"She spoke up?"

"Talked back . . . kept askin' even more questions, trying to defend herself when she was to be silent," Lizzie explained. "Not a gut idea, I should say. And for this she was threatened with the shun."

The air went out of Leah and she began to understand more fully Mamma's tremendous pain during Sadie's seemingly endless shunning. When she had composed herself, she noticed a tear roll down Aunt Lizzie's face.

"Sometimes it's ever so hard. . . ."

Leah reached out a hand to comfort Lizzie. "Did the preachers succeed in putting the *Bann* on Mamma?"

"They came close . . . but Abram managed to get the upper hand with her, at least till all the dust had settled and the bishop wasn't keeping such a close eye on them." Lizzie attempted to blink back more tears but failed.

Leah offered her a handkerchief from beneath her own sleeve, feeling sorry for bringing up such a painful topic.

◆

Leah listened as Lydiann excitedly repeated herself about "goin' to eat supper at Carl's house tonight." The family was all bundled up, and both buggy seats were rather full and spilling over, what with Abe on Leah's lap and Lydiann and Sadie bunched up together so Dat, Aunt Lizzie, and Dawdi John could squeeze into the front seat.

Quite surprisingly, a handwritten invitation had arrived in the mail from Dan and Dottie Nolt on Friday. To Leah's further amazement, Dat had instructed her to accept. How all this had come about, she was unsure, although they had been sufficiently warned by Lydiann, hadn't they? Still, Leah found it interesting that Carl had managed to get his parents to invite Amish folk for a New Year's Eve supper, even with Mary Ruth's help. Leah could only hope they as a family weren't sitting ducks to be influenced toward Mennonite ways. That would not go over whatsoever with Dat.

Suddenly feeling playful, she bounced her knees, and Abe laughed. "Mamma's got awful bony knees," he said as she jostled him.

Dawdi John craned his neck in their direction. "Ya best be thankful you ain't sittin' on *my* knees, young man."

To this Lydiann let out a giggle. "Oh, Abe . . . I say you oughta be glad ya have a place to sit at all. Or maybe you'd rather walk."

"Well, it ain't so far to the Nolts' place," Abe shot back.

"Remember when Abe was a little tyke?" Dat said more to Lizzie than to the rest of them. "I used to balance him and Lydiann both on my knees."

"Oh, I remember," Lydiann said.

Leah had to smile. "I don't think that's quite possible, dear."

"But I *do*!" Lydiann insisted.

Dawdi John chimed in, "Well, now, ya must be a mighty *schmaert* one to recall what happened when you was hardly out of diapers."

"Ach, Dawdi!" Lydiann said a bit too loudly.

"Now, Lyddie," Dat scolded over his shoulder.

"Shh," whispered Leah, patting the heavy woolen robe on top of Lydiann's lap.

Lydiann continued muttering but did not say anything more, and Leah was grateful. It wouldn't do to have a lippy Lydiann on board, not this night. With Dat's word of rebuke, silence reigned but for the muted, yet heavy *thud* of the horses' hooves against encrusted snow. Sleigh bells sounded in the distance, joined, as they passed another Amish farmhouse, by the familiar peal of a supper bell.

When they arrived at the Nolts', Leah noticed Carl was leaning up against the front room window, peering out. For a fleeting moment she recalled her excitement as a girl going to visit young Jonas and her other Mast cousins; then she got out of the enclosed buggy and turned to offer her hand to Lydiann and Sadie as they stepped down and onto the snow.

It took no time at all for Lydiann to also spot Carl. "Lookee there, Mamma," she said, tugging on Leah's arm. "My best friend's waitin' for us." With this, she took off running, embarrassing Leah thoroughly and, no doubt, Aunt Lizzie, as well.

Dat, meanwhile, tied the horse to a boulder as Lizzie helped Dawdi John up the shoveled walkway, both moving nearly as slowly as cold blackstrap molasses.

Chapter Eight

His smile contagious, Carl Nolt told each person where to sit at the long trestle table, which reminded Lydiann of their own at home. When it was her turn, he led her to the place beside Aunt Lizzie. "Denki," she said, and he grinned the way he had when he was Joseph in the Christmas play, leaning near baby Jesus as their teacher had prompted him. She couldn't help but think Carl had a kind face. *Like the real Joseph must've had.*

When Carl seated himself across the table from Lydiann, she was ever so glad, because this way she could observe him without much effort. Her curiosity about his adoption was going to get the best of her sooner or later, though she didn't quite know how to bring up the topic. What *was* it like to be an orphan, anyway? She couldn't imagine it, really, except, of course, she herself could be considered a half orphan, having her sister Leah as a substitute mamma. So, in a way, maybe she did understand Carl's family situation better than she realized. Maybe that was why she liked him as a school chum, although Abe and Carl were also good pals, since the boys played together at recess and ate lunch together at noon.

She wondered if Mary Ruth had taught Carl to read some Pennsylvania Dutch, or . . . was it possible his uncle, the one who enjoyed attending Amish farm sales, had instructed him? If so, maybe *that* was something she could ask Carl about here before too long.

Jah, I will, once school starts up again, she decided.

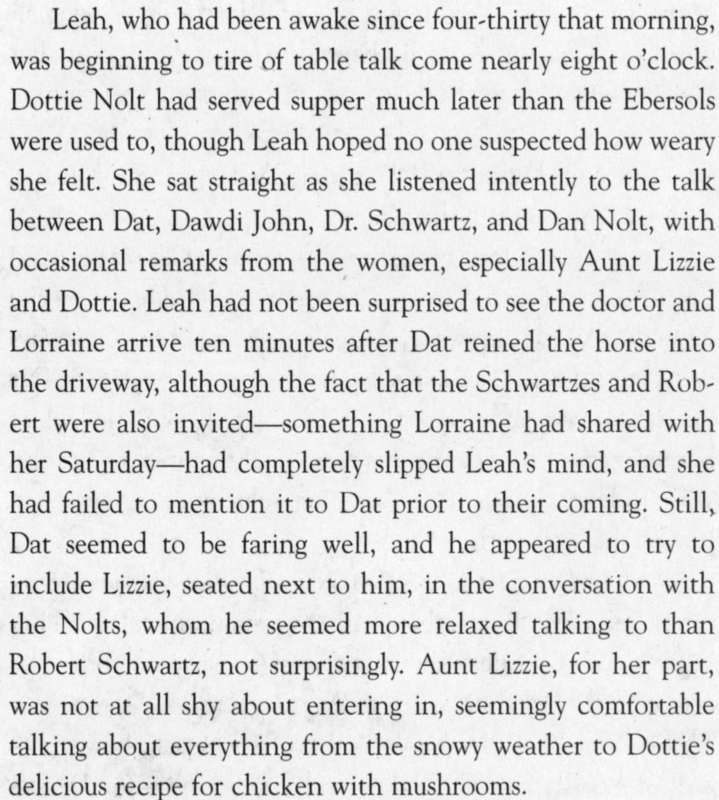

Leah, who had been awake since four-thirty that morning, was beginning to tire of table talk come nearly eight o'clock. Dottie Nolt had served supper much later than the Ebersols were used to, though Leah hoped no one suspected how weary she felt. She sat straight as she listened intently to the talk between Dat, Dawdi John, Dr. Schwartz, and Dan Nolt, with occasional remarks from the women, especially Aunt Lizzie and Dottie. Leah had not been surprised to see the doctor and Lorraine arrive ten minutes after Dat reined the horse into the driveway, although the fact that the Schwartzes and Robert were also invited—something Lorraine had shared with her Saturday—had completely slipped Leah's mind, and she had failed to mention it to Dat prior to their coming. Still, Dat seemed to be faring well, and he appeared to try to include Lizzie, seated next to him, in the conversation with the Nolts, whom he seemed more relaxed talking to than Robert Schwartz, not surprisingly. Aunt Lizzie, for her part, was not at all shy about entering in, seemingly comfortable talking about everything from the snowy weather to Dottie's delicious recipe for chicken with mushrooms.

Dr. Schwartz and Dan discussed something they'd read in

the newspaper about a professional baseball team called the Dodgers and a proposed new stadium for downtown Brooklyn, New York. Leah could merely guess what such an enormous place might look like, having witnessed only their Amish young folk playing baseball or cornerball in meadows at one gathering or another. Meanwhile, she noticed how Sadie's face became drawn, her lips tense, whenever the doctor spoke, and Leah's heart felt especially tender toward her suffering sister.

The talk that most interested her, though, came from Mary Ruth's lips—here lately, she and Dottie had spent an entire day making cottage cheese. "And, not to boast, but Dottie caught on real quick," Mary Ruth said, eyes shining with the telling.

"We made butter, too." Dottie nodded, apparently pleased with the end result of their labor.

Aunt Lizzie's face broke into an even wider smile. And Leah thought Lizzie's heart must surely be gladdened by the news that Mary Ruth was passing along some of the Old Ways to Dottie. *What a nice thing*, Leah thought, wondering if Dat might also be heartened at this domestic talk. But one look at her father made it clear he was now caught up in conversation with Robert, despite Dat's seeming reluctance to approach him at the start of the evening.

How odd for Dat to meet Mary Ruth's beau this way, contemplated Leah. But as the evening wore on, she felt it hadn't been such a bad idea, seeing that Dat and the doctor's elder son were getting along quite well.

She dared not think too hard on that herself, however—each time she pondered how truly odd it was for Derek's brother to be sweet on one of Sadie's sisters, she felt a bit ill.

To think the same union that had given life to thoughtless Derry had also produced well-mannered Robert. She knew firsthand what an upstanding young man Robert was, for she'd had ample opportunity to encounter him while cleaning his mother's house.

Amidst the comfortable talk of the adults, Leah noticed Lydiann smiling at Carl across from her. But, by the time dessert was served, Lydiann's face had become serious, a sharp contrast to her earlier high spirits.

Leah sighed, wondering what might be bothering her dear girl. Was it possible she was dreading the end of a wonderful-good evening? After all, the two youngsters were close friends, although she sometimes wondered how Dat felt about Carl's weekly visits with Lydiann and Abe and, occasionally, Sadie, as well, who had been known to join the children on the floor near the wood stove, playing games. Surely Dat wouldn't want to risk a Mennonite youngster as a close playmate to Lydiann and Abe, and she had recently considered recommending to him that the children not continue attending the one-room Georgetown School, which met the needs of the growing rural population of Plain and fancy children alike. Besides, there had been talk amongst the People of building an Amish one-room school in Gobbler's Knob, following the recent consolidation of public schools. But so far nothing had been done to make this happen, although with the divine appointment falling upon Gid, there might be more interest now, especially if Leah took it upon herself to voice Dat's concern about Carl, Lydiann, and Abe becoming too friendly.

Sadie's first reaction upon laying nervous eyes on Robert Schwartz was of absolute surprise, not because he reminded her of Derry, but because in every way he did not. Mary Ruth's beau was nothing at all like the brother she remembered—even his mannerisms were unlike those of the dark-haired, dark-eyed boy who'd captured her heart, only to smash it to pieces. Robert's thoughtful demeanor and the way his eyes genuinely admired her sister were a marked contrast to the almost leering way Derry had always looked at her.

Recalling her youth, she realized anew what a tease she had been, seeking out fancy English boys to flirt with nearly every Friday night. It was no surprise she'd attracted the unwholesome advances of a young man such as Derry.

All that's behind me, Sadie thought, wishing she might have done things differently, yet recognizing her weakness for male attention. She still found it difficult to live without a man, no matter that she was a widow and drawing close to thirty years old.

◆

"It was nice you could finally meet my father," remarked Mary Ruth as she and Robert sat together in the formal parlor. Such a pleasant room it was, with several windows facing north, toward the vast woods, which could readily be seen during daylight hours. Framing the wide doorway, gleaming wood reflected the light of two reading lamps mounted on the wall behind the settee.

All the good-byes had been said, and Mary Ruth had enjoyed the evening immensely, except that her twin and her newly expanded family had stayed snug at home, which was understandable with a newborn in the house.

"Your dad's quite a talker," said Robert. "I wasn't sure what to expect."

"Once you get acquainted with him, Dat's not one to shy from speaking his mind, that's for sure."

Going to the window, Robert stood silently.

"Everything all right?" she asked, getting up to stand near him.

"Sure," he said, not convincing her.

"There's something on your mind."

As he turned, Robert's eyes seemed to search hers. "I'm falling in love with you, Mary Ruth."

Her heart leaped up at his words, but she felt torn, as well. Robert had yet to learn the terrible truth regarding Sadie and Derek, and she felt compelled to reveal the past and the resulting apprehensions that troubled her at the prospect of an engagement. She must find the courage to share what she had held so close all this time.

"I care deeply for you, too, Robert," she replied softly. "But there is something you must know, if you don't already."

"Dear, what is it?" He reached for her hands. "Have I done something to offend you . . . said something out of turn?"

She assured him that was not the case and let unfold the story of the day she had seen his younger brother running down Georgetown Road. "He was fit to be tied."

"You met Derek?"

She nodded and then continued. "More than once. Your brother and my sister . . . poor Sadie, were . . ." She couldn't bring herself to say the word *lovers*.

Robert was frowning, evidently puzzled. "What is it?"

"Sadie had a baby . . . with Derek."

Robert flinched suddenly and shook his head, as if unable to believe his ears.

"My sister had a wild *rumschpringe*, and she met your brother somehow, somewhere—I don't know much about that." She sighed, sickened at the thought of being the one to inform him, for it was obvious he was not aware of this shocking news. "Their baby . . . was stillborn, and Sadie was unrepentant about her relationship with Derek, which, I was told, was the reason she left to go to Ohio. And why she was eventually shunned."

He looked at her as if astounded. "Oh, Mary Ruth, I had no idea."

She was sorry to upset him, yet relieved he apparently believed her.

He squeezed her hand and held it for a moment, staring down. When at last he looked at her, his eyes were intense. "At the very least, I must apologize for Derek's behavior toward Sadie."

She felt grateful for his words. "Please . . . can we keep this private . . . just between us?" She had almost hesitated to ask this, but he immediately agreed, and she was rather surprised he didn't inquire of her further, asking if there might have been some misunderstanding . . . if another young man might have been the father of her sister's child. But nothing of the kind was mentioned, and Mary Ruth felt he trusted her implicitly.

Still, neither knew how to handle the fact that a marriage between them would have the unintended consequence of also uniting Derek and Sadie once more, if only as in-laws, serving as a lifetime reminder of their regrettable past.

The evening had taken a much different turn than the

romantic moment Robert must surely have had in mind for them. Heart heavy, Mary Ruth accompanied him to the front door. He kissed her cheek before he slipped out into the cold night. "I'll call you soon, dear."

"Good night," she said, the softly spoken word *dear* lingering in her mind long after midnight.

Chapter Nine

Jonas settled back into his favorite chair by the fire with a copy of *The Budget*, enjoying the many accounts of Christmas from various towns around Ohio, sometimes even chuckling aloud in the stillness of the kitchen. He read till his eyes were tired, then stood up to put out the gas lamp.

Sitting back down, he took pleasure in the silence as his eyes slowly became accustomed to the darkness. Emma had long since turned in for the night, having suffered a head cold for a second day. He delighted in recalling the happiness on her sweet face at his gift on Christmas morning—the antique vase.

His mind wandered back to the encounter with the aging fellow he'd met at the recent auction, where he had seen and bid on the colorful vase. He found himself wondering if, indeed, he was the person—the particular Jonas Mast—meant for the old letter, as the elderly gentleman had seemed to indicate. And the more he pondered this, the more he wished he'd spoken up, offered to ride to wherever it was the man was living and see for himself the letter in question.

Not usually curious, he surprised himself by repeating the event in his mind. Tired as he was, Jonas did not wish to see the new year in, as groups of young people were sure to be doing this night—one group, in fact, just down the long dirt lane that passed the farmhouse. He knew there were couples building a bonfire on the frozen lake, probably making ready to roast marshmallows. He and Emma had seen a good many youth gathering there on previous New Year's Eves, and if by chance some of the boys drank too much moonshine, the immature noises of glee carried well over the lake and down this way.

Tonight, however, he didn't care to know how many were shivering in the cold or showing off for their sweethearts—if indeed they were. He wondered if most were in the middle of rumschpringe and if they would end up joining church sooner rather than later.

For a moment he contemplated the Bann put on him by the Gobbler's Knob church. It was peculiar that a revered minister would impose such a ruthless punishment, shunning those who did not stay put in the church of their baptism . . . not to mention those pursuing a livelihood other than farming. All the same, Jonas knew of several other like-minded brethren here locally, some being ultraconservative Swartzentruber Amish.

Inhaling deeply, he was grateful that Emma scarcely ever sought to explore the landscape of his past, though he had responded through the years to any number of questions she'd had about Lancaster County and his family.

Growing weary, Jonas rose to his feet and headed upstairs.

Leah noticed how bright-eyed Abe was as he sat himself down at the breakfast table New Year's Day, after having helped Dat and Sadie with the milking. Lydiann had remained indoors again to help Leah make cornmeal mush, fried eggs, and bacon, something she was doing more and more at both Dat's and Leah's bidding.

"We oughta have some hot cocoa for breakfast, too," Lydiann said, a mischievous smile on her face. "'Tis better tasting than coffee."

"But hot chocolate doesn't go well with fresh-squeezed orange juice, do ya think?" Leah asked, standing at the cookstove.

Lydiann shrugged and continued to set the table. "I don't give a care, really."

"Something botherin' my girl?"

"Jah." Lydiann wandered over and stood next to Leah.

Leah was eager to listen, and by not saying more, she got Lyddie to open up and share her heart.

"'Tween you and me, Mamma, Mary Ruth really annoys me, 'cause she lives over there with the Nolts and not here with us. And she dotes on Carl something awful."

So that's what was troubling her last night. She's jealous of her sister's affection for Carl, Leah decided.

"I thought you and Carl were pals."

"Maybe so, but . . . it's just that . . ." Lydiann hesitated; then she shrugged.

Leah patted Lydiann's arm. "I daresay things'll change as time goes by." She was thinking of how likely it was that Mary Ruth would settle down and marry, and once that happened, their sister wouldn't be so connected to the Nolts—especially to Carl, which was apparently the crux of Lydiann's complaint.

"What if Mary Ruth likes Carl better than me?" Lydiann suddenly burst out, tears pooling in her eyes.

"Ach, Lyddie, come here." She held out her arms to hold her girl and drew her near. "There, there . . . you mustn't fret now. You've got Abe and me . . . and Dat, too." She named off Aunt Lizzie and Dawdi John, as well. "And you've got Sadie," Leah added. "You and your eldest sister have become quite close in a short time."

Lydiann dried her eyes and sat on the long bench on the near side of the table. "But what if Sadie leaves again?" she asked. "Why'd she live somewhere else anyway . . . all those years?"

"Her husband lived in Indiana—you know that."

"No . . . I mean before she was married. How come she ended up out west, 'stead of livin' here in Gobbler's Knob?"

"Perhaps someday you'll know . . . when you're older."

A strained silence fell over the kitchen and was abruptly broken when Dat pushed in through the back door, clunking inside wearing his work boots. Sadie was right behind him, cheeks as red as cherry tomatoes.

Leah rose to welcome them. "Come wash up . . . breakfast is nice 'n' hot." She motioned for Lydiann to scoot over and sit at her usual place, aware of the brooding look on the girl's face. *Lyddie's sullenness mustn't get the best of her*, thought Leah, hoping to find a way to nip it in the bud.

Leah felt in the pit of her stomach that something was amiss, even before Dat and Gid came in the house midmorning to warm up awhile, eager for some hot coffee and freshly baked chocolate-chip cookies. Her dread deepened when Dat and Gid both said they hadn't seen hide nor hair of Abe.

"Not since immediately following breakfast," Dat said.

"We thought he'd run an errand for you—over to my mamma, maybe," Gid said.

Upon hearing this, Leah headed straight for her woolen shawl.

Dat's hand on her arm interrupted her. "I'll go 'n' look for him," he said. "You stay here with the family . . . in case he comes home a-hankerin' for some hot cocoa and cookies."

She let go of her shawl and stood with her back against the hard wall, watching her father shove his big feet into mud-caked work boots. With not a sigh or a word of goodbye, he reached for his heavy coat and scarf and stepped out the back door.

He's worried now, because I am, she thought. Dat could read her, so to speak, from all the years they'd worked side by side in the barn and the fields, no doubt. He knew how she thought, and when moments like this arose, he trusted her instincts. Something was terribly wrong, and now Dat knew it, too.

Chapter Ten

Abram inhaled deeply through his nose lest he chill his lungs as he tramped through the frozen pastureland toward the barren cornfield and eventually Smitty's wide meadow. The path he cut through the ice and snow made a direct line from his house to the Peacheys' back door, where he chose to stop, since Miriam somehow observed most everything that went on from the many windows in her kitchen. When she came to the door and welcomed him inside, she asked right away if he was looking for Abe. He assured her that he was.

"Well, I saw him head out to the pond," and here she pointed and raised her chin a bit, staring hard in the direction of Blackbird Pond, where they'd gone ice fishing three days ago.

"How long ago?"

"Oh, it's been some time." Miriam wore a sudden frown. "A good two hours or more, I'd have to say."

A tremor of foreboding caught Abram off guard, and he turned and swiftly headed down the steps, waving his hand in farewell without looking back.

Two hours . . . in this cold?

He could not imagine what Abe might be doing out in this frigid weather, and he quickened his pace.

Lorraine Schwartz had been rather astonished at how much her husband had seemingly enjoyed himself at the Nolts' house last evening. When Henry had first met the Ebersols there, she'd noticed that he was somewhat standoffish, yet as the ice was broken and people began passing the food, eating and talking, he relaxed and entered into conversation with Abram, who was quite an interesting fellow, Lorraine thought. She had also noticed her husband discreetly studying Sadie, whom Lorraine had recognized with a jolt, to be sure, recalling the urgent look on Sadie's young face when she had unexpectedly come calling for Derek years ago.

Something else had caught Lorraine's interest last evening. It was the way Henry spoke to young Carl Nolt—his gestures, the softness in his voice. She couldn't help but notice the camaraderie between them and wondered how it was that Carl, healthy as he had always been, would have connected so well with Henry on so few clinic visits. Yet Henry was undeniably playful and easily succeeded in drawing out the young boy. *Henry will be a wonderful grandfather someday*, she thought with a smile.

Presently making her way to the kitchen, the recollection of the supper next door caused her to wish the whole group of them might enjoy yet another opportunity to dine together. *Perhaps at Robert's wedding . . . if Robert can indeed win Mary Ruth's heart.*

She would not hold her breath on that matter, however, because Mary Ruth gave the distinct impression she was holding back. Lorraine didn't mind if Robert took his time wooing the former Amish girl, for she was fond of both Mary Ruth and her older sister Leah. Each of the Ebersol girls was sweet in her own unique way, although the pained, sad eyes of their eldest sister, Sadie, caused Lorraine to wonder just what the beautiful girl had ever wanted with Derek that distant night, waiting for hours on their front steps for his return home.

"Abe . . . no!" Abram gasped, sucking cold air into his lungs as he stooped down. There before him lay his son face-down on the ice of Blackbird Pond. He called to him and rolled him over, patting his face at first, and then slapped him one quick smack, becoming even more alarmed when Abe did not respond. Not even an eyelid flickered.

"Abe!" he hollered.

Still no response.

Abram panicked and, not wasting another moment, he scooped his limp child into his arms and carried him back to the Peacheys' house. Somehow or other Abe had been knocked out cold, and the fierceness of the winter weather distressed Abram as he pounded his fist on Smitty's storm door.

This time the blacksmith himself came and opened the door, his eyes growing round when he spied unconscious Abe. "*Himmel,* come in, Abram, come in."

"He was all sprawled out on the ice," Abram said, a catch in his voice as both Smitty and Miriam gathered near.

"Lay him out on the rug here, close to the wood stove," Smitty offered.

Miriam knelt beside Abe, touching his hair and face. "Ach, he's ice-cold."

Abram's heart caught in his throat and he realized he was petrified with fear. As gently as he could, he removed the boy's shoes and socks to check for frostbite, noticing immediately the telltale signs of hard and shiny grayish skin.

"We best not be warmin' him too quickly," advised Miriam, hovering near Abe and wearing a worried frown.

Abram made an attempt to keep his emotions in check, but the strange chalky pallor of his boy's face caused him grave concern. He shook Abe and called to him, "Can ya hear me, son? Wake up!" but to no avail.

"I best be ridin' for the hex doctor," Smitty said, resting his big hand on Abram's shoulder.

The smithy turned and was heading toward the back door to begin the process of hitching up when Miriam let out a moan. She shook her head and was weeping, which brought the smithy back into the kitchen. "Why must ya first think of powwowin'?" she asked. "Why not call for a *real* doctor—Dr. Schwartz, not but a mile down the way? He's ever so much closer, ain't so?"

"Ach, Miriam, can't ya see Abe's in trouble here? There's no sense callin' for Dr. Schwartz when what the boy needs is the *Amish* doctor," Smitty replied, his brow creased with a deep frown.

Abram struggled greatly, going back and forth in his mind, knowing full well the time might be short. *My boy could be dying,* he thought. *My only son . . . I can't let what happened to dear Ida befall my Abe.*

Always before he'd decided for the powwow doctor—it was the best way, the method that made the most sense to him.

But what would Ida want me to do? She sacrificed her life giving birth to our boy. He labored over this, feeling the burden as seconds ticked away. He must hurry and do something . . . think on it later.

Yet he knew the answer—knew it in his innards—for not only had his devout wife made her wishes known in her wholehearted disapproval of the powwow doctors, she'd also left her legacy of beliefs in the form of her own Bible, marked up almost to the point of irreverence. Abram knew this as well as anybody, because, for the past several months, he had been reading every New Testament Scripture Ida had underlined on healing and other issues.

Smitty stepped out to the utility room within Abram's sight and pulled an additional woolen scarf off the wooden peg. "Well, who's it gonna be? Dr. Schwartz or the hex doctor? By the looks of Abe—all conked out like that . . ." Smitty's voice faded.

Abram could just imagine Lizzie having her say if word got to her ears about this, and even though he had always put his trust in the sympathy healers, all of a sudden he experienced a strong desire to please Lizzie, as well as his beloved Ida.

With a conviction that surprised him, he made his choice. "Ride to Dr. Schwartz, and make it quick!"

Miriam sighed, obviously relieved. Then, as if in prayer, she closed her eyes while Smitty rushed out the back door.

Watching Miriam kneeling there beside Abe, he wished Lizzie were here with him, too, for though she had a regular tendency to share her opinions a bit too freely, she might know what to do for Abe's frostbite—at least that. And she was as encouraging as the day was long, which would be of help to Abram at this terrible moment.

Now that Smitty was gone, he hoped against hope he had done the right thing. This being New Year's Day, what chance was there of the doctor being home? A niggling fear crept in at the back of his mind.

He continued to sit cross-legged on the floor next to Abe as worrisome thoughts nagged him. When he thought he might lose the ability to keep his chin from quivering, Leah startled him by flying in the back door.

"Dat . . . what on earth!" Immediately she slid to her knees beside Miriam, close to her little brother lying on the floor . . . in truth, her *son*. "Oh, Abe . . . Abe." Then to Abram she asked, "Whatever happened? Where did ya find him?"

"He must've gone walking out on the pond and tripped . . . fell forward, hitting his head. When I found him, he was knocked clean out . . . near frozen, too." Abram could hardly manage that much.

"Splash some water on him, maybe," Leah suggested, and they tried that, but Abe lay still as death, his breath mighty shallow.

Will he ever open his eyes again? Abram held his own breath, steeling himself against the worst.

Leah was now holding Abe's small hand in her own, cradling it as she took his pulse, glancing up at the round day clock, high on the kitchen wall. "Seems a mite too slow," she whispered, eyes locking on Abram. "Where's Smitty?"

"Gone for Dr. Schwartz," Miriam answered quickly as she reached an arm around Leah and pulled her near.

Ida's death weighed heavily on Abram's mind—after seven long years, images of that night were still vivid: the hushed, sad tone of the midwife; Leah's ashen face and the way she had held Ida's wrist so gently, taking her pulse just as she was this minute lovingly caring for Abe. "Dr. Schwartz'll be here in no time," he heard himself say for Leah's benefit. "We can't lose hope."

"Oh, my sweet, precious Abe," cried Leah, putting her face next to his now. "I love ya so . . ." Her soft crying shook her shoulders.

Placing his hand on Abe's ankle, too aware of the stiffness, Abram wrestled to bring to memory one or two Scripture verses that dealt with troublesome times—so many there were—but why couldn't he recall a single one? And why was it Ida always seemed to have had a fitting verse on the tip of her tongue for nearly every occasion?

Ida had ignored the brethren in all of that, he thought. *She outright disobeyed by studying the Bible, even memorized certain verses, because she couldn't keep herself from it, as she'd always said.* Her yearning had caused her grief—for Abram, too—but somehow or other she'd managed to keep from having the Bann put on her by the bishop, maybe because Ida agreed to keep her opinions on Scripture to herself. Although, in the end, his wife had felt comfortable enough to keep sharing her views on the Bible with him, for she had known him all too well. Never, ever would he have turned her in to the bishop or any of the brethren. His love for Ida had been stronger than his devotion to Bontrager or to the church.

At last the words of the psalmist David crept into his mind: *He shall call upon me, and I will answer him: I will be with him in trouble; I will deliver him, and honour him.*

Reaching now for Abe's other hand, Abram clutched it between his own rough and callused hand and closed his eyes right along with Miriam and Leah.

O Lord God and heavenly Father, hear my desperate prayer. . . .

Leah was astonished to see her father's head bowed as they waited for Smitty to return. Silently, she joined him with a prayer of her own. *Lord, please allow Abe, our dear boy, to live . . . let him open his eyes and suffer no lingering effects from this nasty fall*, she prayed. *I trust your grace and mercy, Lord, your many kindnesses to us.*

The prayer was the best she knew to offer, and she wished either Aunt Lizzie—who'd remained at home with Dawdi John—or Mary Ruth were on hand to offer a spoken prayer of faith. She certainly didn't feel comfortable beseeching the Lord almighty out loud herself, and her heart fell as she again looked at Abe's stony white face.

Sighing deeply, she felt as if her own heart might stop beating if Abe did not soon blink his shining eyes open or twitch one of his childish fingers. Anything at all.

Chapter Eleven

Abe Ebersol, seven years old," the young nurse repeated, writing Abe's vital information on her clipboard. "Date of birth?"

Leah replied quickly, "December 27, 1949."

"Does he have any allergies?"

"None that I know of." Leah glanced over at Dat, who was sitting, slumped in a heap, on one of only two chairs in the semiprivate hospital room. Her father was unable to be of much help after his ride in Dr. Schwartz's front seat, where he'd stiffly braced himself for dear life while Leah and Aunt Lizzie sat in the backseat with unresponsive Abe stretched out between them. Drawn by her growing concern, Lizzie had shown up at the Peacheys' just before Dr. Schwartz's arrival, and by the look on Dat's face, he was ever so grateful to have her here.

Dat was distraught beyond anything Leah could recall in recent years, and she felt terribly sorry for him. Goodness, he hadn't ridden in the front seat of an automobile much at all, and never at such a high speed.

As soon as the nurse left the room, having tended to a doctor-ordered oxygen tent for Abe, Aunt Lizzie said, "He'll be comin' to . . . here 'fore long." But her voice trembled, and Leah noticed Dat glance up at Lizzie, his eyes softening.

"Jah, I daresay he will." Leah retuned her gaze to poor Abe, lying as quiet and motionless as can be. Oh, how small a boy he was, even though he'd grown out of nearly all his school pants lately. She'd teased him just last week that he was shooting up like a weed, "and much too fast at that." At this moment, as unchecked tears rolled down her cheeks, she promised herself she would never, ever again grumble about such things, even in jest.

"Let's talk in Dutch," Dat said suddenly, getting up and leaning on the bed rail closer to Abe.

"A wonderful-gut idea." Lizzie rose to join him.

Softly they reminded Abe of their love for him. Aunt Lizzie even spoke of the day the men had all gone ice fishing and what fun he'd had—and of the fish fry they'd enjoyed that evening. All the while the nurse came in and out of the room to check the boy's vital signs.

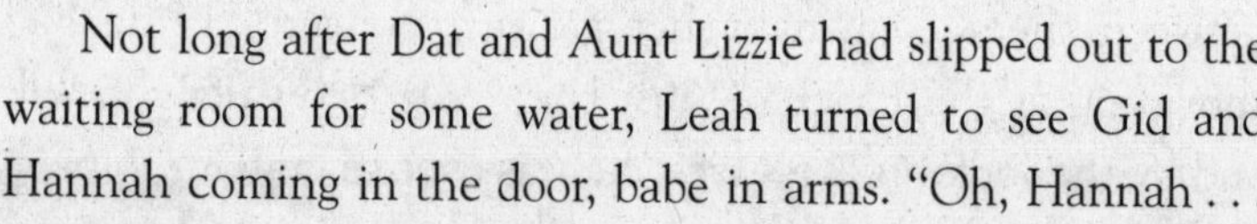

Not long after Dat and Aunt Lizzie had slipped out to the waiting room for some water, Leah turned to see Gid and Hannah coming in the door, babe in arms. "Oh, Hannah . . . Gid!" She ran to her sister and buried her face in Hannah's neck.

"We came as soon as we could get Ida Mae and Katie Ann settled in with my folks," Gid explained, saying Sadie had remained with both Lydiann and Dawdi John.

When Leah had composed herself, she took Mimi from Hannah and saw Gid reach for Hannah's hand. Together, they went and stood at Abe's bedside; he had been wrapped in several warm blankets in an attempt to slowly raise his body temperature, which was low due to prolonged exposure to the elements. The hospital staff had also surrounded his head with an oxygen tent and was watching him closely for signs of a brain concussion.

"Does anybody know what happened?" Hannah whispered. "Did he slip and fall?"

Gid reached around her and drew her near as Hannah began to sob in his arms. "Dear . . . dear," he said.

"Ach, this is just what I saw in my dream," she cried, and Gid, trying his best to soothe her, suggested they join Dat and Lizzie in the waiting area.

This left Leah alone with Abe and the tiny infant asleep in her arms. Her heart went out to Hannah, who seemed terribly fragile today, both physically and emotionally, likely from having given birth so recently. The shock of Abe's accident had no doubt set her back even more.

Slipping quietly to Abe's side, Leah began to sing the song Mamma had taught her so long ago: " 'Jesus loves me, this I know . . . for the Bible tells me so.' "

The baby in her arms stirred slightly, and she leaned her face near to sing to sweet and tiny Mimi, too. " 'Little ones to Him belong . . .' " With each precious word, she realized that these dear ones did, in fact, belong to God; and she was suddenly too overcome to continue singing.

Instead, she found Abe's hand and touched it lightly, hoping she might feel a hint of a stir. Anything to give her hope.

After a while Hannah and Gid returned to the hospital room to get Mimi. They visited with Leah a bit longer, although Leah could see in Hannah's eyes that she wasn't ready to come to town just yet, especially under such distressing circumstances.

Soon Gid looked tenderly at Hannah before nodding his good-bye. "God be with you, Leah," he said, and they turned and waved, leaving the room again nearly as fast as they'd returned.

There was little time between clusters of visits, and Dan and Dottie Nolt arrived soon after with Mary Ruth. Dottie told Leah that Carl had wanted desperately to come, but they'd asked Lorraine Schwartz to look after him because he was under twelve and wouldn't be allowed upstairs to the room anyway. "It was Lorraine who came running over to our house to announce the sad news, asking us to pray for Abe."

Leah clung to Mary Ruth's hand as she listened, ever so glad to see her. "I was hopin' you'd hear somehow and come."

"All during the ride here . . . we were praying," Mary Ruth said of the three of them.

"Denki, oh, thank you," Leah told Dottie, accepting a concerned embrace.

Meanwhile, Dan excused himself to go in search of Dat and Aunt Lizzie, after Leah explained how distressed her father had been earlier. "He's having the hardest time seein' Abe like this. We all are, truly." She stopped, not wanting to go on so for fear Abe in his stupor might hear them talking.

Mary Ruth nodded. "Dan will do Dat some good," she

said, offering a brave smile even in the midst of her tears.

A hush fell over the room, apart from the periodic *swoosh* of the oxygen tent, and Leah and Mary Ruth moved to the foot of Abe's bed. "Let's pray for him together," her sister whispered.

Leah could not speak for the lump in her throat as she gratefully nodded.

Mary Ruth began as if she were humbly addressing a dear and close friend, and as her sister raised her petition to the Throne of Grace, Leah whispered her own prayer. "Dear Lord, thank you for sending Mary Ruth here today. . . ."

Repeatedly Sadie had tried to console Lydiann, who was still crying upstairs in her bedroom. She *had* managed to get Lydiann to lie down—the poor girl was emotionally worn out over Abe's accident.

Downstairs, Sadie paced from the kitchen all the way to the front room and back again, wishing for some word on their brother. Anything at all would help to alleviate her pent-up feelings. She was all too familiar with such frustration, having suffered similarly for hours on the day the startling report of Harvey's fatal accident had come, unable to get to the hospital until too late to say her good-byes to her darling.

The Indiana bishop had been on hand during that dark, sad time, and she wondered again why the bishop here couldn't be more compassionate to her . . . or even encouraging. Clenching her jaw, she recalled how she'd felt upon receiving the harsh letter Bishop Bontrager had sent in response to her request to return home. He had pointedly stated she was a "most vile woman in need of repentance," and he even hinted that he doubted she would have contacted him if not for her widowhood. He had also dared to suggest her husband's untimely death showed she was most likely under God's judgment.

Sadie wondered if she could ever truly forgive the bishop for those words and what he'd forced upon her, yet she had no choice but to walk in obedience to the *Ordnung* lest she fail her second Proving time and be cast out of her father's house.

Truly, she wanted to be found worthy to live amongst the People, and she didn't see herself remaining under Dat's covering for the rest of her life. Although it was much too early for her to think about such things, she hoped to have the chance to marry again someday, perhaps to a widower, once she was past her grieving for Harvey. After all, she had been happiest when married, and happiness was her ambition in life, regardless of Bishop Bontrager's frequent insistence in his sermons that obedience to the church is the highest calling for God's children. "Obey or die"—the words had both discouraged her and, at times, kept her on the straight and narrow, even finding their way into the core of her late-night dreams. And she couldn't help but recall the teachings of the upstanding Ohio bishop she had known back when she was staying with the Mellingers. *Oh, the remarkable wisdom of the ministers of Millersburg!* She knew she ought not let the encouragement of Scripture go unheeded.

Aware of a voice in the Dawdi Haus, she headed through the adjoining door and found her grandfather alone, talking to himself. "Dawdi?" she said so as not to startle him, bending low beside his chair. "Are you all right?"

He lifted his tear-streaked face. "I can hardly stand to

think 'bout what happened to that young'un," he said, voice breaking. "Abe's a right fine boy, he is. Just don't understand what he thought he was doin' going to Blackbird Pond like that."

She rose and pulled up a chair to sit near her grandfather. "Jah, I know it's awful hard on all of us, but we daresn't give up hope."

He nodded slowly, though it seemed with great effort. "That there boy's the apple of your father's eye. He's everything to Abram."

"A son is ever so precious to his father." *And to his mother*, she pondered, having to look away and collect herself a bit.

"I daresay the family will still be away at the hospital come suppertime." He was obviously anxious for some word, just as she was.

Sadie offered to make him some coffee, but Dawdi shook his head.

Making an effort to help him get his mind off young Abe, she picked up *The Budget* and began to read from its pages. Two humorous stories from Sugarcreek, Ohio, got Dawdi quieted down. After all, it wouldn't do to have both Lydiann and Dawdi crying buckets of tears over Abe. What good would it do? Sadie herself had shed too many fruitless tears over things she could not change.

But there were some things that *could* be altered, and she thought again of the letter that had come out of nowhere, as if the Lord God had dropped it into her lap to see if she might actually do the right thing at long last. Of course, she still had no idea how poor Leah would react.

It was after she finished reading to Dawdi that Sadie decided she could no longer wait to fess up to Leah. She must come clean once and for all as soon as Abe was home and feeling better.

It was decided Leah would stay the night in the hospital with Abe, and both she and Aunt Lizzie were now talking this over in the family waiting area while Dat went into Abe's room to sit with him. Her father was still berating himself for having introduced Abe to ice fishing not but a few days ago. "Dat needs his own bed and a nice hot meal besides," Leah said, to which Lizzie agreed.

"I daresay word'll get out quickly enough," Aunt Lizzie said, "and you'll have plenty of visitors here with ya tonight, dear one."

Leah knew this to be true, for Plain relatives and friends often gathered around a family during such times of crisis. She wasn't hesitant to be here alone, though. No, she worried more about what she would do if Abe should take a turn for the worse.

"Lydiann will be awful glad to see you and Dat come home." Leah rose. "Dawdi will be, too."

"And Sadie will have supper on by now." Aunt Lizzie looked up at the clock. "I best be gettin' Abram thinking 'bout headin' home." She went to Leah and slipped her arm through hers. "Are ya sure you'll be all right here?"

She couldn't say outright that she would be, but then again she couldn't openly speak of her fears. "Don't worry over me. Look after Dat . . . get him home for now."

Lizzie nodded, smiling sweetly. "All right, then." And they walked arm in arm down the hall to Abe's room.

Dat was coming out, a look of sadness on his face as they approached him. "Abe's still passed out."

"We must leave him in God's hands," offered Lizzie.

"Easier said than done," Dat replied. "I just hope I did the right thing. . . ." His voice trailed off.

"Whatever do you mean, Dat?"

"By having Smitty get Dr. Schwartz . . . bringing Abe here."

"You did just what Mamma would've wanted," Leah replied.

"Lizzie here would've chewed me out but gut, otherwise," Abram admitted with a fleeting smile. "But that's all right, I guess. She's had her say-so in the past, just as Ida often did."

Dat's acceptance of Lizzie's aversion to hex doctors seemed related in some way to his possible romantic interest. Leah had noticed Lizzie patting Dat's hand today, and just now she felt strongly that if Dat *was* falling for Lizzie after being a widower for this long, then so be it. Leah found the prospects quite interesting, even promising, since Aunt Lizzie had most likely given up on ever being married.

Grateful for the help and heartening Lizzie had offered this day, she hugged her good-bye and waved to Dat as they made their way down the hallway together. Thoughtfully she watched them for a moment before heading back to spend the rest of the night with Abe.

Settling into a chair, she suddenly felt alone and downright melancholy. With Dat and Aunt Lizzie gone, she was the sole caretaker of Mamma's son, who was presently sleeping so soundly inside his oxygen tent, he scarcely moved.

She must have dozed off, although for how long Leah didn't know, till she became aware of a sound in the room and assumed it was the night nurse. She blinked her eyes open to see Abe's eyes opening, too.

"Mamma . . ." he said faintly.

Her heart sped up and she rushed to his side. "Oh, Abe . . . you're awake!"

"Mamma," he whispered again, smiling weakly now.

"Jah, I'm here, dearest boy."

He lifted his hand to meet hers.

"You're better, ain't so?" She wished Dat and Aunt Lizzie were here for this wonderful moment.

Abe tried to sit up but began to moan, putting his free hand to his forehead. "Ach, my head hurts somethin' awful."

"Well, now, sure it does," she said, encouraging him to lie still. "Ya smacked it a gut one on the ice."

He frowned. "I don't remember any such thing. When was this?"

She was quick to tell him he'd conked his head hard, knocking out the memory of his being at Blackbird Pond earlier today.

"No . . . no, I was never there today . . . not since Dat and all went ice fishin'. Why would I be goin' over there alone, anyways?"

Leah's throat went dry and she became anxious, afraid Abe's accident might have caused mental damage. "Try to rest quietlike while I go 'n' get the nurse. I'll be right back."

She returned alone and hovered near him, eager for the nurse to observe him and to help her understand what was causing Abe to talk so.

Promptly her dear boy closed his eyes again, and for a

moment he lay there as still as he had before awakening minutes ago. She felt a strange sensation in the pit of her stomach—something akin to fear.

She stood there beside Abe's bed, helpless to do anything but watch him breathe, when at last the nurse hurried in the door. Leah told of Abe's having come to, and the nurse seemed quite pleased, then touched his arm to awaken him again to take his temperature, pulse, and blood pressure.

When Abe complained more loudly about his headache and a ringing in his ears, the nurse said she would get him some pain medication. She rushed out of the room and returned quickly with a pill and a glass of cold water. "This will make you feel much better."

"Denki," said Abe softly.

Leah got the courage to speak up and say that Abe did not seem to remember having fallen, and the nurse explained that it was normal following a grade-three concussion. "A grade three is determined by a loss of consciousness, and symptoms can continue for a full month or longer," the nurse clarified.

"Do ya mean to say Abe might have to miss school for that long?" Leah asked.

"He'll need bed rest for several weeks, at least. I wouldn't rush him back to school, no." The nurse listed a number of other possible symptoms—memory loss, severe headaches, nausea, slurred speech, vision disturbance, fatigue, and more. She went on to mention that Abe would probably require a follow-up exam in two weeks.

When the sound of the nurse's footsteps faded, Leah sat back in the chair. For now her mind was more at ease.

"You'll stay with me tonight, Mamma?" Abe asked.

She moved her chair next to his bed. "I'll sit beside you all the night through."

In the dim light, she silently began to count her blessings, as well as Abe's. Her boy was alive, able to talk, hear, and see. *Thank you, dear Lord,* she prayed, keeping a watchful eye on her sleeping little brother—the son of her heart.

Chapter Twelve

Hannah finished nursing tiny Mimi and placed her gently on her shoulder till several soft burps escaped the infant's rosy mouth. Then she wrapped Mimi securely in soft blankets and placed her snugly in the cradle handmade by Dawdi Mathias back when Hannah was expecting Ida Mae. Just as dear Mamma had often done, Hannah looked in on the older girls, both soundly sleeping, before tiptoeing to the window of the bedroom she and her husband shared.

This room, which she had enjoyed setting up when she and Gid had first moved into Aunt Lizzie's former home as newlyweds, was altogether comforting in the partial light. Aware of the stillness, she watched as the moon ascended gradually over the faraway hills to the east, wishing Gid would hurry back home. He'd gone down to the Ebersol Cottage on foot after they'd stopped to retrieve Ida Mae and Katie Ann from his parents' house, following the brief hospital visit.

Longingly she watched the candle-lit windows on the main floor of her father's house, particularly the golden light from the kitchen, which shone most brightly. *They're all gathered near the wood stove. . . .* She could just imagine her family together, Dat and Aunt Lizzie having arrived home a short while before, and Dawdi John, Sadie, and Lydiann hungry for word about Abe. Gid, too, was keenly interested in hearing how young Abe was doing, as well as finding out why Abram hadn't called for the hex doctor, as he'd heard his father had suggested.

She recalled Aunt Lizzie telling her that such practices had the power to hinder one's walk with the Lord God, thus hampering the hope of salvation. Truth be known, she didn't so much care for her aunt's take on spiritual things and knew she'd never embrace Lizzie's outspoken faith, nor Mary Ruth's, for that matter. Such boldness went against the Old Ways, she was sure, but she dared not discuss such a touchy subject with her husband, instead writing down her thoughts in her journal as she had been doing for a good many years.

Tonight, however, she had scarcely the energy to stand at the window, feeling dismal and left out here at home with her little ones, missing the current news from Dat and Aunt Lizzie.

Is Abe going to live?

She fought back the tears, fairly certain Leah had stayed behind at the hospital, knowing her sister as she did. Ever so strong . . . and altogether calm in the midst of such a trying time, that was Leah. It had also been so after Mamma's death.

Hannah sighed, recognizing again her lack of similar fortitude. She couldn't have done what Leah had done . . . or what she continued to do, giving up all opportunities to wed. But now, thinking on that, Hannah was altogether happy Leah *had* broken up with Gid, so to speak, although she knew from his mouth that, when all was said and done, *he* had been the cause of their breakup. And rightly so, since he longed for his own household and flesh-and-blood children, which he was certainly having with Hannah—one after another. Yet, thus far, she had failed to give him a son.

Maybe next time the Lord God will see fit to give us a boy, she thought, moving away from the window and heading to bed. Her ears would have to wait till morning for some word on Abe. She was just too tired, and not long from now, in a few hours, Mimi would be crying yet again for nourishment.

A familiar dread of darkness overwhelmed her as it seemed to nearly every night, and Hannah went again to check on her children, ever worried that they might sleep too soundly, never to awaken. Even with her baby safely born, the gnawing fear of death seemed to shadow her every move.

The evening progressed, bringing with it a steady trickle of visitors to the waiting area—Uncle Jesse Ebersol and nearly all his family—and Leah was especially glad to see Adah among those who had come to keep her company through the sunless hours.

"Ya mustn't wear yourself out," Adah advised sweetly, her big eyes revealing the concern of a best friend. "Will ya promise you'll rest when ya can?"

Leah's lip quivered and she said she would.

"This too shall pass," Adah offered, sitting beside her. "A concussion is a worrisome thing, but I have a feelin' you'll see him up and goin' about his work and school in no time."

Leah opened her heart and shared what the nurses had told her to expect about Abe's condition if things went normally. To this Adah frowned, yet she stood her ground. "Trust the Lord God for healing," she whispered, glancing around her lest she be heard and misunderstood.

A bit surprised at this, Leah kept her voice low, saying she had been doing just that, but she was awful glad for Adah's encouragement. "I felt I nearly lost my own son this day," she admitted. "And Dat, oh goodness, you best be prayin' for him, too. He needs it as much as Abe, I'm thinkin'."

Saying she would remember the whole family in her prayers, Adah gripped Leah's hand and added, "Nothin's impossible with the Lord God. Ya have to hold on to that."

When all of this recent faith had sprung up in Adah, Leah didn't know. But she wasn't too surprised to hear such things from Miriam Peachey's daughter, knowing what she did about Mamma's good friend and the way she believed, though quite secretly, in the saving grace of the Lord Jesus. Like Miriam and Adah, a growing number of the People seemed to be embracing the blessing of prayer.

Come ten o'clock, the family waiting room grew empty and quiet, and soon Leah was alone with Abe once again. She was distressed that he seemed disoriented at times, as though he had lost his way in his mind and could not get back to where he belonged. The nurse had talked about accident-related amnesia, something that should fade with time, and hopefully that would be the case with Abe. For now, though, Abe continued to complain about a growing list of symptoms. At first light tomorrow some tests would be done, the nurses assured her.

Leah settled into the oversized leather chair, aware of Abe's steady breathing. *Tomorrow we'll know more.* She wrestled with the thought, hoping the doctor would indeed have more for her to go on, something to help her grasp all the strange things happening with Abe.

A horrendous thirst awakened Abram in the night—a powerful urge to get out of bed and go to the kitchen for some water. Along with the intense craving was the lingering memory of a nightmare. In his dream, Abram had made repeated attempts to reach Abe, yet he had slipped on the ice himself, his arms stretched out before him, unable to save his son.

Attempting to recover from the dreadful sense of helplessness, Abram drank the glass dry in one continuous gulp. The events of the day played in his mind as he padded back to his bedroom, and all he could think of now was that Abe and Leah were far removed from him this night . . . nearly an hour away by horse and carriage. He was beholden to Henry Schwartz, the kindhearted doctor who had probably saved Abe's life. Once Dr. Schwartz had arrived and Abram had carried his unconscious son out to the doctor's car, he'd clung to a measure of hope that Abe was going to be all right in the long run—and without the help of the hex doctor.

But presently, in the dimness of his room, he prayed silently that he'd made the right decision for his son . . . for Leah, too, who was tending to Abe with her heart, no doubt getting precious little sleep herself. Time would tell, Abram knew.

Such a day it's been, he thought.

In time Abram yielded to slumber and was disturbed by yet another dream. Abe had slipped into a hole in a pond created for ice fishing, his small hands thrashing about, his weak voice calling for help as he slipped farther and farther from the opening, at last bumping his head against the frozen pond above him and drowning in the frigid waters.

Breaking out in a cold sweat, Abram awakened, wishing for the dawn. He arose again and sat on the edge of his bed, struggling to control his yearning to see with his own eyes that Abe still lived.

I should've stayed at the hospital. . . .

Going to get another drink, he stood at the kitchen window and looked out across the snowy pastureland, this plot of land owned by his own father and grandfather before him. Had either of them ever spoken to the Almighty the way Lizzie did . . . the way Ida had always done? The way *he'd* silently prayed at his injured son's side?

Again he felt a nudging within to call on the name of the almighty One, if only in a whisper. Inhaling deeply, he began. "O Lord God and heavenly Father, will you hear and honor this prayer I make? Will you look after young Abe this night . . . and Leah, too? Will you shine your light of love kindly upon them while they are so far away from my care? Amen."

He felt altogether odd about the act, yet there was something truly strengthening about speaking this way in prayer. He had never done so before in his life, having been instructed against it, and the actual doing was such an eye-opener, he wondered why on earth Bishop Bontrager was so opposed to something so powerful—something as potent as some of the People viewed a hex doctor's chanting.

But even more than the sense of power in the room was the prevailing peace, an assurance that Abe would indeed survive.

"Father in heaven, hear my prayers for young Abe," whispered Mary Ruth as she walked the length of her bedroom, with only the light of the moon to guide her way. "Touch my father and Sadie and Lydiann . . . and Dawdi John, too, with your saving grace. Minister your abiding strength to Aunt Lizzie and Leah, and call Hannah, my dear twin, and her husband, Gid, and their little ones to the eternal truth of your Word. These things I pray in the name of the Lord Jesus. Amen."

"O Lord God, let Abe live," Sadie prayed silently beneath the coverlet of the bed she normally shared with Leah. "Let young Abe live a long and healthy life."

She wondered if Leah was able to rest at the hospital. But no, more than likely she was keeping watch over Abe. *If I'd raised him as my own, I'd be doing the same*, she contemplated, sighing into the darkness. *If I'd stayed put, I would have been here for Mamma to ask for* my *promise on her deathbed.*

Too often she let her mind wander to this: that had she been living at home, Leah never would have been anywhere near the birthing room with Mamma, Aunt Lizzie, and the midwife. For Sadie had always been Mamma's right-hand girl, and prior to the years of her rumschpringe, they had scarcely ever been apart. She had worked alongside Mamma in most every respect.

She pictured Abe lying still as a stone in a hospital of many strangers—Englishers mostly—and was startled at a keen sense of not wanting to lose him to death. *Just as I lost my only son.*

Weeping now, she felt compelled to continue her prayer to the almighty One.

"Dear God, let my brother live so that I might know him . . . so that he might come to love me in part as he does Leah." Only after praying this would Sadie allow herself to rest.

What's to become of us if Abe dies? Lydiann wondered, lying wide-awake, having cried her eyes dry. *Am I to grow up alone?*

She thought she heard Sadie down the hall and raised herself up in the darkness to listen. The graceful, beautiful sister she'd missed knowing for nearly her whole life was sniffling in her bed, crying over Abe, too, probably. Getting up, she pushed her slippers on and tiptoed to the room her mamma Leah and Sadie shared. She tapped gently on the door. "Sadie, it's me . . . Lyddie."

She was told to come in, which she did gladly, especially thankful when Sadie held open the heavy quilt to welcome her to climb in.

"I could use some company tonight, too," said Sadie, her voice raspy.

"That's gut, 'cause I'm awful sad." Lydiann slipped into bed and felt the warmth of Sadie's arm around her. She nestled down like a kitten in a wicker basket.

"No need for both of us to be lonely tonight," Sadie whispered.

Lydiann smiled through her tears. "Were you ever, well, lonely before . . . ?"

"Before I moved home, ya mean?"

"Jah."

"I'd have to say I was always missing my family . . . especially Mamma . . . the mother who birthed both you and me. We were always ever so close."

Lydiann wondered if she dare ask the question burning within her. Was this the right time to bring up such a thing? She sighed and tried to go to sleep, but rest would not come. Turning over, she lay facing the ceiling.

"What are ya thinkin' now?" Sadie asked.

"Not sure if I oughta say."

"You can ask me whatever ya like. How's that?"

She could just imagine Mamma Leah saying this wasn't a good idea—not tonight, not now, not ever. But Lydiann didn't so much care at the moment what anybody thought. So she asked, "Why were ya treated so, Sadie? Why'd ya have to go away?"

Chapter Thirteen

Two days following New Year's Day, along about midday, Abe was released from the Lancaster hospital. Evidently Dr. Schwartz had been keeping in touch with the attending physician by phone, for he kindly offered to drive both Leah and Abe home—"to avoid further jostling in a buggy" was precisely the way the doctor had put it to Leah. She realized anew what wonderful-good friends and neighbors the Schwartzes were, and she'd gotten up the nerve to tell Dr. Schwartz as much during the ride back to Gobbler's Knob. Together, she and Abe had sat in the backseat, Abe leaning against her and quietly complaining of dizziness the length of the trip.

Once she resumed her work at the clinic, Leah intended to ask Dr. Schwartz privately about Abe's continuing symptoms, including his insistence that he had not returned to the frozen pond. The rest of the family would, no doubt, be just as concerned as she once Abe got settled back at home.

Meanwhile, they—*all* of them—had much to be grateful for, because their boy's injuries could have been far worse.

Lydiann tried to keep herself from bawling as she greeted Abe, she was so happy to see him. "What was it like at the hospital? Did the nurses take gut care of ya? Did they let you eat ice cream?"

"I think we best let your brother rest up before ya ask *too* many questions," Mamma Leah said, to which Dat agreed, nodding his head.

The entire family, including Dawdi John, who'd hobbled over from next door, stood in Mamma's kitchen, awful happy to see Abe again. But it wasn't long before Mamma Leah and Dat were taking him upstairs to lie down.

"Isn't he all better?" Lydiann followed them to the bottom of the stairs and looked up with longing as her brother leaned hard on Dat's arm.

Briefly turning around, Dat chided her, "Hush now."

Lydiann hurried to Sadie's side at the cookstove, where she had cooked up her best corn chowder. "What do ya make of that?" she whispered. "Abe comes home and he can hardly walk. I saw him, Sadie. His balance is off-kilter!"

"Don't ya worry none," Sadie replied. "He'll be as gut as new . . . you'll see."

But Abe wasn't better that evening or the next morning, neither one. And Lydiann worried something truly terrible had happened to him over on Blackbird Pond, something Abe might never recover from.

Then and there, she decided it best not to tell her school friends what she'd seen with her own eyes, even though they were all asking about Abe. Dat had already gone to the school and informed the teacher that Abe would be missing some days—just how many, no one could say.

The day following Leah's return with Abe, Sadie found her in the kitchen sweeping the floor. Silently, she set about cleaning up the wood stove, wondering how to raise the subject of the letter she'd hidden in her bureau drawer. She considered yet again the new barrier it was bound to create between the two of them as she continued her work, rubbing hard at the cookstove's surface. Maybe this still wasn't the best time, but Sadie couldn't wait another minute. Ever since her decision to come clean, the letter had begun to bore a hole in her bureau drawer, as well as in her heart.

So when Leah stopped sweeping to fetch the dustpan, Sadie straightened and inhaled deeply. The second she reappeared, Sadie blurted, "It's time I talk to ya 'bout something, sister."

"Oh?" Leah was obviously innocent to what Sadie had in mind, for she continued with her work, bending low to sweep the floor debris onto the dustpan.

"I hate to upset ya, really I do . . . but I've been wanting to make something right. And for a gut long time now."

At once Leah ceased her work, her eyes red and her face still pale from lack of sleep, most likely. "What's on your mind?" she asked.

Momentarily Sadie reconsidered. *How selfish of me.* Sighing, she knew she must not turn back. "When I was livin' in Millersburg years ago, I did something I must ask your forgiveness for." She pressed on. "It was a horrid thing I did. Unforgivable, truly."

Blinking her eyes, Leah frowned and stood tall with the broom upright in her hand. "I have no idea what you're talking 'bout."

"'Course, you don't." Scarcely could she go on, but she admitted how vexed she had been at the time over what she felt had been an outright betrayal on Leah's part. "I was awful angry you upped and spilled the beans to Mamma and Dat 'bout my wild days . . . me gettin' myself in the family way 'n' all. So one day, when one of your letters to Jonas arrived in the mail, I dropped it in the rubbish as a way to get back at you—it wasn't till it was too late that I realized what a dreadful thing I'd done. By then, it was beyond possibility to retrieve the letter."

Leah's face flushed red with unmistakable ire, but as quickly as she allowed her wrath to show, she stepped back and breathed a great sigh. "I don't care to rehash my resentment during those disturbing days"—she wiped her brow with the back of her hand—"but it does wonder me if that letter might not be the one explainin' some needful things to Jonas."

Meekly Sadie whispered, "You can know that for sure and for certain."

"What do ya mean?"

"It's upstairs . . . tucked away." Sadie quivered. "The mailman delivered it here recently. . . . It must've fallen out of the trash truck all that time ago, although who can be sure just what happened for it to find its way back here now."

Leah's eyes flickered. "Jah, go 'n' get the letter for me."

Hurrying upstairs, Sadie found the concealed letter, her

pulse racing as she hoped against hope her sister might find it in her heart to forgive.

Taking short, quick breaths, Leah placed her hand on her chest. *Why, O Lord, must this be happening now . . . when my thoughts of Jonas are few and far between?*

Faithfully she had been reading Mamma's old Bible, and with her heart wide open, the Scriptures were filling the void left there by her tenderness for Jonas. God's Word offered her strength and even solace for her loneliness.

Yet now she couldn't help but recall how she'd felt so terribly heartbroken, assuming her sister had stolen her dear beau when Sadie had lived near Jonas during the time of his Millersburg cabinetmaking apprenticeship. In her desperation at the perceived deception, Leah had fully given herself up to the mercy of almighty God, drawing courage for her life from the love of her heavenly Father.

Sadie returned, holding out the letter. "It's soiled but unopened all the same."

Leah nodded, unable to speak as she inspected the discolored postmark.

Sadie's voice was soft yet strained. "Can you ever forgive me?"

Intently examining the envelope, Leah could not reply. She could discern the month and year—not the actual day—and went quickly to the utensil drawer and pulled out a table knife, slicing through the top of the envelope . . . and into the long-ago past. Suddenly it all felt so recent.

Opening the letter, she recognized the handwriting as her own and read the first few lines. Immediately she knew this surely *was* the most important letter she'd ever written. To think Jonas had never known . . . never even laid eyes on it!

She glanced up and noticed Sadie turning to leave the kitchen, heading slowly, if not forlornly, toward the stairs. *Can you ever forgive me?* Her request echoed in Leah's ears.

How many secrets must we bear? Leah clutched the letter, grateful for the privacy, and wandered to the window, struggling not to shake as she read through to the end.

When she finished, she refolded it gently and slipped it back into the safety of its envelope. *He never read my answers to his pointed questions about my friendship with Gid. Jonas never knew my heart on this. . . .*

She held it close to her and bowed her head under the burden of her pain. *No wonder his letters stopped,* Leah thought tearfully. *No wonder he never returned home to marry me.*

Chapter Fourteen

Something's awful wrong with Abe," Hannah confided in Mary Ruth, who'd come for a late afternoon visit nearly a week after their brother's discharge from the hospital. "He ain't nearly the same, and I've seen firsthand that it's true." She had to swallow hard as she tried not to cry, still wishing Dat would come to his senses and have the hex doctor work his magic on the boy.

Mary Ruth held little Mimi in her arms, rocking her slowly while Ida Mae and Katie Ann stacked small towers of wooden blocks near the cookstove. "Lorraine told Dottie head injuries of this nature take time to heal . . . and that came from Dr. Schwartz, naturally. Funny how the grapevine works on the outside, too."

Hannah didn't find talk of the grapevine at all amusing. Truth was, Mary Ruth's frequent visits were beginning to annoy Gid, being themselves the subject of tittle-tattle amongst the People. He'd told Hannah before Abe's accident, "Not such a gut idea for an Amishwoman-turned-Mennonite to be comin' round here and fillin' the preacher's wife's head with all kinds of nonsense." He'd also confided the bishop had put him on the spot, questioning Hannah's close ongoing relationship with a Mennonite.

Mary Ruth's my sister, for pity's sake, Hannah had thought at the time, not daring to speak up. After all, having received the divine ordination, Gid was always right—God's choice of a shepherd to this flock. There was to be no questioning the man of God, even though there were times when she did secretly wonder how the Lord God could look on Bishop Bontrager's heart and be pleased. Was it possible for a divine appointment to go off beam . . . for a man reckoned to be the messenger of God to become blind and puffed up with pride?

She could only hope such a thing would always be far from true of her handsome husband, although she had always known him to have an opinion about most everything, just as both of their fathers staunchly did. The two older men had been quite similar in their thinking on most things, except here lately Dat hadn't heeded his friend's advice to call the hex doctor—Gid had said as much. This puzzled her no end, and she was relieved Abe had managed to survive the blow to his head despite what *might've* happened with Dat disregarding the importance, even the sway, of a sympathy healer.

"When did you last see Abe?" she asked Mary Ruth, getting up to take Mimi from her to nurse her.

"Just yesterday, when I took Carl for a visit after school." Mary Ruth said that Carl had been worried to the point of an upset stomach over his friend.

Hannah smiled faintly. "Well, it's mighty sure Carl's become nearly part of the family, seems to me." She wondered what her sister might say to that.

"Dat hasn't always been so keen on Carl's visits, but it seems to me that recently he's been a little more easygoing." Mary Ruth paused, giving Hannah a small smile. "He's surely got a new spring in his step." Mary Ruth rose and went to rescue several blocks the girls had allowed to roll under the corner cupboard. She got down on all fours, laughing as she did, because Ida Mae had come running over and hopped on her back as if Mary Ruth were a horse.

Hannah admitted she'd observed the same thing. "I suspect Dat won't always be a widower . . . though it ain't our place to speculate on his business," Hannah said, lifting baby Mimi onto her shoulder for burping. She wondered if now was the right time to tell Mary Ruth what Gid had said about her visits here, though it pained her to think of doing so. Instead she again brought up the subject of her concern for Abe.

"Leah says our brother has been talkin' nonsense. His balance is off-kilter, too. It's got her mighty anxious."

Mary Ruth sat back down in the chair near the window, the light coming in and resting on her slender shoulders, making her hair look even blonder. "He must've hit his head awful hard."

Hearing Gid's footsteps outside, Hannah felt awful nervous now. *What'll my husband say if he finds Mary Ruth here again?*

She immediately rose and headed to her bedroom to put Mimi in her cradle, hearing Gid's voice as he greeted Mary Ruth out in the front room. Standing behind the bedroom door, she was hesitant to return, so she waited there, eavesdropping.

"Is Hannah here?" Gid asked.

"She's tucking Mimi in" came Mary Ruth's reply.

There was a lull, but soon Gid said, "This ain't easy to say, but I've been thinkin', Mary Ruth, 'bout the People and all. Seems it might be better if ya didn't speak your mind to Hannah so much."

Mary Ruth remained silent.

"Might just be best, too, if ya didn't come round here so often," Gid said flatly. "Hannah bein' the preacher's wife now and you bein' . . . well, Mennonite. Just doesn't set so gut with some folk."

Ach, Gid! Hannah clutched her heart, because she'd never heard her husband talk so, not in that severe tone of voice . . . not even to a stubborn horse. She felt she might burst out crying.

◆

As Mary Ruth walked down the mule road toward her father's house, she could think only of her brother-in-law's stern admonishment. The formerly pleasant Gid had surely changed since his divine appointment. Fact was, Hannah needed loving encouragement—she'd sunk into near despair over Abe's accident, and even life's small concerns seemed to pull hard at her. And now was Mary Ruth to obey Gid's warning and be cut off from her own twin sister? A more intimate friend she'd never known.

She breathed in the wintry air as she made her way out toward the main road, bypassing a visit with Leah and Abe, although her heart longed to stop in for a short while. She wouldn't give in to worry over Abe, though, because she had made up her mind she was going to trust the Lord for her brother's healing. She must stand on the promises of God, let

Him be at work in young Abe. "In all of us," she said aloud.

Soon her thoughts turned to Robert. While they had continued seeing each other since their frank discussion about Derek and Sadie, there had been no marriage proposal. Without a doubt, Robert was an upstanding man, one kind and good in every respect. She had every reason to love him. Robert had all the qualities a good preacher should possess—and all those of a good husband, too.

She found it curious that both she and Hannah were connected to ministers. One who humbly taught the full truth of God's Word, and one who, having been raised a smithy's son, was much more skilled at shoeing horses than at helping folk shod their feet with the preparation of the Gospel of peace. After all Gid Peachey had never had a speck of training. When the lot fell on a man, there were often days and weeks of actual mourning as the newly appointed man accepted the responsibility, even the burden, of the People resting soundly on his shoulders. Mary Ruth could just imagine that weight on Gid now, which might have been the reason for his harsh remarks to her today. Yet she would not allow her encounter with him to bring her discouragement, for a dispirited person was open to even more opposition from the enemy of the soul.

So Mary Ruth marched along the road with head high, ever so confident in the Lord. She was sure that in God's time, He could turn even this for good.

Days had passed since Sadie's revelation, and since then Leah had seemed distracted, encumbered by her continued care of Abe. Or perhaps it was newfound resentment toward Sadie that made Leah so distant, although it seemed unlike her sister to hold a grudge. Still, one thing was altogether sure: no offer of forgiveness had come. *Maybe she's had enough*, thought Sadie.

Meanwhile the original peace she'd experienced at her confession had faded, and old thoughts had returned to haunt her—memories of dear Harvey and her blue babies. Memories, too, of her shunning, Leah's seeming betrayal of her, and of Derry and the terrible sin with him that had set things in motion. *If only dwelling on the past could make things different for me.*

The afternoon weather had turned blustery and cold when Sadie spotted Mary Ruth out on the road. *Maybe Mary Ruth knows something of Derry . . . if he happens to know the fate of our baby*, Sadie thought. But she decided she best not take off running after her, though she surely wanted to. She simply stood there at the front room window, gazing after her sister, wondering just what Mary Ruth might know about Derry Schwartz. *Will she say what she knows?*

Finally, having tried her best to stay calm and not give in to impulsiveness, she told Leah she was going for a short walk and donned her wool coat, black outer bonnet, and snow boots.

"Where are ya headed?" Leah looked a bit surprised at the amount of outer clothing she was piling on.

"Need some air, is all."

"Goin' up to see Hannah, maybe?" Leah pressed, eyes revealing more disquiet as Sadie reached for her muffler and mittens.

"Haven't decided just where," Sadie fibbed, feeling a sting

of guilt, yet not changing her plan as she turned and walked out the back door. A strong wind nearly blew her back into the house, but stubbornly she pushed ahead.

When at last she caught up with Mary Ruth, she was more than a half mile from home, farther away than she had been since the outset of her present Proving. Farther, too, than was allowed on her own, really, but Sadie felt she was safe from Miriam's eyes on such a cold and snowy day. Besides, if she kept her face forward, who'd know it was she beneath the big black winter bonnet?

"I saw you from the window," she told Mary Ruth, matching her stride as they went. "Need to talk to you privately."

Mary Ruth's face was red with the cold, but she didn't mince words. "Shouldn't you head back, what with the rules of your Proving and all?"

Sadie shook her head. "I'll risk that for now."

"Well . . . what's on your mind, then?"

Inhaling, she held in the frigid air before breathing out. "I've been wantin' to ask ya something for the longest time," she began. "It's about your beau's brother."

"Derek?"

"Do ya happen to know him at all?"

Mary Ruth hesitated, as if pondering her response. "I've seen him only twice. Once long ago at the vegetable stand and, later, out on the road at Christmastime some years ago now. Why do you ask?"

Pausing, Sadie worried how her questions might sound, but she persisted. "Do you know he was the father of my first baby?"

Mary Ruth nodded. "In fact, he wasn't shy about telling

me who he was that Christmas Day. I must say, I was mighty surprised."

"Did he ask about the baby . . . or me?"

Mary Ruth said she recalled that afternoon quite clearly. "He seemed to be in a big hurry . . . headed down this same road, toward the house."

"Our house, ya mean?"

"That's right. He was out of sorts, swinging his arms like he was lookin' for a fight."

Sadie didn't care to reflect on the way Derry had behaved when he was irritated; he'd displayed his bad temper too many times for her to forget. "Did you tell him I wasn't livin' at home any longer?"

"Since we'd heard you were married to Jonas Mast back then, I said you were out in Ohio somewhere and married. That was all."

Sadie slowed her pace now. "Anything else?"

"He asked if you'd had a boy or a girl, and I told him your baby son had died at birth. That was pretty much the end of the conversation. He turned and left, headed back toward his parents' house."

Sadie breathed more deeply, taking all this in. *Derry had been heading toward Dat's house. Why was that?*

They fell silent for some time, walking more briskly to keep warm.

When they grew closer to the Nolts' place, Sadie asked if ever Robert talked about his brother.

"Last I heard, Derek's stationed somewhere out in Washington state. He hasn't been home in seven years . . . not since that Christmas." Mary Ruth was frowning. "I'm worried that you're asking all these questions, Sadie. You never should have met him in the first place. Why would you want to know about him now?"

Abruptly, Sadie stopped walking. "I wondered what he knew. I guess I thought it might help me to put the whole thing to rest and forget the past."

"This happened a long time ago. And since I've told you everything you need to know, why not head on home?" Mary Ruth urged. "I'm nervous for you."

Sadie felt she was walking on dangerous ground, too, having wandered this far already. "Jah, s'pose you're right."

Mary Ruth turned and hugged her. "So long for now."

Waving, Sadie turned and started back down the lonely road. She shivered against the fierce cold and, when the weather turned even more blustery, she wished she'd stayed put at home in the kitchen near the wood stove. What did it matter, anyway, that Derry had asked about her or their baby? *So cruel he was*, she thought.

Less than halfway home, a squall of snow came up. She tugged on her coat and drew the muffler around her neck more securely, bracing herself against an afternoon storm that had in short order become a full-blown blizzard.

Sadie tried in vain to see her way, unsure if she was wandering toward the shoulder or out into the middle of the road. But she kept going, hoping she might make it home before Dat or Leah began to worry. Her hands, feet, and face were so cold they were beginning to sting with pain, yet she must not focus on that. Reminded of young Abe's struggles with frostbite, she happened to notice automobile headlights creeping toward her. Moving out of the way, she was surprised to see Robert Schwartz waving at her through the snowy windshield.

Mary Ruth's beau stopped, opened the car door, and

insisted she get inside. "What are you doing out in this?" he asked.

She didn't think twice about accepting his invitation, even though the mandate on her Proving was once again breached the minute she climbed inside the warm car. "Thank you," she said, shivering uncontrollably. "I thought I could make it home. . . ."

"Thank the Lord I saw you."

"Jah." She was grateful indeed and kept her face forward, sitting stiff as can be as he turned the car around and headed toward her father's house. "I'm much obliged," she said, not knowing what else to say now that she was alone with Derry's elder brother.

"Your family will be glad to see you safe," Robert said.

She mentioned she'd just spent some time walking with Mary Ruth. "She sent me on home."

"I'll get word to her by phone that you're safe and sound, once I arrive home."

By phone . . .

Truly, Mary Ruth had all the conveniences of the world—a handsome boyfriend with a fast, warm car; a pretty house to live in with heat, electric, and a telephone.

She was glad for the offer. "I might've lost my way in the storm if you hadn't come along."

"If not that, at least I may have spared your hands and feet from frostbite."

She smiled at that, though her face was so numb she could scarcely feel the muscles move. "There's the lane to the house," she said, pointing to the left.

"Thanks, I would have missed it," he acknowledged with a chuckle. Making the turn, he stopped the car without a warning and set the brake. "Uh, Sadie." He turned to face her. "Mary Ruth shared with me what happened between you and my brother some years ago." His face was solemn, even sad. "I'd like to offer an apology on behalf of Derek."

Sadie was both stunned and moved. "That's kind of you, but it's not for you to say." Still, she greatly appreciated the courteous gesture.

"It's best, I believe, that my brother's long gone. Otherwise, you might be tortured by running into him from time to time."

"Jah" was all she could manage to utter, looking away now.

Without saying more, Robert released the brake and inched the car forward. The tense conversation was behind them, yet she marveled at the timing of her encounter with Mary Ruth's beau. Who would have thought, when she'd set out to catch up with Mary Ruth earlier, she would be hearing apologetic words from no less than Derry's own brother?

However, when they arrived near the back door, she was completely aghast. Bishop Bontrager was walking to his carriage, leaning hard into the wind. But just before he moved to step in, he looked straight at her. Their eyes met and held.

"Oh," she groaned with deepest despair. "I'm surely ruined."

"Beg your pardon?" Robert said.

She shook her head, again muttered a feeble thanks for the ride, and headed out into the elements, toward the house and her certain *Schicksaal*—her fate.

Chapter Fifteen

The bishop motioned for Sadie to follow him back into the house, where she stood, unmoving, in the utility room as the man of God announced to both her father and herself that she was to be sent away for her disobedience.

Sent away? She hung her head not so much in shame as resentment. Surely Bishop Bontrager knew she would never have accepted a ride with a man had it not been for the severe weather. Still, she knew she'd ignored the rules of the Proving and for that deserved what she was getting.

Dat spoke up. "But the blizzard . . ." he said, attempting to defend her. "Sadie wouldn't have—"

"Such has no bearing on the matter at hand," the bishop said, cutting him off. At once the older man turned and pushed out the door, leaving Sadie standing alone with Dat, scarcely able to raise her eyes to his. When she did so at last, she caught his look of both disappointment and aggravation. With a low groan, Dat walked toward the kitchen.

Bishop would've sooner I froze to death, Sadie decided, going to the window to watch his horse and buggy head down the lane toward the main road. The back of the buggy whisked out of sight as it quickly became shrouded in the whiteout of dense, wind-driven snow. Moving from the doorway, she hung her coat on the wooden peg and, feeling dreary, removed her mittens, muffler, and boots. From the kitchen came the low hum of voices—no doubt the rest of the family was talking about the bishop's visit.

Why'd he come on such a dismal, stormy day, anyway?

Suddenly she knew: The bishop had come to see how poor Abe was faring.

She could have kicked herself for having chosen this day to display such open disobedience. The lie she'd told Leah earlier hung on her conscience like a yoke; she'd drifted much too far from the house, not to mention accepted a ride in an automobile with a man. All were clear violations of the Proving.

Sadie sighed deeply. *How foolish I am to have tempted fate so. . . .*

Leah had suspected all along where Sadie had gone, because not but a few minutes before her departure, Mary Ruth had walked past the house, probably coming from a visit with Hannah. *If Sadie didn't flat out lie, saying she didn't know where she was going!* Now her untruthful sister was coming into the kitchen, her cheeks mighty red from the cold in spite of her ride home in Robert Schwartz's car, of all things. What on earth was she thinking?

Sadie didn't stop to say hello or to join in their conversation, all of them having hot cocoa at the table—she simply forced a smile and made her way to the stairs. Leah could hear the quickness of her sister's footsteps as Sadie nearly flew upstairs.

She's been caught again, Leah thought, feeling both sad and worried about what additional church discipline might do to Sadie's emotional state. She found herself tuning out the talk around her, anxious about how the bishop would ultimately handle this transgression, with Sadie already nearly three months into her Proving.

The afternoon after the bishop's visit, while Abram and Leah were out in the barn amidst the cows and the milk buckets, Abram brought up his great frustration, for possibly the third time. "Sadie needs to be livin' with us, not somewhere else. 'Tis not for widows to live apart from family."

Leah was sitting in Sadie's usual place under Ol' Rosie, squeezing the cow's teats for all she was worth, evidently irritated no end. "This could push Sadie into deepest grief yet again. Seems to me she just got home."

"Jah, I was surprised she held up as well as she did yesterday. The bishop talked mighty straight to her. His face was downright purple."

"So . . . do ya think Bishop will hold a firm stand?" Leah asked.

Abram considered this. "Hard to say. I'm hopin' he comes to his senses, and right quick."

Abram went on to mention he'd spoken with Dawdi John about the bishop's harsh stance toward Sadie, and Dawdi agreed they must go along with it, whether they liked it or not. "What about Mary Ruth—could she make room at the Nolts' for Sadie?" he asked.

Leah sighed softly. "How would that set with the brethren,

her livin' with Englishers and all?"

"The Nolts are less fancy than, say, the doctor and his wife. I don't know where else she could go right now." His heart sank as he worried about losing another daughter to the world. He wanted Sadie under *his* roof, or within close riding distance at least, in hopes the bishop might allow them to visit her on occasion. Most folk under church discipline benefited greatly from words of kindness and admonition.

Truth be known, Abram wished he'd spoken up even more to the bishop yesterday when Sadie returned home—the elderly minister was taking this much too far. *Sure, she's broken specific requirements of the Proving, but the discipline doesn't seem to match the offense.* If Robert hadn't come along in his car when he did, who knows where they might've found his eldest daughter. Abram's heart was torn between the Ordnung and his love for Sadie, and there was no getting around it.

Leah's good-byes to Sadie were not nearly as emotional as Lydiann's tearful farewell. Poor Lyddie followed her all the way out to the sleigh, crying her name. Now she stood with nose pressed to the front window, watching Dat take Sadie up to the Nolts'. Dottie herself had surprised them by coming over, once the roads were plowed, to drop Mary Ruth and Carl by to visit Abe, who was still suffering headaches and frequent dizzy spells. Leah had made it a point to follow Dottie out the back door, where she had quickly shared the family's dilemma, taking care not to point fingers at the bishop. Surprisingly Dottie had taken to the idea with enthusiasm, and the arrangements had been made just that quickly. Sadie had crossly gone to pack her bags when Dat had okayed the plan.

Lydiann burst out sobbing to high heavens when she could no longer see the horse and sleigh moving down Georgetown Road. "Dat's takin' my big sister away from me!"

"Ach, don't cry so, Lyddie," said Leah, going and wrapping her arms around her. "Surely the bishop will let us visit Sadie now and then . . . help her get back on the straight and narrow. Surely he will."

"But you don't know that for sure . . . and she's goin' to Mary Ruth now . . . and Carl, too." Lydiann wept in Leah's arms. "Just when I was gettin' to know her. Just when . . ." She cried as if her heart might break.

Leah let Lydiann cling to her. "We can pray this will all work out for the best."

Lydiann leaned back and looked up at her with tear-filled eyes. "What do ya mean?"

"I 'spect I'll be talkin' to God 'bout all this," she whispered to her dear girl. "And you can, too."

Lydiann blinked her eyes and a slight frown crossed her brow. "I don't understand."

"There are times—like right now—when the Lord God wouldn't mind hearin' a prayer from our hearts. One we make up on our own, so to speak."

"Not the prayers we usually say in our heads, then? The ones we think of at dinnertime and before bed?"

"That's just what I'm tellin' you. There are times when, if ya feel as if your heart's breaking, 'tis best to call on the Lord and say what's on your mind."

Lydiann burst into a smile just then and pressed against her, hugging her hard. "I'll just do that, Mamma. I will!"

And deep within herself, Leah knew she, too, must be offering similar prayers more often.

Mary Ruth cried when she saw Sadie standing at the front door. She hurried to greet her sister, and the two fell into each other's arms. "Oh, Sadie, I'm so sorry."

"Ain't your fault," Sadie whimpered. " 'Tis all my doin'. I deserve this . . . I know I do."

Mary Ruth led her upstairs and showed her where she could put her clothes for the time being, saying that Dottie had offered more storage space in a seasonal closet down the hall. "You'll be ever so comfortable here," she said. "You'll see."

Sadie sat on the bed, looking all around. "Mercy sakes, I've never seen such a perty bedroom." Then she smiled a little. "Well, now, how could I, since I've never been inside an Englisher's bedroom before now?"

Mary Ruth didn't want to tell Sadie that it wouldn't take too long and she'd become adjusted to the warmth of the rooms each morning, not to mention the indoor bathroom and other luxuries. But such modern conveniences were not good enough reason to leave Amish life behind. "I'm glad you'll be stayin' here," she said, going to sit next to Sadie on the bed. "Maybe we'll get caught up some now."

Sadie nodded sadly. "Denki, Mary Ruth, for sharin' your room and all."

"I'm glad to do it." She hoped to share more than just the room. Given the time, Mary Ruth was eager to share the Lord Jesus with Sadie, as well.

Dat was a late riser that Saturday, so Leah went to his door and knocked lightly. "Dat? It's Leah . . . are you awake yet?"

"Jah, come in" was his reply.

Feeling right peculiar at his response, she did as she was told. She saw him sitting in the corner of the room near the gas lamp, Mamma's open Bible on his lap. "Leah," he said, "do you happen to know, by chance, when your mamma started markin' up this here Bible?"

A breath caught in her throat, and she saw then that tears filled his eyes. "It was some years ago . . . long before Lydiann was born."

A nearly reverent hush passed between them.

"Are ya certain?" Dat asked.

She nodded her head. "Mamma loved to read God's Word." She hoped she wasn't speaking out of turn, recalling the quiet tones in which Mamma had spoken on the several occasions she and Leah had discussed such matters.

"I awakened at midnight," Dat said. "The wind . . . or maybe it was the Lord God, woke me out of a deep sleep. I've been sittin' here reading near every underlined passage in this here *Biewel* . . . two or three times each."

Leah stood silently, staring at her father.

Dat placed one hand gently on the open pages. "I have to admit that I think I know why your mamma walked the floor nearly ev'ry night, prayin' over her children . . . and me. Jah, believe I do. . . ." His voice faltered.

Leah knew, as well, but she yearned to hear Dat say it, wanting to know if he truly understood just what it was that put a near-holy smile on Mamma's face each and every day.

"Ida grasped the most important things about God. She understood them . . . and she lived them, ain't so?"

Leah nodded. "Oh, Dat, she did that."

He closed the Bible and placed both hands on top. "I want what my precious Ida had. How should I go 'bout getting it?"

Leah glanced over her shoulder, wondering if either Lydiann or Abe had come downstairs yet. "The best I know to tell ya is to do what I did . . . open your heart wide to the Lord Jesus." She wouldn't reveal at this moment that she'd nearly memorized some of the passages in Mamma's Bible.

"The Good Book says to come to Him as a little child," Dat said, wiping his eyes.

Leah felt a lump rise in her throat. "I should say so" was all she could whisper for her joy.

Once the milking and breakfast were finished, Abram wasted no time. He found Lizzie in the small kitchen of the Dawdi Haus.

" 'Tis a brisk mornin', but I'd like to take ya out for some fresh air and maybe a sticky bun," he said quietly, lest her father overhear their conversation from the front room. "How'd that be?"

Her pretty hazel eyes lit up like it was Christmas all over again. "Can ya first spare me a half hour?"

Too eagerly, he bobbed his head. "I'll get the horse hitched up and come for ya right quick."

She beamed her interest, and he headed back through the

tiny front room, where John was starting to snore—or pretending to.

This was no time to give in to his emotions, yet Abram longed to reach for Lizzie's hand as they rode along in the privacy of the family buggy. His heart pounded at the idea, and it was all he could do to redirect his thoughts. Yet the woman he had come to love was sitting next to him, and they were alone, under heaven's canopy.

They talked of Sadie's pitiless ousting by the bishop, and Lizzie pointed out that Sadie had seemed to purposely go beyond the boundaries of the Proving. "Wouldn't ya say so, Abram?"

"Jah, I agree on that, though I don't see it as out-and-out rebellion." He went on to share how troubled he was by their bishop. "It's one thing after 'nother, seems. I almost wonder if Bontrager has it in for me and my household."

Lizzie nodded, stirring as she sat next to him in the carriage. "Dear Sadie's bound to be doubly dejected about now, still mournin' her dead husband and all."

If Abram didn't control himself, he might simply allow the horse to trot along, let go the reins, and take this outspoken but dear woman in his arms right now in broad daylight. And, goodness, wouldn't that be a telling picture if someone came riding along in the opposite direction?

For a fleeting second, he wished he were a young fellow once again and he and his sweetheart-girl were out riding under the covering of night. No wonder young folk courted after sundown. Made plenty of good sense to him, now that the tables were turned and he was the one falling in love . . . for the second time.

But first things first. "Lizzie?" His voice cracked as he held tight the reins.

"Jah, Abram?"

"I want to tell ya 'bout what happened to me this morning while I was readin' Ida's Bible." He found it mighty easy to pour out his heart to his deceased wife's devout younger sister. "I believe I've seen the light . . . a long time comin', I daresay."

He knew Lizzie understood what he meant when she gave him the sweetest smile he'd seen in recent memory. "Ach, 'tis true. I see Jesus in your eyes."

He nodded, eyes filling quickly with tears. "I've resisted much too long, sorry to say. I 'spect heaven's pursuit of me has the Lord himself near tuckered out."

Her soft laugh encouraged him greatly. "I guess you can say you've joined the ranks of the silent believers, ain't so?"

"There ain't a doubtful bone in my body."

"Thank the Lord above," she said.

"Jah, the Lord sought me out, indeed." He drew in a long breath, because what he planned to say next was definitely going to be more difficult. "I've been thinking 'bout something else, too, for quite some time."

Will she welcome this news? he wondered, becoming more hesitant now that he realized how far out he was about to stick his neck. No question, the thought of her rejecting him would do him in. Should he forge ahead?

It was then she surprised him and reached over and placed her hand on his. " 'Tis all right, Abram. Say what's on your mind."

Caressing her hand, he turned to face her. "Lizzie, my dear, I'm head over heels in love with ya."

Her smile was even brighter than before.

He didn't waste any time. "Oh, ya just don't know how awful much. . . ."

They rode along for another good half hour, but before they came to the turnoff to the Ebersol Cottage, Abram asked with confidence, "Will ya accept me as your husband?"

"'Course I will, Abram. I'd be right happy to." Lizzie didn't shilly-shally one bit. By the look on her face, it was evident Lizzie knew, just as he did, that they were meant to be together as husband and wife as soon as possible.

He lifted her small hand to his lips and planted a kiss there, not caring at all now who spied them.

Glory be! Lizzie felt as if she might take off flying, so happy she was as she headed into the Dawdi Haus. "Dat, I've got somethin' to tell ya," she called to her father, who was still snoozing in his favorite chair.

He roused momentarily, eyebrows raising, then eyelids flitting shut.

"No, no, now—stay awake to listen to your maidel daughter," she said, crouching near his knee. "I've got me a beau, Dat: Abram Ebersol, your own son-in-law. Now, what do ya think of that?" She watched his expression closely. How would he take his Ida's being replaced by her sister?

Hearing Abram's name must have awakened him, for now her father was all eyes. "Well, now, what did you say?"

"You heard me, didn't ya? And you're the first to know

something else . . . I'm gettin' married here 'fore too long." She could scarcely keep her voice at a whisper, where it needed to be, at least for now.

An endearing smile spread across her father's craggy face. "Ah, Lizzie . . . my dear girl. I'm mighty glad to hear it." He paused before saying, "I guess I'm not too surprised, really. I've been wonderin' if the old fella wasn't sweet on you."

"So, then, you're all right with it? You can give us your blessing?"

He chuckled—it was a quick little cackle, almost gleeful. "Aw, go on. You's don't need my approval. You're old enough to make up your own minds, for goodness' sake!"

Leaning over, she kissed his rough cheek. "I'm ever so happy . . . really I am."

"Happiness is short-lived, I daresay, so make the most of it while ya can." He was grinning now, and he reached for her hand and squeezed it.

"I just wish my mother had lived to see this day."

He nodded. "It's natural you'd be thinkin' thataway."

She rose and headed for the kitchen, where she set to brewing a nice big kettle of tea—a kind of celebratory pot to be shared between her elderly Dat and herself. *Truly, I've never been so happy!*

Chapter Sixteen

Time dragged. Lydiann watched the minute hand move toward the numeral twelve, ever so anxious for ten-o'clock recess to come this bright and snowy Monday. She knew Carl had some seatwork to complete before he would be allowed to play, so she'd volunteered to help redd up the cloakroom while he worked at his desk and the teacher was outdoors supervising the rest of the children.

At last it was time, and the teacher reminded some of the younger pupils to sharpen pencils and visit the outhouse. When Lydiann got the go-ahead to sweep the cloakroom, she was glad. Once all the children had filed out to recess, she took the broom from the hook and hurriedly swept the dirt from the floor, scooped it up into the dustpan, and dumped it into the trash can near the teacher's desk. That done, she tiptoed over to Carl's desk, where he was dawdling with his pencil, not working his problems.

"Did ya get behind in arithmetic?" she asked.

"A little."

"But you ain't doin' what you're s'posed to, are ya?"

He pulled a face and then put down his pencil. "What're *you* doing inside during recess, anyway?"

"Got somethin' to ask, that's all." She glanced toward the door, hoping none of the other pupils would come bursting in just then. "I've been wonderin'. Can you read Amish even though you don't speak it?"

His face turned red but he nodded. "I know it from my uncle Paul, the one who used to be Amish. He taught me to read Pennsylvania Dutch, which isn't, by the way, called Amish."

"Sure it is."

"No, that's only what Amish folk call it." He looked so determined, she decided to let him have the last word.

"Did your uncle ever join church?" she asked, more softly now.

"Nope. He bought himself a tractor instead."

"Oh." She thought on that. "Seems he must not have thought much of the Old Ways, then."

Carl shrugged. "Not when it comes to farming. Why waste all that time plowing, planting, and harvesting with horse-drawn wagons and whatnot when you can be done with it in short order with a tractor? Seems right silly to me."

"But tractors have inflatable tires, and that's a no-no."

Again he shook his head. "Rubber tires or steel tires, tractors or horses or mules. Isn't it all about getting the job done?"

"You'd have to talk to our bishop 'bout that."

"So you can't think for yourself?" Carl smiled faintly.

She pouted at that. "I've been wonderin' something else."

"What now?"

She didn't like his tone but pressed on. "What's it like bein' adopted?"

"You oughta know that."

"What do ya mean?"

"I don't want to speak out of turn, but aren't you and Abe adopted in a way? Mary Ruth says your real mamma died when Abe was born, so your sister Leah has raised you like you're her own."

Mary Ruth says . . .

Why was her sister's name so quick out of his mouth? Still, she thought on what he'd said till she got up the nerve to ask, "Do you know your true family at all?"

He stared at her. "That's a silly question and you know it, Lyddie. I'm living with my true family. It doesn't matter to me who my birth parents were."

"*Were?* Do ya mean your parents died?"

"I didn't say that."

She could see he was upset, even angry. "I'm sorry, Carl."

"No, I don't think you are." He got up and went to the cloakroom, where he threw on his coat and scarf and hurried outside, slamming the door behind him.

Now what have I done?

Not only had she poked her nose in Carl's life, but he would surely catch what-for since she'd kept him from completing his seatwork.

He's got every right to tattle on me, Lydiann thought, returning to the cloakroom to make sure there was not a speck of dirt on the floor.

The coffee shop in Apple Creek, Ohio, was jam-packed with customers, especially the back room, which was solely populated by Amishmen. Jonas made his way through the maze of tables toward his friend Lester Schlabach, who nodded his head when he caught sight of Jonas.

"Sounds like a crowded hen house in here," Jonas commented amidst the chatter.

Lester laughed. "You oughta come out for coffee more often . . . you'd get used to the racket mighty quick."

"S'pose so, but orders for hope chests keep me downright busy these days—almost more work than I can handle on my own. Must be plenty-a girls turnin' sixteen this year."

"Awful gut for the pocketbook, I'll bet."

Jonas agreed and motioned for the waitress. He ordered a pot of coffee and a raspberry sticky bun for each of them—his and Lester's favorite pastry—insisting today was his treat.

When the waitress had gone, Lester stroked his beard, pulling it into a point. "I saw in *The Budget* that Eli Gingerich is goin' out of the plumbing business and is havin' himself a big sale here 'fore too long."

"I saw that, too. He wants to tear down some of his old shop and rebuild it to make a woodworking one."

"Some competition for ya?"

"Not a problem, really. Ain't enough woodworkers to go round here."

"That old bishop of yours back in Pennsylvania prob'ly wouldn't see eye to eye with ya though, ain't?"

Jonas looked hard at Lester and solemnly nodded his head. The mention of Bishop Bontrager reminded him again why he'd ended up living here in Ohio all these years, estranged from his parents and brothers and sisters. "Doubt I'd agree with much of what Bishop Bontrager thinks anymore."

"Seems to me I recall you sayin' he didn't take too kindly

to fellas who shunned farming."

Shunned. He supposed Lester had completely forgotten that he lived under the Bann himself, although it did not affect Jonas in his daily routine here. Nevertheless, he did have a family in Pennsylvania he missed terribly.

"My old bishop felt it was a fella's duty to follow in his father's footsteps and work the land. He took a mighty strong stand on that." *Among other things*, he thought. Shunning folk for leaving behind the church of their baptism was unheard of in Wayne County, far as he knew. "I wish my people back home could have a chance to sit under the teaching of the Apple Creek bishop. There was a wonderful-gut bishop like that in Millersburg, too," he said, recalling the short time he'd spent with the Mellinger family. It had been David Mellinger who had given him such a strong start in cabinetmaking with a valuable apprenticeship. "Those two Ohio bishops and my former bishop are the difference 'tween night and day, for sure and for certain."

Lester perked up his ears. "You mean to say your Pennsylvania family doesn't hear sermons like ours?"

"Well, it would be awful hard to know that anymore, really." It felt to him as if many decades had come and gone since his last visit to Lancaster County, back when he and Leah Ebersol were engaged and looking ahead to a happy and bright future together. He could only assume that Bishop Bontrager still kept the clamps on the People of Gobbler's Knob and Georgetown, but there was no way to be sure, since all communication had been cut off to him—and *from* him. He cared not to cause trouble for his parents and siblings, or his extended family and former friends, by attempting to make forbidden contact. *What's done is done.*

He hadn't planned to, but he began to tell his new friend how he had a whole batch of siblings, some of whom were grown and probably married by now. "My youngest brother and sister will be ten years old come this April."

"Twins?"

"Jah, and I haven't seen them since they were babies."

"How odd . . . them havin' a big brother they've never known."

Sadly he agreed. But there was nothing he could do about any of that. With the blessing of the heavenly Father and the People here, he'd put his roots down deeply and joyfully in Apple Creek. What more could a man want?

It was a brutally cold afternoon when Mary Ruth suggested she and Sadie go and sit near the fireplace in the Nolts' well-decorated front room. Sadie politely accepted the cup of hot peppermint tea her sister offered, her sad eyes brightening when Carl came to kneel beside her, showing a drawing he'd made at school.

"That's awful perty," Sadie said.

Carl handed the picture to her. "It's for you . . . to keep."

"Well, how nice." Sadie stared down at the crayoned picture of a big brown horse and a small gray buggy. "This looks like the bishop's horse," Sadie said, holding it up for Mary Ruth to see.

"Well, I'm not so sure about that. Seems to me it might just be Dat's horse," Mary Ruth replied, studying the drawing.

Carl frowned. "How can you tell the difference when there are so many horses and buggies?"

"Oh, believe me, we know," Sadie laughed.

Mary Ruth nodded. "Same way an Amishman knows which straw hat belongs to him, even though dozens of hats might be lined up on a bench."

Carl asked about Amish farm life, and Sadie seemed eager to tell him about milking a cow by hand, feeding chickens, and pitching hay to the mules and horses. "Sometime you should talk to Leah 'bout all that," she said. "She knows all there is to know about farm animals."

Mary Ruth found herself daydreaming about next Friday evening, when Robert planned to drive her to Honey Brook, where they would dine at a "very fine restaurant." A tingle of excitement ran up her spine as she wondered if he would again say he loved her. If so, she wondered if it was the right time to say it back to him. Handsome as he was kind, Robert would make any girl's heart glad, yet he had chosen her, and the passage of time had proven that neither of them wanted to let anything prevent their hopes for the future—not even the past foolishness of her sister and Robert's younger brother. In any event, the likelihood of Sadie and Derek ever crossing paths again was quite slim.

She turned her attention back to Sadie and Carl, who were now sitting side by side on the hearth looking at a storybook. Sadie's voice was gentle and low, but the expression she gave to the phrases on the page impressed Mary Ruth so much she wondered if she might invite Sadie to come with her to school as a volunteer tomorrow. She could certainly put someone to work part-time helping with a few struggling pupils. *It might keep Sadie's mind off herself*, Mary Ruth thought. But then she worried that such a thing might put Sadie even more at risk with the Amish brethren, so she decided against it.

What's to become of her?

Sadie had confided to her just today she wouldn't be staying on at the Nolts', wanting to find work outside the Amish community, but Mary Ruth hoped that wouldn't happen, not when it would break the hearts anew of everyone in the Ebersol Cottage to see her leave them once more. If her time here lasted long enough, maybe Sadie might begin to understand more of God's plan for her life, perhaps through the simple Bible stories she was even now reading aloud.

Leah picked her way through the ice and snow to the barn to speak with Gid and Dat, leaving Abe alone at the table with his schoolwork. "I won't be long," she'd told him, rushing out the back door into the dusk.

In the stillness of the stable, she cautiously asked Dat's and Gid's permission to pay a short visit to Sadie tomorrow at the Nolts', telling them she wanted to encourage her to repent to the bishop for her misconduct. Leah also had something else on her mind, but she didn't go so far as to reveal that.

Dat looked at Gid and asked, "Have ya given any more thought to what we discussed?"

Gid shook his head. "Haven't talked to the bishop just yet, no." He paused, glancing at Leah. "I'm the youngest preacher in the district and . . . well . . ." He didn't finish the thought, but Leah knew he must be hesitant to make waves with Bishop Bontrager.

Dat continued. "Well, I can see your point, but it's important we get our girl back home."

Gid nodded thoughtfully, but it was fairly obvious to Leah that he wasn't so keen on the idea, what with the bishop's tough stand on breaking the requirements of a Proving.

But Gid seemed to catch Leah's sense of urgency when she said she'd heard tell from Mary Ruth that Sadie was thinking of getting a job and moving closer to Strasburg.

"Sadie isn't *that* stubborn, is she?" he asked.

"Jah," Leah replied. "But I daresay she's not thinkin' clearly yet . . . still distraught over losin' her husband so awful young."

Gid put down his pitchfork. "I'll go 'n' talk things over with the bishop and see what can be done."

"You're headin' over there *now*?" Dat sounded mighty surprised.

"Time's a-wastin'." Gid looked right at Leah and smiled. "Wouldn't it be mighty nice if this family came together once and for all?"

Leah felt joy in her heart at his words. But would he actually succeed in getting the bishop to change his mind?

After enjoying Dottie's delicious crumb cake with applesauce, Mary Ruth and Sadie slipped away upstairs to the bedroom they now shared, where Mary Ruth offered to brush her sister's hair.

"Aw, you don't have to do that," Sadie said, seemingly touched by the gesture.

"But I want to." She coaxed Sadie to sit on the chair while she stood behind her, whispering a silent prayer.

"Ya know, Leah and I used to take turns brushin' each

other's hair of an evening," Sadie said softly, even sadly.

"We both have happy memories of growing up in Dat and Mamma's big house." Mary Ruth began making long sweeps down Sadie's golden locks with the brush.

Sadie nodded. "Ain't that the truth."

They talked about the endless winter, how cold it was, and how much Mary Ruth loved teaching school.

Out of the blue, Sadie asked, "When will Carl turn ten?"

"This spring."

She was silent for a moment, then—"Same age as my first little one . . ."

Mary Ruth's heart went out to her, and she wondered if being around Carl was an emotional hardship. "Do you find it difficult to be around Carl for that reason?"

"Oh no . . . not at all," she promptly reassured her. "My stay here has been delightful—hardly the punishment the bishop had planned for me. But even so, I need to find my own place and land myself a job."

"You'd really leave the Amish life behind?" Mary Ruth asked. "Is that what your heart's telling you?"

"Oh, I don't know what I want anymore. I can hardly abide the bishop and his rules—I just felt so locked up in Dat's house. There were plenty of days I wished I could hop in the buggy and drive off to Georgetown to run errands or whatnot. And now look where I am. Like a person without a home."

Mary Ruth felt now was the moment to share one of her favorite Scripture passages with Sadie. "I've been wanting to tell you something that's helped me a lot during some of my darkest hours," she said, not waiting for her sister to respond. "It's from the Proverbs: 'Trust in the Lord with all thine heart;

and lean not unto thine own understanding. In all thy ways acknowledge him, and he shall direct thy paths.'"

Sadie turned to face her, chin quivering. "I've heard those verses before."

"Do you remember where?"

Sadie nodded. "From Mamma. She used to recite Scripture while we cooked and baked together. I always wondered, though, why some of her favorite Bible verses weren't ever read at Preachin' service."

"I wondered that, too."

"Out in the Ohio church—and later in Indiana—the preachers stressed different verses than they do here at home."

Mary Ruth listened with interest and then told how terribly she'd struggled at Elias Stoltzfus's funeral and how she'd finally found what she had longed for her whole life at a Mennonite church, not so many days following his death.

"If it's divine guidance you're looking for, Sadie, it can be found in God's holy book." She went to her dresser and picked up the black leather Bible Dottie had given her as a gift. "Everything I need to live my life each day is right here." She held the Bible close. "Sometimes I think I could simply read it instead of eating. That's how dear it is to me."

"Oh, Mary Ruth, bless your heart, you're cryin'." Sadie reached out her hand.

"They're joyful tears," Mary Ruth confessed with a warm smile. *Sadie's opening her heart*, she thought, full of thanksgiving.

Chapter Seventeen

Leah awakened in the morning to the sound of fussing coming from Abe's bedroom. Quickly she scurried into her slippers and made her way down the hallway. When she looked in on Abe, he was all tangled up in his bedclothes, struggling to get loose. "Mamma, Mamma!" he was crying. "The room's spinnin' round and I'm stuck. I have to get out of bed."

Panic seized her heart and she sat down with him. "There, now, lie back, Abe. I'm here . . . just rest." She stroked his forehead gently, her other hand on his chest. His heart was pounding nearly out of his rib cage, and he was breathing ever so fast. "You'll be all right now. Take longer breaths . . . that's right. Jah."

Whatever had caused him so much turmoil this morning? She couldn't imagine, nevertheless she stayed right there with him till he quieted down enough to fall back to sleep.

He's exhausted, she thought, straightening the sheet and blankets, taking care not to awaken him. Dr. Schwartz had kindly suggested she bring Abe in for yet another checkup, and now she was determined to do so . . . as soon as she felt comfortable taking him out in this cold weather.

She hurried back to her bedroom to dress, setting forth on her daily routine. Once her hair was twisted tightly on both sides and the low bun at her neck was secure, she put on her head covering and went to her hope chest at the foot of her bed. There she located Sadie's delicate butterfly handkerchief.

She truly hoped she wasn't making a mistake in taking it to her sister today. Ever since Sadie's confession, Leah had pondered the past—Sadie's and her secret keeping. The whole kettle of secrets had brought a world of hurt. Yet looking fondly now at the pretty handkerchief, she couldn't be sure how Sadie would respond to receiving this physical memory of her first dear baby's birth.

Is this the right time, Lord?

Two hours before she was to arrive at the clinic for work, Leah could hardly wait to head off on foot to see Sadie. A growing urgency to forgive compelled her along as her boots plodded through the snow. She felt she was carrying an unnecessary burden, and it was time to do what she knew she must—what she longed to do.

When Sadie flung wide the front door, Leah blurted, "Ach, sister, I just had to come see ya."

Sadie's eyes narrowed and a brief frown creased her brow. "Come in, come in," she said after a moment, nearly pulling Leah inside. "Here, let me take your wraps and mittens."

"Denki, but I shouldn't be long." She sighed, hurrying into the front room, following Sadie. "I miss ya so much," she said.

Sadie's pretty eyes shimmered with tears. "Oh, Leah . . ." Sadie reached for her hand.

"I've come to say something else, too"—Leah struggled to continue—"something that has been brewin' in my heart."

Sitting next to her on the settee, Sadie said, with trembling lower lip. "I'm awful sorry for what I did against you and Jonas, honestly I am. I don't deserve your forgiveness, Leah. It was plain awful to hurt you the way I did. The letter I took belonged to Jonas. . . ." Her apology trailed away into a sniffle.

When at last Leah was able to speak, her voice sounded thin to her own ears. "Oh, Sadie, I *do* forgive you . . . I do. I came here to set things right 'tween us."

At this Sadie seemed overwhelmed, her eyes welling up with tears. Leah drew her near, and they embraced with fond sisterly affection.

When they broke free, Leah was at a loss to know what to say. Second-guessing her plans to show Sadie the butterfly hankie, she wondered, *Is this really the best time? Will it open new wounds for her?*

Still searching for words, Leah said quickly, "Lydiann wanted me to tell ya hullo."

Sadie sighed. "And you say the same back for me, won't ya?"

" 'Course I will." Leah sat tall and straight—uncomfortably so. "And I'm hopin' you'll think of askin' the bishop to forgive ya . . . soon, maybe?"

Sadie hesitated, and Leah feared she'd perhaps spoken out of turn. "I know 'tis an awful trying thing," Leah said.

Sadie nodded, and her words were soft and labored as she spoke. "I've heard tell—best not say from whom—that the brethren may be payin' me a visit."

Leah's heart rose at the thought. Gid's meeting with the bishop had accomplished *something*.

Sadie folded her hands. "Not so sure what I'll do 'bout it."

"What do ya mean?"

"I daresay I don't deserve a second chance . . . if that's what the ministers are thinkin'."

Leah faced her. "Well, you surely didn't mean to get yourself in such a pickle, did ya?"

"Frankly, I don't know what came over me, wantin' to meander away from the house like that." Sadie paused. "I never should've lied to you."

"This has all been so hard on you," Leah replied. "It'll be all right. You'll see."

Sadie drew in a deep breath. "I thought comin' home would be easy somehow, but . . . oh, Leah, the memories are everywhere for me. I thought they were buried in the past, but . . ." She nearly gasped. "Being here, I still think of my first baby ever so often. Is that so wrong?" Sadie wept softly now, but her gaze held Leah's, as if a newfound trust was developing between them.

It is time, Leah thought hopefully. Touching Sadie's hand gently, Leah reached under her black apron. "I'm hopin' what I have here might help make ya feel some better." She took from her dress pocket a handkerchief. "I thought you might want to have this back," she whispered, holding it up.

"Goodness me," said Sadie, obviously recognizing the cutwork embroidered butterfly. "Isn't this . . . ?"

Leah nodded.

Raising the white cotton hankie to her face, Sadie brushed it against her cheek. "Where on earth did ya find it?"

"On the sidewalk leading to Dr. Schwartz's clinic."

"How'd it get *there?*" Sadie asked, appearing startled.

"I wondered that, too, but it looks as if Dr. Schwartz simply forgot to return it followin' the night of your baby's . . ." There was no need to go on.

Sadie fingered the handkerchief lovingly. "Thank you ever so much, Leah. 'Tis the closest thing on earth to my wee son."

Leah was moved by Sadie's response, and she wished she'd returned the hankie sooner—perhaps upon Sadie's return home last fall. *Still, she's happy to have it now, and that's what matters.*

Minutes later Dottie came in carrying a tray of goodies and hot cocoa. Leah rose and offered to help serve her sister. "No, that's all right. This is what I love to do," said Dottie, setting the large tray on a table near the settee.

"Thank you," Leah said.

"Jah, this'll hit the spot," Sadie added, the handkerchief laid out on her lap.

Dottie pointed to the hankie, a bright look of recognition in her eyes. "Well, now, that looks exactly like the embroidered hankie an acquaintance of mine had and lost."

Leah felt herself frown, but it was Sadie who spoke up. "Here, have a careful look-see," she offered, holding the handkerchief up for Dottie to inspect. "I have a feelin' you must be mistaken, 'cause if you'll look closely you'll see that this is one of a kind. Hannah made it especially for my sixteenth birthday."

Dottie touched the edges of the emerald green butterfly. "No, I'm quite sure I've seen this before today . . . or one exactly like it."

Dottie was so unyielding that for a moment Leah wanted

to ask where she thought she'd seen it, but then they got to talking about the stitching and how Hannah must have a very steady hand to create such beauty.

"Fannie Mast pointed out some of the same lovely features on the butterfly hankie she had. A gift to her," Dottie said matter-of-factly.

Leah's eyes locked with hers. "Fannie, ya say?"

Dottie nodded. "She's an Amishwoman with a set of boy-girl twins the same age as our Carl. Fannie had a hankie like this with her one day. I couldn't help noticing it when she was sitting in the waiting room at Dr. Schwartz's clinic with her twins, just as I was with Carl. We talked quite a lot, exchanged names, and got along famously, I must say." Here she laughed a little, and then she told how she and Fannie had seen each other several other times since. "I purchased a bushel of apples from the Mast orchard this past fall. Real nice folk, they are."

Leah felt slightly queasy hearing talk of her former beau's family.

"Did you say Fannie lost the handkerchief she had like this?" Sadie's question disturbed Leah's thoughts.

Dottie nodded, returning the handkerchief to Sadie. "Quite some time back."

"Well, there's only one like this, that's for sure," Sadie said pointedly.

For a fleeting moment, Leah wondered if this hankie *was* in fact Fannie's, especially since she'd found it lying on the sidewalk just outside the clinic door. Was it possible Cousin Fannie had dropped it on her way to a doctor visit? *How could that be?*

Yet the way Sadie was going on now with Dottie about

this absolutely being Hannah's handiwork, Leah dismissed the notion that there could be two identical hankies.

"God be with you, sister," Leah whispered as she hugged Sadie good-bye. She was relieved to note her sister's spirits had greatly improved.

Outside, though, Leah was unable to forget Dottie's self-assured remarks about the butterfly hankie. *No, I'm quite sure I've seen this before today*, Dottie had said.

Impossible, thought Leah as she headed around the corner to Dr. Schwartz's clinic.

There she began by sweeping and cleaning the floors, and then moved on to dusting the furniture in the waiting area.

After a time she stopped her work and went to see if Dr. Schwartz was in his office. Along with Dottie's supposed memory of that same handkerchief, Leah had also been struck by Sadie's renewed grief for her first baby, born in Aunt Lizzie's former log house on the hill.

Till now Leah had rejected the notion of approaching Dr. Schwartz again on the subject, but today's visit had made her certain it might help Sadie if she knew her baby was buried in the vacant lot below the Peacheys' farmland. Why else would Dr. Schwartz tend the tiny grave?

Another recent storm had blown piles of snow against the north side of the clinic, and she could see the tops of drifts at eye level out the doctor's lone office window as she waited in the doorway. "Mind if I come in?" she asked.

"You certainly may, Leah." He pushed up his glasses and

studied her for a moment. "How's Abe feeling now? Back to school?"

"Not just yet, but Lydiann brings home plenty of schoolwork to keep him out of mischief."

"And the dizzy spells, have they lessened some?"

"Not much just yet and it does worry me. He still has a bit of confusion when he gets to talkin', too."

The doctor's eyes narrowed and he removed his glasses. "Bring him in and I'll check him over for you. No charge." He went on to ask about the follow-up tests made at the hospital. "Anything show up there?"

"Nothin' alarming," she told him. "But he doesn't yet remember a stitch of what happened that day, and it clearly annoys him. His mind used to be ever so sharp."

Dr. Schwartz assured her that the symptoms should diminish over time. "I know it's difficult, but try to be patient and keep Abe as calm as you can."

Leah had to laugh. "Well, he's all boy, so that ain't an easy task." They exchanged small talk for a bit; then Leah decided to ask the thing plaguing her.

"I hesitate to bring this up, really," she began. "It's just that Sadie's strugglin' these days." She quickly explained as best she could something of the Proving requirements and the burden they placed on her sister. When she revealed that Sadie had temporarily moved in with the Nolts, he admitted to having already heard this news from his wife, Lorraine and Dottie having become good friends over the years.

"I hate to ask, but I wondered if it might not help Sadie somehow to know . . . well, ever since I stumbled onto a little grave on your property, I've wondered if, by chance, you might've buried Sadie's baby there."

He started at her words and his eyes squinted nearly shut. "What do you mean to imply?"

"I saw you clipping the grass in one small spot, tending to it, last spring."

The doctor rose suddenly. "You surely recall that your sister's baby was quite premature. You saw him yourself. There was simply no need for a burial."

"But . . . your car was parked nearby, and Lydiann and I saw you while we were walkin' back from Mamma's grave at the Amish cemetery."

His eyes avoided hers for a moment, and then he turned to face her. "What you saw was my attempt at dowsing for water." He indicated there was a small spring-fed pond on the same sweep of meadow—not to mention Blackbird Pond behind the smithy's property, not so far away—and he assumed there might be a well on his land. "And there is."

"But there *was* a grave . . . I know it, for sure and for certain, she insisted."

The telephone rang just then, jolting her nerves, and the doctor excused himself, wasting no time rushing off to the receptionist's desk.

Alone now, Leah thought again about what she had seen that warm day, but she was fairly sure the doctor had not been carrying a forked water-witching stick. No, he had been down on all fours, working close to the ground. Was it possible he had the ability to simply use his hand to dowse for water?

If that were true, neither she nor Aunt Lizzie would want her to be in the employ of someone who had such powers. But since she didn't know for certain just what the doctor had been doing, she ought not be too hasty in judging this man who had been ever so kind to her. Still, the way he'd stood up so suddenly, as if taken aback by her question—apparently anxious to answer the phone—made her shiver, even though the room was plenty warm compared to the frigid weather outdoors.

Chapter Eighteen

Sadie was truly astonished at Dat and Preacher Gid's unexpected visit two days after Leah's. The knock at the Nolts' door came midafternoon Friday, and she was thankful there was no one else in the house at the time.

Dat and Gid agreeably stepped inside when she opened the door and welcomed them, and her father got right to the point. "Our preacher, here, went to plead your case to the bishop this past week . . . and I'm mighty happy to tell ya, I believe his news to be ordained of the Lord God."

"What news?" she asked, eager to know.

Her father turned toward Gid and nodded his head, as if prompting him to reveal all. "Jah, 'tis true . . . it's something of a miracle, I'd have to say." He looked down at his black hat before continuing. "Seems the bishop's willin' to give ya another chance at the Proving, Sadie. But only if you come clean before the brethren."

Carefully she listened as Gid explained further. "The requirements will be even more rigid than before, and you must repent to three of the brethren—the bishop, one preacher, and a deacon."

Dat went on to say that all this must be agreed to before the new time of scrutiny would ever begin. If, and only if, Sadie agreed to adhere to this even stricter Proving, which was to be extended to the beginning of June, instead of to the middle of April, she could return home.

Sadie could scarcely believe her ears. "A longer Proving, ya say?"

"'Tis the price for disobedience."

She hung her head. "Jah, I was awful foolish."

Gid's face brightened, apparently heartened by her words. Dat, on the other hand, moved to her side, and she sensed his zeal for what he'd taken as an admission of her guilt.

"So embarrassing all this is," she said, her mouth dry as can be.

Dat's voice was thick with emotion when he said, "We'll welcome ya home with open arms . . . when the time comes."

She knew she could not now keep making offhand remarks about getting a job out in the world. Truly, she did not desire to leave her life with the People, even though her short time in a modern house *had* been warm and wonderful-good in many ways.

She reckoned Leah's return of the butterfly handkerchief to her to be a symbol of providence ahead. Something far beyond her was calling her back to the straight and narrow, where she felt she might find peace if she simply did not fail in following the Old Ways.

The heavy snowfall partially obscured Leah's view as she watched Dat and Gid from the kitchen window. The men cleared off the buried path to the woodshed, and then dug out the high drifts near the barn doors.

Soon here came Lydiann, piling on outdoor clothes, saying she was going out to help Dat "no matter how deep the snow," and with that was out the back door.

Red-cheeked Dat came in for some hot coffee after a while when Gid ran back up to his house for breakfast. With Lydiann still out in the snow, Leah and Dat found themselves alone in the toasty warm kitchen.

"I best be tellin' you first," he began.

Leah was struck by the radiance of his gray eyes, but she said not a word. "Somewhere along the way, I fell in love with Lizzie, and I plan to marry her come next Saturday." His gaze searched Leah's following this declaration. "I'm hopin' this won't come as a shock, nohow."

"I guess I'm not too surprised," she said, meaning it. "The twinkle in your eye for Aunt Lizzie has been perty obvious at times."

He nodded awkwardly as if there was much more he wanted to say.

"Goodness knows, I couldn't be happier for you two."

To this they both laughed. "Wanted you to know directly from me," Dat said, looking more serious again. "It'll affect you more than any of the others in the family, I 'spect."

She understood what he meant and held her breath as she waited for him to continue.

"Lydiann and Abe look to *you* as their mamma, which mustn't change a'tall because of this," Dat said. "You'll always be that to them. Wouldn't think of meddlin' with that, not one iota, and Lizzie agrees wholeheartedly."

She felt ever so grateful to this man who'd loved and sheltered her as his own during her growing-up years, just as she was now doing for his children. To think he was planning to marry Leah's own natural mother. "Aw, Dat, you'll be ever so happy with Lizzie," she found herself saying. "I know you will be."

There was a merry light in Dat's eyes. "I'm awful glad Lizzie and I don't have to wait till fall to say *our* vows."

"Like the young folk."

He chuckled and added, "Bein' an old widower ain't so bad when it comes to some things, jah?"

Leah went to the wood stove and poured him more coffee, and he sat by the fire drinking it silently. Meanwhile, she headed upstairs to awaken young Abe as joy flooded her heart. She felt she ought to pinch herself at the thought of Aunt Lizzie becoming Dat's wife. At last dear Lizzie would have a husband of her own!

Monday morning Leah hurried upstairs after making the pancake batter and while waiting for the griddle to heat up. Through his doorway, she spied Abe sitting on the edge of his bed, looking up at her with squinting eyes, as if his vision was still blurred. "It's me, Abe," she said, going to sit next to him.

"I'm awful mixed up," he whispered.

"That's all right. The doctors say you'll get better each day, jah?"

"No, I mean 'bout something else."

"Oh, what's that?"

He scratched his head, frowning to beat the band. "Just who's gonna be my mamma when Dat gets married again?"

She smiled and put her arm around him. Dat had announced the happy news to the rest of the family at suppertime last night. "Well, I am, silly. Who'd ya think?"

He shook his head. "I can't figure out how that can be. Won't Aunt Lizzie become my mother?"

She could see how confusing all this would be, even without the lingering effects of a traumatic blow to the head. "Let me tell you again all about the day you were born, Abe."

"Jah, I'm all ears for that."

He settled against her, and she let him relax that way as she shared the precious things Mamma had said, even prayed, over her beautiful baby boy as he was entering the world and she was leaving it for heaven. "Mamma must've surely prayed a special blessing over you at your birth," she told him. "By the sweet look on her face as she lay dying, I believe she did."

"Our mamma loved us, ain't so?"

Leah nodded. She would always think of his mamma as her own and felt sure she was smiling down on all of them as they looked ahead to the happy wedding day.

Monday, January 21
Dear Diary,

I feel as if I must write down my feelings or sink deeper into despondency. Abe doesn't seem to be getting better quickly enough to suit anyone. Leah was here to see Mimi again yesterday afternoon, and she admitted to still being most anxious about him. I've thought of asking Gid to call for the hex doctor one day when Dat and Leah are away from the house, maybe, to put an end to this misery for poor Abe. For Leah, too. I hate to think this, but I wonder if Dat's refusal to have the Amish doctor come hasn't been some sort of a curse on his only son. Yet Gid doesn't think so when I talk to him of this, though I can see he is as wide-eyed with worry as the rest of us.

We've been awful careful not to discuss Abe's ailments in front of our girls. Even so, the notion young Abe will never be right disturbs me round the clock. Maybe all this never-ending worry comes from the baby blues I'm having something awful. I might just need a visit from the hex doctor myself. Oh, I just don't know, really. Mary Ruth seems to think I should throw myself on the mercy of the Lord God, but I honestly don't see how her "saving grace" can help me.

Poor Gid isn't in control of his own household . . . much less the household of faith. But I really can't lessen the amount of tears I shed, sometimes for no real reason at all . . . though I feel just terrible when Gid comes home to find me in a heap on the floor, sobbing while I hold tiny Mimi as Ida Mae and Katie Ann play. Is this what it feels like to lose one's mind, I wonder?

I must keep my tears in check for at least Dat and Lizzie's wedding. Gid's going to marry them in the front room at Dat's house. Since Dat's a widower and Lizzie, at age forty-five, is much older than most brides, this will be a small gathering of family and close friends.

Plenty of changes will take place in the Ebersol Cottage with this new marriage. Sadie has already returned home—on her best behavior and with the blessing of the bishop—and will move to the Dawdi Haus this next week to look after Dawdi John. Leah, of course, will stay put in the main house, because she is helping raise Lydiann and Abe, who will have had the love of three mothers in one lifetime.

Well, I best be tending to Mimi. Truly, her cries slice right through me—at times I am startled, even put out by my own flesh and blood. Whatever is wrong with me?

Respectfully,
Hannah

The deep cold made itself known in the crunching creak of work boots on hard-packed snow as farmers headed for the barnyard, or in the solid thump of horses' hooves on wintry roads. A stiff northern wind swayed the towering trees in Abram's backyard as Gid made his way into the lower level of the bank barn, ready to shovel out the manure and redd up the stable.

Still ringing in his ears was the sound of Mimi's crying into the wee hours of this morning, and he wondered why it was that Ida Mae and Katie Ann had been such easy babies for Hannah to tend to. He recalled Hannah had actually been cheerful when the older girls were but newborns.

Picking up the shovel, he set to work, beginning the smelly yet needful job. All the while, he couldn't get his wife's gloominess out of his mind. The joy of motherhood had flown out the window with the arrival of Mimi. Nearly all Hannah wanted to talk about these days was one worry after another, concerns that revisited her during the dark night hours in her increasingly frequent nightmares.

Gid shoveled all the harder, glad for the quiet of the barn, not looking forward to returning to the log house for lunch. Fact was, he was often tempted to slip in at Abram's table and enjoy the peace of his father-in-law's house and Leah's tidy kitchen, come noon. Naturally he had never succumbed, always heading up the long mule road to the cabin where he'd made a home with Hannah. It wasn't that he regretted his choice in a bride—Hannah had been his all in all, his everything, from the first day he'd invited her for a ride in his courting buggy. He just wished he could somehow lessen her emotional burden. Maybe tonight he'd offer to walk the floor with inconsolable and colicky Mimi, if necessary. A good night's sleep might be all Hannah needed, he thought. Either that or a visit from one of the hex doctors. *Jah, might just do all of us some good along about now, including young Abe.*

He would have to check with Abram on this first, of course, because Abram had not called for a sympathy healer when it had been most critical. What had made Abram change his mind on something he'd long held important? Would Abram, in fact, agree to set things right by having the hex doctor come and work his magic as should have been done in the first place?

Just today Hannah had pleaded with him to ride for the powwow doctor not but four miles away. "Have him calm Mimi down with his potions or chanting. And me, too!" she'd said.

He recalled how uneasy he'd felt around the older man, how he could hardly wait to send him packing once Hannah's baby was born safe and sound. Never in his life had he felt such a cold presence—like a blue haze draped over all of them in the room. He could remember only a handful of times as a boy being taken to visit the man with healing powers . . . and only by his father. Mamma would sooner have seen them all perish than summon the Hexedokder, he knew.

Thinking back on his breakfast conversation with flustered

Hannah, he wondered how she'd gotten to the place where she so strongly desired help from powwowing, especially since both her mother and Aunt Lizzie had resisted it.

That evening following supper, Gid offered to look after the girls. "Hannah, go 'n' rest a bit," he instructed, following her into the bedroom to make sure she did indeed lie down.

Hannah nodded, brushing tears away, and he pulled up a quilt to cover her, hoping she might be able to console herself in the silence of the room.

His wife had caused him alarm on plenty of other occasions—if the ministers knew the full extent of her suffering, just how would it set with them? The preacher's wife was to be an example, not a hindrance to the People, so Gid must see to it that Hannah was surrounded with joyful folk like Leah, Aunt Lizzie, and his own mother and sisters. There was plenty of support awaiting Hannah . . . and himself.

Meanwhile Gid had his first wedding to prepare for, and after morning milking tomorrow, he must pay another visit to the bishop about the procedure. The thought of yet another face-to-face talk with the man of God put a chill in his bones, especially after the grueling encounter he'd borne on behalf of Sadie, but there was no putting it off. Abram Ebersol was mighty eager to wed, and the bride-to-be was happily willing.

Chapter Nineteen

Leah heard Lizzie stirring next door in the Dawdi Haus midmorning Tuesday. She could see the top of her aunt's head near the cookstove in the cozy kitchen, where she found Lizzie leaning down to remove a large sheet of chocolate-chip cookies from the oven. On the way over, she'd noticed the front room was empty. *Dawdi John must be upstairs resting*, she decided.

"Oh, hullo," Aunt Lizzie said, noticing her right then.

Leah joined her as Lizzie sat at the table to scoop warm cookies from the cookie sheet with a spatula, carefully placing them to cool on brown paper. "They smell wonderful-gut," she said.

"Your father's favorite, ain't so?" Aunt Lizzie smiled broadly as she mentioned Dat.

Leah breathed in the tempting aroma. "I'll wait till they cool a bit before having a taste. But I'm having only one."

"Ach, goodness, you could stand to eat a whole handful." Lizzie eyed her curiously. "You ain't tryin' to lose weight, now, are ya?"

In all reality, Leah hadn't gained a single pound in more than ten years; she had been cutting her dress and apron patterns the exact same size since she was coming into her time of rumschpringe. "I just best not be eatin' more than one" was all she said.

"Some sugar will do ya gut," Aunt Lizzie pressed.

"Makes me droopy after a time, though." Leah supposed it did that way with many people. She'd noticed the same in Lydiann when she ate lots of cookies in one sitting or had too much cake or pie. Lydiann had a surge of energy—too much, really—and then she'd become whiny and worn out. The same wasn't true of Abe, though. Like Dawdi John, he could eat and eat desserts and never be bothered.

"We'll have plenty of goodies and pies and things for the wedding," Aunt Lizzie spoke up. "I've asked Miriam and your aunt Mary Ebersol to help with the baking."

Leah's ears perked up. "I didn't realize there would be more than just the immediate family invited."

Lizzie broke out in a wide smile. "Abram and I got to talkin' and we changed our minds 'bout that. Peacheys—Smitty and Miriam—will come, as well as most of your father's siblings. I've mailed handwritten invitations to my brother Noah and his wife, Becky, as well as all my siblings over in Hickory Hollow. We'll see who shows up." Suddenly her smile grew a bit cunning. "I even stuck my neck out and invited Peter and Fannie Mast."

"What on earth?" Leah couldn't believe her ears. "They'll never show their faces, ya know."

"No, prob'ly not. But we can keep extendin' the hand of friendship."

Leah wondered if her father had been in favor of this, but

she was more interested in something else. "Since most people don't know about you and me bein' mother and daughter, I've been wonderin' what we—Sadie, Hannah, and Mary Ruth—oughta call ya, once you and Dat are wed."

"Well, now, I'll always be Aunt Lizzie to you girls, I'm thinkin'. Lydiann and Abe, too, of course." Lizzie's eyes narrowed. "Did ya have something in mind?"

To this Leah had to smile. "I wondered if Dat might want us to call you Mamma, out of respect, maybe." She paused. "I doubt any of us would mind that, but . . ."

Lizzie patted her face. "Nothing much 'tween you and me or your sisters and me will change when I marry your father. There'll always be a shoulder to cry on and plenty of love to go round. No need to alter any of that, right?"

Leah could feel herself relax a bit; she had wanted to honor Lizzie as her father's new wife, yet she longed to keep separate the special place dear Mamma still held in her heart.

Hannah dropped off Ida Mae and Katie Ann at the Peacheys', eager to slip away from the house and go with Mimi to visit one of the hex doctors. She'd gotten to thinking that perhaps all her ceaseless worrying about everyone and everything was more *her* problem, really—something unique to her. She seemed to turn near all the little things in the life of her family, immediate and otherwise, into an overwhelming haystack of issues. As she had tried to rest last night between Mimi's bouts of colic, she couldn't stop thinking about wanting to fall asleep forever, never to wake up. She didn't know why she would think such a thing, when it would appear she had the kind of life any Amishwoman would envy—a handsome, kind, and loving husband and three beautiful little ones. So what was wrong?

Well, she was on her way to find out, and with baby Mimi tucked snugly in a makeshift cloth carryall next to her on the buggy seat. Hannah rode as fast as she could to the only woman powwow doctor in the area: Old Lady Henner, as old as Gobbler's Knob itself, some said.

Hannah's mental road map proved to be absolutely accurate, even though she had visited this doctor only one other time in her life. The place was a quiet and unassuming white three-room cottage, set back from the road and lined on either side by lilac bushes and other flowering shrubs, which, as she recalled, were always more abundant in blossoms than any others in the area come springtime.

She made her way up the short walkway and, holding her baby near, she rapped on the screen door, heart pounding as she did so. The elderly woman hobbled to within a few feet of the door and waved her in, not bothering to come and open it, almost as if she'd been expecting her.

"I hope it's all right to visit today," Hannah ventured.

"Come in, come in." The white-haired woman nodded. "What can I do for ya, Hannah?"

"I'm here for help with three ailments," she replied, thinking of the troubles of baby Miriam, herself, and her brother.

The nearly toothless woman gave a swift smile and peered into the small basket where Mimi, miraculously, was fast asleep. "Oh . . . you've brought your littlest one. Well, now, she looks something like your husband, ain't so?"

Hannah readily agreed. "She has Gid's eyes and hair."

"Ah, our youthful preacher . . ." The old woman looked at her, gray eyes cloudy, and Hannah wondered if she might be going blind. "This one's got herself a quick temper, and so awful young at that. Ain't that a big reason why you've come?"

Hannah removed Mimi from the basket. "I'd hoped Miriam wasn't a bad seed, so to speak. I'd hoped she simply had a long bout with the colic."

The old woman leaned hard on her gnarled walking stick and backed up and lowered herself into a rocking chair. "Now," she sighed, "give the wee babe to me."

Hannah lowered Mimi into the old woman's frail arms and lap. She wasn't exactly sure what Old Lady Henner began to softly utter while holding sweet, sleeping Mimi, but the short chant sounded mighty strange.

As she finished, the baby's eyes flew open, and Mimi reached her tiny hand up to the old woman's face and cooed contently.

"Now, then, Hannah, what can I do for you?"

Reaching down, Hannah picked up Mimi and placed her back in the basket, noticing how limp her daughter felt. Quickly she turned back to the old woman. "I'm afraid I have the mother fits, and there just ain't anything to stop 'em." She struggled with the lump in her throat. "Honestly I think I might be losin' my mind some days."

The old woman looked up at her. "I'll see to all of that. Don't you worry your perty little head." And Old Lady Henner motioned for Hannah to sit cross-legged at her feet.

Eager for relief from the gloom that tenaciously enveloped her, Hannah went willingly to the floor and sat like a child, closing her eyes.

When the chanting was through, Hannah felt so relaxed she wanted to stay sitting there, without budging an inch.

But Old Lady Henner was eager to move ahead to the

third ailment, so Hannah began to describe Abe's symptoms as best she could.

Then, for the longest time, the older woman squeezed her eyes shut, concentrating on something, her lips moving slowly . . . silently. After a while, though, she opened her eyes and shook her head, wearing a look of consternation. "Ach, I'm havin' me an awful time breakin' through for Abe, no matter how hard I try."

Hannah found this to be ever so peculiar, as she'd never heard of such a thing. Evidently Old Lady Henner's powers were fading with her age, but Hannah said not a word about that.

Abram swallowed his intense nervousness. He had never before thought of doing what he'd just done. The strongest urging had come to him—from the Lord God, he felt certain. "What do ya think of me placin' my hands on Abe's head to pray for him?" he'd asked Leah.

"For his healing, ya mean?" Leah's hazel eyes had shone.

He had nodded, reverently whispering the Scripture he'd committed to memory: "They shall lay hands on the sick, and they shall recover. . . ."

With Leah accompanying him, they had gone to Abe's room. There, Dat had knelt beside Abe's bed, placing his hands on his sleeping son, and fervently prayed, "O Lord God and heavenly Father, I come before you to ask for my son's healing, in the name of your Son, the Lord Jesus. . . ."

◆

It was Abe who broke the news to Leah, just as she was encouraging him to lie down for an afternoon rest, following the noon meal. She had been thinking about all the schoolwork Lydiann was gladly carrying home each day for her brother, worried the boy might never catch up, even a little fearful that he might lose a year and have to be held back. She doubted Dat would ever hear of such a thing, not for his bright-eyed and smart son, and she wouldn't let herself cross that bridge till the time came. Truth was, Abe was a determined sort of youngster. He'd not only survived the struggle of his own difficult birth, but he was pronounced to be "as healthy as they come" by Annie, the Amish midwife—something for which Leah was grateful each day.

"I can see better today," Abe told her as they headed up the stairs.

Leah noticed his speech was less garbled, too. "Of course, you're gettin' better. I knew you would." She followed him to his room and stood in the doorway, wanting to share with him what Adah had said in the hospital, that with God all things were possible. "Our heavenly Father's lookin' after you," she told him. "I've been askin' almighty God to heal you. Dat has, too."

He looked at her quizzically. "Ya talk to the Lord God 'bout me? 'Bout my hurt head?"

She couldn't help herself; he was such a dear boy. She rushed to his side and squeezed him good. "Of course I do. You're the apple of His eye, just as you are your earthly father's."

When she released him, he looked up at her, his eyes clearly focused. "God must care for me an awful lot."

"I'd have to say that's ever so true." She pulled back the quilt and top coverlet on his bed, and Abe climbed in, having just removed his shoes. "By takin' it easy and not complaining, I believe you're doin' your part. Now let the Lord do the rest."

He smiled up at her from beneath the blankets. "You're downright smart," he said. "I'm glad you're my mamma."

She leaned over and kissed his forehead gently. "Have a nice sleep now, ya hear?"

Tiptoeing out of the room, she smiled at Abe's sweet remark, ever so glad God had given her the opportunity to care for him and Lydiann. Glad, too, that Sadie was back home and would be on hand for Dat and Lizzie's wedding. She dearly hoped Hannah would be able to attend, as well—Leah was deeply concerned about her sister's present mental state.

Heading to the kitchen to begin preparing supper, she wondered if, like Hannah, Lorraine Schwartz might not also be a melancholy sort of person. There had been times when, upon entering a room, she'd discovered Lorraine's eyes red, a handkerchief in her hand. Leah's heart went out to her and Hannah both. It seemed to her there was much to be joyful about in life, but obviously Lorraine didn't see it that way, at least not since her younger son had forsaken his family. As for Hannah, she had every reason in the world to be happy.

Blushing a bit and wearing her new blue cape dress, Aunt Lizzie stood before Preacher Gid on Saturday morning with Dat near and looking sober yet happy in his clean black Sunday trousers and coat. The front room of the Ebersol Cottage was packed to the windowpanes with wedding guests. Leah watched and listened ever so closely, not wanting to miss a single word as Dat and Lizzie promised "nevermore to depart from each other," but to faithfully care for and cherish each other, till that time when the dear Lord God should separate them by death.

Leah sat between Sadie and Lydiann, glad to see such a large gathering of folk on hand to witness the wedding service, aware of the sunny faces of Dat's relatives and a good many of Lizzie's, too—most coming by horse and sleigh because the roads were packed with plenty of new snow. Sadie was all smiles today, too, a sight Leah hadn't seen in some time, although she and her sister had enjoyed a long heart-to-heart talk upon her return, when Sadie shared that she was going to see it through *this* Proving "no matter what. I won't disappoint my family—or God—this time." Glancing at her now, Leah reached for her dear sister's hand as the People began to sing in unison three wedding hymns from the *Ausbund*.

The one and only thing to cast a faint cloud over the day was the obvious absence of the Masts, though neither Leah nor Lizzie—nor Dat especially—had expected Mamma's cousins to grace them with their presence this day of days.

When the time came Bishop Bontrager rose and took Preacher Gid's spot before Dat and Lizzie. He placed his big hands over theirs and solemnly recited, "I say to you: the God of Abraham, Isaac, and Jacob be present with you and aid you and carry out His blessing abundantly upon you, through Jesus Christ. Amen."

They were pronounced husband and wife moments later, and Leah found herself thinking right then of the mother who'd raised her. *Oh, Mamma, if you're looking down on all of us now, surely you know how happy Dat is this wonderful-good day.*

Lydiann looked up at her, eyes glistening. "This holy moment is ever so special, ain't so?"

Reaching over, Leah clasped her darling girl's hand and nodded slightly. Lord willing, there were not too many more years before young Lyddie and Abe would also be standing before the brethren with the dear young man and woman of their choosing, waiting to say their lifelong vows before God and the People.

Jah, not so many years hence, thought Leah through joyful tears.

Part Two

◆ ◆ ◆ ◆

To appoint unto them that mourn in Zion,
to give unto them beauty for ashes,
the oil of joy for mourning,
the garment of praise for the spirit of heaviness;
that they might be called trees of righteousness,
the planting of the Lord, that he might be glorified.

—Isaiah 61:3

Chapter Twenty

Spring 1963

The sky was barely light and every bird in Gobbler's Knob was warming up for a grand daybreak chorus when Lydiann hurried downstairs, hoping to make it to the kitchen before either Mamma or Aunt Lizzie awakened. She wanted to surprise the family this morning with a great big breakfast, which she was planning to cook all by herself.

Ever since her sixteenth birthday last week, Lydiann had been planning the breakfast, this being the day before her first-ever Sunday singing. After all, if she met the right boy soon, it wouldn't be too many years from now she'd be cooking in her own kitchen. She and Mamma had been talking about this season of her life for quite some time now, Mamma encouraging her to simply "have fun during rumschpringe—get acquainted with plenty of nice fellas."

In other words, don't settle down too quickly with one boy and rush into getting serious.

Lydiann knew Mamma's intended message, all right. It was more than clear where she was going with her concerns. After all, having babies out of wedlock seemed to run in the family, and, well, she wasn't going to make such a mistake with *her* life. Mamma and Aunt Lizzie both had nothing at all to worry about, as she'd told them in so many words. Maybe more words than necessary, truly.

As for Dat, he wanted to get his say in, too, what with all his talk of "now, make sure Abe's the one to be takin' ya to the barn singing come Sunday night." Her first time at a singing was turning into a family concern—definitely not the way things were supposed to be.

Sighing, she contemplated all of this over the sizzling skillet, ready to pour fresh eggs and milk, mixed together and salted, into the pan. Naturally, once she did begin seeing different boys, coming home with them in their spanking-new courting buggies, not a soul under Dat's roof would be privy to anything at all. She just hoped she could tell the difference between a nice boy and one who wasn't so nice. Mamma had talked with her about some of the telltale signs to look for, one being about the way a young man looked at a girl.

She'd felt she had seen the right kind of look in Carl Nolt's eyes over the years, having attended the Georgetown School with him and all until two years ago, when she finished up eighth grade and came home to work alongside Mamma, Sadie, and Aunt Lizzie. Carl had long since forgiven her for her bold remarks about his adoption and happily gone off to high school, because there was no limit put on education by the Mennonites. She knew this from Mary Ruth, who was quite content to have married her preacher husband, Robert Schwartz, three years ago—a bride for the first time at the age of twenty-seven, of all things! The happy couple was living in a small rental house between Quarryville and Gobbler's Knob, and Mary Ruth was teaching Sunday school at the church where Robert was the associate minister, as well as conducting a weekly home-quilting class while waiting for their first baby, due in late October.

Setting the table and hearing footsteps in the bedroom directly above the kitchen, Lydiann was aware of Aunt Lizzie and Dat just getting up. She scurried about, hurrying the pace of her preparations, recalling as she worked how Dawdi John used to make hints about what a good Amish boy was supposed to look, sound, and act like . . . but that was more than a year ago, before he passed on to Glory. With only the memory of her wise grandfather to cherish, she hoped and prayed she might remember everything of utmost importance now that she was courting age and "ripe for the pickin'."

I do hope to have a wonderful-good time, she thought, looking ahead to tomorrow's singing, to be held near Grasshopper Level.

Abram rose out of a deep sleep, stumbling across the room toward his work clothes hanging on the wooden peg rack high on the wall. Such heavy slumbers—stupors, really—always hit him this time of year. He sensed it was going to be one of the warmest days of May thus far, with not a hint of a breeze coming in through the open windows. The dawn felt balmier than any in recent weeks.

Quickly dressing, he looked at Lizzie, still asleep. He grinned to himself and went over and poked her till she was awake. "I smell ham and eggs already." He chuckled, watching her drowsy face as she slowly opened one eye and then the other. "Best be gettin' up, or someone's gonna replace you as the breakfast cook," he teased, then leaned down and kissed the tip of her nose.

"I must've overslept," she said softly, stretching now.

He nodded. "And all well 'n' gut, since we had something of a late night, didn't we?"

"Oh, Abram." She sat up with a big smile on her pretty face, and then reached for the pillow as he backed away. She flung it straight at him anyway.

He tossed the pillow back and, when she caught it and leaned backward onto the bed, he hurried over to her and planted kisses all over her face. "Lizzie, Lizzie . . . look what you've gone and done to me. I feel like a young buck again." These years with his second wife had been joyful ones, despite a few ups and downs. He was altogether surprised they'd gotten along as well as they had, considering the many tiffs they'd had over the years they'd known each other. Lizzie, still his dear bride at fifty-one, kept him smiling, and he would have told almost any John Zook on the street how grateful he was to be so happily married at the ripe old age of fifty-nine.

Of course, there was more to happiness than being with someone who made you feel the way Lizzie did. If only Ida could see him now, she'd be amazed at his spiritual transformation, as well. *She'd be ever so joyful to see the answer to her many prayers*, he thought. Truth was, he and Lizzie were followers of the Lord Jesus in every respect, though they did not parade or air their beliefs. His own faith had helped him to accept Mary Ruth's choice of the Mennonite life . . . and husband. Sure, he wished she'd stayed Amish and married a good man right here amongst the People, but Mary Ruth and Robert delighted in walking with the Lord, adhering to the teachings of His Word, and holding firm to the assurance of salvation—all frowned upon by Bishop Bontrager and others in the Amish church here. Yet such strong faith could be found among the People, Abram's own having come about because of Ida, initially. Truly, the Holy Spirit had been at work in his life all those years.

With a lump in her throat and a sense of foreboding, Leah stood at the edge of the walkway, waving as thirteen-year-old Abe drove Lydiann to her first singing. She wasn't certain just how long she held up her hand in a somewhat motionless wave, but when the horse and carriage reached the end of the lane and made the turn west, she realized her arm was still high over her head. *Goodness me,* she thought, feeling like a persnickety mother hen at thirty-two, worrying her head over Lydiann. But she knew why she felt so hesitant about Lydiann entering the time of rumschpringe—her darling girl was almost too eager to meet boys and begin her courtship years.

Dear Lord, be with her always, Leah prayed, wondering if she might not just stand here and wait for Abe to return from his brotherly duty. Still, she did not wish to behave the way Aunt Lizzie had when Leah and her sisters were courting age, although she knew Lizzie had meant well. She refused to get too caught up in guessing who was seeing whom, even in jest. *I'll treat Lydiann with respect and trust, the way Mamma always did me,* she decided then and there.

Turning toward the house, she felt nearly exhausted. Without a word to either Sadie or Aunt Lizzie, she hurried through the kitchen and to the stairs. She had long since purchased her own Bible, not wanting to borrow Mamma's once Dat and Lizzie had begun to read aloud from it every day, as well as from the old German Bible downstairs in the kitchen.

The latter was still used for evening and morning family prayers, which, not surprisingly, Dat insisted on doing without fail.

In the quiet of her room, having moved back to her childhood bedroom years ago when Dat first married Aunt Lizzie, Leah settled into the chair near the window. Opening her Bible to Psalm Thirty-four, she read silently, *I sought the Lord, and he heard me, and delivered me from all my fears.*

Again she read the fourth verse, wanting to memorize it . . . realizing how essential it was for her to do so. *I must give Lydiann and her running-around years to you, Lord.* She made a conscious effort not to fret another minute from now until the wee hours, when Lydiann would be escorted home by her first beau, whoever that might be.

From where she was working in her little kitchen, Hannah couldn't hear everything being said in the front room, but she'd caught several words and sentences that almost made her wish she'd heard nothing at all. Gid and the bishop were talking about trading Gobbler's Knob young men for some in Ohio. She'd heard tell of switching boys between St. Joseph, Missouri, and places in Pennsylvania for the purpose of bringing fresh blood into the various Amish church districts, but never had she thought such a thing would happen here in Gobbler's Knob. All the same, she knew of several recent instances where babies had been born with severe physical or mental problems because of close intermarrying. As for her own healthy threesome, she and Gid both thanked the Good Lord daily for them, even though she wished she might conceive another child one day soon.

Just now, though, she wanted to inch forward and hear

what on earth Gid was helping the bishop plan for some poor, unsuspecting souls—more than a dozen fellows, is what she'd thought she had heard. But she resisted the temptation and set about making a cake for supper, glad that the girls were off at school and nowhere around to hear the kind of talk their preacher father was involved in. More and more, Gid was succumbing to Bishop Bontrager's spell. It was as if the bishop were God himself to Gid these days—no matter what the older man said, her husband seemed to go along with it. The strangest thing, really, especially since Gid had always been his own man when it came to opinions.

Mixing the flour, sugar, and baking powder for the cream cake and filling, Hannah contemplated what such a trade of men might have meant for her had Gid been offered such an adventure. A chill ran up her spine and she shook her head. "For pity's sake," she whispered.

When she heard the front door close—an altogether odd occurrence when everyone else entered by way of the back door—she kept busy with her cake and hoped Gid might wander out to chat with her. Much to her surprise, he did, though here lately he seemed to be refraining from any church talk with her.

"Makin' supper?" he asked, avoiding her eyes.

She nodded, not so eager to say a word, hoping he wouldn't realize she'd overheard bits and pieces.

"Bishop's downright worried," Gid said.

Not as worried as I am, she thought.

"He thinks what he wants to do might cause a real stir amongst the People." Gid went and stood by the back-door window overlooking the flower beds she and the girls had planted not too many weeks ago.

"Oh?"

Gid came right out and asked her, "Did ya happen to hear any of what we talked 'bout?"

"Only a little."

Gid turned and came to sit at the table, where he watched her blend together an egg, some cornstarch, and milk for the filling. "I can't stand up to him on anything," he admitted. "He has such a powerful way 'bout him. There's just no gettin' through to the man."

"The man of God," she said softly.

"Jah, exactly. How do ya deal with that?" He went on to say exactly what the bishop wanted to do: that he was mighty eager to bring new men into this close-knit community. By the time Gid finished, his hands were over his face, covering his eyes. "This'll bring such heartache to our families. I can't begin to say . . ."

She felt the pain for those boys Gid had just mentioned. "Sweethearts will be torn apart, too, no doubt."

"Jah, with all of them courtin'-age fellas." He rose and went into the front room again without saying another word.

'Tis an awful sad day for the People, Hannah decided then and there, knowing, if the bishop had made his choice, nothing could halt the course of those boys' lives.

An idea popped into her head just then, and she left her cake batter to hurry to Gid's side. "Why not make the tradin' something the boys could choose to do? Appeal to the adventuresome, maybe. Wouldn't that make much better sense than makin' it required?"

Gid was studying her face now, reaching out to embrace

her. "That's a wonderful-gut idea, Hannah. This may be just the answer!" He kissed her cheek and then released her to rush out the back door, no doubt hoping to catch up with the bishop.

Chapter Twenty-One

"That's a right perty sight," Sadie said as she and Abe rode together to market in nearby Bartville on the first day of summer. She motioned to the colorful arrangement of petunias around a large birdbath as they passed one farmhouse.

"Do ya know who lives there?" asked Abe, gawking over his shoulder as they passed.

"Somebody with a green thumb, that's who." She had to laugh, thinking about Aunt Lizzie's amazing talent for coaxing flowers of all colors and kinds to flourish under her tender care.

"*You've* got yourself a green thumb, Sadie."

"That's awful nice of you."

"Well, 'tis true." Abe grinned at her.

It was good of her brother to offer to ride along and help her sell the produce and other items today while Lydiann and Hannah's older girls, Ida Mae and Katie Ann, tended the roadside stand at home. "We'll bring in a gut amount of money for all our work today, Lord willin'."

Abe nodded and hopped down out of the buggy, going to tie up the horse.

Sometimes she couldn't get over the kind and generous helper Abe was. His accident on Blackbird Pond all those years back had worried everyone nearly sick, especially Hannah, but it was clear there was nothing at all wrong with him now.

Abe was quick to unload plenty of fresh-from-the-farm vegetables, including Swiss chard and snap peas. There were also baked goods, dried nuts, and homemade tartar sauce from Aunt Lizzie, along with pepper jam, corn relish, and hand-dipped candles from Leah. Hannah had sent along embroidered handkerchiefs and table linens, and Sadie had canned chowchow and home-cooked stews. Everyone had pitched in the past few days to make this Saturday market day an extra good one.

Sadie was glad they'd gotten themselves settled in long before customers began to arrive. She had always liked to get there well ahead of time, allowing ample opportunity to chat with other standholders, most of them farmers' daughters and wives.

Among the newcomers were several youth from the Grasshopper Level area. One in particular who seemed to hit it off with Abe was a tall and slender young man with dark hair several aisles over from them. Being an outgoing fellow, Abe had gone wandering up and down the rows during a few lulls in the normally steady stream of buyers, talking to nearly everyone at each of the produce tables. Sadie couldn't see if the dark-headed young man was tending his table alone, but she certainly heard his catching laughter and, in the midst of all the marketplace chatter, she thought she heard Abe's, as well.

This is good, she thought, having been a little concerned, along with Leah and Aunt Lizzie, that Abe had been spending far too much time with Carl Nolt rather than other Plain boys.

When the volume of customers picked up again, here came Abe once more, rushing back to help Sadie, taking charge of hand selling and making change. Between customers, Abe mentioned the young man across the way, saying he'd given Abe a homemade peppermint stick made by his twin sister.

"How interesting," Sadie said, lowering her voice so as not to be heard by anyone but Abe. "You might not know this, but Mary Ruth may be having twins come fall."

"Ya don't mean it." Abe laughed. "I might have both a nephew and a niece?"

"Or two of either," she replied.

"Ain't it 'bout time Dat had himself a grandson? Goodness knows how much he'd like that!"

Sadie thought yet again of Dat's one and only grandson thus far, gone to heaven sixteen long years ago. It still surprised her how often she thought of that wee boy, all shriveled and blue, never having made a single sound, not even a whimper. Yet she loved him, he and his stillborn half sisters . . . all being cared for in heaven by Mamma, Harvey, and Dawdi John. *And the angels, too*, she supposed, because Aunt Lizzie had always said God's ministering servants cared for the babies who went to Glory before their parents. "Jah, maybe Mary Ruth will give Dat a grandson or two," she replied, standing to greet the next customer.

"That'd be right nice," Abe replied.

When the end of the day came and it was time to say good-bye to the folk on either side of their table, Abe suggested Sadie go with him to meet his new friend. "No, that's all right. I don't have to meet all your friends, for goodness' sake," she said, feeling suddenly shy. Having observed from afar the way the two boys had gotten along, talking animatedly together, she didn't feel the need to barge in, and she told Abe so.

"But, Sadie, you'd like him. He's the nicest fella and downright easygoing." Abe motioned with his head, nearly insisting Sadie walk over there with him.

"All right, then," she agreed. "If ya do all the talkin'."

Abe said he would, and he led her to the almost empty long table. "This is my oldest sister, Sadie," Abe said. Then, turning to Sadie, he said, "Meet my friend Jacob."

The handsome teen reached out a firm hand and shook hers. "Hullo, Sadie. Most folks call me Jake."

She smiled, surprised by his relaxed manner, just as Abe had described. "Nice to meet you, Jake."

Grinning at them both, Jacob volunteered that his next-oldest and twin sisters had gone to Central Market in Lancaster today, so he'd offered to come tend to the table here. "Tending stand ain't what I do best, though," he said, the color rising in his face. "I'd much rather help my father in our apple orchard."

Suddenly, at that moment, everything clicked. *This must be Peter and Fannie Mast's boy*, she thought. If so, he was right now talking to the cousins his own father had chosen to shun. Well, she didn't dare spoil things for Abe—she simply acted as if she had innocently met an acquaintance of her brother's.

Yet all during the ride home, Sadie couldn't get Jake's

enormous dark eyes and his winning smile out of her mind. He reminded her of someone. A young man in the Millersburg, Ohio, church years ago, perhaps? And there was a certain resemblance to big brother Jonas, too. "Have ya ever met Jake before today?" she asked.

"Seems to me I did, maybe, quite a while back. But honestly, I can't remember where." Abe looked at her curiously. "Did you think you knew him from somewhere?"

She leaned back in the buggy seat, glad Abe held the reins to the horse. "Well, maybe so. Was it that obvious to you?"

He nodded, grinning. "You just were starin' at him," he admitted. "I felt a bit embarrassed, truth be known."

She didn't want to blurt out that they'd just run into Peter Mast's youngest son—at least she hadn't heard that Cousin Fannie had ever birthed more children after her fraternal boy-girl twins, but how would she know? Peter and Fannie had cut themselves off from the tiny world of Gobbler's Knob simply because the Abram Ebersol family lived there.

"I'd hate to embarrass my handsome little brother," she said, reaching up and touching his blond hair.

"Ach, keep your hands to yourself," he said playfully and clicked his tongue, urging the horse to a trot.

She laughed, glad to be heading home even as the memory of Jake's countenance stirred up bewildering feelings.

A nesting robin in the nearby maple tree sang with such clarity, Mary Ruth raised her head from the feather pillow, hearkening to its call. She was keenly aware this morning of the early bird's song, so anxious was she to greet the day. *This*

day! How long had it been since her last Sisters' Day? She had been passed over far too long, yet she understood and had no business questioning why Sadie and Leah—Hannah too—had not included her at Adah Peachey Ebersol's and others' homes for canning bees and work frolics. A lingering sadness had pricked her heart, though she'd never shared any of this with her husband, who now lay asleep next to her. It was obvious why she had been treated so in the past.

It had been years now since Gid had taken it upon himself to ask her to stop coming to his household's little log home. Naturally Dat had felt she had done wrong in leaving her Old Order Amish life behind, yet she knew there was no benefit in rethinking any of that, especially when she would never give up her precious beliefs. Still, she did feel like not only an outcast from the community of the People, but also somewhat estranged from her family—especially her twin. Hannah was not behind the decision by Gid, Mary Ruth was sure, for she often saw the look of sorrow in her sister's eyes when at the Ebersol Cottage, where she *was* permitted to visit with Hannah and the rest of her family. "Just never talk with Hannah alone," Gid had said privately, making things heartbreakingly clear that day so long ago.

So the invitation to attend Sisters' Day at Leah's best friend's place was something of a breakthrough, at least in Mary Ruth's mind. Her heart was gladdened at the thought of seeing her sisters and Aunt Lizzie all in the same kitchen working together.

Getting up quietly so as not to awaken Robert, she gently placed a hand on her stomach and walked downstairs to the kitchen, turning her thoughts to the baby, possibly more than one, growing inside her. She offered a prayer for the safe and normal development of this, their first little one. Or two. And she prayed she might be a cheerful blessing today as she attended the work frolic, sharing in all the talk that grown women—married and single alike—seemed able to prattle on about on such a fine late-June day.

As the sun was breaking over a dark string of trees, Lydiann hurried outside, barefoot and still wearing her night-clothes. She'd awakened with a hankering to spend some time with their new German-shepherd pups, especially sleek and pretty Boo, who reminded her quite a bit of their former dog Sassy. Lydiann sometimes still missed Blackie, King, and Sassy, who'd lived out their lifespans a few years before, but Dat had been eager for more dogs, so they'd purchased another two from Brother Gid.

Presently, Boo was making high-pitched sounds, the way some dogs did when a storm was brewing. Seemed to her that dogs could hear storms in the distance long before people—Dat had always said as much. It had to do with more than their keen hearing; perhaps they had a special sense for such things. From Boo's behavior, Lydiann was ever so sure there'd be a thunderstorm later that day. She just hoped the weather cooperated with her handsome beau's plans for them to meet down Georgetown Road in his open buggy. But knowing him, she was quite sure he'd have the forethought to bring along an umbrella, though if the weather was too bad, he simply wouldn't show up. He *had* thought ahead the last time they'd gone riding in his courting buggy, reaching down and pulling an umbrella out from beneath the front seat just before the first droplets of rain fell on them.

Oh, she could just pinch herself with all this happiness, having met such a wonderful boy at her first-ever Sunday singing back in May. It had been obvious he'd had no interest in any of the other girls that lovely evening. In fact, after her ride home in his open carriage that night, she hadn't really noticed any of the other boys at the following singings, although she was sure they were awful nice and fine looking, too. Already she and Jake had seen each other more times than she could count on one hand, which was quite frequent given that courting couples were really only supposed to see each other every other Sunday night at barn singings and the Saturday nights in between those—usually four times a month. But here it was only one month later and she'd nearly lost track of how many moonlit buggy rides they'd enjoyed.

She and Jake Mast had done a good job of keeping their budding romance hush-hush—difficult to do when many of the young people whispered behind each other's backs about who was seeing whom. But Jake and she were exceedingly cautious, and it was a good thing, too, since neither of them had ever dated and they were, as Dat would surely say, too young to settle down just yet. Of course, there was also the prickly matter that Jake's family had chosen to shun her family—Jake had overheard his older sister Becky telling someone exactly that. Just why this was, Lydiann had no idea, but she took comfort in Jake's emphatic determination to continue seeing her, no matter what. "We'll get my father's blessing in due time," he'd told her recently.

"There ya be, Boo," Lydiann said, discovering the noisy dog in the warm hay of the stable area, not but a few feet from one of the two milk cows, as if he thought he was a new calf.

"What on earth are you doin' whining and fussin' out here? Is a storm comin', do ya think?"

The pup looked up at her with kindly eyes as she knelt next to him, rubbing his neck under his ears. His eyes instantly glazed over as if with pleasure, and she smiled. "You're no help at all!" In a bit she got up and went in search of Brownie.

One of the mules neighed loudly as she moved through the lower level of the barn, which was already warming with the dawn of a new day. *It'll be a hot one today,* she decided, still searching for Mamma Leah's favorite of the two dogs. In fact, just last night Mamma had talked about what a gift of joy all their pets had been—both past and present. Secretly, though, Lydiann wondered if Mamma Leah didn't prefer cats to dogs now, since especially the barn kittens seemed ever so drawn to her.

When she finally located Brownie, he was standing up and pointing his nose toward the north like a living compass. She had to laugh, slapping her leg through her cotton nightgown and robe. "Come here," she said. "You're a silly one." But she knew she'd found her weather forecaster. "It is gonna storm today, ain't so?"

Brownie looked up at her as if he were smiling his answer. "I'll take along my shawl tonight, then . . . in case you're right," she said, deciding it was high time to hurry back to the house and dress for the day before Dat and Abe came trotting out to the barn for milking. What would they think if they found her in her nightclothes, of all things?

Chapter Twenty-Two

Of course I do," Leah answered when, following breakfast, Lydiann asked her if she remembered her own running-around years.

"Then, why are ya worried 'bout me, Mamma?"

Leah paused. Had she mistakenly given that impression to her dear girl, or was it actually true? Was she too concerned about all the nights Lydiann was leaving the house after dusk and returning home before dawn? *Too much like Sadie's wild days*, she had been thinking, hoping Lyddie hadn't met some English boy somewhere. She felt she ought to ask, though, just for good measure. "You're not seein' fancy boys, are ya?"

Lyddie's eyes grew wide at the question. "For goodness' sake, Mamma, what would give ya that idea?"

She didn't want to say she'd had a nagging feeling, but she did wonder how on earth Mamma had faced four daughters' times of rumschpringe. Truly, she felt sympathetic for any mother with a courting-age daughter.

"There are rules to be followed during the running-around years, Lyddie." She reached for her hand. "Spendin' time with a boy following Sunday singings is all well and good. But ya shouldn't see each other too often otherwise."

"But what does it hurt to see each other more than that?" The light of love, or something close to it, was evident on Lydiann's sweet face.

Leah's heart sank. *Just what I've worried about.* "Ach, dear one, I daresay you're a bit young to get serious."

Lyddie's brow knit into a frown. "But didn't you like a boy long before you were sixteen? Sadie told me so once when we were up in the high meadow last spring, gathering willow twigs to weave into wreaths." She stopped a moment. "I . . . I hope I'm not speakin' out of turn, Mamma. You fell in love when you were young, didn't ya?"

This moment Leah wondered why on earth she hadn't gone along to the pastureland when Sadie had invited her that day. What had she been thinking, allowing Lydiann to go off for hours alone with Sadie? She gathered herself, torn between her present feelings and what she knew she ought to be saying about all of this. It wasn't really Sadie's fault that such a sensitive topic had come up. Better Jonas and her romantic tale than for Sadie to have revealed hers with Derry Schwartz.

"Mamma, you all right?" Lydiann asked, staring at her.

"Oh sure, I'm fine. And about bein' in love and all . . . I'd have to say it was such a long time ago I've nearly forgotten." But she had not forgotten how much she'd loved Jonas . . . and how she'd felt the autumn day Sadie had revealed he was not the man her sister had married after all. Leah honestly believed she might never forget the bolt of shock that had ripped through her upon hearing the stunning news.

"Do ya remember how it felt when the first boy you ever

loved reached for your hand and held it for miles on end?" Lydiann's words were coated with honey, but it didn't make them any more pleasant for Leah to hear.

Lyddie and her beau are farther along than I thought. . . .

"Oh, Lydiann, I oughta remind ya to be ever so careful. Don't fall too quick, too soon."

"Fall?" Lyddie gasped. "You make it sound dangerous, Mamma. Don't ya trust me?"

Of course she did—she had believed in her heart that Lyddie was eager for romantic love, though perhaps not the kind that involved devotion and commitment to one person for a lifetime. Leah tried to explain the difference, saying all the things Mamma and Aunt Lizzie had told her back when *she* turned sixteen.

At one point Lydiann seemed a bit peeved, and Leah couldn't help but worry this time of courtship might cause a rift between herself and her girl. Well, she would move heaven and earth to make sure that didn't happen. If it meant stepping back and praying about it more, she'd do that. The fact Lydiann was willing and almost excited to discuss such things was a comfort, a reminder they indeed had as close a mother-daughter relationship now as always. Leah earnestly desired to preserve their good relationship until such a time as the two of them would become equals. More than anything, it was essential for her to keep the talk flowing. She must attempt to keep an open mind, as well—try to know and understand what Lydiann was thinking, if at all possible, even though the People expected the courting years to be secretive.

Just as their dogs had seemed to indicate earlier, the weather began to change around midafternoon, and a storm blew up. Lydiann watched the gale from her bedroom window, high on the second floor in what had been Hannah and Mary Ruth's bedroom when they were her age. She observed the storm whip the row of maples lining the pasture and lift and twirl the barnyard dust. A single bird flew for cover, heading home to the four-sided birdhouse Dat had erected.

Let nature get this out of her system, thought Lydiann, not happy about the prospect of meeting her beau in the midst of such a gust and rain. Surely, though, this fast-moving storm would pass by nightfall. She hoped so, because she wanted so much to ride next to him, talking into the wee hours. And who would've thought she'd like the first boy she'd ever spent time with. Well, that wasn't necessarily true, because she'd developed something of a crush on Carl Nolt a few years ago, and he on her, too. Discussing their differences, his being Mennonite and all, had made for several long walks between his house and hers, but no one in her family knew about them. She'd always felt she wouldn't be happy if she wasn't Amish, unlike Mary Ruth, who seemed to thrive in the Mennonite church.

But since Lydiann had met Jake, there had been very little space in her mind—or her heart—for Carl or for remembering fondly their school years together or his once-frequent visits. Truth was, Carl was the sort of fellow whom any girl might enjoy having as a kind of brother, but she couldn't imagine feeling about him the way she did about Jake, who was not only good-looking and fun-loving, but able to look at her with an expression that made her heart melt but good. She didn't know if falling in love was supposed to feel this way, but scarcely could she wait to ride through the night with Jake, eagerly listening to his voice, feeling secure and ever so happy while leaning her head on his shoulder, her heart nearly bursting.

If this blustery weather continues, Jake won't come for me, she thought sadly. They'd made this agreement early on since there was no way for him to contact her beforehand. So she sat down on her bed and prayed, asking the Lord God to bring a swift end to the wind and rain, dearly hoping she might see her beau this night.

The busyness of the Sisters' Day work frolic in Adah's kitchen was a welcome relief to Mary Ruth. Beginning at midmorning the group of women had gathered at Adah's to put up canned peas. She worked alongside her twin and ten-year-old Ida Mae, pleased to have this time with Hannah and her oldest girl. She listened intently as her sister shared some of her daughters' latest antics, all the while happily anticipating the sound of children in her own home.

"Katie Ann's been collectin' butterflies lately," Hannah said. "Gid and I can't figure out how she catches them without damaging their wings, but she does. And she's got herself quite a collection now."

Ida Mae nodded, her blue eyes smiling. "You oughta see it, Aunt Mary Ruth. Ach, I wish you could . . ."

By the sound of things, evidently young Ida Mae wished her auntie might be allowed to visit their home. Mary Ruth was drawn to Ida's demure face and strawberry blond hair. *So similar to Hannah's*, she thought, wondering whom *her* baby—

or babies—might favor in looks.

"I'll ask Dat if you can come up to the house after the frolic, maybe," said Ida Mae.

To this Hannah frowned quickly and changed the subject. "Where's Lydiann today?"

"Best be askin' Leah," said Mary Ruth. "I thought for sure she'd come, but she may be workin' with Dat."

"She sure seems to like workin' with the barn animals," Hannah replied. "She's a lot like Leah was at that age."

Mary Ruth hadn't thought of that before, but she could certainly see what Hannah meant. Lydiann did love the outdoors, and she liked working alongside Dat and Gid, too, though she hardly did so as often as Leah had.

"I, for one, am glad to keep my girls round the house, especially these summer months," Hannah said, smiling warmly at her Ida Mae as she reached for another jar.

"Not so much falls on your shoulders now, right?" Mary Ruth said.

Hannah nodded. "It's lots more fun, too, than when they're off at school all day long."

Feeling suddenly dizzy, Mary Ruth went to wash her hands at the sink, then stepped outdoors for a breath of fresh air.

Leah wished Lydiann had come along to the Sisters' Day work bee, but she hadn't pressed the issue. If Lyddie wanted to stay behind and help Dat in the barn and the fields, then so be it. Still, she couldn't help but think Lyddie was probably daydreaming about her beau again, though she mustn't let herself get caught up in anxiety over Lydiann's rumschpringe.

Long before Mamma had died, before she'd ever asked Leah to bring up Lydiann and Abe as her own, Leah had often contemplated notions of fate and a person's destiny, wondering if it was possible that a single spoken word or one misdeed could change the course of a person's future. She wasn't so sure about such farfetched youthful thoughts these days. All the same, the notion lingered in the back of her mind that she must step lightly where things of the heart were concerned.

She worked alongside Sadie, Adah, and Adah's younger sister, Dorcas, trying her best to think about other things. She was thankful when Dorcas began telling how her young sons had been going on "adventures," as she put it. "They're havin' themselves a great time roamin' the acres, goin' exploring. But yesterday Little Joe wandered off alone and, when he did finally come home, he said he'd found what looked to be a little grave."

Leah perked up her ears.

"Where on earth was it?" Sadie asked, looking quite surprised.

"Wasn't on Pop's property, that's for sure . . . it was south of us, a way over on that vacant lot. Honestly I think Little Joe must be dreamin' but gut."

Leah had sometimes wondered if someone else might also discover the grave one day. After all, it had been years and years since she and Jonas had first discovered what had then been a tiny mound, clearly trimmed of grass, although they were sure, at the time, that it was simply the well-tended plot of a beloved pet. But Dr. Schwartz had denied it was a grave altogether.

"Little Joe was both upset and confused, truth be told,"

Dorcas was saying. "He couldn't understand why the plot wasn't in the cemetery."

Sadie spoke up. "Best be tellin' Little Joe not to worry. No need to, really, is there?"

Dorcas shrugged her shoulders. "It bothered him . . . 'twas clear."

"Why's that, do ya think?" Hannah asked, having come over just in time to overhear the conversation.

"Not being in the cemetery, for one. And he said he saw flowers on it, like someone had just been there," replied Dorcas.

So Dr. Schwartz did lie to me when I asked, Leah thought, knowing he was the only one who knew the truth. In her heart, she knew she must approach him on this again; this time she would refuse to let him pull the wool over her eyes. *Dowsing for water, indeed!*

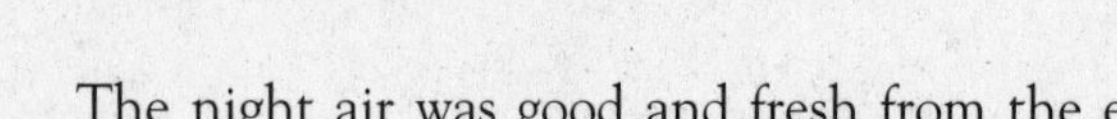

The night air was good and fresh from the earlier storm, and Lydiann was delighted to be sitting next to Jake in his open buggy. "I almost thought we might not see each other tonight, what with the rain 'n' all."

He looked at her, eyes smiling his pleasure. "I'm mighty glad it stopped, too."

They talked about the next singing and how his twin sister, Mandie, had been asking him who he was seeing. "But Mandie's easy to distract," he said, "what with her interested in a couple of boys. I think we can keep her from finding out about us till the time is right."

"Do ya know who the boys are?" she asked.

He bobbed his head. "I have an idea, but I could be wrong."

"Your twin sister mustn't want you to know her business, then?"

He laughed softly. "Ya might say that."

They rode quietly, passing a good many roadside vegetable stands, all of them cleared off for the night. "Ever notice how busy the roads get this time of year?" she said. "They're nearly a public marketplace during daylight hours."

"Well, jah, and isn't it gut for the Plain families up and down Georgetown Road?"

"I don't mind tendin' vegetable stand, but it does get awful hot out there of an afternoon. And there's never a lull, it seems."

"When you're my bride, I'll see to it you have a nice big awning over our roadside stand," he said.

Stunned, she wondered if she'd heard him right. Had he just said what she thought—that he hoped to marry her?

Jake turned to look at her, and then reached over to touch her face. "I didn't scare ya, did I, Lydiann?"

To be truthful, she had been a bit taken aback by his boldness. "My mamma would be concerned." She paused, thinking she needed to say more. "And . . . I think it's best we . . . well, be careful not to get too close, ya know."

He smiled. "I understand, Lyddie. But I want you to think 'bout us being together soon . . . getting married."

None of her family would be much in favor of their wedding anytime soon, particularly since she and Jake were both only sixteen.

"Don't ya think we oughta wait a while before sayin' our

vows?" she asked softly, trying to think the way Mamma would want her to right now.

"I knew when I first laid eyes on ya that you were the girl for me. If you feel the same way 'bout me, why should we wait?"

"I do like you, too, Jake. A lot," she replied, enjoying the nearness of him.

His smile returned. "Well, I happen to *love* you, Lydiann. And I want to marry you come wedding season."

She was further surprised by his outspoken announcement. "Ya mean, this year?"

"In five months . . . an eternity away, wouldn't you say?"

With them having come along this far in just one month, four more months of courting might seem like forever, especially if they kept taking so many nighttime buggy rides.

"This has all come up so quick," she whispered. "Mind if I think on it?"

"You've got yourself, say, ten minutes?" He was grinning to beat the band.

She knew he was teasing her now and was glad for the sweet smell left by the rain and the sounds of chirping insects as they rode under the stars and half moon. If she felt the way she did after such a short time as Jake's girlfriend, how on earth would she feel about him by November's wedding season? Deep in her heart, Lydiann was sure she knew the answer. She already loved him dearly, for sure and for certain.

Chapter Twenty-Three

"Your father says the bishop's got somethin' up his sleeve for some of the menfolk," Aunt Lizzie told Leah as they rolled out pie dough the day following the work frolic. They'd decided to use up the rhubarb on hand and make a dozen strawberry-rhubarb pies to be served at the common meal following Preaching service tomorrow at Jesse Ebersol's house.

"Oh?"

"An unusual plan, really . . . to help bring new blood into our community. And it doesn't seem to be a big secret. At least Abram didn't say it was."

Leah couldn't believe her ears when she heard what was supposed to happen before the harvest—young men from Lancaster County were being swapped with a few from Holmes County, Ohio. "This sounds outlandish. Who'd ever think of goin' along with it?"

Aunt Lizzie raised her eyebrows. "Evidently it's up to individual families which boys go and which stay."

Leah shook her head. "I doubt there'll be anyone volunteering, truly."

"Well, Gid's all for the idea." Lizzie looked up just then, staring right through Leah. "'Tween you and me, there's no way he'll stand up to the bishop." Lizzie didn't continue; she let her expression finish her thought.

Leah wondered if this had all come about because of several babies born with severe handicaps in the past few years . . . and more than a handful with webbed feet, too. She shivered. "Maybe tradin' men isn't such a bad idea, really," she found herself saying.

"Well, no, I can understand the why of it. But think of the heartbreak . . . boys leavin' their families behind only to marry and settle down in a new, faraway place."

Like Jonas. It astonished her that she would suddenly think of him as a prime example. "Obviously the boys who've already joined church won't go, right?"

"Bishop Bontrager wouldn't think of doin' away with his own ruling. Those baptized boys'll stay put or the Bann would be sure to follow."

Very few churches held to such strict guidelines, Leah knew. She was just glad she hadn't ever had any desire to leave the Gobbler's Knob community, wanting to honor her vow—not only because of the bishop's decision, but because she loved her dear family and the People here.

While cleaning up after the Sunday common meal in Aunt Mary Ebersol's kitchen, Leah overheard several older women talking. One particularly gray-haired *Mammi* was saying something about "so-and-so livin' under the shadow of another's sorrow." When the woman turned and caught Leah's eye, she hushed up right quick, looking the other way.

Surely they're not talking about me! But as she minded her own business and helped dry the many plates, she couldn't get the comment she'd heard out of her mind. *Do the People think I'm living under the gloom of Sadie's less-than-spotless life?* For sure and for certain, they could take one look at her and know she was as happy as any mother around here. All the same, the idea of folk whispering about her made her feel uneasy. Were the two older women feeling sorry for her? Did they happen to know of her former connection to Jonas Mast or, later, to Gid?

Leah couldn't abide the notion of anyone's feeling unwarranted sympathy for her, especially when more than anything, she had been determined to be joyful in all she did, serving her family under God all these years. There was no need for such a thing to be whispered, yet she felt sure the comment had been about her, otherwise why the embarrassed look?

Fact was, she was as delighted to be alive as the next person, glad to be witnessing the maturing love between Dat and Aunt Lizzie, for one, as well as the love between Hannah and Mary Ruth and their spouses. If there was any fret showing on her face, she figured it had to do with raising two teenagers at the moment. Lydiann was out all hours and moping around like a love-sick puppy, of all things, and Abe was feeling his oats because Dat had allowed him to go with a group of older boys on a lark, raising a bit of tomfoolery at Root's Country Market.

Even so, the older woman's remark plagued Leah all the way home. She honestly didn't feel alone or lonely, neither one. Surrounded by the extended family she loved so dearly, there was scarcely any time to feel that way.

Once home Leah decided to take the horse and carriage out for a drive, to give herself some quiet time. It would have made sense to simply turn around a full mile or so after she passed the Nolts' and Schwartzes' places, but she felt inclined to drift along on this pleasant and sunny Sunday afternoon, letting the horse pull her farther, not caring where she was headed. For certain, Dat might eventually begin to wonder where the world she'd taken herself off to, but for now she had plenty of time.

Sighing, she leaned back in the buggy seat and watched the clouds float by, feeling nearly as light as a chicken feather. She contemplated the sermons today, having heard similar ones, if not the same, from Bishop Bontrager more times than she could count. But lately Preacher Gid's were somewhat more interesting to her, and she wondered if he'd gotten to reading the Holy Bible, maybe. Since he spent so much time around Dat, that might be a possibility, what with Dat reading God's Word twice a day and even studying it. So just maybe some of that was rubbing off on their young preacher—unbeknownst to the bishop, naturally.

She might have turned around about then and headed home, but she saw two young people walking her way. Without meaning to, she found herself staring at the boy and girl as they walked, who turned now and then to glance at each other and smile or laugh. The girl was shorter than the boy, and Leah might've guessed them to be twins except that the girl was quite blond in comparison to the young man, who had deep brown hair.

As they approached the horse and buggy, she waved to them and they waved back, calling out a greeting to her. "*Wie geht's?*" the boy said, smiling and raising his straw hat. His face seemed rather familiar.

"Good day for walkin', jah?"

"The way from Grasshopper Level is all uphill to here," he called. "But the return trip is much easier."

She slowed the horse, pulling onto the dirt shoulder.

"Are ya goin' far yet?" asked the girl.

"Looks like your horse is awful hot," the boy said, briefly touching the bridle.

At that moment she recognized them. "Say, aren't you Jake and Mandie Mast?"

"I thought ya seemed a mite familiar, too," Jake said with a quick look at his sister. "Didn't we meet once over at Dr. Schwartz's clinic? A long time ago, seems now."

"What a keen memory you have," she said. "And jah, it's ever so nice to see the both of you again."

"Same here," Mandie replied politely, appearing rather shy.

"I always wondered why we never bumped into you and your family again," Jake spoke up, glancing a bit sheepishly at Mandie. "But when I asked Mamma, she said you were the sort of folk who kept to home."

Homebodies, baloney! Leah thought sadly, quite sure the twins knew more than they were saying about their father's imposed shun of the Ebersols.

"Well, have yourselves a nice afternoon walk. I guess I oughta be goin' now."

"So long!" Jake called to her.

"Good-bye, Cousin!" Mandie said.

Even once the horse started moving again and she got him turned around in the narrow road, Leah could scarcely stop looking after the Mast twins.

Something's terribly familiar about Jake. . . .

But she decided it was her memory of his childish face that tugged at her so, and as she rode farther away from the chance meeting, she felt quite sure that Jacob Mast must simply remind her of his father.

Leah wasted no time Monday morning, after the laundry was washed and hung out to dry, heading off to work on foot. Once at the clinic, she went promptly to the waiting room and stood before the lineup of framed photographs on the wall. One in particular caught her eye—Derek Schwartz wearing a sports uniform and holding a baseball bat.

She sucked in her breath as she stared at his face. If she remembered yesterday's encounter correctly, Jake Mast and Derry Schwartz were nearly twins in looks.

But how can that be?

She thought back to the last time she'd seen Peter Mast, recalling his dark brown hair and distinct jawline. Both were akin to Jake's hair and the shape of his mouth and chin.

I'm borrowing trouble, she thought and set to dry-mopping the floors.

Dr. Schwartz noticed Leah standing in the waiting room, intently looking at a picture of his son Derek. That in itself wasn't so odd, perhaps, but her facial expression was one of discovery. He was well aware of the pounding of his own heart, his nerves suddenly on edge.

Turning from the doorway, he hurried back to his private office, closed the door, and began to pace. Would Leah approach him with more questions?

No longer could he attempt to fool himself into thinking his deceitful plan was forever safe. On a subconscious level he had been in a state of perpetual worry for these sixteen years—Sunday mornings spent tending the tiny grave, hoping to atone for this, his worst sin. Yet had he purposely set himself up to be found out? Putting flowers on an obvious grave . . .

Did he, in all actuality, long to be found out, the crime dealt with . . . himself punished?

If Leah was as bright a woman as she had thus far proven herself to be, no telling how long before she'd put two and two together. Or maybe she already had. What *had* he been thinking bringing her into his circle of acquaintances, hiring her to work for him, allowing Lorraine to put her to work as part-time housekeeper? She had even seen Derek in the flesh one Christmas quite a few years back. To think he had been remiss, even reckless, in protecting his awful secret.

The logic behind the treacherous deed he had committed now completely escaped him. Hadn't he thought it best to protect his good name?

What good name? he thought, sick with self-disgust.

A wave of dread seized him and he leaned over, resting on his desk. *Breathe, Henry . . . take slow, deep breaths.*

Mary Ruth perked up her ears when her father-in-law brought up the subject of his land Monday evening at supper. "It's a nice big property south of the Peacheys' farm," he said. "If ever you were thinking of building a house for your growing family, Robert—and now's as good a time as any—it would be ideal." He paused a second, his eyes blinking fast as he continued. "I'd like to offer you this as a gift . . . since your first child is on the way. We could begin excavating right away."

"Why, Dad, this is a surprise," Robert said, eyes wide at the news.

Lorraine spoke up next. "Your father and I have been talking this over for some time now."

Mary Ruth enjoyed watching Robert's handsome face light up at the prospect of owning land and a house, but he quickly went on to say they were comfortable in their small rental home for now.

"Well, if you should ever decide otherwise . . ." his father said.

"We appreciate the offer," Robert assured him.

Mary Ruth agreed. "What a lovely thing to contemplate for our future." She imagined Henry and Lorraine both were hoping for more than the one or two grandchildren they were expecting, and their growing family could surely use more space in years to come.

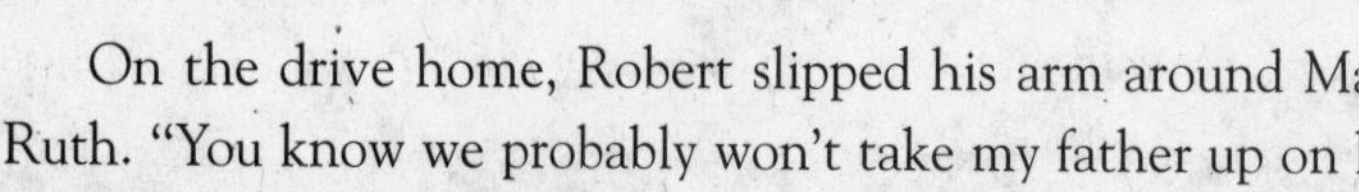

On the drive home, Robert slipped his arm around Mary Ruth. "You know we probably won't take my father up on his generous offer, don't you?"

She was amazed at his response. "Whatever do you mean?"

"I'm not interested in handouts, even from my father."

"Your parents mean well, Robert."

"All the same, we will make our own way, under God. I feel strongly about this, dear."

She could understand Robert's position well enough—after all, she had been raised with a strong work ethic, too. It had been one of the things that attracted her to Robert in the first place. Her husband studied the Scriptures diligently—his first calling—also putting great care into his second job of planting trees and shrubs, beautifully landscaping folks' yards. *A preacher and a gardener both till the soil, in a manner of speaking.*

Smiling, she shared the thought with him.

"Well, aren't you clever?" He gave her shoulder a quick squeeze as he drove.

"Would you marry this Amish girl again if you had the chance?" she teased.

"In a minute I would. And, by the way, you aren't so Amish anymore."

She smiled back at him. "Oh, I don't know about that. They say, 'once Amish, always Amish,' you know."

While Lydiann helped Leah clear the supper dishes, she mentioned having met a girl named Mandie Mast at the singing the night before. "She's the same girl we met years back, Mamma, over at Dr. Schwartz's clinic. I remember her so clearly because her eyes are blue as can be. Do ya know who I'm talking 'bout?"

Leah nodded. "Jah, I believe I do." She found Lydiann's comment about Mandie to be rather curious, because there were too many times when Lyddie simply could not keep track of having fed the chickens of a morning, let alone recall something that had happened years before.

Lyddie went on. "Mandie said she and her twin brother happened to see you out ridin' yesterday afternoon. So she must've remembered *you*, too."

"I stopped the horse and talked with them a bit, jah." She didn't divulge Jake's comment about the Ebersols keeping "to home," though, or how peeved she had felt at hearing Fannie's untruthful explanation.

"Anyway, Mandie told me the most interesting thing."

Leah braced herself for some remark about the rejection Mamma's cousins had made of all of them.

"Mandie said her and Jake's birthdays aren't on the same date, even though they're twins. Isn't that downright peculiar?"

Lyddie had her there. "Whatever do ya mean, dear?"

"Mandie was born a few minutes before midnight on April *ninth* . . . and Jake came along in the wee hours the next day, so his birthday is April *tenth*." Lydiann laughed softly. "Now, what do ya think of that? Bein' twins but not havin' the same birthday."

April ninth?

"Are ya awful sure of this?" Leah asked, her pulse pounding in her temples.

Lydiann appeared confused. "I have no reason to think Mandie's lyin'."

"No . . . I didn't mean . . ."

So . . . Mandie and Jake were born mere hours after Sadie's first baby. The thought tormented Leah, and she couldn't stop her brain from spinning, her mind on her encounter with Cousin Fannie's twins yesterday afternoon—how she'd fixed her gaze on Jake, nearly staring a hole in him. He did not resemble Mandie; she recalled he never had, even as an infant. In fact, he didn't much resemble any of his brothers or sisters, though he did remind her of Peter Mast . . . but only if she thought enough about it.

Helplessly she thought of Jake's nearly black eyes . . . identical to the eyes that haunted her from a recently framed photo of Derek Schwartz as a teen, a favorite of Lorraine's she'd pulled out of an old scrapbook. Leah had dusted it weekly for the past few months, aware of her resentment each time she considered again what he'd done to Sadie . . . to all of them.

The news of Sadie's baby—that he was our grandson—would have caused Lorraine tremendous sadness . . . even embarrassment, Dr. Schwartz had told Leah years before.

Once again she contemplated Jake's dark eyes and shock of hair. But she shook herself and hoped she was imagining things.

◆

That night Leah lay still in her bed, reliving the meeting with the Mast twins. She thought of the striking similarities between Jake and the new photo of Derek, as well as those of his childhood photos she'd been dusting in the front room of the Schwartz home these years.

Tired as she was, she let her mind wander into a whirl. Lyddie's comments about the Mast twins' birthdays had gotten her all stirred up.

In her drowsy yet troubled state, Leah suddenly recalled the butterfly handkerchief Sadie had used to cover her dead baby's face after his premature delivery—and the strange comments Dottie Nolt had made about it years ago, upon its return to Sadie. Hannah had made only one such cutwork embroidered handkerchief, yet Dottie had said she'd seen Fannie Mast with one exactly like it. Was there in fact only one handkerchief . . . and had Fannie dropped it at the clinic, where it was retrieved by Leah?

Was it possible Sadie's baby had not died at all? Could it be that he was actually *alive*? She had seen his lifeless blue body with her own eyes. Had she been deceived? But Dr. Schwartz had left so quickly . . . and why was that?

Leah knew she must pay a private visit to Dr. Schwartz at the next opportunity—there would be no getting around the truth this time. She would not budge from his clinic all night if it took that to get his attention . . . or Lorraine's. She would do what she had to in order to drag an honest answer out of the doctor. She would give it her Amish best.

She tossed about in bed, dreadfully aware of Sadie, probably asleep now in the Dawdi Haus. If any of what she suspected was true . . . *Poor, dear Sadie . . . .*

On the other hand, Leah thought, what if she were completely wrong? Until she knew the truth, she dared not share her misgivings with anyone, even in speculation.

Chapter Twenty-four

From time to time, Jonas ventured out and away from his woodworking shop, especially on auction days like today or when stifling afternoon temperatures and high humidity made it nearly impossible to keep his mind on his work. Today he'd taken himself off to the neighboring town of Berlin, where, due to the sale in town, he knew there'd be plenty of farmers congregating at Boyd and Wurthmann's Restaurant and General Store for a grand slice of pie, if not a generous lunch to go with it. At breakfast he had kindly asked Emma not to bother packing him a sack lunch as he'd had it in his mind that he wanted a chance to chew the fat a bit, needing some male companionship.

He paid the Mennonite driver quickly when he was let out at the stoplight on the main street, and then he headed off on foot toward the old restaurant that looked out onto the road. Inside he found a good many Amishmen already feeding their faces. Glancing about, he happened to see young Preacher Solomon Raber, or Sol for short. At only thirty-three, the newly ordained preacher was as pleasant a man as any he knew, with a contagious smile and big brown eyes.

"Hullo, Jonas!" Sol called to him, leaning up out of his chair a bit at a table not so far from the long wooden counter. "Come 'n' join us."

Jonas nodded and hurried to take the only vacant seat with the preacher and two of his friends, Gravy Dan Miller and Peach Orchard Levi Troyer, their nicknames distinguishing them from the dozens of other Dan Millers and Levi Troyers in the area. "Hullo," Jonas said, removing his straw hat. "What's gut on the menu today?"

"Oh, just everything." Sol tapped the sandwich section of the menu. "Like hot beef with some broth to dip it in?" He fairly grinned at the suggestion.

"Sounds fine to me." Jonas put down the menu, not bothering to look at the price or even what came with the sandwich.

They began to talk of the weather and local happenings, but when Sol commented, "I've heard tell of more than a handful of our young men volunteering to move to Pennsylvania," Jonas paid close attention.

"Just what do ya mean?" he asked.

"Well, now," Preacher Sol explained, "I guess one of the old bishops back east got this crazy idea to trade some of his boys with ours."

Jonas scratched his head, trying to recall if ever he'd heard of such a thing. "Whatever for?"

"Guess there's been too much intermarrying—the blood's gettin' weak or something, and it's affecting babies."

Gravy Dan nodded and spoke up. "Same thing's goin' on in some places out here, too. That's what happens when a fella falls for his first cousin and marries her, I 'spect."

"Jah, makes sense to me," Peach Orchard Levi said, his face blushing red at the sensitivity of the topic, no doubt.

Jonas hardly knew what to make of the idea. "So a few of our teen boys plan to go to Pennsylvania and marry and settle down, in exchange for the same number of fellas from back east?"

"More than a dozen are comin' here," Sol said, "from someplace in Lancaster County."

Lancaster . . . The mere mention of the area set his mind to turning. So many years had come and gone since he'd laid eyes on Leah Ebersol . . . Abram's Leah. And his parents and dear old grandparents—were they even still alive? His brothers and sisters . . . all the happy days, growing up and helping his father in the apple orchard, working the soil, preparing for market day week after week in the summer, the harvest and apple cider making. Remembering the beckoning smell of homemade applesauce, he felt he was right back in his mother's kitchen at this moment, even while he sat here in the heart of Holmes County, Ohio, in this wonderful-good restaurant catering to Plain folk.

He retraced the steps of his boyhood and teen years. Leah had been such a big part of those growing-up days, and for just a moment, he found himself reflecting on her warm and pleasing laugh, her gentle smile—nearly constant, it had seemed.

Although such memories were not improper, he refused to dwell on the past. His life was more than happy here. He had made the best choice for his future.

Still, the thought of young men passing between the states as a way to bring in fresh blood struck him as downright strange, yet he guessed he could see the need for it. He was just glad the Grasshopper Level bishop hadn't thought up this idea back when *he* was sixteen or seventeen. It would have meant having to leave behind his family and the girl he planned to court and marry. He had been quite young then; he and Leah both were. Just how would he have felt if the brethren had decided to start switching men around back then? He might have had even fewer years with his former beloved.

When the waitress came with his sandwich platter, Jonas felt strangely relieved, glad to dive into his lunch and abandon futile memories.

Saturday, July 6
Dear Diary,

Today, while the girls took turns tending the roadside stand with Lydiann, I headed over to see Old Lady Henner. It's been a few weeks since my last visit, but I wanted to check in on her, see how she was feeling, especially since I think she might be dying. She's the oldest person living in the county at the present time, and she looks it, too. When I saw her pale face and frail condition, I asked if there was anything I could do—maybe call on another Amish healer. I wish she might live on forever, though I know that's impossible. She's only human, after all.

Another reason I went to visit her was to make sure all my ailments, physical and mental, were tended to, in case she should die in her sleep here before too long. That might seem selfish, but I've come to depend on her and don't see how I'll manage when she goes. The dear thing has been such a comfort.

Dat and Aunt Lizzie have not been privy to my frequent visits over the years, and I don't plan on telling them. They would not approve, though there are many amongst the People who do put great stock in our Amish hex doctors, Gid and the bishop included. Thankfully Dat has not been able to persuade my husband differently.

Mary Ruth and Robert stopped in at Dat's the other day, and Mary Ruth looks as healthy as I've ever seen her. When I spied them from the rose garden, I called to the girls, and all of us ran down for a nice visit under the shade of the linden tree, where we sipped cold lemonade. It was such fun seeing the way Robert and Mary Ruth smiled so fondly at each other, as if they share a special secret . . . which, of course, they do. Goodness, Dat has made it clear he's just itching for a grandson, holding out hope for Mary Ruth to give him his first. As for me, I've given up on having more than three children, and all girls at that. Seems to me the Lord God has closed up my womb, and probably a good thing, too, after what I went through with Mimi—though, of course, following her first visit to Old Lady Henner, there was never another sleepless night due to colic. I know Gid and the older girls were ever so happy about that. Gid came right out and asked if I'd taken Miriam off to the hex doctor, and I told him the truth. He probably wondered why I'd waited so long.

Well, it's an awful hot July, but I can't complain. Living up here with tall shade trees sheltering the whole back of the house, we enjoy our evening hours on the porch, looking out over the flower gardens and laughing at the girls' cute antics, enjoying one another's company like nobody's business.

Respectfully,
Hannah

Lydiann hung on Jake's every word as they rode slowly together beneath the dark covering of sky and trees. He had a big talk on tonight, telling about the times his mother would read to his twin and himself, both of them squashed into a single large hickory rocker by a flickering fire in the wood stove.

"Mostly she read Bible stories to us, but sometimes she would read poetry about animals and nature by one of Dat's Amish friends," Jake said.

She found that interesting. "A *man* who's a poet, ya say?"

"Jah, and a real gut one, too."

"What sort of poems . . . rhyming ones?"

Jake laughed a little. "What kinds of poems don't rhyme?"

She tried to explain that there were, indeed, poems where the phrases and lines rambled along without any rhyme at all. She had come across them one day when she and some of her school friends had taken themselves off to Strasburg to the library there and stayed for hours reading all different kinds of books. Mamma Leah had never known of it, but Lydiann had happened into Lorraine Schwartz out on the street, and Lydiann remembered feeling as if she'd been caught doing something wrong, even though Mrs. Schwartz had merely eyed her curiously.

Lydiann shared with Jake that she sometimes felt she craved books, just as Mary Ruth told her she had at this age. Sometimes she felt as if she had a little piece of each of her older sisters in her, and, all in all, she was mighty glad the Lord God had made her the way she was. She could scarcely wait to get on with her life, particularly when Jake was ever so near, as he was right this minute. "I love ya, Lyddie," he whispered, reaching for her hand.

She wondered how much longer it would be before he might kiss her cheek, though she knew courting days were a time to "get to know one another," as Mamma always said, and not about smooching.

So when Jake leaned near, their heads almost touching, she held her breath, fearing she might fail Mamma tonight, for sure and for certain.

Just at that moment a hoot owl startled her with its nocturnal cry. "Ach, Jake!" she hollered.

"It's only a barn owl," he laughed.

But the sound from high in the tree had altered the intensity of the moment, and in one way she was glad, thankful she had been careful to stay pure during their courtship. On the other hand, she almost wished his lips *had* found her face. Who was to ever know, after all? In fact, from what she heard from girlfriends and distant cousins, some parents expected their teenagers to do a bit of necking now and then. "It leads to marriage," said one, "which is just what the deacons, preachers, and the bishop hope for."

More marriages mean more babies, she knew—the way the Lord God intended them to populate the community of the People. Thoughts of marriage and babies made plenty of good sense to Lydiann, especially tonight. Except that now the romantic moment had passed and Jake was back to talking about his twin sister.

Puh!

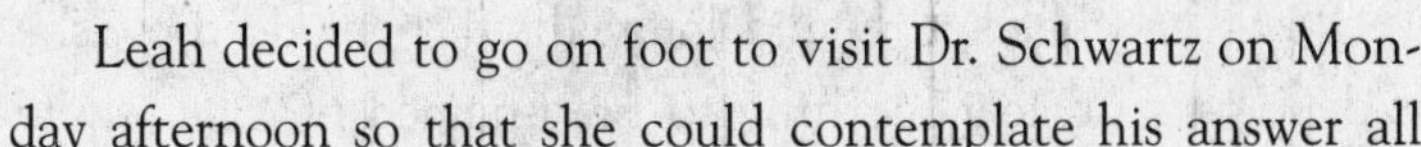

Leah decided to go on foot to visit Dr. Schwartz on Monday afternoon so that she could contemplate his answer all the long walk home. For now, she took her time, listening to the peeping of birds and insects in the dense woods, trying to calm her frayed nerves. She'd planned to arrive at the clinic a full hour before he resumed patient hours, well aware of Dr. Schwartz's daily schedule.

What will he say? she wondered. *Will he brush me off again?* She could only hope she was able to stand her ground this time . . . persevere until she was satisfied that what he revealed was the full story.

She was growing increasingly anxious to get the confrontation behind her. Doing such a thing went against her grain, yet the accumulation of unasked-for clues now made it impossible to avoid.

The road ahead wavered and blurred into watery colors as Leah finally allowed herself to let go angry tears. She felt strongly that if there was any truth at all to what she suspected, she had every right to lash out at Dr. Schwartz. Just how she might reveal her fury, she was undecided, because, fact was, the good doctor was probably not good at all, and she'd been schnookered, working for him and his wife all this time.

Sighing, she raised her head to the sky and tried her utmost to enjoy her morning walk—the birdsong, the gentle rustle of trees, and the vastness of God's world. At this moment she felt as small as the tiniest insect. A feeling of helplessness nearly overtook her, and Leah stopped walking and turned around quickly, staring back at the long road from whence she'd come. *Lord, are you with me in this?*

Her tears ebbed a bit, and she realized then and there she had nothing to fear, nothing to be ashamed of. She would turn herself right around and walk forward . . . for Sadie's sake. No longer did it matter what Dr. Schwartz thought of her. Most important was discovering if Sadie's child was alive or not.

Chapter Twenty-five

As Leah made the turn left off Georgetown Road toward Dr. Schwartz's clinic, the wind gusted, and she found herself thinking of the Scripture in Philippians chapter four, which she had read just this morning: *I can do all things through Christ which strengtheneth me*.

She began to whisper the Scripture, surrounded now by a marked sense of confidence. She felt undeniably convinced she was doing the right thing. *I am my father's daughter. . . . I can do this*, she assured herself, aware of her rising optimism. *With God's help*.

Dr. Schwartz was in his office, poring over a pile of papers, just as she assumed he might be, and when she knocked on the doorjamb of the open door, he looked up immediately. His eyebrows shot up. "Well, good morning, Leah. Aren't you here early?"

"I came to talk something over with you, Dr. Schwartz, if ya don't mind." Somehow she managed to get the whole sentence out without breathing.

The pause between her statement and the time involved

for her to inhale deeply was long enough for the doctor to murmur, "Ah." The way he frowned and rapidly blinked his eyes made her feel somewhat hesitant, but she did not lose heart.

She began by asking right out the most urgent question of all. "What happened to Sadie's baby after you left with him the night he was born?"

The doctor's frown deepened and he rose quickly to close the door. When he turned to face her, he wore an odd look. He sat back down at his desk and gazed intently at the ceiling, seemingly aware of something she could not see. "Leah," he said, lowering his eyes to her, "*you* saw the baby. He was as blue as can be."

"Jah, ever so blue. But is it possible he turned pink sometime between his birth and now?" She breathed again. "What I mean is . . . could it be Sadie's son actually lived that night . . . that he lives even now?"

Calmly, his hands folded on the desk before him, Dr. Schwartz replied, though nearly in a whisper at first. "I'm afraid these may be the most startling words you've ever heard. Absolutely no one else knows this about my own dear grandson—your sister's son—until now. . . ." He paused, looking down at his desk. Then, biting his lip, he began again. "Sadie's premature baby *did* live that night. Quite a miracle, even though I've heard of similar things happening. The night air apparently revived him . . . as phenomenal as anything I've witnessed." He studied her attentively.

Leah breathed hard at the matter-of-fact way in which he had revealed the life-changing news. "You kept Sadie's baby, then?"

"I weighed the consequences, Leah. My son's future . . .

the fact that, at the time, Sadie had kept her pregnancy a secret from her family . . . except for you and your aunt. My reasoning was sadly skewed, you must know. I wanted what was best for my family, our good name . . . the baby's future. I was terribly selfish."

"You should have returned him to Sadie—to us. You never came back and told my grieving sister her baby was alive." Leah was nearly overwhelmed at the reality. "What happened to him? Where did you take my sister's son?"

"A good family gave him a home . . . once he was strong enough to leave this clinic."

"So *you* looked after him? You tended to Sadie's baby until he could be placed in the loving arms of . . . a new family?"

He nodded, eyes glistening. "I was torn between right and wrong . . . didn't consider the ultimate consequences. I didn't know the torment my poor decision would eventually produce in myself. In others . . ."

The doctor wept, not with sobs but with great sighs and tears coursing down his face. "I would go back to that night in a minute, if I could, and I would do everything differently. Believe me, Leah . . . I would change everything."

She sat shaking in the chair across from his desk, trying hard to remain seated, fearing she might simply storm over to Dr. Schwartz and shout at him in Amish.

Holding on to the chair, she attempted to speak her mind without losing her temper. "How could you do such a thing? You stole my sister's baby from her." Suddenly she sprang to her feet. "If Sadie knew this, it would rip her heart in two!"

"My life was altered forever that night," he whispered, seemingly struggling to get the words out.

"*Your* life?"

He remained silent for an awkward span of time. At last he spoke again, "I have offered my continual remorse to God." He brushed sorrowful tears from his face, wiping his chin hard with his folded white handkerchief. "I deserve no mercy. Do as you must with what I have told you." He turned away from her.

You know what I'll do, she thought angrily. *The People don't press charges. It isn't our way.*

Inhaling, she demanded again, "Where'd you put Sadie's son? Where *is* he?"

"Fannie and Peter Mast's youngest son is Sadie's boy. They are raising him as Mandie's twin brother."

Jake Mast . . . the mirror image of Derry Schwartz. Her suspicions had been well founded.

Sighing with a tremendous sense of sadness, Leah stood next to the beautiful desk, leaning her hands flat on its highly polished surface to support her weight, lest her trembling cause her to fall. "Does Fannie know who her young Jake really is?"

Dr. Schwartz picked up a pen and stared at it, then absentmindedly pressed it against a piece of paper. "Neither Peter nor Fannie has any reason to suspect Jake is not their flesh and blood. You see, Fannie did birth twins—the first was born well before midnight, after I returned from delivering Sadie's baby the same night. And up until the moment when Fannie's stillborn second baby came, I had no idea what I would do with Sadie and Derry's frail little one. He was barely alive." He hesitated for a moment, apparently pained at the memory. "You must believe me, Leah. I felt then as if God almighty had made it possible—inexplicably so—for Fannie to nurture and mother Jake, for my grandson to be raised in an Amish family, his rightful heritage. And at the same time I knew sending him home with the Masts would protect my family from shame."

He went on to say that switching Fannie's dead baby son with Sadie's own premature one had seemed sensible, if not the right thing to do at the time, and the Masts had never been the wiser. "In doing this, I've been fortunate enough to watch my grandson grow up . . . a luxury I've denied your sister."

"You took it upon yourself to do that which is only for the Lord God to do!" Leah's rage was fanned by his explanation, and she was helpless to quench it.

The doctor stared blankly at his desk, tear stains evident on his face.

She had to stop to collect herself—so many thoughts assailed her . . . nearly too many to consider. "If I'm understandin' what ya just said, Fannie Mast has given Jake all the love my sister gladly would've offered him. . . ."

Dr. Schwartz forlornly nodded.

She clenched her fists and turned to stare at the wall. "So you must've buried Fannie's dead baby in the grave on your property, then." She swung around to face him again. "Is that what ya did?"

Again he nodded. "The least I could do for the Masts' full-term baby was give him a proper burial."

"And I'll bet you thought it would soothe your conscience."

He rubbed his face and kept his hands over his eyes for the longest time before looking at her again. "I could be arrested . . . sent to jail for this crime, if word gets out."

"Jah, for certain."

"Do as you see fit," he said flatly, as though resigned to his just fate.

"The People are forgiving and generous . . . nearly to a fault." She struggled to continue. "Even if Peter and Fannie came to know this horrible thing, they would not condemn you. I'm quite sure of it." Part of her wanted to see him squirm, but it was evident that the guilt-ridden years had already taken their toll, transforming him into the dejected man he now was.

With a great sigh, she said, "It might be best if I not continue workin' for you and Lorraine." Then, before he could answer, she excused herself from her expected hours of labor this day. Leah hurried out of his office, not looking back at the clinic established by the man the community had wrongly trusted . . . a man who had deceived them all. Sixteen precious years had been lost to Sadie—to all of them—forever.

Hot with anger, Leah headed down the road, plagued by the terrible truth that Mamma's cousins had unknowingly raised Sadie's child—Dat's only grandson.

Jacob Mast.

How bitterly ironic it was that Peter and Fannie's youngest son belonged to the cousins they'd chosen to shun.

As if the news of Jake Mast's being Sadie's only living child wasn't enough, Leah began to feel under the weather. She was painfully aware that she must hold close the disheartening information, lest she weaken and pour out her shock, sadness, and exasperation to either Dat or Aunt Lizzie. *It's*

Sadie who deserves to hear it first. When I can muster the strength. . . .

Sleep refused to come that night, and Leah stared at the dark windows, wishing the moon were out in full to spread its white light into the room—the same bedroom where she had ofttimes wondered where Sadie had taken herself off to back when her sister was in the midst of rumschpringe. As it was, Leah felt the murky room was dreadfully silent with Sadie sleeping next door in the Dawdi Haus.

Sadie surely slept soundly still, having dreams of the little ones she'd lost . . . longing in the very depths of her soul for the babies she'd birthed but never held long enough to truly love or know.

A breeze blew in the open windows, gentle yet strong enough for the shades to flap slightly. *When should I tell her?* Leah wondered, knowing it would be heartless to keep the information from her any longer. Yet she struggled with the idea of coming right out and saying Jake was Sadie's son, especially since the Masts had kept all of them at arm's length and worse. Considering the commotion this could cause between the two estranged families, she shied from revealing such news to anyone. Still, the thought of being privy to what Sadie did not know caused Leah a wakeful and troublesome night.

◆

By the noon meal of the next day, Leah was in such turmoil she could scarcely keep her attention on serving the large pot roast to the family, let alone interact normally with either Lydiann or Abe as they sat chattering at the table, eager to enjoy the dinner she and Sadie had prepared together. All Leah could think of was how she had been kept from the truth about her own birth mother until adulthood, thereby having missed out on the extra-special closeness she might have experienced with Lizzie had she known differently as a little girl. Though her Mamma had always loved her, they had not shared the strong bond Sadie and Mamma had always had, seemingly so closely linked, and understandably so, Sadie being Mamma's firstborn and all. Indeed, had Leah known about Lizzie, she might have had that with her.

At last Leah concluded she could not, *would not*, keep back the near-sacred news about Jake from Sadie, who had been dreadfully wounded so many times over. It was time for her sister to hear the facts of the matter as both Dr. Schwartz and she knew it.

Leah contemplated the afternoon ahead, thinking she might invite Sadie to take a walk someplace where they could be perfectly alone, once their gardening work was complete. Perhaps the woods? But no. How much better it would be to have the sun shining on them as they walked and talked. With the strong emotions that were sure to surface, she definitely wanted to be where they could see the openness of sky and fields.

As she placed the heavy platter of roast and vegetables before her family, Leah settled in her mind on the best place for her most solemn talk with dearest Sadie.

Chapter Twenty-Six

Henry had heaved himself out of bed the day after the grueling confrontation with Leah, floundering to find his robe and house slippers long before Lorraine might awaken. He had then proceeded to the bath, where he'd replayed the conversation as he lathered up his whiskers for shaving, fearing he had done the wrong thing in sharing Jake Mast's identity.

He recalled splashing on some aftershave and dressing before wandering downstairs to the sitting room between the front room and the kitchen. There he'd sat in the stillness for more than a half hour, pondering the probable destruction of his life until the newspaper had thumped against the back door. He had risen slowly to collect it, hungry for news of the outside world to choke out his own agitated thoughts.

All morning long he had gone back and forth about the wisdom of having revealed the truth. Now that he was sitting at his office desk, a sliced apple and a turkey and Swiss-cheese sandwich uneaten before him, he pondered again what he had done. *Such stupidity!*

Yet he had to hope his devastating confession was safe

with Leah. Sighing, he could only imagine what she was going through now. His doing . . . all of it. Torn between the truth and the pain it was sure to inflict on her older sister, Leah was, no doubt, aggravated by the tremendous burden of her knowledge. He had done her a great disservice, and he was ashamed, not only of having revealed the deed, but of having committed it in the first place.

He tried to picture Jake growing up in Abram's household, being looked after and loved by his real mother, surrounded by his rightful family.

Leah won't contact the authorities, will she?

Even if she did not, Henry wondered if word might eventually get to Peter's and Fannie's ears. What then? He would be compelled to be straightforward with the Masts, if it came to that. And what of poor Jake? The innocent young man would be forced to come face-to-face with not only his unsought birth mother but the entire Ebersol family. Would Sadie's family ever accept Jake as their own? Would Jake embrace them?

Questions wrenched him every which way, and he felt as tired when he reached for his sandwich as he had upon slipping into bed last night. Although he had experienced no trouble falling asleep, he had awakened repeatedly throughout the long night, even startling himself with the sound of his own miserable moaning. And Lorraine, saint that she was, had slept through the many thrashings and turnings he felt unable to control.

My life is in ruins, Henry thought, realizing that if his wife discovered *this* offense, he would have to daily atone for every wrongdoing he had ever committed . . . and there were many. Not that she would purposely hold it over him—that wasn't her way. His reluctance for her to know about their grandson now had more to do with Lorraine's keen interest in God, which made him feel even more culpable.

Leah suggested she and Sadie take a walk following noon dinner, to which Sadie heartily agreed. She simply went along, enjoying the wispy clouds softening the rays of the sun, bringing the slightest bit of relief from the hottest part of the afternoon.

"Did ya know that Dat doesn't believe the English know anything 'bout how to gentle a horse?" Sadie had been thinking on this, having heard Dat say to Gid earlier that morning that he thought their approach was an insult to the horse. But the lack of a response from Leah made Sadie doubt she was any too interested in talking about horses. No, it was fairly obvious, now as they'd made the turn onto the main road and were heading southeast toward the Peacheys' place, that there was something very important on Leah's mind.

Leah slowed the pace and turned to face her. "Sadie, I don't honestly know how to tell ya . . . what I must say to you, but I'm gonna try."

She could see Leah was struggling as they continued walking, coming up on the area where the road opened up and the field on the left stretched out to a pretty pond—a small one, to be sure, but one that made for a lovely verdant setting, nonetheless. "What's on your mind, sister?" she asked, feeling breathless and almost perplexed at the tone of Leah's voice.

"Oh, Sadie, this is the hardest thing I've ever had to do . . . but I want you to know that if I could keep this back in order to spare you—if I thought it wouldn't hurt you worse to never know—well, I wouldn't utter a single word." Leah was absolutely shaking with emotion.

"You're frightening me," Sadie said. "What on earth is it?"

They walked for too long in total silence, but Sadie decided not to pressure Leah. It seemed best for her sister to take her time with whatever was troubling her, even though Sadie couldn't begin to think what that might be.

Along the road, a green fringe of pasture flourished where thin feelers on sheaths of grass turned purple, then sapphire, then a deep gray-lavender as the sun shifted in and out of the faint cover of cirrus clouds.

Leah spoke again, a near whisper. "Sadie, your baby . . . the son you birthed in Aunt Lizzie's cabin . . . he didn't die that night."

Sadie stopped walking and felt as if her heart might stop beating. "What are you sayin'?" Her voice cracked.

Leah reached to hold both her hands. "Come with me. I'll tell you all that I've just learned."

They turned a sharp left, and she followed Leah down through a vacant and large piece of land, her mind and heart screaming to know more even as her sister quietly shared the astounding story.

At last they stood at the grave where Dr. Schwartz had buried the Masts' *real* son. Sadie was scarcely able to see for her tears. Leah held her as she sobbed with both sorrow and joy.

My *son's alive!* she thought, and when she turned to look at her sister, she saw on her face a reflection of her own emotions. Sadie hardly knew what to think or say. She felt almost ill, and a cold shiver ran up her spine. "Dr. Schwartz has known all along?"

"Jah, I'm sorry to say."

"Well, I must tell Jake . . . I must meet with him privately. Right away."

"Oh, Sadie, think on this a bit. Think what this knowledge might do to him, to Mandie . . . to the entire Mast family."

Sadie shook her head. Obviously Leah didn't understand and had no idea what she was asking. Jake was a fine young man with a gentle nature—she knew this sure as anything, having watched him with Abe, shaken his hand at market, and witnessed the lighthearted expression in his eyes. "I can't wait any longer, don't you see? I've already lost all this time!"

Leah's head drooped, and when she looked up at Sadie, she was crying. "Please think about your son, Sadie. Peter and Fannie are the only parents he's known. For you to go to him now and reveal this . . . I just think, well, I s'pose I wouldn't have ever told ya if I thought you'd press ahead without thinkin' things through . . . ya know?" Leah reached over and touched Sadie's elbow.

Sighing, Sadie whispered, "Jah," choking back her own tears. "Maybe I'm bein' awful hasty, but I want to get to know him. . . . The years have flown from me."

Why is all this happening? Why now?

The entire story was as strange as can be, yet she would not doubt it for a minute, for Leah could be trusted. And looking into her sister's eyes, seeing her concern, as well as her sadness, Sadie knew something else: She must do Leah's bidding and simply wait. But when would be the right time? She had no idea, and all she could think about now was that she had already looked into the face—and felt the hand—of her only living child. Her son.

Leah was speaking again. "I think it wise to keep this just 'tween us till we carefully consider what we ought to do next, if anything. Till we seek some wisdom from above."

"Jah, from the Lord God."

Leah nodded her head, eyes still glistening. "We mustn't rush into something you'd surely regret later."

"And you don't think we should ask Dat or Aunt Lizzie 'bout this?"

"Not just yet, no."

Sadie, though terribly frustrated, began to slowly understand the reasoning behind Leah's words. At least in this solemn moment she did. Later today she did not know how impulsive she might feel, how eager she might be to hitch up the horse to the buggy and drive over to the Masts' orchard house to tell Jake the good news—that his real mother had come to take him home, where he belonged.

Ach! I mustn't do any such thing! She imagined the potential scene she would make with Jake's family, his close twin, all his older siblings—and him. Sadly she began to think that if she truly loved her flesh and blood, she might need to leave him in ignorance, never knowing he was the illegitimate child of one of the Ebersol cousins his family had shunned.

As they rose and walked back toward the main road, Sadie thought of the night she had told Leah of her youthful pregnancy and how the roles on this day were, in a peculiar way, quite reversed. Today it had been for Leah to share the truth that Sadie's own son was very much alive, instead of Sadie revealing her secret about the wee babe growing inside her. Truly, this child of hers had been veiled in secrecy from the time of his earliest beginnings.

Chapter Twenty-Seven

The days slid together, hot and muggy, the mid-July heat rising like a deep green tide in the open pasture. The intolerable temperatures brought with them sultry, restless nights for all the residents of the Ebersol Cottage, particularly Leah and Sadie, who had agreed that, for now, it was best Jake not be told of his true family roots. At only sixteen, he was too young for such jolting news, they reasoned, and the strained relations between their two families only compounded the problem.

Leah was prayerful, even watchful over her sister, hoping Sadie might somehow manage the emotional trauma she was now experiencing with some seemliness, keeping her feelings in check, at least while in the presence of other family members. And even though Sadie and Leah had endured several rather tense days, going so far as to exchange angry words in the vegetable garden one afternoon, Leah was quite sure no one suspected them of having had a fuss over something as earth-shaking as Jake Mast's being Sadie's son. Such a secret to keep!

With tomorrow a "no-church" Sunday, this Saturday night was an evening when most courting couples were out riding together. The traditional arrangement ensured their staying out all hours didn't cause stress in the family if the daughter or son of a household decided to sleep in a bit on Sunday morning.

Having hunger pangs in the middle of the night, Leah crept downstairs for a glass of milk and a cookie when she happened upon voices in the kitchen. Never having expected to encounter Lydiann entertaining her beau here in the house on a warm and moonlit night, of all things, Leah halted in surprise. She could see both Lyddie and a tall young man in the shadows, over in the corner where Dat's hickory rocker usually sat in the summer, out of the way of the wood stove, which was used for cooking even during the heat of July and August. She could see the two standing quite close together, talking. Not so eager to listen in, she decided to go and sit on the steps leading to the second floor, hoping Lyddie might have the common sense to send the young man on his way fairly soon. Yet even there, she could hear their voices.

"We'll get hitched as soon as the harvest is past," the young man said, startling her. "We'll be the first couple published at Preachin' this year."

Lydiann laughed softly.

"I'd marry ya tomorrow if we could."

"But we're underage," Lydiann said. "Will your father sign for you to marry?"

There was a long pause; then Lyddie's beau replied, "Somehow or other, I'll get him to say he will."

Leah felt terrible sitting there eavesdropping, yet she realized her girl was in over her head with this boy. Just what on earth could she do? Speak to Dat, maybe? But no, thinking back on her courting days with Jonas, she would not have wanted such interference, although there had certainly been enough of that coming from her father, for certain.

She rose and thought of heading back upstairs to simply wait for Lyddie to say good-bye to her fellow and head for bed. Just as she moved to do so, she heard Lydiann talking again. "Oh, I love ya so." And suddenly Lyddie burst out crying, as if her heart might break, saying she didn't see how her father would agree to let her marry so awful young. "You just don't know what you're askin', Jake . . . you don't know Dat."

Jake.

Leah froze in place, unable to make her legs move forward. She knew she'd heard correctly, and her heart was pounding much too hard. Could it be Lydiann was seeing Jake *Mast*?

"Ach . . . Lyddie, don'tcha worry your perty head," Jake was saying. "Things'll work out; you'll see. We're meant to be together."

Calm down, Leah told herself. *There are oodles of Jakes round these parts. Nothing to fret about.*

Even so, she knew she would not be hurrying back upstairs yet. No, she'd wait right here all night long to find out which tall Jake her Lyddie was crying over like there was no tomorrow.

Sadie stared in the little hand mirror on the dresser that quiet Sunday, trembling as she dressed. She looked much as she had a week ago, although she *had* lost some inches, since the waist of her apron was quite loose. Staring at her features, she noticed her eyes had an almost distant look to them. *Will I ever know Jake Mast the way a mother knows her son? Will I ever be allowed to love him . . . share my life with him?*

She feared she might never lay eyes on him again, let alone speak privately with him. The droop of her mouth gave away her fears as she studied herself in the small mirror. Mamma had always said to look at the eyes of a person to know what they were really thinking, but now as she pondered that, Sadie felt sure it was especially the mouth that betrayed the truth about a person's happiness or grief. She let her face sag, without forcing even the slightest smile, and she was surprised at how terribly alone she seemed to appear—alone and weary of life.

I have no choice now but to keep this quiet, she thought. *I gave Leah my word.*

She went downstairs, through the small front room of the Dawdi Haus to the connecting door to the main house. In the corner cupboard of the big kitchen, she pulled from its shelf a large volume, *Martyrs Mirror or The Bloody Theatre*. An account of seventeen centuries of Christian martyrdom, including one of her father's own great-grandmothers, Catharina Meylin, Dat frequently read silently from the book. Leah had been the one to tell Sadie about their special relationship to this courageous woman following Sadie's return home. Not so long after that, Sadie had read for herself the heartrending tale of the great-grandmother who'd given up her life for the Lord Jesus.

Today the final recorded words of this godly woman, mother to many children, comforted Sadie's heart as she held the big book ever so close, almost cradling it.

All that long morning Sadie kept wishing Dawdi John were still alive; she could sit with him and talk about most anything—even, she was sure, about her long-lost son. But Dawdi could no longer lend his kind, listening ear . . . gone to heaven, where Sadie had thought all her little ones were, up until a few days ago. It seemed so strange, nearly like a dream, to think her only son lived—and with Mamma's cousins. She had to remind herself repeatedly of the reality of it.

Since the house seemed deathly still, she decided to visit Hannah and the girls. She hurried out the back door of the Dawdi Haus, wishing she didn't have to reside alone in an addition typically meant for older relatives. Still, she knew she ought to be grateful for a place to live so near to those she loved.

Hurrying across the wide backyard, she walked toward the mule road, waving to Dat, who was stumbling out of the barn, rubbing his eyes like he'd just awakened from a catnap in the haymow. It was so hot she almost wished she'd stayed indoors fanning herself with the colorful paper fans Lydiann had made a while back at school.

Thinking of her own school days past, she was all the more anxious to see Hannah's girls—so cute they were when they stood together all in a row. Young Miriam, already six years old, had become a surprisingly cheerful sort—nothing at all the way she had started out. Though she'd never come right out and asked Hannah, Sadie guessed her sister had taken her youngest to one of the hex doctors for that, since she'd seen such a drastic change in not only the baby but in Hannah herself.

Ida Mae and Katie Ann must have seen her coming from their back porch, because they ran down the steps and hugged her hard. "Mamma, Mamma! Aunt Sadie's here for a visit," they called.

Pretty soon, Hannah and Mimi joined them. "Well, it's gut ya came up today, or we'd start thinkin' you a stranger."

"Never that." She followed the girls to the porch, where they all sat down, full of smiles. "It's sure cooler up here."

"Jah, under all these trees," Hannah replied. "Gid says it's a right nice place for a house."

"Where's Gid today?" Sadie asked.

"Over yonder, visiting an uncle."

Ida Mae asked if Sadie wanted some lemonade or something else cold to drink. "We have sun tea, too . . . sweetened with honey."

"Tea sounds gut," she said, glad to get her mind off herself . . . and Jake.

But when Ida Mae returned with a tall glass of tea for her, she was struck by how very dear each of Hannah's daughters was. *To think what life might have been like without even one of them. . . .* Sadie felt as if she might cry, contemplating each of the wee lives lost to her. Even the one that had just been found was still so far out of her reach.

Following breakfast Monday morning, Leah went out alone and began hoeing weeds in the vegetable and flower gardens, not caring that by now Dr. Schwartz would be missing his former housekeeper. Truth was, she wanted to have nothing to do with the man, and the best way to avoid him was simply to stay as far away from the clinic as possible. *Let him explain to Lorraine why I'm not coming back*, she thought, still beside herself with anger.

Meanwhile, Sadie was inside, moping about, although no one was in the house to inquire of her sister's dark mood—at least not at the present time.

Leah took out her intense frustration, even fear, on the vinelike weeds that had determined to choke out the staked tomato plants. All the while she mulled over what on earth would happen if Jake Mast—who was indeed Lydiann's beau—somehow obtained his father's permission to marry young . . . assuming his father wasn't privy to his son's courtship of one of Abram Ebersol's daughters, that is. Her imagination ran away with her regarding Lydiann and Jake's courting relationship, revealed by Leah's Saturday-night kitchen vigil. Sadly she thought of the strong possibility of deformed and mentally retarded babies such an aunt-nephew union might produce. And dear Lydiann—what would she think if she discovered she was in love with her sister's son? The emotional implications alone were enough to cause serious problems for Lydiann and Jake.

She wished the dilemma might simply disappear, but there was no escaping what she now knew must be swiftly dealt with. Even so, she must carefully contemplate this and ask God for help in knowing what she should or shouldn't do.

And there was the matter of Sadie, too. If Leah were to tell her of Lydiann and Jake, would she become distraught at this devastating news? Leah recalled all too well the hopelessness and the long, sad nights that had beset Sadie following the loss of her son all those years ago. Sadie had sniffled into the wee hours each night, competing with baby Lydiann's own fits of crying. Most likely Sadie was already reliving all of that, the wounds having been reopened by Leah herself. And now this latest discovery . . .

Leah didn't know what to do. She longed to run to the house and check on her sister, embrace her, but maybe it was best she chop away these nasty weeds, though it would likely do Sadie some good if *she* were the one out here hacking away at the pesky vines. *Goodness, how she must need something to pound on right about now!*

Aunt Lizzie wandered over from the barn, looking pink in the face. "It's too hot for weeding, Leah," she said, wiping her brow. "But if I know you, you'll keep on workin' no matter what I say."

Leah had to laugh at that. "I think ya know me too well," she replied, leaning on the hoe. "I don't quit till the job's done."

Lizzie turned and glanced toward the house. "Where's Sadie?"

"Inside."

"Tryin' to keep cool?"

Leah said nothing, hoping Lizzie wouldn't take it upon herself to fetch Sadie just now.

"Is something the matter with your sister?" Lizzie frowned and shielded her eyes with one hand. "For the past couple of days she's been down in the mouth."

"Seems so" was all Leah would say. All she *could* say.

"I'm thinkin' it's time we made us some ice cream. Chocolate, maybe. Might put a smile on all our faces, ain't so?"

Leah nodded and watched Lizzie head toward the house, hoping Sadie might be sheltered away in her bedroom, except with its being so hot, she hardly thought her sister would want to be upstairs in the Dawdi Haus.

Returning to her weeding, she forced her thoughts to the upcoming farewell for the teenage boys headed out to Ohio. She wondered how the mothers, sisters, and even sweethearts would ever manage saying good-bye. Gid had mentioned to her and Dat last week that it would be nice for some of the women to bake cakes and serve them on the first Sunday in August, following the final Lancaster Preaching service for more than two handfuls of boys. Since the church meeting and the subsequent singing would be held at Old Jonathan Lapp's house, Leah had already talked with his unmarried daughter about providing several hot-water sponge cakes for the common meal.

Just then the thought popped into her head that she ought to talk to Gid about somehow getting Jake Mast included in the group of young men headed to Ohio. *A solution, maybe?* she wondered, realizing it would mean having to share the truth about Jake with her brother-in-law. *I'll have to talk to Sadie, too . . . tell her about Lydiann being in love with Jake—wanting to marry a close blood relative!*

But the thought of the awful heartbreak such a plan would cause Lydiann, as well as Sadie, kept her from marching right up to Gid and Hannah's place. How on earth could she be responsible for setting such a thing in motion? With a shudder, she realized that what she was thinking of doing was nearly equal to what Dat had done about Jonas Mast, arranging to have him work in Ohio as a cabinetmaker's apprentice.

Feeling distressed, Leah left the garden and headed back to the house for some ice-cold lemonade.

Chapter Twenty-Eight

Dense storm clouds, which before Tuesday's noon had threatened rain, had all but dissipated when Leah met Sadie on the small porch off the Dawdi Haus, where Sadie was beating rugs.

"Sister, I'm afraid I have something mighty difficult to tell you," Leah began softly, hating to find herself the bearer of sad news as she explained how she'd stumbled onto the late-night conversation in the kitchen between Lydiann and Jake.

Sadie's eyes widened as she promptly abandoned her chore, draping the rugs over the porch railing. "Ach, are ya ever so sure?" Shaking her head in apparent disbelief, Sadie's face turned ashen, as if she might be ill. "This can't be."

"But it is, and we must do something to put a stop to it—and right quick."

"Why must this be happenin'?" Sadie moaned. "On top of everything else!"

Leah leaned on the banister. "If we don't do anything, they prob'ly will end up married. We can't stand by and merely hope they change their minds 'bout each other."

"We have to think more on this," Sadie said. "Let's walk up to the high meadow—go somewhere more private."

Agreeing, Leah hurried off with Sadie, the two of them talking through the ins and outs of this almost unthinkable quandary.

When they'd exhausted all possibilities, including telling Lydiann privately of Jake Mast's parentage—something both feared would come to no good end—Sadie tearfully begged Leah not to mention a word to anyone. "Not even to Gid," she said. "I'm just not ready to think 'bout having Jake sent away."

"Well, honestly, it's the wisest choice we've discussed," Leah said.

"Jah, I see that." Still, Sadie said she couldn't bring herself to agree to anything, least of all something that would take her only living child farther away from her.

All that day and the next, Leah went about her chores and responsibilities, hoping a better solution would present itself. She wasn't too surprised when Lorraine Schwartz stopped by the vegetable stand, asking for her, and Lydiann sent the doctor's wife up to the house, around to the back door.

Lorraine's eyes were full of concern. "We miss you terribly, Leah. We can't be without your wonderful help."

So as not to open up the troublesome topic with the doctor's unsuspecting wife, Leah promised to return to work the following day, saying she had not been feeling well lately—which was entirely true. Surely Dr. Schwartz, wretched man that he was, would understand the source of Leah's illness should Lorraine relay this exchange to him. As justified as her decision had been, Leah felt sorry about having stayed put at home, leaving innocent Lorraine in the lurch.

When Lorraine had gone her way, Leah turned her attention to Sadie. She understood why her sister wanted to keep quiet about Jake, wanting nothing to hamper her chances of bumping into him—a selfish but unsurprising reaction, for sure. Sadie's present grief, along with her hope for at least one more encounter with her son, caused Leah to consent for now to keep mum about Jake and Lydiann's romance. Yet each day that passed brought opportunity for Sadie's sister to fall more deeply in love with Sadie's son.

◆

A full week had passed since Leah had heard Jake's declaration of love for Lydiann, and she felt increasingly anxious. She was aware that this Sunday there was to be another singing across the cornfield at the Peacheys' place, where Dorcas and her husband, Tomato Joe Zook, lived with their young family now that Smitty and Miriam had moved to the Dawdi Haus. There was no question in Leah's mind that Lydiann would go, particularly with the singing this close to home. Lyddie wouldn't even need to bother asking Abe for a ride when she could simply walk over there.

Leah wished she could approach Lydiann with her concerns about Jake, but neither she nor Sadie felt that was wise. Leah in particular had a strong desire to shield Lyddie from the truth about her forbidden courtship with Jake, and undeserving as Dr. Schwartz might be, she felt concern for him and especially his good-hearted wife, as well. Truth be told, Lyddie wasn't so good at keeping secrets, and in the wink of an eye, everyone might know that the doctor, whom so many had trusted, was responsible for this horrible deed. Worse still, Jake's relationship to the only family he had ever known could be placed in jeopardy as Sadie's past reputation was once again brought to light. *Ach, but such a revelation would be a devastating blow to Dat and Aunt Lizzie, too!* Leah dreaded the thought of telling anyone at all, though Gid might actually be able to quietly help do something about the mind-boggling *Druwwel.* And what an entangled problem it was!

She had prayed all week long there might be a better answer. If she could just convince Sadie how essential it was for Jake to leave . . . to help her understand that what Leah assumed her sister wanted most desperately—a private encounter with Jake—most likely wouldn't happen anytime soon, and in a few months the wedding season would be upon them. No, they couldn't simply mark time when something this important was at stake. Leah must act immediately.

The hayloft had often drawn Sadie as a small girl when she was sad or miffed. She much preferred the sweetness of the hay to the lower level of the bank barn, where the enduring reek of the animals saturated the air. But this night, she'd felt terribly alone in the Dawdi Haus; the heat had been stifling as she tossed about in her bed in the room where Aunt Lizzie had slept before she'd married Dat. Sadie had gotten up and stood near the open window, yearning for even the slightest waft of a breeze, and then headed downstairs to the kitchen, where she'd opened the screen door. There she had remained for the longest time on the little square porch, looking out toward the top of the Peacheys' farmhouse and their big barn.

It was close to two o'clock in the morning when she made her way out to their own barn and gingerly climbed the ladder to the haymow just under the eaves. Tired as she was, she wouldn't think of allowing herself to sleep there, with the mice and the insects crawling about. Despite the presence of the barn cats, she was ever so sure the pests were there, just out of view. Late as it was, Lydiann was probably still out riding under the stars with Jake Mast, and Sadie was determined to see for herself exactly how it was between the pair.

Sighing, she thought back to the day she'd first heard her child with Derry was actually alive. How could things have changed so radically for her in one respect, yet nothing else had seemingly changed at all? She sat in the hay, having imaginary conversations with Jake in her head, trying to guess what another face-to-face meeting with him might be like now that she knew he was her flesh and blood. Would he appreciate knowing that she, not Fannie Mast, was his real mother? Would he be upset? Would he even believe her?

Tormented, she rose and began to pace the upper level, going back and forth in her mind. And what of Jake's love for Lydiann? Wasn't it probable he was simply experiencing something akin to puppy love? If Leah would simply bide her time and not speak to Gid, as she'd promised, there was always the possibility Jake might become disinterested in Lydiann and move on to a new girlfriend, as many young men in their middle teens were known to do. Sadie could only hope so, because the thought of Jake's being sent away was almost more than she could bear.

The tickle of kitten fuzz against her bare foot awakened Sadie with a start, and she realized hazily that, despite her intentions, she must have settled down on the threshing floor, amongst the various mother cats and their kittens. But now she was quite awake and aware of the sound of a horse and buggy . . . and voices wafting through the darkness.

"Oh, Jake, I'm nervous 'bout askin' Dat for his permission."

"We mustn't fret, Lyddie. Mamma always said the Lord God moves heaven and earth for those in love." It was Jake's voice, but if Sadie hadn't known better she might've thought Derry was speaking.

Let Jake have pure motives, Lord. . . .

Sadie was ever so anxious to lay eyes on him again, even in the dim light of a half moon—the faintest silhouette would satisfy her heart—so she moved to the window and peered into the night.

Lydiann's voice was muffled now as she pressed her face against Jake's shoulder. Sadie watched them embrace near the buggy and then gaze into each other's eyes.

The scene told Sadie just how serious they were. This was most likely not the puppy love she'd hoped to witness.

With tears in her eyes, she could only wonder what it would mean to her sister and Jake—and their future children—if no one stopped them. *Spared them, truly.*

Sadie knew beyond all doubt she must tell Leah it *was* for

the best to confide in Gid and see that Jake was somehow included among the boys traded.

Poor Lydiann, thought Sadie, moving from the window. *How will she ever survive such a loss? How will I?*

Leah happened upon Gid as he was rounding up the cows for afternoon milking. She felt awkward, his being alone and all, but she knew it was necessary, what with Sadie not feeling up to coming along.

"Nice day, ain't?" She folded her hands in front of her.

Gid nodded. "We could use some rain, but, jah . . . a right fine day."

She stood still just then, realizing she had little time to speak up. "I . . . uh, Gid, there's something awful important on my mind."

He turned his full attention to her.

"As you know, Sadie gave birth to a baby years ago, and she thought the wee one was born dead," Leah began, aware he had heard as much at Sadie's kneeling repentance at Preaching, nearly seven years ago. "Well, it's come to light that her son is actually quite alive."

"He's *alive*?" Gid was frowning as he held her gaze. "Oh, Leah, no wonder ya came to talk to me. Where's Sadie's boy now?"

"Growin' up as Peter Mast's youngest son." She spoke more softly now, explaining all that she knew as quickly as she could. "And worst of all, Jake's seein' our Lydiann . . . and quite seriously."

Looking even more puzzled, Gid squared his shoulders.

"How on God's green earth do ya know he's courtin' Lydiann?"

Somewhat embarrassed, she shared what both she and Sadie had overheard. She sighed, pressing on, hoping she might appeal to Gid's kindliness. "Honestly, what I have in mind will bring Lyddie much sadness, and she won't understand what's happened to her beau . . . but I've been wondering if Jake shouldn't be one of the boys approached about going out to Ohio. Ya know . . . to get him away from Lydiann, his aunt by blood."

Gid nodded his head emphatically. "I sure can see where you're comin' from. I can talk to the bishop about it right quick."

To this Leah shook her head. "Let's keep this 'tween you, me, and Sadie for now."

Willingly, Gid agreed. Leah was ever so sure he understood the impact such a revelation could have on the community of the People. No good thing could ever come of it.

Hitching up his horse and carriage, Gid went straightaway to Grasshopper Level to speak with Peter Mast, mighty concerned. He found Peter in his apple orchard, puffing on his pipe and muttering to himself as he ambled along.

Catching Peter's eye, Gid introduced himself, though being a preacher for the district neighboring Grasshopper Level, he was fairly certain Peter knew who he was—at least by name.

"Jah, I know ya well enough." Peter's eyes narrowed. " 'Tis

a mighty gut thing you got yourself loose from that Leah Ebersol . . . I daresay."

Gid wondered where Peter was going with such a snide remark, but bearing in mind his business there, he held his peace. "Look, I best be gettin' to the point of why I'm here," he said, anxious to put some distance between himself and this coldhearted man. "'Tis a right touchy subject I'm here 'bout, but seems your son Jake is awful serious about Abram's Lydiann."

Peter coughed and removed the pipe from between his chapped lips. "Now, just a minute here. Did ya say one of Abram Ebersol's daughters?"

"Jah, that's what I'm sayin'. Seems Jake's determined to marry her, and as a preacher and Lydiann's brother-in-law, it troubles me that she is thinkin' of marriage at such a young age," said Gid, withholding the sensitive information that Jake was also an Ebersol himself. Being a man of his word, Gid intended to keep his promise to Leah on that.

"Marriage? Well, I'll be puttin' a stop to that!" There was instant fire in Peter's eyes at the mention of a possible wedding involving the two families.

Gid was aghast at Peter's vehement response. Such animosity he had scarcely seen on the face of any man, let alone a God-fearing Amish farmer. The rift between Peter Mast and Abram Ebersol was unmistakably enormous, and Gid cared not to get himself caught in the middle. He was quick to suggest that perhaps Peter might consider including Jake with the Gobbler's Knob boys heading out to Ohio in two weeks' time. "What would ya think of that?"

"Put *my* son in the trade for the Ohio men?" Peter asked, actually seeming to calm a bit as he contemplated the notion.

"Jah, to settle in and work out there . . . find himself a mate," he said, wanting Peter to be clear on what he might agree to.

Peter looked pointedly at him. "If it's true my son's courtin' an Ebersol, I'll be thinking hard on this."

Mighty eager to depart now, Gid remarked that Hannah was waiting supper for him and excused himself to head back to his horse and buggy . . . and home. *Back to the peace of my house*, he thought, shuddering from the intensity of the encounter.

Chapter Twenty-Nine

Lydiann's bedroom was tidy because she could not stand for anything less than perfectly clean. Her bureau was kept dusted, even polished, and the handmade doilies were washed and ironed frequently. She liked to make her bed just as soon as she slipped out of it of a morning, and her floor was free of dust bunnies and cobwebs, even beneath the bed, a fact she was very proud of. She'd often thought what an exceptional housekeeper she would be for her husband and family some fine day—a family she'd hoped to have with Jake. But now, as she held the letter from him in her trembling hands, reading it again for the tenth time since its arrival days ago, she felt that hope was dimmed . . . if not gone.

Dear Lyddie,

I'm sorry to write in a letter the things I want to say to your face, but I have no other choice.

First of all, I apologize that I couldn't attend the singing at your neighbor's place recently. I wanted to . . . really, I did.

Please, you must believe me, Lyddie. I have nothing to do with this painful separation. My father is entirely opposed to my hope of marrying this fall. Somehow he is privy to who you are, although I was not the one to inform him. It has come to his ears that I am seeing one of Abram Ebersol's daughters, and my father, who, as you know, has always looked unkindly on your father and your family, is insisting I go to Ohio. His response was worse than I feared—I see that I was right in wanting to keep our love secret from him till our wedding day, if necessary. I am so sorry.

Lydiann, I love you and always will. I know this as sure as my name is Jacob Mast. Please don't cry for me once I'm gone to Ohio, my dear girl, because I will come back to Pennsylvania someday. For now, though, I am expected to establish myself in the home of an Amish family, begin working, and court girls from that area. I know this is terrible to have to tell you. Truth is, I refuse to either court or marry anyone but you, my darling. You are the bride of my heart. I will simply work hard in Holmes County until I am of age; then I will return for you.

Will you wait for me? I know this is the most awful thing that could have ever happened to two people so in love.

I will not forget you. When I arrive where I'm intended to go, I'll send you another letter. Please pardon my father for this. I must attempt to forgive him, too. Meanwhile I must try to figure out a way to earn his blessing on our future marriage, years from now.

All my love,
Jake

Lydiann stared at the letter through her tears. She already missed him and was feeling on the verge of collapse, as if someone had chopped off a supporting limb. Her heart was wounded and forlorn . . . all because of an ugly problem between Jake's father and her own.

For sure and for certain, she could not begin to comprehend what would have made Jake's father choose to have him join the young men being herded off to Ohio. What sort of father would do such a thing? Would Peter Mast have decided to send his son away if *she* wasn't the girl he loved? Could Jake have been spared this terrible thing if he'd fallen in love with, say, Uncle Jesse Ebersol's daughter, maybe? All too well, she knew the answer.

Lydiann rose and went to the bureau and shoved the letter deep into a drawer, wishing she'd never turned sixteen this past spring . . . wishing she were still as young and naive as the day before she went to her first singing and fell hard for wonderful Jacob Mast.

Hearing of Lydiann's dejection from both Hannah and Aunt Lizzie, Mary Ruth visited Lyddie every other day, offering her company, even going so far as to invite Lydiann to spend some time with Robert and her, "just to get away a bit."

But Lydiann refused, saying she wanted to stay close to home, near Mamma and Abe. Still, Mary Ruth couldn't get over how beside herself Lydiann was for one so young. *Her heart must be broken,* she thought as she sat on Lydiann's bed, looking now at her young sister's tear-streaked face.

"I can scarcely eat," Lyddie told her, sitting in the upright cane chair across the room. "I miss him so."

She sighed sadly, remembering well how troubled she had been when Elias Stoltzfus died. "I felt the same way once," she admitted.

"You did, sister?"

Mary Ruth nodded and began to tell Lydiann of her dear friend and first beau, explaining how he had been killed in an accident, though leaving out the part that Robert had been the one whose car had struck Elias's pony cart.

When she was finished, Lydiann was crying all the harder, and Mary Ruth went to her, reaching down to kiss her cheek. "Oh, Lyddie, I never would've told you all this if I had thought it would upset you so."

"No, no, it's a gut thing ya did, prob'ly." She looked up at Mary Ruth with the saddest, bluest eyes. "I needed to hear that someone else had such a dreadful thing happen to them and yet could still smile, years later." Lydiann got up and put her arms around Mary Ruth, clinging to her as if she might slip from her grasp. "Denki, sister."

Holding Lyddie was the best help she felt she could offer, so she let her sister cry in her arms, for as long as need be . . . just as Leah and Mamma and Aunt Lizzie had always comforted her. All of them would continue to surround Lydiann with their love, if possible making up for the powerful sadness.

"The Lord Jesus cares for you," she whispered.

Lydiann moved her head as if to say she knew that was true. "Mamma Leah prays for me every day," she murmured.

"I do, too," said Mary Ruth, hoping God's love would touch Lydiann during her time of misery.

Chapter Thirty

Halfway to Smitty's, Abram felt the warm breeze on his face and breathed in a whiff of the barnyard. He fixed his gaze on Blackbird Pond, shimmering in the distance, and recalled the winter day he'd found Abe unconscious on the ice. His son had bounced back to normal, which had made him a believer in prayer all those years ago. That and his wonderful-good relationship with Lizzie. No question, the Lord had bestowed blessings upon him . . . upon each member of his family, really.

He just wished God might reach down now and pull up the sides of Lydiann's mouth, helping her to smile again. Abram was aware of her gloominess, yet knew from Lizzie only that a young man had gone off to Ohio, instead of staying home and courting Lyddie as he'd set out to do. Sadie, too, had seemed awfully down in the dumps recently, and although he'd asked Lizzie about that, as well, she hadn't offered any answers.

Truth was, his house was full up with women who had a whole range of emotions, and he'd learned over the years to keep a safe distance at particular times. It did seem, though, that if one woman was tetchy, there was bound to be at least one other of a similar mindset. The hitch was, of course, that he had three adult women and one courting-age daughter all living together under the same roof.

He grinned at the thought as he approached Smitty's pasture now, having reached the edge of the cornfield. It was a very good thing his twins had found themselves fine husbands. For certain, he didn't care to imagine what daily life would be like with all *six* of the women in his life residing at the Ebersol Cottage, for goodness' sake.

Both Leah and Dat preferred to wait until the last possible minute before fetching a gas lamp on summer evenings, waiting till just past dusk for some artificial lighting in the house. Tonight Leah made her way out to the utility room to get one of the tall lamps, scarcely able to see as she went.

She had noticed Lydiann sitting clear back in the dark corner by herself as the rest of the family all sat around the table, enjoying Dat's reading from the Bible and the cake she'd baked for supper. She had been careful not to make hot-water sponge cake, which had been served at the farewell meal for the boys heading off to Ohio. She had no desire to remind Lydiann in any way of that particular Sunday, hard as it had been for all of the People. For the past three weeks she couldn't help but observe how crestfallen Lyddie had looked since Jake Mast had left with the others—all of it her doing. Yet what other choice had she?

Leah had always loathed self-pity, but she completely

comprehended where Lydiann was coming from. The girl seemingly had no interest in battling her emotions, and she could not hide her anguish, especially from those who loved her. Sadie had tried to cheer her up to no avail; even Abe had asked Leah if there was something wrong with Lyddie—"She's just too quiet," he'd said.

She's entitled to be sad, since we pulled the rug out from under her. She, Sadie, and Gid had never bothered to consult with Lydiann but had, instead, taken matters into their hands and acted in what they all agreed was her best interest. Yet right now, looking at her, Leah questioned their approach—it seemed nothing could soothe her girl. And although Leah believed in her heart that Jake's leaving was for the best, she did worry Lyddie might never get over his seeming abandonment of her.

She began to clear away the dishes, thinking all the while of what might bring a smile to Lydiann's face . . . Sadie's, as well. She was reminded of some of the new boys from Ohio; several of them had taken an obvious shining to Lydiann at the first Preaching service after their arrival. Leah had been as sorry as she could be to watch the light in their eyes fade when Lyddie politely looked the other way. Of course, it was too early to encourage her girl in that direction—much too soon.

The glow from the gas lamp was altogether cheery now as it cast large shadows of each of the family members onto the far wall. The steady warmth of the lamp offered security and a bit of comfort.

Just as the presence of God's love lights our pathway, Leah thought.

"O Lord God, help me understand why Jake left me behind," Lydiann prayed beneath the massive branches of the thornless honey-locust tree. She still remembered the first time Mamma had ever brought her and Abe up to these woods, to what she called her "special piece of earth."

"It's one of the most restful spots I know," Mamma had told them. Today Lydiann was finding out for herself yet again that most always what Mamma said was true.

I'm so alone, Lord . . . remembering when Jake was my own, and I was his.

She recalled those things Sadie had shared with her years ago regarding Leah's romance with Jonas Mast—how his joining the Gobbler's Knob church and then not staying put here had caused him to be shunned. Because of Jonas's subsequent estrangement from them, the Masts were still angry with Leah and all of them. Was that the only reason Peter Mast despised the thought of her being Jake's bride?

Lydiann was grateful to receive Jake's love letters—several each week. She answered each one of them often right here, beneath the tree that had so often comforted Mamma Leah in the past.

This day, she took out her stationery and pen and, once again, told Jake of her steadfast love. *I'll love you no matter where you are,* she wrote. *Ohio or Indiana, or Pennsylvania. Where you are doesn't matter as much as the state of our hearts, ain't so?*

She meant every word she wrote beneath the shade of this old and very rare tree, and she could scarcely wait for the years to fly, till Jake would send for her or, better yet, return home for her. An eternity away to be sure.

By the time Jonas redded up his woodworking shop and closed for the day, he was eager to get home. A fine supper would await him, and he happily wondered what delicious dish Emma had cooked for him today. Coming from a long line of terrific cooks, Emma seemed to derive great joy from preparing tasty meals, even feasts, nearly every evening. He had frequently told her that simple fare was fine with him, but Emma thrived on cooking and baking—the fancier the better. Most of their neighbors took their big meal at noon, but since he had quite a ride to his shop, which he rented from an old farmer friend, Jonas was satisfied with a good sandwich or two at that hour. Maybe that was the reason why Emma seemed to want to outdo herself come supper. He smiled, thinking of her affectionately. What a kind and generous woman she was, always considering him.

It was as he reined the horse into the lane that he noticed another buggy parked near the side yard. His good friend Preacher Sol Raber hailed from the house. "Jonas, hullo!" the jolly man called.

Glad to see him, Jonas jumped out of his carriage. "What brings ya all the way to the sticks?"

"Oh, I thought ya might want to take a young man under your wing, is all."

"Why, sure," he said, not waiting to hear just who might be looking for some pointers in cabinetmaking.

Sol continued on to say he'd recently met one of the young men traded from Pennsylvania. "He's just hankerin' for some gut fellowship with a master carpenter, as he says. Naturally I thought of you first, Jonas."

"If he's hardworking, I surely could use some young help."

Sol grinned, showing his teeth. "Fine and dandy," he said. "I'll bring him out first thing tomorrow. How's that?"

"I'll look forward to it."

"I think the two of you will get along fine," Sol said. " 'Specially bein' he's a Mast, same as you."

"How 'bout that?" Jonas found this news altogether interesting. "Where's the youngster from in Pennsylvania, anyway?"

"Lancaster County."

"Plenty of Masts round there." He reached for the bridle. "What's his first name?"

"Jake."

He stood up and scratched his head, suddenly bone weary. "Jake, ya say?"

"Jah, and this one's mighty young to be gone from family." Sol took off his straw hat and wiped his brow with his blue paisley kerchief. "Honestly, he says he's downright miserable—came out here against his will. Guess his pop wanted to get him away from the girl he loves for some reason or other."

Jonas turned just then, deliberately looking at the acres of tall corn across the dirt road.

"You all right, there, Jonas?"

He patted his horse's neck. "I'll look forward to meetin' this Jake fella."

Sol pressed his hat back down on his head and made for his own carriage and horse. "See ya tomorrow, then."

"Have a gut evening, Sol." With that Jonas offered a confident wave and set about unhitching his horse.

Chapter Thirty-One

With the arrival of September, Lydiann found more relief in working alongside Abe outdoors than inside the crowded house. She was glad to help where she could, especially with Dat complaining more often about aches and pains. Besides, the other women of the house were far better at scaring up a dinner. Lydiann preferred to write wonderful-good letters to her faraway beau, reminding him of her love for him as often as he did her.

She found herself continually checking the mailbox, even tuning her ear for their postman, ever so eager for more word from Ohio. Jake had written in his very last letter that he was doing some work with a "right fine woodworker—one with the same last name as my own." He looked on it as quite providential, especially since master woodworkers were few and far between here in Lancaster County. His happiness at this turn of events made Lydiann both pleased and a little sad. Pleased that he was finding plenty to keep his hands busy until such a time as he could return to her . . . and sad because she feared he just might get himself too attached to either

Ohio or the friendly Mast woodworker.

Today she intended to take twenty minutes from her morning chores to write another letter to Jake so she could get it tucked into the mailbox before the mail was picked up this afternoon.

"What're ya thinking 'bout *now*?" Abe asked her when they'd hauled the milk cans to the milk house.

"Nothin' much."

"Like foolin', you're not." He eyed her curiously. "You're thinking 'bout that beau of yours, ain't so? The one who up and left ya."

She sucked in air quickly. "Mind your own business!"

Abe frowned, staring hard at her. "What's a-matter, Lyddie? Ya don't have to bite my head off."

She had a mind to ignore him and she did.

"I've heard things . . . from some of the other fellas, ya know," Abe said.

She nodded. " 'Spect you have." She tensed up, worried he'd come right out and ask her something about Jake specifically—make her admit to his knowing whom it was she loved.

"Some of my friends are asking 'bout ya," he said. "A few are downright sweet on you, Lyddie."

She turned and glared at him, the little brother who'd become a young teenager before her eyes. Tall like Sadie and nearly as blond, Abe was good-looking in anyone's opinion. She didn't know for sure if she ought to say what she was thinking, but she did anyway. "I know our cousin Essie Ebersol is sweet on *you*, but would I have come right out and said it without thinking?" she hollered over her shoulder. Then she blew out a long sigh. "Truth is, when ya start to learn 'bout such things—who likes whom and all of that—it's really not for you to be sayin'. Don't you know anything?"

He stuck out his tongue. "Puh!"

"The day you ever think twice before talkin' . . . well, that'll be a right fine one, if I must say so!"

Before she might up and shed a tear, she started for the potting shed to cry her eyes out in peace. She wouldn't have been so easily upset, except she was missing Jake something awful.

When at last she'd pulled herself together, Lydiann headed for the chicken house, where she felt altogether hopeless as she scattered feed to the clucking hens and the solitary rooster.

On Jake's second visit to Jonas's cabinetmaking shop, unlike the first, the two of them quickly got to talking. Jake seemed less perturbed at having been unwillingly sent so far from home. In fact, it appeared to Jonas that Jake settled in for the day as if he were visiting an old friend. With their mutual Lancaster County connection and same last name, Jonas was curious to know more about Jake's family. "What's your father do?" he asked.

"He owns an apple orchard in a place called Grasshopper Level. Ain't really a town or a village—it's just a raised area between miles of farmland, southeast of Strasburg."

Astonished, Jonas stared at Jake. *This has to be my baby brother!* Looking at his nearly grown sibling, he was painfully aware of the passage of years, having been cut off from his family for nearly sixteen years. Had the Lord God truly brought his youngest brother to his very door?

Jonas said nothing, only watched and listened intently as the sad-eyed teenager went on. "My pop gave me no choice," Jake said, reaching for a hammer and holding it gingerly. "I had to leave home and come here, like it or not."

Jonas found this altogether puzzling. "Did you ever ask why that was?"

Jake laughed quietly. "You don't know my father. He isn't one to be questioned."

Jonas knew someone like that well enough, but the description wasn't one he would have used of his father. Fact was he knew *two* such someones: Abram Ebersol and Bishop Bontrager. But there was no sense bringing up the past with his young friend—his brother!

"I'm here 'cause I lacked courage, I s'pose you could say." Holding the hammer in both hands now and frowning down at it, Jake went to sit on the wooden stool near the table saw. "I'm in love with a girl my father doesn't like . . . doesn't approve of her family." He clenched his jaw. "How am I s'posed to feel 'bout that? I can't just stop loving her at his say-so."

Jonas studied him as he listened to the all-too-familiar account, drinking in the image of this dark-haired teen before him. Jake had been merely an infant when Jonas was still living at home, so he couldn't be of legal age to marry on his own just yet. No doubt he needed their father's permission to marry, something that had been denied.

"She couldn't be prettier, Jonas, with a down-to-earth sort of grace. Ever know someone like that?"

"Jah, I believe I do." He was thinking now of Emma.

"What do you do when love comes along clear out of the

blue and nearly knocks ya off your feet? Do you follow with all of your heart?"

He nodded. "Well, I should say so. Lord willin', of course."

Later, after Jonas had shown Jake several different tricks of the trade, he offered to take him back to the family with whom he was staying near Berlin.

"You sure?" Jake's big brown eyes were alight with the offer.

"Wouldn't mention it if I wasn't."

They had a good chuckle over that and headed out to hitch up the horse and buggy.

Sadie headed on foot to Ivan and Mary Etta Troyers' place, keeping her promise to help with some heavy cleaning, even though several of the older daughters planned to be on hand to help, as well. Thinking about a family of twelve—a perfect dozen—she wondered what it would be like to raise ten youngsters as she made her way toward the Troyers' farmhouse not too far down from the Kauffmans' spread. Not only did it seem unfair that some women had no trouble giving birth to one healthy baby after another, but she had also begun to second-guess Jake's going to Ohio. As far as she was concerned, it might as well be China, or some other country halfway around the world.

She rubbed her neck, realizing anew how upset she still was—finding and losing her precious son all within the space of a few weeks. Every now and then, she recalled how she had "heard" her baby crying all those months after she birthed him. At the time she'd thought she was losing her mind, but presently she wondered if God had been trying to tell her all those years ago that Jake was very much alive.

Now she let her eyes take in the trees and pastureland, sighing crossly. Never would there be another chance to anonymously spend time with her boy, let alone talk with him one-on-one as she longed to. How she wished to share the truth of who she was with him. Who *he* was to her!

She refused to let herself cry—not here on the road in plain view of Englishers driving past in their fancy cars. Today she must be in control of her emotions, not allow her misgivings to take over again. She must try to demonstrate the kind of pluckiness Leah seemed to have cultivated over time, despite her own heartaches. Just last night Sadie had talked with Leah, who indicated that when sorrowful things happen to people who are the children of God, they can either run to the Lord and seek after His presence, or they can pray and plead for God to remove the struggles so their life might be happy once again. "But don't be mistaken," Leah had warned, "it is not the easy or contented life that makes folk hunger hard after the Lord Jesus."

Even so Sadie wasn't sure she was ready to fully surrender her wants and wishes to the Lord God. Feelings of anger and resentment still raged within her—toward Dr. Schwartz and toward God, too, for allowing the doctor to do what he'd done. Sure, she could observe Leah's joyfulness all day long, but she didn't understand where it came from. It seemed the more sorrow Leah encountered in her life, the more peaceful, even content, she was. Sadie wished she, too, might experience such a miraculous reaction to the sad circumstances swirling around her, but she wasn't convinced a closer walk with God was the way for that to happen. When she prayed at all, she much preferred to beseech Him to bring her son home to her. It was only in that event that her happiness would be restored.

The lush green of grassy hills and treed hollows was never tiresome to Jonas, even though he took this way to work each and every weekday, and ofttimes Saturdays. He enjoyed the ride on the back roads of his second home in Apple Creek, though Grasshopper Level would always be first in his heart. The winding dirt roads led to one lumberyard after another, past Amish schoolhouses and white clapboard houses with sometimes three Dawdi Hauses built onto the main house, and clusters of mailboxes for as many Masts as Millers and Yoders. There, vast hayfields were frequently misty with gray fog at dawn, and golden fields were dotted with oat shocks, as well as large well-kept red barns with green roofs and miles and miles of whitewashed horse fencing. He never took a bit of this striking, colorful scenery for granted.

The road to town dipped and turned, making for some interesting conversation as Jake compared the landscape to that in Lancaster County.

"I'm gonna miss the apple harvest back home," Jake commented, and then said that another big reason he had despised being sent out here was having to leave behind his twin sister, Mandie. "Her name's Amanda, really, but she rarely gets called that anymore."

What should I say? Jonas's mind whirled mighty fast as his brother once again happened on the subject of their family. *How much does Jake know about me? Anything?*

Difficult as it was, he decided he would not reveal his identity just yet, for he feared Jake might not even know he existed, due to the Bann imposed by Bishop Bontrager. Even if Jake *had* heard of his wayward older brother, there was a real possibility the lad might not want to fellowship with him any longer, preferring to follow the strict shun slapped on Jonas. There was no way in this world he was going to ruin their growing friendship.

Yet again Jonas wondered what he had done to merit the divine blessing of being reunited with one of his family. So full was his heart, he could scarcely hold on to the reins.

Chapter Thirty-Two

Leah noticed almost immediately Lydiann's freshly scrubbed face and the combed hair neatly tucked beneath her head covering. Watching from the front room window, she was quite aware of the boost of energy in Lydiann's stride this afternoon as she hurried out to the mailbox. *She's surely eager for word from Jake,* thought Leah, wondering how long he would cling to Lydiann, especially when he had been admonished by his bishop, even Gid, to mingle with Ohio girls. No doubt Peter Mast shared the same desire. But if what she suspected was true, Jake had dismissed their urging, steadfastly staying in contact with Lydiann. Often, Leah had seen her, pen and paper in hand, heading off toward the woods after chores, just as she herself had when writing to Jonas so long ago.

When Lydiann came running in the back door, calling for her, Leah anxiously went to see what was on her mind. "Mamma, listen to what my beau wrote to me!"

Surprised, she asked, "Ach, Lyddie, are ya ever so sure you want to share this?"

"'Tis all right, really. I know you'll keep quiet, ain't?" Lydiann began to read from Jake's most recent letter as soon as they'd settled down at the kitchen table.

Leah was taken with the expression in Lyddie's voice as she related one interesting thing after another, pleased that her girl should entrust this very personal moment to her . . . yet sobered that Lyddie's affection for Jake did not appear to have lessened.

As the letter came to a close, Lydiann's voice became softer. Then, she looked up, still holding the letter. "I best not read further."

Leah nodded, struggling with a lump in her throat. She loathed having to pretend as if she didn't know anything about how and why Lyddie's beloved had ended up being sent away.

"He cares for me, Mamma." Lydiann brushed tears from her face. "What am I s'posed to do 'bout that?"

Unable to advise, Leah merely reached out a hand. "I'm awful sorry, dear. Truly I am. I hope you can trust the Lord for your future."

"Is that what you had to do, too, Mamma? After Jonas left here?"

She inhaled sharply. "Jonas?"

"Remember, Sadie told me 'bout him—and you—quite a while back."

Leah didn't care so much to talk about what she'd put behind her. There was no need to rehash the old days, especially when Jonas was the last person she wanted Lydiann to be asking about just now.

Lovely and peaceful, that's what Mary Ruth thought of this particular September morning as she drove the car to visit Lydiann. She hadn't stopped by to see her youngest sister in more than a week, and she wanted to gauge for herself how Lydiann was coping.

More than anything, she wanted to pass on the encouraging things she was learning in Scripture; she'd even tucked into her dress pocket a slip of paper with sermon notes from last Sunday. She wouldn't press the issue, of course, but she certainly hoped the Lord might make it possible for her to speak privately with Lydiann. That and maybe offer a quiet prayer for her.

When she parked the car in the driveway and switched off the ignition, Abe came running out from the barn to greet her. "Hullo!" he called, peering inside the driver's side of the car.

"How are you?" she asked, unable to open the door with Abe now hanging nearly inside the open window, reaching to touch the steering wheel, a curious grin on his face. "I think you best keep your eyes on driving horse and buggy," she said, lest Dat accuse her of promoting worldly interests in his only son.

"Aw, don't worry 'bout that. I know plenty of boys who have cars . . . hide 'em from their fathers."

She didn't like the sound of this at all and was glad when Abe stepped back so she could climb out of the driver's seat and head for the house. But Abe was trailing right behind her, not ready to let the topic drop.

"How fast do ya think your car can go?" he asked. "How quick can it get to top speed from a dead stop, I mean?"

"Now, Abe . . ."

"I'm serious," he replied. "I want to know."

She shook her head. "I have no idea about any of that."

Evidently disappointed, Abe sat down on the back steps, and she made her way inside.

In the kitchen she found Leah and Lydiann working side by side, stirring up two large fruit salads. One was to be served at dinner and the other was to take to Miriam Peachey, she was told.

Mary Ruth wondered about the latter, and Lydiann explained Miriam was under the weather. "That bein' the case, I wanted to do something nice for her and Smitty."

Sitting down on the wood bench, Mary Ruth was glad for a chance to catch her breath. Without asking; Lydiann brought her a glass of iced tea. "Denki," she said, glad for it, even though the day wasn't nearly as hot as it had been in past weeks.

"Won't be long now and school will be startin' up again," Lydiann mentioned, sitting down next to her. "Will you be missin' your students?"

"Well, yes and no."

Leah smiled and came over to the table with some crackers and several varieties of cheese on a plate. "You'll have one of your own little pupils to look after, 'fore too long."

"A new little one in the family," Lydiann said, eyes sparkling with her words. "I'll baby-sit whenever you want—just so long as it isn't twins. I'm not sure I could keep up with two babies the same age." Suddenly a shadow fell over her face, as if something had brought back a sad memory.

Leah quickly changed the subject to plans she had for making several crib quilts for the new baby.

"That's real nice of you," Mary Ruth told Leah—then to

Lydiann, she said, "Rest assured I'm having only *one* baby."

"Oh? When did ya learn this?" Leah asked, keeping her voice low and glancing toward the back door.

"The midwife told me yesterday." Mary Ruth sighed. "I do believe Robert is somewhat relieved, as well."

Just then they heard a sneeze coming from the back steps, and Mary Ruth put her hand on her chest. "Goodness, is Abe still sitting outside?"

Leah hopped up quickly and went to check, only to return with a grin on her face. "You guessed quite right," she said. "Abe took off runnin' toward the barn just now, but you can be sure both Dat and Gid will soon know it's a single baby comin'."

Mary Ruth reached for a second cracker with two small pieces of cheese on top. "That's all right with me." She looked at Lydiann, eager to talk with her alone, but the moment never presented itself, and after a piece of apple pie, she bid her farewell to her sisters.

"Come again soon," Leah called as Mary Ruth made her way out to the car.

"Oh, I will," she replied, noticing Lydiann making a quick dash toward the road.

The familiar squeal of brakes from out on the main road told Mary Ruth it was time for the mail.

Leah heard Lydiann run into the house, and when she turned, she saw her waving a letter, already opened.

"Listen to this!" Lydiann plopped herself back down on the bench and began to read, nearly breathless with excitement. " 'Dear Lydiann,' " she began. " 'I have the most interesting news. You know I've written in the past about the woodworking shop in Apple Creek. Well, I've made quite a discovery—one I think you'll be surprised at, too. You see, I've been working alongside my eldest brother all this time . . . and didn't even know it.'"

"Wait just a minute. Would ya mind readin' that last line again?" Leah interrupted, her heart in her throat.

Lydiann stared at her for a moment, frowning a bit, and then she raised the letter to reread it.

"Oh my . . ." Leah groaned.

"Mamma, did I upset you?"

"No . . . no. Is there more you want to share?"

Lydiann nodded. "I read this on the way in from the mailbox . . . and, honestly, if Jonas Mast isn't the one givin' woodworking pointers to *my* Jake."

Leah felt her hands trembling now. "Well, for goodness' sake," she whispered, not sure how to respond in the least.

"Can ya believe it?" asked Lydiann. "His own shunned brother."

Quickly Leah gathered her composure. "The Bann on Jonas is not for us to speak of." She wanted to say she'd never felt it was his fault . . . yet it wasn't for her to question the man of God, especially not in front of Lydiann. Truly, she had mixed emotions about the whole situation.

Trying to occupy herself, Leah offered Lydiann a glass of iced tea, but she was once again caught up in her letter. Leah sipped her own cold drink and breathed a silent prayer.

Chapter Thirty-Three

Hannah was anxious to write in her journal as her husband and girls lay sleeping soundly, bringing peace to the small house.

Friday, September 28
Dear Diary,

It is nearly nine-thirty tonight, yet I can't sleep—I'm ever so sure I am expecting another baby. We've waited so many years for this day, the thought doesn't frighten me in the least, especially because I made a good number of visits to Old Lady Henner before she died last week. The People turned out in large numbers for the funeral, but it was clear to me who was there paying their respects and who wasn't. Dat and Lizzie did not attend, nor did my sisters, all of them honoring Dat's stand against powwowing except me. Gid did happen to say on the long ride over to the funeral that he was beginning to see Dat's side of things, but he didn't go any further than that. These days it sounds to me as if Dat has much more sway over Gid than his own father does—Gid talks often of "Abram this and Abram that." Seems to me Gid has embraced my father as nearly his own.

All the same, I don't think he knows how much my father and stepmother tend to read the Bible, even study it. But I figure what Gid doesn't know about that won't be a nuisance to him if the bishop should ever ask. It's best to leave things be as they are, just as nobody kept me from going to Old Lady Henner all these years.

If I truly am in the family way, I hope to have yet another baby not so long after this one so he or she can have a close-in-age sibling. But I won't fret about when the Good Lord wants to send along our children to us, though I would like to give Gid a boy this time.

And I am awful happy for Mary Ruth, who is looking forward to her first wee one at the end of next month. What fun it will be to hold my twin's newborn in my arms! Mary Ruth will be a wonderful-good mother, for she has always had a strong leaning toward infants and little children . . . and she had all that practice with Carl Nolt when he was tiny.

Well, with Old Lady Henner gone, I don't believe I'll be seeking out a hex doctor anymore. I never cared much at all for the ones who are men—they give me the jitters. Now it will be for me to simply follow more closely the folk medicine on my own.

Respectfully,
Hannah

An early October throng of ladybugs rose like a great mist and then settled on the sunny-most side of the barn the first Saturday of the month. Leah had observed them in flight while taking down some washing that couldn't wait till Monday, all sun dried and bright from hanging on the line that morning and part of the afternoon. At the sight of the insects, she wondered whether an awful harsh winter might be in store this year.

Lydiann and Ida Mae and Katie Ann were away at Central Market in downtown Lancaster, tending table to a host of yellow, orange, white, and lime gourds, along with piles of prized pumpkins slashed from the vines just yesterday. The trip was a good, long ride by horse and buggy, to be sure. Still, Leah wished someone other than herself might have witnessed the strange sight, knowing Lydiann and the girls would have been equally surprised at hundreds of ladybugs seeking out shelter for the coming winter. No doubt the insects had found it under the loose slats on the south side of the old bank barn.

Hurrying across the backyard with her wicker basket, its contents nearly spilling over, she spied the ladybugs again. Immediately she got to wondering if Dat and Gid had split and stacked ample firewood to carry both families through the cold days come late October and beyond.

October. The word played in her mind with the energy of a brush fire before it quiets down and begins to smolder. Dat and Abe had lit the first such fire of the season just this morning, having spent hours raking up dead tree boughs and limbs in preparation, tidying things up in general. Sunlight seemed to leak out of the first weeks of autumn, and yet the vast woods to the northwest grew brighter by day, especially where the maples were set against ancient hemlocks.

Her thoughts flew to Lydiann, who continued to sulk around the house as though her last friend had died—when there wasn't a new letter to be had, that is. Faithfully Leah spent time in prayer each morning on the subject of Jake Mast, asking that he might stay put in Ohio. Asking, too, that

Lydiann might eventually become interested in a different young man.

With the slowing down winter would bring, Lydiann would soon have plenty of nurturing from the whole family—long fireside chats with Leah, evening prayers with Dat, playing table games with Lizzie and Abe. And knowing Lyddie as Leah did, she had reason to believe the dear girl would not pine for Jake forever. At least she hoped not.

Sadie was astonished when Lydiann came running in the back door saying she'd received another letter in the afternoon mail delivery.

In a whisper, Lydiann told her, "If you keep it quiet, Sadie, I'll tell ya who my beau is. I'll even read ya a bit of his letter."

"Aw, no, that ain't necessary," Sadie said immediately, glancing at Leah, who stood behind Lydiann. Sadie had recently suspected her youngest sister of sharing Jake's letters with Leah, although Leah had not revealed this in anything she'd said. Still, Sadie assumed she was right, as unusually close as Lydiann and Leah were. Certainly Leah had seemed to have more on her mind here lately.

"But I want to tell ya, honestly I do." And Lydiann revealed, right then and there, that the boy she loved was indeed Jake Mast. "And he loves *me*, too," she said, eyes twinkling.

Sadie was speechless at Lydiann's willingness to make known her beloved's identity, though she was grateful to have an opportunity to hear the kinds of things her son wrote and the way he phrased his thoughts. It was a small way to feel nearer to him.

Lydiann was already scanning her letter. At once she stopped reading to herself and announced, "Ach, listen to this. Jake writes that his eldest brother, Jonas, lives clear out in the country, where he boards and rooms with an older lady who is almost completely deaf. I guess he thinks of her fondly . . . as almost a family member, since he's never married and had a family of his own."

"What on earth?" Sadie said, bewildered. "You mean to say Jake knows of Jonas . . . and Jonas isn't married?" She looked now at Leah. Her sister's lips were parted, as if in shock, but she remained silent.

Lydiann refolded the letter. "Sure sounds like it, ain't?"

"Well, I should say this is quite amazing," she breathed. "If it's true."

"Jah, 'tis ever so surprising" was all Leah said.

"You all right?" Sadie placed a hand on Leah's slender shoulder. Evidently overcome with unexpected emotion, Leah bowed her head, and Sadie felt her precious sister tremble at the astonishing news.

Leah slipped away to the Dawdi Haus after Lydiann and Sadie had taken themselves off for a midafternoon walk at her insistence and following her repeated assurances she was going to be quite all right.

Now, in the solitude of Sadie's small house, she looked about her, taking in the tiny front room, the hickory rocker, the simple maple side table and wood settee, all the furnishings reminding her of Dawdi John. This room where she'd spent much time getting to know her grandfather, asking him questions about his courtship days . . . and sharing with him some about her own.

Incapable of grasping the implications of what Lydiann had revealed not thirty minutes ago, Leah felt terribly restless and walked to the open front door, welcoming the scents and gentle breezes of early autumn. There she recalled how Jonas had gently carried her into his father's house after she'd wrenched her ankle playing volleyball, how his strong arms had made her feel cared for and secure. Truly, there was so much to remember: The early years of stolen glances at family get-togethers, the summertime picnics on the lawn, the dear betrothal promise they'd made as youngsters, a love covenant to be sure. She remembered fondly the day of their church baptism, the long afternoon afterward spent sharing intimately while sitting in the grassy meadow, his sweet kiss on her lips. Dozens of Ohio letters had traveled between them . . . followed by the heartache of the years when she had naively believed Sadie had stolen him away.

Early on in those painful days, she had met with the Lord God in a very personal way up in the woods, realizing that she was and always would be God's Leah, that the dear Lord Jesus would mend her heart in due time and fulfill His plans and will for her life. Now the unexpected news that Jonas had remained single, just as she had, was almost more than she could comprehend or bear.

Standing there, Leah was relieved to be alone with her thoughts. Glad, too, that both Dat and Aunt Lizzie had not been present in the kitchen earlier. It had been hard enough to hold her emotions in check with Sadie and Lydiann staring at and making over her.

Sighing into the stillness, she breathed her silent questions. My *beloved, what things do you recall? Will you ever know that I am and always will be your Leah?*

In her heart she knew this was so. She had always loved Jonas, no matter how long she'd tried to fool herself into believing differently.

Yet even in this hushed moment of reflection and inner acknowledgment, she was not so sure Jonas would care that she was still a maidel. How could she possibly know what he was thinking . . . or if he was even aware that she, too, remained unmarried?

Turning, she wandered back into the house, to the kitchen doorway looking out to the barn and up toward the mule road.

All the happy days . . .

Through the simple act of faithful living, Leah had learned the most important thing—not to cling to or to chase after happiness. What she yearned for now was the heaven-sent joy that carried her through, even in the midst of suffering.

Jesus is the joy of my life, she thought anew.

She had come to know and live this truth from reading Mamma's Bible, and she'd attempted to teach it to Lydiann and Abe.

Dropping to her knees beside the small kitchen table, she thanked the heavenly Father for not only her many blessings, but for all of life's difficulties that had led her to this amazing moment . . . although she had no idea what to do with her knowledge of Jonas. But that was not for her to decide. She would do as the Scriptures instructed and wholly trust the Lord.

Chapter Thirty-four

An enormous relief came over Jonas on Monday morning when he opened the door to the woodworking shop and there, once again, stood his youngest brother on the stoop. He had wondered if perhaps Jake had gotten his fill of instruction, so intense Jonas had been the last time Jake spent the workday here. Intense in part because he'd heard things from Jake regarding Leah, whom Jake's girlfriend referred to as Mamma. The notion Leah was now Lydiann's mother had completely baffled Jonas. How was it his former sweetheart could be raising Lydiann, whom Jonas knew to be *Ida's* daughter? Sadly there was only one way that could have come about, and he was anxious to quiz Jake about it today. He must be more patient in awaiting answers about the girl he'd loved in Gobbler's Knob, yet his heart shouted to know all he could about her, especially since he had come to know she was not, in fact, married to Gideon Peachey. Was she Gid's widow, perhaps, helping a similarly widowed Abram raise Lydiann?

Sadie hurried through the connecting door to the main house, to the kitchen, where she made coffee, began to mix eggs and milk for scrambling, and fried up some bacon. She wanted to do something nice for Leah, seeing as how her sister was probably still mulling over the surprising Ohio news.

She waited until the table was laid and Aunt Lizzie had gone outdoors before slipping out of the house herself, wearing only an old sweater for her wrap. Quickly she caught up with Lizzie on the other side of the barn, where she was out taking a short jaunt in the grazing land.

At once she opened her heart to the woman she'd often confided in as a young girl. "I'm hopin' ya might help me get word to Dat's ears somehow . . . about Jonas Mast," she began. She did not plead with fancy words, nor did she fight back the tears that threatened to spill. She prayed silently and spoke honestly, hoping a gentle approach might work more effectively than dramatically beseeching Lizzie to do her bidding . . . for dear Leah's sake.

Abram was dressing around for Tuesday morning chores when Lizzie sidled up to him and said, "I have an idea . . . and I want ya to think on it."

"Oh?" He leaned down and kissed her full on the lips. Then, when she tried to wiggle free from his tight embrace, he kissed her again.

"For goodness' sake, Abram!"

He looked at her, all fresh and sweet from a good night's rest. "How was I to know what you had in mind, dear?"

She smiled and went to sit on their bed, her arms folded

now. "I've heard tell that Peter Mast's eldest son is as unattached as any man ever was."

He felt the frown crease his brow. "Well, how on earth would ya know that?"

Lizzie looked at him with love in her eyes. "My dear Abram, you best be trustin' me on this," she said. "But I know one thing—you could put a smile on more than one person's face round here if you'd be willin' to write one short letter."

He had no idea what she was suggesting and told her so.

"We've heard from someone in Ohio"—and here she looked at him, as if to make her meaning clear—"who knows for sure that Jonas has never married."

"And just who's that?" he asked, beginning to suspect the reason for the sadness in Lydiann's eyes.

"Don't know exactly . . . though I wouldn't tell ya, prob'ly, if I did."

Oh, he loved this spunky wife of his. He walked over to her and raised her up so he could hug the stuffings out of her.

"Think of it, Abram—Jonas not hitched up yet," Lizzie said in his arms. "And Leah still single . . ."

He figured out then he was supposed to put it together that the two of them might yet secretly care for each other. Leah's happiness, according to Lizzie, lay right in his own hands.

Lizzie was adamant. "Peppermint oil in tea *does* fight colds!" She glanced up at Hannah's girls playing in the haymow as she talked with Lydiann below. "My mother and grandmother both said this, and I know from experience it's true."

Lydiann sniffled and then pulled out a handkerchief from her dress pocket and sneezed. "This always happens to me at the beginning of autumn," she complained. "What is it 'bout that?"

"Oh, the change of seasons, I 'spect. Some folk get downright blue when summer turns to fall, and others catch a cold, just like you are. But . . . ya really oughta try some peppermint oil in a cup of tea, I'm tellin' ya."

Obviously uninterested, Lydiann turned up her nose yet again.

"All right, then, but don't say I didn't try 'n' help."

"I won't." Lydiann shrugged and headed for the ladder to join her young nieces.

A stubborn sort, she is, thought Lizzie, wishing Lydiann wasn't so much like Sadie had been at this age. But then again, who was *she* to talk?

Seeing Hannah's girls so playful just now, she thought of Mary Ruth and Robert. She could scarcely wait for their first baby to arrive, another grandchild by marriage for her. She felt so full of joy each day, walking and talking with the Lord Jesus and enjoying the young ones growing up around her. Sometimes she felt she ought to pinch herself to see if all her dreams had really come true, though she knew they surely had.

Only one thing clouded her happiness, however infrequently. Still, she wouldn't let it rob her peace, but it *was* something she could never quite shake. She wondered when she ought to finally bring herself to sit down one-on-one with Leah and be done with it . . . reveal everything about her beginnings. Or at least all she remembered. She had been taking into account the sorrows and disappointments Leah had endured these years, not wanting to further hamper her dear girl's seeming contentment with the potentially burdensome knowledge. She'd thought of asking Abram his opinion on this—if he thought it a good time to consider addressing it with Leah—even though he himself was in the dark about the man who'd fathered her one and only child. Truth was, she couldn't bring herself to reveal this to Abram, either—not just yet.

Leah had by no means endeavored to keep up with the English in the neighborhood. For one thing, talk of daylight savings time coming to an end here pretty quick made her laugh under her breath. Lorraine Schwartz loathed "losing light at the end of the day," as she liked to say, so it always fell to Leah to change back the settings on their clocks to "slow time" come the last Sunday of this month. Seemed odd to her, really, fancy folk wanting to go back and forth like that, especially since the People never observed "fast time" in the first place.

She did as was requested of her all the same, heeding the wants and wishes of her employers. Both Dr. Schwartz and his wife had become accustomed to her being altogether dependable, except for the few days, of course, when she had quit her job out of sheer anger. The problem with working for Dr. Schwartz, whom she'd long seen as an upstanding man, was that she no longer viewed him as so good, after all. Leah sometimes wondered if there was something she might do to help point him toward the Savior his heart undoubtedly longed for.

As Leah set about dusting the many framed family pictures, taking note that the pictures of Derek as a teen had been removed and replaced by wedding pictures of Mary Ruth and Robert, she thought how odd it was that the doctor's second grandchild was also to be an Ebersol by blood, though the circumstances were vastly different.

Sighing, she would not allow herself to feel upset for having approached Dr. Schwartz as she had. There had been extreme frustration and sadness in his eyes that day, but also absolute relief, as if the man had been waiting all these years for someone to condemn him!

Well, now that he had finally owned up to the truth, she felt almost sorry for him. Leah hoped she might share the love of the Lord Jesus with him—if not in words, then by her deeds.

Jonas stared down at the unexpected letter Jake had thrust into his hands, quite stunned to see it was from stubborn Abram Ebersol.

Meanwhile Jake tried to explain. "Tell ya the truth, I was mighty surprised gettin' this letter from Lyddie's father, along with a short one from her, too."

Jonas ran his hand through his hair, saying nothing.

"You all right?" Jake stared at him but good.

"Never better." Jonas had to suppress the urge to chuckle, but nothing of what Abram had written had anything to do with Jake. Except without this mighty handsome brother of his standing here, how long might it have been before Jonas had heard *any* word about Leah . . . let alone that she was still a maidel? He slipped the paper into his pants pocket.

He paused, wanting to get the words out just right. "I think it's high time I find out for myself why you were sent away. Your being here makes no sense to me at all." Jonas placed a firm hand on his brother's shoulder. "Time I heard this straight from the horse's mouth."

Jake expressed his wholehearted enthusiasm for the idea, and Jonas hurried to finish the new desk he'd promised to complete by next week. The more Jonas deliberated on it, the more he pondered how Jake's inclusion with the men who'd been traded—none of the others had any complaints, evidently—appeared much like what had happened to him years ago, just as he was preparing to wed Leah.

While sanding and smoothing out the wood's surface, he recognized that he had no idea what his first step upon his return would be toward Leah. Could he actually show up at Abram's home unannounced and knock on the door? He was a shunned man. Even if he were to be so brazen, Leah would adhere to the Old Ways, he was sure. And knowing Abram, he had not consulted with Leah before writing this brief letter.

Rubbing the wood all the harder, he wondered if Leah would *ever* want to see him again. Abram had hinted as much, yet nagging thoughts continued in Jonas's head. Truth was, the two of them scarcely knew each other anymore. *Is a future for us even possible?*

Unjust as his shunning was, Jonas was suddenly very eager to get home and set things aright. For Leah's sake.

He scrutinized the piece of wood intended for the desk top

and immediately spotted the small yet visible dip where he'd sanded much too hard. Straightening, he stopped his work. *Outcast or not, it's time I correct the foolishness of the past . . . time I did what I should've done long ago.*

"This desk will have to wait for finishing," he announced.

Jake looked up, eyes blank. "What do ya mean?"

"I'm closing up shop for a few days. I'll explain everything when I return."

Feels like a lifetime of waiting, he thought.

Chapter Thirty-five

The sun had already begun to make its way southward in Lancaster County. High in the sugar maple trees, birds preened and twittered contentedly, and, Jonas imagined, perhaps an ornery crow poked at an abandoned wasps' nest.

He was very aware of the many familiar landmarks as he rode in the backseat of the taxicab he'd taken from the train station in downtown Lancaster. Staring out the window, he made up his mind to do things the right way, with some semblance of propriety, at least. On the other hand, since he was a mere visitor, there was no harm done in simply putting off a visit to Bishop Bontrager.

While it was Leah he longed to see, he felt he must head straight to Grasshopper Level to speak with his father before entertaining notions of a visit to Gobbler's Knob. So the cab was traveling through the village of Strasburg, southeast toward Peach Lane with its tall trees and curving road dotted by Amish farms on either side, and then on to the Mast orchard house. He gazed out at roads he and Leah had not only ridden on together in his open buggy, but had walked on numerous times, enjoying the sun, the earthy smell of the fields, and their easygoing talk.

When he arrived at his father's house, Jonas hurried around to the back door, where he saw his mother in a green dress and old black apron standing by the cookstove, stirring a big soup kettle with a long wooden spoon.

Turning to look his way and seeing him just then, she let out a gasp and put her hand to her throat. "Ach, is it you, Jonas?" she said, coming quickly to the door, her eyes shining with happiness and tears both as she stared at his face and beard. "You've come home!"

But almost as fast as she'd expressed joy on her sweet face, the reality of his shunning must have set in, for her eyes darkened and she began to back away.

"Hullo, Mamma. Is Dat home?" His pulse throbbed with every breath, and he felt as though he were sleepwalking.

His mother struggled to hold back her tears, the thinly disguised longing evident on her dear face. "Your father's in the barn," she said softly.

"Believe me, I mean no trouble . . ." he managed to say, knowing full well he was required to speak to his father first, as was their custom when an excommunicated family member returned home.

Jonas hurried across the yard toward the large bank barn. The luster of orange and yellow trees captured his awareness yet again, but only for an instant. His stride was strong and he felt the determined set of his own jaw, his gaze steadfast on the open barn door.

He found Dat tending to the mules, talking low, slow words in Dutch, just as Jonas remembered his father doing when he was a boy. Standing there, he took in the old place and its noticeable barn stench, recalling all the years he'd worked alongside his father and younger brothers . . . the pranks they'd pulled on each other, the times when he was allowed to wear Dat's work boots and he'd gone clunking and falling through the haymow, kicking up a dust to kingdom come.

He waited to speak till Dat's back was no longer turned so he would not startle his aging father. "Dat, it's Jonas."

As tall and brawny as ever, his father inched his head up, taking uneven breaths, his large shoulders rising with each measured heave. "Son?"

"I've come a long way to speak to ya." He wanted to hurry to Dat's side, reach around the familiar burly frame and hug the man he'd missed so terribly.

Dat extended his hand. "Come here to me, Jonas. Let me look at ya."

Obediently he moved across the barn floor; his mouth went dry as the moment hit him hard. "I wish to talk to ya, Dat."

"You're a married man, jah?" His father chewed on a piece of straw he held in his callused hand as he studied Jonas's chin. "Where's your missus?"

Jonas felt the softness of his beard. "Oh that. Well, things are a bit different out in Ohio. We let the whiskers grow right away, followin' baptism. I'm still unhitched."

Dat kept staring, as if what Jonas had just said and what Dat was seeing with his own eyes didn't quite register. "Jake wrote us a letter . . . said he'd run into ya . . . but I never expected him goin' out to Ohio would bring *you* back to us."

How can I tell him otherwise? Jonas wondered, but he didn't have to reveal his plans—not just yet. "I'm home to talk over some things with Bishop Bontrager," he volunteered. "In fact, I'm headed up to Gobbler's Knob after a while."

Dat seemed interested in hearing more, nodding his head quicklike. "Well, now, I sure hope you're goin' to talk about repentin' and returning home . . . where ya belong, after all these long years."

Jonas didn't have the heart to say differently when he took in the look of longing in his dear old father's eyes. "I have some questions to voice, for now." He didn't say what, but he added, "And I'm here to ask something of you, too."

"That's right fine, as long as you're goin' to repent." There it was again. Dat knew he best not be talking for too long with his wayward son unless the Gobbler's Knob bishop allowed it.

"I have to know something from you directly," said Jonas. "Why was my brother sent to Ohio . . . forced to leave behind his sweetheart-girl?"

Dat's eyes grew suddenly small and a deep frown tunneled into his brow. "Not your concern."

"I beg your mercy on this, Dat. Jake's awful *ferhoodled* . . . he loves a girl *here*. He wants to marry her—he told me so."

"Abram Ebersol's daughters are off limits to my sons. No exceptions," Dat bellowed, hands clenched. Jonas heeded the flinching muscles around Dat's mouth and whiskers, the fire in his eyes as he uttered the terse explanation. "The family's tainted. Leah's a bad seed, 'cause of her illegitimate birth. But I don't need to be tellin' you that. Look how she tricked you."

Jonas was shocked that his father could refer to one so lovely in spirit as deceitful, even wicked. "How can you say that?"

"The woman betrayed you by gettin' you to join church

with her over there in Gobbler's Knob, that's what." His father made an attempt to explain his view of the entire problem: that Leah's deception—Jonas's taking the baptismal vow in her church—had set him up for eventual shunning, when "she dumped ya and went for that other fella."

"Gid Peachey, ya mean?" Jonas asked, knowing from Abram's letter to him that Leah had never married Gid. "Leah is, in fact, still a maidel."

The news was evidently not a surprise to Dat.

"You honestly blame Leah for all this?" Jonas asked.

"Abram, the skunk, carries the full weight of blame," his father replied, making it mighty clear that had not Abram opened his home, and Ida her arms, to "that witch of a sister, Lizzie Brenneman, back when she was in the family way without a husband, you would never have been put under the Bann. Never!"

Dat's shout startled the mules, and a small cloud of dust rose into the air as the animals' hooves stamped and dug into the ground. "That's enough talkin' for now. You best be headin' to see the minister!"

With that Dat turned away as one did to the shunned, although doing so did not conceal the rapid rise and fall of his father's shoulders.

Will he turn his back on me . . . yet again?

"Ach, she's as perty as a rosebud," Leah breathed, cradling Mary Ruth's newborn daughter in her arms.

Mary Ruth nodded drowsily in the birthing bed, all smiles. "A gift from our Lord to us," she said, dabbing at her perspired face and neck with a damp towel.

"What's her name?" Leah looked down at this precious tiny person, holding her gently near.

"Ruthie," replied Mary Ruth, glancing up at Robert, who leaned his head against her own.

Leah kissed Ruthie's wee face and reluctantly passed her to Aunt Lizzie, who was clearly itching to get her hands on the sleeping bundle. "Suits her fine, seems to me," Leah said.

"It surely does," said Lizzie, eyes alight.

Leah stepped out into the hallway, glad for such an easy birth for her sister. She was also grateful to Dan and Dottie Nolt, who had insisted Robert and Mary Ruth come to their home for the midwife-assisted birth, although the idea behind that was so Mary Ruth could be within "calling distance" of Dr. Schwartz should anything go wrong.

Whispering a prayer of thanksgiving, Leah donned her shawl and slipped out the back door, pleased to walk beneath the brilliant canopy of colors toward home.

◆

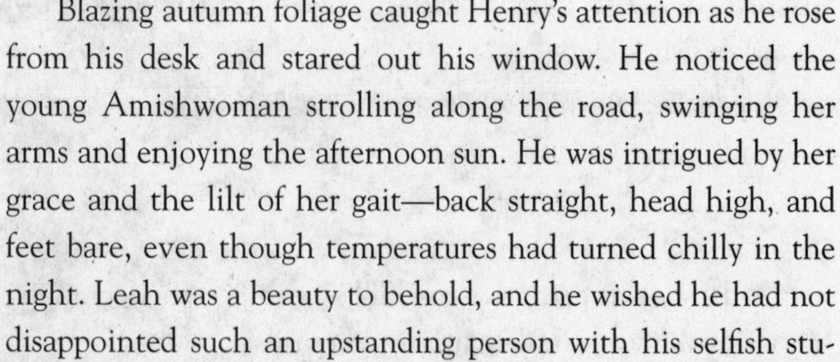

Blazing autumn foliage caught Henry's attention as he rose from his desk and stared out his window. He noticed the young Amishwoman strolling along the road, swinging her arms and enjoying the afternoon sun. He was intrigued by her grace and the lilt of her gait—back straight, head high, and feet bare, even though temperatures had turned chilly in the night. Leah was a beauty to behold, and he wished he had not disappointed such an upstanding person with his selfish stupidity.

The phone rang in his office, and he went to his desk to

pick up the receiver. "Dr. Schwartz speaking."

"Dad, you're a grandpa!"

"Well, what good news, Robert! How's your little missus?" he asked first about Mary Ruth.

"Oh, she's fine . . . happy as can be."

"And the baby?"

"A little girl—six pounds, eight ounces, and only nineteen inches long. But she's real healthy and the prettiest baby I've ever seen."

"No doubt it's true." He chuckled, recalling Robert's own birth and the rapturous feeling of seeing his firstborn child for the first time. "Congratulations, son," he said. "And give Mary Ruth our love."

Robert urged him to come over right away. "Bring Mother along to see little Ruthie . . . her given name. It's not a nickname," he insisted. "This is Mary Ruth's idea, and I like it!"

Henry could certainly hear the joyous cadence of Robert's voice, and he assured him they would soon be over. "Thanks for the phone call," he said before hanging up.

He returned to the window, wondering if Leah was still in view. Staring into the near-neon oranges and golds of the expansive willow oak shade tree and silver maples, his thoughts returned to the secret Abram's second daughter had evidently chosen to keep from the world . . . at least for now.

I dare not press my good luck, he thought.

News of his first granddaughter mingled with his former reflections on Jake, his first *grandson.* In a second of momentous decision, he reached for a pen and wrote two words on his note pad: *Early retirement.*

He determined his future right then—a future that would be his choice no matter what Leah decided to do. He would turn his clinic over to Ron Burkholder, the young intern presently assisting him, and retreat from his faithful patients. He would punish himself, since no one else had . . . effectively locking himself up by withdrawing from his greatest passion in life, however much longer it might endure. He would announce this to Lorraine tonight at supper, after they'd cooed over and held their new grandbaby.

"Ruthie," he whispered, already fond of the name Mary Ruth had selected.

Once more his thoughts returned to Jake . . . and to Derry. *My son will never know either his own son or his niece.* Henry was again humiliated that Derek bore the Schwartz name. Or perhaps, on further recollection, Derek was merely a reflection of the worst part of himself. Henry shuddered.

Chapter Thirty-Six

Jonas was convinced he'd borrowed his father's slowest driving horse, but he wasn't in the mood to gripe, even to himself, though he was in a tremendous hurry. He had left his father in an awful bad way, back there in the barn, Dat having been both glad and reluctant to see him. Regrettably there had been no other way to handle that initial encounter, and the fact remained that he *had* needed transportation to get to Bishop Bontrager's.

The truth came home to him that his father believed Abram's daughters were at the very root of the problem besetting the Masts. First Leah . . . and now Lydiann.

Poor Jake, he thought, wishing he could do something to change things for his brother. But knowing their father . . . and hardheaded Abram, there was only one way to unravel such a thorny matter.

Hurrying the old mare, Jonas leaned forward in the Mast family buggy, as if doing so might encourage the horse onward, up the long, steep grade to Gobbler's Knob.

Years ago Leah had memorized the tree that marked the halfway point between the Nolts' house and the Ebersol Cottage. She looked curiously at the bent old spruce, wondering what had happened to cause its deformity. Surely not lightning or hurricane-gale winds, although they'd had a few scares with such violent weather in past summers. Today the autumn air was as calm as the atmosphere encircling a newborn infant, and she felt as though she could still smell and feel Mary Ruth's new little one. "Ruthie Schwartz," she said, smiling at the memory of Robert's face upon holding his daughter for the first time.

I will enjoy everyone else's babies, she thought, though not sadly, merely accepting her own lot. *I'll love each one . . . spoil 'em, too!*

Watching the birds flit from tree to tree, several groups of them playing chase across the road and back again, she got to thinking about the days, not so long past, when Lydiann and Abe were completely dependent on her loving care. The years had flown away and both children had reached adolescence, eager to stretch their youthful wings. Especially Lydiann . . . *dear, heartbroken girl.*

She could only hope for the best where Lyddie was concerned . . . Abe, as well. She, Dat, and Aunt Lizzie had surely given their all to instill obedience to God and the church, along with a full measure of honesty, kindness, and a humble spirit. The children had heard more Scripture than *she* ever had growing up, and for this she was beholden to Dat. Leah was endlessly thankful he had embraced Mamma's and Lizzie's faith as his own. Really, it had changed his attitude toward a lot of things.

Feeling compelled to wander from the road a ways, she

found a large rock beyond the shoulder and sat there still as could be, enjoying the birdsong that was certain to quiet with deep autumn and, soon to come, the cold winter. She remembered the surprise in Dat's eyes when she had shared about the ladybugs congregating on the side of the barn. "Jah, a right harsh winter this one'll be," he'd said, confirming her suspicions.

Pondering nature's splendor all around, she heard the sound of a horse and buggy but did not turn her head to look. Dozens of carriages and horses came and went up and down this road—sometimes she could almost tell which horse belonged to which family before ever actually laying eyes on it. Presently she concentrated on the rattle of the hard wheels, the *clip-a-clop* and gait of the horse. Whoever it was wasn't from Gobbler's Knob.

When the horse was but several hundred feet away, she turned out of curiosity. Squinting, she saw the features of a bearded man who seemed familiar somehow. She was drawn by his appearance but knew better than to stare at a married man, for pity's sake! Yet there was something more to him—the way he held the reins, the tilt of his head—than simply his looks.

The closer the horse pulled the carriage toward her, the more she stared. She ought to look away, but a sudden knowing flooded her.

Jonas? But surely she must be mistaken. This man had a beard. Had Jake gotten his information off beam in his letters to Lydiann?

Her own indecision was resolved when the man glanced her way, a look of puzzlement on his face.

Suddenly he pulled on the reins and called out, "Whoa!"

When the horse had obeyed and come to a halt, he leaped down and walked toward her. "Leah? Is that you?"

This *was* Jonas. There was no mistaking his voice, or those azure blue eyes.

Removing his hat, he said softly, "I didn't expect to see ya out here on the road."

And I didn't expect to see you ever again, she thought in wonderment. It was her turn to nod, her turn to say something—*anything*—but she was unable to speak. Jonas was *here*! He stood only a few feet away, holding his hat, eyes shining.

"Nice day for a walk, ain't?" he said.

His casual tone took her off guard, and a thousand answers cluttered her mind, none of them making sense at all.

"Jah, a perty day, for sure," she murmured, still staring at his beard.

A long, awkward moment passed as Jonas held his hat in his hands, turning it repeatedly. Neither of them seemed to know what to say.

"I'm on my way to see the bishop," he said at last, gesturing toward the buggy. "Would ya care to ride a ways with me?"

She was again mindful of his beard. "But . . . Jonas, you're married."

He chuckled a bit. "These whiskers don't mean what you think." And he explained the Ohio custom, apparently mighty eager to clear up that niggling detail.

She felt like laughing but squelched her giddiness. She wasn't a bit sure what she was doing . . . couldn't think clearly, not with those adoring eyes of his staring down at her that way.

"You must be mighty surprised to see me, Leah."

"Well, I'd have to say I am. Uh, but I best not ride with you," she said quickly.

He frowned for a moment and then smiled. "I'm here to clear up a few important things."

Jonas is a shunned man. . . .

"Are ya headin' to the bishop's to talk 'bout lifting the Bann on you, maybe?" she asked.

He paused, his eyes locked on hers. "He and I have plenty to discuss." His smile was the next thing to beautiful. "I came back right away when I heard. . . ." He shook his head, as if reconsidering his reply, nearly twirling his hat in his hands now.

Turning, he looked at the horse and carriage. "I say you and I have some catchin' up to do."

She eyed the buggy, wishing she could agree to go along and sit beside him in the first seat the way they used to in his open courting buggy when they were teenagers. *Lydiann's age*, she thought.

Was she willing to risk getting in trouble with the brethren, accepting a ride before the bishop had his say with Jonas?

"If the bishop or one of the ministers should happen along and see me ridin' in your buggy, wouldn't I be considered disobedient?"

He grinned. "All of that . . . and much more."

She couldn't suppress her smile. "I don't mean to be difficult—"

"Then don't." Again, the smile that made her heart flutter. "Please, won't ya get in the carriage, Leah?"

She took a deep breath. *I've waited forever for this moment.*

"I want to talk to ya further," he said more softly. "I've missed you terribly."

All reason flew away when his endearing eyes met hers. "Well, I s'pose it might be all right." She willingly followed Jonas past the horse and to the carriage, where he helped her up.

Once inside, Jonas picked up the reins, his voice suddenly earnest again, a concerned look in his eyes. "How's your family?"

She shared that her father was well. "But Mamma died giving birth to our Abe in 1949," she explained. "I raised my brother and sister Lydiann as my own, with help from Dat . . . and, more recently, Aunt Lizzie, who married my father some six years ago."

He expressed his sadness over the loss of her mother, and Leah was taken by his gentleness. Their talk grew more animated as she attempted to catch him up on the community of the People in Gobbler's Knob.

The years were melting away, as though nothing much had changed. And when her father's house came into view, Jonas didn't halt the horse or offer to make the turn into the long lane to the Ebersol Cottage.

Instead, he kept on, describing his Apple Creek cabinetmaking shop and telling her about Emma Graber, the deaf landlady who rented out an upstairs room to him. He talked of his years alone . . . and the many wonderful-good things the Lord had been teaching him.

Leah hung on to his every word, soaking in his presence, memorizing his every movement and expression . . . lest she wake up and discover this to be a fleeting dream.

When Jonas stopped talking of Ohio, an uncomfortable silence followed. And then, he turned to her, his eyes altogether serious. "Leah . . . I believed all these years . . . you were married to Smithy Gid."

She shook her head slowly. "I sent a letter right back—after you wrote me your questions." She paused, gathering her thoughts, her wits.

Jonas turned to look at her. "What letter do ya mean?"

In all her life, she could not have imagined this conversation and this moment, as the two of them came to grips with all the foolishness that had caused their wedding plans to go awry. She explained the mix-ups and misunderstandings as best she could, careful to keep dear Sadie out of her remarks. "I've honestly forgiven the past," she whispered at last.

Slowly Jonas pulled back on the reins, bringing the buggy to a stop on the dirt road south of the Amish cemetery, off Georgetown Road. "I didn't know for sure till just now," he said, "but I've waited years to tell you this, never daring to believe I'd have the chance."

She stared at his dear face. "What is it?" she asked, nearly breathless to know.

His eyes gently pierced her. "My heart has always belonged to *you*, Leah."

In that tender, yet revealing instant, she knew that no matter how busy her life had become, how important her responsibilities to Lydiann and Abe, or how many times she had been convinced she'd left the past far behind, she had never, ever stopped loving Jonas.

"If you should happen to have any feelings left for me," he said in a near whisper, "I'd like to spend time with you . . . get to know you again. Once the bishop gives me the go-ahead, that is."

She breathed in slowly and held the air in her lungs. Was he indicating he'd returned home to court her . . . was that what he meant to say? "I . . . it's . . . I'd like to get reacquainted, jah, really I would. It's just that . . ." Scarcely could she get the words out.

So many things to consider . . . to work through. The bishop's insensitive ruling on Sadie, for one. Wouldn't Jonas be put through a similar Proving? One even more trying, perhaps? And there was Jonas's father to reckon with, too. Wouldn't Peter Mast and Bishop Bontrager put their heads together and devise a way to keep Jonas and Leah apart? Possibly forever.

"I love you," Jonas whispered, his words close to her ear.

Tears sprang to her eyes, yet she nodded back, desperately trying to tell him that she cared deeply, too.

"I'll never leave you again, Leah. Never."

She could not speak for the rush of emotion, and when he moved closer still, she felt nearly helpless, yielding, at last, to his tender embrace.

Epilogue

I honestly marvel at the amazing things the Lord has done in my life—I sometimes have to pinch myself, for sure. Jonas still loves *me* . . . after all this time. But what is most astonishing, aside from my darling's plan to move back home, is that Sadie—with a little help from Dat—was the one to set the wheels in motion for Jonas to return in the first place. Aunt Lizzie whispered this to me while we were rolling out pie dough today.

The minute I could go and find Sadie in the Dawdi Haus, where she was sitting and reading Mamma's Bible, I leaned down and kissed her cheek.

She looked up at me and said with eyes bright with her own tears, "It was the least I could do for ya, sister, considerin' all the trouble I've caused."

Dear Sadie! She misses Harvey something dreadful, and I pray she might offer up her desires and longings to the Lord, for He alone is the answer to her lonely and broken heart.

Lydiann, too, seems caught in a fog of melancholy. She is miserable and restless, and more times than I can count, I've prayed that something or someone might come along to get her attention off Jake Mast.

It's still heartbreaking for me to think of Sadie's son being clear out in Ohio, though now with Jonas returning home, I also worry Jake might up and decide to come back, too. If so, what a pickle we will be in!

Dr. Schwartz surprised me by announcing his retirement, even though Lorraine says this won't happen for another six months or so—he'll have to turn his loyal patients over to young doctor Burkholder. If I want to, I'll still have plenty to do keeping house for them, though sometimes it's hard to work for Dr. Schwartz, knowing what I know. It does seem peculiar to me that he should want to simply travel round and "see the world," giving up his work at the clinic when he's still a relatively young man. Dat thinks it's an awful shame. "A man oughta work till he dies," my father likes to say. As for me, I think it *is* high time the village doctor packed away his stethoscope.

Thinking of work, Sadie, Lydiann, and I have been busy sewing dresses and aprons for Hannah's girls, as well as crocheting more baby blankets for sweet Ruthie. And it won't be long before Ruthie has herself a new cousin, for Hannah's told me privately that she's expecting another little one, as well.

Abe, the baby of *this* family, has been having plenty of fun at the expense of a good many rats and other farm pests here lately. With the corn harvest in full swing, he's been joining other young fellows round the area, going to pest hunts. So the suppertime talk is frequently filled with his chatter about such rambunctious things, but I do love to watch his expressive eyes light up with all the youthful excitement. And I can see by Dat's eyes that he, too, is delighted and amused.

Dat is also outwardly pleased at the prospect of Jonas's impending return to Gobbler's Knob, although I must admit to being quite fretful in waiting to hear how the bishop and the brethren will view all of this . . . and just when I'll see my beloved again.

For now, I simply thank our dear Lord for His merciful kindness, and I'm trusting Him no matter what the future may hold. I can only hope to marry Jonas one fine day, but even such a sacred end—and a joyous beginning, too—must rest in God's sovereign will, and that alone.

Watch for ABRAM'S DAUGHTERS book five,

The Revelation

in summer 2005 at your local bookstore!

Also by Beverly Lewis

Picture Books

Annika's Secret Wish · *Cows in the House*
Just Like Mama

The Cul-de-sac Kids
(For ages 7 to 10)

The Double Dabble Surprise · *Tarantula Toes*
The Chicken Pox Panic · *Green Gravy*
The Crazy Christmas Angel Mystery · *Backyard Bandit Mystery*
No Grown-ups Allowed · *Tree House Trouble*
Frog Power · *The Creepy Sleep-Over*
The Mystery of Case D. Luc · *The Great TV Turn-Off*
The Stinky Sneakers Mystery · *Piggy Party*
Pickle Pizza · *The Granny Game*
Mailbox Mania · *Mystery Mutt*
The Mudhole Mystery · *Big Bad Beans*
Fiddlesticks · *The Upside-Down Day*
The Crabby Cat Caper · *The Midnight Mystery*

Girls Only (GO!)
(For ages 8 to 13)

Dreams on Ice · *Follow the Dream*
Only the Best · *Better Than Best*
A Perfect Match · *Photo Perfect*
Reach for the Stars · *Star Status*

SummerHill Secrets
(For ages 11 to 14)

Whispers Down the Lane · *House of Secrets*
Secret in the Willows · *Echoes in the Wind*
Catch a Falling Star · *Hide Behind the Moon*
Night of the Fireflies · *Windows on the Hill*
A Cry in the Dark · *Shadows Beyond the Gate*

Holly's Heart
(For ages 11 to 14)

Best Friend, Worst Enemy · *Straight-A Teacher*
Secret Summer Dreams · *No Guys Pact*
Sealed With a Kiss · *Little White Lies*
The Trouble With Weddings · *Freshman Frenzy*
California Crazy · *Mystery Letters*
Second-Best Friend · *Eight Is Enough*
Good-Bye, Dressel Hills · *It's a Girl Thing*

www.BeverlyLewis.com

04C

THREE BEVERLY LEWIS FAVORITES!

October Song

A WELCOME RETURN TO LANCASTER COUNTY!

Colorful and quaint, *October Song* weaves together a captivating peek into the lives of Beverly Lewis's most adored characters. Readers young and old will be thrilled by the continuation of their favorite stories, from *The Shunning* to *The Postcard* and more!

Annika's Secret Wish

A HEARTWARMING TALE MAKES CHRISTMAS MORE MEANINGFUL THAN EVER!

Capture the spirit of Christmas and help your children understand Jesus' gift for us with this cherished tale from Beverly Lewis. Included is a special CD from recording artist Evie Tornquist Karlsson, who narrates the story and sings two Christmas hymns. This is a true holiday treasure!

The Sunroom

REVEL IN THE POWER OF UNCONDITIONAL LOVE

This poignant novella tells the story of Becky Owens, a young girl who makes a desperate pact with God in hopes of keeping her critically ill mother alive. Filled with beautiful illustrations, this is a wonderful gift book to be treasured.

BETHANYHOUSE

The Revelation

BEVERLY LEWIS

The Revelation

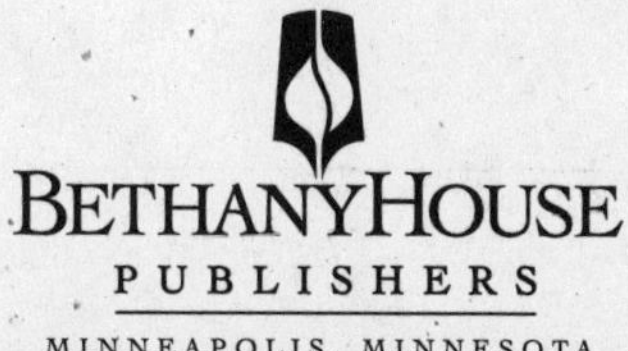

BETHANYHOUSE
PUBLISHERS
MINNEAPOLIS, MINNESOTA

The Revelation
Copyright © 2005
Beverly Lewis

Cover design by Dan Thornberg

Published by Bethany House Publishers
11400 Hampshire Avenue South
Bloomington, Minnesota 55438

Bethany House Publishers is a division of
Baker Publishing Group, Grand Rapids, Michigan.

Printed in the United States of America

ISBN 0-7642-2874-9 (Paperback)
ISBN 0-7642-2881-1 (Hardcover)
ISBN 0-7642-2882-X (Large Print)
ISBN 0-7642-2883-8 (Audio Cassette)

Library of Congress Cataloging-in-Publication Data

Lewis, Beverly, 1949–
The revelation / by Beverly Lewis.
p. cm. — (Abram's daughters ; 5)
Summary: "Conclusion to the series spanning three generations in a quaint Old Order Amish community. A story of love, faith, and second chances featuring five courting-age sisters and their extended family that is both heartrending and uplifting."—Provided by publisher.
ISBN 0-7642-2881-1 (hardback : alk. paper) — ISBN 0-7642-2874-9 (pbk.) — ISBN 0-7642-2882-X (large print pbk.) 1. Amish—Fiction. 2. Sisters—Fiction. 3. Lancaster County (Pa.)—Fiction. I. Title. II. Series: Lewis, Beverly, 1949– . Abram's daughters ; 5.

PS3562.E9383R48 2005
813'.54—dc22

2005004598

Dedication

For

Mary Jo and Helen Jones,

two wunderbaar *aunties.*

By Beverly Lewis

ABRAM'S DAUGHTERS

The Covenant
The Betrayal
The Sacrifice
The Prodigal
The Revelation

❖ ❖ ❖

THE HERITAGE OF LANCASTER COUNTY

The Shunning
The Confession
The Reckoning

❖ ❖ ❖

ANNIE'S PEOPLE

The Preacher's Daughter

❖ ❖ ❖

The Postcard · *The Crossroad*

❖ ❖ ❖

The Redemption of Sarah Cain
October Song · *Sanctuary**
The Sunroom

❖ ❖ ❖

The Beverly Lewis Amish Heritage Cookbook

www.beverlylewis.com

*with David Lewis

05C

BEVERLY LEWIS, born in the heart of Pennsylvania Dutch country, fondly recalls her growing-up years. A keen interest in her mother's Plain family heritage has led Beverly to set many of her popular stories in Lancaster County.

A former schoolteacher and accomplished pianist, Beverly is a member of the National League of American Pen Women (the Pikes Peak branch). She is the 2003 recipient of the Distinguished Alumnus Award at Evangel University, Springfield, Missouri, and her blockbuster novel, *The Shunning*, recently won the Gold Book Award. Her bestselling novel *October Song* won the Silver Seal in the Benjamin Franklin Awards, and *The Postcard* and *Sanctuary* (a collaboration with her husband, David) received Silver Angel Awards, as did her delightful picture book for all ages, *Annika's Secret Wish*. Beverly and her husband make their home in the Colorado foothills.

Prologue

October 24, 1963

Six endless days have come and gone since that wonderful-good crimson-and-gold-speckled day when Jonas returned to Lancaster County to declare his fondest affection for me. Yet I've had no word since—not even following his important visit with the bishop. And as each day passes I am mindful not to give in to fretting, losing myself in needless worry. I must simply bide my time till I know precisely what my beloved is up against. That decision will be made following Preaching service tomorrow, though I don't dread this meeting as much as I did my sister Sadie's kneeling confession, because Jonas did not commit a sin of the flesh, as Sadie did. His only transgression was to disobey Bishop Bontrager's rigid position on never leaving the church of one's baptism, a sin as defined by our *Ordnung*.

The winds of autumn bluster over Dat's frayed fields and Smitty's silver pond, and the sound reminds me of the work remaining to be done before winter sets in fully. Often I feel as if I'm chasing after the daylight, hoping to complete every last chore on my mental list. All the while the mules eagerly dismantle one bale of hay after another, growing thicker coats for the coming cold.

Sadie and I have talked frankly about Jonas's return—I simply had to share my heart lest it burst apart. She is the only one who knows he saw me before he went to visit Bishop Bontrager, as he should have done straightaway. Honestly there are times when I am nearly giddy with anticipation, knowing Jonas is only thirty minutes away, living once again in the orchard farmhouse on Grasshopper Level. The sky seems nearly like a blue jewel on clear days, and I have never been so awestruck by the color and texture of grazing land, windswept dew ponds, or even the shy silhouettes of clouds. What I thought had long since died in me has sprung to vibrant life, surprising me all to pieces.

Truly, it is a rare night when Jonas is not present in my dreams, and he is my cherished first thought at daybreak. I carry within my heart the hope of one day being reunited with my darling beau, if God should see fit.

Still, I must be ever so careful not to let this renewed passion for Jonas distract me from mothering Lydiann and Abe. The dear Lord knows there are enough issues to provide conflict under one roof, including Lydiann's *rumschpringe*, which, despite an unexpected twist, has thus far been innocent compared to Sadie's running-around time long ago.

We have heard by way of Jake Mast's letters to Lydiann that he's chomping at the bit to get home and right the wrong he feels was done to him by his father—not to mention rekindle the flame with Lyddie—even though I am sure Peter Mast will continue to put the nix on things. My heart quivers at the thought of Jake's potential return—a prickly prospect, to be sure. Although he remains in Ohio at the moment,

Sadie and I agonize over what will befall us if his identity should ever be revealed. Truth be told, if the Masts were aware their youngest son is in fact Sadie's, there would be no question in *anyone's* mind that the two youngsters must never marry.

Thinking again of Jonas, I have no way of knowing if he'll be expected to abandon his woodworking. The bishop, in particular, has scorned any livelihood but those related to the soil—sowing and reaping—and blacksmithing or other necessary tasks. For Jonas to be forced to farm would be heartache, what with his keen interest and skill in the area of crafting fine furniture. Just how long his Proving will last is hard to know . . . if the bishop will require one, considering the lesser sin he's committed against the church.

Secretly, though, I fear something will yet keep us apart. I pray not, but alas, ever since first seeing swarms of ladybugs a few weeks back, heralding the advent of winter with its dearth of light, I have been aware of a sense of foreboding. Soon snow as thick as lamb's wool will fall, and if I lose myself in the flurry, the road seems to become a looming tunnel . . . and as I imagine riding horse and buggy through its shadowy center, the eyes of my heart become painfully aware of the confinement. Try though I might, will I ever truly find my way out to the other side?

Part One

◆ ◆ ◆ ◆

Our joys as winged dreams do fly;

Why then should sorrow last?

Since grief but aggravates thy loss,

Grieve not for what is past.

—Thomas Percy

Chapter One

A chill had settled into the rustic planks of the old farmhouse overnight, and Jonas worked quickly to remedy the situation. He crouched near the wood stove and watched the kindling seize hold of dry logs in a burst of flame. Temperatures had unexpectedly dropped to the midthirties in the wee hours, and the wind had crept up, too. His aging mother and his youngest sister, Mandie, Jake's twin, would especially mind the cold.

Jonas had roused himself while it was still dark, enjoying the stillness and a renewed sense of duty since his permanent return from Apple Creek, Ohio. He had taken a mere two days to say good-bye to his longtime church friends and to pack his belongings—passing along his unfulfilled orders for several pieces of fine and fancy furniture to a good friend and seasoned woodworker. Here in Grasshopper Level, his father had given him permission to live at home, working alongside him, till such time as Jonas hoped to marry.

His father had made it mighty plain where *he* stood on the tetchy topic of marrying an Ebersol, but there was nothing he could do now that Jonas was thirty-six years old. Jonas pondered just how difficult Dat might make things, especially for Leah as his daughter-in-law. Would he exclude them from family get-togethers? And what of Jonas and Leah's children, if God so willed it; would they ever know their Mast grandparents?

Hard as it was to envision his and Leah's living with such a situation, Jonas was determined to get on with the business of marriage and having a family of his own. When he was most discouraged with his father's disapproval, he had only to think again how the Lord had kept dearest Leah for him all these years!

But, for the time being, he must convince the bishop by his compliant attitude and willingness to come under the People's scrutiny that he was ready indeed to begin courting Leah immediately following his confession at Preaching today. He suspected Bishop Bontrager of wanting to keep him at arm's length. "There's no need to be thinking 'bout doing much of anything 'cept farmin' now," the revered elderly man had pointedly admonished him at their initial meeting. "If you're not so keen on that, then there's not much for ya to do round these parts." Such was not the case in Ohio, where a good number of Amishmen made their living making and selling furniture. Jonas guessed the reason Bishop Bontrager was so set against his woodworking was because he'd been creating fancy, fine furniture for Englishers, using turned lathe pieces and scrollwork. The bishop likely had in mind to get the hankering for such things out of Jonas's system—even though the Ohio brethren had permitted them.

But Lancaster County was the original settlement of their Amish ancestors and remained by far the most traditional.

Still, even if it meant Jonas could not sell them, he hoped to someday make at least the necessary pieces of furniture for his own house.

Hurrying out to the woodshed, Jonas was glad to be of help at the start of this Lord's Day. He would do whatever it took to change the bishop's mind about allowing furniture making to be his primary source of income, but only once the Proving was past. He was a woodworker through and through, but if required, he would attempt to make a living as a farmer and dairyman, or even perform odd jobs around the community till such time as he was reinstated with the People.

Opening the shed door, he spotted a fat mouse dart across and then under the dry stack of wood. He made note of the critter's fleshiness as he reached down for an armful of logs. *Winter's round the bend. . . .*

He'd also observed patchy clusters of milkweed out in the cow pasture, their thick-walled pods cracked open to reveal hundreds of downy seeds, each attached to its own glossy parachute. A sure sign wedding season was coming up right quick.

Jonas recalled his childhood as he nimbly covered the very ground he'd walked as a lad. He and his younger brothers, especially Eli and Isaac, had often stopped to count the spidery seeds as they floated far and wide, dotting the skies high overhead. The two-story barn and farmhouse and surrounding apple orchard all looked the same to him, except for the trees having grown much taller. At a glance, it might have seemed as if nothing had changed at all . . . when everything had.

So much catching up to do.

He wanted to get reacquainted with his seven married

brothers and sisters—meet their spouses and children, too—as well as keep in touch with Jake, who was in Ohio working with an older apprentice, an arrangement made by the same man who'd taken over Jonas's outstanding orders for fine furniture.

Having enjoyed his all too brief encounter with Jake, Jonas was glad there was still one sibling living at home, though fun-loving Mandie was already courting age. And here she came just this minute, her golden locks hanging loose to her waist, looking *schtruwwlich*, not having bothered to brush her long hair before heading out for milking. Jonas had never witnessed any Amishwoman in such a state, and he found himself wondering how Leah's beautiful thick hair—such a rich brunette it was—looked undone, long and freed from her tight bun. He shook away the inappropriate thought, deciding he must wait to contemplate his soon-to-be-bride's lovely tresses until after he'd married her . . . and not a single moment before.

His arms loaded down with plenty of wood for the cookstove, Jonas called over his shoulder, "'Mornin', Mandie! Forget somethin'?"

She returned his teasing with a silent smirk and a toss of her tousled hair behind her head.

Somewhat amused at the sight of her, he made his way toward the back porch, quite aware of Dat's dog nipping at his heels. "Ya want a hullo, too? Is that what you're askin' for?"

He rushed to stack some wood inside the screened-in porch, mindful of the dog still waiting. When the chore was done, he went and sat on the back stoop, rubbing the golden retriever's neck and beneath his sides. "How's that, ol' boy?" he said before turning his attention to the important Preaching service to be held at smithy Peachey's place, next farm over from Abram Ebersol's. These days Smitty's son-in-law and daughter, Joseph and Dorcas Zook, and their boys occupied the main house, where they evidently had been living for a number of years, tending to most of the farming and looking after Smitty and Miriam in their twilight years.

Jonas smiled at the thought of comical Joe Zook hitching up with Smitty's serious younger daughter. He well recalled Joe's making fast work of ripe tomatoes at barn raisings and corn huskings as a youngster, eating them whole before the women folk could get to slicing them, the red juice dribbling down his neck. While growing up Joe had helped his own father raise truckloads of tomatoes, no doubt the reason for his nickname, Tomato Joe, as the bishop had referred to him when speaking of the location where Preaching was to be held today. Jonas had been reminded once again of how awful long he'd been gone from home—and from Leah.

His thoughts drifted back to his years in Ohio, recalling different nicknames for the young men coming up in the church, Gravy Dan being his favorite. The name brought Jonas back to the present with thoughts of the big Sunday morning breakfast his mother was sure to cook up, and he gave the dog a final pat on the belly and headed inside.

But when the time came for all of them to sit down to the delicious food Mamma had carried to the table, Jonas suddenly felt he ought to skip eating. He was strongly impressed to pray during the breakfast hour, just as he had observed the traditional fast day prior to the fall communion service that had taken place here a week ago. Recognizing the significance of *this* day, Jonas headed to his room, where he knelt to pray at his chair.

Create in me a clean heart, O God, and renew a right spirit within me. . . .

Leah got herself settled on the same backless wooden bench where Sadie, Lydiann, and Aunt Lizzie sat in an attitude of prayer, waiting for the house-church meeting to begin. Her bare feet scuffed softly against the wood floor, and she briefly wondered when the first snow might fly, making it necessary to don shoes again.

Today several hymns from the *Ausbund* would be sung, including the *Lob Lied,* always the second hymn. The introductory sermon would come next, followed by the silent kneeling prayers of the People. The main sermon, which would undoubtedly address obedience to the baptism vow, the Bible, and the honor due to parents, was most likely to be given by Bishop Bontrager. Even now the ministers were upstairs, deciding who should give the sermons.

What will the bishop require of Jonas following his confession?

She had awakened in the night to nerve-racking dreams, and now, as Leah sat surrounded by her family and church friends, she wondered how Jonas was holding up today.

Her gaze fell on Adah Peachey Ebersol, her best friend and cousin by marriage. Fondly Leah looked away to her younger sister Hannah and her three school-age daughters, Ida Mae, Katie Ann, and Mimi, all of them sitting tall in the row directly in front of Leah. She focused especially on Mimi, whose present delightful disposition bore no trace of the fussy, colicky baby she had been, causing Hannah such emotional trauma at the time. Those days were long past, and Leah anticipated the little one Hannah was expecting next spring, curious as to what sort of temperament he or she might have.

Her thoughts of babies led Leah to note a record number of infants in the house of worship this day. *Will I ever have a baby of my own . . . as Jonas's wife?*

Just then Ol' Jonathan Lapp rose from his seat and announced the first hymn in a feeble voice, and the People joined him in unison, filling the farmhouse with the familiar sound. Glad for the opportunity to raise her voice in song, Leah breathed a prayer for God to be near and dear to Jonas throughout this sacred meeting.

Jonas knew Leah was definitely amongst the crowd in Tomato Joe's front room—all voting church members were required to be in attendance. Besides that, he'd caught a blissful glimpse of her outdoors as she, Lydiann, and Lizzie stood together with the other women before the bishop and the preachers had arrived. Oh, the rapture he felt whenever their eyes met, even briefly. When Leah was near—when she was in the selfsame room—it was as if there was no one else in the world. Just seeing her lovely face, her honest, shining eyes, the bit of hair showing outside her head covering, near the middle part . . .

But no, he must set aside thoughts of Leah, even though she was the singular reason why he was here in this place on this day. It did seem strange not sitting next to his longtime Apple Creek friends at Preaching service, where he'd enjoyed the good fellowship of many other believers while living in Wayne County. Yet this was Leah's place, and so where he belonged. Already it seemed difficult to believe that it was only last week he'd swiftly purchased a train ticket and come home once he knew for certain, via Abram Ebersol's letter to him, that Leah was a *maidel*, having never married. His heart had not allowed room for another love, so here he sat, waiting for the moment when Bishop Bontrager would give the nod and present him to the church membership.

His stomach rumbled unexpectedly during the deacon's reading of the Scripture, yet he was thankful to have skipped breakfast in favor of spending time in prayer. Reverently he had once again committed this meeting, as well as his future—and Leah's—to the guidance of the Almighty.

When Leah's brother-in-law Preacher Gid went to stand before the People, Jonas was particularly interested in observing his manner—this man whom he had been fooled into thinking had been the downfall of his and Leah's affection years ago. The brawny man who'd married bashful Hannah instead of Abram's Leah had an unflinching gaze. How ironic that this relatively young man was now one of the Gobbler's Knob preachers!

Slowly, piece by piece, Jonas was taking in all he'd missed during his lengthy absence. But more essential than fitting together details about people and events would be standing humbly before God and the local church this fine autumn day.

Chapter Two

Seeing Jonas kneeling now before the bishop stirred up something Leah hadn't expected to encounter, and she felt as if she might fail to suppress the lump in her throat. Her beloved looked terribly vulnerable, bending low that way, admitting to a transgression that was scarcely sin. At least, she'd never come across such a thing in the pages of the Bible, although she knew the People viewed keeping the Ordnung agreed upon each year at council meeting as equal to holy submission unto God. She could no longer hold back tears as Jonas confessed in hushed tones to having abandoned the church of his baptism.

Sadie reached over and covered Leah's hand with her own, which made Leah's silent tears fall all the faster. There he was, her dearest love, requesting pardon from the brethren and the membership as a whole, having returned here for *her*, in answer to the love he'd carried in his heart for these many years . . . in the hopes of taking her as his bride someday. For sure and for certain, that undying love was the one and only reason behind the genuine penitence that seemed to flow from Jonas's very soul.

Abram had been altogether curious to observe how this aspect of the membership meeting might turn out, but he had not expected the bishop to insist on a six-month Proving before Jonas could be considered a voting member again. Unnecessary, far as he could determine. Of course, it was not nearly as long as Sadie's time of testing had ended up being, though that had been her own doing. The way Abram saw it, Jonas Mast's past disobedience had more to do with not following the whim of one man than God's law, and his record in Ohio was mighty good. It was rather obvious why the young Jonas had remained in Ohio when he'd heard and assumed that Leah had married another—any upstanding Amishman might have done as much, but this was not for Abram to argue. He felt his indignation rising up, even though he was partially responsible for what had befallen.

He sighed inwardly, wondering if he was also to blame for Jonas's Proving. From as far back as Ida's early spiritual questioning, followed by Abram's own coming to faith—and his good friendship with son-in-law Gid—Abram and the bishop hadn't seen eye to eye. Was Bontrager retaliating by punishing the man who had returned to marry Abram's Leah?

The bishop was making a declaration now, and it was clear he was not in any way pleased with Jonas's inclination toward making fancy furniture as a livelihood, "no matter what our brethren are doin' in other places." The man of God placed both hands on Jonas's shoulders and stated, "You must turn your back on that worldly thing."

Abram felt his breath nearly go out of him as he heard with his own ears such narrow-mindedness. During the time of his Proving, Jonas was to earn his living primarily off the land, like the rest of the menfolk present, although he would be allowed to work in the harness or blacksmith shop, as well. The membership had yet to vote on this decision, but Abram felt certain no one would stand in opposition to what they knew Bishop Bontrager wanted.

The bishop continued. "I appoint Preacher Peachey to oversee this important time in your service to God and man." He nodded toward Gid.

What on earth? Surely he must not have thought this one through, Abram thought. But no, the bishop was motioning for the steadfast preacher to come and stand with him, and Gid's unmistakably blushing face distinguished him among the crowd.

A cold shiver ran down Leah's back and she held herself stiffly. The bishop was making a formal pronouncement, saying, "The Lord God heavenly Father of us all is manifest in the nearness to nature, the soil—the good earth—and the best way to stay close to the Maker of heaven and earth is to till and plow the land and harvest its abundance."

There was no doubt now the bishop would not tolerate Jonas's talent and enthusiasm for making desks and other lovely wooden pieces. And with her beau's submissive response came the death of his creative gift; she was helpless to stop what was happening before her eyes. Leah sat straight as a yardstick, willing her breath to come slowly, more evenly. *I can't let Jonas agree to do this for* me . . . *this horrid thing.*

At once she wished she might be more outspoken like Lizzie and Mamma and talk up to the church brethren.

This bishop is beyond reason, Sadie decided as she shoved a clothespin down on the shoulder of the dress while hanging out the wash early Monday morning. She thought back to the Preaching service yesterday and to Jonas's having obviously expected the right hand of fellowship from the bishop and not received it. She'd seen the light of anticipation in his eyes—all of them had. And for what? Only to discover that he must submit himself to a Proving and miss out on marrying Leah this wedding season. Truth was, without being reinstated as a church member, Jonas could not marry Leah or anyone.

Hardly seems fair, Sadie thought, but she'd learned not to question this bishop. It was best to do as you were told and nothing less.

She set her mind to the work of hanging out the wet clothing in an orderly fashion—Dat's and Abe's trousers lined up together, followed by their shirts, and then the women of the family's cape dresses and aprons, each item in a grouping all its own, like the coordinated design of the colorful squares she had been carefully cutting so she and her sisters could stitch up another beautiful quilt this winter.

Around midmorning, Aunt Lizzie returned from a trip to Georgetown to stock up on necessary fabric and other sewing notions at Fishers' General Store, her face purple. When Sadie asked about it, Lizzie held up her thumb, which looked as injured as anything Sadie had ever seen. "Goodness, *Aendi*, what'd you do?" asked Sadie, coming to her side.

"Smashed my thumb in a car door gettin' out," she said. "I rode along with Miriam Peachy and her Adah—we hired us a Mennonite driver."

"Aw, let's have a look-see." Sadie led her quickly to the sink, where they gently rinsed the blood off the bruised thumb.

"Abram won't be happy 'bout this." Lizzie was shaking her head. "Drivers are to be used as a last resort."

"Dat won't care you went thataway," Sadie reassured her. "He's hired a driver plenty of times for longer trips."

"I s'pose there's a reason for everything." Lizzie muttered something about getting more behind the hurrier she went. She stared at her thumb and tried to move it but winced at the pain. "I daresay it's broken."

"Best soak it in cold water," Sadie replied. "I'll go 'n' get Dat."

"No, don't be botherin' your father. I'll be just fine."

"But, Aunt Lizzie—"

"Now, ya heard me. I'll just wrap it with a cold cloth and take myself off to rest a bit."

Sadie tried again to persuade her aunt to let her fetch Dat, but Lizzie was adamant. With a determined glance she hurried toward the stairs, still fretting about riding in a fancy car. "*Ach*, and goin' much too fast."

Heading slowly to the staircase herself, Sadie listened, taking care to determine her aunt had made it safely upstairs. She'd known some folk to pass out from the pain of a broken bone, and women folk were more prone to such fainting spells.

Once she heard the bed creak with the weight of weary Lizzie, Sadie went to the front room and began dusting, glad Leah had gone up to the log house to help Hannah do some fall housecleaning. A right good thing to get Leah's mind off the lack of Jonas's reinstatement.

She could only imagine how Leah must be feeling. Though Sadie knew it to be so, most everyone suspected the reason why Jonas had come back was to marry his childhood sweetheart at long last. That was one secret not to be kept, for the light of love was evident on both of their faces. Sadly, their marriage would not take place *this* year. Jonas wouldn't be recognized as a member till next spring, once his Proving was past . . . and then only if the bishop chose to extend the hand of fellowship at that time.

Stepping out the front door to shake out her dustcloth, Sadie was quite relieved *her* days of close scrutiny were over. Because, just this past week, Leah had begun talking about the thirty-eight-year-old who had come along from Ohio with the other traded men. The redheaded man with the sturdy frame was called Eli Yoder, and Leah seemed rather convinced he might be someone for Sadie, though Sadie couldn't help wondering who would want her for a wife, since she had been unable to give birth to a living, breathing baby—except, of course, for Jake.

Never once had she allowed her eyes to meet Eli's gentle blue ones, even though she *had* observed him furtively. Now and then, while she worked around the house, cooking, hanging out wash, canning, and mending, she did find herself thinking about the possibility of getting to know him, considering Leah's gentle urging.

Since arriving, Eli had been renting a small farmhouse a mile or so away, making his living off the fruit of the land and assisting other farmers and doing odd jobs, as were several of the fine young Ohio men who'd also helped with the harvest and silo filling around Gobbler's Knob and the surrounding areas. The newcomers already appeared well settled into their respective homes—families assigned to them for the time being.

Even after only a few weeks following last summer's trade, Sadie had begun to hear inklings from several of the women at work frolics that Eli was a right nice choice for a "perty girl like Ella Jane Peachey." One of Smitty's nieces, Ella was still an unclaimed treasure at thirty-five. Hearing such "whispers down the lane" through the Amish grapevine made Sadie bristle—this was not at all the way such matters were typically approached during youth's blush of courtship. Yet Sadie knew that if ever the Lord should will her to marry again, she would be ever so grateful, scarcely minding others' gossip. She would be as good and faithful as she had been when she was dear Harvey's wife.

Of course, she did not want to enter into another marital union for the mere purpose of numbing her grief over her husband's death, a grief that ached deeply even still. It simply wouldn't be right, and for that reason alone she must be cautious, protecting her heart.

Sadie sighed. Her tentative curiosity about Eli was nothing akin to what Leah must be feeling now that her Jonas was home. Sadie felt sure that if she were in Leah's shoes, she would have told Jonas she still loved him. But then, she was not nearly as patient as her sister, and she had no desire to get in the middle again. She was, in fact, so nervous about botching things she purposely busied herself these days with additional household chores.

Ready for some fresh air, Sadie wandered out through the stable area to the barnyard, noticing that the animals had worn a narrow path through the paddock. Then and there she hoped to goodness her life living in the *Dawdi Haus* wasn't in any way a parallel to that dreadful rut.

She was undeniably certain she was meant for more than her present existence. And though she thought she would like to help things along, even beseech the Good Lord for a fine husband, she knew she had no choice but to practice the virtue of patience—truly, her biggest area of failing.

Her impulsive tendencies were further reflected in her desire to get to know her son. She found herself wishing to see Jake again, even though she knew there was little hope of that. And even if there was, it would come at the cost of certain jeopardy for Lydiann, who apparently remained besotted with Jake and seemingly lived from one letter to the next.

Locating the butterfly handkerchief in her pocket, her sole connection to Jake, Sadie looked at it fondly. Always she carried it with her, now that this treasure was back in her possession—thanks to Leah.

She thought again of Jake. If he had any idea how closely connected he and Lydiann were blood-wise, wouldn't he be absolutely repulsed at the thought of their courtship?

Their relationship was doomed from the start, Sadie thought sorrowfully, feeling terribly responsible.

Chapter Three

"Well, I would urge you not to consider such a thing," Aunt Lizzie told Leah on the Wednesday following Jonas's confession.

Leah was leaning against the icebox in the kitchen, waiting for her midnight chocolate cake to finish baking. She wasn't surprised at Lizzie's forthright response. "I'm not sayin' I want to raise a stink," Leah said, defending her wish to speak with Bishop Bontrager and his wife about Jonas. "I just feel like my head might burst if I don't do something 'bout how I feel. It's so unfair to Jonas."

Lizzie shook her head and reached out a hand. "You should know by now our bishop is an exception to the rule. He won't budge. Not one smidgen."

"Still . . . wouldn't *you* speak up if the tables were turned?"

"Ain't any of your concern what Jonas agreed to do during his Proving. He gave up makin' furniture and whatnot for you. Don't ya see? This is a man who's in love, really and truly. Be grateful he's willin' to return to farmin'."

Jonas a farmer.

Leah had difficulty contemplating the idea. As a boy, Jonas had never complained about helping with the milking or tending to his father's apple orchard, at least not that she'd ever known. But he wasn't nearly as called to the soil as even she had been as a youngster. He *was* strong and able—hard-working, too—no question about that, but he'd had a gift that had lain dormant all those years before he received his training in Ohio from David Mellinger.

Just yesterday she had received a letter from Jonas asking if he might pick her up at the end of the lane this Saturday night, *at dusk . . . like when we were courting age . . . if you're willing.*

Willing? Smiling, she'd quickly found a pen and a page of stationery and written her answer, placing her note to him in the mail today. By tomorrow he would know she was very happy to see him again, though she had been a bit guarded about signing off *with love*, as he had to her and she had to him in times past. Truly, she wanted to say those important words to his face on this glorious occasion. In many ways, they were starting their courtship all over again.

Aunt Lizzie was regarding her with a gentle expression. "You're daydreamin' again."

"Jah, s'pose I am. But somebody oughta talk up to the bishop."

"Maybe so, but it oughtn't be you, dear one."

Can't accomplish anything if you don't try, Mamma had always said. Even though fourteen years had passed since Mamma had gone to heaven, Leah wondered what her mother might advise her to do. For all she knew, Mamma might admit she had learned a hard lesson about speaking out of turn. *It nearly got her shunned*, thought Leah, remembering what Lizzie had shared privately some years back.

"I just feel it's necessary to voice my opinion," Leah murmured.

"Your mamma got herself in hot water with the bishop. Best you not do the same. Don't take up this topic with such an unyielding man." Lizzie returned to the dirty dishes. "I'm hopin' you'll listen to me . . .'cause, for sure and for certain, your mamma would be sayin' the same thing."

"I'll think on it." Leah headed to the wood stove and opened the oven door to check on the cake baking inside. She would wait till she saw Jonas on Saturday evening to discuss the subject further—let him determine what she ought to do about visiting the bishop.

Hannah was at the back door to greet her before Leah was even halfway up the walkway. "Awful nice to see ya again."

"Feelin' some better?" Leah noted how pale her sister's face was and how frail she looked overall.

"Come sit with me." Hannah waved her into the kitchen and pulled a chair out from the table. "Would ya like some tea?"

"No, you should be the one to sit," Leah insisted. "*I'll* pour the tea or whatever sounds *gut* to you."

"But—"

"I won't be treated as a guest in my sister's house, for pity's sake." She went to the cookstove and picked up the teakettle. "You never said how you're doin', Hannah."

"Oh, I'm all right."

Leah eyed her. "Ain't a wise thing for a preacher's wife to fib."

Hannah sniffled and dabbed at her eyes. "I've been strugglin' something awful . . . can't sleep much at night, not with so much pain."

"Then you best be seein' a medical doctor."

"Aunt Lizzie says the same," Hannah said, coughing.

"Maybe you've got a touch of autumn flu. It's going round, I hear. Abe says plenty of pupils are missin' from school."

Hannah touched her stomach lightly. "I hope it's not something the matter with this baby."

Leah listened but felt she could do no more than continue to entrust Hannah to the hand of the Lord and to His mercy.

"Even Gid suggested I pay a visit to Dr. Schwartz." Hannah looked awful serious. "But only one person can help me," she added, "and *she's* dead."

"Who's that?"

"Old Lady Henner," Hannah said. "I don't care to admit it, knowin' you and I disagree on powwow doctors."

Leah said nothing.

"Our family's seen so much heartache, 'specially when it comes to birthin' babies."

Eager to get off the subject of hex doctors, Leah brought up newborn Ruthie Schwartz, Mary Ruth's baby. From what Leah could tell, Ruthie was thriving under her doting parents' nurturing, which came as no surprise, since, like Leah, Mary Ruth had always displayed an especially gentle way with babies and young children. "She's got a mighty strong set of lungs for such a wee one."

"Jah, I should say. I wouldn't mind hearin' her squeal again real soon. One time wasn't enough to hold baby

Ruthie." She stopped abruptly, and Leah assumed, by the faraway look in Hannah's eyes, she was chafing under Gid's long-ago decision to keep her from spending time alone with her twin, Mary Ruth having turned Mennonite years back. Though Mary Ruth was not welcome in the Peachey home, at least Hannah could visit with her sister at Dat's house and elsewhere when others were around.

"When you'd like to, I'll take ya over to see Mary Ruth and the baby again," Leah volunteered. "Whenever you're up to it."

"If ever I am," Hannah muttered.

"Well, of course you'll be."

"That's easy for you to say, ain't so?"

Leah looked hard at her. "You seem put out with me."

"S'posin' I oughta be ashamed of myself. I have no right to talk so to ya. Not after all you've been through yourself." Hannah hung her head.

Leah remained silent as she sipped more tea. It was rather clear something more than a physical ailment was troubling Hannah, and Leah prayed her sister wouldn't fall back into the gloom that had plagued her in earlier years. The idea occurred to her to get her morose sister out of the house, perhaps for a long ride, but what with a sudden crash of thunder, she knew better than to suggest it this minute.

"You should head on down the hill to home," Hannah urged. "Wouldn't do for you to get caught in the storm . . . then again, for some, maybe it mightn't be such a bad thing."

Leah looked at Hannah, surprised. "What on earth are ya saying?"

"Haven't you ever heard how Old Lady Henner got her powers?"

"I don't care to know, really." She set her teacup aside, rose quickly, and pushed in the chair. Glancing out the window, she looked over the stretch of woods beyond Hannah's many flower gardens, the trees swaying to beat the band. "Seems a big storm's a-brewin'," she said, hurrying for the door.

Hannah hollered at her, as if afraid Leah might not hear in the midst of the rising gale and now the pelting rain. "Old Lady Henner got struck by lightning when she was little! It nearly killed her, but her healing gifts came to her thataway."

Hannah must be off in the head, thought Leah, shivering, never having heard such a tale.

The morning after the storm, the sky was as gray as the old ivy-strewn stone wall alongside Gid and Hannah's house, and the atmosphere was heavy with the threat of more rain to come. The girls chattered as they dressed for school, and Hannah had trouble keeping her mind on preparations for bread baking.

"Nearly time for breakfast," she called to them, hoping Gid might soon return from helping with the milking down yonder in the Ebersol barn.

She stewed about her condition, thinking that if the pain grew worse she'd have to say something to Gid. The last thing she wanted was to disappoint her husband, who was bent on this being their first son. Hannah was seized with the knowledge that, though many months yet from birth, their coming child was in jeopardy, and she felt helpless to prevent it.

With more determination than was necessary, she pounded the bread dough hard, wondering if the possibility of rain was sinking her more deeply into despair.

After she slipped into a clean work dress and apron, the first thing Leah did that Thursday morning was tiptoe downstairs in her bare feet to look out the kitchen door at the barn. From where she stood, her nose nearly against the windowpane, she could see the lightning rod on the top of the barn roof. *Thank goodness for it*, she thought, having witnessed a most astounding event yesterday, following her unsettling visit to Hannah. Queasy with concern over the words Hannah had hurled at her as she darted into the torrent of rain, Leah had lifted her long black apron over her head as a slight shelter. About the time she passed the outhouse, a white lightning bolt had struck its jagged finger at the barn roof, and she saw flashes of electricity. Stunned, she had run helter-skelter to the house, taking cover on the very spot where she stood now.

Even recalling the unforgettable sight caused her heart to race, so she offered a quick prayer. "Thank you, Lord, for sparing Dat's barn and the animals . . . and for giving my father the wisdom to mount the lightning rod in the first place." After saying, "Amen," she opened her eyes and stared again at the roof, still in awe.

Last evening, when she had shared with the rest of the family what she'd seen, their eyes had lit up, though it was clearly Abe who was most interested in hearing how the sparks shot out like "Englishers' fireworks on Independence Day," as he put it. Naturally, this remark encouraged raised eyebrows from Dat, Aunt Lizzie, and even Sadie, what with

Abe's growing curiosity in forbidden things such as fast cars and modern electricity. Neither was to be sought after one iota.

Realizing how busy a day she had ahead of her, Leah decided to put yesterday's excitement behind her, along with Hannah's strange words about Old Lady Henner. Turning back to the house, she went into the kitchen, preparing to make her usual eggs-and-bacon breakfast. *Better for lightning to hit the barn than one of us*, she thought.

As Leah was frying up the eggs, Lydiann wandered into the kitchen, all smiles. "Got me another letter from Ohio," she whispered at the cookstove. "And I couldn't be more pleased."

Fear gripped Leah's heart, but she tried not to let it show on her face.

"Jake says he's savin' up his money, hopin' to come home this year." Lydiann paused a moment before going on. "Besides me, he daresn't tell a soul, though. Promise me you won't, either, Mamma?"

Leah felt her toes curl. "You're not sure just when it might be?"

"He didn't say, but he made it clear he's mighty upset 'bout being sent away. It's got his goat, bein' traded for other men, and he sees no reason to stay in Ohio with Jonas back here. Anyhow, I'm hopin' Jonas might clear the way for Jake's return—with their father, ya know."

Leah struggled to fix her mind on buttering slices of toast for breakfast, all the while shuddering to think what was in store if Jake should happen to come knocking on Lydiann's door.

Time to get Lyddie to Sunday singings again! Gschwind!—*Soon!*

"Why on earth didn't ya tell me you broke your thumb?" Abram scolded Lizzie as they dressed in their room.

"Now, nobody knows that for sure," she countered, hoping he would drop the matter.

Nonetheless, he asked her to unwind the makeshift bandage she'd made on the day of the accident. "I wanna see for myself."

"I'll be fine, Abram. Honest."

He persisted till she had no choice but to show him her wounded thumb, now as purple and green as springtime wild flowers. He peered at it, pushing his bifocals down farther on his nose. "Hmm, this looks awful bad to me."

"I daresay it'll get better right quick." She wanted to stave off any insistence she go to a doctor.

"You can say all ya want, Lizzie, but, truth is, this here thumb's gonna need to be rebroken and set correctly." He waited while she wrapped it up again. "I'll be takin' ya over to see Dr. Schwartz the minute you're dressed for the day."

"Ach, Abram. That ain't necessary at all." She would stand her ground to get her way if it took that. She was a strong woman, after all, with no need for doctor visits and suchlike. *Mercy's sake!*

"Well, I don't know what's come over you, but I'm takin' you, like it or not."

You'll have to carry me to the buggy, then, she thought,

unconsciously locking her knees. "I'll think on it," she mumbled.

With a huff about how "awful stubborn this one is," her husband left the room. Lizzie could hear his needlessly heavy footsteps on the stairs, and she breathed a great sigh of relief.

Chapter Four

"Why do ya s'pose we don't practice bundling anymore?" Lydiann asked Leah clear out of the blue while they were scrubbing potatoes together outdoors, near the well.

Leah took what she hoped was an inconspicuous breath and willed herself not to reply too hastily to her girl's curiosity. "Where'd you ever hear this?"

"Oh, just one of Jake's letters."

"Well, do you know how bed courtship first got started?"

"I think so." Lydiann went on to explain what she knew—how the early colonists lived in unheated farmhouses, so when a young man came to visit his girl, they simply spent time in her bedroom. "For practical reasons."

Leah nodded. "From what I know of this old custom, the couple would lie down on the made bed, fully clothed, and a bundling board was fixed between them as they talked and sometimes held hands late into the night. Later it became a time for the young lady to display her pretty handmade quilts and pillow coverings, as well. At least, that's how it was amongst *our* ancestors."

"A sort of getting-acquainted time?"

"Jah, with much talkin' expected between the twosome." She didn't say what was *not* supposed to happen. No need at the moment to have another talk about the birds and the bees.

"Jake says there are certain Ohio groups that still practice the custom." Lydiann looked rather embarrassed. "And . . . well, I best not be sayin' *all* that Jake knows."

Leah felt suddenly nervous, if not ill, at the thought of this sort of private talk being initiated by Jake; the possibility of his return made it all the more concerning.

"A friend of Jake's says there are some couples that get downright snug as a bug in a rug." Lydiann seemed unable to leave well enough alone. "They slip under the quilts—"

"Lyddie," Leah interrupted. "I daresay 'tis best to turn our attention to other things now."

Lydiann's head bowed. "Sorry, Mamma."

"You surely know there's a time and a place for all things," Leah was quick to add.

"Jah . . . the wedding night, ain't so?" Lydiann wore a fine, sweet smile now.

Wiping her wet hand on her apron, Leah slipped her arm around Lyddie. "You've got plenty of time for smoochin' and whatnot. All good things come to those who wait."

Lydiann looked up at her. "Will *you* ever marry?"

"That's up to the Lord, dear one." She suspected Lydiann had heard enough about Jonas from Sadie, years ago, that her girl would be curious now, although the recent church members' meeting was never to be discussed with folk not yet baptized. Without knowing what Jonas looked like, Lydiann would not have known Jonas Mast was present with the People last Sunday—except for Jake and the incessant grapevine, of course. Such news was hard to squelch.

"I feel awful sad for you sometimes," whispered Lyddie, still standing near.

"Why's that?"

Lyddie shrugged. "You oughta have a husband to hug and kiss ya good night—to cry on his shoulder when need be and laugh with him, too."

"Well, that would be nice, but *this* is the life the Lord God has given me . . . for the time being anyhow." Leah had no desire to be less than forthcoming with Lyddie, but she was thinking of having nearly fulfilled her dying mother's wishes. And if Jonas could regain his eligibility as a church member, they might end up marrying next year.

Fact was, the likelihood of marriage during this wedding season had completely flown out the window with the bishop's decree. Thinking back once more to Sunday made her worry she might lose her peace and march right out to the barnyard to ask Gid what on earth could be done about the unbearable situation, if anything.

Sighing, she looked into Lydiann's trusting blue eyes. She found herself predicting the pain that would surely reside there when, at last, Lydiann was told why Jake Mast could never be her husband. Leah must move heaven and earth to make sure such a union never happened, though just how she didn't know. But she would think of something, even if it meant telling Lydiann the bitter truth at last.

Lydiann bumped into her brother, who was gathering eggs

from the henhouse. "This is *my* chore." She stared at the large wire basket in his hand.

"Well, you weren't out here."

"I am now. Give me the basket!"

"Better be quiet or you'll scare the chickens . . . get them all *ferhoodled*, and your goose'll be cooked."

"Leave me be," she said more softly, struggling to keep her voice down.

Abe gave her a smirk and continued going from one nest to another. "You've done quit attendin' singings, sister."

"Jah, a while back. No need asking 'bout it." She turned on her heels and left, not at all interested in bickering any longer with her obstinate brother. Truth be known, there was no need for her to go to singings when Jake was anxious to see her again—even hoped to marry her the minute she turned eighteen. But she was beginning to wonder if he'd gotten in with a wild bunch out in Berlin. How else would he know so much about bundling and whatnot?

Blushing as she rushed toward the house, Lydiann was surprised to hear Abe calling to her. He'd emerged into the sunshine, his blond hair glinting purest white. "Brothers are s'posed to drive sisters to singings, in case you forgot. So *'tis* my business."

"Puh!"

"Near as I can tell, your beau's comin' home, ain't so? That's why you're not interested in the boys here. I can see right through ya."

"Hush up! You know nothin' at all." She sucked in air and then, when she felt she might burst out saying further unkind words, she bit her lip and simply walked away. How could Abe possibly know any such thing about Jake's plans? Her

Dummkopp brother had committed the sin of eavesdropping, no doubt.

Just wait till Abe's rumschpringe. Then we'll see what happens with him. Already less than three years away from the time, she could easily imagine Abe driving a fast car, seeing lots of different girls, getting himself a modern haircut, and only heaven knew what else—all before he settled down and joined church!

◆

Saturday afternoon Jonas heard his mother calling up the stairs. "Preacher Peachey's here to see ya!"

Hurrying down to greet the ordained man who was overseeing his Proving, Jonas wondered if he'd be able to keep from his brother-in-law-to-be his aim to see Leah tonight, especially since he'd just donned his newest shirt and trousers, wanting to look his very best.

Gid, however, seemed to take no specific interest in Jonas's attire but firmly shook his hand and asked if they could talk privately. Jonas motioned to the front room and they walked there together, taking seats in hardback chairs on opposite sides of the wide room. "I wouldn't be honest with ya if I didn't say this is the most awkward situation I've found myself in," Gid began. "But the bishop has asked me to see how you're doin'."

It occurred to Jonas yet again that the bishop had *intended* the arrangement to be downright uncomfortable. Why else would he have chosen Gid as his overseer? "You're welcome to drop by anytime," he said. "I'm doin' just fine."

"Is there any way I can help durin' this time?"

Momentarily, Jonas thought of making a bit of a joke. He wondered what Gid might say if asked for some solid suggestions on making a living off the land when the harvest was nearly past. Indeed, the bishop's Proving conditions were rather absurd.

"I've been helping my father with orchard and barn work, living here without payin' board and room, but I certainly won't be able to make enough to marry and support a family doing odd jobs."

Gid tilted his head as if to say, *I hope you're not questioning the bishop's decree.*

"Do you know of *any* Amish who make fancy furniture round here?" A courageous question on his part, to be sure.

"There's the one fella from Ohio—Eli Yoder—but it's more of a hobby with him, I think." Gid frowned and glanced out the window. "Honestly I don't know of any who make their living thataway, but we do have our carpenters . . . those who help with raisin' barns and all."

Jonas was not interested in carpentry, although if he had to in order to bring in enough money to marry Leah, he might consider it.

"Are you willing to make your way farming?" Gid asked.

Jonas wasn't keen on giving a flippant retort to this kind-hearted and considerate preacher-man, especially married as he was to Leah's younger sister. Yet with his father so opposed to his marrying Leah, he would not be expecting any help whatsoever from his parents, once he was married. "I'll simply trust the Lord for His leading." *That, and work mighty hard at whatever my hands find to do. . . .*

Gid made a throaty sound and rose suddenly, putting on

his hat. He shook Jonas's hand once more as he took leave. "I'll be checkin' in on you every month or so till the Proving is done. If ever ya need anything, feel free to give a holler."

"*Denki*" was all Jonas said. He followed Gid through the kitchen and utility room and then stood at the back door as the preacher headed for his horse and carriage. Gid was a good man, but already Jonas was missing his wise Ohio bishop and the many times they had openly conversed about Scripture.

Long after the dinner of pork chops with rice, steamed carrots, and broccoli was devoured and the dishes were redd up Saturday evening, Leah slipped away to her bedroom and removed her head covering. *I want to look as neat as can be for Jonas*, she thought as she pulled the hairpins out and shook down her long hair, looking at herself in the tiny hand mirror. *I'm not as young as I used to be.* She sighed. *So many lost years . . .*

She took to brushing out the snarls and then pulled it all back from the middle part. But even as she prepared for their meeting, she dared not allow herself to dwell too much on seeing Jonas tonight, lest she become all scatterbrained and unable to think straight. That would never do, not with the way she'd always felt when they were together. Ever so giddy she was in his presence, though she was fairly sure she could hide this from Jonas—especially on a night like this, when they were permitted to ride in Peter Mast's enclosed family buggy, being they were past the age of riding in an open courting buggy. Such carriages were for young folk Lydiann's age, who whispered dear words to each other under naught but the canopy of heaven.

Her hair smoothed with a comb and knotted in a bun, Leah placed her *Kapp* on her head and offered a silent prayer. *Thank you, O Father, for bringing my beau back home to me.*

She rose to stand at the bedroom window, looking out over the level grazing land that seemed to inch its way to the very edge of the immense forest, her heart suddenly as cheery and hopeful as if she were sixteen all over again.

Chapter Five

The air had a distinct chill to it, and Leah smiled when Jonas took advantage of her slight shiver. "Move closer." He reached around her. "I can't have my girl catchin' cold just 'cause I didn't offer a warm lap blanket."

A little laugh escaped, but Leah didn't say what was on her mind. Truth was, she much preferred his warm embrace to a woolen wrap any day. She'd missed him terribly, more than she'd even realized until now, having pushed any romantic feelings under the rug of domestic chores and family responsibilities.

The horse pulled the Mast family carriage down a few of the most deserted roads she ever remembered taking, and it slowly dawned on her what Jonas was doing. "Why, I think you must be takin' me for a ride down memory lane."

He nodded. "I wondered if ya noticed."

When had she ever felt this happy? It was well past dusk, but the stars twinkling high above seemed to brighten the way as their conversation began to melt the hours, and soon the moon lent its light to them. Jonas pointed out the silvery gleam it cast over ponds and pastures, and she felt as if she'd never before taken sufficient time to soak in its lunar beauty . . . or, if she had, she'd forgotten. *I've overlooked so many things. . . .*

Jonas was telling her of close friends he wanted her to meet one day—Preacher Sol and others, including Emma Graber, the kind woman who'd rented a room to him for so long. "After we're married, I'll take you to Ohio for a visit. What would you think of that?"

After we're married . . .

The lovely words stuck in her head, and she couldn't move past the echo of them. She relished his loving talk, his nearness.

"Leah? Are ya gettin' tired, dear?" He looked fondly at her.

She wasn't one bit tired, but he'd taken her by surprise, speaking about something so important in such a relaxed manner. Then again, Jonas really had no need to propose, did he? After all, he'd asked her years ago to be his wife, and she'd wholeheartedly consented. Maybe he simply assumed he didn't have to ask twice.

"Sorry," she said quickly. "I think a trip to your former stompin' grounds would be interesting."

"After we're wed, of course." There it was again.

She turned to look at him and noted the sparkle of mischief in his eyes. No suppressing *this* giggle. "Oh, Jonas," she said. "I'm so glad you're back. You just don't know . . ."

He reached to coax her nearer. "I've wanted to see your smile, hear your contagious laughter . . . ach, I've missed everything about you." He paused. "And you must know I never loved anyone but you, Leah. Not one time did I think

I'd be happy with anyone else."

She couldn't say the same due to her brief engagement to Preacher Gid. There was plenty of time to talk about her innocent courtship by Smitty's son, now her dear brother-in-law. For now she could say what was burning in her heart and had been from their reunion on Georgetown Road, not too many days ago. "I *love* you, Jonas," she whispered.

"You don't know how much I've wanted to hear you say that again." The earnest tone of his response startled her a bit. "I've dreamed it, Leah—daydreamed it, too—never once truly believing this night . . . us out ridin' like this, could ever be anything more than my own imagination. Till today all the joy and hope of it existed only in my head." He kissed her on both cheeks and then the very tip of her nose. "We belong together. You know that?"

"Yes, for always." She held back the tears of gladness till she could no longer.

"Don't cry, darling. Such a happy night this is." He cradled her face in his hands.

"Ach, I wish . . ." She couldn't go on.

"What is it?"

She leaned her head on his strong shoulder, trying to gather her wits lest she embarrass him or herself, although she felt nearly as helpless as a child. "I feel just awful . . . terrible, really."

"What troubles you so?"

She searched for the right words. "Oh, Jonas . . . you made your livin' with wood. Such a thing is a true gift from God."

"Well, you mustn't be sad."

She sniffled and nodded her head. "All the same, seems so unnecessary for you to have to give it up for your Proving.

I've even thought of sayin' something to the bishop . . . respectfully, of course. I just don't understand."

He straightened suddenly, reaching for her hand. "Leah . . . dearest love, it is not such a hard thing. I gladly do this . . . for *you*. To cherish you as my very own—takin' you as my bride—will be the greatest gift I could have. You must not go to the bishop. Promise me this."

The way he so tenderly stated his affections made tears well up all the more. How she longed for him to be her husband! Jonas cared for her enough to do even this unreasonable thing. "Jah, I promise, but it won't make it any easier keepin' mum," she said.

Her heart was ever so soft toward him, and she was somewhat relieved when he picked up the reins and directed the horse to trot, quickening the pace until they arrived at a turnoff to a narrow dirt road, which led to a small hummock where grazing land sandwiched the way on either side.

Soon Jonas stopped the mare and jumped down out of the buggy. "A mighty nice night for walkin'. All right with you?"

The evening was mild, with only the slightest breeze in the leafless sycamores, oaks, and maples. She breathed in the clean air, feeling like an insignificant dot under the backdrop of heaven's twinkling lights. If only the years could be rolled back and all things done differently, their lives might have been much easier. They'd missed so much time . . . so many experiences had slipped from their grasp. But they had now, *this* most precious time, and she couldn't help wishing everyone might have the chance to feel the way she did—to experience this enduring kind of love.

Jonas helped her down from the carriage, and they strolled to the highest point of the grassy rise as he talked of their future together. When he stopped walking, he turned to take her hands in his. "I hope and pray we'll be able to marry—the minute I finish my Proving, in fact. We aren't youngsters anymore; there'd be no need to wait for the weddin' season next year."

"Even so, we aren't widowed, so who's to know if we'd be permitted to marry earlier than a year from now." She wondered how long Bishop Bontrager would attempt to keep them apart.

Jonas continued. "It would be wonderful, though unlikely, for the bishop to agree to a wedding in late spring, when the older widowed folk get married."

She was ever so glad for the light of the moon and studied his dear face, memorizing every feature. She held her breath as she drank in his presence, almost sure what was coming next.

"I wouldn't ever think of takin' you for granted, Leah—your promise to marry me so long ago, I mean." He paused, lifting her right hand to his lips. "So will ya, Leah? Will you be my bride . . . as soon as we can marry?"

Moved beyond her ability to speak, she silently surrendered to his welcoming arms. Love had truly found her, and she nestled close to his heart.

When at last she had composed herself, she drew back and looked him full in the face. "I will, Jonas. I'll be your wife all the days of my life."

"You'll make me the happiest man ever." He went on to say he would be on the lookout for a small farmhouse for them to rent or purchase.

Joy, oh joy! Setting up housekeeping with Jonas filled her with ideas for things to make or sew during the time being, because her own hope-chest items had already been put to good use all these years, she'd so long ago given up on ever marrying. But now? She could scarcely wait to see the dawn of her wedding day.

They talked of how each had changed since the years when they'd first fallen in love. How strong Jonas thought Leah had been, taking on her much younger siblings as her own children . . . making and keeping such a hard promise to her mother. Leah replied with all the dear things she'd longed to say to his face.

"The years have only served to prove what an upstanding, good man I've always known you to be."

Their chatter slowed some, and it was Jonas who again brought up what Leah knew without a doubt. "As much as I want it, we'll never get the brethren to agree to a springtime wedding since we're first-timers, so to speak. I've never heard of its being done that way, have you?"

"No," she admitted. "Besides, don't we want a full day of festivities like the young folks, with as many of our family attending?"

"You're right, Leah. We've waited this long—why sacrifice such a wonderful-gut day just so we can marry early?"

Still, her heart sank a bit, knowing twelve long months stretched before them. *Yet our love has survived this long*, she thought. *What's another year?*

As they made their way back through the meadow on the slender band of road that led out to the paved highway, she was aware of the gray spread of grassland and the dark outline of trees atop the ridge. Even in the deep of night, Gobbler's Knob had to be the prettiest place on earth, and she told Jonas so. She wondered if he might tell her how beautiful his second home had been in Apple Creek, but he only smiled and kissed her cheek.

On the long ride back to the Ebersol Cottage, Jonas changed the topic. "My brother's thinkin' of returning home once he has enough money to make the trip," he said offhandedly.

Leah's throat turned bone dry. She'd heard this from Lydiann, of course, but hearing it from Jonas made the possibility seem more real. "You must mean Jake."

"Jah, my youngest brother. Truth be known, I'm all for it. No gut reason for him to be clear out there when his family's all here . . . and the girl he loves is, too."

For sure and for certain, she couldn't say what she was thinking. Immediately she wished she could tell him what she knew about Jake's blood tie to Lydiann, but she couldn't bring herself to. She didn't want to spoil the memory of this night, not even for something as important as this.

"What will your father say?" she managed to ask.

"Oh, there'll be plenty of words, but who's to say what he'll actually *do* if Jake does return. And I'll do everything I can to help things to that end. My brother's too young to be gone from home, especially with his heart here. I'm workin' on Dat to let him return, at least for a visit."

She cringed at the thought. *Dear Lord, let Jake stay put in Ohio. Please give us more time!*

Mary Ruth walked the floor with her wee bundle, recalling the delicious meal she'd enjoyed with Robert earlier tonight. His hearty laughter as they had joyfully shared the day together resonated in her memory even now.

At this moment, however, weary Robert was sleeping in their bed, and Mary Ruth was hoping to get Ruthie tucked in once again. By the looks of her dreamy eyes, the infant would yield to slumber soon.

Strolling through the front room, she stopped and looked out one of the east-facing windows at the moon. She was drawn to its light, glad for this moment to reflect on God's goodness in giving darling Ruthie to them. Mary Ruth couldn't stop counting her blessings each day. So many there were!

Looking down into the tiny face, she cooed, "You sweet baby . . . ever so precious to your daddy and me." She quietly stroked Ruthie's forehead and cheek with a single finger before returning her thoughts to God in deepest gratitude. "Thank you, dear Lord, for giving to Robert and me such a healthy little one. Help us raise her to know and love you all the days of her life. Amen."

Mary Ruth did not move away from the window as she basked in the knowledge of God's kindness to them. She was reluctant to leave the spot where ofttimes she had stood to speak the names of her young students in prayer during the years she'd taught school.

She gazed at the rolling landscape awash in moonlight, and when a lone buggy came into view, she assumed the enclosed carriage held a married couple who had been out unusually late visiting relatives.

Bless them, Father, whoever they are.

How can I possibly be thinking straight? Leah nearly panicked. The more she considered the sticky matter, the more she wondered if she was doing the wrong thing by not sharing with Jonas what she knew about Jake. But her darling had *just* proposed marriage this wonderful-good night! What was she thinking, second-guessing her decision to keep mum?

They rode past a familiar house, and looking more closely, she saw that it was Robert and Mary Ruth's place. She suddenly realized how far—and how long—she had been riding around the countryside with Jonas.

As for revealing to him that his baby brother was not his blood sibling, she must not be either foolish or hasty. But as soon as possible, she would talk to Sadie. Together, they would have to decide what to do with this exceedingly knotty problem once and for all.

Chapter Six

What can we do?" asked Sadie, ashen faced and still nestled beneath her quilt.

Leah had hurried to the Dawdi Haus and up the steps to sit quietly on the edge of her sister's bed, waiting there only a few minutes before confiding in her, so anxious was she to discuss the dilemma. And this with but a small amount of sleep, because Jonas had cheerfully forgotten they weren't courting age any longer, bringing her home mere hours before daybreak, though she wasn't complaining one bit.

"I've wracked my brain and can't come up with anything, except fessin' up to Lydiann 'bout Jake," admitted Leah.

Sadie sighed, frowning hard. "Awful risky . . . unless ya think she'd honestly keep it to herself." Then, looking a bit sheepish, she said, "I have to confess something to you."

"What is it, sister?"

Sadie drew a long breath and pulled the covers up to her neck. "I s'pose you'll be unhappy 'bout this, but I sometimes pray for Jake to come home. Maybe something inside me is tuggin' him back here." Sadie's sleepy blue eyes revealed a mingling of emotions that seemed to merge into guilty hope, and Leah knew if she were in the same position, she'd feel the same way.

"I can't blame ya, really," Leah replied. "I just wish Jake wasn't still in love with our Lydiann. It makes everything so complicated."

"Jah, and if only she wasn't head over heels for *him*." Sadie went on to say how she'd run into Lydiann up in the woods not but a day ago. "I found her sitting under a tree, cryin' like all get-out. She had herself a pen and tablet and looked to be writing . . . no doubt to Jake." Sadie stirred and then in one quick motion pushed the covers back and got out of bed. She wandered over to the wooden pegs on the wall and pulled down her bathrobe. Slipping it on, she slowly tied a loop in the cloth belt and stood there, looking as forlorn as can be. "I can't get certain things out of my head."

Leah sat still on the bed, not daring to try to comfort her, although it seemed Sadie was distraught about more than the news regarding her son.

Sadie turned and faced the window, staring out at what, Leah didn't know—maybe the forest, or the snug log house at the edge of it. Sadie's chest was heaving.

"I'm so sorry," whispered Leah, going to her.

"Ain't for you to say." Sadie buried her head in Leah's shoulder. "None of what I'm feelin' is your doing."

"Still, I can't help but bear it, too." She wanted to remind her of all the good things the Lord had brought their way—all the blessings she saw as clearly coming from their heavenly Father's hand—but she thought better of it. *Best to simply let Sadie cry. . . .*

Moments later Sadie pulled a hankie out of the pocket of

her bathrobe. "We should've told Lyddie right away," she said through sniffles. "Back when we first knew Jake was seein' her. We wouldn't be in this mess now."

Leah nodded, feeling terribly overwhelmed, even helpless. "What on earth were we thinkin'?"

Sadie shrugged. "We thought Lyddie would've forgotten him by now—found someone new—him being her first beau and all. Guess we were sorely wrong."

Guess so, Leah thought, contemplating the calamity the news of Sadie's "baby" come back from the dead would bring to the entire Plain community. Dat and Peter Mast would be fit to be tied. *Oh, I can just see it.*

Truly, there was no love lost between the Masts and the Ebersols, though if Mamma were still alive, she'd dispute that notion entirely. *Got to keep showing kindness whether they accept our love or not,* she'd often said, which meant you never wanted to sever family ties. With these years of awful silence between them and Grasshopper Level, there was no telling what Mamma might've been willing to do to bring an agreeable end to it.

But with their mother long departed, it was for them to make amends. Of course, with Jonas home and working through his Proving, there was no telling what might come of the Mast-Ebersol standoff, especially with Jonas planning to marry her.

Now is not the time for Peter and Fannie to discover Jake actually belongs to us, Leah thought, cracking a pained smile at the irony. If anyone was to be told, she felt strongly that it should be Lydiann, but only provided she promised to keep the truth absolutely silent.

Leah waited for Hannah to get settled into the carriage before picking up the reins late morning on Monday. "You'll enjoy another visit with Mary Ruth and little Ruthie," she told her gloomy sister, hoping the outing would do them both some good.

"You must've forgotten I don't so much care to be round strangers," Hannah replied, folding her arms across her chest.

" 'Tis all right to be timid with Mary Ruth's quiltin' ladies. That's just how you are."

"They're all Mennonites, ain't?"

"I hadn't heard that. Just a few neighbors and others who want to learn how to quilt."

Hannah let out a *harrumph*, still acting like a child.

"What's gotten into ya? You seem out of sorts," Leah said, eyeing her sister, who sat all rigid and straight.

"I'll tell ya what's ailin' me," Hannah snapped, surprising Leah. It was as if she was desperate for a chance to give voice to her pent-up frustrations. "I'm tired of bein' looked down on by my family." Not waiting for Leah to answer, she added, "It's all 'bout my interest in folk medicine, I daresay."

Leah was surprised to hear Hannah spout off so. "There's nothin' wrong with using home remedies and whatnot. Aunt Lizzie and I've never felt there was, and Mamma never did, neither . . . as you surely know." She paused for a moment and then continued when she saw Hannah was sitting with arms crossed even higher up on her bosom than before. "What bothers some of the People is dabbling in areas that are best left alone."

"Jah, Gid says the People are split down the middle on powwowing, some saying it's straight from the pit of hell—though I don't see why when it helps those who are ailin'."

"Mamma always said there was no point steppin' as close as possible to the wrong side," Leah reminded her. "So I'd have to say we ought to stay far away from things that don't set well in one's spirit."

"Now you sound like Mary Ruth. She was always reciting Scripture and suchlike all those years back when Gid told her to stop comin' over to see me."

"But don't you agree there's something downright spooky 'bout the hex doctors' way with chants and buryin' dead chickens and whatnot?"

Hannah groaned and shook her head. "No . . . you don't know what you're sayin', Leah. That's all part of the earthy nature of things. Take people, for example, who can't wear a wristwatch because they have a special type of energy coursing through their bodies."

"I don't know anyone like that."

"Old Lady Henner could never wear a watch."

Leah didn't care one iota to hear more of Hannah's thin reasoning behind her obvious curiosity with the sympathy healers' dark, even evil, secret practices. "Sounds like an old wives' tale to me."

They rode along without saying much more, although Leah made occasional comments about various trees or so-and-so's well-tended landscape. But when they arrived at Mary Ruth's house and Hannah noticed the many Englishers' cars parked outside, she uttered in disdain, "Looks like a bunch of fancy folk to me."

Leah hopped out of the carriage and began tying the horse

to the hitching post. "I expect we'll *all* have a wonderful-gut time."

Hannah shrugged her shoulders and stepped out of the buggy on the opposite side, moving as slowly as if she were nigh unto eighty years old, instead of her sprightly thirty.

It was altogether pleasing to Leah seeing the eight ladies sitting around the kitchen table in Mary Ruth's modest kitchen, all chattering about intricate stitching and the creative combination of design and color.

Several looked up from where they sat, scissors in hand, smiles on bright faces, waiting expectantly as Mary Ruth happily introduced both Leah and Hannah as "two of my dear sisters." After that Leah and Hannah sat at the table, as well, cutting squares for the project: a nine-patch quilt.

Leah couldn't help but notice how unusually expressive Mary Ruth's blue eyes were as she spoke with one student after another. Her sister had seemingly discovered a way to channel her gift for teaching right here in her own cozy kitchen. Each lady present—three obviously very English, wearing gold scatter pins on blouse collars, and one with big, round red earrings—seemed to lap up the techniques much as a kitten does fresh milk.

Meanwhile, Ruthie slept snug in her cradle amidst the contented hum of the industrious women, whose busy hands flew to doing piecework and cutting squares for the pretty side border.

When it came time for the noon meal, each woman opened a sack lunch containing an extra sandwich or piece of fruit to share, which was exactly what they did. They broke bread together, with Mary Ruth saying the mealtime blessing before a single morsel was eaten.

Spreading God's love in her own way, thought Leah, touched not only by Mary Ruth's sweetness but by her enthusiasm for holding such classes. Even though there was a small charge for the weekly instruction, it struck Leah as a delightful way for Mary Ruth to have a pleasant and meaningful social outlet after being accustomed to teaching and enjoying the company of children all day long. Goodness, she knew how isolating it could be to tend to a new baby. She couldn't have imagined raising Lydiann and Abe without the emotional support of Aunt Lizzie and, at the time, Hannah. In those days, she had even looked forward to doing housework for Dr. Schwartz and his wife, Lorraine.

Sighing, she caught herself glancing around the long table, once the dinner hour was past, drinking in the sounds and sight of the quilters trimming off the *Schnibbles* from many squares.

It was after the last quilter had thanked Mary Ruth at the back door and headed on her way that Leah and her sisters went and sat in the front room, taking turns holding Ruthie. Hannah couldn't seem to get over how small her niece's fingers were, and how "awful tiny the moons are on her fingernails." To this Mary Ruth remarked that she had put tiny mitts on Ruthie's hands at night. "So she doesn't scratch her face."

Hannah offered quickly that she'd done the same for Mimi. "She had a way of thrashin' her arms in her sleep . . . but only before a visit to the sympathy healer."

Leah's breath caught in her throat.

"Why on earth did you take your baby daughter to a powwow doctor?" Mary Ruth asked, unable to hide a look of astonishment.

Hannah didn't bother to answer. "I've been thinkin' quite a lot here lately. Ain't it time we had another woman doctor in the area?"

"You mean similar to an Amish midwife?" asked Mary Ruth.

"No, someone to carry on the healing gifts, like Old Lady Henner."

Mary Ruth stood right up and went over to Hannah to take sleeping Ruthie from her arms. "I'd rather you not talk about such things within the hearing of my firstborn." Pacing the floor, Mary Ruth glanced every so often at Hannah, who merely sat in the hickory rocker, a bewildered look on her face.

"Why is it you're so against our doctors, anyways?" asked Hannah at last.

Though Leah flinched inwardly, she hoped Mary Ruth might speak up and share what she'd learned about the matter. She was secretly pleased when Mary Ruth carried Ruthie to the kitchen and returned with a Bible. "Here's why I believe we must call upon the name of the Lord for healing and not seek out the powers of certain ones in our community."

Before Mary Ruth could thumb through the thin pages of the Scriptures, Hannah spoke up again. "Doesn't the Lord God give good gifts to His children? Just look at water dowsers and folks who can find the depth and flow of a well—and they can locate other things, too—do ya mean to say those things ain't from the hand of God?"

"The sort of healing used by sympathy healers is done mostly by chantings and charms," argued Mary Ruth. "My Robert has been doing some research as an outgrowth of a church debate two years ago, and he's discovered that pow-wowing uses chants and formulas from a book of spells that traces back to the thirteenth century—some of it comes from even farther back than that."

Hannah frowned. "I've never heard tell of that. Old Lady Henner never needed a book. She knew exactly what to say and do to help a sick person . . . or even an animal."

"But she did things in secret, didn't she?" Mary Ruth pressed, the Bible in her lap.

"I guess she did."

Leah couldn't keep still any longer. "We *know* she did."

Looking as though she had been cornered, Hannah said, "Are ya gonna read the Bible now, Mary Ruth?" She gave Leah an annoyed look.

"Will you heed God's Word on this matter . . . *this* time?"

Hannah nodded her head and sighed. "I'm still here, ain't I?"

"All right, then, I'll read from the eighteenth chapter of Deuteronomy, verses ten through part of twelve. 'There shall not be found among you any one that maketh his son or his daughter to pass through the fire, or that useth divination, or an observer of times, or an enchanter, or a witch, or a charmer, or a consulter with familiar spirits, or a wizard, or a necromancer. For all that do these things are an abomination unto the Lord.' "

Hannah's face dropped and she looked like the air had gone out of her. The sisters endured a long and awkward silence.

Softly, yet confidently, Mary Ruth volunteered something Leah had not heard previously. "Believe it or not," she said, "I've heard some of the diseases are supposedly transferred at the time of the healing." Her shoulders rose and fell, and she went on. "Following such a treatment, the sympathy healer must go and rest to recover from taking on the toxic part from the sick person."

Leah wasted no time in responding. "For pity's sake, that doesn't sound like God's doing, does it?"

Hannah remained silent.

Leah rose and went to check on Mary Ruth's sleeping baby. Kneeling on the kitchen floor, she rocked the cradle and prayed silently that Hannah might ponder the goodness and grace of the Lord and take the Scripture reading to heart instead of yearning for the hex doctors' powers.

Please, Lord, help Mary Ruth finally get through Hannah's thick head on this matter.

On the ride home Leah was heartened by Hannah's rather relaxed demeanor. And because she hoped something good had been accomplished for Hannah today, Leah began to hum softly.

"Must be feelin' happy," her sister commented.

"S'pose I am." She couldn't go so far as to say just why, but another look at Hannah's serene face left Leah wondering what she was truly thinking.

"Mary Ruth seems quite contented, ain't so? All cozy in her house . . . with her first baby 'n' all."

"Ruthie is so cuddly and dear." *Makes me want one of my own*, she thought.

They rode along, Leah humming all the while, and

Hannah leaning back against the front seat as if taking in the countryside, not saying much.

Will she consider the Bible verses Mary Ruth shared? Leah wondered. After all, there had been numerous other times when Hannah's twin had tried to link their concern to God's Holy Word for her sake.

Leaving the matter once again to the Lord, Leah was tempted to give in to aimless musing, but an open *courting* buggy—in broad daylight, of all things—was headed their way.

As the carriage drew closer, she looked over at the young couple, expecting perhaps to wave and greet familiar faces. Instead, she drew in a sharp breath.

Jake?

Hannah sat up quickly. "Wasn't that our Lyddie?"

Leah was speechless.

Jake had surprised all of them, possibly even Lydiann, too, by coming home so soon. Witnessing yet again how smitten Sadie's boy was over Lydiann—his arm draped around her—all of nature seemed at once topsy-turvy. The terrible sight led Leah's imagination to run ahead of her to the hour the day would die away into twilight. And all the while, Jake and Lydiann would be out riding alone.

Chapter Seven

I *must turn this horse and carriage around!* Leah panicked and checked to see if anyone was coming from behind. On impulse, she reined the horse hard to the left.

Hannah gasped. "What the world, sister? You're gonna wreck us!"

Hannah was surely right; there was no turning as sharply as Leah had attempted to do. Besides, the poor horse was thoroughly confused, pawing at the ground and neighing something fierce. "Leah? You all right?"

Truth was, she was downright upset and determined to put a stop to Jake's obvious arrogance. What sort of young man simply showed up unannounced? He hadn't even waited till after sundown to come calling on Lyddie, the traditional way.

She could not get the memory of Lydiann's blissful smile out of her head—her girl riding next to her dark-haired beau. It spurred Leah to get on home, but the horse was presently not in a cooperative mood.

"Best be more cautious, Leah." Well she deserved it, but how strange for Hannah to be chiding *her*.

She thought ahead to those things that must be said to Jake. Not so willing to get the entire family involved—although what choice did she have—she rehearsed in her mind a make-believe conversation with Lydiann, followed by another with Gid. Thrown in there somewhere, as well, would be at least a question or two or more from Dat and Aunt Lizzie.

"Ach, such a mess we're in," she said flat out.

"What're you muttering?"

Leah caught herself and explained quietly, "Just talkin' to myself." She hoped Jake Mast hadn't gotten any wild ideas about running off with Lydiann. Because if so, all of Gobbler's Knob would hear her sobbing, and she'd send a group of the People after them, or even go out looking for Jake herself . . . anything to rescue her Lyddie from certain heartache.

◆

"I was up in the woods writing a letter to you this very mornin'," Lydiann told Jake as they rode toward Ninepoints. "There's a beautiful old tree not so deep into the forest, and I like to sit under it and dream of you."

He smiled and touched his forehead to hers. "No need for that anymore. Because of Jonas, I'm here . . . right where I belong. With you."

She liked the sound of this. "I missed you terribly. Saved every single letter you wrote," she whispered, afraid she might cry, so happy she was to be riding in his courting buggy. "I thought my heart might break in two if I didn't lay eyes on ya again."

He reached for her hand. "If Jonas hadn't talked to my father, I'd still be in Ohio. It was a downright dirty trick my father did, sendin' me away. I 'spect he's thinkin' I'm only home for a visit, but I'm never goin' back, not if I don't have to."

"Ya mean, you might?" She fretted at the latter.

"That's not for you to worry your perty head over, Lyddie."

"But you said—"

"I know what I want. That's why I'm here."

She looked down at their entwined fingers. She'd yearned to sit right next to him again this way. All their painful time apart had vanished with the morning mist.

"What is it, love?" He leaned closer.

She hadn't realized she'd spoken anything, but perhaps she had. "I'm thinkin' that maybe I love ya more than I oughta," she told him, brushing tears away.

"*Himmel* . . . that just ain't possible!" He squeezed her tight.

She could hardly wait to become his bride—Jake's Lyddie!

Leah helped Hannah unhitch the carriage and said goodbye as she led the horse up to the stable.

Down at the house, Sadie met Leah, solemn faced, standing in the doorway of the kitchen. "Awful bad news," she whispered. "Jake's back. I saw him come for Lyddie not too long ago."

"I know. Hannah and I saw them out on the road."

"What on earth are they doin' . . . out before dark?" Sadie frowned. "What can it mean?"

"He's flaunting his return, I daresay." Leah hurried past her. "I won't stand here guessin' what your son's got on his mind. I say we go out and find 'em."

Sadie followed Leah into the kitchen. "And if we do—what then? Flat out tell them what's what?"

Leah shook her head. "No, we get Lyddie away from him . . . and tell her privately. That's the only way to handle the pickle we're in."

"But we'll cause a big scene if we do it that way, and Jake will wonder why we're interfering. Is that what ya want?" Sadie went to the sink to pour water into a glass. "Sounds like a terrible plan to me."

Leah knew it wasn't a good idea, but what else could they do? "Then I guess we wait till she comes home," she said slowly.

"What if she doesn't?"

Terror flooded Leah's heart anew. "Do ya think Lydiann would fall for doin' such a dumb thing?"

"She's bent on bein' with him, same as I was with Derry . . . and I knew better, too." Sadie went and sat on the table bench. "Love's powerful, I'd have to say. 'Specially at Lyddie's age, when youthful, fanciful ideas get all mixed up inside and confuse you into thinking wrongs are right."

"Jake would surely think twice 'bout taking her away, wouldn't he?" Feeling nearly overcome with worry, Leah joined Sadie at the table. She turned and looked up at the day clock, high on the wall behind her. "I say we give her till supper. If she isn't home by then . . ." She honestly didn't know what she'd do. "What an awful test of a mother's endurance!" She twisted the hem of her apron till she'd made a wrinkled mess of it. "I can't help but wonder what Mamma might do."

Sadie leaned forward. "Mamma *prayed*," she said,

surprising Leah. "Sometimes nearly all night . . . she walked the floors and talked to God 'bout everything on her mind and in her heart. She told me so."

Mamma had done something vital back then, and Leah wanted to do the same. *Ach, but I wish Sadie hadn't prayed for Jake's return.* It looked as if God had answered her sister's heart's cry. She rose and headed for the stairs. "I'll be in my room," she said, glancing back over her shoulder.

Evidently Sadie wanted to follow Mamma's wise example, as well, for she had already folded her hands and bowed her head at their mother's old trestle table.

A sob caught in Leah's throat. *Lord Jesus, please keep Lydiann safe . . . and bring her home right quick!*

Chapter Eight

In the early evening light, Plain children often stayed outdoors playing until the sound of the supper bell or their mothers' voices called them into the house to wash up. Henry Schwartz took note of quite a number of such youngsters on this day . . . young boys clad in broadfall trousers, Amish-green shirts, and straw hats, as well as barefooted girls chasing after one another in pale blue or lavender dresses, white caps perched on their small heads. They seemed to move in slow motion at times, leaning on the white yard gate, giggling, tossing a ball high over the martin birdhouse, playing ring-around-the-rosy near the springhouse, apparently unaware of autumn's end, nearly in sight.

Henry had been out driving for a time after picking up a few groceries for tomorrow's breakfast, as Lorraine had requested. The sun had been falling fast, but he did not rush his pace, not concerned with getting home promptly at suppertime, although his wife would hope that he might. So relaxed was he that he pulled off the road onto the shoulder when he noticed a broken-down carriage, its hitch undone from the lone horse. An Amish boy and girl—both not more than sixteen or so—were flagging him down.

Getting out of his car, he saw Jake Mast and the youngest Ebersol girl. "Well, hello there, young man." He waved to them, his pulse pounding nearly out of control.

Jake removed his hat and smiled. "Good to see ya, Dr. Schwartz. It's been a while, ain't?"

He nodded, feeling almost breathless as Jake quickly introduced his girlfriend. "This here's Lydiann—Abram Ebersol's daughter."

"Hello, Lydiann. How's your family?" he managed to ask, extending his hand to shake her small one. She, however, was obviously not interested in making a good impression, saying something soft and too low for him to hear before looking away to fasten her eyes on Jake, avoiding Henry's inquisitive gaze.

"Would ya mind givin' us a lift?" Jake asked.

Henry agreed and asked, "Where to?"

Jake hesitated momentarily, glancing at Lydiann, as if unsure. Then quickly, he said, "Take us to Gobbler's Knob, if you would . . . to Abram's place."

Lydiann seemed almost passive, as though expecting Jake to make this decision.

"Denki, doctor." Jake went and tied up the horse before reaching for Lydiann's hand to lead her to the car.

Henry felt as dispirited as the day he had exposed to Leah the truth about Jake's origin and his atrocious mishandling of the situation. How could it be that his flesh-and-blood grandson was seeing his birth mother's own sibling? The idea that this young couple, noticeably taken with each other, was now seated behind him—even whispering under their breath—

made him feel like an inexperienced swimmer without a life jacket, rushing headlong down the Susquehanna River.

He gripped the steering wheel and drove as carefully as ever he had in his life, willing himself forward through the dense fog that enveloped him on this evening free of cloud or mist.

"Turn here," he heard Jake say, and Henry did so, mechanically clicking on his turn signal and tapping on the brake.

Sadie called to Leah at the sound of the automobile coming up the lane, and the two of them flew down the stairs. Scarcely ever did anyone drive a car onto their property, though she fleetingly recalled the freak snowstorm and her kind brother-in-law Robert's attempt to spare her frostbite by driving her home. Such distress her actions that day had brought, resulting in yet another Proving period.

She ran to the window and saw Dr. Schwartz, Lydiann, and Jake getting out of the car. To think the missing couple was with the doctor, of all people! "Jake's horse and buggy must've broken down somewhere," she told Leah, who was hovering near. "The minute we can get our hands on Lydiann, we need to take her for a long walk," she added.

"Why not go next door with her," Leah suggested, to which Sadie agreed.

Just as she was about to push open the back door, Sadie heard Jake's voice coming from the yard. She had wished to see her wonderful boy once again, to gaze at him for as long as she dared. Inhaling deeply, she made herself slowly step out the back door and down the stoop, moving toward the automobile.

Dat emerged from the barn and waved at Dr. Schwartz, a strange look settling on his face at the sight of his youngest daughter holding hands with her beau in broad daylight.

Sadie could hear Leah breathing hard behind her, or maybe she was mumbling a quiet prayer. Whichever it was, Sadie knew for certain she and Leah must not let Lydiann out of their sight until they had spoken ever so frankly with their sister. *Dear, poor girl!* As much as Sadie cared for Jake, she was horrified at the way he continued to look so fondly at Lydiann, still keeping her hand in his as he explained to Dat how the two of them had come to be riding with the doctor in his car.

Soon Gid came across the yard, more than likely to see what was going on. Right away he offered to help Jake go back and work on rehitching the carriage to the horse, briefly returning to the barn to retrieve an old, rusted toolbox before climbing with Jake into the doctor's car. *Bless Gid for taking Jake away for now,* Sadie thought, breathing more easily.

She watched in silence as Dr. Schwartz backed up the vehicle repeatedly, making several attempts to turn around in the narrow lane. Gid looked out the back window, his face turning shades of red, while Jake sat up front, smiling and waving like a boy on Christmas morning.

Leah broke the stillness. "Lyddie, why don't you come with Sadie and me to the Dawdi Haus? We best be talkin' some things over."

The pointed way Leah had put it just now brought a sudden frown to Lydiann's pretty face, and Sadie felt awfully tense. Yet she followed her sisters down the walkway, bypassing the back door of the main house to head straightaway to her own kitchen next door.

In the quiet and very private room that was Sadie's bedroom, Leah prayed silently for wisdom. "Please listen, Lydiann," she began. "What I must tell you, I should've said right from the start, when Jake and you first started courtin'."

Sadie stood quietly, her solemn blue eyes blinking a mile a minute. Lydiann, on the other hand, held herself like a child caught snitching a handful of cookies, her arms folded tightly against her slight chest, the way Hannah had done earlier this afternoon when Leah had sided with Mary Ruth against powwow doctors. Leah could see unmistakably in Lydiann's eyes this was not to be the easiest conversation she'd ever set out to have with the girl she viewed as her daughter.

"Ach, I don't see why you are so upset," Lyddie burst out. "Your eyes looked like they might pop out of your head when we drove up, and Jake did nothin' wrong." She was shaking her head. "My beau just arrives home . . . comes over to surprise me ever so nicely, and *this* is what happens." She let out a huff and looked away toward the wall.

Sadie eyed Leah helplessly and then shrugged one petite shoulder. "We wouldn't be talkin' like this to you," she said, "if we didn't think it terribly necessary."

"Talkin' like what? Sayin' *what* to me?" Lydiann's eyes flashed with what appeared to be resentment.

Leah moved closer to her on Sadie's bed, aware of Lydiann's sweet-smelling perfume, an alluring fragrance she hadn't noticed till now.

Sadie stepped nearer the door, as if guarding it against Lydiann's possible attempt to flee midrevelation.

In hushed tones Leah said, "Even though I'm opposed to secret keepin'—I've learned some hard lessons 'bout that—

you must never tell anyone what I'm goin' to say. And I mean not a single soul . . . ever."

"If the family Bible were nearby, we'd ask you to put your hand on it and promise," Sadie cut in.

Still staring at them with defiance in her eyes, Lydiann sat quietly, not making an effort to pledge anything at all.

"Oh, my dear girl," Leah said softly, "it would affect you terribly, and most probably any future children, if you and Jake were to marry because of being ignorant of what we know." Leah felt she was stumbling over her words . . . wishing there was a better way than to speak this horrid truth that was going to shatter Lydiann's heart.

Lydiann's shoulders dropped and she appeared to wilt at the mention of Jake's and her marriage—or perhaps she was reacting to the comment about their being ignorant. "I'm listenin'," she said.

"And promising, too?"

"Whatever it is, I won't share with anyone. You have my word."

Tears glistened in Sadie's eyes. "Not Jake, neither."

Lydiann grimaced when she caught sight of her eldest sister's tears. "What on earth?"

"Years ago," Leah began again, "when Sadie gave birth to her son, she thought he had died . . . his comin' too early into the world and all."

Sadie sniffled and moved away from the door, coming to sit beside Lydiann. "My sin resulted in a beautiful dark-haired boy . . . who did not go to heaven that night as I'd thought." She stopped, clearly unable to finish.

Lydiann looked first at Sadie and then at Leah and then back at Sadie, as if to ask, *What are you saying?* She opened her mouth to speak but shook her head instead. Finally she ventured, "Surely, you don't mean . . ."

Sadie's eyes met Lydiann's.

"But Jake is Mandie's twin . . . Peter and Fannie Mast's son!" Lydiann insisted.

Leah, still sitting on the other side of Lydiann, reached for her hand, but Lydiann pulled away, her breath coming in short gasps.

Leah quickly explained how Dr. Schwartz had switched Fannie's stillborn twin son with Sadie's premature babe. "He was just barely alive."

"Dr. Schwartz did this?" Lydiann asked in obvious disbelief.

Leah nodded sadly.

Lydiann's lower lip began to tremble, and she covered her face with both of her hands. "If this is a lie, it's the cruelest scheme in the world to keep us apart."

"We would never think of saying a word 'bout this to you if things were otherwise," Sadie said. "We *love* you."

"Ever so dearly," Leah added. "And we want what's best for you and for Jake."

"For your future children, too." Sadie handed Lydiann a handkerchief.

"But Jake loves me and I care for him. Tellin' me this doesn't change the way I feel," Lydiann sobbed.

Leah waited a moment before going on. "We were terribly unfair to you and Jake. We did you wrong by not sayin' something immediately." She told how she'd first stumbled onto Jake with Lydiann in the kitchen last summer. "Once Jake left for Ohio, we thought your affection for him might fade with time."

"How can I just stop carin' for someone so wonderful?" Lydiann was staring now at Leah. "You . . . you knew this for that long? How could you keep it from me?" She bent her head low. "Honestly I don't believe my *first* mamma would've let something like this happen!" With that she headed straight for the door and flew out.

I can't bear to watch her heart breaking so, thought Leah. *How I wish I could do everything differently . . . for Lyddie's sake most of all.*

Sadie wrapped an arm around her. "I won't let her treat you this way."

"No . . . no, just leave her be. There's nothin' more we can do." Leah rested her head on her sister's shoulder and gave in to anguished tears.

Chapter Nine

Lydiann had been only five or six when she first realized that folk looked on her and Abe differently than other children, especially women at Preaching service whose eyes shone with sympathy—and pity. Leah had been a wonderful-good mother to them both, no question, but while Abe obviously considered Leah his mamma, Lydiann had always thought of Leah as both a mother and a sister. And when she'd fallen for the first boy who made eyes at her, she wondered if God was somehow making up for taking her mother to heaven early.

Jake was everything I wanted in a beau . . . in a husband and father for my children, she mourned as she headed away from the house. She wept angry tears, infrequently brushing them away with the back of her hand, letting most fall freely. She felt she was rebelling somehow against nature and the Lord God who'd fashioned her in His own image, with tears and emotions beyond her control. She walked as fast as she could to try to drive away the painful feelings, unable to escape them no matter how swiftly she went. "Jake . . . oh, Jake."

She passed the woods on her right and Dr. Schwartz's

clinic on the left as she came up on the crest of the hill where the road fell slowly yet decidedly toward the area known as Grasshopper Level. She slowed her pace somewhat, contemplating just where it was she wanted to go—or if she really wanted to go anywhere at all.

Stopping now, she thought what it would be like to walk all the way to the Masts' orchard house. But what good would that do? Jake would wonder why she was there . . . ask why she looked so disheveled, with swollen eyes and a face streaked with tears. He would press for answers and she might give in, breaking her promise to Mamma Leah and Sadie. Nothing good could possibly come of that . . . could it?

Standing there in the road, she brooded further on the possible consequences of Jake's hearing from her—his own aunt, of all things—that he was not his parents' son at all, but the child of a woman he did not know and had been kept from knowing since Sadie and her family had always been off limits to him. *Out-and-out shunned.*

Things don't add up, she thought sorrowfully. *Why does one family reject another?*

All in, she turned to go back home, hardly able now to make her legs move. If what Sadie and Mamma Leah had shared with her was true—and she knew better than to doubt their word—she had no choice but to break things off with Jake.

She knew she could not do that today, nor tomorrow. Just *when* she would bring herself to turn her back on him, she didn't know. She almost wished his dear face repulsed her, but as she again considered the shocking news that he was indeed Sadie's own son, she was moved to further tears. She also felt an unexpected sorrow for Sadie, who had never been able to know her only living child.

Why, O God, should something this dreadful happen to me? To all of us?

Henry gathered up all the trash from the house and dragged it out to the receptacle in the garage. He shuffled back to the clinic, aware of some movement in the air, more subtle than a breeze, and he wondered if it was a figment of his imagination. *The ghost of Henry past, perhaps.* He deserved any haunting he might encounter, even welcomed the notion of rebuke by an accusing spirit.

Inside his office, he picked up the small waste basket and went from examining rooms to the patients' waiting room, not looking forward to Leah's arrival at work tomorrow. He speculated on what she might have to say about his giving Lydiann and Jake a lift.

The sight of the young Amish couple together on the road earlier today had put him in something of a panic, even though he was convinced he had concealed it well. However, he *had* experienced a sensation of nausea, and the more he became aware of the pair's animated whispering in the backseat behind him, the more discouraged he'd become.

All my doing . . .

It seemed as if he had mentally repeated the logic, or lack thereof, in choosing Peter and Fannie Mast to raise and nurture Sadie and Derek's illegitimate infant thousands of times. Had it been the wrong thing to place Derek's firstborn in the arms of birth-weary Fannie . . . tricking her into thinking she had indeed birthed the gangly and gaunt boy? A counterfeit twin to Amanda, with not a scrap of resemblance to her in build or facial features. Truth be known, Jake was the spitting image of his biological father, Henry's second son.

So Henry had committed the riskiest act he had ever elected to do; one he had concurrently lamented and praised, unknown to anyone but Leah—or so he hoped. Now, as he returned from disposing of the last of the clinic rubbish, he happened to look up and see Lydiann walking alone, appearing somewhat agitated.

Sighing loudly, he strode down the sidewalk toward the house. Whatever was weighing on the Ebersol girl was none of his business.

For as long as Leah remembered, she had been careful to follow the rules, doing as she was told by Mamma, by Dat . . . and, once she'd known to, by God. She'd always looked forward to being considered a faithful church member, and now, these many years away from having made her life covenant, she knew she must continually reach for that mark. Even when no one was looking, she was striving to be all that she ought to be before God and the church. The one thing she had done to disobey the Ordnung, though not blatantly, had been to read the Bible more often than she supposed was necessary, and more passages than were ever preached on of a Sunday.

But today, this miserable day, she would have given anything not to have told Lydiann the appalling truth. She felt nearly as if she'd sinned, and she wished there might have been some reasonable way for her to remain silent, especially after witnessing the pain she'd inflicted upon her darling girl. Yet the strong possibility that a marriage between the two might occur; to the potentially disastrous effect such a thing would have on Jake and Lyddie's babies, should any survive; as well as the shame such devastating knowledge would have eventually brought upon Jake and Lydiann themselves had been enough to push her into speaking so plainly to Lyddie.

It was distressingly apparent how much Lydiann cared for Jake. Her affection for him was all over her face—dwelling in her brooding eyes, pulling down the corners of her mouth even as she was hit with the startling facts.

Yet this heartbreaking dilemma was not Leah's doing, nor her fault. When all was said and done, it was Dr. Schwartz's deception that had brought them to this troublesome place when God, in His sovereignty, allowed Jake to breathe his first breath and live.

If the truth had not been revealed to Lydiann, the door would have remained open for more close contact between Sadie and her son. Yet with Jake unaware of his true roots, how satisfying could such a relationship have been for Sadie? Leah could only contemplate such things after the fact.

In the space of one heart-to-heart talk, the what-ifs had been settled. Today the agonizing truth had been laid open to one more person, and Lydiann's heart was surely breaking.

Sadie wandered aimlessly around the large plot that had been last summer's charity garden, feet pressing into the tilled-up earth as she talked to herself. "What have we done?" she whispered, still caught up in the sorrowful scene that had taken place a few hours ago. "I'll never know my son now."

She spoke to the dirt, but she suddenly raised her head. It was dreadfully quiet here past the side yard, not so far from the woodshed and the outhouse—so much so that she thought she could hear the beating of her own heart.

She stared at the rolling lawn that swept up to the front of the house, the location of countless happy family gatherings over these many years. *Family . . . love . . . unity. Have we ruined that?* She shrugged helplessly. Likely Lydiann was experiencing something similar to the grief she herself had felt when the stunning news of Harvey's death arrived at her door. The surge of sadness, even emptiness that had enveloped her had nearly drowned her as each minute ticked by. At times she had yearned for it to do just that—submerge her into oblivion so she might not have to suffer such pain.

Yet with the dawning of harsh reality came a slow but sorrowful acceptance. Harvey was gone from her, never again to knock the mud off his work boots at the stoop, chuckling as he came into the house at suppertime, eager to wrap her in his big, strong arms with an "Ach, I missed ya so."

In her mind she saw the years ahead for Lydiann, her poor sister possibly feeling queasy every time she thought of her hand being held so tenderly by her own nephew. *Will she be able to put this out of her mind? Perhaps even forgive us for not saying something sooner?* Sadie wondered as she noticed Aunt Lizzie coming toward her.

"Dorcas is having a few of the women folk over for a cornhuskin' bee tomorrow," Lizzie announced. "Would you want to go and help?"

Opening her mouth to answer, Sadie suddenly spotted Lydiann walking toward the house, making her way across the side yard. Anxious as to where she'd gone, Sadie watched her sister, trying to think what she ought to be saying to Lizzie. "She . . . I . . . jah, I don't see why I couldn't help with the huskin."

"All right, then," Aunt Lizzie replied, eyeing her curiously.

Sadie was terribly aware of the lump in her throat as she noticed Lydiann sit down on the back step, hands covering her face. *Where'd she go?* Sadie wondered. *Did she keep her promise not to tell anyone?*

Chapter Ten

Tuesday morning, November 5

Dear Diary,

The children are still fast asleep, as is Gid. I have been walking the floors all night, just as I did when Mimi was a baby, since sleep escapes me—my pain is unbearable at times. I am beginning to feel like I'm bobbing along on a dark sea, my head scarcely above water.

I truly believe I must see a hex doctor—if I could just get some help, I know I'd feel much better. No matter what my family thinks of me, I must do this for myself . . . and for the baby. Nothing else has ever worked for me.

The more I think on it, the more I have a desire to seek out the healing gift myself. Surely that would drive away my sadness, and it would make many others who desire to be touched happy, too. How I long for this gift to come to me! Would that it could be so.

Respectfully,
Hannah

Peace had come to rest on the countryside around the Ebersol Cottage, and autumn's cyclical touch was unmistakable in every direction as Leah walked with Sadie across the meadow to the corn-husking frolic. "I should've stayed home with Lyddie," Leah said softly. She shivered at the gamut of emotions Lydiann was no doubt experiencing—from sadness and disbelief, to intense grief, even probable disgust at the courting relationship she'd unknowingly shared with her own nephew.

"Well, Aunt Lizzie's there, so if Lydiann needs anything . . ." Sadie stopped short.

"Jah, and that's what I'm worried 'bout. What if Lizzie asks what's botherin' her . . . and Lydiann spills the beans?" Leah wished every last one of the family secrets could be boxed up and the lid closed tightly, never to be troublesome again.

"Should I go back to the house?" asked Sadie. "I'd be more than happy to."

Leah sighed. "No, that might signal something's amiss. Let's just pray that all is well."

"Do ya think she'll ever be tempted to talk 'bout this with anyone—besides us, I mean?"

"For now Lyddie's best left alone to consider all that was at stake for her."

"Not to mention findin' it in her heart to forgive us," Sadie added.

"Our being the ones to give her the sorry news will make that difficult, jah."

"But once it fully dawns on her who Jake is to me . . . and to her, won't she feel relieved that someone stepped in?"

"I can't imagine otherwise." Looking down at her feet, Leah realized she'd worn shoes for one of the first times this fall. This coming Thursday the People would celebrate one of the earliest weddings of the season down at the Kauffmans' farm, where Naomi's youngest cousin was marrying her second cousin, a Zook. Leah wondered how Lydiann would manage the three-hour wedding service, or if she would even go.

"I'm not so sure we're out of the woods with this, to tell ya the truth," Sadie murmured.

Leah nodded. "Well, just give her some time. She'll do the right thing, I'm sure. She won't want to keep being courted by her nephew, for pity's sake."

Sadie put out a hand to stop her. "Frankly I think one of us will end up havin' to tell Jake the truth before all's said and done. If he's anything like me, he won't go away quietly."

"Besides, you're still holdin' out hope to get to know him, ain't so?"

Sadie began walking again, though quite slowly, as if her pace were indicative of her pattern of thought. "I just think we haven't tapped the root of it yet. Jake will want to know why Lydiann doesn't want to see him anymore, and she'll have to give some answer to satisfy him. It's an awful can of worms."

Leah pitied Sadie, because even though she'd ignored her pointed question, she was right in thinking the threads of Jake and Lydiann's predicament were just as entangled as ever before—and each strand twisted back to Sadie.

Lydiann sat down in the chair near the window of her bedroom, her light frame feeling as heavy as she'd ever known it. *Oh, Jake, I already miss you.*

Running her hands over the cane beneath her, she could not get him out of her mind, in spite of the fact their good-bye this time must be permanent and said very soon. Yet if he were truly Sadie's son, why didn't he at least resemble her in some respect? Even his personality was nothing at all like her sister's. Of course, Jake looked and acted nothing like Mandie, either, but fraternal twins often seemed more like regular brother and sister, or even cousins, than twins. Still, she couldn't help but wonder who Jake's real father was. *Could it be Jake looks like* him?

She had not thought quickly enough when Leah and Sadie had sat her down and spoken so confidentially. At least a dozen or more questions had come to mind after the fact, taking a toll on her ravaged brain. In truth, she was plain exhausted, the reason she'd stayed home from today's husking bee. All she could think about was her need for sleep.

She went to her bed and lay down, not bothering to cover herself. She whispered Jake's name again and declared to the air how much she had loved him, till her tears found their way across her nose and onto her pillow.

"I'll never love anyone again. I'll stay a maidel my whole life long if need be." She was convinced of her feelings, as well as her words, and she gave in to sleep, wishing she were a little girl again and might remain so. Wishing, too, there might be a gentle way to break off her relationship with unsuspecting Jake.

Abram knew full well how much Lizzie enjoyed walking through the meadow and up to the edge of the woods and back, sometimes three times a week, getting her fill of nature. Once winter arrived and hunting season came to an end, she'd be back to wandering through the woods, making him mighty uneasy, even though she knew the forest better than most anyone around.

Maybe too well, he decided, sitting next to her in the family carriage as they headed up the road to Dr. Schwartz's clinic. She'd once again insisted that this visit was unnecessary, putting up an awful fuss, saying it didn't matter to her if her thumb mended crooked or not.

"Well, it matters to me," he'd said at last. Like it or not, Lizzie had climbed into the carriage as he'd stood right behind her, nudging her inside like an obstreperous heifer.

She'd let him have it, too, coming close to blessing him out but good as she repeated that she had no need for a doctor. So strong were her objections that Abram began to wonder if she had some sort of beef with the doctor.

"When's the last time you had yourself a checkup?" He looked at her as she pouted up a storm, and reached around her to try to give her a hug.

She pushed him away playfully. "Ach, Abram, ya just don't listen, do you?"

He chuckled and let her be. "Your thumb will look right fine come Christmas, if ya don't slam it in a car door again."

"I don't plan on gettin' near another automobile."

"If ya hadn't broke it, you'd be over at the Peacheys' place huskin' corn with the rest of the women folk."

"Better I stayed put at home with Lydiann, poor girl. Something awful's happened to her . . . haven't you noticed? 'Tis written all over her sad face."

"Her beau's back home, so she oughta be smilin', ain't?" He was growing too old to keep up with his teenage children and their friends. Fact was, young Abe was in and out of the house so much these days, Abram was beginning to wonder if his boy only cared to show up for supper. Soon to be fourteen, Abe was nearly finished with his education at the one-room Amish school, a right fine building if Abram said so himself. Led by their two preachers, including Gid, all the men who were able had pitched in a few years back, after the public elementary schools were consolidated, raising the schoolhouse in a day much like a small-scale barn raising.

Just then Lizzie said, "Peter Mast is bound to be irate about Jake's seein' Lyddie, ya know."

"Serves him right, don't it? I mean . . . look at the standoff he's made with his family. All for what?"

"Our Leah got their Jonas shunned."

Abram nodded. "That's how *they* see it."

"So . . . what's keepin' Peter from pulling the rug out from under Jake with Lydiann?"

"Assuming he even *knows* they're seein' each other."

"How could he not know with how those two were carryin' on for all to see?" Lizzie reminded him.

"Reckless and in love," Abram offered. "Remember how we were? Not carin' what anybody thought—holdin' hands in public?"

"Jah, I remember." This woman had a deliciously spunky sweetness to her.

"You ain't mad at me, then?" he asked.

"For marryin' me?"

He snorted, trying to contain his laughter and not succeeding. "No, for draggin' you off to see Dr. Schwartz today."

Her smile faded quickly, as if she wished he hadn't brought *that* up again. "Just never you mind 'bout my broken thumb . . . Abram Ebersol."

From the look on her face, he was in the doghouse or woodshed, one.

All Dr. Schwartz wanted to talk about when he greeted Abram in the patients' waiting room was the beautiful six-point buck his son Robert had bagged with a bow and arrow. "Right over there in those woods across the road," the doctor said, pointing north.

Abram listened, eager to tell him about Tomato Joe's deer. "The smithy's son-in-law got himself a nice deer yesterday, too. He said he saw four doe and two rack bucks, but he finally got the five-pointer he'd had his eye on." Abram looked at Lizzie. "We're s'posed to be gettin' some canned and cubed meat from Dorcas . . . don't ya forget."

Lizzie nodded and said she'd be expecting it. "Wouldn't surprise me if Leah or Sadie come home with some after the corn-huskin' today," she spoke up.

Abram's mouth watered at the thought of what a fine supper the delicious venison would provide. But his concern for Lizzie renewed as she rose from the chair in the reception area to follow the doctor into one of the examining rooms. Abram was thankful she could be seen today without waiting too long, since there seemed to be only a few patients. "You'll be all right, dear," he said, reassuring her as she glanced over her shoulder. "Dr. Schwartz will take gut care." He winced at the thought of Lizzie enduring the pain of having her thumb rebroken if necessary, but he was mighty glad Dr. Schwartz was the man doing it. He'd been relieved to hear the doctor was still seeing patients till his planned retirement some months away yet.

Reaching for a *Time* magazine, Abram settled back in a chair and looked at the cover, which featured a man and his horse. It seemed this Goldwater fellow hailed from Arizona and was planning to ride east, though just why that was, Abram didn't know. Even so, he was interested enough to flip through the pages to find the article about this man, who was not just a cowboy but also a member of the United States senate.

"Englishers sure must like havin' their pictures taken," he muttered, somewhat taken with the magazine all the same, though more accustomed to the format of his favorite publication, *The Budget*.

He looked up now and then to see if Lizzie was coming out of the patients' room, thinking he should've gone in with her, especially since she'd never been sick enough to come here before today, far as he knew. *We all should be so healthy*, he thought.

Lizzie felt a bit awkward having a man other than her husband probe her hand, even if he was a doctor. The X-rays soon showed exactly what Abram had suspected, but having her thumb straightened and reset was not as painful as she might've thought, although at the moment the throbbing had a strong pulse of its own. Still, she was of good, strong stock and wouldn't let this get the best of her. Goodness, she'd been through much worse in her lifetime. Afflictions of the heart, to her thinking, were more difficult to bear.

When it came time for the sling Dr. Schwartz insisted she must wear, he helped guide her arm through it. "You'll need to rest some while your thumb heals," he urged her.

She thanked him but did not agree to take it easy. Truth was, she wasn't the sort to simply put her feet up and slow down, broken bone or not. As far as she was concerned, it was much better all around to keep busy.

She glanced about the room, noticing how tidy Leah kept the place. *Neat as a pin.* And she wondered what it was like working for this man whose dark brown eyes probed her own. Far as she could tell, Dr. Schwartz was in his midfifties by now, even though he could easily have been mistaken for much older. Worry lines crinkled his brow—the sort of frown that made her wonder if the village doctor ever slept soundly.

Her jaw tightened when he patted her arm. "Come back in six weeks. We'll see how you're doing," he said with a winning smile. "And you might want to consider sticking with horses and buggies."

His uncommonly gracious manner provoked her all of a sudden, and she felt it was wrong of him to speak to her that way. She was not a regular patient of his, nor a child to be admonished. But she *was* anxious to return to the waiting room and be on her way, back to the Ebersol Cottage and the life she cherished with Abram and his family.

Chapter Eleven

As far as Jonas could tell, he was the only person from Grasshopper Level present at the all-day Kauffman-Zook wedding. He'd wanted to be on hand to celebrate with the People and look ahead to his own wedding one day, but there was an even stronger motivation—to steal glimpses of Leah.

While the women prepared to serve the wedding feast indoors, he enjoyed standing and talking outside with the men. He even hoped to visit some with Abram Ebersol, who, unbeknownst to Jonas at the time, had arranged for Jonas's woodworking apprenticeship in Millersburg, Ohio, years ago. The hidebound man who'd once so opposed Jonas's courting Leah had softened considerably over the years.

He wandered over near the barn, where several men, including Smitty and Tomato Joe, stood chewing the fat. No breeze to speak of, two of the men lit their pipes, puffing the sweet-smelling smoke into the air. He caught a whiff or two as he stood there enjoying the sunshine on this early November day, getting a kick out of watching a whole group of Jesse Ebersol's teenaged grandsons standing in a conspiratorial huddle, some of them with visibly fancy leanings.

Old Jonathan Lapp seemed to notice the boys, too, and remarked about the youngest Ebersol boy. "He's the spittin' image of his grandpa Jesse, ain't?"

This brought a chorus of jahs from the men. "The youngster's just as hardworkin', too," the smithy spoke up. "Why, I heard he worked alongside his Dat in the wheat field from sunup to sundown till the harvest was done. Now, that's a *fleissich* young man!"

Jonas agreed, nodding his head with the others. *I was that sort of diligent lad*, he thought, pleased to be of good help once again at his father's farm and apple orchard. But there was no getting around his hankering to work with wood—he missed the distinct tang of sawdust, the feel of the smooth grain in his callused hands. At times he even awakened from dreams at night that had him back making fine furniture in his shop near Apple Creek. To think he'd initially convinced himself he would *not* chafe under the stern discipline of Bishop Bontrager. In the short time since his return, he had already failed miserably.

Leah foresaw this. How well she knows me. . . .

Leah—as pretty at thirty-three as any of the courting-age young women present here today, he decided. He supposed he might be a smidgen partial because he just so happened to love her with every ounce of his being. Seeing her sitting with Sadie, Hannah, Lizzie, and the other women folk during the wedding ceremony had stirred up even greater affection for his intended, to the extent it had even crossed his mind to ask her to ride with him afterward today in his father's buggy. Though he wanted to in the worst way, he knew better than to break with tradition, especially now when he needed to adhere to the Old Ways of the Gobbler's Knob church more than ever before.

"Jonas—hullo!"

He spied Abram and Gid strolling up.

"Gut to see ya," called Gid.

"And *you*, Preacher," he said, mighty glad to see them both. He wanted to say something about the enthusiastic way Gid had delivered one of the wedding sermons but decided not to embarrass his brother-in-law-to-be. Besides, talking about sermons and such just wasn't done here as it was in Apple Creek. There he'd often stood around with the men after a Preaching service, discussing the sermons and even some of the Scripture references, something he'd enjoyed immensely.

"Awful nice day, ain't?" Abram said to the group of men, giving Jonas a bit of a nod.

First time I've encountered Leah's father since my return. . . .

Gid glanced at the sky. "This sort of weather won't hold out much longer."

Several of the older men stepped closer, and one began to tell a story. Jonas listened and watched with interest as Abram stood frowning quite hard until it was said a man named Noah Fisher had lost his dentures in his outhouse a day ago.

"Well, what'd he do?" Abram asked, laughing and pulling on his long beard.

"The old fella just let 'em be. Said, after looking down the hole, 'I'll be gummin' it the rest of my life,'" the storyteller answered. "And just who's to blame him?"

That got Gid going with a story he'd heard while harvesting corn. "A fella from Ninepoints has a cousin out in Walnut Creek, Ohio, who has twelve children and a hobby of workin' with wood"—here, Gid looked right at Jonas. "But honestly, if he didn't have all four legs put on a new *high chair* before he reckoned what his wife wanted it for!"

"Now, that's a thickheaded fella, ain't?" Abram grinned, making eye contact with Jonas for the third time.

Removing his hat, Jonas ran his fingers through his hair, feeling like he was beginning to fit in somewhat. He opened his mouth and offered his two cents' worth. "I'd say after four or five young'uns, he would've figured that one out."

The men who were smoking removed their pipes to let out a belly laugh, and Abram put his hand on Jonas's shoulder. "That's a right gut one, son," he said.

Son . . . He had not mistaken what he'd heard. Such a bold attempt on Abram's part, and in front of so many other men, too. Jonas had no doubt now: He would approach Leah's father when the Proving time was over, and Abram would receive him—even offer his blessing to Jonas and Leah.

A long time coming. Even in spite of all that had transpired between them, he had every good reason to be obliged to this man. Truth was, Abram had been the one to write a letter of invitation, making the first welcoming gesture to Jonas, sending it to Ohio by means of Jake not so many weeks back.

The fences are mended, he thought, mighty glad to have come here on this bright and clear, wonderful-good wedding day.

Sadie busied herself indoors, helping set the very special corner table—the *Eck*—for the bridal party. There in the most prominent place in the front room, the bride, bridegroom, and their attendants were soon to be seated. As she was placing a folded napkin on the bride's white plate, she happened to glance out one of the west-facing windows and spied Eli Yoder wandering over to a group of men that included Jonas, Gid, and Dat. She was heartened by the warm smile and decidedly firm handshake her father and brother-in-law seemed to be giving the handsome widower just now.

What could Dat be saying to Eli? she wondered, lowering her eyes to the table. She would not be caught gawking. Sadie sighed and willed herself to keep moving down the table, putting out the utensils and napkins as quickly as possible.

Even so, she couldn't help but speculate as to where Eli might end up sitting for the noon feast. If given the opportunity to get acquainted, she must be careful not to reveal how fond she was inclined to be of him.

She found herself daydreaming about what it might be like to talk with him, although she knew from overhearing some of the older women in the kitchen again today that an elderly matchmaker had arranged for a private meeting for Eli with Ella Jane Peachey. This news had saddened Sadie a bit, but she would not let on to a soul.

She hurried now to the kitchen, where she and Leah and several other women had been asked by the bride's mother to serve the roast duck and chicken, mashed potatoes, gravy, and stuffing. She opened the gas-operated refrigerator, a newfangled addition to the community. Surprisingly, the bishop had given his blessing for this convenience, and a few families had replaced their old iceboxes.

"Nice big crowd of folk," Leah said when she saw her.

"Seems everyone's turned out for *this* wedding."

"And there's someone here from elsewhere, too," her sister whispered.

Sadie flushed pink. "Best not be sayin' that now." With

Bishop Bontrager in attendance, she felt they should be especially cautious, the way it seemed he'd chosen to point fingers at their family. "Do ya plan to walk home, by any chance?" Sadie asked, changing the subject.

"Hadn't thought of it, really."

"Now, sister . . ."

"Sadie, *please*!" said Leah, an embarrassed smile on her face.

Touching her sister's hand, Sadie let things be for now. She could only hope, even pray a bit, that Jonas might drive his buggy right past Leah as she walked along the road and exchange a few thoughtful words before heading on his way. Even though Sadie pretended to be ignorant of their secret meetings, she was sure Leah and Jonas were seeing each other again, and the thought pleased her to no end.

Sadie felt like a matchmaker in her own right—had so much to make up for, truly.

It wasn't hard to locate Old Lady Henner's grandson Zachariah among the menfolk, although Hannah couldn't just go and approach him out near the tobacco shed, where he stood puffing on a pipe. As a general rule, the women didn't mingle with the men outdoors at weddings or on Sundays. This day, of course, the women—relatives and friends of the bride from her church district—busied themselves with setting out the spread of food, so there was no time for Hannah to peek out the window and wish for a way to relay a message to Zachariah. On second thought, she supposed she could say something to his wife, Mary Ann. *Jah, that might work. . . .*

Fact was, ever since her visit to Mary Ruth on the day of the beginner quilting class, where both Leah and Mary Ruth had talked awful straight against hex doctors, Hannah had grown more determined than ever in her desire to pursue the healing arts. Getting better acquainted with either Mary Ann or the newest Amish doctor in the area, Zachariah himself, seemed the best way to do that. More and more, she honestly coveted having the type of know-how Old Lady Henner had once possessed—an ability to heal with hands and words that the elderly woman had transferred to Zachariah prior to her death.

I'll invite Zachariah and Mary Ann for supper next week. She made up her mind before even thinking of asking Gid, something she knew she would get around to sooner or later. For now, though, she hoped she could sit next to Mary Ann during the meal out here in the Kauffmans' long kitchen.

◆

"So, did ya end up on foot *all* the way home today?" Sadie prodded quietly because she and Leah were sitting in the kitchen of Dat's house.

Leah ignored the question and motioned for her to slip back toward the screened-in porch, a frown on her face. "I ought not be sayin' this, prob'ly, but Jonas says Jake's awful put out with our bishop."

"Why's that?"

"Well, for slappin' an unnecessary Proving on Jonas. Evidently Jake threatened to see the bishop 'bout getting it lifted early—one of the reasons, supposedly, he saved up money to come all the way back home."

"For goodness' sake! Jake hasn't any influence on our

bishop, does he? He's very young."

Leah put her finger to her lips. "Shh, just listen." She leaned toward the doorway, checking to see if Dat or Aunt Lizzie was anywhere near. When she seemed satisfied they were indeed alone, she continued. "Jonas told me his little brother is up in arms 'bout plenty of things. For one, Jake doesn't understand how young men can be sent off 'to a foreign land,' as he put it. He knows Gid went to see Peter Mast back last summer. Perhaps he expects the bishop's behind that."

"I wonder how word of *that* got out." Sadie felt pressure in her shoulders and at the back of her neck as she contemplated whether Jake might discover she and Leah were behind his being sent to Ohio.

"Jake is also bent on findin' out why Jonas isn't allowed to earn a livin' by making desks and hope chests and other furniture. He says up and down that Jonas was given the go-ahead by the Grasshopper Level bishop to learn the trade back when."

"Jonas said *all* this to you?"

Leah was nodding hard. "Jah, and he's tryin' to talk Jake out of doing such a rash thing. Says it's not his place to approach the bishop . . . 'tis *rilpsich*—rude."

"But since Jake ain't baptized yet and likely won't be joinin' the Gobbler's Knob church after all, there's nothin' to lose, really."

"I hope Jonas wins out on this, since I expect he knows best." Then her face clouded. "I hate to see strife 'tween two brothers who scarcely know each other."

Sadie touched Leah's arm. "You mustn't fret, sister."

Leah stared off into nothingness, as if pondering it all. "It does seem Lydiann's kept her promise to us, which is a relief."

"Thank goodness for that," Sadie whispered, although secretly wishing there might come a day when Jake could learn the truth about his past without causing a calamity. If they could simply bypass the wretched mess it was bound to create if the Masts found out Jake was not their boy and move right to Sadie's getting to know her son, that would be fine and dandy. Of course, she knew that was completely impossible.

Leah spoke again ever so softly. "Time will tell 'bout Lydiann, but I'm wishin' she might simply send Jake a letter to break off their courtship."

"But how miserable would that be for him? Not hearin' it to his face . . ." Truly, Sadie was thinking like a mother again, caught in the middle as she was.

Leah shook her head. "You can't have things both your way *and* the best way, Sadie."

She knew this well enough. *Ach, what a frustrating state we're in!* Jake would be terribly dejected once he heard the news from Lydiann, and what reason would she give for the sudden and hurtful turn of events? Lydiann had been put in a most difficult, even awkward situation. No wonder she was spending so much time in her room between chores, brooding around the house as if her last friend on earth had upped and died.

Naturally, she feels that way. Sadie sensed misery ahead for both her precious sister and for Jake.

From the present conversation, she knew now that Jonas had indeed invited Leah into his carriage and taken her quite a ways toward home. Sadie couldn't be happier for them, being able to spend time alone today, no matter the subject of conversation.

What Sadie would not reveal to Leah was her momentary disappointment when she'd spotted Eli and Ella Jane sitting across the table from each other at the wedding feast, randomly paired according to age—the oldest men and women being seated and served first. She was too aware of the twinkle in Eli's eyes when he smiled, as if Ella were the prettiest woman in the very crowded room.

Chapter Twelve

More than anything else, Abram enjoyed reading the Bible aloud to his family. This evening was no exception as Lizzie and the others in his household gathered around him in the kitchen, beneath the circle of gaslight. He also planned to pray aloud tonight, having eliminated the former silent prayers of each and every night a good many years ago.

Truth be told, he drew tremendous joy from his regular reading of God's Word. Scarcely could he keep his nose out of his old German Bible—or the English one, as well.

Just this past week he'd spoken again with Gid about some of the wondrous things he was learning, cautiously sharing chapter and verse with his preacher son-in-law, though no longer caring what might happen if Gid reported him to the bishop for "studying" certain books or chapters that had never been referred to or preached on during his lifetime here in Gobbler's Knob. No, he was willing to take the chance of being called in by the church brethren if it came to that. But he had been praying, even beseeching the Lord to help him share openly with Gid from the Holy Scriptures. Gid, after all, had been showing more signs recently of being interested in seeking out spiritual truths, just as Abram delighted in his and Lizzie's holy hunger for the Lord God.

After all, the years were flying away. One quick look at the growing Abe, and Abram could see his son heading too quickly toward rumschpringe. Was Abe ever mindful of God's mercy and love? Would he receive the great sacrifice of God's one and only Son?

All this and much more weighed utterly on Abram, and he ofttimes found himself contemplating the purpose of his own life—even thinking ahead to his days as an old, old man—considering all the years he had been the protector of this family.

What will I leave behind for the sake of Christ? Who among my kinfolk will know the love of the Father because of my courage to speak up?

He had a fervent hankering to pass on his beliefs, so following the Bible reading, he closed the Good Book and asked his family to bow their heads while he prayed to their heavenly Father. He paused. "And if any of you want to join in followin' me, that's just fine, too."

He was conscious of a deep reverence in the room, a sense of peace and somberness. Raising his voice first in thanksgiving, a deep assurance welled up in him and he went on to utter his few petitions, making his requests known to God, as Philippians chapter four, verse six, had taught him to do.

When he lifted his head, he saw that Lydiann's eyes were glistening, and an hour or so later, when everyone had scattered and headed off to bed, she crept back into the kitchen, pulling a chair up near him.

He wondered why Lydiann had come. What had caused

the concern on her face and dread in her eyes?

"Will you pray for *me*, Dat?" she asked, eyes intent on the Bible he held on his knee.

His heart went out to her, although he was befuddled as to why she seemed blue, especially with Jake Mast back home. "Jah, I'll pray." He rose to return the Bible to its resting place in the corner cupboard.

"No . . . I mean right now."

Taken aback by her urgency, he realized she wanted him to take her seriously—here and now. "Are ya feelin' sick?" he asked.

"In my heart, jah. Terribly ill I am."

Is she heartbroken? If that was true, just how was he to go about approaching the Lord with that news? Most daughters drew strength from their mothers or older sisters, and Lydiann was blessed to have Leah, Sadie, and Lizzie near. Why on earth she'd sought him out, he didn't know.

Going back to his rocking chair, Abram nodded and sat down, making his familiar whispered grunt, as he always had prior to a silent prayer. But his young Lydiann had asked specifically, so he breathed in, asking God for divine strength, and began. "Father in heaven, I come before you with my dear daughter Lydiann in mind. She's downright heartsick and in need of your help, and I humbly ask for your presence to come now and fill her with divine peace and joy . . . even understandin'. In the holy name of our Lord Jesus, I ask this. Amen."

He heard Lydiann's sniffles and was hesitant to open his eyes lest he embarrass her. But she surprised him by reaching to touch the back of his hand. "What I must do is the worst and best thing I'll ever do in my life," she whispered. "Keep on prayin' for me, Dat. Every single day. I need it something awful."

Well, now she had his interest but good, and his heart beat double time. "I promise I will continue talking to the Lord God about your sadness, daughter."

"Denki, Dat." She stood and kissed his forehead before hurrying out of the kitchen.

He might've stayed put there, soaking in the sweetness of his youngest daughter in the stillness, but he got himself up and lumbered across the room to the stairs. He meant to help Lizzie take down her long brown hair from its bun again tonight, knowing she would be grateful, given her broken and painful thumb, even though his *dabbich* fingers and the hairpins didn't mix so well.

Making his way to the stairs, Abram offered up another prayer, this one silent, for whatever was ailing Lydiann, dear girl that she was.

Shoe polishing was a regular occurrence every other Saturday night, and Hannah quickly lined up each of her daughters' black Sunday-go-to-meeting shoes alongside her husband's big ones, placing them on waxed paper on the kitchen table. She could hear Ida Mae and Katie Ann and Mimi playing happily together in the front room, where Mimi was saying *she* was the Amish doctor, "for pretend." On any other Saturday Hannah might've stopped to ask her eldest, ten-year-old Ida, for help with the chore, but she wished to be alone with her thoughts, still reeling as she was from Gid's firm no to her request to invite Zachariah and Mary Ann Henner over for supper.

His refusal makes no sense, she thought, wondering why he'd objected to having a nice hot meal with good folk from a neighboring church district. She suspected his response was somehow related to having gotten another earful from Dat not too many days ago, because he was now saying things like they best be looking to the Lord God for their family's healing, as well as other things. "'Tis time we relied more on the Word of God."

She knew better than to speak out of turn to her husband, being that she was his helper, not his equal. But now that Gid was down working at the barn again with her Bible-reading father, she was stewing plenty.

He's one of the preachers, for pity's sake!

She must respect the divine ordination of her husband, yet she was eager to get better acquainted with the Henners. Had Gid put his foot down because of studying the Bible? He had even been reciting Scripture here lately, which was considered a serious form of pride. She recalled the bishop stating yet again at Preaching service recently that the Bible was not to be freely read and explored except by those ordained of God: in short, bishops and preachers. *And since Gid is a preacher, it must be all right,* Hannah decided. All the same, she couldn't help but wonder if Dat's influence wasn't steadily spilling over onto him.

Being an obedient woman, she set about shining her husband's church shoes, hoping the rubbing and polishing might keep her mind busy, as well as her hands.

If not supper here with the Henners, then maybe a visit to Mary Ann instead, decided Hannah. She wanted to pay close attention to whatever it was growing mighty strong in her these days. Lest she be consumed with her desire to know the secrets of the healers, she began to hum a song from the Ausbund, suddenly aware that she no longer was experiencing a single pain related to her difficult pregnancy. The realization made her hum all the louder.

The handsome cherry writing desk caught Jonas's attention as he entered the front room of Eli Yoder's house. Eli had kindly latched on to him when Jonas was awaiting the feast at the Kauffman farm, and both men had found great satisfaction in discussing familiar landmarks in Holmes County, even discovering mutual friends in and around Millersburg and Berlin. Here it was a week later and Jonas had already taken Eli up on his offer to "drop by sometime," asking about Eli's woodworking hobby.

"To tell ya the truth," Eli was saying, "cutting and sawing wood, stainin' it and all, well, it's in my blood."

Jonas nodded. *A kindred soul*, he thought, withholding an enthusiastic response.

Eli ran his thick fingers through his red hair. "Seems woodworkin' ain't so accepted here in Lancaster County as it was in Holmes. . . ."

"Well, that decision's left to the bishop and the particular church district" was all Jonas said—all he best be saying, too. This topic was something he would do well to steer clear of, although more and more that was becoming difficult. He was altogether drawn to the only livelihood he'd ever really known.

"That there desk was one of the first pieces I ever made," Eli said, eyes alight with the memory. "I wasn't but twenty-five, I guess, when my father and I laid out the plans for it."

Jonas was all ears. "You must keep in close touch with your family."

Eli's face broke into a wide grin. "My brothers and sisters are itchin' for me to find myself a bride. They think a man my age is too young to give up on ever marryin' again."

"Well, seems to me there's some fine pickin's here." Since he had his heart set only on Leah, he didn't know precisely which girls were courting age and which were older and already considered maidels.

"Got my eye on a couple of perty ones, for sure. And I s'pose I could be married again and livin' back in Ohio within a year's time." He went on to share that he'd been a widower for nearly two years already. "I had a right happy eighteen years with my Nancy Mae, kindest woman there ever was."

Jonas hadn't heard that a traded man could expect to return to his original church district, once married, but Eli was old enough to decide such a thing. "Seems we're in somewhat similar situations, both bein' older and hoping to marry."

"But you've remained single . . . after all this time." The question in Eli's eyes was evident, but he didn't press further.

Jonas felt no obligation to say why he'd never married. After all, he didn't know this fellow all that well, although he did know the Ohio bishop Eli had grown up under. Surely Eli was also a man of integrity, and a fine husband for any young woman in Gobbler's Knob.

Just then Eli asked if he could pour him some coffee, and Jonas was much obliged to accept. He followed his new friend back into the kitchen and thought unexpectedly of Emma Graber, his former, longtime landlady. His enduring interest in Apple Creek had much to do with the loss of his wonderful-good friends and the weekly Bible studies he had always looked forward to—a place of ongoing and keen spiritual interest, where he had regularly enjoyed the bonds of faith. Yet he must not allow his yearnings for his former life to thwart his Proving time, because the reward for fulfilling Bishop Bontrager's stern commands would be the go-ahead to make Leah his bride—and not a single Ohio friend was more important.

Chapter Thirteen

Jake stormed out of the barn following his attempt to speak to his father about the ridiculous notion of his returning to Ohio. Dat was determined for Jake to have nothing to do with the Ebersols, but no matter what Dat thought of his choice of a bride, Jake planned to marry Lydiann, *like it or not*!

The fury in Dat's eyes and the sound of the pitchfork scraping hard against the concrete floor of the barn had seared into Jake's memory, and all he could think of was running off his anger as hard and fast as he could, hoping to wipe the entire scene from his mind. The words flung at him by his father were as terrible as any he'd ever heard.

Running north, he headed toward the vast apple orchard, the site of numerous joyful days. *Much happier times*, he thought, not stopping to rest even when pain shot through his lower right side.

To make matters worse, he was befuddled with Lydiann, who'd surely fibbed to him yesterday, saying she was too ill to go riding with him last night when she'd looked hale and hearty standing there in the side yard, shaking her head as he pleaded with her to reconsider.

His mind in a whirl, Jake dashed through his father's orchard, his feet pounding against the dirt path in a relentless rhythm that nearly matched the beat of his heart.

Lydiann knew the longer she waited to break things off with Jake, the harder it would be for both of them. *It's horribly unfair,* she told herself in the privacy of her bedroom. *He needs to court a girl he can actually marry. . . .*

Thinking how innocent Jake was to the predicament they were in made her feel like crying, but if she gave in to tears, she'd never complete this terrible yet necessary task. The way things had been progressing, Jake would want them to start baptismal instruction next spring and then join church in the fall to be ready for the wedding season. She had seen the intensity of his affection growing in his eyes when he looked her way as they rode together beneath a sky dotted by silver-white stars and a shining moon, an affection that had in no way been quelled by their time apart. She'd also observed his discouragement last Saturday evening when she'd claimed she was too ill to go riding with him.

"It must be done this minute . . . I must figure out a way to do this gently," she whispered, taking out her best white stationery. Hardest of all was not telling him the real reason.

Moving toward the window, she looked out over the farmland and the east side of the meadow, wishing to goodness it wasn't hunting season so that she might have donned her heavy shawl and hiked up to the woods in search of the rare and beautiful honey locust tree she called her own. But no, she must simply write a few well-thought lines to Jake right here where she sat on the cane chair with Mamma Leah's Bible in her lap. She could not allow herself to think too hard about what she must write. Whatever her words, her letter would be sent on its way, along with her broken heart.

Monday, November 18
Dear Jake,
I hope you won't despise me for what you're about to read in this letter. . . .

Early Tuesday afternoon Jonas and Jake had been out pruning apple trees before the snow flew when Jake suggested they return to the house to fill up several large Thermoses with cold water. Since it didn't take two of them to carry water, Jonas wondered what could possibly be on his brother's mind.

"Nobody knows it, but I hurried off to see your bishop first thing this mornin'," Jake confessed as they walked along the dirt path.

Jonas's jaw immediately tensed. "You didn't!"

"He's one perturbed man, I'd have to say."

"Well, I'm not sure we should be discussin' this."

Jake rolled his eyes. "If you ask me, sounds like he's got it in for both you *and* Abram Ebersol's family."

"You brought up my Proving?"

"I asked why it was all right for you to sell the furniture

you made in Ohio but not here. Guess what he said to that? 'We follow the letter of the law here.'" Jake snorted.

"I wish you hadn't gone. It can only make matters worse."

Jake removed his hat and swatted it against his backside. "Well, then, why haven't you gone and talked to him yourself?"

"Because I'm followin' the Proving carefully, regardless of what is involved. Receiving the right hand of fellowship come spring is what *I'm* after!" Jonas felt sure his brother had stirred up a hornets' nest in his efforts to help. "Best not to say any more to anyone 'bout this."

"I thought you oughta know what you're up against, is all," Jake replied. "I came all the way home to speak my mind. That, and for one other important reason."

Jake didn't let on what he was thinking, but Jonas was certain Jake's main reason for returning was to get Dat's permission to marry Lydiann. "Time to get that water we came for," he said now, walking faster.

With a shrug, Jake followed.

I wish Jake had bided his time and kept his mouth shut, thought Jonas, heading glumly toward the well.

The afternoon mail had just arrived, and Jonas could hear Mandie hollering to Jake. "There's a letter for you!" Somehow or other, she always managed to be the first one out to the road this late in the afternoon, and she seemed to take great delight in calling out the names of those who had received mail.

A large russet squirrel scampered across the barnyard and began filling his pouches with food for the winter. Jonas kept his eye on the bushy-tailed critter and headed for the well to pump a glass of water, too dirty from his barn work to enter Mamma's clean kitchen. All the while, he thought about the audacity of Jake, thinking it was his place to set the bishop straight. On the other hand, Leah had wanted to do nearly the same thing, though she'd had the sense to talk it over with him first . . . and to respect his wishes.

Some time later he spied Jake rushing out the back door, face as red as a beet. "What the world?" he muttered, turning to watch his brother make haste up the hill toward the springhouse. He decided to catch up.

What's got into him? Surely Jake could see him following, but he made no attempt to acknowledge Jonas. No getting around it, Jake was pigheaded when he wanted to be. *Much like Dat.* Jonas grimaced, but his impression softened when he was close enough to notice Jake's stiff jaw and trembling hands.

"All I ever did was love her. . . ." Jake stared at the ground.

Without speaking, Jonas placed his big hand on Jake's slender shoulder, immediately aware of the blow his brother had obviously been dealt. *Lydiann must have found herself another beau,* he thought, hoping he was wrong. *There's nothing worse than losing your sweetheart to another man . . . or assuming it to be so.*

Not wanting to pry, he squatted down to eye level with his brother, who'd perched himself on an old milk can, tears welling, lip quivering.

It must be a misunderstanding. He'd heard Jake speak fondly of Lydiann and assumed she cared similarly for him. So what had gone wrong?

At last Jake wiped his face on the sleeve of his shirt and raised his eyes. "I can't just let her walk away," he said. "She's the dearest, most beautiful girl I know."

Jonas listened, wondering if perhaps Dat had thrown a wrench in things.

Standing abruptly, Jake announced, "I have to talk to her. I won't let someone else come between us."

"Is it possible you're jumpin' to conclusions?" Jonas felt he should say this to help Jake think more clearly. *There's too much at stake to do otherwise.*

"No, there can't be any other reason. Someone's come along and put doubts in *my* girl's mind. That has to be it!"

There was no talking sense to Jake now. "When did ya see her last?" Jonas asked.

Ignoring the question, Jake pulled out a folded letter from his pocket and slapped it against his hand. "It's all right here. Lydiann doesn't want to see me ever again. We're through."

Jonas inhaled deeply and felt as if the clock had been turned back to another time and place. "I'm awful sorry."

Jake coughed as if he was trying to choke back more tears. "I know she has every right to see who she wants . . . but we were gonna be married. We were in love. I'm sure of it."

"Best to let some time pass before you say or do anything," he suggested. "It won't be easy, but it's better to wait."

"We'll see 'bout that." Jake shook his head and slapped his hand on his thigh. "I'm not nearly as patient a man as you, Jonas."

Jonas wasted no time falling into step with Jake. They headed back toward the barn for afternoon milking, and along the way Jonas noticed a squirrel, possibly the same one as before, nibbling away on a seed or a nut. *Once winter sets in, Jake will be terribly lonely*, he thought, recalling the lengthy days and the long, long winters he had endured till surprising word had come of Leah's singleness.

Too bad their father would most likely be a thorn in Jake's side, jumping for joy when word reached his ears—if it hadn't already—which would *not* sit well with tetchy Jake. And perhaps Dat would still eventually insist on Jake's returning to Ohio. Now that Jonas thought on it, such a thing might not be such a bad idea.

Chapter Fourteen

At breakfast the morning after receiving Lydiann's letter, Jake refused to reveal his anger or disappointment as he slid onto the bench next to Mandie at the table. Lacking an appetite, he did his best to eat the food Mamma served: fried eggs and potatoes, cornmeal mush, toast, butter, and strawberry jam.

He glanced across the table at his father. *Has Dat interfered with Lydiann and me? Is that what happened?*

Jonas mentioned something about helping their father shovel manure in the barn following breakfast.

"Jake'll help us." Dat nodded his head in Jake's direction.

Jonas and their father carried the conversation for the next few minutes, and Jake noticed an interesting camaraderie between the two. What sort of agreement had Jonas and Dat worked out, allowing Jonas to live here, yet court Leah? And Jake was mighty sure Jonas was doing just that, seeing Leah at least once a week. There would have been no other reason for him to move home from Ohio.

When it came time for the prayer following the meal, they

bowed their heads for the silent blessing, waiting for Dat to make the guttural sound that signaled the end.

Mamma and Mandie talked of going to the mill near Grasshopper Level to have some corn ground into cornmeal as Dat, Jonas, and Jake headed out to the barn.

The minute I can break free, I'm going to Gobbler's Knob, Jake thought.

By the time Jake was able to get away, it was well after supper, but Jake was rather glad of the hour. This way he could stand out in Lyddie's side yard, a ways back from the farmhouse, and observe Abram and his family gathered in the kitchen for Bible reading and prayers. He *was* quite shocked when it came time for the silent prayer, since it was obvious Abram's lips were moving. Was he praying aloud? If so, this was something Jake had never heard of in their Old Order community, let alone witnessed, although he did recall Lydiann saying her father was most interested in reading aloud from the Bible every night.

He waited awhile till he thought Lydiann might be alone in the kitchen doing a bit of sewing, but when he gingerly knocked on the back door, it was Leah who came to open it and peer out at him.

"Could I . . . uh, talk to Lyddie right quick?"

Leah turned and glanced momentarily over her shoulder before turning back to him. "Is she expectin' you?" she asked softly.

"Well, no, she ain't."

She sighed loudly. "Honestly, Jake"—her voice was almost a whisper now—"I daresay it's too late tonight for an unexpected visitor." With that she lowered her head, as if pained; then she slowly pulled the door shut.

He felt as grief stricken as when he'd first laid eyes on the wretched letter. *Lyddie doesn't want to have anything to do with me!*

He wandered without a purpose now, shining his flashlight to find his way back to where he'd left his horse and open buggy parked some distance down Abram's lane.

◆

Leah suspected from Jake's demeanor the night of his attempted visit that Lyddie must have put an end to their courtship—certainly Lyddie herself appeared morose and kept close to home in the days that followed. Leah, meanwhile, attended to her housecleaning duties for Dr. Schwartz at the medical clinic and for his wife, Lorraine, at their big two-story house. She took her responsibilities seriously—dusting, mopping, and running the sweeper, as well as cleaning the bathrooms, leaving everything as sparkling clean as she and Aunt Lizzie strove to do at home.

It was midafternoon when she happened to see Mary Ruth coming in the door of the clinic, bringing tiny Ruthie for a one-month checkup. "Hullo, sister," said Mary Ruth right away.

Leah hurried over to peek at the sleeping bundle. "Aw, she's so sweet."

Mary Ruth smiled. "I think Robert's been spoilin' her."

"Ach, that's not possible with one so small." Leah took the baby in her arms. "Now, is it?" she whispered down to the infant.

Mary Ruth laughed and said her husband had decided there was no need for their firstborn to cry herself to sleep. "Not ever." Mary Ruth shook her head. "Which means one of us is either rocking her or walking the floor every night."

"I hope she doesn't have the colic like Mimi did."

"Oh no, our Ruthie's not suffering any pain. Just getting pampered but good," Mary Ruth said.

"I'd be tempted to do the same, such a doll baby she is. Do ya ever just stare at her—so perfect and all—and nearly cry for joy?"

"Sometimes I do that." Mary Ruth stroked the wisps of hair on top of Ruthie's soft little head and began to share about the work Robert was doing with the young people at their church in Quarryville, mentioning that her close friend Dottie Nolt's son, Carl, was among them. "Carl's had quite the time of it recently. It seems his high-school girlfriend has jilted him."

Nodding her head in sympathy, Leah thought immediately of Lydiann and her sad situation. "Was Carl serious 'bout her, do ya think?" she asked.

Mary Ruth frowned momentarily, as if thinking what she best ought to say. "To be frank, I think Dottie is somewhat relieved, since this was Carl's first girlfriend and all. Still, as I understand, Carl's taking the breakup rather hard."

"Jah, where the heart's involved . . . there can be awful pain." Leah remembered Mary Ruth's grief after *her* first beau, young Elias Stoltzfus, was killed, fifteen years ago now—ironically by a car Robert Schwartz was driving.

But Mary Ruth's thoughts must have turned to Lydiann, because she suddenly asked how their youngest sister was doing. "Has she been going to Sunday singings again?"

"I have no idea, but I doubt it," Leah said, wondering if Lydiann had indeed broken up with Jake, yet not comfortable volunteering more about so private a matter. Instead, she settled back with Ruthie nestled in her arms to listen to Mary Ruth chatter on pleasantly about the weather, church activities, and what color the tiny booties and blankets were she was crocheting for Ruthie.

It was as her sister was reaching for her baby, with Leah being careful to support Ruthie's head just so, that a thought crept into Leah's mind. Before she could even mull over the idea, she said it right out. "What would happen if Carl and Lydiann were reintroduced to each other?"

Mary Ruth's eyes widened and she began to blink fast. "What did you just say?"

"I was only thinkin' it might be nice for two childhood friends to meet up with each other again somehow. They used to have quite a bond when they were schoolmates at the Georgetown School. Remember?"

"Well, I never thought I'd hear such a suggestion from you, Leah. Carl's most definitely preparing to join Oak Shade Mennonite Church—Dottie's said as much."

Leah had expected this sort of reaction from Mary Ruth, but she had no wish to explain her reasoning. "It might be nice for them to renew their friendship, is all. Nothin' serious, mind you."

Mary Ruth chuckled, touching Leah's hand. "Well, if you're sure about this . . ."

"You could start by puttin' a bug in Dottie's ear," Leah

said. "Let her handle it the way she sees fit."

Mary Ruth agreed. "I think this just might put a smile on Carl's face."

Wish I could say the same about Lyddie, thought Leah, hoping none of this matchmaking would backfire.

Anything to take her mind off Jake Mast!

Chapter Fifteen

Mary Ruth was going about her usual preparations for a Friday evening meal when her husband came in the back door, looking pale as can be. "The president's been shot!"

"What?"

"Killed by an assassin's bullet."

"Oh, Robert!"

He reached for her hand. "People were standing around the sidewalks near our church, crying . . . a few came in and knelt at the altar. I suppose some will even think the end of the world is coming." He paused. "I can see why they might think that."

Tears sprang to her eyes. "This is just terrible."

"He was much too young to die. . . ."

"Makes me think how awful short life is." Mary Ruth brushed away tears and went to check on her little one, sound asleep in her cradle. She didn't bother to tell Robert she had noticed Lydiann walking alone on the road earlier today, looking rather forlorn. At the time Mary Ruth had been running an errand with a friend and had merely waved, but she wondered now if it was possible Lydiann had somehow heard of the president's death. But how could that be with no radios in the house? Even with Lydiann in the midst of rumschpringe, Dat would never allow such worldly things.

"The vice president will take over President Kennedy's duties, of course," Robert was saying, "but our president was so well liked that his death will certainly leave a political hole for years, maybe even decades."

She recalled having studied the line of succession in high school, but understanding it and realizing its dire necessity were two separate issues. She could scarcely bear to listen as Robert described the sad scene in Dallas, Texas, today as relayed by an obviously shaken Walter Cronkite.

She recalled how President Kennedy's approach to war had disturbed her father, who, back during the election, had been rather outspoken against such a man leading the country, although he had refrained from voting. "I wonder what Dat will think when he hears this sad news," she said softly.

"I expect he won't say much but rather spend time in prayer for the Kennedy family," Robert offered. "And the nation as a whole."

They did the same as they sat down to eat their supper. Robert's eyes seemed to fall on Ruthie more often than usual throughout the meal, Mary Ruth noticed, and her own spirit felt numb, saddened anew by humanity's need of the Savior.

Lydiann rode with Abe to Saturday market in Georgetown, ready to keep occupied with customers. She, along with

Sadie and Hannah, had stitched up oodles of pretty pillowcases and crocheted doilies and even some rather fancy placemats. Once Aunt Lizzie and Mamma Leah had contributed over a dozen pies, the enclosed family carriage was laden down with plenty of items to sell.

She tried her best not to communicate anything about her mood to her brother as they rode along. Truth was, she wanted to kick herself for sending off a letter to Jake instead of doing the kinder thing and breaking up with him in person. *He must think I've got myself another fellow!* That he might believe this of her hurt even more, and she thought again of how Jake must have opened the envelope in anticipation of a loving note, only to read words that had surely brought him heartache. How she wished she had never promised Mamma and Sadie to keep this secret to herself! Without his knowing the truth, her good-bye to Jake cast her in a heartless light, and poor Jake could never begin to understand her reasoning otherwise. Sometimes Lydiann wondered just how she would find it in herself to celebrate Christmas this year.

"What did ya think when ya heard 'bout the president gettin' shot?" Abe asked, reins held tightly in both hands.

"It's just horrifying, that's what."

He looked hard at her. "Ach, I wasn't the one doin' the shootin', ya know."

"I'm sorry, Abe." She dared not let on what was really bothering her or what she was contemplating just now. Abe would never begin to understand, and aside from the one time she and Jake had shown up at the house in the middle of the day, she was pretty sure her brother didn't know beans from applesauce about the state of their courtship. Maybe he'd put two and two together, though.

Abe spoke up. "Do ya want me to stay and help make change for customers?"

"That'd be right nice . . . if ya want." Time to talk less pointedly. After all, this was her only brother and she must show him some respect, even though he was younger. Besides that, it was good of him to offer, as lippy as she'd been.

"Okay, then, I'll stay till noon or so and then come back for ya. How's that?"

"Dat will be glad for your help shreddin' cornstalks, I'm sure." That was all she said to him in answer, so quick was she to lose herself in gazing at the countryside. More weddings were coming up next week, both Tuesday and Thursday, and she tried not to think about how miserable she'd been the day of the one down at the Kauffman farm. At the time she'd begged off going, knowing she couldn't possibly plaster a smile on her face when it was all she could do to simply breathe.

When they arrived at market Abe helped her carry in the pies, but once the stand was set up and ready, he wandered about, talking to different friends and waiting for the doors to open to the general public.

It was during the first bustling hour that she happened to see Carl Nolt, along with his mother. Lydiann noticed their baskets were already full up with handmade aprons and other linens.

"I'm buying ahead for Christmas," Dottie told her when the two of them came over to say hello. She turned to her tall, slender son. "You remember Abe and Lydiann?"

"Hi," Carl said.

Lydiann felt a bit embarrassed for her old friend and nodded, saying, "Hullo, Carl," as did Abe.

It was clear to Lydiann that Carl was miserable, and not

from awkwardness. He looked as dejected as any boy she had ever seen—as bad as she felt, really—but she refused to stare.

Sometime later, when his mother was nowhere in sight, Carl came wandering back to see her. Abe shooed her off for a walk with her old friend, though her heart wasn't in it at all.

"Where have you been keeping yourself?" asked Carl, once they were outside and away from the stream of customers. Suddenly his smile was as big as it had been in the days before she'd stuck her neck out some years ago and insensitively questioned him about being adopted. He must have erased that conversation from his mind.

"I haven't seen you round much, neither." She felt uncomfortable around him, despite the fact they'd gone walking together plenty of times during seventh grade.

"How've you been, Lydiann?"

"Oh, fine, I guess."

"You don't sound so sure."

She avoided his eyes and made small talk, speaking only of insignificant things like the weather and all the folk at market. And she also mentioned how pleased she was with her new baby niece, Ruthie Schwartz.

Carl was kind, but he seemed almost too eager to visit with her, telling of his interesting experiences in high school while seemingly cautious not to be too excited about his adventure into higher education. He was no doubt well aware of the Amish stance on schooling past eighth grade. "I made a big mistake in the past year, though," he confessed. "I started seeing a girl I should've never given a second look."

She waited for him to continue, turning to glance his way. It was then she saw the hurt in his eyes.

"She and I . . . well, we're through."

"I'm sorry for you," she said, meaning it.

"What 'bout you, Lyddie? Are you seein' anyone?"

How to tell him without bursting into tears? "I was . . . jah, for quite a while. But no more." The lump in her throat threatened to make it impossible for her to speak, so she quit talking altogether. Carl wouldn't have known Jake, anyway, since Jake had attended the Amish school over on Esbenshade Road.

He stopped walking and grinned. "I have an idea," he said more softly now. "How would you like to go on a hayride with me . . . for old time's sake?" He immediately added that it was a church-sponsored youth activity. "Just so you know."

She was caught off guard, not knowing what to say—she was still too pained over Jake to think of spending time with anyone else, even with a former friend like Carl. "That's awful nice of you, but I best not." She also knew her father, if he got wind of it, would not take kindly to the idea, no matter that she, Abe, and Carl had grown up playing together, thanks to Mary Ruth. Dat would want her to be courted by an Amish boy and eventually join the Gobbler's Knob church, not spend time with a Mennonite.

After Carl said a kind good-bye, she wandered back inside to find Abe acting glad to see her. "We've sold more than a third of our goods, snatched up in no time." He gave her a sly smile. "Out chummin' with Carl, ol' buddy, old friend . . . as they say?"

"No need to get any ideas in your head 'bout that, little brother," she shot back.

But on the ride home, Lydiann thought again of Abe's reaction to her visit with Carl, and she began to wonder if she shouldn't consider going to singings again, if only for a little innocent fun. She hoped she wouldn't run into Jake there, but she truly needed the comfort of her many friends.

Hannah stooped low to pull out several of her numerous notebooks from the bedroom bookcase. Flipping through the pages of the makeshift journals, where she'd recorded bits and pieces of her life from the early teen years on, she felt unexpectedly self-conscious. As a wife and mother of three daughters with yet another baby on the way, she found herself amused at the childish things she'd written and wondered what she had been thinking back then, pouring out her immaturity onto these pages. Some of her own private thoughts struck her now as rather worthless, causing her to consider whether she shouldn't cease keeping a journal presently, although most of what she noted these days was about the cute antics of her girls or goings-on down at the Ebersol Cottage. She found herself wishing she might pass along the notion of keeping a diary to at least Ida Mae, who was showing some interest in writing, especially short notes to friends.

Glad for the stillness pervading the house on a Saturday of all things, the girls having gone over yonder to their Peachey grandparents', Hannah felt freed up to sort, taking the time to organize the notebooks according to year before she dusted the lower shelf.

That done, she moved on to dust the large bureau and the small table on Gid's side of the bed. Noticing a Bible there, she picked it up and opened it to the bookmarked page. She was surprised to see two underlined Scripture verses: *Is any sick among you? Let him call for the elders of the church; and let them pray over him, anointing him with oil in the name of the Lord: And the prayer of faith shall save the sick, and the Lord shall raise him up; and if he have committed sins, they shall be forgiven him.*

Reading the verses made her stop and think. The fact Gid had apparently marked these for a reason counted for something, although she was shocked to see such markings in the Holy Bible, of all places. Suddenly Hannah worried her husband might put a stop to her growing interest in powwowing. The idea made her almost frantic, and she was anxious to move forward with her planned visit to the Henners' as soon as possible. The minute, then, she finished dusting, Hannah would be on her way. *Nothing must stop me!*

Chapter Sixteen

From the vantage point of the buggy, Hannah could see the Henners' white clapboard farmhouse clearly from the road, despite the lofty sycamore trees and clusters of maples that created a formidable windbreak.

She turned into the long, narrow lane, stepped down, tied the horse to the post, and then made her way around to the back door. She knocked lightly, feeling hesitant, hoping not to interfere, yet desiring to have an opportunity to observe a healing. Despite the weeks she had anticipated such a visit with Zachariah or another healer, she didn't know if she would be acceptable to a seasoned *Brauchdokder*. If all went well and she was welcomed, she might learn about herbal potions, various chants, and formulas known only by local hex doctors.

Mary Ann came to the door with three small towheaded children at her skirt, her eyes bright. "Well, come in, Hannah." Over her shoulder, she called, "Zach, it's Preacher Gid's wife come to visit!"

"Hope I'm not a bother," Hannah said as she stepped

inside. "I've been wantin' to get better acquainted with yous."

"Well, now's as gut a time as any." Mary Ann smiled warmly and motioned for her to follow, leading her through the long kitchen and into the front room, where the green shades were drawn, making the space extremely dark for midday. Zachariah was seated on a straight-backed chair, wearing gray trousers, black suspenders, and a long-sleeved white shirt, dressed as if for Sunday Preaching service. He looked up, somewhat bleary-eyed.

"You remember Hannah Ebersol, dear?" said Mary Ann, evidently assuming it was her husband whom Hannah was most interested in seeing.

"Come in." The healer waved to her.

"Hullo," said Hannah shyly, suddenly quite nervous in the presence of the man she had sought after, though still ready to receive as much as Zachariah might be willing to impart.

"Are ya in need of healin'?" he asked.

She shook her head. "Well, no, not today." She went on to explain. "I was a devoted patient of your *Grandmammi*'s—several times I visited her."

Zachariah's head bobbed up and down slowly. "I believe she spoke of you, jah." But the light went out of his eyes and he seemed preoccupied once again.

Now that she was here, she felt almost reluctant to stay as her eyes grew accustomed to the dimness. "I've been wantin' to ask you some things."

An uncomfortable silence ensued. Finally, without looking at her, he spoke again. "Along the lines of powwowing, do you mean?"

This is my chance, she thought. *Might be the only time I catch him alone*. She knew he had a good many patients all hours of the day and night.

"I've been curious," she said, asserting herself, "not in a prying way . . . but about becomin' a healer . . . like you."

He looked at her again, holding her gaze this time, as if sizing her up. For a long while she felt uneasy, but when he asked her to sit down she did. "Tell me more."

At last she had his attention. Glancing over at Mary Ann, she saw the young woman standing alone in the doorway, her small children having left the room, though exactly when Hannah did not know. "I don't know much 'bout sympathy healin', but I have a yearning to help others, startin' with my own little ones. I must say I do hunger after the gift."

Zachariah's blue eyes shone. "Your children, ya say. Are they sickly?"

"Not anymore, and with all thanks to your Grand-mammi." She continued on, telling how Old Lady Henner had cured both herself and Mimi. "The ailments disappeared instantly. I was completely in awe."

Zachariah rose from his seat and beckoned for Hannah to do the same. Then, turning to Mary Ann, he asked if he might be alone with "the seeking woman."

Hannah was only now aware of a draft in the room as Zachariah moved closer to stand near her. "As a rule, the gift is passed to a younger relative, from man to woman, or woman to man, but in this case—since you are a willing vessel—I will consider you."

"Oh, I'm ready *now*."

"Not just yet," he said. "'Tis important for me to observe you amongst the People . . . in a crowd . . . see if folk are drawn to you, which is necessary."

Her heart sank. *Not a smidgen of hope for me, then.*

"Well . . . I've never been one to turn heads." She hadn't drawn attention the way Mary Ruth and Sadie had in their youth.

"You're a creature of heaven—anyone can see that." He smiled, but it seemed out of place.

"What happens when the transfer comes . . . if I'm to receive it?" This she felt she must know, for she'd heard whispered talk indicating frightening things.

"When the moment comes," Zachariah said in a monotone, "you'll experience a sensation . . . some say like an electrical current from head to toe. I can assure you it is not unpleasant. In due time I will know if you are the one."

Standing in his presence, Hannah felt a great fatigue sweep over her.

"If it is to be so and you are to receive the healing gift, you will be given the necessary instruction, once the transference is made."

If it is to be so . . .

She bade him and his wife good-bye and made her way out of the house and around to the horse and buggy, aware now of an odd tranquility. Her breathing seemed slower and steadier than before she'd encountered Zachariah Henner alone. Deep down, she wondered, *Will they consider me special enough?*

Leah was startled out of sleep by a stone hitting her window. Looking up, she watched a streak of light pass over her bedroom wall. For a moment she felt as if she were a teenager again, being courted by Jonas. *Well, of course, I'm being courted,* she thought, sitting up in bed. *Just ain't a girl anymore.*

Having been asleep for more than an hour already, she climbed out of bed, scurrying across the room. Quietly she lifted the window and leaned her head out. Jonas stood down in the yard, his flashlight shining brightly against the frosty ground. "Jonas? Are you all right?"

"Can ya come down?" he asked immediately, adding, "I'll wait at the end of the lane."

"I'll only be a minute." Closing the window, she slipped out of her long nightclothes and took down from its peg one of several clean work dresses, hurrying to dress in the dark. *What on earth would bring Jonas here at this hour?*

She hoped the unanticipated visit wasn't going to involve Jake or his interest in Lydiann, particularly as Jake himself had shown up here unannounced just last Wednesday night. With how miserable her girl had been the past few days, it did seem Lyddie had put the nix on things at last. She prayed it was so, yet she could not be sure, as Lyddie had stopped sharing with her as she used to—truth be told, her girl had nearly stopped talking to her altogether. As it stood, it was terribly awkward for her or Jonas, or both of them, to get thrown into the middle.

Tiptoeing down the long staircase, she wished she weighed even less than she did—every creak seemed amplified so late at night. She hurried through the kitchen and out to the utility room, where she slipped on some shoes to protect her feet from the frost.

When she met up with Jonas, his flashlight was off and his horse and carriage were parked quite a ways up the main road.

He pulled her into his arms and hugged her till she thought she might pop. "I missed ya, Leah."

I can tell! She was awful glad to see him, too, and told him so.

When he released her, he reached for her hand. "I *had* to see ya tonight. Jake's out of his mind distraught over Lydiann. She wants to break up."

She felt herself stiffen. "Was there a letter from her?"

"Apparently . . . and there's no consolin' my brother. He's a mess, 'tween you and me."

Sighing, she fully understood Jonas's concern.

"I'm worried 'bout Jake. He's never seen anyone else—first love is quite intense, for sure, as we oughta know." He forged ahead without skipping a beat. "He's awful angry, like I've never seen him. Even so, I'm mighty sure Dat would be right happy, if he had any idea. Can't say that he does, though."

Knowing what she did and not being able to reveal it to her darling put Leah in an awful quandary. Feeling truly dreadful, she said as little as possible while offering her sympathy to his despairing brother. *Jake's behaving like Sadie did when she was a youth . . . and no doubt Derry, too,* she happened to think. Torn as she was on the matter, she wished she were not out here on the road with Jonas, juggling a rather one-sided conversation as she struggled to keep a terrible secret from the man she'd been separated from for so long. She despised being less than forthright, but what choice did she have? If she revealed Jake was Sadie's son, what might Jonas decide to do about his promise of love to *her*? Besides, such upsetting news was not hers to tell—not without talking first to Sadie—even though she wished she could be completely truthful with Jonas.

No, I must remain silent. 'Tis best he never know.

Chapter Seventeen

Despite repeated calls from Mamma, Jake was late for breakfast. Presently Dat was hollering for the missing boy as Jonas stood near the wood stove, watching the scene unfold. Finally Dat went stomping up the stairs, but when Jake didn't respond to even that, Jonas assumed he was hiding out in the barn or elsewhere.

"What's gotten into him?" Mandie asked, getting up from the table where she had been sitting with a longing glance at the sausage and waffles, which were growing cooler by the minute. She headed for the back door and peered out. "I saw him outside earlier."

"Too cold out for him to just be wanderin' round," Mamma said, her face rather drawn.

"Ach, he'll come in when he's hungry," said Dat as he came to the table and pulled out his chair. He sat down with a disgusted harrumph. "I say we go ahead and eat."

Mamma sat quickly and bowed her head when Dat did. The silent blessing was shorter than ever before, and Jonas wasn't pleased at the thought of feeding his face when he had visions of Jake out in the haymow somewhere, or clear up in the back meadow, bawling like a wounded pup. Of course, it was his right to wail if need be. Jonas remembered too well the disillusionment that had come from being jilted, though in his own case the breakup had turned out to be the result of a complicated misunderstanding.

Some time later Jonas found Jake in the meadow clear on the other side of the orchard, where from the house, the sky appeared to meet the hillock. "Mamma's worried 'bout you."

Jake stared up at him from the ground, where he'd planted himself. "I don't feel like eatin' or anything else. Lydiann's called it quits with me. How do ya expect me to be hungry?"

Jonas sat down next to him on the frosty earth. "I say it's time you wrote her back—ask how it happened that she changed her mind."

"What gut will *that* do?" Jake got up and brushed off the back of his work pants. "She doesn't want to see me, so I doubt she'd even read my letter." He explained how he'd gone to Gobbler's Knob some days ago now, only to be turned away.

"Listen to me." Jonas's ire was building, and he felt it was his duty to persuade Jake to pursue his girl. "Disregard her letter." He grabbed Jake by the shoulder. "I've walked in your shoes. When you love someone the way you care for Lydiann, you must never just stand idly by."

Jake shrugged him away. "I ain't gonna beg her."

"Jake, I mean to help. I missed out on knowin' you all your life, for pete's sake. The most I can do is pound some smarts into your head." He stared at his stubborn little brother. "I know why you came back home. Think on it, Jake. It wasn't so much to give the bishop a piece of your mind 'bout *me*. You returned for Lydiann."

Jake looked down at his feet. "You're right. I know what I want." His head came up and his gaze met Jonas's. "And I won't let one letter change the direction of my life. I know what I'll do."

Amazed and relieved at Jake's sudden change of heart, Jonas headed with him down the wide brown pasture, brittle grass crunching beneath their work boots.

When the last plate was washed and dried that Sunday evening and Hannah felt too tired to stand any longer, she went to Gid's favorite rocker near the wood stove and sank into it. Sighing, she thought back somewhat discouragedly on her visit to the Henners'. To think she might not be "chosen," as Zachariah put it, made her even more desperate to secure the gift.

She'd nearly given in to sleep when Gid came into the kitchen, looking for some more coffee. "Oh," she said, getting up, "let me pour it for ya."

He looked at her, frowning slightly. "You're all in, Hannah. Go and sit some more."

"No, I best not rest too much 'fore bedtime."

"Soon it'll be time for evening prayers," he said. "And, just so ya know, tonight I plan to say some out loud."

Even though she didn't admit it, Hannah was right

startled, and had she been a strong woman who thrived on speaking her mind, she might've asked, *What on earth for?* But she bit her lip and decided this strange announcement was further reason to keep her encounter with Zachariah to herself, at least for now. Thinking again of Zachariah's words, Hannah wondered if his observations of her with others would leave her wanting. She could try all she wanted to put her best foot forward, but the truth of the matter was, she had never been the sort of woman people were drawn to. She had few friends and was as shy a person as anyone she knew. And just now, with the cares of her own world and family responsibilities resting heavily on her shoulders, she could only hope she might impress either of the Henners the next time they were at the same church gathering or whatnot.

Breathing deeply, she tilted her head back against the chair and let herself go into the hazy realm of presleep, relieved to be free of pain where her wee babe grew beneath her heart.

Thank goodness, she thought, though not directing her gratefulness toward anyone in particular.

Blinking her eyes open, Hannah saw by the day clock on the wall that twenty minutes had already passed. Feeling guilty for having herself a catnap too late in the day, she rose swiftly and headed to the front room. There Gid was playing checkers with Ida Mae while Katie Ann read a storybook to Mimi. *My contented and happy family*, she thought, standing silently.

At last Gid looked up. "Come and watch Ida Mae's king finish me off!" he invited. To this Ida and Katie both laughed and clapped their hands. Their father was clearly cutting up with them, even clowning a bit—the man was such a good father.

Once the game was finished and put away, the family gathered around Gid for the Bible reading. This night he read in English, from the New Testament epistle of James—the very underlined verses Hannah had seen earlier. In fact Gid read from verse thirteen all the way to the end of chapter five, emphasizing the words " 'The effectual fervent prayer of a righteous man availeth much.' " He went on to explain, after he finished the reading, what he thought it meant to pray fervently, and Hannah was taken aback by the break in routine, as well as the eagerness on the faces of their elder daughters. It was as if they were soaking up their father's every word—except Mimi, who had a most unpleasant look on her usually sweet face.

"Dawdi Abram prays out loud," Gid was saying now, "and I aim to do the same. I believe the Lord God has this in mind for us, no matter what the bishop might say."

Hannah wondered what the bishop might think if he knew of her husband's rather rebellious opinion, but when the time came, she bowed her head and hoped Gid would never ask *her* to speak a prayer in front of the whole family. She doubted she could pray in such a fashion by herself, let alone with people listening. If Gid knew the truth, he might be surprised to learn she had ceased her silent rote praying years ago.

"O Lord God and heavenly Father," Gid began, "I come before you in the name of the Lord Jesus, who spilled His blood on Calvary's tree for each of us. Humbly I ask for the Holy Spirit to guide us every day . . . to teach us your ways . . . that we might wholly belong to you. I beseech you for the strength and health of our bodies and minds. Make our hearts your dwelling place so that we may be found worthy on that holy day to stand before you without spot or wrinkle. In the name of Jesus our Lord, I make these petitions known. Amen."

Befuddled as she was, Hannah was quite sure she knew who must have encouraged her husband to pray this way: Gid had revealed himself that her own father, under the influence of Aunt Lizzie—and much earlier, Mamma—had brought him to this curious spiritual place. She would not think of inquiring further about such private matters of her husband, though, being that he was not only the patriarch of this house, but God's appointed one.

Much later, once the girls were tucked into one big feather bed, Gid sat down at the kitchen table and asked for a second helping of lemon meringue pie. Hannah was happy to serve him a generous slice, but the tone in his voice made her uneasy.

"We best be talking 'bout your visit to Henners'," he said, his face rather stern.

She came to stand near the table, her hands all of a sudden clammy. How did he know of this?

"Won't ya sit, Hannah?"

Quickly she did so.

"I s'pose you didn't understand why I said not to invite Zach and Mary Ann over for supper." He folded his hands on the table and regarded them for a moment before going on. "Frankly, Hannah, I've come to understand why there are folk among the People who won't go to a powwow doctor. And I believe most firmly now that my mother, your father, and Lizzie have been right all these years in stayin' clear of them."

Her heart sank. "I should've known you wouldn't approve of me goin'," she confessed softly, knowing she ought to offer an apology. "I just felt like I was bein' pulled there . . . wanting to be a healer myself 'n' all."

Gid's eyes widened, his eyebrows shooting up into his forehead. "No, Hannah. That's not what you oughta be seekin' after."

"I guess I haven't told ya because I was worried you'd feel this way." She must not go on trying to explain herself, even though it was all she could do to sit there and realize how much he disapproved of her. The concerned way he continued to frown made her wonder if his demeanor was beginning to change, his affection wane, maybe. But then, her own father had actually softened quite a lot since getting all caught up in Aunt Lizzie's view of God.

"You know I never cared one way or the other about powwowing," Gid said, "but now I've come to believe the teachings of the Holy Scriptures, 'which are able to make thee wise unto salvation.'"

"It surprises me that you're quotin' the Bible so freely," she said meekly. "Even Mimi looked troubled by your talk tonight . . . and she has no idea what's expected of us from the bishop."

He offered a smile, obviously unfazed by her comment. "Between you and me, I've memorized quite a lot of verses here lately—whole chapters—though not to boast. I do it because I've come to know the God of the Bible, Hannah, really know Him and something of what it means to be a servant of Christ Jesus, my Lord and Savior. And ain't it awful strange this should happen to me since becomin' a preacher?"

She wondered what on earth Bishop Bontrager might say to this admission, but she continued to listen as Gid shared his "unexpected faith," as he called it.

Then he said something else that truly caught her off guard. "I've been thinking, and I'd like to say this outright: Your twin sister is welcome to visit here with you anytime." He reached for her hand. " 'Tis high time to make amends on that count. I'm sure my harsh decision hurt both you and Mary Ruth terribly, and I'm sorry for that."

She was astonished at this change of heart. "You're sayin' it's all right for her to visit with me alone?"

He nodded and kissed her hand. "You've missed out on some important sisterly chats, I daresay. And the girls need to see both her and their uncle Robert more often, too."

She felt nearly scatterbrained with joy, and she smiled her gratitude back at her husband, letting the pleasant expression on *his* face quiet her heart. In one short span of time she had been both reprimanded and rewarded.

"Mary Ruth might not know what to think, if she doesn't hear this directly from you," she ventured.

"Then we'll have them over for supper this week. How'd that be?"

"I'll drop a note to her tomorrow, first thing—invite her and Robert and little Ruthie." Hannah couldn't help wondering if Gid had gone a tad ferhoodled, forgetting the initial reason he'd given for her not to spend time alone with Mary Ruth: talk amongst the People. Supposedly, some were bothered by a preacher's wife having frequent fellowship with a Mennonite who claimed to have received salvation.

So what changed? That Gid was seeing things much differently these days was obvious. He'd admitted to a newfound faith. Was it the sort of one Mary Ruth and Robert also shared?

With all that Gid had opened up to her about, Hannah felt she ought to at least say something more about her trip to see the Henners. "I honestly wish I could say I'm sorry for visitin' Zachariah and Mary Ann," she said at last. "Shouldn't have gone without your consent, I know."

Gid finished off the last bite of his pie before he spoke. "Next time you have a hankerin' to visit a sympathy healer, come and talk to me first, won't ya?"

Quite unexpectedly Hannah began to feel awfully blue again as a wave of depression nearly toppled her in spite of her best attempts to stand. All this intense yearning for the gift—how could she simply turn it off? And what would happen if she were to be chosen, after all? Would Gid forbid her to accept?

Chapter Eighteen

Finding out which Sunday night singing Lydiann would attend, if she was going at all, felt like searching for a lost boot in the depths of a forest. But Jake thought it through carefully, backward and forward, until he'd decided on what he felt was a good plan.

He waited till dusk to ride to Gobbler's Knob, about the time he assumed Abe would be taking his sister. Once in the vicinity of the Ebersol house, he tied up his horse within running distance and hid in the thicket not far from the entrance to the long lane. Waiting was the hardest part of all.

It was not but ten minutes later and here came Abe at the reins, driving fast, with Lydiann alongside.

Nearly breathless, Jake watched. His dear girl was in the Ebersol family buggy with her brother.

Which direction will they go?

He kept himself concealed as best he could till Abe turned onto the main road, heading west. Jake breathed more easily, knowing they wouldn't spy an abandoned horse and courting buggy just east of them.

His instincts had paid off, and he felt a boost of energy as he dashed back, ready to follow Abe and Lydiann, wherever they were headed.

When Lydiann noticed Jake sitting with a group of fellows from the Grasshopper Level church at the singing, she was at once surprised and instantly disheartened.

What's he doing here? she wondered, thinking surely he wasn't ready to begin looking for a new girlfriend. *Oh, how terribly awkward if that's true. . . .*

Quickly she determined not to look his way a single time more all evening long. She would have kept to that if he hadn't come walking right up to her following the actual singing part of the get-together. Different couples were already pairing up and walking or talking together within the large expanse of the swept barn floor. She even spied four young people sitting high in the haymow, one girl cuddling a midnight black cat.

"Hullo, Lydiann," said Jake, standing much too close to her.

She stepped back slightly, heart in her throat. Oh, she'd missed him something awful! Yet seeing him now, she felt she saw something of Sadie in Jake's face for the first time, and she found herself all but too shy to speak.

"I got the letter you sent, and I don't believe I see eye to eye with ya at all." He looked down, fidgeting with his thumb. "Tell ya the truth, I think the whole thing is baloney, plain and simple, and I won't have any of it. So there." He was grinning now, holding out his hand to her. "Let's just let bygones be by—"

"No, you don't understand. I . . . *we* can't go on courtin'."

"Why not? I love you." He reached again to hold her hand, and she felt her body shiver.

She looked at him, hoping he hadn't seen in her eyes the apprehension she'd felt. She had planned this moment so differently, having already decided what she might say if she encountered him again . . . knowing she must speak the truth on her heart. But it was too late for that.

"Why are you looking at me that way?" He released her hand, the pain on his face unconcealed.

"I love you, too, Jake," she whispered. "What I mean is . . . I *did*. And if you listen carefully, I can explain why."

He grimaced. "What're ya sayin'?"

The promise she'd made to Mamma Leah and Sadie now struck her full in the face. How much easier to simply tell him the truth outright and let things fall into place as they eventually must!

She managed to move back, even turned away from him momentarily, hoping he might walk away from her and be done with it. But no, she felt his hand on her shoulder, spinning her around to face him yet again.

"If there's someone else for you, just say it to my face, Lydiann Ebersol!" He was talking much too loudly, and several of the other young people turned to stare their way.

"Jake—please!"

"There *is* another beau, ain't?" he said more softly. "Why else would ya write such a letter?"

"That's not the reason at all." She searched his eyes, his face. "If you knew the truth, you wouldn't be raisin' your voice." Tears spilled down her cheeks. "You'd be sayin' to me: 'Ach, Lyddie, I'm ever so sorry to hear this . . . and I hate it, too, something awful.' That's what you'd be sayin'."

Jake was shaking his head now, staring as if he thought she was a crazy woman. She should have backed away right then and run, but she couldn't make her legs move.

"What do you mean, that's what *I'd* be sayin'?"

"Oh, Jake . . . it's no use. . . ." She began to inch away, but he grabbed her arm, literally pulling her out of the barn with him, his face red.

"You're hurting me." She tried yanking away, and he tightened his grip.

"I won't let you go! I'll *never* let you go, don't ya see? How can you forget the promises we made . . . the love I thought we shared? Is it that easy to walk away?"

When they reached the tobacco shed, he loosened his grasp and stood there facing her in the light of the moon.

"It's not easy at all, Jake. I still care for you."

He reached for her and pulled her close. "What do you mean when you say such things? Tell me, what's in your head?"

Lydiann had no choice. Promise or no, she felt she would never be able to get Jake to understand unless he heard the whole story. So she pleaded with him to go and sit on the fence nearby, and she crossed her arms in front of her, breathing hard.

In that moment she remembered how Mamma Leah often asked God for wisdom, even under her breath sometimes. Drawing in lungfuls of air, she asked the Lord God above to help her say what she knew she must.

"We're both Ebersols, Jake" came the words.

His eyes narrowed, but he held her gaze without blinking or speaking.

"It's a long and knotty tale, but according to what I've just learned, you are not Mandie's twin brother, nor the natural son of Peter and Fannie Mast."

Jake began to shake his head, no doubt bewildered. She shivered, horrified by the things she had shared. She had broken her promise, but there was no turning back.

"Your mother is my sister Sadie." She sighed, not caring her tears were falling fast. "We can never, ever marry . . . 'cause I'm your aunt."

Then, as if it had finally sunk in, he gasped. "I've heard of girls makin' up stories to suit their fancy, but this? Lydiann, you best just come right out and say we're through for any other reason under the sun than *this* crazy, mixed-up one." He jumped down off the fence and began to pace in front of her. "I daresay you're as flighty as my father says all you Ebersols are." The tone of his voice had changed.

Quite unexpectedly, he turned to look at her again, coming too close for her liking. "But if you ever decide to stop tellin' fibs and want to fulfill your promise to me, I'll be waitin' for ya." With that he began to hightail it toward the barn.

"No! Wait, Jake!" She ran hard to catch up, nearly plowing into him when he stopped. "If ya don't believe me, go 'n' pay a visit to the doctor."

"Dr. Schwartz?"

"He'll tell you what's what." She turned away.

"All right." His voice grew stronger again, as if he was challenging her. "I'll do that. Right away tomorrow, in fact."

Her heart felt like the heavy stones Dat, Gid, and Abe

dug up out of the fields this time of year, but Lydiann knew she must not look back. She had to keep walking all the way home, hoping against hope Jake would follow through with seeing Dr. Schwartz.

Before first light Jonas hurried out to the barn to get things rolling for milking, wondering how Jake felt after seeing Lydiann, if that was indeed where he had gone. He was mighty sure Jake had taken himself off somewhere last night, most likely to one of the barn singings, looking all spiffed up in his for-good trousers, white shirt, and black vest.

So when Jake came dragging into the barn, looking down in the mouth, Jonas knew he had his work cut out, either getting Jake to talk or trying to lift his spirits while they hand-milked their several cows.

The morning had gotten off to a cold and windy start with the tinny tap of sleet on the windowpanes long before it was time to arise. With the approaching nasty weather and the knowledge that yet another November had come and was nearly gone without his marrying Leah, he wasn't in the mood for a sorry ending to Jake's courtship with Leah's youngest sister, as she was in most folks' eyes. Truly, Lydiann was Leah's first cousin, and he had never forgotten the surprising account of Leah's beginnings Abram had given him deep in the cornfield seventeen long years ago. Not a whit of it bothered Jonas enough to ever unduly ponder Lizzie's having conceived Leah without being married. People—young and old alike—made dire mistakes, ofttimes paying dearly for them their entire lives. Eventually Lizzie had become an upstanding woman in the eyes of the People, and what mattered most to him was that Leah had grown from a sweet girl into a precious and honorable woman.

All the same, if Jake had a hankering to talk now, Jonas would do his utmost to listen and encourage him to try and move forward with whatever good things his life had to offer, whether here or in Ohio. The pursuit of a wife, while important, was only a part of that. *Anyway, he's too young to marry even next year,* thought Jonas as he recalled his own midteen years and his near-constant yearning to spend time with Leah. *Seems like just yesterday. . . .*

With that thought, he turned his attention to somber-faced Jake, lest his own longings for marriage overtake and distract him.

Studying Jake, he realized again what a strong and gritty young man he had become, one who understood and thrived in the adult world of farming, tending to orchards and barn animals alongside their father these many years.

"I don't s'pose you'd care to hear a downright dreadful story," Jake said from his place on the old, three-legged milking stool.

Jonas cocked his head. "Speak your mind."

"I'll say it straightaway, but you'll never believe this. Still, it's the reason Lydiann's givin' for our breakup."

Such a long pause ensued that Jonas nearly spoke, but a glance over at Jake's frowning, pinched face made him hold his tongue.

"According to Lyddie, I don't belong to this here family. *She* says I'm Sadie's baby son, all grown up . . . ain't a Mast at all." Jake looked right at him—clear through him, really.

"Have you ever heard such a ridiculous thing?"

"There's no way she can believe that." Puzzled, Jonas wondered at the source of this tale. "Did you ask her how she came to think such a peculiar thing?"

"She seemed altogether sure it's fact—even said I ought to go 'n' see Dr. Schwartz 'bout it."

"What on earth?" Jonas mumbled, considering what this odd suggestion might mean.

"Truth is, Lydiann declares up and down she's my aunt, and 'cause of that, we can't court anymore."

Jonas glanced at Jake again. *Why would she say such a thing?* The thought disturbed him, but he forced himself to set the question aside for the time being. "The whole notion's absurd," he said.

"And a right *dumm* way to end our courtship if there's another boy she'd rather be seein'." Jake said this in such a fiery manner, the cows swooshed their tails and bellowed.

Jonas scarcely knew what to offer as consolation. "What are ya goin' to do?"

There was an awkward silence, and it seemed Jake might not answer. At last he replied, "I'm honestly thinking 'bout paying a visit to the doctor . . . just to show her up and make her give me the real reason."

"Ya really want to go 'n' do that?"

"I need to put all this to rest—and quick." He rose and walked to the barn door but looked back at Jonas. "Best not be sayin' a word of this to Dat and Mamma."

Jonas nodded, watching him leave. *It can't be true,* he thought.

Yet in the back of his mind, he recalled how Leah had shared her aching heart over her sister's sin—and Sadie herself had confided in him, as well, out in Millersburg the summer after she'd given birth to a supposedly stillborn baby. Come to think of it, he realized Jake *was* the age Sadie's son would have been, had he survived.

O Lord God in heaven, may this all blow over!

Chapter Nineteen

The frosty weather printed roses on Abe's and Lydiann's cheeks as the two headed briskly toward the house, leaving afternoon milking chores behind. Sadie watched them from the window of the back door, smiling as they fell into step, their breath wafting up from their heads as they talked. The wind puffed Lyddie's long skirts out behind her, and Abe leaned his black felt hat into the wind, steadying it with his hand.

While she couldn't hear what was being said, she observed the lively exchange and fondly wondered what her own still-born babies might've grown up to look like, had they lived. The memory of meeting her sole living child at market, the one and only time they had spoken, had emblazoned itself in her mind, though at the time she had been unaware of their relationship. *What would happen if Jake knew I was the mother who birthed him? What if he knew how much he was loved by a silent stranger?*

She opened the door for her younger sister and brother as they came up the back steps. Once inside, they began to remove their work boots and hang up coats and scarves, and she headed into the kitchen to make some hot cocoa. "Anybody need warmin' up?"

"I do!" Abe said, hurrying to the cookstove to thaw out. "It's too early for weather this cold, ain't?"

Lydiann, on his heels, responded with merely a nod of her head, though when Sadie served up two large coffee mugs of hot chocolate, Lydiann wasted no time in reaching for hers and blowing gently. She was so quiet Sadie wondered if she wasn't feeling well, but the brightness of her eyes and the flush of health on her cheeks told another tale.

Abe brightened when a second mug was offered, asking for whipped cream this time, to which Sadie happily obliged.

Sitting with them in her regular place at the table, she was taken with Abe's animated talk. "I'm goin' on a pest hunt here in a few days," he said, face alight. "We're gonna see who can catch the most rats and prove it."

"Ew!" Lydiann said suddenly, shaking her head. "You and your friends oughta find something better to do with your time than choppin' off rat tails."

"Why should you care?" he shot back. "I don't complain 'bout the quiltin' frolics and whatnot you hurry off to."

Lydiann scrunched up her face. "But pest hunts are disgusting."

Sadie spoke up, enjoying the banter between them. "Dead rats do mean less work for barn cats."

"So there!" Abe said, glowering in jest at Lydiann. "Wouldn't want them cats to have too many rodents runnin' loose, now, would we?"

"I don't care in the least," Lydiann whispered.

Abe continued, oblivious to his sister's solemn demeanor.

"I daresay some of the fellas from Ohio are goin' with us—now, ain't that right fine?" He started rattling their names, and Sadie's ears perked up when Abe mentioned Eli Yoder. Evidently it was he who'd asked for some help from the young folk with the barn pests.

Abe leaned over and grinned right in Lydiann's face. "We'll make short work of 'em."

Lydiann simply slid her cocoa away from her and rose to her feet, leaving the room without saying a word.

Sadie wanted to get up and follow her in the worst way, but Lyddie probably needed some time alone upstairs, which was where she was headed, and mighty fast, too, by the sound of her feet on the steps.

Abe was quick to verbalize concern. "What's gotten into her?"

Sadie raised her eyebrows. "You know her best, jah?"

"I'd have to say she's crazy in love," he spouted off. "But don't ask me how I know."

Sadie rose and began rinsing the mugs at the sink.

"I'm serious," Abe insisted, coming over to her. "Lyddie's a walkin', breathin' mess over the youngest Mast boy, if ya ask me."

"Nobody's askin' you, Abe." Just then she remembered Abe and Jake were acquaintances—no wonder Abe was so adamant about Lydiann's emotions. Turning, she placed a gentle hand on her brother's shoulder. "Don't be too hard on your sister, all right?"

He nodded, more serious now. "Jah, I s'pose."

Sadie sighed. "Ain't nothin' easy 'bout love sometimes."

Seeing the envelope with her name printed in Hannah's hand, Mary Ruth sliced it open with a table knife. She was pleased to discover a supper invitation from Gid and Hannah. "Well, *this* is interesting," she said, placing the note on the kitchen table for Robert to see when he returned from the church.

Just then a knock came at the back door, and she hurried to see who was there. "Dottie! Come in, won't you?" She took her friend's wrap and hung it on the row of wooden wall pegs. "So good to see you again."

"I can't seem to keep myself away from your baby," Dottie said, following her into the kitchen, where Ruthie's cradle was pulled close to the table. "Oh, just look at her." She stooped low and made over the sleeping infant.

"She got herself a clean bill of health from her grandfather at her checkup," volunteered Mary Ruth. "She's as healthy as the day is long."

"I'm not one bit surprised." Dottie eyed the little one longingly.

"She's still at that stage where she sleeps through most anything," Mary Ruth said. "Go ahead and pick her up if you wish."

Dottie sat in the rocker with Ruthie and began to hum softly.

"Babies bring out the hum in all of us." Mary Ruth laughed. "You should hear Robert sing to her while he rocks. It's the dearest thing."

Dottie nodded, yet it was as if she was paying Mary Ruth little or no mind, her gaze was focused so wholly on Ruthie's peaceful face.

"How's your family?" Mary Ruth asked.

"Oh, Dan's keeping real busy; you know how he is. And Carl . . . well, he's some perkier here lately."

"Oh?"

Dottie looked up at her. "Between you and me, I think he had a nice, long walk with your little sis."

"When was this?"

Dottie told about the Georgetown Saturday market. "I just so happened to show up there with Carl."

"You didn't!"

Dottie smiled mischievously. "What can it hurt? The two of them were good friends until Carl went on to high school, you know."

"I wonder if Leah has any idea they talked."

"I say we leave things be. In time who knows what might come of their renewed friendship."

"True." Suddenly Mary Ruth remembered the note from Hannah and picked it up to show Dottie. "I honestly think my twin and I are about to renew *our* close relationship, as well."

Dottie took the note and read it. "Oh, how wonderful!"

"It's an answer to prayer, to be sure. The old bishop must have changed his mind—either that or Gid is simply doing what he believes is best for Hannah . . . and for me."

"Well, it's good news whatever the reason." Dottie rose from the rocker and began walking the length of the kitchen as Ruthie began to stir.

"Here, I'll take her. It's time she nurses again."

Smiling, Dottie handed Ruthie to her. "You're a fine mother, Mary Ruth. I hope you have a half dozen more wee ones."

"That's nice of you to say." She settled into the rocker

while Dottie sat at the table, picking up the note from Hannah. "Isn't it interesting how the Lord works?"

"Especially when we don't try to rush things."

Dottie agreed. "Patience is more than a virtue, I'd have to say."

Mary Ruth thought of Leah. "For some, it's a way of life."

The breathy sound of Ruthie's suckle rose and fell in the quietude of the house, and Mary Ruth smiled, thinking of Hannah yet again, eager to write an answer to her twin's kind supper invitation.

Henry saw Jake Mast coming up the drive, his feet pounding hard against the pavement in the way Derek had always run. He moved away from the window and walked to the door of the clinic, opening it for his grandson.

"Dr. Schwartz, I must talk to ya!" Jake announced as he came rushing inside.

It was virtually closing time, and Henry noticed Leah was pushing a dry mop over the hallway. By the intense look on Jake's handsome face, Henry was relieved the lad hadn't burst in thirty minutes before, when a patient or two might still have been in the waiting room. "Let's step into my office," he suggested as calmly as possible.

He closed the door and motioned for Jake to have a seat. Then, sitting at his desk, he noted again the intense concern registered on Jake's face and guessed what had precipitated this visit.

"I had to come here, Doctor . . . and I'm awful sorry, not

makin' an appointment 'n' all."

"Quite all right." Henry felt his entire body go stiff.

"I'm having trouble believing what someone told me Sunday, so downright ridiculous it is." Jake's face was red. "I was told I should hear what you have to say about it, which is why I'm here."

"Go on, son." He felt the fire in his bones as he anticipated what was coming. He had lived this moment in his mind, projecting forward in time to this inevitable day. It was ground he had already walked with Leah, presently down the hall as she completed her cleaning duties.

Carefully he observed Jake, whose upper torso remained rigid as he sat inert but for his callused, restless fingers, which seemed unable to be still. Henry was caught by the sight, finding it curious that Derek's son should be so similar to Derek himself in this small way—superbly composed in one area, yet obviously out of control in another.

Jake got right to the matter. "Am I a Mast or an Ebersol?"

"I beg your pardon?" Henry asked. He'd expected to face that very question, but hearing Jake voice it here in his office still took him off guard.

"Who *am* I, sir? Someone told me I ain't who I think I am."

"Why, you're Jake Mast . . . you know that." But no, he must backtrack and start over, lest he cower and fall into his old, devious pattern. "What I mean to say is . . ." He stopped. This was not going well. "Jake, I have been terribly deceitful," he tried again. "For too long I have kept from you . . . and those who love you . . . the most vital information."

He paused to breathe deeply before continuing. "You are both an Ebersol and a Schwartz." His jaw was so tight he had trouble forming the words. "Let's begin with the night you were born, not so far from here."

Jake listened, eyes flickering open and shut, as Henry confessed the truth about everything, including Jake's connections to Sadie, Derek, and even Henry himself. He did not spare a single detail, describing the apparent stillbirth and the astonishing miracle that had occurred during the drive to the clinic, as well as his wrenching decision to give Jake to the Masts instead of to his rightful mother.

When he finished, Jake was frowning harder than when he had first arrived. "But . . . this—how can it be?" He stood abruptly, shaking his head. "My parents are Peter and Fannie Mast. Mandie's my twin." He paused a moment, looking around the room as if trying to get his bearings. "You must've gotten this wrong—ach, awful mixed-up. I'm not that boy. Surely you must have someone else in mind."

Henry rose to go to him. "You *are* my flesh-and-blood grandson, Jake—that's why I've kept you within arm's reach. But I also needed to know you were being nurtured by good Amish folk—Sadie's people." His throat locked up, leaving him with only his compassionate expression to attempt to atone for his sins.

"What proof is there of this?"

Henry reached for a framed picture of young Derek, turning it around. "This is your natural father. You're the spitting image of him at this age."

Jake held the picture and stared at it for a long time before speaking. "And . . . my parents don't know this?" His voice was thick with emotion.

Henry sighed. "No."

Jake shook his head sorrowfully. "What'll they say . . . or

think?" He returned his gaze to Henry. "They must be told . . . soon as I get home."

It's unraveling, just as I feared, he realized. *I have no one to blame but myself.* He wanted to apologize again, to say he'd had no right to play God, but he couldn't utter the words at the look of distrust in Jake's eyes.

"No wonder Lyddie says I can never marry her," the boy said. "Himmel, no wonder!"

Henry continued, "If I could change what I did that night, I would. I *should* have returned you to your mother. Instead, I cruelly allowed her to believe her baby had died."

Jake's eyes gleamed with angry tears. "I met her once, did ya know? And I thought she was Abe Ebersol's sister, nothin' more." He shook his head, eying Henry with disdain before hurrying to open the office door. "Ach, my poor parents!"

Then, just as loudly as he'd come in, Jake turned around and declared, "I've never known what it means to hate another person till today—nor did I think I could be rude enough to say so!" At that he dashed down the hall.

Henry stepped out of his office as the clinic door slammed shut, and he almost bumped into Leah, who looked both pale and astonished. He required fresh air, not another painful discussion, but he lingered long enough for her to say, "Maybe you should follow him home, Doctor."

He looked at her incredulously. "Yes, that's absolutely the right thing to do." He tried to collect his wits. Leah was a bright woman, yet if he went to the Masts' home, as she suggested, what would he say? Henry glanced at her again, the unspoken question looming in his mind.

As if perceiving the reason for his hesitancy, she repeated,

"Follow him. Please . . . don't let Jake attempt this revelation alone."

He hurried to grab his coat and hat off the coat tree. *My sins have more than found me out. It's long past time to come clean.*

Part Two

◆ ◆ ◆ ◆

For the Lord God is a sun and shield:

the Lord will give grace and glory:

no good thing will he withhold

from them that walk uprightly.

—Psalm 84:11

Chapter Twenty

Leah had once heard it said that, especially in late autumn, a person's cheerfulness was in direct proportion to the amount of daylight one might expect. Yet in spite of the sun's brilliance, she was worried nearly sick as she trudged home.

She opened the back door of the Dawdi Haus, calling for Sadie, whom she found folding a pile of clothes. "Ya best stop what you're doin'."

"What is it, sister?"

Leah looked about her to see if they were indeed alone. She felt uneasy telling Sadie what she must, but there was no need to withhold what she knew. "Lydiann broke her promise. She told Jake 'bout you."

Sadie held the dish towel she was folding in midair, her face turning nearly ashen as she stood like a slight statue.

"Jake knows who you are to him . . . that the Masts aren't his parents by blood." Leah paused to catch her breath, suddenly winded.

"How'd ya hear this?" Sadie's voice sounded unnaturally high.

Leah sighed. "I put two and two together," she said, telling how she'd overheard Jake's heated comment as he left Dr. Schwartz's clinic.

Sadie's lip quivered and she put her hand on her chest, as if fighting back tears. "Ya mean . . . ?"

"Jah, dear one. Jake knows the doctor's secret . . . and ours."

"At long last." Sadie reached for Leah's hand. "Time for rejoicing. The truth is out at last!"

Shrinking back, Leah shook her head. "No, this is a terrible thing . . . for all of us."

"It's the best news *I've* had in a long, long time—truly 'tis." Sadie stood tall, eyes shining with what Leah knew to be tears of gladness.

Leah, on the other hand, was terribly worried. Jake and Dr. Schwartz were on their way to tell the truth to Peter and Fannie Mast, and she couldn't help wondering how long before the news might overtake the whole community. What would this mean for the Mast family? For herself? How would all of this set with Jonas—that she had known for some time, even the night he'd asked pointed questions about Lydiann's letter to Jake? Yet she had kept the truth from her beloved, as well as, for a time, from her own dear Lydiann.

Emotionally torn, Leah dreaded what was to befall them, and the day and the season seemed darker to her than ever before.

Lydiann was out on the road with the team, running a sewing errand for Aunt Lizzie to Deacon Stoltzfus's wife, when she saw a cluster of bundled-up children walking home from the one-room schoolhouse. It seemed like only last week that she, too, had been among the youngsters returning home from a long day in the classroom.

She slowed the horse and called to them. "Any of yous care for a ride?"

All eight of them came running. "Can ya squeeze in tight?" she said, smiling as she remembered how cold it could be walking this time of year.

The children jostled into the buggy, several of them thanking her right away, before she realized she wouldn't be getting to the Stoltzfuses' anytime soon—not if she was to deliver the children to their individual homes.

"So . . . how many sets of brothers and sisters do I have here?" she asked, which brought a burst of laughter, the children catching on that she'd taken on more than she might have originally set out to do.

"Two Zooks," said one of the girls.

"Four Kings," said another.

"Mast twins," said one boy softly.

That comment befuddled her, and just when she was finally hoping to get her mind off Jake Mast. "That's three stops," she said, glancing over her shoulder. "Where to first?"

The oldest Zook girl spoke up again. "We aren't but a half mile from here."

When asked, the others said they were "just a bit farther." Lydiann didn't mind, really. She enjoyed listening in as the children chattered in Pennsylvania Dutch about their school day.

She heard one of the boys mention Carl Nolt. "He's taking some of us sleddin' when the first big snow comes."

She almost blurted out, *How do you know Carl?* but kept quiet, taking in the fond remarks about Carl, who seemed to be someone special to the children.

Well, and of course he is. She hadn't thought of his invitation to include her in his church autumn hayride much at all, but as considerate as Carl had always been, she shouldn't have been surprised at his offer. Still, it was much too soon to think about another boy.

Carl was only trying to get my mind off my woes, she decided, dismissing the notion he might have actually been asking her for a date.

At Leah's gentle yet wise suggestion, Henry had gotten into his car and had driven merely a short distance when he spied Jake running along the road. Stopping, he insisted Jake not travel on foot all the way home in the chilly air. "Let me drive you," he offered.

Jake shook his head, holding his ground. Henry continued to entreat him all the same, ever conscious of his own churning emotions—despising the confession that had led to such obvious antagonism in his own grandson.

After much persistence and suggesting that he, too, go and talk with Jake's parents, he was finally able to coax him into the comfort and warmth of the car.

Jake seemed to cling to the far right side of the front seat. "I have no need of your help with my family," he mumbled.

Henry drove without speaking, trying to overlook Jake's obvious antagonism. He imagined how incensed Derek would have been at hearing such earth-shattering news, comparing it to Jake's more tempered, yet plainly icy demeanor.

Since Henry could not begin to anticipate how the next

few minutes might unfold, he concentrated on turning into the driveway.

"This ain't somethin' that oughta be kept quiet any longer," Jake said suddenly. "I've reconsidered: I'm thinkin' you ought to see firsthand what findin' out about your trickery will do to my parents . . . if they believe it."

Henry realized that no amount of spoken regret would remove the pain from Jake's face, nor the justifiable sting from his words.

They got out of the car and headed toward the back door, Henry trudging along behind Jake.

"You and your family bein' English makes all this even more complicated, ya must surely know," Jake said, nervously touching the brim of his hat.

Again Henry was appalled at his own lack of judgment. Had he never envisioned the excruciating scene about to take place here in Jake's childhood home? Why hadn't he foreseen this present heartbreak?

Vaguely he was aware of Jake telling his mother, "There's something important to be said to you and Dat and Jonas." Then Jake, terse yet evidently wanting to exhibit good manners, kept his wits about him and insisted Mandie go upstairs, "for the time being." To Henry's surprise she went willingly, glancing down at them several times as she ascended the long staircase. That done, Jake left the kitchen and hurried out to the barn to fetch his father and Jonas.

The awkward moments that followed seemed nearly endless as Henry stood near the wood stove with Fannie, who appeared to be trying her best to keep her attention on ironing Peter's long-sleeved shirts while waiting for Jake to return with the two men.

All too soon, though, what Henry had confidentially shared with Jake in the privacy of his office was being voiced aloud in the hearing of Peter, Fannie, and Jonas.

"Outrageous . . . if true," Peter said, the anger in his eyes speaking volumes.

"I'm afraid it is," said Henry, "though it's much too late now to offer an apology for my misguided attempt. I primarily had my family's potential embarrassment in mind." He struggled to keep his emotions in check, tempted to hide his long-ago decision behind some kind of purposeful rationale. "When Fannie gave birth to her stillborn twin boy, I knew both of you would be heartsick at the loss . . . and since Sadie had already experienced what she had assumed was the death of *her* baby—all in the same night—it seemed right, somehow, to place premature Jake in Fannie's welcoming arms."

Peter glared at him. "A deceitful deed."

Henry continued, digging himself deeper into a pit of his own making. "It was a most selfish act, one I wish could be undone."

Peter breathed loudly, as if he was about to erupt into a heated retort, but it was Fannie who began to weep.

After some time Henry offered to direct the dismayed couple to the location of their deceased son's grave, but Peter declared the notion "idiotic."

Turning toward the window, Peter inhaled loudly, and an uncomfortable silence fell on the kitchen.

Jake stood alone, his eyes forlorn, like those of a child suddenly displaced, and Henry was aware of the pulse pounding in his own aching temples.

Jonas stepped forward, going to stand with Jake, his arm

resting on Jake's shoulder. "I say we're brothers, no matter what."

To this Peter deliberately turned, his face grave. "No, not brothers. And not my *son*." He frowned briefly, eyes focusing on Jake, whose face was drawn. "You're an Ebersol," he said brusquely, as if making a pronouncement of evil. "Pack your clothes and get out of my house immediately."

Jonas appeared stunned. "But, Dat!"

"Do not defy me." Peter moved quickly to Fannie, who was sobbing. "Come with me," he said to her, not looking back a single time at the young man whom they'd raised as their own. Clearly, he was theirs no longer.

"Dat, mayn't I speak to Mandie?" pleaded Jake. "Can't I have a minute to say good-bye?"

"Hurry up with it," said Peter, his back still to Jake and Jonas.

Henry's heart sank and his blood boiled, but he dared not utter a word: This mess was his doing. Even so, he could not fathom Peter's decision. *No, you ignorant man, you cannot renounce your son!*

"Listen, Dat," said Jonas. "If ya mean what you say, then I'll be goin', too . . . with Jake."

Abruptly Peter turned in the doorway between the long kitchen and the front room, his countenance surprised but no less unyielding. "Do as you must, Jonas." Then, looking Henry's way, he motioned with his head to indicate that he was also expected to exit now.

Bewildered at the unforeseen turn of events, Henry wasted no time in plodding toward the back door, making his way outside, tormented by what he had just witnessed . . . and the responsibility he bore for it.

What wretched thing have I done to this family?

Chapter Twenty-One

As discouraged as he'd ever been, Jonas headed out on foot with Jake. Both of them politely refused Dr. Schwartz's proffered lift, and they made their trek up the hill to Gobbler's Knob, toward the home of Eli Yoder, with only a pillowcase each, filled with a few essential items of clothing. The sun behind them, they discussed the tumultuous scene in their mamma's kitchen as the wind kicked up from a breeze to full-blown gusts.

On the way Jake expressed his disbelief at their cold-hearted ousting by Dat, his voice quaking. "He can't be thinkin' straight . . . he just can't be." Their father had given them scarcely any time to gather up work trousers and an extra shirt or two, socks, and underwear. In fact, Dat had outright barked at them from the bottom of the steps, to Jonas's disbelief. This was a man he suddenly felt he did not know.

Jonas offered some halfhearted encouragement to his brother. "Dat's beside himself with anger, but I would hope he might come round in time." But after what they'd just experienced, he was not absolutely sure of that.

Jake's face remained taut and expressionless. "Got Schwartz and Ebersol blood in my veins . . . but it's Abram's blood that's the culprit in Dat's eyes," he muttered.

Jonas listened quietly as his brother ranted, his own head reeling. He could only imagine the enormous pain Jake was feeling.

"So this means I'm not part of my own family, then? Just like that, everything I've known 'bout my life and who I thought I was is dead wrong."

"Not everything, Jake."

"Aren't ya believing Dr. Schwartz?"

"It's a mighty hard thing, but I can't say differently." *What other reason would the doctor have for telling such a tale?* Jonas thought to himself.

" 'Tis unbelievable." Jake blew out an angry breath. "And to think I'm not welcome at the orchard house anymore . . ."

Jonas had long since come to both accept and ignore his father's intolerance toward Abram Ebersol and his family, though he wondered how Jake's being kicked out of the house might affect Leah when she found out—and surely she would—since she had become quite close to Sadie in recent years. With Jake's being Sadie's son, Jonas considered how such a relationship might play out over time. Still, he was hopeful for a sensible resolution to his father's initial reaction, unreasonable and shortsighted as it was.

"The worst of it is I can never marry Lyddie." Grief registered powerfully on Jake's face. "If only Dr. Schwartz had told the truth when Sadie gave me birth . . ." His voice trailed off to nothing.

They remained silent for a time, their shoes making the only sound as they plodded along the frozen road. Jonas didn't intend to bring up the idea of pressing forward with one's life—not at this difficult moment. There would be time for that later.

Jake glanced at him now, his jaw set. "I've never seen Dat so irate, 'specially not in front of Mamma . . . and Dr. Schwartz, too. What am I s'posed to do, Jonas?"

Jonas clenched his hands. All facts considered, Jake was going to have a rough time of it, starting with walking away from Sadie's little sister. "Well, we can only pray something gut will come out of the whole mess," Jonas said, wishing Jake might seek spiritual counsel from one of the brethren. But from whom? Gid, or even Abram? He would think on that and do a heap of praying on his own.

When at long last they arrived at Eli Yoder's, they were welcomed with a warm smile, even though Jonas told Eli precious little as to why they needed a place to stay for a while. He would share more later, if need be, but for now he was mighty grateful for the hand of friendship and a roof over their heads.

In the meantime Jonas was all too aware he was seeing Jake in a completely different light—which couldn't be helped as he struggled to get his mind bent around a Jake who was Sadie's son, as well as both Abram's and Dr. Schwartz's grandson.

I need to get away, thought Henry. Too many years without a vacation had taken their toll, too many years of waiting for the inevitable revelation of his sin—too many years, as well, of trying to protect his good name, only to lose it with his own disclosures.

And when the truth finally filtered out to all his patients—*if* it did—he preferred not to be in town. It crossed his mind that, if worse came to worst, he might end up being forced to take a vacation at an entirely unwelcome location, and he shuddered at the thought.

He trudged up the porch steps and entered the side door of the house. Instead of calling out, "Lorraine, I'm home," as he normally did upon returning, he went directly to the formal parlor, where he stood before the tall bookcase and opened the glass door. Pulling out the world atlas, he thumbed through the section for Switzerland, Italy, and Austria, deciding to take Lorraine on an extended getaway, a sort of second honeymoon.

It might be our last chance, he thought morosely.

Standing at the window, he looked across the way to the woods, noting a small clearing someone had made near the road where chopped wood had been neatly stacked. Seeing the firewood drove his thoughts back to hardworking Jake, who had cut firewood for him on several occasions.

I'll begin making travel arrangements tomorrow, he thought, taking the atlas with him into the kitchen. There he found a somewhat disheveled Lorraine cooking supper. "How would you like to go on a trip with me, dear?"

Her smile was unexpectedly spontaneous. "Really? Where to?"

"Does Europe interest you?"

"Oh, Henry . . . I'd like that quite a lot." She was silent for a moment, as if she wished to make a request but was reluctant to do so.

"What is it, dear?"

"Would you be interested in Florence, Italy?" she asked. "I'd like to see the cathedral and Michelangelo's famous sculpture of David."

He hurried to her side and wrapped his aching arms around her. "We'll go as soon as I can contact a travel agent to line everything up."

She looked surprised but pleased.

"Yes, it's high time we go somewhere special together. It could be an early Christmas present, come to think of it." But Henry dreaded spoiling his wife's happiness with the distressing truth he was compelled to reveal while they were gone from home. At least she would have ample time to process what he must tell her once they arrived in the Renaissance city, which was more than he could say for the now-cynical Jake and infuriated Peter Mast. It did not take any great intellectual enlightenment to understand that the mind-numbing news they had received today would take the Mast family a lifetime to recover from.

Such destruction I've wrought.

Word of Jonas and Jake's hasty move came to Leah's surprised ears at the Friday quilting frolic at Dorcas's house. Women folk sat around the large frame making small stitches to join together the colorful design they had pieced together some time ago when someone quietly mentioned that Eli Yoder had visitors.

"Jah, Jake Mast's been sent away," an older woman said.

"By his own father," added another.

At first Leah wondered why Jonas hadn't contacted her directly, though she assumed he was busy and would be sending word soon enough. Earlier in the week she'd heard from Dorcas that he was helping Tomato Joe with the removal of large rocks in the fields for pay and that he had been doing odd jobs for others, including her uncle Jesse Ebersol. Whatever had befallen him, Leah could not imagine why both he and Jake were now staying with the Ohio widower, and she tried not to show undue interest as she listened.

Leah glimpsed Sadie, who appeared distressed, and then looked at Lydiann, whose pretty face was screwed up as she pushed her needle into the quilt. *Such a trying time for poor Lyddie, especially,* she thought.

"Jonas is ever so kindhearted to go along to stay with Jake at Widower Yoder's place," Dorcas spoke up, making it apparent she knew somewhat more than the others.

Leah felt her chest tighten but was determined not to fret, even though, most likely, Jake's and Jonas's leaving the orchard farmhouse presumably had much to do with the doctor's confession. *Could it be Dr. Schwartz spoke openly with the Masts?* If so, it was surely the last straw for Peter Mast.

Where will it end? Leah worried, thinking of Jonas and what he must be pondering. The secret, kept only out of concern for others, was flying in their faces.

That afternoon after the frolic, Abe announced to both Leah and Dat that he and a group of boys were going on another pest hunt. "We'll be back after dark tonight," he said.

"We're all going over to Uncle Jesse's to visit tomorrow, so it'd be a gut idea if you're not out too late," Leah gently reminded her excited boy.

Dat nodded in agreement. "Don't get too rowdy, like some of the youngsters I've been hearing 'bout lately."

Abe flashed his winning smile and pushed his hands through his hair. "I won't be *that* late, you'll see."

"Well, nobody's gonna wait up for ya, son," Dat said, rustling this week's edition of *The Budget* as he looked up from his rocking chair.

Dat having had his say, Leah went about her work, putting the finishing touches on the apple betty she was making. Sadie had settled in beside her to peel potatoes, not saying a word.

After Abe had disappeared out the back door, Dat cleared his throat, as though to request their attention. When Leah turned to look, he said, "I want to talk about whatever is goin' on with Jake and Jonas Mast."

The direct reference to her beau took Leah momentarily off guard, but she quickly composed herself. "I've heard nothin' from Jonas, if that's what you mean. But I'd think he'll fill me in soon."

"Seems Jake was not only asked to leave his father's house but also told never to return," Dat said, as if he somehow knew firsthand.

She wanted to ask where he'd heard such a thing but waited to speak, not wishing to interrupt her father's pattern of thought.

Dat continued. "I have a mind to go over there to Eli's and see what's what." He shook his head. "Truth be told, it's bothered me no end this rift 'tween Peter and me. Ain't right." He paused. "All these years, well, it's just a shame."

"I think I know why Cousin Peter would send Jake away," Leah offered softly, motioning to include Sadie in the conversation.

"Jah, we both know," Sadie spoke up. "It's time to open the floodgates, I daresay."

Sadie's right. The secret's as good as out, Leah thought. *No point pretending otherwise.*

Sadie's voice remained at a whisper as she shared with their father the truth about Jake Mast, his own grandson.

When at last she had revealed every jot and tittle, Dat rose swiftly from his chair. His paper shook as he attempted to fold it, but he gave up struggling to do so and pushed the whole bunch of it onto the table. "I'm mighty shocked at this news. You mean to tell me I have a grandson I've never known?" He inhaled loudly. "Sadie, your son is alive?"

"Jah, Dat . . . 'tis quite true." Sadie's eyes were bright with tears.

Leah spoke up. "We should have told you earlier, but—"

"Jah, you should've," Dat muttered, and Leah looked down at the floor, ashamed. "But what's done is done. And . . . it's best to leave every part of this in God's hands. He alone knows the end from the beginning."

Leah and Sadie nodded respectfully.

It was obvious how shaken their father was. He wandered through the kitchen and mutely came back to sit down as if the shocking news had impaired his ability to speak his mind.

The room was still as stone until he smiled. "Well, now, ain't it something? This might be precisely what we Ebersols and Masts need to bring us all together again."

Before either Leah or Sadie could respond, he headed outside for the barn, leaving much changed.

Leah rushed to Sadie's side and squeezed her but good. "You heard him, didn't ya? Your son—your Jake—might just be the one to cross the chasm of years."

Sadie bobbed her head slowly, apparently awestruck at the idea. "Well, ya know, Mamma always said, 'the tarter the apple, the tastier the cider.'"

To this both sisters burst into laughter. When Leah had wiped her face of bittersweet tears, she returned to her baking, adding the icing to the apple betty while it was still warm.

With nearly a week having passed since he and Jake took up residence with bighearted Eli, Jonas was quite eager to see Leah again. He sat down at the desk Eli had made years before and wrote a brief note, asking if he might visit her soon. He was reasonably sure the grapevine had begun to spread its creepers and Leah might already have heard of his and Jake's relocation.

Jonas had been mulling over what part, if any, Leah might have played in keeping the doctor's and Sadie's secret, at times even feeling the immediate need to ask her straight out why she hadn't shared with him her possible knowledge of Jake's roots. He recalled having asked Leah what had prompted Lydiann to write a letter breaking things off with Jake for seemingly no reason, yet Leah had remained silent on the matter that night, giving no indication of what was to come.

Now, if only she might be able to see him Saturday evening, it wouldn't be long before he and his darling would be able to clear the air on the matter, the Lord willing.

One week to the day following his visit to Dr. Schwartz's office, Jake received a letter from Mandie.

Dear Jake,

How are you? I simply had to write!

Mamma told me the sad news a few days ago, though I can hardly believe it. How is it possible you and I aren't twins or even brother and sister? I've cried myself to sleep and gone through the motions of my days as if in a nightmare. This has to be the worst thing that could ever befall me—a cruel joke.

In case you don't know it already, you'll always be my brother, no matter what. How can anyone change the fact we grew up picking apples in the orchard together, sledding down the steep hill in winter, playing volleyball, husking corn—all of that? Except for those long months you were in Ohio, we've shared all our lives so far together.

I know where you're living, because Jonas has written to both Dat and Mamma twice already. I wish I didn't have to bear the pain in our parents' eyes, especially Mamma's. Dat isn't himself, either. I can tell he's as upset as the rest of us, yet he is as stubborn as any man I know. Sending you away can't have made it easier on him.

And you, dear Jake? How on earth must you be feeling?

I hope you'll write to me and say what you're thinking these days. Will you go and see your first mother sometime? I would if I were you. Jonas will go along, maybe. He's the perfect choice for a visit to the Ebersols, seems to me.

With love—and I miss you something awful,

Your twin sister (in heart),
Mandie Mast

Jake handed the letter to Jonas, who was outside working on the shed behind Eli's house. "Read this when you have the chance." He turned away, not wanting to stand there and see the hurt on Jonas's face. He had already pictured Mandie's red and swollen eyes—Mamma's, too.

His *poor* mother, innocent as a daylily—what terrible things must be going through her mind! He longed to console her, to reassure her things would soon return to normal. Yet he wondered if that was even true, so topsy-turvy his life had become.

Mingled with grief over the doctor's deplorable deed, the misery of breaking up with the only girl he'd ever loved, and the loss of his family was the budding realization that eventually he must seek out Sadie Ebersol. Mandie was right that he needed to meet her: A few short minutes on market day were never going to be enough.

Leah was not one to jump too hastily to conclusions, but when a letter from Jonas arrived in the mailbox with her name clearly written on it, she assumed this was the word she had been awaiting. Opening the envelope out in the barn, high in the haymow, she discovered quickly that he wanted to see her again, "to talk."

There was no question in her mind that Jonas was out of sorts with her, because there was little else written, except a single comment about the weather having been awful cold—

enough that he felt he should come for her in a borrowed, enclosed buggy.

Leah wished again that she and Sadie might have handled Jake and Lyddie's courtship differently. Dr. Schwartz must surely be thinking along similar lines where Jake was concerned, and she'd heard from Lorraine they were planning a rather long getaway overseas. *I'm not surprised he desires an escape*, she thought, assuming the doctor's conscience must be gnawing away at him.

Thinking back to Jonas, she realized he now deserved to hear her side of the story—with Sadie's permission, of course. Such a thorny problem all of this was. And would Jonas react like Lydiann, who, since hearing the truth, had been quite cold toward her? The detached state of affairs between her and her girl tore at her heart, but what could she do now?

Weary of secret keeping, Leah felt like calling for a meeting of the People to get the news completely out in the open as quickly as possible.

She rose from the corner of the hayloft, where she'd sat on the window ledge, and stumbled over a burlap bag covered with straw. When she opened it and looked inside, she was astonished. It was half filled with rat tails! *Proof of Abe's recent pest hunt triumph.* The discovery brought both a small smile to her face and a bit of trepidation to her heart. She would continue to pray for Abe's safety, since it seemed he was bent more on satisfying his curiosity than using his head. *He's all boy, that one.*

With the hope of marrying Jonas a year from now, once he was past his Proving, Leah wondered how both Lyddie and Abe would manage without her here in Dat's house. She had considered asking Jonas his opinion on the matter but hadn't brought it up just yet, recalling the stumbling block the question of Mamma's children had been for Gid so long ago.

Yet, now that she thought on it, she supposed she *had* indeed followed through on her loving promise to Mamma. With Dat remarried and Sadie living next door in the Dawdi Haus, surely Leah would be free to marry her dearest love.

Chapter Twenty-Two

Abram preferred the sounds in his house to fade to nothing come eight o'clock or so of an evening. He welcomed the tranquility and thought about making ready to retire for the night, but before doing so, he went and knocked on the neighboring door between the big house and the smaller one.

Grateful that Sadie was still up and dressed, he asked if he might come in and talk a bit.

"Why sure." Sadie took a seat after offering him one.

He brought up the weather and the numerous weddings coming fast and furious all this month, as many as fifteen on the same day. Then, at last, what he really wanted to say—the question foremost in his thoughts—came out. "Well, daughter, just how are you doin' with all that's swirlin' round you these days?"

Her lips broke into a gentle smile. "Findin' out Jake's my very own?"

"Jah, that's what I'm meanin' to ask."

"Honestly, I'm as delighted as ever I've been. Jake's the grown baby son I thought I'd lost, and now he knows it. Jah,

I'm right fine with that." She stopped for a moment and then continued, saying she was hoping—"even prayin' "—she might have a chance to get to know him one day.

Abram nodded, unable to stop looking at her lovely face, so peaceful she seemed. They talked quietly of all that had transpired since her return as a widow, until Sadie's yawns became so frequent he took them as a signal that he, too, ought to call it a night. "Well, s'pose I'll be seein' you at the breakfast table, first thing tomorrow, ain't?"

She stood when he got up from his chair and followed him to the doorway. "Denki, Dat . . . talking with me 'bout this means a lot."

Abram wasn't too much on fussing with compliments or niceties—he left that for the women folk. "Good night, then," he said before taking leave of his eldest.

Making his way up the staircase in the main house, he headed toward the spacious room he shared with Lizzie. His wife was already propped up in bed with pillows, wearing her long cotton nightgown, hair brushed out and hanging gracefully past her shoulders.

He slipped on his pajamas quickly and hurried to her side, reaching for the covers and top quilt before bringing up the subject still on his mind. "I shouldn't be sayin' this to you, prob'ly, particularly not at night . . . before fallin' asleep 'n' all."

She reached over and brushed his hair from his face. "What's on your mind, dear?"

"Seems we've got ourselves a grandson we didn't even know existed." He began to share with her the news of Jake Mast's true identity, telling all he understood about the situation.

"Ach, Abram . . ."

"Quite surprising, ain't it?"

"Oh, but how's our Sadie with all of this?"

"Chickens come home to roost, I daresay." He chuckled softly.

Lizzie nodded her head. "I of all people should know this. We're so blessed, *all* of us, with Leah's precious life. Seems the Good Lord can turn a sad and traumatic circumstance into something exceptionally beautiful, just as He promises. I don't see why it can't be the same for Sadie and Jake—over time, of course," she concluded.

"I would think they'd both want to get acquainted," Abram agreed.

"Hopefully, for Sadie's sake, they will." Lizzie squeezed his hand. "If she's anything like me, she'll be holdin' her breath for the day she and Jake can sit down together and talk. I pray, too, that Jake will forgive Dr. Schwartz for keepin' him from his rightful mother. Such a grievous thing."

Abram pondered his wife's tenderhearted words. "As the Scripture says, 'Judge not, and ye shall not be judged: condemn not, and ye shall not be condemned: forgive, and ye shall be forgiven. . . .'" Leaning over, he planted a lingering kiss on her cheek.

They talked for a while longer about what this revelation meant to them and to their family . . . and, eventually, all of the People. At last, too weary to continue, Abram put out the lantern and held Lizzie close till they both fell asleep.

Leah felt her heart in her throat as she waited at the end of the long lane for Jonas to arrive Saturday night. She purposely had come a bit early, knowing she might need time out here on the road to gather her wits before she saw him again. Except for after Preaching service, she had not been alone with him since his unexpected nighttime visit on behalf of poor, pining Jake.

Waiting in the cold, the darkness seemed to envelop her as she looked toward the vast woods, fixing her gaze on the amber blush of windows—Gid and Hannah's log house. The blackness of the forest seemed exceptionally menacing tonight, and she shivered, turning to face the road.

Oh, Jonas, please understand. . . .

She heard a horse and carriage coming and braced herself, tightly winding her woolen scarf around the collar of her long winter coat.

Jonas halted the horse after making a slight turn into the drive to the house, and he rushed to her side. "Hullo, Leah. An awful brisk evening, jah?"

"*Wie geht's,* Jonas," she replied. "Wouldn't surprise me if it snows."

He admitted to expecting the same. "The air hangs heavy, ain't?" He helped her into the carriage and walked around to hop in on the opposite side, offering her the heavy lap robe as soon as he sat down.

She was aware of its warmth, Jonas having covered himself with it as he'd driven here. "Denki," she said softly, struggling already with tears that threatened to spill.

She was thankful he did not immediately bring up the topic of Jake, although she felt terribly tense awaiting it. They made small talk for a while and then Jonas asked, "How's everyone at your house?"

"Oh, 'bout the same," she replied, pausing a moment before forging ahead. "Except for Sadie, who's on edge since . . . since . . ." She couldn't go on.

Jonas finished for her. "Since Jake discovered the truth 'bout who she is to him?"

She sighed, her hands clasped beneath the lap robe. "Jah," she said simply.

"Were you ever going to tell me?" he asked, his words gentle but probing. "Surely you've known longer than Jake."

" 'Tis as you say. Honestly . . . Sadie and I, we didn't think it through. When we found out last summer, we decided it should be kept quiet." She could scarcely go on.

"Seems unfair to Jake, considerin' his strong feelings for Lydiann."

She nodded. Her face felt numb, even frozen, not so much from the cold but from the pressure she endured within. "We didn't intend to cause him pain. Sadie wanted to get to know her son, but it was I who argued with her, wanting to spare your family all the pain they're goin' through now. In so doin', I hurt Sadie and everyone else."

Jonas fell silent for a time. When he spoke again, his voice was almost too low to hear. "You meant well. I can see that."

Leah felt like crying again. "But we should've told the truth right when we knew it was Sadie's son who was courtin' Lyddie," she said, adding, "I'm sure your parents and Jake must be havin' a terrible time."

"Terrible's one word for it," he said. "But sooner or later, if things had kept on, they likely would have suffered learnin' the truth. Placing Jake with them was Dr. Schwartz's doin', not yours."

"True . . . though, actually, Jake was sent to Ohio because of Sadie and me, because I confided in Gid what we knew 'bout Jake's courtin' Lydiann. Oh, Jonas, we were so terribly worried they might fall in love and want to marry."

They rode for a time without saying more, and finally, when they reached the edge of Gobbler's Knob, before the road wound down the long hill toward Grasshopper Level, Jonas pulled off, heading north a ways. This being a less-traveled road, she wondered if he might find a place to stop, but he didn't, and she was relieved.

Some time later, he turned to her. His eyes searched hers, and his slow and kind smile made her wonder, *Has he forgiven me?*

Lightly he covered her gloved hand with his own. "I have to say one more thing, love."

She held her breath, listening intently.

"If Jake hadn't been sent away to Ohio, I never would've had the chance to meet him, and you and I would still be separated by hundreds of miles."

Leah swallowed hard. "Oh, Jonas, I'm awful sorry I didn't tell you the night when ya came inquirin' about Jake and Lyddie. So many things were goin' through my mind." She stopped to catch her breath, longing to be in his arms once again.

"You mustn't blame yourself." Then, as if reading her mind, he reached for her, gathering her into his welcoming embrace. "We'll muddle through what's ahead, helpin' Jake all we can. We'll pray, too, for a healing 'tween our families, ain't?"

To this Leah agreed wholeheartedly, glad they'd had this frank talk after all.

Jonas veered the horse around and headed back to the Ebersol Cottage, while Leah continued to ponder.

Chapter Twenty-Three

Monday, December 9
Dear Diary,

Today I had to string up a line in the kitchen to dry the washing because of the sleet making down outside. Not sure how many days we'll have like this, seeing as how winter's arrived early in Gobbler's Knob.

The cold, wet weather draws our little family round the wood stove every night now. Gid reads from his big Bible and talks to the girls about Old Testament stories, taking time to read from the New Testament, as well—sometimes even reciting nearly a whole chapter from memory before sharing his thoughts on various verses. Ever so strange this is, but I've kept my lips closed. It's painfully clear that some of what Gid's been teaching us will contradict what happened yesterday, following the common meal after Preaching. That's when Zachariah and his wife came over to me and whispered that I've been chosen to receive the healing gift by the laying on of hands. I must either dismiss this and never say a word to my husband or accept it as God's will for me and keep mum.

I'm in something of a quandary, because I know Gid

would be mighty upset if I went ahead without his blessing. Still, I am tempted to follow through, with the hope he might someday come to see things the way I do . . . and the way his own father does. But though I long for the gift Zachariah Henner is eager to pass on to me, accepting it would be disobedient. Yet how will I ever overcome my depression without such power?

At least the wee one within me is active, kicking hard at times. I am greatly relieved to feel as strong in body as ever I did with both Ida Mae and Katie Ann. Come April, there will be another little Peachey in this house. I do hope it's a boy, and so does Mary Ruth. She said as much when she and Robert came with their own darling bundle for supper at our house recently. Gid was ever so good to allow my dear sister and me to go off by ourselves awhile to talk quietly, even if "the love of the Lord Jesus" was nearly all Mary Ruth wanted to chat about. All the same, I feel so happy to have Mary Ruth smack-dab in the middle of my home—and life—again.

Respectfully,
Hannah

No matter where he happened to be when the first snow of the season flew, Jonas was immediately called back to his boyhood, when he would watch the timid flecks' descent through the pallid sky from the wide windows of the milk house or barn. And as winds stirred the tops of trees—a sudden and steady squall out of the north—falling snow would soon become a flurry of white, making the view of his father's farmhouse murky.

This day and the heavy snow it brought reminded him of

some of the worst blizzards ever to hit Lancaster County. But when his youngest sister showed up at Eli's in Dat's open market wagon, he felt certain something more terrible than a snowstorm was threatening his family's orchard house.

"Come in from the cold!" He held open the back door as Mandie hurried inside.

"Ach, you best be returnin' home with me, Jonas . . . something's wrong with Mamma," she cried, her distress plain on her face. "She's up in bed, sobbin' her eyes out."

"Sit down and talk more slowly," he said, glad that, at least for the moment, Jake was out in the shed with Eli. "Take a deep breath and begin again."

She placed her hand on her chest. "'Tween you and me, Jonas, I heard Dat and Mamma quarreling somethin' awful early this morning . . . over Jake and, well . . . all of that."

"What happened?"

"Mamma was sayin' it was wicked to send a boy away they'd raised as their own, 'don't matter the circumstances.'" Mandie wiped a tear from her cheek. "But Dat said this is all 'bout trickery, and there's no getting round it. Jake simply doesn't belong to us, and what's more, he's one of Abram Ebersol's grandchildren . . . and that's that."

She stopped to dab her eyes with a handkerchief. "Mamma's beside herself missin' Jake, but Dat's standin' firm on his decision." She hiccupped twice. "I'm scared Mamma's gonna be sick over this . . . I fear she is already."

"What're ya sayin', Mandie?"

"She's got herself an awful cough and a fever, and I've heard tell of folk comin' down with a bad flu when, well . . ."

"I understand." He recalled his own emotional upheavals

following his loss of Leah years back. "Do ya want me to try talkin' to Dat, maybe?"

"No need for that now," she replied. "Dat left after breakfast . . . said he was goin' down to the Beilers' farm auction."

"Jah, I went for a time myself but don't recall seein' him there."

"Well, that's where he was headin' hours and hours ago."

He sat down next to Mandie on the kitchen bench.

"Oh, this is just horrid!" She was wailing now, and he put his arm around her shoulder.

"You mustn't take this on yourself, sister . . . ya just can't."

"But what can be done?" She raised her head and looked at him. "Dr. Schwartz's switchin' babies has touched each of us, and I don't see how we'll ever get over it."

"The Lord God sees this here mess from on high." He patted her arm and led her to the sink, where she flung cold water on her tear-streaked face. "I daresay we oughta be prayin', beseeching God for His mercy on us all," he said.

Mandie turned around and stared at him. "I want my twin brother back, is what I want. What can God do about that?" With this she headed for the front room and stood at the window for a while, still weeping.

Jonas refused to interfere with what he hoped was a silent prayer for Mamma, Dat, and Jake. He went to the utility room and pulled on his boots, pushing down his old black felt hat on his head. Soon he heard Mandie's footsteps coming his way. "I'll follow ya home," he said, "and I'll try to console Mamma . . . and help with milkin', too."

"Denki." She gave him a little smile and threw her woolen scarf around her neck.

Jonas didn't bother to take the time to tell either Jake or Eli where he was headed. "Let's get goin', then."

By suppertime temperatures had fallen at least fifteen degrees, and the cold seeped into Jonas's bones as he finished carrying the milk cans to the milk house. He, along with Mandie, had looked in on Mamma, who was still upstairs in bed, sound asleep, completely exhausted from having wept much too long, Jonas guessed. Mandie had placed a hand on Mamma's forehead and was convinced her fever, if she'd had one, was nearly gone.

Mandie made him a supper of corn chowder and corn bread, also setting out a variety of jams and his favorite apple butter, too. He was grateful to sit down at the large family table and warm up a bit before his ride back to Eli's. "I'm sure Dat will be home before it's too dark," he said.

"What if he doesn't return?" Her eyes began to glisten again.

"Dat isn't one to shirk his duty," Jonas offered. "I could go lookin' for him if you're worried."

"No, he'll come back when he, well . . . gets here."

Jonas frowned, studying her. "Has he done this before?"

With what seemed to be grave reluctance on her part, she nodded her head. "Dat's got himself a weakness for moonshine," she whispered. "It's caused Mamma her share of sadness. He started drinkin' after he sent Jake off to Ohio . . . once he learned another son was in love with an Ebersol girl. The news must've opened some old wounds."

Jonas had never known his father to have trouble with alcohol and found Mandie's point of view to be quite perceptive for her age. Then again, she had lived here in this house for all the years of his absence. Since his return home, he had occasionally suspected such of his father, but he'd hoped he was wrong.

"The hate Dat carries for the Ebersols has been eatin' away at him, I think. He gets miserable 'bout how he's treated Mamma's cousins; then he goes and drinks."

"Where, though? Where does he go?"

"Who's to know, but there *are* plenty-a male cousins who like to imbibe. Our bishop might not know this, but it's quite true."

He thought on this and realized where his father might possibly go to guzzle liquor—Dat's Amish doctor friend, Zachariah Henner. The man was some years younger but had a keenness for spirits, both whiskey and otherwise—Dat himself had told Jonas as much. Perhaps strong drink was the reason for the rumors that Zachariah was linked to white witchcraft, as some in the area referred to Henner's powwowing. "I'm sure Dat will be home, and soon," said Jonas.

Mandie thanked him repeatedly for helping with the milking and for sitting down to supper with her. "You don't know how much I appreciate it." She walked him to the back door and out to the horse and carriage.

"Will you be all right?" he asked. "Or do ya want me to stay till Dat returns?"

Mandie shook her head. "It's fine, really. But he'll be mean as ever. Mamma and I have learned to keep to ourselves till he sleeps the stupor away," she confided in a near whisper.

Jonas's heart ached to hear of the dark times his mother

and sister suffered. "I'll check on you and Mamma tomorrow at dawn."

Mandie's lower lip quivered. "Ach . . . Jonas. What on earth did we ever do before you moved home?"

"Now, let's not be thinkin' backward, jah?" He leaned down and kissed the top of her head. "Go be with Mamma. When she wakes up, tell her I love her."

She bobbed her head in agreement, and Jonas clumped out to his cold horse and now-white carriage through the ankle-deep snow, concern for his family bending him low.

Jonas found Eli in the kitchen with Jake, both men cleaning up the supper dishes in total silence. He was especially grateful for Eli's reading of God's Word as the three of them gathered near the wood stove afterward. When Eli closed the Bible and bowed for a silent prayer, Jonas prayed for his father, who was out somewhere in the bitter cold, possibly traveling home intoxicated. He also prayed for both Mamma and Mandie, so vulnerable there at home alone.

Later, when Jake had gone upstairs to bed, Jonas began reminiscing with Eli about a few mutual friends in Ohio, as well as his memories of joyous Sunday-go-to-meetings. "I admit to missin' the brethren in Apple Creek, too," he said. "And what a man of the Word our bishop was . . . studied it like he might kick the bucket tomorrow, he was that spiritually hungry."

Eli pulled on his wiry, thick beard. "Jah, I'd have to agree on that—missin' solid preaching, and all." He went on to relate one of the more lively discussions on Scripture he and several of the ministers had enjoyed, "not too long before I joined up with the group of men to be swapped with those from here."

"You must've been eager to marry again, deciding to do such a thing—leaving your home 'n' all."

"I'd hate to go through the rest of my life without a wife." Eli paused, squinting his eyes. "I miss Nancy Mae a whole lot, and if I can be so blunt, the nights can be awful long at times."

"What caused your wife's death?"

"Leukemia . . . it took her mighty fast, which was a blessing, really. She didn't suffer like some."

"This life can be full up with misery." Jonas reflected on the trial this good man had endured. "But it makes us mighty anxious for the next, ain't so?"

To this Eli nodded emphatically, and Jonas felt a growing fondness for the ruddy-faced widower. The woman who would become his new bride would be blessed indeed.

Chapter Twenty-Four

Saturday dawned with a stony sky and icy showers of rain mixed with snow. In spite of the dismal day, Lydiann volunteered to run an errand to Georgetown for Leah and Aunt Lizzie—anything to get out of the house and breathe the brisk morning air to clear her head. It had been nearly three weeks since her encounter with Jake at the singing, and she'd not heard from him since.

Just as well. No sensible reason to hang on to a love that was never meant to be. She was actually looking forward again to attending singings and seeing old friends and making new ones. More than ever before, she needed the social connection with other courting-age young people, and she recognized that she was beginning to slowly make a turn in her mind—and in her heart. Even though her soul felt void of hopefulness as far as romantic attachments were concerned, she knew she must go ahead somehow with her life. And stopping in to visit with cheery Mary Ruth and her pretty baby was one way to do so.

While they sat visiting in Mary Ruth's cozy house,

Lydiann laid eyes on the first real piece of evidence that her former school chum Carl Nolt *did* want to get to know her better. The proof came in the form of a handwritten invitation sent to Mary Ruth, who said she'd been wishing Lydiann might drop by to see her.

"He sent it here?" She found this curious and for a moment felt her cheeks warm with the knowledge. A quick scan of the short note left her secretly pleased—Carl was asking her to consider going with him to a church activity, a get-together on the Saturday evening following Christmas.

When Lydiann revealed to her sister what he'd written, Mary Ruth wore a fine smile. "Well, why don't you go? You might have the best time."

"Just why do ya think that, sister?"

"He's a wonderful boy, and the two of you used to have such a good friendship. One evening with him and his friends is nothing serious, mind you."

Sipping her warm tea sweetened with raw honey, Lydiann listened as Mary Ruth continued to sing Carl's praises, finding it a bit amusing. Still, if she were forthright with her sister, she would tell her not to hold her breath on this invitation. Lydiann would not be accepting, because she was not at all ready to forge a new relationship, old friends notwithstanding.

In the heart of the ancient town of Florence, Henry and Lorraine Schwartz had come across a picturesque restaurant with only a half dozen tables visible through its windows. The menu posted outside the door boasted of several courses of superb Italian dishes, pasta a staple with each meal.

"What do you say, dear? Shall we?" Henry asked, hoping his wife might agree, so appealing was the tiny place set back on the narrow, winding street tucked between rows of Gothic-style buildings.

"Why, it's just delightful." Lorraine was obviously pleased, and he was relieved.

They made their way inside, the smiling hostess ushering them to a table for two near an inviting fire. "*Buon appetito!*"

Enjoy the meal, the woman had just said, but Henry could not imagine it. Not unless he changed his mind and did not reveal his long-held secret to his wife as planned. Despite their charming surroundings, at the present he was feeling rather wretched, knowing their vacation was drawing to a possibly disastrous close.

Wine bottles of every conceivable vintage and from every region perched on shelves above a narrow mirror encircling the room just above the chair rail. His gaze caught the reflected glints of candlelight from each table, like miniature echoes in the mirror. *Haunting reverberations of the past* . . .

After he had ordered for both his wife and himself, Henry sat straight as a board in his chair, eyes fixed on Lorraine. She looked particularly lovely in her favorite ruby red two-piece day dress as she sat smiling across the linen tablecloth. He inhaled deeply. "I've been wanting to tell you about Derek's illegitimate son for quite some time."

Lorraine frowned. "Beg your pardon?"

The plunge taken, he returned to the beginning of the story, recounting Leah Ebersol's frantic knocking at their door, followed by the delivery of their very own grandson—apparently stillborn. That is, until a miracle occurred. . . .

Lorraine listened quietly, her composure seemingly intact, even though the shock of his tale was registered in the seriousness of her expression. When he had finished, she leaned forward and, instead of censuring him as he thoroughly deserved, said, "I never forgot the sight of that forlorn Plain girl sitting out on the porch steps, waiting for Derek."

He nodded. Neither had he.

"Ah, Henry . . . you know, I always suspected Derek had an ulterior motive for enlisting in the army the minute he turned eighteen."

Woman's intuition, he thought. Evidently Lorraine had sensed something amiss on a subconscious level all this time. He said, "I'm sure you've seen Jake Mast coming with Fannie and his twin sister, Mandie, for annual checkups and such."

"Maybe so," she replied, still remarkably composed.

She inquired about his reason for giving baby Jake to the Masts instead of revealing the sad truth that their son was stillborn. He struggled to explain his thoughts that night, his panicked decisions, until finally she reached across the table and covered his hand with her own. "I wish you had confided in me. Perhaps between the two of us, we might have come up with a more satisfactory solution. One that might have had poor Sadie's blessing."

Again he nodded, ashamed by her calm reaction. Why *hadn't* he sought the advice of his sensible wife? Sadie could have been told the truth and spared much heartache, and she might have desired to raise her baby. Or perhaps a legal adoption could have been arranged, such as the one Henry had made on behalf of a young patient who'd also found herself in the family way around the same time. That baby had ultimately been placed with their close neighbors, Dan and Dottie Nolt.

"You crossed the line, Henry," she said softly, her gaze on their entwined fingers. With a look of sudden concern, she raised her eyes to meet his. "Might you be arrested for this?"

"It's a worry, yes," he admitted, sorry to have put his wife in such a dreadful position.

Lorraine squeezed his hand and glanced away, and when the waiter came around with the first course, Lorraine shrugged as if unwilling to continue further discussion.

Henry sighed. Though years too late, he had at last apprised his wife of the truth.

Even if she forgave him, he knew the worst remained ahead. He must live each day unaware of what the present, or the future, might hold. And if word of his offense reached the ears of the wrong people . . . *Or the right people*, he thought sorrowfully.

He shuddered, attempting to dismiss his fears. Having just toured the Cathedral of Santa Maria del Fiore and seen with his own eyes the awe-inspiring genius of Michelangelo, he would have much preferred to pretend the problems he'd created at home did not exist. There would be plenty of time to contemplate the disturbing prospects in Gobbler's Knob upon his return.

Jonas and Gid worked closely in the blacksmith shop, Jonas paying careful attention to Gid's patient instruction on shoeing a horse. He watched as Gid pulled each horse's leg up through his own and held it clamped between his knees. Jonas was fairly sure that if he could prove himself a reliable worker, he might be asked to continue his temporary employment here, because Tomato Joe was too busy with the work of farming and butchering to attend to all the steady blacksmithing help his father-in-law required.

Jonas kept the bellows going steadily, all the while observing even the smallest details of the trade as, one by one, the horses came through. As he did, he wondered how things were at his father's house at this hour. When he'd returned to visit with Mandie and Mamma earlier this morning, he had encountered his father, whose bloodshot eyes and overall rumpled appearance confirmed Mandie's suspicions. Jonas did not ask where Dat had disappeared to the day before, but Mandie whispered that he had indeed stumbled into the house awful late, quite *gsoffe*—drunk—at that.

His drinking surely feeds his animosity toward Abram, thought Jonas. On this he could only speculate, but the fact remained that Dat had a serious problem in his inability to forgive and accept Abram and his family, as well as in his obvious need to drown his troubles in alcohol.

I wish I could help somehow, Jonas thought, wondering, too, how long before his father might come to realize he *must* receive Jake back into the fold of his household. But if or when that might take place, Jonas had no way of knowing. After all, Dat's rift with Abram and his family had dragged on for nearly two decades.

The day was almost indistinct from all the others Sadie

had spent doing heavy cleaning for Dorcas—this time the family was preparing for out-of-town company from Berlin, Ohio. Cousins on Tomato Joe's mother's side were coming in by train on Monday; a Mennonite driver would meet them at the station. Since Dorcas hadn't been feeling well, Sadie had volunteered to help redd up, even going so far as to wash down walls and mopboards and cook ahead several meals.

Weary now, Sadie picked her way through the snow and ice on the shoulder of the main road, always on the watch for horses and sleighs or buggies, a number of which were certainly out this Saturday night before a no-church Sunday tomorrow.

She kept a steady pace, her thoughts on her son and what he might be dealing with. What she wouldn't give to hear his voice again, to see him! A nagging worry skittered through her mind, and she feared Jake might up and return to Ohio, never to be heard from again. If so, she would not have the chance to know him at all.

Several horse-drawn sleighs passed by, each carrying young courting couples. She tried not to let the pain of wishing show on her face . . . the *we* of them and the loneliness of herself. The trees ahead stood black and shadowy against the steadily falling snow as she plodded along, one heavy foot following the other.

She whispered to heaven, petitioning the Lord not so much for her own happiness as for Jake's. *Let him someday know not only my love but the acceptance of those who raised him, as well.* A lump rose in her throat and she found herself fighting back tears.

Just then, like a distant echo in the darkness, she heard a man call her name. "Sadie?"

She did not turn to look because she thought she might be daydreaming. Was this the memory of her precious son's voice? Was it her mind playing tricks, as it had so long ago?

"Is that you, Sadie?" This time the call came more urgently.

She turned to see a slow-moving enclosed buggy with two people inside.

Eli Yoder? She squinted to see through the snow. The driver was indeed the handsome widower.

"Hullo?" she returned, hoping her voice might carry to where he held the reins.

"Care for a ride?" Eli asked as the carriage all but stopped right where she stood, trembling with cold and with the awareness that not only was Eli offering her a ride when the Ebersol Cottage was not so far away, but Ella Jane Peachey was sitting there next to him, prim and proper.

What an odd thing for him to do, she thought, but she found herself accepting and saying, "Denki," before she thought over what on earth she truly ought to say.

Eli hopped down and came around to help her to the left side of the carriage, lending his hand. Her heart sped up as she placed her own gloved hand in his, suddenly very aware of his attentiveness to her.

Eli stood outside the buggy, waiting for her to get settled into the seat next to his date. He made a quiet comment about Sadie's remembering Ella Jane, and with that went back around to the right side to climb in and move them forward.

Sitting there, Sadie wondered why she'd said yes to the ride. But no, she knew all too well. She had hardly dared dream such a thing might happen, assuming she'd already had her share of male attention during her lifetime.

She found it painfully humorous that Eli should proffer a ride, no doubt prompting as much uneasiness on Ella Jane's part as excitement on hers. Yet Eli was obviously interested in spending the evening with Ella Jane. *Eli and Ella . . . won't the People get their tongues tied if they marry?* She smiled at her foolish thought, rejecting it just as quickly; she must be respectful, even in her private thoughts.

When Eli directed the horse to turn right onto her father's long lane, piled high with snow, she wondered what she ought to say when the carriage came to a halt. How far would Eli bid his horse to go?

"There we are, now," he said, bringing the mare right up to the shoveled walkway that led to the back door. He stepped down to come around and help her out, standing for a moment at the end of the walk as she managed to extend her thanks before turning to make her way toward the door.

All the while, her heart continued its euphoric new rhythm, and she wondered what Ella Jane must be thinking . . . or feeling.

Chapter Twenty-five

Tuesday, December 17, saw the return of Henry and Lorraine from their ten-day excursion. Tired from their long flights, they unpacked and ate supper, scarcely speaking a word to each other. Both retired to bed before twilight, relatively disoriented from having traveled through several time zones.

Henry was unable to immediately fall asleep, however, again recalling the calm nature of his wife's reaction to the news of Derek's son. Henry had been completely astounded when he realized she was not at all condemning or taken aback by the revelation. *Lorraine's so much more than I imagined her to be.*

Nodding off at last, he gave in to a fitful slumber. His dreams had him lost in a cornfield maze, the distorted stalks taking on the shape of Amishmen who whispered accusations as he attempted to find his way out. With no exit in sight, Henry fell and landed on the ground, his hands pressing deep into a freshly dug grave.

Sadie wasted not a speck of time worrying how Ella Jane Peachey might feel if she knew Eli Yoder had sent the letter Sadie was reading this minute. *He wants to see me again . . . alone!*

Though she was torn on whether to share the exciting news with Leah, Sadie felt it best not to respond too quickly to Eli's invitation. For her own sake, he must not think of her as overly hasty in replying, but rather she would take several days before she wrote a polite answer. This meant the earliest she would be riding with him again would be the Saturday after Christmas, a day that now felt an eternity away. *All in God's timing,* she told herself, most joyful at this unexpected turn of events.

Ascending to her bedroom, she removed her head covering and each of the hairpins holding her bun to let down her hair, so long she could sit on it. *Am I still pretty enough to be courted?* She began to brush her hair, counting the strokes as she and Leah often had as youngsters.

When she finished, she sat on the bed and purposed in her heart not to get her hopes too high about Eli, although she knew she already was in danger of exactly that.

Breathing a prayer for guidance, she rose and went to the dresser. The small hand mirror lay on top, and she reached for it, holding it up to her face. "I will not let pride get in the way of God's will," she whispered to her reflection. "I will follow Leah's path . . . askin' for the blessing of the Lord."

No matter what happens. . . .

That Wednesday Lydiann made five loaves of bread—

including two for Dorcas Zook and her family, and one for Hannah's—never once uttering a word to Mamma Leah all morning, although she truly wanted to. She longed to tell Mamma of her visit with Mary Ruth and of feeling a twinge of enthusiasm for Carl's invitation, even though she'd declined it. But an impenetrable wall prevented her from saying what was on her heart, as if her disappointment and aggravation at not having been told sooner of Jake's connection to Sadie kept her from saying anything now.

All that aside, Lydiann busied herself in her work, recalling how delighted she'd felt while little Ruthie lay in her arms, aware of the stirrings within her heart toward her beautiful niece. It was then the terrible truth struck her that Jake Mast was as directly related to her as was darling Ruthie.

Shuddering, she was more than relieved Jake had not contacted her again. Glad, too, that he must be settling into his own awareness of their kinship . . . and realizing there were many other girls to pick from at singings and other social gatherings.

She glanced up and caught Mamma's eye. The right words skipped through her mind, but she remained mute, simply unable to make herself say them.

"I love ya, Lyddie," Mamma said, eyes bright now with tears.

Nodding helplessly, she felt more and more ridiculous as she stood there, silently gawking.

"I best be sayin' this again, dear one. I was wrong not to tell ya right away, and I'm terribly sorry."

The dam broke inside, and a sob caught in Lydiann's throat as she flung her forgiving arms around her. "Oh, Mamma. I never should've treated you so."

Jonas was grateful for the hope of steady work at smithy Peachey's blacksmithing shop, especially as Christmas was fast approaching and he had not decided what to give Leah. Having never fulfilled his promise to her of an oak sideboard for a wedding gift, he decided on that, knowing he could easily pay his weekly room and board to Eli, as well as purchase the necessary wood and stain to make Leah's keepsake. But before he took the time to gather up the materials to create the piece, he must seek out the Grasshopper Level bishop, Simon Lapp, to inform Dat's bishop about his family's potentially dangerous home situation.

The minute he completed his work for the day, he headed straightaway to the older gentleman's abode. Halting the horse in the side lane, he was surprised to see Bishop Lapp emerge from the house. "Ach, ya must come in, and quickly, Jonas. Get yourself out of this cold," the man said, greeting him. The stocky bishop apparently remembered seeing him following Jonas's return from Ohio, and Jonas was thankful to have grown up under this highly respected man's leadership.

"I won't beat round the bush," Jonas said quietly once the bishop had shooed his wife out of the kitchen. "I'm here about my father." Warming his hands by the fire, he continued on to tell about his father's recent drunken late-night return home.

The bishop acknowledged his awareness of the standoff between the Mast and Ebersol families, but he didn't indicate he knew of Dat's hankering for strong drink.

"I don't want to speak out of turn, but I'm concerned."

Jonas explained some of what Mandie had observed, as well as testifying to having seen with his own eyes his father's obvious hangover. "It may be that liquor has made my father do things he might never have thought of doin' if sober, or maybe his rage and unacceptance has caused him to dull his sensibilities in drink. One way or the other, he has a problem. Actually, *all* of us do, because of it."

Bishop Lapp tugged his long, untrimmed beard. "If he drinks as much as you assume he does, I wouldn't be surprised if there's something he's tryin' to forget." He paused. "Now, Abram Ebersol, he's kin to your father, ain't so?"

"Actually, it's my mother who's the blood relation . . . to Ida, Abram's deceased wife. Abram has since married Ida's younger sister, Lizzie Brenneman."

"Ah, Lizzie . . . the name rings a bell." The bishop's ears seemed to perk up. "There was a-plenty of tittle-tattle flyin' round about this Lizzie years back, but Bishop Bontrager and I squelched it right quick . . . with some help from Abram and Ida."

Jonas knew precisely what he meant: Lizzie's pregnancy with Leah. "Well, I'm wonderin' what can be done to bring peace to the families."

"Hard to say." The bishop fell silent, folding his hands as if in prayer. Then he continued. "I'm reluctant to say this, but I've heard comments from your father that he believes one of Abram's daughters is . . . well, something of a bad seed."

Bishop Lapp was thinking of Leah, of course, because of Lizzie's sin. "He has no right to say such a thing, but, jah, I know what he thinks," Jonas replied, his neck hot. "Truth is, Leah is just the opposite of that. She's everything gut, and I hope my father might know this someday."

"Someday meaning you plan to marry the woman?" No doubt Bishop Lapp had been adequately filled in by Dat.

"I'm more than happy to say that, jah, I am." Jonas eyed him a bit suspiciously. The thought had crossed his mind on several occasions, but now that he was faced with the opportunity to pose the question, he pressed on. "Would you also happen to know anything 'bout the Proving I'm under?"

Bishop Lapp appeared grim. "Well, sadly, I believe I do. Maybe I oughtn't admit it, but there were quite a few heads put together on that. Your bishop and your father—"

"My *father*, you say?" Jonas interrupted, startled. His parents were not even members of the Gobbler's Knob church district, which he'd chosen to join as a teenager preparing to marry Leah. That his father should confer with Bishop Bontrager made not one whit of sense.

"Might be best to leave things be, then."

"Keep me in the dark, you mean?" Jonas felt terribly bold. "Please, I must know more. It's important—has been for years. The hard feelings between my father and Abram have gone on too long . . . and now the problem's even thornier." He didn't feel as if he should blurt out the news about Jake, but he'd obviously gotten the bishop's attention, for the man leaned forward now, frowning, his blue eyes intent on him.

"If you must know . . . it was your father who went to Bishop Bontrager nearly the minute after you presented yourself that first day you returned home. He was the one who put the idea of a lengthy, if not nearly endless Proving in Bontrager's mind, hoping to break your will to marry as you wished by takin' away your ability to work with wood. Naturally, that fell right into Bontrager's way of thinkin'. And now with the church membership having voted to give their approval, I'm afraid you'll have to bide your time."

Jonas was aghast. "My *father's* behind much of this?"

"You asked, and I told ya . . . a mistake, I can see now."

"But I wish to make Leah my bride next fall, which is one of the reasons why I want to see things set right between our families."

"Your father thought he could thwart your marryin' her. If you break under the demands of your Proving, you'll never be reinstated as a member and thus be unable to marry in your church district . . . separated forever from this woman." The bishop sighed loudly and shook his head. "With both your father and Bontrager in cahoots . . . well, it's a shame for you. That's what." He eyed Jonas. "Oughtn't to be this way."

Jonas understood fully for the first time what he was up against—the stern Gobbler's Knob bishop had found a like mind in Jonas's own conniving father.

Frustrated by what he had learned, Jonas attempted to put his feelings aside for the time being, as there was something else he wished to discuss with the sincere man. Putting his hands in his pockets, he pondered how he should say it. "Things being as they are, I wonder if it wouldn't help my sister and mother if you paid frequent visits to Dat . . . maybe beginning as soon as you can ride over there." As he saw it, the only clear way to prevent his father's habitual imbibing was to keep him far away from the drink that looked like water but kicked like a mule.

The bishop gave his word he'd go and see what could be done.

Jonas thanked him and hurried back to his waiting horse and carriage. The animal had more than a dusting of snow

Chapter Twenty-Six

Immediately following breakfast on Friday, once the children were sent off to school in Gid's big sleigh and the kitchen was spotless, Hannah sat quietly to write in her diary. She began by recording the weather, but try as she might, she simply could not keep her mind on it, so she headed back into the kitchen to bake a two-layer spice cake and several dozen chocolate-chip cookies.

That done, she felt lonely yet again and went to the bedroom window to peer down the hill at the Ebersol Cottage. Was Gid off working with Dat today, or perhaps Tomato Joe and Jonas Mast? She'd heard from her husband that Jonas was spending lots of time lately at the smithy's shop, helping out for pay.

If Gid's occupied for now, I'll go and visit the Henners, she decided then and there. Not daring to give it a second thought, lest she change her mind out of respect for her husband, she hurried to find her warmest coat, snow boots, and knitted mittens. She hoped she could borrow her father's enclosed buggy for the trip, having noticed from afar the covering his mane and back. "Let's get goin'." He reached for the reins.

As he rode over the deserted, snow-packed roads, he was aware of increasing tension in his neck and jaw. *Dat and Bishop Bontrager have joined forces to keep Leah and me apart?*

He could scarcely get past Simon Lapp's words. His own father had gone behind his back, suggesting such a difficult Proving—one tailor-made to trip him up but good.

Abe was the first one downstairs for breakfast, and Leah greeted him with a delighted smile. "Happy Christmas Day!"

"To you, too, Mamma!" He surprised her by kissing her cheek. "I smell waffles."

"Jah, and not just any waffles—chocolate waffles served with hot syrup or whipped cream, take your pick."

"That's easy. I'll have both." He went and sat right down at the table.

" 'Let patience have her perfect work.' " Leah smiled.

"You're the most patient person I know." Abe picked up his fork and knife and clunked them on the table. "I ain't even half as long-suffering, Mamma. I've been waitin' all night for a taste of your Christmas waffles."

How could she deny such a wonderful boy? "All right, then. Get yourself over here." She motioned him over.

"Really, Mamma? You're goin' to tempt me, ain't so?"

She removed a freshly made waffle and placed it on the large serving platter. "Count to five slowly and pull off a piece. Tell me if there's too much chocolate or not."

The twinkle in his eye surely reflected hers. "Aw, you can *never* have too much chocolate!"

"All right, then. Go 'n' call your father and Aunt Lizzie . . . and Lyddie, too. I'm ready for our Christmas breakfast."

She watched him dash to the stairs, thinking all the while what a wonderful-good day this would be. But it was knowing she would see her beloved beau in a few hours that made Leah's heart beat faster.

Leah held her breath as Jonas's buggy fairly flew up the lane. *He's here!* She hurried down the steps and tried to contain her exuberance, but it couldn't be helped.

"Come in, son," Dat said in his big voice, greeting Jonas at the back door. "Leah's in the front room."

That was all she could make out as Aunt Lizzie also offered soft words of welcome. Soon Jonas was coming through the doorway and into the large room, not nearly as toasty warm as the kitchen, but more private at least.

He rushed to her, giving her a squeeze. "Blessed Christmas to you, love."

"Happy Christmas, Jonas."

He comically pulled her away from the view of anyone who might be peering into the doorway, grinning at her as he reached for her hands. "I've missed you something terrible. And I have a surprise for you, but you'll have to ride with me somewhere to see it."

"Oh? Where to?"

"You must wait 'n' see."

"All right." She nodded, but she could scarcely wait, feeling as thrilled as a young girl.

"Should I give you a hint?" he teased.

"I thought you said I had to wait. What's this guessin' game?"

"I love you to pieces, that's what."

Her heart pounded with his nearness. "We best go 'n' see what pies are left, jah?"

A flicker of disappointment came and went on his face,

but she knew he would enjoy one of the tasty pies she, Aunt Lizzie, and Sadie had busied themselves making. Pecan, apple mincemeat, pumpkin, lemon sponge, and chocolate cream all awaited, so she took him by the hand and led the way to the kitchen.

They spent time visiting with the rest of the family, some of whom sat at the table for second and third helpings of dessert, not minding at all sampling the many sweets.

Sometime later, when afternoon milking rolled around, Dat, Abe, and Lydiann excused themselves, and Jonas mentioned he and Leah were "goin' for a quick ride." Leah rose and kissed Aunt Lizzie and Sadie on the cheek before rushing to find her warmest wraps, cheerfully following her beloved out the back door.

On the ride to Eli's place, Jonas recounted for Leah the day he'd gone to visit the bishop. Leah's heart went out to him as he described the hazardous search and the ultimately terrible discovery. He shook his head as though reliving the ordeal.

"A car struck him . . . that's what you think?" Leah was horrified.

"Well, there's no way to check that—no skid marks, not with all the snow." He reached around her. "But it's Christmas, my dearest, so let's not talk of this anymore. I'm sorry."

"'Tis all right. Poor man . . . it was his time." She believed in the sovereignty of the Lord. What came to bear on a person's life was simply the will of the Almighty One.

They rode along, Leah sitting smack-dab next to Jonas, surrounded by the crisp late afternoon air and the serenity of snowy white.

Jonas pointed out some deer tracks along the roadside. "They must know 'tis hunting season."

"The clatter of gunshot must frighten them," Leah said, wondering if Jonas, who was not a hunter, was aware of the old shack where local men, particularly the English, went for shelter or to reload their rifles and fill their stomachs with food and drink. It had been a long time since she'd roamed the woods high above the Ebersol Cottage, and even longer since her last visit to the old shanty, where she'd heard the surprising tale of her beginnings from Aunt Lizzie, who'd happened upon her there. But she did not utter a word about the place just now—not on the Lord's birthday.

"My father and brothers had been planning to go huntin'," Jonas said out of the blue. "But I doubt they will now."

"Leah, there's something on my mind, but I hesitate to bring it up." Her interest piqued, she waited for him to go on. "It seems Jake has an idea . . . and I'm only sayin' this on his behalf."

"Oh?"

"He'd like to visit with Sadie sometime. What do you think of that?"

The words inched into Leah's mind, but she didn't have to think too hard, knowing her sister as she did . . . and the cry of her heart. "Honestly? I say it's a perfectly wonderful idea. When should it be?"

"Well, you might think this too sudden, but Jake was hopin' it might happen yet today, bein' it's Christmas and all."

"Tonight?" She could scarcely believe her ears.

Jonas nodded. "You and I could bring Jake back with us, if you think it wise, and you could go and see how Sadie feels 'bout it."

She almost laughed but squelched it. "Oh my, Jonas. Let me tell ya . . . there's no need to be askin' Sadie anything beforehand. I know what she'd say." She sighed. What an amazing turn of events. "There's not a single doubt in my mind." She became so excited she could hardly sit still.

"I wanted to do the right thing, you know. Be mighty cautious."

She fully understood. "Thank you for being so considerate, but I'm sure nothing would please my sister more."

When they arrived at Eli's, Jonas took her around the back to the shed, where, when he opened the door and lit the lantern, she gazed at a most beautiful furniture piece.

"This is for you, Leah." He slipped his arm around her.

"Oh . . . it's ever so perty!" She assumed it was an engagement gift, but he quickly told her it was for Christmas. To this she said, "Ach, are ya sure?"

He pulled her into his arms. "It's been the longest time since I promised it to you."

She leaned her head against his strong chest. "I don't think I've ever been so happy."

"Jah, I know that feelin', too, my dear."

She stepped back and went to explore the wood and sheen of the lovely sideboard, Jonas right by her side as she touched it and peered into its drawers. "You should be makin' furniture like this all the time, ya know." Instantly she realized what she'd said and wished to take back her remark, hoping against hope she had not been thoughtless.

"Maybe I will again someday." He reached for her hand. "I'm biding my time."

She leaned into his tender embrace. "Denki, Jonas . . . for the lovely present."

After she'd inspected every inch of the sideboard, Jonas asked if she wanted to go to the house to talk with Jake. She was a bit reluctant to leave behind her Christmas surprise, but quite eager to see Jake, as well. To think of Sadie spending time with her son on this most blessed day made Leah feel ever so joyful.

What will dear Sadie say when she sees her son?

Chapter Twenty-Nine

Just when Sadie was thinking she might feel a bit lonely tonight, she heard the back door spring open and became aware of Leah's voice. She also heard Jonas and assumed he was coming in to get warm before heading back into the cold.

Leah came running into the front room, her cheeks flushed and eyes wider than usual, and Sadie immediately wondered what was up. "Stay sittin' right there, Sadie . . . I have a surprise for you!" Then she turned and headed toward the kitchen.

In a few moments she was back in the front room again. "Sister, ya best close your eyes, all right?"

She would play along with Leah's game, whatever it was, but she felt nearly like a child doing so, what with Leah's goings-on. "I've got my eyes covered, you silly."

After a moment's wait she heard the sound of footsteps—and a young man's voice. "Hullo, Sadie . . . a happy Christmas to ya."

When she opened her eyes, there stood Jake, tall and

smiling. She could not speak, so astonished she was. "Oh goodness!" she sputtered.

"I've been wantin' to meet you." His brown eyes shone and he looked slightly embarrassed.

Leah and Jonas, who had been standing in the doorway, inched back, leaving her alone with her son. "Please sit with me," she said at last, her heart racing with absolute gladness.

"I hope I didn't startle you by comin' uninvited."

"Well, jah . . . you certainly did. But never a more welcomed fright!" She literally stared, taking in every aspect of his handsome face—eyes, brow, nose, cheeks, mouth, chin—until she realized he was just as curious about her, too. "Well, I guess it's not polite to stare, is it?"

They both laughed, and she blinked back tears, nearly overcome with emotion.

He looked at her fondly. "Ever since I heard 'bout you from Dr. Schwartz . . . well, my grandfather, I knew I had to see you again." He paused before continuing. "I wouldn't have known of you if it hadn't been for Lydiann."

"Most important is we're here now, Jake, sittin' and talking together, ain't so?" She opened her heart wide and began to tell him many of the things she had longed to say all this time. "Losing you the night you were born was out of my hands. I would've kept you, because I wanted you so desperately . . . to raise you and love you dearly, in spite of my unmarried state."

She felt the tears running down her cheeks. "I always felt in my heart you might be alive somehow. I truly did." She didn't refer to her recurring dreams in those first months of a baby's cries, but her remembrance of them caused her to weep.

"I didn't want to barge in on you tonight . . . but I'm

cause her to be put under the shun, as well, which would never do. And as close as she was to Lydiann and Abe, as well as her other sisters and father, it was unlikely Leah would ever consent to leave. He loved her too much to present such a maddening choice, so Jonas was keenly aware he was in something of a dilemma at the moment, and the knowledge left him miserable.

Gid commented on the blizzard as he moved toward the door. "An awful ugly day out."

"Best be careful goin' home."

Despite the nasty weather, Jonas made his way to the house to put on his heaviest coat and muffler as soon as Gid was gone. He went and hitched up Eli's sleigh to the only remaining horse, as both Eli and Jake were down the road, visiting friends in Eli's buggy. *No sense waiting for a sunny day to tell on myself*, he decided.

The road was snow-packed, with drifts on either side, and the white stuff was thick in the air as a fierce wind whipped it, making seeing nearly impossible twenty minutes or so into the trip. He had a mind to turn around, but another five minutes would get him to the Dawdi Haus where Bishop Bontrager and his elderly wife resided, next door to their married grandson Luke and his wife, Naomi, and family. Jonas recalled it had been Naomi who was Sadie's troublemaking sidekick back when they were both caught up in rumschpringe, though Naomi had obviously become a good and faithful church member over the years. And he knew from Leah that Sadie had gotten herself straightened out for the better, as well.

Pulling into the lane now, Jonas could hardly make out the Bontrager farmhouse till he got right up next to it. *I'll stay just long enough to tell about the sideboard and then hurry back to Eli's.*

Tying the horse to the hitching post, he clumped up the walkway that led to the smaller addition built onto the main house. Suddenly he felt unexpected anger well up in him as he realized how put out he was with Bishop Bontrager . . . not to mention his own father. To think the two had conspired against him!

If he didn't get ahold of himself and settle down, he might say some things he'd later regret. So he briefly hesitated at the back door, inhaling the frigid air several times before knocking firmly.

The bishop's wife answered, all bent over, leaning on her cane. "Oh, hullo, Jonas." Her eyes and nose were puffy and red. "Are ya here with bad news for this ol' woman?" She shook her head, tears welling. "Didja happen to find him?"

"Who?"

"Why, *der Mann* . . . he's gone missin' out in this terrible blizzard."

Jonas stepped inside as she motioned for him to do so. "I'm here to pay him a visit. I thought surely he would be at home."

She studied him; no doubt she'd overheard her husband speak not so fondly of him through the years. "He's been gone for hours out somewhere in this storm. But . . . there are others already lookin' for him." Hobbling over to the wood stove, she picked up the coffeepot. "Wouldn't ya like some hot coffee? Warm yourself a bit?"

"No, I best be goin', but denki!" He opened the door and waved his good-bye. "If the bishop is lost, I'll join the search."

Sadie was thankful for the tranquility of the Dawdi Haus, especially this snowy evening. Having completed all her chores, she curled up on a rug near the wood stove and read mighty glad I did," he said gently.

When Sadie had composed herself, she went on. "I believe you're much like I was at your age. Nothing stood in my way if I had my heart set on it." She reached for his hand. "Denki, ever so much, for takin' this brave, even awkward step. I can't tell you what it means to me."

"Thank *you* . . . for sharin' what you did."

"I am very happy." She said it with the utmost reverence.

"We daresn't wait so long to see each other again, jah?"

"Why, sure, as soon as you'd like."

He placed his free hand on hers. "Happiest Christmas, jah?"

"Oh my . . . the best ever, Jake. Truly."

He rose slowly, and she felt compelled to stand, as well, wishing she might hold him near, wanting to protect him from further pain, desiring only what was best for him, but she spared him more choked-up words and tears.

With a deep breath, she put on her brightest, most delighted smile, following him through the kitchen, where her family sat around the table playing quiet games, their heads politely bowed. She happened to notice Lydiann's head bob up quickly before going down again.

Poor, dear girl. She thought of the unfortunate short-lived courtship with Jake, thankful she'd heard recently from Leah that the worst of Lyddie's sadness was already past.

Soon both Sadie and Jake found Jonas and Leah in the utility room, holding hands and looking as happy as she'd ever seen them.

"Good night, Leah, and happy Christmas," Jonas said.

When it seemed appropriate, Sadie thanked Jonas—and Leah—for making it possible to meet with her son. She found it difficult to keep her eyes on anyone but Jake, hardly able to get her fill. "A most wonderful night!" she declared.

Leah came and stood near, and together they watched Jake and Jonas head outside, the two men turning to wave their good-byes yet again.

Seems like nothing short of a miracle, thought Sadie, her heart brimming with joy.

Cozy in her log home, Hannah sipped hot cocoa as she watched the girls play with their new games. Gid sat nearby in the front room, close to the fireplace. Such a fine day they'd all enjoyed together, having made the short trek across barren fields to Gid's parents' to partake of the Christmas feast with Tomato Joe and Dorcas and their children, as well. A later visit to the Ebersol Cottage in the early afternoon had treated them to more pie and cookies. A busy sort of Christmas Day, yet Hannah would not have traded their comings and goings for anything.

Out of the blue, Gid spoke of the bishop's death and how there would most likely be an ordination for a new bishop come spring. "We'll draw from the older, more established preachers from both the Georgetown district and here."

"Who'll oversee us in the meantime?" she asked.

"The Grasshopper Level bishop is the nearest, so I'm sure it will be Simon Lapp—a most compassionate man, I must say."

"You won't be considered for bishop, then?" Hannah said.

"People would look on me as too young, which is quite all right by me."

She was glad to hear this, because when the ministerial lot fell on a man, it was a most solemn thing. To back away he did not utter another word; the look in his eyes made plain his utter disdain.

"What are you talking about?" Henry shot back. "Abram is as innocent as you were. And as ignorant of Sadie's pregnancy as you were to Jake and Lydiann Ebersol's courtship."

Peter deliberately turned and walked to the bar, apparently snubbing him. Henry stayed seated, reflecting on their blunt conversation. Peter was clearly a wounded and angry man, and when Henry saw him returning with a shot glass of whiskey, he decided he cared for not an ounce more of either Peter's company or strong drink.

Getting up from the table, Henry left without offering even a good-night.

News of Derek's death swept through the village from the west end to the eastern side of Gobbler's Knob. Friends and neighbors of the family and schoolmates of Derek who remembered him from before he enlisted called the Schwartzes or sent their condolences in the form of flowers, cards, and hot dishes. Even the Ebersols sent a sympathy card, signed by Leah on behalf of the family, and both Leah and Sadie dropped by for a short visit with a large fruit basket, not saying much more than how sorry they were.

On the day of the family viewing, Robert and Mary Ruth accompanied Henry and Lorraine to the Strasburg funeral home, along with, at Henry's personal invitation, Jake Mast. Now, as Henry stood in the portal to the visitation room, his eyes focused on the open, flag-draped coffin. His breath caught in his throat and his chest felt as if it might cave in.

Struggling, he made an attempt to compose himself lest his grief overtake him. He looked at Lorraine, slumped in one of the formal-looking wingback chairs, with Mary Ruth hovering near. Yet before he could make his way to her, Robert motioned to him. His son was standing next to Jake, whose usually ruddy complexion was now as pale as a white sheet, and the two spoke quietly to each other.

Henry went to them, and the three moved slowly to stand before the casket together. Henry's throat closed at the sight of Derek's face. *How much older he looks*, he thought, recalling the youthful days before Derek's enlistment.

Jake stood silently, hands folded. "I daresay I didn't expect to meet him . . . like this," he said, his voice cracking.

Robert put his hand on Jake's shoulder. "None of us could have imagined it." He gave a slight smile. "Your being here today is a gift to our family."

"I wish I might've known Derek . . . somehow or other." Then, clearly shaken, Jake stepped away, going to sit by Lorraine.

Henry followed him. "I want you to know . . . your natural father was a fun-loving young man."

Robert pulled out a folded handkerchief from the inside pocket of his suit coat, coming to Jake's side again. "My brother had a real spirit of adventure, too. You would've enjoyed that."

Henry suddenly realized they were attempting to offer thoughtful comments—even going overboard somewhat—largely for Jake's benefit. He felt sorry the boy had been placed in such an awkward position, attending a viewing for a father he'd never known. Making the best of it, Henry encouraged

Jake to go with him to the small alcove, where a guest book lay open on a marble podium.

Henry picked up the plumed pen and handed it to Jake. "Why don't you sign your name first?"

After Jake did so, Henry scrawled his and Lorraine's names on the line beneath. *Dr. and Mrs. Henry Schwartz.* His hand shook slightly as he returned the pen to its holder.

His heart sank as he watched Robert and Mary Ruth encircle Lorraine, who was crying softly. *Dear Lorraine.* She had taken the startling news about Jake in her stride. But now, here in this hushed, floral-laden place, she had completely lost her composure over Derek.

He felt torn between wanting to comfort his beloved wife and a sense of duty to remain with Jake. Henry was, after all, responsible for bringing the boy here—a day to say hello and good-bye in a single, overwhelming breath.

Sadie needed time to think, but she didn't want either Leah or Aunt Lizzie to know what was bothering her. She paced in front of her bedroom window, wondering why she felt numb when she thought of Derek Schwartz's death. *He was my first love. Shouldn't I feel sad?*

She recalled the unspeakable grief she'd suffered when Harvey had died, how she'd fallen into a deep pit of despair but concealed it as best she could.

Not so now. With Derek she felt only the sadness one might when hearing of a stranger's death. In all truth, it had seemed as if Derek had already been dead to her for years on end, his abandonment had been so complete.

And now he *was* dead, never to reconcile the loose ends of his life here at home, or to know his son, which, as she pondered it, might be better for Jake. At the same time, though, Derek would never have the opportunity to make amends with her—nor his parents, whom he had continually rejected, according to Leah, who'd on several occasions lent a sympathetic ear to a dismayed Lorraine.

No, Derek's time to make peace has simply run out.

Chapter Thirty-Two

All of Gobbler's Knob experienced winter's brazen settling in, and there wasn't anything anyone could do to stop it. Often from January through early March, the dark and distant hills would be shrouded in banks of haze nearly every dawn. The People would endure frigid temperatures and howling winds, warming themselves by drinking hot apple cider and cocoa, or black coffee, the brew of choice, and taking comfort in cobblers, apple dumplings and crisps, and the ever-popular creamed, chipped beef served at church gatherings.

Leah would long, as she did every winter, for the fairest season of all. This year the spring thaw would precede the solemn period of fasting and prayer as baptized church members examined their lives and motives in hopes of finding blessed unity. Then, and only then, would the spirit be right for the ordination of another bishop. Everyone knew that disharmony and friction during these days would mean postponing an ordination. Only once it was determined the People of Gobbler's Knob were in one accord could they "make a bishop," according to the qualifications of their Ordnung.

It was well into February when Lydiann confided in Leah about having attended "several Mennonite Bible studies." Despite the source, Leah felt she could hardly discourage her girl from learning more about God's Word. After all, Mary Ruth's unique experience had changed her life for the better, just as faith had altered the lives of Mamma and Aunt Lizzie and, eventually, Dat. And by the number of quilting bees Lydiann was taking part in with Mary Ruth lately, Leah believed Lydiann had found additional comfort in spending time with her older sister, as well as baby Ruthie. A blessing, indeed.

The month of March brought various sales and property auctions for retiring farmers, and Smitty Peachey let it be known officially that he was turning over his blacksmithing work to both Gid and Jonas. Leah was reasonably pleased for her husband-to-be, although she held to her secret hope that Jonas might one day be allowed to return to woodworking. For now, however, the work of a smithy in a well-established shop seemed both rewarding and financially smart for a man about to take a bride.

Leah wasn't the only one of Abram's daughters with matrimony on her mind. Sadie, too, had whispered recently of Eli Yoder's keen interest in her. "I wonder if he might just ask me to marry him," she said to Leah, her face glowing as they worked together in the kitchen.

Leah pinched the rim of dough on a pie plate. "What'll you say if the time comes?"

Sadie put her head down, speechless now, her cheeks blushing, and her uncharacteristic reaction spoke volumes.

Leah leaned her head against her sister's. "I'm ever so happy for you . . . for both of us, really." She thought of how things had begun to settle down in their lives—for the most part, just since the bishop's death, sadly enough. At present Jonas was looking for a house to rent or buy, though both knew they would not marry till the wedding season began . . . still nearly eight months away. The demanding work of plowing, planting, and harvesting prevented anyone from enjoying the privilege of an all-day celebration until November.

"What would you think if I moved to Ohio . . . if Eli and I were to marry?" Sadie asked unexpectedly.

"Goodness' sakes, I didn't think I was goin' to lose you again." Leah sighed, not wanting to think about the dismal notion. "Does Eli want to return home?"

"His family expects him to go back to them with a bride. Honestly, it was the only way he would consider comin' here in the first place."

Leah didn't want to overreact, but she was already starting to feel glum. "Is there no other way—I mean, if you were to accept Eli's proposal?"

"Ach, we haven't gotten that far. It's just a feelin' I have that he might propose . . . but I could be wrong."

"Well, I hope you're not," Leah said, meaning it. "Time for you to have some ongoing happiness."

Sadie laughed. "Look who's talkin'!"

Leah smiled back. "Oh, Sadie, I've always been happy . . . just in a different way, I 'spect. Serving my family has brought me the greatest joy, even in the midst of difficult times."

"You ain't tellin' me anything there," Sadie said. "I've seen ya pourin' out your life, and it's been lonely and nearly exhausting for ya even during the best of times. Because of that, I've been askin' our Lord to return some of the selfsame kindness back to you."

"Ya must quit prayin' for blessings when the greatest reward is simply doin' for others."

Sadie shrugged. "Still, can't I ask God to give you and Jonas a whole houseful of children? That'd be wonderful-gut, ain't so?"

Opening the oven door, Leah checked on her pies. "First things first. Let's just pray Jonas will be voted in as a church member once again."

"Surely he will."

"You'd think so after all he's sacrificed to follow the Proving."

The sisters fell into a companionable silence until Sadie left the room for the Dawdi Haus, saying she wanted to finish her monthly letter to her former sister-in-law in Indiana.

Leah turned her attention to setting the table, thoughts of cooking and baking for Jonas filling her head. *Thank you, dear Lord, for bringing us this far.*

Saturday, March 14

Dear Diary,

Tomorrow marks the day of the council meeting when the People will vote to reinstate Jonas or not—and the day we cast lots for a new bishop. Bishop Simon Lapp of the Grasshopper Level district will be on hand, of course, as he has been overseeing our church since the death of our former bishop. Such a difference there is between him and Bishop Bontrager!

Bishop Lapp is more open-minded, I'd have to say, and Gid has become interested in discussing his opinion on church matters with me. All in all, much has changed in my husband since he became Preacher, and I have come to respect his wishes, even on matters I never dreamt we'd see eye to eye on. Truly, there is no longer any desire in me for the powwowing gift. And I have dear Gid to thank . . . him and the way the hair on my neck stood up the last time I visited Henners.

With baby soon to arrive, I've been sewing some infant sleeping gowns here lately. They'll do fine for either a boy or a girl. Oh, how we all look forward to having a new little one in the house!

Respectfully,
Hannah

Years ago Henry had decided he much preferred the outdoors and the wide, open sanctuary of nature to the stuffy walls of a church edifice. But months had passed since he had last gone to look after the Mast baby's grave on a Sunday morning, and the snows had drifted high over the vacant meadow.

The more he considered it, the more he recognized that coming clean with Jake and Peter and Fannie Mast had appeased his conscience somewhat, although Henry still felt appallingly responsible for the boy's current displacement. He had even contacted his grandson to let him know that, if at any time he was in need of accommodations, he was always welcome to occupy Derek's former bedroom, the current guest room of the house.

He and Lorraine had been elated when, in January, Jake had accepted an invitation to supper. What a fine time they'd had together. In some surprising way, it was almost as if they had Derek himself back in the youthful form of his only child.

Robert and Mary Ruth, too, had opened their home to their nephew for the first time, with Henry and Lorraine looking on while Jake held his cousin Ruthie, his eyes wide with happiness as he had comically talked in Dutch to her. Little Ruthie had seen fit to coo back "in English," as Robert had joked.

But it was Lorraine's obvious affection for Jake that impressed Henry most of all when, one day, she'd revealed that she had included her grandson in her book of prayer requests. Her kindhearted reaction to Jake made Henry feel he was beginning to fall in love with her again, even at this late stage of their lives. So much so, in fact, that he had given in to her repeated invitations to attend church. It seemed everything pulled them closer these days, even their shared grief over Derek.

For these reasons, then, Henry planned to go with his wife this Easter Sunday, willingly accepting the confinement of a conventional house of worship.

I've actually come to anticipate it, he thought, knowing how pleased Lorraine would be . . . and was already.

Danny Stoltzfus, who ran the general store over near Ninepoints, was a jolly, stout fellow who'd never met a stranger. He called out his usual cheerful greeting when Eli held the door open for Sadie, its bell jingling to beat the band. They slipped inside to warm up some before indulging in a root beer from the large box of ice-cold soft drinks found in the corner of the store. "Hullo, Eli!" called Daniel, eyeing them both.

"How's business today?" Eli removed his black felt hat and pushed his hand through his hair.

"On the downturn, I'd say. Most everybody's home gettin' themselves ready for Preaching tomorrow."

"Jah . . . most." Eli turned to smile at Sadie.

She felt a thrill rush through her, all the way down to her toes. She followed him to a small table and sat down while he went to the deep icebox to retrieve their sodas.

"Been gettin' all your mail delivered these days?" Daniel asked Eli, coming around from the counter.

Sadie nearly laughed at Daniel's remark.

"Well, now, how would I know *that*?" Eli replied.

"S'pose you're right. How would ya know?" Now Daniel was the one giving it a chuckle.

Eli was grinning as he brought a frosty root beer to her, placing the opened bottle on the table in front of her. "There ya be." He sat across from her on the delicate matching chair, nearly too small for Sadie, let alone a husky man like him.

Daniel had the good sense to leave them be, turning to step behind the counter.

"How's he know you, Eli?" she whispered.

"Oh, I helped put up those shelves behind the counter," he said. "Long 'bout the third week after I arrived in Gobbler's Knob, I heard tell of Daniel's need, so I got myself down here and helped out."

She found this interesting. "And our former bishop didn't give you a tongue-lashin' for it?"

"I doubt he even heard." Eli smiled, setting down his root beer and curving his hand around it. "Figured I wasn't staying round here longer than to find me a wife and return to Ohio. Least, that's what I thought back then," he said, his voice softer.

"Oh?" She felt she might need to hold her breath.

"Now I'm lookin' to settle down in these parts . . . that is, if you'll have me for your husband, Sadie."

Surely he knows how I feel! But no, she best not make her response quite like that. "Will I have ya?" she repeated, scarcely able to keep a straight face when this was all she'd been hoping for.

"Jah, that's what I said, Missy Sadie."

She smiled her sweetest smile. "Well, jah, I think marryin' you'd be real fine and dandy." Then, right away, she said what she'd been pondering for some time. "Since Leah's never married, well . . . what would ya say if we wait till she and Jonas get hitched first?"

Eli's grin filled his whole face. "First of December, maybe?"

"Whenever you say." She nearly startled herself, sounding so compliant. But Sadie knew this man across from her with the most appealing twinkle in his eye was surely God's will for the rest of her life.

Chapter Thirty-Three

Leah felt as if the pony and cart were flying, not making contact at all with the reality of pavement. The church vote was in. They'd had their unanimous say: Jonas was now permitted to fellowship with the People—to participate in every respect as a full-fledged voting member.

The membership meeting following the Preaching service this Easter Sunday had been a true relief from the past six months, and Leah savored the vision of Jonas wearing a broad smile as he was given the hand of fellowship by the ministers.

The whole Ebersol family was overjoyed and had stayed behind for seconds on dessert at Deacon Stoltzfus's house, where Preaching had been held. Undoubtedly they would soon head home in the family buggy.

For the moment Leah needed some time alone. Time to think and talk to God, thanking Him for this most wondrous blessing. *Jonas and I can be married for sure*, she thought, urging the pony to full speed.

She wondered when to bring up with her father the subject of Abe and Lydiann and where they ought to live.

Should they join Jonas and Leah, or remain with Dat and Aunt Lizzie at home? With the rift between her and Lyddie fully healed, Leah certainly didn't want to appear to turn her back on either Lydiann or Abe, even though they were both well on their way to becoming young adults.

She delighted in her homeward thoughts, almost pinching herself at the remembrance of the People's vote for Jonas today.

Aware now of a team coming toward her, right down the middle of the road, Leah slowed the pony a bit.

What on earth?

She leaned forward, straining to see if the driver was at the reins, but she couldn't tell because the enclosed gray buggy was too far away. The horse looked to be galloping recklessly out of control, and the closer it came, the harder she tried to see if there was a driver inside. Or was this runaway horse pulling an empty carriage?

"Whoa!" She drew back on the reins of her pony. Once she'd come to a complete stop, she got out and swiftly tied him to a tree trunk right quick before going to stand in the road, waiting, hoping to flag down the horse.

Straightaway this time she saw the driver was slumped over in the front seat, his head bobbing as the carriage raced along. *He must be terribly ill . . . maybe unconscious.*

She knew she had to be extremely cautious and quick or she could easily get tangled up in the buggy wheels and be run over. Recently there had been an account in *The Budget* about a mishap where a church bench wagon had zigzagged down a hill. The driver had been thrown, and the wagon wheels had run him over, causing his death.

Yet with no one else to turn to, Leah must try her best to

bring the horse and carriage to a stop, lest the man inside be terribly hurt or even killed. *Dear Lord, help me!*

But as the animal approached, it did not slow at her command. She noticed one of the reins dangling loose, dragging on the road. *If I can just grab it,* she thought.

With desperate resolve, she lifted her skirt with one hand and stooped and snatched the rein off the road with the other.

"Ach!" she groaned, and was immediately snatched off her feet, losing her balance. She fell to the ground, clinging to the rein as she was dragged along, screaming out in pain.

"Whoa!" she called again and again, sobbing as she did, yet refusing to let go of the rein.

The horse, whose head was pulled hard to the left, began to slow, and then, as if by a miracle, came to an abrupt stop.

Thanks be to God, she prayed silently, thankful to be alive.

She lay whimpering in the road, catching her breath. Then, little by little, she cautiously inched up to stand and saw that her dress and apron were tattered and filthy. Instantly she was terribly aware of a sharp, shooting pain in her rib cage, and she held her side.

Hobbling up to the sweating and panting horse, she spoke softly to him, hoping to keep him still. Then she reached for the bridle and slowly led the animal off the road and tied him to a tree trunk. *I can't let this horse go wild again!*

Turning, she crept to the buggy and gingerly climbed inside to check on the man, who was clearly dazed and still limp in his seat. "You all right?" she asked.

He muttered something she couldn't make out, and as he raised his head, the glazed look in his eyes suggested he might be intoxicated. She gasped. "Why, you're Cousin . . . Peter Mast, aren't you?"

The man nodded slowly, trying to sit up straight now. "Jah, I'm Peter. Who might *you* be?"

What with the ongoing ill will between this man and her family, she didn't know whether she should say. But just when she gathered enough courage to do just that, Cousin Peter's eyelids drooped closed once again.

Surely he's drunk. She'd heard something of Peter's weakness for strong drink from Jonas, and a whiff of the man's breath confirmed her suspicions. Quickly she pinched her nose at the reeking odor.

Leah took another long look at Peter, who'd caused so much trouble for herself and her family, and knew there was only one place to take him. *Dat will know what to do*, she decided, taking charge of both reins while Peter leaned like a sack of potatoes toward the right side of the buggy.

She got down and untied the horse and then returned to the carriage. She slapped the reins against the horse's haunches and managed to get it turned around and headed back toward the Ebersol Cottage. All the while Leah prayed she might not pass out from the sharp pain in her throbbing left side.

It'll never do to have two of us fainted away as if dead—not with this horse!

Mary Ruth delighted in the fellowship around her and Robert's table as their guests lingered long after the Easter feast was finished. Along with Robert's parents, they had included Dan and Dottie Nolt and their jovial Carl. And although she would have loved to have her entire family there, as well, Mary Ruth understood how important the Amish Preaching service and common meal following was to

Dat and Leah and the family—especially on this most important day, when it was expected Jonas would be reinstated.

"The meal was absolutely delicious," Robert whispered to her. In her opinion, however, it was not so much the tenderness or the flavor of the roast leg of lamb and springtime vegetables that mattered, but the lively table discussion regarding today's sermon. To her amazement and delight, even her father-in-law, who in the past had shown no interest in Scripture or sermons, spoke up about the disciples' renewed zeal in spreading the Gospel following the death and resurrection of Christ.

But it was the profound comment made just now by her dear Robert that stood out most to her. "The power that brought Jesus Christ back from the grave is the same power that today can meet our every need—body, mind, and spirit."

Lorraine was nodding her head and smiling. "Yes, and I don't believe the Lord ever calls us to accomplish tasks greater than that very power."

Mary Ruth wanted to say something, but she held back, listening now as Carl spoke up. "I say it's our purpose as Christians to use God's strength to extend His love to others—to everyone we meet."

They talked awhile longer, Robert taking out his Bible to look up several verses as Mary Ruth poured more coffee for everyone.

At one point Dottie clasped her hands together, glancing around the room. "God is at work in so many hearts."

Mary Ruth knew exactly what she meant, and, later in the kitchen, she whispered as much to Dottie. "It excites me to see hungry souls being drawn to God's saving grace. To have my father-in-law at church . . . what a blessed Easter!"

If only there was some slight indication on Hannah's part of yearning toward the Lord, Mary Ruth thought. Still, it wasn't necessary for anyone but God to know the condition of her sister's spirit, for He alone was the discerner of heart and intention. Mary Ruth knew she must continually put her faith and trust in that.

By the time Leah arrived home with Peter and his horse and carriage, she could scarcely get out of the buggy for the pain. She inched her way out, very aware of the snoring gray-haired man slouched in the front seat.

Teetering up the walkway, she reached for the back door, pulling it open with all her might. Once she'd caught her breath, each one an agony, she called as loudly as she could. "Dat! Aunt Lizzie! Somebody help!"

Immediately Dat came running out. "What's a-matter, Leah?" But one glance at her and he was hollering for Lizzie. "Come right quick!" Then to Leah, he said, "Daughter, you're awful hurt!"

"I'll manage," she said, pointing toward the carriage. "There. Cousin Peter's out cold."

Dat rushed over to have a look-see.

By then Aunt Lizzie and Lydiann were outside, as well, looking worried sick. "Oh, honey-girl, you're all *skun* up . . . what happened to ya?" Aunt Lizzie asked.

"I tried to stop Cousin Peter's runaway horse. Wasn't so easy."

"Well, for goodness' sake!" Aunt Lizzie motioned wide-eyed Lydiann to support Leah's other side, and they helped her into the house before Lydiann ran to find Abe.

Meanwhile, Dat stayed in the carriage with Peter, trying

to get him to come to, no doubt. Leah could hear him talking rather loudly even from where she stood in the kitchen. Cautiously she eased herself down, settling onto the wood bench with some assistance.

She tried not to cry, but she just hurt so badly. "Someone needs to go 'n' get the pony and cart," she gasped. "Left 'em out on the road a bit east of here. The pony's tied to a tree."

"Ach, don't worry yourself," Aunt Lizzie chided, dabbing Leah's face with a cool rag and calling for Sadie, who was in the Dawdi Haus.

"What the world?" Sadie exclaimed, joining them in the kitchen. When she was told what had happened, she said, "We best be gettin' Leah off to Dr. Schwartz."

"No . . . no, I'll be all right," Leah whispered, but she wasn't so sure.

" 'Tis for your own gut," Sadie insisted.

About that time Dat came into the kitchen nearly carrying Peter, who remained in a stupor. "Here's a man in dire need of a warm bed and a good night's sleep," Dat grunted.

Sadie gawked at Peter and looked back at Leah. "Where'd ya find *him* like this, and on Easter Sunday yet?"

"Does seem just awful . . . what a thing to be doin' on such a blessed day!" Lizzie whispered.

Lydiann returned with Abe now, who soon was helping Dat to navigate Peter to the downstairs bedroom. In short order Leah heard them easing him onto Abe's bed, both shoes clunking to the floor, and she imagined Dat's frustration at having their drunk and bad-tempered cousin here in this peaceful haven of a house.

But when he returned to the kitchen, Dat appeared not at all angry but thanked Abe for a "strong set of arms" before sending him off to bring back the pony and cart.

"Maybe Abe should go 'n' let Fannie know Peter's stayin' the night here," suggested Aunt Lizzie.

Dat agreed. "Jah, Abe, do just that, but first get the pony and cart home and then take one of my drivin' horses and a regular carriage, since it's makin' down rain now. 'Course, maybe this means Fannie'll actually let you in."

An unspoken message passed between the two, and Leah thought Dat must be wondering if Fannie would agree to hear what Abe had to say about her husband's situation.

Abe went out the back door, and Dat said to Lizzie, "When Peter awakens in the mornin', I want Leah nearby." He went and sat beside Leah, touching her bruised face in several places. "It pains me to see ya like this."

"I'll be all right," she said.

Dat looked directly at Aunt Lizzie. "Our daughter's a brave one, she is." He sighed too loudly. "Riskin' her life to save the old man's . . ." He might well have said "the old scoundrel's," but there was no resentment in his voice. "You women look after Peter, here—see that he doesn't roll out of bed and hit his noggin."

More caringly, Dat said to Leah, "You and I are goin' to go 'n' see if anything's broken. There'll be no puttin' up a fuss."

With the stinging pain in her side growing ever worse, Leah went willingly.

"This here horse's gonna get himself a mighty gut workout tonight," Dat declared as he and Lizzie helped Leah into the Mast family buggy, its being already hitched up and ready to go.

"Be ever so careful, Abram," said Lizzie.

"I'll take care of her . . . and so will Dr. Schwartz," reassured Dat.

Aunt Lizzie waved as the horse turned at the top of the lane and headed back toward the road.

"I hope they won't fret over me," Leah said, trembling now.

"Well, sure they will." Dat glanced at her and adjusted his black hat. He grunted. "Just think. We get Jonas voted back in, and somethin' like this happens."

Leah held herself together around the ribs, unable to quiet her shaking. She fought to steady herself on the ride up the road to the clinic, already pained at the buggy's jostling. *Dear Lord, help me bear this in silence.*

Lizzie and Sadie sat with Lydiann near the wood stove, leaning an ear toward the downstairs bedroom, but all they heard was the sound of loud snoring. "He'll sleep it off and not know where he is, come mornin'," Lizzie said.

"It's kinda funny Peter Mast should awaken here, ain't so?" Lydiann squelched a giggle as she opened the family Bible. Since attending Mennonite meetings, she liked to read first in German and then in English.

"Well, Mamma should be smilin' above, don't ya think?" Sadie said.

"I should say so." Lizzie rose to pour herself another cup of hot coffee. "Care for more?"

Sadie shook her head. "I've had my fill."

They worried aloud over Leah—all brush-burned and scraped up—yet marveled how she had been spared dire injury and even death. "The Lord was with her, that's for sure," said Lizzie.

"Ain't that the truth," agreed Sadie, a tear in her eye.

After a time, they began to recount the Preaching service and the members' meeting in soft tones, careful not to mention anything that shouldn't be discussed before Lydiann, as she had not yet joined church. But Leah and Jonas were foremost on Lizzie's mind. "Our girl's gonna have herself a weddin', seems to me," she declared.

"'Bout time," Lydiann spoke up, eyes bright and a smile on her face.

"Too bad November's seven months away yet," Sadie said.

Lizzie nodded, wishing it weren't so. "But there's plenty of farm work to be done . . . sowing and reapin' come first round here. The time of celebration will arrive soon enough." She sighed, thinking ahead to the smile of sweet bliss on Leah's face as she stood next to her Jonas. "A mighty happy day for us all."

Sadie was nodding. "Happiest ever."

Would be even more so if the Masts gave us the time of day, thought Lizzie.

Chapter Thirty-Four

Frustrated to be stuck in the corner of the kitchen, away from the cookstove, Leah twiddled her thumbs while Sadie and Lizzie made breakfast. Dr. Schwartz's X-rays last evening had shown a fractured rib, and he'd ordered her to take it easy. Leah was trying her best to follow through on his advice, and she felt terribly confined at being wrapped securely around the middle. There was no way for her to help much with spring housecleaning now, either at home or the Schwartzes'.

Aunt Lizzie poured coffee and brought her a full cup with a heaping teaspoon of sugar and a few drops of rich cream already added. "Who can know what a day will bring, jah?"

"Jah, for sure," whispered Leah, breathing carefully, glad for the delicious coffee—something hot to sip on a rainy day.

Lizzie stood near. "I'm awful sorry you're hurt, honey-girl."

"Ach, I should be much better in six or seven weeks, Dr. Schwartz says."

"Till you're mended, I'll tend to all of your chores," Aunt Lizzie insisted.

"Oh, you mustn't fuss. I'll be bakin' and cleanin' in no time, you'll see."

"I say you let yourself heal first."

Leah smiled despite the painful spasms in her chest. Dear Aunt Lizzie, always looking out for everyone else. Just listening to the lull of Lizzie's gentle chatter made her relax some—that and the pills Dr. Schwartz had given, urging her not to wait until the pain crept up again before taking more.

She was thankful that other than the broken rib she had been merely bruised and scraped up on her arms, since, according to the doctor, there would be no scarring.

Aunt Lizzie kept glancing at her with pity.

"You're too worried 'bout me," Leah chided.

"Oh, now . . . I'll worry if I want to."

Just then, breaking the stillness, Dat rushed into the kitchen. "Peter's wakin' up," he announced in a hushed tone. "Come with me, daughter," he said to Leah, helping her up.

She did as she was told, slipping her arm through the crook of his as they made their way to Abe's bedroom.

They found Cousin Peter sitting up in bed, still fully dressed in wrinkled clothes, his hair standing on end.

"*Gude Mariye!*" Dat leaned over to offer a handshake.

Peter ignored Dat's good morning and his extended hand. He looked first at Leah and then at Dat. "What am I doin' *here?*" he growled.

Dat paused, inhaling slowly. "Sleepin' off your drunken stupor, looks like to me."

"In *your* house?" Peter's face turned red as he swung his long legs over the side of the bed.

"Ain't a single foe under this roof," Dat said calmly.

A flicker of recognition crossed Peter's eyes as he fixed his gaze on Leah and frowned. "You were in my carriage yesterday."

She nodded.

Dat spoke up. "Leah might've been a goner if she hadn't stopped your runaway horse. It was a true miracle of God she wasn't run over by the buggy wheels!" He went on to describe her fractured rib and many scrapes and bruises, embarrassing Leah no end. He surprised her even more by saying, "Here's your Good Samaritan, Peter." Dat motioned for her to come closer. "I'd have to say my Leah spared your hide."

The three of them stood looking at one another, but mostly Peter stared at Leah, which made her feel utterly uncomfortable. At last Dat motioned for her to leave, and she went gladly, wondering if her father's sharp words to Cousin Peter would help or hinder the long-standing feud between them. Time would surely tell.

She hobbled out to the kitchen and sat at the table to rest. She was both surprised and pleased to hear Jonas's voice as he entered the back door.

"Ach, be gentle with her," Aunt Lizzie warned him.

That didn't stop him from coming near, wet through though he was from the rain. Lightly he touched Leah's bruised face.

"You best be stayin' for breakfast if you want to hear all 'bout it," Aunt Lizzie said, carrying a second large platter of bacon and eggs to the table.

"Mandie told Jake and me late last night you were hurt. I prayed as soon as I heard."

"Everything happened so fast. And Dat took me off to the clinic right away." She mentioned his father was still here.

"He's talkin' to Dat now," Leah whispered as they went to sit together at the long table.

"Well, isn't *this* progress?" said Jonas, smiling. "They're talkin' to each other at least—all 'cause of what you did."

She shook her head. "Anybody would've tried."

Aunt Lizzie laughed. "I ain't exactly sure of that." She went back to tend to her pancakes. "Plenty of women folk wouldn't have taken on a wild horse *and* a drunk man."

"Oh, Aendi!" said Leah. "Ya mustn't go on so."

"We'll have to look after you better. Can't have my bride-to-be chasin' down stallions." Jonas grinned playfully.

She returned his smile, enjoying his company. "You're such a tease."

"You're just noticin'?"

Aunt Lizzie coughed slightly and looked their way. "You two best be takin' your lovey-dovey talk out to the barn."

"Jah, a gut idea"—Jonas eyed the serving dishes of piping hot food—"right after breakfast, maybe."

They discussed quietly between them what could be done to help his father. "I'm thinkin' Bishop Lapp isn't the *only* one who can befriend Dat," Jonas said. "In time your Dat might just be someone to come alongside him, too."

Leah agreed, listening as Jonas mentioned other men who might lead his father to lasting peace.

Just then Leah heard her father's voice, and then Peter's, too. "Well, what do ya know," she whispered. "Maybe their grudge *is* comin' to an end."

"I sure hope so," Jonas whispered.

Leah agreed. *What better thing to happen on Easter Monday?*

Jonas led the way in the pouring rain to Eli's, eager for his father to visit with Jake. Evidently Leah's risking her life for his had made a startling difference in his father. Jonas had seen it firsthand in the way his Dat had talked almost agreeably with Abram and Aunt Lizzie at the breakfast table not but an hour ago, even remaining at his place well after he'd finished eating.

Could it be he's softening toward the Ebersols?

When they arrived at the small farmhouse, Jonas rushed to the house for a raincoat for his father and then they hurried together through the puddles to the back door.

Inside the outer room, Jonas called into the kitchen, "Jake, you've got yourself a visitor."

Jake's eyes popped wide at the sight of Dat, and before he could speak, their father was already saying, "Hullo, son."

"Come in," Jake said, eyes alight. He pulled up a chair for Dat and then went to pour coffee, his movements belying an undoubted sudden case of nerves. "We fellas have to fend for ourselves . . . cookin' and whatnot. A jolting experience, to say the least." Quickly he offered both Jonas and Dat biscuits and some apple butter. "Eli baked these up this mornin'."

Jonas reached for one and took a single bite, eating it plain, keenly reminded of Eli's mediocre baking skills.

Jake volunteered to pour more coffee for Dat the moment he finished his first cup and encouraged him to have another biscuit.

"Mighty gut seein' you, Jake," said Dat, looking at his son for the longest time. Jonas nearly dropped his coffee cup, and his father shifted his weight in the chair, sighing. "It was foolish and wrong of me to send you away. I knew it then . . . know it now, too."

After receiving no response from Jake, who was obviously at a loss for words, Dat turned to Jonas. "I was out of order, talkin' the way I did to you . . . that day Dr. Schwartz came to the house."

Jake spoke up at last. "It takes some getting used to, seein' you here. That's all."

Dat's eyes watered and his expression was somber. He gazed at both of them as if he had lost them for too long and was bound and determined to get them back. "You'll be seein' a lot more of me, if you're willin'."

Jake frowned and plunked down at the head of the table, where Eli always sat. "If you're sayin' I'm welcome at home, I don't mean to be rilpsich—rude—but I don't think I can agree to it, unless . . ." Jake hesitated, glancing at Jonas.

"What is it?" Dat asked.

"Well, are you and Mamma agreeable to attendin' Jonas's wedding?" Jake's tone was respectful, but his face was painfully sincere.

Jonas felt the urge to give in to a chuckle but quickly squelched it. He was touched by Jake's obvious loyalty and wanted to help his brother along, eager to hear what his father might say, as well. He addressed Dat himself. "*Will* ya come and witness my marriage to Abram's Leah?"

Dat's eyes locked with his. "An Ebersol, ya say?"

"A peach of a girl." Jonas did not breathe.

A shroud of silence hung over the room as his father appeared to consider Jonas's request. Then, shaking his head, he replied, "No . . . I'd have to say a young woman who risks her life for an old man like this is not a piece of fruit so much as she is an angel in disguise." He rose unexpectedly. "Just say when and where, and the whole family will be there with our blessing."

Jonas went to shake his father's extended hand and bumped into Jake, who was headed like an arrow to its mark. Dat wrapped his burly arms around both of them before standing to offer the sort of genuine smile Jonas hadn't seen on his face since before he'd returned for good from Ohio. He couldn't help wondering what Bishop Lapp might think if he were observing this small reunion.

"Tell Mamma and Mandie I'll be home in time for supper," said Jake, walking Dat to the door.

Jonas took up the rear, deciding not to say a word just now about his plans to stay on here with Eli till Leah and he were married. What mattered now was that his little brother had been welcomed home and, seemingly, all was well.

Chapter Thirty-five

In the weeks that followed, Abram marveled at the loving care Jonas demonstrated toward Leah. Without fail he walked over from the blacksmith shop each day, carrying his brown lunch bag to sit next to her at the table, doting while he benefited from helpings of Lizzie's tasty fruit pies or chocolate cakes. Seeing Leah and Jonas cooing at each other like turtledoves made Abram's heart mighty glad.

Adah Peachey Ebersol stopped by to see Leah several times a week, as well, but it was Sadie who spent nearly every free moment with her sister, doing for her even when she protested. There were times when Abram saw them whispering like young girls, their heads close together, eyes bright with their newest secret.

Most surprising to Abram, though, were Peter Mast's visits. The man came over often, saying he was "on his way somewhere," but really—or so Abram thought—he was coming to see about Leah, concerned she was mending properly. Peter took each opportunity to apologize anew to Abram, declaring up and down he was *"es Schlimmscht vun Narre"*—the worst of fools.

Abram had insisted there was more than one *Glotzkopp* between them. He'd apologized more than once for having been deceitful enough nearly eighteen years ago to let Peter think Gid was courting Leah while she was engaged to Jonas. Both Abram and Peter agreed they had plenty of lost years to make up for, and it was Peter who said, " 'Tis a gut thing we didn't go to our graves shunnin' each other." Abram wholeheartedly agreed, mighty glad to have renewed the kinship.

Following Peter's overnight stay, Abram made the decision to help him get his drinking under control, hoping Peter might remain consistently sober for as long as it might take till he had the willpower on his own. Both Jonas and Jake were helping their father keep a good distance from strong drink, too—Jake especially, now that he was living at home again.

On this particular morning, however, when Peter dropped in to visit, both men got to talking. "What say you to having a reunion between our families, and right soon?" asked Peter.

Abram leaned on his shovel. "Sounds fine to me. Come to think of it, Lydiann and Abe have never met Fannie and most of your children."

"Likewise our Mandie and . . ." Peter paused for a second. "But would it be too uncomfortable for Jake and Lydiann, do ya think?"

"Oh, it's bound to be tickly, but it'll have to happen sometime. Anyway, Jake was over here for a short visit on Christmas Day . . . talked to Sadie for a while. Lydiann stayed put in the kitchen the whole time." Abram scratched his head, surprised at Peter's thoughtful consideration. "I'll have Leah see how Lyddie feels 'bout it." He didn't say he himself wished to spend some time getting acquainted with his only grandson. That day would come, he felt sure.

"All right, then." Peter headed for the barn door. "Talk to Lizzie, and I'll say something to Fannie."

"Well, I'll be seein' ya. Have a wunderbaar day!" he called, still getting used to *this* cousin's stopping by to chew the fat.

Lydiann caught up with Mamma Leah, who was walking very slowly back from the outhouse. "Sure's a nice day, ain't?"

"The weather's teasin' us, I think." Mamma smiled faintly. "Somethin' on your mind, dear?"

Lydiann looked warily at the sky. "Cousin Peter and Dat . . . they sure have been spendin' quite a lot of time together, visitin' and walking round the barn and such."

"Jah, the way it used to be."

She sighed. "It's right nice, them talkin' to each other again, but . . . to tell the truth, it's got me worried some."

"Why's that, Lyddie?"

"Well, with me havin' cared for Jake as my beau, it seems kind of awkward, them no longer being at odds." She felt she ought to come right out and say what she was thinking. "And since you're goin' to marry Jonas come fall, it just seems the families will be gettin' together more and more often."

Mamma stopped right there on the narrow path. "You don't have feelings for Jake yet, do ya?"

"Well, no, ain't that. . . ."

"I guess it's a gut thing we're havin' this chat, Lyddie, 'cause Dat tells me he and Peter want to have a get-together with both families on one of the no-church Sundays, comin' up fairly soon."

Lyddie nodded. "Makes sense. Abe and I don't know the Mast cousins." *Except for Jake and Mandie*, she thought.

She looked at the tender young grass shoots pushing through the soil and the bright blue of the springtime sky. "Will it still be strange, uh . . . when Jake's married someday, and I'm married to someone else? Will he and I sit across the table, remembering our first singing and ride together under the moon? Will we always see that in each other's eyes?"

Mamma was quiet for a moment. "You wouldn't want to start seein' someone else as long as you have those thoughts of Jake."

Even now Lyddie didn't see how she could erase the past.

"I daresay it'll take some time, but you and a *new* beau—if he can make you forget you cared so deeply for Jake—will build your own lovely memories together. And when those most precious thoughts and hopes and recollections fill up all the spaces in your mind, there will be scarcely any room for the ones you made before."

"Oh, that's dear of you!" Lyddie replied as they turned to walk toward the house. "I can't wait for all those things to come true . . . one day."

They headed into the house, and right away Lydiann smelled how clean the kitchen was, the walls and floor having been scrubbed down by Sadie. And something delicious was baking in the oven—probably one of Aunt Lizzie's favorite desserts, apple crispett.

"God's ways are higher than ours," Mamma Leah

whispered to her as they hung their shawls on the wooden pegs.

"That's for sure," she agreed.

Mamma kissed her on the forehead, and as she did, Lydiann noticed a tear. She was filled again with gratitude as she slipped off her shoes to help keep the floor shining clean.

Following the noon meal Leah was tickled to see her friend Adah arrive, and she welcomed her inside. "I'm all done in, so I have a gut excuse to sit and enjoy a cup of tea," Leah said.

Adah looked a bit tuckered out, as well, but her green eyes twinkled as she spoke. "Don't go to any trouble for me."

"Aw, tea's no bother." Leah carried two of her prettiest teacups and saucers to the table and sat down, waiting for the water to boil in the teakettle. "So nice of you to come by again."

They talked of how the weather had been cooperating with the farmers, and Adah said how busy her husband was sterilizing the tobacco beds and plowing the fields. "Sam and the boys will be plantin' potatoes here perty quick, ya know," Adah said. "They're actually a little behind."

Leah enjoyed the serene talk, listening as Adah spoke of the things to be done before she planted her vegetable garden.

When she had poured hot chamomile tea for both of them and offered honey to Adah, who preferred it to sugar, they settled down to visiting in earnest.

"So how *are* you doin'?" Adah asked with a mischievous look.

Chapter Thirty-Six

A full month had come and gone since the Ebersol and Mast family reunion, and Lizzie was anxious to plant the charity garden in the small plot of land offered by Abram. She, Sadie, Leah, and Lydiann all settled in for a long morning of work, laughing and talking as they planted lettuce, kohlrabi, Brussels sprouts, endive, eggplant, and carrots. Come July, they would be planting three hundred celery sets in another garden plot set aside for that vegetable, creamed celery being a traditional necessity for wedding feasts. At times Lizzie had to pinch herself to believe things were happening as they were for her darling girl. *Long time comin'*. . . .

Today, following noon dinner, she needed to run an errand over to Fishers' General Store for several bolts of fabric and sewing notions. She invited Leah to ride along, thinking it would be nice to have a mother-daughter chat.

When they were out on the road, a mile or so from the house, Lizzie said, "Whenever you want to sit down and talk 'bout who to assign to the work on your wedding day, we can start makin' our lists."

"I've begun doin' some of that already," Leah admitted.

"Knowin' you, I figured as much. There's goin' to be plenty to do, what with three hundred and fifty or more folk comin'."

"Uncle Jesse and Aunt Mary's children and grandchildren alone make for over sixty guests. And I want to invite all of Mamma's and your Brenneman side over in Hickory Hollow, too."

"Absolutely. Maybe we should plan for closer to four hundred guests. What do ya say?"

"Maybe so." Leah turned and looked at her. "Do ya think Uncle Noah and Aunt Becky will want to come?"

"Aw, I'm surprised you'd be askin', after all this time."

Leah nodded. "I'd like to invite them." She was silent for a while before adding, "And Jonas wants to send written invitations to several of his closest friends in Ohio, as well. Can you help me with that, too?"

Lizzie smiled, noticing the pure radiance on Leah's face. "Sadie might enjoy doin' some of the writing and addressing, too, since you both have a right nice hand."

"I 'spect she'll be thinkin' ahead to her own wedding here 'fore too long. She and Eli plan to wait till early December for that, though. Hannah says Gid thinks their waitin' till us first-timers are married is a very gut idea."

Lizzie laughed a little. "Well, then, it seems everyone knows everyone else's business, ain't so?" Of course, both girls' plans were quite different than those of the younger couples, who kept quiet about who they were even courting till the bishop published them two Sundays before the wedding day. Jonas and Leah, as well as Eli and Sadie, were certainly exceptions to the rule.

"Most of all, it's wonderful to know Peter and Fannie will be comin'. Jonas is 'specially glad."

"And havin' you as his bride-to-be makes him more than happy, I'd imagine." Lizzie leaned her shoulder against Leah, and they both laughed.

"My only challenge is choosing two single girls to be my wedding attendants," Leah said. "I truly wish Adah or Hannah or Sadie could be standin' up next to me, but, of course, that's impossible now." She was laughing again. "Everyone even close to my age has been long married."

"That's all right." Lizzie patted her hand. "You're havin' your special time just as our dear Lord planned it."

"Do you honestly believe God picks out husbands and matches them up with the right woman?"

"Well, now, I think I do, Leah."

Leah listened as Aunt Lizzie explained herself, saying she'd once read of a mother praying for the young man who would become her daughter's husband, even as the infant slept in her arms. "She asked the Lord to protect him and keep him till such time as the two would meet."

"That's the sweetest thing," Leah said.

At that Lizzie opened her heart in a most unexpected way. "You know, dear girl, since you're goin' to be a wife in the comin' months, I thought it might be the time to tell you . . . 'bout your natural father." She seemed hesitant, yet her words had a ring of determination. "I know there was a time when you felt it wasn't important to know, but how do you feel now?"

Watching her lovely hazel eyes, Leah knew deep love for the woman who'd birthed her under such dreadful circumstances. "Honestly . . . I *have* been wonderin' again here lately."

Lizzie's eyes glistened. "You're sure?"

"Jah, I'd like to know."

Slowly, quietly, Lizzie began to tell her the last piece in the story of a rumschpringe gone reckless—thankfully for Leah, skipping over many of the details. "It may be difficult to believe, but it was Henry Schwartz who was the spruced-up young man drivin' his fast automobile that New Year's Eve . . . the day I was bound to hitchhike my way to town."

"What?" Leah could scarcely believe her ears. "Our doctor?"

Lizzie bowed her head. "Sad, but true."

"Never would I have thought this. . . . Oh, Aunt Lizzie."

They sat without speaking for the longest time before Lizzie continued, "I s'pose he doesn't suspect who *you* are, neither."

The truth slowly trickled into Leah's brain. "Then he doesn't know about me at all?"

Lizzie shook her head, tears threatening to spill. "He never knew I birthed you. Didn't even know who I was, or that I was Amish . . . I looked far different back then." She reminded Leah of how she'd cut her hair and donned English clothes, turning her back on her Plain upbringing. "Rebellious as can be, I was."

Rebellious.

The word stung like a nettle, and Leah suddenly wondered about poor Lorraine. "What was Dr. Schwartz thinkin', for pity's sake? At the time he had to have been married with young sons, for sure!"

Lizzie put her hand over her heart. "'Tis so. I'm awful

sorry to say, but later that night, when he was beginning to sober up, he had the urge to confess to me that he'd been separated from his family for over a year. Lorraine and the boys had gone home to live with her parents while he finished his studies to become a doctor. He told me it was a trying time for them, but that was all I knew. Bein' from Hickory Hollow, I had no idea I'd ever see him again." Lizzie stopped to catch her breath. "When I found out I was in the family way, well, I was just stunned. And I wouldn't have known where to find him, even if I'd wanted to. I felt just awful, in every which way you can imagine." She added that it was then she'd felt compelled to make things right with God and the church.

Leah's heart broke anew for Lizzie—and for the man who was her natural father. "Seems like Dr. Schwartz made things even worse for himself with his doings. But . . . as you say, he has no idea I'm his daughter." She couldn't help wondering if Lorraine had been aware of the extent of her husband's betrayal. *She seems like the kind of woman who might love a man in spite of himself.*

Leah wondered if the doctor's immoral tendencies had been passed along to Derry, the boy who'd gotten Sadie in trouble—the boy who had been, in fact, Leah's own half brother. The realization was startling.

Lizzie let the reins fall onto her lap. "What I've just shared should be for your ears only, Leah. Dr. Schwartz need never know."

Wholeheartedly Leah agreed. "Nothing gut can come of tellin', for sure and for certain. But I won't be keepin' any secrets from Jonas. I'll tell him once he becomes my husband."

"You're wise in that, I should say, provided he keeps it under his hat."

"No question 'bout it, Jonas can be trusted."

Moments later Leah realized she had another half brother in Robert. And, come to think of it, she was both cousin *and* aunt to Jake, and the same for baby Ruthie. Strange as it seemed, she was even more closely related on the Schwartz side than the Ebersol!

Her mind in a whirl now as she pondered the many connections, she said more to herself than to Lizzie, "I s'pose it might be best for me not to think too hard 'bout all this."

Lizzie seemed to understand. "Why don't you give this to the Lord, just as I've had to."

"Oh, I'll be talkin' to God 'bout this, all right." She would also set her heart to pray even more often for Dr. Schwartz and Lorraine in the coming days. Recently the couple had actually talked of doing some volunteer work overseas, possibly getting involved with a mission organization—and this after the doctor had appeared to nearly give up on life. *God can work such miracles*, she thought.

Happy to be able to say it, she told Lizzie, "Mary Ruth says Dr. Schwartz has been attendin' church with his wife every Sunday since Easter."

"Well, that's glorious news." Lizzie clapped her hands. "Praise be!"

They rode along in the buggy, smiling into each other's faces, soaking up all the love their hearts could hold.

With admiration, Leah reached to pat Aunt Lizzie's hand, thinking of the many honorable and godly traits her natural mother daily demonstrated.

have overheard, because her face burst into a jubilant smile. Lizzie knew exactly how she felt.

Abram mentioned he'd never used the shanty, it having been built by Englishers years ago. "But that doesn't mean there oughtn't to be a place for shelter from the elements come huntin' season," he said, and Abe agreed.

Her husband had a point, and there was time between now and deer hunting season to get other hunters interested in pitching in money for lumber and whatnot. Just a few menfolk could easily construct a replacement in a single day.

Lizzie went about her cooking chores, well aware of Sadie's zipped lip—and, bless her heart, if she didn't wear a grin clean past supper and on into eventide, when Abram read from the old Bible to all of them.

Listening intently to the Word of Life, Lizzie pressed the stubby splinter of wood deep in her pocket—a somber reminder that only the dear Lord could see . . . and understand.

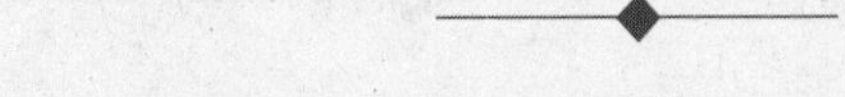

Mid-September brought a distinct coolness to the night air, and Abram much preferred such temperatures for sleeping. Since a boy, he had eagerly anticipated the coming of autumn, and with Leah's coming marriage, this year was no exception.

Lizzie cut a piece of carrot cake for both Jonas and Leah while Abram cheerfully told of his plan. "I'd like my new son and his bride to live here in this house, once you're wed," he told them.

Leah's smile widened and Jonas reached out a hand to shake Abram's. "You have no idea how grateful Leah and I are 'bout this. Denki, Abram . . . thank you!"

"Jah," Leah said, eyes bright with tears, "we appreciate this so much, Dat . . . and Lizzie."

Abram inhaled and felt good all over. "With Lizzie and me settled into the Dawdi Haus, Abe and Lydiann can come and go 'tween it and the main house as they please," he suggested.

Leah looked at Jonas, nodding her head. "This answers the question I've been ponderin' for some time now."

Jonas slipped his arm around her. "You'll be keepin' your word to your mamma and then some, jah?"

Abram went on to say there were a number of bedrooms to choose from, as far as Lydiann and Abe were concerned. By this he was letting Leah know she didn't have to fret about his children's welfare. Abe could continue to sleep in the first-floor bedroom in this house, and Lydiann could sleep upstairs next door in the second bedroom. "There's plenty of room for everyone . . . includin' any little ones to come, the Lord willin'."

Leah spoke up. "Sadie may want to stay in one of the Dawdi Haus bedrooms till she's married, which would mean Lyddie could have my old room upstairs for a while."

Abram didn't need to pretend surprise about Sadie and Eli Yoder, for the news was common knowledge among the family . . . and the grapevine. "Jah, my eldest daughters will both be happily hitched before year's end." He looked kindly at Lizzie, who'd just planted herself down next to him at the table.

"The Lord's been gut to us all," she said, eyes smiling.

"And for that we give Him all the glory and praise." Abram would have reached over and clasped Lizzie's hand but for the young lovebirds present.

Later, he thought, anxious to hold his Lizzie near.

Chapter Thirty-Eight

By the time late October rolled around, there were radiant hues of reds, oranges, and gold in every direction and things were shaping up nicely for Leah's wedding.

A week before, Lizzie, Sadie, Leah, and Lydiann, along with a half-dozen other women, washed down all the upstairs bedroom walls and the hallway, too, scrubbing woodwork and windows in preparation for painting, as each room in the house would be put to good use during the daylong festivities.

Meanwhile, the menfolk were building a temporary enclosure for the front porch, to provide additional space.

Toward the end of the hectic afternoon, Lizzie sought out Leah and found her in the kitchen of the Dawdi Haus, where she and Sadie were catching their breath, having some hot tea and strawberry jam on toast. "Oh, I hope I'm not interruptin'," she said, standing back from the table.

"Not at all, Aunt Lizzie . . . please, come join us." Leah rose to pull out a chair.

"Well, denki, but I came to show you some hope-chest items I've put aside." Not to exclude Sadie, she added quickly,

"I have keepsakes for your sister, too . . . when the time comes."

To this Sadie smiled, waving Leah on. "I'll warm up your tea when you return."

Lizzie led the way back to the main house and up the steps to the bedroom she shared with Abram—for now. Opening the long chest at the foot of the bed, Lizzie removed several quilts. "I want you to have these," she said, presenting first a purple, red, and green diamond-in-the-square quilt and then two others, both the sixteen-patch pattern. "My mother and her mother—your great-grandmammi—made these when she was eighteen . . . for her own wedding."

"Oh, Lizzie, they're beautiful!" Leah ran her fingers down the wide binding that served to identify the quilt's Lancaster County origin.

"You won't see that width in other places round the state . . . nor in the Midwest," Lizzie reminded her.

Leah was obviously pleased and gave her a quick hug. "Mammi Brenneman was a new quilter when she made these?"

"No, she started much earlier . . . at fourteen, I believe."

"Well, I'll take good care of them." There was absolute delight on Leah's face.

"Maybe one day you'll hand them down to your own daughter."

Leah squeezed her hand. "Denki ever so much." Then she paused, studying her for a quiet moment. "You were always Aunt Lizzie to my sisters and me," she said, "and I've never called you Mamma . . . but I'd like to start. Today—from now on."

Her joy spilling from her lips, Lizzie whispered, "Oh, Leah . . . my dear, dear girl."

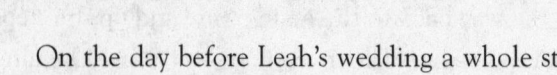

On the day before Leah's wedding a whole string of helpers, like so many sparrows, worked steadily to remove the wall partitions between the front room, downstairs bedroom, and kitchen, before unloading the bench wagon and setting up the seating.

By midmorning Jonas had already wrung the necks of a good three-dozen chickens, aided by Abe in the chopping off of heads. Aunt Lizzie, Sadie, and Lydiann plucked and cleaned the fowl and baked them for the roast, which was similar to stuffing but with finely chopped pieces of chicken mixed in. It would be served as the main dish at tomorrow's wedding feast.

The creaking of the windmill had long since replaced the pleasant song of birds and raspy crickets, and the ladybugs and other insects were nestled deep in their underground hideaways. The recent snow flurries had resulted in no accumulation, making travel to the Ebersol Cottage tomorrow easier for the People. And for this Leah was thankful.

Immediately following the noon meal, at Aunt Lizzie's urging, Leah and Sadie set out for a walk to the high meadow behind the barn, in the grassland, away from the buzz of wedding preparations. One last sisterly walk before Leah became Jonas's bride.

Arm in arm, Leah matched Sadie's lengthy strides. "I can't tell ya how glad I am that Eli's stayin' put in Gobbler's Knob," she said.

Leah assumed she wanted to talk about the prospects for a wedding. "You're askin' when I'm gonna be Jonas's bride, ain't?"

Adah's face reddened slightly at her admission. "Oh, I'm so happy for ya, Leah! Can it be that you two will be husband and wife after all?"

"Well, the Lord willin' and the creek don't rise," Leah joked, going on to say that she and Jonas had already decided they'd like theirs to be one of the first weddings of the season.

"When's the date?" Adah rose to look at the calendar on the back of the cellar steps.

"November third."

With her finger, Adah found the month and day. Her eyes sparkled as she turned and came back to the table, wearing the biggest smile as she sat down. "What a wonderful-gut day that'll be." Adah frowned suddenly. "Seems there's a goings-on amongst Englishers that day, isn't there?"

Leah nodded. "When I told Mary Ruth the date, she said she and Robert would have to get out and vote for America's next president right quick after the weddin' feast."

"Jah, I heard there's a man from Arizona who's runnin' against President Johnson. My Mennonite cousin keeps sayin' we need this Goldwater for president, since he's very conservative, but I daresay we should let the English fret over all of that."

"Prob'ly so." Leah raised her teacup and thought back over all the happy years she'd had with her best friend, Adah, and here they were, talking at last of Leah and Jonas's wedding, months away though it was.

Adah stirred more honey into her tea and sighed. She eyed Leah. "You're still young enough to have babies."

Leah had contemplated that very notion, especially lately. Being she would turn thirty-four in October, she could still hope to birth several children before the change crept up on her. "If I'm anything like the Brenneman women, surely I will, but who's to know, really."

"Your dearest dream, jah?"

Leah agreed. "Jonas and I will trust the Lord for our family."

Adah nodded, and Leah felt warmed by the sweet and knowing look on her dearest friend's face.

Abram was jubilant over his and Peter's plan for a family reunion on this, the third Sunday in April. Peter, Fannie, and as many of their family as could make it had come for dinner, which meant all but two of the married Mast daughters—Katie and Martha—had come from Grasshopper Level for the feast on this no-church day.

Abram supervised as Gid and Abe, and Jonas and his brother Eli set up two long extra tables in the kitchen, as well as a medium-sized one in the room next to the front room for the children. Lizzie, Sadie, Lydiann, and Mary Ruth had done most all of the cooking, with Leah pitching in as much as she could, even though she was still moving a bit cautiously.

Abram and Peter stood outside talking and watching the dogs romp back and forth over the yard while Peter puffed on his pipe. "Seems Fannie's taken right up with Lizzie, and vice versa," Peter was saying.

"Oh jah, the women folk have no trouble pickin' up

where they left off." Abram could hear the chatter coming from the house; the happy sound of kinfolk was downright pleasing to his ears.

"And it looks like Jake and Lydiann hardly even notice each other. A gut sign." Abram had taken note of this the moment the Mast family arrived.

"Jah, I have a feelin' he might be lookin' for a new girl . . . heard he's goin' to singings again." Peter drew on his pipe for a moment, a faraway look in his eye, as if he had something else on his mind. "Say, I've been thinkin' . . . wouldn't ya like to meet Jake officially? I mean, as your grandson?"

"Why, sure. When's a gut time?"

Before Abram could stop him, Peter hurried to the house, returning in less than a minute with Jake following him.

"Hullo," Jake said warmly, extending his hand.

Abram nodded, firmly gripping the lad's hand. "*Willkumm*, Jake. Mighty nice to meet ya."

Jake ran his thumbs up and down his suspenders, glancing first at Peter and then at Abram. "Seems I've got me two families now. Not a bad spot to be in."

Peter grinned and placed his hand on Jake's shoulder. "That you have. Two of everything, I daresay."

"Best of all is us comin' back together on a day like this, ain't?" Jake said, smiling at both men.

Abram agreed, aware of a growing sense of satisfaction as he looked at his handsome and mannerly grandson. "Can't think of anything better!"

It was much later, in the midst of pie serving and coffee

pouring, when Hannah leaned over and whispered to Lizzie at the table, the usual roses in Hannah's cheeks fading. As if he sensed something, Gid immediately got up from the table, helping Hannah do the same. "We best be heading home right quick."

Lizzie told Abe to ride to summon the midwife, and Gid agreed. "No hex doctor."

Sadie rose to assist Hannah out the back door, followed by Lizzie and Gid, who told his girls to "stay put with Dawdi Abram." The girls seemed glad for a chance to enjoy their newfound cousins and indulge in more dessert.

About the time Abe was getting ready to head out for afternoon milking, word came back from the log house that yet another baby girl Peachey had made her entrance into the world.

Abram was relieved to learn Hannah had not insisted on a hex doctor for this baby. It was becoming apparent Gid was having his way on that issue. A *mighty good thing for them all*, he felt.

"We named her Ada, without an *h*," Gid told them.

Leah spoke up. "Named after your sister?"

Gid nodded and chuckled a bit. "I s'pose if we keep on havin' girls, *both* my sisters' names and all of Hannah's will end up in our family Bible."

Abram took the comment humorously, even though he caught the slightest hint of disappointment, which flickered . . . then faded, on Gid's face.

Jake certainly hadn't been staring, or at least he didn't think so. Still, he could not ignore the way Abram gestured as he spoke even now with a measure of tenderness about Gid and Hannah's newest baby girl up yonder. Jake had been fascinated to meet the ruddy-faced man his father had despised for Jake's entire lifetime—his own grandfather.

This day the blood association brought with it a tangible sense of happiness, especially because Jake wanted to believe that his existence—and the acknowledgment of his identity—was in some way responsible for bringing the two families together. And for this, he was glad to have borne the pain of rejection.

A peculiar way to mend fences, he thought as he helped his older brother Eli carry the extra tables from the kitchen to a storage shed behind the henhouse.

Returning to the yard, he saw Mandie and Lydiann walking on the mule road a short distance away, talking and laughing. His eye caught Lydiann's, but he felt only the slightest pull of discontent—more regret than anything. No getting around it, she was the prettiest girl he'd ever known, which was in her favor. Any young man would take a shine to her, and as long as she wore that winning smile, she need never worry about being a maidel. He hoped for her sake that she would find a beau who would treat her with the love and kindness he observed in Jonas's interactions with Leah.

Continuing on, he saw Sadie waving to him from the well, and he hurried to her to insist on pumping the water for her glass, moved again by her sweetness and obvious fondness for him.

"There's a volleyball game 'bout to start," she said, her blue eyes shining.

He could hear the voices drifting from the other side of the house and nodded, tipping his straw hat. "You gonna come play, too?" he asked.

"I'll catch up in a bit."

He found Jonas and Abe setting up a net amidst a group of eager players on the narrow stretch of yard along the lane. When asked to join in the game of boys against girls, Jake removed his straw hat and hung it on a low branch, aware of Dat and Abram leaning against the tree's trunk, still deep in conversation, Abram's expressive hands moving like slow waves in a wheat field as he talked.

Jake forced his attention back to the players, amazed afresh at the sight of his newly extended family enjoying one another's company here on Ebersol soil, as if the partition of years had fully collapsed.

It was toward the latter part of August, and Hannah had tucked four-month-old baby Ada into her crib for a morning nap. The weeks since this wee one's birth had seemed nearly endless to Hannah, and she needed to get out of the house for a bit. Since the older girls were already back in school, she'd asked Gid if, on his way to the blacksmith's shop, he could see whether either Leah or Lizzie could watch Ada for a couple of hours this morning.

It wasn't long before Leah came with her needlework, wearing a bright smile. "Go out for a mornin' ride, Hannah, and don't worry 'bout a thing. I'll take care of Ada as if she were my own," she said, nearly shooing her out the door.

"I won't be long. It's lookin' to be another scorcher of a day without a speck of rain."

Leah waved good-bye, and Hannah thought again that it was too bad her sister was getting married so late in life. *Leah would've made a loving mother to quite a brood, given the chance.* Here lately Leah had told her that she believed the Lord had kept Jonas just for her, though Hannah didn't quite know what to think about that.

Eager to get going, she took her father's horse and carriage down east a ways, heading for the cemetery. Soon she found herself alone beneath the sleek blue sky and knobby trunks of trees, the breezes surrounding her like sultry whispers. The day would soon be blistering hot, and she wouldn't want to be outdoors once the sun rose high overhead. But she had needed to come here, to this hushed and tranquil place where so many of her dear ones lay in their graves, awaiting the Judgment Day.

Wandering along the rows of headstones, she was cautious not to step on the grassy plots. As a young girl, she'd felt nearly ill when she had accidentally tripped and planted one bare foot right in the middle of a newly laid grave, feeling as guilty as if she'd committed the worst possible of sins. It wouldn't do to make that mistake again.

Presently she spied the small white markers for Dawdi and Mammi Ebersol's graves and dear Mamma's, too. She blinked back tears as Dawdi John and Mammi Brenneman's gravestones also came into view. Overcome with an immense burden of sadness, she sat on an old tree stump cut nearly level with the ground. "Why must anybody die?" she spoke aloud.

She had long decided there were no sensible answers when it came to this final circumstance; all were helpless against the sting of death.

Numerous times over the years she had longed to rush to Dat's house and talk to Mamma about everything from how the baby blues seemed to catch some women unawares to why it seemed the Lord God heavenly Father listened intently to some folk's prayers and not at all to others. Such thoughts ofttimes made her feel as gloomy as she did this moment.

Aware of the heaviness in the air and the ache in her heart, Hannah sat there watching the birds, some in flight and others perched and calling back and forth in the many trees surrounding the cemetery. *Can it really be true that God cares for each of them, just as Gid says?*

When at last she rose to stroll down yet another row of tombstones, she heard someone sneeze. Turning to look, she saw Deacon Stoltzfus's wife, Sarah, painstakingly making her way through the wild ferns and up the slope toward the cemetery.

"Hullo," Hannah called so as not to alarm her.

The older woman was startled nonetheless, eyes wide at the sight of her. "Ach, I didn't expect to see Preacher Peachey's wife here on such a fine summer's day."

Hannah might've said the same of her. "Oh, I come here every so often," she admitted. "I miss my relatives terribly . . . 'specially Mamma."

Tears sprang up in the woman's eyes, and Hannah felt sorry for having said the wrong thing altogether.

"I've never told a soul, but I visit this place quite often." Sarah leaned against a tree trunk to steady herself, her lip quivering. After a time she moved onward without saying more, her gaze intent on a grave marker not far from Bishop Bontrager's own.

Her son Elias, Mary Ruth's first beau . . . dead fifteen years.

Hannah recognized the same sort of unresolved grief in Sarah as herself—the heartrending anguish she'd felt at the loss of each and every relative who'd passed away from her earliest teen years till now. Every passing had left her feeling more and more alone to struggle with her fear—even abhorrence—of death. "I think I know how you must feel," she suddenly called after Sarah.

The woman turned, her face wet with tears. "Oh, Hannah, you surely do, losin' your mamma 'n' all."

"Jah, such wretched turmoil . . . feelin' trapped in one place, unable to forget the pain." She stopped to catch her breath, aware now of the sun's rays beating hard against her back. "Why is it the Lord God chooses to take some young and healthy ones and let others suffer long past their time of usefulness?" Hannah asked. "I don't understand ever so many things—the ins and outs of the Ordnung we're s'posed to take at face value, or the divine lot fallin' on an austere man, making *him* bishop, instead of a kinder, more compassionate man." She felt the words pour out of her, powerless to stop even though she was on dangerous ground, talking this way about the Lord's anointed.

Sarah made no answer and Hannah reached out, impulsively clasping her wrinkled hand. "You aren't alone, Sarah. I promise ya that."

They walked together through the thick grass, slowly moving toward Elias's grave. When they found it, they stood silently, two ministers' wives, both tormented by long-held grief.

Hannah considered the burial services she'd attended from her childhood on—the endless funeral sermons and processions of horses and carriages creeping down back roads to this burial place, the earthy smell of freshly dug graves, her fear as the first shovelful of dirt struck against a wooden coffin. She remembered having often felt guilty to be among the living, yet never wanting to experience death herself.

Sarah was crying now, her stooped shoulders heaving and her hand over her face as the two of them stood beneath the arching branches of an ancient oak tree.

In that instant Hannah pitied Sarah more than she pitied herself. This poor woman must never again be alone in her sorrow, not if Hannah had any say in it. "Come, I'll take you home," she said gently, thinking it was dangerous for her to be walking alone on the road. "No one needs to know you were here today . . . no one but me."

"Oh, denki . . . such a *liewe*—dear girl."

Hannah helped Elias's brokenhearted mamma creep down the grassy hill toward the waiting horse and buggy, tending to her as if she were her own mother.

Sunday morning Lydiann got herself settled on a bench on the side with the women folk, glad Dat had decided to have Preaching service here in the barn, where occasional breezes could be felt this late August morning. The sun hadn't been up but three hours, and already it was nearly unbearable out, the bugs thicker than ever. Grateful for the pretty flower hankie Hannah had made for her last Christmas, she waved it back and forth in front of her face, hoping for some relief, but anxious lest she breathe in a fly. *Best not to do any yawnin' during the second sermon*, Lydiann thought.

She'd chosen to sit with some of the girls her own age for these summer Preaching services, and Mamma hadn't minded at all. Deep into courting age now, Lydiann had discovered as many nice Mennonite boys—and good-looking ones, too—as Amish fellas. Cute boys aside, lately she'd been leaning in the direction of the Mennonites, mostly because the sermons made a whole lot of sense to her. Besides that, she liked to understand what was being talked about, something that wouldn't be the case with the sermons given today in High German, here in Dat's bank barn.

She looked over at her sisters and Aunt Lizzie and Mamma Leah, all of them sitting together, with Hannah's girls nearby and baby Ada snuggled in Aunt Lizzie's arms. Lydiann's heart was full with joy for Mamma Leah. She would never forget the way Mamma's pretty eyes had lit up at Jonas's return from Ohio. And now Mamma was in a perpetual state of anticipation, waiting to be united with her beloved—the boy Mamma had always loved, or so the story went.

Lydiann felt sure she'd be one of Mamma's bride attendants. And most likely, Jonas would ask one of his teenaged nephews, perhaps one of his sister Anna's sons and Leah's Uncle Jesse Ebersol's younger boys.

But she oughtn't be pondering such things as who she might be paired up with at Mamma and Jonas's wedding, not with the ministers making their entrance and the Preaching service about to begin. Yet it was next to impossible to sweep such exciting thoughts of love away. How could she, when she longed for the same kind of love Mamma and Jonas shared? That precious, narrow distance between two innocent hearts. . . .

They were well into the three-hour meeting and Deacon Stoltzfus's reading of a chapter from the Bible when a horsehair floated past Lydiann, soaring horizontally over the heads of the People.

Right away she knew what her brother and his friends were up to, all of them sitting in the back row of benches on the men's side, where they could conceal their assembly line and usual antics. One of the boys, probably Abe, mischief maker that he was, had put a long horsehair or two in his pocket this morning for this stunt. Several times now she'd witnessed her brother catch a fly between his thumb and forefinger, baiting it first with his own disgusting spit. Another boy would make a small, open loop in the end of the horsehair, and the captured insect, still alive, would have its head strung through the horsehair with the loop closing skillfully around its neck. Abe and his friends would repeat the process till four or five flies were tied to a single horsehair, finally releasing the clever creation to buzz and dip and dive over the entire assembly.

Abe never gets caught, she thought, assuming many of the flock were already dozing off due to the heat and the length of the meeting.

The airborne horsehair was about to soar past Jonas Mast, who was wide awake. He glanced up and saw the boys' prank, and the biggest grin appeared on his face.

She watched the flies drift farther toward the front, right over the deacon's head, but he never paid any mind and droned on as he read the Scripture in High German.

Lydiann sighed and fanned her handkerchief harder, wishing Abe's practical joke might flutter *her* way. If so, she'd catch it but good and show Dat what sort of things his only son was doing during Preaching these days. *Wouldn't that be a fine howdy do?*

Chapter Thirty-Seven

When Leah finished drying the last plate following the common meal of the first Preaching service in September, she was altogether willing to accept an afternoon ride with Jonas. She never tired of his company. Listening to his infectious laughter, or to whatever happened to be on his mind, was such a delight. They had truly become the best of friends again. The admiration she found in his eyes whenever she looked his way was even more profound than before he'd left Lancaster County.

"Dat says he wants to talk with us sometime fairly soon," Leah mentioned when they were well on their way.

Jonas glanced at her, his eyebrows raised in obvious curiosity.

"Neither he nor Aunt Lizzie said what's on his mind, so I won't be guessin'."

A smile stretched across his tan face. "Could it be your father wants to offer his blessing on our marriage?"

"Well, I doubt that's necessary anymore, knowin' how he's come to regard you, Jonas." For sure and for certain, her father had dropped plenty of hints this past year indicating how pleased he was with Jonas's return home . . . and into her life, too.

Jonas let the reins lay across his knees and reached for her hand. "Then we best be waitin'."

"Jah, we've become real gut at *that.*" She was unable to suppress a titter, and he joined in, their laughter blending with the melodies of birds and insects surrounding them.

Lizzie always did her best praying in the woods, speaking out loud into the air, saying what was on her heart and mind. She felt she needed to do exactly this today, as she and Leah had been hard at it for hours on end, deciding who of their many relatives and friends should be asked to help on the day of the wedding. With such a large celebration, there was need for a great many cooks, servers, men to set up benches, and teenage boys to tend to the numerous horses when guests arrived.

Presently she made her way up the long hill, past the stone wall surrounding the side of the log house, the snug abode where she'd spent so many years living alone, growing in the nurture and admonition of the Lord while watching little Leah become a kind and thoughtful young woman.

She waved to Gid, who was up working on his roof, nailing down the shingles that had blown off in last night's fierce wind. Abe and Jonas were doing the same at the main house. Such a gale had come up in the wee hours. *Like to waken the dead*, she recalled, picking up her pace.

Deliberately she pushed her feet hard into the grassy path that led to the crest of the glimmering hillock a good ways from here. As she went, she took in all the various hues of dark green brushwood, reddening sumac, and hints of gold and orange from oak, maple, and locust, all soon to be ablaze with the brilliance of autumn. Deeply she breathed in the sweet smells.

The sky began to disappear as the woods closed in around her. Multitudes of blackbirds soared above, fluttering from tree to tree—nature's resonance bringing peace to her mind.

The sun-drenched outcroppings signaled she was approaching the densest part of the forest, not so far from the hunters' shack where Leah had had her beginnings. The place had become more and more rundown over the years, though Lizzie had been keeping herself so busy she scarcely ever ventured into the woods this far. Still, something within her urged her onward.

At last she arrived at the summit, and, catching her breath, she turned to look at the ramshackle structure. There, strewn on the ground, lay so many rickety boards like cast-off lumber. "Well, I declare." She put her hands on her hips and began to laugh. "The effect of a single night's storm!" she said right out.

Lest by some miracle she be heard, she ceased her hilarity and went over and tugged on a sliver of the decaying wood. "A stark reminder of God's forgiveness and grace." She pushed it down into her pocket. "Help me never forget all your tender mercies, Lord."

Later, when she returned home, she told Abram about all the rotting firewood up yonder, and he said he'd ask Jonas, Gid, and Abe to go up and haul back the debris. Sadie must

"And to think his Ohio bishop sent permission some weeks ago to transfer his membership here."

Leah nodded. "This means we'll be seein' each other quite a lot, even after you're married."

"Livin' close enough to borrow a cup of sugar now and then." Sadie's smile was warm, even playful. "Remember the way you and I always talked when we were little girls?"

"Jah . . . and I still can hardly believe Dat gave the main house to Jonas and me."

Sadie let go of Leah and leaned down to pull up a slender piece of dry, wild grass. She twirled it around between her fingers, surely lost in thought. "Makes sense, really—the way it ought to be—'specially after Dat was so opposed to Jonas back when."

"Seems like nearly a lifetime ago." Leah couldn't help but smile. "I have to say, the Lord has blessed Jonas and me. Not just because of Dat's present generosity . . . it goes so much further than that."

Sadie reached over and tickled Leah's face with the grassy shoot. "You deserve every happiness, sister. And don't forget, I'm askin' the Lord God to give you a houseful of children."

Leah laughed softly. "Speakin' of that, you'll be seein' Jake again today, jah?"

"I'm excited the entire Mast clan is comin' for the weddin' . . . and staying all day, too, is what Dat says."

" 'Tis true," Leah replied. "Jonas is nearly jumpin' up and down 'bout it."

"Well, no wonder."

They walked all the way to the edge of the property and turned to look back at the gray stone farmhouse built by Dat's bishop-grandfather. "Just think, Dat and Mamma weren't even born yet when the foundation was laid for the Ebersol Cottage," Leah said thoughtfully.

"And such a large, comfortable place it is." Sadie let the blade of grass fall from her fingers, a gentle breeze stirring the loose hairs at her temple. "I've never understood why you called our house a cottage."

"Well, it's a cozy abode, ain't? It just seemed right somehow to call it that." Leah sighed. "So many happy days . . . and years spent here."

"And many more to come, the Lord willin'." Sadie offered her prettiest smile. "I've learned so much about God's love in Dat's big house. Beginning with Mamma and then from you, Leah—the way you give and give, expecting nothin' in return."

"Well, now, we've both been through a-plenty."

Sadie looked at the sky, squinting up. "Watching you live your life has been better for me than a sermon, sister."

Leah felt her face blush at that. "Oh, now."

"No . . . I'm serious. I wish I might've walked the narrow way earlier in my life."

"Well, you are now and that's what matters."

They reminisced about their childhood days, including their fondest memories of dear Mamma. "I hope there's a way she knows how happy we are."

"Oh, surely there is," Sadie said quickly. "Mamma would be the first person to wish you well . . . I just know it. She always liked Jonas, don't forget."

Leah knew that to be true. A bittersweet feeling came and went like a feather fluttering past her in the breeze, and she and Sadie made their way back toward the house, keenly aware of the many changes ahead.

Chapter Twenty-Eight

The days following the bishop's death included the strenuous process of digging out from persistent, heavy snows, as well as getting word to the People of the bishop's fatal accident. Then, the funeral itself. While there was still plenty of snow on the ground, the day was sunny with no breeze at all, as if the wind had blown itself out. Folk from both the Georgetown and Gobbler's Knob church districts turned out in droves for the Preaching service and the burial, though Jonas hadn't noticed Bishop Simon Lapp anywhere in the crowd of men who waited outside before filing into the Bontrager homestead or who stood together at the graveside.

But he *had* seen and talked with Preacher Gid, spending a few private moments with him during the time the large pine box was carried from the front room of the house out to the wide front porch for the public viewing. Gid took the opportunity to thank Jonas. "'Twas a kind and generous deed, riskin' your life to search for the bishop."

Jonas said that, despite the circumstances of his Proving, he felt it was only right for him to have located the minister.

toward Eli's sleigh. With all the energy he could muster, Jonas hoisted Bishop Bontrager up and onto it, laying him out, face up. *Toward the heavens.*

The ride was insufferably cold as the exhausted horse pulled the sleigh back toward the Bontrager home. *Our long-time bishop . . . dead three days before Christmas.*

There was no way to know precisely what had transpired this bleak and ferocious night, and Jonas was downcast about returning the dead man to the bishop's frail wife. The darkness of the evening and the merciless gale seemed to thrust him through the long, snowy tunnel, and he sent a plea for help heavenward.

Chapter Thirty-Nine

N*ovember third.*

Leah awakened hours before daybreak, lying in bed still as can be, needing to return to sleep, but thoughts of Jonas and their wedding keeping her much too alert to rest.

She pushed back the blankets and quilt coverlet and rose to greet the day, getting herself dressed, not yet in her newly sewn blue cape dress and full white apron, but in a green everyday dress and black apron.

As she brushed through her long hair, preparing to wind it up into the customary bun, she thought again of Mamma, remembering a summer's day when she and Sadie had taken themselves off on a hiking adventure through the woods after having been repeatedly warned to stay away. The two of them had gotten lost, though not for long, and both had fallen, badly banging up their elbows and ripping their dresses. Leah recalled Mamma bursting into tears at the sight of them all *lumbich*, and she smiled now at the recollection, recalling how very loving Mamma had been, taking them in her arms to soothe away the hurts.

She was glad for the memory, though she cringed now at what a dreadful wait Mamma had endured. Breathing a prayer of thanksgiving for the lessons of obedience she'd learned along the way, Leah was wholly grateful for her loving family, and for God's hand on her life . . . and on Jonas's.

Abram headed for the milk house to deposit the morning's fresh milk, whispering to himself, "Leah's gettin' herself a husband today." The realization had been long coming, yet it was not until this moment that he had fully embraced it.

Jonas will care for her, just as I have all these years, he thought, lifting the heavy door to the cooler.

Once he'd put in the milk cans, he went and stood at the window, peering out. Had he ever really forgiven himself for the part he'd played in keeping the adoring couple apart?

He removed his black hat and shook his head, astounded that Leah regarded him at all as her father. True, he was not her natural parent, and Lizzie had shared with him some time back that Leah now knew the truth on that matter. Abram had asked Lizzie not to reveal it to him, to which Lizzie had screwed up her face into a hard frown and asked if he wasn't dealing with "the green-eyed monster." Well, sure, he was, or had been. But life went on, and one's time allotted to living on earth was entirely too brief to be harboring enmity.

Abram's Leah, he thought, thinking over all the years Lizzie's only child had been described that way. No longer. Jonas had somehow managed to wait for what he did not know would ever come to him. *A bit like faith in the Lord Jesus—not seeing, yet believing.*

Heading toward the barn, Abram breathed in the crisp air, glad for the glistening, snowy coating of powdery white that covered fields, barnyard, and the yards. All was still, and the sky was nearly as white as the ground, the clouds seemingly suspended motionless there. "Such a fine day. . . ."

Jonas sat tall and handsome directly across from Leah, wearing his new black suit and a little black bow tie that stood out nicely against his pressed white shirt. Nathaniel King Jr., Jonas's nephew, and Zeke Ebersol, Uncle Jesse's eldest grandson, sat on either side of Leah's groom, wearing similar suits and bow ties, faces shiny from scrubbing.

Leah wondered what Lydiann was thinking, knowing she would be paired up with blond, good-looking Nathaniel for the blessed day of celebration. Lydiann and Mandie Mast were her two beaming attendants.

The house was filled with not only every Ebersol family member age sixteen and up, but also the Mast family adults. And members from both the Gobbler's Knob and Grasshopper Level church districts, and even a handful of Jonas's friends from Ohio—Preacher Sol Raber and Emma Graber—were present. Henry and Lorraine Schwartz came and sat in the back with all the other invited Englishers, including the Nolts and a host of other neighbors who had frequented the Ebersol roadside stand through the years.

Leah caught Jonas's loving gaze and his unexpected wink, and her heart thrilled to his playful expression. She sat still, her eyes never wavering from her darling, hoping he might see the affection in her own heart written on her face.

She pondered all she'd come to know and understand

through the years about relationships, especially between a man and a woman. In her mind, the sort of trust she and Jonas had tested over time went far beyond what anyone around them might notice. The tender care they'd had for each other even as youngsters had made the many years of their separation all the more bitter for them.

Yet here they were. She could hardly wait to stand before the bishop and the nearly four hundred guests, ever so ready to say she believed Jonas's and her marriage was definitely from God, that she accepted her brother in the fellowship as her husband.

When the ministers began to file slowly into the room, Leah lowered her head as was customary. *Thank you, Lord, for keeping Jonas only for me . . . and me for him.*

The song leader—*der Vorsinger*—began the third verse of the Lob Lied from the Ausbund. Sitting between his attendants, Jonas lifted his voice in song as he looked across to his bride and her half of the wedding party.

Preacher Gid presented the opening sermon, recounting the stories of creation, Adam and Eve in the garden, the birth of the first children, the sacrifice of burnt offerings, all the way to the great flood and Noah's praiseworthiness for having descendants who did not marry unbelievers. Jonas was again impressed at his detailed telling; Gid had certainly grown in his knowledge of Scripture since becoming a Preacher.

Levi King, the newly ordained Gobbler's Knob bishop, gave the main sermon. It would be he who put forth the important questions when the time came for them to be pronounced as husband and wife.

At this moment, however, Jonas looked fondly at his

bride. Would he lose all sense of time, not to mention his own good sense, while Bishop King continued the chronicling of Bible stories from the love of Isaac and Rebekah to the marriage of Jacob and Rachel?

Leah is beautiful, he thought, observing her face and radiant expression. He could no longer resist staring at her loveliness—her pretty lips, the color of her hazel-gold eyes, and the rich brunette hue of her hair. He contemplated Leah's waist-length tresses, now tucked devoutly beneath her Kapp.

Tonight . . . he chided himself.

"Husbands, love your wives, even as Christ also loved the church, and gave himself for it," the bishop was saying.

Sadie caught a glimpse of Eli sitting with the other men on this most holy day. *Can it be that I, too, will soon stand where Leah is, beside my husband-to-be?*

She could scarcely believe how richly God had answered her prayers, giving her the chance to get to know and be known by her son and the opportunity to wed again in a mere month.

For whither thou goest, I will go; and where thou lodgest, I will lodge: thy people shall be my people, and thy God my God. . . .

Eli had quoted that same Scripture not so many nights ago as they were discussing where they should live—whether to continue renting the present farmhouse, where Eli had been living with Jonas, or to purchase a house of their own. "Or we could build one," he'd said, seemingly eager to do the latter.

But just now the bishop was asking Jonas if he would be loyal and tend to Leah's needs. "Will you care for her as a God-fearing husband?"

"Jah," Jonas answered in a clear, strong voice.

When the bishop looked at Leah and asked the same question, Sadie saw there were tears welling up in her sister's eyes.

May God bless their happy union.

Sadie was almost overwhelmed by the tenderness and love between Leah and Jonas. Composing herself, she wondered when she'd ever seen Leah's face glow with such happiness. Perhaps once, on the Sunday afternoon following Leah's and Jonas's baptisms. They'd gone off riding together and Leah had confided in her later that she'd never been happier in her whole life. At the time Sadie had secretly guessed Jonas might've stolen a kiss or two—no doubt Leah's first ever.

The bishop further addressed the couple, particularly Jonas. "Do you stand in the assurance that this sister is intended of the Lord God to be your wedded wife?"

"Jah," Jonas answered with confidence.

"Do you promise before God and His church gathered here today that you will nevermore depart from her, but will look after her, care for her needs, and cherish her until our dear God and Father will separate you one from the other?"

Jonas paused ever so briefly, and Sadie wondered if the mention of separation through death was the reason, but as his resounding "jah" came forth, Leah broke into another smile.

The same questions were asked of Leah, and soon the bishop was offering the final words, so familiar to Sadie and to all of the People. Jonas reached for Leah's hands, their locked gaze evident to all.

Sadie held her breath lest she sob with joy, reaching under her sleeve to find the butterfly hankie she always kept tucked away there. For sure and for certain, this incredibly hopeful day encompassed all that dear Leah had ever dreamed of, both for Jonas . . . and for herself.

Do you promise before God *and* His *church* . . .

Lydiann stood tall as can be next to Mamma Leah, her precious mother. Truly, her sister was that to her. Attending the woman who'd loved and nurtured her all these years, Lydiann felt as warm and good as ever she could remember. She hoped if or when the day came for her to marry, she, too, might look as lovely and *in love* as Mamma did this very instant.

Indeed, she could dream, and she surely did, that *her* dearest beau would come along and find her soon—or, as Mamma often said, when it was God's time.

The bishop went on. "The God of Abraham, of Isaac, and of Jacob be ever with you. And may He grant you His divine and abundant blessing and grant you mercy through Jesus Christ. Amen."

Together with her handsome partner, Lydiann followed Jonas and Mamma out of the front room to the upstairs, where they were to wait privately—she and Mandie in one bedroom, the young men in another—till the wedding feast was ready to be served. All Lydiann could think of was the wonder of love, hardly able to wait for such a day to dawn for her.

"Jonas, your eyes are shining," Leah whispered when they were alone in the room where they would spend their wedding night.

Her husband seemed to be saying many things with his eyes today. His strong, warm fingers curled around hers, and he pulled her into his arms. "You're right where you belong, love."

She leaned her head against his heart, and after a time, she looked up at him. Slowly he cupped her face in his hands and his lips found hers.

I could fly, she thought, eager for more of his tender kisses.

He held her close and she never wanted to let go. "I know why I was born . . . it was for you, Leah. Always for you."

She gave him her best smile and then let out a little giggle. They both laughed, though trying their best not to be heard by the bridal attendants down the hall. Certainly, their laughter would not reach the ears of the People, already busy with work below. The men assigned to setting up tables were placing three benches side by side to create one table, elevating it with a special trestle beneath. White tablecloths would be distributed and placed on the many tables soon to be laden with the wedding feast: roast chicken with bread stuffing, mashed potatoes and gravy, coleslaw, celery sticks, creamed celery, peaches, prunes, pickles, freshly made bread, jams and jellies, cherry pies, and cream-filled doughnuts galore.

Leah could scarcely wait to sit at the Eck, the extra-special corner table reserved for Jonas and her and their wedding attendants, where the bride was expected to sit to the left of the groom, just as they would sit in their family buggy from now on as husband and wife.

Jonas took her hand and led her to the window. There he kissed her again, his lips lingering longer this time.

"I'm Leah Mast," she whispered, coming up for air. She turned to look out at the forest and the sky with her darling. A sudden multitude of birds soared up into the spacious blue sky, and she lifted her face once again to Jonas's. "Together for always."

Epilogue

Although it has been nearly two years since Jonas and I said our vows to God and each other, I feel as dearly cherished by him as I did on our wedding day. We talk over everything at the end of each day, never allowing a single thing to come between us.

We were both delighted when our new bishop gave permission for Jonas to make and sell fine furniture. So far it's only a part-time job, and in the rest of his working hours he continues to assist Gid in the blacksmith shop, but Jonas does seem to have a near-constant grin on his handsome face. Someday I wouldn't be surprised if he is able to be full-time in his woodworking shop as word about his gift gets out not only amongst the People but also with Englishers.

As is our custom, I quit working for Dr. Schwartz and his wife several weeks before I got married, and it is Lydiann who now earns a bit of pin money by checking on the house when the Schwartzes are overseas helping with their church-related mission projects. Especially because of the change in the doctor's heart, I was relieved to hear from Lorraine that Peter

Mast vowed never to press charges against him for what he did so long ago, which was awful good of Peter to go and say, seeing how Dr. Schwartz lived in fear of that very thing.

A few weeks following Jonas's and my wedding, Eli and Sadie were married. About a hundred family members were on hand for the half-day affair, and Sadie was the prettiest bride I've ever seen. Now she's the happy mother of blue-eyed, fair-haired Leah—my sweet little namesake. Goodness knows Sadie has longed for this baby! To think I'll be hearing my own name for many years to come when they visit or on Sunday-go-to-meeting days.

Jake still lives in Grasshopper Level, working at home, having taken over many of the duties of the orchard and farm from Peter. He happily takes Mandie to singings, as brothers do. And he's seeing a serious "sweetheart," too, I hear. Sadie says he spends much of his leisure time visiting her and Eli, often playing blocks with his wee half sister, who reportedly has learned to stick out her tiny tongue on command when he is near.

A few months ago Hannah surprised Gid with his first-born son—named Gideon, of course. So tiny Ada has a close-in-age playmate, and their big sisters keep out a watchful eye, acting as live-in baby-sitters, Hannah says. Thankfully my sister is more settled than she's been in years, regularly enjoying quilting bees and other work frolics, even though she has more children than ever before.

Mary Ruth is expecting her second baby late spring of next year, and she and Robert are as busy as ever in the work of their church. When she and Hannah and their families get together, it's most enjoyable for all of us to watch their children frolic, Ruthie and Ada in particular playing much as the twins themselves once did.

As for dear Lydiann, she has decided to follow in Mary Ruth's footsteps and join the Mennonite church, and I gather from her recent confidences in me that she plans to become Mrs. Carl Nolt not long after her church baptism. There is that certain bounce to her step, giving us all cause to smile—even Dat, I daresay.

Well, it's nearly time for Jonas to come home for the noon meal, and I look forward to his company. What with cooing twin boys to make over, I sometimes forget how to talk like a grown-up.

Jonas is as gentle a father as ever was with our little ones. Having *two* babies instead of one was quite a big surprise, but Jonas believes it's the Lord's way of making up for lost time. That just may be, and I'd have to say tiny Abraham and Peter are the joy of our lives. They look ever so much like both Jonas *and* me, our families say, but truly I think both boys bear a strong likeness to Jonas and his father. I had wondered, even worried a bit while carrying them close to my heart, how I'd feel if either of them bore a resemblance to Dr. Schwartz, just as Jake has always looked so much like Derek—as if the secret was determined to be known, stamped as it is upon his face—but that fretting was needless in the end.

And then there is our Abe, who unnerves all of us when he says he's "livin' in his rumschpringe," and this with a mischievous grin. At present he is thrilled to have two *boys* in the Ebersol Cottage, and both he and Jonas like to get right down close and jabber in Dutch to our babies.

As for me, I like to whisper to my sons while holding

them near, one in each arm. Always I begin with that day of days—Second Christmas on Grasshopper Level—when I first caught the blue-eyed gaze of the dearest boy ever. "I'm talking 'bout your father," I say, leaning down and kissing each downy head.

Just today Dat came into the kitchen while I was relating to my babies how I'd fallen for Jonas back before I was old enough to know better. "Well," he said right out, "just listen to you go on so." He was smiling to beat the band, and when I waited to hear what was on his mind, he said, "I can only hope I live long enough to tell these young'uns how wonderful-gut it is that their mamma ended up married to their Dat."

"Oh, now . . . for goodness' sakes," I said.

"No . . . no, 'tis quite a love story." His gray head bobbed up and down, as if to emphasize the words.

I couldn't help but thank God anew for the enduring love strands, divine and otherwise, that brought Jonas and me together, strands that bind us together even now.

Dat stood near where I sat in the rocking chair, gazing down at the matching bundles in my arms. "Bless the Lord and Father of us all," he said, a catch in his voice.

"You're not becomin' *weechhatzich*, are ya?" I looked up at him.

"Softhearted?" To this he waved casually. "Well, ain't such a terrible thing, I don't think."

I rose from the rocker with his help and went and tucked my babies into the double-wide wooden cradle crafted by their father. Then I followed Dat into the front room, walking past the spot where Jonas and I had stood and promised to love each other all the days of our lives.

Dat bade farewell as he walked through the doorway connecting the Dawdi Haus to this one, and I stood at the window and stared out at the multicolored patchwork squares of fertile fields stretching out in all directions. After a while I turned and walked the length of the room, recalling the several times Jonas and I had hosted Preaching service here as husband and wife, thankful for the way Jonas's heart was turned toward the Lord and His Word.

The familiar creak of the kitchen door signaled my darling's arrival, and I hurried to greet him, always eager for his strong embrace and fervent kisses.

"How's my perty wife?" he asked, holding me ever so tight.

"Busy as a honeybee, I s'pose."

"Must be why you're so sweet."

I laughed softly, not wanting to wake the babies. That brought another smile to his handsome face . . . and a kiss for me. Then, hand in hand, we tiptoed over to the wide cradle to gaze at our most precious gifts, ever grateful to God.

Acknowledgments

My first debt of gratitude is to my husband, Dave, for making it possible for me to skip meals and work late in order to create a saga-style series like this from idea to publication. There would be no ABRAM'S DAUGHTERS without the encouragement, love, and constant support of our family, as well. Thanks to Julie for reading the first draft with such enthusiasm . . . and for making all those healthy snacks. I also always appreciate Janie's and Jonathan's earnest prayers. And my gratefulness goes to my son-in-law, Kenny, for his research assistance.

This final book could never have come together in the amazing way it did without the fine attention to detail from my editors: Carol Johnson, Rochelle Glöege, and David Horton. I also wish to thank Julie Klassen and Cheri Hansen for their editorial input; Jerad Milgrim for his military research assistance; Fay Landis, Priscilla Stoltzfus, and Hank Hershberger for their answers to Amish-related questions; and Carol Johnson for her description of the café in Florence, Italy.

My heartfelt appreciation goes to Monk and Marijane

Troyer for their contribution of the "flying horsehair escapade," and for permitting me to include it. To the anonymous Lancaster County research assistants who wish to remain so, I offer my ongoing debt of gratitude and love.

For readers interested in making the Amish roast referred to in this book, the recipe is found on page 82 of *The Beverly Lewis Amish Heritage Cookbook*.

As always, I offer earnest thanks to my loyal readers for the thoughtful e-mail (and snail mail) notes and comments—so encouraging to me. To my faithful partners in prayer, may the Lord Jesus bless each one.

"And I pray that you, being rooted and established in love, may have power, together with all the saints, to grasp how wide and long and high and deep is the love of Christ, and to know this love that surpasses knowledge—that you may be filled to the measure of all the fullness of God." —Ephesians 3:17b–19, NIV

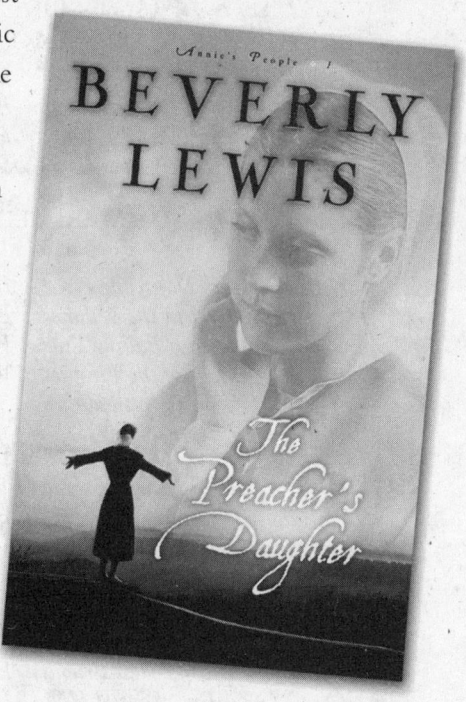

Also by Beverly Lewis

PICTURE BOOKS

Annika's Secret Wish *Cows in the House*
Just Like Mama

THE CUL-DE-SAC KIDS
(For ages 7 to 10)

The Double Dabble Surprise
The Chicken Pox Panic
The Crazy Christmas Angel Mystery
No Grown-ups Allowed
Frog Power
The Mystery of Case D. Luc
The Stinky Sneakers Mystery
Pickle Pizza
Mailbox Mania
The Mudhole Mystery
Fiddlesticks
The Crabby Cat Caper
Tarantula Toes
Green Gravy
Backyard Bandit Mystery
Tree House Trouble
The Creepy Sleep-Over
The Great TV Turn-Off
Piggy Party
The Granny Game
Mystery Mutt
Big Bad Beans
The Upside-Down Day
The Midnight Mystery

GIRLS ONLY (GO!)
(For ages 8 to 13)

Dreams on Ice
Only the Best
A Perfect Match
Reach for the Stars
Follow the Dream
Better Than Best
Photo Perfect
Star Status

SUMMERHILL SECRETS
(For ages 11 to 14)

Whispers Down the Lane
Secret in the Willows
Catch a Falling Star
Night of the Fireflies
A Cry in the Dark
House of Secrets
Echoes in the Wind
Hide Behind the Moon
Windows on the Hill
Shadows Beyond the Gate

HOLLY'S HEART
(For ages 11 to 14)

Best Friend, Worst Enemy
Secret Summer Dreams
Sealed With a Kiss
The Trouble With Weddings
California Crazy
Second-Best Friend
Good-Bye, Dressel Hills
Straight-A Teacher
No Guys Pact
Little White Lies
Freshman Frenzy
Mystery Letters
Eight Is Enough
It's a Girl Thing

www.BeverlyLewis.com

04C

to speaking of Ohio. "Did you happen to get over to the Swiss cheese factory near Berlin?"

"No, I didn't stay in the area for long. One young fella from the Millersburg church district introduced me to the Indiana man I eventually married."

Their conversation was slow and quiet, and she found herself perfectly content to sit with him, conscious of the heat in the belly of the stove, as well as the gentle warmth of the hot coffee she drank.

During a lull in their conversation, she presented him with her homemade card and was surprised when he handed her one, too. "Why, thank you," she said, feeling her cheeks warm at his attention.

When they'd finished their coffee and Sadie had taken the cups and saucers to the sink, she reached for her heaviest coat. Quickly Eli offered to hold it while she slid her arms inside.

They walked to his enclosed buggy, and she was thankful they were no longer youngsters. No need to endure this brisk night in an open courting buggy!

"Awful nice spendin' time with you, Sadie," he said.

As Eli helped her into his carriage, she felt as if her heart might burst with joy.

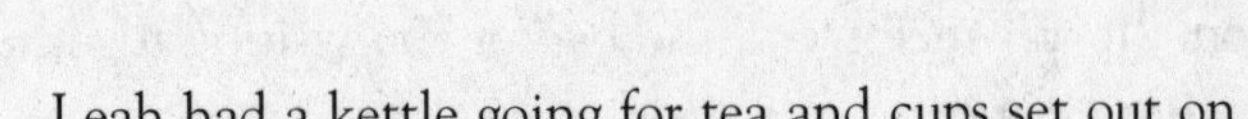

Leah had a kettle going for tea and cups set out on a tray when she went in search of Sadie Saturday evening.

She found her sister happily humming as she worked by gaslight in her tiny kitchen. "We must talk," Leah said softly.

"I'll bring us some tea over here if you'd like."

Sadie looked up from the pot of vegetable soup she was making. "Sure, I'll be glad for some hot tea." She added shyly, "I had a visit with Eli Yoder today."

"Oh, what lovely news!" Then and there Leah knew she had to admit to having seen Sadie and Eli make their way out to his carriage. "I hoped, all the while you were gone, that you'd have yourself a real nice time. Did ya?"

"Oh my . . . jah." Sadie did not volunteer anything else, and Leah guessed she wanted to hold this memory close for a while before revealing more. "Well, sister, what's on your mind?" she asked after a brief lull.

Leah hesitated, not wanting to spoil Sadie's present contentment. "It's just that I've been considerin' Jake quite a lot." She paused. "I'm wonderin' if you think it might be time for folk to know he's your son."

Sadie folded her hands on the table. "All the People, ya mean?"

"Mary Ruth and Hannah and their spouses in particular."

Turning her head, Sadie looked at the cookstove and icebox. "I've thought the same, to tell the truth. 'Tis next to impossible livin' with the knowledge of something so . . . well, wonderful, and havin' to keep it to myself." Sadie looked back at her, tears glistening. "Jake's such a fine boy, Leah. Truly, he is. I can't tell you how happy I am."

Leah felt she understood at least something of her sister's emotion. "It was nice seein' the two of you visiting together. Did my heart gut."

"One of the best moments of my life." Sadie got up for the honey jar and asked, "How do you think we should go 'bout telling Hannah and Mary Ruth and Abe? I don't want

ing if he's ever to attend Jonas and Leah's wedding," Robert said, surprising her.

She looked at him, not sure what to say. "You sincerely think Peter and Fannie would not attend the marriage of their eldest son?"

Robert shrugged. "Something's got to give, sooner or later. People shouldn't willingly go to their graves filled with such hate—at least not if I can help it."

"What can you do, Robert? Seriously."

"I don't know what the Lord has in mind, but I've felt compelled to pray about it more frequently, and I won't stop until I get an answer, one way or the other. Prayer changes circumstances, you know."

"And people, too." She found Robert's sudden concern about the longtime clash between the Masts and the Ebersols to be quite curious. "I felt so sad when Cousins Peter and Fannie didn't come to Mamma's funeral . . . sad for them and for Dat."

"At this point, I doubt Peter even remembers what triggered his aggravation with Abram in the first place."

"Perhaps." Mary Ruth wished something could be done about it. Just what, she had no idea, but she would join her husband in praying for God's answer.

"Which is just the way I like you."

They sat gazing into the face of their precious sleeping daughter, reminiscing on the day spent between Dat's house and the Schwartzes'. "Your parents seemed quite taken with Ruthie," she said, touching her baby's dainty hand.

"Yes, and with each other, as well," said Robert. "Did you happen to notice?"

"I did, actually." She hadn't said anything before but was glad Robert brought it up. "What is different between them, do you think?"

"With Dad that can't be easy to know. He's as tight-lipped as they come. But they must've had a wonderful time on their trip overseas."

"There's a shared something or other . . . a special *knowing* between them."

"All for the good, I trust," Robert said.

Feeling tired, Mary Ruth was content to simply lean her head on her husband's shoulder, aware of the occasional crackle in the fireplace and the sighs of their little one, nestled in Robert's embrace.

"I know it's a long way off, but I'd like to have our families here for dinner next Easter," said Robert.

She sat up at the suggestion. "Maybe we should invite the Masts, too. See if they'll surprise all of us and accept an invitation for a change."

Robert chuckled. "After all these years, I wonder what it would take for Peter Mast to change his mind about your father."

"I think his grudge has more to do with Leah . . . and Aunt Lizzie, maybe."

"Well, he'll have to come around quite a lot in his think-

the Bible. She didn't want to break the peaceful stillness of the moment, so she sang a gentle lullaby. The traditional carol was one the children sang at church.

"Infant holy, infant lowly, for His bed a cattle stall . . . oxen lowing, little knowing Christ, the babe, is Lord of all."

As she sang, she thought of Hannah, who, while seeming to have experienced relief from depression and despondency for some time now, still appeared to be spiritually lost. *Will my twin ever open her heart to the Lord?*

She knew she would not cease praying for just that—not as long as she was living and breathing. Surely Hannah would come to find Jesus real and near to her someday. Mary Ruth sighed. She knew too many Amishwomen, several of whom Hannah was well acquainted with, who suffered from a melancholy spirit. Often she prayed for Hannah to be free of the darkness that seemed to surround her, so she might spread light to others in similar need, perhaps. *Too many such women live in bondage.* She was glad her twin at least was blessed with a kind, God-fearing husband. It was for Mary Ruth to simply put her trust in God's sovereignty, praying each of her family members would experience saving grace in the Lord's perfect way and time.

When Robert closed the Bible, he patted the pillow next to him. "Come sit with me, love."

She went willingly, placing Ruthie in his arms and snuggling close to him. "What a special day, jah?" She laughed softly as the Dutch word slipped out unexpectedly.

"Once Amish, always Amish, you used to say." Robert kissed her head.

"I daresay," she replied. "Well, maybe just simple and Plain."

and not receive the ordination was to meddle with the sovereignty of God and seen by some as a bad omen.

Gid reached for her hand. "Don't worry over the ordination, Hannah, but be in an attitude of prayer."

In that moment she wanted to say once more how sorry she was for her recent disobedience. "I was ever so wrong, Gid."

"No need to cover old ground," he replied. "All's forgiven."

She nodded, tears unexpectedly springing to her eyes. She would not seek out Zachariah further, having promised Gid she would not. "I don't know what got into me that day, goin' to the Henners."

"Well, I think *I* do. You're much too curious, that's what." He was teasing her, but now his face grew more serious. "And it's high time for me to apologize to *you*, dear."

"Whatever for?"

"I s'pose it must've seemed I was more concerned 'bout Mary Ruth's Mennonite influence on you and our family over the years than I was the powwowing you were so bent on. But I was sorely wrong on that point."

She was quite surprised to hear such a thing coming from Gid. "Mary Ruth brings joy to everyone."

"Jah, your twin's cheerful nature is bound to raise a person's spirit."

"For sure and for certain." She was most grateful for her husband's understanding and love this blessed Christmas . . . and all year through.

Mary Ruth sat by the fire, rocking Ruthie to sleep. She smiled across the room at Robert, who sat on the sofa reading

horse and carriage already hitched up at the end of the mule road. Now all she must do was make her way down the long, lonesome hill through the ice and snow to the carriage.

She overheard Gid's voice in the barn when she arrived, but it was Dat who was coming out and heading toward the house with something of a limp. "Mind if I take the buggy for a little bit?" she called to him.

"Just be sure 'n' be back before dinner."

I'll be home plenty before noon, she thought, climbing into the right side of the buggy. *And if all goes well, I'll return with the healing gift.*

Having sat at the same table as Zachariah and Mary Ann, enjoying sticky buns and hot coffee for a good half hour, Hannah was eager to get on with talk of powwowing. She didn't want to seem forward, but she was curious to know exactly how the power was transferred from one person to another, and she was anxious to move ahead before she lost her resolve. Already she'd begun to feel prickles at the back of her neck—as though she was doing something wrong.

Zachariah began to speak affectionately of his grandmother and her lifelong fascination with powwowing. "She received the transfer from her elderly uncle, a bad-tempered deacon," he said with a slight chuckle. "Or so the story goes."

Mary Ann was frowning slightly, as if to say, *Don't tell all you know, Zach.*

Yet he continued. "*Mammi* Henner kept many diaries . . . hundreds of pages of 'em. Recently I looked back and

discovered she kept a record of who came for healing, how often, who left money on the table, and suchlike. Mighty remarkable it was, seein' there were plenty of preachers—even local bishops—who frequented her place, night and day."

Hannah took this in, thinking of her own journal writing.

" 'Tis interesting you're so keen on havin' the gift," said Zachariah. He did not ask her why she should desire it so, but he studied her, and the intensity of his gaze made her feel weak. It was as if his eyes spoke their own secret language, and she shivered.

He leaned forward, his elbows on the table. "You can be one of us."

The haunting words seemed to hang in the air.

"Are you ready to receive from me, Hannah Ebersol Peachey?"

Why is there such force behind his eyes? Just now she felt truly frightened—nothing like she'd expected. Maybe it was because she had always been somewhat unnerved by male Brauchdokders.

She trembled within, feeling panicky . . . even sick. The thought of Zachariah's hands touching her head or her shoulders—or whatever he had in mind to do to pass the gift to her—made her almost frantic. She'd come here for understanding and for the gift she had so respected in Old Lady Henner, only to feel as if she was being led down a long gray burrow that was closing in around her spirit.

The prayer of faith shall save the sick and the Lord shall raise him up. . . .

That Gid believed this wholeheartedly, there was no doubt in her mind. *I've gone against my husband in this. I've sinned against my dear Gid!*

"No," she whispered, barely able to utter the word. "I'm *not* ready." She rose abruptly, mumbling, "I changed my mind," and forgetting to offer her pardon for leaving the table that way.

She made a beeline to the back door, pushed it open, and headed out just as it dawned on her she'd left her wrap, scarf, gloves, and even boots indoors.

"Puh!" she said to herself, catching her breath.

At that moment she spied her husband at the end of the walkway. Gid stood with his back to his horse and sleigh, frowning in disbelief. "Hannah, what the world are ya doin' *here*?"

She nodded, acknowledging his presence, yet was incapable of speech.

Scarcely was Hannah able to make out the silhouette of Gid and his sleigh ahead on the road, the squall of snow was so dense. She followed him in Dat's enclosed buggy, thankful for the slightly warmer carriage but still suffering the sting of her shame.

She was as low as she'd ever felt in her life, defying her husband as she had. And she had no idea how Gid would go about disciplining her—surely he could do just that, being the anointed man he was.

Leah carefully topped each mug of hot cocoa with a dollop of whipped cream before carrying the tray of steaming

cups over to the table. "Here we are."

When Lyddie spied the special treat, a full smile appeared on her face. "This looks delicious!"

"I daresay it'll warm us up a bit." Leah settled down where she normally sat at mealtime, looking fondly at her girl. "You seem so peaceful today."

Lyddie nodded. "I've had some time to think 'bout what happened with Jake. The shock of all this knowin' . . ." Her voice grew softer. "I know he'll find himself a nice wife someday, but I wouldn't be surprised if he returns to Ohio for that."

Leah listened, wishing she could absorb every speck of pain still evident in Lydiann's voice, although her countenance wore a noticeable resolve. "Maybe it'd be a smart idea for Jake to put down some roots in a new place."

"Except then he wouldn't be anywhere near either the Masts or Sadie." She sighed. "And I think he'd miss Mandie terribly."

"Jah . . . that *would* be painful for him," Leah said, knowing firsthand how it felt to lose connection with a loved one.

"It's kinda strange, really," Lydiann said. "To think the girl he thought was his twin is actually someone he *could* marry—but, pity's sake, who'd want to, them growin' up together! Meantime the girl he loved turns out to be an aunt, of all things. Why, there must be times he wishes this was all a mixed-up dream . . . just as I do."

"I know . . . that's why, however necessary, it was so difficult, knowin' what a mess this would make for both you and Jake—and to think of stirring up such pain for him, as well as his family. Imagine raising a boy, only to discover he wasn't yours at all!"

They sipped their hot cocoa and continued to talk heart-

to-heart. All the while Leah kept thinking how thankful she was for Lydiann's ability to share her thoughts this way. *Very grateful, indeed.*

At dusk Jonas pulled off the main road onto the Henners' treelined lane, hoping to goodness he might not be seen and mistakenly assumed to be a patient of Zachariah's. Coming this late had been a good choice, he decided as he headed to the back door and knocked.

When Zachariah greeted him, Jonas made note of the man's scrutinizing milky blue eyes and the way he carried himself . . . as if he thought he was rather important.

Not wanting to stay longer than necessary, Jonas preferred to ask his questions while standing in the outer room connected to the kitchen, and he politely refused Zachariah's invitation to come in and have some black coffee. He could hear the voices of young children and Zachariah's wife's gentle prodding. But so as not to detain the family from their evening time together, he simply asked outright about his father's visits here. "Does he come regularly?"

Zachariah nodded without hesitation. "Both for back treatments and otherwise."

"For fellowship, too?"

"Oh, we like to talk whilst enjoyin' a drink, jah."

Obviously, Zachariah was not attempting to hide anything. "I believe my father has a problem, and I'm here to ask you not to encourage him further by offerin' him whiskey when he visits in the future."

Zachariah sighed loudly, folding his arms across his wide chest. "Well, now, I can always recommend coffee if you'd rather." His reply gave the impression he wasn't too interested in kowtowing to a nosy son's demands.

"This is hardly a joking matter," Jonas said. "I'll take you at your word on the coffee. Much obliged!" He turned to dart down the back steps, mighty glad to breathe in the crisp night air and hoping Zachariah was trustworthy.

Mamma's old Bible. She enjoyed the Old Testament love stories, especially the one of Isaac and Rebekah. Actually, she liked reading all the biblical accounts of courtship and marriage and found herself daydreaming once more. *If God wills, I'd like to be a wife again. . . .*

She contemplated Rebekah and Isaac's meeting that fine day out in the countryside as Rebekah came riding on her camel. *What things were in her heart and on her mind? Did she wonder if Isaac would find her pleasing . . . even pretty? Had she ever wished to be cherished by a man?* Sadie remembered how dearly loved Harvey had made her feel during their short marriage.

Nearly embarrassing herself with such idle thoughts, she wondered if Eli was thinking ahead to one week from today, when he was to pick her up right at her door—and not under the covering of night, but during the afternoon.

Sadie couldn't deny how excited she was. Since their meeting was to be the Saturday right after Christmas, she thought about making a card for him, with tatting gently glued on. *Jah, I'll do something nice like that.*

Snug by the fire, she turned again to the first book of Moses to reread the heartwarming account of Isaac and Rebekah's marriage arrangement.

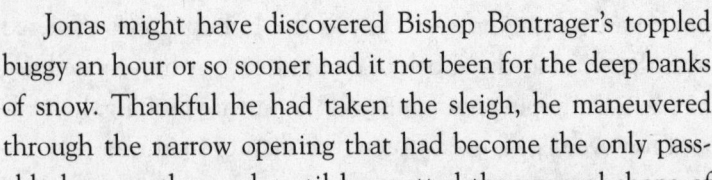

Jonas might have discovered Bishop Bontrager's toppled buggy an hour or so sooner had it not been for the deep banks of snow. Thankful he had taken the sleigh, he maneuvered through the narrow opening that had become the only passable lane on the road, until he spotted the unusual shape of

one particular drift. From what he could tell, it was not as tall and windswept as others he'd scrutinized while riding through the blinding snowstorm. Halting his horse, he went to investigate, pushing mounds of snow away. A shattered carriage lay buried beneath.

Desperately he searched for the elderly bishop, seeing no evidence of either a man or an injured horse thus far. Further investigation caused him to conclude that the broken hitch, as well as the smashed carriage, must have occurred when an automobile struck from behind. Jonas hoped the driver of the car had stopped to assist the bishop, taking him to get medical assistance, if necessary. He couldn't imagine anything less on the part of their English neighbors, although there was no way to know who had been out driving in this storm. Still, he continued searching for more clues, his face, hands, and feet growing more numb by the minute.

Moving snow away with his gloved hands, he was determined to find evidence this *truly* was the minister's carriage. And when, at last, he came upon a red Thermos with the initials *B.B.* printed on the side, Jonas assumed he'd found exactly that.

Not so eager to go on with his search, except for the possibility of finding a wounded bishop, he turned to head back toward his horse and sleigh and stumbled over something large—a piece of the buggy, maybe?

Stooping, he swept more than a foot of snow away and let out a gasp—lying on his side was the bishop. Jonas shivered into the wind at the shock of seeing him, yet he touched the man's neck, hoping for a pulse. Upon further probing, he realized how very stiff, even frozen, the man of God was.

Not waiting another moment, he began to drag him

to wait and have word leak out through the grapevine . . . which it could, ya know."

"Ask Dat," Leah suggested. "Either he or Aunt Lizzie will have something to say 'bout it."

Sadie smiled, although her chin still trembled slightly. "The worst is behind us, jah?"

Reaching for her hand, Leah closed her eyes. "Oh my, let's pray so."

Every corner of the morning sky twinkled gold as Jake and Jonas worked methodically in the kitchen on New Year's Day, chopping vegetables and cutting up stew beef for their noon-time meal with Eli. Jake was fired up and eager to say what was on his mind, and as Eli was gone from the house, now was as good a time as any. "I say *everyone* ought to know the truth 'bout me."

Jonas didn't immediately respond, although his quick intake of breath and the serious look in his eyes made it clear he had an opinion.

"Seems like a falsehood to me for folk to continue thinkin' I'm Peter Mast's son, don't ya think?"

Jonas regarded Jake quietly, nodded his head, and then unexpectedly went and adjusted the flame under the black kettle. "Too bad the secret was ever kept at all . . . but then, I wouldn't have known you as my brother, would I?" he said at last. "I can't imagine what Mandie or Mamma or any of our siblings would think if you weren't a part of our family. I do mean this, Jake. What's done is done and should be left

alone." He paused to reach for the lid and placed it firmly on the kettle. "And something else . . ." He turned toward Jake. "You must forgive Dat. The sooner you do, the sooner you'll get past all your disappointment toward him. That's not to say I blame you for feelin' the way you do."

Jake shook his head and sat down at the table. "I would never think of doin' such a thing to my son—true kin or not. It helps some knowin' that Sadie never would've given me up if she'd had any say."

"I believe you're right."

Jake stared at the tray filled with the sourdough sticky buns a neighbor lady had brought over earlier as a New Year's surprise. He muttered to himself, not persuaded that he shouldn't go about telling the world—*his* world, at least—the news.

Jonas spoke up again. "Maybe Dr. Schwartz is the one you need to consider forgiving first."

Jake wasn't surprised at Jonas's pointed words. Unfortunately, both the doctor and their father had been terribly at fault in his case, though the latter was of more concern at present. A month had come and gone since Dat had asked him to leave, with nary a note or visit all this time.

How long will the silence continue? Jake wondered with a heavy heart.

When a knock came at the door, Henry jumped, startled from where he had dozed off while reading the newspaper, enjoying the tranquility of the house.

It had been that sort of afternoon—one in which to recover from having overindulged in Lorraine's fine New Year's Day dinner of prime rib with all the trimmings. His wife had not gone to all that trouble simply for him, however. Robert, Mary Ruth, and their peach of a baby girl had come to spend a good portion of the day, much to both Lorraine's and Henry's delight.

He rose gradually to see who might be stopping by for a visit, and upon opening the door saw three uniformed men. He instantly tensed and thought Peter Mast had decided to press charges, having abandoned the nonaggressive posture Leah had been so adamant was the Amish way.

So this is it, he thought, imagining how Lorraine would react to his being handcuffed and arrested today, and just when the two of them had begun to click far better than they had in many years. No doubt in his mind, his luck had run out.

"Are you Henry Schwartz, father of Sergeant Major Schwartz, Derek L.?" one of the men asked.

His breath caught in his throat. These men were not here to charge him with a crime; they weren't policemen but military personnel. "I beg your pardon?"

The man asked again, "Is your son Sergeant Major Schwartz?"

Henry trembled, realizing at that instant why this man with intense gray eyes wore the badge of a military chaplain. He stood like a piteous sage of sorrow right here on the front porch.

"Yes, Derek is my son," he said as terror filled his soul.

"On behalf of the U.S. Army, we regret to inform you . . ."

Henry clutched his chest, scarcely able to breathe. *Derek . . . my boy . . . dead.*

More words cut through the fog fast descending on him. "Your son's body will be sent home with a full military escort within four days." It registered in Henry's brain that the military was already doing an investigation into Derek's accident, but the thought seemed somehow unrelated to him. Henry's sense of things and the world as he knew it had utterly changed.

One late-summer evening when Derek had begged permission to spend the night in the highest crook of a towering tree in their backyard, Henry had taken Derek's side against the more protective Lorraine, and in the end the boy had gotten his way. Their son had hoisted an old pillow and a blanket to the uppermost branches, where he had slept blissfully beneath the leaves.

Henry wondered what sort of relationship they might have had if Derek had made even the slightest attempt to keep in touch as an adult. What if his son *had* responded to letters from home instead of ignoring them since the Christmas of 1949, the last time either Henry or Lorraine had seen him? Henry had continued to write, only to be pierced afresh by Derek's indifferent silence.

The chaplain had indicated Derek had never married, his next of kin being his parents. Henry had no reason to doubt it, but this brief glimpse into his son's life had come as a surprise, especially because of Derek's previous fondness for the ladies.

He thought of Lorraine again. Not wanting to leave her alone too long, he was rising to leave when he noticed Peter Mast sitting across the room, the only Amishman present. Wandering over somewhat hesitantly, he offered a greeting. "Happy New Year, Peter."

He was only partially convinced Peter had motioned for him to sit at the table, but Henry pulled out a chair to do so and the bearded man frowned. "I wouldn't have expected to see *you* here, Doctor."

"Likewise, you." Henry nodded, eyeing Peter's nearly empty glass. "Alcohol appears to be the drug of choice. Folk delaying their resolutions for one more day."

"I daresay you carry enough guilt around for two or three men." Peter raised his tumbler.

Henry stared at this man, incredulous at his contempt. He recalled that Derek had actually worked for him as a teenager, often bringing home Fannie's excellent jams to Lorraine at her request. Peter had changed for the worse over the years; his rudeness was unlike the polite, even dignified manner of the Plain folk Henry treated up and down the Georgetown Road and beyond. "I'm here because Jake's father is said to be dead," he muttered at last.

Peter leaned back in his chair and let out an odd chuckle. "I shouldn't be surprised . . . there are prob'ly more than a few who wish me an early end."

Stunned, Henry looked at him. "Not *you.* My son Derek . . . the father Jake never knew. Nor, scarcely, did I." He formed the last words with difficulty.

"Well, then, we've both lost sons, seems to me. Mine's as gut as dead."

Henry shook his head. "You and Fannie raised Jake as your own. He *is* yours."

"I'm no fool, Doctor. Jake's got your blood in his veins—Abram's, too. He ain't mine at all."

Henry was appalled. "Jake has your values . . . he accepts your principles as his own. What more could a man want?" He wished the same could be said of Derek. *If only he had embraced a sense of family loyalty, if nothing else. . . .*

"I was deceived and my family's in shambles for it." Peter got up and stood at the table, fire in his eyes. "I don't know who to blame more—you or that scoundrel Abram." He planted his fists on the tabletop, his head lunging forward, but

Chapter Thirty-One

The Bullfrog Inn was smoke-filled and noisy with men making merry. Henry had slipped out of the house some time after breaking to Lorraine the news of Derek's tragic death at his army base in Ft. Carson, Colorado, where he had been assisting in conducting predawn live-fire exercises. Not at all familiar with the military and its war games and drills, Henry could not envision the scenario, and the pieces of information the chaplain had given him did nothing to quell the string of questions from Lorraine's trembling lips. They would have to wait two weeks for the official account to understand more fully how their son had died.

Henry's chest ached now as the devastating knowledge of their loss seeped into his mind and soul. Before ever telling Lorraine, he had gone alone to the clinic, grieving there in the privacy of his office for a while, dry heaves shaking him to the core.

When, at last, he was able to return to the house, he found his wife awaking from a nap. He went to her and said the painful words, holding her near as she wept.

After quite some time, they talked a little of Derek's disconnection from them in recent years, so complete he had ceased answering even his father's letters. Now they would never know what unforgivable deed they had committed against him, if indeed the fault lay with them at all. When Henry voiced this thought to Lorraine, she shook her head and pleaded with him not to say such things. "Derek chose his way . . . his own path. You mustn't torment yourself for the choices our son made." Yet Henry was shaken in knowing the day of reconciliation for which he had long held out hope would never be.

Even as they talked of funeral plans—Henry insisting the service be small, with a private viewing for family members only—he was scarcely able to grasp that their long-estranged son was gone from them forever. Henry had felt an urgent need to "breathe some fresh air," and Lorraine kindly encouraged him to do so. His feet had led him here.

Now that he stood inside the door of the local tavern, he was beginning to feel guilty for having left his wife to mourn alone. Not having any appetite whatsoever, he slipped into a chair at a corner table to order a single beer. His emotions—a vast array this night—ran deep, and for the first time in his life he was uncertain how to repress his reaction to despair.

Henry sipped beer from a tall glass and recalled the day he and Lorraine had brought their second baby home from the hospital. He allowed himself to remember the joy—and his great pride—at welcoming another son into the family.

He recalled Derek's childhood days as a curly-haired tot, inquisitive and playful. Derek had always been so clever and bright, though somewhat boastful about his accomplishments as a Tenderfoot in the Boy Scouts.

When all was said and done, he harbored no malice toward Bishop Bontrager. *No point in that.*

"I wanted you to know, too, that I haven't said a word to the other preacher, nor Deacon Stoltzfus, neither . . . 'bout the sideboard you made."

Jonas perked up his ears. "But I thought—"

"It's clear you have no intention to earn money from it—a Christmas present to your soon-to-be bride, plain and simple." Gid's breath was like a spiral of smoke. "All that Proving business will need to be discussed at the next ministers' council, I'm thinkin'."

Jonas was relieved to hear it. "Denki."

"No need to thank me." With that Gid walked away, waving his black hat.

It had been a long and tiresome day by the time Jonas and Eli returned home from the bishop's funeral, and the fire in the wood stove was dying down to embers. Now it was long past time to turn in for the night, but Jonas was still sitting in the kitchen listening to Jake pour out his feelings. It was apparent he had been brooding for some time, although he only this minute had declared that he wanted to meet Sadie. He said it with much certainty, as if his grief at their father's rejection of him had turned into an iron-willed determination to forge new ties.

Jake raked his hand through his dark hair. "Don't ya think that if Sadie had known I lived the night I was born, she would've kept me?" He was staring a hole in Jonas. "Just think

how everything would've been different if she had."

"What makes you say this?"

Jake stared at the braided rug for a while before he spoke. "You should know what I'm gettin' at. You love her sister Leah, who's a kindhearted woman, raisin' Lydiann and Abe like they're her own. So I'm thinkin' something of Leah must surely be in Sadie." He paused again, frowning. "If I could have even just a short time with her."

Jonas wondered if Jake's interest stemmed from their being here at Eli's, missing out on their own family Christmas dinner and gift exchange. Mandie had been the only one to hint at them coming over for Christmas, and Jonas felt it wise not to simply show up unwelcome. Like Jake, he also felt somewhat displaced this cold and wintry evening.

"I'll be seein' Leah tomorrow," Jonas offered. "I could ask her what she thinks of you visitin' with Sadie."

Jake leaned forward, nearly falling out of his chair. "Ach, would ya? I'll take a bath and put on my for-gut clothes."

"I have no doubt you'll tidy up, but I think it best if you not get your hopes set on this. It's such short notice . . . and I'd hate to see your feelings smartin' on Christmas."

"Oh, I'm sure Sadie will *want* to see me again." Jake rose and walked to the window. "What a mighty *feiner* day!"

Not certain what to say to his overly eager brother, Jonas got up and went to the window, peering out at the stars. "I pray this isn't a mistake."

But Jake insisted it was not. "The mistakes are in the past, don't ya see? Old things are passed away. . . ."

"In more ways than one," whispered Jonas, thinking now of Bishop Bontrager, gone to his eternal reward.

Chapter Thirty

"Listen to this," Jake said on Friday as he read to Jonas another letter from Mandie.

Jonas was all ears where he stood clearing the breakfast dishes from the table. He, Eli, and Jake had been taking turns redding up the kitchen, each drawing lots to see who would cook which day, as well.

"Seems Dat's got himself a 'certain visitor' every evening now, followin' supper . . . and sometimes right after the noon meal, too." Jake looked up from the letter. "Can ya guess who?"

Jonas was sure he knew. "Bishop Lapp?"

"Well, now, how did ya know that?"

Jonas wasn't about to say. Fact was, Bishop Lapp was apparently interested in dealing with problems head-on, whereas it seemed Bishop Bontrager had been more inclined to create them, at least where some folk were concerned.

Jonas had told Jake nothing concerning the frank visit with the Grasshopper Level bishop, and maybe he never would. At least it sounded like some progress was being made

at the Mast orchard house, especially if Dat wasn't riding off to get his daily quota of the hard stuff, what with the man of God showing up to keep him regular company.

Sadie couldn't have suppressed her smile even if she'd wanted to when Eli Yoder showed up at her back door the Saturday afternoon after Christmas. "Hullo," she greeted him. "Would ya like to come in and warm up a bit?"

"Mighty nice of you," he said, a twinkle in his eye.

Once he was seated at her table, she poured hot coffee for them both, all the while utterly aware of his endearing smile—like a moonbeam on newly fallen snow. She noticed the notched cut of his red hair, slightly squared off at the ears, evidence of his Ohio roots.

They exchanged comments about his enthusiasm for woodworking, as well as their individual time spent in places in Ohio familiar to both, discovering several people they knew in common from the Millersburg area. "Ever get a chance to walk along Killbuck Creek?" he asked.

"Oh jah, and it ain't such a little creek, either, is it?"

"Well, in some places, it is plenty wide and deep—nearly like a small river." He lifted his coffee cup to his lips and drank. Then, setting it down again, he smiled. "This is right gut coffee."

"Denki."

They talked of Christmas, and Eli described how both Jonas and Jake had helped "cook up a fine feast." Hearing Jake's name mentioned made her miss him, but Eli was back

Chapter Twenty-Seven

Upon moving in with Eli, Jonas and Jake had learned of Bishop Bontrager's special allowance regarding the shed behind the widower's house. The small space had been converted into a makeshift woodworking shop, something that was of little consequence to the People here, since Eli had long ago joined his Ohio church district and wasn't planning to stay put in Gobbler's Knob, anyway.

It was nearly two o'clock on the Saturday before Christmas when Jonas stepped back from his handiwork, crossing his arms as he admired the attractive sideboard he'd put together in a matter of days. "A fine gift indeed," he said in the quietude of the shed. "Nearly as perty as Leah is herself."

A knock came at the door and he jumped. Turning, he saw Gid at the window, waving and wearing a tentative smile. "Ach, it can't be locked . . . must be stuck," Jonas called out, hurrying through the wood shavings to yank open the door.

"Hullo," Gid said right quick. "It's been a while since we talked privatelike."

"Jah, and it's gut to see you," said Jonas.

Gid eyed Eli's fancy tools . . . and the sideboard. "What's this you're makin', Jonas?"

"A Christmas gift for my bride-to-be."

Gid nodded, scratching his beard. "Can't help but wonder what the bishop might say to this."

"I wouldn't think it's a problem, but I s'pose I should've gotten the go-ahead all the same." Jonas felt rising frustration. "Guess I assumed since it's a present, and plain as can be, it would be all right."

Gid looked around Eli's shop. "Must be a mighty big temptation livin' here."

Jonas wished he could convince Gid he hadn't moved in with Jake for the purpose of using Eli's fine tools. There was no denying he was irresistibly drawn to woodworking—cherry, oak, walnut, maple, and cedar for lining chests—every variety of wood caught his eye, and in a big way. Yet he'd promised to put all that behind him during his Proving, both as a means to earn money and a regular hobby—anything to find favor with the Gobbler's Knob church, and all for the sake of marrying Leah.

"I'm afraid I have no choice but to mention this to Bishop," Gid was saying. "Much to my dismay."

Jonas would not plead with Gid to keep quiet. It wasn't as if he'd forgotten his promise or wanted to disrupt the Proving in any way; he'd simply let his great eagerness to please Leah at Christmas overtake him. "I understand," he said.

"On second thought, might be best if *you* went to him 'bout this. The consequences might be less severe thataway."

"Not a bad idea." Prior to today, Jonas had thought that if things didn't work out here in Lancaster, he might try to convince Leah to marry him out in Ohio—except that would